THE CLARENDON EDITION OF THE
NOVELS OF GEORGE ELIOT

ROMOLA

GEORGE ELIOT

ROMOLA

EDITED BY
ANDREW BROWN

CLARENDON PRESS · OXFORD
1993

Oxford University Press, Walton Street, Oxford OX2 6DP

Oxford New York Toronto
Delhi Bombay Calcutta Madras Karachi
Kuala Lumpur Singapore Hong Kong Tokyo
Nairobi Dar es Salaam Cape Town
Melbourne Auckland Madrid
and associated companies in
Berlin Ibadan

Oxford is a trade mark of Oxford University Press

Published in the United States
by Oxford University Press Inc., New York

British Library Cataloguing in Publication Data
Data available

Library of Congress Cataloging in Publication Data
Eliot, George, 1819–1880.
Romola | George Eliot: edited by Andrew Brown.
(The Clarendon edition of the novels of George Eliot)
Includes bibliographical references.
I. Brown, Andrew, 1950– . II. Title. III. Series: Eliot,
George, 1819–1880. Novels. 1980.
PR4668.A2B76 1993   821'.8-dc20   92–14326
ISBN 0–19–812594–1

Set by Hope Services (Abingdon) Ltd.
Printed in Great Britain
on acid-free paper by
Bookcraft Ltd.,
Midsomer Norton, Bath

PREFACE

THAT *Romola* should have become the least read of her novels would have saddened George Eliot but probably not surprised her. From the first she was resigned to its being less popular, and less understood, than her other novels. Set outside England, and in the distant past, it has struck generations of her readers as something of an anomaly, but it always claimed a special place in her own affections: 'there is no book of mine', she remarked in 1877, 'about which I more thoroughly feel that I could swear by every sentence as having been written with my best blood'.

She began writing on New Year's Day 1862, after fully six months of concentrated research on the background to the story—a period of such single-minded absorption in the history of late fifteenth-century Florence that George Henry Lewes was moved to wonder whether, having buried herself for so long in 'musty old antiquities', she had got into 'the idea of a Romance being the product of an Encyclopaedia'. The range and intensity of her studies are evident on almost every page of the novel, and perhaps more than any other factor it is this—what one contemporary review termed the 'instructive antiquarianism' of the book—that has sealed *Romola*'s fate as the least accessible of her works of fiction.

Romola is also notable as the only one of George Eliot's novels to have appeared as a serial, in monthly parts. To secure it for the *Cornhill Magazine* the publisher George Smith made her the extraordinary offer of £10,000 for the copyright, a sum quite without precedent at the time. As it turned out, however, serial publication suited her neither artistically nor temperamentally. The pressure of monthly deadlines, together with a deep anxiety at essaying so different a work from her previous novels, led to bouts of severe depression and ill-health throughout the period of composition. She was later to confess that none of her books had as painful a gestation as *Romola*: in her own words 'I began it a young woman,—I finished it an old woman'.

Romola is a formidably learned book, and to edit it has required the assistance of a whole host of kind colleagues. I am glad to take this opportunity to acknowledge the invaluable help of the following scholars, but for whom my own efforts would have been sadly lacking in crucial respects: Katharina Brett, David Carroll, Jane Hodgart, Jonathan Hunt, E. J. Kenney, the late Uberto Limentani, Andrew Sanders, Lindeth Vasey, and John Worthen.

Many others have also provided expert advice on all manner of specific problems: William Baker, Gillian Beer, Michael Black, Françoise Bolton, Felicia Bonaparte, James Boulton, Pat Boyde, Roger Coleman, Victoria Cooper, Mark Davie, John Deathridge, David Ekserdjian, Nadine Ekserdjian, Simonetta de Filippis, Colin Hardie, Pauline Hire, Ian Jack, U. C. Knoepflmacher, Brian Lake, Maureen Leach, David McKitterick, Nicholas Mann, Terence Moore, Virginia Murray, George Pigman III, Barry Qualls, Lawrence Rainey, Arden Reed, Arthur Sale, Terence Sculley, John Stevens, Charles Swann, John Trevitt, Eric van Tassell, Alexander Wainwright, Michael Wheeler, Robert Williams, Hugh Witemeyer, and Richard Ziemacki.

I have had cause to work in a number of libraries, whose staff have fielded my queries with unfailing courtesy: the Beinecke Library at Yale, the Bodleian Library, the British Library, Cambridge University Library, Princeton University Library, the National Library of Scotland, the New York Public Library, the Harry Ransom Humanities Research Center at the University of Texas, the Sadleir Collection at UCLA, the University of Virginia Library, and Dr Williams's Library in London where so many of George Eliot's own books are deposited.

At Oxford University Press I have been fortunate to deal with John Bell (in the 1970s) and Frances Whistler (in the 1990s). In between it has been my pleasure to have as an editor Kim Scott Walwyn, who has preserved an astonishingly sympathetic attitude in the face of a whole decade of more or less plausible excuses for the late delivery of copy.

I should like to express my gratitude to Jonathan Ouvry for granting me permission to quote unpublished George Eliot manuscript material, and like everyone else with any pretensions to working on George Eliot I must acknowledge the late Gordon Haight, without whose encouragement this book would not have been. Amidst all these thanks, though, the palm goes to my wife Lorna—for putting up with the twin co-respondents of Marian Evans and Romola de' Bardi.

A.B.

Cambridge,
1991

GENERAL CONTENTS

LIST OF ILLUSTRATIONS

Frederic Leighton's twenty-four illustrations to *Romola* in the *Cornhill Magazine* are reproduced in the text at the equivalent points to their original appearance in the serial, as follows:

For Leighton's illustrated capitals to the start of each serial part, the tailpiece to the Proem, and the vignette on the title-page of the Illustrated edition, see Appendix D.

REFERENCES AND ABBREVIATIONS

BL	Autograph notebook in the British Library (Add. MSS 40768).
Bod	Autograph notebook in the Bodleian Library, Oxford (MS Don. g. 8).
CM	*Cornhill Magazine* serialization (14 parts, July 1862–August 1863).
Cross	*George Eliot's Life as Related in Her Letters and Journals*, ed. J. W. Cross (3 vols., 1885).
GE	George Eliot
GHL	George Henry Lewes
Haight	G. S. Haight, *George Eliot* (London, 1968).
Letters	*The George Eliot Letters*, ed. G. S. Haight (9 vols., New Haven, Conn., 1954–78).
MS	Romola, British Library, Add. MSS 34027–9.
Pf	*Some George Eliot Notebooks: An Edition of the Carl H. Pforzheimer Library's George Eliot Holograph Notebooks* (vol. ii: MS 708), ed. William Baker (Salzburg, 1984).
Q	'Quarry for Romola', autograph notebook in the Parrish Collection, Princeton University Library (AM 14959).
WN	*George Eliot: A Writer's Notebook 1854–1879*, ed. Joseph Wiesenfarth (Charlottesville, Va., 1981).
1	1st edition, 3 vols., 1863.
2	Illustrated edition, 1 vol., 1865.
3C	Author-marked-up setting copy for *3*, Harry Ransom Humanities Research Center, University of Texas at Austin.
3P	Author-corrected proof of *3*, Harry Ransom Humanities Research Center, University of Texas at Austin.
3	Cabinet edition, 2 vols., 1878.
⟨ ⟩	Deleted in *MS*
{ }	Added in *MS*

INTRODUCTION

GENESIS

On 21 March 1860, having written the final few paragraphs of *The Mill on the Floss*, George Eliot noted in her journal 'We hope to start for Rome on Saturday, 24th. *Magnificat anima mea!*'[1] This was to be her second visit to Italy. In the summer of 1849, just after the death of her father, she had travelled on the continent with her friends Charles and Cara Bray, and had visited Genoa, Milan, and Lakes Como and Maggiore before settling for an extended stay in Switzerland. Though her spirits had been at a desperately low ebb (she later recalled 'How wretched I was then—how peevish, how utterly morbid!'),[2] the image of Italy remained bright in her mind, and in 1860 she confessed 'I had looked forward for years to the journey to Italy . . . with the hope of the new elements it would bring to my culture'.[3]

When she set out with George Henry Lewes on 24 March, then, it was with high enthusiasm, if with few illusions about the comforts of European travel. This was just as well, for it proved an exhausting journey: seventy-two hours from Paris to Genoa by train, diligence, and—at one point, high in the Alps—by sledge; then by steamer via Leghorn to Civitavecchia, and finally by train to Rome. Their first impressions of the Eternal City, like those of many other visitors before and since, were of dirty streets, noisy tourists, and the outrageous cost of accommodation. Disappointment, however, soon gave way to 'an intoxication of delight', not only at the ancient glories of Rome but at the living spirit of Italy: 'Oh, the beautiful men and women and children here! Such wonderful babies with wise eyes!— such grand-featured mothers nursing them! As one drives along the streets sometimes, one sees a madonna and child at every third or fourth upper window'.[4]

After four weeks of sightseeing and acclimatization, they travelled south to Naples, arriving on 30 April. The weather was glorious and they made several excursions, including one to Pompeii: 'a thing never to be forgotten—that walk through the silent city of the past'.[5] On 15 May they were on the move again, by sea to Leghorn and thence to Florence, where they took lodgings at the Pension Suisse in the Via Tornabuoni—'the quietest hotel in Florence, having sought it

[1] Cross, ii. 159. [2] *Letters*, iii. 321. [3] Journal: Cross, ii. 164.
[4] *Letters*, iii. 286, 288. [5] Ibid. iii. 293.

out for the sake of getting clear of the stream of English and
Americans in which one finds oneself in all the main tracks of travel,
so that one seems at last to be in a perpetual noisy pic-nic, obliged to
be civil though with a strong inclination to be sullen'.[6]
Notwithstanding, they set about the business of sightseeing with a
will. On their first evening they attended an indifferent performance
of *Il Trovatore*: as Lewes noted, 'a screaming opera screamingly
given'.[7] On the second they drove out to Fiesole to view the city
from afar, and on the next to San Miniato and Bellosguardo for less
distant panoramas, the description of which in George Eliot's journal
anticipates that in the Proem to *Romola*:

There is Brunelleschi's mighty dome, and close by it, with its lovely colours
not entirely absorbed by distance, Giotto's incomparable Campanile, beautiful
as a jewel. Farther on, to the right, is the majestic tower of the Palazzo
Vecchio, with the flag waving above it; then the elegant Badia and the
Bargello close by; nearer to us, the grand campanile of Santo Spirito, and that
of Santa Croce.[8]

From their conveniently central hotel they visited most of Florence's
major buildings, churches, and museums. When not actually sightseeing, they were assiduously reading about the sights and their historical context. Four days after their arrival, on 21 May, Lewes recorded
in his journal that 'while reading about Savonarola it occurred to me
that his life and times afforded fine material for an historical romance.
Polly at once caught at the idea with enthusiasm'.[9] The next day they
visited San Marco, the building most closely associated with
Savonarola. Since it was still a Dominican monastery, entrance was
forbidden to women, so while Lewes toured the interior and took
notes George Eliot remained in the chapter house, studying Fra
Angelico's fresco of the Crucifixion (see p. 155). On the way back to
their hotel they bought a copy of Savonarola's poems and of F. T.
Perrens's recent biography *Jérôme Savonarole, sa vie, ses prédications,
ses écrits*. A few days later, on 27 May, George Eliot wrote to William
Blackwood: 'There has been a crescendo of enjoyment in our travels,
for Florence, from its relation to the history of modern art, has
roused a keener interest in us even than Rome, and has stimulated me
to entertain rather an ambitious project.'[10]

That 'ambitious project', of course, was *Romola*. Though there is
some circumstantial evidence that George Eliot may have already
been considering a work of fiction set in Italy (in a letter to her of
June 1858 John Blackwood had referred, intriguingly, to 'the Italian

[6] *Letters*, iii. 294–5.   [7] GHL Journal (Yale).

[8] 'Recollections of Italy' (Yale MS IV. 2).

[9] *Letters*, iii. 295 (corrected from MS (Yale)).   [10] Ibid. iii. 300.

story you have in view'),[11] it would seem that the immediate inspiration for *Romola* dates from her fortnight's stay at Florence in 1860.

The remainder of that stay was spent visiting further places of historical and artistic interest, including several specially associated with Savonarola: for example the Great Hall of the Palazzo Vecchio, 'built under Savonarola's direction'; the Palazzo Corsini, to see Pollaiuolo's painting of Savonarola's death at the stake ('a curious and to us interesting 'bit of history'); and the Magliabecchian Library, where they examined a manuscript volume by him, 'written in a minute, short-sighted hand, but very clear'.[12] They left Florence on 1 June and travelled in northern Italy and Switzerland before finally returning home on July 1—an absence of over three months in all. As their trip drew to a close George Eliot wrote to John Blackwood 'We ought to be for ever ashamed of ourselves if we don't work the better for this great holiday. We both feel immensely enriched with new ideas and new veins of interest.'[13]

In May, when first hinting at her new project to William Blackwood, George Eliot had added that she meant to keep it a secret from everyone but himself and his brother John. A month later, in Switzerland, she was still less forthcoming. In reply to John's request for further information, she politely refused to supply any, explaining rather mysteriously: 'I don't think I can venture to tell you what my great project is by letter, for I am anxious to keep it a secret. It will require a great deal of study and labour, and I am athirst to begin'.[14] This guardedness seems to have intensified with the passage of time—or with her distance from Florence. If she returned to England in July with her enthusiasm for the idea of an Italian novel undimmed, it was with rising uncertainty at her ability to carry it off; and when she eventually revealed the idea to her publishers, in late August, her misgivings had become so serious that her plans for its immediate prosecution had changed dramatically:

I think I must tell you the secret, though I am distrusting my power to make it grow into a published fact. When we were in Florence I was rather fired with the idea of writing a historical romance—scene, Florence—period, the close of the fifteenth century, which was marked by Savonarola's career and martyrdom. Mr. Lewes has encouraged me to persevere in the project, saying that I should probably do something in historical romance rather different in character from what has been done before. But I want first to write another English story, and the plan I should like to carry out is this: to publish my next English novel when my Italian one is advanced enough for us to begin its publication a few months afterwards in Maga. It would appear without a name in the Magazine, and be subsequently reprinted with the name of

[11] Ibid. ii. 463.   [12] GHL journal: Haight, p. 326.   [13] *Letters*, iii. 307.
[14] Ibid.

George Eliot. I need not tell you the wherefore of this plan—You know well enough the received phrases with which a writer is greeted when he does something else than what was expected of him.

But just now I am quite without confidence in my future doings, and almost repent of having formed conceptions which will go on lashing me now until I have at least tried to fulfil them.[15]

As things turned out, this scheme of staggered publication proved short-lived, but it is interesting both for the light it casts on George Eliot's diffidence and defensiveness about *Romola*, and for its indication of the pressures which may have contributed to the genesis of her 'next English novel', namely *Silas Marner*. There is no evidence that when she wrote the above letter to John Blackwood on 28 August she had any clear notion of what that novel might be. Her famous remark that the idea for *Silas* 'thrust itself between me and the other book I was meditating' can refer to a date no earlier than 24 September, when the Leweses moved from Wandsworth to 10 Harewood Square, Marylebone, for her journal states that it 'came to me after our arrival in this house'.[16] She later wrote that *Silas* 'came *across* my other plans by a sudden inspiration'.[17] Given the nature of those plans, however, as set out in her letter of 28 August, it would appear that the inspiration was at least as timely as it was sudden. Unless, which is unlikely, she was 'meditating' a quite different English novel during August and September 1860—a novel subsequently supplanted by *Silas Marner*, and one to which no corroborative reference has survived—her sudden inspiration for *Silas* came as something of a self-fulfilling prophecy as regards her declared intention of postponing *Romola*.

The Leweses stayed only three months in their new house before moving again, this time just a few hundred yards to 16 Blandford Square, where they were to remain for three years. Such upheavals were plainly distracting to George Eliot, who had always begrudged time spent in domestic activities. 'To crown my sorrows', she confided after the second move, 'I have lost my pen—my old favourite pen with which I have written for eight years'.[18] Her sorrows during the autumn of 1860 were indeed considerable; in November she complained to Sara Hennell of 'extreme languor and unbroken fatigue from morning to night—a state which is always accompanied in me psychically by utter self-distrust and despair of ever being equal to the demands of life'.[19] Periods of physical debility and mental depression were to become alarmingly regular over the next few years. To a certain extent they can be explained by her thorough dislike of living in London: on visits to the country her spirits

---

[15] *Letters*, iii. 339.   [16] Ibid. iii. 360.   [17] Ibid. iii. 371.
[18] Ibid. iii. 364   [19] Ibid. iii. 359.

and her strength would revive virtually overnight. More specifically, as Gordon Haight has suggested,[20] they were probably due in no small measure to the continued irregularity of her marital status, which she felt to be more painfully conspicuous in the public gaze of the metropolis. It was at this time that Lewes investigated the possibility of obtaining a divorce abroad, but was advised that it would have no standing in English law. George Eliot put on a brave face, but it scarcely masked her bitterness: 'I am not sorry . . . I prefer excommunication. I have no earthly thing that I care for, to gain by being brought within the pale of people's personal attention.'[21]

For all her sorrows, she started work on *Silas Marner* soon after her arrival in Harewood Square. Writing slowly and with numerous interruptions, she had managed only three chapters by the end of November. Thereafter, though further delayed by the move to Blandford Square in December—and presumably with a new pen— she quickened her pace, and on 15 February 1861 she was able to send the first thirteen chapters to John Blackwood, followed by the next five on 4 March, and the final pages on 10 March. She received an advance copy on 25 March at Hastings, where Lewes had taken her to recuperate. The day after their arrival she wrote to John Blackwood 'I feel already a new creature with a day's draught of sea-air'.[22] As her spirits revived her thoughts turned again to the 'great project' which *Silas Marner* had supplanted for the past six months. On 24 March Lewes recorded in his journal that they had been walking along the coast 'talking of the Italian Romance Polly is contemplating'.[23] The day before, George Eliot had confided to Blackwood 'We are meditating (do you know it?) another visit to Florence with grave purposes'.[24]

PREPARATION

They set out for Italy on 19 April 1861 and after a leisurely journey arrived in Florence on the evening of 4 May. This time they chose rather grander accommodation: first at the Hôtel de l'Europe in the Piazza Santa Trinità, and subsequently at the Hôtel de la Victoire, overlooking the river on the Lung'Arno. Almost immediately, they both came down with feverish colds, and spent much of their first week nursing each other through headaches, chills, and sore throats. Still, they had come with 'grave purposes'—to seek further inspiration and background colour for George Eliot's 'Italian Romance'—and even before they were fully recovered they were out and about,

[20] Haight, p. 338.   [21] *Letters*, iii. 366–7.   [22] Ibid. iii. 391.
[23] Haight, p. 342.   [24] *Letters*, iii. 392–3.

eagerly revisiting the sights and enlarging their sense of Florence and its history. To augment this latter they spent several days working in the Magliabecchian Library. Remarkably, at least some of their borrowing slips have survived, so it is possible to reconstruct the course of much of their research.

On their first visit, on 15 May, they consulted the volumes dealing with Italy in Giulio Ferrario's encyclopaedic *Il costume antico e moderno*. The following day they asked for Lorenzo Lippi's seventeenth-century comic poem *Il malmantile racquistato* (a burlesque parody of Tasso's *La Gerusalemme liberata*), and two books on the ancient customs and topography of the city: Leopoldo del Migliore's *Firenze illustrata* and Modesto Rastrelli's *Firenze antica e moderna*. On the 17th and 18th, besides browsing in the *Opere volgari* of the fifteenth-century poet and scholar Angelo Poliziano, they worked their way through the early histories of Florence by Buonaccorsi, Capponi, Cavalcanti, and Nerli.[1] On the 19th they turned to Agostino Ademollo's *Marietta de' Ricci*, a historical novel set in early sixteenth-century Florence, in Luigi Passerini's edition of 1845 with its copious notes on various aspects of Florentine social history and mores. They returned on 24 May to consult *Marietta de' Ricci* again, as well as Pompeo Litta's massive and as yet unfinished genealogical survey *Celebri famiglie italiane*.

For most of the time, however, they were content simply to explore the city, avoiding the crowds when possible and 'looking at streets, buildings, and pictures'—or as Lewes put it in a letter to his son Charles, 'we trot out, visit a church or two, or a picture gallery, look over bookstalls, and poke into the curiosities of old Florence'.[2] One evening they risked another production of *Il Trovatore*, only to find it 'bawled at the top of the voice'; they left at the end of Act II.[3] Their only major excursion was a three-day trip with their friend Thomas Adolphus Trollope (Anthony Trollope's older brother), by carriage and on horseback, into the hills to the east of Florence to visit the ancient monasteries of Camaldoli and La Vernia. Before they left for home, Trollope presented George Eliot with a copy of his novel *La Beata: A Tuscan Romeo and Juliet*, which he had recently completed. As for her own Italian romance, she wrote to John Blackwood 'I feel very brave just now and enjoy the thought of work—but don't set your mind on my doing just what I have dreamed. It may turn out that I can't work freely and fully enough in the medium I have chosen, and in that case I must give it up'.[4] Lewes felt rather more confident; ten days later he wrote to

---

[1] For full details of all the books GE read in her preparations for *Romola*, see App. B.
[2] GE journal: Cross, ii. 305; *Letters*, iii. 414.
[3] GHL journal (Yale).   [4] *Letters*, iii. 417.

Blackwood 'She is "drinking in" Florence, and as far as the old past life can be restored she will, I am certain, restore it, if only from that wonderful intuition with which genius throws itself into all forms of life'.[5] In her journal she reflected:

We arrived at Florence on the 4th May, and left it on the 7th June—thirty-four days of precious time spent there. Will it be all in vain? . . . I am in excellent health, and long to work steadily and effectively. If it were possible that I should produce *better* work than I have yet done! At least there is a possibility that I may make greater efforts against indolence and the despondency that comes from too egoistic a dread of failure.[6]

They returned to England via Switzerland, arriving on 14 June, and George Eliot settled down to a period of intense study on the background to her novel. By the end of July she had read Hallam, Sismondi, and Comte on the middle ages; Hélyot, Montalembert, and Renan on ecclesiastical history; and Gibbon, Buhle, and Tenneman on the revival of learning—together with Savonarola's treatise on government, several volumes of his sermons, and Audin de Rians's edition of his poems (the copy she had purchased in Florence the previous year). As lighter fare she went through Franco Sacchetti's *Trecentonovelle* (a collection of comic tales from the late fourteenth century) and T. A. Trollope's *La Beata*—a singularly undistinguished novel, but whose principal male character, interestingly, is named Tito. It was at this time, also, that she began to read Marco Lastri's *Osservatore fiorentino* (1776–8), a survey of Florentine social history, topography, and monuments from the thirteenth to seventeenth centuries, which was to prove one of her most important sources.

None of this enthusiastic study, however, could stave off the headaches or fits of depression of which she was to complain almost continually during her work on *Romola*. By 30 July, in fact, she was so despondent as to have 'struck out two or three thoughts towards an English novel'[7]—presumably having considered abandoning or at least further postponing her Italian one—but she soon returned with a will to the work on hand. By the middle of August she had made her way through *Le istorie della città di Fiorenza* by the sixteenth-century historian Jacopo Nardi, whom she describes in *Romola* as 'one of the very few who . . . have written about [Savonarola] with the simple desire to be veracious';[8] Antonio Doni's *I marmi* (1552: a series of imaginary conversations on social and political issues supposedly overheard on the steps of the Duomo in Florence); Boccaccio's

---

[5] Ibid. iii. 420.   [6] Cross, ii. 305.

[7] Unless otherwise specified, all subsequent quotations are from GE's journal, now at the Beinecke Library, Yale (MS IV. 3).

[8] See p. 584.

Decameron, from which she made copious notes on idiomatic and colloquial usages; Roscoe's *Life of Lorenzo de' Medici*, 'with much disgust at his shallowness and folly'; Edward Bulwer Lytton's best-selling novel *Rienzi: The Last of the Tribunes*, 'to examine his treatment of an historical subject'; and the two most important biographies of Savonarola—the contemporary account attributed to Pacifico Burlamacchi, and Pasquale Villari's new and definitive study *Storia di Fra Girolamo Savonarola e de' suoi tempi* (1859–61).

As usual, her hard work was accompanied by persistent headaches and poor spirits, and by 12 August she had 'got into a state of so much wretchedness in attempting to concentrate my thoughts on the construction of my story, that I became desperate, and suddenly burst my bonds, saying, I will not think of writing!' On the 15th, however, after two days spent reading Villari on Savonarola, things took a turn for the better, as she noted in her journal: 'Discussed the plot of my novel with G. and in the course of our conversation I struck out an idea with which he was thoroughly satisfied as a "backbone" for the work'. Precisely what this idea was we have no way of knowing, but it evidently took hold for a while, and on 20 August she recorded 'This morning I conceived the plot of my novel with new distinctness'. The same day Lewes wrote to John Blackwood that her plans were 'slowly crystallising into what will be a magnificent programme. Until quite lately I thought she would relinquish altogether in despair, her singular diffidence being exaggerated in this case. But now I think it will really be written. If only I could see the first chapter!'[9] For the time being, though, she simply continued her omnivorous research: between 15 and 30 August she read, among other things, Mrs Jameson's *Sacred and Legendary Art*; Tiraboschi's history of Italian Literature; the *Hymni et Epigrammati* of the fifteenth-century Graeco-Florentine poet Marullus, to whom Tito Melema bears certain obvious similarities (see p. 29); Daniel Rock's *Hierurgia; or the Holy Sacrifice of the Mass*, from which she made notes on ecclesiastical vestments; and Domenico Manni's *Le veglie piacevoli*, in which she found accounts of four of the supporting historical characters in *Romola*: the barber-poet Burchiello, on whom Nello is based, the mountebank Vaiano Vaiani, the pedlar Bratti Ferravecchi, and the eccentric painter Piero di Cosimo.

The sheer quantity of her reading during July and August 1861 is the more remarkable when one considers that she was by no means living the life of a solitary student. There was a daily procession of guests and visitors at Blandford Square throughout these weeks; there were regular walks with Lewes in Regent's Park and to the Zoological

---

[9] *Letters*, iii. 446.

Gardens; there were excursions, visits to exhibitions, to concerts, and to the theatre; there was church-going, letter-writing, and piano-playing (and shopping at Broadwood's for a new grand piano). Above all, apart from her own ailments, there was mounting anxiety at the state of Lewes's health, which deteriorated rapidly during the month of August. On 5 September they left for ten days at Malvern, where he was to take the waters. The escape from London proved thoroughly beneficial to George Eliot herself, and she was much invigorated by long walks in the surrounding countryside. She had taken books with her, though, and between the walks she put in long hours reading Mrs Jameson's *Legends of the Monastic Orders* and the eulogistic biography of Savonarola in Vincenzo Marchese's *Storia di San Marco*. They returned to London on 17 September, whereupon she promptly went down with a series of acute headaches.

It was not until 30 September that she 'Took up again the MSS. connected with my Italian novel, and made various arrangements towards work'. This implies that she had already made some preliminary sketches or outlines, but if so they have not survived. On 2 October she spent the morning 'arranging the plot'—apparently without much success, for two days later she notes 'My mind still worried about my plot—and without any confidence in my ability to do what I want'. On 5 October she read *Le vite d'uomini illustri del secolo XV* by the fifteenth-century biographer Vespasiano da Bisticci, and began to make her way through the *Archivio storico italiano*—a multi-volume compendium of archival sources in which she consulted Jacopo Pitti's history of Florence; Vincenzio Acciajoli's biography of Piero Capponi, the prominent politician whose exploits are described in chapter 29 of the novel; and the *Cedrus Libani*, an account of Savonarola's life by his contemporary and fellow-monk Fra Benedetto da Firenze. On 7 October she wrote in her journal 'Began the first chapter of my novel'—another false start, followed by a further period of voracious reading. Two days later Lewes wrote to John Blackwood that 'Mrs Lewes is very well and buried in musty old antiquities, which she will have to vivify. I am a sort of Italian Jackal, hunting up rare books, and vellum bound unreadabilities in all the second hand bookstalls of London'.[10] On 23 October, after a fortnight's concentrated study, George Eliot announced to Mrs Congreve 'I am in the happiest, most contented mood . . . I have hardly any trouble nearer to me than the American [Civil] War and the prospects of our poor cotton weavers'.[11] To express things thus boldly was clearly tempting fate; the very next day, a nagging sore throat developed into 'a severe catarrh' and she took to her bed.

[10] Ibid. iii. 457.   [11] Ibid. iii. 460.

Her journal entry for 28–30 October reads simply 'Not very well. Utterly desponding about my book'; and on 31 October: 'Still bilious with an incapable head—trying to write, trying to construct, and unable'. The early part of November saw little improvement, though she kept up her reading—in works as diverse as Cicero's *De Officiis* (see p. 591), Petrarch's *Rerum Familiarium* (see pp. 51 and 54), and Monteil's *Histoire des Français des divers états*, which she described as 'a marvellous book: crammed with erudition, yet not dull or tiresome'. On 5 November she 'Walked with G. into town, and looked at old books. *Dreadfully depressed about myself and my work*'; and the following day 'So utterly dejected that in walking with G. in the Park, I almost resolved to give up my Italian novel'. Mercurial as ever, on 10 November she was able to record 'New sense of things to be done in my novel, and more brightness in my thoughts. Yesterday, I was occupied with ideas about my next English novel; but this morning the Italian scenes returned upon me with fresh attraction'. The next day she went to see Charles Fechter in *Othello*, which she thought 'lamentably bad . . . it seems to move only titters among the smart and vulgar people who always make up the bulk of a theatre audience'.[12] On 14 November she paid her first visit to the reading room of the British Museum (she had previously used only the London Library, and had written to Joseph Munt Langford, Blackwood's London agent, that 'unhappily, with my temperament I fear it would be next to impossible for me to go to the British Museum').[13] She does not say what she read there, but the following day she awoke with a headache which lasted until the 19th.

For the next few weeks she worked at home, but her reading ranged ever more widely: Juvenal's *Satires*, the *Encheiridion* of Epictetus, Filelfo's letters, and Luigi Pulci's comic epic *Il morgante maggiore* (all of which are quoted in the novel); Benedetto Varchi's sixteenth-century *Storia fiorentina*, an important source from which she made extensive notes; W. A. Becker's popular novel of ancient Greek life *Charikles* (see p. 640); the life of Marullus in Humphrey Hody's *De Graecis Illustribus*; and Savonarola's *Compendium Revelationum* and *De Veritate Prophetica*, which she bought from a second-hand bookshop for £4. Throughout, her health remained frail, and her morale correspondingly low. On 6 December she wrote to Sara Hennell 'I am particularly grumbling, and disagreeable to myself, just now . . . I think no one bears physical pain so ill as I do, or is so thoroughly upset by it mentally'.[14] A few days later she sketched out a revised plot, but added cautiously 'I must make several other draughts before I begin to write'. It was now fully five months since

---

[12] *Letters*, iii. 467.   [13] Ibid. iii. 393–4.   [14] Ibid. iii. 468.

they had returned from Italy, and Lewes's impatience at her failure to start writing was becoming acute. On 14 December he wrote to John Blackwood, who was planning a visit to London:

Polly is still deep in her researches. Your presence will I hope act like a stimulus to her to make her begin. At present she remains immovable in the conviction that she *can't* write the romance because she has not knowledge enough. Now as a matter of fact I know that she has immensely more knowledge of the particular period than any writer who has touched it; but her distressing diffidence paralyses her.

This between ourselves. When you see her, mind your care is to discountenance the idea of a Romance being the product of an Encyclopaedia.[15]

When Blackwood called at Blandford Square, he found that Lewes's account was no exaggeration. Five years later George Eliot herself recalled 'I took unspeakable pains in preparing to write Romola—neglecting nothing I could find that would help me to what I may call the "Idiom" of Florence, in the largest sense one could stretch the word to'.[16] The pains she took to establish this idiom—to construct an unimpeachably authentic historical backdrop to her story—were remarkable. As Blackwood reported in December 1861, she studied her subject 'as subject never was studied before'.[17]

As she studied her sources, George Eliot made copious notes. Five of her surviving notebooks contain material relevant to *Romola*, though only two of them are devoted exclusively to it and it is impossible to determine the precise sequence, if any, in which they were compiled. Perhaps the most important is the one she titled 'Quarry for Romola' (now in the Parrish Collection at the Princeton University Library: AM 14959). Its 106 folios are filled with all manner of information on the social and political history of the period. In no particular order, there are notes from Nardi, Cambi, and Varchi; from Nerli, Litta, and Ammirato; from Burlamacchi, Marchese, and Villari; from Lastri and Muratori, Guingémé and Laborde. There are notes, for example, on the credence given to prophetic powers, on the portents which preceded the death of Lorenzo the Magnificent, on Charles VIII's arrival in Florence, and on the ceremonial procession of the Madonna dell'Impruneta. There are notes on the topography of fifteenth-century Florence, on its customs and costumes, prices and incomes, famines and funerals, state officials, religious societies, and sumptuary laws. There are lists, with dates, of prominent politicians, scholars, artists, and poets. There is an eight-page chronology of Savonarola's life from 1494 to 1498, and a 138-item alphabetized subject-index to Lastri's *Osservatore fiorentino*.

---

[15] Ibid. iii. 473–4.   [16] Ibid. iv. 301.   [17] Ibid. iii. 474.

The other notebook given over entirely to *Romola* is now in the British Library (Add. MSS 40768); it is labelled 'Florentine Notes'. Its 55 folios are similarly crammed with a host of details from a variety of sources. There are notes on early Florentine printers, on the city's wool-trade, taverns and churches, fairs and prisons, on the Ferravecchi and Compagnacci, on usury, the invention of spectacles, and the culture of the mulberry tree. There are notes on scholars such as Filelfo, Platina, and Guarino, and several pages on the barber-poet Burchiello, with quotations from his works. There is a chronology of Florentine history from 1076 to 1498 and another of Savonarola's life, this time from 1492 to 1495. There are lists of Italian Christian names and their diminutives (among them Tessa, Brigida, Nofrio, and Ghita), of the relative value of Florentine coins, and of the titles of the seventy-five 'dissertations' which make up Muratori's *Antichità italiane*. There is a note that the expression 'la vacca muglia' was used of the sounding of the great bell of the Palazzo Vecchio. There is a table of fifteenth-century Florentine weights and measures with their modern equivalents (specifying, for example, that a *barile* of wine contained 12 gallons but one of oil only 8). By and large, there are rather fewer passages copied out from contemporary historians than in the Princeton 'Quarry', and rather more biographical references and *aides-mémoires*. Among these last, in a list headed 'Mountains round Florence', is the name 'Romola'.

The notebook, at the Beinecke Library at Yale, published under the title *George Eliot: A Writer's Notebook 1854–1879*, ed. Joseph Wiesenfarth (1981) contains a good deal of material (on 75 or so of its 311 folios) relevant to *Romola*—as well as to *Felix Holt*, *The Spanish Gypsy*, *Middlemarch*, and *Daniel Deronda*. It includes, in particular, copious notes 'from Paris's *Pharmacologia*, Rock's *Hierurgia*, King's *Antique Gems*, Hélyot's *Histoire des ordres religieux*, and Mrs Jameson's *Sacred and Legendary Art*. The notebook now in the Bodleian Library at Oxford (MS Don. g. 8) has some 60 folios of *Romola* material, the balance mostly comprising preparatory notes for *The Spanish Gypsy*. Much of it takes the form of quotations from classical and Italian authors: from Hesiod, Horace, Ovid, Quintilian, Martial, Juvenal, Tacitus, and Pliny; from Dante, Boccaccio, Pulci, Sacchetti, Firenzuola, Filelfo, Pontanus, Panhormita, Poliziano, Machiavelli, Buondelmonte, and Savonarola. Finally, there is the notebook published as volume ii of *Some George Eliot Notebooks: An Edition of the Carl H. Pforzheimer Library's George Eliot Holograph Notebooks*, ed. William Baker (1984); the first 35 of its 110 folios contain further quotations from classical and contemporary Italian authors, a good proportion of which are used in the novel. Both this and the Bodleian notebook also include lists of Italian proverbs and sayings.

Amidst all this accumulation and storage of information, the authors on whom she drew most heavily for the novel were Villari and Lastri. Pasquale Villari's *Storia di Fra Girolamo Savonarola e de' suoi tempi* was by some way the most complete and authoritative account then available, far surpassing those of Rastrelli (1781), Barsanti (1782), Rudelbach (1835), Meier (1836), Perrens (1854), and Madden (1855). It was based on exhaustive archival research, and quoted extensively from contemporary manuscript sources—notably those of Parenti, Cerretani, Cinozzi, Violi, and Fra Benedetto. As such it represented something of a compendium of primary historical sources for George Eliot: a recapitulation, with important additions, of her own reading of the major chroniclers of the period: Villani, Varchi, Nerli, Nardi, and so on. Moreover, Villari's attitude to Savonarola himself was broadly in sympathy with her own. Though less inclined to criticize than George Eliot, even implicitly, he saw the Frate as a heroic figure whose pursuit of high moral ideals was compromised by a narrow insistence upon supernatural visions; whose religious mysticism proved his undoing in a world which, 'in the unrest of a new growth',[18] was increasingly inimical to the concept of divine intervention in human affairs. In his account, therefore, both of Savonarola and his times, Villari proved a ready source for George Eliot; her own copy of his book is heavily marked and underlined throughout.

Marco Lastri's colourfully encyclopaedic *Osservatore fiorentino* is made up of several hundred articles, each mostly comprising extracts from a wide range of earlier writers, on the history and associations of particular streets, buildings, and monuments in Florence from the middle ages to the seventeenth century. George Eliot had acquired a copy of the revised edition (16 vols., 1831) on her second visit to Florence. Her dependence on it for all manner of socio-historical details is signalled by her thematic index to it in the Princeton 'Quarry'; the following are just some of the entries which found their way into the novel in one form or another: Arte di Calimara, Baptisms, Bargello, Buonuomini di San Martino, Calcio, Corso di Barberi, Giostre, Laudi, Lingua di Mercato, Monte, Nozze, Loggia di Orcagna, Orsanmichele, Osteria delle Bertucce, Pinzochera, Standards, Stinche, Umiliati, Via del Garbo, Zecca. Of the many sources she consulted about the customs and traditions of Florentine life, it was the compendious Lastri to whom she turned most often.

---

[18] The phrase is from the proem to *Romola*: '. . . that human conscience which, in the unrest of a new growth, was filling the air with strange prophecies and presentiments' (p. 8). Compare the following passage from Villari—also describing the intellectual climate of the period: 'un presentimento di strani casi, di grandi mutamenti . . . era comune a tutti gli uomini, ma più specialmente agl'Italiani'.

Her use of such sources in the novel was sometimes on a simple word-for-word basis. The description in chapter 14 of the votive wax images in the Santissima Annunziata talks of 'famous condottieri with plumed morion seated on their chargers' (p. 147); the phrase is borrowed from the *Osservatore*: 'Condottieri, Soldati, e gente d'arme la piu famosa . . . su destrieri, armata con morioni'. The distinctive phrase used of the Fierucoloni, 'with their paper lanterns, howling their hymns to the Virgin' (p. 135) is taken from one of Passerini's notes to Ademollo's novel *Marietta de' Ricci* ('cantare rozzamente le laudi della Vergina al lume di fanali di certa') which is itself very probably derived from Lastri ('Cantan Inni alla Vergine nel loro rozzo volgare'). Tito's account to Bardo of the dangers of scholars visiting Ottoman Athens—'it was impossible for us to venture near the Acropolis, for the sight of men eager in examining "old stones" raised the suspicion that we were Venetian spies' (p. 67)—is plainly drawn from Léon de Laborde's history of the city: 'Quant aux archéologues, s'ils eûssent existé, ils auraient été malvenus à Athènes, on les eût traités comme des espions vénitiens, nul alors n'eût compris qu'un homme de sens se détournât de la route suivie pour venir voir ce qui était déjà pour les Turcs, et ce qu'ils n'ont cessé d'appeler de *vieilles pierres*.'

More often, one can trace a piece of historical commentary in the novel back to a source which, though not quoted directly, is clearly the origin of the passage. Take, for example, the description in chapter 20 of the mayhem in the city at Carnival-time:

For the boys and striplings, always a strong element in Florentine crowds, became at the height of Carnival-time as loud and unmanageable as tree-crickets, and it was their immemorial privilege to bar the way with poles to all passengers, until a tribute had been paid towards furnishing those lovers of strong sensations with suppers and bonfires: to conclude with the standing entertainment of stone-throwing, which was not entirely monotonous, since the consequent maiming was various, and it was not always a single person who was killed.

Compare this with Villari's account of the proceedings:

E, come è ben naturale, quelli che più affezione avevano per quelle feste, erano i fanciulli. In quei giorni, essi usavano di fermare continuamente la gente per via, chiudendo loro il cammino con certi lunghi pali, che non venivano rimossi, se prima essi non avevano ricevuta qualque moneta, per far, poi, la sera i loro pazzi desinari. Dopo de' quali, accendavano grandi fuochi nelle piazze, vi ballavano e cantavano intorno; e finalmente, facevano ai sassi con tanta violenza, che ogni anno più di loro restava morto per le vie.[19]

[19] GE read Villari's biography in Italian (it was not transl. into English until 1863). In the explanatory notes to this edn., for convenience, I quote the work in Linda Villari's authoritative transl. of 1888, which renders the above passage as follows: 'And,

A passing reference in Varchi's *Storia fiorentina* to the fact that gentlemen rarely raised their hats to others affords her an equally passing
opportunity to illustrate Tito's ingratiating manner (see p. 137). On
the larger scale, Tito's dramatic arrival on horseback, olive-branch in
hand, with the news that French galleys had landed safely at Leghorn
(pp. 383–4), follows exactly the original account of the scene in
Nardi's *Istorie della città di Fiorenza*—except, of course, that Nardi
conveniently fails to mention the name of the actual messenger.
Anonymous to history, but historically verifiable, the bringer of the
momentous news is fair game for appropriation by a novelist who
would no more invent a public scene for one of her fictional characters to take prominent part in than she would invent a minor character when a real one could usefully be pressed into service (when we
gather that Mariotto, the 'merry-eyed youth of seventeen', who
appears for all of 10 lines in chapter 14, is an artist, and we find in
the Princeton 'Quarry' a jotting to the effect that the Florentine
painter Mariotto Albertinelli was aged 17 in 1492, the conclusion is
inescapable). As the explanatory notes to this edition will further indicate, there are very few such historical details in *Romola* which cannot
in the end be traced back to George Eliot's voluminous preparatory
reading.

COMPOSITION

As 1861 drew to a close, the encyclopaedic research which so frustrated Lewes showed no sign of abating. Even on Christmas Eve we
find George Eliot out book-hunting, and coming home with prized
copies of Lippi's *Malmantile* and Ammirato's *Delle famiglie nobili
fiorentine*. On Christmas Day, as she records appreciatively in her
journal, there was turkey and plum pudding; on 26 December she
turned her attention to Luigi Pulci's *Novella dello sciocco senese* (see
p. 346) and the Carnival songs of Lorenzo de' Medici (see p. 600).
Then, almost out of the blue, but with exquisite timing, on New
Year's Day 1862 she announced '*I began my novel of Romola*'. This
was the first occasion on which she had referred to the book by name,
and this time it was no false start.

During the first three weeks of January she worked on the Proem
and first chapter—and complained almost incessantly of 'dreadful

as was only natural, the boys of Florence took special delight in these revels. They
were accustomed, during those days, to continually stop people in the streets by barring the road with long poles, and refusing to remove them until they had extorted
enough money to pay for their mad feastings by night. After these carousals they made
bonfires in the squares, round which they danced and sang, and finally pelted one
another with stones in so brutal a fashion that no year passed without some of the
combatants being left dead on the ground.'

headaches' and 'terrible depression'. Then on the 23rd she noted that 'Mr. Smith the publisher called and had an interview with G. He asked if I were open to "a magnificent offer"'. Lewes had known George Smith for twenty years and had been invited by him to contribute to the *Cornhill Magazine* when it was founded in 1860. His Darwinian essays 'Studies in Animal Life', however, were discontinued after only six numbers. The apparent reason for Smith's interview with Lewes was to suggest the publication in the *Cornhill* of a further series of zoological essays, which Lewes declined, and to discuss the publication in book form of the earlier series, to which Lewes was obliged to agree according to the terms of his original contract. Smith, though, clearly had larger game in his sights. He had launched the *Cornhill* with the serialization of Trollope's *Framley Parsonage*, which had been extremely successful throughout its run (concluding in April 1861) and had helped raise the monthly circulation to 100,000 copies. Its successor, Thackeray's *The Adventures of Philip* (January 1861–August 1862), was proving a good deal less popular, and Smith was eager to secure the services of a new star to revive the fortunes of his magazine. Dickens, of course, was committed to his own magazine *All the Year Round*, which in January 1862 was scaling new heights of success with Bulwer Lytton's *A Strange Story* (which had itself followed *Great Expectations* and *The Woman in White*). Smith plainly required a major catch to increase his circulation; hence, presumably, the 'magnificent offer' to George Eliot. Precisely what response he got on this visit we do not know, but it was sufficiently encouraging for him to return a month later and propose actual terms.

Meanwhile George Eliot continued her work. On 24 and 25 January she went to the British Museum, where she made notes from the fifteenth-century chronicler Giovanni Cambi (see p. 239) and copied out Antonio Pucci's poem 'La proprietà di mercato vecchio' (see p. 13). Next came two comic dramas of the period: Machiavelli's *La mandragola* (a 'second reading for the sake of Florentine expressions') and Bernardo Dovizi's *La calandria*. On 26 January she reported in her journal that she had been 'detained from writing by the necessity of gathering particulars: 1st about Lorenzo de' Medici's death; 2nd about the possible retardation of Easter; 3rd about Corpus Christi day; 4th about Savonarola's preaching in the Quaresima of 1492'. That she found information about the said particulars is clear from the text of the novel; that she derived small cheer from doing so is evidenced by her journal entry for 31 January:

This evening I have been reading to G. some entries in my note-book of past times in which I recorded my *malaise* and despair. But it is impossible to me to believe that I have ever been in so unpromising and despairing a state as I now feel.—After writing these words, I read to G. the Proem and opening scene of my novel and he expressed great delight in them.

Lewes's delight did little to inspirit her, and throughout the following week she was 'very ill with headache and sickness'.

On 11 February Lewes took her off to Dorking, a favourite bolt-hole in times of stress. They spent only two days there, but both felt revived by the country air; George Eliot also managed to make her way through Heinrich von Sybel's history of the Crusades. By 17 February she had completed chapter 2; on the 19th, despite appalling weather, she ventured out to the British Museum, where she made notes from Domenico Manni's Life of Bartolommeo Scala (see chapter 7) and Vincenzo Borghini's historical Discorsi (1584)—'about the simplicity of the Florentine table equipage' (see p. 127). During the course of the next week she managed only a further 15 manuscript pages, i.e. to the mid-point of chapter 3. Her journal entry for 26 February tells an all too familiar story:

I have been very ailing all this last week and have worked under impeding discouragement. I have a distrust in myself, in my work, in others' loving acceptance of it which robs my otherwise happy life of all joy. I ask my self, without being able to answer, whether I have ever before felt so chilled and oppressed . . . I have written now about 60 pages of my romance. Will it ever be finished?—ever be worth anything?

The next day George Smith called again, bringing with him the proofs of Lewes's *Studies in Animal Life*, as well as a quite remarkable offer to George Eliot. Lewes records the exchange in his journal:

he made a proposal to purchase Polly's new work for £10,000. This of course includes the entire copyright. It is the most magnificent offer ever yet made for a novel; and Polly, as usual was disinclined to accept it, on the ground that her work would not be worth the sum! Moreover she felt it impossible to begin publication in April or May—the period when Smith wishes it to begin to appear in the 'Cornhill Mag.' Unless she sees her book nearly completed and such as she considers worthy of publication she objects to begin printing it. I went down to Smith to tell him of her difficulties. He was much put out, April or May being the months when the Magazine will stand in need of some reinforcement as Thackeray's story is quite insufficient to keep up the sale. Smith then proposed to print her story of *Brother Jacob*,[1] written in 1860, if it can be split up into three numbers, and thus tide over the three months; and then to commence in August or September with the new work.

---

[1] It appears that Smith was here repeating an earlier offer for 'Brother Jacob'. In her journal for 7 Feb. George Eliot reports that he had called 'the other day' and offered her 250 guineas for her 'story of the Idiot Brother' (which Lewes had mentioned to him), but that she had not decided whether or not to accept.

She has consented to let him see the story to see if this arrangement will do.[2] If not some other proposal will be made by him.[3]

By any reckoning it was indeed a magnificent offer: Trollope had received £1,000 for the serial rights to *Framley Parsonage*, Bulwer Lytton £1,500 for *A Strange Story* (with the guarantee of a further £1,200 for publication in book form), and even Thackeray only £2,100 (itself an almost unprecedented sum) for the six-part serial *Lovel the Widower*. One can well imagine that Smith was 'much put out' at its rejection. When he called again on 1 March, Lewes records that

On examining his engagements he finds it impracticable to delay the publication of Polly's new work in the Magazine till August or September. This project is therefore finally abandoned. But he is very anxious to publish her book and we discussed the plan of a sixpenny serial, also of publishing the book at once at 6/. On these points he is to make calculations and then make a new proposal. Although I regret the loss of such an opportunity of £10,000, I am just as well pleased that Polly should not be hurried and flurried, by being bound to appear at an earlier date than she would like.[4]

In her own journal for the same day, George Eliot reports bluntly 'The idea of my novel appearing in the Cornhill is given up, as G. Smith wishes to have it commenced in May, and I cannot consent to begin publication until I have seen nearly to the end of the work'.

The end must have seemed a very long way off when she wrote those words. After six months of concentrated study, and two of desultory composition, she had managed only 60 pages of the novel. March was to prove no more productive. It began auspiciously enough with a relaxing week at the Barley Mow Inn at Englefield Green in Surrey, where she read Luigi Pulci to herself and Dumas père aloud to Lewes. As usual, however, she returned 'to protracted headache and discomfort'. Lewes too was in poor health, which depressed her further. By the 23 March she had done no more than finish chapter 3. On 27 March she wrote to Sara Hennell congratulating her 'on being out of London, which is more like a Pandemonium than usual. The fog and rain have been the more oppressive because I have seen them through Mr Lewes's almost constant discomfort'.[5] In the entire month she managed only 17 manuscript pages. On 2 April she announced that (for the first time) she had been 'writing with enjoyment'. The enjoyment was short-lived. Her next journal entry is not until the 16th, and it comes as no surprise that during the intervening fortnight she had been 'very ailing'. That same day they set off for three weeks recuperation at Dorking, whence they returned on

---

[2] In the event, it would not do. 'Brother Jacob' was published in the *Cornhill Magazine*, but not until July 1864 and then in a single instalment.
[3] *Letters*, iv. 17–18.   [4] Journal: *Letters*, iv. 19–20.   [5] *Letters*, iv. 22–3.

6 May, 'feeling much better and stronger for our furlough from town, and hoping to work well'.

Thackeray, who had never been entirely happy as editor of the *Cornhill*, had finally resigned in March 1862, whereupon Smith offered the position to Lewes. At first Lewes turned him down, but in due course he agreed to act as consulting editor, selecting the articles and suggesting subjects, if Smith would hire a suitable assistant to look after the more mundane matters. George Eliot reports in her journal that when Smith called at Blandford Square on 8 May 'it was agreed that George should assist with his advice in the administration of the Cornhill, at £50 per number'. Having successfully cemented this relationship, Smith turned his attention once more to George Eliot's novel in progress. Lewes apparently favoured the idea of publishing it in weekly parts; Smith plainly still wanted it for the *Cornhill*. At all events, on 12 May Smith came round so that George Eliot could read him extracts (she had by then written a further 70 pages, taking her well into chapter 8) 'in order that before finally making any proposals he should know the kind of work it was to be'.[6] His verdict, not inconveniently for his own designs, was that it 'would not *tell* in small portions',[7] and that the scheme of weekly parts was therefore inappropriate. Instead, he again proposed publication in the *Cornhill*, in sixteen numbers of 24 pages each (a *Cornhill* page generally running to *c*.600 words), for which he repeated his offer of £10,000, though this time asking only for 'a limited right to subsequent publication'.[8] After some reflection, however, George Eliot decided that 'she could not properly divide the book into as many as sixteen parts'. Smith's account of the subsequent exchange reports that

I took exception to this . . . and pointed out that my offer was based on the book being in sixteen parts, and that my calculations were made with regard to the MAGAZINE being able to afford a payment of so much a number. She said that she quite understood that the alteration would make a difference to me, but that she supposed the amount of the difference could easily be calculated. George Lewes and I did all we possibly could to persuade her to

---

[6] GHL journal: *Letters*, iv. 33. Lewes subsequently recorded that 'She read Smith a few chapters before making the arrangement with him, because she naively thought, "he might not like it." He was in raptures' (*Letters*, iv. 37).

[7] GHL journal: *Letters*, iv. 33. Smith's reaction suited Lewes's designs too. Lewes later recalled that his 'main object in persuading her to consent to serial publication, was not the unheard-of magnificence of the offer, but the advantage to such a work of being read slowly and deliberately, instead of being galloped through in three volumes' (*Letters*, viii. 304).

[8] George Smith, 'Our Birth and Parentage', *Cornhill Magazine*, NS 10 (1901), 10. Recording Smith's offer in his journal for 17 May 1862, Lewes refers to 'considerable instalments—of 45 or 40 pages each number', by which he presumably means MS pp.

xxxINTRODUCTION

reconsider her decision, but in vain. We pointed out to her that the publication in the MAGAZINE was ephemeral, and that the work would be published in a separate form afterwards and be judged as a whole. However, nothing could move her, and she preferred receiving £7,000 in place of £10,000 for the book.[9]

A few days later the terms were settled:[10] George Eliot would receive £7,000 for the serialization, beginning in July; in respect of that sum the firm of Smith, Elder & Co. would also, following the appearance of the last part in the *Cornhill*, have a six-year period of exclusivity for the novel in book form, including the disposal of all foreign rights, and a continuing right to reprint it thereafter in a single format to be determined by them. Though substantially less than the initial 'magnificent offer', these terms were still princely: £7,000 was almost twice what she earned from *The Mill on the Floss*, and not much less than she had hitherto made from all her previous novels put together.

The House of Blackwood, under whose imprint all her previous novels had appeared, and which had every reason to assume that it would be offered *Romola*, had always been the most courteous and accommodating of publishers. One imagines that her decision to desert it was not made without sharp feelings of remorse. One assumes, also, that Lewes's influence in the matter was considerable: after all, if he was to edit the *Cornhill* it was in both their interests that she should publish in it. Above all, though, in purely financial terms Smith's was a offer she could not reasonably refuse.[11] On 19 May she broke the news to John Blackwood:

I fear this letter will seem rather abrupt to you but the abruptness is unavoidable.

Some time ago I received an offer for my next novel which I suppose was handsomer than almost any terms ever offered to a writer of Fiction. As long as I hesitated on the subject I contemplated writing to you to ascertain your views as to the arrangement you would be inclined to make for the publica-

[9] George Smith, 'Our Birth and Parentage', *Cornhill Magazine*. That is, she preferred receiving £7,000 for 12 parts of 32 pp. each in place of £10,000 for the book in its originally proposed form of 16 parts of 24 pp. each.

[10] The memorandum of agreement (see *Letters*, viii. 301) was between 'Messrs. Smith Elder & Co.' on the one side and 'Mrs Marian Evans Lewes and George Henry Lewes Esq.' on the other. Smith had left a space between 'Mrs' and 'Lewes' which George Eliot then filled in as above. Gordon Haight suggests, quite reasonably, that this was because he was uncertain precisely how to name her in a formal document. That the contract was with them both, however, does rather imply Smith's estimation of Lewes's importance in the affair.

[11] For an exhaustive account of GE's business dealings with Blackwood, including a suggestion that she was in any case dissatisfied with the sort of terms he was offering to her at this time, see R. F. Anderson, '"Things Wisely Ordered": John Blackwood, George Eliot, and the Publication of *Romola*', *Publishing History*, 11 (1982).

tion of the same work; since I was not willing to exchange my relations with you for any new ones without overpowering reasons. Ultimately I declined the offer (on various grounds) and there was therefore no need to write.

But another offer, removing former objections, has been made, and after further reflection, I felt that, as I was not at liberty to mention the terms to you, and as they were hopelessly beyond your usual estimate of the value of my books to you, there would be an indelicacy in my making an appeal to you before decision. I have consequently accepted the offer, retaining however a power over my copyright at the end of six years so that my new work may then be included in any general edition.

I know quite well from the feeling you have invariably shewn, that if the matter were of more importance to you than it is likely to be, you would enter fully into the views of the case as it concerned my interests as well as your own.[12]

If the abruptness was indeed inevitable under the circumstances, the hint of condescension was less so. Blackwood's reply, dated 20 May, was a masterpiece of forbearance and good nature (in her journal George Eliot referred to it as 'a letter in the most perfect spirit of gentlemanliness and good feeling'):

I am of course sorry that your new Novel is not to come out under the old colours but I am glad to hear that you have made so satisfactory an arrangement.

Hearing of the wild sums that were being offered to writers of much inferior mark to you, I thought it highly probable that offers would be made to you, and I can readily imagine that you are to receive such a price as I could not make remunerative by any machinery that I could resort to.

Rest assured that I feel fully satisfied of the extreme reluctance with which you would decide upon leaving your old friend for any other publisher, however great the pecuniary consideration might be, and it would destroy my pleasure in business if I knew any friend was publishing with me when he thought he could do better for himself by going elsewhere. We have had several most successful enterprises together and much pleasant correspondence and I hope we shall have much more.[13]

Insult followed close upon injury: two days later Blackwood's London Office received from Smith, Elder & Co. copy for an advertisement to be run in the June issue of *Blackwood's Edinburgh Magazine* announcing 'A New Novel by the Author of "Adam Bede"' to commence in the next issue of the *Cornhill*. Langford sent this off to John Blackwood with a covering note that 'in the first flirt of temper I thought you should refuse insertion, but it will certainly be more dignified to insert it. I shall have an opportunity of talking over with you this disgusting transaction, which certainly does not surprise me on her part, but does rather on the part of Mr Smith'.[14] It would seem that Langford, so often the errand-runner for his firm's star

---

[12] *Letters*, iv. 34–5.   [13] Ibid. iv. 35–6.   [14] Ibid. iv. 38 n.

novelist (he would, on request, go out and buy parcels of books for her researches, and even opera tickets for her and Lewes), had accumulated a parcel of resentment over the years. It seems also that he believed in honour among publishers. In his reply Blackwood dropped the tone of sympathetic good will that had characterized his letter to George Eliot, but remained remarkably even tempered:

The conduct of our friends in Blandford Square is certainly not pleasing nor in the long run will they find it wise however great the bribe may have been. It is too bad after all the kindness she has experienced but I am sure she would do it against her inclination. The going over to the enemy without giving me any warning and with a story on which from what they both said I was fully entitled to calculate upon, sticks in my throat but I shall not quarrel—quarrels especially literary ones are vulgar.

In reality I do not care about the defection and it has not disturbed me a bit. From the voracity of Lewes I saw that there would be great difficulty in making the arrangement with them and marchanding or bidding against any one else is a thing I could not stand, so 'let them go'. Besides if the story is the one I suppose, I have no doubt it will be a fine thing but it was doubtful in my mind how far it would bear being given in fragments in the Magazine and certainly it would not suit the readers of the Cornhill. I intended to have decided on the form of publication when I had read the M.S.[15]

That, of course, was to an employee. It was in a subsequent letter to his nephew William that he probably came closest to revealing his true feelings: 'I am sorry for and disappointed in her but with their extortionate views we could not have made an arrangement so all is for the best. She does not know how strongly her desertion and going over to the enemy will tell upon the public estimate of her character and most justly'.[16] On 17 June he called at Blandford Square. Neither George Eliot nor Lewes mentions the visit in their journals, but the interview was recorded by Blackwood in another letter to William:

She said that 'under all the circumstances she had felt that she must accept the enormous offer that had been made—that she could never feel to another publisher as she felt towards me—that pleasure to her was gone in the matter and she did not feel sure now whether she had acted right'—whether she meant this last as towards me or as wisely regarding herself I could not tell. She also said that she 'hoped another time would arise', apparently meaning that she would then show how strong her feeling was. I . . . looked her full in the face and shaking hands said, 'I'm fully satisfied that it must have been a very sharp pang to you' and came away.[17]

As it turned out, his dignity and generosity served him well; all of George Eliot's subsequent major publications were with the House of Blackwood.

[15] *Letters*, iv. 38.   [16] Ibid. iv. 38 n.   [17] Ibid. iv. 44.

However one accounts for George Eliot's decision to accept Smith's offer, one cannot ignore the fact that when she did so she had completed only eight chapters of the novel—enough for just one and a half of the 12 parts specified in the agreement, though the book was due to commence publication within two months. Clearly, the paralysing doubts and delays had to be put behind her. Indeed, it may be that this pressing practical obligation was exactly what she needed. The contract was signed, and public announcements made; now she had to deliver the goods. She was certainly now writing with unprecedented energy: by 31 May she had completed the second part (i.e. to the end of chapter 10), and by 24 June she had added the third (chapters 11–14).

Among her more pleasurable distractions during this period were her discussions and correspondence with Frederic Leighton, whom Smith had retained to illustrate *Romola* at £40 per number.[18] Described by Lewes as 'by far the *best* man to be had in England',[19] Leighton, who had lived and studied in Florence, had in his early work made something of a speciality of Florentine historical subjects with paintings such as *The Plague in Florence* (1851), *The Death of Brunelleschi* (1852), and *Cimabue's Celebrated Madonna is Carried in Procession through the Streets of Florence* (1855, a canvas purchased by Queen Victoria for 600 guineas). On 20 May, a couple of days before he was to call at Blandford Square to discuss his commission, the Leweses went to the Royal Academy to view his most recent work. Of the half-dozen of his paintings on display the one that especially 'surpassed expectation' for them was on another Florentine historical subject: *Michael Angelo Nursing His Dying Servant*.[20] Immediately after his visit on 22 May he was provided by Smith with a set of proofs of the first part of the novel, and wrote to George Eliot with suggestions for possible illustrations. His letter has not survived, but her reply, dated 26 May, gives a clear indication of the way his thoughts were tending:

Your letter comforts me particularly. I am so glad to think that you find subjects to your mind. I have no especial desire for the view from S. Miniato, and indeed a plan we started in conversation with Mr. Smith this morning, namely, to have moderately sized initial letters—the opening one being an old Florentine in his *Lucco* and generally the subjects being bits of landscape or Florentine building—seems to do away with any reason for having the

---

[18] For a fuller account of Leighton's work on the novel see Hugh Witemeyer, *George Eliot and the Visual Arts* (New Haven, Conn., 1979).

[19] *Letters*, iv. 37.

[20] GHL Journal: *Letters*, iv. 37 n. As it happened, among the other pictures in the same exhibition was Phoebus Levin's *Alexander VI Signing the Death-Warrant of Savonarola*.

landscape to begin with. The idea of having Tessa and the mules, or Nello's sanctum, smiles upon me, so pray feel free to choose the impression that urges itself most strongly.[21]

The plan of having illustrated initial letters was taken up: chapter I and the opening chapter of each subsequent part begins with one, while the old Florentine in his *lucco* was in the event used as a tail-piece to the Proem. As for the alternative subjects for the main illustrations, the artist settled on Tito and Nello in the barber's shop (chapter 3); Tessa and the mules (chapter 2) do not appear. It would seem, however, that Leighton's letter was not restricted to matters of illustration. George Eliot's reply continues: 'Your observation about the "che, che" is just the aid I besought from you. With that exception, I have confined myself, I believe, to such interjections as I find in the writers of the fourteenth and fifteenth centuries, and in them, curiously enough, this exclamation now said to be so constant . . . does not seem to occur.'[22] Leighton was presumably referring to the passage towards the end of chapter 2 (p. 26) which in the *Cornhill* text reads '*Che, che* . . . the fact is . . .'. (In the first edition, following Leighton's intervention, it reads simply 'The fact is . . .'). Plainly, she appreciated the artist's expert contribution in such matters, apprehensive as she was at writing in a colloquial idiom so unfamiliar to herself. Her letter of 26 May concludes 'Pray let me have as many criticisms of that kind as you can. I am more gratified, I think, by your liking these opening chapters than I have yet been by anything in these nervous anxious weeks of decision about publication'.[23]

Leighton's method was to sketch his designs in black and white chalk on grey paper, and then redo them in pen and ink on woodblocks before turning them over to the engravers, Joseph Swain and W. J. Linton. At the beginning of June he sent George Eliot his preliminary chalk sketch for the first illustration for the opening number, 'The Blind Scholar and His Daughter'. Her letter of acknowlegement reveals how closely she scrutinized it, and with what feeling:

I feel for you as well as myself in this inevitable difficulty—nay, impossibility of producing perfect correspondence between my intention and the illustrations.

I think your sketch is charming, considered in itself, and I feel now with regret that if we had seen each other and talked a little together after you had read the proof, the only important discrepancy might have been prevented. It is too late for alterations now. If it had not been, I should have wished Bardo's head to be raised with the chin thrust forward a little—the usual attitude of the blind head, I think—and turned a little towards Romola, 'as if he were looking at her.'[24]

---

[21] *Letters*, iv. 39.   [22] Ibid. iv. 39–40.   [23] Ibid. iv. 40.   [24] See p. 48.

Romola's attitude is perfect, and the composition is altogether such as gives me a very cheering prospect for the future, when we have more time for preparation. Her face and hair, though deliciously beautiful, are not just the thing—how could they be? Do not make yourself uneasy if alteration is impossible, but I meant the hair to fall forward from behind the ears over the neck, and the dress to be without ornament.[25]

Leighton might be forgiven for getting Romola's coiffure slightly wrong, for its precise arrangement is not entirely clear from the text, but he has certainly departed from George Eliot's description of her dress: Romola's gown of 'black rascia, or serge' (p. 48), presumably intended to imply the asceticism of her character, is represented by him as being of a much lighter colour and with considerable ornamentation. It is interesting, though, that George Eliot does not mention the other obvious discrepancy between the drawing and the text. In the novel we are given to understand that the room is dark and gloomy: we are told that 'the sun was not yet high enough to send gleams of brightness through the narrow windows', and that the 'only spot of colour in the room' was generated by the nimbus-like effect of Romola's 'reddish gold' hair (p. 48). In the drawing the lighting is quite different: sunlight streams in from outside to fill the room, while Romola's hair is plainly of a darker hue than her dress. However, it was indeed 'too late for alterations', and the drawing was engraved much as George Eliot had seen it.[26]

The following day Leighton sent her his second sketch for part 1, 'Suppose you let me look at myself'; her response, though no less forthright, was more considered:

Unmitigated delight! Nello is better than my Nello. I see the love and care with which the drawings are done.

After I had sent away my yesterday's note, written in such haste that I was afterwards uncomfortable lest I had misrepresented my feelings, the very considerations you suggest had occurred to me and I had talked them over with Mr. Lewes—namely that the exigencies of your art must forbid perfect correspondence between the text and the illustration; and I came to the conclusion that it was these exigencies which had determined you as to the position of Bardo's head and the fall of Romola's hair. You have given her attitude

---

[25] *Letters*, iv. 40.

[26] In fact the engravers did not reproduce the drawings as closely as either author or artist had expected. Writing to Sara Hennell about the illustrations to the opening number, George Eliot noted that Leighton 'has suffered an artist's agonies at the misrepresentation—(it is almost that) which the engravers have made of these first two drawings', while to Smith she reported 'poor Mr. Leighton's chagrin at the engraver's rendering of Nello', adding that 'Bardo, too, is far less feeble in the original than in the translation' (*Letters*, iv. 49, 48). It seems unlikely, however, that the discrepancy between text and illustration concerning the lighting in Bardo's study results from any alteration introduced by the engraver.

transcendently well, and the attitude is more important than the mere head-dress. I am glad you chose Nello's shop; it makes so good a variety with Bardo and Romola. In a day or two you will have the second part, and I think you will find there a scene for Tessa 'under the Plane Tree.'[27]

The next day, 6 June, she wrote again, to say that the 'Vignettes' (i.e. the tailpiece to the Proem and the illustrated capital at the start of chapter 1 showing Bratti finding Tito asleep under the Loggia de' Cerchi) were 'satisfactory'; to lavish further praise on the 'delicious drawing' of the scene in Nello's shop; and finally to request another meeting—suggesting that 'we shall both benefit by a little talk after you have read the second proof'.[28] At that meeting Leighton evidently ventured further criticisms of the kind she had invited concerning points of historical detail, for on 10 June she wrote to him:

Since I saw you I have confirmed by renewed reference my conclusion that *gamurra* was the equivalent of our *gown*, i.e. the constant outer garb of femininity, varying in length and cut according to rank and age. Perhaps it would have been better to call Tessa's gown a *gamurrina*, the word sometimes used and indicating, I imagine, just that abbreviation of petticoat that active work demands.[29]

(In chapter 2 Monna Ghita is described as wearing a 'green serge gamurra or gown' (p. 25), and Tessa simply a 'green serge mantle' (p. 24).) George Eliot's letter continues:

If you are going to see Ghirlandajo's frescoes—the engravings of them I mean—in the choir of Santa Maria Novella, I wish if you would especially notice if the women in his groups have not that plain piece of opaque drapery over the head which haunts my memory. We were only allowed to see those frescoes once, because of repairs going on; but I am strongly impressed with a belief—which, *au reste*, may be quite false—in the presence of my "white hood" there.[30]

If we are to infer that Leighton had contested the authenticity of the white hood which Tessa wears in chapters 8 and 10 (pp. 92, 103)—though in chapter 2, interestingly, it had been a red one (p. 22)—his doubts were ill-founded. George Eliot's memory of Ghirlandaio's women wearing white hoods was an accurate one; they are prominent in a number of his frescoes in the church of Santa Maria Novella in Florence, most notably in *The Birth of the Virgin* and *The Visitation of the Virgin to St Elizabeth* (in the former of which one of the women is wearing an outer garment which might well be described as a 'green serge gamurra'). She goes on to refer to 'the garb of the luxurious

---

[27] *Letters*, iv. 41. This scene provided the subject for the second illustration to the second part (ch. 10).

[28] Ibid. iv. 42.   [29] Ibid.   [30] Ibid. iv. 43.

classes at that time', noting that 'We have in Varchi[31] a sufficiently fit and clear description of the ordinary male costume of dignified Florentines in my time; but for the corresponding feminine costume the best authority I have seen is the very incomplete one of a certain Ginevra's *trousseau* in the Ricordi of the Rinuccini family of rather an earlier period, but marking even there the rage for embroidery and pearls which grew instead of diminishing'.[32] George Eliot is evidently referring to her description of Monna Brigida's costume in chapter 12, for which her source was the *Ricordi storici di Filippo di Cino Rinuccini dal 1282 al 1460*, which gives details of the trousseau of Ginevra d'Ugolino di Niccolò Martelli, who married Cino di Filippo Rinuccini in Florence in 1461 (see pp. 629 and 663).

On 25 June Lewes took the completed part 3 off to the printers, and on the next day George Eliot began part 4. By 30 June she had finished the scene between Romola and Dino at San Marco (chapter 15). That same day she received 'a delightful generous letter' from Anthony Trollope, who wrote

I have just read the first number of Romola and I cannot refrain from congratulating you . . . The description of Florence,—little bits of Florence down to a close nail, and great facts of Florence up to the very fury of life among those full living nobles,—are wonderful in their energy and in their accuracy. The character of Romola is artistically beautiful, a picture exceeded by none that I know of any girl in any novel. It is the perfection of pen painting,—and you have been nobly aided by your artist. I take it for granted that it is Leighton. The father also of Romola is excellent.[33]

Trollope went on, however, to caution her in terms that must surely have struck a chord, given the nature of some of Lewes's earlier apprehensions:

Do not fire too much over the heads of your readers. You have to write to tens of thousands, and not to single thousands. I say this, not because I would have you alter aught of your purpose. That were not worth your while, even though the great numbers were to find your words too hard. But because you may make your full purpose compatible with their taste. I wonder at the toil you must have endured in getting up your work,—wonder and envy.[34]

Excessive 'getting up', of course, was precisely what had alarmed Lewes. There is no evidence, though, that she acted on the advice of either of them. Indeed, when Sara Hennell sent her another appreciative letter about part 1 she replied in terms which suggest that she

---

[31] i.e. in the *Storia fiorentina* (ch. 9).   [32] *Letters*, iv. 43.
[33] Bradford A. Booth (ed.), *The Letters of Anthony Trollope* (Oxford, 1951), p. 174.
[34] Ibid. 174–5.

had deliberately decided to reject any such advice as inappropriate to
the artistic design of the book:

Of necessity, the book is addressed to fewer readers than my previous works,
and I myself have never expected—I might rather say *intended*—that the book
should be as "popular" in the same sense as the others. If one is to have freedom to write out one's own varying unfolding self, and not be a machine
always grinding out the same material or spinning the same sort of web, one
cannot always write for the same public. I forewarned the proprietor of the
Cornhill on that point, read a large portion to him, and made him fully aware
what the book was to be—but he is confident and happy—so I am acquitted
of all scruple or anxiety except the grand anxiety of doing my work worthily.
Alas, I want to do something very much better than I ever *can* do it—if fasting and scourging oneself would make one a fit organ, there would be more
positive comfort.[35]

In the event there was little immediate comfort: on 6 July she
recorded in her journal that 'The past week has been unfruitful from
various causes . . . I am no further in my MSS. and have lost the
excellent start my early completion of the 3rd part had given me'.
The situation deteriorated, and on 10 July she noted that 'A dreadful
palsy has beset me for the last few days—I have scarcely made any
progress'. As usual, when she felt unable to write the novel she 'got
up' more for it, in this instance reading Christoph Meiners's lives of
Poliziano and Pico della Mirandola, commenting 'They have German
industry and are succinctly and clearly written'. The following day
she completed the first half of chapter 16. On 17 June Lewes set out
for a fortnight in Belgium, to take the waters at Spa; later that day
she dropped a line to Smith announcing that 'The two chapters [i.e.
15 and 16] from which I wish the illustrations for Part IV to be taken
might now be put in type for Mr Leighton, if you would be kind
enough to send for the MS.'[36] By the 21st she had added chapter 17,
and by the 31st chapters 18–20, bringing her to the end of part 4.
    On 6 August she noted in her journal that 'Having had a new
scene to insert in Part IV, and not having been well, I have not yet
begun Part V'. Circumstantial evidence of repagination in the manuscript suggests that the scene in question was probably Tito's unexpected encounter with Tessa on his way to his betrothal ceremony
(chapter 20, pp. 197–200); indeed, her alteration in the manuscript of
the title of this chapter—from 'The Hiding of the Crucifix' to 'The
Betrothal' and then to 'The Day of the Betrothal'—may well reflect
the new balance of narrative priorities in the chapter brought about
by the added scene. When she did finally start work on part 5 (chapters 21–6) she wrote quite rapidly, completing it on 2 September. On

[35] *Letters*, iv. 49.   [36] Ibid. iv. 50.

4 September she set out with Lewes for a stay in the country—first by the sea at Littlehampton, and then for a few days at Dorking again—where instead of 'fuming in imperfect resignation under London smoke' there was 'the wide sky of the coast above me and every comfort positive and negative around me, even to the absence of staring eyes and crinolines'.[37] In the quiet and comfort of the Beach Hotel at Littlehampton, Lewes wrote to his son Charles, 'all is so peaceful that [she] drinks in enjoyment, and scribbles away in perpetual thanksgiving'.[38] The scribbling was productive; by the time they returned to London, on 23 September, she was half-way through chapter 30.

While at Littlehampton, on 10 September, she heard again from Leighton, with whom she kept in close contact—often apprising him of likely subjects for illustration in advance of actually writing the scene concerned. On this occasion he asked for guidance about the representation of Niccolò Caparra in part 5 ('Niccolò at Work') and of Piero di Cosimo in part 6 ('The Painted Record') and then went on to raise the issue of how Romola should be portrayed. Following George Eliot's criticism of her portrayal in part 1, Leighton's next attempt ('The First Kiss', in part 3) had been rather different: in a simpler gown, and wearing neither necklace nor head-dress, Romola there is less 'pretty' (see below) almost to the point of being plain, and one infers from George Eliot's reply to Leighton on 20 September that this revised image had come no closer to realizing her own conception of the heroine's appearance than had the original:

If you feel any doubt about the *new* Romola, I think it will be better for you to keep to the original representation, the type given in the first illustration, which some accomplished people told me they thought very charming. It will be much better to continue what is intrinsically pretty than to fail in an effort after something indistinctly seen . . . I am quite convinced that illustrations can only form a sort of overture to the text. The artist who uses the pencil must otherwise be tormented to misery by the deficiencies or requirements of the one who uses the pen, and the writer, on the other hand, must die of impossible expectations.[39]

One presumes that the '*new* Romola' under discussion here was the figure who appears in 'Coming Home' (the second illustration to part 6), though as things turned out that figure resembled the Romola of 'The First Kiss' rather more closely than her 'original representation' in 'The Blind Scholar and His Daughter'. Leighton's letter had concluded with yet another query concerning Italian usage, to which George Eliot responded with customary respect: 'I am very much obliged to you for your critical doubts. I will put out the questionable

---

[37] Ibid. iv. 57.   [38] Ibid. iv. 54.   [39] Ibid. iv. 55–6.

"Ecco!" in deference to your knowledge. I have a tremulous sense of my liability to error in such things'.[40] Questionable the usage may have been, but there is no evidence of her removing any of the several instances of the exclamation 'Ecco!' that occur in the text—either from the manuscript or in subsequent proof revisions.

Back in London, on 25 September, she received a letter from T. A. Trollope 'full of encouragement for me. *Ebenezer!*' By the end of the month she had reached the half-way point of chapter 31; her journal entry for 30 September reads 'not yet at the end of my December part. After three days of fog and rain, a clear sky. We walked towards Hamsptead, but were overtaken by rain. Read Savonarola on Amos'. She finished part 6 on 3 October and immediately started planning part 7 (chapters 33–7). To begin with, things went well, and between 6 and 12 October she managed two of the part's five chapters. Chapter 35, though brief, took the whole of the next week; on 22 October she confided 'My work would make me very happy if there were not always the presence of something that *might* be done to make me dissatisfied with what is, or is likely to be, done'.[41] On the 25th she held a dinner party, and the following day reported 'An unfruitful morning, consequent on the excitements of the evening'. She finished part 7 on 31 October. Part 8 (chapters 38–41) was to take the whole of the next month, during which she also spent a good deal of time reading—in the *Decameron* and the poetical works of Poliziano (including *Orfeo*, from which Tito quotes in chapter 39: p. 354). On 18 November she had reached the point toward the end of chapter 39 where Baldassarre is tested with the edition of Homer, and by the 25th she had added chapter 40. That same day she wrote to Leighton about his preliminary drawings for the illustrations to part 7, declaring herself 'enchanted' and 'purely delighted',[42] both with the solitary figure of Romola in 'Escaped' and with Tessa showing her baby to Baldassarre in 'You didn't think it was so pretty did you?'

She completed part 8 on 30 November. Part 9 (chapters 42–6) was to take still longer: a full five weeks, during which her health and spirits declined still further. Her journal for the first half of December reports a succession of headaches; on 17 December, while struggling with chapter 43, she noted 'I am extremely spiritless—dead, and hopeless about my writing. The long spate of headache and disordered liver has left me in depression and incapacity. The constantly heavy, clouded and often wet weather, tends to increase the depression. I am inwardly irritable and unvisited by good thoughts'. Feeling unable to write, she took up Dante and Savonarola again, prompting Lewes to remark to a friend that 'Marian lives entirely in the fifteenth cen-

---

[40] *Letters*, iv. 56.   [41] Ibid. iv. 62.   [42] Ibid. iv. 63.

tury'.[43] Her journal entry for 19 and 20 December reads bleakly 'Wretched hemicrania beset me again and prevented me from working', with the result that by 22 December she was barely half-way through chapter 44. On Christmas Eve they went to hear *Messiah* at Her Majesty's Theatre, which she enjoyed 'greatly in spite of a rather unsatisfactory performance—no organ and an ill-trained chorus', and about which she wrote to Sara Hennell 'What pitiable people those are who feel no poetry in Christianity! Surely the acme of poetry hitherto is the conception of the suffering Messiah—and the final triumph, "He shall reign for ever and for ever." '[44] She finished part 9, which she thought 'the dullest that has yet come', on 4 January 1863; that evening she read it aloud to Lewes, thereby provoking 'a dreadful headache, which lasted nearly all the next day'. It was at this juncture that she realized she could not after all complete the book in the 12 parts she had earlier insisted on limiting it to. With Smith's agreement, but no suggestion of increasing her fee, she decided to extend it to 14 parts. (In fact, as printed in the *Cornhill*, the novel runs to 436 pages—some 13 per cent more than originally contracted for.)

On 6 January she started to plan part 10 (chapters 47–51). On the 7th they went to a performance of Handel's *Judas Maccabaeus* at the Exeter Hall to hear the celebrated tenor Sims Reeves. The following evening Lewes met Arthur Helps at a dinner party and came home with 'the encouraging word that he highly enjoys Romola, and thinks it the finest thing I have done'. Suitably encouraged, she began work on part 10 but initially made little progress. On 22 January Browning and Anthony Trollope came to dinner. The next morning, 'Feeling very poorly', she escaped once more to Dorking, where her spirits immediately revived. When she returned to London on 26 January she noted that she had only 'about 25 pages' of part 10 still to write. On the 30th, however, she reported that 'Having referred a portion of what I have written I am thrown back a little in my Part.' The portion concerned was probably chapter 51 ('Monna Brigida's Conversion'), which it seems she originally intended to follow on directly from 'The Pyramid of Vanities' (chapter 49). Indeed if, as she records in her journal, on 2 February she was still working on chapter 50, then what became chapter 51 must surely have already been written by that date, since the entire part was completed by 4 February.

On 2 February she had replied to another letter of praise from Sara Hennell:

I have had a great deal of pretty encouragement from immense big-wigs— some of them saying 'Romola' is the finest book they ever read; but the

---

[43] Ibid. viii. 308.   [44] Ibid. iv. 71.

opinion of big-wigs has one sort of value, and the fellow-feeling of a long-known friend has another. One can't do quite well without both.—*En revanche*, I am a feeble wretch, with eyes that threaten to get blood-shot on the slightest provocation. We made a rush to Dorking for a day or two, and the quiet and fresh air seemed to make a new creature of me; but when we get back to town, town-sensations return.[45]

That very day she had heard from Smith that the painter Millais had reported 'that at a party at Lady de Grey's she said [*Romola*] was the finest book she had ever read: the expression of opinion passed round the company and it was unanimous in the same sense. Ebenezer!' As usual, however, the encouragement of others failed conspicuously to alleviate the pains of composition. Part 11 (chapters 52–6) took the whole of February, a month again marked by persistent ill health. Between 6 and 23 February there are nine entries in her journal; seven of them complain of headaches, frailty, vomiting, 'malaise', or 'uneasy incapacitating sensations'. In between there were further visits from Browning and Herbert Spencer among others, a visit to the National Gallery, a drive to Wimbledon to see the Congreves, walks with Lewes to the zoo and Hampstead Heath, a trip to the bank 'to receive a dividend', some proof correction, a little reading, and a good deal of letter-writing. On 24 February they went to Dorking for a week; the day of their return, 3 March, she recorded 'I had a headache as usual as my introduction to town life. Finished Part XI.'

On 16 March she completed the second of part 12's five chapters, but confessed herself 'Wretchedly oppressed and ailing—feeling as if I should never get my work done so as to satisfy me'. Another week at Dorking revived her somewhat, and while there she added chapters 59 and 60. She returned, however, to a 'violent sick headache', and for several days thereafter she was 'in incessant malaise from indigestion producing Hemicrania'. She finally completed part 12 on 5 April. The end was now almost in sight, but composition proved harder than ever. Part 13 (chapters 62–7) took her almost six weeks, despite a further therapeutic break at Dorking, this time for a whole fortnight. On 6 May she noted in her journal 'I am backward with my July number', and on 12 May she wrote to Barbara Bodichon, who was planning a visit, 'I have been a mere wretch for several months past. You will come to me like the morning sunlight, and make me a little less of a flaccid cabbage plant'.[46] It was with reference to this period that J. W. Cross famously recalled

I remember my wife telling me . . . how cruelly she had suffered at Dorking from working under a leaden weight at this time. The writing of 'Romola' ploughed into her more than any of her other books. She told me she could

---

[45] *Letters*, iv. 75.   [46] Ibid. iv. 84.

put her finger on it as marking a well-defined transition in her life. In her own words, 'I began it a young woman,—I finished it an old woman.'[47]

On 10 May she began 'The Trial by Fire' (chapter 65). On 16 May she 'Killed Tito in great excitement!', thus finishing part 13; in the afternoon she and Lewes looked over a new house, the Priory, by the side of the Regent's Canal, which they subsequently bought for £2,000.

George Eliot began the fourteenth and final part of *Romola* on 18 May. By 25 May she had finished chapter 68 ('Romola's Waking'). The day before, a Sunday, they had attended a performance of Beethoven's Mass in C and gone on to hear Cardinal Wiseman's 'wretched Sermon on the Day of Pentecost'. On 1 June she finished chapter 70. On the 6th she wrote in her journal 'We had a little evening party, with music, intended to celebrate the completion of Romola, which however is not absolutely completed, for I have still to alter the Epilogue'. Entirely in character, the final touches had to be postponed for 48 hours: on the 7th she was 'Ill with hemicrania, unable to do anything all day', while the next day found her still afflicted by 'cough and headache'. Finally, on Tuesday 9 June 1863 she 'Put the last stroke to Romola'—and commented, not without justification, 'Ebenezer'.

PUBLICATION

Looking back many years later on *Romola*'s serialization in the *Cornhill* (July 1862–August 1863), George Smith recalled that though it certainly failed to increase the sale of the magazine, he found it 'difficult to say what, if any, effect it had in sustaining the sale'.[1] What evidence we have, circumstantial and somewhat partial though it is, suggests that the effect was minimal. On 12 July 1862, soon after the publication of the first instalment, William Blackwood wrote from Edinburgh to his uncle John in London to report with undisguised glee 'the going down sale of the Cornhill . . . and no fresh stir from Romola'. In an attempt to counter this, he noted, 'The publishers have been writing to all their agents who get copies stating that for every dozen they sell beyond last month's they will get another 5% off! Did you ever hear anything like this. I think they are beginning to tremble for their money. I hope the beasts will be made to pay the piper.'[2] A week later he wrote again, announcing that '*Romola* has not

---

[47] Cross, ii. 352.

[1] 'Our Birth and Parentage' (see 'Composition', n. 8 above), 10.

[2] National Library of Scotland (NLS) MS 4167, fos. 175–6 (quoted in Anderson: see 'Composition', n. 11 above).

raised the sale in the very slightest and that they are going to have a novel by Trollope set agoing at once. I wonder how G.E. will like that!'[3]

Romola was published in book form, in three volumes at one and a half guineas, on 6 July 1863 (i.e. before the appearance of the final part in the *Cornhill*, and just four weeks after George Eliot had finished writing). On hearing of its disappointing subscription, John Blackwood confessed to 'a pious feeling that things are wisely ordered'.[4] Smith himself was to remark laconically that 'As a separate publication it had not, I think, the success it deserved'.[5] Certainly, as compared with her most recent three-decker (*The Mill on the Floss*, which had sold over 6,000 sets in its first two months), its performance was disappointing. Smith, Elder & Co.'s publication ledgers show that 2,288 copies were printed, of which 1,714 were disposed of over the next 12 months. At least some of these were sold in the guise of a second edition, which, remarkably, was announced as 'now ready' in the *Publishers' Circular* for 16 July 1863—a mere ten days after the book's first publication. Whether this tactic was designed to encourage the trade to infer that *Romola* was proving a runaway success, we can only speculate. In fact, the so-called second edition was bound up from the same sheets (and in the same cloth) as the first, except for cancel titles specifying 'SECOND EDITION' in each volume. At best, therefore, it should properly be termed a second *issue*. Though there is no record of how many of the 2,000 or so sets printed were thus designated, the rareness of surviving copies relative to those of the first issue suggests that the proportion was small.[6]

Toward the end of August Lewes noted that *Romola* 'has been flatly received by the general public though it has excited a deep enthusiasm in almost all the élite'.[7] In none more so, surely, than Robert Browning, who, though initially unable to get hold of a copy at Mudie's, wrote to George Eliot at 5 o'clock one morning after reading the first two volumes 'to express my gratitude for the noblest and most heroic prose-poem that I have ever read'.[8] Among others of

---

[3] NLS MS 4167, fo. 183 (quoted in Anderson). Trollope's novel *The Small House at Allington* commenced its publication in the Sept. issue of the *Cornhill*.

[4] NLS MS 4177, fo. 67 (quoted in Anderson).

[5] 'Our Birth and Parentage', 10.

[6] Smith, Elder & Co.'s ledgers indicate that the first printing was of 1,500 copies only; a further 788 were run off on 14 July, and it is likely that some of these constituted the 'Second Edition'. No fewer than 1,300 sets were sold to various libraries, 550 of them to Mudie's alone. After the first year the sale tailed off dramatically; in June 1865 there were still 502 sets of sheets in stock, at least some of which were subsequently bound up in single vols. and sold as remainders at 6s. (see below, 'Descriptive List of Editions', p. lxxv).

[7] *Letters*, iv. 102.   [8] Ibid. 96.

'the élite' (the 'immense big-wigs' about whom George Eliot had written to Sara Hennell) who expressed admiration for the book were Tennyson and Gladstone, F. D. Maurice, Monckton Milnes, Millais, Mazzini, and the Trollope brothers. On receiving a presentation copy, Anthony Trollope wrote to George Eliot 'You will know what I mean when I say that Romola will live after you. It will be given to but very few latter day novels to have any such life. The very gifts which are most sure to secure present success are for the most part antagonistic to permanent vitality'.[9] Trollope's words were carefully chosen: 'present success' was proving decidedly limited, though Lewes's later remark that Romola was greeted 'with a universal howl of discontent'[10] was certainly an exaggeration.

Most of the contemporary reviews, in fact, made much the same point as Trollope. 'It will never be George Eliot's most popular book', wrote R. H. Hutton in the Spectator; 'it seems to us, however, much the greatest she has yet produced'.[11] 'It cannot be denied that "Romola" is less popular than its predecessors', suggested the Westminster Review, 'but we do not hesitate to say that it is the author's greatest work'.[12] 'As a novel', concluded the Athenaeum, '"Romola" cannot be called entertaining . . . but those who do not seek the mere amusement of an exciting story will find noble things in "Romola"—eloquent and beautiful pages—subtle utterances and lovely thoughts'.[13] Three years later, in a review of Felix Holt, the Christian Remembrancer took a similar line: 'It will never be popular like "Adam Bede" . . . but "Romola" adds largely to our sense of the author's powers, and gives weight to her own works'.[14]

In turn, most of the reviews agreed that the main reason why it would not be popular was what the Saturday Review termed its 'instructive antiquarianism', for 'sometimes the antiquarian quite drowns the novelist'.[15] The Westminster Review was quite clear on this point:

[9] Letters of Trollope (see 'Composition', n. 33 above), 200.
[10] Letters, vi. 312.   [11] 36 (18 July 1863), 2267.   [12] 80 (Oct. 1863), 344.
[13] 11 July 1863, p. 46.   [14] 52 (1866), 478–9.
[15] 16 (25 July 1865), 124. At least one notice shared no such qualms. Writing in post-bellum Charlotte, North Carolina, an enthusiastic reviewer in The Land We Love ('A Monthly Magazine devoted to Literature, Military History, and Agriculture') found in GE's evocation of renaissance Italy an inspiring parallel to the proud but shattered civilization of the American South, commenting: 'Possessed of such a connected chain of intellectual trophies; bearing in her bosom the ruins of the mighty monuments of her by-gone power—sad witnesses to a glory overthrown; linked as her history is with the destinies of those nations who most fitly represent the progressive portion of the human race; blessed with a lovely sky and a delicious climate, with enchanting scenery and a picturesque peasantry, no wonder that beautiful Italy should be sought by our great artists in every department in which the efforts of genius take rank, as classic ground and fit scene for muse-inspired labor' (1 (1866), 135).

No care and labour have been spared to give an objective character to the portraiture of ancient Florence, but this care has resulted only in an accumulation of details . . . This historical background, too, somewhat oppresses the human interest of the tale, and in its ultimate impression affects us like a mediaeval painted window, in which the action has to be disentangled from the blaze of colour and overwhelming accessories. To this source may be traced that want of appreciation with which the book has met. The general novel-reader is impatient at such details.[16]

The *Athenaeum* was only slightly less critical in its conclusion:

The amount of reading that the author must have achieved to get up the minute details of time, place, circumstance and costume, down even to the old proverbs, jokes and squibs of the passing moment . . . is marvellous;—a monument of patience and easy walking in heavy fetters, which commands the reader's wonder. But then, the jokes are dried; the appearance of vitality given to politics and pageants long since dead and passed away is remarkable; but neither the politics nor the people are really alive,—they are only well dried, preserved and coloured, and the reader feels as though he were ungrateful, in not being better entertained by all that has cost so much time and labour.[17]

E.-D. Forgues in the *Revue des deux mondes* observed that 'Les moindres détails y sont d'une précision historique et locale qui étonne parfois l'esprit et parfois aussi le fatigue', and argued that too much of the book comprised

broderies savamment et trop minutieusement travaillées, hors d'œuvres d'une recherche excessive, superfluités laborieuses, qu'on peut admirer à froid en les détachant du sujet principal, mais qui très certainement auront dû nuire au succès d'un ouvrage d'ailleurs si bien conçu, si soigneusement et si passionnément exécuté.[18]

The *British Quarterly Review* was still blunter; the distracting minutiae of Florentine history, it insisted, 'have no interest for the general reader, and a very subdued one even for the historical student . . . Let us trust that in her next novel George Eliot will place her scene upon English ground'.[19]

Adverse criticism always affected George Eliot badly, and criticism of *Romola* was no exception. In September 1862 Lewes reported to T. A. Trollope that she was 'in an extra state of the *dumps*' following the visit of a friend (very likely Herbert Spencer) who had expressed appreciation of the novel 'only as an "immense feat"—a racer carrying a hundredweight'.[20] And when, a few weeks later, Sara Hennell wrote mentioning some unfavourable comments she had heard, Lewes conveniently 'lost' the letter before George Eliot could read it, explaining

---

[16] 80, pp. 346–7.   [17] 11 July 1863, p. 46.   [18] 48 (Dec. 1863), 943, 945.
[19] 38 (Oct. 1863) 462, 465.   [20] *Letters*, viii. 305.

that 'With regard to "Romola" she has all along resisted writing it on the ground that no one would be interested in it; but a general sense of its not being possibly popular would not be half so dispiriting to her as the knowledge that any particular reader did not like it'.[21] Two years earlier George Eliot had told François d'Albert-Durade that since newspaper reviews were generally written by incompetents, and were 'utterly indecisive as to the ultimate rank of any book', she made it a rule never to read any 'except such as occur in the "Times"'.[22] If she stuck to these principles in the case of *Romola*, she would at least have seen a representative notice: on 5 September 1863 the *Times* pronounced that 'It is an imperfect work, not likely to be popular, nevertheless it impresses one . . . with a sense of sublime power'.

By September 1865 the three-decker had been remaindered and the one-volume 'Illustrated Edition' was published at 6s. In fact, only four of the original twenty-four Leighton illustrations were reproduced: 'Will his eyes open?' (frontispiece), 'The Dying Message', 'The Visible Madonna', and 'A Dangerous Colleague'. An illustrated title-page was newly commissioned from Leighton (and engraved by Swain), showing a young couple looking over the Arno from the Ponte Vecchio (see Appendix D). Just 1,519 copies were printed, and sales were correspondingly modest: barely 800 in the first year, and a further 350 in the second. (A reprint of 500 copies was set in hand in January 1869, which lasted until 1872.)[23] The stereotype plates cast for this edition were subsequently reused throughout the 1870s to print a 'New Edition', selling at 2s. 6d.—the format selected by Smith, Elder & Co. according to the terms of the original contract. The illustrated title-page was dropped, and only the frontispiece retained; 3,000 copies were printed in June 1869, and a further 2,082 four months later; 3,620 had been sold by the beginning of 1870; 1,000 more were printed in November 1870 and another 2,030 in May 1871. By 1 January 1872 something over 7,000 had been sold; further reprints, of 2,000 each, followed in September 1872, October 1873, and October 1874. Clearly, the 2s. 6d. format was a successful one.[24]

Smith, Elder & Co.'s period of exclusivity had lapsed in August 1869, but it was not until late 1876 that Blackwoods gave serious consideration to issuing the novel themselves, and even then only at the

---

[21] *Letters*, iv. 58.   [22] Ibid. iii. 302.

[23] By way of comparison one might note that Blackwoods' 6s. edn. of *The Mill on the Floss* in one vol. sold *c*.1,700 copies between 1862 and 1873.

[24] It was rather more successful, in fact, than Blackwoods' 3s. 6d. edns. of her other novels during much the same period. For example, *The Mill on the Floss* (published in 1867) had sold 8,500 copies by 1874, *Scenes of Clerical Life* (1868) 5,800, and *Felix Holt* (1869), *c*.6,000.

author's suggestion.[25] In January 1877, following a preliminary inquiry from Lewes, George Eliot wrote to John Blackwood asking 'What are we to do about "Romola"? It ought to range with the cheap [i.e. 'Stereotyped'] edition of my books . . . as well as any handsomer series which the world's affairs may encourage us to publish'.[26] Blackwood agreed, expressing the hope that a 'handsome and uniform' edition of *Romola* at 3s. 6d. would hold its own despite the fact that 'Smith and Elder's 2/6 edition, which I suppose they are entitled to go on with, will doubtless interfere with the sale'.[27] Three weeks later, however (during which period George Eliot unsuccessfully tried to interest Helen Allingham, the wife of the poet William Allingham, in illustrating a cheap edition of *Romola*), Lewes wrote to John Blackwood with a rather different proposal:

I have been 'dallying with faint surmise' of a new and uniform edition of the works of G.E. to begin with Romola . . . Each volume to be six shillings (except Silas—Middlemarch and Deronda)—the type of the present edition would do very well but a larger margin and a new cover, would disguise this. My belief is that the public is always attracted by novelty—be it only that of the binding!—and that six shillings would be just as freely paid as 2/6 by a great many people.[28]

Blackwood immediately saw the business sense of this idea. In his reply he noted that 'there is too little being made out of these admirable books and we must try something to give a semblance of novelty to a complete edition of George Eliot's Works'.[29] He suggested an edition, starting with *Romola*, at 6s. a volume, using larger and better-quality paper than the cheap edition, without illustrations but with engraved vignettes as frontispieces. In the event, what came to be called the 'Cabinet Edition' had no frontispieces,[30] used a rather smaller page size than the Stereotyped edition, and sold for 5s. a volume. Instead of reprinting from existing plates, the volumes were reset in a more generous format. George Eliot herself chose the colour of the binding, a 'rich olive green' which she thought

---

[25] As early as Nov. 1866 GE had pointed out to John Blackwood that 'It may be an item for consideration that "Romola" will be at my disposal at the end of three years from the beginning of last June . . . so that from the beginning of June, 1869, it can be included in the series of my books' (*Letters*, iv. 313). There is evidence that Lewes reread the novel in the summer of 1869, presumably with an eye to a reissue by Blackwoods, though nothing came of it at the time.

[26] *Letters*, vi. 335.   [27] Ibid. vi. 339.   [28] Ibid. vi. 345.
[29] Ibid. vi. 349.

[30] Interestingly, it appears that at an early stage it was planned to reproduce photographs of Florence in the Cabinet edn. of *Romola*. Though this came to nothing, the photographs were duly acquired by Blackwoods (for 4s.) and logged accordingly in the publication ledger.

admirably set off the gold lettering and black foliage decoration.[31]
The result, she felt, was 'handsome—and handy'.[32] The Cabinet
edition of *Romola* was in two volumes, the first published in
December 1877 (though with 1878 on the title-page) and the second
in February 1878; the initial printing was of 1,050 sets. By the middle
of July, 892 copies of volume i had been sold and 810 of volume ii. A
further 630 copies of volume i and 525 of volume ii were run off in
September and October 1878, 525 of each volume in April 1880, and
another 1,050 of each in March 1881.[33]

The plan for a one-volume cheap edition of *Romola* from
Blackwoods resurfaced once the scheme for the Cabinet edition had
been set in train. On 5 November 1877 George Eliot wrote to John
Blackwood that 'If you think it is not inconsistent with prudence or
any wise consideration to print a 3/6 edition of "Romola" under the
existing right of Smith and Elder to continue their 2/6 edition, I shall
like much to see it ranging with our handsome 3/6 volumes'.[34]
Blackwood replied that though Smith's cheap edition would be 'a formidable competitor' (he had earlier expressed the forlorn hope that it
might be withdrawn and its plates transferred to him),[35] he would
indeed go ahead with the 3s. 6d. edition.[36] The 'Stereotyped Edition'
of *Romola* was duly published in August 1878, newly typeset as
volume 6 of 'The Novels of George Eliot'.[37] Except for a striking
(and unsigned) vignette of the Palazzo Vecchio on the series title-
page, it was unillustrated; 2,100 copies were printed, followed by
2,100 more in October. By October 1879, 3,520 had been sold, which
prompted another reprint of 2,100 the following month. Three subsequent reprints added a further 7,875 copies by May 1881.[38]

The last English edition of *Romola* to appear in George Eliot's lifetime was published by Smith, Elder & Co. in October 1880: a lavish
limited edition in two imperial octavo volumes (each of its 1,000 sets
individually numbered) with all of Leighton's *Cornhill* illustrations,

---

[31] *Letters*, vi. 422–3.   [32] Ibid. vi. 435.

[33] The agreement with Blackwoods specified that George Eliot should receive a royalty of 1s. 3d. on each volume sold after the first 2,000; a rough calculation shows that
at the time of her death, therefore, her earnings from the Cabinet edn. of *Romola* were
still negligible, though its sales were slightly above average for the series as a whole.

[34] *Letters*, vi. 414.   [35] Ibid. vi. 411.   [36] Ibid. vi. 422.

[37] *Middlemarch* and *Daniel Deronda* were already selling in separate, one-vol. edns.
at 7s. 6d. each, and were never formally added to the 'Stereotyped Edition', though
they were subsequently issued in bindings uniform with it.

[38] There is no record of the precise royalty she received for this edn. Assuming, however, that it was in line with those negotiated earlier for the other five vols. in the series,
the sum involved was probably substantial. The smallest payment for any of the previous
titles was 27s. 6d. per 100 copies sold (for *The Mill on the Floss*), and the largest (for
Felix Holt) 37s. 6d. Even if the royalty on *Romola* was calculated at the lower rate, she
would have earned from it something in the order of £1,500 by the time of her death.

including the illustrated capitals at the beginning of each part, pasted in by hand. Full-page advertisements in the *Athenaeum* on 25 September and in the *Publishers' Circular* for 1 October 1880 announced that the letterpress was to be printed by the firm of Richard Clay 'on paper of the finest quality, made expressly for the Work by Messrs. John Dickinson & Co.'; that the illustrations were to be on '*real China Paper*'; and that the type would be broken up and distributed after each sheet had been printed. No price was specified, but Smith, Elder & Co.'s ledgers show that the majority of copies were sold to the trade at a discounted price of 73s. 6d., which would suggest a retail price of around five guineas a set. Smith suggested the idea to George Eliot in February 1880, offering her an honorarium of £100. In reply she remarked 'you have already paid me so handsomely for the work and I have so valued a remembrance of the sympathy you gave me in the course of its production, that I would rather not receive more until the complete success of the undertaking has been assured'.[39] Notwithstanding, when he sent her six advance copies on 23 September Smith attached a cheque for £100, commenting 'Now that the work is completed I have no doubt of its success'.[40] His confidence was well placed: the edition sold out in under six months.

THE TEXTS

1. The Manuscript

The autograph manuscript of *Romola* is in the British Library (Add. MSS 34027-9). It is bound in three volumes, of 370, 378, and 316 folios respectively. Volume i comprises the Proem and opening 20 chapters of the·novel (parts 1-4 of the *Cornhill* serialization); volume ii consists of chapters 21-47 (parts 5-9 of the serialization, together with the opening chapter of part 10); volume iii contains chapters 48-72 and the Epilogue. The system of pagination changes as the novel progresses. Following the Proem, which is numbered [I]-XIV in roman caps, the opening fourteen chapters (parts 1-3 of the serial) are paginated in arabic numerals in a single consecutive sequence. At the start of chapter 15 (headed 'Part IV'—the first time George Eliot thus indicates a division in the serial) a new sequence starts from

[39] *Letters*, vii. 247. The day Smith called on her to finalize the arrangements, GE wrote to William Blackwood, with whom she had evidently already broached the scheme, 'You will probably now recall your having concurred in the idea that such an edition would be rather an advantage to the already existing editions, as bringing the work into relief and adding in its advertisement' (*Letters*, vii. 250).

[40] *Letters*, vii. 328 n. Smith's publication ledger for the edn. specifies the sum as 'To Amount paid Mrs J. W. Cross for permission to print 1000 copies'.

p. 1, running through to the end of the volume. In volumes ii and iii each part is independently paginated—except for part 10, whose opening chapter (no. 47, the last in the second volume) runs on with the sequence started for part 9. It may be that she originally intended the chapter to be included in part 9, but that she then decided to carry it over to the next instalment, or was perhaps requested to do so by the publisher on grounds of lack of space in the March 1863 issue; volume iii of the manuscript starts again (with chapter 48) at p. 1, with the instruction 'Cont. of Part X beginning at Ch. 47. *April*'.

The first two volumes and the first 168 folios of volume iii use a dull, creamy-white paper with 24 grey ruled lines to the page; five separate watermarks can be identified, two of them with dates (1860 and 1861), mixed fairly evenly throughout. The balance of the third volume is on a slightly brighter paper, with only 23 grey lines per page, and with a different watermark (bearing the date 1862). All six of the paper stocks are of a uniform size, measuring 225×185 mm. George Eliot wrote in black ink throughout, on one side of the page only. The names of compositors are written in pencil in the margins, but are barely legible. (In the following pages the compositors are referred to collectively as 'the printer'.)[1] The first leaf of volume i bears the inscription 'To the Husband whose perfect Love has been the best source of her insight and strength, this manuscript is given by his devoted Wife, the writer'.

Circumstantial physical evidence (the neatness of the hand, the lack of any alterations, and so on) suggests that up to a fifth of the manuscript is a fair copy; the bulk, however, shows all the signs of being a working draft, and contains plentiful deletions, revisions, and additions (marginal and interlinear); changes in the chapter divisions (the breaks at what are now chapters 4, 10, 12, 23, 39, and 69 were all afterthoughts); page renumbering, short pages, and extra material squeezed in at the head or foot to make pages run on. George Eliot often went to considerable lengths to ensure that her deletions would be indecipherable, turning her pen sideways and scoring through the words concerned with a broad line. With care and persistence, however, most of the cancellations can in the end be recovered, and are recorded in the Clarendon edition; at a rough estimate only 10 per cent of them remain illegible.

The manuscript was shot through with all manner of minor orthographic irregularities and inconsistencies of presentation. For example, if one discounts terms denoting place or station (see below, p. lxix),

---

[1] It should be noted that neither the manner nor the degree of styling imposed on the MS copy varies perceptibly between the several compositors.

there are in all 431 Italian words and phrases in the manuscript; 221 are underlined, 210 are not. The position is much the same when one turns to the use of capitals: selecting almost at random, one finds Cathedral and cathedral, Confessor and confessor, Government and government; Divine Mother but Divine child, Holy Mother but holy Virgin. George Eliot's use of hyphens was equally unsystematic: 'well-spiced' but 'well scented', 'shaving cloth' but 'shaving-chair', 'fellow-being', but 'fellow man'; 'shoe maker' and 'shoe-maker', 'fore-finger' and 'fore finger'. As for spelling, along with various internal inconsistencies, there are a number of archaic, idiosyncratic, or simply incorrect forms: for example, acolyth, ancle, burthen, chesnuts, cieling, cloke, drest, ecstacy, forestal, gorjeous, intreat, inuendo, meersschaum, prophecies (as a verb), weazel, and wo. Finally, there are many hundreds of inadequacies and lacunae in the punctuation, most notably when she alters the wording of a passage but fails to revise the punctuation accordingly—for example, on p. 30 she originally wrote 'like one, in fact, who sins', but when she cancelled the words 'in fact' she scored through only the first of the two commas, leaving the incorrect reading 'like one, who sins'. All in all, then, the setting copy she delivered to the printer left a good deal to be desired.

2. The Cornhill Magazine

Considering the detail in which George Eliot records in her journal each stage of *Romola*'s composition, it is strange that she makes so few mentions of her proof-reading of the novel for publication in the *Cornhill*. It is clear, though, that she was generally able to deliver copy for each part around six weeks in advance of its scheduled appearance, and that she did indeed then read proof for each episode. Unfortunately, none of these proofs has survived. This presents a serious problem for the editor of the novel, for between the manu-script and the *Cornhill* versions of the text there are some 8,000 points of difference. Almost 1,000 of these are substantive changes, some of them involving the recasting of entire sentences. The major-ity, however, concern changes to the accidentals: spelling, hyphen-ation, capitalization, italicization, and above all (c.6,000 instances) punctuation. Without the evidence of the proofs one can never be sure how many and which of these differences were the result of house-styling or miscopying by the printer, and how many were George Eliot's own decision and marked by her as such on the proofs. The vital intermediate stage is missing, and we must rely on probability and informed guesswork.

The strong probability is that George Eliot herself was responsible for most of the substantive changes. These fall into several categories. One finds a good deal of Italian in the manuscript translated into

English in the *Cornhill* (a process she was to continue at each subsequent stage of revision): 'Collegi' is changed to 'magistracy', 'visaccio' to 'visage', 'cerretano' to 'conjuror', 'Lioverno' to 'Leghorn', and
so on. There are minor but distinct alterations of factual details; for
example, 'an Apulian Greek' becomes 'a Calabrian Greek', the reference to eyeglasses as 'wondrous Florentine device of the last generation' is corrected to simply 'wondrous Florentine device' (see p. 637),
the title of 'Proposto' is rendered as 'spokesman' of the city council in
place of 'foreman'. And there are changes to narrative and descriptive
details such as one might expect from an author revising a complex
but hurriedly written story: the 'pale terror' in Tito's face when Piero
di Cosimo asks if he can paint him as Sinon deceiving Priam becomes
merely 'pale astonishment'; when persuading himself that it would be
pointless to abandon his new-found fortune in Florence to go in
search of Baldassarre, Tito's 'right to feel the omnipresence of casualties that seemed to impeach all projects' becomes his 'good cause for
feeling the omnipresence of casualties that threatened all projects with
futility'; the observation that the open hostility between Tito and
Romola in chapter 46 was the first 'since the disclosure about the
library' is, understandably, revised to read the first 'since her flight
and return'. By and large, the substantive changes between the manuscript and the *Cornhill* might be characterized as running repairs—
occasional adjustments, made with a degree of hindsight, to a text she
had been obliged to produce under unaccustomed and uncomfortable
pressure. A number of new footnotes are added; chapter titles are
altered, and supplied for those chapters (28, 40, 41, 66, and 68) which
were untitled in the manuscript; the names of some of the minor
characters are changed—Piero Cennini to Pietro, the mountebank
Vaio to Vaiano—as are the spellings or forms of others: Demetrius
Calcondyla to Demetrio Calcondila, Arggropolo to Argiropulo; the
acceptable but unusual Lorenzo dei Medici to the more familiar
Lorenzo de' Medici, the Latinism or archaism 'Sanctissima' to the
more common Italian form 'Santissima'. To be sure, some of the
above examples (the last in particular) could be the result of miscopying by the printer, and there are many instances where a substantive variant in the *Cornhill* should be regarded with extreme
suspicion:[2] the 'rapping' on Piero di Cosimo's door becoming 'tapping',

---

[2] That GE's proof-reading was not exhaustive is clear from the number of compositorial miscopyings and misprints in the *Cornhill* text. On p. 518 e.g. we find 'Via Cocornero'
for *MS*'s poorly written 'Via Cocomero'; on p. 514 'Savonarola' is misprinted as
'Savanarola'; on p. 300 'didn't' appears as 'did't'; what should be ch. 31 is numbered 30
in the *Cornhill* (i.e. there are two ch. 30s and no ch. 31). The *Cornhill* text includes at
least a dozen such errors, and it is unreasonable to account for them all as having been
introduced between the corrected proofs and the printed sheets. The probability is that
both GE and the printer's proof-reader failed to notice them on the proofs.

'drivelling rain' becoming 'drizzling rain', Savonarola's 'promises and threats' transposed to 'threats and promises', singulars becoming plurals, tenses changing, 'further' becoming 'farther', 'among' changed to 'amongst', and so on. No general rule can be adduced for determining the authority of substantive variants in the *Cornhill* text, and each instance must be considered strictly on its own merits. On balance, though, my opening statement bears repetition: the majority of such variants were *probably* introduced by George Eliot on the lost proofs. There is no evidence that she was edited, as opposed to styled, by her publishers, and if she was by Lewes (it is not unlikely that he assisted her in reading proof) it is reasonable to assume that she approved his revisions.

When one turns to the accidentals, the situation alters dramatically, for here the strong probability is that most of the changes were introduced by the printer. Presented with setting copy as erratic as I have indicated, any printer of the time would naturally have sought to tidy up and normalize as he saw fit and had been trained to do. By far the largest group of variants between the manuscript and *Cornhill* texts involves the punctuation: innumerable commas are introduced (and a very few deleted); dashes are replaced by commas, commas by colons or semi-colons; missing full stops are supplied at the end of sentences, as are inverted commas around direct speech; appropriate new marks are provided when she changes the words of a passage in the manuscript but omits to revise its punctuation accordingly. Many of these instances amount to a skilled and intelligent reaction on the part of the printer to manifest inadequacies in the setting copy. Many more, however, involve a decision being made as to what constituted an inadequacy in the existing punctuation. There are literally thousands of occasions when the manuscript punctuation, though extremely spare or informal (sometimes just a sequence of dashes) does still hold the words together in recognizable syntax. On these occasions the printer's decision to emend is, editorially, contentious, and I will discuss the full implications of this below. It is reasonable to assume, however, that the majority of punctuation changes between the manuscript and the *Cornhill* were indeed made on the printer's initiative. What evidence we have suggests that George Eliot concerned herself little with such matters, even when proof-reading under less unfavourable circumstances, and it is surely inconceivable that either she, or Lewes, should have marked what amounts to an average of ten new commas per *Cornhill* page on the proofs.

3. The First Edition

It is unclear whether the typesetting and proofing of the three-volume first edition was staggered over a period of several weeks (the first two volumes dealt with, perhaps, before she had actually finished writing the third), or effected at one go after she had delivered the final part of the serial in the second week of June 1863. Neither is there any corroborative documentary evidence that George Eliot herself read proof for the edition. The evidence of the text, however, is fairly conclusive as concerns this latter point. There are some 250 substantive variants between the *Cornhill* and the three-decker, at least two-thirds of which are surely authorial. There is more Italian translated or recast: for example, the authentically idiomatic 'you come like *cacio alla lasagna*' becomes the rather cryptic 'you come like cheese ready grated'; the manuscript's '*gravezze*', which in the *Cornhill* had been expanded to '*gravezze* (burdens, *i.e.* taxes)', is changed again, this time simply to 'burdens'. There are further factual, descriptive, and narrative adjustments: the observation that Politian's epigram about the *culex* was 'unhappily founded on the zoological mistake that the flea, like the gnat, was born from the waters' is corrected to read 'founded partly on the zoological fact that the gnat, like Venus, was born from the waters' (see p. 621); the statement that 'The signs of the fair were present here too' becomes 'Here, too, the signs of the fair were present'; Fra Luca's closing words to Tito, 'I cannot say more at present', are changed to 'I am unable to talk now'. A handful of compositorial miscopyings and interventions in the *Cornhill* are corrected and overturned: for example, on p. 47 the rooms 'fitted with precious stores' reverts to the manuscript reading of 'filled with precious stores'; on p. 28 the word 'Paradiso', wrongly italicized in the *Cornhill* (it refers to the location rather than to Dante's poem), is properly restored to roman.[3] Though the substantive changes are generally small, one or two of them are especially interesting. For example, in the very first sentence of the novel the striking and original adjective describing the angel of the dawn as 'star-quenching' is removed. Also removed, *passim*, are no fewer than six of the ten occasions on which, in the manuscript and serial texts, Romola is described as 'flushing' or as having a 'flush' on her face. There are in addition some 600 changes to the accidentals from the *Cornhill* text, most of them involving punctuation; 50 new paragraph breaks are introduced (see Appendix C), several of them probably in reaction to

---

[3] Inevitably, new errors were also introduced at the printers, and a number found their way through to the printed text. For examples see below, 'Descriptive List of Editions', p. lxxiv. It is of course possible that some of the errors were introduced after GE had corrected her set of proofs.

the smaller number of words per page in the three-decker—*c.*300 as compared with the *Cornhill's c.*600.

4. The Illustrated Edition

That George Eliot read proof for the Illustrated edition of 1865 is clear from her journal, though as in the case of earlier states of the text no proofs have survived. As printed, there are some 100 substantive variants between the three-decker and the Illustrated edition. In this instance, however, one hesitates to attribute such changes primarily to the author—if only for the fact that no more than half a dozen of them could not reasonably be ascribed to miscopying or intervention by the printer. The circumstantial evidence is overwhelming. Tenses change for no apparent reason, singulars become plurals and vice versa, contractions are opened out, prepositions are altered; 'should' becomes 'would', 'these' changes to 'those', 'their' to 'the', 'farther' to 'further'. Unusual usages are 'normalized' to their more common forms: 'philosophic treatises' to 'philosophical treatises', 'Funereal mourners' to 'Funeral mourners', 'cut-and-thrust northerns' to 'cut-and-thrust northerners'. Other, simpler words are changed to similar-sounding ones: 'wild multitude' to 'wide multitude', 'a show of armour' to 'a shower of armour', 'newly furbished' to 'duly furbished'. Still other words are transposed or simply dropped: 'not what she had at all thought' becomes 'not at all what she had thought'; 'arms, legs, hands, and other members' becomes 'arms, legs, and other members'; 'he never thought of doing anything base' becomes 'he never thought of anything base'; 'if I were certain—yes, if I were certain that' becomes simply 'if I were certain that'. There are over 90 instances of substantive changes which may plausibly be ascribed to compositorial carelessness or intervention not picked up by George Eliot as she read proof. Such evidence is circumstantial and suppositious, but it is none the less powerful: it seems at least likely that up to 95 per cent of the substantive changes in the Illustrated edition were introduced not by the author but by the printer. That George Eliot did herself mark a handful of changes on the proofs is equally likely. For example, the italicization of Tito's dramatic dismissal of Baldassarre on p. 222 as '*Some madman, surely*' is very probably authorial, as, surely, is the alteration in chapter 8 to the introductory remarks about 'the car of the Zecca' (see p. 89), and the correction of the spelling of Via dell' Oriuolo on p. 235 (which in both the *Cornhill* and first edition had been wrongly printed as Via dell' Orinolo, following poorly written manuscript copy). There are *c.*350 changes to the accidentals between the first and Illustrated editions, the majority, as before, involving punctuation. There is also the customary clutch of misprints which George Eliot evidently failed to spot: 'any' for 'and', 'mamed' for 'named', 'Trinitiâ' for 'Trinità' (an error she later corrected on the proofs of the Cabinet edition), and so on—further indication that her reading of these proofs was less than exhaustive.

5. The Cabinet Edition

The Cabinet edition was set from a copy of the 'New Edition' (itself printed from the plates cast for the Illustrated edition), which George Eliot marked up and sent to John Blackwood for this purpose in February 1877, and which is now in the Harry Ransom Humanities Research Center in Austin, Texas. In her covering letter to Blackwood she noted that she had 'only made a few alterations of an unimportant kind—the printing being unusually correct'. I take it this last remark refers to literals; certainly, it would be unsafe to regard it as a retrospective validation of the substantive changes introduced into this setting back in 1865. Indeed, she goes on to acknowledge quite how unfamiliar she had become with the text in the interim: 'I think it must be nearly ten years since I read the book before . . . It has made me often sob with a sort of painful joy as I have read the sentences which had faded from my memory'.[4]

In the event she marked fewer than 150 changes on the Cabinet setting copy, most of them very small. She corrected a number of literals, but missed others; made some minor adjustments to the punctuation, usually adding or cancelling commas; and translated a further dozen Italian words into English. She tinkered periodically with close details of word, style, or structure: changing 'but' to 'yet', 'monk' to 'friar', 'resolutions made' to 'resolutions taken', 'a dagger that hung up' to 'a dagger hanging up'; the phrase 'valuable alike in sieges and shows' becomes 'valuable alike in sieges and in shows'; the observation 'That was a question to which it would be difficult for Baldassarre to discover the answer' is altered to 'It would be difficult for Baldassarre to discover the answer to that question'. She also marked a handful of changes which more significantly modify sense or emphasis. For example, the adjective 'majestic' used to describe the heroine on pp. 95 and 120 is deleted on both occasions, while on p. 179 Romola's 'radiant majesty' becomes her 'radiant beauty'. On p. 251 the narrator's explanation that Romola was labouring to subdue her nature to that of her husband, 'as every loving woman must', is revised to 'as a loving woman must'.

The proofs of the Cabinet edition which Blackwoods subsequently sent to George Eliot (she had specifically requested a set, explaining that she felt 'bound to take care of my text')[5] are also now in the

---

[4] *Letters*, vi. 335–6.   [5] Ibid. vi. 335.

Harry Ransom Humanities Research Center. They incorporate all the changes she had called for on the setting copy, together with several hundred which she had not. Almost all these latter concern accidentals and are the result of house-styling, most notably of her punctuation and spelling. For example, her habitual *ize* word endings, which Smith, Elder & Co. had followed in their printings of the novel, are all changed to *ise*, as was Blackwoods' standard practice. By a similar token, the variety of punctuation marks which previous states of the text had employed as the lead-in to direct speech are mostly standardized to a simple dash. The proofs also contain a number of miscopyings or misprints of substantives: 'creditable historians' for 'credible historians', 'Romola's fervent nature' for 'Romola's fervid nature', 'old painter' for 'odd painter'. There are some 20 such instances, but George Eliot corrected none of them on the proofs. All, therefore, were included in the Cabinet edition—and have been reproduced in subsequent printings. One of them in particular, though involving the displacement of just a single letter, could be distinctly misleading. When Baldassarre strangles Tito by the side of the Arno, he clings to the corpse waiting for 'Justice' to send a witness to his deed—'He would never lose his hold till some one came and found them'. So runs the Cabinet edition. 'Loss' is a state closely associated with Baldassarre: his fortune, family, and occupation gone, he dimly perceives his intellectual powers too as 'Lost, lost!' (p. 357). At this climactic moment he has but one thing left to him: his just revenge as signified by his grasp on the traitor's neck. Here is one last thing he will not lose—'He would never *lose* his hold'. So, perhaps, reflects the reader of the Cabinet text. In fact, what George Eliot wrote was the more obvious word *loose*. This is how it appears in the manuscript, and in the *Cornhill*, first, and Illustrated editions. The printer of the Cabinet edition dropped the second 'o', and one assumes that George Eliot simply did not notice.

Though she failed to correct these miscopyings, and overturned none of Blackwoods' house-styling, George Eliot did mark 150 or so other changes on the proofs. She translated still more Italian, and made minor alterations both to the punctuation (usually with the effect of making structures more formal) and to the words: 'commenced' to 'began', 'fevered' to 'feverish', 'remarks at' to 'remarks on', 'feel its edge' to 'try its edge', 'that young ambition covets' to 'that attracts young ambition'. Again, there are a handful of slightly more significant adjustments and fine-tuning of detail: for example, Tito's 'brown curls' are now 'dark curls'; his admission 'I may rather be called a Graeculus than a Greek' is recast as 'I am a Greek very much as your peaches are Persian' (see p. 29); his 'hypothetic talent, constructing from subtle indications' becomes his 'constructive talent, guided by subtle indications'; the concluding assertion of Savonarola's greatness—'*But therefore he may the more fitly be called a martyr by his fellow-men to all time*'—is given added force by being marked, thus, to go into italics.

Finally, a further 250 or so changes (more house-styling, mostly to the punctuation and hyphenation) were introduced between the corrected proofs and the Cabinet edition as finally printed. These perhaps derive from a set of revises read in-house only; George Eliot herself saw only the one stage of proof.

6. The Stereotyped and Deluxe Editions

George Eliot read proof for neither of the two subsequent editions to appear during her lifetime. The first of these, Blackwoods' Stereotyped edition of 1878, was set from a copy of the Cabinet edition and differs from it on a mere 100 occasions. Almost all the variants involve punctuation and hyphenation; most were probably deliberate changes by the printer, continuing the process of standardization to house conventions, rather than copying errors. Smith & Elder's deluxe edition of 1880 was the last new setting to be published before the author's death. Interestingly, it follows the Stereotyped edition rather than one of Smith's own, earlier ones. It may be that George Eliot requested this when Smith called on her in February 1880 to discuss the project, or that the publishers simply used the most recent available version.

7. Overseas Editions

Five American editions of *Romola* were published during George Eliot's lifetime, though she read proof for none of them. The first, set from a copy of the *Cornhill* serialization, was published in August 1863 by the New York firm of Harper and Brothers, at $1.50. The text occupies 241 closely printed double-column pages, and includes all but the last (see p. lxxxi) of Leighton's illustrations and illustrated capitals at the start of serial instalments. This was followed by Fields, Osgood, & Co.'s Household edition (Boston, 1869) at $1; Harper's Library edition (New York, 1869; reprinted 1870, 1873, 1875, and 1877) at 75 cents; Fields's Illustrated Library edition (Boston, 1870), bound with *The Mill on the Floss* and *Silas Marner* and selling for $1.75; and finally George Munro's Seaside Library edition (New York, 1877), a triple-column setting, in paperback, squeezed into 80 12" × 9" pages, at the remarkable price of 10 cents.

The only English-language continental edition was published in December 1863 in two volumes by the firm of Bernhard Tauchnitz in Leipzig—as volumes 682 and 683 of Tauchnitz's 'Collection of British Authors'. Smith, Elder & Co. received £60 for the rights. It was set from a copy of the three-decker rather than the serial; George Eliot did not read proof.

A German translation by A. E. Wollheim was issued in six volumes in 1864 by the firm of G. Pätz of Naumberg; and a French translation, by George Eliot's friend François d'Albert-Durade, was published by Hachette in two volumes in 1878 in both Paris and Geneva under the title *Romola, ou Florence et Savonarola*.

CHOICE OF COPY TEXT

To recap, there were twelve separate settings of *Romola* during George Eliot's lifetime, but she herself exercised some control over only four of them: the *Cornhill* serialization (*CM*), the three-volume first edition (*1*), the Illustrated edition (*2*), and the Cabinet edition (*3*). These four printed states, together with the manuscript (*MS*) and the setting copy (*3C*) and proofs (*3P*) of the Cabinet edition, constitute the primary materials from which the Clarendon edition is assembled.

The manuscript, of course, is the only state of the text for which the author alone was responsible. It was not, however, a state which she would have expected to be laid before the public exactly as it had been written. As an experienced author, she had every reason to anticipate its being styled and normalized prior to publication, for to do so was no more than standard printing practice at the time. There is no evidence that she actively objected to this,[1] though we cannot tell whether—in so far as she thought of it at all—she regarded it as an imposition to which she was bound to resign herself, or as a convenient check on what she had drafted. It is fair to say, however, that in practice the manuscript setting copy represented a final draft rather than a finalized text. As concerns the accidentals, it was left to the printer, whose business it was to do so, to make such details more appropriate to the conventions of a printed text—even though this inevitably meant flattening out certain particularities and idiosyncrasies of her style. The text as printed, in other words, represented a collaborative effort between author and printer. Of course she knew she would see proof, which in theory afforded her the opportunity of overturning any house-styling to which she objected on critical

---

[1] As it happens, one of the very few occasions on which she expressed any view on the subject was in Sept. 1861, when she took a break from her preparatory work on *Romola* to correct copy for Blackwoods' cheap edns. of her previous novels, and wrote to the printer concerning *Adam Bede* that 'Unmistakeable is to be spelt with an *e*' though two years earlier, in *The Mill on the Floss*, she had herself thrice written 'unmistakable' without it. In the MS of *Romola* the following year she spelt the word with an 'e', but failed to overturn the *Cornhill* printer's revision of it to 'unmistakable'.

grounds, or which actually distorted the sense. For the most part, though, proofs gave her the chance to revise what she herself had written, and thus would have been doubly welcome in the case of *Romola*—a novel written under less than ideal conditions for a form of publication she was unused to and found hard to come to terms with.[2] We should remember that she was sent proofs of no fewer than twelve of the book's fourteen instalments before she had actually completed *MS*. There is a strong case that many of the substantive revisions she marked on the proofs of *CM* were of the kind she would probably have made to the manuscript of a non-serial novel before sending the *complete* manuscript to the printer; that *MS*, therefore, should be seen as an almost-finished draft, and only with *CM* does the novel stand for the first time as a completed work.

Each of the following three editions for which she read proof constitutes a different, authorially approved state of the text, and a plausible case might be made for preferring either *1* or *3* to *CM* as copy text. Whichever state is chosen will to a degree anchor the Clarendon edition at a particular moment of the text's developing history, though by emending as appropriate and recording significant variants one can obviate most of the problems inherent in fixing on a single point in a dynamic process. Under the circumstances, it seems safest and, as I shall argue below, most logical to choose *CM* as copy text.

EMENDATION OF COPY TEXT

1. Substantives

Between the completed manuscript and the last setting for which George Eliot read proof, some 1,500 substantive alterations were made to the text of the novel, involving a total of over 10,000 words in all. The largest number of alterations (*c*.1,000) were introduced between *MS* and *CM*. Even in the absence of the intervening stage of proof, it is fairly clear that the majority of these were authorial, being of a kind which a printer was most unlikely to have made independently: sentences rewritten, new phrases inserted, Italian translated into English, and so on. In such cases the *CM* (i.e. copy text) reading is allowed to stand, and the *MS* variant recorded in the textual apparatus. There is, however, another group of *MS/CM* changes, whose origin it is harder to attribute with confidence. These mostly concern minor alterations to individual words, such as might plausibly stem

---

[2] In 1875, looking back on her experience with *Romola* (which, it should be noted, she had conceived from the first as a serial novel (see above, p. xiii)), she averred 'I have the strongest objection to cutting up my work into little bits . . . if I could gain more [money] by splitting my writing into small parts, I would not do it, because the effect would be injurious as a matter of art' (*Letters*, vi. 179).

from miscopying or stylistic intervention by the printer. Some, for example, may be the result of his misreading George Eliot's hand: 'stepping' for 'slipping' (p. 144), 'coldest' for 'coolest' (p. 476). Others may perhaps represent the printer, whether deliberately or unconsciously, adjusting what George Eliot had actually written to what he thought she had meant to write: thus substituting 'dull philosophic' dinners in the Rucellai Gardens for the unusual composite 'dull-philosophic' (p. 337), the 'much-praised' Tito for the more convincingly rhetorical 'much-bepraised' (p. 169), 'milk and victuals' for Monna Ghita's idiomatically specific 'milk and victual' (p. 25), an 'insoluble problem' for the less common form 'unsolvable' (p. 471). With regard to singular nouns becoming plural and vice versa, the superiority of the *MS* reading, and the corresponding unlikeliness of George Eliot having altered it on the proofs of *CM*, is occasionally attested by external evidence. For example, *CM*'s change of the 'fortresses' of Naples to 'fortress' (p. 371) introduces a historical error, as, almost certainly, does that from 'confessors' to 'confessor' on p. 505. (More intriguing is *CM*'s description of Tito on p. 108 as 'resting on his elbows', for Leighton's illustration of the scene in 'Under the Plane-Tree' plainly shows him leaning on one 'elbow'—as *MS* has it; since Leighton took his cue from the proofs of *CM* rather than from *MS*, this seems to argue for the change having been made by George Eliot on her set of proofs.) In a handful of cases the probability of a *CM* variant being an unauthorized printer's change is strengthened by the *MS* reading then being restored in *1*: 'come' for 'some' (p. 107), 'name' for 'names' (p. 236), 'St' for 'Saint' (p. 426). For the most part, though, such variants remain obstinately resistant to simple solutions—as do those involving transpositions, contractions, and single words dropped from phrases—the problem being further compounded by the fact that, so far as we can tell, George Eliot did not read proof against copy. As I noted above, no blanket rule can safely be applied; rather, each instance must be tried on its own merits—and in its own context. For example, *CM*'s second 'her' in 'She put her thumb and her forefinger to her betrothal ring' (p. 324) seems a likely miscopying: three 'her's in seven words is uncharacteristically clumsy. On the other hand, consider the passage at the end of chapter 23 where the true baseness of Tito's nature is revealed. It is a passage which, as the revisions to the manuscript show, caused George Eliot some difficulties. One of these revisions was to the statement that 'the only strength he trusted to lay in his ingenuity and his dissimulation' (p. 225). She originally wrote 'the only strength he trusted to now was his ingenuity and his dissimulation' but then replaced 'was' with 'lay in'. In *CM*, as quoted above, the word 'now' is dropped. In determining whether this was an author's proof correction or a miscopying by the printer, one is bound to take account not only of the extent of her *MS* revisions to the passage as a whole (signifying the difficulty she had in fixing on a final version), but of the fact that the very next sentence opens with the word 'Now' and that a dozen lines below a further sentence begins 'The question now was'. All in all, there is a persuasive circumstantial case for regarding the change as authorial, and in this instance allowing the *CM* reading to stand. More often than not, however (in fact in 75 of around 100 such instances), the *MS* reading is reinstated—and the *CM* variant recorded in the apparatus.

Of the 250 or so substantive changes introduced between *CM* and *1*, fewer than 100 are of the kind which one feels confident in attributing to George Eliot on the grounds that they are too large or too deliberate for a printer to have made without instructions. The remainder fall into the same contentious categories as outlined above: alterations to case, number, and tense, transpositions, single words dropped or added, etc. Since setting copy this time was a printed text, the legibility of George Eliot's hand is not an issue. Some miscopying, however, is virtually inevitable in a 300,000 word novel, and such, it seems probable, accounts for a number of the *CM/1* variations. For example, on p. 118 the *CM* reading 'larger and more radically natural view' seems, with its balanced comparatives, more congruous than *1*'s 'large and more radically natural view'. On p. 379 *CM*'s 'opened door' is contextually more logical than the 'open door' in *1*, while on p. 562 *CM*'s 'With nimble movements she seated the baby on the ground' is clearly preferable to *1*'s 'With nimble movement . . .'. In Dino's prophetic vision of his sister's marriage, cast throughout in a self-consciously rhetorical idiom, the inversion 'you went all three down the stone steps' (p. 161) is so entirely in character that the transposition in *1* to 'you all three went' must be viewed with considerable suspicion. Another group of changes may well result from the printer instinctively normalizing certain particularities of George Eliot's style: thus altering the 'gossips and debates' of the street corner to 'gossip and debates' (p. 9), the 'supernal and heavenly' atmosphere of the Nunziata to 'supernatural and heavenly' (p. 147), Bernardo del Nero's 'extended family connections' to the more usual but less precise locution 'extensive family connections' (p. 255). In all such instances (about 40 in total) the reading of the copy text is allowed to stand, and the variant in *1* recorded in the apparatus. There are a further 120 or so cases in which the revised reading in *1* seems more likely to have been an authorial change: 'dislike' for 'don't like' (p. 169), 'spinning itself' for 'spinning' (p. 304), 'date' for 'day' (p. 306), 'rounded' for 'round' (p. 312), 'enough of' for 'enough' (p. 353), 'held it up' for 'held it' (p. 440), and so on. In these cases the copy text is emended and the superseded *CM* reading recorded in the apparatus.

As I have already suggested, most of the substantive changes in *2* are probably copying-errors by the printer. The few which seem to be authorial are incorporated in the copy text, and the majority recorded as variants. By a similar token, the text is emended to include the changes marked by George Eliot on *3C* and *3P*, while those for which the printer of *3* was responsible are rejected.

As concerns substantives, then, the Clarendon edition presents an eclectic text, arrived at by emending the *CM* copy text to include all later readings which we know (or have sound reason to believe) were authorial, together with those of *MS* which it seems probable the *CM* printer changed without authority. In practice, therefore, it makes little difference in terms of the substantives which of the seven relevant states is designated as copy text, for the final emended version would be the same whichever provided the starting-point. It is when we turn to the accidentals that the choice of *CM* assumes critical significance.

2. Accidentals

(a) *Punctuation*

Of the changes to the accidentals 85 per cent concern punctuation, and 80 per cent of these occur between *MS* and *CM*. If, as seems very likely, the overwhelming majority were introduced by the printer, why choose *CM* as copy text in preference to *MS*? By way of answering this question, let us first consider the claims of *MS*.

MS, of course, starts with the distinct advantage of being the one state of the text for which the author and the author alone was responsible. It would not, however, be an acceptable option to reproduce the *MS* punctuation exactly as it stands, for, as I have already indicated, this is plainly deficient or actually lacking on many hundreds of occasions. If *MS* were copy text the editor would on such occasions (for example, when George Eliot rewrites a passage but fails to revise the punctuation accordingly) be obliged to repoint as he saw appropriate—presumably in line with the author's preferred method (one hesitates to call it a system) as inferred from the bulk of *MS*. Any readable edition of *Romola* must inevitably include a good deal of punctuation that is not George Eliot's own, for an entirely 'authorial' text would not make sense. On the other hand, the bulk of the *MS* punctuation, though extremely light and informal, is for the most part serviceable, if occasionally so sparse as to render the sense ambiguous. It recalls a speaking voice—such as that, perhaps, in which George Eliot read sample passages aloud to Lewes—though one whose precise inflexions are not always clear to a third party. To reproduce it unmediated would be an adventurous course, for the novel would read more rapidly, breathlessly even, and in larger periods. It would startle readers, but rarely baffle them.

Why then prefer the *CM* version, with its several thousand interventions, interpolations, and interpretations from the printer's hand? The answer is that *CM* is preferable on historical rather than aesthetic grounds, for it is the version which George Eliot accepted for *publication. MS*, on the other hand, was a final draft; its punctuation, lightweight and unconventional throughout, occasionally inadequate or incomplete, actively required a measure of interpretive normalization before it could realistically be set before the novel-reading public. Such was the function of the printing-house, and such was what George Eliot would have expected Smith's printer to do for *Romola*, as Blackwoods' had for her previous novels. Virtually all her contemporary novelists were similarly restyled and, so far as we can tell, accepted this as standard publishing practice. (The evidence of other Smith, Elder & Co. authors of the early 1860s such as Thackeray and Hawthorne indicates that the degree of repointing in *Romola* was unexceptional.) It should not be supposed that George Eliot did not care about formal punctuation, but rather that she was ready to delegate responsibility for this, and that she was therefore unconcerned at supplying as setting copy the rapid, abbreviated, and provisional version that came most naturally as she wrote. The punctuation of *Romola* in the text as first printed, as in the case of most nineteenth-century novels, represented a collaborative effort between author and printing-house. George Eliot had expected such a collaboration, and she accepted its results as appropriate to the published form of the book. When choosing a state on which to base the Clarendon edition, *CM* thus has a historical authority which the draft *MS* version cannot claim.

On purely critical grounds one could wish that the printer had compensated rather less emphatically for the sparseness of the setting copy, for his systematic imposition of a more conventional style of pointing tends to weigh down sections of the text with punctuation that can seem unnecessarily fussy. In the absence of proofs, of course, we cannot tell how often George Eliot may in fact have overturned other of his changes. There are, however, a number of instances where the punctuation in *1* reverts to that of *MS*—most probably as the result of an authorial proof correction. The *CM* printer's most frequent contribution was to insert commas, and a handful of his less satisfactory additions, though allowed to stand in *CM*, were removed in *1*. For example

(p. 48) one long white hand] *MS 1 2 3* one long, white hand *CM*
(p. 155) the emaciated face of Fra Luca . . . with deep-sunken

hazel eyes fixed on a small crucifix] *MS 1 2 3* . . . eyes, fixed . . .
CM

(p. 204) He was mounted on a high car completely covered with
black] *MS 1 2 3* . . . car, completely . . . *CM*

One suspects that the printer's insertion of commas in such instances
was made almost without thinking. In any case, on the assumption
that George Eliot called for their removal on the proofs of *1*, I have
emended the copy text to exclude them. By a similar token, there are
(rather fewer) occasions when *CM* drops commas from *MS* which are
then restored in *1*. For example

(p. 403) But, himself in shadow, he had seen] *MS 1 2 3* But himself . . . *CM*

(p. 143) I will be at your shop, if nothing hinders] *MS 1 2 3* . . .
shop if . . . *CM*

Here again the copy text is emended, as it is to prefer a handful of
MS commas and colons which were changed to semi-colons in *CM*,
thereby altering the flow of the passage concerned, but then restored
in *1* (e.g. on pp. 115, 117, and 119). That George Eliot did care, at
least intermittently, about the effect of commas added or removed by
the *CM* printer is further evidenced by her restoration of certain *MS*
readings in *3P*. For example:

(p. 8) That very Quaresima or Lent of 1492 in which he died] *MS
3P* That very Quaresima, or Lent, of 1492, in which he died *CM
1 2*

(p. 29) I come of a Greek stock planted in Italian soil] MS *3P* . . .
stock, planted . . . *CM 1 2*

(p. 324) There was still something else to be stript away from her,
belonging to that past on which she was to turn her back for
ever] *MS 3P* . . . her belonging . . . *CM 1 2*

It is clear that when, for whatever reason and however long after the
event, she was struck by instances such as these, where the printer's
interventions were unnecessarily cumbersome, or wrongly shifted the
emphasis of a phrase, she was quite prepared to revise accordingly. I
have emended the copy text in all such cases in line with the *MS 3P*
reading. More problematic are those instances where she failed to
overturn what I take to be a printer's punctuation change which
materially affected the sense. In a dozen or so of these I have restored
the *MS* reading. Take, for example, the reference to the younger of
the Cennini brothers on p. 85: 'Piero, the erudite, corrector of proof

sheets, not Domenico the practical'. *CM*'s removal of the comma after 'erudite' changes the function of the word from an adjectival noun in apposition to 'Piero' to a simple adjective modifying 'corrector'. (By implication, it has a similar effect on the word 'practical'.) Or again, on p. 137 *CM*'s omission of the comma in Brigida's remark that Romola 'has that way of walking, like a procession' flattens out the oral particularity of the observation. In both cases one suspects that the *CM* printer thought he was normalizing a minor stylistic eccentricity. In both, however, the result was almost certainly a misconstruction of what George Eliot had written.

Several hundred punctuation changes were subsequently made between *CM* and *1*, the majority representing an extension of the formalization process started in *CM*. While, however, the *MS* setting copy actively required a measure of repointing to bring it into line with conventional standards, the *CM* text did not. Its punctuation was in the main sufficiently regular and complete to require no further attention of this kind. The fact that the printer of *1*, notwithstanding, introduced so many new changes is not in itself surprising, for, as a general rule, it was part of his professional function to restyle what he set as he saw fit. Taken as a whole, though, his contribution cannot realistically be claimed as a necessary stage in the transformation of the novel from manuscript draft to printed text. For the most part, therefore, I have not preferred the revised punctuation in *1* to that of *CM*. Rather, I have emended the copy text only on those very few occasions (*c*.35 in all) when it seems likely that George Eliot herself marked the change on the proofs. Some of these, as already indicated, involve the restoration of a *MS* reading. Others overturn the common reading of both *MS* and *CM*: for example the removal of the comma from Nello's description of himself as 'a barber⟨,⟩ unsnared by authorship' (p. 37), which makes syntactically more precise the allusion which he plainly intends to the barber-poet Burchiello. Or take the narrator's remark that 'At the end of 1492, the year in which Lorenzo de' Medici died⟨,⟩ and Tito Melema came as a wanderer to Florence, Italy was enjoying . . . peace and prosperity' (p. 210). Here it seems less likely that the printer deleted the comma as part of his self-determined normalizing brief than that George Eliot decided more deliberately to emphasize the historical conjunction of Lorenzo's death and the arrival in Florence of a man like Tito.

The copy text is further emended to incorporate the 50 or so punctuation changes which George Eliot herself marked on *3C* and *3P*; those introduced between *1* and *2* (*c*.150) or made without authority by the printer of *3* (*c*.250) are rejected. In practice this means that the Clarendon edition follows the punctuation of the *CM* copy text except when we know, or have persuasive circumstantial reasons to believe, that subsequent changes to it were made by the author, or when it seems that the *CM* reading actually runs counter to the sense intended in *MS*.

(b) *Spelling and Hyphenation*

As I noted above, George Eliot's own spelling was at times archaic, idiosyncratic, or simply wrong, and was normalized to more conventional forms by the printer. Following the practice of the Clarendon series, I have here emended the copy text to restore those of her MS spellings which are sanctioned by *OED*. Her hyphenation was still more irregular than her spelling, and was similarly restyled by the printer; here again I have restored the MS forms where the combinations concerned are sanctioned by *OED*.

(c) *Capitalization*

George Eliot's use of capitals was inconsistent throughout, and evidently caused the printer a good deal of trouble (the *CM* text, in fact, is more uneven in this respect than *MS*). It may be that her handwriting was partly to blame for the confusion. Her letter 'c', for example, is especially difficult to size accurately, and this might have contributed to the discrepancy over a word such as 'Cardinal': ten instances in all, eight with a capital 'C' in *MS* (as I read it) but only two in *CM*. On the other hand, when one turns to the word 'Carnival' one finds that *MS* has an initial capital on 26 out of 28 occurrences and *CM* on 25 of them. It would seem that the printer's own judgement as to how a word ought to be written was a more decisive factor than his ability to decipher how the author herself had written it. 'King' and 'Kingdom' appear a total of 25 times, in *MS* always with an initial capital, in *CM* always in lower case. 'Anathema' is given a capital 'A' throughout in *CM*, but never in *MS*. The treatment of most recurring nouns, however, is something of a lottery in *MS* and *CM* alike. Simple words like 'cathedral' and 'palace', 'council' and 'government', 'paradise' and 'plague', or more historically specific usages such as 'signor' and 'madonna', 'loggia' and 'piazza', all appear regularly in both upper and lower case (but in differing ratios from text to text) without the distinction apparently signifying any variation of meaning, emphasis, or application. Like most authors, George Eliot was careless of such details as she wrote; the *CM* printer restyled selectively, and case by case only, thereby replacing the author's inconsistency with his own. To reproduce either state exactly as it stands would be to preserve patent and often confusing irregularities which it is surely unreasonable to suppose that George Eliot intended or expected to be carried through into the published text.

Under the circumstances the most sensible course seems to be to normalize afresh on the basis of MS majority practice, taking care to
make all possible allowance for what may be deliberate variations from
the predominant pattern.

(d) *Italicization*

The underlining of Italian words in *MS* seems largely haphazard.
Though a hint of a pattern emerges with nouns denoting place
('piazza', 'loggia', 'mercato', etc.) or station ('padre', 'signor',
'Messer', etc.), which are hardly ever underlined, for the most part no
discernible system can be inferred. There are, for example, 55
instances of single-word exclamations ('Ecco', 'Lasso', 'Santiddio',
etc.); 24 of them are underlined, 31 are not. Of a total of 32 spoken
addresses ('buona donna', 'bel erudito', 'Romola mia', etc.) 15 only
are underlined. The word 'sajo' (tunic) is underlined but 'gamurra'
(gown) is not, while 'beretta' (cap) is underlined on just two of its
five occurrences and 'lucco' (garment) on seven out of nine. We find
'*ragazza*' but 'damigella', '*bambino*' but 'bimbo', '*Priori*' but
'Segretario'. Of 33 occurrences of 'grosso', 'quattrino', and 'danari'
(all coins) 15 are underlined and 18 are not; words such as 'cero',
'corso', 'cugina', 'leggio', 'marmi', 'palio', 'poverina', and 'zazzera' are
each underlined, on average, on every second occurrence only. The
CM printer tended to italicize rather more often than George Eliot
had underlined, but with results that are only marginally less inconsistent. Indeed, at times he merely compounded the problem: where
MS had underlined 'festa' on two out of nine occasions, *CM* italicizes
on five; the word 'confetti', though always underlined in *MS*, is now
given in roman on two of its seven occurrences. Words such as 'dottore', 'pazzarella', 'polenta', and 'rascia', which are never underlined
in *MS*, are italicized throughout in *CM*. If the printer was working to
a plan, it is no clearer than that of the author.

As in the case of capitalization then, and quite distinct from that of
punctuation, we are faced with two equally arbitrary and confusing
methods. And again, though the printer's intervention proved inadequate in the event, there is no good reason to suppose that George
Eliot had intended or expected her own inconsistency in composition
to be carried through into the published text. Deliberately to reproduce the inconsistency of either state as concerns italicization, though
it might preserve the 'historical integrity' of the text, would be a form
of bibliographic pedantry and an abdication of editorial responsibility.
Accordingly, I have chosen to normalize afresh on the basis of majority *MS* usage. In practice this has often meant regularizing by *category* of word—for example, it would seem perverse to settle on '*Piero
mio*' but '*Nello mio*' (as one would on a simple case-by-case majority

count)—though I have made every effort to be sensitive to what may constitute deliberate and meaning-bearing variations. I have sought, not to impose a blanket system, but sympathetically to interpret and complete George Eliot's own rudimentary system in *MS*.

RECORDING OF VARIANTS

All substantive variants from the *CM* copy text are recorded in the textual apparatus. When, as in the majority of cases, the Clarendon reading follows that of *CM*, the source of the variant only is listed. So, for example, the entry 'stranger] youth *MS*' signifies that *CM* and all other states except *MS* read 'stranger' while *MS* has 'youth'. The entry 'gossips] gossip *1 2 3*' indicates that 'gossips' (in the plural) is the reading in both *MS* and *CM*. It should be noted that, when used in isolation, *3* refers to a reading introduced without authority (i.e. not marked by George Eliot on *3C* or *3P*) in the Cabinet edition: hence 'loose] lose *3*' indicates that 'loose' was the reading in all states through 2 and that it was then changed to 'lose' by the Cabinet printer. When the Clarendon text differs from *CM* the source of the emendation is listed immediately after the square bracket, as in 'angel] *1 2 3* star-quenching angel *MS CM*', or 'pretty parrot] *3C papagallo MS CM 1 2*' (*3C* signifies that the change was marked by George Eliot on the setting copy of the Cabinet edition, *3P* that it was made by her on the Cabinet proofs; when either is designated as the source of a preferred reading it should be assumed that the reading concerned was repeated in *3*).

All emendations of punctuation (where readings from *MS 1 3C* or *3P* are preferred to those in *CM*) are also recorded, following the same system, together with a handful of significant but rejected *MS* variants. No attempt is made to record the mass of rejected punctuation variants either in *MS* (*c.*6,000) or in *1 2* and *3* (*c.*1,100). By a similar token, to list all emendations relating to the minutiae of spelling, hyphenation, capitalization, and italicization (arrived at according to the principles outlined above) would add several hundred entries to an already large apparatus. Moreover, since these categories are generally normalized to *MS* majority usage, a list of the Clarendon text's variations from *CM* would present only a partial record of the editorial intervention involved. Under the circumstances I have chosen to omit such details from the apparatus. A full list of paragraphing emendations and variants is given in Appendix C. The occasional error in *CM* (a punctuation mark omitted, a self-evident misprint, etc.) is silently corrected, as are one-off variants or mistakes in the spelling of proper names—e.g. 'Machiavelli' (which is usually given with a double 'c'), 'Sienna' with an extra 'n', etc. The much-

used title 'Messer' is generally changed to 'Messere' in *1*; I have
emended in all such instances without a note.

The commonest category of entry in the apparatus concerns *MS*
deletions and additions. Deletions are indicated by angled brackets:
for example, '⟨doublet⟩ tunic *MS*' signifies that George Eliot originally wrote the word 'doublet' but then crossed it out and substituted 'tunic' (the placing of the revision—whether in the margin, or
immediately after or above the cancellation—is not shown). Whenever
feasible the length of the pick-up phrase from the Clarendon text
indicates the precise nature of the revision. For example, on p. 391
MS originally read 'Romola had never uttered a word to her godfather on the subject'; George Eliot then deleted 'subject' and substituted 'circumstances of the sale'. The entry, accordingly, reads
'⟨subject⟩ circumstances of the sale *MS*', signifying that the four
words quoted from the Clarendon text replaced the single cancelled
word. In the case of longer deletions, however, this method would
lead to unhelpfully cumbersome entries. For example, on p. 248
George Eliot first wrote 'And that self doubt was urged to activity in
Romola by the necessity', but then revised this to 'And Romola was
urged to doubt herself the more by the necessity'. For the sake of
concision, the entry here reads 'And ⟨that self doubt was urged to
activity in Romola⟩ *MS*'.

On numerous occasions, of course, a *MS* deletion represents a false
start that has no direct correspondence to the final version, and in
such cases the pick-up word from the Clarendon text simply indicates
where the cancelled passage was located—see, for example, p. 155:
'and ⟨clad in his white tunic with the black rosary falling by his side
and the black mantle falling around him⟩ *MS*'. This last example
conveniently leads on to the issue of the order in which cancellations
were made. It is possible that George Eliot intended the words 'the
black mantle falling around him' as a replacement for 'the black
rosary falling by his side'. The physical evidence of *MS* is unclear on
this; it *seems*, however, that she struck out both phrases at one go
(together with the preceding half-dozen words), and I have therefore
recorded them, as above, as equal parts of a single clause. When, on
the other hand, it is plain (whether from the placing of the words on
the page, from the physical variations of the crossings out, or, most
likely, from the sense) that there was a distinct sequence of cancellation, substitution, cancellation, and further revision, I have reproduced this sequence in the apparatus, e.g. on p. 236: '⟨more plebeian⟩
⟨poorer⟩ less aristocratic *MS*'.

Very occasionally there are significant deletions of a word or two
within large deletions of a phrase or sentence; these are recorded by
means of double angled brackets ⟪ ⟫, as on pp. 358 and 579. When a

few words in a deletion cannot be read they are indicated with square
brackets: [*three words*]. If most of the words in a deletion are undecipherable, it is not recorded. Deleted words are preceded by a question mark when the readings are likely but not definitive. Words
deleted and immediately repeated are not recorded; but words
deleted, revised, cancelled again, and then repeated are given. In the
recording of deletions ampersands are replaced by 'and'; *MS* punctuation, spelling, hyphenation, capitalization, and italicization are reproduced exactly, though on occasions of course they differ from the
Clarendon text. (It will be noted, also, that substantive *MS* variants
sometimes involve differences in accidentals from the copy text—since
MS is always reproduced exactly in the apparatus.)

Additions in *MS*, indicated by braces { }, are not separately
recorded when they simply replace a deletion, or when they correct
an obvious error of sense, but only when they represent a new
thought in themselves. For example, at the climactic moment in
chapter 52 when Romola rises in mental turmoil from the altar-step
in the Badia, George Eliot originally wrote 'She rose from her knees
that she might hasten to her sick people in the courtyard, and by
some beneficent action, revive that sense of worth in life which at this
moment was unfed by any wider faith'. Subsequently she went back
and added the word 'immediate': hence the often-quoted phrase
'some immediate beneficent action'. The entry here reads '{immedi-
ate} beneficent action *MS*'. Sometimes a single entry records both
additions and deletions within the same passage; sometimes additions
are recorded within deletions or vice versa, so as to make the exact
order of revision clearer. Occasionally (e.g. pp. 418 and 422) minor
additions or deletions are included within an entry whose main purpose is to record a *MS* variant reading. When recording additions, as
with cancellations, *MS* accidentals are reproduced exactly and ampersands are replaced by 'and'. Neither additions nor deletions are
recorded when, as part of the reordering of a first draft, they concern
the insertion or removal of material at the head or foot of a page in
order to make the sense run on.

DESCRIPTIVE LIST OF EDITIONS
1863–1880

Romola was first published in the *Cornhill Magazine* in fourteen monthly parts between July 1862 and August 1863, in each case comprising the opening pages of the part concerned.

Parts 1–6 appeared in vol. vi of the magazine (nos. 31-6), as follows: 1 (July 1862: Proem, chs. 1–5) pp. [1]–43; 2 (August 1862: chs. 6–10) pp. [145]–86; 3 (September 1862: chs. 11–14) pp. [289]–318; 4 (October 1862: chs. 15–20) pp. [433]–70; 5 (November 1862: chs. 21–6) pp. [577]–604; 6 (December 1862: chs. 27–32) pp. [721]–57.

Parts 7–12 appeared in vol. vii (nos. 37–42): 7 (January 1863: chs. 33–7) pp. [1]–30; 8 (February 1863: chs. 38–41) pp. [145]–71; 9 (March 1863: chs. 42–6) pp. [282]–309; 10 (April 1863: chs. 47–51) pp. [417]–40; 11 (May 1863: chs. 52–6) pp. [553]–76; 12 (June 1863: chs. 57–61) pp. [681]–705.

Parts 13 and 14 appeared in vol. viii (nos. 43 and 44): 13 (July 1863: chs. 62–7) pp. [1]–34; 14 (August 1863: chs. 68–72, Epilogue) pp. [129]–53.

Frederic Leighton produced twenty–four illustrations for the *Cornhill* serialization: two in each part except for parts 10, 12, 13, and 14, which contained only one each. (It was when she was working on part 9 that GE decided to extend the work from twelve parts to fourteen, whereupon it would seem that the publishers decided to ration the appearance of the illustrations, Leighton's commission having been for twenty-four only.) They were placed as follows: (part 1) THE BLIND SCHOLAR AND HIS DAUGHTER facing vi. [1], Proem, "SUPPOSE YOU LET ME LOOK AT MYSELF" facing vi. 27, ch. 3; (part 2) A RECOGNITION facing vi. [145], ch. 6, UNDER THE PLANE-TREE facing vi. 184, ch. 10; (part 3) THE FIRST KISS facing vi. [289], ch. 11, THE PEASANTS' FAIR facing vi. 311, ch. 14; (part 4) THE DYING MESSAGE facing vi. [433], ch. 15, A FLORENTINE JOKE facing vi. 450, ch. 16; (part 5) THE ESCAPED PRISONER facing vi. [577], ch. 21, NICCOLÒ AT WORK facing vi. 603, ch. 26; (part 6) THE PAINTED RECORD facing vi. [721], ch. 27, COMING HOME facing vi. 726, ch. 27; (part 7) "YOU DIDN'T THINK IT WAS SO PRETTY DID YOU?" facing vii. [1], ch. 33, ESCAPED facing vii. 29, ch. 37; (part 8) "FATHER, I WILL BE GUIDED" facing vii. [145], ch. 38, A SUPPER IN THE RUCELLAI GARDENS facing vii. 161, ch. 39; (part 9) THE VISIBLE MADONNA facing vii. [281], ch. 42, A DANGEROUS COLLEAGUE facing vii. 306, ch. 46; (part 10) MONNA BRIGIDA'S CONVERSION facing vii. [417], ch. 47; (part 11) "BUT YOU WILL HELP ME" facing vii. [553], ch. 52, TESSA AT HOME facing vii. 569, ch. 56; (part 12) DRIFTING AWAY facing vii. [681], ch. 57; (part 13) "WILL HIS EYES OPEN?" facing viii. [1], ch. 62; (part 14) AT THE WELL facing viii. [129], ch. 68.

1   *First Edition, 3 volumes octavo, July 1863, 190 × 115 mm.*

ROMOLA. | BY | GEORGE ELIOT, | AUTHOR OF | "ADAM BEDE," "THE MILL ON THE FLOSS," "SILAS MARNER," | AND "SCENES OF CLERICAL LIFE." | IN THREE VOL-UMES. | VOL. I. [II.] [III.] | LONDON: | SMITH, ELDER AND CO., 65, CORNHILL. | [*rule*] | M.DCCC.LXIII.

Collation:

VOL. I.

π^2 1–21^8; pp. iv + 336

[i] title-page; [ii] [*The Right of Translation is reserved.*]; [iii]–iv CONTENTS | TO THE FIRST VOLUME.; [1]–336 text; 336 text | END OF VOL. I. | [*rule*] | London: SMITH, ELDER and Co., Little Green Arbour Court, Old Bailey, E.C.

VOL. II.

π^2 22–42^8 χ1; pp. iv + 333 + [3]

[i] title-page; [ii] [*The Right of Translation is reserved.*]; [iii]–iv CONTENTS | TO THE SECOND VOLUME.; [1]–333 text; 333 text | END OF VOL. II.; [334] LON-DON: | PRINTED BY SMITH, ELDER AND Co., | LITTLE GREEN ARBOUR COURT, OLD BAILEY, E.C. | [335]–[336 (numbered 2)] publisher's advertisement: NEW NOVELS, | PUBLISHED BY | SMITH, ELDER & Co., 65, Cornhill.

VOL. III

π^2 43–60^8 61^2; pp. iv + 292

[i] title-page; [ii] [*The Right of Translation is reserved.*]; [iii]–iv CONTENTS | TO THE THIRD VOLUME.; [1]–292 text; 292 text | THE END. | [*rule*] | London: SMITH, ELDER and Co., Little Green Arbour Court, Old Bailey, E.C.

Binding: Dark green cloth, dot-and-line grain, ornamental frame blocked in blind on front and back boards; spine lettering, reversed out of elaborate ornamental device in gilt: ROMOLA | BY | THE AUTHOR | OF ADAM BEDE. | then in gilt: VOL. I. [II.] [III.] | LONDON | SMITH ELDER & C? Pale yellow end-papers.

Publication: 6 July 1863, one and a half guineas, 2,288 copies.

Copies: (1) British Library; (2) editor; (3) University of Virginia Library; (4)–(7) Princeton University Library: (4) Sir Edward Burne-Jones's copy, (5) Anthony Trollope's copy presented by GE; (8) and (9) Cambridge University Library; (10) F. D. Maurice's copy, Sadleir Collection UCLA.

Notes: The following misprints and errors occur in all ten copies examined: (i) the title-page of vol. iii lacks the comma after GEORGE ELIOT; (ii) i. 131, l. 8, the semi-colon is omitted after 'tested', leaving the line one character–space short at the right-hand margin; (iii) i. 154, l. 2, the words 'giovane mio' are run together into a single word; (iv) iii. 199, l. 4 up, the 'e' is omitted from the word 'He' and a gap left; (v) iii. 287, l. 13, 'air' for 'hair'. In all copies except nos. 3 and 10 the initial 'e' on the word 'expe-rience' is missing at the start of l. 17 on ii. 212 and a gap left in its place. In all copies except nos. 2 and 4 there is a space instead of the letter 'k' on the word 'think' 6 ll. up on i. 183; the word 'can' 1 l. above is misaligned in all copies, though to varying degrees. In all copies except nos. 1 and 9 the title-page of vol. i lacks the inverted com-

mas before ADAM BEDE. In copies 5, 6, and 7 the 'C.' is omitted from 'OLD
BAILEY, E.C.' in the printer's colophon on p. [334] of vol. ii.

1a   *Second Edition, 3 volumes octavo, July 1863, 190 × 115 mm.*

ROMOLA. | BY | GEORGE ELIOT, | AUTHOR OF | "ADAM
BEDE," "THE MILL ON THE FLOSS," "SILAS MARNER," |
AND "SCENES OF CLERICAL LIFE." | IN THREE VOL-
UMES. | VOL. I. [II.] [III.] | SECOND EDITION. | LONDON:
| SMITH, ELDER AND CO., 65, CORNHILL. | [*rule*] |
M.DCCC.LXIII.

Collation: as for *1*, except for cancel title in each volume. The publisher's advertisement
is included in vol. ii. In the copy examined, the 'C.' is omitted from the printer's
colophon in vol. ii.

Binding: As for *1*.

Publication: Announced as 'now ready' in *The Publishers' Circular*, 16 July 1863 (see
above, p. xliv), one and a half guineas.

Copy: British Library.

Notes: Though describing itself as a second *edition*, this was in fact simply a second
issue and was bound from the same sheets as the first, though with the addition of a
cancel title. The inverted commas are present before ADAM BEDE on the title-page
of vol. i, as is the comma after GEORGE ELIOT on the title-page of vol. iii. On
i. 183 the 'k' is missing from 'think' and the word 'can' above is misaligned. All the
other misprints and errors described above in the notes to *1* are present also in *1a*.

1b   *First Edition Remainder, 3 volumes in 1, octavo, 1864,*
192 × 119 mm.

ROMOLA. | BY GEORGE ELIOT, | AUTHOR OF "ADAM
BEDE," "THE MILL ON THE FLOSS," | "SILAS MARNER,"
AND "SCENES OF CLERICAL LIFE." | THREE VOLUMES IN
ONE. | LONDON: | SMITH, ELDER AND CO., 65, CORN-
HILL. | [*rule*] | M.DCCC.LXIV.

Collation:

π^1 χ^2 1–60^8 61^2; pp. vi + 336 + 333 + [1] + 292

[i] blank; [ii] frontispiece; [iii] title-page; [iv] [*The Right of Translation is reserved.*];
[v]–'vi' CONTENTS.; [1]–336 text; 336 text | END OF VOL.I. | [*rule*] | (*printer's
colophon as in* 1); [1]–333 text; 333 text | END OF VOL. II. | [334] (*printer's colophon
as in* 1); [1]–292 text | THE END. | [*rule*] | (*printer's colophon as in* 1)

Illustration: the frontispiece, on the verso of a single leaf tipped on to χ1, is Leighton's
illustration to part 9 of the *Cornhill* serialization, THE VISIBLE MADONNA, reproduced the same size as in the magazine (153 × 100 mm.).

Binding: Smooth dark-brown cloth, front blocked with gilt and black lines forming a
frame, back blocked with same pattern but in blind. Gilt lettering on spine: ROMOLA
| BY | GEORGE ELIOT | 6/-; gilt and black bands head and tail. End-papers dark
green.

Publication: though the title-page specifies 1864, Smith, Elder & Co.'s records imply
that publication was in 1865, perhaps in order to clear sheet stock of the three-decker

before the appearance (in September) of the one-volume Illustrated edition (2), which sold for the same price of 6s.

Copy: Princeton University Library.

Notes: Bound from the same sheets as *1* though with new prelims at the beginning and, naturally, without prelims to vols. ii and iii. The misprints and errors noted in *1* on i. 131, i. 154, iii. 199, and iii. 287 are all present. On i. 183 the 'k' is missing from 'think' and the word 'can' above is badly misaligned, but the initial 'e' on 'experience' (ii. 212) and the 'C.' in the printer's colophon on ii. [334] are both present.

2   *Illustrated Edition, 1 volume octavo, September 1865, 186 × 118 mm.*

ROMOLA. | BY | GEORGE ELIOT, | AUTHOR OF | "ADAM BEDE," "THE MILL ON THE FLOSS," "SILAS MARNER," | AND "SCENES OF CLERICAL LIFE." | ILLUSTRATED EDI-TION. | LONDON: | SMITH, ELDER AND CO., 65, CORN-HILL. | 1865.

Collation:

a^4 (a1 + χ2) 1–33^8 34^4; pp. xii + 535 + [1]

[i] half-title: ROMOLA.; [ii]–[iii] blank; [iv] frontispiece; [v] illustrated title-page [vignette, 89 × 139 mm., of a young man and woman leaning over the Ponte Vecchio]: ROMOLA | BY | GEORGE ELIOT. | SMITH, ELDER, & Co. | 65, CORNHILL, | 1865.; [vi] blank; [vii] title-page; [viii] [*The Right of Translation is reserved.*]; [ix]–'vi', 'vii' CONTENTS.; [xii] LIST OF ILLUSTRATIONS.; [1]–535 text; 535 text | THE END.; [536] LONDON: | PRINTED BY SMITH, ELDER AND CO., | OLD BAILEY, E.C.

Illustrations: (all printed on heavier, smoother paper): four of Leighton's illustrations from the *Cornhill Magazine*: WILL HIS EYES OPEN? (frontispiece); THE DYING MESSAGE (facing p. 142, verso blank); THE VISIBLE MADONNA (facing p. 355, recto blank); A DAN-GEROUS COLLEAGUE (facing p. 370, verso blank). The subtitle vignette (also by Leighton, and engraved by Swain) was commissioned for this edition.

Binding: Dark-red morocco cloth, blocked in blind on front and back with framing lines and fleurons; in the centre (front and back) an elaborate armorial device comprising a decorated shield with scrolls above and below, all superimposed upon three ears of corn; lettering within scrolls: SMITH ELDER & Co. | CORNHILL | LONDON. Spine lettering within gilt ornament, in gilt on red background: ROMOLA | BY | GEORGE ELIOT.; reversed out of gilt in diagonal bands: ILLUSTRATED | EDI-TION; at tail reversed out of gilt band with ornament: SMITH ELDER & Co.; blind rules head and tail. End-papers pale yellow.

Publication: September 1865, 6s. 1,519 copies; 500 copies reprinted January 1869.

Copies: Sadleir Collection UCLA; Princeton University Library; British Library; editor.

Notes: The following misprints and errors occur in all copies examined: (i) p. 12, l. 22, the space between the words '*chi*' and '*abbaratta*' is too small; (ii) p. 47, l. 16, the single inverted comma after '*junguntur*' is missing; (iii) p. 87, l. 2 up, inverted commas are wrongly placed before 'But'; (iv) p. 95, l. 5, the word 'ingenuousness' lacks the first 'u'; (v) p. 97, l. 33, the full stop is missing between 'go' and 'I'; (vi) p. 126, l. 5 up, inverted commas are extraneously placed before 'No one'; (vii) p. 218, l. 18, 'this' for 'his'; (viii) p. 258, l. 27, the 'a' is missing from the word 'cause' and a gap left; (ix) p. 307, l. 5, the sentence ends with a comma rather than a full stop; (x) p. 362, l. 7, 'amost' for 'amongst'; (xi) p. 448, l. 8 up, there is an extraneous set of closing inverted commas after 'other'; (xii) p. 478, l. 2, 'audiance' for 'audience'; (xiii) p. 503,

l. 1, 'Trinitâ' for 'Trinità'; (xiv) p. 516, l. 11 up, 'any' for 'and'; (xv) p. 530, l. 20, 'mamed' for 'named'.

2a   New Edition, 1 volume octavo, June 1869, 167 × 113 mm.

ROMOLA. | BY GEORGE ELIOT. | A NEW EDITION. | LON-DON: | SMITH, ELDER & CO., 15, WATERLOO PLACE. | 1871 [*though this edition was first published in 1869, I have been unable to locate a copy of that date*].

Collation:

π^4 1–33^8 34^4; pp. x + 535 + [1] (frontispiece after π1)

[i] half-title: ROMOLA.; [ii]–[iii] blank; [iv] frontispiece [on single leaf]; [v] title-page; [vi] blank; [vii]–'vi', 'vii' CONTENTS.; [x] blank; [1]–535 text; [536] LONDON: | PRINTED BY SMITH, ELDER AND CO., | OLD BAILEY, E.C.

Illustration: Leighton's *Cornhill Magazine* illustration "WILL HIS EYES OPEN?" (frontispiece).

Binding: Dark green cloth, sand grain, blocked front and back with elaborately ornamental framing device in black; in gilt at head of front board ROMOLA (centred, between gilt fleurons); in gilt at foot of front board GEORGE ELIOT. (centred, between gilt fleurons); in gilt at centre of front board an oval monogram device bearing the initials S&E (for Smith & Elder). Spine blocked with black and gilt ornaments; ROMOLA (reversed out of gilt) | GEORGE·ELIOT (in gilt on green background) | SMITH ELDER & C? (reversed out of gilt band at the tail). Cream end-papers.

Publication: (printed from the stereotype plates cast for *2*) price 2s. 6d.; 3,000 copies were run off in June 1869, and a further 2,082 in October 1869; 1,000 copies were reprinted in November 1870 and 2,030 more in May 1871; further reprints followed in 1872, 1873, 1874, and (the last during George Eliot's lifetime) 1878. Four dates have been identified on the title-pages of 'New' editions during George Eliot's lifetime: [1869], 1871, 1874, 1878 (The National Union Catalogue records an edition dated 1875 in the Beinecke Library at Yale, but there is no such copy there—nor any record of one ever having been there).

Copies: (1871) British Library; (1874) editor; (1878) editor. It seems very likely, from circumstantial evidence, that the text marked up by George Eliot as setting copy for the Cabinet edition (*3C*, now at the Harry Ransom Humanities Research Center in Austin, Texas) was a copy of the 1869 (i.e. first) printing. Since, however, the title-page is lacking, this identification must remain provisional.

Notes: All the misprints and errors above in the notes to *2* also occur in *3C* and the 1871 issue of *2a*; all but (viii) occur in the 1874 and 1878 issues. All three issues examined, together with *3C*, contain one error which was not in *2*: on the first line of p. 148 the word 'father' is given as 'rather'; all except that of 1878 lack the 'f' on 'for' on l. 2 of p. 75. *3C* alone omits the single inverted comma before '*ingenia*' on the last line of p. 168. The publisher's colophon at the foot of the title-page of the 1874 and 1878 issues omits the comma in '15, WATERLOO PLACE'. In the 1874 issue the printer's colophon is given at the foot of p. 535 and reads '*Printed by William Moore & Co.*'; p. [536] is blank. In the 1878 issue it is similarly located but reads 'LONDON: PRINTED BY | SPOTTISWOODE AND CO., NEW-STREET SQUARE | AND PARLIAMENT STREET'. There is no caption to the frontispiece in the 1874 and 1878 issues.

3. *Cabinet Edition, 2 volumes octavo, December 1877 and February 1878, 176 × 113 mm.*

THE WORKS | OF | GEORGE ELIOT | ROMOLA | VOL.I. [II.] | WILLIAM BLACKWOOD AND SONS | EDINBURGH AND LONDON | MDCCCLXXVIII | *All Rights reserved*

Collation:

VOL. I.

π^4 A–2E^8; pp. viii + 445 + [3]

[i] blank; [ii] publisher's advertisement: THE | WORKS OF GEORGE ELIOT. | *in Five-Shilling Monthly Volumes.* | [list of other volumes in the series]; [iii] series title: THE WORKS | OF | GEORGE ELIOT | [*rule*] | Cabinet Edition; [iv] blank; [v] title-page; [vi] blank; [vii]–'vi' CONTENTS OF THE FIRST VOLUME.; [1]–444 text; 444 text | END OF THE FIRST VOLUME.; [445] NOTE. | [*rule*] | SAVONAROLA'S SERMON, p. 350. The sermon here given is not a translation, but a free repre- | sentation of Fra Girolamo's preaching in its more impassioned | moments.; [446] PRINTED BY WILLIAM BLACKWOOD AND SONS.; [447]–[448] blank.

VOL. II.

π^4 A–2E^8; pp. viii + 447 + [1]

[i] blank; [ii] publisher's advertisement, as for vol. i; [iii] series title; [iv] blank; [v] title-page; [vi] blank; [vii]–'vi' CONTENTS OF THE SECOND VOLUME.; [1]–447 text; 447 text | THE END.; PRINTED BY WILLIAM BLACKWOOD AND SONS.

Binding: Olive cloth, diagonal fine rib grain, stamped in black: front, a scroll leaf design within a line frame, WORKS | OF | GEORGE ELIOT; back, circular leaf design within a line frame. Spine: black leaf ornaments and, in gilt: WORKS | OF | GEORGE | ELIOT | ROMOLA | I. [II.] | CABINET | EDITION. Russet end–papers.

Publication: Vol. i, December 1877 (though with 1878 on the title-page), vol. ii, February 1878; price 5s. per volume. The initial printing was 1,050 sets; 630 copies of vol. i and 525 of vol. ii were reprinted in September and October 1878 respectively, and a further 525 of each volume in April 1880. These last, together with post-1880 reprints, have no date on the title-page.

Copies: (1), (2), and (3) editor; (4) British Library; (5) Cambridge University Library.

Notes: The following misprints and errors have been noted in all copies examined: (i) i. 11, l. 3 up, the dot is missing from the 'i' in '*marmi*'; (ii) i. 103, l. 10 up, the apostrophe is missing in 'father's'; (iii) i. 193, l. 11 up, 'Romolo' for 'Romola'; (iv) i. 391, l. 1, inverted commas missing before 'What'; (v) ii. 33, bottom line, full stop instead of comma after 'tenderness'; (vi) ii. 89, l. 13, double instead of single inverted commas around '*Orfeo*'; (vii) ii. 190, l. 14, hyphen instead of full stop after 'hair'; (viii) ii. 242, l. 16, question mark omitted after 'scholarship'; (ix) ii. 361, l. 9 up, single instead of double inverted commas after 'others?'. In copies 1 and 4, which, from the evidence of the publisher's advertisement on p. [ii], appear to be the earliest in date of the five copies examined, the word 'martyrs' on l. 7 of ii. 256 is misprinted 'maryrs'; copies 2 and 5 have corrected the error. (Copies 1 and 4 appear to be from the first printing, copy 2 from the October 1878 reprint, and copies 3 and 5 from post-1880 printings.)

4.　*Stereotyped Edition, 1 volume octavo, August 1878, 188 × 125 mm.*

ROMOLA | BY | GEORGE ELIOT | STEREOTYPED EDITION | WILLIAM BLACKWOOD AND SONS | EDINBURGH AND LONDON

Collation:

π⁴ A–2I⁴ χ1; pp. x + 504 + [2] (illustrated title after π1)
[i] blank; [ii] publisher's advertisement for the Cabinet edition of George Eliot's Works; [iii] illustrated title-page: NOVELS | OF | GEORGE ELIOT | VOL.VI. | ROMOLA | [oval vignette (81 × 64mm.) of the Palazzo Vecchio viewed from the Piazzale degli Uffizi] | WILLIAM BLACKWOOD AND SONS | EDINBURGH AND LONDON; [iv] blank; [v] title-page; [vi] blank; [vii]–'iv', 'v' CONTENTS.; [x] blank; [1]–504 text; 504 text | THE END.; [505] NOTE. | [*rule*] | SAVONAROLA'S SERMON, p. 199. | [as in Cabinet edition: see above]; [506] PRINTED BY WILLIAM BLACKWOOD AND SONS.

Binding: Red cloth, sand grain, blocked in blind on front and back boards, with medallion of Savonarola's head (probably based on Fra Bartolommeo's portrait at San Marco in Florence) in gilt on front. Spine ruled at top and tail in gilt, lettered in gilt: ROMOLA | BY | GEORGE | ELIOT | Wᵐ. BLACKWOOD & SONS | EDINBURGH & LONDON. End-papers dark chocolate.

Publication: August 1878, 2,100 copies, 3s. 6d.; 2,100 reprinted in October 1878 and a further 2,100 in November 1879. Several reprintings post–1880.

Copies; (1) British Library; (2), (3), and (4) editor.

Notes: The following misprints and errors have been noted in the first issue: (i) p. 9, l. 2, inverted commas omitted before 'when'; (ii) p. 98, 10 ll. up, 'give' for 'gave'; (iii) p. 175, l. 15, 'allusions' for 'illusions'; (iv) p. 224, 4 ll. up, the dot is missing on the 'i' in 'like'; (v) p. 232, 11 ll. up, the 'i' is missing from 'image' and a gap left; (vi) p. 306, 8 ll. up, a question mark is extraneously placed after 'Tito'; (vii) p. 307, l. 7, single instead of double inverted commas following 'here', though a space left for the missing comma; (viii) p. 312, l. 20, 'Romolo' for 'Romola'; (ix) p. 343, 3 ll. up, 'stanch' for 'staunch'; (x) p. 375, 19 ll. up, the top half of the 'l' in 'Romola' has failed to print; (xi) p. 395, l. 5, the line-breaking hyphen is omitted in 'em-/phasis' though a space is left for it; (xii) p. 440, 15 ll. up, full stop omitted between 'him' and 'He' though a space is left for it. Nos. v, vii, x, and xi are corrected in later issues. Since the Stereotyped edition never carried a date on the title-page, the date of a given copy must be inferred from circumstantial evidence such as publisher's advertisements bound in. (Copies 1 and 2 appear to be from the first issue and copies 3 and 4 from post-1880 reprints.)

5.　*'Deluxe Edition', 2 volumes quarto, October 1880, 266 × 185 mm.*

ROMOLA | BY | GEORGE ELIOT | WITH ILLUSTRATIONS BY SIR FREDERICK LEIGHTON, P.R.A. | IN TWO VOLUMES | VOL.I [II.] | LONDON | SMITH, ELDER, AND CO., 15, WATERLOO PLACE | 1880

Collation:

VOL. I.

π⁴ b² B–3E⁴; pp. xiv + 397 + [3] (frontispiece after π²)
[i] publisher's announcement: *Only One Thousand Copies of this Edition have been printed for Sale* | THIS COPY IS NUMBER . . . ; [ii] blank; [iii] half-title: ROMOLA;

[iv]–[v] blank; [vi] frontispiece; [vii] title-page; [viii] LONDON: | R. CLAY, SONS, AND TAYLOR, | BREAD STREET HILL.; [ix]–'viii', 'ix', 'x' CONTENTS.; [xiii] LIST OF PLATES.; [xiv] blank; [1]–396 text; 396 text | END OF VOL. I.; [397] NOTE. | SAVONAROLA'S SERMON, p. 313. [as in Cabinet edition: see above]; [398] LONDON: | R. CLAY, SONS, AND TAYLOR, | BREAD STREET HILL, E.C.; [399]–[400] blank.

VOL. II.

π^4 b^2 B–3E^4 3F^2; pp. xiv + 403 + [1] (frontispiece after π2)

[i] publisher's announcement, as for vol. i; [ii] blank; [iii] half-title; [iv]–[v] blank; [vi] frontispiece; [vii] title-page; [viii] LONDON: | R.CLAY, SONS, AND TAYLOR, | BREAD STREET HILL.; [ix]–'viii', 'ix', 'x', 'xi' CONTENTS.; [xiv] LIST OF PLATES.; [1]–403 text; 403 text | THE END.; [404] LONDON: | R CLAY, SONS, AND TAYLOR, | BREAD STREET HILL.

Illustrations: all 24 of Leighton's illustrations for the *Cornhill Magazine* (12 per volume, placed alongside the page of text to which they refer), together with the illustrated capitals to each serial part and the tailpiece to the Proem (this last placed in the centre of the Proem's penultimate page [p. 10] rather than at the end of the Proem [p. 11]), printed on China paper and pasted in by hand on to tipped-in leaves of plate paper (unnumbered, with the rectos or versos blank). The frontispiece to vol. i ("SUPPOSE YOU LET ME LOOK AT MYSELF") is in fact the 2nd illustration to the first part of the serial; the frontispiece to vol. ii ("YOU DIDN'T THINK IT WAS SO PRETTY DID YOU?") is the 13th in the *Cornhill* sequence. Three of the illustrations in vol. ii have different titles in the List of Illustrations from the actual captions (which follow those of the *Cornhill*): ROMOLA AND SAVONAROLA for "FATHER, I WILL BE GUIDED"; BALDASSARRE AND ROMOLA for "BUT YOU WILL HELP ME"; DEATH OF TITO for "WILL HIS EYES OPEN?".

Binding: Cream glazed calico cloth. Spine (on light-brown paper labels): ROMOLA | BY | GEORGE ELIOT | VOLUME I. [II.] Chocolate end-papers.

Publication: 15 October 1880, print run limited to 1,000 individually numbered sets, offered to the trade at a discounted price of 73s. 6d. *Athenaeum*, 25 September 1880; *The Publisher's Circular*, 1 October 1880:

'MESSRS. SMITH, ELDER, & CO. have the pleasure of announcing the Publication of an Edition of ROMOLA, by GEORGE ELIOT, in Two Volumes, Imperial 8vo.

The Letterpress of this Edition will be printed by Messrs. RICHARD CLAY, SONS, & TAYLOR, on paper of the finest quality, made expressly for the Work by Messrs. JOHN DICKINSON & Co.

The Illustrations for the Work, which were drawn by Sir FREDERICK LEIGHTON, the President of the Royal Academy, will all be printed on *real China Paper* by Messrs. RICHARD CLAY, SONS, & TAYLOR, and mounted on Plate paper; the Initial Letters will be mounted with the Letterpress of the Book.

The Edition will be limited to *One Thousand Copies*, and the type will be distributed after each sheet has been printed.

The Work will be published on the 15th October, 1880.

Subscriptions will be received *through Booksellers*; each copy will be numbered, and copies will be delivered to Subscribers in the order in which Subscriptions are received.

The Publishers reserve to themselves the option of at any time increasing the Subscription price.

The Publishers also reserve to themselves the right of printing a few copies beyond the Edition of One Thousand Copies, for the purpose of presentation to the Author and Reviewers. Such additional copies will not be numbered or sold; the Edition for sale being strictly limited to One Thousand Copies.

Prospectuses and Specimen Pages, with information as to the price at which

Booksellers will receive Subscriptions, may be obtained on application to the principal Booksellers in London and the Provinces.
    15 WATERLOO PLACE, LONDON:
        September 20, 1880.'

Copies: Princeton University Library (copy no. 415 in the sequence of 1,000); editor (no. 498); British Library (no. 593); British Library (limitation leaf removed during rebinding).

Notes: The following errors and unauthorized changes have been noted in all copies examined: (i) vol. i, p. 68, l. 3, 'fallows' for 'furrows'; (ii) i. 320, l. 9, 'self-mastering' for 'self-martyring'; (iii) ii. 31, l. 2, 'looks' for 'look'; (iv) ii. 45, l. 12 up, 'presented' for 'presents'; (v) ii. 125, l. 13, 'needs' for 'need'; (vi) ii. 165, l. 1, 'have not' for 'not have'; (vii) ii. 199, l. 6, 'learn' for 'learn more'; (viii) ii. 284, l. 2, 'thought' for 'felt'; (ix) ii. 378, l. 6 up, 'I had' for 'I'd'.

First American Edition, 1 volume octavo, 1863, 235 × 145 mm.

ROMOLA. | A NOVEL. | BY GEORGE ELIOT, | AUTHOR OF | "ADAM BEDE," "THE MILL ON THE FLOSS," "SCENES OF CLERICAL LIFE," AND | "SILAS MARNER." | WITH ILLUSTRATIONS. | NEW YORK: | HARPER & BROTHERS, PUBLISHERS, | FRANKLIN SQUARE. | 1863.

Collation:

π^4 A–P^8 Q^6; pp. viii + 242 + [10]

[i] title-page; [ii] blank; [iii]–vi CONTENTS.; [vii] LIST OF ILLUSTRATIONS.; [viii] blank; [9]–250 text (double column); 250 text | THE END.; [251]–[252 (numbered 2)] publisher's advertisement: HARPER'S | LIBRARY OF SELECT NOVELS.; [253]–[254, 255 (numbered 2, 3)] HARPER & BROTHERS' | LIST OF NEW BOOKS.; [256] publisher's advertisement: GEORGE ELIOT'S NOVELS.; [257]–[260] blank.

Illustrations: all but one of Leighton's 24 illustrations for the *Cornhill Magazine* (the final illustration, AT THE WELL, is omitted), located at the appropriate points in the text. Each is reproduced exactly the same size as in the *Cornhill*, and therefore takes up approximately three-quarters of the text area of the page concerned, spread across both columns. In addition, all but the last of the illustrated capitals to the opening of the novel's fourteen serial parts are reproduced, again same size (*c*.75 × 50 mm., so the width of a single column only). These are reproduced as in-text illustrations, always on the first page of the part-opening chapter, but without the actual capital letters which the vignettes frame in the *Cornhill*. Each is given a caption (not always an entirely appropriate one) in the list of illustrations, though not in the text, as follows: part I, ch. 1 (p. 12 of First American Edition) THE SHIPWRECKED STRANGER; part II, ch. 6 (p. 33) A STREET IN FLORENCE; part III, ch. 11 (p. 56) THE CLOISTER GATE; part IV, ch. 15 (p. 73) SAN MARCO, FLORENCE; part V, ch. 21 (p. 94) IN THE VIA LARGA, FLORENCE; part VI, ch. 27 (p. 109) ROMOLA WAITING; part VII, ch. 33 (p. 130) IN FLORENCE; part VIII, ch. 38 (p. 147) TO ROME; part IX, ch. 42 (p. 162) THE FLORENTINE GALLEY; part X, ch. 47 (p. 179) THE PORCH; part XI, ch. 52 (p. 192) THE CHILD OF THE OTHER WIFE; part XII, ch. 57 (p. 206) THE OLD PALACE; part XIII, ch. 62 (p. 219) THE PULPIT IN SAN MARCO. The illustrated capital to part XIV (ch. 68), showing Romola in the plague village, is omitted. The tailpiece to the Proem in the *Cornhill* appears before the text on the opening page of the Proem (p. [9]), the caption in the List of Illustrations reading simply FLORENCE. The omission of the main illustration and illustrated capital from the final part of the *Cornhill* serialization was probably caused by timing problems, the First American Edition being published in the same month (August 1863).

Binding: (1) purple cloth, (2) brownish purple cloth, (3) black cloth, (4) brown cloth, (5) black cloth, all bead grain, blocked in blind on front and back boards with elaborate framing device. Spine ruled in gilt at head and tail, ornamental gilt lettering: ROMOLA | BY | GEORGE ELIOT | AUTHOR OF | ADAM BEDE | &c. | ILLUSTRATED | HARPERS.

Publication: August 1863, $1.50 in cloth, $1.25 in paper.

Copies: (1) editor; (2) British Library; (3) Princeton University Library; (4) Cambridge University Library; (5) University of Virginia Library.

Notes: All copies examined contain the list of HARPER'S LIBRARY OF SELECT NOVELS on pp. [251–2]. The remaining pages in copies 2 and 4 are identical to those in 1; copies 3 and 5 have different publisher's advertisements bound in. Copy 5 lacks the date on the title-page. Copy 1 bears the following handwritten inscription on the fly-leaf: 'Bought at Louisville Ky August 1863. During the War This Book has heard the thunder of the guns'.

Copyright Edition, 2 volumes octavo, December 1863, 150 × 115 mm.

ROMOLA. | BY | GEORGE ELIOT, | AUTHOR OF "ADAM BEDE" ETC. | *COPYRIGHT EDITION.* | IN TWO VOLUMES. | VOL. I. [II.] | LEIPZIG | BERNHARD TAUCHNITZ | 1863. | *The Right of Translation is reserved.*

Collation:

VOL. I.

$\pi^1 \chi^2 20^8 21^4 \chi\chi^1$; pp. vi + 328 + [2]

[i] sub-title: COLLECTION | OF | BRITISH AUTHORS. | VOL. 682. | [*rule*] | ROMOLA BY GEORGE ELIOT. | IN TWO VOLUMES. | VOL.I.; [ii] publisher's advertisement: TAUCHNITZ EDITION. | BY THE SAME AUTHOR, | [list of George Eliot's works: SCENES OF CLERICAL LIFE, ADAM BEDE, THE MILL ON THE FLOSS, SILAS MARNER]; [iii] title-page; [iv] blank; [v]–vi CONTENTS | OF VOLUME I.; [1]–328 text; 328 text | END OF VOL.I.; [329] PRINTING OFFICE OF THE PUBLISHER.; [330] blank.

VOL. II.

$\pi^1 \chi^2 1–19^8 20^4$; pp. vi + 310 + [2]

[i] sub-title: COLLECTION | OF | BRITISH AUTHORS. | VOL. 683. | [*rule*] | ROMOLA BY GEORGE ELIOT. | IN TWO VOLUMES. | VOL. II.; [ii] blank; [iii] title-page; [iv] blank; [v]–vi CONTENTS | OF VOLUME II.; [1]–310 text; 310 text [*rule*] | PRINTING OFFICE OF THE PUBLISHER.; | [311]–[312] blank.

Copies British Library; Princeton University Library; editor.

ROMOLA

The Blind Scholar and His Daughter

PROEM

[1]MORE than three centuries and a half ago, in the mid spring-time of 1492, we are sure that the angel[2] of the dawn, as he travelled with broad slow wing from the Levant to the Pillars of Hercules,* and from the summits of the Caucasus across all the snowy alpine ridges to the dark nakedness of the western isles, saw nearly the same outline of firm land and unstable sea—saw the same great mountain shadows on the same valleys as he has seen to-day—saw olive mounts, and pine forests, and the broad plains green[3] with young corn or rain-freshened grass—saw the domes and spires of cities rising by the river sides or mingled with the sedge-like masts on the many-curved sea coast, in the same spots where they rise to-day. And as the faint light of his course pierced into the[4] dwellings of men, it fell, as now, on the rosy warmth of nestling children; on the haggard waking of sorrow and sickness; on the hasty uprising of the hard-handed labourer; and on the late sleep of the night-student, who had been questioning the stars or the sages, or his own soul, for that hidden knowledge which would break through the barrier of man's brief life, and show its dark path, that seemed to bend no whither, to be an arc in an immeasurable circle of light and glory. The great river-courses which have shaped the lives of men have hardly changed; and those other streams, the life-currents that ebb and flow in human hearts, pulsate to the same great needs, the same great loves and terrors. As our thought follows [5]close in the slow wake of the dawn, we are impressed with the broad sameness of the human lot, which never alters in the main headings of its history—hunger and labour, seed-time and harvest, love and death.

Even if, instead of following the dim daybreak, our imagination pauses on a certain historical spot and[6] awaits the fuller morning, we may see a world-famous city, which has hardly changed its outline since the days of Columbus, seeming to stand as an almost unviolated symbol, amidst the flux of human things, to remind us that we still resemble the men of the past more than we differ from them, as the great mechanical principles on which those domes and towers were

---

1 〈More〉 〈Nearly four centuries〉 More *MS*
2 angel] *1 2 3* star-quenching angel *MS CM*
3 plains green] *MS 3P* plains, green *CM 1 2*   4 pierced {into} the *MS*
5 〈slowly〉 close *MS*   6 spot and] *MS 3P* spot, and *CM 1 2*

raised must make a likeness in human building that will be broader and deeper than all possible change. And doubtless, if the spirit of a Florentine citizen, whose eyes were closed[7] for the last time while Columbus was still waiting and arguing for the three poor vessels with which he was to set sail from the port of Palos[8],* could return from the shades and[9] pause where[1] our thought is pausing, he would believe that there must still be fellowship and understanding for him among the inheritors of his birthplace.

Let us suppose that such a Shade has been permitted to revisit the glimpses* of the golden morning, and is standing once more on the famous hill of San Miniato, which overlooks Florence from the south.

The Spirit is clothed in his habit as he lived: the folds of his well-lined black silk garment or *lucco* hang in grave unbroken lines from neck to ancle; his plain cloth cap, with its *becchetto*, or long hanging strip of drapery, to serve as a scarf in case of need, surmounts a penetrating face, not, perhaps, very handsome, but with a firm, well-cut mouth, kept distinctly human by a close-shaven lip and chin. It is a face charged with memories of a keen and various life passed below there on the banks of the gleaming river[2]; and as he looks at the scene before him, the sense of familiarity is so much stronger than the perception of change, that he thinks it might be possible to descend once more among[3] the streets, and take up that busy life where he left it. For it is not only the mountains and the westward-bending river that he recognizes; not only the dark sides of Mount Morello opposite to him, and the long valley of the Arno that seems to stretch its grey low-tufted luxuriance to the far-off ridges of Carrara; and the steep height of Fiesole, with its crown of monastic walls and cypresses; and all the green and grey slopes sprinkled with villas which he can name as he looks at them. He sees other familiar objects much closer to his daily walks. For though he misses the seventy or more towers that once surmounted the walls, and encircled the city as with a regal diadem,* his eyes will not dwell on that blank; they are drawn irresistibly to the unique tower springing, like a tall flower-stem drawn towards the sun, from the square turreted mass of the Old Palace* in the very heart of the city—the tower that looks none the worse for the four centuries that have passed since he used to walk under it. The great dome, too, greatest in the world, which, in his early boyhood, had been only a daring thought* in the mind of a small quick-eyed man—there it raises its large curves still, eclipsing the hills. And the

7 whose eyes were closed] who closed his eyes *MS*
8 still waiting . . . Palos] still rising early to visit his unfinished galleries in the ⟨bay⟩ port of ⟨Cadiz⟩ Palos *MS*
9 shades and] *MS 3P* shades, and *CM 1 2*   1 where ⟨we are⟩ *MS*
2 {gleaming} river *MS*   3 among] *MS* amongst *CM 1 2 3*

well-known bell-towers—Giotto's,* with its distant hint of rich colour, and the graceful-spired Badia,* and the rest—he looked at them all from the shoulder of his nurse.

"Surely," he thinks, "Florence can still ring her bells with the solemn hammer-sound that used to beat on the hearts of her citizens and strike out the fire there. And here, on the right, stands the long dark mass of Santa Croce, where we buried our famous dead,* laying the laurel on their cold brows and fanning them with the breath of praise and of banners.[4] But Santa Croce had no spire then:* we Florentines were too full of great building projects to carry them all out in stone and marble; we had our frescoes and our shrines to pay for, not to speak of rapacious condottieri, bribed royalty, and purchased territories, and our façades and spires must needs wait. But what architect can the Frati Minori* have employed to build that spire for them? If it had been [5]built in my day, Filippo Brunelleschi[6] or Michelozzo* would have devised something of another fashion than that—something worthy to crown the church of Arnolfo[7]."*

At this the Spirit, with a sigh, lets his eyes travel on to the city walls, and now he dwells on the change there with wonder at these modern times. Why have five out of the eleven convenient gates been closed?* And why, above all, should the towers have been levelled that were once a glory and defence?* Is the world become so peaceful, then, and do Florentines dwell in such harmony, that there are no longer conspiracies to bring ambitious exiles home again with armed bands at their back? These are difficult questions: it is easier and pleasanter to recognize the old than to account for the new. And there flows Arno, with its bridges just where they used to be—the Ponte Vecchio, least like other bridges in the world, laden with the same quaint shops where[8] our Spirit remembers lingering a little, on his way, perhaps, to look at the progress of that great palace which Messer Luca Pitti had set a-building with huge stones got from the Hill of Bogoli* close behind, or, perhaps, to transact a little business with the cloth-dressers in Oltrarno.* The exorbitant line of the Pitti [9]roof is hidden from San Miniato; but the yearning of the old Florentine is not to see Messer Luca's too ambitious palace* which he built unto himself; it is to be down among those narrow streets and busy humming Piazze where he inherited the eager life of his fathers. Is not the anxious voting with black and white beans* still going on

4 banners. ⟨Yes, it is a great thing to dwell under the shadow of common ancestral monuments—*Magnum est eadem habere monumenta, eisdem uti sacris, sepulchra habere communia.*⟩ But *MS**

5 ⟨done⟩ built *MS*   6 Filippo Brunelleschi] Filippo *MS*
7 something worthy to crown the church of Arnolfo] something as grand as the campanile of San Spirito *MS*
8 shops where] *3P* shops, where *MS CM 1 2*   9 ⟨palace⟩ roof *MS*

down there? Who are the *Priori** in these months, eating soberly-
regulated official dinners in the Palazzo Vecchio, with removes of
tripe and boiled partridges, seasoned by practical jokes against the ill-
fated butt among those potent signors? Are not the significant banners
still hung from the windows—still distributed with decent pomp
under Orgagna's Loggia* every two months?

Life had its zest for the old Florentine when he, too, trod the marble
steps and shared in those dignities. His politics had an area as wide as
his trade, which stretched from Syria to Britain, but they had also the
passionate intensity, and the detailed practical interest, which could
belong only to a narrow scene of corporate action; only to the members of a community shut in close by the hills and by walls of six
miles' circuit, where men knew each other as they passed in the
street, set their eyes every day on the memorials of their common-
wealth, and were conscious[1] of having not simply[2] the right to vote,
but the chance of being voted for. He loved his honours and his
gains, the business of his counting-house, of his guild, of the public
council-chamber; he loved his enmities too[3], and fingered the white
bean which was to keep a hated name out of the *borsa** with more
complacency than if it had been a golden florin. He loved to
strengthen his family by a good alliance, and went home with a triumphant light in his eyes after concluding a satisfactory marriage[4] for
his son or daughter under[5] his favourite loggia in the evening cool; he
loved his game at chess* under that same loggia, and his biting jest,
and even his coarse joke, as not beneath the dignity of a man eligible
for the highest magistracy. He had gained an insight into all sorts of
affairs at home and abroad: he had been of the "Ten" who managed
the war department, of the "Eight" who attended to home discipline,
of the *Priori* or *Signori* who were the heads of the executive government; he had[6] even risen to the supreme office of *Gonfaloniere*[7];* he
had[8] made one in embassies to the Pope and to the Venetians; and he
had been commissary to the hired army of the Republic, directing the
inglorious bloodless battles in which no man died of brave breast-
wounds—*virtuosi colpi*—but only of casual falls and tramplings.* And
in this way he had learned to distrust men without bitterness; looking
on life mainly as a game of skill, but not dead to traditions of heroism
and clean-handed honour. For the human soul is hospitable, and will
entertain conflicting sentiments and contradictory opinions with much

1 conscious ⟨not only of the right⟩ MS   2 simply] 3C only MS CM 1 2
3 enmities too] MS 1 2 3 enmities, too CM
4 satisfactory marriage] 1 2 3 satisfactory *parentado*, or marriage MS CM
5 daughter under] 3P daughter, under MS CM 1 2
6 government; he had] government, and had MS
7 the {supreme} office of Gonfaloniere ⟨, the highest in the Republic⟩ MS
8 he had] had MS

impartiality. It was his pride, besides, that he was duly tinctured with the learning of his age, and judged not altogether with the vulgar, but in harmony with the ancients: he, too, in his prime, had been eager for the most correct manuscripts, and had paid many florins for antique vases and for disinterred busts of the ancient immortals—some, perahps, *truncis naribus*,* wanting as to the nose, but not the less authentic; and in his old age he had made haste to look at the first[9] sheets of that fine Homer* which was [1]among the early glories of the Florentine press. But he had not, for all that, neglected to hang up a waxen image* or double of himself under the protection of the Madonna Annunziata, or to do penance for his sins in large gifts to the shrines of saints whose lives had not been modelled on the study of the classics; he had not even neglected making liberal bequests towards buildings for the *Frati*, against whom he had levelled many a jest.

For the Unseen Powers were mighty. Who knew—who was sure—that there was *any*[2] name given to them behind which there was no angry force to be appeased, no intercessory pity to be won? Were not gems medicinal, though they only pressed the finger?* Were not all things charged with occult [3]virtues? Lucretius might be right*—he was an ancient, and[4] a great poet; Luigi Pulci,* too, who was suspected of not believing anything from the roof upward (*dal tetto in su*),* had very much the air of being right over the supper-table, when the wine and jests[5] were circulating fast, though he was only a poet in the vulgar tongue. There were even learned personages who maintained that Aristotle, wisest of men (unless, indeed, Plato were wiser?), was a thoroughly irreligious philosopher;* and a liberal scholar must entertain all speculations. But the negatives might, after all, prove false; nay, seemed manifestly false, as the circling hours* swept past him, and turned round with graver faces. For had not the world become Christian? Had he not been baptized in San Giovanni, where the dome is awful with the symbols of coming judgment,* and where the altar bears a crucified Image[6] disturbing to perfect complacency in oneself and the world? Our resuscitated Spirit was not a pagan philosopher, nor[7] a philosophizing pagan poet, but a man of the fifteenth century, inheriting its strange web of belief and unbelief; of Epicurean levity and fetichistic dread; of pedantic impossible ethics [8]uttered by rote, and crude passions acted out with childish impulsiveness; of inclination towards a[9] self-indulgent paganism, and

9 first] *1 2 3* early *MS CM*
2 *any*] *1 2 3* any *MS CM*
4 ancient, and] *3P* ancient and *MS CM 1 2*
6 a crucified Image] an image *MS*
8 ⟨acted⟩ uttered *MS*

1 ⟨one of⟩ among *MS*
3 ⟨forces⟩ virtues *MS*
5 jests] *3P riboboli MS CM 1 2*
7 nor] or *MS*
9 inclination towards a] velleities towards *MS*

inevitable subjection to that[1] human conscience which, in the unrest
of a new growth, was filling the air with strange prophecies and presentiments.

He had smiled, perhaps, and shaken his head dubiously, as he
heard simple folk talk of a Pope Angelico,* who was to come by and
by and bring in a new order of things, to purify[2] the Church from
simony, and the lives of the clergy from scandal—a state of affairs too
different from what existed under Innocent the Eighth* for a shrewd
merchant and politician to regard the prospect as worthy of entering
into his calculations. But he felt the evils of the time, nevertheless;
for he was a man of public spirit, and public spirit can never be
wholly immoral, since its essence is care for a common good. That
very Quaresima or Lent of 1492* in[3] which he died, still in his erect
old age, he had listened in San Lorenzo, not without a mixture of satisfaction, to the preaching of a Dominican Friar, named Girolamo
Savonarola, who[4] denounced with a rare boldness the worldliness and
vicious habits of the clergy, and insisted on the duty of Christian men
not to live for their own ease when wrong was triumphing in high
places, and not to spend their wealth in outward pomp even in the
churches, when their fellow-citizens were suffering from want and
sickness. The *Frate* carried[5] his doctrine rather too far for elderly
ears; yet it was a memorable thing to see a preacher move his audience to such a pitch that the women even took off their ornaments,
and delivered them up to be sold for the benefit of the needy.[6*]

"He was a noteworthy man, that Prior of San Marco," thinks our
Spirit; "somewhat arrogant and extreme, perhaps, especially in his
denunciations of speedy vengeance.* Ah, *Iddio non paga il
Sabato**—the wages of men's sins often linger in their payment, and I
myself [7]saw much established wickedness of long-standing prosperity.
But a Frate Predicatore[8*] who wanted to move the people—how
could he be moderate? He might have been a little less defiant and
curt, though, to Lorenzo de' Medici, whose family had been the very
makers of San Marco:* was that quarrel ever made up? And our
Lorenzo himself, with the dim outward eyes and the subtle inward
vision, did he get over that illness at Careggi?* It was but a sad,
uneasy-looking face that he would carry out of the world which had
given him so much, and there were strong suspicions that his handsome son would play the part of Rehoboam.* How has it all turned

---

1 that ⟨new human conscience which was⟩ *MS*   2 to purify] purify *MS*
3 Quaresima or Lent of 1492 in] *MS 3P* Quaresima, or Lent, of 1492, in *CM 1 2*
4 Friar, named Girolamo Savonarola, who] *1 2 3* friar, who *MS CM*
5 The *Frate* carried] He carried *MS*   6 sickness. {He carried . . . needy.} *MS*
7 ⟨have seen⟩ saw *MS*
8 Frate Predicatore] *MS 3P Frate Predicatore CM 1 2*

out? Which party is likely to be banished and have its houses sacked just now? Is there any successor of the incomparable Lorenzo, to whom the Great Turk is so gracious as to send over presents of rare animals, rare relics, rare manuscripts, or fugitive enemies,* suited to the tastes of a Christian Magnifico who is at once lettered and devout—and also slightly vindictive? And what famous scholar is dictating the Latin letters of the Republic—what fiery philosopher is lecturing on Dante in the Duomo, and going home to write bitter invectives* against the father and mother of the bad critic who may have found fault with his classical spelling? Are our wiser heads leaning towards alliance with the Pope and the *Regno*,* or are they rather inclining their ears to the orators of France and of Milan?

"There is knowledge of these things to be had in the streets below, on the beloved *Marmi* in front of the churches, and under the sheltering Loggie, where surely our citizens have still⁹ their gossips¹ and debates, their bitter and merry jests as of old. For are not the well-remembered buildings all there? The changes have not been so great in those uncounted years. I will go down and hear—I will tread the familiar pavement, and hear once again the speech of Florentines."

Go not down, good Spirit! for the changes are great, and the speech of Florentines would sound as a riddle in your ears. Or, if you go, mingle with no politicians on the *Marmi*, or elsewhere; ask no questions about trade in the Calimala;* confuse yourself with no inquiries into scholarship, official or monastic. Only look at the sunlight and shadows on the grand walls that were built solidly, and have endured in their grandeur; look at the faces of the little children, making another sunlight amid the shadows of age; look, if you will, into the churches, and hear the same chants, see the same images as of old—the images of willing anguish for a great end, of beneficent love and ascending glory; see upturned living faces and lips moving to the old prayers for help. These things have not changed. The sunlight and shadows bring their old beauty and waken the old heart-strains at morning, noon, and even-tide; the little children are still the symbol of the eternal marriage between love and duty; and men still yearn for the reign of peace and righteousness—still own *that* life to be the highest, which is a conscious voluntary sacrifice. For the Papa² Angelico is not come yet.

9 have {still} *MS*   1 gossips] gossip *1 2 3*
2 Papa] *MS* Pope *CM 1 2 3*

BOOK I

*

CHAPTER I.

THE SHIPWRECKED STRANGER

THE Loggia de' Cerchi stood in the heart of old Florence, within a labyrinth of narrow streets behind the Badia, now rarely threaded by the stranger, unless in a dubious search for a certain severely simple door-place, bearing this inscription:

QUI NACQUE IL DIVINO POETA.

To the ear of Dante, the same streets rang with the shout and clash of fierce battle between rival families; but in the fifteenth century, they were only noisy with the unhistorical quarrels and broad jests of wool-carders in the cloth-producing quarters of San Martino and Garbo.

Under this loggia, in the early morning of the 9th of April, 1492, two men had their eyes fixed on each other: one was stooping slightly, and looking downward with the scrutiny of curiosity; the other, lying on the pavement, was looking upward with the startled gaze of a suddenly-awakened dreamer.

The standing figure was the first to speak. He was a grey-haired, broad-shouldered man, of the type which, in Tuscan phrase, is moulded with the fist and polished with the pickaxe; but the self-important gravity which had written itself out in the deep lines about his brow and mouth seemed intended to correct any contemptuous inferences from the hasty workmanship which Nature had bestowed on his exterior. He[1] had deposited a large well-filled bag, made of skins, on the pavement, and before him hung a pedlar's basket, garnished partly with small woman's-ware, such as thread and pins, and partly with fragments of glass, which had probably been taken in exchange for those commodities.

"Young man," he said, pointing to a ring on the finger of the reclining figure, "when your chin has got a stiffer crop on it, you'll know better than to take your nap in street corners with a ring like that on your forefinger. By the holy 'vangels[2]! if it had been anybody but me standing over you two minutes ago—but Bratti Ferravecchi* is not the man to steal. The cat couldn't eat her mouse if she didn't catch it alive, and Bratti couldn't relish gain if it had no taste of a

---

1 He ⟨carried a bag made of skins on his back⟩ MS   2 'vangels] Vangel MS

bargain. Why, young man, one San Giovanni,* three years ago, the Saint sent a dead body in my way—a blind beggar, with his cap well lined with pieces—but, if you'll believe me, my stomach turned against the money[3]* I'd never [4]bargained for, till it came into my head that San Giovanni owed me the pieces for what I spend yearly at the Festa: besides, I buried the body and paid for a mass—and so I saw it was a fair bargain. But how comes a young man like you, with the face of Messer San Michele, to be sleeping on a stone bed with the wind for a curtain?"

The deep guttural sounds of the speaker were scarcely intelligible to the newly-waked, bewildered listener, but he understood the action of pointing to his ring: he[5] looked down at it, and, with a half-automatic obedience to the warning, took it off and thrust it within his doublet, rising at the same time and stretching himself.

"Your [6]tunic and hose match ill with that jewel, young man," said Bratti, deliberately. "Anybody might say the saints had sent *you* a dead body; but if you took the jewels, I hope you buried him—and you can afford a mass or two for him into the bargain."

Something like a painful thrill appeared to dart through the frame of the listener, and arrest the careless stretching of his arms and chest. For an instant he turned on Bratti with a sharp frown; but he immediately recovered an air of indifference, took off the red Levantine cap which hung like a great purse over his left ear, pushed back his long dark-brown curls, and glancing at his dress, said, smilingly,

"You speak truth, friend: my garments are as weather-stained as an old sail, and they are not old either, only, like an old sail, they have had a sprinkling of the sea as well as the rain. The fact is, I'm a stranger in Florence, and when I came in foot-sore last night I preferred flinging myself in a corner of this hospitable porch to hunting any longer for a chance hostelry, which might turn out to be a nest of blood-suckers of more sorts than one."

"A stranger in good sooth," said Bratti, "for the words come all melting out of your throat, so that a Christian and a Florentine can't tell a hook from a hanger.* But you're not from Genoa? More likely from Venice, by the cut of your clothes?"

"At this present moment," said the stranger, smiling, "it is of less importance where I come from than where I can go to for a mouthful of breakfast. This city of yours turns a grim look on me just here: can you show me the way to a more lively quarter, where I can get a meal and a lodging?"

---

3 money] *3P testoni MS CM 1 2*   4 ⟨paid⟩ bargained *MS*
5 he ⟨took it off⟩ *MS*   6 ⟨doublet⟩ tunic *MS*

"That I can," said Bratti, "and it is your good fortune, young man, that I have happened to be walking in from Rovezzano* this morning, and turned out of my way to Mercato Vecchio* to say an Ave at the Badia. That, I say, is your good fortune. But it remains to be seen what is *my*[7] profit in the matter. Nothing for nothing, young man. If I show you the way to Mercato Vecchio, you'll swear by your patron saint to let me have the bidding for that stained suit of yours, when you set up a better—as doubtless you will."

"Agreed, by San Niccolò[8],"* said the other, laughing. "But now let us set off to this said Mercato, for I feel[9] the want of a better lining to this doublet of mine which you are coveting."

"Coveting? Nay," said Bratti, heaving his bag on his back and setting out. But he broke off in his reply, and burst out in loud, harsh tones, not unlike the creaking and grating of a cart-wheel: "*Chi abbaratta—baratta—b'ratta—chi abbaratta cenci e vetri—b'ratta ferri vecchi?*"*

"It's worth but little," he said presently, relapsing into his conversational tone. "Hose and altogether, your clothes are worth but little. Still, if you've a mind to set yourself up with a lute worth more than any new one, or with a sword that's been worn by a Ridolfi,* or with a paternoster of the best mode, I could let you have a great bargain, by making an allowance for the clothes; for, simple as I stand here, I've[1] got the best-furnished shop in the Ferravecchi, and it's close by the Mercato. The Virgin be praised! it's not a pumpkin I carry on my shoulders. But I don't stay caged in my shop all day: I've got a wife and a raven to stay at home and mind the stock.* *Chi abbaratta—baratta—b'ratta?*. . . . And now, young man, where do you come from, and what's your business in Florence?"

"I thought you liked nothing that came to you without a bargain," said the stranger. "You've offered me nothing yet in exchange for that information."

"Well, well; a Florentine doesn't mind bidding a fair price for news: it stays the stomach a little, though he may win no hose* by it. If I take you to the prettiest damsel in the Mercato to get a cup of milk[2] —that will be a fair bargain."

"Nay; I can find her myself, if she be really in the Mercato; for pretty heads are apt to look forth of doors and windows. No, no. Besides, a sharp trader, like you, ought to know that he who bids for nuts and news, may chance to find them hollow."

7 *my*] *1 2 3* my *MS CM*   8 San Niccolò] San Giovio *MS*
9 I feel] *1 2 3* I promise you I feel *MS CM*
1 here, I've] *1 2 3* here (*così fatto come tu mi vedi*), I've *MS CM*
2 milk] milk from *MS*

"Ah! young man," said Bratti, with a sideway glance of some admiration, "you were not born of a Sunday—the salt shops were open* when you came into the world. You're not a Hebrew, eh?—come from[3] Spain or Naples, eh? Let me tell you the Frati Minori are trying to make Florence as hot as Spain for those dogs of hell that want to get all the profits[4] of usury* to themselves and leave none for Christians; and when you walk the Calimala with a piece of yellow cloth in your cap, it will spoil your beauty more than a sword-cut across that smooth olive-cheek of yours.—*Abbaratta, baratta—chi abbaratta?*—I tell you, young man, grey cloth is against yellow cloth;* and there's as much grey cloth in Florence as would make a gown and cowl for the Duomo, and there's not so much yellow cloth as would make hose for Saint Christopher—blessed be his name, and send me a sight of him* this day!—*Abbaratta, baratta, b'ratta—chi abbaratta?*"

"All that is very amusing information you are [5]parting with for nothing," said the stranger, rather scornfully; "but it happens not to concern me. I am no Hebrew."

"See, now!" said Bratti, triumphantly; "I've made a good bargain with mere words. I've made you tell me something, young man, though you're as hard to hold as a lamprey. San Giovanni be praised! a blind Florentine is a match for two one-eyed men. But here we are in Mercato[6]."

They had now emerged from the narrow streets into a broad piazza, known to the elder Florentine writers as the Mercato Vecchio, or the Old Market[7]. This piazza, though it had been the scene of a provision market from time immemorial, [8]and may perhaps, says fond imagination, be the very spot to which the Fesulean ancestors* of the Florentines descended from their high fastness to traffic with the rustic population of the valley, had not been shunned as a place of residence by Florentine wealth. In the early decades of the fifteenth century, which was now near its end, the Medici and other powerful families of the *popolani grassi*, or commercial nobility, had their houses there, not, perhaps, finding their ears much offended by the loud roar of mingled dialects, or their eyes much shocked by the butchers' stalls, which the old poet Antonio Pucci accounts a chief glory, or *dignità*,* of a market that, in his esteem, eclipsed the markets of all the earth beside. But the glory of mutton and veal (well attested to be the flesh of the right animals; for were not the skins, with the heads attached, duly displayed, according to the decree of the

3 from ⟨Venice or⟩ Spain ⟨or Naples⟩ MS   4 profits] profit *2 3*
5 ⟨giving me⟩ parting with MS   6 in Mercato] in the Mercato *1 2 3*
7 as the Mercato Vecchio ⟨or the old Market⟩ MS
8 ⟨being traditionally⟩ and may perhaps, says fond ⟨tradition⟩ imagination MS

Signoria?) was just now wanting to the Mercato, the time of Lent not being yet over. The proud corporation, or "Art," of butchers was in abeyance, and it was the great harvest-time of the market-gardeners, the cheesemongers, the vendors of macaroni, corn, eggs, milk, and dried fruits: a change which was apt to make the women's voices predominant in the chorus. But in all seasons there was the experimental ringing of pots and pans, the chinking of the money-changers, the tempting offers of cheapness at the old-clothes' stalls, the challenges of the dicers, the vaunting of new linens and woollens, of excellent wooden-ware, kettles, and frying-pans; there was the choking of the narrow inlets with mules and carts, together with much uncomplimentary remonstrance in terms remarkably identical with the insults in use by the gentler sex of the present day, under the same imbrowning and heating circumstances. Ladies and gentlemen, who came to market, looked on at a larger amount of amateur fighting than could easily be seen in these later times, and [9]beheld more revolting rags, beggary, and rascaldom, than modern householders could well picture to themselves. As the day wore on, the hideous drama of the gaming-house might be seen here by any chance open-air spectator—the quivering eagerness, the blank despair, the sobs, the blasphemy, and the blows: –

> "E vedesi chi perde con gran soffi
> E bestemmiar colla mano alla mascella,
> E ricever e dar dimolti[1] ingoffi."*

But still there was the relief of prettier sights: there were brood-rabbits, not less innocent and astonished than those of our own period; there were doves and singing-birds to be bought as presents for the children; there were even kittens for sale, and here and there a handsome *gattuccio*, or "Tom,"* with the highest character for mousing; and, better than all, there were young, softly rounded cheeks and bright eyes, freshened by the start from the far-off castello* at daybreak, not to speak of older faces with the unfading charm of honest goodwill in them—such as are never quite wanting in scenes of human industry. And high on a pillar in the centre of the place—a venerable pillar, fetched from the church of San Giovanni—stood Donatello's stone statue of Plenty,* with a fountain near it, where, says old Pucci,* the good wives of the market freshened their utensils, and their throats also[2]—not because they were unable to buy wine, but because they wished to save the money for their husbands.[3]

---

9 ⟨saw⟩ beheld *MS*   1 dimolti] di molti *2 3*   2 throats {also} *MS*
3 industry. And high . . . husbands.] *1 2 3* industry. {Set high . . . husbands—*"Ma pe' mariti voglian risparmiare."*} *MS CM*

But on this particular morning a sudden change seemed to have come over the face of the market. The *deschi*, or stalls, were indeed partly dressed with their various commodities, and already there were purchasers assembled, on the alert to secure the finest, freshest vegetables and the most unexceptionable butter. But when Bratti and his companion entered the piazza, it appeared that some common preoccupation had for the moment distracted the attention both of buyers and sellers from their proper business. Most of the traders had turned their backs on their goods, and had joined the knots of talkers who were concentrating themselves at different points in the piazza. A vendor of old clothes, in the act of hanging out a pair of long hose, had distractedly hung them round his neck in his eagerness to join the nearest group; an oratorical cheesemonger, with a piece of cheese in one hand and a knife in the other, was incautiously making notes of his emphatic pauses on that excellent specimen of *marzolino*; and elderly market-women, with their egg-baskets in a dangerously oblique position, contributed a wailing fugue of invocation.

In this general distraction, the Florentine boys, who were never wanting in any street scene, and were of an especially mischievous sort—as who should say, very sour crabs* indeed—saw a great opportunity. Some made a rush at the [4]nuts and dried figs, others preferred the farinaceous delicacies at the cooked-provision stalls—delicacies to which certain four-footed dogs also, who had learned to take kindly to Lenten fare, applied a discriminating nostril, and then disappeared with much rapidity under the nearest shelter; while the mules, not without some kicking and plunging among impeding baskets, were stretching their muzzles towards the aromatic green-meat.

"*Diavolo!*" said Bratti, as he and his companion came, quite unnoticed, upon the noisy scene; "the Mercato is gone as mad as if the Most Holy Father had excommunicated us again.* I must know what this is. But never fear[5]: it seems a thousand years to you till* you see the pretty Tessa, and get your cup of milk; but keep hold of me, and I'll hold to my bargain. Remember, I'm to have the first bid for your suit, specially for the hose, which, with all their stains, are the best *panno di garbo*—as good as ruined, though, with mud and weather stains."

"*Olà*, Monna Trecca," Bratti proceeded, turning towards an old woman on the outside of the nearest group, who for the moment had[6] suspended her wail to listen, and shouting close in her ear, "Here[7] are

---

4 ⟨unripe fruit and early mountain strawberries⟩ nuts *MS*
5 is. But never fear] is, but ⟨don't be abashed⟩ never fear *MS*
6 had] *1 2 3* has *MS CM*
7 ear, "Here] ear, ⟨"Chè Diavolo⟩ "Che domin, Monna Trecca! here *MS*

the mules upsetting all your [8]bunches of parsley: is the world coming
to an end, then?"

"Monna Trecca" (equivalent to "Dame Greengrocer") turned
round at this unexpected trumpeting in her right ear, with a half-
fierce, half-bewildered look, first at the speaker, then at her dis-
arranged commodities, and then at the speaker again.

"A bad Easter and a bad year* to you, and may you die by the
sword!" she burst out, rushing towards her stall, but directing this
first volley of her wrath against Bratti, who, without heeding the
malediction, quietly slipped into her place, within hearing of the narrative which had been absorbing her attention; making a sign at the
same time to the young[9] stranger to keep near him.[1]

"I tell you I saw it myself," said a fat man, with a bunch of newly-
purchased leeks in his hand. "I was in Santa Maria Novella, and saw[2]
it myself. The woman started up* and threw out her arms, and cried
out and said she saw a big bull with fiery horns coming down on the
church to crush it. I saw it myself."

"Saw what, Goro?" said a man of slim figure, whose eye twinkled
rather roguishly. He wore a close jerkin, a skull-cap lodged carelessly
over his left ear as if it had fallen there by chance, a delicate linen
apron tucked up on one side, and a razor stuck in his belt. "Saw the
bull, or only the woman?"

"Why, the woman, to be sure; but it's all one, [3]mi pare: it doesn't
alter the meaning—va!" answered the fat man, with some contempt.

"Meaning? no, no; that's clear enough," said several voices at once,
and then followed a confusion of tongues,[4] in which "Lights shooting
over San Lorenzo for three nights together"—"Thunder in the clear
starlight"—"Lantern of the Duomo struck with the sword of St.
Michael"—"Palle"*—"All smashed"—"Lions[5] tearing each other to
pieces"*—"Ah! and they might well"—"Boto* caduto in Santissima
Nunziata![6]"—"Died like the best of Christians"—"God will have
pardoned him"—were often-repeated phrases, which shot across each
other like storm-driven hailstones, each speaker feeling rather the
necessity of utterance than of finding a listener. Perhaps the only
silent members of the group were Bratti, who, as a new-comer, was
busy in mentally piecing together the flying fragments of information;
the man of the razor; and a [7]thin-lipped, eager-looking personage in
spectacles, wearing a pen-and-ink case at his belt.

8 ⟨green gooseberries⟩ bunches of parsley MS   9 young] younger 2 3
1 absorbing her attention—{making a sign . . . him.} MS   2 saw] I saw MS
3 ⟨I suppose⟩ mi pare MS
4 at once {and then followed a confusion of tongues,} MS
5 smashed"—"Lions] 1 2 3 smashed"—"Lasso!"—Lions MS CM
6 Nunziata!—⟨"morto come ottimo Cristiano"—Dio l'abbia perdonato"—chè
[?dermo] per Firenze!⟩ "Died MS   7 thin ⟨pale-⟩lipped MS

"*Ebbene*, Nello", said Bratti, skirting the group till he was within hearing of the barber. "It appears the Magnifico is dead—rest his soul! and the price of wax will rise?"

"Even as you say," answered Nello; and then added, with an air of extra gravity, but with marvellous rapidity[8], "and his waxen image in the Nunziata fell at the same moment, they say; or at some other time, whenever it pleases the Frati Serviti,* who know best. And several cows and women have had still-born calves this Quaresima; and for the bad eggs that have been broken since the carnival, nobody has counted them! Ah! a great man—a great politician—a greater poet than Dante.* And yet the cupola didn't fall, only the lantern. *Che miracolo!*"

A sharp and lengthened "Pst!" was suddenly heard darting across the pelting storm of gutturals. It came from the pale man in spectacles, and had the effect he intended; for the noise ceased, and all eyes in the group were fixed on him with a look of expectation.

"'Tis well said you Florentines are blind,'* he began, in an incisive high voice. "It appears to me, you need nothing but a diet of hay to make cattle of you. What! do you think the death of Lorenzo is the scourge God has prepared for Florence? Go! you are sparrows chattering praises[9] over the dead hawk. What! a man who was trying to slip a noose over every neck in the Republic that he might tighten it[1] at his pleasure! You like that; you like to have the election of your magistrates turned into closet-work, and no man to use the rights of a citizen unless he is a Medicean. That is what is meant by qualification now: *netto di specchio** no longer means that a man pays his dues to the Republic: it[2] means that he'll wink[3] at robbery of the people's money—at robbery of their daughters' dowries; that he'll play[4] the chamberer and the philosopher by turns—listen to bawdy songs at the Carnival,* and cry 'Bellissimi[5]!'—and listen to sacred [6]Lauds, and cry again, 'Bellissimi[7]!' But this is what you love: you grumble and raise a riot over your *quattrini bianchi"** (white farthings)[8]; "but you take no notice when the public treasury has got a hole in the bottom for the gold to run into Lorenzo's drains. You like to pay for footmen[9] to walk before and behind one of your citizens, that he may be affable and condescending to you. 'See, what a tall Pisan we

8 gravity {but with marvellous rapidity} *MS*

9 praises] *MS* praise *CM 1 2 3*   1 tighten {it} *MS*

2 means that . . . Republic: it] *1 2 3* means a man with his proper limbs and ⟨his⟩ with reason in his eye: it *MS* means a man who pays his dues to the Republic: it *CM*

3 means that he'll wink] *1 2 3* means a man who'll wink *MS CM*

4 that he'll play] *1 2 3* who'll play *MS CM*

5 Bellisimi] *1 2 3* Bellisimo *MS CM*   6 ⟨Laudesi⟩ Lauds *MS*

7 Bellisimi] *1 2 3* Bellisimo *MS CM*   8 *quattrini bianchi* {(white farthings)} *MS*

9 footmen] *3C staffieri MS CM 1 2*

keep,"[1] say you, 'to march before him with the drawn sword flashing
in our eyes; and yet Lorenzo smiles at us. What goodness!' And you
think the death of a man, who[2] would soon[3] have saddled and bridled
you as the Sforza has saddled and bridled Milan*—you think his
death is the scourge God is warning you of by portents. I tell you
there is another sort of scourge in the air."

"Nay, nay, Ser Cioni,* keep astride your politics, and never mount
your prophecy; politics is the better horse," said Nello. "But if you
talk of portents, what portent can be greater than a pious notary?
Balaam's ass* was nothing to it."

"Ay, but a notary out of work, with his ink-bottle dry," said
another bystander, very much out at elbows. "Better don a cowl at
once, Ser Cioni; everybody will believe in your fasting."

[4]The notary turned and left the group with a look of indignant
contempt, disclosing, as he did so, the sallow but mild face of a short
man who had been standing behind him, and whose bent shoulders
told of some sedentary occupation.

"By San Giovanni, though," said the fat purchaser of leeks, with
the air of a person rather shaken in his theories, "I'm[5] not sure there
isn't some truth in what Ser Cioni says. For I know I've[6] good reason
to find fault with the *quattrini bianchi* myself. Grumble, did he say?
Suffocation! I should think we do grumble; and, let anybody say the
word, I'll turn out into the piazza[7]* with the readiest, sooner than
have our money altered in our hands as if the magistracy[8] were so
many necromancers. And it's true Lorenzo might have hindered such
work if he would—and for the bull with the flaming horns, why, as
Ser Cioni says, there may be many meanings to it, for the matter of
that; it may have more to do with the taxes than we think. For when
God above[9] sends a sign, it's not to be supposed he'd have only one
meaning."

"Spoken like an oracle, Goro!" said the barber. "Why, when we
poor mortals can pack two or three meanings into one sentence, it
were mere blasphemy not to believe that your miraculous bull[1] means
everything that any man in Florence likes it to mean."

"Thou art pleased to scoff, Nello," said the sallow, round-
shouldered man, [2]no longer eclipsed by the notary, "but it is not the
less true that every revelation, whether by visions, dreams, portents,

---

1 keep," ⟨?look Lorenzo how grand he looks with⟩ *MS*
2 man, who] man who *MS*   3 would {soon} *MS*
4 ⟨"By San Giovanni, though", said⟩ The *MS*   5 I'm] I am *3*
6 I've] I have *3*   7 into the piazza] *1 2 3 in piazza MS CM*
8 magistracy] *Collegi MS*
1 bull ⟨may⟩ *MS*   9 God above] Messer Domeneddio *MS*
                                                 2 ⟨when⟩ no longer *MS*

or the written word, has many meanings, which it is given to the illuminated only to unfold."

"[3]Assuredly," answered Nello. "Haven't I been to hear the Frate in
San Lorenzo? But then, I've been to hear Fra Menico[4]* in the
Duomo too; and according to him, your Fra Girolamo, with his
visions and interpretations, is running after the wind of Mongibello,*
and those who follow him are like to have the fate of certain swine*
that ran headlong [5]into the sea—or some hotter place. With San
Domenico roaring *è vero* in one ear, and San Francisco screaming *è
falso* in the other, what is a poor barber to do—unless he were illuminated? But it's plain our Goro here is [6]beginning to be illuminated,
for he already sees that the bull with the flaming horns means first
himself, and secondly all the other aggrieved taxpayers of Florence,
who are determined to gore the magistracy on the first opportunity."

[7]"Goro is a fool!" said a bass voice, with a note that dropped like
the sound of a great bell in the midst of much tinkling. "Let [8]him
carry home his leeks and shake his flanks over his wool-beating. He'll
mend matters more that way than by showing his tun-shaped body in
the piazza[9], as if everybody might measure his grievances by the size
of his paunch. The burdens[1] that harm him most are his heavy car-
cass and his idleness."

[2]The speaker had joined the group only in time to hear the conclusion of Nello's speech, but he was one of those figures for whom all
the world instinctively makes way, as it would for a battering-ram. He
was not much above the middle height, but the impression of enormous force which was conveyed by [3]his capacious chest and brawny
arms bared to the shoulder, was deepened by the keen sense and
quiet resolution expressed in his glance and in every furrow of his
cheek and brow. He had often been an unconscious model to
Domenico Ghirlandajo, when that great painter was making the walls
of the churches reflect the life of Florence,* and translating pale aerial
traditions into the deep colour and strong lines of the faces he knew.
The naturally dark tint of his skin was additionally bronzed by the
same powdery deposit that gave a polished black surface[4] to his leathern apron—a deposit which habit had probably made a necessary condition of perfect ease, for it was not washed off with punctilious
regularity.

3 ⟨?Sicuro⟩ Assuredly *MS*
4 Fra Menico] *3P* Fra Menico da Ponzo *MS CM 1 2*
5 ⟨down⟩ into *MS*   6 ⟨going⟩ beginning *MS*
7 "⟨*Bajè*!⟩ Goro *MS*   8 ⟨Goro⟩ him *MS*
9 in the piazza] *1 2 3 in piazza MS CM*
1 burdens *1 2 3 gravezze MS gravezze* (burdens, *i.e.* taxes) *CM*
2 ⟨Niccolò Grosso surnamed Caparra⟩* The speaker *MS*
3 ⟨the⟩ his *MS*   4 ⟨black⟩ surface *MS*

Goro turned his fat cheek and glassy eye on the frank speaker with
a look of deprecation rather than of resentment.

"Why, Niccolò," he said, in an injured [5]tone, "I've heard you sing
to another tune than that, often enough, when you've been laying
down the law at San Gallo* on a festa. I've heard you say yourself,
that a man wasn't a mill-wheel, to be on the grind, grind, as long as
he was driven, and then stick in his place without stirring[6] when the
water was low. And you're as fond of your vote as any man in
Florence—ay, and I've heard you say, if[7] Lorenzo—"

"Yes, yes," said Niccolò. "Don't you be bringing up my speeches
again after you've swallowed them, and handing them about as if they
were none the worse. I vote and I speak when there's any use in it: if
there's hot metal on the anvil, I lose no time before I strike; but I
don't spend good hours in tinkling on cold iron, or[8] in standing on
the pavement as thou dost, Goro, with snout upward, like a pig under
an [9]oak-tree. And as for Lorenzo—dead[1] and gone before his time—
he was a man who had an eye for curious iron-work; and if anybody
says he wanted to make himself a tyrant, I say, 'Sia; I'll not deny
which way the wind blows when every man can see the weathercock.'
But that only means that Lorenzo was a crested hawk, and there are
plenty of hawks without crests whose claws and beaks are as good for
tearing. Though if there was any chance of a real reform, so that
Marzocco* might shake his mane and roar again, instead of dipping
his head to lick the feet of anybody that will mount and ride him, I'd
strike a good blow for it."

"And that reform is not far off, Niccolò," said the sallow, mild-
faced[2] man,[3] seizing his opportunity like a missionary among the too
light-minded heathens, "for a time of tribulation is coming, and the
scourge is at hand. And when the Church is purged of cardinals and
prelates who traffic in [4]her inheritance that their hands may be full to
pay the price of blood and[5] to satisfy their own lusts, the State will
be purged too—and Florence will be purged of men who love to see
avarice and lechery under the red hat and the mitre because it gives
them the screen of a more hellish vice than their own."

"Ay, as Goro's broad body would be a screen for[6] my narrow person in case of missiles," said Nello; "but if that excellent screen happened to fall, I were stifled under it, surely enough. That is no bad

---

5 ⟨voice⟩ tone *MS*   6 place {without stirring} *MS*   7 say {if} *MS*
8 or ⟨with⟩ *MS*   9 ⟨?acorn⟩ oak-tree *MS*
1 Lorenzo—dead] *3P* Lorenzo—who's dead *MS CM 1 2*
2 sallow, mild-faced] sallow *MS*
3 man, ⟨earnestly,⟩ {seizing his opportunity . . . heathens.} "for *MS*
4 ⟨its⟩ her *MS*   5 blood and] *MS 1 2 3* blood, and *CM*
6 for ⟨me when⟩ *MS*

image of thine, Nanni—or rather, of[7] the Frate's; for I fancy there is no room in the small cup of thy understanding for any other liquor than what he pours into it."

"And it were well for thee, Nello," replied Nanni, "if thou could'st empty thyself of thy scoffs and thy jests, and take in that liquor too. The warning is ringing in the ears of all men: and it's no new story; for the Abbot Joachim* prophesied of the coming time three hundred years ago, and now Fra Girolamo has got the message afresh. He has seen it in a vision, even as the prophets of old: he has seen the sword hanging from the sky."

"Ay, and thou wilt see it thyself, Nanni, if thou wilt stare upward long enough," said Niccolò; "for that pitiable tailor's work of thine makes thy noddle so overhang thy legs, that thy eyeballs can see nought above the stitching-board but the roof of thy own skull."

The honest tailor [8]bore the jest without bitterness, bent on convincing his hearers of his doctrine rather than of his dignity. But Niccolò gave him no opportunity for replying; for he turned away to the pursuit of his market business, probably considering further dialogue as a tinkling on cold iron.

"*Ebbene*," said the man with the hose round his neck, who had lately migrated from another knot of talkers, "they are safest who cross themselves and jest at nobody. Do you know that the Magnifico sent for the Frate at the last,* and couldn't die without his blessing?"

"Was it so—in truth?" said several voices. "Yes, yes—God will have pardoned him." "He died like the best of Christians." "Never took his eyes from the holy crucifix." "And the Frate [9]will have given him his blessing?"

"Well, I know no more," said he of the hosen; "only Guccio there met a footman[1] going back to Careggi, and he told him the Frate had been sent for yesternight, after the Magnifico had confessed and had the holy sacraments."

"It's likely enough the Frate will tell the people something about it in his sermon this morning; is it not true, Nanni?" said Goro. "What do you think?"

But Nanni had already turned his back on Goro, and the group was rapidly thinning; some being stirred[2] by the impulse to go and hear "new things" from the Frate ("new things"[3] were the nectar of Florentines); others by the sense that it was time to attend to their

---

7 or rather, of] *MS* or, rather of *CM 1 2* or, rather, of *3*
8 ⟨took⟩ bore *MS*   9 ⟨gave⟩ will have given *MS*
1 footman] *3C* staffiere *MS 1 2 staffiere CM*
2 {being} stirred *MS*   3 "new things"] *cose nuove MS*

private business. In this general movement, Bratti got close to [4]the
barber, and said,—

"Nello, you've a ready tongue of your own, and are used to worm-
ing secrets out of people when you've once got them well-lathered. I[5]
picked up a stranger this morning as I was coming in from
Rovezzano, and I can spell him out no better than I can the letters on
that scarf I bought from the French cavalier. It isn't my wits are at
fault,—I want no man to [6]help me tell peas from paternosters,*—but
when you come to foreign fashions, a fool may happen to know more
than a wise man."

"Ay, [7]thou hast the wisdom of Midas, who could turn rags and
rusty nails into gold, even as thou dost," said Nello, "and he had also
something of the ass about him. But where is thy bird of strange
plumage?"

Bratti was looking round, with [8]an air of disappointment.

"*Diavolo!*" he said, with some vexation. "The bird's flown. It's
true he was hungry, and I forgot him. But we shall find him in the
Mercato, within scent of bread and savours[9], I'll answer for him."

"Let us make the round of the Mercato, then," said Nello.[1]

"It isn't his feathers that puzzle me," continued Bratti, as they
pushed their way together. "There isn't much in the way of cut and
cloth on this side the Holy Sepulchre that can puzzle a Florentine."

"Or frighten him, either," said Nello, "after he has seen an
Englander or a German[2]."

"No, no," said Bratti, cordially; "one may never lose sight of the
Cupola and yet know the world, I hope. Besides, this stranger's
clothes are good Italian merchandise, and the hose he wears were
dyed in Ognissanti* before ever they were dyed with salt water, as he
says. But the riddle about him is—"

Here Bratti's explanation was interrupted by some jostling as they
reached one of the entrances of the piazza, and before he could
resume it, they had caught sight of the enigmatical object they were
in search of.

4 ⟨Nello⟩ the barber *MS*   5 I] I've *MS*   6 ⟨tell⟩ help me tell *MS*
7 ⟨you have⟩ thou hast the wisdom of Midas, ⟨Bratti of thy⟩ ⟨who even ?poverty⟩
who *MS*
8 ⟨a bewildered air⟩ an air of disappointment *MS*
9 savours] savours (*pane e companatico*) *MS*
1 "Let us . . . Nello.] "Bembè," said Nello. "Let us make the round of the Mercato,
then." *MS*
2 seen an Englander or a German] *3P* seen {an Inglese or} a Tedesco *MS CM 1 2*

CHAPTER II.

A BREAKFAST[1] FOR LOVE

AFTER Bratti had joined the knot of talkers, the young stranger, hopeless of learning what was the cause of the general agitation, and not much caring to know what was probably of little interest to any but born Florentines[2], soon became tired of waiting for Bratti's escort; and chose to stroll round the piazza, looking out for some vendor of eatables who might happen to have less than the average curiosity about public news. But as if at the suggestion of a sudden thought, he thrust his hand into a purse or wallet that hung at his waist, and explored it again and again with a look of frustration.

"Not an obolus,* by Jupiter!" he murmured, in a language which was not Tuscan or even Italian. "I thought I had one poor piece left. I must get my breakfast for love, then!"

He had not gone many steps farther before it seemed likely that he had found a quarter of the market where that medium of exchange might not be rejected.

In a corner, away from any group of talkers, two mules were standing, well adorned with red tassels and [3]collars. One of them carried[4] wooden milk-vessels, the other a pair of panniers filled with herbs and salads. Resting her elbow on the neck of the mule that carried the milk, there leaned a young girl, apparently not more than sixteen, with a red hood surrounding her face, which was all the more baby-like in its prettiness from the entire concealment of her hair. The poor child, perhaps, was weary after[5] her labour in the morning twilight in preparation for her walk to market from some castello three or four miles off, for she seemed to have gone to sleep in that half-standing, half-leaning posture. Nevertheless, [6]our stranger had no compunction in awaking her, but the means he chose were so gentle that it seemed to the damsel in her dream as if a little sprig of thyme had touched her lips while she was stooping to gather the herbs. The dream was broken, however, for she opened her blue baby-eyes, and started up with astonishment and confusion to see the young stranger standing close before her. She heard him speaking to her in a voice which[7] seemed so strange and soft, that even if she had been more collected she would have taken it for granted that he said something

---

1 A BREAKFAST] BREAKFAST 3   2 Florentines ⟨did not choose to wait⟩ MS
3 ⟨belled⟩ collars MS
4 carried ⟨panniers and the other had wooden {milk} vessels and close by them⟩ MS
5 after ⟨a long walk⟩ MS   6 ⟨the young⟩ our MS   7 which] that MS

hopelessly unintelligible to her, and her first movement was to turn her head a little away, and lift up a corner of her green serge[8] mantle as a screen. He repeated his words—

"Forgive me, pretty one, for awaking you. I'm dying with hunger, and the scent of milk makes breakfast seem more desirable than ever."

He had chosen the words "*muoio di fame*," because he knew they would be familiar to her ears; and he had uttered them playfully, with the intonation of a mendicant. This time he was understood; the corner of the mantle was dropped, and in a few moments a large cup of fragrant milk[9] was held out to him. He paid no further compliments before raising it to his lips, and while he was drinking, the little maiden found courage to look up at the long dark[1] curls of this singular-voiced stranger, who had asked for food in the tones of a beggar, but who, though his clothes were much damaged, was unlike any beggar she had ever seen.

While this process of survey was going on, there was another current of feeling that carried her hand into a bag which hung by the [2]side of the mule, and when the stranger set down his cup, he saw a large piece of bread held out towards him, and caught a glance of the blue eyes that seemed intended as an encouragement to him to take this additional gift.

"But perhaps that is your own breakfast," he said. "No, I have had enough without payment. A thousand thanks, my gentle one."

There was no rejoinder in words; but the piece of bread was pushed a little nearer to him, as if in impatience at his refusal; and as the long dark eyes of the stranger rested on the baby face, it seemed to be gathering more and more courage to look up and meet them.

"Ah, then, if I must take the bread," he said, laying his hand on it, "I shall get bolder still, and beg for another kiss to make the bread sweeter."

His speech was getting wonderfully intelligible in spite of the strange voice, which had at first almost seemed a thing to make her cross herself. She blushed deeply, and lifted up a corner of her mantle to her mouth again. But just as the too presumptuous stranger was leaning forward, and had his fingers on the arm that held up the screening mantle, he was startled by a harsh voice close upon his ear.

"Who are *you*—with a murrain to you? No honest buyer, I'll warrant, but a hanger-on of the dicers—or something worse. Go! dance off, and find fitter company, or I'll give you a tune to a little quicker time than you'll like."

The young stranger drew back and looked at the speaker with a glance provokingly free from alarm and deprecation, and his slight expression of saucy amusement broke into a broad beaming smile as he surveyed the figure of his threatener. She was a stout but brawny woman, with a man's jerkin slipped over her green serge gamurra or gown, and the peaked hood of some departed mantle fastened round her sunburnt face, which, under all its coarseness and premature wrinkles, showed a half-sad, half-ludicrous maternal resemblance[3] to the tender baby face of the little maiden—the sort of resemblance which often seems a more croaking, shudder-creating prophecy than that of the death's head.

There was something irresistibly propitiating in that bright young smile, but Monna Ghita was not a woman to betray any weakness, and she went on speaking[4], apparently with [5]heightened exasperation.

"Yes, yes, you can grin as well as other monkeys in cap and jerkin. You're a minstrel or a mountebank, I'll be sworn; you look for all the world as silly as a tumbler when he's been upside down and has got on his heels again. And what fools'[6] tricks hast thou been after, Tessa?" she added, turning to her daughter, whose frightened face was more inviting to abuse. "Giving away the milk and victual[7], it seems; ay, ay, thou'dst carry water in thy ears for any idle vagabond that didn't like to stoop for it, thou silly staring rabbit! Turn thy back, and lift the herbs out of the panniers, else I'll make thee say a few Aves without counting."

"Nay, Madonna," said the stranger, with a pleading smile, "don't be angry with your pretty Tessa for taking pity on a hungry traveller, who found himself unexpectedly without a quattrino. Your handsome face looks so well when it frowns, that I long to see it [8]illuminated by a smile."

"*Va via*[9]! I know what paste you are made of. You may tickle me with that straw a good long while before I shall laugh, I can tell you. Get along, with a bad Easter! else I'll make a beauty spot or two on that face of yours that shall spoil your kissing on this side Advent."

As Monna Ghita lifted her formidable talons by way of complying with the first and last requisite of eloquence,* Bratti, who had come up a minute or two before, [1]had been saying to his companion, "What think you[2] of this pretty parrot[3], Nello? Doesn't[4] his tongue smack of Venice?"

"Nay, Bratti," said the barber in an under-tone, "thy wisdom has much of the ass in it, as I told thee just now; especially about the

3 {maternal} resemblance *MS*
5 ⟨increased⟩ heightened *MS*
7 victual] *MS* victuals *CM 1 2 3*
9 *Va via*] *1 2 3* Baje *MS Va, va CM*
2 think you ⟨Nello⟩ *MS*
4 Does{'nt} *MS*

4 went on {speaking} *MS*
6 fools'] *MS* fool's *CM 1 2 3*
8 ⟨with⟩ illuminated by *MS*
1 ⟨was⟩ had been *MS*
3 pretty parrot] *3C pappagallo MS CM 1 2*

ears. This stranger[5] is a Greek, else I'm not the barber who has had the sole and exclusive shaving of the excellent Demetrio[6],* and drawn more than one sorry tooth from his learned jaw. And this youth might be taken to have come straight from Olympus—at least [7]when he has had a touch of my razor."

"*Orsù!*[8] Monna Ghita!" continued Nello, not sorry to see some sport; "what has happened to cause such a thunder-storm[9]? Has this young stranger been misbehaving himself?"

"By San Giovanni!" said the cautious Bratti, who had not[1] shaken off his original suspicions concerning the shabbily-clad possessor of jewels, "he did right to run away from *me*, if he meant to get into mischief. I can swear that I found him under the Loggia de' Cerchi, with a ring on his finger such as I've seen worn by Bernardo Rucellai* himself. Not another rusty nail's worth do I know about him."

"The fact is," said Nello, eying the stranger good-humouredly, "this[2] *bello giovane* has been a little too presumptuous in admiring the charms of Monna Ghita, and has attempted to kiss her while her daughter's back [3]is turned; for I observe that the pretty Tessa is too busy to look this way at present. Was it not so, Messer?" Nello concluded, in a tone of courtesy.

"You have divined the offence like a soothsayer," said the stranger, laughingly. "Only that I had not[4] the good fortune to find Monna Ghita here at first. I begged a cup of milk from her daughter, and had accepted this gift of bread, for which I was making a humble offering of gratitude, before I had had[5] the higher pleasure of being face to face with[6] these riper[7] charms which I was perhaps too bold in admiring."

"*Va, va!* be off, every one of you, and stay in purgatory till I pay to get you out, will you?[8]" said Monna Ghita, fiercely, elbowing Nello, and leading forward her mule so as to compel the stranger to jump aside. "Tessa, thou simpleton, bring forward thy mule a bit—the[9] cart will be upon us."

5 stranger] youth *MS*   6 Demetrio] Demetrius *MS*   7 ⟨if⟩ when *MS*
8 *Orsù!*] Chè, chè, *MS* *Orsú!* *3*
9 cause such a thunder-storm] cause this hurrasca *MS*
1 not ⟨quite⟩ shaken *MS*
2 "The fact is . . . this] *1 2 3* "Pooh, pooh", said Nello, good humouredly, "the fact is, this *MS* "*Che, che*," said Nello, eyeing the stranger good-humouredly, "the fact is, this *CM*
3 ⟨was⟩ is *MS*   4 had not] *1 2 3* had not had *MS CM*
5 had had] had *1 2 3*   6 with ⟨the ripe charms of⟩ *MS*
7 riper] *1 2 3* ripe *MS CM*
8 you, {And stay . . . will you?}" said Monna Ghita . . . jump aside. ⟨"And stay . . . will you?⟩ *MS*
9 bit—the] *MS* bit, the *CM* bit: the *1 2 3*

As Tessa turned to take the mule's bridle, she cast one timid glance at the stranger, who was now moving with Nello out of the way of an approaching market-cart; and the glance was just long enough to seize the beckoning movement of his hand, which indicated that he had been ¹watching for this opportunity of an adieu.

"*Ebbene*," said Bratti, raising his voice to speak across the cart; "I leave you with Nello, young man, for there's no pushing my bag and basket any farther, and I have business at home. But you'll remember our bargain, because if you found Tessa without me, it was not my fault. Nello will show you my shop in the Ferravecchi, and I'll not turn my back on you."

"A thousand thanks, friend!" said the stranger, laughing, and then turned away with Nello up the narrow street which led most directly to the Piazza del Duomo.

1 ⟨waiting⟩ watching *MS*

CHAPTER III.

THE BARBER'S SHOP

"To tell you the truth," said the young stranger to Nello, as they got a little clearer of the entangled vehicles and mules, "I am not sorry to be handed over by that patron of mine to one who has a less barbarous accent, and a less enigmatical business. Is it a common thing among you Florentines for an itinerant trafficker in broken glass and rags to talk of a shop where he sells lutes and swords?"

"Common? No: our Bratti is not a common man. He has a theory, and lives up to it, which is more than I can say for any philosopher I have the honour of shaving," answered Nello, whose loquacity, like an over-full bottle, could never pour forth a small dose. "Bratti means to extract the utmost possible amount of pleasure, that is to say, of hard bargaining, out of this life; winding it up with a bargain for the easiest possible passage through purgatory, by giving Holy Church his winnings when the game is over. He has had his will made to that effect on the cheapest terms a notary could be got for. But I have often said to him, 'Bratti, thy bargain is a limping one, and thou art on the lame side of it. Does it not make thee a little sad to look at the pictures of the Paradiso? Thou wilt never be able there to chaffer for rags and rusty nails: the saints and angels want neither pins nor tinder; and except with San Bartolommeo, who carries his skin* about in an inconvenient manner, I see no chance of thy making a bargain for second-hand clothing.' But God pardon me[1]," added Nello, changing his tone, and crossing himself, "this light talk ill beseems a morning when Lorenzo lies dead, and the Muses are tearing their hair*— always a painful thought to a barber; and you yourself, Messere, are probably under a cloud, for when a man of your speech and presence takes up with so sorry a night's lodging, it argues some misfortune to have befallen him."

"What Lorenzo is that whose death you speak of?" said the stranger, appearing to have dwelt with too anxious an interest on this point to have noticed the indirect inquiry that followed it.

"What Lorenzo? There is but one Lorenzo, I imagine, whose death could throw the Mercato into an uproar, set the lantern of the Duomo leaping in desperation, and cause the lions of the Republic to feel under an immediate necessity to devour one another. I mean Lorenzo de' Medici, the Pericles of our Athens—if I may make such a comparison in the ear of a Greek."

1 God pardon me] *1 2 3 Dio mi perdoni MS CM*

"Why not?" said the other, laughingly; "for I doubt whether Athens, even in the days of Pericles, could have produced so learned a barber."

"Yes, yes; I thought I could not be mistaken," said the rapid Nello, "else I have shaved the venerable Demetrio Calcondila to little purpose; but pardon me, I am lost in wonder: your Italian is better than his, though he has been in Italy forty years—better even than that of the accomplished Marullo, who may be said to have married the Italic Muse in more senses than one, since he has married our learned and lovely Alessandra Scala."*

"It will lighten your wonder to know that I come of a Greek stock planted[2] in Italian soil much longer than the mulberry-trees which have taken so kindly to it. I was born at Bari, and my—I mean, I was brought up by an Italian—and, in fact, I am a Greek very much as your peaches are Persian.* The[3] Greek dye was subdued in me, I suppose, till I had been dipped over again by long abode and much travel in the land of gods and heroes. And, to confess something of my private affairs to you, this same Greek dye, with a few ancient gems I have about me, is the only fortune shipwreck has left me. But—when the towers fall, you know, it is an ill-business for the small nest-builders—the death of your Pericles makes me wish I had rather turned my steps towards Rome, as I should have done, but for a fallacious Minerva* in the shape of an Augustinian monk. 'At Rome,' he said, 'you will be lost in a crowd of hungry scholars; but at Florence, every corner is penetrated by the sunshine of Lorenzo's patronage: Florence is the best market in Italy for such commodities as yours.'"

"*Gnaffè*, and so it will remain, I hope," said Nello. "Lorenzo was not the only patron and judge of learning in [4]our city—heaven forbid! Because he was a large melon, every other Florentine is not a pumpkin, I suppose[5]. Have we not Bernardo Rucellai, and Alamanno Rinuccini,* and plenty more? And if you want to be informed on such matters, I, Nello, am your man. It seems to me a thousand years till I can be of service to a *bel erudito* like yourself. And, first of all, in the matter of your hair. That beard, my fine young man, must be parted with, were it as dear to you as the nymph of your dreams. Here at Florence, we love not to see a man with his nose projecting over a cascade of hair. But, remember, you will have passed the Rubicon, when once you have been shaven: if you repent, and let your beard grow after it has acquired stoutness by a struggle with the razor, your

2 stock planted] *MS 3P* stock, planted *CM 1 2*
3 in fact . . . Persian. The] *3P* in fact, ⟨I am rather⟩ may rather be called a Graeculus than a Greek. The *MS CM 1 2*
4 ⟨Florence⟩ our city *MS*   5 I suppose] *3C mi pare MS CM 1 2*

mouth will by and by show no longer what Messer Angelo* calls the
divine prerogative of lips, but will appear like a dark cavern fringed
with horrent brambles."

"That is a terrible prophecy," said the Greek, "especially if your
Florentine maidens are many of them as pretty as the little Tessa I
stole a kiss from this morning."

"Tessa? she is a rough-handed contadina[6]: you will rise into the
favour of dames who[7] bring no scent of the mule-stables with them.
But to that end, you must not have the air of a *sgherro*, or a man [8]of
evil repute:* you must look like a courtier, and a scholar of the more
polished sort, such as our Pietro Crinito*—like one[9] who[1] sins among
well-bred, well-fed people, and not one who sucks down vile *vino di
sotto* in a chance tavern."

"With all my heart," said the stranger. "If the Florentine Graces
demand it, I am willing to give up this small matter of my beard,
but—"

"Yes, yes," interrupted Nello. "I know what you would say. It is
the *bella zazzera*—the hyacinthine locks,* you do not choose to part
with; and there is no need. Just a little pruning—ecco!—and you will
look not unlike the illustrious prince Pico di Mirandola* in his prime.
[2]And here we are in good time in the Piazza San Giovanni, and at the
door of my shop. But you are pausing, I see: naturally, you want to
look at our wonder of the world, our Duomo, our Santa Maria del
Fiore. Well, well, a mere glance; but I beseech you to leave a closer
survey till you have been shaved: I am quivering with the inspiration
of my art even to the very edge of my razor. Ah, then, come round
this way."

The mercurial barber seized the arm of the stranger, and led him
to a point, on the south side of the piazza, from which he could see
at once the huge dark shell of the cupola, the slender soaring grace of
Giotto's campanile, and the quaint octagon of San Giovanni in front
of them, showing its unique gates of storied bronze,* which still bore
the somewhat dimmed glory of their original gilding[3]. The inlaid
marbles were then fresher in their pink and white and purple than[4]
they are now, when the winters of four centuries have turned their
white to the rich ochre of well-mellowed meerschaum; the façade of
the Cathedral did not stand ignominious in faded stucco,* but had
upon it the magnificent promise of the half-completed marble inlaying

6 "Tessa? she is a rough-handed contadina] "Pah! Tessa is a contadina *MS*
7 dames who] *MS 1 2 3* dames, who *CM*   8 ⟨*mal affare*⟩ of evil repute *MS*
9 {such as our Pietro Crinito}—like one ⟨, in fact,⟩ who *MS*
1 one who] *MS 1 2 3* one, who *CM*
2 ⟨But you are pausing, I see: naturally, you⟩ And *MS*
3 bronze {which still . . . gilding} *MS*
·4 pink and white and purple than] *MS* pink, and white, and purple, than *CM 1 2 3*

and statued niches, which Giotto had devised a hundred and fifty years before; and as the campanile in all its harmonious variety of colour and form led the eyes upward, high into the clear air of this April[5] morning, it[6] seemed a prophetic symbol, telling that human life must somehow and some time shape itself into accord with that pure aspiring beauty.

But this was not the impression it appeared to produce on the Greek. His eyes were irresistibly led upward, but as he stood with his arms folded and his curls falling backward, there was a slight touch of scorn on his lip, and when his eyes fell again, they glanced round with a scanning coolness which was rather piquing to Nello's Florentine spirit.

"Well, my fine young man[7]," he said, with some impatience, "you seem to make as little of our Cathedral as if you were the angel Gabriel come straight from paradise. I should like to know if you have ever seen finer work than our Giotto's tower, or any cupola that would not look[8] a mere mushroom by the side of Brunelleschi's there, or any marbles finer or more cunningly wrought than these that our Signoria got from far-off quarries, at a price that would buy a dukedom. Come, now, have you ever seen anything to equal them?"

"If you asked me that question with a scimitar at my throat, after the Turkish fashion, or even your own razor," said the young Greek, smiling gaily, and moving on towards the gates of the Baptistery, "I daresay you might get a confession of the true faith from me. But with my throat free from peril, I venture to tell you that your [9]buildings smack too much of Christian barbarism for my taste. I have a shuddering sense of what there is inside—hideous smoked Madonnas; fleshless saints in mosaic[1], staring down idiotic astonishment and rebuke from the apse; skin-clad skeletons hanging on crosses, or stuck all over with arrows, or stretched on gridirons; women and monks with heads aside in perpetual lamentation. I have seen enough of those wry-necked favourites of heaven at Constantinople. But what is this bronze door rough with imagery[2]?* These women's figures seem moulded in a different spirit from those starved and staring saints I spoke of: these heads in high relief speak of a human mind within them, instead of looking like an index to perpetual spasms and colic."

"Yes, yes," said Nello, with some triumph. "I think we shall show you by and by that our Florentine art is not in a state of barbarism.

5 clear air of this April] *1 2 3* pure air of that April *MS CM*
6 it ⟨must surely have spoken⟩ *MS*
7 "Well, my fine young man] *1 2 3* "*Ebbene, bel giovane MS CM*
8 look ⟨like⟩ a *MS*   9 ⟨building smacks⟩ buildings smack *MS*
1 saints {in mosaic} *MS*
2 imagery—⟨signio exstantibus asper [1 word]⟩ These *MS*

These gates, my fine young man, were moulded half a century ago, by our Lorenzo Ghiberti, when he counted hardly so many years as you do."*

"Ah, I remember," said the stranger, turning away, like one whose appetite for contemplation was soon satisfied. "I have heard that your Tuscan sculptors and painters have been studying the antique a little. But with monks for models, and the legends of mad hermits and martyrs for subjects, the vision of Olympus itself would be of small use to them."

"I understand," said Nello, with a significant shrug, as they walked along. "You are of the same mind as Michele Marullo, aye, and as Angelo Poliziano himself, in spite of his canonicate,* when he relaxes himself a little in my shop, after his lectures, and talks of the gods awaking from their long sleep and making the woods and streams vital once more. But he rails against the Roman scholars who want to make us all talk Latin again: 'My ears,' [3]he says, 'are sufficiently flayed by the barbarisms of the learned, and if the vulgar are to talk Latin I would as soon have been in Florence the day they took to beating all the kettles in the city because the bells were not enough to stay the wrath of the saints.' Ah, [4]Messer Greco, if you want to know the flavour of [5]our scholarship, you must frequent my shop: it is the focus of Florentine intellect, and in that sense the navel of the earth—as my great predecessor, Burchiello,* said of *his* shop, on the more frivolous pretension that his street of the Calimala was the centre of our city. And here we are at the sign of 'Apollo and the Razor.' Apollo, you see, is bestowing the razor on the Triptolemus* of our craft, the first reaper of beards, the sublime *Anonimo*, whose mysterious identity is indicated by a shadowy hand."

"I see thou hast had custom already, Sandro," continued Nello, addressing a solemn-looking dark-eyed youth, who made way for them on the threshold. "And[6] now make all clear for this signor to sit down. And prepare the finest-scented lather, for he has[7] a learned and a handsome chin."

"You have a pleasant little adytum* there, I see," said the stranger, looking through a latticed screen which divided the shop from a room of about equal size, opening on to[8] a still smaller walled enclosure, where a few bays and laurels surrounded a stone Hermes. "I suppose your conclave of *eruditi* meets there?"

3 ⟨says Messer Angelo⟩ he says *MS*   4 ⟨sir Greek⟩ Messer Greco *MS*
5 ⟨Florentine⟩ our *MS*
6 "I see thou . . . threshold. "And] "Ebbene, ⟨Cecco⟩ Sandro", continued Nello, addressing a solemn looking dark-eyed youth, who made way for them on the threshold, "thou hast had custom already, I see. And *MS*
7 has] hath *MS*   8 on to] *MS* into *CM 1 2 3*

"There, and not less in my shop," said Nello, leading the way into the inner room[9], in which were some benches, a table, [1]with one book in manuscript and one printed in capitals lying open upon it, a lute, a few oil-sketches, and a [2]model or two of hands and ancient masks. "For my shop is a no less fitting haunt of the Muses, as you will acknowledge when you feel the sudden illumination of understanding and the serene vigour of inspiration that will come to you with a clear chin. Ah! you can make that lute discourse, I perceive. I, too, have some skill that way, [3]though the serenata is useless when daylight discloses a visage[4] like mine, looking no fresher than an apple that has stood the winter[5]. But look at that sketch—it is[6] a fancy of Piero di Cosimo's, a strange freakish painter, who says he saw it by long looking at a mouldy wall."*

The sketch Nello pointed to represented three masks—one a drunken laughing Satyr, another a sorrowing Magdalen, and the third, which lay between them, the rigid, cold face of a Stoic: the masks rested obliquely on the lap of a little child, whose cherub features rose above them with something of the supernal promise in the gaze which painters had by that time learned to give to the Divine Infant.

"A symbolical picture, I see," said the young Greek, touching the lute while he spoke, so as to bring out a slight musical murmur. "The child, perhaps, is the Golden Age, wanting neither worship nor philosophy. And the Golden Age can always come back as long as men are born in the form of babies, and don't come into the world in cassock or furred mantle. Or the child may mean the wise philosophy of Epicurus, removed alike from the gross, the sad, and the severe."

"Ah! everybody has his own interpretation for that picture," said Nello; "and if you ask Piero himself what he meant by it, he says his pictures are an appendix which Messer Domeneddio has been pleased to make to the universe, and if any man is in doubt what they mean, he had better inquire of Holy Church. He has been asked to paint a picture after the sketch, but he puts his fingers to his ears and shakes his head at that: the fancy is past, he says—a strange animal, our Piero. But now all is ready for your initiation into the mysteries of the razor."

"Mysteries they may well be called," continued the barber, with rising spirits at the prospect of a long monologue, as he imprisoned

9 room ⟨which was furnished with⟩ *MS*
1 ⟨two or three books⟩ with one book *MS*   2 ⟨?cast⟩ model *MS*
3 ⟨but⟩ though *MS*   4 visage] *visaccio MS*
5 mine {looking ⟨like an apple that⟩ no fresher . . . winter} *MS*
6 But look at that sketch—it is] But see you there, that sketch of three masks: that is *MS*

the young Greek in the shroud-like shaving-cloth; "mysteries of Minerva[7] and the Graces. I get the flower[8] of men's thoughts, because I seize them in the [9]first moment after shaving. (Ah! you wince a little at the lather: it tickles the outlying limits of the nose, I admit.) And that is what makes the peculiar fitness of a barber's shop to become [1]a resort of wit and learning. For, look now at a druggist's shop: there is a dull conclave at the sign of 'The Moor,'[2] that pretends to rival mine; but what sort of inspiration, I beseech you, can be got from the scent of nauseous vegetable decoctions?—to say nothing of the fact that you no sooner pass the threshold than you see a doctor of physic[3],* like a gigantic spider disguised[4] in fur and scarlet, waiting for his prey; or even see him blocking up the doorway seated on a bony hack, inspecting saliva. (Your chin a little elevated, if it please you: contemplate that angel who is blowing the trumpet at you from the ceiling. I had it painted expressly for the regulation of my clients' chins.) Besides, your druggist, who herborises and decocts, is a man of prejudices: he has poisoned people according to a system, and is obliged to stand up for his system to justify the consequences. Now a barber can be dispassionate; the only thing he necessarily stands[5] by is the razor, always providing he is not an author. That [6]was the flaw in my great predecessor Burchiello—he was a poet, and had [7]consequently a prejudice about his own poetry. I have escaped that; I saw very early that authorship is a narrowing business, in conflict with the liberal art of the razor, which demands an impartial affection for all men's chins. Ecco, Messer! the outline of your chin and lip is[8] as clear as a maiden's; and now fix your mind on a knotty question—ask yourself whether you are bound to spell Virgil with an *i* or an *e*, and say if you do not feel an unwonted clearness on the point. Only, if you decide for the *i*, keep it to yourself till your fortune is made, for the *e* hath the stronger following in Florence.* Ah! I think I see a gleam of still [9]quicker wit in your eye. I have it on the authority of our young Niccolò Macchiavelli,* himself[1] keen enough to discern *il pelo nell' uovo*,* as we say, and a great lover of delicate shaving, though his beard is hardly of two years' date,[2] that no sooner

7 "Mysteries they may . . . Minerva] "Yes, yes", continued the barber, with rising spirits at the prospect of a long monologue, as he imprisoned the young Greek in the shroud like shaving-cloth, "mysteries they may well be called—mysteries of Minerva *MS*

8 flower] very flower *MS*   9 ⟨very⟩ first *MS*
1 ⟨the heart⟩ a resort *MS*   2 'The Moor,'] *3P Il Moro, MS CM 1 2*
3 a doctor of physic] a medicus {or doctor of physic} *MS*
4 spider disguised] *MS 1 2 3* spider, disguised *CM*
5 {necessarily} stands *MS*   6 ⟨is⟩ was *MS*
7 ⟨necessarily⟩ consequently *MS* 8 is] *1 2 3* are *MS CM*
9 higher⟩ quicker *MS*   1 himself ⟨so keen a wit that he can⟩ *MS*

do the hairs begin to push themselves, than he perceives a certain grossness of apprehension creeping over him."

"Suppose you let me look at myself," said the stranger, laughing. "The happy effect on my intellect is perhaps obstructed by a little doubt as to the effect on my appearance."

"Behold yourself in this mirror, then; it is a Venetian mirror from Murano, the true *nosce teipsum*,* as I have named it, compared with which the finest mirror of steel or silver is mere darkness. See now, how by diligent shaving, the nether region of your face may preserve its human outline, instead of presenting no distinction from the physiognomy of a bearded owl or a Barbary ape. I have seen men whose beards have so invaded their cheeks, that one might have pitied them as the victims of a sad, brutalizing chastisement befitting our Dante's *Inferno*, if they had not seemed to strut with a strange triumph in their extravagant hairiness."

"I seems to me," said the Greek, still looking into the mirror, "that you have taken away some of my capital with your razor—I mean a year or two of age, which might have won me more ready credit for my learning. Under the inspection of a patron whose vision has grown somewhat dim, I shall have a perilous resemblance to a maiden of eighteen in the disguise of hose and jerkin."

"[3]Not at all," said Nello, proceeding to clip the too extravagant curls; "your proportions are not those of a maiden. And for your age, I myself remember seeing Angelo Poliziano[4] begin his lectures on the Latin language when he had a younger beard than yours;* and between ourselves, his juvenile ugliness was not less signal than his precocious scholarship. Whereas you—no, no, your age is not against you; but between ourselves, let me hint to you that your being a Greek, though it be only an Apulian[5] Greek,* is not in your favour. Certain of our scholars hold that your Greek learning is but a wayside degenerate plant until it has been transplanted into Italian brains, and that now there is such a plentiful crop of the superior quality, your native teachers are mere propagators of degeneracy. Ecco! your curls are now of the right proportion to neck and shoulders; rise, Messer, and I will free you from the encumbrance of this cloth. *Gnaffè!* I almost advise you to retain the faded jerkin and hose a little longer; they give you the air of a [6]fallen prince."

"But the question is," said the young Greek, leaning against the high back of a chair, and returning Nello's contemplative admiration

---

2 {though his beard is hardly of two years' date}—that no sooner ⟨does his beard begin to push itself⟩ *MS*

3 ⟨Niente⟩ Not at all *MS*

4 Angelo Poliziano] Messer Angelo {Poliziano} *MS*

5 an Apulian] a Calabrian *MS*   6 ⟨faded⟩ fallen *MS*

'Suppose you let me look at myself'

with a look of inquiring anxiety; "the question is, in[7] what quarter I am to carry my princely air, so as to rise from the said fallen condition. If your Florentine patrons of learning share this scholarly [8]hostility to the Greeks, I see not how your city can be a [9]hospitable refuge for me, as you seemed to say just now."

"[1]*Pian piano*—not so fast," said Nello, sticking his thumbs into his belt and nodding to [2]Sandro to restore order. "I will not conceal from you that there is a prejudice against Greeks among us[3]; and though, as a barber unsnared[4] by authorship, I share no prejudices, I must admit that the Greeks are not always such pretty youngsters as yourself: their erudition is often of an uncombed, unmannerly aspect, and encrusted with a barbarous utterance of Italian, that makes their converse hardly more euphonious than that of a Tedesco in a state of vinous loquacity. And then, again, excuse me—we Florentines have liberal ideas about speech, and consider that an instrument which can flatter and promise so cleverly as the tongue, must have been partly made for those purposes; and that truth is a riddle for eyes and wit to discover, which it were a mere spoiling of sport for the tongue to betray. Still we have our limits beyond which we call dissimulation treachery. But it is said of the Greeks that their honesty begins at what is the hanging-point with us, and that since the old Furies* went to sleep, your Christian Greek is of so easy a conscience that he would make a stepping-stone of his father's corpse."

The[5] flush on the stranger's face indicated what seemed so natural a movement of resentment, that the good-natured Nello[6] hastened to atone for his want of reticence.

"Be not offended, *bel giovane*; I am but repeating what I hear in my shop; as you may perceive, my eloquence is simply the cream which I skim off my clients' talk. Heaven forbid I should fetter my impartiality by entertaining an opinion. And for that same scholarly objection to the Greeks," added Nello, in a more mocking tone, and with a significant grimace, "the fact is, you are heretics, Messer; jealousy has nothing to do with it: if you would just change your opinion about leaven[7], and alter your Doxology* a little, our Italian scholars would think it a thousand years till they could [8]give up their chairs to you. Yes, yes; it is chiefly religious scruple, and partly also the authority of a great classic,—Juvenal, is it not?[9] He, I gather, had his bile as much

---

7 {the question is,} in *MS*

9 ⟨very⟩ hospitable *MS*

2 ⟨Cecco⟩ Sandro *MS*

4 barber unsnared] *1 2 3* barber, unsnared *MS CM*

5 The ⟨alternate⟩ flush ⟨and paleness⟩ on *MS*

7 leaven] *MS 3P* Leaven *CM 1 2*

9 not?—⟨who, as I gather from Messer Angelo⟩ *MS*

8 ⟨prejudice against⟩ hostility to *MS*

1 ⟨Not so fast—⟩Pian piano *MS*

3 Greeks {among us} *MS*

6 {the good-natured} Nello *MS*

8 ⟨offer you⟩ give up *MS*

stirred by the swarm of Greeks[1] as our Messer Angelo, who is fond of quoting some passage about their incorrigible impudence—*audacia perdita*."

"Pooh! the passage is a compliment," said the Greek, who had recovered himself, and seemed wise enough to take the matter gaily—

"'Ingenium velox, audacia perdita, sermo
Promptus, et Isæo torrentior.'*

A rapid intellect and ready eloquence may carry off a little impudence."

"[2]Assuredly," said Nello. "And since, as I see, you know Latin literature as well as Greek, you will not fall into the mistake of [3]Giovanni Argiropulo, who ran full tilt against Cicero,* and pronounced him all but a pumpkin-head. [4]For, let me give you one bit of advice, young man[5]—trust a barber who has shaved the best chins, and kept his eyes and ears open for twenty years—oil your tongue well when you talk of the ancient Latin writers, and give it an extra dip when you talk of the modern. A wise Greek may win favour among us; witness our excellent Demetrio, who [6]is loved by many, and not hated immoderately even by the most renowned scholars."

"I discern the wisdom of your advice so clearly," said the Greek, with[7] the bright smile which was continually lighting up the fine form and colour of his young face, "that I will ask you for a little more. Who now, for example, would be the most likely patron for me? Is there a son of Lorenzo who inherits his tastes? Or is there any other wealthy Florentine specially addicted to purchasing antique gems? I have a[8] fine Cleopatra cut in sardonyx[9], and one or two other[1] intaglios and cameos[2],* both curious and beautiful, worthy of being added to the cabinet of a prince. Happily, I had[3] taken the precaution of fastening them within the lining of my doublet before I[4] set out on my voyage. Moreover, I should like to raise a small sum for my present need on this ring of mine" (here he took out[5] the ring and replaced it on his finger), "if you could recommend me to any honest trafficker."

"Let us see, let us see," said Nello, perusing the floor, and walking

1 greeks ⟨in his day⟩ *MS*   2 ⟨?Sicuro⟩ Assuredly *MS*
3 ⟨our⟩ Giovanni *MS*   4 ⟨And let⟩ For, let *MS*
5 young man] bel giovane *MS*   6 ⟨is⟩ ⟨was⟩ is *MS*   7 with ⟨his usual⟩ *MS*
8 a ⟨few worth adding to the cabinet of a prince⟩ *MS*
9 sardonyx] sapphire *MS*   1 {one or two} other *MS*
2 intaglios and cameos] *1 2 3* intagli and camei *MS CM*
3 {Happily} I had *MS*
4 before I ⟨committed myself to the ⟨⟨deceitful⟩⟩ treacherous ⟨⟨waves⟩⟩ [?archipelago] *MS*
5 took {out} *MS*

up and down the length of his shop. "This is no time to apply to Piero de' Medici, [6]though he has the will to make such purchases if he could always spare the money; but I think it is another sort of Cleopatra that he covets most.* . . . Yes, yes, I have it. What you want is a man of wealth, and influence, and scholarly tastes—not one of your learned porcupines, bristling all over with critical tests, but one whose Greek and Latin are of a comfortable laxity. And that man is Bartolommeo Scala, the secretary of our Republic. He came to Florence as a poor adventurer himself—a miller's son—a 'branny monster,'* as he has been nicknamed by our honey-lipped [7]Poliziano, who agrees with him as well as my teeth agree with lemon-juice. And, by the by, that may be a reason why the secretary may be the more ready to do a good turn to a strange scholar. For, between you and me, *bel giovane*—trust a barber who has shaved the best scholars— friendliness is much such a steed as Ser Benghi's:* it will hardly show much alacrity unless it has got the thistle of hatred under its tail. However, the secretary is a man who'll keep his word to you, even to the halving of a fennel seed;* and he is not unlikely to buy some of your [8]gems."

"But how am I to get at this great man?" said the Greek, rather impatiently.

"I was[9] coming to that[1]," said Nello. "Just now everybody of any public importance will be full of Lorenzo's death, and a stranger may find it difficult to get any notice. But in the meantime, I could take you to a man who, if he has a mind, can help you to a chance of a favourable interview with Scala sooner than anybody else in Florence—worth seeing for[2] his own sake too, to say nothing of his collections, or of his daughter Romola[3], who is as fair as the Florentine lily before it got quarrelsome, and turned red."*

"But if this father of the beautiful Romola[4] makes collections, why should he not like to buy some of my gems himself?"

Nello shrugged his shoulders. "For two good reasons—want of sight to look at the gems, and want of money to pay for them. Our old Bardo[5] de' Bardi is so blind that he can see no more of his daughter than, as he says, a glimmering of something bright when she comes very near him: doubtless her golden hair, which, as Messer

Luigi Pulci says of his Meridiana's[6], '*raggia come stella per sereno.*'*
Ah! here come some clients of mine, and I shouldn't wonder if one of
them could serve your turn about that ring."

6 says {of his Meridiana's} *MS*

CHAPTER IV.

FIRST IMPRESSIONS

"GOOD DAY, Messer Domenico," said Nello to the foremost of the two visitors who entered the shop, while he nodded silently to the other. "You come[1] as opportunely as cheese on[2] macaroni. Ah! you are in haste—wish to be shaved without delay—ecco! And this is a morning when every one has grave matter on his mind. Florence orphaned—the very pivot of Italy snatched away—heaven itself at a loss what to do next. *Oimè*[3]*!* Well, well; the sun is nevertheless travelling on towards dinner-time again; and, as I was saying, you come like cheese ready grated[4].* For this young stranger was wishing for an honourable trader who would advance him a sum on a certain ring of value, and if I had counted every goldsmith and money-lender in Florence on my fingers, I couldn't have found a better name than Menico Cennini. Besides, he hath other ware in which you deal—Greek learning, and young eyes—a double implement which you printers are always in need of."

The grave elderly man, son of that Bernardo Cennini,* who, [5]twenty years before, having heard of the new process of printing carried on by Germans, had cast his own types in Florence, remained necessarily in lathered silence and passivity while Nello showered this talk in his ears, but turned a slow sideway gaze on the stranger.

"This fine young man[6] has unlimited Greek, Latin, or Italian at your service," continued Nello, fond of interpreting by very ample paraphrase. "He is as great a wonder of juvenile learning as Francesco Filelfo* or our own incomparable Poliziano. A second Guarino, too, for he has had the misfortune to be shipwrecked,* and has doubtless lost a store of precious manuscripts that might have contributed some correctness even to your correct editions, Domenico. Fortunately, he has rescued a few gems of rare value. His name is—you said your name, Messer, was—?"

"Tito Melema," said the stranger, slipping the ring from his finger, and presenting it to Cennini, whom Nello, not less rapid with his razor than with his tongue, had now released from the shaving-cloth.

Meanwhile the man who had entered the shop in company with the goldsmith—a tall figure, about fifty,* with a short trimmed beard,

---

1 come ⟨like⟩ as opportunely as *MS*   2 on] to *MS*
3 *Oimè*] *1 2 3 Lasso MS CM*
4 like cheese ready grated] *1 2 3* like *cacio alla lasagna MS CM*
5 ⟨thirty⟩ twenty *MS*   6 fine young man] bel giovane *MS*

wearing an old felt hat and a threadbare mantle—had kept his eye fixed on the Greek, and now said abruptly,

"Young man, I am painting a picture of Sinon deceiving old Priam,* and I should be glad of your face for my Sinon, if you'd give me a sitting."

Tito Melema[7] started and looked round with a pale astonishment[8] in his face as if at a sudden accusation; but Nello left him no time to feel at a loss for an answer[9]: "Piero," said the barber, "thou art the most extraordinary compound of humours and fancies ever packed into a human skin. What trick wilt thou play with the fine visage of this young scholar to make it suit thy traitor? Ask him rather to turn his eyes upward, and thou may'st make[1] a Saint Sebastian of him that will draw troops of devout women,* or, if thou art in a classical vein, put [2]myrtle about his curls and make him a young Bacchus, or say rather a Phœbus Apollo, for his face is as warm and bright as a summer morning; it made me his friend in the space of a 'credo.'[3]"

"Aye, Nello," said the painter, speaking with abrupt pauses; "and if thy tongue can leave off its everlasting chirping long enough for thy understanding to consider the matter, thou may'st see that thou hast just shown the reason why the face of Messere[4] will suit my traitor. A perfect traitor should have a face which vice can write no marks on—lips that will lie[5] with a dimpled smile—eyes of such agate-like brightness and depth that no infamy can dull them—cheeks that will rise from a murder and not look haggard. I [6]say not this young man is a traitor: I mean, he has[7] a face that would make him the more perfect traitor if he had the heart of one, which is saying neither more nor less than that he has[8] a beautiful face, informed with rich young blood, that will be nourished enough by food, and keep its colour without much help of virtue. He may have the heart of a hero along with it; I aver nothing to the contrary. Ask Domenico there if the lapidaries can always tell a gem by the sight alone. And now I'm going to put the tow in my ears, for thy chatter and the bells together* are more than I can endure;[9] so say no more to me, but trim my beard."

With these last words Piero (called "di Cosimo," from his master, Cosimo Rosselli) drew out two bits of tow, stuffed them in his ears, and placed himself in the chair before Nello, who shrugged his

7 Melema ⟨looked round with some surprize at this sudden [4 or 5 words]⟩ MS
8 astonishment] terror MS   9 to {feel at a loss for an} answer MS
1 make ⟨him a Saint Sebastian⟩ MS   2 ⟨?bay⟩ myrtle MS
3 'credo.'] 1 2 3 credo MS CM
4 the face of Messere] 1 2 3 Messer's face MS the face of Messer CM
5 {will} lie MS   6 ⟨said⟩ say MS   7 has] hath MS   8 has] hath MS
9 ears: {for thy chatter . . . endure:} MS

shoulders and cast a grimacing look of intelligence at the Greek, as much as to say, "A whimsical fellow, you perceive! Everybody holds his speeches as mere jokes."

Tito, who had stood transfixed, with his long dark eyes resting on the unknown man who had addressed him so equivocally, seemed recalled to his self-command by Piero's change of position, and, apparently satisfied with his explanation, was again giving his attention to Cennini, who presently said,—

"This is a curious and a valuable[1] ring, young man. This intaglio of the fish with the crested serpent above it, in the black stratum of the onyx, or rather nicolo, is well shown by the surrounding blue of the upper stratum. The ring has[2], doubtless, a history?" added Cennini, looking up keenly at the young stranger.

"Yes, indeed," said Tito, meeting the scrutiny very frankly. "[3]The ring was found in Sicily, and I have understood from those who busy themselves with [4]gems and sigils, that both the stone and intaglio are of virtue to make the wearer fortunate, especially at sea, and also to restore to him whatever he may have lost.* But," he continued, smiling[5], "though I have worn it constantly since[6] I quitted Greece, it has not made me altogether [7]fortunate at sea, you perceive, unless I am to count escape from drowning as a sufficient proof of its virtue. It remains to be seen whether my lost chests[8] will come to light; but to lose no chance of such a result, Messer, I will pray you only to hold the ring for a short space as pledge for a small sum far beneath its value, and I will redeem it as soon as I can dispose of certain other gems which are secured within my doublet, or indeed as soon as I can earn something by any scholarly employment, if I may be so fortunate as to meet with such."

"That may be seen, young man, if you will come with me," said Cennini[9]. "My brother Pietro[1], who is a better judge of scholarship than I, will perhaps be able to supply you with a task that may test your capabilities. Meanwhile, take back your ring until I can hand you the necessary florins, and, if it please you,[2] come along with me."

"Yes, yes,[3]" said Nello, "go with Messer Domenico, you cannot go in better company; he was born under the constellation that gives a man skill, riches, and integrity, whatever that constellation may be, which is of the less consequence because babies can't choose their

---

1 a valuable] valuable *2 3*   2 has] hath *MS*   3 ⟨It⟩ The ring *MS*
4 ⟨the virtues of⟩ gems *MS*
5 continued, smiling] *MS 3* continued smiling *CM 1 2*
6 {constantly} since *MS*   7 ⟨fortunate⟩ ⟨lucky⟩ fortunate *MS*
8 {lost} chests *MS*   9 Cennini ⟨, returning the ring⟩. *MS*
1 brother Pietro] brother {Piero} *MS*
2 and {if it please you} come along with me ⟨, if it please you⟩ *MS*
3 yes, ⟨bel giovane,⟩ *MS*

own horoscopes, and indeed, if they could, there might be an inconvenient rush of babies at particular epochs. Besides, our Phœnix, the
incomparable Pico, has shown that your horoscopes are all a nonsensical dream[4]*—which is the less troublesome opinion. *Addio! bel giovane!* don't forget to come back to me."

"No fear of that," said Tito, beckoning a farewell, as he turned
round his bright face at the door. "You are to do me a great service:—that is the most positive security for your seeing me again."

"Say what thou wilt, Piero," said Nello, as the young stranger disappeared, "I shall[5] never look at such an outside as that without taking it as a sign of a loveable nature. Why[6], thou wilt say next that
Lionardo, whom thou art always raving about, ought to have made[7]
his Judas as beautiful as St. John!* But thou art as deaf as the top of
Mount Morello with that accursed tow in thy ears. Well, well: I'll get
a little more of this young man's history from him before I take him
to Bardo Bardi[8]."

---

4 Besides, our Phœnix . . . dream] Besides, {our Phoenix,} the incomparable Pico
has shown that ⟨the whole affair⟩ is a nonsensical ⟨illusion⟩ dream *MS*

5 "Say what . . . I shall] "Ebbene", said Nello, as the young stranger disappeared,
{"Say what thou wilt, Piero,} I shall *MS*

6 nature. Why] *1 2 3* nature. Suffocation! why *MS CM*

7 to have made] to make *MS*   8 Bardo Bardi] Bardo de' Bardi *MS*

CHAPTER V.

THE BLIND SCHOLAR AND HIS DAUGHTER

THE Via de' Bardi, a street noted in the history of Florence, lies in Oltrarno, or that portion of the city which clothes the southern bank of the river. It extends from the Ponte Vecchio to the Piazza de' Mozzi[1] at the head of the Ponte alle Grazie; its right-hand line of houses and walls being backed by the rather steep ascent which in the fifteenth century was known as the Hill of Bogoli, the famous stone-quarry whence the city got its pavement—[2]of dangerously unstable consistence when penetrated by rains; its left-hand buildings flanking the river and making on their northern side a length of quaint, irregularly-pierced façade, of which the waters give a softened loving reflection as the sun begins to decline towards the western heights. But quaint as these buildings are, some of them seem to the historical memory a too modern substitute for the famous houses of the Bardi family, destroyed by popular rage in the middle of the fourteenth century.

They were a proud and energetic stock, these Bardi: conspicuous among those who clutched the sword in the earliest world-famous quarrels* of Florentines with Florentines, when the narrow streets were darkened with the high [3]towers of the nobles,* and when the old tutelar god Mars, as he saw the gutters reddened with neighbours' blood, might well have smiled at the centuries of lip-service paid to his rival, the Baptist.* But the Bardi hands were of the sort that not only clutch the sword-hilt with vigour, but love the more delicate pleasure of fingering [4]minted metal: they were matched, too, with true Florentine eyes, capable of discerning that power was to be won by other means than by rending and riving, and by the middle of the fourteenth century we find them risen from their original condition of *popolani** to be possessors, by purchase, of lands and strongholds, and the feudal dignity of Counts of Vernio, disturbing to the jealousy of their republican fellow-citizens. These lordly purchases are explained by our seeing the Bardi disastrously signalized only a few years later as standing in the very front of European commerce—the Christian Rothschilds of that time—undertaking to furnish specie for the wars of our Edward the Third,* and having revenues "in kind" made over to them; especially in wool, most precious of freights for Florentine

---

1 Piazza de' Mozzi] Piazza Mozzi *MS*
2 Bogoli, {the famous . . . pavement—} *MS*   3 ⟨?houses⟩ towers *MS*
4 ⟨the⟩ minted metal *MS*

Galleys. Their august debtor left them with an august deficit, and
alarmed Sicilian creditors made a too sudden demand for the payment
of deposits, causing a ruinous shock to the credit of the Bardi and
that of[5] associated houses, which was felt as a commercial calamity
along all the coasts of the Mediterranean. But, like more modern
bankrupts, they did not, for all that, hide their heads in humiliation;
on the contrary, they seemed to have held them higher than ever, and
to have been among the most arrogant of those grandees[6], who under
certain noteworthy circumstances,* open to all who will read the honest[7] pages of Giovanni Villani,* drew upon themselves the exasperation of the armed people in 1343. The Bardi, who[8] had made
themselves fast in their street between the two bridges, kept these
narrow inlets, like panthers at bay, against the oncoming gonfalons of
the people, and were only [9]made to give way by an assault from the
hill behind them. Their houses by the river, to the number of
twenty-two (*palagi e case grandi*),* were sacked and burnt, and many
among the chief of those who bore the Bardi name were driven from
the city. But an old Florentine family was many-rooted, and we find
the Bardi maintaining importance and rising again and again to the
surface of Florentine affairs in a more or less creditable [1]manner,
implying an untold family history that would have included even
more vicissitudes and contrasts of dignity and disgrace, of wealth and
poverty, than are usually seen on the background of wide kinship.*
But the Bardi never resumed their proprietorship in the old street on
the banks of the river, which in 1492 had long been associated with
other names of mark, and especially with the Neri, who possessed a
considerable range of houses on the side towards the hill.

In one of these Neri houses[2] there lived, however, a descendant of
the Bardi, and of that very branch which a century and a half before
had become Counts of Vernio: a descendant who had inherited the
old family pride and energy, the old love of pre-eminence, the old
desire to leave a lasting track of his footsteps on the fast-whirling
earth. But the family passions lived on in him[3] under altered conditions: this descendant of the Bardi was not a man swift in street warfare, or one who loved to play the signor, fortifying strongholds and
asserting the right to hang vassals, or a merchant and usurer of keen
daring, who delighted in the generalship of wide commercial schemes:
he was a man with a deep-veined hand cramped by much copying of
manuscripts, who ate sparing dinners, and wore threadbare clothes, at
first from choice and at last from necessity; who sat among his books

5 and that of] and of *1 2 3*   6 grandees] *3C grandi MS 1 2 3*
7 honest] clear honest *MS*   8 Bardi, who] Bardi who *MS*
9 ⟨overcome⟩ made to give way *MS*   1 ⟨way⟩ manner *MS*
2 houses ⟨,however,⟩ *MS*   3 lived on {in him} *MS*

and his marble fragments of the past, and saw them only by the light of those far-off younger days which still shone in his memory: he was a moneyless, blind old scholar—the Bardo de' Bardi to whom Nello, the barber, had promised to introduce the young Greek, Tito Melema.

The[4] house in which Bardo lived was situated on the side of the street nearest the hill, and was one of those large sombre masses of stone building pierced by comparatively small windows, and surmounted by what may be called a roofed terrace or loggia[5], of which there are many examples still to be seen in the venerable city. Grim doors, with conspicuous [6]scrolled hinges, having high up on each side of them a small window defended by iron bars, opened on a groined entrance court, empty of everything but a massive lamp-iron suspended from the centre of the groin. A smaller grim door on the left hand admitted to the stone staircase, and the rooms on the ground floor. These last were used as a warehouse by the proprietor; so was the first floor; and both were filled[7] with precious [8]stores, destined to be carried, some perhaps to the banks of the Scheldt, some to the shores of Africa, some to the isles of the Egean, or to the banks of the Euxine.* Maso,* the old serving-man, when he returned[9] from the Mercato, with the stock of cheap vegetables, had to make his slow way[1] up to the second story before he reached the door of his master, Bardo, through which we are about to enter only a few mornings after Nello's conversation with the Greek.

We follow Maso across the antechamber to the door on the left hand, through which we pass as he opens it. He merely looks in and nods, while a clear young voice says, "Ah, you are come back, Maso. It is well. We have wanted nothing."

The voice came from the farther end of a long, spacious room, surrounded with shelves, on which books and antiquities were arranged in scrupulous order. Here and there, on separate stands in front of the shelves, were placed a beautiful feminine torso; a headless statue, with an uplifted muscular arm wielding a bladeless sword; rounded, dimpled, infantine limbs severed from the trunk, inviting the lips to kiss the cold marble; some well-preserved Roman busts; and two or three vases from[2] Magna Græcia.* A large table in the centre was covered with antique bronze lamps and small vessels in dark pottery. The colour of these objects was chiefly pale or sombre: the vellum bindings, with their deep-ridged backs, gave little relief to the marble livid with long burial; the once splendid patch of carpet at the farther

4 {¶}The *MS*   5 terrace or loggia] terrace *MS*   6 ⟨iron⟩ scrolled hinges *MS*
7 filled] *MS 1 2 3* fitted *CM*   8 ⟨woollens⟩ stores *MS*
9 when he returned] *3C* who returned *MS CM 1 2*
1 {slow} way *MS*
2 from] *3C* of *MS CM 1 2*

end of the room had long been worn to dimness; the dark bronzes
wanted sunlight upon them to bring out their tinge of green, and the
sun was not yet high enough to send gleams of brightness through
the narrow windows that looked on the Via de' Bardi.

The only spot of bright colour in the room was made by the hair
of a tall maiden of[3] seventeen or eighteen, who was standing before a
carved *leggio*, or reading-desk, such as is often seen in the choir[4] of
Italian churches. The hair was of a reddish gold colour, enriched by
an unbroken small ripple, such as may be seen in the sunset clouds
on grandest autumnal evenings. It was confined by a black fillet[5]
above her small ears, from which it rippled forward again, and made
a natural veil for her neck above her square-cut gown of black rascia,
or serge[6]. Her eyes were bent on a large volume placed before her:
one long white[7] hand rested on the reading-desk, and the other
clasped the back of her father's chair.

The blind father sat with head uplifted and turned a little aside
towards his daughter, as if her were looking at her. [8]His delicate pale-
ness, set off by the black velvet cap which surmounted his drooping
white hair, made all the more perceptible the likeness between his
aged features and those of the young maiden, whose cheeks were also
without any tinge of the rose. There was the same refinement of brow
and nostril in both, counterbalanced by a [9]full though firm mouth and
powerful chin, which gave an expression of proud tenacity and latent
impetuousness: an expression carried out in the backward poise of the
girl's head, and the grand line of her neck and shoulders. It was a
type of face of which one could not venture to say whether it would
inspire love or only that unwilling admiration which is mixed with
dread: the question must be decided by the eyes, which often seem[1]
charged with a more direct message from the soul. But the eyes of
the father had long been silent, and the eyes of the daughter were
bent on the Latin pages[2] of Politian's *Miscellanea*,* from which she
was reading aloud at the eightieth chapter, to the following effect[3]:—

"There was a certain nymph of Thebes named Chariclo, especially
"dear to Pallas; and this nymph was the mother of Teiresias. But
"once when in the heat of summer, Pallas, in company with
"Chariclo, was bathing her disrobed limbs in the Heliconian
"Hippocrene, it happened that Teiresias coming as a hunter to
"quench his thirst at the same fountain, inadvertently beheld Minerva
"unveiled, and immediately became blind. For it is declared in the

3 of {⟨Romola de Bardi⟩} *MS*   4 choir] *MS* choirs *CM 1 2 3*
5 fillet] band *MS*   6 rascia {or serge} *MS*
7 long white] *MS 1 2 3* long, white *CM*   8 ⟨The⟩ His *MS*
9 ⟨firm full mouth⟩ full ⟨but⟩ though firm mouth *MS*   1 {often} seem *MS*
2 Latin pages] pages *MS*   3 chapter, to the following effect] chapter *MS*

"Saturnian laws, that he who beholds the gods against their will, shall
"atone for it by a heavy penalty. . . . When Teiresias had fallen into
"this calamity, Pallas, moved by the tears of Chariclo, endowed him
"with prophecy and length of days, and even caused his prudence and
"wisdom to continue after he had entered among the shades, so that
"an oracle spake from his tomb: and she gave him a staff, wherewith,
"as by a guide, he might walk without stumbling. . . . And hence
"Nonnus, in the fifth book of the *Dionysiaca*, introduces Actæon
"exclaiming that he calls Teiresias happy, since, without dying, and
"with the loss of his eyesight merely, he had beheld Minerva
"unveiled, and thus, though blind, could for evermore carry her
"image in his soul."*

At this point in the reading, the daughter's hand slipped from the
back of the chair and met her father's, which he had that moment
uplifted; but she had not looked round, and was going on, though
with a voice a little altered by some suppressed feeling, to read the
Greek quotation from Nonnus, when the old man said—

"Stay, Romola; reach me my own copy of Nonnus. It is a more
correct copy than any in Poliziano's hands, for I made emendations in
it[4] which have not yet been communicated to any man. I finished it
in [5]1477, when my sight was fast failing me."

Romola walked to the farther end of the room, with the queenly
step which was the simple action of her tall, finely-wrought frame,
without the slightest conscious adjustment of herself.

"Is it[6] in the right place, Romola?" asked Bardo, who was perpetually seeking the assurance that the outward fact [7]continued to correspond with the image which lived to the minutest detail in his mind.

"Yes, father; at the west end of the room, on the third shelf from
the bottom, behind the bust of Hadrian,[8] above Apollonius[9] Rhodius
and Callimachus, and below Lucan and Silius Italicus."

As Romola said this, a fine ear would have detected in her clear
voice and distinct utterance, a faint suggestion of weariness struggling
with habitual patience. But as she approached her father and saw his
[1]arms stretched out a little with nervous excitement to seize the volume[2], her hazel eyes filled with pity; she hastened to lay the book on
his lap, and kneeled down by him, looking up at him as if she
believed that the love in her face must surely make its way through
the dark obstruction that shut out everything else. At that moment the
doubtful attractiveness of Romola's face, in which pride and passion

4 emendations {in it} *MS*   5 147⟨8⟩7 *MS*   6 Is it] It is *MS*
7 ⟨corresponded⟩ continued to correspond *MS*
8 bottom {behind the bust of Hadrian,} *MS*
9 above Apollonius] between the Apollonius *MS*   1 ⟨hands⟩ arms *MS*
2 volume ⟨that he might feel the [4 or 5 words]⟩ *MS*

seemed to be quivering in the balance with native refinement and
intelligence, was transfigured to the most loveable womanliness by
mingled pity and affection: it was evident that the deepest fount of
feeling within her had not yet wrought its way to the less changeful
features, and only found its outlet through her eyes.

But the[3] father, unconscious of that soft radiance, looked flushed
and agitated as his hand explored the edges and back of the large
book.

"The vellum is yellowed in these thirteen years, Romola."

"Yes, father," said Romola, gently[4]; "but your letters at the back
are dark and plain still—[5]fine Roman letters; and the Greek character," she continued, laying the book open on her father's knee, "is
more [6]beautiful than that of any of [7]your bought manuscripts."

"Assuredly, child," said Bardo, passing his finger across the page,
as if he hoped to [8]discriminate line and margin. "What hired amanu-
ensis can be equal to the scribe who loves the words that grow under
his hand, and to whom an error or indistinctness in the text is more
painful than a sudden darkness[9] or obstacle across his path? And even
these mechanical printers who threaten to make learning a base and
vulgar thing—even they must depend on the manuscripts[1] [2]over
which we scholars have bent with that insight into the poet's meaning
which is closely akin to the *mens divinior** of the poet himself; unless
they would flood the world with grammatical falsities and inexplicable
anomalies[3] that would turn the very fountains[4] of Parnassus into a
deluge of poisonous mud. But find the passage in the fifth book, to
which Poliziano refers[5]—I know it very well."

Seating herself on a low stool, close to her father's knee, Romola
took the book on her lap and read[6] the four verses* containing the
exclamation of Actæon.

"It is true, Romola," said Bardo, when she had finished; "it is a[7]
true conception of the poet; for what is that grosser, narrower light
by which men behold merely the petty scene around them, compared

3 the ⟨old man's features were lit up by an agitation that was no response to that
gentle look⟩ MS
4 "Yes, father; {said Romola, gently} MS   5 ⟨beautiful⟩ fine MS
6 ⟨perfect⟩ beautiful MS   7 ⟨the manuscripts⟩ your bought manuscripts MS
8 ⟨discern⟩ discriminate MS   9 {a sudden} darkness MS
1 manuscripts] MS manuscript CM 1 2 3   2 ⟨at⟩ over MS
3 {inexplicable} anomalies ⟨which⟩ that MS   4 fountains] fountain 2 3
5 passage {in the fifth book} to which Poliziano refers: ⟨I know it very well⟩ ⟨"Ολβιε
Τειρεσα⟩ MS*
6 Seating herself . . . read] Romola {seating herself on a low stool close to her
father's knee took the book on her lap and} read MS
7 Romola {"said Bardo, when she had finished}—"it is a ⟨fine⟩ true conception of
the poet: ⟨it is better to be blind⟩ for what is that grosser narrower light ⟨which men
rise every morning to behold⟩ ⟨which men behold every day⟩ by which men behold MS

with that far-stretching, lasting light which spreads over centuries of thought, and over the life of nations, and makes clear to us the minds of the immortals who have reaped the great harvest and left us to glean in their furrows? For me, Romola, even when I could see, it was with the great dead that I lived; while the living often seemed to me mere spectres—shadows dispossessed of true feeling and intelligence; and unlike those Lamiæ,* to whom Poliziano, with that superficial ingenuity which I do not deny to him, compares our inquisitive Florentines[8], because they put on their eyes when they went abroad, and took them off[9] when they got home again, I have returned from the converse of the streets as from a forgotten dream, and have sat down among my books, saying with Petrarca, the modern who is least unworthy to be named after the ancients, 'Libri medullitus delectant, colloquuntur, consulunt, et viva quadam nobis atque arguta familiaritate junguntur.' "*

"And[1] in one thing you are happier than your favourite Petrarca, father," said Romola, affectionately humouring the old man's disposition to dilate in this way; "for he used to look at his copy of Homer and [2]think sadly that the Greek was a dead letter to him:* so far, he had the inward blindness that you feel is[3] worse than your outward blindness[4]."

"True, child; for I carry within me the fruits of that fervid study which I gave to the Greek tongue under the teaching of the younger Crisolora,* and Filelfo, and Argiropulo, though that great work in which I had desired to gather, as into a firm web, all the threads [5]that my research had laboriously disentangled, and which would have been the vintage of my life, was cut off by the failure of my sight and my want of a fitting coadjutor. For the[6] sustained zeal and unconquerable patience demanded from those who would tread the unbeaten paths of knowledge are still less reconcileable with the wandering, vagrant propensity of the feminine mind than with the feeble powers of the feminine body."

"Father," said Romola, with a sudden flush and in an injured tone, "I read anything you wish me to read; and I will look out any passages for you, and make whatever notes you want."

Bardo shook his head, and smiled with a bitter sort of pity. "As well try to be a pentathlos and perform all the five feats of the palæstra[7] with the limbs of a nymph.* Have I forgotten thy fainting in the

---

8 {inquisitive} Florentines *MS*   9 off ⟨again⟩ *MS*
1 And ⟨you are in one way⟩ *MS* 2 ⟨feel⟩ think *MS* 3 that {you feel} is *MS*
4 outward blindness] *1 2 3* outward *MS CM*
5 ⟨which I⟩ that my research *MS*
6 coadjutor. For the] *1 2 3* coadjutor; for ⟨that⟩ the *MS CM*
7 pentathlos {and perform all the five feats of the palaestra} *MS*

mere search for the references I needed to explain a single passage of
Callimachus?"

"But, father, it was the weight of the books, and Maso can help
me,—it was not want of attention and patience."

Bardo shook his head again. "It is not mere bodily organs that I[8]
want: it is the sharp edge of a young mind to pierce the way for my
somewhat blunted faculties. For blindness acts like a dam, sending
the streams of thought backward along the already-travelled channels
and hindering the course onward. If my son had not forsaken me,
[9]deluded by debasing fanatical dreams, worthy only of an energumen*
whose dwelling is among tombs, I might have gone on and seen my
path broadening to the end of my life; for he was a youth of great
promise. . . . But it has closed in now," the old man continued, after
a short pause; "it has closed in now;—all but the narrow track he has
left me to tread—alone, in my blindness."

Romola started from her seat, and carried away the large volume to
its place again, stung too acutely by her father's last words to remain
motionless as well as silent; and when she turned away from the shelf
again, she remained standing at some distance from him, stretching
her arms downward[1] and clasping her fingers tightly as she looked
with a sad dreariness in her young face at the lifeless objects around
her—the parchment backs, the unchanging mutilated marble, the bits
of [2]obsolete bronze and clay.

Bardo, though usually susceptible to Romola's movements and
eager to trace them, was now too entirely preoccupied by the pain of
rankling memories to notice her departure from his side.

"Yes," he went on, "with my son to aid me, I might have had my
due share in the triumphs of this century: the names of the Bardi,
father and son, might have been held reverently on the lips of scholars in the ages to come; not on account of frivolous verses or philosophic[3] treatises, which are superfluous and presumptuous attempts to
imitate the inimitable, such as allure vain men like Panhormita, and
from which even the admirable Poggio* did not keep himself
sufficiently free; but because we should have given a lamp whereby
men might have studied the supreme productions of the past. For
why is a young man like Poliziano (who[4] was not yet born when I
was already held worthy to maintain a discussion with Thomas of
Sarzana)[5]* to have a glorious memory as a commentator[6] on the
Pandects*—why is Ficino, whose Latin is an offence to me, and who

8 {that} I *MS*   9 ⟨and been⟩ deluded *MS*   1 downward] downwards *2 3*
2 ⟨moulded⟩ obsolete *MS*   3 philosophic] philosophical *2 3*
4 who ⟨when⟩ *MS*
5 Poliziano (who . . . Sarzana)] *2 3* Poliziano, who . . . Sarzana, *MS CM 1*
6 {a} commentator *MS*

wanders purblind among the superstitious fancies that marked the decline at once of art, literature, and philosophy, to descend to posterity as the very high priest of Platonism,* while I, who am more than their equal, have not effected anything but scattered work, which will be appropriated by other men? Why? but because my son, whom I had brought up to replenish my ripe learning with young enterprise, left me and all liberal pursuits that he might lash himself and howl at midnight with [7]besotted friars—that he might go wandering on pilgrimages befitting men who know of no past older than the missal and the crucifix?—left me when the night was already beginning to fall on me."

In these last words the old man's voice, which had risen high in indignant protest, fell into a tone of reproach so tremulous and plaintive that Romola, turning her eyes again towards the blind aged face, felt her heart swell with forgiving pity. She seated herself by her father again, and placed her hand on his knee—too proud to obtrude consolation in words that might seem like a vindication of her own value, yet wishing to comfort him by some sign of her presence.

"Yes, Romola," said Bardo, automatically letting his left hand, with its massive prophylactic rings,* fall a little too heavily on the delicate blue-veined back of the girl's right, so that she bit her lip to prevent herself from starting. "If even Florence only is to remember me, it can but[8] be on the same ground that it will remember Niccolò Niccoli*— because I forsook the vulgar pursuit of wealth in commerce that I might devote myself to collecting the precious remains of ancient art and wisdom, and leave them, after the example of the munificent Romans, for an everlasting possession to my fellow-citizens. But why do I say Florence only? If Florence remembers me, will not the world remember me? . . . Yet," added Bardo, after a short pause, his voice falling again into a saddened key, "Lorenzo's untimely death has raised a new difficulty. I had his promise—I should have had his bond—that my collection should always bear my name and should never be sold, though the harpies might clutch everything else; but there is enough for them—there is more than enough—and for thee, too, Romola, there will be enough. Besides, thou wilt marry; Bernardo reproaches me that I do not seek a fitting *parentado* for thee, and we will delay no longer, we will think about it."

"No, no, father; what could you do? besides, it is useless: wait till some one seeks me," said Romola, hastily.

"Nay, my child, that is not the paternal duty. It was not so held by the ancients, and in this respect Florentines have not degenerated from their ancestral customs."

7 ⟨Franciscan⟩ besotted *MS*   8 but] only *MS*

"But I will study diligently," said Romola, her eyes dilating with anxiety. "I will become as learned as [9]Cassandra Fedele:* I will try and[1] be as useful to you as if I had been a boy, and then perhaps some great scholar will want to marry me, and will not mind about a dowry; and he will like to come and live with you, and he will be to you in place of my brother . . . and you will not be sorry that I was a daughter."

There was a rising sob in Romola's voice as she said the last words, which touched the fatherly fibre in Bardo. He stretched his hand upward a little in search of her golden hair, and as she placed her head under his hand, he gently stroked it, leaning towards her as if his eyes discerned some glimmer there.

"Nay, *Romola mia*[2], I said not so: if I have pronounced an anathema on a degenerate and ungrateful son, I said not that I could wish thee other than the sweet daughter thou hast been to me. For what son could have tended me so gently in the frequent sickness I have had of late? And even in learning thou art not, according to thy measure, contemptible. Something perhaps were to be wished in thy capacity of attention and memory, not incompatible even with the feminine mind. But as Calcondila bore testimony, when he aided me to teach thee, thou hast a ready apprehension, and even a wide-glancing intelligence. And thou hast a man's nobility of soul: thou hast never fretted me with thy petty desires as thy mother did. It is true, I have been careful to keep thee aloof from the debasing influence of thy own sex, with their sparrow-like frivolity and their enslaving superstition, except, indeed, from that of our[3] cousin Brigida, who may well serve as a scarecrow and a warning. And though—since I agree with the divine Petrarca, when he declares[4], quoting the *Aulularia* of Plautus, who again was indebted for the truth to the supreme Greek intellect, 'Optimam fœminam nullam esse, alia licet alia pejor sit'*—I cannot boast that thou art entirely lifted out of that lower category to which Nature assigned thee, nor even that in erudition thou art on a par with the more learned women of this age; thou art nevertheless—yes, *Romola mia*," said the old man, his pedantry again melting into tenderness, "thou art my sweet daughter, and thy voice is as the lower notes of the flute, 'dulcis, durabilis, clara, pura, secans aëra et auribus sedens,' according to the choice words of Quintilian;* and Bernardo tells me thou art fair, and thy hair is like the brightness of the morning, and indeed it seems to me that I discern some radiance from thee. Ah! I know how all else looks in this room, but thy form I only guess at. Thou art no longer

---

9 ⟨Alessandra Scala, as [1 word] as Caterina Fedele⟩ Cassandra Fedele *MS*
1 try and] try to *MS*   2 *Romola mia*] Romola *MS*
3 our] thy *MS*   4 declares] says *MS*

the little woman six years old, that faded for me into darkness: thou art tall, and thy arm is but little below mine. Let us walk together."

The old man rose, and Romola, soothed by these beams of tenderness, looked happy again as she drew his arm within hers, and placed in his [5]right hand the stick which rested at the side of his chair. While Bardo had been sitting, he had seemed hardly more than sixty: his face, though pale, had that refined texture in which wrinkles and lines are never deep; but now that he began to walk he looked as old as he really was—rather more than seventy; for his tall spare frame had the student's stoop of the shoulders, and he stepped with the undecided gait of the blind.

"No, Romola," he said, pausing against the bust of Hadrian, and passing his stick from the right to the left that he might explore the familiar outline with a "seeing hand." "There will be nothing else to preserve my memory and carry down my name as a member of the great republic of letters[6]—nothing but my library and my collection of antiquities. And [7]they are choice," continued Bardo, pressing the bust and speaking in a tone of insistance. "The collections of Niccolò I know were larger: but take any collection which is the work of a single man—that of the great Boccaccio* even—mine[8] will surpass it. That of Poggio was contemptible compared with mine. It will be a great gift to unborn scholars. And there is nothing else. For even if I were to yield to the wish of Aldo Manuzio when he sets up his press at Venice,* and give him the aid of my annotated manuscripts, I know well what would be the result: some other scholar's name would stand on the title-page of the edition—some scholar who would have fed on my honey and then declared[9] in his preface[1] that he had gathered it all himself fresh from Hymettus.* Else, why have I refused the loan of many an annotated codex? why[2] have I refused to make public any of my translations? why? but because scholarship is a system of licensed robbery, and your man in scarlet and furred robe who sits in judgment on thieves, is himself a thief of the thoughts and the fame that belong to his fellows. But against that robbery Bardo de' Bardi shall struggle—though blind and forsaken, he shall struggle. I too have a right to be remembered—as great a right as Pontanus or [3]Merula,* whose names will be foremost on the lips of posterity, because they sought patronage and found it; because they had tongues that could flatter, and blood that was used to be nourished from the client's basket.* I have a right to be remembered."

5 ⟨left⟩ right MS   6 memory {and carry . . . letters} MS
7 ⟨it is⟩ they are MS
8 even—mine] 1 2 3 even, which Niccolò bought ⟨or that⟩—mine MS CM
9 declared] ⟨declared⟩ declare MS   1 {in his preface} MS
2 why ⟨?⟩ ⟨but because⟩ MS   3 ⟨Platina⟩ Merula MS*

The old man's voice had become at once loud and tremulous, and a pink flush overspread his proud, delicately-cut features, while the habitually raised attitude of his head gave the idea that behind the curtain of his blindness he saw some imaginary high tribunal to which he was appealing against the injustice of Fame.

Romola was moved with sympathetic indignation, for in her nature too there lay the same large claims, and the same spirit of struggle against their denial. She tried to calm her father by a still prouder word than his.

"Nevertheless, father, it is a great gift of the gods to be born with a hatred and contempt of all injustice and meanness. Yours is a higher lot, never to have lied and truckled, than to have shared honours won by dishonour. There is strength in scorn, as there was in the martial fury by which men became insensible to wounds."

"It is well said, Romola. It is a Promethean word* thou hast uttered," answered Bardo, after a little interval in which he had begun to lean on his stick again, and to walk on. "And I indeed am not to be pierced by the shafts of Fortune. ⁴My armour is the *æs triplex** of a clear conscience, and a mind nourished by the precepts of philosophy. 'For men,' says Epictetus,* 'are disturbed not by things themselves, but by their opinions or thoughts concerning those things.' And again, 'whosoever will be free, let him not desire or dread that which it is in the power of others either to ⁵deny or inflict: otherwise, he is a slave.' And of all such gifts as are dependent on the caprice of fortune or of men, I have long ago learned to say, with Horace—who, however, is too wavering in his philosophy,* vacillating between the precepts of Zeno and the less worthy maxims of Epicurus, and attempting, as we say, 'duabus sellis sedere'*—concerning such accidents, I say, with the pregnant brevity of the poet—

'Sunt qui non habeant, est qui non curat habere.'*

He is referring to gems, and purple, and other insignia of wealth; but I may apply his words not less justly to the tributes men pay us with their lips and their pens, which are also matters of purchase, and often with base coin. Yes, '*inanis*'*—hollow, empty—is the epithet justly bestowed on Fame."⁶

They made the tour of the room in silence after this; but Bardo's lip-born maxims were as powerless over the passion which had been moving him, as if they had been written on parchment and hung round his neck in a sealed bag;* and he presently broke forth again in a new tone of insistance.

4 ⟨For men, says Epictetus⟩ My *MS*   5 ⟨inflict or⟩ deny or inflict *MS*
6 coin. {Yes—'Inanis' . . . fame."} *MS*

"*Inanis?* yes, if it is a lying fame; but not if it is the just meed of labour and a great purpose. I claim my right: it is not fair that the work of my brain and my hands should not be a monument to me—it is not just that my labour should bear the name of another man. It is but little to ask," the old man went on, bitterly, "that my name should be over the door—that men should own themselves debtors to the Bardi library in Florence. They will speak coldly of me, perhaps: 'a diligent collector and transcriber,' they will say, 'and also of some critical ingenuity, but one who could hardly be conspicuous in an age so fruitful in illustrious scholars. [7]Yet he merits our pity, for in the latter years of his life he was blind, and his only son, to whose education he had devoted [8]his best years—' Nevertheless, my name will be remembered, and men will honour me: not with the breath of flattery, puchased by mean bribes, but because I have laboured, and because my labour[9] will remain. Debts! I know there are debts; and there is thy dowry, Romola, to be paid. But there must be enough—or, at least, there can lack but a small sum, such as the Signoria might well provide. And if Lorenzo had not died, all would have been secured and settled. But now. . . ."

At this moment Maso opened the door, and advancing to his master, announced that Nello, the barber, had desired him to say, that he was come with the Greek scholar whom he had asked leave to introduce.

"It is well," said the old man. "Bring them in."

Bardo, conscious that he looked more dependent when he was walking, liked always to be seated in the presence of strangers, and Romola, without needing to be told, conducted him to his chair. She was standing by him at her full height, in quiet majestic self-possession,[1] when the visitors entered; and the most penetrating observer would hardly have divined that this proud pale face, at the slightest touch on the fibres of affection or pity, could become passionate with tenderness, or that this woman, who imposed a certain awe on those who approached her, was in a state of girlish simplicity and ignorance concerning the world outside her father's books.

---

7 ⟨Nevertheless⟩ Yet *MS*   8 ⟨the best years of his⟩ best years *MS*
9 labour] labours *2 3*   1 height {⟨and⟩ in quiet majestic self-possession,} *MS*

A Recognition

CHAPTER VI.

DAWNING HOPES

WHEN Maso opened the door again, and ushered in the two visitors, Nello, first making a deep reverence to Romola, gently pushed Tito before him, and advanced with him towards her father.

"Messer Bardo," he said, in a more measured and respectful tone than was usual with him, "I have the honour of presenting to you the Greek scholar, who has been eager to have speech of you, not less from the report I made[1] to him of your learning and your priceless collections, than because of the furtherance your patronage may give him under the transient need to which he has been reduced by shipwreck. His name is Tito Melema, at your service."

Romola's astonishment could hardly have been greater if the stranger had worn a panther-skin and carried a thyrsus;* for the cunning barber had said nothing of the Greek's age or appearance; and among her father's scholarly visitors, she had hardly ever seen any but middle-aged or grey-headed men. There was only one masculine face, at once youthful and beautiful, the image of which remained deeply impressed on her mind: it was that of her brother, who long years ago had taken her on his knee, kissed her, and never come back again: a fair face, with sunny hair, like her own. But the habitual attitude of her mind towards strangers—a proud self-dependence and determination to ask for nothing even by a smile—confirmed in her by her father's complaints against the world's injustice, was like a snowy embankment hemming in the rush of admiring surprise. Tito's bright [2]face showed its rich-tinted beauty without any rivalry of colour above his black *sajo* or tunic[3] reaching to the knees. It [4]seemed like a wreath of spring, dropped suddenly into[5] Romola's young but wintry life, which had inherited nothing but memories—memories of a dead mother, of a lost brother, of a blind father's happier time—memories of far-off light, love, and beauty, that lay embedded[6] in dark mines of books, and could hardly give out their brightness again until they were kindled for her by the torch of some known joy.

---

1 made] have made *2 3*   2 ⟨young features⟩ face showed ⟨their⟩ its *MS*

3 {*sajo* or} tunic ⟨and short cloak assumed by Nello's advice in deference to the general mourning of Florence⟩ *MS*

4 ⟨was⟩ seemed *MS*   5 into] in *1 2 3*   6 {that lay} embedded *MS*

[7]Nevertheless, she returned Tito's bow, made to her on entering, with the same pale proud face as ever; but, as he approached, the snow melted, and when he ventured to look towards her again, while Nello was speaking, a pink flush overspread her face, to vanish again almost immediately, as if her imperious will had recalled it. [8]Tito's glance, on the contrary, had that gentle, beseeching admiration in it which is the most propitiating of appeals to a proud, shy woman, and is perhaps the only atonement a man can make for being too handsome. The finished fascination of his air came chiefly from the absence of demand and assumption. It was that of a fleet, soft-coated, dark-eyed animal that delights you by not bounding away in indifference from you, [9]and unexpectedly pillows its chin on your palm, and looks up at you desiring to be stroked—as if it loved you.

"Messere, I give you welcome,[1]" said Bardo, with some condescension; "misfortune wedded to learning, and especially to Greek learning, is a letter of credit that should win the ear of every instructed Florentine; for, as you are doubtless aware, since the period when your countryman[2], Manuelo[3] Crisolora,* diffused the light of his teaching in the chief cities of Italy, now nearly a century ago, no man is held worthy of the name of scholar who has acquired merely the transplanted and derivative literature of the Latins; rather, such inert students are stigmatized as *opici* or barbarians, according to the phrase of the Romans themselves, who frankly replenished their urns at the fountain-head. I am, as you perceive, and as Nello has doubtless forewarned you, totally blind: a calamity to which we Florentines are held especially liable, whether owing to the cold winds which rush upon us in spring from the passes of the Apennines, or to that sudden transition from the cold gloom of our houses to the dazzling brightness of our summer sun, by which the *lippi** are said to have been made so numerous among the ancient Romans[4]; or, in fine, [5]to some occult cause which eludes our superficial surmises. But I pray you be seated: Nello, my friend, be seated."

Bardo paused [6]until his fine ear had assured him that the visitors were seating themselves, and that Romola was [7]taking her usual chair at his right hand. Then he said:

"From what part of Greece do you come, Messere? I had thought that your unhappy country had been [8]almost exhausted of those sons

---

7 ⟨Yet⟩ Nevertheless *MS*   8 ⟨His⟩ Tito's *MS*   9 ⟨but⟩ and *MS*

1 welcome] good welcome *MS*   2 when {your countryman} *MS*

3 Manuelo] *3P* Emmanuel *MS* Manuello *CM 1 2*

4 sun, by which . . . Romans] sun, which is said to have made the lippus a common disease with the ancient Romans *MS*

5 ⟨from⟩ to *MS*   6 ⟨while his fine ear assured⟩ until *MS*

7 ⟨placing herself on⟩ taking *MS*   8 ⟨nearly⟩ almost *MS*

who could cherish in their minds any image of her original glory, though indeed the[9] barbarous Sultans have of late shown[1] themselves not indisposed to engraft on their wild stock the precious [2]vine which their own fierce bands have hewn down[3] and trampled under foot. From what part of Greece do you come[4]?"

"I sailed last from Nauplia,"* said Tito; "but I have resided both at Constantinople and Thessalonica, and have travelled in various parts little visited by Western Christians[5] since the triumph of the Turkish arms. I should tell you, however, Messere, that I was not born in Greece, but at Bari. I spent the first [6]sixteen years of my life in Southern Italy and Sicily."

While Tito was speaking, some emotion passed, like a breath on the waters, across Bardo's delicate features; he leaned forward, put out his right hand towards Romola, and turned his head as if about to speak to her; but then, correcting himself, turned away again, and said, in a subdued voice,—

"Excuse me; is it not true—you are young?"

"I am three and twenty,"[7] said Tito.

"Ah," said Bardo, still in a tone of subdued excitement, "and you had, doubtless, a father who cared for your early instruction—who, perhaps, was himself a scholar?"

There was a slight pause before Tito's answer came to the ear of Bardo; but for Romola and Nello it began[8] with a slight shock that seemed to pass through him, and cause a momentary quivering of the lip; doubtless at the revival of a supremely painful remembrance.

"Yes," he replied; "at least, a father by adoption. He was a [9]Neapolitan, and of accomplished scholarship both Latin and Greek. But," added Tito, after another slight pause, "he is lost to me—was lost on a voyage he too rashly undertook to Delos."

Bardo sank backward again, too delicate to ask another question that might probe a sorrow which he divined to be recent. Romola, who knew well what were the fibres that Tito's voice had stirred in her father, felt that this new acquaintance had with wonderful suddenness got within the barrier that lay between them and the alien world. Nello, thinking that the evident check given to the conversation offered a graceful opportunity for relieving himself from silence, said—

"In truth, it is as clear as Venetian glass that this fine young man[1]

9 the] these *MS*

2 ⟨branches of knowledge⟩ vine *MS*

4 come, ⟨Messer⟩ *MS*

6 ⟨fourteen⟩ sixteen *MS*

8 began] *3P* commenced *MS CM 1 2*

1 fine young man] *1 2 3 bel giovane MS CM*

1 shown ⟨a desire to engraft⟩ *MS*

3 hewn {down} *MS*

5 {western} Christians *MS*

7 twenty,"] twenty, Messer," *MS*

9 ⟨?scholar⟩ Neapolitan *MS*

has had the best[2] training; for the two Cennini have set him to work
at their Greek sheets already, and it seems to me they are not men to
begin cutting before they have felt the edge of their tools;[3] they tested
him[4] well beforehand, we may be sure, and if there are two things
not to be hidden—love and a cough*—I say there is a third, and that
is ignorance, when once a man is obliged to do something besides
wagging his head. The *tonsor inequalis** is inevitably betrayed when he
takes the shears in his hand; is it not true, Messer Bardo? I speak
after the fashion of a barber, but, as Luigi Pulci says—

> 'Perdonimi s'io fallo: chi m'ascolta
> Intenda il mio volgar col suo latino.' " *

"Nay, my good Nello," said Bardo, with an air of friendly severity,
"you are not altogether illiterate, and might doubtless have made a
more respectable progress in learning if you had abstained somewhat
from the *cicalata* and gossip of the street-corner, to which our
Florentines are excessively addicted; but still more if you had not
clogged your memory with those frivolous[5] productions of which
Luigi Pulci has furnished the most peccant exemplar—a compendium
of extravagancies[6] and incongruities[7] the farthest removed from the
models of a pure age, and resembling rather[8] the *grylli** or conceits of
a period when mystic meaning was held a warrant for monstrosity of
form; with this difference, that while the monstrosity is retained[9], the
mystic meaning is absent; in contemptible contrast with the great
poem of Virgil, who, as I long held with Filelfo, before Landino* had
taken upon him to expound the same opinion, embodied the deepest
lessons of philosophy in a graceful and well-knit fable. And I cannot
but regard the multiplication of these babbling, lawless productions,
albeit countenanced by the patronage, and in some degree the example of Lorenzo* himself, otherwise a friend to true learning, as a sign
that the glorious hopes of this century are to be quenched in gloom;
nay, that they have been the delusive prologue to an age worse than
that of iron*—the age of tinsel and gossamer, in which no thought has
substance enough to be moulded into consistent and lasting form."

"Once more, pardon," said Nello, opening his palms outward[1], and
shrugging his shoulders, "I find myself knowing so many things in
good Tuscan before I have time to think of the Latin for them; and
Messer Luigi's rhymes are always slipping off the lips of my cus-

2 best] *1 2 3* finest *MS CM*
3 and it seems . . . tools;] *1 2 3* and they are not men to begin cutting before they
have felt the edge of their tools, *mi pare*; *MS CM*
4 him] Messer *MS*   5 frivolous ⟨and monstrous⟩ *MS*
6 extravagancies] extravagances *2 3*   7 incongruities ⟨which are⟩ *MS*
8 rather ⟨those ?monstrous⟩ *MS*   9 retained ⟨there is not⟩ *MS*
1 outward] outwards *1 2 3*

tomers:—that is what corrupts me. And, indeed, talking of customers, I have left my shop and my reputation too long[2] in the custody of my slow Sandro, who does not deserve even to be called a *tonsor inequalis*, but rather to be [3]pronounced simply a bungler in the vulgar tongue. So with your permission, Messer Bardo, I will take my leave—well understood that I am at your service whenever Maso calls upon me. It seems a thousand years till I dress and perfume the damigella's hair, which deserves to shine in the heavens as a constellation, though indeed it were a pity for it ever to go so far out of reach."

Three voices made a fugue of friendly farewells to Nello, as he retreated with a bow to Romola and a beck to Tito. The acute barber saw that the pretty youngster, who had crept into his liking by some strong magic, was well launched in Bardo's favourable regard; and satisfied that his introduction had not miscarried so far, he felt the propriety of retiring.

The little burst of [4]wrath, called forth by Nello's unlucky [5]quotation, had diverted Bardo's mind from the feelings which had just before been hemming in further speech, and he now addressed Tito again with his ordinary calmness.

"Ah! young man, you are happy in having been able to unite the advantages of travel with those of study, and you will be welcome among us as a bringer of fresh tidings from a land which has[6] become sadly strange to us, except through the agents of a now restricted commerce and the reports of hasty pilgrims. For those days are in the far distance which I myself witnessed, when men like Aurispa and Guarino went out to Greece as to a storehouse, and came back laden with manuscripts* which every scholar was eager to borrow—and, be it owned with shame, not always willing to restore*; nay, even the days when erudite Greeks flocked to our shores for a refuge,* seem far off now—farther off than the on-coming of my blindness. But, doubtless, young man, research after the treasures of antiquity was not alien to the purpose of your travels?"

"Assuredly not," said Tito. "On the contrary, my companion—my father—was willing to risk his life in his zeal for the discovery of inscriptions and other traces of ancient civilization."

"And I trust there is a record of his researches and their results," said Bardo, eagerly, "since they must be even more precious than those of Ciriaco,* which I have diligently availed myself of, though they are not always illuminated by adequate learning."

"There *was*[7] such a record," said Tito, "but it was lost, like

2 too long] over long *MS*
4 ⟨indignation caused⟩ wrath called forth *MS*
6 has ⟨now⟩ become *MS*

3 ⟨called⟩ pronounced *MS*
5 ⟨allusion⟩ quotation *MS*
7 *was*] was *MS*

everything else, in the shipwreck I suffered below Ancona.* The only record [8]left is such as remains in our—in my[9] memory."

"You must lose no time in [1]committing it to paper, young man," said Bardo, with growing interest. "Doubtless you remember much, if you aided in transcription; for when I was your age, words wrought themselves into my mind as if they had been fixed by the tool of the graver; wherefore I constantly marvel at the capriciousness[2] of my daughter's memory, which grasps certain objects with tenacity, and lets fall all those minutiæ [3]whereon depends accuracy, the very soul of scholarship. But I apprehend no such danger with you, young man, if your will has seconded the advantages of your training."

When Bardo made this reference to his daughter, Tito ventured to turn his eyes towards her, and at the accusation against her memory his face broke into its brightest smile, which was reflected as inevitably as sudden sunbeams in Romola's. Conceive the soothing delight of that smile to her! Romola had never dreamed that there was a scholar in the world who would smile at a[4] deficiency for which she was constantly made to feel herself a culprit. It was like the dawn of a new sense to her—the sense of comradeship[5]. They did not look away from each other immediately, as if the smile had been a stolen one; they looked and smiled with frank enjoyment.

"She is not really so cold and proud," thought Tito.

"Does *he*[6] forget too[7], I wonder?" thought Romola. "Yet[8] I hope not, else he will vex my father."

But Tito was obliged to turn away[9], and answer Bardo's question.

"I have had much practice in transcription," he said, "but in the case of inscriptions copied in memorable scenes, rendered doubly impressive by the sense of risk and adventure, it may have happened that my retention of written characters has been weakened. On the plain of the Eurotas, or among the gigantic stones of Mycenæ and Tyrins*—especially[1] when the fear of the Turk hovers over one like a vulture—the mind wanders, even though the hand writes faithfully what the eye dictates. But something doubtless I have retained," added Tito, with a modesty which was not false, though he was conscious that it was politic—"something that might be of service if illustrated and corrected by a wider learning than my own."

"That is [2]well-spoken, young man," said Bardo, delighted. "And I

8 ⟨remaining⟩ left *MS*   9 in {our—in} my *MS*
1 ⟨writing⟩ committing *MS*   2 capriciousness ⟨and uncertainty⟩ *MS*
3 ⟨on which⟩ whereon *MS*   4 smile at a] *3C* smile at her for a *MS CM 1 2*
5 comradeship ⟨which⟩. They *MS*   6 *he*] he *MS*
7 forget too] *MS 1 2 3* forget, too *CM*   8 Yet] *3C* But *MS CM 1 2*
9 turn {away} *MS*
1 Tyrins—especially] Tyrins, or under the columns of Elis—espcially *MS*
2 well ⟨said⟩ spoken *MS*

will not withhold from you such aid as I can give, if you like to communicate with me concerning your recollections. I foresee a work which will be a useful supplement to the *Isolario* of Cristoforo[3] Buondelmonte,* and which may take rank with the *Itineraria* of Ciriaco and the admirable Ambrogio Traversari.* But we must prepare ourselves for calumny, young man," Bardo went on with energy, as if the work were already growing so fast that the time of trial was near; "if your book contains novelties you will be charged with forgery; if my elucidations should clash with any priciples of interpretation adopted by another scholar, our personal characters will be attacked, we shall be impeached with foul actions; you must prepare yourself to be told that your mother was a fish-woman, and that your father was a renegade priest or a hanged malefactor. I myself, for having shown error in a single preposition, had [4]an invective written against me wherein I was[5] taxed with treachery, fraud, indecency, and even hideous[6] crimes.* Such, my young friend[7]—such are the flowers with which the glorious path of scholarship is strewed! But tell me, then: I have learned much concerning Byzantium and Thessalonica long ago from Demetrio Calcondila, who has but lately departed from Florence; but you, it seems, have visited less familiar scenes?"

"Yes; we made what I may call a pilgrimage full of danger, for the sake of visiting places which have almost died out of the memory of the West, for they lie away from the track of pilgrims; and my father used to say that scholars themselves hardly imagine them to have any existence out of books. He was of opinion that a new and more glorious era would open[8] for learning when men should begin to look for their commentaries on the ancient writers in the remains of cities and temples, nay, in the paths of the rivers, and on the face of the valleys and mountains.[9]"

"Ah!" said Bardo, fervidly, "your father, then,[1] was not a common man. Was he fortunate, may I ask? Had he many friends?" These last words were uttered in a tone charged with meaning.[2]

"No; he made enemies—chiefly, I believe, by a certain impetuous candour; and they hindered his advancement, so that he lived in obscurity. And he would never stoop to conciliate: he would never forget an injury."

"Ah!" said Bardo again, with a long, deep intonation.

"Among our hazardous expeditions," continued Tito, willing to prevent further questions on a point so personal, "I remember with

---

3 Cristoforo] Christoforo *2 3*   4 ⟨a philippic⟩ an invective *MS*
5 was ⟨called⟩ *MS*   6 hideous] unnatural *MS*
7 my young friend] Messer *MS*   8 open] begin *MS*
9 mountains] the mountains *1 2 3*   1 father {then,} *MS*
2 These last . . . meaning.] (These last . . . meaning.) *MS*

particular vividness a hastily snatched visit to Athens[3]. Our hurry[4], and the double danger of being seized as prisoners by the Turks, and of our galley raising anchor before we could return, made it seem like a fevered vision of the night—the wide plain, the girdling mountains, the ruined porticos and columns, either standing far aloof, as if receding from our hurried footsteps, or else jammed in confusedly among the dwellings of Christians degraded into servitude, or among the forts and turrets of their Moslem conquerors, who have their stronghold on the Acropolis."

"You fill me with surprise," said Bardo. "Athens, then, is not utterly destroyed and swept away, as I had imagined?[5]"

"No wonder you should be under that mistake, for few even of the Greeks themselves who live beyond the mountain boundary of Attica know[6] anything about the present condition[7] of Athens, or *Setine*,* as the sailors call it. I remember, as we were rounding the promontory of Sunium, the Greek pilot we had on board our Venetian galley pointed to the mighty columns that stand on the summit of the rock—the remains, as you know well, of the great temple erected to the goddess Athena, who looked down from that high shrine with triumph at her conquered rival Poseidon;—well, our Greek pilot, pointing to those columns said, 'That was the school of the great philosopher Aristotle.'* And at Athens itself, the monk who acted as our guide in the hasty view we snatched, insisted most on showing us the spot where St. Philip[8] baptized the Ethiopian eunuch,* or some such legend[9]."

"Talk not of monks and their legends, young man!" said Bardo, interrupting Tito impetuously. "Is it enough to overlay human hope and enterprise with an eternal frost to think that the ground which was trodden by philosophers and poets is crawled over by those insect-swarms of besotted fanatics or howling hypocrites."

"*Perdio*, I have no affection for them," said Tito, with a shrug; "servitude agrees well with a religion like theirs, which lies in the renunciation of all that makes life precious to other men. And they carry the yoke that befits them: their matin chant is drowned by the voice of the muezzin, who, from the gallery of the high tower on the Acropolis, calls[1] every Mussulman to his prayers.* That tower springs from the Parthenon itself; and every time we paused and directed our eyes towards[2] it, our guide set up a wail, that a temple which had

3 a hastily snatched visit to Athens] *1 2 3* a visit we snatched to Athens *MS CM*
4 hurry] *1 2 3* haste *MS CM*   5 imagined?] imagined. *MS*
6 themselves who . . . Attica know] *MS* themselves, who . . . Attica, know *CM 1 2 3*
7 {present} condition *MS*   8 {St} Philip *MS*
9 legend ⟨, and whenever we directed our eyes towards the Parthenon he called upon us to bear in mind that that was the temple of the Unknown God⟩ *MS**
1 calls ⟨the faithful⟩ *MS*   2 towards] *MS 3* toward *CM 1 2*

once been won from the diabolical uses of the pagans to become the temple of another virgin than Pallas—the Virgin Mother of God—was now again perverted to[3] the accursed ends of the Moslem.* It was the sight of those walls of the Acropolis, which disclosed themselves in the distance as we leaned over the side of our galley when it was forced by contrary winds to anchor in the Piræus,* that fired my father's mind with the determination to see Athens at all risks, and in spite of the sailors' warnings[4] that if we lingered till a change of wind they would depart without us: but after all, it was impossible for us to venture near the Acropolis, for the sight of men eager in examining 'old stones' raised the suspicion that we were Venetian spies,* and we had to hurry back to the harbour."

"We will talk more of these things," said Bardo, eagerly. "You must recall everything, to the minutest trace left in your memory. You will win the gratitude of after times by leaving a record of the aspect Greece bore while yet the barbarians had not swept away every trace of the structures that Pausanias and Pliny described:* you will take those great writers as your models; and such contribution of criticism and suggestion as my riper mind can supply shall not be wanting to you. There will be much to tell; for you have travelled, you said, in the Peloponnesus?"

"Yes; and in Bœotia also: I have rested in the groves of [5]Helicon, and tasted of the fountain Hippocrene.* But on every memorable spot in Greece conquest after conquest has set its seal, till there is a confusion of ownership even in ruins, that only close study and comparison could unravel. High over every fastness, from the plains of Lacedæmon to the straits of Thermopylæ, there towers some huge Frankish fortress, once inhabited by a French or Italian marquis,* now either abandoned or held by Turkish bands."

"Stay!" cried[6] Bardo, whose mind was now too thoroughly preoccupied by the idea of the future book to attend to Tito's further narration. "Do you think of writing in Latin or Greek? Doubtless Greek is the[7] more ready clothing for your thoughts, and it is the nobler language. But, on the other hand, Latin is the tongue in which we shall measure ourselves with the larger and more famous number of modern rivals. And if you are less at ease in it, I will aid you—yes, I will spend on you that long-accumulated study which was to have been thrown into the channel of another work—a work in which I myself was to have had a helpmate."

Bardo paused a moment, and then added,—

"But who knows[8] whether that work may not be executed yet? For you, too, young man, have been brought up by a father who poured

3 to] for *MS*   4 {sailors'} warnings *MS*   5 ⟨Parnassus⟩ Helicon *MS*
6 cried] said *MS*   7 the ⟨nobler language⟩ *MS*   8 knows] knows now *MS*

into your mind all the long-gathered stream of his knowledge and experience. Our aid might be mutual."

Romola, who had watched her father's growing excitement, and divined well the invisible currents of feeling that determined every question and remark, felt herself in a glow of strange anxiety: she turned her eyes on Tito continually, to watch the impression her father's words made on him, afraid lest he should be inclined to [9]dispel these visions of co-operation which were lighting up her father's face with a new hope. But no! He looked so bright and gentle: he must feel, as she did, that in this eagerness of blind age there was piteousness enough to call forth inexhaustible patience. How much more strongly he would feel this if he knew about her brother! A girl of eighteen[*] imagines the feelings behind the face that has moved her with its sympathetic youth, as easily as primitive people imagined the humours of the gods in fair weather: what is she to believe in, if not in this vision woven from within?

And Tito was really very far from feeling impatient. He delighted in sitting there with the sense that Romola's attention was fixed on him, and that he could occasionally look at her. He was pleased that Bardo should take an interest in him; and he did not dwell with enough seriousness on the prospect of the work in which he was to be aided, to feel moved by it to anything else than that easy, good-humoured acquiescence which was natural to him.

"I shall be proud and happy," he said, in answer to Bardo's last words, "if my services can be held a meet offering to the matured scholarship of Messere.[1] But doubtless"—here he looked towards Romola—"the lovely damigella, your daughter, makes all other aid superfluous; for I have learned from Nello that she has been nourished on the highest studies from her earliest years."

"You are mistaken," said Romola; "I am by no means sufficient to my father: I have not the gifts that are necessary for scholarship."

Romola did not make this self-depreciatory statement in a tone of anxious humility, but with a proud gravity.

"Nay, my Romola," said her father, not willing that the stranger should have too low a conception of his daughter's powers; "thou art not destitute of gifts; rather, thou art endowed beyond the measure of women; but thou hast withal the woman's delicate frame, which ever craves repose and variety, and so begets a wandering imagination. My daughter"—turning to Tito—"has been very precious to me, filling up to the best of her power the place of a son. For I had once a son . . ."

Bardo checked himself: he did not wish to assume an attitude of complaint in the presence of a stranger, and he remembered that this

young man, in whom he had unexpectedly become so much interested, was still a stranger, towards whom it became him rather to
keep[2] the position of a patron. His pride was roused to double activity by the fear that he had forgotten his dignity.

"But," he resumed[3], in his original tone of condescension, "we are
departing from what I believe is to you the most important business.
Nello informed me that you had certain gems which you would fain
dispose of, and that you desired a passport to some man of wealth
and taste who would be likely to become a purchaser."

"It is true; for, though I have obtained employment[4] as a corrector
with the Cennini, my payment leaves little margin beyond the [5]provi-
sion of necessaries, and would leave less but that my good friend
Nello insists on my hiring a lodging from him, and saying nothing
about the rent till better days."

"Nello is a good-hearted prodigal," said Bardo; "and though, with
that ready ear and ready tongue of his, he is too much like the ill-
famed Margites*—knowing many things and knowing them all badly,
as I hinted to him but now—he is nevertheless[6] 'abnormis sapiens,'*
after the manner of our born Florentines. But have you the gems
with you? I would willingly know what they are—yet it is useless: no,
it might only deepen regret. I cannot add to my store."

"I have one or two intaglios[7] of much beauty," said Tito, proceeding to draw from his wallet a small case.

But Romola no sooner saw the movement than she looked at him
with significant gravity, and placed her finger on her lips,

"Con viso che tacendo dicea, Taci."[8]*

[9]If Bardo were made aware that the gems were within reach, she
knew well he would want a minute description of them, and it would
become pain to him that they should go away from him, even if he
did not insist on some device for purchasing them in spite of poverty.
But she had no sooner made this sign than she felt rather guilty and
ashamed at having virtually confessed a weakness of her father's to a
stranger. It seemed[1] that she was destined to a sudden confidence and
familiarity with this young Greek, strangely at variance with her

2 {rather} to keep *MS*

3 dignity. ¶ "But," he resumed] dignity ⟨and he resumed in his original tone of con-
descension⟩ ¶ "But, young man" he resumed *MS*

4 employment] some employment *MS*   5 ⟨payment⟩ provision *MS*

6 is nevertheless] is *MS*   7 two intaglios] *1 2 3* two *MS* two *intagli CM*

8 *The quotation does not appear in MS*

9 ⟨She knew that⟩ If Bardo ⟨became⟩ were made aware ⟨of⟩ that the gems were
⟨there⟩ within reach *MS*

1 seemed ⟨as if⟩ that she ⟨were⟩ was *MS*

deep-seated[2] pride and reserve; and this consciousness again brought the unwonted colour to her cheeks.

Tito understood her look and sign, and immediately withdrew his hand from the case, saying, in a careless tone, [3]so as to make it appear that he was merely following up his last words, "But they are usually in the keeping of Messer Domenico Cennini, who has strong and safe places for these things. He estimates them as worth at least five hundred ducats[4]."

"Ah, then, they are fine intagli," said Bardo. "Five hundred ducats! Ah, more than a man's ransom!"[5]

Tito gave a slight, almost imperceptible start, and opened his long dark eyes with questioning surprise at Bardo's blind face, as if his words—a mere phrase of common parlance, at a time when men were often being ransomed from slavery or imprisonment—had had some special meaning for him. But the next moment he looked towards Romola, as if her eyes must be her father's interpreters. She[6], intensely preoccupied with what related to her father, imagined that Tito was looking to her again for some guidance, and immediately spoke.

"Alessandra Scala delights in gems, you know, father; she calls them her winter flowers; and [7]the Segretario would be almost sure to buy any gems that she wished for.[8] Besides, he himself sets great store by rings and sigils, which he wears as a defence against pains in the joints."

"It is true," said Bardo. "Bartolommeo has overmuch confidence in the efficacy of gems—a confidence wider than what is[9] sanctioned by Pliny,* who clearly shows that he regards many beliefs of that sort as idle superstitions; though not to the utter denial of medicinal virtues in gems. Wherefore, I myself, as you observe, young man, wear certain rings, which the discreet Camillo Leonardi* prescribed to me by letter when two years ago I had a certain infirmity of sudden numbness. But thou hast spoken well, Romola. I will dictate a letter to Bartolommeo, which Maso shall carry. But it were well that Messere should notify to thee what the gems are, together with the intagli they bear, as a warrant to Bartolommeo that they will be worthy of his attention."

"Nay, father," said Romola, whose dread lest a paroxysm of the

2 deep-seated] *3C* deeply-seated *MS CM 1 2*   3 ⟨as if merely⟩ so as *MS*

4 estimates . . . ducats] estimates one of them alone ⟨as worth⟩, an intaglio in sardonyx, as worth four hundred ducats *MS*

5 "Ah, then, they . . . ransom!"] "Ah, then it is a fine intaglio," said Bardo. "Four hundred ducats—ah—a man's ransom." *MS*

6 She ⟨imagined⟩ *MS*

7 ⟨Bartolommeo⟩ ⟨Messer Bartolommeo⟩ the Segretario *MS*

8 buy any gems that she wished for.] *1 2 3* buy some of Messere's gems if she wished it. *MS CM*

9 than what is] *3C* than is *MS CM 1 2*

collector's mania should seize her father, gave her the courage to resist his proposal. "Your word will be sufficient that Messere is a scholar and has travelled much. The Segretario will need no further inducement to receive him."

"True, child," said Bardo, touched on a chord that was sure to respond. "I have no need to add proofs and arguments in confirmation of my word to Bartolommeo. And I doubt not that this young man's presence is in accord with the tones of his voice, so that, the door being once opened, he will be his own best advocate."

Bardo paused a few moments, but his silence was evidently charged with some idea that he was hesitating to express, for he once leaned forward a little as if he were going to speak, then turned his head aside towards Romola and sank backward again. At last, as if he had made up his mind, he said in [1]a tone which might have become a prince giving the courteous signal of dismissal,—

"I am somewhat fatigued this morning, and shall prefer seeing you again to-morrow,[2] when I shall be able to give you the secretary's answer, authorizing you to present yourself to him at some given time. But before you go"—here the old man, in spite of himself, fell into a more faltering tone—"you will perhaps permit me to touch your hand? It is long since I touched the hand of a young man."

Bardo had stretched out his aged white hand and Tito immediately placed his dark but delicate and supple fingers within it. [3]Bardo's cramped fingers closed over them, and he held them for a few minutes in silence. Then [4]he said,—

"Romola, has this young man the same complexion as thy brother—fair and pale?"

"No, father," Romola answered, with determined composure, though her heart began to beat violently with mingled emotions. "The hair of Messere[5] is dark—his complexion is dark." Inwardly she said[6], "Will he mind it? will it be disagreeable? No, he looks so gentle and good-natured." Then aloud again,

"Would Messere permit my father to touch his hair and face?"

Her eyes inevitably made a timid entreating appeal [7]while she asked this, and Tito's met them with soft brightness as he said, "Assuredly," and, leaning forward, raised Bardo's hand to his curls, with a readiness of assent which was the greater relief to her because it was unaccompanied by any sign of embarrassment.

Bardo passed his hand again and again over the long curls and grasped them a little, as if their spiral resistance made his inward

---

1 ⟨the tone of a⟩ a tone *MS*   2 to-morrow,] to-morrow, Messer, *MS*

3 ⟨Bardo's⟩ ⟨The⟩ Bardo's *MS*   4 ⟨Bardo⟩ he *MS*

5 The hair of Messere] Messer's hair *MS*   6 said] said to herself *MS*

7 ⟨as⟩ while she ⟨said⟩ asked *MS*

vision clearer; then he passed his hand over the brow and cheek, tracing the profile with the edge of his palm and fourth finger, and letting the breadth of his hand repose on the rich oval of the cheek.

"Ah!" he said, as his hand glided from the face and rested on the young man's shoulder. "He must be very unlike thy brother, Romola: and it is the better. You see no visions, I trust, my young friend?"

At this moment the door opened, and there entered, unannounced, a tall elderly man in a handsome black silk *lucco*, who, unwinding his *becchetto* from his neck and taking off his cap, disclosed a head as white as Bardo's. He cast a keen glance of surprise at the group before him—the young stranger leaning in that filial attitude, while Bardo's hand rested on his shoulder, and Romola sitting near with eyes dilated by anxiety and agitation. But there was an instantaneous change: Bardo let fall his hand, Tito raised himself from his stooping posture, and Romola rose to meet the visitor with an alacrity which implied all the greater intimacy, because it was unaccompanied by any smile.

"Well, god-daughter[8]," said the stately man, as he touched Romola's shoulder; "Maso said you had a visitor, but I came in nevertheless."

"It is thou, Bernardo," said Bardo. "Thou art come at a fortunate moment. This, young man," he continued, while Tito rose and bowed, "is one of the chief citizens of Florence—Messer[9] Bernardo del Nero, my oldest, I had almost said my only friend—[1]whose good opinion, if you can win it, may carry you far. He is but three and twenty, Bernardo, yet he can doubtless tell thee much which thou wilt care to hear; for though a scholar, he has already travelled far, and looked on other things besides the manuscripts for which thou hast too light an esteem."

"Ah, a Greek, as I augur," said Bernardo, returning Tito's reverence but slightly, and surveying him with that sort of glance which seems almost to cut like fine steel. "Newly arrived in Florence, it appears. The name of Messere[2]—or part of it, for it is doubtless a long one?"

"On the contrary," said Tito, with perfect good humour, "it is most modestly free from polysyllabic pomp. My name is[3] Tito Melema."

"Truly?" said[4] Bernardo, rather scornfully, as he took a seat, "I had expected it to be at least as long as the names of a city, a river, a province and an empire all put together[5]. We Florentines mostly use

---

8 Well, god-daughter] *3C Ebbene, figlioccina MS CM* Well, *figlioccina 1 2*

9 Florence—Messer] *MS* Florence, Messer *CM 1 2 3*

1 Nero {my oldest—I had almost said my only friend—}*MS*

2 The name of Messere] Messer's name *MS*   3 name is] name, Messer, is *MS*

4 "Truly?" said] *MS 1 2 3* "*Davvero? (Indeed?)*" said *CM*

5 empire {all put together} *MS*

names as we do prawns, and strip them of all flourishes before we trust them to our throats."

"Well, Bardo," he continued, as if the stranger were not worth further notice, and changing his tone of sarcastic suspicion for one of sadness, "we have buried him!"

"Ah!" replied Bardo, with corresponding sadness, "and a new epoch has come for Florence—a dark one, I fear. Lorenzo has left behind him an inheritance that is but like the alchemist's laboratory when the wisdom of the alchemist is gone."

"Not altogether so," said Bernardo. "Piero de' Medici has abundant intelligence; his faults are only the faults of hot blood. I love the lad—lad he will always be to me, as I have always been 'little father'[6] to him."

"Yet all who want a new order of things are likely to conceive new hopes," said Bardo. "We shall have the old strife of parties, I fear."

"If we could have a new order of things that was something else than knocking down one coat of arms to put up another," said Bernardo, "I should be ready to say, 'I belong to no party: I am a Florentine.' But as long as parties are in question[7], I am a Medicean, and will be a Medicean till I die. I am of the same mind as Farinata degli Uberti: if any man asks me what is meant by siding with a party, I say, as he did, 'To wish [8]ill or well, for the sake of past wrongs or kindness.[9]'"*

During this short dialogue, Tito had been standing, and now took his leave.

"But come again at the same hour to-morrow," said Bardo, graciously, before Tito left the room, "that I may give you Bartolommeo's answer."

"From what quarter of the sky has this pretty Greek youngster alighted so close to thy chair, Bardo?" said Bernardo del Nero, as the door closed. He spoke with dry emphasis, evidently intended to convey something more to Bardo than was implied by the mere words.

"He is a scholar who has been shipwrecked and has saved a few gems, for which he wants to find a purchaser. I am going to send him to Bartolommeo Scala, for thou knowest it were more prudent in me to abstain from further purchases."

Bernardo shrugged his shoulders and said, "Romola, wilt thou see if my servant [1]is without? I ordered him to wait for me here." Then, when Romola was at a sufficient distance, he leaned forward and said to Bardo in a low, emphatic tone:—

---

6 'little father'] *3C padricciuolo* (little father) *MS CM 1 2*

7 "If we could . . . question] "Be it so", said Bernardo. "If parties are in question *MS*

8 ⟨well or ill⟩ ill or well *MS*   9 kindness] *MS* kindnesses *CM 1 2 3*

1 ⟨waits⟩ is *MS*

"Remember, Bardo, thou hast a rare gem of thy own; take care no man[2] gets it who is not likely to pay a worthy price. That pretty Greek has a lithe sleekness about him, that seems marvellously fitted for slipping easily into any nest he fixes his mind on."

Bardo was startled:[3] the association of Tito with the image of his lost son had excluded instead of suggesting the thought of Romola. But almost immediately there seemed to be a reaction which made him grasp the warning as if it had been a hope.

"But why not, Bernardo? If the young man approved himself worthy—he is a scholar—and—and there would be no difficulty about the dowry, which always makes thee gloomy."

2 no man] no one 2 3   3 startled: ⟨in spite of⟩ *MS*

CHAPTER VII.

A LEARNED SQUABBLE

BARTOLOMMEO SCALA, secretary of the Florentine Republic, on whom Tito Melema had been thus led to anchor his hopes, lived in a handsome palace close to the Porta Pinti, now known as the Casa Gherardesca.* His arms—an azure ladder transverse on a golden field, with the motto *Gradatim** placed over the entrance—told all comers that the miller's son held his ascent to honours by his own efforts a fact to be proclaimed without wincing. The secretary was a vain and pompous man, but he was also an honest one: he was sincerely convinced of his own merit, and could see no reason for feigning. The topmost round of his azure ladder had been reached by this time: he had held his secretaryship these twenty years—had long since made his orations* on the *ringhiera*, or platform, of the Old Palace, as the custom was, in the presence of princely visitors, while Marzocco, the republican lion, wore his gold crown on the occasion, and all the people cried, "Viva Messer Bartolommeo!"—had been on an embassy to Rome, and had there been made titular Senator, Apostolical Secretary, Knight of the Golden Spur; and had, eight years ago, been Gonfaloniere*—last goal of the Florentine citizen's ambition. Meantime he had got richer and richer, and more and more gouty, after the manner of successful mortality; and the Knight of the Golden Spur had often to sit with helpless cushioned heel ¹under the handsome loggia he had built for himself, overlooking the spacious gardens and lawn at the back of his palace.

He was in this position on the day when he had granted the desired interview to Tito Melema. The May afternoon sun was on the flowers and the grass beyond the pleasant shade of the loggia; the too stately silk *lucco* was cast aside, and a² light loose mantle was thrown over his tunic; his beautiful daughter Alessandra and her husband, the Greek soldier-poet Marullo, were seated on one side of him: on³ the other, two friends, not oppressively illustrious, and, therefore, the better listeners. Yet, to say nothing of the gout, Messer Bartolommeo's felicity was far from perfect: it was embittered by the contents of certain papers that lay before him, consisting chiefly of a correspondence between himself and Politian. It was a human foible at that period (incredible as it may seem) to recite quarrels, and favour scholarly visitors with the communication of an entire and lengthy correspondence; and this was neither the first nor the second

1 ⟨on⟩ under *MS* 2 a] the *2 3* 3 him: on] him and on *MS*

time that Scala had asked the candid opinion of his friends as to the
balance of right and wrong in some half score Latin letters between
himself and Politian, all springing out of certain epigrams written in
the most playful tone in the world. It was the story of a very typical
and pretty quarrel,* in which we are interested, because it[4] supplied
precisely that thistle of hatred necessary, according to Nello, as a
stimulus to the sluggish paces of the cautious steed, Friendship.

Politian, having been a rejected pretender to the love and the hand
of Scala's daughter, kept a very sharp and learned tooth in readiness
against the too prosperous and presumptuous secretary, who had
declined the greatest scholar of the age for a son-in-law. Scala was a
meritorious public servant, and, moreover, a lucky man*—naturally
exasperating to an offended scholar; but then—O beautiful balance of
things!—he had an itch for authorship, and was a bad writer—one of
those excellent people who, sitting in gouty slippers, "penned poetical
trifles" entirely for their own amusement, without any view to an audience, and, consequently, sent them to their friends in letters, which
were the literary periodicals of the fifteenth century. Now Scala had
abundance of friends who were ready to praise his writings: friends like
Ficino and Landino—amiable browsers in the Medicean park along
with himself—who found his Latin prose style elegant and masculine;
and the[5] terrible Joseph Scaliger,* who was to pronounce him totally
ignorant of Latinity, was at a comfortable distance in the next century.
But when was the fatal coquetry inherent in superfluous authorship
ever quite contented with the ready praise of friends? That critical,
supercilious Politian—a fellow-browser, who was far from amiable—
[6]must be made aware that the solid secretary showed, in his leisure
hours, a pleasant fertility in verses, which[7] indicated pretty clearly how
much he might do in that way if he were not a man of affairs.

Ineffable moment!* when the man you secretly hate sends you a
Latin epigram with a false gender—hendecasyllables with a questionable elision, at least a toe too much—attempts at poetic figures which
are manifest solecisms. That moment had come to Politian: the secretary had put forth his soft head from the official shell, and the terrible
lurking crab was down upon him. Politian had used the freedom of a
friend, and[8] pleasantly, in the form of a Latin epigram, corrected the
mistake of Scala in making the *culex*[9] (an insect too well known on
the banks of the Arno)[1] of the inferior or feminine gender.* Scala

4 it ⟨turned out to be⟩ *MS*   5 the] a *MS*
6 Politian {, a fellow-browser who was far from amiable,} *MS*
7 which] *3C* that *MS CM 1 2*
8 friend, and] friend (egi liberius cum te, ita enim soleo)* and *MS*
9 the *culex*] *culex MS*
1 insect too well known on the banks of the Arno)] *1 2 3* insect well known at the
revival of learning) *MS CM*

replied by a bad joke, in suitable Latin verses, referring to Politian's unsuccessful suit. Better and better. Politian found the verses very pretty and highly facetious: the more was the pity that they were seriously incorrect, and inasmuch as Scala had alleged that he had written them in imitation of a Greek[2] epigram, Politian, being on such friendly terms, would enclose a Greek epigram of his own, on the same interesting insect—not, we may presume, out of any wish to humble Scala, but rather to instruct him; said epigram containing a lively conceit about Venus, Cupid, and the *culex*,* of a kind much tasted at that period, founded partly on the zoological fact that the gnat, like Venus, was born[3] from the waters. Scala, in reply, begged to say that his verses were never intended for a scholar with such delicate olfactories as Politian, nearest of all living men[4] to the perfection of the ancients, and of a taste so fastidious that sturgeon itself must seem insipid to him; defended his own [5]verses, nevertheless, though indeed they were written hastily, without correction, and intended as an agreeable distraction during the summer heat[6] to himself and such friends as were satisfied with mediocrity, he, Scala, not being like some other people, who courted publicity through the booksellers. For the rest, he had barely enough Greek to make out the sense of the epigram so graciously sent him, to say nothing of tasting its elegancies[7]; but—the epigram was Politian's: what more need be said? Still, by way of postscript, he feared that his incomparable friend's comparison of the gnat[8] to Venus, on account of its origin from the waters, was in many ways ticklish. On the one hand, Venus might be offended; and on the other, unless the poet intended an allusion to the doctrine of Thales,* that cold[9] and damp origin seemed doubtful to Scala[1] in the case of a creature so fond of warmth: a fish were perhaps the better comparison, or, [2]when the power of flying was in question, an eagle, or, indeed, when the darkness was taken into consideration, a bat or an owl were a less obscure and more apposite parallel, &c. &c. Here was a great opportunity for Politian. He[3] was not aware, he wrote, that when he had Scala's verses placed before him,

---

2 Greek] *1 2 3* certain Greek *MS CM*

3 period, founded partly . . . born] *1 2 3* period, but unhappily founded partly on the zoological mistake that the flea, like the gnat, was born *MS CM*

4 {living} men *MS*   5 ⟨Latin⟩ verses *MS*

6 distraction {during the summer heat} *MS*

7 elegancies] elegances *3*   8 gnat] *1 2 3* flea *MS CM*

9 ticklish. On the one . . . cold] *1 2 3* ticklish. {Venus might be offended, and} that cold *MS CM*

1 doubtful to Scala] *1 2 3* doubtful *MS CM*   2 ⟨if⟩ when *MS*

3 He ⟨was ashamed, he wrote, to answer such trivialities, the bad spirit O stomachus et ironia, that animated them ⟨⟨was⟩⟩ being too evident⟩ was not aware {, he wrote,} that *MS*

there was any question of sturgeon, but rather of frogs and gudgeons:
made short work [4]with Scala's defence of his own Latin, and mangled
him terribly on the score of the stupid criticisms he had ventured on
the Greek epigram kindly forwarded to him as a model. Wretched
cavils, indeed! for as to the damp origin[5] of the gnat[6], there was the
authority of Virgil himself, who had called it the "*alumnus* of the
waters;"* and as to what his dear dull friend had to say about the fish,
the eagle, and the rest, it was "nihil ad rem;"* for because the eagle
could fly higher, it by no means followed that the gnat could not fly
at all, &c. &c.[7] He was ashamed, however, to dwell on such trivialities, and thus to swell a gnat[8] into an elephant; but, for his own part,
would only add that he had nothing deceitful or[9] double about him,
neither was he to be caught when present by the false blandishments
of those who slandered him in his absence, agreeing rather with a
Homeric sentiment* on that head—which furnished a Greek quotation
to serve as powder to his bullet.

The quarrel could not end there. The logic could hardly get worse,
but the secretary got more pompously self-asserting, and the scholarly
poet's temper more and more venomous. Politian had been generously
willing to hold up a mirror, by which the too-inflated secretary,
beholding his own likeness, might be induced to cease setting up his
ignorant defences of bad Latin against ancient authorities whom the
consent of centuries had placed beyond question,—unless, indeed, he
had designed to sink in literature in proportion as he rose in honours,
that by a sort of compensation men of letters might feel themselves
his equals. In return, Politian was begged to examine Scala's writings:
nowhere would he find a more devout admiration of antiquity. The
secretary was ashamed[1] of the age in which he lived, and blushed for
it. *Some*, indeed, there were who wanted to have their own works
praised and exalted to a level with the divine monuments of antiquity;
but he, Scala, could not oblige them. And as to the honours which
were offensive to the envious, they had been well earned: witness his
whole life since he came in penury to Florence. The elegant scholar,
in reply, was not surprised that Scala found the Age distasteful to
him, since he himself was so distasteful to the Age; nay, it was with
perfect accuracy that he, the elegant scholar, had called Scala a
branny monster, inasmuch as he was formed from the offscourings of
monsters, born amidst the refuse of a mill, and eminently worthy the

---

4 ⟨of⟩ with *MS*   5 {damp} origin of the flea ⟨from the waters⟩ *MS*

6 gnat] *1 2 3* flea *MS CM*

7 for because . . . &c. &c.] *1 2 3* for, because the eagle could fly, it by no means followed that the flea could not fly, &c. &c. *MS CM*

8 gnat] *1 2 3* flea *MS CM*   9 or] *1 2 3* and *MS CM*

1 to examine Scala's . . . ashamed] to draw forth Scala's writings: who so great an
admirer of antiquity as the secretary? He was ashamed *MS*

long-eared office of turning the paternal millstones (*in pistrini sordibus natus, et[2] quidem pistrino dignissimus*)![3*]

It was not without reference to Tito's appointed visit that the papers containing this correspondence were brought out to-day. Here was a new Greek scholar whose accomplishments were to be tested; and on nothing did Scala more desire a dispassionate opinion from persons of superior knowledge than on that[4] Greek epigram of Politian's. After sufficient introductory talk concerning Tito's travels, after a survey and discussion of the gems, and an easy passage[5] from the mention of the lamented Lorenzo's eagerness in collecting such specimens of ancient art to the subject of classical tastes and studies in general and[6] their present condition in Florence, it was inevitable to mention Politian, a man of eminent ability indeed, but a little too arrogant—[7]assuming to be a Hercules, whose office it was to destroy all the literary monstrosities of the age, and writing[8] letters to his elders without signing them, as if they were miraculous revelations* that could only have one source. And after all, were not his own criticisms often questionable and his taste[9] perverse?[1] He was fond of saying pungent things about the men who thought they wrote like Cicero because they ended every sentence with "esse videtur:"* but while he was boasting of his freedom from servile imitation, did he not fall into the other extreme, running after strange words and affected phrases? Even in his much-belauded *Miscellanea* was every point tenable? And Tito, who had just been looking into the *Miscellanea*, found so much to say that was agreeable to the secretary—he would have done so from the mere disposition to please, without further motive— that he showed himself quite worthy to be made a judge in the notable correspondence concerning the *culex*. Here was the Greek epigram which Politian had doubtless thought the finest in the world, though he had pretended to believe that the "transmarini," the Greeks themselves, would make light of it: had he not been unintentionally speaking the truth in his false modesty?

Tito was ready, and scarified the epigram to Scala's content. O wise young judge!* He could doubtless appreciate satire even in the vulgar tongue, and Scala—who, excellent man, not seeking publicity through the booksellers, was never unprovided with "hasty uncorrected trifles," as a sort of sherbet for a visitor on a hot day, or, if the weather were cold, why then as a cordial—had a few little matters in

2 *natus, et*] MS *natus et* CM *1 2 3*
3 millstones! {(in pistrini . . . dignissimus.)} *MS*
4 than on that] *3*C than that *MS* CM *1 2*   5 passage] lapse *MS*
6 art to . . . general and] *MS 1 2 3* art, to . . . general, and *CM*
7 ⟨proclaiming himself⟩ assuming *MS*
8 and writing] writing *MS*   9 taste] *MS* tastes CM *1 2 3*
1 perverse? ⟨Pray, was every point in the Miscell[anea]⟩ *MS*

the shape of sonnets, turning on well-known foibles of Politian's, which he would not like to go any farther, but which would, perhaps, amuse the company.

Enough: Tito took his leave under an urgent invitation to come again. His gems were interesting; especially the agate, with the *lusus naturæ* in it—a most wonderful semblance of Cupid riding on the lion; and the "Jew's stone," with the lion-headed serpent* enchased in it; both of which the secretary agreed to buy—the latter as a reinforcement of his preventives against the gout, which gave him such severe twinges that it was plain enough how intolerable it would [2]be if he were not well supplied[3] with rings of rare virtue, and with an[4] amulet worn close under the right breast. But Tito was assured that he himself was more interesting than his gems. He had won his way to the Scala Palace by the recommendation of Bardo de' Bardi, who, to be sure, was Scala's old acquaintance and a worthy scholar, in spite of his overvaluing himself a little (a frequent foible in the secretary's friends); but he must come again on the ground of his own manifest accomplishments.

The interview could hardly have ended more auspiciously for Tito, and as he walked out at the Porta Pinti[5] that he might laugh a little at his ease over[6] the affair of the *culex*, he felt that Fortune could hardly mean to turn her back on him again at present, since she had taken him by the hand in this decided way.

2 ⟨have been⟩ be *MS*   3 {well} supplied *MS*   4 with an] an *MS*
5 Porta Pinti] *MS 3C* Porta a Pinti *CM 1 2*   6 over] *1 2 3* at *MS CM*

CHAPTER VIII.

A FACE IN THE CROWD

It is easy to northern people to rise early on Midsummer morning, to see the dew on the grassy edge of the dusty pathway, to notice the fresh shoots among the darker green of the oak and fir in the coppice, and to look over the gate at the shorn meadow, without recollecting[1] that it is the Nativity of Saint John[2] the Baptist.

Not so to the Florentine—still less to the Florentine of the fifteenth century: to him on that particular morning the brightness of the eastern sun on the Arno had something special in it; the ringing of the bells was articulate, and declared it to be the great summer festival of Florence, the Day of San Giovanni.

San Giovanni had been the patron saint of Florence for at least eight hundred years—ever since the time when the Lombard Queen Theodolinda had commanded her subjects to do him peculiar honour; nay, says old Villani,* to the best of his knowledge, ever since the days of Constantine the Great and Pope Sylvester,* when the Florentines deposed their Idol Mars, whom they were nevertheless careful not to treat with contumely; for while they consecrated their beautiful and noble temple to the honour of God and of the "Beato Messere Santo Giovanni," they placed old Mars respectfully on a high tower near the River Arno, finding in certain ancient memorials that he had been elected as their [3]tutelar deity under such astral influences that if he were broken, or otherwise treated with indignity, the city would suffer great damage and mutation. But in the fifteenth century that discreet regard to the feelings of the man-destroyer* had long vanished: the god of the spear and shield had ceased to frown by the side of the Arno, and the defences of the Republic were held to lie in its craft and its coffers. For spear and shield could be hired by gold florins, and on the gold florins there had always been the image of San Giovanni.

Much good had come to Florence since the dim time[4] of struggle between the old patron and the new: some quarrelling and bloodshed, doubtless, between Guelf and Ghibelline, between Black and White, between orthodox sons of the Church and heretic Paterini;* some floods, famine, and pestilence; but still much wealth and glory. Florence had achieved conquests over walled cities once mightier than

---

1 recollecting] ever recollecting *MS*   2 Saint John] John *MS*
3 ⟨patron⟩ tutelar *MS*   4 {dim} time *MS*

itself[5], and especially over hated Pisa,* whose marble buildings were
too high and [6]beautiful, whose masts were too much honoured on
Greek and Italian coasts. The name of Florence had[7] been growing
prouder and prouder in all the courts of Europe, nay, in Africa itself,
on the strength of purest gold coinage, finest dyes and textures, pre-
eminent scholarship and poetic genius, and wits of the most serviceable sort for statesmanship and banking: it was a name[8] so
omnipresent that a Pope with a turn for epigram had called
Florentines "the fifth element."* And for this high destiny, though it
might partly depend on the stars and Madonna dell' Impruneta,* and
certainly depended on other higher Powers less often named, the
praise was greatly due to San Giovanni, whose image was on the fair
gold florins.

Therefore it was fitting that the day of San Giovanni—that ancient
Church festival[9] already venerable in the days of St. Augustine—
should be a day of peculiar rejoicing to Florence, and should be ushered in by a vigil duly kept in strict old Florentine fashion, with
much dancing, with much street jesting, and perhaps with not a[1] little
stone-throwing and window-breaking, but emphatically with certain
street sights such as could only be provided by[2] a city which held in
its service a clever Cecca,* engineer and architect, valuable alike in
sieges and in shows[3]. By the help of Cecca, the very saints, surrounded with their almond-shaped glory, and floating on clouds with
their joyous companionship of winged cherubs, even as they may be
seen to this day in the pictures of Perugino,* seemed, on the eve of
San Giovanni, to have brought their piece of the heavens down into
the narrow streets, and to pass slowly through them; and, more wonderful still, saints of gigantic size, [4]with attendant angels, might be
seen, not seated, but moving in a slow mysterious manner along the
streets, like[5] a procession of colossal figures come down from the high
domes and tribunes of the churches. The clouds were made of good
woven stuff, the saints and cherubs were unglorified mortals supported by firm bars, and those mysterious giants were really men of
very steady brain, balancing themselves on stilts, and enlarged, like
Greek tragedians, by huge masks and stuffed shoulders; but he was a
miserably unimaginative Florentine who thought only of that—nay,
somewhat impious, for in the images of sacred things was there not

5 glory. Florence . . . itself] glory: conquest over walled cities once mightier than
Florence itself MS
   6 ⟨grand⟩ beautiful MS
   7 coasts. The name of Florence had] coasts: a name that had MS
   8 banking: it was a name] banking—a name MS   9 {church} festival MS
   1 perhaps with not a] perhaps a MS   2 by] in MS
   3 in shows] 3C shows MS CM 1 2   4 ⟨surrounded⟩ with MS
   5 {along the streets} like MS

some of the virtue of sacred things themselves? And if, after that, there came a company of merry black demons well-armed with claws and thongs, and other implements of sport, ready to perform impromptu farces of bastinadoing and clothes-tearing, why, that was the demons' way of keeping a vigil, and they, too, might have descended from the domes and the tribunes. The Tuscan mind slipped from the devout to the burlesque, as readily as water round an angle; and the saints had already had their turn, had gone their way, and made their due pause before the gates of San Giovanni, to do him honour on the eve of his [6]Festa. And on the morrow, the great day thus ushered in, it was fitting that the tributary symbols paid to Florence by all its dependent cities, districts, and villages, whether conquered, protected, or of immemorial possession, should be offered at the shrine of San Giovanni in the old octagonal church, once the Cathedral, and now the Baptistery, where every Florentine had had the sign of the cross made with the anointing chrism on his brow; that all the city, from the white-haired man to the stripling, and from the matron to the lisping child, should be clothed in its best to do honour to the great day, and see the great sight; and that again, when the sun was sloping and the streets were cool, there should be the glorious race or Corso, when the unsaddled horses, clothed in rich trappings, should run right across the city, from the Porta al Prato on the north-west, through the Mercato Vecchio, to the Porta Santa Croce on the south-east, where the richest of *Palii*, or velvet and bro-cade banners with silk linings and fringe of gold, such as became a city that half clothed the well-dressed world, were mounted on a tri-umphal car awaiting the winner or winner's owner.

And thereafter followed more dancing; nay, through the whole day, says an old chronicler* at the beginning of that century, there were weddings and the grandest gatherings, with so much piping, music and song, with balls and [7]feasts and gladness and ornament[8], that this earth might have been mistaken for paradise!

In this year of 1492, it was, perhaps, a little less easy to make that mistake. Lorenzo the magnificent and subtle was dead, and an arro-gant, incautious Piero was come in his room; an evil change for Florence, unless, indeed, the wise horse prefers the bad rider, as more easily thrown from the saddle; and already the regrets for Lorenzo were getting less predominant over the murmured desire for govern-ment on a broader basis[9], in which corruption might be arrested, and there might be that free play for everybody's jealousy and ambition,

6 ⟨great⟩ Festa *MS*   7 ⟨gladness⟩ feasts and gladness *MS*
8 balls and feasts and gladness and ornament] *MS 1 2 3* balls, and feasts, and glad-ness, and ornament *CM*
9 broader basis ⟨⟨*meno ristretto*⟩⟩ *MS*

which made the ideal liberty of the good old quarrelsome, struggling times[1], when Florence raised her great buildings, reared her own soldiers, drove out would-be tyrants at the sword's point, and was proud to keep faith at her own loss. Lorenzo was dead, Pope Innocent was dying, and a troublesome Neapolitan succession, with an intriguing, ambitious Milan, [2]might set Italy by the ears* before long: the times were likely to be difficult. Still, there was all the more reason that the Republic should keep its religious festivals.

And [3]Midsummer morning, in this year 1492, was not less bright than usual. It was betimes in the morning that the symbolic offerings to be carried in grand procession were all assembled at their starting-point in the Piazza della Signoria[4]—that famous piazza, where stood then, and stand now, the massive turreted Palace of the People, called the Palazzo Vecchio, and the spacious Loggia, built by Orgagna—the scene of all grand State ceremonial. The sky made the fairest blue tent, and under it the bells swung so vigorously that every evil spirit with sense enough to be formidable, must long since have taken his flight; windows and terraced roofs were alive with human faces; sombre stone houses were bright with hanging draperies; the boldly soaring palace tower, the yet older square tower of the Bargello,* and the spire of the neighbouring Badia, seemed to keep watch above; and below, on the broad polygonal flags of the piazza, was the glorious show of banners, and horses with rich trappings, and[5] gigantic *ceri*, or tapers, that [6]were fitly called towers—strangely aggrandized descendants of those torches by whose faint light the Church worshipped in the catacombs. Betimes in the morning all processions had need to move under the midsummer sky of Florence, where the shelter of the narrow streets must every now and then be exchanged for the glare of wide spaces; and the sun would be high up in the heavens before the long pomp had ended its pilgrimage in the Piazza di San Giovanni.

But here, where the procession was to pause, the magnificent city, with its ingenious Cecca, had provided another tent than the sky; for the whole of the Piazza del Duomo[7], from the octagonal Baptistery in the centre to the façade of the Cathedral and the walls of the houses on the other sides of the quadrangle, was covered, at the height of forty feet or more, with blue drapery, adorned with well-stitched yellow lilies and the familiar coats of arms, while sheaves of many-coloured banners drooped at fit angles under this superincumbent

---

1 {struggling} times *MS*   2 ⟨was likely enough to⟩ might *MS*
3 ⟨the⟩ Midsummer morning ⟨of⟩ in *MS*   4 della Signoria] de' Signori *MS*
5 banners, and horses with rich trappings, and] *3P* banners and horses with rich trappings and *MS* banners and horses, with rich trappings and *CM 1 2*
6 ⟨might well be⟩ were fitly *MS*
7 the whole of the Piazza del Duomo] the whole Piazza *MS*

blue—a gorgeous rainbow-lit shelter to the waiting spectators who leaned from the windows, and made a narrow border on the pavement, and wished for the coming of the show.

One of those[8] spectators was Tito Melema. Bright, in[9] the midst of brightness, he sat at the window of the room above Nello's shop, his right elbow resting on the red drapery hanging from the window-sill, and his head supported in a backward position by the right hand, which pressed the curls against his ear. His face wore that bland liveliness, as far removed from excitability as from heaviness or gloom, which marks the companion popular alike amongst men and women—the companion who is never obtrusive or noisy from uneasy vanity or excessive animal spirits, and whose brow is never contracted by resentment or indignation. He[1] showed no other change from the two months and more that had passed since his first appearance in the weather-stained tunic and hose, than that added radiance of good fortune, which is like the just perceptible perfecting of a flower after it has drunk in[2] a morning's sunbeams. Close behind him, ensconced in the narrow angle between his chair and the window-frame, stood the slim figure of Nello in holiday suit, and at his left the younger Cennini—Piero, the erudite, corrector[3] of proof-sheets, not Domenico the practical. Tito was looking alternately down on the scene below, and upward at the varied knot of gazers and talkers immediately around him, some of whom had come in after witnessing the commencement of the procession in the Piazza della Signoria[4]. [5]Piero di Cosimo was raising a laugh among them by his grimaces and anathemas at the noise of the bells, against which no kind of ear-stuffing was a sufficient barricade, since the more he stuffed his ears the more he felt the vibration of his skull, and declaring that he would bury himself in the most solitary spot of the Valdarno* on a festa, if he were not condemned, as a painter, to lie in wait for the secrets of colour that were sometimes to be caught from the floating of banners and the chance grouping of the multitude.

Tito had just turned his laughing face away from the whimsical painter to look down at the small drama going on among the chequered border of spectators, when at the [6]angle of the marble steps in front of the Duomo, nearly opposite Nello's shop, he saw a [7]man's face upturned towards him, and fixing on him a gaze that seemed to have more meaning in it than the ordinary passing observation of a

8 those] these *1 2 3*   9 Bright, in] Bright in *MS*

1 He] It *MS*   2 drunk in] drunk *2 3*

3 the erudite, corrector] *MS* the erudite corrector *CM 1 2 3*

4 della Signoria] de' Signori *MS*   5 ⟨Amongst them⟩ Piero *MS*

6 ⟨angle of the wall opposite Nello's shop which stood just at the entrance of the piazza⟩ ⟨edge⟩ angle *MS*

7 ⟨strange face⟩ man's face *MS*

stranger. It was a face[8] with tonsured head, that rose above the black mantle and white tunic of a Dominican friar—a very common sight in Florence; but the glance had something [9]peculiar in it for Tito. There was a faint suggestion in it, certainly not of an unpleasant kind. Yet what pleasant association had he ever had with monks? None. The glance and the suggestion hardly took longer[1] than a flash of lightning.

"Nello!" said Tito, hastily, but immediately added in a tone of disappointment, "Ah, he has turned round. It was that tall, thin friar who is going up the steps. I wanted you to tell me if you knew aught of him?"

"One of the Frati Predicatori," said Nello, carelessly; "you don't expect me to know the private history of the crows."

"I seem to remember something about his face," said Tito. "It is an uncommon face."

"What? you thought it might be our Fra Girolamo? Too tall; and he never shows himself in that chance way."

"Besides, that loud-barking 'hound of the Lord'* is not in Florence just now," said Francesco Cei,* the popular poet; "he has taken Piero de' Medici's hint, to carry his railing prophecies on a journey for a while."

"The Frate neither rails nor prophesies against any man," said a middle-aged personage seated at the other corner of the window; "he only prophesies against vice. If you think that an attack on your poems, Francesco, it[2] is not the Frate's fault."

"Ah, he's gone into the Duomo now," said Tito, who had watched the figure eagerly. "No, I was not under that mistake, Nello. Your Fra Girolamo has a high nose and a large under-lip. I saw him once—he is not handsome;[3] but this man . . ."

"Truce to your descriptions!" said Cennini. "Hark! see! Here come the horsemen and the banners. That standard," he continued, laying his hand familiarly on Tito's shoulder,—"that carried on the horse with white trappings—that with the red eagle holding the green dragon between his talons, and the red lily over the eagle—is the Gonfalon of the Guelf party, and those cavaliers close round it are the chief officers of the Guelf party. That is one of our proudest banners, grumble as we [4]may; it means the triumph of the Guelfs, which means the triumph of Florentine will, which means triumph of the *popolani*."

8 face ⟨[?encased] [?in] the black Dominican cowl—a very ordinary sight⟩ MS
9 ⟨very⟩ peculiar MS
1 hardly took longer] *1 2 3* were hardly longer MS CM
2 it] *1 2 3* that MS CM   3 once{—he is not handsome:} MS
4 ⟨will⟩ may MS

"Nay, go on, Cennini," said the middle-aged man, seated at the window, "which means triumph of the fat *popolani* over the lean, which again means triumph of the fattest *popolano* over those who are less fat."

"Cronaca, you are becoming sententious," said the printer; "Fra Girolamo's preaching will spoil you, and make you take life by the wrong handle. Trust me, your cornices will lose half their beauty if you begin to mingle bitterness with them; that is the *maniera Tedesca* which you used to declaim against when you came from Rome. The next palace you build we shall see you trying to put the Frate's doctrines[5] into stone."*

"That is a goodly show of cavaliers," said Tito, who had learned by this time the best way to please Florentines; "but are there not strangers[6] among them? I see foreign costumes."

"Assuredly", said Cennini; "you see there the Orators* from France, Milan, and Venice, and behind them are English and German nobles; for it is customary that all foreign visitors of distinction pay their tribute to San Giovanni in the train of that gonfalon. For my part, I think our Florentine cavaliers sit their horses as well as any of those cut-and-thrust northerns[7], whose wits lie in their heels and saddles[8]; and for yon Venetian, I fancy he would feel himself more at ease on the back of a dolphin.* We ought to know something of horsemanship, for we excel[9] all Italy in the sports of the *Giostra*, and the money we spend on them. But you will see a finer show of our chief men by and by, Melema; my brother himself will be among the officers of the Zecca."

"The banners[1] are the better sight," said Piero di Cosimo, forgetting the noise in his delight at the winding stream of colour as the tributary standards advanced round the piazza. "The Florentine men are so so; they make but a sorry show at this distance with their patch of sallow flesh-tint above the black [2]garments; but those banners with their velvet, and satin, and minever, and brocade, and their endless play of delicate light and shadow!—*Va!* your human talk and doings are a tame jest; the only passionate life is in form and colour."

"Ay, Piero, if Satanasso could paint, thou wouldst sell thy soul to learn his secrets," said Nello. "But there is little likelihood of it, seeing the blessed angels themselves are such poor hands at chiaroscuro, if one may judge from their capo-d'opera, the Madonna Nunziata."*

"There go the banners of Pisa and Arezzo," said Cennini. "Ay[3],

5 doctrines] MS doctrine CM *1 2 3*
6 but are there not strangers] but surely there are strangers MS
7 northerns] northerners *2 3*   8 northerns {whose wits . . . saddles} MS
9 We ought . . . excel] We excel MS
1 banners ⟨and horses⟩ MS   2 ⟨lucco⟩ garments MS   3 Ay] Yes MS

Messer Pisano, it is no use for you to look sullen; you may as well carry your banner to our San Giovanni with a good grace. 'Pisans false, Florentines blind'*—the second half of that proverb will hold no longer. There come the ensigns of our subject-towns and signories, Melema; they will all be suspended in San Giovanni until this day next year, when they will give place to new ones."

"They are a fair sight," said Tito; "and San Giovanni will surely be as well satisfied with that produce of Italian looms as Minerva with her peplos,* especially as he contents himself with so little drapery. But my eyes are less delighted with those whirling towers, which would soon make me fall from the window in sympathetic vertigo."

The "towers" of which Tito spoke were a part of the procession esteemed very glorious by the Florentine populace; and being perhaps chiefly a kind[4] of hyperbole for the all-efficacious wax taper, were also[5] called *ceri*. But inasmuch as hyperbole[6] is impracticable in a real and literal fashion, these gigantic *ceri*, some of them so large as to be of necessity carried on wheels[7], were not solid but hollow, and had their surface made not solely of wax, but of wood and pasteboard, gilded, carved, and painted, as real sacred tapers often are, with successive circles of figures—warriors on horseback, foot soldiers with lance and shield, dancing maidens, animals, trees and[8] fruits, and in fine, says the old chronicler, "all things that could delight the eye and the heart;"* the hollowness having the further advantage that men could stand inside these hyperbolic tapers and whirl them continually, so as to produce a phantasmagoric effect, which, considering[9] the towers were numerous, must have been calculated to produce dizziness on a truly magnificent scale.

"*Pestilenza!*" said Piero di Cosimo, moving from the window, "those whirling circles one above the other are worse than the jangling of all the bells. Let me know when the last taper has passed."

"Nay, you will surely like to be called when the contadini come carrying their [1]torches," said Nello; "you would not miss the country folk[2] of the Mugello and the Casentino,* of whom your favourite Lionardo would make a hundred grotesque sketches."*

"No," said Piero resolutely; "I will see nothing till the car of the Zecca comes. I have seen clowns enough holding tapers aslant, both with and without cowls, to last me for my life."

"Here it comes, then, Piero—the car of the Zecca," called out

4 and being perhaps chiefly a kind] *3C* and being doubtless in their origin a kind *MS* and having their origin, perhaps, in a confused combination of the tower-shaped triumphal car which the Romans borrowed from the Etruscans, with a kind *CM 1 2*
5 also] still *MS*   6 hyperbole] *3C* all hyperbole *MS CM 1 2*
7 wheels] cars *MS*   8 trees and] *MS 1 2 3* trees, and *CM*
9 considering ⟨there were a "hundred towers"⟩ *MS*
1 ⟨tapers⟩ torches *MS*   2 country folk] *3C* men *MS CM 1 2*

Nello, after an interval during which towers and tapers in a descending scale of size had been making their slow transit.

"*Fediddio!*" exclaimed Francesco Cei, "that is a well-tanned San Giovanni! some sturdy Romagnole* beggar-man, I'll warrant. Our Signoria[3] plays the host to all the Jewish and Christian scum that every other city shuts its gates against, and lets them fatten on us like Saint Anthony's swine."*

The car of the Zecca* or Mint, which had just rolled into sight, was[4] originally an immense wooden tower or *cero* adorned after the same fashion as the other tributary *ceri*, mounted on a splendid car, and drawn by two mouse-coloured oxen, whose mild heads looked out from rich trappings bearing the arms of the Zecca. But the latter half of the century was getting rather ashamed of the towers with their circular or spiral paintings, which had delighted the eyes and the hearts of the other half, so that they had become a contemptuous proverb, and[5] any ill-painted figure looking, as will sometimes happen to figures in the best ages of art, as if it had been boned for a pie, was called a *fantoccio da cero*,* a tower-puppet; consequently improved[6] taste, with Cecca to help it, had devised for the magnificent Zecca a triumphal car like a pyramidal catafalque, with ingenious wheels warranted to turn all corners easily. Round the base were living figures of saints and angels arrayed in sculpturesque fashion; and on[7] the summit, at the height of thirty feet, well bound to an iron rod and holding an iron cross also firmly infixed, stood a[8] living representative of St. John[9] the Baptist, with arms and legs bare, a garment of tiger-skins about his body, and a golden nimbus fastened on his head—as [1]the Precursor was wont to appear in the cloisters and churches, not having yet revealed himself to painters as the brown and sturdy boy who made one of the Holy Family.[2]* For where could the image of the patron saint be more fitly placed than on the symbol of the Zecca? Was not the royal prerogative of coining money the surest token that a city had won its independence? and by the blessing of San Giovanni this [3]"beautiful sheepfold"* of his had

3 Signoria] *1 2 3* Signory *MS CM*

4 The car of . . . was] *2 3* To make clear this exclamation of Cei's, it must be understood that the car of the Zecca, or Mint, was *MS CM 1*

5 and ⟨if⟩ *MS*

6 consequently improved] consequently, improved *MS*

7 easily. Round . . . on] easily, with living figures of saints and angels arranged in sculpturesque fashion round the base, and on *MS*

8 stood a] a *MS*   9 {St} John *MS*   1 ⟨he⟩ the Precursor *MS*

2 churches, not yet having revealed . . . Family.] churches {for he had not yet revealed himself to painters ⟨in⟩ as the brown and sturdy boy ⟨making⟩ who made one of the Holy Family—} *MS*

3 ⟨sheepfold⟩ "beautiful sheepfold" *MS*

shown that token earliest among the Italian cities. Nevertheless, the annual function of representing the patron saint was not among the high prizes of public life; it was paid[4] for with something like ten shillings[5], a cake weighing fourteen pounds, two bottles of wine, and a handsome supply of light eatables; the money being furnished by the magnificent Zecca, and the payment in kind being by [6]peculiar "privilege" presented in a basket suspended [7]on a pole from an upper window of a private house, whereupon the eidolon of the austere saint at once invigorated himself with a reasonable share of the sweets and wine, threw the remnants to the crowd, and embraced the mighty cake securely with his right arm through the remainder of his passage. This was the attitude in which the mimic San Giovanni presented himself as the tall [8]car jerked and vibrated on its slow way round the piazza to the northern gates[9] of the Baptistery.

"There go the masters of the Zecca, and there is my brother—you see him, Melema?" cried[1] Cennini, with an agreeable stirring of pride at showing a stranger what was too familiar to be remarkable to fellow-citizens. "Behind come the members of the corporation of Calimala,* the dealers in foreign cloth, to which we have given our Florentine finish; men of ripe years, you see, who were matriculated before you were born; and then comes the famous Art of money-changers."*

"Many of them matriculated* also to the noble art of usury before you were born," interrupted Francesco Cei, "as you may discern by a certain fitful glare of the eye and sharp curve of the nose which manifest their descent from the ancient harpies, whose portraits you saw supporting[2] the arms of the Zecca. Shaking off old prejudices now, such a procession as that of some four hundred[3] passably ugly men carrying their tapers in open daylight, Diogenes-fashion,* as if they were looking for a lost quattrino, would make a merry spectacle for the Feast of Fools."*

"Blaspheme not against the usages of our city," said Piero Cennini, much offended. "There are new wits who think they see things more truly because they stand on their heads to look at them, like tumblers and mountebanks, instead of keeping the attitude of rational men. Doubtless it makes little difference to Maestro Vaiano's monkeys whether they see our Donatello's statue of Judith* with their heads or their tails uppermost."

4 paid ⟨simply by⟩ MS
5 with something like ten shillings] 3C with ten lire MS CM 1 2
6 ⟨prescription⟩ peculiar "privilege" MS   7 ⟨from⟩ on MS
8 ⟨tower⟩ car MS   9 gates] MS gate CM 1 2 3
1 cried] said MS   2 you saw supporting] {you saw} support MS
3 {some} four hundred MS

[4]"Your solemnity will allow some quarter to playful fancy, I hope," said Cei, with a shrug, "else what becomes of the ancients, whose example you scholars are bound to revere, Messer Piero? Life was never anything but a perpetual see-saw between gravity and jest."*

"Keep your jest then till your end of the pole is uppermost," said Cennini, still angry, "and that is not when the great bond of our Republic is expressing itself in ancient symbols, without which the vulgar[5] would be conscious of nothing beyond their own petty wants of back and stomach, and never rise to the sense of community in religion and law. There has been no great people without processions, and the man who thinks himself too wise to be moved by them to anything but contempt is like the puddle that was proud of standing alone while the river rushed by."

No one said anything after this indignant burst of Cennini's till he himself spoke again.

"Hark! the trumpets of the Signoria: now comes the last stage of the show, Melema. That is our Gonfaloniere in the middle, in the starred mantle, with the sword carried before him. Twenty years ago we used to see our foreign *Podestà*,* who was our judge in civil causes, walking on his right hand; but our Republic has been over-doctored by clever *medici*[6]. That is the Proposto* of the *Priori* on the left; then come the other seven *Priori*; then all the other magistracies and officials of our Republic. You see your patron the Segretario?"

"There[7] is Messer Bernardo del Nero also," said Tito; "his visage is a fine and venerable one, though it has worn rather a petrifying look towards me."

"Ah," said Nello, "he is the dragon that guards the remnant of old Bardo's gold,* which, I fancy, is chiefly that virgin gold that falls about the fair Romola's head and shoulders; eh, my Apollino?" he added, patting Tito's head.

Tito had the youthful grace of blushing, but he had also the adroit and ready speech that prevents a blush from looking like embarrassment. He replied [8]at once:—

"And a very Pactolus* it is—a stream with golden ripples. If I were an alchemist—"

4 ⟨Che? you will allow some⟩ ⟨Che, Che, said Cei with a shrug⟩ "Your *MS*
5 the vulgar] *3C* the vulgar—the *popolo minuto*—*MS CM 1 2*
6 *medici*] *Medici 1 2 3*
7 him. Twenty years ago . . . ¶ "There] him, and this on his right hand is the Podestà, our judge in civil causes, and on the left is the Proposto of the Priors: then come the other seven Priors, then all the other magistracies and officials of our republic:—you see your patron the Segretario? Ah, the Secretaryship is a snug nest, and Messer Bartolommeo has had it these twenty years—not like our Piero and the rest who have no sooner got warm at the end of two months than they have to turn out into the cold again'. ¶ There *MS*
8 ⟨immediately⟩ at once *MS*

He was saved from the need for further speech by the sudden for-
tissimo of drums and trumpets and fifes,[9] bursting into the breadth of
the piazza in a grand storm of sound—a roar, a blast, and a whistling,
well befitting a city famous for its musical instruments, and reducing
the members of the closest group to a state of deaf isolation.

During this interval Nello observed Tito's fingers moving in recognition of some one in the crowd below, but not seeing the direction
of his glance he failed to detect the object of this greeting—the sweet
round blue-eyed face under a white hood—[1]immediately lost in the
narrow border of heads, [2]where there was a continual eclipse of round
contadina cheeks by the harsh-lined features or bent shoulders of an
old spadesman, and where profiles turned as sharply from north to
south as weathercocks under a shifting wind.

But when it was felt that the show was ended—when the twelve
prisoners released in honour of the day, and the very *barberi* or racehorses, with the arms of their owners embroidered on their cloths,
had followed up the Signoria, and been duly consecrated to San
Giovanni, and[3] every one was moving from the window—Nello,
whose Florentine curiosity was of that lively canine sort which thinks
no trifle too despicable for investigation, put his hand on Tito's
shoulder and said,—

"What acquaintance was that you were making signals to, eh, *giovane mio*[4]?"

"Some little contadina who probably mistook me for an acquaintance, for she had honoured me with a greeting."

"Or who wished to begin an acquaintance," said Nello. "But you
are bound for the Via de' Bardi and the feast of the Muses: there is
no counting on you for a frolic, else we might have gone in search of
adventures together in the crowd, and had[5] some pleasant fooling in
honour of San Giovanni. But your high fortune has come on you too
soon: I don't mean the professor's mantle—*that* is[6] roomy enough to
hide a few stolen chickens, but—Messer Endymion minded his manners after that singular good fortune* of his; and what says our Luigi
Pulci?

> 'Da quel giorno in quà ch' amor m' accese
> Per lei son fatto e gentile e cortese.'"*

9 drums and {trumpets and} fifes bursting ⟨from⟩ into *MS*

1 ⟨which⟩ immediately *MS*   2 ⟨in which⟩ where *MS*

3 ended{—when the twelve prisoners released in honour of the day and ⟨when⟩ the
very Barberi or racehorses ⟨had followed up the Signoria⟩ with the arms . . . San
Giovanni—}and *MS*

4 *giovane mio*] *1 2 3* giovane *MS CM*   5 had] have *MS*
6 *that* is] that's *MS*

"Nello, *amico mio*, thou hast an intolerable [7]trick of making life stale by forestalling it with thy talk," said Tito, shrugging his shoulders, with a look of patient resignation, which was his nearest approach to anger: "not to mention that such ill-founded babbling would be held a great offence by that same goddess whose humble worshipper you are always professing yourself."

"I will be mute," said Nello, laying his finger on his lips, with a responding shrug. "But[8] it is only under our four eyes that I [9]talk* any folly about her."

"Pardon! you were on the verge of it just now in the hearing of others. If you want to ruin me in the minds of Bardo and his daughter—"

"Enough, enough!" said Nello. "I am an absurd old barber. It all comes[1] from that abstinence of mine, in not making bad verses in my youth: for want of letting my folly run out that way when I was eighteen, it runs out at my tongue's end now I am at[2] the unseemly age of fifty[3]. But Nello[4] has[5] not got his head muffled for all that; he can see a buffalo in the snow.* *Addio, giovane mio*[6]."

---

7 ⟨way⟩ trick *MS*   8 But, ⟨as I⟩ *MS*   9 ⟨tell⟩ talk *MS*
1 comes ⟨of my having abstained from making bad verses⟩ *MS*
2 {now I am} at *MS*   3 fifty] *1 2 3* forty *MS CM*
4 Nello ⟨is not so muffle-headed that he⟩ *MS*   5 Nello has] thy Nello has *MS*
6 *giovane mio*] *1 2 3 giovane MS CM*

CHAPTER IX.

A MAN'S RANSOM

TITO was soon down among the crowd, and, notwithstanding his indifferent reply to Nello's question about his chance acquaintance, he was not without a passing wish[1], as he made his way round the piazza to the Corso degli Adimari,* that he might encounter the pair of blue eyes which had looked up towards him from under the square bit of white linen drapery that formed the ordinary hood of the contadina at festa time. He was perfectly well aware that that face was Tessa's; but he had not chosen to say so. What had Nello to do with the matter? Tito had an innate love of reticence—let us say a talent for it—which acted as other impulses do, without any conscious motive, and, like all people to whom concealment is easy, he would now and then conceal something which had as little the nature of a secret as the fact that he had seen a flight of crows.

But [2]the passing wish about pretty Tessa was almost immediately eclipsed by the recurrent recollection of that friar whose face had some irrecoverable association for him. Why should a sickly fanatic, worn with fasting, have looked at *him* in particular, and where in all his travels could he remember encountering that face before? Folly! such vague memories hang about the mind like cobwebs, with tickling importunity—best to sweep them away at a dash: and Tito had pleasanter occupation for his thoughts. By[3] the time he[4] was turning out of the Corso degli Adimari into a side street he was caring only that the sun was high[5], and that the procession had kept him longer than he had intended[6] from his visit to that room in the Via de' Bardi, where his coming, he knew, was anxiously awaited. He felt the scene of his entrance beforehand: the joy beaming diffusedly in the blind face like the light in a semi-transparent lamp; the transient pink flush on Romola's face and neck, which subtracted nothing from her majesty, but only gave it the exquisite charm of womanly sensitiveness, heightened still more by what seemed the paradoxical boy-like frankness of her look and smile. They were the best comrades in the world during the hours they passed together round the blind man's chair: she was constantly appealing to Tito[7], and he was informing her, yet he felt himself strangely in subjection to Romola with that

---

1 wish ⟨that⟩ *MS*   2 ⟨that⟩ the *MS*
3 dash: and . . . thoughts. By] dash. And . . . thoughts: by *MS*
4 he ⟨had got into the Corso degli Adimari and was turning out of it⟩ *MS*
5 high] rather high *MS*   6 {had} intended *MS*
7 Tito ⟨as if he had been⟩ *MS*

simplicity[8] of hers: he felt for the first time, without defining it to himself, that loving awe in the presence of noble womanhood, which is perhaps something like the worship paid of old[9] to a great Nature-Goddess, who was not all-knowing, but whose life and power were something deeper and more primordial than knowledge. They had never been alone together, and he could frame to himself no probable image of love scenes between them: [1]he could only fancy and wish wildly—what he knew was impossible—that Romola would some day tell him that she loved him. One day in Greece, as he was leaning over a wall in the sunshine, a little black-eyed peasant girl, who had rested her water-pot on the wall, crept gradually nearer and nearer to him, and at last shyly asked him to kiss her, putting up her round olive cheek very innocently. Tito was used to love that came in this unsought fashion. But Romola's love would never come in that way: would it ever come at all?—and yet it was that topmost apple on which he had set his mind. He was in his fresh youth—not passionate, but impressible: it was as inevitable that he should feel lovingly towards Romola as that the white irises should be reflected in the clear sun-lit stream; but he had no coxcombry[2], and he had an intimate sense that Romola was something very much above him. Many men have felt the same before a large-eyed, simple child.

Nevertheless, Tito had had the rapid success which would have made some men presuming, or would have warranted him in thinking that there would be no great presumption in entertaining an agreeable confidence that he might one day be the husband of Romola—nay, that her father himself was not without a vision of such a future for him. His first auspicious interview with Bartolommeo Scala had proved the commencement of a growing favour on the secretary's part, and had led to an issue which would have [3]been enough to make Tito decide on Florence as the place in which to establish himself, even if[4] it had held no other magnet. Politian[5] was professor of Greek as well at Latin at Florence, professorial chairs being maintained there, although the university had been removed to Pisa;[6] but for a long time Demetrio Calcondila, one of the most eminent and respectable among the emigrant Greeks, had also held a Greek chair, simultaneously with the too predominant Italian. Calcondila was now

8 simplicity] *3C* majestic simplicity *MS CM 1 2*   9 paid of old] paid *MS*
   1 ⟨but there was [?one] fancy which had [2 words] formulation for him because he felt it to be wildly impossible [3 words] in love with him and tell him [1 or 2 words] in spite of herself⟩ he *MS*
   2 coxcombry ⟨in him⟩ *MS*
   3 ⟨made⟩ been enough to make Tito ⟨decide unhesitatingly⟩ ⟨desire to⟩ decide *MS*
   4 if ⟨there had been no other magnet there⟩ *MS*
   5 Politian ⟨held a Greek as well as Latin chair⟩ *MS*
   6 Florence, {professorial chairs . . . removed to Pisa;} *MS*

gone to Milan, and there was no counterpoise or rival to Politian such
as was desired for him by the friends who wished him to be taught a
little propriety and humility. Scala was far from being the only friend
of this class, and he found several who, if they were not among those
thirsty admirers of mediocrity [7]that were glad to be refreshed with his
verses in hot weather, were yet quite willing to join him in doing that
moral service to Politian. It was finally agreed that Tito should be
supported in a Greek chair, as Demetrio Calcondila had been by
Lorenzo himself, who, being at the same time the affectionate patron
of Politian, had shown by precedent that there was nothing invidious
in such a measure, but only a [8]zeal for true learning and for the[9]
instruction of the Florentine youth.

Tito was thus sailing under the fairest breeze, and besides convincing fair judges that his talents squared with his good fortune, he wore
that fortune so easily and unpretentiously that no one had yet been
offended by it. He was not unlikely to get into the best Florentine
society: society where there was much more plate than the circle of
enamelled silver in the centre of the brass dishes, and where it was
not forbidden by the Signory to wear the richest brocade.* For where
could a handsome young scholar not be welcome when he could
touch the lute and troll a gay song? That bright face, that easy smile,
that liquid voice, seemed to give life a holiday aspect; [1]just as a strain
of gay music and the hoisting of colours make the work-worn and the
sad rather ashamed of showing themselves[2]. Here was a professor
likely to [3]render the Greek classics amiable to the sons of great
houses.

And that was not the whole of Tito's good fortune; for he had sold
all his jewels, except the ring he did not choose to part with, and he
was master of full[4] five hundred gold florins.

Yet the moment when he first had this sum in his possession was
the crisis of the first serious struggle his facile, good-humoured nature
had known. An importunate thought, of which he had till now
refused to see more than the shadow as it dogged his footsteps, at last
rushed upon him and grasped him: he was obliged to pause and
decide whether he would surrender and obey, or whether he would
give the refusal that must carry irrevocable consequences. It was in
the room above Nello's shop, which Tito had now hired as a lodging,
that the elder Cennini handed him the last quota of the sum on
behalf of Bernardo Rucellai, the purchaser of the two most valuable
gems.[5]

7 ⟨who⟩ that *MS*
8 ⟨love of⟩ zeal for *MS*   9 for the] *1 2 3* the *MS CM*   1 ⟨like⟩ just as *MS*
2 {showing} themselves *MS*   3 ⟨make⟩ render *MS*   4 full] nearly *MS*
5 the two most valuable gems.] *1 2 3* the Cleopatra. *MS CM*

"*Ecco, giovane mio*[6]*!*" said the respectable printer and goldsmith, "you have now a pretty little fortune; and if you will take my advice, you will let me place your florins in a safe quarter, where they may increase and multiply, instead of slipping through your fingers for banquets and other follies which are rife among our Florentine youth. And it has been too much the fashion of scholars, especially when, like our Pietro Crinito, they think their scholarship needs to be scented and broidered, to squander with one hand till they have been fain to beg with the other. I have brought you the money, and you are free to make a wise choice or an unwise: I shall see on which[7] side the balance dips. We Florentines hold no man a member of an Art till he has[8] shown his skill and been matriculated; and no man is matriculated to the art of life till he has been well tempted. If you make up your mind to put your florins out to usury, you can let me know to-morrow. A scholar may marry, and should have something in readiness for the *morgen cap*.* Addio."

As Cennini closed the door behind him, Tito turned round with the smile dying out of his face, and fixed his eyes on the table where the florins lay. He made no other movement, but stood with his thumbs in his belt, looking down, in that transfixed state which accompanies the concentration of consciousness on some inward image.

"A man's ransom!"—[9]who was it that had said five hundred florins was more than a man's ransom?* If now, under this midday sun, on some hot coast far away, a man somewhat stricken in years—a man not without high thoughts and with the most passionate heart—a man who long years ago had rescued a little boy from a life of beggary, filth, and cruel wrong, had reared him tenderly, and been to him as a father—if that man were now under this summer sun toiling as a slave, hewing wood and drawing water, perhaps being smitten and buffeted because he was not deft and active? If he were saying to himself, "Tito will find me: he had but to carry our manuscripts and gems to Venice; he will have raised money, and will never rest till he finds me out"? If that were certain, could he, Tito, see the price of the gems lying before him, and say, "I will stay at Florence, where I am fanned by soft airs of promised love and prosperity: I will not risk myself for his sake"? No, surely not, *if it were certain*. But nothing could be farther from certainty. The galley had been taken by a Turkish vessel on its way to Delos: *that* was known by the report of the companion galley, which had escaped. But there had been resistance, and probable bloodshed; a man had been seen falling overboard: who were the survivors, and what had befallen them amongst

6 *giovane mio*] giovane *MS*   7 on which] which *MS*
8 has ⟨been matriculated and shown his skill⟩ *MS*   9 ransom!"—] ransom—
MS

all the multitude of possibilities? Had not he, Tito, suffered shipwreck, and narrowly escaped drowning? He had good cause for feeling the omnipresence of casualties that threatened all projects[1] with
futility. The rumour that there were pirates who had a settlement in
Delos was not to be depended on, or might be nothing to the purpose. What, probably enough, would be the result if he were to quit[2]
Florence and go to Venice; get authoritative letters—yes, he knew
that might be done—and set out for the Archipelago? Why, that he
should be himself seized, and[3] spend all his florins on preliminaries,
and be again a destitute wanderer—with no more gems to sell.

Tito had a clearer vision of that result than of the possible moment
when he might find his father again, and carry him deliverance. It
would surely be an unfairness that he, in his full ripe youth, to whom
life had hitherto had some of the stint and subjection of a school,
should turn his back on promised love and distinction, and perhaps
never be visited by that promise again. "And yet," he said to himself,
"if I were certain—yes, if I were certain that[4] Baldassarre Calvo was
alive, and that I could free him, by whatever exertions or perils, I
would go now—now I have the money: it was useless to debate the
matter before. I would go now to Bardo and Bartolommeo Scala, and
tell them the whole truth." Tito did not say to himself so distinctly[5]
that if those two men had known the whole truth he was aware there
would have been no[6] alternative for him but to go in search of his
benefactor, who, if alive, was the rightful owner of the gems, and
whom he had always equivocally spoken of as "lost;"[7] he did[8] not say
to himself—what he was not ignorant of—that[9] Greeks of distinction
had made sacrifices, taken voyages again and again, and sought help
from crowned and mitred heads for the sake of freeing relatives from
slavery to the Turks. Public opinion did not regard that[1] as an exceptional[2] virtue.

This was his first real colloquy with himself: he had gone on following the impulses of the moment, and one of those impulses had
been to conceal half the fact: he had never considered this part of his
conduct long enough to face the consciousness of his motives for the

concealment. What was the use of telling the whole? It was true, the thought had crossed his mind several times since he had quitted Nauplia that, after all, it was a great relief to be quit of Baldassarre, and[3] he would have liked to know *who* it was that had fallen overboard. But such thoughts spring inevitably out of a relation that is irksome. Baldassarre was exacting, and had got stranger as he got older: he was constantly scrutinizing Tito's mind to see whether it answered to his own exaggerated expectations; and age—the age of a thick-set, heavy-browed, bald man beyond sixty[4], whose intensity and eagerness in the grasp of ideas have long taken the character of monotony and repetition, may be looked at from many points of view without being found attractive. Such a man, stranded among new acquaintances, unless he had the philosopher's stone, would hardly find rank, youth, and beauty at his feet. The feelings that gather fervour from novelty will be of little help towards making the world a home for dimmed and faded human beings; and if there is any love of which they are not [5]widowed, it must be the love that is rooted in memories and distils perpetually the sweet balms of fidelity and forbearing tenderness.

"But[6] surely such memories were not absent from Tito's mind? Far in the backward vista of his remembered life, when he was only seven years old, Baldassarre had rescued him from blows, had taken him to a home that seemed like opened paradise, where there was sweet food and soothing caresses, all had on Baldassarre's knee; and from that time till the hour[7] they had parted, Tito had been the one centre of Baldassarre's fatherly cares.

And he[8] had been docile, pliable, quick of apprehension, ready to acquire: a very bright, lovely[9] boy, a youth of even splendid grace, who seemed quite without vices, as if that beautiful form represented a vitality so exquisitely poised and balanced that it could know no uneasy desires, no unrest—a radiant presence for a lonely man to have won for himself. If he were silent when his father expected some response,[1] still he did not look moody; if he declined some labour— why, he flung himself down with such a charming, half-smiling, half-pleading air, that the pleasure of looking at him made amends to one who had watched his growth with a sense of claim and possession: the curves of Tito's mouth had ineffable good humour in them. And then, the quick talent to which everything came readily, from philosophic[2] systems to the rhymes of a street ballad caught up at a

3 Baldassarre, and] Baldassarre—that *MS*

4 man beyond sixty] man of ⟨sixty⟩ beyond sixty *MS*

5 ⟨withered⟩ widowed *MS*   6 {¶} But *MS*   7 till {the hour} *MS*

8 And he] *1 2 3* Well, he *MS CM*

9 bright, lovely] *MS* bright lovely *CM 1 2 3*   1 response, ⟨why⟩ *MS*

2 philosophic] philosophical *2 3*

hearing! Would any one have said that Tito had not[3] made a rich return[4] to his benefactor, or that his gratitude and affection would fail on any great demand? He[5] did not admit that his gratitude had failed; but *it was not certain* that Baldassarre was in slavery, not certain that he was living.

"Do I not owe something to myself?" said Tito, inwardly, with a slight movement of his shoulders, the first he had made since he had turned to look down at the florins. "Before I quit everything, and incur again all the risks of which I am even now weary, I must at least have a reasonable hope. Am I to spend my life in a wandering search? *I believe he is dead.* Cennini was right about my florins: I will place them in his hands to-morrow."

When, the next morning, Tito put this determination into act he had chosen his colour in the game, and had given an inevitable bent to his wishes. He had made it impossible that he should not from henceforth desire it to be the truth that his father was dead; impossible that he should not be tempted to baseness rather than that the precise facts of his conduct should not remain for ever concealed.

Under every guilty secret there [6]is hidden a brood of guilty wishes, whose unwholesome infecting life is cherished by the darkness. The contaminating effect of deeds often [7]lies less in the commission than in the consequent adjustment of our desires—the[8] enlistment of our self-interest on the side of falsity; as, on the other hand, the purifying influence of public confession springs from the fact, that by it the hope[9] in lies is for ever swept away, and the soul recovers the noble attitude of simplicity.

Besides, in this first distinct colloquy[1] with himself the ideas which had previously been scattered and interrupted had now concentrated themselves: the little rills of selfishness had united and made a channel, so that they could never [2]again meet with the same resistance. Hitherto Tito had left in vague indecision the question whether, with the means in his power, he would not return, and ascertain his father's fate; he had now made a definite excuse to himself for not taking that course; he had avowed to himself a choice which he would have been ashamed to avow to others, and which[3] would have made him ashamed in the resurgent presence of his father. But the inward shame, the reflex of that[4] outward law which the great heart of

---

3 not ⟨repaid⟩ *MS*   4 a rich return] *1 2 3* due return *MS CM*
5 He] Tito *MS*   6 ⟨lies⟩ is *MS*
7 ⟨lies less in⟩ ⟨depends less on⟩ lies less in the commission than ⟨in⟩ ⟨on⟩ in *MS*
8 the] than in the *MS*
9 falsity; as, on . . . hope] falsity; and ⟨on this ground rests⟩ on this depends the purifying influence of public confession—that the hope *MS*
1 {distinct} colloquy *MS*   2 ⟨meet again⟩ again meet *MS*
3 others, and which] others—which *MS*   4 that] the *MS*

mankind makes for every individual man, a[5] reflex which will exist even in the absence of the sympathetic impulses that need no law, but rush[6] to the deed of fidelity and pity as inevitably as the brute mother shields her young from the attack of the hereditary enemy—that inward shame was showing its blushes in Tito's determined assertion to himself that his father was dead, or that at least search was hopeless.

5 law {which the great . . . man—}a *MS*
6 impulses that need no law, but rush] impulse that needs no law, but rushes *MS*

CHAPTER X.

UNDER THE PLANE-TREE

ON the day of San Giovanni it was already three weeks ago that Tito had handed his florins to Cennini, and we have seen that as he set out towards the Via de' Bardi he showed all the outward signs of a mind at ease. How should it be otherwise? He never jarred with what was immediately around him, and his nature was too joyous, too unapprehensive, for the hidden and the distant to grasp him in the shape of a dread. As he turned out of the hot sunshine into the shelter of a narrow street, took off the black cloth berretta, or simple cap with upturned lappet, which just crowned his brown curls, pushing his hair and tossing his head backward to court the cooler air, there was no brand of duplicity on his brow;[1] neither was there any stamp of candour: it was simply a finely formed, square, smooth young brow. And[2] the slow absent glance[3] he cast round[4] at the upper windows of the houses had neither more dissimulation in it, nor more ingenuousness, than belongs to a youthful well-opened eyelid with its unwearied breadth of gaze; to perfectly pellucid lenses; to the undimmed dark of a rich brown iris; and to pure cerulean-tinted angle of whiteness streaked with the delicate shadows of long eyelashes. Was it that Tito's [5]face attracted or repelled according to the mental attitude of the observer? Was it a cipher with more than one key? The strong, unmistakable expression in his whole air[6] and person was a negative one, and it was perfectly veracious; it declared the absence of any uneasy claim, any restless vanity, and it made the admiration that followed him as he passed among the troop of holiday-makers a thoroughly willing tribute.

For by this time the stir of the Festa was felt even in the narrowest side streets[7]; the throng which had at one time been concentrated in the lines through which the procession had to pass, was now streaming out in all directions in pursuit of a new object. Such intervals of a festa are precisely the moments when the vaguely active animal spirits of a crowd are likely to be the most petulant and most ready to sacrifice a stray individual to the greater happiness of the greater number. As Tito entered the neighbourhood of San Martino, he found the throng rather denser; and near the hostelry of the *Bertucce*,[*]

---

1 brow;] *MS 1 2 3* brow, *CM*   2 brow. And] *1 2 3* brow; and *MS CM*
3 {absent} glance *MS*   4 round] around *1 2 3*   5 〈person〉 face *MS*
6 {whole} air *MS*
7 {the stir of the Festa was felt} even in the narrowest side streets 〈the stir of the Festa was felt〉 *MS*

or Baboons, there was evidently some object which was arresting the passengers and forming them into a knot. It needed nothing of great interest to draw aside passengers unfreighted with a purpose, and Tito was preparing to turn aside into an adjoining street, when, amidst the loud laughter, his ear discerned a distressed childish voice crying, "Loose me! Holy Virgin, help me!" which at once determined him to push his way into the knot of gazers. He had just had time to perceive that the distressed voice came from a young contadina, whose white hood had fallen off in the struggle to get her hands free from the grasp of a man in the particoloured dress of a *cerretano*, or conjuror, who was making laughing attempts to soothe and cajole her, evidently carrying with him the amused sympathy of the spectators. These, by[8] a persuasive variety of words, signifying simpleton, for which the Florentine dialect is rich in equivalents, seemed to be arguing with the contadina against her obstinacy. At the first moment the girl's face was turned away, and he saw only her light brown hair plaited and fastened with a long silver pin; but in the next, the struggle brought her face opposite Tito's[9], and he saw the baby features of Tessa, her blue eyes filled with tears, and her under-lip quivering. Tessa, too, saw *him*[1], and through the mist of her swelling tears there beamed a sudden hope, like that in the face of a little child, when, held by a stranger against its will, it sees a familiar hand stretched out.

In an instant Tito had pushed his way through the barrier of bystanders, whose curiosity made them ready to turn aside at the sudden interference of this handsome young signor, had grasped Tessa's waist, and had said, "Loose[2] this child[3]! What right have you to hold her against her will?"

The conjuror[4]—a man with one of those faces in which the angles of the eyes and eyebrows, of the nostrils, mouth, and sharply defined jaw, all tended[5] upward—showed his small regular teeth in an impish but not ill-natured grin, as he let go Tessa's hands, and stretched out his own backward, shrugging his shoulders, and bending them forward a little in a half-apologetic, half-protesting manner.

"I meant[6] the *ragazza* no evil in the world, Messere: ask this respectable company. I was only going to show them a few samples of my skill, in which this little damsel might have helped me the better because of her kitten-face, which would have assured them of open dealing; and I had promised her a lapful of *confetti* as a reward. But

8 spectators. These, by] *3P* spectators, who by *MS CM 1 2*
9 opposite Tito's] *3C* opposite to Tito's *MS CM 1 2*   1 *him*] him *MS*
2 Loose ⟨?you⟩ this *MS*   3 child] *1 2 3* maiden *MS CM*
4 conjuror] *cerretano MS*   5 tended] *MS* tend *CM 1 2 3*
6 meant] mean *3*

what then? Messer has doubtless better *confetti* at hand, and she
knows it."

A general laugh among the bystanders accompanied these last
words of the conjuror, raised, probably, by the look of relief and
confidence with which Tessa clung to Tito's arm, as he drew it from
her waist and placed her hand within it. She only cared about the
laugh as she might have cared about the roar of wild beasts from
which she was escaping, not attaching any meaning to it; but Tito,
who had no sooner got her on his arm than he [7]foresaw some embarrassment in the situation, hastened to get clear of observers who[8],
having been despoiled of an expected amusement, were sure to re-
establish the balance by jests.

"See, see, little one! here is your hood," said the conjuror, throwing the bit of white drapery over Tessa's head. "*Orsù*, bear me no
malice; come back to me when Messere can spare you."

"Ah! Maestro Vaiano,* she'll come back presently, as the toad said
to the harrow,"* called out one of the spectators, seeing how Tessa
started and shrank at the action of the conjuror.

Tito pushed his way vigorously towards the corner of a side street,
a little vexed at this delay in his progress to the Via de' Bardi, and
intending to get rid of the poor little contadina as soon as possible.
The next street, too, had its passengers inclined to make holiday
remarks on[9] so unusual a pair; but they had no sooner entered it than
he said, in a kind but hurried manner, "Now, little one[1], where were
you going? Are you come by yourself to the Festa?"

"Ah, no!" said Tessa, looking frightened and distressed again; "I
have lost my mother in the crowd—her and my father-in-law.* They
will be angry—he will beat me. It was in the crowd in San
Pulinari*—somebody pushed me along and I couldn't stop myself, so
I got away from them. Oh, I don't know where they're gone! Please,
don't leave me!"

Her eyes had been swelling with tears again, and she ended with a
sob.

Tito hurried along again: the church of the Badia was not far off.
They could enter it by the cloister that opened at the back, and in the
church he could talk to Tessa—perhaps leave her. No! it was an hour
at which the church was not open; but they paused under the shelter
of the cloister, and he said, "Have you no cousin or friend in
Florence, my little Tessa, whose house you could find; or are you
afraid of walking by yourself since you have been frightened by the
conjuror? I am in a hurry to get to[2] Oltrarno, but if I could take you
anywhere near—"

---

7 ⟨felt⟩ foresaw *MS*   8 observers who] *MS 3P* observers, who *CM 1 2*
9 on] *3P* at *MS CM 1 2*   1 little one] fancuillina mia *MS*   2 to] into *MS*

"Oh, I *am* frightened: he was the devil—I know he was. And I don't know where to go—I[3] have nobody: and my mother meant to have her dinner somewhere, and I don't know where. Holy Madonna[4]! I shall be beaten."

The corners of the [5]pouting mouth went down piteously, and the poor little bosom with the beads on it above the green serge gown[6] heaved so, that there was no longer any help for it: a loud sob *would* come, and the big tears fell as if they were making up for lost time. Here was a situation! It would have been brutal to leave her, and Tito's nature was all gentleness. He wished at that moment that he had not been expected in the Via de' Bardi. As he saw her lifting up her holiday apron to catch the hurrying tears, he laid his hand, too, on the apron, and rubbed one of the cheeks and kissed the baby-like roundness.

"My poor little Tessa! leave off crying. Let us see what can be done. Where is your home—where do you live?"

There was no answer, but the sobs began to subside a little and the drops to fall less quickly.

"Come! I'll take you a little way, if you'll tell me where you want to go."

The apron fell, and Tessa's face began to look as contented as a cherub's budding from a cloud. The diabolical conjuror, the anger and the beating seemed a long way off.

"I think I'll go home, if you'll take me," she said, in a half whisper, looking up at Tito with wide blue eyes, and with something sweeter than a smile—with a child-like calm.

"Come, then, little one," said Tito, in a caressing tone, putting her arm within his again. "Which way is it?"

"Beyond Peretola*—where the large pear-tree is."

"Peretola? Out at which gate, pazzarella? I am a stranger, you must remember[7]."

"Out at the Por del Prato," said Tessa, moving along with a very fast hold on Tito's arm.

He did not know all the turnings well enough to venture on an attempt at choosing the quietest streets; and besides, it occurred to him that where the passengers were most numerous there was, perhaps, the [8]most chance of meeting with Monna Ghita and finding an end to his knight-errantship. So he made straight for Porta Rossa, and on to Ognissanti, showing his usual bright propitiatory face to the

3 go—I] go. I *3C [2 omits the punctuation between go and I; GE supplies a full stop in 3C]*

4 Holy Madonna] ⟨O⟩ Santa Madonna *MS*   5 ⟨little⟩ pouting *MS*

6 gown] *1 2 3* gamurra *MS CM*   7 {must} remember *MS*

8 ⟨most⟩ ⟨greatest⟩ most *MS*

mixed observers who threw their jests at him and his little heavy-shod maiden with much liberality. Mingled with the more decent holiday-makers there were frolicsome apprentices, rather envious of his good fortune; bold-eyed women with the badge of the yellow veil;* beggars who thrust forward their caps for alms, in derision at [9]Tito's evident haste; dicers, sharpers, and loungers of the worst sort; boys whose tongues were used to wag in concert at the most brutal street games: for the streets of Florence were not always a moral[1] spectacle in those times, and Tessa's terror at being lost in the crowd was not wholly unreasonable.

When they reached the Piazza d'Ognissanti, Tito slackened his pace: they were both heated with their hurried walk, and here was a wider space where they could take breath. They sat down on one of the stone benches[2] which were frequent against the walls of old Florentine houses.

"Holy Virgin[3]!" said Tessa; "I am glad we have got away from those women and boys; but I was not frightened, because you could take care of me."

"Pretty little Tessa!" said Tito, smiling at her. "What makes you feel so safe with me?"

"[4]Because you are so beautiful—like the people going into Paradise—they are all good."

"It is a long while since you had your breakfast, Tessa," said Tito, seeing some stalls[5] near, with fruit and sweetmeats upon them. "Are you hungry?"

"Yes, I think I am—if you will have some too."

Tito bought some apricots, and cakes, and comfits, and put them into [6]her apron.

"Come," he said, "let us walk on to the Prato, and then perhaps you will not be afraid to go the rest of the way alone."

"But you will have some of the apricots and things," said Tessa, rising obediently and gathering up her apron as a bag for her store.

"We will see," said Tito aloud; and to himself he said, "Here is a little contadina who might inspire a better idyl than Lorenzo[7] de' Medici's *Nencia da Barberino*,* that Nello's friends rave about; if I were only a Theocritus,* or had time to cultivate the necessary experience by unseasonable walks of this sort! However, the mischief is done now: I am so late already that another half hour will make no difference. Pretty little pigeon!"

"We have a garden and plenty of pears," said Tessa, "and two

9 ⟨his⟩ Tito's *MS*   1 moral] highly moral *MS*

2 benches] *1 2 3 panche* or benches *MS CM*

3 Holy Virgin] *1 2 3 Vergine santissima MS CM*   4 ⟨O⟩ Because *MS*

5 stalls] *deschi MS*   6 ⟨Tessa's⟩ her *MS*   7 Lorenzo⟨'s⟩ de Medici's *MS*

cows, besides the mules; and I'm very fond of them. But my father-in-law[8] is a cross man: I wish my mother had not married him. I think he is wicked; he is very ugly."

"And does your mother let him beat you, poverina? You said you were afraid of being beaten."

"Ah, my mother[9] herself scolds me: she loves my young sister better, and thinks I don't do work enough. Nobody speaks kindly to me, only the Pievano (parish priest) when I go to confession[1]. And the men in the Mercato laugh at me and make fun of me. Nobody ever kissed me and spoke to me as you do; just as I talk to my little black-faced kid, because I'm very fond of it."

It seemed not to have entered Tessa's mind that there was any change in Tito's appearance since the morning he begged the milk from her, and that he looked now like a personage for whom she must summon her little stock of reverent words and signs[2]. He had impressed her too differently from any human being who had ever come near her before, for her to make any comparison of details: she took no note of his dress; he was simply a voice and a face to her, something come from Paradise into a world where [3]most things seemed hard and angry; and she prattled with as little restraint as if he had been an imaginary companion born of her own lovingness and the sunshine.

They had now reached the Prato, which at that time was a large open space within the walls, where the Florentine youth played at their favourite *Calcio*—a peculiar kind of foot-ball—and otherwise exercised themselves. At this midday time it was forsaken and quiet to the very gates, where a tent had been erected in preparation for[4] the race. On the border of this wide meadow, Tito paused and said,

"Now, Tessa, you will not be frightened if I leave you to walk the rest of the way by yourself. Addio. Shall I come and buy a cup of milk from you in the Mercato to-morrow morning, to see that you are[5] quite safe?"

He added this question in a soothing tone, as he saw her eyes widening sorrowfully, and the corners of her mouth falling. She said nothing at first; she only opened her apron and looked down at her apricots and sweetmeats. Then she looked up at him again, and said complainingly,—

"I thought you would have some[6], and we could sit down under a tree outside the gate, and eat them together."

"Tessa, Tessa, you little siren, you would ruin me," said Tito,

8 my father-in-law] *3C* the *patrigno MS CM 1 2*   9 my mother] the *madre MS*
1 confession ⟨once a year⟩ *MS*   2 {reverent} words and signs ⟨of reverence⟩ *MS*
3 ⟨all⟩ most things *MS*   4 {in preparation} for *MS*
5 you are] you're *MS*   6 some] *MS 1 2 3* come *CM*

laughing and kissing both her cheeks. "I ought to have been in the
Via de' Bardi long ago. No! I must go back now; you are in no danger. There—I'll take an apricot. Addio!"

He had already stepped two yards from her when he said the last
word. Tessa could not have spoken; she was pale, and a great sob was
rising; but she turned round as if she felt there was no hope for her,
and stepped on, holding her apron so forgetfully that the apricots
began to roll out on the grass.

Tito could not help looking after her, and seeing her shoulders rise
to the bursting sob, and the apricots fall—could not help going after
her and picking them up. It was very hard upon him: he was a long
way off the Via de' Bardi, and very near to Tessa.

"See, my silly one," he said, picking up the apricots. "Come, leave
off crying, I will go with you, and we'll sit down under the tree.
Come, I don't like to see you cry; but you know I must go back some
time."

So it came to pass that they found a great plane-tree not far outside the gates, and they sat down under it, and all the feast was
spread out on Tessa's lap, she leaning with her back against the trunk
of the tree, and he stretched opposite to her, resting his elbows[7] on
the rough green growth cherished by the shade, while the sunlight
stole through the boughs and played about them like a [8]winged thing.
Tessa's face was all contentment again, and the taste of the apricots
and sweetmeats seemed very good.

"You pretty bird!" said Tito, looking at her as she sat eyeing the
remains of the feast with an evident mental debate about saving them,
since he had said he would not have any more. "To think of any one
scolding you! What sins do you tell of at confession, Tessa?"

"Oh, a great many. I am often naughty. I don't like work, and I
can't help being idle, though I know I shall be beaten and scolded;
and I give the mules the best fodder when nobody sees me, and then
when the *madre* is angry I say I didn't do it, and that makes me
frightened at the devil. I think the conjuror was the devil. I am not so
frightened [9]after I've been to confession. And see,[1] I've got a *Breve**
here that a good father, who came to Prato* preaching this Easter[2],
blessed[3] and gave us all." Here Tessa drew from her bosom a [4]tiny
bag carefully fastened up. "And I think the Holy Madonna will take
care of me; she looks as if she would; and perhaps if I wasn't idle, she
wouldn't let me be beaten."

"If they are so cruel to you, Tessa, shouldn't you like to leave

7 elbows] elbow *MS*   8 ⟨living⟩ winged *MS*   9 ⟨now⟩ after *MS*
1 And {see}, *MS*   2 Easter] Pasqua *MS*
3 father, who . . . Easter, blessed] *3P* father who . . . Easter blessed *MS CM 1 2*
4 ⟨little⟩ tiny *MS*

them, and go and live with a beautiful lady who would be kind to you, if she would have you to wait upon her?"

Tessa seemed to hold her breath for a moment or two. Then she said doubtfully, "I don't know."

"Then should you like to be *my* little servant, and live with me?" said Tito, smiling. He meant no more than to see what sort of pretty look and answer she would give.

There was a flush of joy immediately. "Will you take me with you now? Ah! I shouldn't go home and be beaten then." She paused a little while, and then added[5] more doubtfully, "But I should like to fetch my black-faced kid."

"Yes, you must go back to your kid, my Tessa," said Tito, rising, "and I must go the other way."

"By Jupiter!" he added[6], as he went from under the shade of the tree, "it is not a pleasant time of day to walk from here to the Via de' Bardi; I am more inclined to lie down and sleep in this shade."

It ended so. Tito had an unconquerable aversion to anything unpleasant, even when an object very much loved and desired was on the other side of it. He had risen early; had waited; had seen sights, and had been already walking in the sun: he was inclined for a siesta, and inclined all the more because little Tessa was there, and seemed to make the air softer. He lay down on the grass again, putting his cap under his head on a green tuft by the side of Tessa. That was not quite comfortable; so he moved again, and asked Tessa to let him rest his head against her lap; and in that way he soon fell asleep. Tessa sat quiet as a dove on its nest, just venturing, when he was fast asleep, to touch the wonderful dark curls that fell backward from his ear. She was too happy to go to sleep—too happy to think that Tito would wake up, and that then he would leave her, and she must go home. It takes very little water to make a perfect pool for a tiny fish, where it will find its world and paradise all in one, and never have a presentiment of the dry bank. The fretted summer shade, and stillness, and the gentle breathing of some loved life near—it would be paradise to us all, if eager thought, the strong angel with the implacable brow, had not long since closed the gates.

It really was a long while before the waking came—before the long dark eyes opened at Tessa, first[7] with a little surprise, and then with a smile, which was soon quenched by some preoccupying thought. Tito's deeper sleep had broken into a doze, in which he felt himself in the Via de' Bardi, explaining his failure to appear at the appointed time. The clear images of that doze urged him to start up at once to a

5 then added] ⟨then⟩ added *MS*   6 added] said *MS*
7 first] *3P* at first *MS CM 1 2*

Under the Plane-Tree

sitting posture, and as he stretched his arms and shook his cap he said,—

"Tessa, little one, you have let me sleep too long. My hunger and the shadows together tell me that the sun has done much travel since I fell asleep. I must lose no more time. Addio," he ended, patting her cheek with one hand, and settling[8] his cap with the other.

[9]She said nothing, but there were signs in her face which made him speak again in as serious and chiding[1] a tone as he could command,—

"Now, Tessa, you must not cry. I shall be angry; I shall not love you if you cry. You must go home to your black-faced kid, or if you like you may go back to the gate and see the horses start. But I can stay with you no longer, and if you cry, I shall think you are troublesome to me."

The rising tears were checked by terror at this change in Tito's voice. Tessa turned very pale, and sat in trembling silence, with her blue eyes widened by arrested tears.

"Look now," Tito went on, soothingly, opening the wallet that hung at his belt, "here is a pretty charm that I have had a long while—ever since I was in Sicily, a country a long way off."

His wallet had many little matters in it mingled with small coins, and he had the usual difficulty in laying his finger on the right thing. He unhooked his wallet, and turned out the contents on Tessa's lap. Among them was his onyx ring.

"Ah, my ring!" he exclaimed,[2] slipping it on the forefinger of his right hand. "I forgot to put it on again this morning. Strange, I never missed it! See, Tessa," he added, as he spread out the smaller articles[3], and selected the one he was in search of. "See this pretty little pointed bit of red coral—like your goat's horn, is it not? and here is a hole in it, so you can put it on[4] the cord round your neck along with your *Breve*, and then the evil spirits can't hurt you: if you ever see them coming in the shadow round the corner, point this little coral horn at them, and they will run away. It is a 'buon[5] fortuna,'* and will keep you from harm when I am not with you[6]. Come, undo the cord."

Tessa obeyed with a tranquillizing sense that life was going to be something quite new, and that Tito would be with her often. [7]All

8 cheek with one hand, and settling] cheek, and ⟨then⟩ ⟨rising to his feet⟩ settling *MS*

9 ⟨Tessa⟩ She *MS*   1 chiding] as chiding *3*

2 "Ah, {my ring} he exclaimed, ⟨"there is my onyx ring.⟩ slipping it on the ⟨third finger⟩ fore-finger *MS*

3 articles ⟨with his finger⟩ *MS*   4 put it on] *MS CM 3C* put on *1 2*
5 buon] buona *2 3*   6 run away. {It is . . . you} *MS*
7 ⟨Everyone who remembers his childhood remembers⟩ All *MS*

who remember their childhood remember [8]the strange vague sense,
when some new experience came, that everything else was going to be
changed[9], and that there would be no lapse into the old monotony.
So the bit of coral was hung beside the tiny bag with the scrap of
scrawled parchment in it, and Tessa felt braver.

"And now you will give me a kiss," said Tito, economizing time by
speaking [1]while he swept in the contents of the wallet and hung it at
his waist again, "and look [2]happy, like a good girl, and then——"

But Tessa had obediently put forward her lips in a moment, and
kissed his cheek as he hung down his head.

"Oh, you [3]pretty pigeon!" cried[4] Tito, laughing, [5]pressing her
round cheeks with his hands and crushing her features together so as
to give them a general impartial kiss.

Then he started up and walked away, not looking round till he was
ten yards [6]from her, when he just turned[7] and gave a parting beck.
Tessa was looking after him, but he could see that she was[8] making
no signs of distress. It was enough for Tito if she did not cry while
he was present. The softness of his [9]nature required that all sorrow
should be hidden away from him.

"I wonder when Romola will kiss my cheek in that way?" [1]thought
Tito, as he walked along. It seemed a tiresome distance now, and he
almost wished he had not been so soft-hearted, or so tempted to
linger in the shade. [2]No other excuse was needed to Bardo and
Romola than saying simply that he had been unexpectedly hindered;
he felt confident[3] their proud delicacy would inquire no farther. He
lost no time in getting to Ognissanti, and hastily taking some food
there, he crossed the Arno by the Ponte alla Carraja, and made his
way as directly as possible towards the Via de' Bardi.

But it was the hour[4] when all the world who meant to be in particularly good time to see the Corso were returning from the *Borghi*, or
villages just outside the gates, where they had dined and reposed
themselves[5]; and the thoroughfares leading to the bridges were of
course the issues towards which the stream of [6]sightseers tended. Just
as Tito reached the Ponte Vecchio and the[7] entrance of the Via de'

---

8 ⟨that⟩ the strange vague sense ⟨that bliss was coming whenever⟩ when *MS*
9 changed ⟨instead of lapsing⟩ *MS*   1 ⟨as⟩ while *MS*
2 ⟨pleased⟩ happy *MS*   3 ⟨little⟩ pretty *MS*   4 cried] said *MS*
5 ⟨and⟩ pressing *MS*   6 ⟨away⟩ from *MS*
7 turned ⟨round and made the sign of parting with his fingers⟩ *MS*
8 was ⟨looking calm⟩ *MS*   9 ⟨nature⟩ ⟨heart⟩ nature *MS*   1 ⟨said⟩ thought *MS*
2 ⟨He determined to attempt no excuse to Bardo and Romola beyond⟩ No *MS*
3 confident ⟨that⟩ *MS*   4 the hour] just ⟨the time of day⟩ the hour *MS*
5 themselves, ⟨under the leafy porches or [?frasche] that⟩ *MS*
6 ⟨passengers⟩ sightseers *MS*
7 the ⟨angle at⟩ entrance of the Via de' Bardi ⟨where the passengers were especially
numerous⟩ *MS*

Bardi, he was suddenly urged back towards the angle of the intersecting streets. A company on horseback, coming[8] from the Via
Guicciardini, and turning up the Via de' Bardi, had compelled the
foot passengers to recede [9]hurriedly. Tito had been walking, as his
manner was, with the thumb of his right hand[1] resting in his belt;
and as he was thus forced to pause, and was looking carelessly at the
passing cavaliers, he felt a very thin cold hand laid on his[2]. He started
round, and saw the Dominican friar whose upturned face had so
struck him in the morning. Seen closer, the face looked more evidently worn by sickness and not by age; and again it brought some
strong but indefinite reminiscence[3] to Tito.

"Pardon me, but—from your face and your ring,"—said the friar,
in a faint voice, "is not your name Tito Melema?"

"Yes," said Tito, also speaking faintly, doubly jarred by the cold
touch and the mystery. He was not apprehensive or timid through his
imagination, but through his sensations and perceptions he could easily be made to shrink and turn pale like a maiden.

"Then I shall fulfil my commission."

The friar put his hand under his scapulary, and drawing out a
small linen bag which hung round his neck, took from it a bit of
parchment, doubled and stuck firmly together with some black adhe-
sive substance, and placed it in Tito's hand. On the outside was written in Italian, in a small but distinct character—

"*Tito Melema, aged twenty-three, with a dark, beautiful face, long
dark curls, the brightest smile, and a large onyx ring on his right
forefinger[4].*"

Tito did not look at the friar, but tremblingly broke open the bit of
parchment. Inside, the words were—

"*I am sold for a slave: I think they are going to take me to[5] Antioch.
The gems alone will serve to ransom me.*"

Tito looked round at the friar, but could only ask a question with
his eyes.

"I had it at Corinth," the friar said, [6]speaking with difficulty, like
one whose small strength[7] had been over-taxed[8], "I had it from a man
who was dying."

"He is dead, then?" said Tito, with a bounding of the heart.

"Not the writer. The man who give it me was a pilgrim, like

8 coming ⟨from the Piazza Pitti⟩ ⟨up⟩ from the *MS*   9 ⟨suddenly⟩ hurriedly *MS*
1 {the thumb of} his right hand *MS*
2 his] his own *MS*   3 reminiscence] *MS* reminiscences *CM 1 2 3*
4 {right} forefinger *MS*
5 {I think} they are going to take me to ⟨Antioch⟩ ⟨somewhere on the coast of Asia
Minor⟩ Antioch *MS*
6 ⟨apparently⟩ speaking *MS*   7 {small} strength *MS*
8 over-taxed] 1 2 sorely taxed *MS CM* overtaxed 3

myself, to whom the writer had entrusted it, because he was journeying to Italy."

"You know the contents?"

"I do not know them[9], but I conjecture them. Your friend is in slavery—you will go and release him. But I am unable to talk now[1]." The friar, whose voice had become feebler and feebler, sank down on the stone bench against the wall from which he had risen to touch Tito's hand, adding,[2]

"I am at San Marco; my name is Fra Luca[3]."

9 I do not know them] *1 2 3* I know them not *MS CM*
1 I am unable to talk now] *1 2 3* I cannot say more at present *MS CM*
2 hand, adding,] *1 2 3* hand, *MS CM*
3 Marco; my name is Fra Luca] Marco—Fra Luca *MS*

CHAPTER XI.

TITO'S DILEMMA

WHEN Fra Luca had ceased to speak, Tito still stood by him in irresolution, and it was not till, the pressure of the passengers being removed, the friar rose and walked slowly into the church of Santa Felicità, that Tito also went on his way along the Via de' Bardi.

"If this monk is a Florentine," he said to himself—"if he is going to remain at Florence, everything must be disclosed." He felt that a new crisis had come, but he was not, for all that, too evidently agitated[1] to pay his visit to Bardo, and apologize for his previous non-appearance. Tito's talent for concealment was being fast developed into something less neutral. It was still possible—perhaps it might be inevitable—for him to accept frankly the altered conditions, and avow Baldassarre's existence—but hardly without casting an unpleasant light backward on his original reticence as studied equivocation, in order to avoid the fulfilment of a secretly recognized claim, to say nothing of his quiet settlement of himself and investment of his florins, when, it would be clear, his benefactor's fate had not been certified. It was at least provisionally[2] wise to act as if nothing had happened, and, for the present, he would suspend decisive thought; there was all the night for meditation, and no one [3]would know the precise moment at which he had received the letter.

So he entered the room on the second story—[4]where Romola and her father sat among the parchment and the marble, aloof from the life of the streets on holidays [5]as well as on common days—with[6] a face only[7] a little less bright than usual, from regret at appearing so late:[8] a regret which wanted no testimony, since he had given up the sight of the Corso in order to express it; and then set himself to throw extra animation into the evening, though all the while his consciousness was at work like a machine with complex action, leaving deposits quite distinct from the line of talk; and by the time he descended the stone stairs and issued from the grim door in the

1 evidently agitated] *3P* agitated *MS CM 1 2*
2 was at least provisionally] *MS 1 2 3* was, at least, provisionally *CM*
3 ⟨need⟩ would *MS*   4 ⟨the room⟩ where *MS*
5 ⟨not less than⟩ as well as *MS*
6 story—where . . . days—with] *MS 3P* story, where . . . days, with *CM 1 2*
7 only] *1 2 3* just *MS CM*   8 late:] *MS 1 2 3* late; *CM*

The First Kiss

starlight, his mind had really reached a new stage in its formation of a purpose.

And when, the next day, after he was free from his professorial [9]work, he turned up the Via del Cocomero,* towards the convent of San Marco, his purpose was fully shaped. He was going[1] to ascertain from Fra Luca precisely how much he conjectured of the truth, and on what ground[2] he conjectured it; and, further, how long he was[3] to remain at San Marco. And on that fuller knowledge he hoped to mould a statement which would in any case save him from the necessity of quitting Florence. Tito had never had occasion to fabricate an ingenious lie before: the occasion was come now—the occasion which circumstance never fails to beget on tacit falsity; and his ingenuity was ready. For he had convinced himself[4] that he was not bound to go in search of Baldassarre. He had once said that on a fair assurance of his father's existence and whereabout[5], he would unhesitatingly go after him. [6]But, after all, *why* was he bound to go? What, looked at closely, was the end of all life, but to extract the utmost sum of pleasure? And was not his own blooming life a promise of incomparably more pleasure, not for himself only, but for others, than the withered wintry life of a man who was past the time of keen enjoyment, and whose ideas had stiffened into barren rigidity? [7]Those ideas had all been sown in the fresh soil of Tito's mind, and were lively germs there:[8] that was the proper order of things—the order of Nature, which treats all maturity as a mere nidus* for youth. Baldassarre had done his work, had had his draught of life: Tito said it was *his* turn now.

And the prospect was so vague:—"I think they are going to take me to Antioch:" here was a vista! After a long voyage, to spend months, perhaps years, in a search for which even now there was no guarantee that it would not prove vain: and to leave behind at starting a life of distinction and love: and to find, if he found anything, the old exacting companionship which was known by rote beforehand. Certainly the gems and therefore the florins were, in a sense, Baldassarre's: in the narrow sense by which the right of possession is

---

9 ⟨duties⟩ work *MS*

1 going ⟨to speak to Fra Luca: he was going to ascertain from him⟩ *MS*

2 ground] *MS* grounds *CM 1 2 3*　　　3 was ⟨going⟩ to *MS*

4 convinced himself ⟨by the most cogent reasoning⟩ *MS*

5 whereabout] *MS 2 3* whereabouts *CM 1*

6 ⟨The assurance was come.⟩ But *MS*

7 ⟨For taking the most fortunate result—supposing the sacrifice ended in the utmost possible good to Baldassarre, what was the amount of that good or enjoyment compared with the possibilities of enjoyment to Tito. It was a choice between a plant which had shed its seed and a plant still teeming with a hundred buds. Baldassarre's⟩ Those *MS*

8 there:] *MS 1 2 3* there; *CM*

determined in ordinary affairs; but in that larger[9] and more radically
natural view by which the world belongs to youth and strength,[1] they
were rather [2]his who could extract the most pleasure out of them.
That, he was conscious, was not the sentiment which the complicated
play of human feelings had engendered in society. The men around
him would expect that he should immediately apply those florins to
his benefactor's [3]rescue. But what was the sentiment of society?—a
mere tangle of anomalous traditions and opinions, that[4] no wise man
would take as a guide, except so far as his own comfort was concerned. Not that he cared for the florins, save perhaps for Romola's
sake: he would give up the florins readily enough. It was the joy that
was due to him and[5] was close to his lips, which he felt he was not
bound to thrust away from him and so[6] travel on, thirsting. Any
maxims that required a man to fling away the good that was needed
to make existence sweet were only the lining of human selfishness
turned outward: they were made by men who wanted others to
sacrifice themselves for their sake. He would rather that Baldassarre
should not suffer: he liked no one to suffer: but could any philosophy
prove to him that he was bound to care for another's suffering more
than for his own? To do so, he must have loved Baldassarre devot-
edly, and he did *not* love him: was that his own fault? Gratitude! seen
closely, it made no valid claim: his father's life would have been
dreary without him: [7]are we convicted of a debt to men for the pleasures they give themselves?

[8]Having once begun to explain away Baldassarre's claim, Tito's
thought showed itself as active as a virulent acid, eating its rapid way
through all the tissues of sentiment. His mind was destitute of that
dread which has been erroneously decried as if it were[9] nothing
higher than a man's animal care for his own skin: that awe of the
Divine Nemesis which was felt by religious pagans, and, though it
took a more positive form under Christianity, is still felt by the mass
of mankind simply as a vague fear at anything which is called wrong-
doing. Such terror of the unseen is so far above mere sensual cowardice that it will annihilate that cowardice: it is the initial recognition
of a moral law restraining desire, and checks the hard bold scrutiny of
imperfect thought into obligations which can never be proved to have
any sanctity in the absence of feeling. "It is good," sing the old

---

9 larger] large *1 2 3*   1 youth, {and strength,} *MS*   2 ⟨Tito's⟩ his *MS*
3 ⟨uses⟩ rescue *MS*   4 that] which *2 3*   5 and ⟨that⟩ was *MS*
6 and so] *3C* and *MS CM 1 2*   7 ⟨do we feel⟩ are we convicted of *MS*
8 ⟨Tito's mind was destitute of that dread which⟩ Having *MS*
9 were] was *MS*

Eumenides, in Æschylus[1],* "that fear should sit as the guardian of the soul, forcing it into wisdom—good that men should carry a threatening shadow in their hearts under the full sunshine; else, how shall[2] they learn to revere the right?" That guardianship may become needless; but only when all outward law has become needless—only when duty and love have united in one stream and made a common force.

As Tito entered the outer cloister of San Marco, and inquired for Fra Luca, there was no shadowy presentiment in his mind: he felt himself too cultured and sceptical for that: he had been nurtured in contempt for the tales of priests whose impudent lives were a proverb,[3] and in erudite familiarity with disputes concerning the chief good, which had after all, he considered, left it a matter of taste. Yet fear was a strong element in Tito's nature—the fear of what he believed or saw was likely to rob him of pleasure; and he had a definite fear that Fra Luca might be the means of driving him from Florence.

"Fra Luca? ah, he is gone to Fiesole—to the Dominican monastery there. He was taken on a litter in the cool of the morning. The poor brother is very ill. Could you leave a message for him?"

This answer was given by a *fra converso*, or lay brother, whose accent told plainly that he was a raw contadino, and whose dull glance implied no curiosity.

"[4]Thanks; my business can wait.[5]"

Tito turned away with a sense of relief. "This friar is not likely to live," he said to himself. "I saw he was worn to a shadow. And at Fiesole there will be nothing to recall me to his mind. Besides, if he should come back, my explanation will serve as well then as now. But I wish I knew what it was that his face recalled to me."

---

1 sing the old Eumenides, in Æschylus] ⟨sang the old Eumenides⟩ ⟨the old Eumenides sang⟩ sang the old Eumenides {in the ear of Aschylus} *MS*

2 shall] should *2 3*

4 ⟨Nay⟩ ⟨*Grazie*⟩ Thanks *MS*

3 proverb,] *MS 1 2 3* proverb; *CM*

5 wait. ⟨Addio.⟩ *MS*

CHAPTER XII.

THE PRIZE IS NEARLY GRASPED

[1]TITO walked along with a light step, for the immediate fear had vanished[2]; the usual joyousness[3] of his disposition reassumed its predominance, and he was going to see Romola. Yet Romola's life seemed an image of that loving, pitying devotedness,[4] that patient endurance of irksome tasks, from which he had shrunk and excused himself. But he was not out[5] of love with goodness, or prepared to plunge into vice: he was in his fresh youth, with soft pulses for all charm and loveliness;[6] he had still a healthy appetite for [7]ordinary human joys, and the poison could only work by degrees. He had sold himself to evil, but at present life seemed so nearly the same to him that he was not conscious of the bond. He meant all things to go on as they had done before, both within and without him: he meant to win golden opinions by meritorious exertion, by ingenious learning, by amiable compliance: he was not going to do anything that would throw him out of harmony with the beings he cared for. And he cared supremely for Romola; he wished to have her for his beautiful and loving[8] wife. There might be a wealthier alliance within the ultimate reach of successful accomplishments like his, but there was no woman in all Florence like Romola. When she was near him, and looked at him with her sincere hazel eyes, he was subdued by a delicious influence as strong and inevitable as those musical vibrations which take possession of us with a rhythmic empire that no sooner ceases than we desire it to begin again.

As he trod the stone stairs, [9]when he was still outside the door, with no one but Maso near him, the influence seemed to have begun its work by the mere nearness of anticipation.

"Welcome, *Tito mio*," said the old man's voice, before Tito had spoken. There was a new vigour in the voice, a new cheerfulness in the blind face, since that first interview[1] more than two months ago.

---

1 ⟨He⟩ Tito *MS*   2 had vanished] was banished *MS*

3 {usual} joyousness of his ⟨nature⟩ disposition *MS*

4 devotedness, ⟨which his own nature had not yielded: he might have felt sure that she would have rushed to the painful⟩ ⟨of⟩ that *MS*

5 out] therefore out *MS*

6 loveliness; ⟨with all the refinement that belonged to learned culture and natural cleverness, with all the ready inoffensive sociability which belonged to a good humoured nature:⟩ he *MS*

7 ⟨all⟩ ordinary *MS*

8 beautiful and loving] *3C* majestic, beautiful, and loving *MS CM 1 2*

9 ⟨even⟩ when *MS*   1 interview ⟨with⟩ *MS*

"You have brought fresh manuscript, doubtless; but since we were talking last night I have had new ideas: we must take a wider scope—we must go back upon our footsteps."

Tito, paying his homage[2] to Romola as he advanced, went, as his custom was, straight to Bardo's chair, and put his hand in the palm that was held to receive it, placing himself on the cross-legged leather seat with scrolled ends, close to Bardo's elbow.

"Yes," he said, in his gentle way; "I have brought the new manuscript, but that can wait your pleasure. I have young limbs, you know, and can walk back up the hill without any difficulty."

He did not look at Romola as he said this, but he knew quite well that her eyes were fixed on him with delight.

"That is well said, my son." Bardo had already addressed Tito in this way once or twice of late. "And I perceive with gladness that you do not shrink from labour, without which, the poet has wisely said,* life has given nothing to mortals. It is too often the 'palma sine pulvere,'* the prize of glory without the dust of the race, that attracts young ambition[3]. But what says the Greek?* 'In the morning of life, work; in the midday, give counsel; in the evening, pray.' It is true, I might be thought to have reached that helpless evening; but not so, while I have counsel within me which is yet unspoken. For my mind, as I have often said, was shut up as by a dam; the plenteous waters lay dark and motionless;[4] but you, my Tito[5], have opened a duct for them, and they rush forward with a force that surprises myself. And now, what I want is, that we should go over [6]our preliminary ground again, with a wider scheme of comment and illustration; otherwise I may lose opportunities which I now see retrospectively, and which may never occur again. You mark what I am saying, Tito?"

He[7] had just stooped to reach his manuscript, which had rolled down, and Bardo's jealous ear was alive to the slight movement.

[8]Tito might have been excused for shrugging his shoulders at the prospect before him, but he was not naturally impatient; moreover, he had been bred up in that laborious erudition, at once minute and copious, which was the chief intellectual task of the age; and with Romola near, he was floated along by waves of agreeable sensation that made everything seem easy.

"Assuredly," he said; "you[9] wish to enlarge your comments on certain passages we have cited."

2 homage] smiling homage *MS*

3 that attracts young ambition] *3C* that young ambition covets *MS CM 1 2*

4 motionless;] *3P* motionless, *MS CM 1 2*   5 my Tito] *1 2 3* Tito mio *MS CM*

6 ⟨the⟩ our *MS*   7 He] Tito *MS*

8 ⟨"Assuredly; you wish to enlarge your comments on certain passages we have cited".⟩ ⟨He⟩ Tito *MS*   9 "Assuredly," he said; you] "Assuredly; you *MS*

"Not only so; I wish to introduce an occasional excursus, where we have noticed an author to whom I have given special study; for I may die too soon to achieve any separate work. And this is not a time for scholarly integrity and well-sifted learning to lie idle, when it is not only rash ignorance that we have to fear, but when there are men like Calderino, who, as Poliziano has well shown, have recourse to impudent falsities of citation to serve the ends of their vanity and secure a triumph to their own mistakes.* Wherefore, my Tito[1], I think it not well that we should let slip the occasion that lies under our hands. And now we will turn back to the point where we have cited the passage from Thucydides, and I wish you, by way of preliminary,[2] to go with me through all my notes on the Latin translation[3] made by Lorenzo Valla,* for which the incomparable Pope Nicholas[4] V.—with whose personal notice I was honoured while I was yet young, and when he was still Thomas of Sarzana—paid him (I say not unduly) the sum of five hundred gold scudi. But inasmuch as Valla, though otherwise of dubious fame, is held in high honour for his severe scholarship, whence[5] the epigrammatist has jocosely said of him that since he went among the shades, Pluto himself has not dared to speak in the ancient languages, it is the more needful that his name should not be as a stamp warranting false wares; and therefore I [6]would introduce an excursus on [7]Thucydides, wherein my castigations of Valla's text[8] may find a fitting place. My Romola[9], thou wilt reach the needful volumes—thou knowest them—on the fifth shelf of the cabinet."

Tito rose at the same moment with Romola, saying, "I will reach them, if you will point them out," and followed her hastily[1] into the adjoining small room, where the walls were also covered with ranges of books in perfect order.

"There they are," said Romola, pointing upward; "every book is just where it was when my father ceased to see them."

Tito stood by her without hastening to reach the [2]books. They had never been in this room together before.

"I hope," she continued, turning her eyes full on Tito, with a look of grave confidence—"I hope he will not weary you; this work makes him so happy."

"And me too, Romola—if you will only let me say, I love you—if you will only think me worth loving a little."

His [3]speech was the softest murmur, and the dark beautiful face,

---

1 my Tito] *1 2 3* Tito mio *MS CM*   2 you {by way of preliminary,} *MS*
3 {Latin} translation *MS*   4 {Pope} Nicholas *MS*
5 whence] *3C* so that *MS CM 1 2*   6 ⟨wish to⟩ would *MS*
7 ⟨the history of⟩ Thucydides *MS*   8 Valla{'s text} *MS*
9 My Romola] *1 2 3* Romola mia *MS CM*   1 her hastily] her ⟨hastily⟩ *MS*
2 ⟨steps⟩ books *MS*   3 ⟨voice⟩ speech *MS*

nearer to hers than it had ever been before, was looking at her with beseeching tenderness.

"I do love you," [4]murmured Romola; she looked at him with the same simple majesty as ever, but her voice had never in her life before sunk to that murmur. It seemed to them both[5] that they were looking at each other a long while before[6] her lips moved again; yet it was but a moment till she said, "I know *now*[7] what it is to be happy."

The faces just met, and the dark curls mingled for an instant with the rippling gold. Quick as lightning after that, Tito set[8] his foot on[9] a projecting ledge of the book-shelves and reached down the needful volumes. They were both contented to be silent and separate,[1] for that first blissful experience of mutual consciousness was all the more exquisite for being unperturbed by [2]immediate sensation.

It had been as rapid as the irreversible mingling of waters, for even the eager and jealous Bardo had not become impatient.

"You have the volumes, my Romola?" [3]the old man said, as they came near him again. "And now you will get your pen ready; for, [4]as Tito marks off the scholia we determine on extracting, it will be well for you to copy them without delay—numbering them carefully, mind, to correspond with the numbers in the text which he[5] will write."

Romola always[6] had some task which gave her a share in this joint work. Tito took his stand at the *leggio*, where he both wrote and read, and she placed herself at a table just [7]in front of him, where she was ready to give into her father's hands anything that he might happen to want, or relieve him of a volume that he had done with. They had always been in that position since the work began, yet[8] on this day it seemed new; it [9]was so different now for them to be opposite each other; so different for Tito to take a book from her, as she lifted it from her father's knee. Yet there was no finesse to secure an additional look or touch. Each woman creates in her own likeness the [1]love tokens that are [2]offered to her; and Romola's deep calm happiness encompassed Tito like the rich but quiet evening light which dissipates all unrest.

They had been two hours at their work, and were just desisting because of the fading light, when the door opened and there entered a

4 ⟨said⟩ murmured *MS*   5 both ⟨some time before she spoke again⟩ *MS*
6 before ⟨she spoke⟩ *MS*   7 *now*] now *MS*   8 set] just set *MS*
9 on ⟨the projecting base⟩ *MS*   1 separate, ⟨?speechless⟩ *MS*
2 ⟨any [?mingling] of⟩ immediate *MS*   3 ⟨said⟩ the *MS*
4 ⟨when we have⟩ as Tito marks off the ⟨part ?that⟩ ⟨?position⟩ scholia *MS*
5 numbers in the text which he] *3C* numbers he will put in the text he *MS CM 1 2*
6 always] almost always *MS*   7 ⟨below⟩ in front of *MS*
8 yet ⟨it seemed new this morning⟩ *MS*   9 ⟨seemed⟩ was *MS*
1 ⟨love that is⟩ love tokens that are *MS*   2 ⟨made⟩ offered *MS*

figure strangely incongruous with the current of their thoughts and
with the suggestions of every object around them. It was the figure of
a short stout black-eyed woman, about[3] fifty, wearing a black velvet
berretta, or close cap, embroidered with pearls, under[4] which surprisingly massive black braids surmounted the little bulging forehead, and
fell in rich plaited curves over the ears, while an equally surprising
carmine tint on the upper region of the fat cheeks contrasted with the
surrounding sallowness. Three rows of pearls and a lower necklace of
gold reposed on the horizontal cushion[5] of her neck; the embroidered
border of her trailing black velvet gown and her embroidered long-
drooping sleeves of rose-coloured damask were[6] slightly faded, but
they conveyed[7] to the initiated eye the satisfactory assurance that they
were the splendid result of six months' labour by a skilled workman;
and the rose-coloured petticoat, with its dimmed white[8] fringe and
seed-pearl arabesques, was duly exhibited in order to suggest a similar
pleasing reflection. A handsome coral rosary hung from one side of an
inferential belt, which emerged into certainty with a large clasp of silver wrought in *niello*;* and, on the other side, where the belt again
became inferential, hung a scarsella, or large purse of crimson velvet,
stitched with pearls. Her little fat right hand, which looked as if it
had been made of paste, and had risen out of shape under partial bak-
ing, held a small book of devotions, also splendid with velvet, pearls,
and silver.

The figure was already too familiar to Tito to be startling, for
Monna Brigida was a frequent visitor at Bardo's, being excepted from
the sentence of banishment passed on feminine triviality, on the
ground of her cousinship to his dead wife and her early care for
Romola, who now looked[9] round at her with an affectionate smile,
and rose to draw the leather seat to a due distance from her father's
chair, that the coming gush of talk might not be too near his ear.

"*La cugina?*" said Bardo, interrogatively, detecting the short steps
and the sweeping drapery.

"Yes, it is your cousin[1]," said Monna Brigida, in an alert voice,
raising[2] her fingers smilingly at Tito, and then lifting up her face to
be kissed by Romola. "Always the troublesome cousin[3] [4]breaking in
on your wisdom," she [5]went on, seating herself and beginning to fan
herself with the white veil hanging over her arm.[6] "Well, well; if I
didn't bring you some news of the world now and then, I do believe

---

3 about] *1 2 3* nearly *MS CM*   4 under] from under *MS*
5 {horizontal} cushion *MS*   6 damask were] *MS* damask, were *CM 1 2 3*
7 {were slightly faded, but they} conveyed *MS*   8 {dimmed} white *MS*
9 {now} looked *MS*   1 your cousin] the cugina *MS*
2 {in an alert voice}, raising *MS*   3 cousin] *1 2 3 cugina MS CM*
4 ⟨coming⟩ breaking *MS*   5 ⟨added⟩ went on *MS*
6 beginning to fan . . . arm.] beginning to use her veil as a fan. *MS*

you'd forget there was anything in life but these mouldy ancients, who want sprinkling with holy water if all I hear about them is true. Not but what the world is bad enough nowadays, for the scandals that turn up under one's nose at every corner—*I* don't want to [7]hear and see such things, but one can't go about with one's head in a bag; and it was only yesterday—well, well, you needn't burst out at me, Bardo, I'm not going to tell anything; if I'm not as wise as the three kings, I know how many legs go into one boot.* But, nevertheless, Florence is a wicked [8]city—is it not true, Messer Tito? for you go into the world. Not but what one must sin a little—Messer Domeneddio expects that of us, else what are the blessed sacraments for? And what I say is, we've got to reverence the saints, and not to set ourselves up as if we could be like them, else life would be unbearable; as it will be if things go on after this new fashion. For what do you think? I've been at the wedding to-day*—Dianora Acciajoli's with the young Albizzi that there has been so much talk of—and everybody wondered at its being to-day instead of yesterday; but, *cieli!* such a wedding as it was might have been put off till the next Quaresima for a penance. [9]For there was the bride looking like a white nun—not so much as a pearl about her—and the bridegroom as solemn as [1]San Giuseppe.* It's true![2] And half the people invited were Piagnoni—they call them Piagnoni* now, these new saints of Fra Girolamo's making. And to think of two families like the Albizzi and the Acciajoli taking up such notions, when they could afford to wear the best! Well, well, they invited me—but they could do no other, seeing my husband was Luca Antonio's uncle by the mother's side—and[3] a pretty time I had of it while we waited under the canopy in front of the [4]house, before they let us in. I couldn't stand in my clothes, it seemed, without giving offence; for there was Monna Berta, who has had worse secrets in her time than any I could tell of myself, looking askance at me from under her hood like a Pinzochera,* and telling me to read the Frate's book about widows,* from which she had found great guidance. Holy Madonna! it seems as if widows had nothing to do now but to buy their coffins, and think it a thousand years till they get into them, instead of enjoying themselves a little when they've got their hands free for the first time. And what do you think was the music we had to make [5]our dinner lively? A long discourse from Fra Domenico of San Marco, about the doctrines of their blessed Fra Girolamo—the three doctrines* we are all to get by heart;

7 ⟨know⟩ hear and see *MS*   8 ⟨place⟩ city *MS*
9 ⟨It seemed to me a thousand years till I got away⟩ For *MS*
1 ⟨St. Joseph⟩ San Giuseppe *MS*   2 It's true! ⟨what I tell you⟩ *MS*
3 making—{And to think . . . side}—and *MS*
4 ⟨Casa Albizzi for the bride to come⟩ house *MS*   5 ⟨us⟩ our dinner *MS*

and he kept marking them off on his fingers till he made my flesh
creep: and the first is, Florence, or the Church—I don't know which,
for first he said one and then the other[6]—shall be scourged; but if he
means the pestilence, the Signory ought to put a stop to such preaching, for it's enough to raise the swelling under one's arms with fright;
but then, after that, he says Florence is to be regenerated; but what
will be the good of that when we're all dead of the plague, or something else? And then, the third thing, and what he said oftenest, is,
that it's all to be in our days: and he marked that off on his thumb,
till he made me tremble like the very jelly before me. They had jellies,
to be sure, with the arms of the Albizzi and the Acciajoli raised on
them in all colours; they've not turned the world quite upside down
yet. But all their talk is, that we are to go back to the old ways: for up
starts Francesco Valori, that I've danced with in the Via Larga when
he was a bachelor and as fond of the Medici* as anybody, and he
makes a speech about the old times, before the Florentines had left off
crying 'Popolo' and begun to cry 'Palle'—as if that had[7] anything to
do with a wedding!—and how we ought to keep to the rules the
Signory laid down heavens knows when, that we were not to wear this
and that, and not to eat this and that—and how our manners were
corrupted and we read bad books; though he can't say that of *me*—"

"Stop, cousin[8]!" said Bardo, in his imperious tone, for he had a
remark to make, and [9]only desperate measures could arrest the rattling lengthiness of Monna Brigida's discourse. But now she gave a
little start, pursed up her mouth and looked at him with round eyes.

"Francesco Valori is not altogether wrong," Bardo went on.[1]
"Bernardo, indeed, rates him not highly, and is rather of opinion
that[2] he christens private grudges by the name of public zeal; though
I must admit that my good Bernardo is too slow of belief in that
unalloyed patriotism which was found in all its lustre among[3] the
ancients.[4] But it is true, Tito, that our manners have degenerated
somewhat from that noble frugality which, as has been well seen in
the public acts of our citizens, is the parent of true magnificence. For
men, as I hear, will now spend on the transient show of a *giostra**
sums which would suffice to found a library, and confer a lasting possession on mankind. Still, I conceive, it remains true of us Florentines
that we have more of that magnanimous sobriety which abhors a trivial lavishness that it may be grandly open-handed on grand occasions,
than can be found in any other city of Italy; for[5] I understand that

6 Florence {or the Church . . . other} *MS*   7 had] *MS CM 1 3P* has 2
8 cousin] *1 2 3 cugina MS CM*   9 ⟨none but⟩ only *MS*
1 went on "⟨though⟩ Bernardo {indeed} rates *MS*
2 that ⟨his new-born zeal is fed by private grudges⟩ *MS*
3 among] amongst *1 2 3*   4 zeal, {though I . . . ancients.} *MS*
5 occasions {than can be found in any other city of Italy}. For *MS*

the [6]Neapolitan and Milanese courtiers laugh at the scarcity of our plate, and think scorn of our great families for borrowing from each other that furniture of the table* at their entertainments. But in the vain laughter of folly wisdom hears half its applause."

"Laughter, indeed!" burst forth Monna Brigida again, the moment Bardo paused. "If anybody wanted to hear laughter at the wedding to-day they were disappointed, for when young Niccolò Macchiavelli tried to make a joke, and told stories out of Franco Sacchetti's book,* how it was no use for the Signoria to make rules for us women, because we were cleverer than all the painters, and architects, and doctors of logic in the world, for we could make black look white, and yellow look pink, and crooked look straight, and, if anything was forbidden, we could find a new name for it—Holy Virgin! the Piagnoni looked more dismal than before, and somebody said Sacchetti's book was wicked. Well, I don't read it—they can't accuse *me* of reading anything. Save me from going to a wedding[7] again, if[8] that's to be the fashion; for all[9] of us who were not Piagnoni were as comfortable as wet chickens[1]. I was never caught in a worse trap but once before, and that was when I went to hear their precious Frate last Quaresima [2]in San Lorenzo.* Perhaps I never told you about it, Messer Tito?— [3]it almost freezes my blood when I think of it. How he rated us poor women! and the men, too, to tell the truth, but I didn't mind that so much. He called us cows, and lumps of flesh, and wantons, and mischief-makers—and I[4] could just bear that, for there were plenty others more[5] fleshy and spiteful than I was—though every now and then his voice shook the very bench under me like a trumpet; but then he came to the false hair[6], and, O misericordia! he made a picture—I see it now—of a young woman[7] lying a pale corpse, and us light-minded widows—of course he meant me as well as the rest, for I had my plaits on, for if one is getting old, one doesn't want to look as ugly as the Befana,*—us[8] widows rushing up to the corpse, like bare-pated vultures as we were, and cutting off its young dead hair to deck our old heads with. Oh, the dreams I had after that! And then he cried, and wrung his hands at us, and I cried too. And[9] [1]to go home, and to take off my jewels, this very clasp, and everything, and to

---

6 ⟨Roman⟩ Neapolitan *MS*   7 a wedding] *Nozze MS*
8 again, if] *3P* again if *MS CM 1 2*   9 fashion; for all] fashion: all *MS*
1 wet chickens] wet ⟨fowls⟩ chickens (*ci stava bene come a pulcini bagnati*) *MS**
2 ⟨at⟩ in *MS*   3 ⟨Cieli!⟩ It *MS*   4 and I] ⟨well⟩ *ebbene* I *MS*
5 plenty others more] plenty ⟨worse⟩ more *MS*
6 false hair] *1 2 3 capelli morti* (dead, *i.e.* false hair) *MS CM*
7 {young} woman *MS*   8 us] *ebbene,* us *MS*
9 too. And] *1 2 3* too—*piagnoni!* indeed, they may well be *piagnoni*—and *MS* too (*piagnoni,* indeed! they may well be *piagnoni*). And *CM*
1 ⟨I went home and took⟩ to go home *MS*

make them into a packet, *fù²* *tutt'uno*; and I was within a hair of sending them to the good men of St. Martin* to give to the poor, but, by heaven's mercy, I bethought me of going first to my confessor, Fra Cristoforo, at ³Santa Croce,* and he told me how it was all the work of the devil, this preaching and prophesying of their Fra Girolamo, and the Dominicans were trying to turn the world upside down, and I was never to go and hear him again, else I must do penance for it; for the great preachers⁴ Fra Mariano and Fra Menico* had⁵ shown how Fra Girolamo preached lies—and that was true, for I heard them both in the Duomo—and how the Pope's dream* of San Francesco propping up the Church with his arms was being fulfilled still, and the Dominicans were beginning to pull it down. Well and good⁶: I went ⁷away *con Dio*, and made myself easy. I am not going to be frightened by a Frate Predicatore again. And all I say is, I wish it hadn't been the Dominicans that poor Dino joined years ago, for then I should have been glad ⁸when I heard them say he was come back—"

"Silenzio!" said Bardo, in a loud agitated voice, while Romola half started from her chair, clasped her hands, and looked round at Tito, as if now⁹ she might appeal to him. Monna Brigida gave a little scream, and bit her lip.

"Donna!" said Bardo, again, "hear once more my will. Bring no reports about that name to this house; and thou, Romola, I forbid thee to ask. My son is dead."

Bardo's whole frame seemed vibrating with passion, and no one dared to break silence again. Monna Brigida lifted her shoulders and her hands in mute dismay;¹ then she rose as quietly as possible, gave many significant nods to Tito and Romola, motioning to them that they were not to move, and stole out of the room like a culpable fat spaniel who has barked unseasonably.

Meanwhile, Tito's quick mind had been combining ideas with lightning-like rapidity. Bardo's son was not really dead, then, as he had supposed: he was a monk; he was "come back:" and Fra Luca— yes! it was the likeness to Bardo and Romola that had made² the face seem half-known to him. If he were only dead at Fiesole at that moment! This importunate selfish wish inevitably thrust itself before every other thought. It was true that Bardo's rigid will was a sufficient safeguard against any intercourse between Romola and her brother; but *not* against the betrayal of what he knew to others, espe-

2 *fù*] fu *MS*   3 ⟨San Miniato⟩ Santa Croce *MS*
4 preachers] preachers of the Frati Minori *MS*
5 Fra Menico had] *MS 2 3* Fra Menico, had *CM 1*
6 Well and good] *Va bene MS*   7 ⟨home and⟩ away *con Dio* and *MS*
8 ⟨to hear⟩ when I heard *MS*   9 now] *MS 1 2 3* now *CM*
1 dismay; ⟨and jerking⟩ ⟨rising⟩ *MS*   2 {had} made *MS*

cially when the subject was suggested by the coupling of Romola's name with that of the[3] very Tito Melema whose description he had carried round his neck as an index. No! nothing but Fra Luca's death could remove all danger; but [4]his death was highly probable, and after the momentary shock of the discovery, Tito let his mind fall back in repose on that confident hope.

They had sat in silence, and in a deepening twilight for many minutes, when Romola ventured to say—

"Shall I light the lamp, father, and shall we go on?"[5]

"No, my Romola, we will work no more to-night. Tito, come and sit by me here."

Tito moved from the reading-desk and seated himself on the other side of Bardo, close to his left elbow.

"Come nearer to me, *figliuola mia*," said Bardo again, after a moment's pause. And Romola seated herself on a low stool and let her arm rest on her father's right knee, that he might lay his hand on her hair, as he was fond of doing.

"Tito, I never told you that I had once a son," said Bardo, forgetting what had fallen from him in the emotion raised by their first interview. The old man had been deeply shaken and was forced to pour out his feelings in spite of pride. "But he left me—he is dead to me—I have disowned him for ever. He was a ready scholar, [6]as you are, but more fervid and impatient, and yet sometimes rapt and self-absorbed, like a flame fed by some fitful source; showing a disposition from the very first to turn away his eyes from the clear lights of reason and philosophy, and to prostrate himself under the influences of a dim mysticism which eludes all rules of human duty as it eludes all argument. And so it ended. We will speak no more of him: he is dead to me. I wish his face could be blotted from that world of memory in which the distant seems to grow clearer and the near to fade."

Bardo paused, but neither Romola nor Tito dared to speak—his voice was too tremulous, the poise of his feelings too doubtful. But he presently raised his hand and found Tito's shoulder to rest it on, while he went on speaking with an effort to be calmer.

"But *you* have come to me, Tito—not quite too late. I will lose no more time[7] in vain regret. When you are working by my side I seem to have a son again."

The old man, preoccupied with the governing interest of his life, was only thinking of the much-meditated book which had quite thrust into the background the suggestion, raised by Bernardo del Nero's warning, of a possible marriage between Tito and Romola. But Tito could not allow the moment to pass unused.

3 that of the] that *MS*   4 ⟨that⟩ his *MS*   5 on? ⟨Or are you too tired?⟩" *MS*
6 ⟨like you⟩ as you are *MS*   7 no more time] no time *1 2 3*

"Will you let me be always and altogether your son? Will you let me take care of Romola—be her husband? I think she will not deny me[8]. She has said she loves me. I know I am not equal to her in birth—in anything; but I am no longer a destitute stranger."

"Is it true, my Romola?" said Bardo, in a lower tone, an evident [9]vibration passing through him[1] and dissipating the saddened aspect of his features.

"Yes, father," said Romola, firmly. "I love Tito—I wish to marry him, that we may be both[2] your children and never part."

[3]Tito's hand met hers in a strong clasp for the first time, while [4]she was speaking, but their eyes were fixed anxiously on [5]her father.

"Why should it not be?" [6]said Bardo, as if arguing against any opposition to his assent, rather than assenting. "It would be a happiness to me; and thou, too, Romola, wouldst be the happier for it."

He stroked her long hair gently and bent towards her.

"Ah, I have been apt to forget that thou needest some other love than mine. And thou wilt be a noble wife. Bernardo thinks I shall hardly find a husband fitting for thee. And he is perhaps right. For thou art not like the herd of thy sex: thou art such a woman as the immortal poets had a vision of, when they sang the lives of the heroes—tender but strong, like thy voice, which has been to me instead of the light in the years of my blindness. . . . And so thou lovest him?"

He sat upright again for a minute and then said, in the same tone as before, "Why should it not be? I will think of it; I will talk with Bernardo."

Tito felt a disagreeable[7] chill at this answer, for Bernardo del Nero's eyes had retained their keen suspicion whenever they looked at him, and the uneasy remembrance of Fra Luca [8]converted all uncertainty into fear.

"Speak for me, Romola," he said, pleadingly. "Messer Bernardo is sure to be against me."

"No, Tito," said Romola, "my godfather will not oppose what my father firmly wills. And it is your will that I should marry Tito—is it not true, father? Nothing has ever come to me before that I have wished for strongly: I did not think it possible that I could care so much for anything that could happen to myself."

---

8 me ⟨that happiness⟩: she *MS*   9 ⟨thrill⟩ vibration *MS*
1 through him] through him {like a new stimulus} *MS*
2 we may be both] we may both be *1 2 3*
3 ⟨The young hands met in⟩ Tito's *MS*   4 ⟨Romola⟩ she *MS*
5 ⟨Bardo⟩ her father *MS*   6 ⟨he said⟩ said Bardo *MS*
7 disagreeable] unpleasant *MS*
8 ⟨infected all uncertainty with fear⟩ converted *MS*

It was a brief and simple[9] plea; but it was the condensed [1]story of Romola's self-repressing colourless young life, which had thrown all its passion into sympathy with aged sorrows[2], aged ambition, aged pride[3] and indignation. It had never occurred to Romola that she should not speak as directly and emphatically [4]of her love for Tito as of any other subject.

"[5]*Romola mia!*" said her father fondly, pausing on the words, "it is true thou hast never urged on me any wishes of thy own. And I have no will to resist thine; rather, my heart met Tito's entreaty at its very first utterance. Nevertheless, I must talk with Berenardo about the measures needful to be observed. For we must not act in haste, or do anything unbeseeming my name. I am poor, and held of little acount by the wealthy of our family—nay, I may consider myself a lonely man—but I must nevertheless remember that generous birth has its obligations. And I would not be reproached by my fellow-citizens for rash haste in bestowing my daughter. Bartolommeo Scala gave his Alessandra to the Greek Marullo, but Marullo's lineage was well known, and Scala himself is of no extraction. I know Bernardo will hold that we must take time: he will, perhaps, reproach me with want of due forethought.[6] Be patient, my children: you are very young."

No more could be said, and Romola's heart was perfectly satisfied. Not so Tito's. If the subtle mixture of good and evil prepares suffering for human truth and purity, there is also suffering prepared for the wrong-doer[7] by the same mingled conditions. As Tito kissed Romola on their parting that evening, the very strength of the thrill that moved his whole being at the sense that this woman, whose [8]beauty it was hardly possible to think of as anything but the necessary consequence of her noble nature, loved him with all the tenderness that spoke in her clear eyes, brought a strong reaction of [9]regret that he had not kept himself free from that first deceit which had dragged him into this[1] danger of being disgraced before her. There was[2] a spring of bitterness mingling with that fountain of sweets. Would the death of Fra Luca arrest it? He hoped it would.

9 {brief and} simple *MS*   1 ⟨expression⟩ story *MS*
2 {sympathy with} aged sorrows *MS*   3 {aged} pride *MS*
4 ⟨on this subject⟩ of *MS*   5 ⟨My Romola⟩ Romola mia *MS*
6 time: {he will . . . forethought.} *MS*

7 If the subtle . . . wrong-doer] If ⟨there is one tragedy prepared⟩ the subtle mixture of good and evil prepares suffering for human {truth and} purity ⟨and goodness⟩ by the young outflow of its affections towards the unworthy, there is also ⟨a tragedy⟩ suffering prepared for ⟨vice⟩ ⟨wrong-doing⟩ the wrong-doer *MS*

8 ⟨physical⟩ beauty *MS*   9 ⟨bitter⟩ regret *MS*   1 this] the *1 2 3*
2 there was ⟨bitterness in⟩ *MS*

CHAPTER XIII.

THE SHADOW OF NEMESIS

IT was the lazy afternoon time on the seventh of September, more than two months after the day on which Romola and Tito had confessed their love to each other.

Tito[1], just descended into Nello's shop, had found the barber stretched on the bench with his cap over his eyes: one leg was drawn up, and the other had slipped towards the ground, having apparently carried with it a manuscript volume of verse, which lay with its leaves crushed. In a corner sat Sandro, playing a game at *mora** by himself, and watching the slow reply of his left fingers to the arithmetical demands of his right with solemn-eyed interest.

Treading with the [2]gentlest step, Tito snatched up[3] the lute, and bending over the barber, touched the strings lightly while he sang,—

> "Quant' è bella giovinezza,
> Che si fugge tuttavia!
> Chi vuol esser lieto sia,
> Di doman non c'è certezza."*

Nello was as easily awaked as a bird. The cap was off his eyes in an instant, and he started up.

"Ah, my Apollino! I am somewhat late with my siesta on this hot day, it seems. That comes of not going to sleep in the natural way, but taking a potion of potent poesy. Hear you, how I am beginning to match my words by the initial letter, like a *trovatore?** That is one of my bad symptoms: I am sorely afraid that the good wine of my understanding is going to run off at the spigot of authorship, and I shall be left an empty cask with an odour of dregs, like many another incomparable genius of my acquaintance. What is it, my Orpheus?" here Nello stretched out his arms to their full length, and then brought them round till his hands grasped Tito's curls, and drew them out playfully. "What is it you want of your well-tamed Nello? For I perceive a coaxing sound in that soft strain of yours. Let me see the very needle's eye of your desire, as the sublime poet says,[4]* that I may thread it."

"That is but a tailor's image of your sublime poet's," said Tito, still letting his fingers fall in a light dropping way on the strings. "But you have divined the reason of my affectionate impatience to see

1 Tito ⟨had⟩ just descended into Nello's shop, ⟨where⟩ had *MS*
2 ⟨lightest⟩ gentlest *MS*   3 snatched {up} *MS*
4 desire, {as the sublime poet says,} *MS*

your eyes open. I want you to give me an extra touch of your art—not on my chin, no; but on the *zazzera*, which is as tangled as your Florentine politics. You have an adroit way of inserting your comb, which flatters the skin, and stirs the animal spirits agreeably in that region; and a little of your most delicate orange scent would not be amiss, for I am bound to the Scala palace, and am to present myself in radiant company. The young Cardinal Giovanni de' Medici is to be there, and he brings with him a certain young Bernardo Dovizi of Bibbiena,* whose wit is so rapid, that I see no way of outrivalling it save by the scent of orange-blossoms."

Nello had already seized and flourished his comb, and pushed Tito gently backward into the chair, wrapping the cloth round him.

"Never talk of rivalry, *bel giovane mio*: Bernardo Dovizi is a keen youngster, who will never carry a net out to catch the wind;* but he has something of the same sharp-muzzled look as his brother [5]Ser Piero[6],* the weasel that Piero de' Medici keeps at his beck to slip through small holes for him. No! you distance all rivals, and may soon touch the sky with your forefinger.* They tell me you have even carried enough honey with you to sweeten the sour Messer Angelo; for he has pronounced you less of an ass than might have been expected[7], considering there is such a good understanding between you and the secretary."

"And between ourselves, *Nello mio*, that Messer[8] Angelo has more genius and erudition than I can find in all the other Florentine scholars put together. It may answer very well for them to cry me up now, when Poliziano is beaten down with grief, or illness, or something else;* I can try a flight with such a sparrow-hawk as Pietro Crinito, but for Poliziano, he is a large-beaked eagle who would swallow me, feathers and all, and not feel any difference."

"I will not contradict your modesty there, if you will have it so[9]; but you don't expect us clever Florentines to keep saying the same things over again every day of our lives, as we must do if we always told the truth. We cry down Dante, and we cry up Francesco Cei, just for the sake of variety; and if we cry you up as a new Poliziano, heaven has taken care that it shall not be quite so great a lie as it might have been. And are you not a pattern of virtue in this wicked city? with your ears double-waxed* against all siren invitations that would lure you from the Via de' Bardi, and the great work which is to astonish posterity?"

"Posterity in good truth[1], whom it will probably astonish as the

5 his brother Ser Piero ⟨da Bibbiena whom⟩ *MS*
6 Ser Piero] *MS 1 2 3* Ser Piero da Bibbiena *CM*   7 expected ⟨from⟩ *MS*
8 that Messer] that same Messer *MS*   9 there {if you will have it so} *MS*
1 truth {if it {ever} astonishes anybody⟩ *MS*

universe does, by the impossibility of seeing what was the plan of it."

"Yes, something like that was being prophesied here the other day. Cristoforo Landino said that the excellent Bardo was one of those scholars who lie overthrown in their learning, like cavaliers in heavy armour,* and then get angry because they are over-ridden—which pithy remark, [2]it seems to me, was not a herb out of his own garden; for of all men, for feeding one with an empty spoon* and gagging one with vain expectation by long discourse, Messer Cristoforo is the pearl. Ecco! you are perfect now." Here Nello drew away the cloth. "Impossible to add a grace more![3] But love is not always to be fed on learning, eh? I shall have to dress the *zazzera* for the betrothal before long—is it not true?"

"Perhaps," said Tito, smiling, "unless Messer Bernardo should next recommend Bardo to require that I should yoke a lion and a wild boar to the car of the Zecca before I can win my Alcestis.* But[4] I confess he is right in holding me unworthy of Romola; she is a Pleiad that may grow dim by marrying any mortal."*

"*Gnaffè*, your modesty is in the right place there. Yet Fate seems to have measured and chiselled you for the niche that was left empty by the old man's son, who, by the way, Cronaca was telling me, is now at San Marco. Did you know?"

A slight electric shock passed through Tito as he rose from the chair, but it was not outwardly perceptible, for he immediately stooped to pick up the fallen book, and busied his fingers with flattening the leaves, while he said,

"No: he was at Fiesole, I thought. Are you sure he is come back to San Marco?"

"Cronaca is my authority," said Nello, with a shrug. "I don't frequent that sanctuary, but he does. Ah," he added, taking the book from Tito's hands,[5] "my poor Nencia da Barberino! It jars your scholarly feelings to see the pages dog's-eared. I was lulled to sleep by the well-rhymed charms of that rustic maiden—'prettier than the turnip-flower,' 'with a cheek more savoury than cheese.'* But to get such a well-scented notion of the contadina, one must lie on velvet cushions in the Via Larga—not go to look at the Fierucoloni stumping in to the Piazza della Nunziata this evening after sundown[6]."

"And pray who are the Fierucoloni?" said Tito, indifferently, settling his cap[7].

"The contadine who come[8] from the mountains of Pistoia,* and the

2 ⟨I fancy⟩ it seems to me *MS*   3 pearl. {Ecco! you are . . . more} *MS*
4 Alcestis. But] *1 2 3* Alcestis; though *MS CM*
5 Ah", {he added . . . hands} *MS*   6 {evening after} sundown *MS*
7 {indifferently} settling his cap ⟨with a careless air⟩ *MS*   8 come] came *2 3*

Casentino, and heaven knows where, to keep their vigil in the church of the Nunziata and sell their yarn and dried mushrooms at the Fierucola*, as[9] we call it. They make a queer show, with their paper lanterns, howling their hymns to the Virgin on this eve of her nativity—if you had the leisure to see them. No?—well, I have had enough of it myself, for there is wild work in the Piazza. One may happen to get a stone or two about one's ears or shins without asking for it, and I was never fond of that pressing attention. Addio."

Tito carried a little uneasiness with him on his [1]visit, which ended earlier than he had expected, the boy-cardinal[2] Giovanni de' Medici, youngest of red-hatted Fathers, who has since presented his broad dark cheek very conspicuously to posterity as Pope Leo the Tenth,* having been detained at his favourite pastime of the chase, and having failed to appear. It still wanted half an hour of sunset as he left the door of the Scala palace, with the intention of proceeding forthwith to the Via de' Bardi; but he had not gone far when, to his astonishment, he saw Romola advancing towards him along the Borgo Pinti.

She wore a thick black veil and black mantle, but it was impossible to mistake her figure and her walk; and by her side was a short stout form which he recognized as that of Monna Brigida, in spite of the unusual plainness of her attire. Romola had not been bred up to devotional observances, and the occasions on which she took the air elsewhere than under the loggia on the roof of the house, were so rare and so much dwelt on beforehand, because of Bardo's dislike to be left without her, that Tito felt sure there must have been some sudden and urgent ground for an absence of which he had heard nothing the day before. She saw him through her veil and hastened her steps.

"Romola, has anything happened?" said Tito, turning to walk by her side.

She did not answer at the first moment, and Monna Brigida broke in.

"Ah, Messer Tito, you do well to turn round, for we are in haste. And is it not a misfortune?—we are obliged to go round by the walls and turn up the Via del Maglio,* because of the Fair[3]; for the contadine coming in block up the way by the Nunziata, which would have taken us to San Marco in half the time."

Tito's heart gave a great bound, and began to beat violently.

"Romola," he said, in a lower tone, "are you going to San Marco?"

They were now out of the Borgo Pinti and were under the city walls, where they had wide gardens on their left hand, and all was

9 Fierucola, as] *3P* Fierucola (petty fair), as *MS CM 1 2*
1 ⟨way to⟩ visit *MS*   2 boy-cardinal] young Cardinal *MS*
3 Fair] *1 2 3* Fiera *MS CM*

quiet. Romola put aside her veil for the sake of breathing the air, and he could see the subdued agitation in her face.

"Yes, *Tito mio*," she said, looking directly at him with sad eyes. "For the first time I am doing something unknown to my father. It comforts me that I have met you, for at least I can tell *you*. But if you are going to him, it will be well for you not to say that you met me. He thinks I am only gone to my cousin[4], because she sent for me. I left my godfather with him: *he* knows where I am going, and why. You remember that evening when my brother's name was mentioned and my father spoke of him to you?"

"Yes," said Tito, in a low tone. There was a strange complication in his mental state. His heart sank at the probability that a great change was coming over his prospects, while at the same time his thoughts were darting over a hundred details of the course he would take when the change had come,—and yet he returned Romola's gaze with a hungry sense that it might be the last time she would ever bend it on him with full unquestioning confidence.

"The *cugina* had heard that he was come back, and the evening before—the evening of San Giovanni—as I afterwards found, he had been seen by our good Maso near the door of our house; but when Maso went to inquire at San Marco, Dino, that is, my brother—he was christened[5] Bernardino, after our godfather, but now he calls himself Fra Luca—had[6] been taken to the monastery at Fiesole, because he was ill. But this morning a message came to Maso, saying that he was come back to San Marco, and Maso [7]went to him there. He is very ill, and he has adjured me to go and see him. I cannot refuse it, though I hold him guilty: I still remember how I loved him when I was a little girl, before I knew that he would forsake my father. And perhaps he has some word of penitence to send by me. It cost me a struggle to act in opposition to my father's feeling, which I have always [8]held to be just. I am almost sure you will think I have chosen rightly, Tito, because I have noticed that your nature is less rigid than mine, and nothing makes you angry[9]: it would cost you less to be forgiving; though, if you had seen your father forsaken by one to whom he had given his chief love—by one in whom he had planted his labour and his hopes—forsaken when his need was becoming greatest—even you, Tito, would find it hard to [1]forgive."

What could he say? He was not equal to the hypocrisy of telling

4 my cousin] *3P* the *cugina MS CM* the cugina *1 2*

5 had been seen . . . christened] had been to the door of our house and desired our good Maso to visit him at San Marco; but when Maso went, Dino—that is, my brother: he was ⟨called⟩ christened *MS*

6 had] he had *MS*   7 ⟨has been⟩ went *MS*   8 ⟨felt⟩ held *MS*

9 mine {and nothing makes you angry} *MS*

1 ⟨stretch out your hand⟩ ⟨pardon⟩ forgive *MS*

Romola that such offences ought not to be pardoned; and[2] he had not the courage to utter any words of dissuasion.

"You are right, my Romola; you are always right, except in thinking too well of me."

There was really some genuineness in those last words, and Tito looked very beautiful as he uttered them, with an unusual pallor in his face, and a slight quivering of his lip. Romola, interpreting all things largely, like a mind prepossessed with high beliefs, had a tearful brightness in her eyes as she looked at him, touched with keen joy that he felt so strongly whatever she felt. But without pausing in her walk, she[3] said—

"And now, Tito, I wish you to leave me, for the *cugina*[4] and I shall be less noticed[5] if we enter the piazza alone."

"Yes, it were better you should leave us," said Monna Brigida; "for to say the truth, Messer Tito, all eyes follow you, and let Romola muffle herself as she will, every one wants to see what there is under her veil, for she has that way of walking, like[6] a procession. Not that I find fault with her for it, only it doesn't suit my steps. And, indeed, I would rather not have us seen going to San Marco, and that's why I am dressed as if I were one of the Piagnoni themselves, and as old as Sant' Anna;* for if it had been [7]anybody but poor Dino, who ought to be forgiven if he's dying, for what's the use of having a grudge against dead people?—make them feel while they live, say I—"

[8]No one made a scruple of interrupting Monna [9]Brigida, and Tito, [1]having raised Romola's hand to his lips, and said, "I understand, I obey you," [2]now turned away, lifting his cap—a sign of reverence rarely[3] made* at that time by native Florentines, and which excited Bernardo del Nero's contempt for Tito as a fawning Greek, while to Romola, who loved homage[4], it gave him an exceptional grace.

He was [5]half glad of the dismissal, half disposed to cling to Romola to the last moment in which she would love him without suspicion. For it seemed to him certain that this brother would before all things want to know, and that Romola would before all things confide to him, what was her father's position and her own after the years which must have brought so much change. She would tell him that she was

---

2 and ⟨that she ought not to⟩ *MS*   3 she ⟨put out her hand to him⟩ *MS*

4 *cugina*] *3P* cugina *MS CM 1 2*

5 less noticed ⟨when we walk alone and I wish not to be seen entering San Marco⟩ *MS*

6 walking, like] *MS* walking like *CM 1 2 3*   7 ⟨anything⟩ anybody *MS*

8 ⟨Tito did not scruple to pause and⟩ No one *MS*   9 Brigida⟨'s speech⟩ *MS*

1 ⟨just lifted⟩ having just raised *MS*

2 ⟨turned and left⟩ ⟨turned and⟩ now turned away *MS*

3 reverence ⟨never⟩ rarely made] *MS 1 2 3* reverence, rarely made *CM*

4 Romola {who loved homage} *MS*   5 ⟨really thankful⟩ half glad *MS*

soon to be publicly betrothed to a young scholar, who was to fill up
the place left vacant long ago by a wandering son. He foresaw the
impulse that would prompt Romola to dwell on that prospect, and
what would follow on the mention of the future husband's name. Fra
Luca would tell all he knew and conjectured, and Tito saw no possible falsity by which he could now ward off the worst consequences
of his former dissimulation. It was all over with his prospects in
Florence. There was Messer Bernardo del Nero, who would be
delighted[6] at seeing confirmed the wisdom of his advice about deferring the betrothal[7] until Tito's character and position had been established by a longer residence; and the history of the young Greek
professor, whose[8] benefactor was in slavery, would be the talk under
every loggia. For the first time in his life he felt too fevered and agitated to trust his power of self-command; he gave up his intended
visit to Bardo, and walked up and down under the walls until the yellow light in the west had quite faded, when, without any distinct purpose, he took[9] the first turning, which happened to be the Via[1] San
Sebastiano,* leading him directly towards the Piazza dell' Annunziata.
He was at one of those [2]lawless moments which come to us all if we
have no guide but desire, and if the[3] pathway where desire leads us
[4]seems suddenly closed; he was ready to follow any beckoning that
offered him an immediate purpose.

---

6 delighted ⟨to find⟩ MS   7 betrothal] espousals MS
8 professor, whose] 3P professor whose MS CM 1 2
9 and {walking up . . . when} without any distinct purpose {, he} took MS
1 Via ⟨dell' Annunziata⟩ San Sebastiano MS
2 ⟨crises⟩ lawless moments MS   3 if the] 3P the MS CM 1 2
4 ⟨is⟩ seems suddenly ⟨hemmed in⟩ closed MS

CHAPTER XIV.

THE PEASANTS' FAIR

THE moving crowd and the strange mixture of noises that burst on him at the entrance of the piazza, reminded Tito of what Nello had said to him about the Fierucoloni, and he pushed his way into the crowd with a sort of pleasure in the hooting and [1]elbowing, that[2] filled the empty moments, and dulled that calculation of the future which had [3]so new a dreariness for him, as he foresaw himself wandering away solitary in[4] pursuit of some unknown fortune[5], that his thought had even glanced towards going in search of Baldassarre after all.

At each of the opposite inlets he saw people struggling into the piazza, while above them paper lanterns, held aloft on sticks, were waving[6] uncertainly to and fro. A rude monotonous chant made a distinctly traceable strand of noise, across which[7] screams, whistles, gibing chants in piping boyish voices, the beating of drums[8], and the ringing of little bells, met each other in confused din. Every now and then one of the dim floating lights disappeared with a smash from a stone launched[9] more or less [1]vaguely in pursuit of mischief, followed by a scream and renewed shouts. But [2]on the outskirts of the whirling tumult there were[3] groups who were keeping this vigil of the Nativity of the Virgin[4] in a more [5]methodical manner than by fitful stone-throwing and gibing. Certain ragged men, darting a hard sharp glance around them while their tongues rattled merrily, were inviting country people to game with them on fair and open-handed terms; two masquerading[6] figures on stilts, who had snatched lanterns from the crowd, were swaying the lights to and fro in meteoric fashion, as they strode hither and thither: a sage trader was doing a profitable

---

1 elbowing ⟨which⟩ ⟨for they⟩ that *MS*
3 ⟨a strange⟩ ⟨such⟩ so new *MS*
5 fortune] fortune for his solitary self *MS*
6 piazza, while above . . . waving] piazza with paper lanterns held aloft on sticks waving *MS*
7 across which ⟨darted⟩ screams, whistles, {gibing chants in piping boyish voices,} *MS*
8 drums] *3C nacchere* or drums *MS CM 1 2*
9 launched] *3P* lanced *MS CM 1 2*

2 that] which *2 3*
4 solitary in] in *MS*

1 ⟨vigorously⟩ vaguely *MS*
2 ⟨amidst⟩ on the outskirts of *MS*
3 were ⟨all round the piazza certain⟩ groups *MS*
4 Nativity of the Virgin] *Natività della Vergine MS*
5 ⟨stationary and⟩ methodical *MS*
6 {two} masquerading *MS*

business, at[7] a small covered stall, in hot *berlingozzi*, a favourite farinaceous delicacy; one man standing on a barrel, with his back firmly
planted against a pillar of the loggia in front of the Foundling
Hospital (Spedale degl' Innocenti)[8], was selling efficacious pills,
invented by a doctor of Salerno, warranted to prevent toothache and
death by drowning; and not far off, against[9] another pillar, a tumbler
was showing off his tricks on a small platform; while a handful
of prentices, despising the slack entertainment of [1]guerilla stone-
throwing, were having a private concentrated match of that favourite
Florentine sport at the narrow entrance of the Via de' Febbrai.*

Tito, obliged to make his way through chance openings in the
crowd, found himself at one moment close to the trotting procession
of bare-footed, hard-heeled contadine, and could see their sun-dried,
bronzed faces, and their strange fragmentary garb, dim with hereditary dirt, and of obsolete stuffs and fashions, that made them look, in
the eyes of the city people, like a way-worn ancestry returning from a
pilgrimage on which they had set out a century ago. Just then it was
the hardy, scant-feeding peasant-women[2] from the mountains of
Pistoia, who were entering with a year's labour in a moderate bundle
of yarn[3] on their backs, and in their hearts that meagre hope of good
and that wide dim fear of harm, which were somehow to be cared for
by the Blessed Virgin, whose [4]miraculous image, painted by the
angels, was to have the curtain drawn away from it on this Eve of her
Nativity, that its potency might stream forth [5]without obstruction.

At another moment he was forced away towards the boundary of
the piazza, where the more stationary[6] candidates for attention and
small coin had judiciously placed themselves, in order to be safe in
their rear. Among these Tito recognized his [7]acquaintance Bratti, who
stood with his back against a pillar and[8] his mouth pursed up in dis-
dainful silence, eying every one who approached him with a cold
glance of superiority, and keeping his hand fast on a serge covering,
which concealed the contents of the basket slung before him. Rather
surprised at [9]a deportment so unusual in an anxious trader, Tito went
nearer and saw two women go up to Bratti's basket with a look of
curiosity, whereupon the pedlar drew the covering tighter, and looked
another way. It was quite too provoking, and[1] one of the women was
fain to ask what there was in his basket?

7 business, at] *MS* business at *CM 1 2 3*
8 Hospital {Spedale degl' Innocenti} *MS*   9 off, against] off him against *MS*
1 ⟨occasional⟩ guerilla *MS*   2 peasant-women] ⟨?mortals⟩ peasants *MS*
3 bundle of yarn *3C* bundle *MS CM 1 2*   4 ⟨dark mysterious⟩ miraculous *MS*
5 ⟨unobstructedly⟩ without obstruction *MS*   6 {more} stationary *MS*
7 ⟨old⟩ acquaintance *MS*   8 and ⟨his basket slung before him with⟩ *MS*
9 ⟨this⟩ a *MS*   1 and ⟨the women were⟩ *MS*

"Before I answer that, Monna, I must know whether you mean to buy. I can't show such wares as mine in this fair for every fly to settle on and pay nothing. My goods are a little too choice for that. Besides, I've only two left, and I've no mind to sell them; for with the chances of the pestilence that wise men talk of, there is likelihood of their being worth their weight in gold. No, no: *andate con Dio.*"

The two women looked at each other.

"And what may be the price?" said the second.

"Not within what you are like[2] to have in your purse, buona donna," said Bratti, in a compassionately supercilious tone. "I recommend you to trust in Messer Domeneddio and the saints: poor people can do no better for themselves."

"Not so poor!" said the second woman, indignantly, drawing out her money-bag. "Come, now! what do you say to a grosso?"

"I say you may get twenty-one quattrini for it," said Bratti, coolly; "but not of me, for I haven't got that small change."

"Come; two, then?" said the woman, getting exasperated, while her companion looked at her with some envy. "It will hardly be above two, I think."

After further bidding, and further mercantile coquetry, Bratti put on an air of concession.

"Since you've set your mind on it," he said, slowly raising the cover, "I should[3] be loath to do you a mischief; for Maestro Gabbadeo* used to say, when a woman sets her mind on a thing and doesn't get it, she's in worse danger of the pestilence[4] than before. Ecco! I have but two left; and let me tell you, the fellow to them is on the finger of Maestro Gabbadeo, who is gone to Bologna—as wise a doctor as sits at any door."

The precious objects were two clumsy iron rings, beaten into the fashion of old Roman rings such as were sometimes disinterred. The rust on them, and the entirely hidden character of their potency, were so satisfactory, that the grossi were paid without grumbling, and the first woman, destitute of those handsome coins, succeeded after much show of reluctance on Bratti's part in driving a bargain with some of her yarn, and carried off the remaining ring in triumph. Bratti covered up his basket, which was now filled with miscellanies, probably [5]obtained under the same sort of circumstances as the yarn, and moving from his pillar, came suddenly upon Tito, who, if he had had time, would have chosen to avoid recognition.

"By the head of San Giovanni, now," said Bratti, drawing Tito

2 like] *MS* likely *CM 1 2 3*

3 "Since you've . . . should] "*Ebbene*," he said, slowly raising the cover, "since you've set your mind on it, I should *MS*

4 pestilence] pest *MS*   5 ⟨collected⟩ obtained *MS*

back to the pillar; "this is a piece of luck. For I was talking of you this morning, Messer Greco; but, I said, he is mounted up among the *signori* now—and I'm glad of it, for I was at the bottom of his fortune—but I can rarely get speech of him, for he's not to be caught lying on the stones now—not he! But it's your luck, not mine, Messer Greco, save and except some small trifle to satisfy me for my trouble in the transaction."

"You speak in riddles, Bratti," said Tito. "Remember, I don't sharpen my wits, as you do, by driving hard bargains for iron rings: you must be plain."

"By the Holy 'Vangels! it was an easy bargain I gave them. If a Hebrew gets thirty-two per cent., I hope a Christian may get a little more. If I had not borne a conscience, I should have got twice the money and twice the yarn. But, talking of rings, it is your ring—that very ring you've got on your finger—that I could get you a purchaser for—ay, and a purchaser with a deep money-bag."

"Truly[6]?" said Tito, looking at his ring, and listening.

"A Genoese who is going straight away into Hungary, as I understand. He came and looked all over my shop to see if I had any old things I didn't know the price of; I warrant you, he thought I had a pumpkin on my shoulders.* He had been rummaging all the shops in Florence. And he had a ring on—not like yours, but something of the same fashion; and as he was talking of rings, I said I knew a fine young man, a[7] particular acquaintance of mine, who had a ring of that sort. And he said, 'Who is he, pray? Tell him I'll give him his price for it.' And I thought of going after you to Nello's tomorrow; for it's my opinion of you, Messer Greco, that you're not one who'd see the Arno run broth, and stand by without dipping your finger."*

Tito had lost no word of what Bratti had said, yet his mind had been very busy all the while. Why should he keep the ring? It had been a mere sentiment, a mere fancy[8], that had prevented him from selling [9]it with the other gems; if he had been wiser and had sold it, he might perhaps have escaped that identification by Fra Luca. It was true that it had been taken from Baldassarre's finger and put on to his[1] as soon as his young hand had grown to the needful size; but there was really no valid good to anybody in those superstitious scruples about inanimate objects. The ring had helped towards the recognition of him. Tito had begun to dislike recognition, which was a claim from the past. This [2]foreigner's offer, if he would really give a

6 Truly] *In vero MS*   7 man, a] *3P* man ⟨of my⟩ who was a *MS CM 1 2*
8 fancy—⟨piety and an unreasoning bias towards⟩ *MS*   9 ⟨the ring⟩ it *MS*
1 on to his] *MS* on his *CM 1 2* on his own *3*
2 ⟨Frenchm[an's]⟩ foreigner's *MS*

good price, was an opportunity for getting rid of the ring without the trouble of seeking a purchaser.

"You speak with your usual wisdom, Bratti," said Tito. "I have no objection to hear what your Genoese will offer. But when and where shall I have speech of him?"

"To-morrow, at three hours after sunrise, he will be at my shop, and if your wits are of that sharpness I have always taken them to be, Messer Greco, you will ask him a heavy price. For he minds not money; it's my belief he's buying for somebody else, and not for himself—perhaps for some great Signor."

"It is well[3]," said Tito. "I will be at your shop, if[4] nothing hinders."

"And you will doubtless deal nobly by me for old acquaintance'[5] sake, Messer Greco, so I will not stay to fix the small sum you will give me in token of my service in the matter[6]. It seems to me a thousand years now till I get out of the piazza, for a fair is a dull, not to say a wicked thing, when one has no more goods to sell."

Tito made a hasty sign of assent and adieu, and moving away from the pillar, again found himself pushed towards the middle of the piazza and back again, without the power of determining his own course. In this zigzag way he was carried along to the end of the piazza opposite the church, where, in a deep recess formed by an irregularity in the line of houses, [7]an entertainment was going forward which seemed to be especially attractive to the crowd. Loud bursts of laughter interrupted a monologue which was sometimes slow and oratorical[8], at others rattling and buffoonish. Here a girl was being pushed forward[9] into the inner circle with apparent reluctance, and there a loud-laughing minx[1] was finding a way with her own elbows. It was a strange light that was spread over the piazza. There were the pale stars breaking out above, and the dim waving lanterns below, leaving all objects indistinct except when they were seen close under the fitfully moving lights; but in this recess there was a stronger light, against which the heads of the encircling spectators stood in dark relief as Tito was [2]gradually pushed towards them, while above them rose the head of a man wearing a [3]white mitre with yellow cabalistic figures upon it.

"Behold, my children!" Tito heard him saying, "behold your

3 It is well] _1 2 3 Sta bene MS CM_   4 shop, if] _MS 1 2 3_ shop if _CM_
5 acquaintance'] acquaintance _MS_   6 matter, ⟨for it seems⟩ _MS_
7 ⟨there seemed to be an entertainment going forward which was⟩ an _MS_
8 {slow and} oratorical _MS_
9 forward ⟨with⟩ _MS_   1 minx ⟨was elbowing a way for herself⟩ _MS_
2 ⟨impelled⟩ gradually pushed towards them ⟨. The light was from tapers burning on an altar-like table raised on a small platform⟩ while _MS_
3 ⟨yellow⟩ white mitre with ⟨black⟩ yellow _MS_

opportunity! neglect not the Holy Sacrament[4] of matrimony when it can be had for the small sum of a white quattrino—the cheapest matrimony ever offered, and dissolved by special bull beforehand at every man's own will and pleasure. Behold the bull!" Here the speaker held up a piece of parchment with huge seals attached to it. "Behold the indulgence granted by his Holiness Alexander the Sixth,[5] who, being newly elected Pope for his peculiar piety,* intends to reform and purify the Church, and wisely begins by abolishing that priestly abuse which keeps too large a share of this privileged matrimony to the clergy and stints the laity. Spit once[6], my sons, and pay a white quattrino! This is the whole and sole price of the indulgence[7]. The quattrino is the only difference the Holy Father allows to be put any longer between us and the clergy—who spit and pay nothing."

Tito thought he knew the voice, which had a peculiarly sharp ring, but the face was too much in shadow from the lights behind for him to be sure of the features. Slipping[8] as near as he could, he saw within the circle behind the speaker an altar-like table raised on a small platform, and covered with a red drapery stitched all over with yellow cabalistical figures. Half-a-dozen thin tapers burned at the back of this table, which had a conjuring apparatus scattered over it, a large open book in the centre, and at one of the front angles a monkey fastened by a cord to a small ring and holding[9] a small taper, which in his incessant fidgety movements[1] fell more or less aslant, while[2] an impish boy in a white surplice occupied himself chiefly in cuffing the monkey, and adjusting the taper. The man in the mitre also wore a surplice, and over it a chasuble on[3] which the signs of the zodiac were rudely marked in black upon a yellow ground. Tito was sure now that he recognized the sharp upward-tending angles of the face under the mitre: it was that of Maestro Vaiano, the mountebank[4], from whom he had rescued Tessa. Pretty little Tessa! Perhaps she too had come in among the troops of contadine?[5]

"Come, my maidens! This is the time for the pretty who can have many chances, and for the ill-favoured who have few. Matrimony to be had—hot[6], eaten, and done with as easily as *berlingozzi!* And see!" here the conjuror held up a cluster of tiny bags. "To every bride I

4 {Holy} Sacrament *MS*   5 Sixth, ⟨whereby he piously abolis[hes]⟩ *MS*
6 once ⟨over your shoulder,⟩ *MS*
7 This is . . . the indulgence] That is . . . this indulgence *MS*
8 Slipping] *MS* Stepping *CM 1 2 3*   9 holding ⟨more or less aslant a small⟩ *MS*
1 {fidgety} movements *MS*   2 while] whilst *2 3*
3 surplice, and over it a chasuble on] surplice with a chasuble over it, on *MS*
4 mountebank] *3C* cerretano *MS CM 1 2*
5 Perhaps she . . . contadine?] ⟨Might not she be⟩ Perhaps she was among the lantern-⟨bearing contadine⟩ bearers? *MS*
6 had—hot] *3C* had {hot} *MS CM 1 2*

The Peasants' Fair

give a *Breve* with a secret in it—the secret alone worth the money
you pay for the matrimony. The secret how to—no, no, I will not tell
you what the secret is about, and that makes it a double secret. Hang
it round your neck if you like, and never look at it; I don't say that
that[7] will not be the best, for then you will see many things you don't
expect: [8]though if you open it (you may break your leg—*è vero*),[9] but
you will know a secret! Something nobody knows but me! And
mark—I give you the *Breve*, I don't sell it, as many another holy man
would: the quattrino is for the matrimony, and the *Breve* you get for
nothing. *Orsù*, [1]*giovanetti*, come like dutiful sons of the Church and
buy the indulgence of his Holiness Alexander the Sixth."

This buffoonery just fitted the taste of the audience: [2]the *fierucola*
was but a small occasion, [3]so the townsmen might be contented with
jokes that were rather less indecent than those they were accustomed
to hear at every carnival, put into easy rhyme by the Magnifico and
his poetic satellites; while the women, over and above any relish of
the fun, really began to have an itch for the *Brevi*. Several couples
had already gone through the ceremony, in which the conjuror's
solemn gibberish[4] and grimaces over the open book, the antics of the
monkey, and even the preliminary spitting, had called[5] forth peals of
laughter; and now a well-looking, merry-eyed youth of seventeen, in a
loose tunic and a red[6] cap, pushed forward, holding by the hand a
plump brunette, whose scanty ragged dress displayed her round arms
and legs very picturesquely.

"Fetter us without delay, maestro!" said the youth, "for I have got
to take my bride home and paint her under the light of a lantern."

"Ha! Mariotto,* my son, I commend your pious observance. . . ."
The conjuror was going on, when a loud chattering behind him[7]
warned him that an unpleasant crisis had arisen with his monkey.

The temper of that imperfect acolyth was a little tried by the over-
active discipline of his colleague in the surplice, and a sudden cuff
administered[8] as his taper fell to a horizontal position, caused him to
leap back with a violence that proved too much for the slackened knot
by which his cord was fastened. His first leap was to the other end of
the table, from which position his remonstrances were so threatening
that the [9]imp in the surplice took up a wand by way of an equivalent

7 say {that} *that*] MS say *that* CM *1 2 3*   8 ⟨but⟩ though MS

9 it (you may break your leg—*è vero*)] it you may break your leg, *è vero 1 2 3*

1 ⟨my⟩ *giovanetti* MS   2 ⟨this⟩ the MS

3 ⟨therefore they⟩ so the townsmen MS

4 gibberish ⟨uttered⟩ and grimaces over the open book, ⟨were hardly a source of
greater amus[ement]⟩ MS

5 {had} called MS   6 a red] red *1 2 3*

7 behind him] MS behind CM *1 2 3*

8 administered ⟨to one of them⟩ MS

9 ⟨younger⟩ imp MS

threat, whereupon the monkey leaped on to the head of a tall woman in the foreground, dropping his taper by the way, and chattering with increased emphasis from that eminence. Great was the screaming and confusion, not a few of the spectators having a vague dread of the maestro's monkey, as capable of more hidden mischief than mere teeth and claws could inflict; and the conjuror himself was in some alarm lest any harm should happen to his familiar. In the scuffle to seize the monkey's string, Tito got out of the circle, and, not caring to contend for his place again, he allowed himself to be gradually pushed towards the church of the Nunziata, and to enter amongst the worshippers.

The brilliant illumination within seemed to press upon his eyes with palpable force after the pale scattered lights and broad shadows of the piazza, and for the first minute or two he could see nothing distinctly. That yellow splendour was in itself something supernal[1] and heavenly to many[2] of the peasant-women, for whom half the sky was hidden by mountains, and who went to bed in the twilight; and the uninterrupted chant from the choir was repose to the ear after the hellish hubbub of the crowd outside. Gradually the scene became clearer, though still there was a thin yellow haze from incense mingling with the breath of the multitude. In a chapel on the left hand of the nave, wreathed with silver lamps,[3] was seen unveiled the miraculous fresco of the Annunciation,* which, [4]in Tito's oblique view of it from the right-hand side of the nave, seemed dark with the excess of light* around it. The whole area of the great church was filled with [5]peasant-women, some kneeling, some standing; the coarse bronzed skins, and the dingy clothing of the rougher dwellers on the mountains, contrasting with the softer-lined faces and white or red head-drapery of the well-to-do dwellers in the valley, who were scattered in irregular groups. And spreading high and far over the walls and ceiling there was another multitude, also pressing close against each other, that they might be nearer the potent Virgin. It[6] was the crowd of votive waxen images,* the effigies of great personages, clothed in their habit as they lived: Florentines of high name in their black silk *lucco*, as when[7] they sat in council: popes, emperors, kings, cardinals, and famous condottieri with plumed morion seated on their chargers; all notable strangers who passed through Florence or had aught to do with its affairs—Mohammedans[8], even, in well-tolerated companionship with Christian cavaliers; some of them with faces blackened and

---

1 supernal] supernatural *1 2 3*   2 many] *2 3* some *MS CM 1*
3 lamps, ⟨and dark with the excess of light around it⟩ *MS*
4 ⟨to⟩ in *MS*   5 ⟨kneeling⟩ peasant women *MS*
6 Virgin. It] *1 2 3* Virgin: it *MS CM*   7 as {when} *MS*
8 Mohammedans] *3P* Mahometans *MS CM* Mahomedans *1 2*

robes tattered by the corroding breath of centuries, others fresh and bright in new red mantle or steel corslet, the exact doubles of the living. And wedged in with all these were detached arms, legs, hands, and[9] other members, with only here and there a gap where some image had been removed for public disgrace, or had fallen ominously, as Lorenzo's had done six months before. It was a perfect resurrection-swarm of remote mortals and fragments[1] of mortals, reflecting, in their varying degrees of freshness, the sombre dinginess and sprinkled brightness of the crowd below.

Tito's glance wandered over the wide[2] multitude in search of something. He had already thought of Tessa, and the white hoods suggested the possibility that he might detect her face under one of them. It was at least a thought to be courted, rather than the vision of Romola looking at him with changed eyes. But he searched in vain; and he was leaving the church, weary of a scene which had no variety, when, just against the doorway, he caught sight of Tessa, only two yards off him. She was kneeling with her back against the wall, behind a group of peasant-women, who were standing and looking for a spot nearer to the sacred image. Her head hung a little aside with a look of weariness, and her blue eyes were directed rather absently towards an altar-piece* where the archangel Michael stood in his armour, with young face and floating hair, amongst bearded and tonsured saints. Her right hand, [3]holding a bunch of cocoons, fell by her side listlessly, and her round cheek was paled, either by the light or by the weariness that was expressed in her attitude: her lips were pressed poutingly together, and every now and then her eyelids half fell: she was a large image of a sweet sleepy child. Tito felt an irresistible desire to go up to her and get her pretty trusting looks and [4]prattle: this creature who was without moral judgments[5] that could condemn him, whose little loving ignorant soul made a world apart, where he might feel in freedom from suspicions and exacting demands, had a new attraction for him [6]now. She seemed a refuge from the threatened isolation[7] that would come with disgrace. He glanced cautiously round, to assure himself that Monna Ghita was not near, and then, slipping quietly to her side, kneeled on one knee, and said, in the softest voice, "Tessa!"

She [8]hardly started, any more than she would have started at a soft breeze that fanned her gently when she was needing it. She turned her head and saw Tito's face close to her: it was very much[9] more beautiful than the archangel Michael[1], who was so mighty and so

9 arms, legs, hands, and] arms, legs, and *2 3*   1 fragments] remnants *MS*
2 wide] wild *2 3*   3 〈held〉 holding *MS*   4 〈words〉 prattle *MS*
5 judgements] judgement *2 3*   6 〈at this moment〉 now *MS*
7 isolation 〈of〉 *MS*   8 〈did not〉 hardly *MS*
9 her: it was very much] *1 2 3* her, very much *MS CM*   1 Michael] Michael's *3*

good that he lived with the Madonna and all the[2] saints, and was prayed to along with them. She smiled in happy silence, for that nearness of Tito quite filled her mind.

"My little Tessa! you look very tired. How long have you been kneeling here?"

[3]She seemed to be collecting her thoughts for a minute[4] or two, and at last she said—

"I'm very hungry."[5]

"Come, then; come with me."

He lifted her from her knees, and led her [6]out under the cloisters surrounding the atrium, which were then open, and not yet adorned with the frescoes of Andrea del Sarto.*

"How is it you are[7] all by yourself, and so hungry, Tessa?"

"The madre is ill; she has very bad pains in her legs, and sent me to bring these cocoons to the Santissima Nunziata, because they're so wonderful; see!"—she held up the bunch of cocoons, which were arranged with fortuitous regularity on a stem,—"and she had kept them to bring them herself, but she couldn't, and so she sent me because she thinks the Holy Madonna may take away her pains[8]; and somebody took my bag with the bread and chestnuts in it,[9] and the people pushed me back, and I was so frightened coming in the crowd,[1] and I couldn't get anywhere near the Holy Madonna[2], to give the cocoons to the *padre*, but I must—oh, I must."

"Yes, my little Tessa, you shall take them; but first come[3] and let me give you some *berlingozzi*. There are some to be had not far off."

"Where did you come from?' said Tessa, a little bewildered. "I thought you would never come to me again, because you never came to the Mercato for milk any more. I set myself *Aves* to say, to see if they would bring you back, but[4] I left off, because they didn't."

"You see I come when you want some one to take care of you, Tessa. Perhaps the *Aves* fetched me, only it took them a long while. But what shall you do if you are here all alone? Where shall you go?"

"Oh, I shall stay and sleep in the church—a great many of them do—in the church and[5] all about here—I did once when I came with my mother; and the *patrigno* is coming with the mules in the morning."[6]

<hr>

2 {all} the *MS*   3 ⟨Tessa⟩ She *MS*   4 minute] moment *MS*

5 hungry." ⟨The madre has got the bag with her and she's ever so far off up the church because⟩ ¶ "Come, then, come with me." ¶ ⟨He took her hand and she rose ⟨⟨in a moment⟩⟩ without hesitation⟩ He ⟨put his⟩ lifted her *MS*

6 ⟨from⟩ out *MS*   7 you are] you're *MS*

8 sent me {because . . . pains} *MS*   9 and {somebody took . . . it,} *MS*

1 back, {and I was . . . crowd,} *MS*   2 the {Holy} Madonna *MS*

3 first come] *3P* come first *MS CM 1 2*   4 but] till *MS*

5 and ⟨the cloisters⟩ *MS*   6 mother {: and the *patrigno* . . . morning."} *MS*

They were out in the piazza now, where the crowd was rather less riotous than before, and the lights were fewer,[7] the stream of pilgrims having ceased. Tessa clung fast to Tito's arm in satisfied silence, while he led her towards the stall[8] where he remembered seeing the eatables. Their way was the easier because there was just now a great rush towards the middle of the piazza, where the masqued figures on stilts had [9]found space to execute a dance. It was very pretty to see the guileless thing giving her cocoons into Tito's hand and then eating[1] her *berlingozzi* with the relish of a hungry child. Tito had really come to take care of her[2], as he did before, and that wonderful happiness of being with him had begun again for her. [3]Her hunger was soon appeased, all the sooner for the new stimulus of happiness that had roused her from her languor, and as they turned away from the stall, she said nothing about going into the church again, but looked round as if the sights in the piazza were not without attraction to her now she was safe under Tito's arm.

"How can they do that?" she exclaimed, looking up at the dancers on stilts. Then, after a minute's silence, "Do you think Saint Christopher helps them?"

"Perhaps. What do you think about it, Tessa?" said Tito, slipping his right arm[4] round her, and looking down at her fondly.

"Because Saint Christopher is so very tall; and he is very good: if anybody looks at him he takes care of them all day. He is on the wall of the church—too tall to stand up there—but I saw him walking through the streets one San Giovanni, carrying the little *Gesù*."*

"You pretty pigeon! Do you think anybody could help taking care of *you*, if you looked at them?"

"Shall you always come and take[5] care of me?" said Tessa, turning her face up to him, as he crushed her cheek with his left hand. "And shall you always be a long while [6]first?"

Tito was conscious that some bystanders were [7]laughing at them, and though the licence of street fun, among[8] artists and young men of the wealthier sort as well as among the populace, made [9]few adventures exceptional, still less disreputable, he chose to [1]move away towards the [2]end of the piazza.

7 before {and the lights were fewer,} *MS*
8 the stall ⟨he remembered seeing with⟩ *MS*   9 ⟨now⟩ found *MS*
1 {giving her cocoons . . . then} eating *MS*   2 her ⟨again⟩ *MS*
3 ⟨She⟩ Her hunger *MS*   4 {right} arm *MS*   5 {come and} take *MS*
6 ⟨between⟩ first *MS*   7 ⟨observing them⟩ laughing at them *MS*
8 fun, among] *3P* fun among *MS CM 1 2*
9 ⟨scarcely anything exceptional, still less [1 or 2 words]⟩ few adventures exceptional {still less disreputable} *MS*
1 ⟨turn⟩ move *MS*
2 ⟨other⟩ end *MS*

"Perhaps I shall come again to you very soon, Tessa," he answered, rather dreamily, when they had moved away. He was thinking, that when all the rest had turned their backs upon him, it would be pleasant to have this little creature adoring him and nestling against him. The absence of presumptuous self-conceit in Tito made him feel all the more defenceless under prospective obloquy: he needed soft looks and caresses too much ever to be impudent.

"In the Mercato?" said Tessa. "Not to-morrow morning, because the *patrigno* will be there, and he is so cross. Oh! but you have money, and he will not be cross if you buy some salad. And there are some chestnuts. Do you like chestnuts?"

He said nothing, but continued to look down at her with a dreamy gentleness, and Tessa felt herself in a state of delicious wonder; everything seemed as new as if[3] she were being carried on a chariot of clouds.

"Holy Virgin[4]!" she exclaimed again, presently; "there is a holy Father like the Bishop I saw at Prato."

Tito looked up too, and saw that he had unconsciously advanced to within a few yards of the conjuror, Maestro Vaiano, who, for the moment, was forsaken by the crowd. His face was turned away from them, and he was occupied with the apparatus on his altar or table, preparing a new diversion by the time the interest in the dancing should be exhausted. The monkey was imprisoned under the red cloth, out of reach of mischief, and the youngster in the white surplice was holding a sort of dish[5] or salver, from which his master was taking some ingredient. The altar-like table, with its gorgeous cloth, the row of tapers, the sham episcopal costume, the surpliced attendant, and even the movements[6] of the mitred figure, as he alternately bent his head and then raised something[7] before the lights, were a sufficiently near parody of sacred things to rouse poor little Tessa's veneration; and there was some additional awe produced by[8] the mystery of their apparition in this spot[9], for when she had seen an altar in the street before, it had been on Corpus Christi Day, and there had been a procession to account for it. She crossed herself, and looked up at Tito, but then, as if she had had time for reflexion, said, "It is because of the Natività."

Meanwhile Vaiano had turned round, [1]raising his hands to his mitre with the intention of changing his dress, when his quick eye

3 as if ⟨the clouds had opened⟩ *MS*
4 Holy Virgin] *1 2 3 Sanctissima Vergine MS Santissima Vergine CM*
5 {sort of} dish *MS*   6 movements] *1 2 3* very movements *MS CM*
7 something ⟨to look at it⟩ *MS*
8 by ⟨the unexpectedness of the apparition⟩ *MS*   9 spot ⟨in the street⟩ *MS*
1 ⟨and had raised⟩ raising *MS*

recognized Tito and Tessa who were both looking at him, their faces being shone upon by the light of his tapers, [2]while his own was in shadow.

"Ha! my children!" he said, instantly, [3]stretching out his hands in a benedictory attitude, "you are come to be married. I commend your penitence—the blessing of Holy Church can never come too late."

But whilst he was speaking, he had taken in the whole meaning of Tessa's attitude and expression, and he discerned an opportunity for a new kind of joke which required him to be cautiously solemn[4].

"Should you like to be married to me, Tessa?" said Tito, softly, half enjoying the comedy, as he saw the pretty childish seriousness on her face, half prompted by [5]hazy previsions which belonged to the intoxication of despair.

He felt her vibrating[6] before she looked up at him and said, timidly, "Will you let me?"

[7]He answered only by a smile, and by leading her forward in front of the *cerretano*, who seeing an excellent jest in Tessa's evident delusion, assumed [8]a surpassing sacerdotal solemnity, and went through the mimic ceremony with[9] a liberal expenditure of *lingua furbesca* or thieves' Latin. But some symptoms of a new movement in the crowd urged him to bring it to a speedy conclusion and dismiss them with hands outstretched in a benedictory attitude over their kneeling figures. Tito,[1] disposed always to cultivate goodwill, though it might be[2] the least select, put a piece of four grossi[3] into his hand as he moved away, and was thanked by a look which, the conjuror felt sure, conveyed a perfect understanding of the whole affair.

But Tito himself was very far from that understanding, and did not, in fact, know whether, the next moment, he should tell Tessa of the joke and laugh at her for a little goose, or whether he should let her delusion last, and see what would come of it—see what she would say and do next.

"Then you will not go away from me again," said Tessa, after they had walked a few steps, "and you will take me to where you live." She spoke meditatively, and not in a questioning tone. But, presently, she added, "I must go back once to the madre, though, to tell her I brought the cocoons, and that I'm[4] married, and [5]shall not go back again."

---

2 ⟨but⟩ while *MS*   3 ⟨raising⟩ stretching out *MS*
4 cautiously solemn] *MS* cautious and solemn *CM 1 2 3*
5 ⟨intoxicated⟩ hazy *MS*   6 vibrating ⟨,under his⟩ *MS*
7 ⟨At any former moment in his life ⟨⟨not⟩⟩ never to have had ⟨⟨the⟩⟩ hard recklessness enough to make an⟩ He *MS*
8 ⟨more than⟩ a *MS*   9 with ⟨much impromptu gibberish.⟩ *MS*
1 Tito, ⟨accustomed to propitiate the good will⟩ *MS*
2 though {it might be} *MS*   3 a piece of four grossi] a *lira MS*
4 I'm] I am *1 2 3*   5 ⟨shan't⟩ shall not *MS*

Tito felt the necessity of speaking now; and, in the rapid thought prompted by that necessity, he saw that by undeceiving Tessa he [6]should be robbing himself of some at least of that pretty trustfulness which might, by and by[7], be his only haven from contempt. It would spoil Tessa to make her the least particle wiser or more suspicious.

"Yes, my little Tessa," he said, caressingly, "you must go back to the madre; but you must not tell her you are married—you must keep that a secret from everybody; else some very great harm would happen to me, and you would never see me again."

She looked up at him with fear[8] in her face.

"You must go back and feed your goats and mules, and do just as you have always done before, and say no word to any one about me."

The corners of her mouth fell a little.

"[9]And then, perhaps, I shall come and take care of you again when you want me, as I did before. [1]But you must do just what I tell you, else you will not see me again."

"Yes, I will, I will," she said, in a loud whisper, frightened at that blank prospect.

[2]They were silent a little while; and then Tessa, looking at her hand, said,—

"The madre wears a betrothal-ring. [3]She went to church and had it put on, and then after that, another day, she was married. And so did the cousin Nannina. But then *she* married Gollo," added the poor little thing, entangled in the difficult comparison between her own case and others within her experience.

"But you must not wear a betrothal-ring, my Tessa, because no one must know you are married," said Tito, feeling some insistance necessary. "And the[4] *buon*[5] *fortuna* that I gave[6] you did just as well for betrothal. Some people are betrothed with rings[7] and some are not."

"Yes, it is true, they would see the ring," said Tessa, trying to convince herself that a thing she would like very much was really not good for her.

They were now near the entrance of the church again, and she remembered her cocoons which were still in Tito's hand.

"Ah, you must give me the *Boto*," she said; "and[8] we must go in, and I must take it to the *padre*, and I must tell the rest of my beads, because I was too tired before."

6 ⟨might⟩ should *MS*   7 might {by and by} *MS*

8 fear] *1 2 3* pale fear *MS CM*   9 ⟨But⟩ And then {perhaps} *MS*

1 ⟨And⟩ But *MS*   2 ⟨She was⟩ They were *MS*   3 ⟨She told me⟩ She *MS*

4 the ⟨ring can be put on afterwards—it makes no difference⟩ *MS*

5 *buon*] *MS* buona *CM 1 2 3*   6 that I gave] *1 2 3* I gave *MS CM*

7 betrothed {with rings} *MS*   8 and ⟨I must go in and take⟩ *MS*

"Yes, you must go in Tessa; but I will not go in. I must leave you now[9]," said Tito, too feverish[1] and weary to [2]re-enter that stifling heat, and feeling that this was the least difficult way of parting with her.

"And not come back? Oh, where do you go?" Tessa's mind had[3] never formed an image of his whereabout or his doings when she did not see him: he had vanished[4], and her thought, instead of following him, had stayed in the same spot where he was with her.

"I shall come back some time, Tessa," said Tito, taking her under the cloisters[5] to the door of the church.[6] "You must not cry—you must go to sleep, when you have said your beads. And here is money[7] to buy your breakfast. Now kiss me, and look happy; else I shall not come again."

She made a great effort over herself as she put up her lips to kiss him, and [8]submitted to be gently turned round, with her face towards the door of the church. Tito saw her enter; and then, with a shrug at his own resolution, leaned against [9]a pillar, took off his cap, rubbed his hair backward, and wondered where Romola was now, and what she was thinking of him. Poor little Tessa had disappeared behind the curtain among the crowd of peasants[1]; [2]but the love which formed one web with all his worldly hopes—with the ambitions and pleasures that must make the solid part of his days—the love that was identified with his larger self—was not to be banished from his consciousness. Even to the man who presents the most [3]elastic resistance to whatever is unpleasant, there will come moments when the pressure from without is too strong for him, and he must feel the smart and the bruise in spite of himself. Such a moment had come to Tito. There was no possible attitude of mind, no scheme of action, by[4] which the uprooting of all his newly-planted hopes could be made otherwise than painful.

9 now ⟨?really⟩ MS   1 feverish] 3P fevered MS CM 1 2

2 ⟨enter into that stifling heat again⟩ re-enter MS   3 Tessa{'s mind} had MS

4 {had} vanished MS   5 cloisters] loggia MS

6 Tessa {said Tito . . . church}. MS   7 money, ⟨if you want food⟩ MS

8 ⟨then⟩ submitted MS   9 ⟨the wall⟩ a pillar MS

1 peasants] 3C contadine MS CM contadine 1 2

2 ⟨but⟩ ⟨and⟩ but the love which ⟨made⟩ formed MS   3 ⟨facile⟩ elastic MS

4 action, by] CM action by MS 1 2 3

CHAPTER XV.

THE DYING MESSAGE

WHEN Romola arrived at the entrance of San Marco she found one of the Frati waiting there in expectation of her arrival. Monna Brigida retired into the adjoining church, and Romola was conducted to the door of the chapter-house in the outer cloister, whither the invalid had been conveyed; no woman being allowed admission* beyond this precinct.

When the door opened, the subdued external light blending with that of two tapers placed behind a truckle-bed showed the emaciated face of Fra Luca, with the tonsured crown of golden hair above it, and with deep-sunken hazel eyes fixed[1] on a small crucifix which he held before him. He was propped up into nearly a sitting posture; and[2] Romola was just conscious, as she threw aside her veil, that there was another monk standing by the bed, with the black cowl drawn over his head, and that he moved towards the door as she entered[3]; just conscious that in the background there was a crucified form rising high and pale on the frescoed wall, and pale faces[4] of sorrow looking out from it below.

The next moment her eyes met [5]Fra Luca's as they looked up at her from the crucifix, and she was absorbed in that pang of recognition which identified this monkish emaciated form with the image of her fair young brother.

"Dino!" she said, in a voice like a low cry of pain. But she did not bend towards him; she held herself erect, and paused at two yards' distance from him. There was an unconquerable repulsion for her in that monkish aspect; it seemed to her the brand of the dastardly undutifulness which had left her father desolate—of the grovelling superstition which could give such undutifulness the name of piety. Her father, whose proud sincerity and simplicity of life had made him one of the few frank pagans of his time, had brought her up with a silent ignoring of any claims the Church could have to regulate the belief and action of beings with a cultivated reason; the Church, in

---

1 eyes fixed] *MS 1 2 3* eyes, fixed *CM*

2 and ⟨clad in his white tunic with the black rosary falling by his side and the black mantle falling around him⟩ *MS*

3 head {and that . . . entered} *MS*　　　　4 {frescoed} wall and {pale} faces *MS*

5 ⟨her brother's⟩ Fra Luca's *MS*

The Dying Magenta

her mind, belonged to that actual life of the mixed multitude from which [6]they had always lived apart, and she[7] had no ideas that could render her brother's course an object of any other feeling[8] than incurious, indignant contempt. Yet the [9]lovingness of Romola's soul had clung to that image in the past, and while she stood rigidly aloof, there was a yearning search in her eyes for something too faintly discernible.

But there was no corresponding emotion in the face of the monk. He looked at the little sister returned to him in her full womanly beauty, with the far-off gaze of a revisiting spirit.

"My sister!" he said, with feeble[1] and interrupted but yet distinct[2] utterance, "it is well thou hast not longer delayed[3] to come, for I have a message to deliver to thee, and my time is short."

Romola took a step nearer: the message, she thought, would be one of affectionate penitence to her father, and her heart began to open. Nothing could wipe out the long years of desertion; but the culprit, looking back on those years with the sense of irremediable wrong committed, would call forth [4]pity. Now, at the last, there would be understanding and forgiveness. Dino would pour out some natural filial feeling; he would ask questions about his father's blindness—how rapidly[5] it had come on? how the long dark days had been filled? what the life was now in the home where he himself had been nourished?—and the last message from the dying lips would be one of tenderness and regret.

"Romola," Fra Luca began again[6], "I have had a vision concerning thee. Thrice I have had it in the last two months: each time it has been clearer. Therefore I came from Fiesole, deeming it a message from heaven that I was bound to deliver. And I gather a promise of mercy to thee in this, that my breath is preserved in order to—"

The difficult breathing which continually interrupted him would not let him finish the sentence.

Romola had felt her heart chilling again. It was a vision, then, this message—one of those visions she had so often heard her father allude to with bitterness. Her indignation[7] rushed to her lips.

"Dino, I thought you[8] had some words to send to my father. You forsook him when his sight was failing; you made his life very desolate. Have you never cared about that? never repented? What is this religion of yours, that places visions before natural duties?"

6 ⟨her father⟩ they *MS*   7 she ⟨thought⟩ *MS*   8 {other} feeling *MS*
9 ⟨young⟩ lovingness *MS*   1 feeble] a feeble *2 3*
2 feeble {and interrupted,} but {yet} distinct *MS*
3 {longer} delayed *MS*   4 ⟨some⟩ pity *MS*   5 how {rapidly} *MS*
6 began again] began *2 3*
7 indignation ⟨—a strong feeling in Romola's nature—⟩ *MS*
8 you ⟨would have sent some⟩ *MS*

The deep-sunken hazel eyes turned slowly towards her, and rested upon her in silence for some moments, as if he were meditating whether he should answer her.

"No[9]," he said at last; speaking, as before, [1]in a low passionless tone, as of[2] some spirit not human, speaking through dying human organs. "No; I have never repented fleeing from the stifling poison-breath of sin that was hot and thick around me, and threatened to steal over my senses like besotting wine. My father could not hear the voice that called me night and day; he knew nothing of the demon-tempters that tried to drag me back from following it. My father has lived amidst human sin and misery without believing in them: he has been like one busy picking shining stones in a mine, while there was a world dying of plague above him. I spoke, but he listened with scorn. I told him the studies he wished me to live for were either childish trifling—dead toys—or else they must be made warm and living by pulses that beat to [3]worldly ambitions and fleshly lusts: for worldly ambitions and fleshly lusts made all the substance of the poetry and history he wanted me to bend my eyes on continually."

"Has not my father led a pure and noble life, then?" Romola burst forth, unable to hear in silence this implied accusation against her father. "He has sought no worldly honours; he has been truthful; he has denied himself all luxuries; he has lived like one of the ancient sages. He never wished you to live for worldly ambitions and fleshly lusts; he wished you to live as he himself has done, according to the purest maxims of philosophy, in which he brought you up."

Romola spoke partly by rote, as all ardent and sympathetic young creatures do; but she spoke with intense belief. The pink flush was in her face, and she quivered from head to foot. Her brother was again slow to answer; looking at her passionate face with strange passionless eyes.[4]

"What were the maxims of philosophy to me? They told me to be strong, when I felt myself weak; when I was ready, like the blessed Saint Benedict, to roll myself among thorns,* and court smarting wounds as a deliverance from temptation. For the Divine Love had sought me, and penetrated me, and created a great need in me; like a seed that wants room to grow. I had been brought up in carelessness of the true faith; I had not studied the doctrines of our religion; but it seemed to take possession of me like a rising flood. I felt that there was a life of perfect love and purity for the soul; in which there would be no uneasy hunger after pleasure, no tormenting questions,

---

9 No, ⟨Romola⟩ MS   1 ⟨with⟩ in MS
2 as of] 3C as if his voice were that of MS CM 1 2
3 ⟨the⟩ worldly ambitions and ⟨the⟩ fleshly lusts ⟨which made⟩: for MS
4 answer; {looking at her passionate face with ⟨a⟩ strange passionless eyes.} MS

no fear of suffering. Before I knew the history of the saints, I had a foreshadowing of their ecstasy. For the same truth had penetrated even into pagan philosophy:[5] that it is a bliss within the reach of man to die to mortal needs, and live in the life of God as the Unseen Perfectness. But to attain that I must forsake[6] the world: I must have no affection, no hope, wedding[7] me to that which passeth away; I must live with my fellow-beings only as human souls related to the eternal unseen Life. That need was urging me continually: it came over me in visions when my mind fell away weary from the vain words which record the passions of dead men; it came over me after I had been tempted into sin, and had turned away with loathing[8] from the scent of the emptied cup. And in visions I saw the meaning of the Crucifix."

He paused, breathing hard for a minute or two: but Romola was not prompted to speak again. It was useless for her mind[9] to attempt any contact with the mind of this unearthly brother: as useless as for her hand to try and grasp a shadow. When he spoke again his[1] heaving chest was quieter.

"I felt whom I must follow: but I saw that even among the servants of the Cross who professed to have renounced the world, my soul would be stifled with the fumes of hypocrisy, and lust, and pride. God had not chosen me, as he chose Saint Dominic and Saint Francis, to wrestle with evil in the Church and in the world. He called upon me to flee: I took the sacred vows and I fled—fled to lands where danger and scorn and want bore me continually,[2] like angels, to repose on the bosom of God. I have lived the life of a hermit, I have ministered to pilgrims; but my task has been short: the veil has worn very thin that divides me from my everlasting rest. I came back to Florence that—"

"Dino, you *did* want to know if my father was alive[3]," interrupted Romola, the picture of that suffering life touching her again with the desire for union and forgiveness.

"—that before I die[4] I might urge others of our brethren to study the eastern tongues, as I had not done, and go out to greater ends than I did, and I find them already bent on the work. And since I came, Romola, I have felt that I was sent partly to thee—not to renew the bonds of earthly affection, but to deliver the heavenly warning conveyed in a vision. For I have had that vision thrice. And through all the years since first the Divine voice called me, while I was yet in

---

5 philosophy:] *3C* philosophy—*MS* philosophy; *CM 1 2*
6 forsake] ⟨forsake⟩ attain *MS*   7 wedding] *3C* that wedded *MS CM 1 2*
8 turned away {with loathing} *MS*   9 useless {for her mind} *MS*
1 When he spoke again his] *3C* He went on as soon as his *MS CM 1 2*
2 continually, ⟨aloft,⟩ *MS*   3 alive"—⟨you⟩ *MS*   4 die] died *1 2 3*

the world[5], I have been taught and guided by visions. For in the painful linking together of our waking thoughts we can never be sure that we have not mingled our own error with the light we have prayed for; but in visions and dreams we are passive, and our souls are as an instrument in the Divine hand. Therefore listen, and speak not again—for the time is short."

Romola's mind recoiled strongly from listening to this vision. Her indignation had subsided, but it was only because she had felt the distance between her brother and herself widening. But while Fra Luca was speaking, the figure of another monk had entered, and again stood on the other side of the bed, with the cowl drawn over his head.

"Kneel, my daughter, for the Angel of Death is present, and waits while the message of heaven is delivered: bend thy pride before it is bent for thee by a yoke of iron," said a strong rich voice, startlingly[6] in contrast with Fra Luca's. The tone was not that of imperious command, but of quiet self-possession and assurance of the right, blended with benignity. Romola, vibrating to the sound, looked round at the figure on the opposite side of the bed. His face was hardly discernible under the shadow of the cowl, and her eyes fell at once on his hands, which were folded across his breast and lay in relief on the edge of his black mantle. They had a marked physiognomy which enforced the influence of the voice: they were very beautiful and almost of transparent delicacy. Romola's disposition to rebel against command, doubly active in the presence of monks, whom she had been taught to despise, would have fixed itself on any repulsive detail as a point of support. But the face was hidden, and the hands seemed to have an appeal in them against all hardness. The next moment the right hand took the crucifix to relieve the fatigued grasp of Fra Luca, and the left touched his lips with a wet sponge which lay near. In the act of bending, the cowl was pushed back, and [7]the features of the monk had the full light of the tapers on them. They were very marked features, such as lend themselves to popular description. There was the high arched nose, the prominent under-lip, the coronet of thick dark hair above the brow, all [8]seeming to tell of energy and passion; there were the blue-grey eyes[9], shining mildly under auburn eyelashes, seeming, like the hands, to tell of acute sensitiveness. Romola[1] felt certain they were the features of Fra Girolamo Savonarola, the prior of San Marco, whom she had chiefly thought of as more offensive

5 world] world (*nel secolo*) *MS*   6 startlingly] startingly *1 2 3*
7 ⟨the monk⟩ the features of the monk ⟨were full in the light⟩ had *MS*
8 ⟨telling⟩ seeming to tell *MS*   9 eyes ⟨with⟩ *MS*
1 Romola ⟨had heard them described more than once⟩ ⟨knew them at once⟩ *MS*

than other monks because[2] he was more noisy. Her rebellion was rising against the first impression, which had almost forced her to bend her knees.

"Kneel, my daughter," the penetrating voice said again, "the pride of the body is a barrier against the gifts that purify the soul."

He was looking at her with mild fixedness while he spoke, and again she felt that subtle mysterious influence of a personality by which it has been given to some rare men to move their fellows.

Slowly Romola fell on her knees, and in the very act a tremor came over her; in the renunciation of her proud erectness, her mental attitude seemed changed, and she found herself in a new state of passiveness. Her brother began to speak again.

"Romola, in the deep night, as I lay awake, I saw my father's room—the library—with all the books and the marbles and the *leggio*, where I used to stand and read; and I saw you—you were revealed to me as I see you now, with fair long hair[3], sitting before my father's chair. And at the *leggio* stood a man whose face I could not see—I looked, and looked, and it was a blank to me, even as a painting effaced; and I saw him move and take thee, Romola, by the hand; and then I saw thee take my father by the hand; and you went all three[4] down the stone steps into the streets, the man whose face was a blank to me leading the way. And you stood at the altar in Santa Croce[5], and the priest who married you had the face of death; and the graves opened, and the dead in their shrouds rose and followed you like a bridal train. And[6] you passed on through the streets and the gates into the valley, and it seemed to me that he who led you hurried you more than you could bear, and the dead were weary of following you, and turned back to their graves. And at last you came to a stony place where there was no water, and no trees or herbage; but instead of water, [7]I saw written parchment unrolling itself everywhere, and instead of trees and herbage I saw men of bronze and marble springing up and crowding round you.[8] And[9] my father was faint for want of water and fell to the ground; and the man whose face was a blank loosed thy hand and departed; and as he went I could see his face; and it was the face of the Great Tempter. And thou, Romola, didst wring thy hands and seek for water, and there was none. And the bronze and marble figures seemed to mock thee and hold out cups of

---

2 monks because] *MS* monks, because *CM 1 2 3*
3 with fair long hair] *1 2 3* pale, with long hair *MS CM*
4 you went all three] you all three went *1 2 3*   5 altar {in Santa Croce} *MS*
6 And ⟨it seemed to me⟩ *MS*   7 ⟨gradually⟩ I saw *MS*
8 you; ⟨and the man whose face was a blank loosed thy hand and I could see his face and it was the face of the Great Tempter⟩ *MS*
9 you. And] *1 2 3* you; and *MS CM*

water, and when thou didst grasp them and put them to my father's lips, they turned to parchment. And the bronze and marble figures seemed to turn into demons and snatch my father's body from thee, and the parchments shrivelled up, and blood ran everywhere instead of them, and fire upon the blood, till they all vanished, and the plain was bare and stony again, and thou wast alone in the midst of it. And then it seemed that the night fell and I saw no more. . . . Thrice I have had that vision, Romola. I believe it is a revelation meant for thee—to warn thee against marriage as a temptation of the enemy—it calls upon thee to dedicate thyself—"

His pauses had gradually become longer and more frequent, and he was now compelled to cease by a severe fit of gasping, in which his eyes were turned on the crucifix as on a light that was vanishing. Presently he found strength to speak again, but in a feebler, scarcely audible tone.

"To renounce the vain philosophy and corrupt thoughts of the heathens: for in the hour of sorrow and death their pride will turn to mockery, and the unclean gods will—"

The words died away.

In spite of the thought that was at work in Romola, telling her that his vision was no more than a dream, fed by youthful memories and ideal convictions, a strange awe had come over her. Her mind was not apt to be assailed by sickly fancies; she had the vivid intellect and the healthy human passion, which are too keenly alive to the constant relations of things to have any morbid craving after the exceptional. Still, the[1] images[2] of the vision she despised jarred and distressed her like painful and cruel cries. And it was the first time she had witnessed the struggle with approaching death: her young life had been sombre, but she had known nothing of the utmost human needs; no acute suffering—no heart-cutting sorrow; and this brother, come back to her in his hour of supreme agony, was like a sudden awful apparition from an invisible world. The pale faces of sorrow in the fresco[3] on the opposite wall seemed to have come nearer, and to make one company with the pale face on the bed.

"Frate," said the dying voice.

Fra Girolamo leaned down. But no other word came for some moments.

"Romola," it said next.

She leaned forward too: but again there was silence. The words were struggling in vain.

"Fra Girolamo, give her—"

1 Still, the] *MS* Still the *CM 1 2 3*
2 over her. {Her mind was not ⟨liable⟩ apt . . . exceptional. Still,} the images *MS*
3 faces of sorrow {in the fresco} *MS*

"The crucifix," said the voice of Fra Girolamo.

No other sound came from the dying lips.

"Dino!" [4]said Romola, with a low but piercing[5] cry, as the certainty came upon her that the silence[6] of misunderstanding could never be broken.

"Take the crucifix, my daughter," said Fra Girolamo, after a few minutes. "His eyes behold it no more."

Romola stretched out her hand to the crucifix, and this act appeared to relieve the tension[7] of her mind. A great sob burst from her. She bowed her head by the side of her dead brother, and wept aloud.

It seemed to her as if this first vision of death must alter the daylight for her for ever more.

Fra Girolamo moved towards the door, and called in a lay Brother[8] who was waiting outside. Then he went up to Romola and said in a tone of gentle command, "Rise, my daughter, and be comforted. Our brother is with the blessed. [9]He has left you the crucifix, in remembrance of the heavenly warning—that it may be a beacon to you in the darkness."

She rose from her knees, trembling, folded her veil over her head, and hid the crucifix under her mantle. Fra Girolamo then led the way out into the cloistered court, lit now only by the stars and by a lantern which was held by some one near the entrance. Several other figures in the dress of the dignified laity were grouped about the same spot. They were some of the numerous frequenters of San Marco, who had come to visit the Prior, and having heard that he was in attendance on the dying brother in the chapter-house, had awaited him here.

Romola was dimly conscious of footsteps and rustling forms moving aside: she heard the voice of Fra Girolamo, saying, in a low tone, "Our brother is departed;" she felt a hand laid on her arm. The next moment the door was opened, and she was out in the wide piazza of San Marco, with no one but Monna Brigida, and the servant carrying the lantern.

The fresh sense of space[1] revived her, and helped her to recover her self-mastery. The scene which had just closed upon her was terribly distinct and vivid, but it began to narrow under the returning [2]impressions of the life that lay outside it. She hastened her steps,

4 ⟨cried⟩ said *MS*   5 low {but} piercing *MS*
6 silence ⟨of a disembodied spirit, "I have never repented⟩ *MS*
7 and this act appeared to relieve the tension] and it seemed as if the act relieved the tension *MS*
8 lay Brother] *1 2 3 fra converso MS CM*   9 ⟨And⟩ He *MS*
1 space ⟨around her⟩ *MS*   2 ⟨images⟩ impressions *MS*

with nervous anxiety to be again with her father—and with Tito—for were they not together in her absence? The images of that vision, while they clung about her like a hideous dream not yet to be shaken off, made her yearn all the more for the beloved faces and voices that would assure her of her waking life.

Tito, we know, was not with Bardo; his destiny was being shaped by a guilty consciousness, urging on him the despairing belief that by this time Romola possessed the knowledge which would lead to their final separation.

And the lips that could have conveyed that knowledge were for ever closed. The [3]prevision that Fra Luca's words had imparted to Romola had been such as comes from the shadowy region where human souls seek wisdom apart from the human sympathies which are the very life and substance of our wisdom; the revelation that might have come from the simple questions of filial and brotherly affection had been carried into irrevocable silence.

3 ⟨warning⟩ prevision {that Fra Luca's words had} imparted *MS*

CHAPTER XVI.

A FLORENTINE JOKE

[1]EARLY the next morning Tito was returning from Bratti's shop in the narrow thoroughfare of the Ferravecchi. The Genoese stranger had carried away the onyx ring, and Tito was carrying away fifty[2] florins. It did just cross his mind that if, after all, Fortune, by one of her able devices, saved him from the necessity of quitting Florence, it would be better for him not to have parted with his ring, since he had been understood to wear it for the sake of peculiar memories and predilections; still, it was a slight matter, not worth dwelling on with any emphasis, and in those moments he had lost his confidence in Fortune. The feverish excitement of the first alarm which had impelled his mind to travel into the future had given place to a dull, regretful lassitude. He cared so much for the pleasures that could only come to him through the good opinion of his fellow-men, that he wished now he had never risked ignominy by shrinking from what his fellow-men called obligations. But our deeds are like children that are born to us; they live and act apart from our own will.[3] Nay, children may be strangled, but deeds never: they have an indestructible life both in and out of our consciousness[4]; and that dreadful vitality of deeds was pressing hard on Tito for the first time.

He was going back to his lodgings in the Piazza di San Giovanni, but he [5]avoided passing through the Mercato Vecchio, which was his nearest way, lest he should see Tessa. He was not in the humour to seek anything; he could only await the first sign of his altering lot.

The piazza with its sights of beauty was lit up by that warm morning sunlight under which the autumn dew still lingers and which invites to an idlesse undulled by fatigue. It was a festival morning too, when the soft warmth seems to steal over one with a special invitation to lounge and gaze. Here, too, the signs of the fair were present[6]; in the spaces round the octagonal Baptistery, stalls were being spread with fruit and flowers, and here and there laden mules were standing quietly absorbed in their nose-bags, while their [7]drivers were perhaps gone through the hospitable sacred doors to kneel before the Blessed Virgin on this morning of her Nativity. On the broad marble steps of

1 {Early} The *MS*
2 fifty] seventy-five *MS*
3 will: {nay,} children *MS*
4 never {: they have . . . consciousness} *MS*
5 〈purposely〉 avoided *MS*
6 Here, too, the signs of the fair were present] *1 2 3* The signs of the fair were present here too *MS CM*
7 〈masters〉 drivers *MS*

the Duomo there were scattered groups of beggars and [8]gossiping talkers; here an old crone with white hair and hard sunburnt face encouraging a round-capped baby to try its[9] tiny bare feet on the warmed marble, while a dog sitting near snuffed at the performance suspiciously; there a couple of shaggy-headed boys leaning[1] to watch a small pale cripple who was cutting a face on a cherry-stone; and above them on the wide platform men were making changing knots in laughing desultory chat, or else were standing in close couples gesticulating eagerly.

But the largest and most important company of loungers was that towards which Tito had to direct his steps. It was the busiest time of the day with Nello, and in this warm season and at an hour when clients were numerous, most men preferred being shaved under the pretty red and white awning in front of the shop rather than within narrow walls[2]. It is not a sublime attitude for a man to sit with lathered chin thrown backward, and have his nose made a handle of; but to be shaved was a fashion of Florentine respectability, and it is astonishing how gravely men look at each other when they are all in the fashion. It was the hour of the day too when yesterday's crop of gossip was freshest, and the barber's tongue was always in its glory when his razor was busy; the deft activity of those two instruments seemed to be set going by a common spring. Tito foresaw that it would be impossible for him to escape being drawn into the circle; he must smile and retort, and look perfectly at his ease. Well! it was but the ordeal of swallowing bread and cheese pills* after all. The man who let the mere anticipation of discovery choke him was simply[3] a man of weak nerves. But just at that time[4] Tito felt a hand laid on his shoulder, and no amount of previous resolution could prevent the very unpleasant sensation with which that sudden touch jarred him. His face, as he turned it round, betrayed the inward shock; [5]but the owner of the hand that seemed to have such evil magic in it broke into a light laugh. He was a young man about Tito's own age[6], with keen features, small close-clipped head, and close-shaven lip and chin, giving the idea of a mind as little encumbered as possible with material that was not nervous. The keen eyes were bright with hope and friendliness, as so many other young eyes have been that have afterwards closed on the world in bitterness and disappointment; for at that time there were none but pleasant predictions about Niccolò

---

8 ⟨knots of talkers⟩ gossiping talkers *MS*   9 its ⟨[?brief] steps⟩ *MS*
1 leaning ⟨with somewhat curious admiration⟩ to watch a {small} pale⟨-faced⟩ cripple *MS*
2 shop {rather than within narrow walls} *MS*   3 was {simply} *MS*
4 time] moment *MS*   5 ⟨and⟩ but *MS*   6 {own} age *MS*

Macchiavelli[7], as a young man of promise, who was expected to mend the broken fortunes of his ancient family[8].

[9]"Why, Melema, what evil dream did you have last night, that you took my light grasp for that of a *sbirro*, or something worse?"

"Ah, Messer Niccolò!" said Tito, recovering himself immediately; "it must have been an extra amount of dulness in my veins this morning that shuddered at the approach of your wit. But the fact is, I have had a bad night."

"That is unlucky, because you will be expected to shine without any obstructing fog to-day in the Rucellai Gardens. I take it for granted you are to be there."

"Messer Bernardo did me the honour to invite me," said Tito; "but I shall be engaged elsewhere."

"Ah! I remember, you are in love," said Macchiavelli, with a shrug, "else you would never have such inconvenient engagements. Why, we are to eat a peacock and ortolans* under the loggia among [1]Bernardo Rucellai's rare trees;* there are to be the choicest spirits in Florence and the choicest wines. Only as Piero de' Medici is to be there, the choice spirits may happen to be swamped in the capping of impromptu verses. I hate that game; it is a device for the triumph of small wits, who are always inspired the most by the smallest occasions."

"What is that you are saying about Piero de' Medici and small wits, Messer Niccolò?" said Nello,[2] whose light figure was at that moment predominating over the Herculean frame of Niccolò Caparra. That famous worker in iron, whom we saw last with bared muscular arms and leathern apron in the Mercato Vecchio, was this morning dressed in holiday suit, and as he sat submissively while Nello skipped round him, lathered him, seized him by the nose, and scraped him with magical quickness, he looked much as a lion might if it had donned linen and tunic, and was preparing to go into society.

[3]"A private secretary will never rise in the world if he couples great and small in that way," continued Nello. "When great men are not allowed to marry their sons and daughters as they like, small men must not expect to marry their words as they like.[4] Have you heard

7 Machiavelli—⟨a youth⟩ *MS*

8 {ancient} family *MS*

9 ⟨"Ah, Messer Niccolò!" said Tito, recovering himself immediately, it must have been an extra amount of dulness in my veins this morning⟩ "Why *MS*

1 ⟨Messer⟩ Bernardo *MS*

2 said Nello, ⟨"A private secretary will never rise in the world if he couples great and small in that way," said Nello⟩ *MS*

3 ⟨"That is sagely spoken, Nello," said Machiavelli⟩ "A *MS*

4 not {expect to} marry their words as they like," ⟨Nello went on.⟩ "Have you heard the news ⟨Messer Bernardo Cennini⟩ Bernardo *MS*

the news Domenico[5] Cennini, here, has been telling us?—that
Pagolantonio Soderini has given Ser Piero da Bibbiena a box on the
ear for setting on Piero de' Medici to interfere with the marriage
[6]between young Tommaso Soderini and Fiammetta Strozzi, and is to
be sent ambassador to Venice as a punishment?"*

"I don't know which I envy him most," said Macchiavelli, "the
offence or the punishment. The offence will make him the most popular man in all Florence, and the punishment will take him among
the only people in Italy who have known how to manage their own
affairs."

"Yes, if Soderini stays long enough at Venice," said Cennini, "he
may chance to [7]learn the Venetian fashion, and bring it home with
him. The Soderini have been fast friends of the Medici, but what has
happened is likely to open Pagolantonio's eyes to the good of our old
Florentine trick of choosing a new harness when the old one galls us[8];
if we have not quite lost the trick in these last fifty years."

"Not we," said Niccolò Caparra, who was rejoicing in the free use
of his lips again. "Eat eggs in Lent and the snow will melt. That's
what I say to our people when they get noisy over their cups at San
Gallo, and talk of raising a *romor* (insurrection): I say, never do you
plan a *romor;* you may as well try to fill Arno with buckets. When
there's water enough Arno will be full, and that will not be till the
torrent is ready."

"Caparra, that oracular speech of yours is due to my excellent
shaving," said Nello. "You could never have made it with that dark
rust on your chin. Ecco, Messer Domenico, I am ready for you now.
By the way, my *bel erudito*," continued Nello, as he saw Tito moving
towards the door, "here has been old Maso seeking for you, but your
nest was empty. He will come again presently. The old man looked
mournful, and seemed in haste. I hope there is nothing wrong in the
Via de' Bardi."

"Doubtless, Messer Tito knows that Bardo's son is dead," said
Cronaca, who had just come up.

Tito's heart gave a leap—had the death happened before Romola
saw him?

"No, I had not heard it," he said, with no more discomposure than
the occasion seemed to warrant, [9]turning and learning against the
door-post, as if he had given up his intention of going away. "I knew
that his sister had gone to see him. Did he die before she arrived?"

"No," said Cronaca; "I was in San Marco at the time, and saw her
come out from the chapter-house with Fra Girolamo, who told us

5 Domenico] *1 2 3* Bernardo *MS CM*   6 ⟨of⟩ between *MS*
7 ⟨bring⟩ learn *MS*   8 galls us] is too tight *MS*
9 ⟨as he turned⟩ turning *MS*

that the dying man's breath had been preserved as by a miracle, that he might make a disclosure to his sister."

Tito felt that his fate was decided. Again his mind rushed over all the circumstances of his departure from Florence, and he conceived a plan of getting back his money from Cennini before the disclosure had become public. If he once had his money he need not stay long in endurance of scorching looks and biting words. He would wait now, and go away with Cennini and get the money from him at once. With that project in his mind he stood motionless—his hands in his belt, his eyes fixed absently on the ground. Nello, glancing at him, felt sure that he was absorbed in anxiety about Romola, and thought him such a pretty image of self-forgetful[1] sadness, that he just perceptibly pointed his razor at him, and gave a challenging look at Piero di Cosimo, whom he had never forgiven for his refusal to see any prognostics of character in his favourite's handsome face. Piero, who was leaning against the other door-post, close to Tito, shrugged his shoulders: the frequent recurrence of such challenges from Nello had changed the painter's first declaration of neutrality into a positive inclination[2] to believe ill of the much-bepraised[3] Greek.

"So you have got your Fra Girolamo back again,* Cronaca? I[4] suppose we shall have him preaching again this next Advent[5]," said Nello.

"And not before there is need," said Cronaca, gravely. "We have had the best testimony to his words since the last Quaresima; for even to the wicked wickedness has become a plague; and the ripeness of vice is turning to rottenness [6]in the nostrils even of the vicious. There has not been a change since the Quaresima, either in Rome or at Florence, but has put a new seal on the Frate's words—that the harvest of sin is ripe, and that God will reap it with a sword."

"I hope he has had a new vision, however," said Francesco Cei, sneeringly. "The old ones are[7] somewhat stale. Can't your Frate get a poet to help out his imagination for him?"

"He has no lack of poets about him," said Cronaca, with quiet contempt, "but they are great poets and not little ones; so they are contented to be taught by him, and no more think the truth stale which God has given him to utter, than they think the light of the moon is stale. But, perhaps, certain high prelates and princes who dislike[8] the Frate's denunciations, might be pleased to hear that, though Giovanni Pico and Poliziano and[9] Marsilio Ficino, and[1] most other men of

---

1 {self-}forgetful *MS*   2 inclination ⟨against Tito⟩ *MS*
3 bepraised] *MS* praised *CM 1 2 3*
4 Cronaca? I] *1 2 3* Cronaca?" said Nello. "I *MS CM*   5 {next} Advent *MS*
6 ⟨even⟩ in *MS*   7 are ⟨getting⟩ *MS*   8 dislike] *1 2 3* don't like *MS CM*
9 Pico and Poliziano and] *MS* Pico and Poliziano, and *CM* Pico, and Poliziano, and *1 2 3*
1 and {Marsilio Ficino and} *MS*

mark in Florence reverence Fra Girolamo, Messer Francesco Cei despises him."

"Poliziano?" said Cei, with a scornful laugh. "Yes, doubtless he believes in your new Jonah;* witness the fine oration[2]* he wrote for the envoys of Siena, to tell Alexander the Sixth that the world and the Church were never so well off as [3]since he became Pope."

"Nay, Francesco," said Macchiavelli, smiling, "a various scholar must have various opinions. And as for the Frate, whatever we may think of his saintliness, you judge his preaching too narrowly.[4] The secret of oratory lies, not in saying new things, but in saying things with a certain power that moves the hearers—without which, as old Filelfo has said[5], your speaker deserves to be called, 'non *o*ratorem, sed *a*ratorem.'* And, according to that test, Fra Girolamo is a great orator."

"That is true, Niccolò," said Cennini, speaking from the shaving-chair, "but part of the secret lies in the prophetic visions. Our people —no offence to you, Cronaca—will run after anything in the shape of a prophet, especially if he prophesies terrors and tribulations."

"Rather say, Cennini", answered Cronaca, "that the chief secret lies in the Frate's pure life and strong faith, which stamp him as a messenger of God."

"I admit it—I admit it," said Cennini, opening his palms, as he rose from the chair. "His life is spotless: no man has impeached it."

"He is satisfied with the pleasant lust of arrogance," Cei burst out, bitterly. "I can see it in that proud lip and satisfied eye of his. He hears the air filled with his own name—Fra Girolamo Savonarola, of Ferrara; the prophet, the saint, the mighty preacher, who frightens the very babies of Florence into laying down their wicked baubles."

"Come, come, Francesco, you are out of humour with waiting," said the conciliatory Nello. "Let me stop your mouth with a little lather. I must not have my friend Cronaca made angry: I have a regard for his chin; and his chin is in no respect altered since he became a Piagnone. And for my own part, I confess, when the Frate was preaching in the Duomo last Advent, I got into such a trick of slipping in to listen to him, that I might have turned Piagnone too, if I had not been hindered by the liberal nature of my art—and also by the length of the sermons, which are sometimes a good while before they get to the moving point. But as Messer Niccolò here says, the Frate lays hold of the people by some power over and above his prophetic visions. Monks and nuns who prophesy are not of that rareness. For what says Luigi Pulci?* 'Dombruno's sharp-cutting

2 oration] *CM* *1* orations *MS* *2* *3*   3 ⟨when⟩ since *MS*
4 And as for . . . narrowly.] And as for the Frate, you judge him too narrowly. *MS*
5 {has} said *MS*

scimitar had the fame of being enchanted; but,' says Luigi[6], 'I am rather of opinion that it cut sharp because it was of[7] strongly-tempered steel.'[8] Yes, yes; paternosters may shave clean, but they must be said over a good razor."

"See, Nello!" said Macchiavelli, "what doctor is this advancing on his Bucephalus? I thought your piazza was free from those furred and scarlet-robed lacqueys of death. This man looks as if he had had some such night adventure as[9] Boccaccio's Maestro Simone,* and had his bonnet and mantle pickled a little in the gutter; though [1]he himself is as sleek as a miller's rat."

"A-ah!" said Nello, with a low, long-drawn intonation, as he looked up towards the advancing figure—a round-headed, round-bodied personage, seated on a raw young horse, which held its nose out with an air of threatening obstinacy, and by constant effort to back and go off in an oblique line showed free views about authority very much in advance of the age.

"And I have a few more adventures in pickle for him," continued Nello, in an under-tone, "which I hope will drive his inquiring nostrils to another quarter of the city. He's a doctor from Padua; they say he has been at Prato for three months, and now he's come to Florence to see what he can net. But his great trick is making rounds among the contadini. And do you note those great saddle-bags he carries? They are to hold the fat capons and eggs and meal[2] he levies on [3]silly clowns with whom coin is scarce. He vends his own secret medicines, so he keeps away from the doors of the druggists[4]; and for this last week he has taken to sitting in my piazza for two or three hours every day, and making it a resort for asthmas and squalling *bambini*. It stirs my gall to see the toad-faced quack fingering the greasy quattrini, or bagging a pigeon in exchange for his pills and powders. But I'll put a few thorns in his saddle, else I'm no Florentine. Laudamus! he is coming to be shaved; that's what I've waited for. Messer Domenico[5], go not away—wait; you shall see a rare bit of fooling, which I devised two days ago. Here, Sandro!"

Nello whispered in the ear of Sandro, who rolled his solemn eyes, nodded, and following up these signs of understanding with a slow smile, took to his heels with surprising rapidity.

"How is it with you, Maestro Tacco?"* said Nello, as the doctor, with difficulty, brought his horse's head round towards the barber's

6 Luigi] *1 2 3* Messer Luigi *MS CM*   7 was {of} *MS*
8 'Dombruno's . . . steel.'] *There are no inverted commas in MS*
9 as ⟨that of⟩ *MS*   1 ⟨the leech⟩ he *MS*
2 capons and eggs and meal] *MS 1 2 3* capons, and eggs, and meal *CM*
3 ⟨patients⟩ silly clowns *MS*   4 druggists] *1 2 3 speziali* (druggists) *MS CM*
5 Domenico] *1 2 3* Bernardo *MS CM*

shop. "That is a fine young horse of yours, but something raw in the mouth, eh?"

"He is an accursed beast, the *vermocane* seize him!" said Maestro Tacco, with a burst of irritation, descending from his saddle and fastening the old bridle, mended with string, to an iron staple in the wall. "Nevertheless," he added, recollecting himself, "a sound beast and a valuable, for one who wanted to purchase, and get a profit by training him. I had him cheap."

"Rather too hard riding for a man who carries your weight of learning: eh, maestro?" said Nello. "You seem hot."

"Truly, I am likely to be hot," said the doctor, taking off his bonnet, and giving to full view a bald low head and flat broad face,[6] with high ears, wide lipless mouth, round eyes, and deep arched lines above the projecting eyebrows, which altogether made Nello's epithet "toad-faced" dubiously complimentary to the blameless batrachian. "Riding from Peretola, when the sun is high, is not the same thing as kicking your heels on a bench in the shade, like your Florence doctors. Moreover, I have had not a little pulling to get through the carts and mules into the Mercato[7], to find out the husband of a certain Monna Ghita, who had had a fatal seizure before I was called in; and if it had not been that I had to demand my fees—"

"Monna Ghita!" [8]said Nello, as the perspiring doctor interrupted himself to rub his head and face. "Peace be with her angry soul! The Mercato will want a whip the [9]more if her tongue is laid to rest."

Tito, who had roused himself from his abstraction, and was listening to the dialogue, felt a new rush of the vague half-formed ideas about Tessa, which had passed through his mind the evening before: if Monna Ghita were really taken out of the way, it would be easier for him to see Tessa again—[1]whenever he wanted to see her.

"*Gnaffè*, [2]maestro," Nello went on, in a sympathizing tone, "you are the slave of rude mortals, who, but for you, would die like [3]brutes, without help of pill or powder. It is pitiful to see your learned [4]lymph oozing from your pores as if it were mere vulgar moisture. You think my shaving will [5]cool and disencumber you? One moment and I have done with Messer Francesco here. It seems to me a thousand years till I wait upon a man who carries all the science of Arabia in his head and saddle-bags[6]. Ecco!"

Nello held up the shaving-cloth with an air of invitation, and Maestro Tacco advanced and seated himself under a preoccupation

6 face, ⟨in which the⟩ *MS*   7 mules {into the Mercato} *MS*
8 ⟨interrupted⟩ said Nello as {. . . head and face.} *MS*   9 ⟨less⟩ more *MS*
1 ⟨if⟩ whenever *MS*   2 ⟨doctor⟩ Maestro *MS*   3 ⟨beasts⟩ brutes *MS*
4 ⟨moisture⟩ lymph *MS*   5 ⟨refresh⟩ cool and disencumber *MS*
6 {head and} saddle-bags *MS*

with his heat and his self-importance, which made him quite deaf to the [7]irony conveyed in Nello's officiously polite speech[8].

"It is but fitting that a great medicus like you," said Nello, adjusting the cloth, "should be shaved by the same razor that has shaved the illustrious Antonio Benevieni,* the greatest master of the chirurgic art."

"The chirurgic art!" interrupted the doctor, with an air of contemptuous disgust. "Is it your Florentine fashion to put the masters of the science of medicine on a level with men who [9]do carpentry on broken limbs, and sew up wounds like tailors, and carve away[1] excrescences as a butcher trims meat? *Via!* A manual art, such as any artificer might learn, and which has been practised by simple barbers like yourself—on a level with[2] the noble science of Hippocrates, Galen, and Avicenna, which penetrates into the occult influences of the stars, and plants and gems!—a science [3]locked up from the vulgar!"

"No, in truth, maestro," said Nello, using his lather very deliberately, as if he wanted to prolong the operation to the utmost[4], "I never thought of placing them on a level: I know your science comes next to the miracles of Holy Church for mystery. But there, you see, is the pity of it"—here Nello fell into a tone of regretful sympathy— "your high [5]science is sealed from the profane and the vulgar, and so you become an object of envy and slander. I grieve to say it, but there are low fellows in this city—mere *sgherri*, who go about in night-caps and long beards, and make it their business to sprinkle gall in every man's broth who is prospering. Let me tell you—for you are a stranger—this is a city where every man had need carry a large nail ready to fasten in[6] the wheel of Fortune* when his side happens to be uppermost. Already there are stories—mere fables doubtless—beginning to be buzzed about concerning you, that make me wish I could hear of your being well on your way to Arezzo. I would not have a man of your metal stoned, for though San Stefano was stoned, he was not great in medicine like San Cosmo and San Damiano.* . . . "

"What stories? what fables?" stammered Maestro Tacco. "What do you mean?"

"*Lasso!* I fear me you are come into the trap for your cheese, maestro. The fact is, there is a company of evil youths who go prowling about the houses of our citizens carrying sharp tools in their pockets;—no sort of door, or window, or shutter, but they will pierce it.

7 ⟨slight⟩ irony *MS*   8 polite speech] *3P* friendly tones *MS CM 1 2*
9 ⟨carpenter⟩ do carpentry on *MS*   1 carve {away} *MS*
2 {—on a level} with *MS*   3 ⟨inaccessible to⟩ locked up from *MS*
4 Maestro {said Nello . . . utmost} *MS*
5 ⟨calling⟩ science *MS*   6 in] *MS* on *CM 1 2 3*

They are possessed with a diabolical patience to watch the doings of people who fancy themselves private. It must be they who have done it—it must be they who have spread the stories about you and your medicines. Have you by chance detected any small aperture in your door, or window shutter? No? Well[7], I advise you to look—for it is now commonly talked of that you have been seen in your dwelling at the Canto di Paglia,* making your secret specifics by night: pounding dried toads in a mortar, compounding a salve out of mashed worms, and making your pills from the dried livers of rats which you mix with saliva emitted during the utterance of a [8]blasphemous incantation—which indeed these witnesses profess to repeat."

"It is a pack of lies!" exclaimed the doctor, struggling to get utterance, and then desisting in alarm at the approaching razor.

"It is not to me, or any of this respectable company that you need to say that, doctor[9]. We[1] are not the heads to plant such carrots as those in. But what of that? What are a handful of reasonable men against a crowd with stones in their hands? There are those among us who think Cecco d'Ascoli* was an innocent sage—and we all know how he was burnt alive for being wiser than his fellows. Ah, doctor, it[2] is not by living at Padua that you can learn to know Florentines. My belief is, they[3] would stone the Holy Father himself, if they could find a good excuse for it; and they are persuaded that you are a necromancer[4], who is trying to raise the pestilence by selling secret medicines—and[5] I am told your specifics have in truth an evil smell."

"It is false!" burst out the doctor, as Nello moved away his razor. "It is false! I will show the pills and the powders[6] to these [7]honourable signori—and the salve—it has an excellent odour—an odour of—of salve." He started up with the lather on his chin, and the cloth round his neck, to search in his saddle-bag for the belied medicines, and Nello in an instant adroitly shifted the shaving-chair till it was in the close vicinity of the horse's head, while Sandro, who had now returned, at a sign from his master, placed himself near the bridle.

"Behold, messeri!" said the doctor, bringing a small box of medicines and opening it before them. "Let any signor apply this box to his nostrils and he will find an honest odour of medicaments—not indeed of pounded gems, or rare vegetables from the East, or stones found in the bodies of birds; for I practise on the diseases of the vul-

7 Well] *1 2 3 Ebbene MS CM*
9 doctor] *1 2 3 dottore MS CM*
2 Ah, doctor, it] *1 2 3 Deh! It MS It CM*
3 My belief is, they] It is my belief they *MS*
4 necromancer] *1 2 3 nigromante MS CM*
5 and ⟨, in truth,⟩ *MS*
6 powders ⟨and the salve⟩ *MS*
7 ⟨excellent⟩ honourable *MS*
8 ⟨diabolical⟩ blasphemous *MS*
1 *We*] We *MS*

gar, for whom heaven has provided cheaper and less powerful remedies according to their degree: and there are even remedies known to
our science which are entirely free of cost—as the new *tussis** may be
counteracted[8] in the poor, who can pay for no specifics, by a resolute
holding of the breath. And here is a paste which is even of savoury
odour, and is infallible against melancholia[9], being concocted under
the conjunction of Jupiter and Venus—and I have seen it allay
spasms."

"Stay, maestro," said Nello, while the doctor had his lathered face[1]
turned towards the group near the door, eagerly holding out his box,
and lifting out one specific after another; "here comes a crying contadina[2] with her baby. Doubtless she is in search of you; it is
perhaps[3] an opportunity for you to show this honourable company a
proof of your skill. Here, *buona donna*! here is the famous doctor.
Why, what is the matter with the sweet *bimbo*[4]?"

This question was addressed to a sturdy-looking, broad-shouldered
contadina, with her head-drapery folded about her face so that little
was to be seen but a bronzed nose and a pair of dark eyes and eyebrows. She carried her child packed up in the stiff mummy-shaped
case in which Italian babies have been from time immemorial introduced into society, turning its face a little towards her bosom, and
making[5] those sorrowful grimaces which women are in the habit of
using as a sort of pulleys to draw down reluctant tears.

"Oh, for the love of the Holy Madonna!" said the woman in a wailing voice; "will you look at my poor bimbo[6]? I know I can't pay you
for it, but I took it into the Nunziata last night, and it's turned a
worse colour than before; it's the convulsions. But when I was holding
it before the Santissima Nunziata, I remembered they said there was a
new doctor come who cured everything; and so I thought it might be
the will of the Holy Madonna[7] that I should bring it to you."

"Sit down, maestro, sit down," said Nello. "Here is an opportunity
for you; here are honourable witnesses who will declare before the
Magnificent Eight[8] that they have seen you practising honestly and
relieving a poor woman's child. And then if your life is in danger, the
Magnificent Eight will put you in prison a little while just[9] to ensure
your safety, and after that[1] their *sbirri* will conduct you out of
Florence by night, as they did the zealous Frate Minore who

---

8 counteracted ⟨in those destitute of⟩ *MS*

9 melancholia ⟨and spasms and convulsions⟩ *MS*   1 {lathered} face *MS*

2 {crying} contadina *MS*   3 is {perhaps} *MS*

4 *bimbo*] *1 2 3* bambino *MS CM*   5 making ⟨the sort⟩ *MS*

6 bimbo] *1 2 3* bambinetto *MS CM*

7 Holy Madonna] *1 2 3* Madonna *MS CM*

8 Magnificent Eight] *1 2 3* Magnificent ⟨Otto⟩ Council of Eight *MS CM*

9 {a little while} just ⟨for the sake⟩ to *MS*   1 after that] then *MS*

preached against the Jews.* What! our people are given to stone-throwing; but we have Magistrates."

The doctor, unable to refuse, seated himself in the shaving-chair, trembling, half with fear and half with rage, and by this time quite unconscious of the lather which Nello had laid on with such profuseness. He deposited his medicine-case on his knees, took out his precious spectacles (wondrous Florentine device!)[2*] from his wallet, lodged them carefully above his flat nose and high ears, and lifting up his brows, turned towards the applicant.

"O Santiddio! look at him," said the woman with a more piteous wail than ever, as she held out the small mummy, which had its head completely concealed by dingy drapery wound round the head of the portable cradle, but seemed to be struggling and crying in a demoniacal fashion under this imprisonment. "The fit is on him! [3]*Ohimè!* I know what a colour[4] he is; it's the evil eye—oh!"

The doctor, anxiously holding his knees together to support his box, bent his spectacles towards the baby, and [5]said cautiously, "It may be a new disease; unwind these rags, Monna!"

The contadina, with sudden energy, snatched off the encircling linen, when out struggled—scratching, grinning, and screaming—what the doctor in his fright[6] fully believed to be a demon, but what Tito recognized as Vaiano's monkey, made more formidable by an artificial blackness, such as might have come from a hasty rubbing up the chimney.

Up started the unfortunate doctor, letting his medicine box fall, and away jumped the no less terrified and indignant monkey, finding the first resting-place for his claws on the [7]horse's mane, which he used as a sort of rope-ladder till he had fairly found his equilibrium, when he continued to clutch it as a bridle. The horse wanted no spur under such a rider, and, the already loosened bridle offering no resistance, darted off cross the piazza, with the monkey clutching, grinning and blinking, on his neck.

"*Il cavallo! Il Diavolo!*"[8] was now shouted on all sides by the idle rascals who had gathered[9] from all quarters of the piazza, and was echoed in tones of alarm by the stall-keepers, whose vested interests seemed in some danger;[1] while the doctor, out[2] of his wits with

2 (wondrous Florentine device!)] (wondrous Florentine device of the last generation) *MS*

3 ⟨Oh⟩ Ohimè *MS*   4 what a colour] what colour *1 2 3*
5 ⟨saying⟩ said *MS*   6 doctor {in his fright} *MS*
7 {mane of Maestro Tacco's} horse's mane *MS*
8 *Il Diavolo!*"] *Il diavolo*⟨!⟩ {*a bardosso!* (the devil riding without a saddle)} *MS*
9 who had gathered] who gathered *1 2 3*
1 piazza {and was echoed . . . danger}; ⟨and⟩ while the ⟨maestro⟩ doctor *MS*
2 doctor, out] *MS 1 2 3* doctor out *CM*

A Florentine Joke

confused terror at the devil, the possible stoning, and the escape of his horse, took to his heels with spectacles on nose, lathered face, and the shaving-cloth about his neck, crying—"Stop him! stop him! for a powder—a florin—stop him for a florin!"[3] while the lads, outstripping him, clapped their hands and shouted encouragement to the runaway.

The *cerretano*, who had not bargained for the flight of his monkey along with the horse, had caught up his petticoats with much celerity, and showed a pair of particoloured hose above his contadina's shoes, far in advance of the doctor. And away went the grotesque race up the Corso degli Adimari—the horse with the singular jockey, the contadina with the remarkable hose, and the doctor in lather and spectacles, with furred mantle outflying.

It was a scene such as Florentines loved,* from the [4]potent and reverend signor* going to council in his *lucco*, down to the grinning youngster, who felt himself master of all situations when his bag was filled with smooth stones from the convenient dry bed of the torrent. The grey-headed Domenico[5] Cennini [6]laughed no less heartily than the younger men, and Nello was triumphantly secure of the general admiration.

"Aha!" he exclaimed, snapping his fingers when the first burst of laughter was subsiding. "I have cleared my piazza of that unsavoury flytrap, *mi pare*[7]. Maestro Tacco will no more come here again[8] to sit for patients than he will take to licking marble* for his dinner."

"You are going towards the Piazza della Signoria, Messer Domenico[9]," said Macchiavelli. "I will go with you, and we shall perhaps see who has deserved the *palio* among these racers. Come, Melema, will you go too?"

It had been precisely Tito's intention to accompany Cennini, but before he had gone many steps, he was called back by Nello, who saw Maso approaching.

Maso's message was from Romola. She wished Tito to go to the Via de' Bardi as soon as possible. She would see him under the loggia, [1]at the top of the house, as she wished to speak to him alone[2].

---

3 florin! ⟨¶ The *cerretano* who had not bargained for the⟩—while the lads, oustripping him, clapped their hand ⟨and hissed encouragement to the⟩ and *MS*

4 ⟨grave signor⟩ ⟨grave looking⟩ potent and reverend *signor MS*

5 Domenico] *1 2 3* Bernardo *MS CM*   6 ⟨?shook⟩ laughed *MS*

7 flytrap {*mi pare*} *MS*   8 here {again} *MS*

9 Domenico] *1 2 3* Bernardo *MS CM*

1 ⟨at the top of the⟩ ⟨in the garden at the back of the house⟩ at the top *MS*

2 him alone] him *MS*

CHAPTER XVII.

UNDER THE LOGGIA

THE loggia at the top of Bardo's house rose above the buildings on each side of it, and formed a gallery round quadrangular walls. On the side towards the street the roof was supported by columns; but on the remaining sides, by a wall pierced with arched openings, so that at the back, looking over a crowd of irregular, poorly-built dwellings towards the Hill of Bogoli, Romola could at all times have a walk sheltered from observation. Near one of those arched openings, close to the door by which he had entered the loggia, Tito awaited her, with a sickening sense of the sunlight that slanted before him and mingled itself with the ruin of his hopes. He had never for a moment relied on Romola's passion for him as likely to be too strong for the repulsion created by the discovery of his secret; he had not the presumptuous vanity which might have hindered him from feeling that her love had [1]the same root with her belief in him. But as he imagined her coming towards him in her [2]radiant beauty[3], made so loveably mortal by her soft hazel eyes, he fell [4]into wishing that she had been something lower, if it were only that she might let him clasp her and kiss her before they parted. He had[5] had no real caress from her—nothing but now and then a long glance, a kiss, a pressure of the hand; and he had so often longed that they should be alone together. They were going to be alone now; but he saw her standing inexorably aloof from him. His heart gave a great throb as he saw the door move: [6]Romola was there. It was all like a flash of lightning: he felt, rather than saw, the [7]glory about her head, the tearful appealing eyes; he felt, rather than heard, the cry of love with which she said, "Tito!"

And in the same moment she was in his arms, and sobbing with [8]her face against his.

How poor Romola had yearned through the watches of the night to see that bright face! The new image of death; the strange bewildering doubt infused into her by the story of a life removed from her understanding and sympathy; the haunting vision, which she seemed not only to hear uttered by the low gasping voice, but to live[9] through, as

---

1 ⟨a common⟩ ⟨but one⟩ the same *MS*

2 ⟨proud⟩ ⟨fair⟩ radiant *MS*

3 beauty] *3C* majesty *MS CM 1 2*

4 ⟨to⟩ into *MS*

5 had ⟨never yet had a⟩ had no *MS*

6 ⟨The next instant⟩ Romola *MS*

7 ⟨bright⟩ glory *MS*

8 ⟨his⟩ her *MS*

9 seemed not only . . . live] seemed at once to hear uttered by the low gasping voice and to live *MS*

if it had been her own dream, had made her more conscious than
ever that it was Tito who had first brought the warm stream of [1]hope
and gladness into her life, and who had first turned away the keen
edge of pain [2]in the remembrance of her brother. She would tell Tito
everything; there was no one else to whom she could tell it. She had
been restraining herself in the presence of her father all the morning;
but now, that long pent-up sob might come forth. Proud and self-
controlled to all the world beside, Romola was as simple and unre-
served as a child in her love for Tito. She had been quite contented
with the days when they had only looked at each other; but now,
when[3] she felt the need of clinging to him, there was no thought that
hindered her.

"My Romola! my goddess!" Tito murmured with passionate fondness, as he clasped her gently, and kissed the thick golden ripples on
her neck. He was in paradise: disgrace, shame, parting—there was no
fear of them any longer. This happiness was too strong to be marred
by the sense that Romola was deceived in him; nay, he could only
rejoice in her delusion; for, after all, concealment had been wisdom.
The only thing he could regret was his needless dread; [4]if, indeed,
the dread had not been worth suffering for the sake of this sudden
rapture.

The sob had satisfied itself, and Romola raised her head. Neither of
them spoke; they stood looking at each other's faces with that sweet
wonder which belongs to young love—she with her long white hands
on the dark brown curls, and he with his dark fingers bathed in the
streaming gold. Each was so beautiful to the other; each was experiencing that undisturbed mutual consciousness for the first time. The
cold pressure of a new sadness on Romola's heart made her linger the
more in that silent soothing sense of nearness and love; and Tito
could not even seek to press his lips to hers, because that would be
change.

"Tito," she said, at last, "it has been altogether painful. But I must
tell you everything. Your strength will help me to resist the impressions that will not be shaken off by reason."

"I know, Romola—I know he is dead," said Tito; and the long lustrous eyes told nothing of the many wishes that would have brought
about that death long ago if there had been such potency in mere
wishes. Romola only read her own pure thoughts[5] in their dark
depths, as we read letters in happy dreams.

"So changed, Tito! It pierced me to think that it was Dino. And so
strangely hard: not a word to my father—nothing but a vision that he
wanted to tell me. And yet it was so piteous—the struggling breath,

and the eyes that seemed to look towards the crucifix, and yet not to
see it. I shall never forget it; it seems as if it would come between me
and everything I shall look at."

Romola's heart swelled again, so that she was forced to break off.
But the need she felt to disburthen her mind to Tito urged her to
repress the rising anguish. [6]When she began to speak again, her
thoughts had travelled a little.

"[7]It was strange, Tito. The vision was about our marriage, and yet
he knew nothing of you."

"What was it, my Romola? Sit down and tell me," said Tito, leading her to the bench that stood near. A fear had come across him lest
the vision should somehow or other relate to Baldassarre; and this[8]
sudden change of feeling prompted him to seek a change of position.

Romola told him all that had passed from her entrance in San
Marco, hardly leaving out one of her brother's words which had
burnt themselves into her memory as they were spoken. But when
she [9]was at the end of the vision, she paused; the rest came too
vividly before her to be uttered, and she sat looking at the distance,
almost unconscious for the moment that Tito was near her. *His* mind
was at ease now; that vague vision had passed over him like white
mist, and left no mark. But he was silent, expecting her to speak
again.

"I took it," she [1]went on, as if Tito had been reading her thoughts;
"I took the crucifix; it is down below in my bedroom."

"And now, my Romola[2]," said Tito, entreatingly; "you will banish
these ghastly thoughts. The vision was an ordinary monkish vision,
bred of fasting and fanatical ideas. It surely has no weight with you."

"No, Tito; no. But poor Dino, *he*[3] believed it was a divine message.
It is strange,[4]" she went on meditatively, "this life of men possessed
with fervid beliefs that seem like madness to their fellow-beings. Dino
was not a vulgar fanatic; and that Fra Girolamo, his very voice seems
to have penetrated me with a sense that there is some truth in what
moves them—some truth of which I know nothing."

"It was only because your feelings were [5]highly wrought, my
Romola. Your brother's state of mind was no more than a form of
that theosophy which has been the common disease of excitable
dreamy minds in all ages; the same[6] ideas that your father's old

6 ⟨But⟩ When *MS*
7 ⟨My Romola! you shall have no more grief," said Tito, kissing the trembling lips,
"Life shall be all love to you and me."⟩ ¶ It *MS*
8 this] the *MS*   9 ⟨came to⟩ was at *MS*   1 ⟨said⟩ went on *MS*
2 my Romola] *1 2 3 angiol mio MS CM*   3 *he*] he *MS*
4 strange, ⟨this⟩ *MS*   5 ⟨in that highly wrought condition⟩ highly wrought *MS*
6 same ⟨as the⟩ ideas {that} *MS*

antagonist, Marsilio Ficino, pores over in the New Platonists; only your brother's passionate nature drove him to act out what other men write and talk about. And for Fra Girolamo, he is simply a narrow-minded monk, with a gift for[7] preaching and infusing terror into the multitude. Any words or any voice would have shaken you at that moment. When your mind has had a little repose, you will judge of such things as you have always done before."

"Not about poor Dino," said Romola. "I [8]was angry with him; my heart seemed to close against him while he was speaking; but since then I have thought less of what was in my own mind and more of what was in his. Oh, Tito! it was very piteous to see his young life coming to an end in that way. That yearning look at the crucifix when he was gasping for breath—I can never forget it. Last night I looked at the crucifix a long while, and tried to see that it would help him, until at last it seemed to me by the lamplight as if the suffering face shed pity."

"My Romola[9], promise me to resist such thoughts; they are fit for sickly nuns, not for my golden-tressed Aurora,* who looks made to scatter all such twilight fantasies. Try not to think of them now; we shall not long be alone together."

The last words were uttered in a tone of [1]tender beseeching, and he turned her face towards him with a gentle touch of his right hand.

Romola had had her eyes fixed absently on the [2]arched opening, but she had not seen the distant hill; she had all the while been in the chapter-house, looking at the pale images of sorrow and death.

Tito's touch and beseeching voice recalled her, and now in the warm sunlight she saw that rich dark beauty which seemed to gather round it all images of joy—purple vines festooned between the elms, the strong corn perfecting itself under the vibrating heat, bright winged creatures hurrying and resting among the flowers, round limbs [3]beating the earth in gladness, with cymbals held aloft; light melodies chanted to the thrilling rhythm of strings—all objects and all sounds that[4] tell of Nature revelling in her force. Strange, bewildering transition from those pale images of sorrow and death to this bright youthfulness, as of a sun-god who knew nothing of night! What thought could reconcile that worn anguish in her brother's face[5]—that straining after something invisible—with this satisfied strength and beauty, and make it intelligible that they belonged to the same world?

7 for] of *3*   8 ⟨spoke indignantly to⟩ was angry with *MS*
9 My Romola] *1 2 3 Romola mia MS CM*   1 ⟨gentle⟩ tender *MS*
2 ⟨distance⟩ arched opening, but she had ⟨all the while⟩ not seen the ⟨?sunlit⟩ distant hill; she had all the while been ⟨seeing the pale images of sorrow⟩ *MS*
3 ⟨pulsing⟩ beating *MS*   4 that ⟨seem⟩ *MS*
5 anguish in her brother's face] anguish *MS*

Or was there never any reconciling of them—but only a blind wor-ship of clashing deities, first in mad joy and then in wailing? Romola for the first time felt this[6] questioning need like a sudden uneasy dizziness and want of something to grasp; it was an experience [7]hardly longer than a sigh, for the eager[8] theorizing of ages is com-pressed, as in a seed, into[9] the momentary want of a single mind. But there was no answer to meet the need, and it vanished before the returning rush of young sympathy with the glad loving beauty that beamed upon her [1]in new radiance, like the dawn after we have looked away from it to the grey west.

"Your mind lingers apart from our love, my Romola," Tito said, with a soft reproachful murmur. "It seems a forgotten thing to you."

She looked at the beseeching eyes in silence, till the sadness all melted out of her own.

"My joy[2]!" she said[3], in her full clear voice.

"Do you really care for me enough, then, to banish those chill fan-cies, or shall you always be suspecting me as the Great Tempter?" said Tito, with his bright smile.

"How should I not care for you more than for everything else? Everything I had felt before in all my life—about my father, and about my loneliness—was a preparation to love you. You would laugh at me, Tito, if you knew what sort of man I used to think I should marry—some scholar[4] with deep lines in his face, like Alamanno Rinuccini, and with rather grey hair, who would agree with my father in taking the side of the Aristotelians, and be willing to live with him. I used to think about the love I read of in the poets, but I never dreamed that anything like that could happen to me here in Florence in our old library. And then *you* came, Tito, and were so much to my father, and I began to believe that life could be happy for me too."

"My goddess! is there any woman like you?" said Tito, with a mix-ture of fondness and wondering admiration at the blended majesty and simplicity in her.

"But, dearest," he went on, rather timidly, "if you minded more about our marriage, you would persuade your father and Messer Bernardo not to think of any more delays. But you seem not to mind about it."

"Yes, Tito, I will, I do mind. But I am sure my godfather will urge more delay now, because of Dino's death[5]. He has never agreed with my father about disowning Dino, and you know he has always said that we ought to wait until you have been at least a year in Florence.

6 this] that *MS*   7 ⟨no⟩ hardly *MS*   8 eager] hungry *MS*
9 into] *MS* in CM *1 2 3*   1 ⟨with⟩ in *MS*   2 My joy] *Gioa mia MS*
3 said ⟨then⟩ *MS*   4 scholar ⟨?going ?grey⟩ *MS*   5 Dino{'s death} *MS*

Do not [6]think hardly of my godfather. I know he is prejudiced and narrow, but yet he is very noble. He has often said that it is folly in my father to want to keep his library apart, that it may bear his name; yet he would try to get my father's wish carried out. That seems to me very great and noble—that power of respecting a feeling which [7]he does not share or understand."

"I have no rancour against Messer Bernardo for thinking you too precious for me, my Romola," said Tito; and that was true. "But your father, then, knows of his son's death?"

"Yes, I told him—I could not help it[8]—I told him where I had been, and that I had seen Dino die; but nothing else; and he has commanded me not to speak of it again. But he has been very silent this morning, and has had those restless movements which always go to my heart; they look as if he were trying to get outside the prison of his blindness. Let us go to him now. I had persuaded him to try to sleep, because he slept little in the night. Your voice will soothe him, Tito; it always does."

"And not one kiss? I have not had one," said Tito, in his [9]gentle reproachful tone, which gave him an air of dependence very charming in a creature with those rare gifts that seem to excuse presumption.

The sweet pink blush[1] spread itself with the quickness of light over Romola's face and neck as she bent towards him. It seemed impossible that[2] their kisses could ever become common things.

"Let us walk once round the loggia," said Romola, "before we go down."

"There is something grim and grave to me always about Florence," said Tito, as they paused in the front of the house, where they could see over the opposite roofs to the other side of the river, "and even in its merriment there is something shrill and hard—biting rather than gay[3]. I wish we lived in Southern Italy[4], where thought is broken not by weariness, but by delicious languors such as never seem to come over the 'ingenia acerrima Florentina.'* I should like to see you under that southern sun, lying among the flowers, subdued into mere enjoyment, while I bent over you and touched[5] the lute and sang to you [6]some little unconscious strain that seemed all one with the light and the warmth. You have never known that happiness of the nymphs, my Romola."

6 ⟨feel⟩ think *MS*   7 ⟨we do⟩ he does *MS*
8 him{—I could not help it} *MS*   9 ⟨pretty⟩ gentle *MS*
1 blush] *1 2 3* flush *MS CM*
2 impossible that] impossible to them that *MS*
3 river {and even . . . gay} *MS*   4 Italy] Italy, Romola *MS*
5 {bent over you and} touched *MS*
6 ⟨the⟩ some *MS*

"No; but[7] I have dreamed of it often since you came. I am very thirsty for a deep draught of joy—for a life all bright like you. But we will not think of it now, Tito; it seems to me as if there would always be pale sad faces among the flowers, and eyes that look in vain. Let us go."

7 No; but] *3P* No, Tito; but *MS CM 1 2*

CHAPTER XVIII.

THE PORTRAIT

WHEN Tito left the Via de' Bardi that day in exultant satisfaction at finding himself thoroughly free[1] from the threatened peril, his thoughts, no longer claimed by the immediate presence of Romola and her father, recurred to those futile hours of dread in which he was conscious of having not only felt but acted as he would not have done if he had had a truer foresight. He would not have parted with his ring; for Romola, and others to whom it was a familiar object, would be a little struck with the apparent sordidness of parting with a gem he had professedly cherished, unless he feigned as a reason the desire to make some special gift with the purchase-money; and Tito had at that moment a nauseating [2]weariness of simulation. He was well out of the possible consequences that might have fallen on him from that initial deception, and it was no longer a load on his mind; kind fortune had brought him immunity, and he thought it was only fair that she should. Who was hurt by it? The[3] results to Baldassarre were too problematical to be taken into account. But he wanted now to be free from any hidden shackles that would gall him, though ever so little, under his ties to Romola. He was not aware that that very delight in immunity which prompted resolutions not to entangle himself again, was deadening the sensibilities which alone could save him from entanglement.

But, after all, the sale of the ring was a slight matter. Was it also a slight matter that little Tessa was under a delusion which would doubtless fill her small head with expectations doomed to disappointment? Should he try to see the little thing alone again and undeceive her at once, or should he leave the disclosure to time and chance? Happy dreams are pleasant, and they easily come to an end with daylight and the stir of life. The sweet, pouting, innocent, round thing! It was impossible not to think of her. Tito thought he should like some time to take her[4] a present that would please her, and just learn if her step-father treated her more cruelly now her mother was dead. Or, should he at once undeceive Tessa, and then tell Romola about her, so that they might find some happier lot for the poor thing? No: that unfortunate little incident of the *cerretano* and the marriage, and

---

1 {thoroughly} free *MS*   2 ⟨feeling⟩ weariness *MS*
3 The] *3C* Any *MS CM 1 2*
4 like{—some time—}to take her ⟨some⟩ a present that would please her ⟨—some time—⟩*MS*

his allowing Tessa to part from him in delusion, must never be known to Romola, and since no enlightenment could expel it from Tessa's mind, there would always be a risk of betrayal; besides, even little Tessa might have some gall in her when she found herself disappointed in her love—yes, she *must* be a little in love with him, and that might make it well that he should not see her again. Yet it was a trifling adventure such as a country girl[5] would perhaps ponder on till[6] some ruddy contadino made acceptable love to her, when she would break her resolution of secrecy and get at the truth that she was free. *Dunque*—good-by, Tessa! kindest wishes! Tito had made up his mind that the silly little affair of the *cerretano* should have no further consequences for himself; and people are apt to think that resolutions taken[7] on their own behalf will be firm. As for the [8]fifty-five florins, the purchase-money of the ring, Tito had made up his mind what to do with some of them[9]; he would carry out a pretty ingenious thought which would set[1] him more at ease in accounting for the absence of his ring to Romola, and would also serve him as a means of guarding her mind from the recurrence of those monkish fancies which were especially repugnant to him; and with this thought in his mind, he went on to the Via Gualfonda* to find Piero di Cosimo, the artist who[2] at that time was pre-eminent in the fantastic mythological design* which Tito's purpose required.

Entering the court on which Piero's dwelling opened, Tito found the heavy iron knocker on the door thickly bound round with wool and ingeniously fastened with cords. Remembering the painter's practice of stuffing his ears against obtrusive noises, Tito was not much surprised at this mode of defence against visitors' thunder, and betook himself first[3] to rapping[4] modestly with his knuckles, and then to a more importunate attempt to shake the door. In vain! Tito was moving away, blaming himself for wasting his time on this visit, instead of waiting till he saw the painter again at Nello's, when a little girl entered the court with a [5]basket of eggs* on her arm, went up to the door, and standing on tip-toe, pushed up a [6]small iron plate that ran in grooves, and putting her mouth to the aperture thus disclosed, called out in a piping voice, "Messer Piero!"

In a few moments Tito heard the sound of bolts, the door opened, and Piero presented himself in a red night-cap and a loose brown-serge tunic[7], with sleeves rolled up to the shoulder. He darted a look

5 {country} girl *MS*   6 till ⟨the temptation came⟩ *MS*
7 taken] *3C* made *MS CM 1 2*   8 ⟨seventy⟩ fifty *MS*
9 {some of} them *MS*   1 set] *3C* make *MS CM 1 2*
2 who ⟨excelled all others of his time in that⟩ *MS*   3 himself {first} *MS*
4 rapping] *MS* tapping *CM 1 2 3*   5 ⟨large⟩ basket *MS*
6 ⟨little⟩ small *MS*   7 cap, {and} a loose brown-serge tunic ⟨and⟩ with *MS*

of surprise at Tito, but without further notice of him stretched out
his hand to take the basket from the child, re-entered the house, and
presently returning with the empty basket, said, "How much to pay?"

"[8]Two grossoni, Messer Piero; they are all ready boiled, my mother
says."

Piero took the coin out of the leathern scarsella at his belt, and the
little maiden trotted away, not without a few upward glances of awed
admiration at the surprising young signor[9].

Piero's glance was much less complimentary as he said,

"What do you want at my door, Messer Greco? I saw you this
morning at Nello's; if you had asked me then, I could have told you
that I see no man in this house without knowing his business and
agreeing with him beforehand."

"Pardon, Messer Piero," said Tito, with his imperturbable good
humour; "I acted without sufficient reflection. I remembered nothing
but your admirable skill in inventing pretty caprices, when a sudden
desire for something of that sort prompted me to come to you."

[1]The painter's manners were too notoriously odd to all the world
for this reception to be held[2] a special affront; but even if Tito had
suspected any offensive intention, the impulse to resentment would
have been less strong in him than the desire to conquer goodwill.

Piero made a grimace which was habitual with him when he was
spoken to with flattering sauvity. He grinned, stretched out the corners of his mouth, and pressed down his brows, so as to defy any
divination of his feelings under that kind of stroking.

"And what may that need be?" he said, after a moment's pause. In
his heart he was tempted by the hinted opportunity of applying his
invention.

"I want a very delicate miniature device taken from certain fables of
the poets, which you will know how to combine for me. It must be
painted on a wooden case—I will show you the size—in the form of a
triptych. The inside may be simple gilding: it is on the outside I want
the device. It is a favourite subject with you Florentines*—the triumph
of Bacchus and Ariadne; but I want it treated in a new way—a story in
Ovid* will give you[3] the necessary hints. The young Bacchus must be
seated in a ship, his head bound with clusters of grapes, and a spear
entwined with vine-leaves in his hand: [4]dark-berried ivy must wind
about the masts and sails, the oars must be thyrsi, and flowers must
wreathe themselves about the poop; leopards and tigers must be
crouching before him, and dolphins must be sporting round. But I
want to have the fair-haired Ariadne with him, made immortal with

8 ⟨Three grossoni⟩ ⟨One lira⟩ Two grossoni *MS*   9 signor] *signore MS*
1 ⟨Pier[o's]⟩ The painter's *MS*   2 held ⟨as⟩ *MS*   3 give {you} *MS*
4 ⟨the⟩ dark-berried *MS*

her golden crown—that is not in [5]Ovid's story, but no matter, you will conceive it all—and above there must be young loves, such as you know how to paint, shooting with roses at the points of their arrows—"

"Say no more!" said Piero. "I have Ovid in the vulgar tongue. Find me the passage. I love not to be choked with other men's thoughts. You may come in."

Piero led the way through the first room, where a basket of eggs was deposited on the open hearth, near a heap of broken egg-shells and a bank of ashes. In strange keeping with that sordid litter, there was a low bedstead of carved ebony, covered carelessly with a piece of rich oriental carpet, that looked as if it had served to cover the steps to a Madonna's throne; and a carved *cassone*, or large chest, with painted devices on its sides and lid. There was hardly any other furniture in the large room, except casts, wooden steps, easels and rough boxes, all festooned with cobwebs.

The next room was still larger, but it was also much more crowded[6]. Apparently Piero was keeping the festa, for the double door[7] underneath the window which admitted the painter's light from above, was thrown open, and showed a garden or rather [8]thicket in which fig-trees and vines grew in tangled, trailing[9] wildness* among nettles and hemlocks, and a tall cypress lifted its dark head[1] from a stifling mass of yellowing[2] mulberry-leaves. It seemed as if that dank luxuriance had begun to penetrate even within the walls of the wide and lofty room; for in one corner, amidst a confused heap of carved marble[3] fragments and rusty armour, tufts of long grass and dark feathery[4] fennel had made their way, and a large stone vase, tilted on one side, seemed to be pouring out the ivy that streamed around. All about the walls hung pen and oil sketches of fantastic sea-monsters; dances of satyrs and mænads[5]; Saint Margaret's [6]resurrection out of the devouring dragon;* Madonnas with the supernal light upon them; studies of plants and grotesque heads;* and on irregular rough shelves a few books were scattered among great drooping bunches of corn, bullock's horns[7], pieces of dried honeycomb, stones with patches of rare-coloured lichen, skulls and bones, peacocks' feathers, and large birds' wings[8]. Rising from amongst the dirty litter of the floor [9]were lay figures—one in the frock of a Vallombrosan monk, strangely

---

5 ⟨the story in Ov[id]⟩ Ovid's story *MS*   6 crowded ⟨with⟩ *MS*
7 door] doors *MS*   8 ⟨wilderness⟩ thicket *MS*   9 {tangled} trailing *MS*
1 {dark} head *MS*   2 yellowing] yellowish *1 2 3*   3 {carved} marble *MS*
4 {dark} feathery *MS*   5 mænads] *3C* Menads *MS* menads *CM 1 2*
6 ⟨rising⟩ resurrection, out of the {devouring} dragon, Madonnas ⟨looking upwards to the divine light⟩ with *MS*
7 corn, {bullocks' horns} *MS*
8 {peacocks'} feathers and {large} birds' wings *MS*
9 ⟨was a lay figure in⟩ were lay figures—one in the ⟨grey⟩ frock *MS*

surmounted by a helmet with barred visor, another smothered with brocade and skins hastily tossed over it. Amongst this heterogeneous still life, several speckled and white pigeons were perched or strutting, too tame to fly at the entrance of men; three corpulent toads were crawling in an intimate friendly way near the door-stone; and a white rabbit, apparently the model for that which was frightening Cupid in the picture of Mars and Venus,* placed on the central easel, was twitching its nose with much content on a box full of bran.

"And now, Messer Greco," said Piero, making a sign to Tito that he might sit[1] down on a low stool[2] near the door, and then[3] standing over him with folded arms, "don't be trying to see everything at once, like Messer Domeneddio, but let me know how large you would have this same triptych."

Tito indicated the required dimensions, and Piero marked them on a piece of paper.

"And now for the book," said Piero, reaching down a manuscript volume.

"There's nothing about the Ariadne there," said Tito, giving him the passage; "but you will remember I want the crowned Ariadne by the side of the young Bacchus[4]: she must have golden hair."

"Ha!" said Piero, abruptly, pursing up his lips again. "And you want them to be likenesses, eh?" he added, looking down into Tito's face.

Tito laughed and blushed. "I know you are great at portraits, Messer Piero; but I could not ask Ariadne to sit for you, because the painting is a secret."

"There it is! I want her to sit to me. [5]Giovanni Vespucci wants me to paint him a picture of Œdipus and Antigone at Colonos,* as he has expounded it to me: I have a fancy for the subject, and I want Bardo and his daughter to sit for it. Now, you ask them; and then I'll put the likeness into Ariadne."

"Agreed, if I can prevail with them. And your price for the Bacchus and Ariadne?"

"*Baie!* If you get them to let me paint them, that will pay me. I'd rather not have your money: you may pay for the case."

"And when shall I sit for you?" said Tito, "for if we have one likeness, we must have two."

"I don't want *your* likeness—I've got it already[6]," said Piero, "only I've made you look frightened. I must take the fright out of it for Bacchus."

As he was speaking, Piero laid down the book and went to look

---

1 making a sign . . . sit] *3P* signing to Tito to sit *MS CM 1 2*
2 {low} stool *MS*   3 and {then} *MS*   4 {the young} Bacchus *MS*
5 ⟨I want to⟩ Giovanni *MS*   6 it {already} *MS*

among some paintings, propped with their faces against[7] the wall. He returned with an oil-sketch in his hand.

"I call this as good a bit of portrait as I ever[8] did," he said, looking at it, as he advanced. "Yours is a face that expresses fear well, because it's naturally a bright one. I noticed it the first time I saw you. The rest of the [9]picture is hardly sketched; but I've painted *you* in thoroughly."

Piero turned the sketch, and held it towards Tito's eyes. He saw himself with his right hand uplifted, holding a wine-cup, in the attitude of triumphant joy, but with his face turned away from the cup with an expression of such intense fear in the dilated eyes and pallid lips, that he felt a cold stream through his veins, as if he were being thrown into sympathy with his imaged self.

"You are beginning to look like it already," said Piero, with a short laugh, moving the picture away again. "He's seeing a ghost—that fine young man.[1] I shall finish it some day, when I've settled what sort of ghost is the most terrible—whether it should look solid, like a dead man come to life, or half transparent, like a mist."

Tito, rather ashamed of himself for a sudden sensitiveness, strangely opposed[2] to his usual easy self-command, said carelessly—

"That is a subject after your own heart, Messer Piero—a revel interrupted by a ghost. You seem to love the blending of the [3]terrible with the gay. I suppose that is the reason your shelves are so well furnished with death's-heads, while you are painting those roguish loves who are running away with the armour of Mars. I begin to think you are a Cynic philosopher in the pleasant disguise of a cunning painter."

"Not I, Messer Greco; a philosopher is the last sort of animal I would[4] choose to resemble. I find it enough to live, without spinning lies to account for life. Fowls cackle, asses bray, women chatter, and philosophers spin false reasons—that's the effect the sight of the world brings out of them. Well, I am an animal that paints instead of cackling, or braying, or spinning lies. And now, I think, our business is done; you'll keep to your side of the bargain about the Œdipus and Antigone?"

"I will do my best," said Tito—on this strong hint, immediately moving towards the door.

"And you'll let me know at Nello's. No need to come here again."

"I understand," said Tito, laughingly, lifting his hand in sign of friendly parting.

7 {with their faces} against *MS*
9 ⟨sketch⟩ picture *MS*
2 for a sudden sensitiveness, strangely opposed] *1 2 3* for this strange and sudden sensitveness, so opposed *MS CM*
3 ⟨horrible⟩ terrible *MS*

8 I ever] *MS CM 1 3P* ever I *2*
1 again." {He's seeing . . . man.} *MS*

4 would] should *2 3*

CHAPTER XIX.

THE OLD MAN'S HOPE

MESSER BERNARDO DEL NERO was as inexorable as Romola had expected in [1]his advice that the marriage should be deferred till Easter, and [2]in this matter Bardo was entirely under the ascendancy of his sagacious and practical friend. Nevertheless, Bernardo himself, though he was as far as ever from any susceptibility to [3]the personal fascination in Tito which[4] was felt by others, could not altogether resist that argument of success which is [5]always powerful with men of the world. Tito was making his way rapidly in high quarters. He was especially growing in favour with the young Cardinal Giovanni de' Medici, who had even spoken of Tito's forming part of his learned retinue on an approaching journey to Rome; and the bright young Greek, who had a tongue that was always ready [6]without ever being quarrelsome, was more and more wished for at gay suppers in the Via Larga, and at Florentine games in which he had no pretension to excel, and could [7]admire the incomparable skill of Piero de' Medici in the most graceful manner in the world. By an unfailing sequence[8], Tito's reputation as an agreeable companion in "magnificent" society made his learning and talent appear more lustrous; and he was really accomplished enough to prevent an exaggerated estimate from being [9]hazardous to him. Messer Bernardo had old prejudices and attachments which now began to argue down the newer and feebler prejudice against the young Greek stranger who was rather too supple[1]. To the old Florentine it was impossible to despise the recommendation of standing well with the best Florentine families, and since Tito began to be thoroughly received into that circle whose views were the unquestioned standard of social value,[2] it seemed irrational not to admit that there was no longer [3]any check to satisfaction in the prospect of such a son-in-law for Bardo, and such a husband for Romola. It was undeniable that Tito's coming had been the dawn of a new life for both father and daughter, and the first promise had even been surpassed. The blind old scholar—whose proud truthfulness would never enter into that commerce of feigned and preposterous

1 ⟨advising Bardo⟩ his advice *MS*   2 ⟨on⟩ in *MS*   3 ⟨that⟩ the *MS*
4 which ⟨attracted⟩ *MS*   5 ⟨all-powerful⟩ always powerful *MS*
6 ⟨and never⟩ without ever *MS*   7 ⟨therefore⟩ admire *MS*
8 sequence] *1 2 3* law of sequence *MS CM*   · 9 ⟨too⟩ hazardous *MS*
1 {rather} too supple ⟨for a stiff-necked Florentine⟩. *MS*
2 value, ⟨there was no longer any⟩ *MS*   3 ⟨anything to⟩ any *MS*

admiration which, [4]varied by a corresponding measurelessness in vitu-
peration, made the woof of all learned intercourse—had fallen into
neglect even among his fellow-citizens, and when he was [5]alluded to
at all, it had long been usual to say that though his blindness and the
loss of his son were pitiable misfortunes,[6] he was tiresome in con-
tending for the value of his own labours; and that his discontent was
a little inconsistent in a man who had been openly regardless of religious rites, and who in days past had refused offers made to him
from various quarters on the slight condition that he would take[7]
orders, without which it was not easy for patrons to provide for every
scholar. But since Tito's coming, there was no longer the same
monotony in the thought that Bardo's name suggested; the old man,
it was understood, had left off his plaints, and the fair daughter was
no longer to be shut up in dowerless pride, waiting for a *parentado*.
The winning manners and growing favour of the handsome Greek
who was expected to enter into the double relation of son and husband helped to make the new interest a thoroughly friendly one, and
it was no longer a rare occurrence when a visitor enlivened the quiet
library. Elderly men came from that indefinite prompting to renew
former intercourse which [8]arises when an old acquaintance begins to
be newly talked about; and young men whom Tito had asked leave to
bring once, found it easy to go again when they overtook him on his
way to the Via de' Bardi, and, resting their hands on his shoulder, fell
into easy chat with him. For it was pleasant to look at Romola's
[9]beauty: to see her, like[1] old Firenzuola's type of womanly majesty,
"sitting with a certain grandeur, speaking with gravity, smiling with
modesty, and casting around, as it were, an odour of queenliness;"*
and she seemed to unfold like a strong white lily under this genial
breath of admiration and homage; it [2]was all one to her with her new
bright life in Tito's love.

Tito had even been the means of strengthening the hope in Bardo's
mind that he might before his death receive the longed-for security
concerning his library: that it should not be merged in another collection; that it should not be transferred to a body of monks, and be
called by the name of a monastery; but that it should remain for ever
the Bardi Library, for the use of Florentines. For the old habit of
trusting in the Medici could not die out while their influence was still
the strongest lever in the State; and Tito, once possessing the ear of

---

4 ⟨intermitted⟩ varied *MS*   5 ⟨thought of⟩ alluded to *MS*
6 that ⟨though his blindness . . . misfortunes,⟩ *MS*
7 and who in . . . take] *3C* and in days passed had refused offers made to him from
various quarters, if he would only take *MS CM 1 2*
8 ⟨?readily⟩ arises *MS*   9 ⟨great⟩ beauty *MS*   1 like ⟨the⟩ *MS*
2 ⟨seemed⟩ was *MS*

the Cardinal Giovanni de' Medici, might do more even than Messer
Bernardo towards winning the desired interest, for he could demonstrate to a learned audience the peculiar value of Bardo's[3] collection.
Tito himself talked sanguinely of such a result, willing to cheer the
old man, and conscious that Romola repaid those gentle words to her
father with a sort of adoration that no direct tribute to herself could
have won from her.[4]

This question of the library was the subject of more than one discussion with Bernardo del Nero when Christmas was turned and the
prospect of the marriage was becoming near—but always out of
Bardo's hearing. For Bardo nursed a vague belief, which they dared
not disturb, that his property, apart from the library, was adequate to
meet all demands. He would not even, except under a momentary
pressure of angry despondency[5], admit to himself that the will by
which he had disinherited Dino would leave Romola the heir[6] of
nothing but debts; or that he needed anything from patronage beyond
the security that a separate locality should be assigned [7]to his library,
in return for a deed of gift by which he made it over to the
Florentine Republic.

"My opinion is," said Bernardo to Romola, in a consultation they
had under the loggia, "that since you are to be married, and Messer
Tito will have a competent income, we should begin to wind up the
affairs, and ascertain exactly the sum that would be necessary to save
the library from being touched, instead of letting the debts accumu-
late any longer. Your father needs nothing but his shred of mutton
and his macaroni[8] every day, and I think Messer Tito may engage to
supply that for the years that remain; he can let it be in place of the
morgen-cap."

"Tito has always known that my life is bound up with my
father's," said Romola[9]; "and he is better to my father than I am: he
delights in making him happy."

"Ah, he's not made of the same clay as other men, is he?" said
Bernardo, smiling. "Thy father has thought of shutting woman's folly
out of thee by cramming thee with Greek and Latin; but thou hast
been as ready to believe in the first pair of bright eyes and the first
soft words that have come within reach of thee, as if thou couldst say
nothing by heart but paternosters, like other Christian men's daughters."

"Now, godfather," said Romola, shaking her head playfully, "as if
it were only bright eyes and soft words that made me love Tito! You

3 Bardo's] Bardi's *1 2 3*   4 her. ⟨For⟩ {¶} This *MS*
5 even {except under . . . despondency} *MS*   6 heir] heiress *MS*
7 ⟨for⟩ to *MS*   8 macaroni] *1 2 3* maccaroni *MS CM*
9 said Romola] *1 2 3* said Romola, flushing *MS CM*

know better. You know I love my father and you because you are both good; and I love Tito, too, because he is so good. I see it, I feel it, in everything he says and does. And if he is handsome, too, why[1] should I not love him the better for that? It seems to me beauty is part of the finished language by which goodness speaks. You know *you* must have been a very handsome youth, godfather"—she looked up with one of her happy, loving smiles at the stately old man—"you were about as tall as Tito, and you had very fine eyes; only you looked a little sterner and prouder, and—"

"And Romola likes to have all the pride to herself[2]?" said Bernardo, not inaccessible to this pretty coaxing. "However, it is well that in one way Tito's demands are more modest than those of any Florentine husband of fitting rank that we should have been likely to find for you; he wants no dowry."

So it was settled in that way between Messer Bernardo del Nero, Romola, and Tito. Bardo assented with a wave of the hand when Bernardo told him that he thought it would be well now to begin to sell property and clear off debts—being accustomed to think of debts and property as a sort of thick wood that his imagination never even penetrated, still less got beyond. And Tito set about winning Messer Bernardo's respect by inquiring, with his ready faculty, into Florentine money matters, the secrets of the *Monti*[3] or public funds, the values of real property, and the profits of banking.

"You will soon forget that Tito is not a Florentine, godfather," said Romola. "See how he is learning everything about Florence!"

"It seems to me he is one of the *demoni*, who are of no particular country, child," said Bernardo, smiling. "His mind is a little too nimble to be weighted with all the stuff we men carry about in our hearts."

Romola smiled too, in happy confidence.

---

1 And if he is handsome, too, why] *3C* And he is handsome, too: why *MS CM 1 2*
2 herself] herself, eh *MS*
3 {the} *Monti MS*

CHAPTER XX.

[1]THE DAY OF THE BETROTHAL

IT was the last week of the Carnival, and the streets of Florence were at their fullest and noisiest: there were the masqued processions, chanting songs, indispensable now they had once been introduced by Lorenzo the Magnificent[2]; there was the favourite *rigoletto*, or round dance, footed "in piazza"[3] under the blue frosty sky; there were practical jokes of all sorts, from throwing comfits to throwing stones—especially stones. For the boys and striplings, always a strong element in Florentine crowds, became at the height of Carnival time as loud and unmanageable as tree-crickets, and it was their immemorial privilege to bar the way with poles[4] to all passengers, until a tribute had been paid[5] towards furnishing these[6] lovers of strong sensations with suppers and bonfires; to conclude with the standing entertainment of stone-throwing, which was not entirely monotonous, since the consequent maiming was various, and it was not always a single person who was killed.* So that the pleasures of the Carnival were of a chequered kind, and if a painter were called upon to represent them truly, he would have to make a picture in which there would be so much grossness and barbarity that it must be turned with its face to the wall, except when it was taken down for the grave historical purpose of justifying a reforming zeal which, in ignorance of the facts, might be unfairly condemned for its narrowness. Still there was much of that more innocent picturesque merriment which is never wanting among a people with quick animal spirits and sensitive organs: there was not the heavy sottishness which belongs to the thicker northern blood, nor the stealthy fierceness which in the more southern regions of the peninsula makes the brawl lead to the dagger-thrust.

It was the high morning, [7]but the merry spirits of the Carnival were still inclined to lounge and recapitulate the last night's jests, when Tito Melema was walking at a brisk pace on the[8] way to the Via de' Bardi. Young Bernardo Dovizi, who now looks at us out of Raphael's portrait as the keen-eyed Cardinal da Bibbiena,[9] was with him; and, as they went, they held animated talk about some subject [1]that had evidently no relation to the sights and sounds through

---

1 ⟨The Hiding of the Crucifix⟩ The {day of the} Betrothal *MS*
2 Lorenzo the Magnificent] *3C* Lorenzo *MS CM 1 2*
3 "in piazza"] *1 2 3 in piazza MS CM*   4 way {with poles} *MS*
5 paid ⟨which was⟩ *MS*   6 these those *2 3*   7 ⟨when⟩ but *MS*
8 the] his *MS*   9 Dovizi {who now . . . Cardinal Bibbiena, }*MS*
1 ⟨which⟩ that *MS*

which they were pushing their way along the Por' Santa Maria. Nevertheless, as they discussed, smiled, and gesticulated, they both, from time to time, cast quick glances around them, and at the turning towards the Lung' Arno, leading to the Ponte Rubaconte[2],* Tito had become aware, in one of these rapid surveys, that there was some one not far off him by whom he very much desired not to be recognized at that moment. His time and thoughts were thoroughly preoccupied, for he was looking forward to a unique occasion in his life—he was preparing for his betrothal, which was to take place [3]on the evening of this very day. The ceremony had been resolved upon rather suddenly; for although preparations towards the marriage had been going forward for some time—chiefly in the application of Tito's florins to the fitting-up of [4]rooms in Bardo's dwelling, which, the library excepted, had always been scantily furnished—it had been intended to defer both the betrothal and the marriage until after Easter[5], when Tito's year of probation, insisted on by Bernardo del Nero, would have been complete. But when an express proposition had come, that Tito should follow the Cardinal Giovanni to Rome to help Bernardo Dovizi with his superior knowledge of Greek in arranging a library, and there was no possibility of declining what lay so plainly on the road to advancement, he had become urgent in his entreaties that the betrothal might take place before his departure: there would be the less delay[6] before the marriage, on his return, and it would be less painful to part if he and Romola were outwardly as well as inwardly pledged to each other—if he had a claim which defied Messer Bernardo or any one else to nullify it. For the betrothal, at which rings were exchanged and mutual contracts were signed, made more than half the legality of marriage, to be completed[7] on a separate occasion by the nuptial benediction. Romola's feeling had met Tito's in this wish, and the consent of the elders had been won.

And now Tito was hastening, amidst arrangements for his departure[8] the next day, to snatch a morning visit to Romola, to say and hear any last words that[9] were needful to be said before their meeting for the betrothal in the evening. It was not a time when any recognition could be pleasant that was at all likely to detain him; still less a recognition by Tessa. And it was unmistakably Tessa whom he had caught sight of moving along, with a timid and forlorn look, towards that very turn of the Lung' Arno which he was just rounding. As he continued his talk with the young Dovizi, he had an uncomfortable

2 Arno, {leading to the Ponte Rubaconte} *MS*

3 ⟨that⟩ on the evening of this *MS*   4 ⟨additional⟩ rooms *MS*

5 after Easter] *1 2 3* Easter *MS CM*   6 delay] delay then, *MS*

7 to be completed] *3C* which was completed *MS CM 1 2*

8 departure ⟨to Rome⟩ *MS*   9 that ⟨might⟩ *MS*

under-current of consciousness which told him that Tessa had seen him and would certainly follow him: there was no escaping her along this direct road by the Arno, and over the Ponte Rubaconte. But she would not dare to speak to him or approach him while he was not alone, and he would continue to keep Dovizi with him till they reached Bardo's door. He quickened his pace, and took up new threads of talk; but all the while the sense that Tessa was behind him, though he had no physical evidence of [1]the fact, grew stronger and stronger; it was very irritating—perhaps all the more so because a certain tenderness and pity for the poor little thing made the determination to escape without any visible notice of her, a not altogether agreeable resource. Yet Tito persevered and carried his companion to the door, cleverly managing his "addio"[2] without turning his face in a direction where it was possible for him to see [3]an importunate pair of blue eyes; and as he went up the stone steps, he tried to get rid of unpleasant thoughts by saying to himself that after all Tessa might not have seen him, or, if she had, might not have followed him.

But—perhaps because that[4] possibility could not be relied on strongly—when the visit was over, he came out of the doorway with a quick step and an air of unconsciousness as to anything that might be on his right hand or his left. Our eyes are so constructed, however, that they take in a wide angle without asking any leave of our will; and Tito knew[5] that there was a little figure in a white hood standing near the doorway—knew it quite well, before he felt a hand laid on his arm. It was a real grasp, and not a light, timid touch; for poor Tessa, seeing his rapid step, had started forward with a desperate effort. But when he stopped and turned towards her, her face wore a frightened look, as if she dreaded the effect of her boldness.

"Tessa!" said Tito, with more sharpness in his voice than she had ever heard in it before. "Why are you here? You must not follow me—you must not stand about door-places waiting for me."

Her blue eyes widened with tears, and she said nothing. Tito was afraid of something worse than ridicule, if he were seen in the Via de' Bardi with a girlish contadina looking pathetically at him. It was[6] a street of high silent-looking dwellings, not of traffic; but Bernardo del Nero, or some one almost as dangerous, might come up at any moment. Even if it had not been the day of his betrothal, the incident would have been awkward and annoying. Yet it would be brutal—it was impossible—to drive Tessa way with harsh words. That accursed folly of his with the *cerretano*—that it should have lain buried in a

---

1 ⟨it⟩ the fact *MS*   2 "addio"] *1 2 3 addio MS CM*
3 ⟨a pair⟩ an importunate pair *MS*   4 {perhaps because} that *MS*
5 knew ⟨quite well⟩ *MS*   6 was ⟨not⟩ a street ⟨of traffic, but⟩ of *MS*

quiet way for months, and now start up before him as[7] this unseasonable crop of vexation! He could not speak harshly, but he spoke hurriedly.

"Tessa, I cannot—must not talk to you here. I will go on to the bridge and wait for you there. Follow me slowly."

He turned and walked fast to the Ponte Rubaconte, and there leaned against the wall of one of the quaint little houses that rise at [8]even distances on the bridge, looking towards the way by which Tessa would come. It would have [9]softened a much harder heart than Tito's to see the [1]little thing advancing with [2]her round face much paled and saddened, since he had parted from it at the door of "the Nunziata."[3] Happily[4] it was the least frequented of the bridges, and there were scarcely any passengers on it at this moment. He lost no time in speaking as soon as she came near him.

"Now, Tessa, I have very little time. You must not cry. Why did you follow me this morning? You must not do so again."

"I thought," said Tessa, speaking in a whisper, and struggling against a sob that *would* rise immediately at this new voice of Tito's— "I thought you wouldn't be so long before you came to take care of me again. And the *patrigno* beats me, and I can't bear it any longer. And always when I come for a holiday I walk about to find you, and I can't.[5] Oh, please don't send me away from you again! It has been so long, and I cry so now, because you never come to me. I can't help it, for the days are so long, and I don't mind about the goats and[6] kids, or anything—and I can't—"

The sobs came fast now, and the great tears. Tito felt that he could not do otherwise than comfort her. Send her away—yes; that he *must* do, at once. But it was all the more impossible to tell her anything that would leave her in a state of hopeless grief. He [7]saw new trouble in the background, but the difficulty of the moment was too pressing for him to weigh distant consequences.

"Tessa, my little one," he said, in his old [8]caressing tones, "you must not cry. Bear with the cross *patrigno* a little longer. I will come back to you. But I'm going now to Rome—a long, long way off. I shall come back in a few weeks, and then I promise you to come and see you. Promise me to be good and wait for me."

It was the well-remembered voice again, and the mere sound was half enough to soothe Tessa. She looked up at him with wide

7 him as] *MS 1 2 3* him, as *CM*   8 ⟨wide⟩ even *MS*
9 ⟨propitiated⟩ softened a much harder ⟨anger⟩ heart *MS*
1 {⟨pretty⟩} little *MS*   2 ⟨a face⟩ her round face *MS*
3 "the Nunziata."] *MS* the "Nunziata." *CM 1 2 3*
4 Happily ⟨there were scarcely any passengers on the bridge and⟩ *MS*
5 longer. {And always . . . can't.} *MS*   6 and] *1 2 3* or *MS CM*
7 ⟨foresaw⟩ saw *MS*   8 ⟨kind⟩ caressing *MS*

trusting[9] eyes, that still glittered with tears[1], sobbing all the while, in spite of her utmost efforts to obey him. Again, he said, in a gentle voice:

"Promise me, my Tessa."

"Yes," she whispered. "But you won't be long?"

"No, not long. But I must go now. And remember what I told you, Tessa. Nobody must know that you ever see me, else you will lose me for ever. And now, when I have left you, go straight home, and never follow me again[2]. Wait till I come to you. Good-by, my little Tessa: I *will* come."

There was no help for it; he must turn and leave her without looking behind him to see how she bore it, for he had no time to spare. When he did look round he was in the Via de' Benci, where there was no seeing what was happening on the bridge; but Tessa was too trusting and obedient not to do just what he had told her.

Yes,[3] the difficulty was at an end for that day; yet this return of Tessa to him, at a moment when it was impossible for him to put an end to all difficulty with her by undeceiving her, was an unpleasant incident to carry in his memory. But Tito's mind was just now thoroughly penetrated with a hopeful first love, associated with all happy prospects flattering to his ambition; and that future necessity of grieving Tessa could be scarcely more to him than the far-off cry of some little suffering animal buried in the thicket, to a merry cavalcade in the sunny plain. When, for the second time that day, Tito was hastening across the Ponte Rubaconte, the thought of Tessa caused no perceptible diminution of his happiness. He was well muffled in his mantle, less, perhaps, to protect him from the cold than from the additional notice that would have been drawn upon him by his dainty apparel. He leaped up the stone steps by two at a time, and said hurriedly to Maso, who met him,

"Where is the damigella?"

"In the library; she is quite ready, and Monna Brigida and Messer Bernardo are already there with Ser Braccio, but none of the rest of the company."

"Ask her to give me a few minutes alone; I will await her in the *salotto*."

Tito entered a room which had been fitted up in the utmost contrast with the half-pallid, half-sombre tints of the library. The walls were brightly frescoed with "caprices" of nymphs and loves sporting under the blue among flowers and birds. The only furniture besides the red leather seats and the central table were two [4]tall white vases,

9 wide trusting] trusting *1 2 3*   1 tears ⟨while she gasped and⟩ *MS*
2 again ⟨and never go into the Via de' Bardi⟩ *MS*   3 Yes,] Yes! *MS*
4 ⟨long necked⟩ tall *MS*

and a young faun playing the flute, modelled by a promising youth*
named [5]Michelangelo Buonarotti. It was a room that gave a sense of
being in the sunny open[6] air.

Tito kept his mantle round him, and looked towards the door. It
was not long before Romola entered, all white and gold, more than
ever like a [7]tall lily. Her white silk garment[8] was bound by a golden
girdle, which fell with large tassels; and above that was the rippling
gold of her hair, surmounted by the white mist of her long[9] veil,
which was fastened on her brow by a band of pearls, the gift of
Bernardo del Nero, and was now parted off her face so that it all[1]
floated backward.

"*Regina mia!*" said Tito, as he took her hand and kissed it, still
keeping his mantle round him. He could not help going backward to
look at her again, while she stood in calm delight,[2] with that exquisite
self-consciousness which rises under the gaze of admiring love.

"Romola, will you show me the next room now?" said Tito, checking himself with the remembrance that the time might be short. "You
said I should see it when you had arranged everything."

Without speaking, she led the way into a long narrow[3] room,
painted brightly like the other, but only with birds and flowers. The
furniture in it was all old; there were old faded objects [4]for feminine
use or ornament, arranged in an open cabinet between the two narrow
windows; above the cabinet was the portrait of Romola's mother; and
below this, on the top of the cabinet, stood the crucifix which Romola
had brought from San Marco.

"I have brought something under my mantle," said Tito, smiling;
and throwing off the large loose garment, he showed the little tabernacle which had been painted by Piero di Cosimo. The painter had
carried out Tito's intention charmingly, and so far had atoned for his
long delay. "Do you know what this is for, my Romola?" added Tito,
taking her by the hand, and leading her towards the cabinet. "It is a
little shrine, which is to hide away from you for ever that remembrancer of sadness. You have done with sadness now; and we will
bury [5]all images of it—bury them in a tomb of joy. See!"

A slight quiver passed [6]across Romola's face as Tito took hold of
the crucifix. But she had no wish to prevent his purpose; on the contrary, she herself wished to subdue certain importunate [7]memories

5 ⟨Michael Angelo⟩ Michelangelo Buonarotti *MS*   6 {sunny} open *MS*
7 ⟨stately⟩ tall *MS*   8 garment] gamurra *MS*
9 {white} mist of her long ⟨white⟩ veil *MS*   1 {it} all *MS*
2 delight, ⟨one exquisite form of⟩ *MS*
3 {long} narrow *MS*   4 ⟨of⟩ for *MS*   5 ⟨every image⟩ all images *MS*
6 ⟨through⟩ across *MS*   7 ⟨memories⟩ ⟨images⟩ memories *MS*

and questionings which still flitted like unexplained shadows across
her happier thought.

He [8]opened the triptych and placed the crucifix within [9]the central
space; then [1]closing it again, taking out the key, and setting the little
tabernacle in the spot where the crucifix had stood, said,

"Now, Romola, look[2] and see if you are satisfied with the portraits
old Piero[3] has made of us. Is it not a dainty device? and the credit of
choosing it is mine."

"Ah, it is you—it is perfect!" said Romola, looking with moist joyful eyes at the miniature Bacchus, with his purple clusters. "And I
am Ariadne, and you are crowning me! Yes, it is true, Tito; you have
crowned my poor life."[4]

They held each other's hands while she spoke, and both looked at
their imaged selves. But the reality was far more beautiful; she[5] all
lily-white and golden, and he with his dark glowing beauty above the
purple red-bordered tunic.[6]

"And it was our good strange Piero who painted it?" said Romola.
"Did you[7] put it into his head to paint me as Antigone, that he might
have my likeness for this?"

"No, it was he who made[8] my getting leave for him to paint you
and your father, a condition of his doing this for me."

"Ah, I see now what it was you gave up your precious ring for. I
perceived you had some cunning plan to give me pleasure."

Tito did not blench. Romola's little illusions about himself had
long ceased to cause him anything but satisfaction. He only smiled
and said,

"I might have spared my ring; Piero will accept no money from
me; he thinks himself paid by painting you. And now, while I am
away, you will look every day at those pretty symbols of our life
together—the ship on the calm sea, and the ivy that never withers,
and those loves that have left off wounding us and shower soft petals
that are like our kisses; and the leopards and tigers, they are the
troubles of your life that are all quelled now; and the strange sea-
monsters, with their merry eyes—let us see—they are the dull passages
in the heavy books, which have begun to be amusing since we have
sat by each other."

8 ⟨took the crucifix in⟩ opened *MS*   9 ⟨its⟩ the *MS*

1 ⟨closed the doors⟩ closing it again {taking out the key}, ⟨he said⟩ ⟨and placing⟩ and
setting *MS*

2 Now, {Romola,} look *MS*   3 {old} Piero *MS*

4 life." ⟨And those roguish loves and those⟩ ¶ They *MS*

5 she ⟨in her pale majesty with her pure white raiment⟩ *MS*

6 {red-bordered} tunic. ⟨With its border of red and white below the round white-
tinted neck⟩ ¶ And *MS*

7 you ⟨get him⟩ *MS*   8 made ⟨the leave to paint⟩ *MS*

"*Tito mio!*" said Romola, in a half laughing voice of love; "but you will give me the key?" she added, holding out her hand for it.

"Not at all!" said Tito, with playful decision, opening his scarsella and dropping in the little key. "I shall drown it in the Arno."

"But if I ever wanted to look at the crucifix again?"

"Ah! for that very reason it is hidden—hidden by these images of youth and joy."

He pressed a light kiss on her brow, and she said no more, ready to submit, like all strong souls, when she felt no valid reason for resistance.

And then they joined the waiting company, which made a dignified little procession[9] as it passed along the Ponte Rubaconte towards Santa Croce. Slowly it passed, for Bardo, unaccustomed for years to leave his own house, walked with a more timid step than usual; and that slow pace suited well with the gouty dignity of Messer Bartolommeo Scala, who graced the occasion by his presence, along with his daughter Alessandra. It was customary to have very long troops of kindred and friends[1] at the *sposalizio*, or betrothal, and it had even been found[2] necessary in time past to limit the number by law to no more than *four hundred*—two hundred on each side;* for[3] since the guests were all feasted after this initial ceremony, as well as after the *nozze*, or marriage, the very first stage of matrimony had become a ruinous expense, as that scholarly Benedict[4], Leonardo Bruno,* complained in his own case. But Bardo, who in his poverty had kept himself proudly free from any appearance of claiming the advantages attached to a powerful family name, would have no invitations given on the strength of mere friendship[5]; and the modest procession of twenty that followed the *sposi* were, with three or four exceptions, friends of Bardo's and Tito's, selected on personal grounds.

Bernardo del Nero walked as a vanguard before Bardo, who was led on the right by Tito, while Romola held her father's other hand. Bardo had himself been married at Santa Croce, and had insisted on Romola's being betrothed and married there,[6] rather than in the little church of Santa Lucia* close by their house, because he had a complete mental vision of the grand church where he hoped that a burial might be granted him among the Florentines who had deserved well.[7] Happily, the way was short and direct, and lay aloof from the loudest

---

9 {little} procession *MS*   1 {kindred and} friends *MS*
2 been {found} *MS*   3 {two hundred on each side} for ⟨as⟩ since *MS*
4 scholarly Benedict] grave scholar *MS*   5 friendship] kinship *MS*
6 {betrothed and} married there, ⟨because⟩ *MS*
7 him {among the Florentines who had deserved well}. *MS*

riot of the Carnival, if only they could return before any dances or shows began in the great piazza of Santa Croce. The west was red as they passed the bridge, and shed a mellow light on the [8]pretty procession, which had a touch of solemnity in the presence of the blind father. But when the ceremony was over, and Tito and Romola came out on to the broad steps of the church, with the golden links of destiny on their fingers, the evening had deepened into struggling starlight, and the servants had their torches lit.

While[9] they came out a strange dreary [1]chant, as of a *Miserere*, met their ears, and they saw that at the extreme end of the piazza there seemed to be a stream of people impelled by something approaching from[2] the Borgo de' Greci.

"It is one of their masked processions, I suppose," said Tito, who was now alone with Romola, while Bernardo took charge of Bardo.

And as he spoke there came slowly into view, at a height far above the heads of the on-lookers, a huge and ghastly image of Winged Time with his scythe and hour-glass, surrounded by his winged children, the Hours. He was mounted on a high car completely covered[3] with black, and the bullocks that drew the car were also covered with black, their horns alone standing out white [4]above the gloom; so that in the sombre shadow of the houses it seemed to those at a distance[5] as if Time and his children were apparitions floating through the air. And behind them came what looked like a troop of the sheeted dead gliding above blackness. And as they glided slowly, they chanted in a wailing strain.

A cold horror seized on Romola, for at the first moment it seemed as if her brother's vision, which could never be effaced from her mind, was being half fulfilled. She clung to Tito, who, divining what was in her [6]thoughts, said—

"What dismal fooling sometimes pleases[7] your Florentines! Doubtless this is an invention of Piero di Cosimo,* who loves [8]such grim merriment."

"Tito, I wish it had not happened. It will deepen the images of that vision which I would fain be rid of."

"Nay, Romola, you will look only at the images of our happiness now. I have locked all sadness away from you."

"But it is still there—it is only hidden," said Romola, in a low tone, hardly[9] conscious that she spoke.

8 ⟨?crimson⟩ pretty *MS*   9 While] *3C* as *MS CM 1 2*

1 ⟨music⟩ chant *MS*   2 from] towards *MS*

3 car completely covered] *MS 1 2 3* car, completely covered *CM*

4 ⟨in⟩ above *MS*   5 seemed {to those at a distance} *MS*

6 ⟨mind⟩ thoughts *MS*   7 {sometimes} pleases *MS*

8 ⟨this⟩ such *MS*   9 hardly ⟨thinking of what she said⟩ *MS*

"See, they are all gone now!" said Tito. "You will forget this ghastly mummery when we are in the light, and can see each other's eyes. My Ariadne must never look backward now—only forward to Easter, when she will triumph with her Care-dispeller."*

END OF BOOK I

The Escaped Prisoner

BOOK II

*

CHAPTER XXI.

FLORENCE EXPECTS A GUEST

I<small>T</small> was the seventeenth of November, 1494: more than eighteen months since Tito and Romola had been finally united in the joyous Easter time, and had had a rainbow-tinted shower of comfits thrown over them, after the ancient Greek fashion,* in token that the heavens would shower sweets on them through all their double life.

Since that Easter[1] a great change had come over the prospects of Florence; and as in the tree that bears a myriad of blossoms, each single bud with its fruit is dependent on the primary circulation of the sap, so the fortunes of Tito and Romola were dependent on certain grand political and social conditions which made an epoch in the history of Italy.

In this very November, little more than a week ago, the spirit of the old centuries seemed to have re-entered the breasts of Florentines. The great bell in the Palace tower had rung out the hammer-sound of alarm, and the people had mustered with their rusty arms, their tools and impromptu cudgels, to drive out the Medici. The gate of San Gallo had been fairly shut on the arrogant, exasperating Piero,* galloping away towards Bologna with his hired horsemen frightened behind him, and shut on[2] his keener young brother, the cardinal, escaping in the disguise of a Franciscan monk: a[3] price had been set on both their heads[4]. After that, there had been some sacking of houses, according to old precedent; the ignominious images, painted on the public buildings, of the men who had conspired against the Medici in days gone by, were effaced; the exiled enemies of the Medici were invited home. The half-fledged tyrants were fairly out of their splendid nest in the Via Larga, and the Republic had recovered the use of its will again.

But now, a week later, the great palace in the Via Larga had been prepared for the reception of another tenant; and if drapery roofing the streets with unwonted colour, if banners and hangings pouring

1 Easter] *3P* Easter time *MS CM 1 2*   2 shut on] *3C* on *MS CM 1 2*
3 monk: a] *3P* monk; and a *MS CM 1 2*
4 both their heads] *3C* their heads *MS CM 1 2*

out from[5] the windows, if carpets and tapestry stretched over all steps and pavement on which[6] exceptional feet might tread, were an unquestionable proof of joy, Florence was very joyful in the expectation of its new guest. The stream of colour flowed from the Palace in the Via Larga round by the Cathedral, then by the great Piazza della Signoria, and across the Ponte Vecchio to the Porta San Frediano— the gate that looks towards Pisa. There, near the gate, a platform and canopy had been erected for the Signoria; and Messer Luca Corsini, doctor of law, felt his heart palpitating a little with the sense that he had a Latin oration to read; and every chief elder in Florence had to make himself ready, with smooth chin and well-lined silk *lucco*, to walk in procession; and the well-born youths were looking at their rich new tunics after the French mode,* which was to impress the stranger as having a peculiar grace when worn by Florentines; and a large body of the clergy, from the archbishop in his effulgence to the train of monks[7], black, white, and grey, were consulting betimes[8] in the morning how they should marshal themselves, with their burthen of relics, and sacred banners, and consecrated jewels, that their movements might be adjusted to the expected arrival of the illustrious visitor, at three o'clock in the afternoon.

An unexampled visitor! For he had come through the passes of the Alps with such an army as Italy had not seen before: with thousands of terrible Swiss, well used to fight for love and hatred as well as for hire; with a host of gallant cavaliers proud of a name; with an unprecedented infantry, in which every man in a hundred carried an harquebuss; nay, with cannon of bronze shooting not stones but iron balls, drawn not by bullocks but by horses, and capable of firing a second time before a city could mend the breach made by the first ball.* Some compared the new comer to Charlemagne, reputed rebuilder of Florence,* [9]welcome conqueror of degenerate Kings, regulator and benefactor of the Church; some preferred the comparison to Cyrus, liberator of the chosen people, restorer of the Temple.* For he had come across the Alps with the most glorious projects: he was to march through [1]Italy amidst the jubilees of a grateful and admiring people; he was to satisfy all conflicting complaints at Rome; he was to take possession, by virtue of hereditary right* and a little fighting, of the kingdom of Naples; and from that convenient starting-point he was to set out on the conquest of the Turks, who were partly to be cut to pieces and partly converted to the faith of Christ. It was a scheme that seemed to [2]befit the Most Christian King,* head of a

5 from] of *2 3*   6 on which] *1 2 3* where *MS CM*
7 monks ⟨in a broad [?sober] mass⟩ *MS*   8 betimes] *MS 1 2 3* by times *CM*
9 ⟨beneficent⟩ welcome conqueror {of degenerate Kings,} *MS*
1 ⟨Lombardy and Tuscany⟩ Italy *MS*   2 ⟨become⟩ befit *MS*

nation which, thanks to the devices of a subtle Louis the Eleventh, who had died in much fright as to his personal prospects ten years [3]before, had become the strongest of Christian monarchies; and this antitype of Cyrus and Charlemagne was no other than the son of that subtle Louis—the young Charles the Eighth of France.

Surely, on a general statement, hardly anything could seem more grandiose, or fitter to revive in the breasts of men the memory of great dispensations by which new strata had been laid in the history of mankind. [4]And there was a very widely spread conviction that the[5] advent of the French King and his army into Italy was one of those events at which marble statues might well be believed to perspire, phantasmal fiery warriors to fight in the air, and quadrupeds to bring forth monstrous births*—that it did not belong to the usual order of Providence, but was in a peculiar sense the work of God. It was a conviction that rested less on the necessarily momentous character of a powerful foreign invasion than on certain moral emotions to which the aspect of the times gave the form of presentiments—emotions which had found a very remarkable utterance in the voice of a single man.

[6]That man was Fra Girolamo Savonarola, Prior of the Dominican convent of San Marco in Florence[7]. On a September morning, when men's ears were ringing with the news that the French army had entered Italy, he had preached in the Cathedral of Florence from the text, "Behold, I[8], even I, do bring a flood of waters upon the earth."* He believed it was by supreme guidance that he had reached just so far in his exposition of Genesis the previous Lent; and he believed the "flood of waters[9]"—emblem at once of avenging wrath and purifying mercy—to be the divinely indicated symbol of the French army. His audience, some of whom were held to be among the choicest spirits of the age—the most cultivated men in the most cultivated of Italian cities—believed it too, and listened with shuddering awe. For this man had a power, rarely paralleled, of impressing his beliefs on others, and of swaying[1] very various minds. And as long as four years ago he had proclaimed from the chief pulpit of Florence that a scourge was about to descend on Italy, and that by this scourge the Church was to be purified. Savonarola appeared to believe[2], and his hearers more or less waveringly believed, that he had a mission like

3 ⟨ago⟩ before *MS*

4 ⟨It is true, that on a closer survey, this heir of a mighty monarchy did not bear altogether the aspect⟩ And *MS*

5 the] this *MS*

6 ⟨That man was the Dominican monk, Fra⟩ That *MS*

7 Prior . . . Florence] Prior of San Marco *MS*   8 Behold, I] Behold I *1 2 3*

9 waters] water *2 3*   1 {of} swaying ⟨the most⟩ very *MS*

2 appeared to believe] *1 2 3* believed *MS CM*

that of the Hebrew prophets, and that the Florentines amongst whom
his message was delivered were in some sense a second chosen[3]
people. The idea of prophetic gifts* was not a remote one in that age:
seers of visions, circumstantial heralds of things to be, were far from
uncommon either outside or inside the cloister; but this very fact
made Savonarola stand out the more conspicuously as a grand exception. While in others the gift of prophecy [4]was very much like a far-
thing candle illuminating small corners of human destiny with
prophetic gossip, in Savonarola it [5]was like a mighty beacon shining
far out for the warning and guidance of men. And to some of the
soberest minds the supernatural character of his insight into the
future[6] gathered a strong attestation from the peculiar conditions of
the age.

[7]At the close of 1492, the year in which Lorenzo de' Medici died
and[8] [9]Tito Melema came as a wanderer to Florence, Italy was enjoying a peace and prosperity unthreatened by any near and definite danger. There was no fear of famine, for the seasons had been plenteous
in corn, and wine, and oil; new palaces had been rising in all fair
cities, new villas on pleasant slopes and summits; and the men who
had more than their share of these good things were in no fear of the
larger number who had less. For the citizens' armour was getting
rusty, and populations seemed to have become tame, licking the
hands of masters who paid for a ready-made army when they wanted
it, as they paid for goods of Smyrna. Even the fear of the Turk had
ceased to be active,* and the Pope found it more immediately
profitable to accept bribes from him for a little prospective poisoning*
than to form plans either for conquering or for converting him.

Altogether, this world, with its partitioned empire and its roomy
universal Church, seemed to be a handsome establishment for the few
who were lucky or wise enough to reap the advantages of human
folly: a world in which lust and obscenity, lying and treachery,
oppression and murder, were pleasant, useful, and, when properly
managed, not dangerous. And as a sort of fringe or adornment to the
substantial delights of tyranny, avarice, and lasciviousness, there was
the patronage of polite learning and the fine arts, so that flattery
could always be had in the choicest Latin to be commanded at that
time, and sublime artists were at hand to paint the holy and the
unclean with impartial skill. The Church, it was said, had never been
so disgraced in its head, had never[1] shown so few signs of renovating,

---

3 {second} chosen *MS*   4 ⟨seemed⟩ was *MS*   5 ⟨seemed⟩ was *MS*
6 future ⟨appeared to receive a strong presumption⟩ *MS*
7 ⟨In the year when⟩ At *MS*   8 died and] *1 2 3* died, and *MS CM*
9 and ⟨when⟩ *MS*   1 never ⟨been with⟩ *MS*

vital belief in its lower members; nevertheless[2] it was much more prosperous than in some past days. The heavens were fair and smiling above; and below there were no signs of earthquake.

Yet at that time, as we have seen, there was a man in Florence who for two years and more had been preaching that a scourge was at hand; that the world was certainly not framed for the lasting convenience of hypocrites, libertines, and oppressors. From the midst of those smiling heavens he had seen a sword hanging*—the sword of God's justice—which was speedily to descend with purifying punishment on the Church and the world. In brilliant Ferrara, seventeen years before, the contradiction between men's lives and their professed beliefs had pressed upon him with a force that had been enough to destroy his appetite for the world, and at the age of twenty-three had driven him into the cloister. He believed that God had committed to the Church the sacred lamp of truth for the guidance and salvation of men, and he saw that the Church, in its corruption, had become a[3] sepulchre to hide the lamp. As the years went on scandals increased and multiplied, and hypocrisy seemed to have given place to impudence. Had the world then ceased to have a righteous Ruler? Was the Church finally forsaken? No, assuredly: in the Sacred Book there was a record of the past in which might be seen as in a glass what would be in the days to come, and the Book showed that when the wickedness of the chosen people, type of the Christian Church, had become crying, the judgments of God had descended on them. Nay, reason itself declared that vengeance was imminent, for what else would suffice to turn men from their obstinacy in evil? And unless the Church were reclaimed, how could the promises be fulfilled, that the heathens should be converted and the whole world become subject to the one[4] true law? He had seen his belief reflected in visions—a mode of seeing which had been frequent with him from his youth up.[5]

But the real force of demonstration for Girolamo Savonarola lay in his own burning indignation at the sight of wrong; in his [6]fervent[7] belief in an unseen Justice that would put an end to the wrong, and in an unseen Purity to which lying and uncleanness were an abomination. To his ardent, power-loving soul, believing in great ends, and longing to achieve those ends by the exertion of its own strong will[8], the faith in a supreme and righteous Ruler became one with the faith in a speedy divine interposition that would punish and reclaim.

2 nevertheless] *1 2 3* yet *MS CM*
3 a] *3C* as a *MS CM 1 2*
4 {the} one *MS*
5 law? {He had . . . up.} *MS*
6 ⟨ardent⟩ fervid *MS*
7 fervent] *1 2 3* fervid *MS CM*
8 of its own strong will] *1 2 3* of a mighty and generous will *MS CM*

[9]Meanwhile, under that splendid masquerade of dignities sacred and secular which seemed to make the life of lucky churchmen and princely families so luxurious and amusing, there were certain conditions at work which slowly tended to disturb the general festivity. Ludovico Sforza—copious in gallantry, splendid patron of an incomparable Lionardo de Vinci—holding the ducal crown of Milan in his [1]grasp, and wanting to put it on his own head rather than let it rest[2] on that of a feeble nephew who would take very little to poison him, was much afraid of the Spanish-born old King Ferdinand and the Crown Prince Alfonso of Naples, who, not[3] liking cruelty and treachery which were useless to themselves, objected to the poisoning of a near relative for the advantage of a Lombard usurper;* the royalties of Naples again were afraid of their suzerain, Pope Alexander Borgia[4]; all three were anxiously watching Florence, lest with its midway territory it should determine the game by[5] underhand backing; and all four, with every small state in Italy, were afraid of Venice—Venice the cautious, the stable, and the strong, that wanted to stretch its arms not only along both sides of the Adriatic but across to the ports of the western coast.

Lorenzo de'[6] Medici, it was thought, did much to prevent the fatal outbreak of such jealousies, keeping up the old Florentine alliance with Naples and the Pope, and yet persuading Milan that the alliance was for the general advantage. But young Piero de' Medici's rash vanity had quickly nullified the effect of his father's wary policy, and Ludovico Sforza, roused to suspicion of a league against him, thought of a move which would checkmate his adversaries: he determined to invite the French King to march into Italy and, as heir of the house of Anjou, take[7] possession of Naples. Ambassadors—"orators," as they were called in those haranguing times—went and came; [8]a recusant Cardinal* determined not to acknowledge a Pope elected by bribery (and his own particular enemy),[9] went and came also, and seconded[1] the invitation with [2]hot rhetoric; and the young King seemed to lend a willing ear. So that in 1493 the rumour spread and became louder and louder that Charles the Eighth of France was about to cross the Alps with a mighty army; and the Italian populations, accustomed, since

9 ⟨He had seen his belief reflected in visions—a mode of seeing ⟨⟨very common⟩⟩ not uncommon in those times; and the conviction thus wrought in him was in itself a vocation to announce the coming scourge, and call men to repentance. ¶ It was this man wherein the first week of⟩ Meanwhile *MS*

   1 ⟨hands⟩ grasp *MS*   2 than {let it rest} *MS*   3 not ⟨much⟩ *MS*
   4 Alexander {Borgia} *MS*   5 by ⟨a too decided⟩ *MS*   6 de'] dei *MS*
   7 take] *3C* to take *MS CM 1 2*   8 ⟨Neapolitan exiles and⟩ a *MS*
   9 bribery (and his own particular enemy),] *3P* bribery, and his own particular enemy, *MS CM 1 2*
   1 {went and came also, and} seconded *MS*   2 ⟨hot⟩ ⟨warm⟩ hot *MS*

Italy had ceased to be the heart of the Roman empire, to look for an arbitrator from afar, began vaguely to regard his coming as a means of avenging their wrongs and redressing their grievances.

And in that rumour Savonarola had heard the assurance that his prophecy was being [3]verified. What was it that filled the ear[4] of the prophets of old but the distant tread of foreign armies, coming to do the work of justice? He no longer looked vaguely to the horizon for the coming storm: he pointed to the rising cloud. The French army was that new deluge which was to purify the earth from iniquity; the French King, Charles VIII., was the instrument elected by God, as Cyrus had been of old, and all men who desired good rather than evil were to rejoice in his coming. For the scourge would fall destructively on the impenitent alone. Let any city of Italy, let Florence above all—Florence beloved of God, since to its ear the warning voice had been specially sent—repent and turn from its ways, like Nineveh* of old, and the storm-cloud would roll over it and leave only refreshing rain-drops[5].

[6]Fra Girolamo's word was powerful; yet now that the new Cyrus had already been three months in Italy, and was not far from the gates of Florence[7], his presence was expected there[8] with mixed feelings, in which fear and distrust certainly predominated. At present it was not understood that he had redressed any grievances; and the Florentines clearly had nothing to thank him for. He held their strong frontier fortresses, which Piero de' Medici had given up to him without securing any honourable terms in return; he had done nothing to quell the alarming revolt of Pisa, which had been encouraged by his presence to throw off the Florentine yoke; and "orators," even with a prophet at their head,* could win no assurance from him, except that he would settle everything when he was once within the walls of Florence. Still, there was the satisfaction of knowing that the exasperating Piero de' Medici[9] had been fairly pelted out for the ignominious

---

3 ⟨fulfilled⟩ verified *MS*   4 ear] ears *2 3*
5 alone. {Let any city . . . rain drops} *MS*
6 ⟨To judge fairly of such preaching, which ⟨⟨falls with a shock on minds⟩⟩ may shock minds ⟨⟨accustomed to⟩⟩ nurtured in the strong feeling of national independence, we must remember, not only the analogies of Jewish history in which Savonarola sought the key to all actual life, but also the long habit of Italy, since it had ceased to be the heart of the Roman empire, to look for an arbitrator from afar. The greatest of Italian poets* ⟨⟨has⟩⟩ recorded in his vitriolic verse his hope of a deliverer for Italy, and the deliverer was the German Emperor, Henry VII. How could it be otherwise? A nation of divided and jealous interests must always want an umpire with an army at its back. ¶ And now, on the seventeenth of November, 1494⟩ Fra *MS*
7 Florence ⟨But here though the belief in his high mission was stronger than any where else,⟩ his *MS*
8 expected {there} *MS*   9 Piero {de' Medici} *MS*

surrender of the fortresses,* and in that act of energy the spirit of the Republic[1] had recovered some of its old fire.

The preparations for the equivocal guest were not entirely those of a city resigned to submission. Behind the bright drapery and banners symbolical of joy, there were preparations of another sort made with common accord by government and people. Well hidden within walls there were hired soldiers of the Republic, hastily called in from the surrounding districts; there were old arms newly[2] furbished, and sharp tools and heavy cudgels laid carefully at hand, to be snatched up on short notice; there were excellent boards and stakes to form barricades upon occasion, and a good supply of stones to make a surprising hail from the upper windows[3]. Above all, there were people very strongly in the humour for fighting any personage who might be supposed to have designs of hectoring over them, they having[4] lately tasted that new pleasure with much relish. This humour was not diminished by the sight of occasional[5] parties of Frenchmen, coming beforehand[6] to choose their quarters, with a hawk, perhaps, on their [7]left wrist, and, metaphorically speaking, a piece of chalk in their right hand to mark Italian doors* withal; especially as credible[8] historians imply that many sons of France were at that time characterized by something approaching to a swagger, which must have whetted the Florentine appetite[9] for a little stone-throwing.

And this was the temper of Florence on the morning of the seventeenth of November, 1494.

1 {spirit of the} Republic *MS*   2 newly] duly *2 3*   3 {upper} windows *MS*
4 they having] *3C* having *MS CM 1 2*   5 occasional ⟨?hawkers⟩ *MS*
6 beforehand ⟨into⟩ *MS*   7 ⟨right⟩ left *MS*   8 credible] creditable *3*
9 {Florentine} appetite *MS*

CHAPTER XXII.

THE PRISONERS

THE sky was grey, but that made little difference in the Piazza del Duomo,[1] which was covered with its holiday sky of blue drapery, and its constellations of yellow lilies and coats of arms. The sheaves of banners were unfurled at the angles of the Baptistery, but there was no carpet yet on the steps of the Duomo, for the marble was being trodden by numerous feet that were not at all exceptional. It was the hour of the Advent sermons, and the very same reasons which had flushed the streets with holiday colour were reasons why the preaching in the Duomo could least of all be dispensed with.

But not all the feet in the piazza were[2] hastening towards the steps. People of high and low degree were moving to and fro with the brisk [3]pace of men who had errands before them; groups of talkers were thickly scattered, some willing to be late for the sermon, others[4] content not to hear it at all.

The expression on the faces of these apparent loungers was not that of men who are enjoying the pleasant laziness of an opening holiday. Some were in close and eager discussion; others were listening with keen interest to a single spokesman, and yet from time to time [5]turned round with a scanning glance at any new passer-by. At the corner, looking towards the Via de' Cerretani—just where the artificial rainbow light of the piazza ceased, and the grey morning fell on the sombre stone houses—there was a remarkable cluster of the working people, most of them [6]bearing on their dress or persons the signs of their daily labour, and almost all of them carrying some weapon, or some tool[7] which might serve as a weapon upon occasion. Standing in the grey light of the street, with bare brawny arms and soiled [8]garments, they made all the more striking the transition from the brightness of the piazza. They were listening to the thin notary, Ser Cioni,[9] who had just paused on his way to the Duomo. His biting words could get only a contemptuous reception two years and a half before in the Mercato, but now he spoke with the more complacent humour of a man whose party is uppermost, and who is conscious of some influence with the people.

1 Duomo, ⟨for the piazza⟩ *MS*
2 But {not} all the feet in the Piazza were ⟨not⟩ *MS*   3 ⟨step⟩ pace *MS*
4 others] and others *2 3*
5 ⟨glanced⟩ ⟨looked⟩ turned round with a scanning ⟨look⟩ glance *MS*
6 ⟨carrying⟩ bearing *MS*   7 {some} tool *MS*   8 ⟨dress⟩ garments *MS*
9 {the thin notary} Ser Cioni, ⟨the thin notary⟩ *MS*

"Never talk to me," he was saying, in his incisive voice, "never talk to me of bloodthirsty Swiss or fierce French infantry: they might as well be in the narrow passes of the mountains as in our streets; and peasants have destroyed the finest armies of our condottieri in time past, when they had once got them between steep precipices. I tell you, Florentines need be afraid of no army in their own streets."

"That's true, Ser Cioni," said a man whose arms and hands were discoloured by crimson dye, which looked like bloodstains, and who had a small hatchet stuck in his belt; "and those French cavaliers, who came in squaring themselves in their smart doublets the other day, saw a sample of the dinner we could serve up for them. I was carrying my cloth in Ognissanti, when I saw my fine *Messeri* going by, looking round as if they thought the houses of the Vespucci and the Agli a poor pick of lodgings for them, and eying us Florentines, like topknotted cocks as they are, as if they pitied us because we didn't know how to strut. 'Yes, my fine *Galli*,'* says I, 'stick out your stomachs, I've got a meat-axe in my belt that will go inside you all the easier;' when presently the old cow lowed,* and I knew something had happened—no matter what. So I threw my cloth in at the first doorway, and took hold of my meat-axe and ran after my fine cavaliers towards the Vigna Nuova. And, 'What is it, Guccio?' said I, when he came up with me. 'I think it's the Medici coming back,'* said Guccio. *Bembè!* I expected so! And up we reared a barricade, and the Frenchmen[1] looked behind and saw themselves in a trap; and up comes a good swarm of our *Ciompi*,* and one of them with a big scythe he had in his hand mowed off one of the fine cavalier's feathers:—it's true! And the lasses peppered a few stones down to frighten them. However, Piero de' Medici wasn't come after all; and it was a pity; for we'd have left him neither legs nor wings to go away with again."

"Well spoken, Oddo," said a [2]young butcher, with his knife at his belt, "and it's my belief Piero will be a good while before he wants to come back, for he looked as frightened as a hunted chicken, when we hustled and pelted him in the piazza[3]. He's a coward, else he might have made a better stand when he'd got his horsemen. But we'll swallow no Medici any more, whatever else the French King wants to make us swallow."

"But I like not those French cannon[4] they talk of," said Goro, none the less fat for two years' additional grievances. "San Giovanni defend us! If Messer Domeneddio means so well by us as your Frate

---

1 Frenchmen] *3P Francesi MS CM* Francesi *1 2*
2 ⟨brawny man⟩ young butcher *MS*   3 in the piazza] *1 2 3 in piazza MS CM*
4 {French} cannon *MS*

says he does, Ser Cioni, why shouldn't he have sent the French another way to Naples?"

"Ay[5], Goro," said the dyer, "that's[6] a question worth putting. Thou art not such a pumpkin-head as I took thee for. Why, they might have gone to Naples by Bologna, eh, Ser Cioni? or if they'd gone to Arezzo—we wouldn't have minded their going to Arezzo."

"[7]Fools! It will be for the good and glory of Florence," Ser Cioni began. But he was interrupted by the exclamation, "Look there[8]!" which burst from several voices at once, while the faces were all turned to a party who were advancing along the Via de' Cerretani.

[9]"It's Lorenzo Tornabuoni,* and one of the French noblemen who are in his house," said Ser Cioni, in some contempt at this interruption. "He pretends to look well satisfied—that deep Tornabuoni—but he's a Medicean in his heart: mind that."

The advancing party was rather a brilliant one, for there was not only the distinguished presence of Lorenzo[1] Tornabuoni, and the splendid costume of the Frenchman with his elaborately displayed white linen and gorgeous embroidery; [2]there were two other Florentines of high birth in handsome dresses donned for the coming procession, and on the left hand of the Frenchman was a figure that was not to be eclipsed by any amount of intention or brocade—a figure we have often seen before. He wore nothing but black, for he was in mourning; but the black[3] was presently to be covered by a red mantle, for he too was to walk in procession[4] as Latin Secretary to the Ten[5]. Tito Melema had become conspicuously serviceable in the intercourse with the French guests, from his familiarity with Southern Italy[6], and his readiness in the French tongue, which he had spoken in his early youth; and he had paid more than one visit to the French camp at Signa.* The lustre of good fortune was upon him; he was smiling, listening, and explaining, with his[7] usual graceful unpretentious ease, and only a very keen eye bent on studying him could have marked a certain amount of change in him which was not to be accounted for by the lapse of eighteen months. It was that change which comes from the final departure of moral youthfulness [8]—from the distinct self-conscious adoption of a part in life. The lines of the face were as [9]soft as ever, the eyes as pellucid; but

---

5 Ay] *1 2 3 Madèsi* (yes, indeed) *MS CM*   6 that's] *1 2 3* and that's *MS CM*
7 ⟨Pazzi⟩ Fools *MS*   8 Look there] Ecco *MS*
9 ⟨It was a rather brilliant party.⟩ "Its *MS*   1 Lorenzo] the young Lorenzo *MS*
2 ⟨but⟩ there *MS*   3 black ⟨dress⟩ *MS*
4 procession ⟨with the professed scholars of Florence⟩ *MS*
5 Ten] *1 2 3 Dieci MS CM*   6 Italy {⟨on which their purposes bent⟩} *MS*
7 his] the *MS*   8 ⟨and from⟩—from *MS*   9 ⟨round and⟩ soft *MS*

something was gone—something as indefinable as the changes in the morning twilight.

The Frenchman was gathering instructions concerning ceremonial before riding back to Signa, and now he was going to have a final survey of the Piazza del Duomo, where the royal procession was to pause for religious purposes. The distinguished party attracted the notice of all eyes as it entered the piazza, but [1]the gaze was not entirely cordial and admiring; there were remarks not altogether allusive and mysterious to the Frenchman's hoof-shaped shoes—delicate flattery of royal superfluity in toes;* and there was no care that certain snarlings at "Mediceans" should be strictly inaudible. But Lorenzo Tornabuoni possessed that power of dissembling annoyance which is demanded in a man who courts popularity, and Tito, besides his natural disposition to overcome ill-will by good-humour, had the unimpassioned feeling[2] of the alien towards names and details that move[3] the deepest passions of the native.[4] Arrived where they could get a good oblique view of the Duomo, the party paused. The festoons and devices placed[5] over the central doorway excited some demur, and Tornabuoni[6] beckoned to Piero di Cosimo, who, as was usual with him at this hour, was lounging in front of Nello's shop. There was soon an animated discussion, and it became[7] highly amusing from the Frenchman's astonishment at Piero's odd pungency of statement, which Tito translated literally. Even snarling on-lookers became curious, and their faces began to wear the half-smiling, half-humiliated expression of people who are not within hearing of the joke which is producing infectious laughter. It was a delightful moment for Tito, for he was the only one of the party who could have made so amusing an interpreter, and without any disposition to triumphant self-gratulation, he revelled in the sense that he was an object of liking—he basked in approving glances. The rainbow light fell about the laughing group, and the grave church-goers had all disappeared within the walls. It seemed as if the piazza had been decorated for a real Florentine holiday.

Meanwhile in the grey light of the unadorned streets[8] there were

---

1 ⟨the remarks that accompanied⟩ the gaze ⟨were⟩ was not entirely cordial and admiring; {there were remarks . . . superfluity in toes;} and {there was no care that} certain *MS*

2 and Tito, besides . . . feeling] *3C* and to Tito's natural disposition to overcome ill-will by good-humour, there was added ⟨that⟩ the unimpassioned feeling *MS CM 1 2*

3 towards names and details that move] towards all that moves *MS*

4 native. ⟨He grew all the more radiant for the grave looks that were bent on him. But when the party had arrived⟩ Arrived *MS*

5 placed] *3C* that had been placed *MS CM 1 2*

6 Tornabuoni] young Tournabuoni *MS*

7 and it became] *1 2 3* which became *MS CM*   8 {unadorned} streets *MS*

on-comers who made no show of linen and brocade, and whose humour was far from merry. Here, too, the French dress and hoofed shoes were conspicuous, but they were being pressed upon by a larger and larger number of non-admiring Florentines. In the van of the crowd were three men in scanty clothing; each had his hands bound together by a cord, and a rope was fastened round his neck and body, in such a way that he who held the extremity of the rope might easily check any rebellious movement by the threat of throttling. The men who held the ropes were French soldiers, and by broken Italian phrases and strokes from the knotted end of the rope, they from time to time stimulated their prisoners to beg. Two of them were obedient, and to every Florentine they had encountered had held out their bound hands and said in piteous tones,

"For the love of God and the Holy Madonna, give us something towards our ransom! We are Tuscans: we were made prisoners in Lunigiana."*

But the third man remained obstinately silent under all the strokes from the knotted cord. He was[9] very different in aspect from his two fellow-prisoners. They were young and hardy, and, in the scant clothing which the avarice of their captors had left them, looked like vulgar, sturdy mendicants. But he had passed the boundary of old age, and could hardly be less than four or five and sixty. His beard which had grown long in neglect, and the hair which fell thick and straight round his baldness, were nearly white. His thickset figure was still firm and upright, though emaciated, and seemed to express energy in spite of age—an expression that was partly carried out in the dark eyes and strong dark eyebrows, which had a strangely isolated intensity of colour in the midst of his yellow, bloodless, deep-wrinkled face with its lank grey hairs. And yet there was something fitful in the eyes which contradicted the occasional flash of energy: after looking round with quick fierceness at windows and faces, they fell again with a lost and wandering look. But his lips were motionless, and he held his hands resolutely down. He would not beg.

This sight had been witnessed by the Florentines with growing exasperation. Many standing at their doors or passing quietly along had at once given money—some in half automatic response to an appeal in the name of God, others in that unquestioning awe of the French soldiery which had been created by the reports of their cruel warfare, and on which the French themselves counted as a guarantee of immunity in their acts of insolence. But as the group had [1]proceeded farther into the heart of the city, that compliance had gradually disappeared, and the soldiers found themselves escorted by a

9 He was ⟨of a very different aspect⟩ MS   1 ⟨entered⟩ proceeded MS

gathering troop of men and boys, who kept up a chorus of exclamations sufficiently intelligible to foreign ears without any interpreter. The soldiers themselves began[2] to dislike their position, for with a strong inclination to use their weapons, they were checked by the necessity for keeping a secure hold on their prisoners, and they were now hurrying along in the hope of finding shelter in a hostelry.

"French dogs!" "Bullock-feet!" "Snatch their pikes from them!" "Cut the cords and make them run for their prisoners. They'll run as fast as geese—don't you see they're web-footed?" These were the cries which the soldiers vaguely understood to be jeers, and probably threats. But every one seemed disposed to give invitations of this spirited kind rather than to act upon them.[3]

"*Santiddio!* here's a sight!" said the dyer, as soon as he had divined the meaning of the advancing tumult, "and the fools do nothing but hoot. Come along!" he added, snatching his axe from his belt, and running to join the crowd, followed by the butcher and all the rest of his companions, except[4] Goro, who hastily retreated up a narrow passage.

The[5] sight of the dyer, running forward with blood-red arms and axe uplifted, and with his cluster of rough companions behind him, had a stimulating effect on the crowd. Not that he did anything[6] else than pass [7]beyond the soldiers and thrust himself well among his fellow-citizens, flourishing his axe; but he served as a stirring symbol[8] of street fighting, like the waving of a well-known gonfalon. And the first sign that fire was ready to burst out was something as rapid as a little leaping tongue of flame: it was an act of the conjuror's[9] impish [1]lad Lollo, who was dancing and jeering in front of the ingenuous boys that made the majority of the crowd. [2]Lollo had no great compassion for the prisoners, but, being conscious of an excellent knife which was his unfailing companion, it had seemed to him from the first that to jump forward, [3]cut a rope, and leap back again before the soldier who held it could use his weapon, would be an amusing and dexterous piece[4] of mischief. And now, when the [5]people began to hoot and jostle more vigorously, Lollo felt that his moment was come—he was close to the eldest prisoner: in an instant he had cut the cord.

2 soldiers themselves began] *1 2 3* soldiers had themselves begun *MS* soldiers themselves had begun *CM*
3 this spirited kind . . . them.] this kind rather than to accept them. *MS*
4 companions, except] *3C* companions except *MS CM 1 2*
5 passage. ¶ The] passage. The notary was already gone into the Duomo. ¶ The *MS*
6 ⟨anything but⟩ anything else than *MS*   7 ⟨well⟩ beyond *MS*
8 {stirring} symbol *MS*   9 conjuror's] *1 2 3 cerretano's MS CM*
1 ⟨boy⟩ ⟨?satellite⟩ lad *MS*   2 ⟨It had seemed to that⟩ Lollo *MS*
3 ⟨and⟩ cut a rope {and leap back again} before *MS*
4 piece] *1 2 3* bit *MS CM*   5 ⟨crowd⟩ people *MS*

"Run, old one[6]!" he piped in the prisoner's ear, as soon as the cord was in two; and himself set the example of running as if he were helped along with wings, like a scared fowl.

The prisoner's sensations were not too slow for him to seize the opportunity: the idea of escape had been continually present with him, and he had gathered fresh hope from the temper of the crowd. He ran at once; but his speed would hardly have sufficed for him if the Florentines had not instantaneously rushed between him and his captor. He ran on into the piazza, but he quickly heard the tramp of feet behind him, for the other two prisoners had been released, and the soldiers were struggling and fighting their way after them, in such tardigrade fashion* as their hoof-shaped shoes would allow—[7] impeded, but not very resolutely attacked, by the people. One of the two younger prisoners turned up the Borgo di San Lorenzo, and thus [8]made a partial diversion of the hubbub; but [9]the main struggle was still towards[1] the piazza, where all eyes were turned [2]on it with alarmed curiosity. The cause could not be precisely guessed[3], for the French dress was screened by the impeding crowd.

"An escape of prisoners," said Lorenzo Tornabuoni, as he and his party turned round[4] just against the steps of the Duomo, and saw a prisoner rushing by them[5]. "The people are not content with having emptied the Bargello the other day. If there is no other authority in sight they must fall on the *sbirri* and secure freedom to thieves. Ah! there is a French soldier: that is more serious."

The soldier he saw was struggling along on the north side of the piazza, but the object of his pursuit had taken the other direction. That object was the eldest prisoner, who had wheeled round the Baptistery and was running towards the Duomo, determined to take refuge in that sanctuary rather than trust to his speed. But in mounting[6] the steps, his foot received a shock; he was precipitated towards the group of Signori, whose backs were turned to him, and was only able to recover his balance as he clutched one of them by the arm.

It was Tito Melema who felt that clutch. He turned his head, and saw the face of his adoptive father, Baldassarre[7] Calvo, close to his own.

The two men looked at each other, silent as death: Baldassarre,

6 old one] *vecchione* MS   7 them {in such tardigrade . . . allow—} MS
8 〈caused〉 made MS   9 〈the main〉 〈half the〉 the main MS
1 {still} towards MS   2 〈towards〉 on MS   3 {precisely} guessed MS
4 round 〈from〉 MS
5 Duomo {and saw 〈the younger〉 a prisoner rushing by them} MS
6 in mounting] in the change of muscular action required for mounting MS
7 of his adoptive father, Baldassarre] *1 2 3* of Baldassarre MS of his adopted father, Baldassarre CM

with dark fierceness and a tightening grip of the soiled worn hands[8] on the velvet-clad arm; Tito, with cheeks and lips all bloodless, fascinated by terror. It seemed a long while to them—it was but a moment.

The first sound Tito heard was the short laugh of Piero di Cosimo, who stood close by him and was the only person that could see his face.

"Ha, ha! I know what a ghost should be now."[9]

"This is another escaped prisoner", said Lorenzo Tornabuoni. "Who is he, I wonder?"

"*Some madman, surely*[1]," said Tito.

He hardly knew how the words had come to his lips: there are moments when our passions speak and decide for us, and we seem to stand by and wonder. They carry in them an inspiration of crime, that in one instant does the work of long premeditation.

The two men had not taken their eyes off each other, and it seemed to Tito, when he had spoken, that some[2] magical poison had darted from Baldassarre's eyes[3], and that he felt it rushing through his veins. But the next instant the grasp on his arm had relaxed, and Baldassarre had disappeared within the church.

8 grip {of the soiled worn hands} *MS*
9 now." ⟨I must⟩ ¶ "This is ⟨the⟩ another *MS*
1 *Some madman, surely*] Some madman, surely *MS*   2 that some] as if some *MS*
3 Baldassarre{'s eyes} *MS*

CHAPTER XXIII.

AFTER-THOUGHTS

"You are easily frightened, though," said Piero, with another scornful laugh. "My portrait is not as good as the original. But the old fellow *had* a tiger look: I must go into the Duomo[1] and see him again."

"It is not pleasant to be laid hold of by a madman, if madman he be", said Lorenzo Tornabuoni, in polite excuse of Tito, "but perhaps he is only a ruffian. We shall hear. I think we must see if we have authority enough to stop this disturbance between our people and your countrymen," he added, addressing the Frenchman.

They advanced towards[2] the crowd with their swords drawn, all the quiet spectators making an escort for them. Tito went too: it was necessary that he should know what others knew about Baldassarre, and the first palsy of terror was being succeeded by the rapid devices to which mortal danger will stimulate the timid.

The rabble of men and boys, more inclined to hoot at the soldier and torment him than to receive or inflict any serious wounds, gave way at the approach of *signori* with drawn swords, and the French soldier was interrogated. He and his companions had simply brought their prisoners into the city that they might beg money for their ransom: two of the prisoners were Tuscan soldiers taken in Lunigiana; the other, an elderly man, was with a party of Genoese, with whom the French foragers had come to blows near Fivizzano.* He might be mad, but he was harmless. The soldier knew no more, being unable to understand a word the old man said[3]. Tito heard so far, but he was deaf to everything else till he was specially addressed. It was Tornabuoni who spoke.

"Will you go back with us, Melema? Or, since Messere is going off to Signa now, will you wisely follow the fashion of the times and go to hear the Frate, who will be like the torrent at its height this morning? It's what we must all do, you know, if we are to save our Medicean skins. *I* should go if I had the leisure."

Tito's face had recovered its colour now, and he[4] could make an effort to speak with gaiety.

"Of course I am among the admirers of the inspired orator," he said, smilingly; "but, unfortunately, I shall be occupied with the Segretario till the time of the procession."

1 go {into the Duomo} *MS*   2 towards] toward 2 3
3 Fivizzano. {⟨He knew no more⟩ He might . . . old man said} *MS*
4 he ⟨spoke⟩ *MS*

"*I* am going into the Duomo to look at that savage old man again," said Piero.

"Then have the charity to show him to one of the hospitals for travellers, *Piero mio*," said Tornabuoni. "The monks may find out whether he wants putting into a cage."

The party separated, and Tito took his way[5] to the Palazzo Vecchio, where he was to find Bartolommeo Scala. It was not a [6]long walk, but, for Tito, it was [7]stretched out like the minutes of our morning dreams: the short spaces of street and piazza held [8]memories, and previsions, and torturing fears, that might have made the history of months. He felt as if a serpent had begun to coil round his limbs. Baldassarre living, and in Florence, was a living revenge, which would no more rest than a winding serpent would rest until it had crushed its prey. It was not in the nature of that man to let an injury pass unavenged: his love and his hatred were of that passionate fervour which subjugates all the rest of the being, and makes a man sacrifice himself to his passion as if it were a deity to be worshipped with self-destruction. Baldassarre had relaxed his hold, and had disappeared. Tito knew well how to interpret that: it meant that the vengeance was to be studied that it might be sure. If he had not uttered those decisive words—"He is a madman"—if he could have summoned up the state of mind, the courage, necessary for avowing his recognition of Baldassarre, would not the risk have been less? [9]He might have declared himself to have had what he believed to be positive evidence of Baldassarre's death; and the only persons who could ever have had positive knowledge to contradict him were Fra Luca, who was dead, and the crew of the companion galley, who had brought him the news of the encounter with the pirates. The chances were infinite against Baldassarre's having met again with any one of that crew, and Tito thought with bitterness that a timely, well-devised falsehood might have saved him from any fatal consequences. But to have told that falsehood would have required perfect self-command in the moment of a convulsive shock: he seemed to have spoken without any preconception—the words had leaped forth like a sudden birth that has[1] been begotten[2] and nourished in the darkness.

Tito[3] was experiencing that inexorable law of human souls, that we prepare ourselves for sudden deeds by the reiterated choice of good or evil which[4] gradually determines character.

That was but one chance for him now: the chance of Baldassarre's

5 way ⟨through the narrow streets leading⟩ to *MS*   6 ⟨very⟩ long *MS*
7 ⟨as⟩ stretched out ⟨as⟩ like the minutes ⟨that are filled with long⟩ *MS*
8 ⟨?earlier⟩ memories *MS*   9 ⟨He thought with bitterness now that if⟩ he *MS*
1 has] had *2 3*   2 begotten] prepared *MS*   3 darkness. {¶} Tito *MS*
4 which] *3C* that *MS CM 1 2*

failure in finding his revenge. And—Tito grasped at a thought more actively cruel than any he had ever encouraged before: might not his own unpremeditated words have some truth in them?—enough truth, at least, to bear him out in his denial of any declaration Baldassarre might make about him? [5]The old man looked strange and wild: with his eager heart and brain, suffering was likely enough to have produced madness. If it were so, the vengeance that strove to inflict disgrace might be [6]baffled.

But there was another form of vengeance not to be baffled by ingenious lying. Baldassarre[7] belonged to a race to whom the thrust of the dagger seems almost as[8] natural an impulse as the outleap of the tiger's talons. Tito shrank with shuddering dread from disgrace; but he had also that physical dread which is inseparable from a soft pleasure-loving nature, and which prevents a man from meeting wounds and death[9] as a welcome relief from disgrace. His thoughts flew at once to some hidden defensive armour that might save him from a vengeance which no subtlety could parry.

He wondered[1] at the power of the passionate fear that possessed him. It was as if he had been smitten with a blighting disease that had suddenly turned[2] the joyous sense of young life into pain.

There was still one resource open to Tito[3]. He might have turned back, sought Baldassarre again, confessed everything to him—to Romola—to all the world. But he never thought of that. [4]The repentance which cuts off all moorings to evil, demands something more than selfish fear. He had no sense that there was strength and safety in truth; the only strength he trusted to lay[5] in his ingenuity and his dissimulation. Now that[6] the first shock, which had called up the traitorous signs of fear, was well past, he hoped to be prepared for all emergencies by cool deceit—and defensive armour.

It was a characteristic fact in Tito's experience at this crisis, that no direct measures for ridding himself of Baldassarre ever occurred to him. [7]All other possibilities passed through his mind, even to his own flight from Florence; but he never thought of any scheme for removing his enemy. His dread generated no active malignity, and he[8]

---

5 ⟨He⟩ The old man *MS*

6 ⟨easily⟩ baffled. {⟨To such a pass had Tito been brought by that choice of selfish ease which three years ago had seemed so excusable. He could think with satisfaction of the keenest misery in the lot of the man who had cherished him⟩} ¶ But *MS*

7 Baldassarre] And Baldassarre *MS*

8 the {thrust of the} dagger seems {almost} as *MS*   9 {wounds and} death *MS*

1 wondered] wondered himself *MS*   2 {suddenly} turned *MS*

3 Tito ⟨but he never thought of⟩ *MS*   4 ⟨For that⟩ The *MS*

5 lay] now ⟨was⟩ lay *MS*   6 Now that] *1 2 3* Now *MS CM*

7 ⟨He contemplated all other possibilities⟩ All *MS*

8 malignity, and he] malignity. He *MS*

would still have [9]been glad not to give pain to any mortal. He had simply chosen to make life easy to himself—to carry his human lot, if possible, in such a way that it should pinch him nowhere; and [1]the choice had, at various times, landed him in unexpected positions. [2]The question now was, not whether he should divide the common pressure of destiny with his suffering fellow-men; it was whether all the resources of lying would save him from being crushed by the consequences of that habitual choice.

9 ⟨willingly⟩ been *MS*   1 ⟨that⟩ the *MS*
2 ⟨And now ⟨⟨it⟩⟩ the question was no longer whether he should consent. It had [?landed] him now⟩ The question {⟨with him⟩} now *MS*

CHAPTER XXIV.

INSIDE THE DUOMO

WHEN Baldassarre, with his hands bound together, and the rope round his neck and body, pushed his way behind the curtain, and saw the interior of the Duomo before him, he gave a start of astonishment, and stood still against the doorway. He had expected to see a vast nave empty of everything but lifeless emblems—side altars with candles unlit, dim pictures, pale and rigid statues—with perhaps a few worshippers in the distant choir following a monotonous chant. That was the ordinary aspect of churches to[1] a man who never went into them with any religious purpose.

And he saw, instead, a vast multitude of warm, living faces, upturned in breathless silence towards the pulpit, at the angle between the nave and the choir. The multitude was of all ranks, from magistrates and dames of gentle nurture to coarsely clad artisans and country people. In the pulpit was a Dominican[2] friar[3], with strong features and dark hair, preaching with the crucifix in his hand[4]. For the first few minutes Baldassarre noted nothing of his preaching.[5] Silent as his entrance had been, some eyes near the doorway had been turned on him with surprise and suspicion[6]. The rope indicated plainly enough that he was an escaped prisoner, but in that case the church was a sanctuary which he had a right to claim; his advanced years and· look of wild misery were fitted to excite pity rather than alarm, and as he stood motionless, with eyes that soon wandered absently from the wide scene before him to the pavement at his feet, those who had observed his entrance presently ceased to regard him, and became absorbed again in the stronger interest of listening to the sermon. Among the eyes that had been turned towards him were Romola's: she had entered late through [7]one of the side doors, and was so placed that she had a full view of the main entrance. She had looked long and attentively at Baldassarre, for grey hairs made a peculiar appeal to her, and the stamp of some unwonted suffering[8] in the face, confirmed by the cord round the[9] neck, stirred[1] in her those sensibilities towards the sorrows of age, which her whole life[2] had

---

1 to ⟨chance visitors⟩ *MS*   2 a {Dominican} *MS*
3 friar] *3C* monk *MS CM 1 2*
4 preaching, {with the} crucifix in {his} hand *MS*
5 preaching ⟨: he felt that eyes⟩. Silent *MS*   6 suspicion ⟨as he entered⟩ *MS*
7 ⟨a side door⟩ one of *MS*   8 {some unwonted} suffering *MS*
9 the] his *2 3*   1 stirred ⟨sensibilities in her⟩ *MS*
2 {whole} life *MS*

tended to develop³. She fancied that his ⁴eyes had met hers in their
first wandering gaze; but Baldassarre had not, in reality⁵, noted her;
he had only had a startled consciousness of the general scene, and the
consciousness was a mere flash that ⁶made no perceptible break in the
fierce tumult of ⁷emotion which the encounter with Tito had created.
Images from the past kept urging themselves upon him like delirious
visions strangely blended with thirst and anguish. No distinct thought
for the future could shape itself in the midst of that fiery passion: the
nearest approach to such thought was the bitter sense of enfeebled
powers, and a vague determination to universal distrust and suspicion.
Suddenly he felt himself vibrating to loud tones, which seemed like
the⁸ thundering echo of his own passion. A voice that penetrated his
very marrow with its accent of triumphant certitude was saying—
"The day of vengeance is at hand!"

Baldassarre quivered and looked up. He was too distant to see
more than the general aspect of the preacher standing⁹ with his right
arm outstretched, lifting up the crucifix; but he panted for the threatening voice again as if it had been a promise of bliss. There was a
¹pause before the preacher spoke again. He gradually lowered his
arm². He deposited the crucifix on the edge of the pulpit, and crossed
his arms over his breast, looking round at the multitude as if he
would meet the glance of every individual face.

"All ye in Florence are my witnesses, for I spoke not in a corner.
Ye are my witnesses, that ³four years ago, when there were yet no
signs of war and tribulation, I preached the coming of the scourge.
I lifted up my voice as a trumpet to the prelates and princes and
people of Italy and said, The cup of your iniquity is full. Behold, the
thunder of the Lord is gathering, and it shall fall and break the cup,
and your iniquity, which seems to you as pleasant wine, shall be
poured out upon you, and shall be as molten lead. And you, O
priests, who say, Ha, ha! there is no Presence in the sanctuary—the
Shechinah* is nought—the Mercy-seat is bare; we may sin behind the
veil, and who shall punish us? To you, I said, the presence of God
shall be revealed in his temple as a consuming fire, and your sacred
garments shall become a winding-sheet of flame, and for sweet music
there shall be shrieks and hissing, and for soft couches there shall be
thorns, and for the breath of wantons shall come the pestilence. Trust

---

3 develop ⟨to a degree that others would have felt to be exaggerated. It seemed to
her⟩ MS

4 ⟨wandering⟩ eyes MS   5 not {in reality} MS

6 ⟨hardly made a⟩ made no MS   7 ⟨thought and⟩ emotion MS

8 the] a MS   9 standing] as he stood MS   1 ⟨moment's⟩ pause MS

2 arm ⟨and having⟩ ⟨crossed his hands with⟩ ⟨leaning forward like⟩ ⟨looked round at
the multitude as if he would meet the glance of every individual face⟩ He MS

3 ⟨?five⟩ four MS

not in your gold and silver, trust not in your high fortresses; for though the walls were of iron, and the fortresses of adamant, [4]the Most High shall put terror into your hearts and weakness into your councils, so that you shall be confounded and flee like women. He shall break in pieces mighty men without number, and put others in their stead. For God will no longer endure the pollution of his sanctuary: he will thoroughly purge his Church.

"And forasmuch as it is [5]written* that God will do nothing but he revealeth it to his servants the prophets, he has chosen me his unworthy servant, and[6] made his purpose present to my soul in[7] the living word of the Scriptures; and in the deeds of his Providence; and by the ministry of angels he has revealed it to me in visions. And his word possesses me so that I am but as the branch of the forest when the wind of heaven penetrates it, and it is not in me to keep silence, even though I may be a derision to the scorner. And for four years I have preached in obedience to the Divine will: in the face of scoffing I have preached three things, which the Lord has delivered to me: that *in these times God*[8] *will regenerate His Church*, and that *before the regeneration must come the scourge over all Italy*[9], and that *these things will come quickly*[1]. [2]But hypocrites who cloak their hatred of the truth with a show of love have said to me 'Come now Frate, leave your prophesyings: it is enough to teach virtue.' [3]To these[4] I answer: 'Yes, you[5] say in your hearts, God lives afar off, and his word is as a parchment written by dead men, and he deals not as in the days of old,[6] rebuking the nations, and punishing the oppressors, and smiting the unholy priests as he smote the sons of Eli.* But I cry again in your ears[7]: God is near and [8]not afar off; his judgments change not. He is the God of armies; the strong men who go up to battle are his ministers, even as the storm, and fire, and pestilence. He drives them by the breath of his angels, and they come upon the chosen land which has forsaken the covenant. And thou, O Italy, art the chosen land: has not God [9]placed his sanctuary within thee, and thou hast polluted it? Behold! the ministers of his wrath are upon thee—they are at thy very doors!' "

Savonarola's voice had been rising in impassioned force up to this

---

4 ⟨He⟩ the Most High *MS*   5 ⟨declared⟩ written *MS*
6 and ⟨by the ministry of his angels he has⟩ made *MS*   7 in ⟨visions⟩ *MS*
8 {I have preached three things . . . me:} that {in these times} God ⟨would⟩ will *MS*

9 scourge {over all Italy} *MS*
1 *in these times . . . quickly*] 3P in these times . . . quickly *MS CM 1 2*
2 ⟨And the [1 word] of goodness⟩ But *MS*   3 ⟨And⟩ To *MS*
4 these] them *MS*   5 you ⟨like to think that⟩ *MS*
6 old, ⟨but⟩ *MS*   7 ears ⟨and [?spare] not⟩ *MS*   8 ⟨is⟩ not *MS*
9 ⟨placed his sanctuary within thee⟩ ⟨made thee the seat of⟩ placed *MS*

point, when he became suddenly silent, let his hands fall, and clasped them quietly before him. His silence, instead of being the signal for small movements amongst his audience, seemed to be as strong a spell to them as his voice. Through the vast area of the Cathedral men and women sat with faces upturned, like breathing statues, till the voice was heard again in clear low tones.[1]

"Yet there is a pause—even as in the days when Jerusalem was destroyed there was a pause* that the children of God might flee from it. There is a stillness before the storm: lo,[2] there is blackness above, but not a leaf quakes: the winds are stayed, that the voice of God's warning may be heard. Hear it now, O Florence, chosen city in the chosen land! Repent and forsake evil: do justice: love mercy: put away all uncleanness from among you, that the spirit of truth and holiness may fill your [3]souls and breathe through all your streets and habitations, and then the pestilence[4] shall not enter, and the sword shall pass over you and leave you unhurt.

"For the sword is hanging from the sky; it is quivering; it is about to fall! *The Sword of God[5] upon the earth, swift and sudden![6]* Did I not tell you, [7]years ago, that I had beheld the vision and heard the voice? And Behold, it is fulfilled! Is there not [8]a King with his army at your gates? Does not the earth shake with the tread of horses and the wheels of swift cannon? Is there not a fierce multitude that can lay bare the land as with a sharp razor? I tell you [9]the French King with his army is the minister of God: God shall guide [1]him as the hand guides a sharp sickle, and the [2]joints of the wicked shall melt before [3]him, and they shall be [4]mown down as stubble: he that fleeth of them shall not flee away, and he that escapeth of them shall not be delivered. And the tyrants who have made[5] to themselves a throne out of the vices of the multitude, and the unbelieving priests who traffic in the souls of men and fill the very sanctuary with fornication, shall be hurled[6] from their soft [7]couches into burning hell[8]; and the pagans and they who sinned under the old covenant shall stand aloof

1 doors." {Savonarola's voice had . . . tones.} *MS*   2 lo,] *MS 1 2 3* lo! *CM*
3 ⟨selves⟩ ⟨souls⟩ ⟨?spirits⟩ souls and breathe ⟨like the soft air⟩ through *MS*
4 the pestilence] pestilence *MS*
5 God ⟨{upon the earth} quick and sudden shall descend ⟨⟨upon the earth⟩⟩ with swiftness⟩ upon the earth, swift and sudden! ⟨In these last words Savonarola's voice had risen to its utmost pitch again. His eyes and his clasped hands were ⟨⟨directed upward⟩⟩ ⟨⟨stretched out⟩⟩ uplifted.⟩ Did *MS*
6 *The sword . . . sudden!*] *3P* The sword . . . sudden! *MS CM 1 2*
7 ⟨four⟩ years *MS*   8 ⟨an army⟩ a King *MS*
9 ⟨that King and⟩ the French King with *MS*   1 ⟨him⟩ ⟨them⟩ him *MS*
2 ⟨knees⟩ joints *MS*   3 ⟨them⟩ him *MS*   4 ⟨?hewed⟩ mown *MS*
5 have made] *2 3* make *MS CM 1*   6 hurled ⟨into⟩ *MS*
7 ⟨places⟩ couches *MS*   8 {burning} hell *MS*

and say: 'Lo! these men have brought the stench of a new wickedness into [9]the everlasting fire.'

"But thou, O Florence, take the offered mercy. See! the Cross is held out to you: come and be healed. Which among the nations of Italy has had a token like unto yours? The tyrant is driven out from among you: the men who held a bribe in their left hand and a rod in their[1] right are gone forth, and no blood has been spilled. And now put away every other abomination from among you, and you shall be strong in the strength of the living God. Wash yourselves from the black pitch of your vices, which have made you even as the heathens: put away the envy and hatred that have made your city as a nest of wolves. And there shall no harm happen to you: and the passage of armies shall be to you as the[2] flight of birds, and rebellious Pisa shall be given to you again, and famine and pestilence shall be far from your gates, and you shall be as a beacon among the nations. But, mark! while you suffer the accursed thing to lie in the camp* you shall be afflicted and tormented, even though a remnant among you may be saved."

These admonitions and promises had been spoken in an incisive tone of authority; but in the next sentence the preacher's voice melted into a strain[3] of entreaty.

"Listen, O people, over whom my heart yearns, as the heart of a mother over the children she has travailed for! God is my witness that but for your sakes I would willingly live as a turtle in the depths of the forest, singing low to my Beloved, who is mine and I am His. [4]For you I toil, for you I languish, for you my nights are spent in watching, and my soul melteth away for very heaviness. O Lord, thou knowest I am willing—I am ready. Take me, stretch me on thy cross: let the wicked who delight in blood, and rob the poor, and defile the temple of their bodies, and harden themselves against thy mercy—let them wag their heads and shoot out the lip at me: let the thorns press upon my brow, and let my sweat be anguish—I desire to be made like thee in thy great love. But let me see of[5] the fruit of my travail—let this people be saved! Let me see them clothed in purity: let me hear their voices rise in concord as the voices of the angels: let them see no wisdom but in thy eternal law, no beauty but in holiness. Then they shall lead the way before the nations, and the people from the four winds shall follow them, and be gathered into the fold of the blessed. For it is thy will, O God, that the earth shall be converted unto thy law: it is thy will that wickedness shall cease and love shall reign. Come, O blessed promise! and behold, I am willing—lay me on

9 ⟨hell⟩ the everlasting fire *MS*   1 their] the *2 3*   2 the] a *2 3*
3 strain] tone *MS*   4 ⟨But⟩ For *MS*   5 see of] see *2 3*

the altar: let my blood flow and the fire consume me; but let my witness be remembered among men, that iniquity shall not prosper for ever."*

During the last appeal, Savonarola had stretched out his arms and lifted up his eyes to heaven; his strong voice had alternately trembled with emotion and risen again in renewed energy; but the passion with which he offered himself as a victim became at last too strong to allow of further speech, and he ended in a sob. Every changing tone, vibrating through the audience, shook them into answering emotion. There were plenty among them who had very moderate faith in the Frate's prophetic mission, and who in their cooler moments loved him little; nevertheless, they too were carried along by the great wave of feeling which gathered its force from sympathies that lay deeper than all theory. A loud responding sob rose at once from the wide multitude, while Savonarola had fallen on his knees and buried his face in his mantle. He felt in that moment the rapture and glory of martyrdom without its agony.

In that great sob of the multitude Baldassarre's had mingled. Among all the human beings present, there was perhaps not one whose frame vibrated more strongly than his to the tones and words of the preacher; but it had vibrated like a harp of which all the strings had been wrenched[6] away except one. That threat of a fiery inexorable vengeance—of a future into which the hated sinner might be pursued and held by the avenger in an eternal grapple, had come to him like the promise of an unquenchable fountain to unquenchable thirst. The doctrines of the sages, the old contempt for priestly superstitions, had fallen away from his soul like a forgotten language: if he could have remembered them, what answer could they have given to his great need like the answer given by this voice of energetic conviction? The thunder of denunciation fell on his passion-wrought [7]nerves with all the force of self-evidence: his thought never went beyond it[8] into questions—he was possessed by it as the war-horse is possessed by the clash of sounds. No word that was not a threat touched his consciousness; he had no fibre to be thrilled by it. But the fierce exultant delight to which he was moved by the idea of perpetual vengeance found at once a climax and a relieving outburst in the preacher's words of self-sacrifice. To Baldassarre those words only brought the vague triumphant sense that he too was devoting himself—signing with his own blood the deed by which he gave himself over to an unending fire, that would seem but coolness to his burning hatred.

"I rescued him—I cherished him—if I might clutch his heart-strings for ever! Come, O blessed promise! Let my blood flow; let the fire consume me!"

The one cord vibrated to its utmost. Baldassarre clutched his own palms, driving his long nails into them, and burst into a sob with the rest.

CHAPTER XXV.

[1]OUTSIDE THE DUOMO

[2]WHILE Baldassarre was possessed by the voice of Savonarola, he had not noticed that another man had entered through the doorway behind him, and stood not far off, observing him. It was Piero di Cosimo, who took no heed of the preaching, having come solely to look at[3] the escaped prisoner. During the pause, in which the preacher and his audience had given themselves up to inarticulate emotion, the new comer advanced and touched Baldassarre on the arm. He looked round with the tears still slowly rolling down his face, but with a vigorous sigh, as if he had done with that outburst. The painter spoke to him in a low tone:—

"Shall I cut your cords for you? I have heard how you were made prisoner."

Baldassarre did not reply immediately: he glanced suspiciously at the officious stranger. At last he said, "If you will."

"Better come outside," said Piero.

Baldassarre again looked at him suspiciously; and Piero, partly guessing his thought, smiled, took out a knife, and cut the cords. He began to think that the idea of the prisoner's[4] madness was not improbable, there was something so peculiar in the expression of his face. "Well," he thought, "if he does any mischief, he'll soon get tied up again. The poor devil shall have a chance, at least."

"You are afraid of me," he said again, in an under-tone; "you don't want to tell me anything about yourself".

Baldassarre was folding his arms in enjoyment of that[5] long-absent muscular sensation. He answered Piero with a less suspicious look and a tone which had some quiet decision in it.

"No, I have nothing to tell."

"As you please," said Piero, "but perhaps you want shelter, and may not know how hospitable we Florentines are to visitors with torn doublets and empty stomachs. There's a[6] hospital for poor travellers outside all our gates,* and, if you liked, I could put you in the way to one. There's no danger from your French soldier. He has been sent off."

Baldassarre nodded, and turned in silent acceptance of the offer, and he and Piero left the church together.

"You wouldn't like to sit to me for your portrait, should you?" said

1 ⟨The Prophet⟩ Outside the Duomo *MS*
2 ⟨During the period in which⟩ While *MS*   3 at ⟨Baldassarre⟩ *MS*
4 the prisoner's] Baldassarre's *MS*   5 that] the *2 3*   6 a] *MS* an *CM 1 2 3*

Piero, as they went along [7]the Via dell' Oriuolo, on the way to the gate of Santa Croce.* "I am a painter: I would give you money to get your portrait."

The suspicion returned to Baldassarre's glance, as he looked at Piero, and said decidedly, "No."

"Ah!" said the painter, curtly[8]. "Well, go straight on, and you'll find the Porta Santa Croce, and outside it there's a[9] hospital for travellers. So you'll not accept any service from me?"

"I give you thanks for what you have done already. I need no more."

"It is well," said Piero, with a shrug, and they turned away from each other.

"A mysterious old tiger!" thought the artist[1], "well worth painting. Ugly—with deep lines—looking as if the plough and the harrow[2] had gone over his heart. A fine contrast to my bland and smiling Messer Greco—my *Bacco trionfante*, who has married the fair Antigone in contradiction to all history and fitness. Aha! his scholar's blood curdled uncomfortably at the old fellow's clutch."

When Piero re-entered the Piazza del Duomo the multitude who had been listening to Fra Girolamo were pouring out from all the doors, and the haste they made to go on their several ways was a proof how important they held the preaching which had detained them from the other occupations of the day. The artist leaned against an angle of the Baptistery and watched the departing crowd, delighting in the variety of the garb and of the keen characteristic faces— faces such as Masaccio had painted* more than fifty years before: such as Domenico Ghirlandajo had not yet quite left off painting.

This morning was a peculiar occasion, and [3]the Frate's audience, always multifarious, had represented even more completely than usual the various classes and political parties of Florence. There were men of high birth, accustomed to public charges at home and abroad, who had [4]become newly conspicuous not only as enemies of the Medici and friends of popular government, but as thorough Piagnoni, espousing to the utmost the doctrines and practical teaching of the Frate, and frequenting San Marco as the seat of another Samuel;*[5]some of them men of authoritative and handsome presence, like Francesco Valori, and perhaps also of a hot and arrogant temper, very much gratified by an immediate divine authority for bringing about freedom in their own way; others, like Sodernini,* with less of the ardent

7 ⟨towards⟩ the MS   8 curtly] 1 2 3 shortly MS CM
9 a] MS an CM 1 2 3   1 artist] painter MS   2 {the} harow MS
3 ⟨the congregation⟩ the Frate's audience MS
4 ⟨lately risen into new ascendancy⟩ become newly conspicuous MS
5 ⟨men sometimes⟩ some of them men MS

Piagnone, and more of the wise politician. There were men, also of family, like Piero Capponi—simply brave undoctrinal lovers of a sober republican[6] liberty, who preferred fighting to arguing, and had no particular reasons for thinking any ideas false that kept out the Medici* and made room for public spirit. At[7] their elbows were doctors of law whose studies of Accursius* and his brethren had[8] not so entirely consumed their ardour as to prevent them from becoming enthusiastic Piagnoni—Messer Luca Corsini himself, for example, who on a memorable occasion yet to come was to raise his learned arms[9] in street stone-throwing for the cause of religion, freedom, and the Frate.* And among these[1] dignities who carried their black *lucco* or furred mantle with an air of habitual authority, there was an abundant sprinkling of men with more contemplative and sensitive faces; scholars inheriting such high names[2] as Strozzi and Acciajoli, who were already minded to take the cowl and join the community of San Marco;* artists, wrought to a new and higher ambition by the teaching of Savonarola—like that young painter who had lately surpassed himself in his fresco of the Divine child on the wall of the Frate's bare cell—unconscious yet that he would one day himself wear the tonsure and the cowl, and be called Fra Bartolommeo.* There was the mystic poet Girolamo Benevieni hastening, perhaps, to carry tidings of the beloved Frate's speedy coming to his friend Pico della Mirandola, who was never to see the light of another morning.* There were well-born women attired with such scrupulous plainness that their more refined grace was the chief distinction between them and their [3]less aristocratic sisters. There was a predominant proportion of the genuine *popolani* or middle class, belonging both to the Major and Minor Arts, conscious of purses threatened by war-taxes[4]. And more striking and various, perhaps, than all the other classes of the Frate's disciples, there was the long stream of poorer tradesmen[5] and artisans, whose faith and hope in [6]his Divine message varied from the rude undiscriminating[7] trust in him as the friend of the poor and the enemy of the luxurious oppressive rich, to that eager tasting of all the subtleties of biblical interpretation, which [8]takes a peculiarly strong hold on the sedentary artisan, [9]illuminating the long dim

6 a sober republican] republican *MS*   7 At] And at *MS*
8 studies of Accursius and his brethren had] studies in Accursius and ⟨his brethren⟩ Bartolo had *MS*
9 learned arms] arms *MS*   1 these] the *2 3*
2 names] *MS 1 2 3* name *CM*   3 ⟨more plebeian⟩ ⟨poorer⟩ less aristocratic *MS*
4 sisters. {There was . . . war-taxes} *MS*
5 {poorer} tradesmen *MS*   6 ⟨the divine message of the Frate⟩ his *MS*
7 rude undiscriminating] rude and undiscriminating *2 3*   8 ⟨often⟩ takes *MS*
9 ⟨lighting up⟩ illuminating *MS*

spaces beyond the board[1] where he stitches, with a[2] pale flame that seems[3] to him the light of Divine science.

But[4] among these various disciples of the Frate were scattered many who were not in the least his disciples. Some were Mediceans who had already, from motives of fear and policy, begun to show the presiding spirit of the popular party a feigned deference. Others were sincere advocates of a free government, but regarded Savonarola simply[5] as an ambitious monk—half-sagacious, half-fanatical—who [6]had made himself a powerful instrument with the people, and must be accepted as an important social fact. There were even some of his bitter enemies: members of the [7]old aristocratic anti-Medicean party—determined to try and get the reins once more tight in the hands of certain chief families; or else licentious young men, who detested him as the kill-joy of Florence. For the sermons in the Duomo had already become political incidents, attracting the ears of curiosity and malice, as well as of faith. The men of ideas, like young Niccolò Macchiavelli, went to observe and write reports to [8]friends* away in country villas; the men of appetites, like Dolfo Spini,* [9]bent on hunting down the Frate as a public nuisance who made game scarce, went to feed their hatred and lie in wait for grounds of accusation.

Perhaps, while no preacher ever had a more massive influence than Savonarola, no preacher ever had more heterogeneous materials to work upon. And one secret of the massive influence lay in the highly mixed character of his preaching. Baldassarre, wrought into an ecstasy of self-martyring revenge, was only an extreme case among the partial and narrow sympathies of that audience. In Savonarola's preaching there were strains that appealed to the very finest susceptibilities of men's natures, and there were elements that gratified low egoism, tickled gossiping curiosity, and fascinated [1]timorous superstition. His need[2] of personal predominance, his labyrinthine allegorical interpretations of the Scriptures, his enigmatic visions, and his false certitude about the Divine intentions, never ceased, in his own large soul, to[3] be ennobled by that fervid piety, that passionate sense of the infinite, that [4]active sympathy, that clear-sighted demand for the subjection of selfish interests to the general good, which he had in common with the greatest of mankind. But for the mass of his audience all the

---

1 spaces {beyond the board} *MS*
2 stitches, with a] stitches his sleeve or his last with ⟨his⟩ a *MS*
3 seems ⟨?adance⟩ *MS*   4 But ⟨sprinkled⟩ ⟨scattered⟩ among *MS*
5 simply ⟨as a man⟩ *MS*   6 ⟨having made⟩ had made *MS*
7 ⟨elder⟩ old *MS*   8 ⟨their⟩ friends {away} in *MS*
9 ⟨resolved to⟩ bent on *MS*   1 ⟨trivial⟩ timorous *MS*
2 His need] In his own large soul his ⟨inner⟩ need *MS*
3 ceased, in his own large soul, to] ceased to *MS*   4 ⟨ardent⟩ active *MS*

pregnancy of his preaching lay in[5] his strong assertion of supernatural claims, in his[6] denunciatory visions, in the false certitude which gave his sermons the interest of a political bulletin; and having once held that audience in his mastery, it was necessary to his nature—it was necessary for their welfare—that he should *keep* the mastery. The effect was inevitable. No man ever struggled to retain power over a mixed multitude without suffering vitiation: his standard must be their lower needs, and not his own best insight.

The mysteries of human character have seldom been presented in a way more fitted to check the judgments of facile knowingness than in Girolamo Savonarola; but we can give him a reverence that needs no shutting of the eyes to fact[7], if we regard his life as a drama in which there were [8]great inward modifications accompanying the outward changes. And up to this period, when his more direct [9]action on political affairs had only just begun, it is probable that his imperious need of ascendancy had burned undiscernibly in the strong flame of his zeal for God and man.

It was the fashion of old, when [1]an ox was led out for sacrifice to Jupiter, to chalk the dark spots, and give the offering a false show of unblemished whiteness. Let us fling away the chalk, and boldly say,— the victim is[2] spotted, but it is[3] not therefore in vain that his mighty heart is[4] laid on the altar of men's highest hopes.

---

5 in ⟨the supernatural claims⟩, his strong . . . claims, {in} the denunciatory visions, {in} the false *MS*

6 his] *1 2 3* the *MS CM*

7 that needs no shutting of the eyes to fact] *1 2 3* that need shut its eyes to no fact *MS CM*

8 ⟨very⟩ great *MS*   9 ⟨political activity⟩ action *MS*   1 ⟨a mighty⟩ an *MS*

2 is] *1 2 3* was *MS CM*   3 is] *1 2 3* was *MS CM*   4 is] *1 2 3* was *MS CM*

CHAPTER XXVI.

THE GARMENT OF FEAR

AT six o'clock that evening most people in Florence were glad the entrance of the new Charlemagne[1] was fairly over. Doubtless when the roll of drums, the blast of trumpets, and the tramp of horses along the Pisan road began to mingle with the pealing of the excited bells, it was a grand moment for those who were stationed on turreted roofs, and could see the long-winding terrible pomp on the background of the green hills and valley. There was no sunshine to light up the splendour of banners, and spears, and plumes, and silken surcoats, but there was no thick cloud of dust to hide it, and as the picked troops advanced into close view they could be seen all the more distinctly for the absence of dancing glitter. Tall and [2]tough Scotch archers, Swiss halberdiers fierce and ponderous, nimble Gascons ready to wheel and climb, cavalry in which each man looked like a knight-errant with his indomitable spear and charger—it was satisfactory to be assured that they would injure nobody but the enemies of God! With that confidence at heart it was a less dubious pleasure to look at the array of strength and splendour in nobles and knights, and youthful pages of choice lineage[3]—at the bossed and jewelled sword hilts, at the satin scarfs embroidered with strange symbolical devices of pious or gallant meaning,* at the gold chains and jewelled aigrettes, at the gorgeous horse-trappings and brocaded mantles, and at the transcendent canopy carried by select youths above the head of the Most Christian King. To sum up[4] with an old diarist, whose spelling and diction halted a little behind the wonders of this royal visit,—"*fù gran magnificenza.*"*

But for the Signoria, who had been waiting on their platform against the gates, and had to march out at the right moment, with their orator in front of them, to meet the mighty guest, the grandeur of the scene[5] had been somewhat screened by unpleasant sensations. If Messer Luca Corsini could have had a brief Latin welcome depending from his mouth in legible characters, it[6] would have been less confusing when the rain came on, and created an impatience in men and horses that broke off the delivery of his well-studied periods, and reduced the representatives of the scholarly city to offer a make-

---

1 {new} Charlemagne *MS*   2 ⟨?rough⟩ tough *MS*
3 splendour {in nobles . . . lineage} *MS*   4 To sum up] In short, to sum up *MS*
5 scene] moment *MS*
6 characters, it] characters, like a frescoed saint, it *MS*

shift welcome in impromptu French. But that sudden confusion had
created a great opportunity for Tito. As one of the secretaries he was
among the officials who were stationed behind the Signoria, and with
whom these [7]highest dignities were promiscuously thrown when
pressed upon by the horses.

"Somebody step forward and say a few words in French," said
Soderini. But no one of high importance chose to risk a second failure. "You, Francesco Gaddi[8]—you can speak." But Gaddi, distrusting
his own promptness, hung back, and, pushing Tito, said, "You,
Melema."*

Tito stepped forward in an instant, and with the air of profound
deference that came as naturally to him as walking, said the few needful words in the name of the Signoria; then gave way gracefully, and
let the King pass on. His presence of mind, which had failed him in
the terrible crisis of the morning, had been a ready[9] instrument this
time. It was an excellent livery servant that never forsook him when
danger was not [1]visible. But when he was complimented on his
opportune service, he laughed it off as a thing of no moment, and to
those who had not witnessed it, let Gaddi have the credit of the
improvised [2]welcome. No wonder Tito was popular: the touchstone
by which men try us is most often their own vanity.

Other things [3]besides the oratorical welcome had turned[4] out rather
worse than had been expected. If everything had happened according
to ingenious preconceptions, the Florentine procession of clergy and
laity would not have found their way choked up and been obliged to
take a make-shift course[5] through the back streets[6], so as to meet the
King at the Cathedral only. Also, if the young monarch under the
canopy, seated on his charger with his lance upon his thigh, had
looked more[7] like a Charlemagne and less like a hastily modelled
grotesque, the imagination of his admirers would have been much
assisted[8]. It might have been wished that the scourge of Italian
wickedness and "Champion of the honour of women" had had a less
miserable leg, and only the normal sum of toes; that his mouth had
been of a less reptilian width of slit, his nose and head of a less exorbitant outline.* But the thin leg rested on cloth of gold and pearls,
and the face was only an interruption of a few square inches in the
midst of black velvet and gold, and the blaze of rubies, and the brilliant tints of the embroidered and bepearled canopy—"*fù gran
magnificenza.*"

7 ⟨high dignitaries⟩ highest dignities *MS*   8 Francesco Gaddi] Gaddi *MS*
9 ready ⟨[?servitor] to him⟩ *MS*   1 ⟨at hand⟩ visible *MS*
2 ⟨answer⟩ welcome *MS*   3 ⟨also⟩ besides *MS*   4 {had} turned *MS*
5 take a make-shift course] *1 2 3* improvise a course *MS CM*
6 the back streets] back streets *MS*   7 more] a little more *MS*
8 the imagination . . . assisted] it would have assisted the imagination *MS*

And the people had cried *Francia! Francia!* with an enthusiasm proportioned to the splendour of the canopy which they had torn to pieces as their spoil, according to immemorial custom; royal lips had duly kissed[9] the altar; and after all mischances the royal person and retinue were lodged in the Palace of the Via Larga, the rest of the nobles and gentry were dispersed among the great houses of Florence, and the terrible soldiery were encamped in the Prato and other open quarters. The business of the day was ended.

But the streets still presented a [1]surprising aspect, such as Florentines had not seen before under the November stars. Instead of a gloom unbroken except by a lamp burning feebly here and there before a saintly image at the street corners, or by a stream of redder light from an open doorway, there were lamps suspended at the windows of all houses, so that men could walk along no less securely and commodiously than by day—"*fù gran magnificenza.*"

Along those illuminated streets Tito Melema was walking at about eight o'clock in the evening, on his way homeward. He had been exerting himself throughout the day under the pressure of hidden anxieties, and had at last made his escape unnoticed from the midst of after-supper gaiety. Once at leisure thoroughly to face and consider his circumstances, he hoped that he could so adjust himself to them and to all probabilities as to [2]get rid of his childish fear. If he had only not been wanting in the presence of mind necessary to recognize Baldassarre under that surprise!—it would have been happier for him on all accounts; for he still winced under the sense that he was deliberately inflicting[3] suffering on his father: he would very much have preferred that Baldassarre should be prosperous and happy. But[4] he had left himself no second path now: there could be no conflict any longer: the only thing he had to do was to take care of himself.

While these thoughts were in his mind he was advancing from the Piazza di Santa Croce along the Via dei Benci, and as he [5]neared the angle turning into the Borgo Santa Croce his ear was struck by [6]a music which was not that of evening revelry, but of vigorous labour— the music of the anvil. Tito gave a slight start and quickened his pace, for the sounds had suggested a welcome thought. He knew that they came from the workshop of Niccolò Caparra, famous resort of all Florentines who cared for curious and beautiful iron-work.*

"What makes the giant at work so late?" thought Tito. "But so much the better for me. I can do that little bit of business to-night instead of to-morrow morning."

---

9 {duly} kissed *MS*   1 ⟨very⟩ surprizing *MS*   2 ⟨rid himself⟩ get rid *MS*
3 deliberately inflicting] inflicting *MS*   4 But ⟨the die was cast now⟩ *MS*
5 ⟨reached⟩ neared *MS*   6 ⟨sounds⟩ a music *MS*

Preoccupied as he was, he could not help pausing a moment in admiration[7] as he came in front of the workshop. The wide doorway, standing at the truncated angle of a great block or "isle" of houses,* was surmounted by a loggia roofed with fluted tiles, and supported by stone columns with roughly carved capitals. Against the red light framed in by the outline of the fluted tiles and columns stood in black relief the grand figure of Niccolò, with his huge arms in rhythmical[8] rise and fall, first hiding and then disclosing the profile of his firm mouth and powerful brow. Two slighter [9]ebony figures, one at the anvil, the other at the bellows, served to set off his superior massiveness.

Tito darkened the doorway with a very different outline, standing in silence, since it was useless to speak until Niccolò should deign to pause and notice him. That was not until the smith had beaten the head of an axe to the due sharpness of edge and dismissed it from his anvil. But in the meantime Tito had satisfied himself by a glance round the shop that the object of which he was in search had not disappeared.

Niccolò gave an unceremonious but good-humoured nod as he turned from the anvil and rested his hammer on his hip.

"What is it, Messer Tito? Business?"

"[1]Assuredly, Niccolò; else I should not have ventured to interrupt you when you are working out of hours, since I take that as a sign that your work is pressing."

"I've been at the same work all day—making axes and spear-heads. And every fool that has passed my shop has put his pumpkin-head in to say, 'Niccolò, wilt thou not come and see the King of France and his soldiers?' and I've answered, 'No: I don't want to see their faces—I want to see their backs.'"

"Are you making arms for the citizens, then, Niccolò?—that they may have something better than rusty scythes and spits in case of an uproar?"

"We shall see. Arms are good, and Florence is likely to want them. The Frate tells us we shall get Pisa again, and I hold with the Frate; but I should be glad to know how the promise is to be fulfilled, if we don't get plenty of good weapons forged? The Frate sees a long way before him; that I believe. But he doesn't see birds caught with winking at them, as some of our people try to make out. He sees sense, and not nonsense. But you're a bit of a Medicean, Messer Tito Melema. *Ebbene!* so I've been myself in my time, before the cask began to run sour. What's your business?"

"Simply to know the price of that fine coat of mail I saw hanging

7 moment {in admiration} *MS*   8 rhythmical] rhythmic *1 2 3*
9 ⟨figures⟩ ⟨black figures⟩ ebony figures *MS*   1 ⟨Yes⟩ Assuredly *MS*

Niccolò at Work

up here the other day. I want to buy it for a certain personage who needs a protection of that sort under his doublet."

"Let him come and buy it himself, then," said Niccolò, bluntly. "I'm rather nice about what I sell, and whom I sell to. I like to know who's my customer."

"I know your scruples, Niccolò. But that is² only defensive armour: it can hurt nobody."

"True: but it may make the man who wears it feel himself all the safer if he should want to hurt somebody. No, no: it's not my own work; but it's fine work of Maso of Brescia:* I should be loth for it to cover the heart of a scoundrel. I must know who is to wear it."

"Well, then, to be plain with you, *Niccolò mio*, I want it myself," said Tito, knowing it was useless to try persuasion. "The fact is, I am likely to have a journey to take—and you know what journeying is in these times. You don't suspect *me* of treason against the Republic?"

"No, I know no harm of you," said Niccolò, in his blunt way again. "But have you the money to pay for the coat? For you've passed my shop often enough to know my sign: you've seen the burning account-books—I trust nobody. The price is twenty florins, and that's because it's second hand. You're not likely to have so much money with you. Let it be till to-morrow."

"I happen to have the money," said Tito, who had been winning at play the day before, and had not emptied his purse. "I'll carry the armour home with me."

Niccolò reached down the finely wrought coat, which fell together into little more than two handfuls.

"There, then," he said,³ when the florins had been told down on his palm. "Take the coat. It's made to cheat sword or poniard or arrow. But, for my part, I would never put such a thing on. It's like carrying fear about with one."

Niccolò's words had an unpleasant intensity of meaning for Tito. But he smiled and said,—

"Ah, Niccolò, we scholars are all cowards. Handling the pen doesn't thicken the arm as your hammer-wielding does. Addio!"

He folded the armour under his mantle, and hastened⁴ across the Ponte Rubaconte.

---

2 that is] that's *MS*   3 said, ⟨giving it to Tito,⟩ *MS*
4 hastened] *1 2 3* hastened homeward *MS CM*

CHAPTER XXVII.

THE YOUNG WIFE

WHILE Tito was hastening across the bridge with the new-bought armour under his mantle, Romola was pacing up and down the old library, thinking of him and longing for his return.

[1]It was but a few fair faces that had not looked forth from windows that day to see the entrance of the French King and his nobles[2]. One of the few was Romola's. She had been present at no festivities since her father had died—died quite suddenly in his chair, [3]three months before.

"Is not Tito coming to write?" he had said, when the bell had long ago sounded the usual hour in the evening. He had not asked before, from dread of a negative; but Romola had seen by his listening face and restless movements that nothing else was in his mind.

"No, father, he had to go to a supper at the Cardinal's: you know he is wanted so much by every one," she answered, in a tone of gentle excuse[4].

"Ah! then perhaps he will bring some positive word about the library; the cardinal* promised last week," said Bardo, apparently pacified by this hope.

He was silent a little while; then, suddenly flushing, he said,—

"I must go on without him, Romola. Get the pen. He has brought me no new text to comment on; but I must say what I want to say about the New Platonists. I shall die and nothing will have been done. Make haste, my Romola."

"I am ready, father," she [5]said, the next minute, holding the pen in her hand.

But there was silence. Romola took no note of this for a little while, accustomed to pauses in dictation; and when at last she looked round inquiringly, there was no change of attitude.

"I am quite ready, father!"

Still Bardo was silent, and his silence was never again broken.

Romola looked back on that hour with[6] some indignation against

---

1 ⟨It was but a few⟩ ⟨Few⟩ It *MS*
3 ⟨two⟩ three *MS*
5 ⟨had⟩ said *MS*

2 nobles ⟨, but one⟩. One *MS*
4 {a tone of} gentle excuse *MS*
6 with ⟨a sense of guilt, for⟩ *MS*

The Painted Record

herself, because even with the first [7]outburst of her sorrow there had mingled the irrepressible thought, "Perhaps my life with Tito will be more perfect now."

For the dream of a triple life with an undivided sum of happiness had not been quite fulfilled. The rainbow-tinted shower of sweets, to have been perfectly typical, should have had some invisible seeds of bitterness mingled with them; the crowned Ariadne,[8] under the snowing roses, had felt[9] more and more the presence of unexpected thorns. It was not Tito's fault, Romola had continually assured herself. He was still all[1] gentleness to her, and to her father also. But it was in the nature of things—she saw it clearly now—it was in the nature of things that no one but herself could go on month after month, and year after year, [2]fulfilling patiently all her father's monotonous exacting demands. Even she, whose sympathy with her father had made all the passion and religion of her young years, had not always been patient, had been inwardly very rebellious. It was true that before their marriage, and even for some time after[3], Tito had seemed more unwearying than herself; but then, of course, the effort had the ease of novelty. We assume a load with confident readiness, and up to a certain point the growing irksomeness of pressure is tolerable; but at last the desire for relief[4] can no longer be resisted. Romola said to herself that she had been very foolish and ignorant in her girlish time: she was wiser now, and would make no unfair demands on the man to whom she had given her best woman's love[5] and worship. The breath of sadness that still cleaved to her lot [6]while she saw her father month after month sink from elation into new disappointment as Tito gave him less and less of his time, and made bland excuses for not continuing his own share of the joint work—that sadness was no fault of Tito's, she said, but rather[7] of their inevitable destiny. If he stayed less and less with her, why, that was because they could hardly ever be alone. His caresses were no less tender: if she pleaded timidly on any one evening that he should stay with her father instead of going to another engagement which was not peremptory, he excused himself with such charming gaiety, he seemed to linger about her with such fond [8]playfulness before he could quit her, that she could only feel a little heart-ache in the midst of her love, and then go to her father

7 ⟨moments⟩ outburst *MS*   8 Ariadne, ⟨as the shower of⟩ *MS*
9 {had} felt *MS*   1 all ⟨love and⟩ gentleness *MS*
2 ⟨bearing⟩ fulfilling *MS*   3 marriage, {and even for some time after} *MS*
4 relief ⟨becomes irresistible⟩ *MS*   5 {woman's} love *MS*
6 ⟨as⟩ while *MS*

7 work—that sadness . . . rather] work—she said it was no fault of Tito's, but rather *MS*

8 ⟨playful caresses⟩ playfulness *MS*

and try to soften his vexation and disappointment. But all the while[9] inwardly her imagination was busy trying to see how Tito could be as good as she had thought he was, and yet find it impossible to sacrifice those pleasures of society which were necessarily more vivid to a bright creature like him than to the common run of men. She herself would have liked more gaiety, more admiration: it was true, she gave it up willingly for her father's sake—she would have given up much more than that for the sake even of a slight wish on Tito's part. It was clear that their natures differed widely; but perhaps it was no more than the inherent difference between man and woman, that made her affections more absorbing. If there were any other difference she tried to persuade herself that the inferiority was on her side. Tito was really kinder than she was, better-tempered, less proud and resentful; he had no angry retorts, he met all complaints with perfect sweetness; he only escaped as quietly as he could from things that were unpleasant.

It belongs to every large nature, when it is not under the immediate power of some strong unquestioning emotion[1], to suspect itself, and [2]doubt the truth of its own impressions, conscious of possibilities beyond its own horizon. And[3] Romola was urged to doubt herself the more by the necessity of interpreting her disappointment in her life with Tito so[4] as to satisfy at once her love and her pride. Disappointment? Yes, there was no other milder word that would tell the truth. Perhaps all women had to suffer the disappointment of ignorant hopes, if she only knew their experience. Still, there had been something peculiar in her lot:[5] her relation to her father had claimed unusual sacrifices from her husband. Tito had once thought that his love would make those sacrifices easy; his love had not been great enough for that. She was not justified in resenting a self-delusion. No! resentment must not rise: all endurance seemed easy to Romola rather than a state of mind in which she would admit to herself that Tito [6]acted unworthily. If she had felt a new heart-ache, in the solitary hours with her father through the last months of his life, it had been by no inexcusable fault of her husband's; and now—it was a hope that would make its presence felt even in the first moments when her father's [7]place was empty—[8]there was no longer any impor-

<hr>

9 disappointment. But all the while] *3P* disappointment, while *MS CM 1 2*

1 nature {when . . . emotion} *MS*   2 ⟨question⟩ doubt *MS*

3 And ⟨that self doubt was urged to activity in Romola⟩ *MS*

4 Tito so] *MS 3C* Tito, so *CM 1 2*

5 lot: ⟨it was only a few wives whose⟩ ⟨few wives had a blind and aged father whose presence claimed continual sacrifices⟩ *MS*

6 ⟨had⟩ acted *MS*   7 ⟨chair⟩ place *MS*

8 ⟨she had no longer that importunate duty that⟩ ⟨and the duty that had divided her from her husband⟩ there *MS*

tunate claim to divide her from Tito; their young lives would flow in one current, and their true marriage would begin.

But the sense of something like guilt towards her father, in a hope that grew out of his death, [9]gave all the more force to the anxiety with which she dwelt on the means of fulfilling his supreme wish. That piety towards his memory was all the atonement she could make now for a thought that seemed akin to joy at his loss. The laborious simple life, pure from vulgar corrupting ambitions, [1]embittered by the frustration of the dearest hopes, imprisoned at last in total darkness[2]—a long seed-time without a harvest—was at an end now, and all that remained of it besides the tablet in Santa Croce and the unfinished commentary[3] on Tito's text, was the [4]collection of manuscripts and antiquities, fruit[5] of half a century's toil and frugality. The fulfilment of her father's life-long ambition about this library was[6] a sacramental obligation for Romola.

The precious relic was safe from creditors, for when the deficit towards their payment had been ascertained, Bernardo del Nero, though he was far from being among the wealthiest Florentines, had advanced the necessary sum of about a thousand[7] florins—a large sum in those days—accepting a lien on the collection as a security.*

"The State will repay me," he had said to Romola, making light of the service which had really cost him some inconvenience. "If the Cardinal finds a building, as he seems to say he will, our Signoria may consent to do the rest. I have no children, I can afford the risk."

But within the last ten days all hopes in the Medici had come to an end: and the famous Medicean collections in the Via Larga were themselves in danger of dispersion. French agents had already begun to see that such very fine antique gems as Lorenzo had collected[8] belonged by right to the [9]first nation in Europe; and the Florentine State[1], which had got possession of the Medicean library, was likely to be glad of a customer for it. With a war to recover Pisa hanging over it, and with the certainty of having to pay large subsidies to the French King, the State was likely to prefer money to manuscripts.

To Romola these grave political changes had gathered their chief interest from their bearing on the fulfilment of her father's wish. She had been brought up in learned seclusion from the interests of actual

---

9 ⟨threw all the more intensity into⟩ gave *MS*

1 ⟨overshadowed⟩ embittered *MS*   2 {total} darkness *MS*

3 unfinished commentary] *1 2 3* unfinished manuscript, long rambling commentary *MS CM*

4 ⟨precious⟩ collection of ⟨books⟩ manuscripts *MS*   5 fruit] the fruit *1 2 3*

6 was ⟨an object that had acquired a sacramental⟩ a sacramental ⟨sanctity for⟩ obligation for *MS*

7 a thousand] eight hundred *MS*   8 collected ⟨were properly⟩ *MS*

9 ⟨strongest⟩ first *MS*   1 State ⟨had had to make haste in⟩ *MS*

life, and had been accustomed to think of heroic deeds and great
principles as something antithetic to the vulgar present, of the Pnyx
and the Forum as something more worthy of [2]attention than the
councils of living Florentine men. And now the expulsion of the
Medici meant little more for her than [3]the extinction of her best hope
about her father's library. The times, she knew, were[4] unpleasant for
friends of the Medici, like her godfather and Tito: superstitious shopkeepers, and the stupid rabble, were full of suspicions; but her new
keen interest in[5] public events, in the outbreak of war, in the issue of
the French King's visit, in the changes that were likely to happen in
the State, was kindled solely by the [6]sense of love and duty to her
father's memory. All [7]Romola's ardour had been concentrated in her
affections. Her share in her father's learned pursuits had been for her
little more than a toil which was borne for his sake; and Tito's airy
brilliant[8] faculty had no attraction for her that was not merged in the
deeper sympathies that belong to young love and trust. Romola had
had contact with no mind that[9] could stir the larger possibilities of
her nature[1]; they lay folded and crushed like embryonic wings, making no element in her consciousness beyond an occasional vague[2]
uneasiness.

But this new personal interest of hers in public affairs had made
her care at last to understand precisely what influence Fra Girolamo's
preaching was likely to have on the turn of events. Changes in the
form of the State were talked of, and all she could learn from Tito,
whose secretaryship and serviceable talents carried him into the heart
of public business, made her only the more eager to fill out her lonely
day by going to hear for herself what it was that was just now leading
all Florence by the ears. This morning, for the first time, she had
been to hear one of the Advent sermons in the Duomo. When Tito[3]
had left her, she had formed a sudden resolution, and[4] after visiting
the spot where her father was buried in Santa Croce, had walked on
to the Duomo. The memory of that last scene with Dino was still
vivid within her whenever she recalled it, but it had receded behind

2 ⟨enthusiasm⟩ attention *MS*

3 ⟨the frustration of⟩ ⟨the extinction of an [?influence]⟩ the extinction *MS*

4 times, she knew, were] times were *MS*   5 in ⟨what the State was⟩ *MS*

6 ⟨hopes and⟩ sense *MS*

7 ⟨the ardour of Romola's nature⟩ Romola's ardour *MS*

8 Her share . . . brilliant] *1 2 3* Her father's learning had remained for her a
pedantry that was tolerable for his sake; and Tito's more airy brilliant *MS CM*

9 had had contact with no mind that] had had no contact that *MS*

1 nature, ⟨which lay⟩ they lay {folded and} crushed *MS*

2 an occasional vague] a vague {occasional} *MS*

3 Duomo. When Tito] Duomo: after Tito *MS*   4 and ⟨first⟩ *MS*

the [5]experience and anxieties of her married life. The new sensibilities and questions which it had half awakened in her were quieted again by that subjection to her husband's mind which is felt by every wife who loves her husband with passionate devotedness and full reliance. She remembered the effect of Fra Girolamo's voice and presence[6] on her as a ground for [7]expecting that his sermon might move her in spite of his being a narrow-minded monk. But the sermon did no more than slightly deepen her previous impression, that this fanatical preacher of tribulations was after all a man [8]towards whom it might be possible for her to feel personal regard and reverence. The denunciations and exhortations simply arrested her attention. She felt no terror, no pangs of conscience: it was the roll of distant thunder, that seemed grand, but could not shake her. But when she heard Savonarola invoke martyrdom, she sobbed with the rest: she felt herself penetrated with a new sensation—a strange sympathy with something apart from all the definable interests of her life. It was not altogether unlike the thrill which had accompanied certain rare heroic touches in history and poetry; but the resemblance was as that between the memory of music, and the sense of being possessed by actual vibrating harmonies.

But that transient emotion, strong as it was, seemed to lie quite outside the inner chamber and sanctuary of her life. She was not thinking of Fra Girolamo now; she was listening anxiously for the step of her husband. During these three months of their double solitude she had thought of each day as an epoch in which their union might begin to be more perfect. She was conscious of being sometimes a little too sad or too urgent about what concerned her father's memory—a little too critical or coldly silent when Tito narrated the things that were said and done in the world he frequented—a little too hasty in suggesting that by living quite simply as her father had done, they might become rich enough to pay Bernardo del Nero, and reduce the difficulties about the library. It was not possible that Tito could feel so strongly on this last point as she did, and it was asking a great deal from him to give up luxuries for which he really laboured. The next time Tito came home she would be careful to [9]suppress all those promptings that seemed to isolate her from him. Romola was labouring, as a loving[1] woman must, to subdue her nature to her husband's. The great need of her heart compelled her to strangle, with desperate resolution, every rising impulse of suspicion, pride, and resentment; she felt equal to any self-infliction that would save her from ceasing to love. That would have been like the hideous night-

5 ⟨new⟩ experience *MS*   6 voice {and presence} *MS*
7 ⟨believing⟩ expecting *MS*   8 ⟨for⟩ towards *MS*
9 ⟨overcome⟩ suppress *MS*   1 a loving] *3C* every loving *MS CM 1 2*

mare in which the world had seemed to break away all round her, and leave her feet overhanging the darkness. Romola had never distinctly imagined such a future for herself; she was only beginning to feel the presence of effort in that clinging trust which had once been mere repose.

She waited and listened long, for Tito had not come straight home after leaving Niccolò Caparra, and it was [2]more than two hours after the time when he was crossing the Ponte Rubaconte that Romola heard the great door of the court turning on its hinges, and hastened to the head of the stone steps. There was a lamp hanging over the stairs, and they could see each other distinctly as he ascended. The eighteen months had produced a more definable change in Romola's face than in Tito's: the expression was more subdued, less cold, and more beseeching, and, as the pink flush overspread her face now, in her joy that the long waiting was at an end, she was much lovelier than on the day when Tito had first seen her. On that day, any onlooker would have said that Romola's nature was made to command, and Tito's to bend; yet now Romola's mouth was quivering a little, and there was some timidity in her glance.

He made an effort to smile, as she said,

"My Tito, you are tired; it has been a fatiguing day: is it not true?"

Maso was there, and no more was said until they had crossed the antechamber and closed the door of the library behind them. The wood was burning brightly on the great dogs; that was one welcome for Tito, late as he was, and Romola's gentle voice was another.

He just turned and kissed her when she took off his mantle; then he went[3] towards a high-backed chair placed for him near the fire, threw himself into it, and flung away his cap, saying, not peevishly, but in a fatigued tone of remonstrance, as he gave a slight shudder,

"Romola, I wish you would give up sitting in this library. Surely our own rooms are pleasanter in this chill weather."

Romola felt hurt[4]. She had never seen Tito so indifferent in his manner; he was usually full of lively solicitous attention. And she had thought so much of his return to her after the long day's absence! He must be very weary.

"I wonder you have forgotten, Tito," she answered, looking at him anxiously[5], as if she wanted to read an excuse for him in the signs of bodily fatigue. "You know I am making the catalogue on the new plan that my father wished for; you have not time to help me, so I

---

2 ⟨nearly three⟩ more than two *MS*

3 kissed her . . . went] *3C* kissed her, when she took off his mantle, then went *MS CM 1 2*

4 hurt] deeply wounded *MS*   5 him anxiously] *MS 3C* him, anxiously *CM 1 2*

Coming Home

must work at it[6] closely."

Tito, instead of meeting Romola's glance, closed his eyes and rubbed his hands over his face and hair. He felt he was behaving unlike himself, but he would make amends to-morrow. The terrible resurrection of secret fears, which, if Romola had known them, would have alienated her from him for ever, caused him to feel an alienation already begun between them—caused him to feel a certain repulsion towards a woman from whose mind he was in danger. The feeling had taken hold of him unawares, and he was vexed with himself for behaving in this new cold way to her. He could not suddenly command any affectionate looks or words; he could only[7] exert himself to say what might serve as an excuse.

"I am not well, Romola; you must not be surprised if I am peevish."

"Ah, you have had so much to tire you to-day," said Romola, kneeling down close to him, and laying her arm on his chest while she put his hair back caressingly.

Suddenly she drew her arm away with a start, and a gaze of alarmed inquiry.

"What have you got on[8] under your tunic, Tito? Something as hard as iron."

"It *is* iron—it is chain armour," he said at once. He was prepared for the surprise and the question, and he spoke quietly, as of something that he was not hurried to explain.

"There was some unexpected danger to-day, then?" said Romola, in a tone of conjecture. "You had it lent to you for the procession?"

"No; it is my own. I shall be obliged to wear it constantly, for some time."

"What is it that threatens you, [9]my Tito?" said Romola, looking terrified, and clinging to him again.

"Every one is threatened in these times, who is not a rabid [1]enemy of the Medici. Don't look distressed, my Romola—this armour will make me safe against covert attacks."

Tito put his hand on her neck and smiled. This little dialogue abut the armour had broken through the new crust, and made a channel for the sweet[2] habit of kindness.

"But my godfather, then," said Romola; "is not he, too, in danger? And he takes no precautions—ought he not? since he must surely be in more danger than you, who have so little influence compared with him."

"It is just because I am less important that I am in more danger," said

6 it ⟨for some months⟩ MS   7 only ⟨make an⟩ MS
8 got on] got *1 2 3*   9 ⟨*Tito mio*⟩ my Tito MS
1 ⟨Medicean⟩ enemy MS   2 sweet] *1 2 3* old sweet MS CM

Tito, readily. "I am suspected constantly of being an envoy. And men like Messer Bernardo are protected by their position and their extended[3] family connections, which spread among all parties, while I am a Greek that nobody would avenge."

"But, Tito, is it a fear of some particular person, or only a vague sense of danger that has made you think of wearing this?" Romola was unable to repel the idea of a degrading fear in Tito, which mingled itself with her anxiety.

"I have had special threats," said Tito, "but I must beg you to be silent on the subject, my Romola. I shall consider that you have broken my confidence, if you mention it to your godfather."

"Assuredly I will not mention it," said Romola, blushing[4], "if you wish it to be a secret. But, dearest Tito," she added, after a moment's pause[5], in a tone of loving anxiety, "it will make you very wretched."

"What will make me wretched?" he said, with a scarcely perceptible movement across his face, as from some darting sensation.

"This fear—this heavy armour. I can't help shuddering as I feel it under my arm. I could fancy it a story of enchantment—that some malignant fiend had changed your sensitive human skin into a hard shell. It seems so unlike my bright, light-hearted Tito!"

"Then you would rather have your husband exposed to danger, when he leaves you?" said Tito, smiling. "If you don't mind my being poniarded or shot, why need I mind? I will give up the armour—shall I?"

"No, Tito, no. I am fanciful. Do not heed what I have said. But such crimes are surely not common in Florence? I have always heard my father and godfather say so. Have they become frequent lately?"

"It is not unlikely they will become frequent, with the bitter hatreds that are being bred continually."

Romola was silent a few moments. She shrank from insisting further on the subject of the armour. She tried to shake it off.

"Tell me what has happened to-day," she said, in a cheerful tone. "Has all gone off well?"

"Excellently well. First of all, the rain came and put an end to Luca Corsini's oration, which nobody wanted to hear, and a ready-tongued personage—some say it was Gaddi, some say it was Melema, but really it was done so quickly no one knows who it was—had the honour of giving the Cristianissimo the briefest possible welcome in bad French."

"Tito, it was you, I know," said Romola, smiling brightly, and kissing him. "How is it you never care about claiming anything? And

3 extended] extensive *1 2 3*   4 blushing] *1 2 3* flushing *MS CM*
5 added, {after a moment's pause} *MS*

after that?"

"Oh! after that, there was a show[6] of armour, and jewels, and trappings, such as you [7]saw at the last Florentine *giostra*, only a great deal
more of them. There was strutting, and prancing, and confusion, and
scrambling, and the people shouted, and the Cristianissimo smiled
from ear to ear. And after that there was a great deal of flattery, and
eating, and play. I was at Tornabuoni's. I will tell you about it to-
morrow."

"Yes, dearest—never mind now. But is there any more hope that
things will end peaceably for Florence—that the Republic will not get
into fresh troubles?"

Tito gave a shrug. "Florence will have no peace but what it pays
well for—that is clear."

Romola's face saddened, but she checked herself, and said, [8]cheer-
fully, "You would not guess where I went to-day, Tito. I went to the
Duomo, to hear Fra Girolamo."

Tito looked startled; he had immediately thought of Baldassarre's
entrance into the Duomo: but Romola[9] gave his look another meaning.

"You are surprised, are you not? It was a sudden thought. I want
to know all about the public affairs now, and I determined to hear for
myself what the Frate promised the people about this French invasion."

"Well, and what did you think of the prophet?"

"He certainly has[1] a very mysterious power, that man. A great deal
of his sermon what was I expected; but once I was strangely moved—
I sobbed with the rest."

"Take care, Romola," said Tito, playfully, feeling relieved that she
had said nothing about Baldassarre; "you have a touch of fanaticism
in you. I shall have you seeing visions, like your brother."

"No; it was the same with every one else. He carried them all with
him; unless it were that gross[2] Dolfo Spini, whom I saw there making
grimaces. There was even a wretched-looking man, with a rope round
his neck—an escaped prisoner, I should think, who had run in for
shelter—a very [3]wild-eyed old man: I saw him with great tears rolling
down his cheeks, as he looked and listened quite eagerly."

There was a slight pause before Tito spoke.

"I saw the man," he said, "the prisoner. I was outside the Duomo
with Lorenzo Tornabuoni when [4]he ran in. He had escaped from a

6 show] shower *2 3*
7 ⟨have seen at a⟩ saw at the last *MS*   8 ⟨in a cheerful tone⟩ cheerfully *MS*
9 Romola ⟨interpreted his look differently⟩ *MS*   1 {certainly} has *MS*
2 gross] gross-looking *MS*   3 wild⟨-looking⟩-eyed *MS*   4 ⟨the man⟩ he *MS*

French soldier. Did you see him when you came out?"

"No, he went out with our good old Piero di Cosimo. I saw Piero come in and cut off his rope, and take him out of the church. But you want rest, Tito? You feel ill?"

"Yes," said Tito, rising. The horrible sense that he must live in continual ⁵dread of what Baldassarre had said or done pressed upon him like cold weight.

5 ⟨suspense as to what⟩ dread of what *MS*

CHAPTER XXVIII.

THE PAINTED RECORD

FOUR days later, Romola was on her way to the house of Piero di Cosimo, in the Via Gualfonda. Some of the streets through which she had to pass were lined with Frenchmen who were gazing at Florence, and with Florentines who were gazing at the French, and the gaze was not on either side entirely friendly and admiring. The first nation in Europe, of necessity finding itself, when out of its own country, in the presence of general inferiority, naturally assumed an air of conscious pre-eminence; and the Florentines, who had taken such pains to play the host amiably[1], were getting into the worst humour with their too superior guests.

For [2]after the first smiling compliments and festivities were over—after wondrous Mysteries* with unrivalled machinery of floating clouds and angels had been presented in churches—after the[3] royal guest had honoured Florentine dames with much of his Most Christian ogling at balls and suppers, and business had begun to be talked of—it appeared that the new Charlemagne regarded Florence as a conquered city, inasmuch as he had entered it with his lance in rest,[4]* talked of leaving his viceroy behind him, and had thoughts of bringing back the Medici. Singular logic this appeared to be on the part of an elect instrument of God! since the policy of Piero de' Medici[5], disowned by the people, had been the only offence of Florence against the Majesty of France. And Florence was determined not to submit. The determination was being expressed very strongly in consultations of citizens inside the Old Palace, and it was beginning to show itself on the broad flags of the streets and piazze[6] wherever there was an opportunity of flouting an insolent Frenchman. Under these circumstances the streets were not altogether a pleasant promenade for well-born women; but Romola, shrouded in her black veil[7] and mantle, and with old Maso by her side, felt secure enough from impertinent observation.

And she was impatient to visit Piero di Cosimo. A copy of her father's portrait as Œdipus, which he had long ago undertaken to make for her, was not yet finished; and Piero was so uncertain in his work—sometimes, when the demand was not peremptory, laying aside a picture for months; sometimes thrusting it into a corner or coffer, where it was likely to be utterly forgotten—that she felt it necessary

---

1 play the host amiably] receive them amiably *MS*   2 ⟨now⟩ after *MS*
3 churches {after} the ⟨mighty⟩ royal *MS*   4 rest, ⟨intended to leave⟩ *MS*
5 Piero de' Medici] Piero *MS*   6 piazze] piazza *2 3*   7 {her} black veil *MS*

to watch over his progress. She was a favourite with the painter[8], and he was inclined to fulfil any wish of hers, but no general inclination could be trusted as a safeguard against his sudden whims. He had told her the week before that the picture would perhaps be finished by this time; and Romola was nervously anxious to have in her possession a copy of the only portrait existing of her father in the days of his blindness, lest[9] his image should grow dim in her mind. The sense of defect in her devotedness to him made her cling with all the force of compunction as well as affection to the duties of memory. Love does not aim simply at the conscious good of the beloved object:[1] it is not satisfied without perfect loyalty of heart; it aims at its own completeness.

Romola, by special favour, was allowed to intrude upon[2] the painter without previous notice[3]. She lifted the [4]iron slide and called Piero in a flute-like tone, as the little maiden with the eggs had done in Tito's presence. Piero was quick in answering, but when he opened the door he accounted for his quickness in a manner that was not complimentary.

"Ah, Madonna Romola, is it you?[5] I thought my eggs were come; I wanted them."

"I have brought you something better than hard eggs, Piero. Maso has got a little basket full of cakes and *confetti* for you," said Romola, smiling, as she put back her veil. She took the basket from Maso, and stepping into the house, said,

"I know you like these things when you can have them without trouble. Confess you do."

"Yes, when they come to me as easily as the light does," said Piero, folding his arms and looking down at the sweetmeats as Romola uncovered them and glanced at him archly. "And they are come along[6] with the light now," he added, lifting his eyes to her face and hair with a painter's admiration, as her hood, dragged by the weight of her veil, fell backward.

"But I know what the sweetmeats are for," he went on; "they are to stop my mouth while you scold me. Well, go on into the next room, and you will see I've done something to the picture since you saw it, though it's not finished yet. But I didn't promise, you know: I take care not to promise:

> 'Chi promette e non mantiene
> L'anima sua non va mai[7] bene.' "*

8 the painter] Piero *MS*
9 blindness, lest] blindness—anxious that it should be as successful as the original, lest *MS*

1 object:] *MS 1 2 3* object; *CM*   2 upon] *1 2 3* on *MS CM*
3 {previous} notice *MS*   4 ⟨little⟩ iron *MS*
5 is it you?] *1 2 3* it is you. *MS CM* 6 come {along} *MS* 7 mai] mai *1 2 3*

The door opening on the wild garden was closed now, [8]and the
painter was at work. Not at Romola's picture, however. That was
standing on the floor,[9] propped against the wall, and Piero stooped to
lift it, that he might carry it into the proper light. But in lifting away
this picture, he had disclosed another—the oil-sketch of Tito, to
which he had made an important addition within the last few days. It
was so much smaller than the other picture that it stood far within it,
and Piero, apt to forget where he had placed anything, was not aware
of what he had revealed as, peering at some detail in the painting
which he held in his hands, he went to place it on an easel. But
Romola exclaimed, flushing with astonishment,

"That is Tito!"

Piero looked round, and gave a silent shrug. He was vexed at his
own forgetfulness.

She was still looking at the sketch in astonishment; but presently
she turned towards the painter, and said with puzzled alarm,

"What a strange picture! When did you paint it? What does it
mean?"

"A mere fancy of mine," said Piero, lifting off his skull-cap,
scratching his head, and making the usual grimace by which he
avoided the betrayal of any feeling. "I wanted a handsome young face
for it, and your husband's was just the thing."

He went forward, stooped down to the picture, and lifting it away
with its back to Romola, pretended to be giving it a passing examination, before putting it aside as a thing not good enough to show.

But Romola, who had the fact of the armour in her mind, and was
penetrated by this strange coincidence of things which associated Tito
with the idea of Fear, went to his elbow and said,—

"Don't put it away; let me look again. That man with the rope
round his neck—I saw him—I saw you come to him in the Duomo.
What was it that made you put him into a picture with Tito?"

Piero saw no better resource than to tell part of the truth.

"It was a mere accident. The man was running away—running up
the steps, and caught hold of your husband: I suppose he had stumbled. I happened to be there, and saw it, and I thought the savage-
looking old fellow was a good subject. But it's worth nothing—it's
only a freakish daub of mine," Piero[1] ended, contemptuously, moving
the sketch away with an air of decision, and putting it on a high
shelf. "Come and look at the Œdipus."

He had shown a little too much anxiety in putting the sketch out
of her sight, and had produced the very impression he had sought to

8 ⟨for⟩ and *MS*   9 was {standing on the floor,} *MS*
1 mine," Piero] mine." Piero 2 3

prevent—that there was really something unpleasant, something dis-
advantageous to Tito, in the circumstances out of which the picture
arose. But this impression silenced her: her pride and delicacy shrank
from questioning farther[2], where questions might seem to imply that
she could entertain even a slight suspicion against her husband. She
merely said, in as quiet a tone as she could,

"He was a strange piteous-looking man, that prisoner. Do you
know anything more of him?"

"No more: I showed him the way to the hospital, that's all. See
now, the face of Œdipus is pretty nearly finished; tell me what you
think of it."

Romola now gave her whole attention to her father's portrait,
standing in long silence before it.

"Ah!" she said at last, "you have done what I wanted. You have
given it more of the listening look. My good Piero"—she turned
towards him with bright moist eyes—"I am very grateful to you."

"Now, that's what I can't bear in you women," said Piero, turning
impatiently, and kicking aside the objects that littered the floor—"you
are always pouring out feelings where there's no call for them. Why
should you be grateful to me for a picture you pay me for, especially
when I make you wait for it? And if I paint a picture, I suppose it's
for my own pleasure and credit to paint it well, eh? Are you to thank
a man for not being a rogue or a noodle? It's enough if he himself
thanks Messer Domeneddio, who has made him neither the one nor
the other. But women think walls are held together with honey."

"You crusty Piero! I forgot how snappish you are. Here, put this
nice sweetmeat in your mouth," said Romola, smiling through her
tears, and taking something very crisp and sweet from the little
basket.

Piero accepted it very much as that proverbial bear that dreams of
pears might accept an exceedingly mellow "swan-egg"*—really liking
the gift, but accustomed to have his pleasures and pains concealed[3]
under a shaggy coat.

"It's good, Madonna Antigone," said Piero, putting his fingers in
the basket for another. He had eaten nothing but hard eggs for a fortnight. Romola stood opposite him, feeling her new anxiety suspended
for a little while by the sight of this naïve enjoyment.

"Good-by, Piero," she said, presently, setting down the basket. "I
promise not to thank you if you finish the portrait soon and well. I
will tell you, you were bound to do it for your own credit[4]."

2 farther] *MS* further *CM 1 2 3*   3 concealed] undramatically concealed *MS*
4 credit] pleasure and credit *MS*

"Good," said Piero, curtly, helping her with much deftness to fold her mantle and veil round her.[5]

"I'm glad she asked no more questions about that sketch," he thought, when he had closed the door behind her. "I should be sorry for her to guess that I thought her fine husband a good model for a coward. But I made light of it; she'll not think of it again."

Piero was too sanguine, as open-hearted men are apt to be when they attempt a little clever simulation. The thought of the picture pressed more and more on Romola as she walked homeward. She could not help putting together the two facts of the chain armour and the encounter mentioned by Piero, between her husband and the prisoner, which had happened on the morning of the day when the armour was adopted. That look of terror which the painter had given Tito, had he seen it? What could it all mean?

"It means nothing," she tried to assure herself. "It was a mere coincidence. Shall I ask Tito about it?" Her mind said at last, "No: I will not question him about anything he did not tell me spontaneously. It is an offence against the trust I owe him." Her heart said, "I dare not ask him." There was a terrible flaw in the trust: she was afraid of any hasty movement, as men are who hold something precious and want to believe that it is not broken.

5 helping her . . . her.] *1 2 3* helping her to fold her mantle and veil round her with much deftness. *MS CM*

CHAPTER XXIX.

A MOMENT OF TRIUMPH

"The old fellow has vanished; went on towards Arezzo the next morning; not liking the smell of the French, I suppose, after being their prisoner. I went to the hospital to inquire after him; I wanted to know if those broth-making monks had found out whether he was in his right mind or not. However, they said he showed no signs of madness—only took no notice of questions, and seemed to be planting a vine* twenty miles off. He was a mysterious old tiger. I should have liked to know something more about him."

It was in Nello's shop that Piero di Cosimo was speaking, on the twenty-fourth of November, just a week after the entrance of the French. There was a party of six or seven assembled at the rather unusual hour of three in the afternoon; for it was a day on which all Florence was excited by the prospect of some decisive political event. Every lounging-place was full, and every shopkeeper who had no wife or deputy to leave in charge stood at his door with his thumbs in his belt; while the streets were constantly sprinkled with artisans pausing or passing lazily like floating splinters, ready to rush forward impetuously if any object attracted them.

Nello had been thrumming the lute as he half sat on the board against the shop window, and kept an outlook towards the piazza.

"Ah," he said, laying down the lute, with emphasis, "I would not for a gold florin have missed that sight of the French soldiers waddling in their broad shoes after their runaway prisoners! That comes of leaving my shop to shave magnificent chins. It is always so: if ever I quit this navel of the earth something takes the opportunity of happening in my piazza."

"Yes, you ought to have been there," said Piero, in his biting way, "just to see your favourite Greek look as frightened as if Satanasso had laid hold of him. I like to see your ready-smiling *Messeri* caught in a sudden wind and obliged to show their lining in spite of themselves. What colour do you think a man's liver is, who looks like a bleached deer as soon as a chance stranger lays hold of him suddenly?"

"Piero[1], keep that vinegar of thine as sauce to thine own eggs! What[2] is it against my *bel erudito* that he looked startled when he felt a pair of claws upon him and saw an unchained madman at his

1 Piero ⟨mio⟩ *MS*
2 thine own eggs! What] *1 2 3* thy own eggs! Suffocation! What *MS CM*

elbow? Your scholar is not like those beastly Swiss and Germans, whose heads are only fit for[3] battering-rams, and who have such large appetites that they think nothing of taking a cannon-ball before breakfast. We Florentines count some other qualities in a man besides that vulgar stuff called bravery, which is to be got by hiring dunderheads at so much per dozen. I tell you, [4]as soon as men found out that they[5] had more brains than oxen they set the oxen to draw for them, and when we Florentines found out that we had more brains than other men we set them to fight for us."

"Treason, Nello!" a voice called out from the inner sanctum, "that is not the doctrine of the State. Florence is grinding its weapons; and the last well-authenticated vision announced by the Frate was Mars standing on the Palazzo Vecchio with his arm on the shoulder of San Giovanni Battista, who was offering him a piece of honeycomb."*

"It is well, Francesco," said Nello. "Florence has a few thicker skulls that may do to bombard Pisa with; there will still be the finer spirits left at home to do the thinking and the shaving. And, as for our Piero here, if he makes such a point of valour, let him carry his [6]biggest brush for a weapon and his palette for a shield, and challenge the widest-mouthed Swiss he can see in the Prato to a single combat."

"*Va*, Nello," [7]growled Piero, "thy tongue [8]runs on as usual, like a mill[9] when the Arno's full—whether there's grist or not."

"Excellent grist, I tell thee. For it would be as reasonable to expect a grizzled painter like thee to be fond of getting a javelin inside thee as to expect a man whose wits have been sharpened on the classics to like having his handsome face[1] clawed by a wild beast."

"There you go, supposing you'll get people to put their legs into a sack because you call it a pair of hosen," said Piero. "Who said anything about a wild beast, or about an unarmed man rushing on battle? Fighting is a trade, and it's not my trade. I should be a fool to run after danger, but I could face it if it came to me."

"How is it you're so afraid of the thunder[2] then, my Piero?" said Nello, determined to [3]chase down the accuser. "You ought to be able to understand why one man is shaken by a thing that seems a trifle to others—you who hide yourself with the rats as soon as a storm comes on."*

"That is because I have a particular sensibility to loud sounds; it has[4] nothing to do with my courage or my conscience."

---

3 only fit for] *3C* fit for nothing but *MS CM 1 2*   4 ⟨when⟩ as soon as *MS*
5 that they] *3C* they *MS CM 1 2*   6 ⟨brushes and his pallet⟩ biggest brush *MS*
7 ⟨said⟩ growled *MS*   8 ⟨goes⟩ runs *MS*   9 mill ⟨with no grist⟩ *MS*
1 {handsome} face *MS*   2 thunder ⟨and lightning⟩ *MS*
3 ⟨avenge his friend Tito⟩ ⟨run⟩ chase *MS*
4 sounds; it has] sounds—that has *MS*

"Well[5], and Tito Melema may have a peculiar sensibility to being laid hold of unexpectedly by prisoners who have run away from French soldiers. Men are born with antipathies; I myself can't abide the smell of mint. Tito was born with an antipathy to old prisoners who stumble and clutch. Ecco!"

There was a general laugh at Nello's defence, and it was clear that Piero's disinclination towards Tito was not shared by the company. [6]The painter, with[7] his undecipherable grimace, took the tow from his scarsella and stuffed his ears in indignant[8] contempt, while Nello went on triumphantly,

"No, my Piero, I [9]can't afford to have my [1]*bel erudito* decried; and Florence can't afford it either, with her scholars moulting off her at the early age of forty. Our Phœnix Pico just gone straight to Paradise, as the Frate has informed us; and the incomparable Poliziano[2], not two months since,* gone[3]—well, well, let us hope he is not gone to the eminent scholars in the Malebolge."

"[4]By the way," said Francesco Cei, "have you heard that Camilla Rucellai* has outdone the Frate in her prophecies? She prophesied two years ago that Pico would die in the time of lilies. He has died in November. 'Not at all the time of lilies,' said the scorners. 'Go to!' says Camilla; 'it is the lilies of France I meant, and it seems to me they are close enough under your nostrils.' I say, 'Euge,* Camilla!' If the Frate can prove that any one of his visions has been as well fulfilled, I'll declare myself a Piagnone to-morrow."

"You are something too flippant about the Frate, Francesco," said Pietro Cennini, the scholarly. "We are all indebted to him in these weeks for preaching peace and quietness, and the laying aside of party quarrels. They are men of small discernment who would be glad to see the people slipping the Frate's leash just now.[5] And if the Most Christian King is obstinate about the treaty to-day, and will not sign what is [6]fair and honourable to Florence, Fra Girolamo is the man we must trust in to[7] bring him to reason."

"You speak truth, Messer Pietro," said Nello, "the Frate is [8]one of the firmest nails Florence has to hang on—at least, that is the opinion of the most respectable chins I have the honour of shaving. But[9] young Messer Niccolò was saying here the other morning—and,

5 Well] Ebbene *MS*   6 ⟨Nello went on triumphantly while⟩ The *MS*
7 with ⟨a grimace⟩ *MS*
8 ears in indignant] *1 2 3* ears, as a sign of indignant *MS CM*
9 ⟨must not⟩ can't afford to *MS*   1 ⟨pretty scholar⟩ *bel erudito MS*
2 Poliziano] Messer Angelo *MS*   3 gone] *MS* gone to *CM 1 2 3*
4 ⟨No Nello⟩ By *MS*   5 quarrels. {They are . . . now.} *MS*
6 ⟨reasonable⟩ fair and honourable {to Florence}, ⟨the Frate⟩ Fra Girolamo *MS*
7 trust in to] look to to *MS*   8 ⟨the only firm⟩ one of the firmest *MS*
9 But ⟨as our⟩ *MS*

doubtless, Francesco means the same thing—there is as wonderful a power of stretching in the meaning of visions as in Dido's bull's hide.* It seems to me a dream may mean whatever comes after it.[1] As our Franco Sacchetti says,* a woman dreams over night of a serpent biting her[2], breaks a [3]drinking-cup the next day, and cries out, 'Look you, I thought something would happen—it's plain now what the serpent meant.' "

"But the Frate's visions are not of that sort," said Cronaca. "He not only says what will happen—that the Church will be scourged and renovated, and the heathens converted—he says it shall happen quickly. He is no slippery pretender who provides loopholes for himself, he is—"

"What is this? what is this?" exclaimed Nello, jumping off the board[4], and putting his head out at the door. "Here are people streaming into the piazza[5], and shouting. Something must have happened in the Via Larga. Aha!" he burst [6]forth with delighted astonishment, stepping out, laughing, and waving his cap[7].

All the rest of the company[8] hastened to the door. News from the Via Larga was just what they had been waiting for. But if the news had come into the piazza, they were not a little surprised at the form of its advent. Carried above the [9]shoulders of the people, on a bench apparently snatched up in the street, sat Tito Melema, in smiling amusement at the compulsion he was under. His cap had slipped off his head, and hung by the *becchetto* which was wound loosely round his neck; and as he saw the group at Nello's door he lifted up his fingers in beckoning recognition. [1]The next minute he had leaped from the bench on to a cart filled with bales, that stood in the broad space between the Baptistery and the steps of the Duomo, while the people swarmed round him with the noisy eagerness of poultry expecting to be fed. But there was silence when he began to speak, in his clear mellow voice—

"[2]Citizens of Florence! I have no warrant to tell the news except your will. But the news is good, and will harm no man in the telling. [3]The Most Christian King is signing a treaty that is honourable to

---

1 It seems . . . it.] *1 2 3* A dream may mean whatever comes after it, *mi pare. MS CM*

2 serpent {biting her} *MS*   3 ⟨candlestick⟩ drinking cup *MS*

4 board] *1 2 3 desco MS CM*   5 in{to the Piazza} *MS*

6 ⟨out⟩ forth with ⟨[?strong] surprize⟩ delighted astonishment *MS*

7 cap, ⟨above his head⟩ *MS*   8 rest {of the company} *MS*

9 ⟨heads⟩ shoulders *MS*

1 ⟨They all left the door and followed the road⟩ The *MS*

2 ⟨Florentines!⟩ Citizens of Florence! *MS*

3 ⟨His Most Christian Majesty⟩ The *MS*

Florence. But you owe it to one of your citizens, who spoke a word
worthy of the ancient Romans—you owe it to Piero Capponi!"

Immediately there was a roar of voices.

"Capponi! Capponi! What said our Piero?" "Ah! he wouldn't stand
being sent from Herod to Pilate!"* "We knew Piero!" "*Orsù!* Tell us,
what did he say?"

When the roar of insistence had subsided a little, Tito began
again—

"The Most Christian King demanded a little too much—was obstinate—said at last, 'I shall order my trumpets to sound.' Then,
Florentine citizens! your Piero Capponi, speaking with the voice of a
free city, said, 'If you sound your trumpets, we will ring our bells!' He
snatched the copy of the dishonouring conditions from the hands of
the secretary, tore it in pieces, and turned to leave the royal presence."

Again there were loud shouts—and again impatient demands for
more.

"Then, Florentines, the high majesty of France felt, perhaps for
the first time, all the majesty of a free city. And the Most Christian
King himself hastened from his place to call Piero Capponi back. The
great spirit of your Florentine city did its work by a great word,
without need of[4] the great actions that lay ready behind it. And the
King has consented to sign the treaty, which preserves the honour, as
well as the safety, of Florence. The banner of France will float over
every Florentine galley in sign of amity and common privilege, but
above that banner will be written the word 'Liberty!'

"That is all the news I have to tell; is it not enough?—since it is
for the glory of every one of you, citizens of Florence, that you have
a fellow-citizen who knows how to speak your Will."

As the shouts rose again, Tito looked round with inward amusement at the variouis crowd, each of whom was elated with the notion
that Piero Capponi had somehow represented him—that he was the
mind of which Capponi was the mouthpiece. He enjoyed the humour
of the incident, which had suddenly transformed him, an alien and a
friend of the Medici, into an orator who tickled the ears of the people
blatant for some unknown good which they called liberty.[5] He felt
quite glad that he had been laid hold of and hurried along by the
crowd as he was coming out of the palace in the Via Larga with a
commission to the Signoria. It was very easy, very pleasant, this exercise of speaking to the general satisfaction: a man who knew how to
persuade need never be in danger from any party; he could convince
each that he was feigning with all the others. The gestures and faces

4 of] for *MS*

5 mouthpiece. {He enjoyed . . . liberty.} Tito ⟨enjoyed the⟩ felt quite glad . . .
Signoria. ⟨He enjoyed . . . liberty.⟩ It *MS*

of weavers and dyers were certainly amusing when looked at from
above in this way.[6] Tito was beginning to get easier in his armour,
and at this moment was quite unconscious of it. He stood with one
hand holding his recovered cap, and with the other at his belt, the
light of a complacent smile in his long lustrous eyes, as he made a
parting reverence to his audience, before springing down from the
bales—when suddenly his glance met that of a man who had not at all
the amusing aspect of the exulting weavers, dyers, and wool-carders.[7]
The face of this man was clean-shaven, his[8] hair close-clipped, and he
wore a decent felt hat. A single glance would hardly have sufficed to
assure any one but Tito that this was the face of the escaped prisoner
who had laid hold of him on the steps. But to Tito it came not
simply as the face of the escaped prisoner[9], but as a face with which
he had been familiar long, long years[1] before.

It[2] seemed all compressed into a second—the sight of Baldassarre
looking at him, the sensation shooting through him like a fiery arrow,
and the act of leaping from the cart. He would have leaped down in
the same instant, whether he had seen Baldassarre or not, for he was
in a hurry to be gone to the Palazzo Vecchio: this time he had not
betrayed himself by look or movement, and he said inwardly that he
should not be taken by surprise again; he should be prepared to see
this face rise up continually like the intermittent blotch that comes in
diseased vision. But this reappearance of Baldassarre so much more in
his own likeness, tightened the pressure of dread: the idea of his
madness lost its likelihood now he was shaven and clad like a decent
though poor[3] citizen. Certainly, there was a great change in his face;
but how could it be otherwise? And yet, if he were perfectly sane—in
possession of all his powers and all his learning—why was he lingering in this way before making known his identity? It must be for the
sake of making his scheme of vengeance more complete. But he did
linger: that at least gave an opportunity for flight. And Tito began to
think that flight was his only resource.

But while he, with his back turned on the Piazza del Duomo, had
lost the recollection of the new part he had been playing, and was no
longer thinking of the many things which a ready brain and tongue
made easy, but of a few things which destiny had somehow made[4]
very difficult, the enthusiasm which he had fed contemptuously was
creating a scene in that piazza in grand contrast with the inward
drama of self-centred fear which he had carried away from it.

6 others. {The gestures . . . way.} *MS*
7 weavers ⟨and⟩ dyers {and wool-carders.} *MS*   8 his] the *MS*
9 prisoner ⟨on the steps⟩ *MS*   1 long, long years] long years *1 2 3*
2 before. {¶} It *MS*   3 decent {though poor} *MS*
4 destiny had somehow made] somehow destiny had made *MS*

The crowd, on Tito's disappearance, had begun to turn their faces towards the outlets of the piazza in the direction of the Via Larga, when the sight of *mazzieri*, or mace-bearers, entering from the Via de' Martelli, announced the approach of dignitaries. They must be the syndics, or [5]commissioners charged[6] with the effecting of the Treaty; the Treaty must be already signed, and they had come away from the royal presence. Piero Capponi was coming—the brave heart that had known how to speak for Florence. The effect on the crowd was remarkable; they parted with softening, dropping voices, subsiding into silence,—and the silence became so perfect that the tread of the syndics on the broad pavement, and the rustle of their black silk garments, could be heard, like rain in the night[7]. There were four of them; but it was not the two learned doctors of law, Messer Guidantonio Vespucci and Messer Domenico[8] Bonsi,* that the crowd waited for; it was not Francesco Valori, popular as he had become in these late days. The moment belonged to another man, of firm[9] presence, as little inclined to humour the people as to humour any other [1]unreasonable claimants—loving order, like [2]one who by force of fortune had been made a merchant, and by force of nature had become a soldier. It was not till he was seen at the entrance of the piazza that the silence was broken, and then one loud shout of "Capponi, Capponi! Well done, Capponi!" rang through the piazza.

The simple, resolute man looked round him with grave joy. His fellow-citizens gave him a great funeral two years later, when he had died in fight:* there were torches carried by all the magistracy, and torches again[3], and trains of banners. But it is not known that he felt any joy in the oration that was delivered in his praise, as the banners waved over his bier. Let us be glad that he got some thanks and praise while he lived.

5 ⟨procurators⟩ commissioners *MS*
6 commissioners charged] *MS 1 2 3* commissioners, charged *CM*
7 heard {like rain in the night} *MS*
8 {Messer} Guidantonio Vespucci and {Messer} Domenico *MS*
9 firm ⟨and resolute⟩ *MS*   1 ⟨exorbitant⟩ unreasonable *MS*
2 ⟨a man⟩ one *MS*
3 torches {carried by all the magistracy} and torches {again} *MS*

CHAPTER XXX.

THE AVENGER'S SECRET

IT was the first time that Baldassarre had been in the Piazza del Duomo since his escape. He had a strong desire to hear the remarkable monk preach again, but he had shrunk from reappearing in the same spot where he had been seen[1] half naked, with neglected hair, with a rope round his neck—in the same spot where he had been called a madman. The feeling, in its freshness, was too strong to be overcome by any trust he had in the change he had made in his appearance; for when the words "*some madman, surely*[2]," had fallen from Tito's lips, it was not their baseness and cruelty only that had made their viper sting—it was Baldassarre's instantaneous bitter consciousness that he might be unable to prove the words false. Along with the passionate desire for vengeance which[3] possessed him had arisen the keen sense that his power of achieving the vengeance was doubtful. It was as if Tito had been helped by some diabolical prompter, who had whispered Baldassarre's saddest secret in the traitor's ear. He was not mad; for he carried within him that piteous stamp of sanity—the clear consciousness of shattered faculties: he measured his own feebleness. With the first movements[4] of vindictive rage awoke a vague caution, like that of a wild beast that is fierce but feeble—or like that of an insect whose little fragment of earth has given way, and made it pause in a palsy of distrust. It was this distrust, this determination to take no step which might betray anything concerning himself, that had made Baldassarre reject Piero di Cosimo's friendly advances.

He had been equally cautious at the hospital, only telling, in answer to the questions of the brethren there, that he had been made a prisoner by the French on his way from Genoa. But his age, and the indications in his speech and manner that he was of a different class from the ordinary mendicants and poor travellers who were entertained in the hospital, had induced the monks to offer him extra charity—a coarse woollen tunic to protect him from the cold, a pair of peasant's shoes, and a few *danari*, smallest of Florentine coins,[5] to help him on his way. He had gone on the road to Arezzo early in the morning; but he had paused at the first little town, and had used a

1 seen ⟨with⟩ *MS*
2 *some madman, surely*] *2 3* some madman, surely *MS CM 1*
3 which] *1 2 3* that *MS CM*   4 movements] movement *2 3*
5 *danari*, smallest of Florentine coins,] *danari MS*

couple of his *danari* to get himself shaved, and to have his circle of hair clipped short, in his former fashion. The barber there had a little hand-mirror of bright steel: it was a long while, it was years, since Baldassarre had looked at himself, and now, as his eyes fell on that hand-mirror, a new thought shot through his mind. "Was he so changed that Tito really did not know him?" The thought was such a sudden arrest of impetuous currents, that it was a painful shock to him: his hand shook like a leaf, as he put away the barber's arm and asked for the mirror. He wished to see himself before he was shaved. The barber, noticing his tremulousness, held the mirror for him.

No, he was not so changed as that. He himself had known the wrinkles as they [6]had been three years ago; they were only deeper now: there was the same rough, clumsy skin, making little superficial bosses on the brow, like so many cipher marks; the skin was only yellower, [7]only looked more like a lifeless rind. That shaggy white beard—it was no disguise to eyes that had looked closely at him for sixteen years—to eyes that ought to have searched for him with the expectation of finding him changed, as men search for the beloved among the bodies cast up[8] by the waters. There was something different in his glance, but it was a difference that should only have[9] made the recognition of him the more startling; for is not a known voice all the more thrilling when it is heard as a cry? But the doubt was folly: he had felt that Tito knew him. He put out his hand and pushed the mirror away. The strong currents were rushing on again, and the energies of hatred and vengeance were active once more.

He went back on the way towards Florence again, but he did not wish to enter the city till dusk; so he turned aside from the high-road, and sat down by a little pool shadowed on one side by alder-bushes still sprinkled with yellow leaves. It was a calm November day, and he no sooner saw the pool than he thought its still surface might be a mirror for him. He wanted to contemplate himself slowly, as he had not dared to do in the presence of the barber. He sat down on the edge of the pool, and bent forward to look earnestly at the image of himself.

Was there something wandering and imbecile in his face—something like what he felt in his mind[1]?

Not now; not when he was examining himself with a look of eager inquiry: on the contrary, there was an intense purpose in his eyes. But at other times? Yes, it must be so: in the long hours when he had the vague aching of an unremembered past within him—when he

---

6 ⟨were⟩ had been *MS*   7 ⟨and⟩ only *MS*
8 the bodies cast up] those who are cast up *MS*   9 {only} have *MS*
1 mind. ⟨Would anybody who considered him attentively say, "It is likely enough he raves?"⟩ *MS*

seemed to sit in dark loneliness, visited by whispers which died out
mockingly as he strained his ear after them, and by forms that
seemed to approach him and float away as he thrust out his hand to
grasp them—in those hours, doubtless, there must be continual frustration and amazement in his glance. And, more horrible still, when
the thick cloud parted for a moment, and, as he [2]sprang forward with
hope, rolled together again, and left him helpless as before; doubtless,
there was then a blank[3] confusion in his face, as[4] of a man suddenly
smitten with blindness.

Could he prove anything? Could he even begin to allege anything,
with the confidence that the links of thought would not break away?
Would any believe that he had ever had a mind filled with rare
knowledge, busy with close thoughts, ready with various speech? It
had all slipped away from him—that laboriously gathered store. Was
it utterly and for ever gone from him, like the waters from an urn
lost in the wide ocean? Or, was it still within him, imprisoned by
some obstruction that might one day break asunder?

It[5] might be so; he tried to keep his grasp on that hope. For, since
the day when he had first walked feebly from his couch of straw[6], and
had felt a new darkness within him under the sunlight, his mind had
undergone changes, partly gradual and persistent, partly sudden and
fleeting. As he had recovered his strength of body, he had recovered
his self-command and the energy of his will; he had recovered the
memory of all that part of his life which was closely inwrought with
his emotions; and he had felt more and more constantly and painfully
the uneasy sense of lost knowledge. But more than that—once or
twice, when he had been strongly excited, he had seemed momentar-
ily to be in entire possession of his past self, as old men doze for an
instant, and get back the consciousness of their youth: he seemed
again to see Greek pages and understand them, again to feel his mind
moving unbenumbed among familiar ideas. It had been but a flash,
and the darkness closing in again seemed the more horrible; but
might not the same thing happen again for longer periods? If it would
only come and stay long enough for him to achieve a revenge—
devise[7] an exquisite suffering, such as a mere right arm could never
inflict!

He raised himself from his stooping attitude, and, folding his arms,
attempted to concentrate all his mental force on the plan he must
immediately pursue. He had to wait for knowledge and opportunity,

---

2 ⟨leaped⟩ sprang forward *MS*
3 doubtless, there was then a blank] *3P* doubtless then, there was a blank *MS CM 1*
2
4 as ⟨in that⟩ of *MS*   5 asunder? {¶} It *MS*
6 straw ⟨out under the sky⟩ *MS*   7 devise ⟨and inflict⟩ *MS*

and while he waited he must have the means of living without beggary. What he dreaded of all things now was, that any one should
think him a foolish, helpless old man. No one must know that half
his memory was gone: the lost strength might come again; and if it
were only for a little while, *that*[8] might be enough.

He knew how to begin to get the information he wanted about
Tito. He had repeated the words "Bratti Ferravecchi"[9] so constantly
after they had been uttered to him, that they never slipped from him
for long together. A man at Genoa, on whose finger he had seen
Tito's ring, had told him that he bought that ring at Florence[1], of a
young Greek, well drest, and with a handsome dark face, in the shop
of a *rigattiere* called Bratti Ferravecchi[2], in the street also called
Ferravecchi. This discovery had caused a violent agitation in
Baldassarre. Until then he had clung with all the tenacity of his
fervid[3] nature to his [4]faith in Tito, and had not for a moment
believed himself to be [5]wilfully forsaken. At first he had said, "My bit
of parchment has never reached him; that is why I am still toiling at
Antioch. But he is searching: he knows where I was lost; he will trace
me out, and find me at last." Then, when he was taken to Corinth,
he induced his owners, by the assurance that he should be sought out
and ransomed, to provide securely against the failure of any inquiries
that might be made about him at Antioch; and at Corinth he thought
joyfully, "Here, at last, he must find me. Here he is sure to touch,
whichever way he goes."[6] But before another year had passed the illness had come from which he had risen with[7] body and mind so shattered that he was worse than worthless to his owners except for the
sake of the ransom that [8]did not come. Then, as he sat helpless in the
morning sunlight, he began to think, "Tito has been drowned, or
they have made *him* a prisoner too.[9] I shall see him no more. He set
out after me, but misfortune overtook him. I shall see his face no
more." Sitting in his new feebleness and despair, supporting his head
between his hands, with blank eyes and lips that moved uncertainly,
he looked so much like a hopelessly imbecile old man, that his owners
were contented to be rid of him, and allowed a Genoese merchant,
who [1]had compassion on him as [2]an Italian, to take him on board his
galley. In a voyage of many months in the Archipelago, and along the

8 *that*] *1 2 3* that *MS CM*
9 "Bratti Ferravecchi"] *1 2 3* Bratti Ferraveccj *MS CM*   1 ring {at Florence} *MS*
2 Ferraveccj—⟨probably from⟩ *MS*   3 fervid] fervent *3*
4 ⟨belief⟩ faith *MS*   5 ⟨willingly⟩ wilfully *MS*
6 me {"Here he . . . goes."} *MS*
7 with ⟨shattered faculties and so feeble body⟩ ⟨a⟩ body *MS*
8 ⟨never came⟩ did not come *MS*
9 drowned {or they have made him a prisoner too—} *MS*
1 ⟨took⟩ had *MS*   2 ⟨a fellow Italian⟩ an Italian *MS*

sea-board of Asia Minor, Baldassarre had recovered his bodily strength, but on landing at Genoa he had so weary a sense of his desolateness that he almost wished he had died of that illness at Corinth. There was just one possibility that hindered the wish from being decided: it was that Tito might not be dead, but living in a state of imprisonment or destitution; and if he lived, there was still a hope for Baldassarre[3]—faint, perhaps, and likely to be long deferred, but still a hope, that he might find his child, his cherished son again; might yet again clasp hands and meet face to face with the one who remembered him as he had been before his mind was broken.

In this state of feeling he had chanced to meet the stranger who wore Tito's onyx ring, and though Baldassarre would have been unable to describe the ring beforehand, the sight of it stirred the dormant fibres, and he recognized it. That Tito nearly a year after[4] his father had been parted from him should have been living in apparent prosperity at Florence, selling the gem which he ought not to have sold till the last extremity, was a fact that Baldassarre shrank from trying to account for:[5] he was glad to be stunned and bewildered by it, rather than to have any distinct thought; he tried to feel nothing but joy that he should behold Tito again. Perhaps Tito had thought that his father was dead; somehow the mystery would be explained. "But at least I shall meet eyes that will remember me.[6] I am not alone in the world."

And now again Baldassarre said, "I am not alone in the world; I shall never be alone, for my revenge is with me."

It was as the instrument of that revenge, as something merely external and subservient to his true life, that he bent down again to examine himself with hard curiosity—not, he thought, because he had any care for a withered, forsaken old man, whom nobody loved, whose soul was like a deserted home, where the ashes were cold upon the hearth, and the walls were bare of all but the marks of what had been. It is in the nature of all human passion,[7] the lowest as well as the highest, that there is a point where[8] it ceases to be properly egoistic, and is like a fire kindled within our being to which everything else in us is mere fuel.

He looked at the pale black-browed image in the water till he identified it with that self from which his revenge seemed to be a thing apart; and he felt as if the image too [9]heard the silent language of his thought.

"I was a loving fool—I worshipped a woman once, and believed she

3 hope {for Baldassarre} *MS*   4 after ⟨he had lost his adopted father⟩ *MS*
5 for:] *3P* for; *MS CM 1 2*   6 me.] *3P* me; *MS CM 1 2*
7 passion, ⟨even the lowest⟩ *MS*   8 where] *3C* at which *MS CM 1 2*
9 ⟨had⟩ heard *MS*

could care for me; and then I took a helpless child and fostered him; and I watched him as he grew, to see if he would care for me only a little—care for *me* over and above the good he got from me. I would have torn open my breast to warm him with my life-blood if I could only have seen him care a little for the pain of my wound. I have laboured, I have strained to crush out of this hard life one drop of unselfish love. Fool! men love their own delights*—there is no delight to be had in me[1]. And yet I watched till I believed I saw what I watched for. When he was a child he lifted soft eyes towards me, and held my hand willingly: I thought, this boy will surely love me a little: because I give my life to him and strive that he shall know no sorrow, he will care a little when I am thirsty—the drop he lays on my parched lips will be a joy to him. . . . Curses on him! I wish I may see him lie with those red lips[2] white and dry as ashes, and when he looks for pity I wish he may see my face rejoicing in his pain. It is all a lie—this world is a lie—there is no goodness but in hate. Fool! not one drop of love came with all your striving—life has not given you one drop. But there are deep draughts in this world for hatred and revenge. I have memory left for that, and there is strength in my arm—there is strength in my will—and if I can do nothing but kill him—[3]"

But Baldassarre's mind rejected the thought of that brief [4]punishment. His whole soul had been thrilled into immediate unreasoning belief in that eternity of vengeance where he, an undying hate, might clutch for ever an undying traitor, and hear that fair smiling hardness cry and moan with anguish. But the primary need and hope was to see a slow revenge under the same sky and on the same earth where he himself had been forsaken and had fainted with despair. And as soon as he tried to concentrate his mind on the means of attaining his end, the sense of his weakness pressed upon him like a frosty ache. This despised body, which was to be the instrument of a sublime [5]vengeance, must be nourished and decently clad. If he had to wait he must labour, and his labour must be of a humble sort, for he had no skill. He wondered whether the sight of written characters would so stimulate his faculties that he might venture to try and find[6] work as a copyist: *that* might win him some credence for his past scholarship. But no! he dared trust neither hand nor brain. He must be content to do the work that was most like that of a beast of burthen: in this mercantile city many porters must be wanted, and he could at least carry weights. Thanks to the justice that struggled in this confused

1 Fool! men . . . me] "Fool! men . . . you" *MS*
2 red lips] red smiling lips *MS*
3 him—⟨I shall follow him where he goes⟩ *MS*   4 ⟨revenge⟩ punishment *MS*
5 ⟨punish[ment]⟩ vengeance *MS*   6 {try and} find *MS*

world in behalf of vengeance, his limbs had got back some of their
old sturdiness. He was stripped of all else that men would give coin
for.

But the new urgency of this habitual thought brought a new suggestion. There was something hanging by a cord round his bare neck;
something apparently so paltry that the piety of Turks and
Frenchmen had spared it—a tiny parchment bag blackened with age.
It had hung round his neck as a precious charm when he was a boy,
and he had kept it carefully on his breast, not believing that it contained anything but a tiny scroll of parchment rolled up hard. He
might long ago have thrown it away as a relic of his dead mother's
superstition; but he had thought of it as a relic of her love, and had
kept it. It was part of the piety associated with such *Brevi*, that they
should never be opened, and at any previous moment in his life
Baldassarre would have said that no sort of [7]thirst would prevail upon
him to open this little bag for the chance of finding that it contained,
not parchment, but an engraved amulet which would be worth
money. But now a thirst had come like that which makes men open
their own veins to satisfy it, and the thought of the possible amulet
no sooner crossed Baldassarre's mind than with nervous fingers he
snatched the *Breve* from his neck. It all rushed through his mind—
the long years he had worn it, the far-off sunny balcony at Naples
looking towards the blue waters, where he had leaned against his
mother's knee; but it made no moment of hesitation: all piety now
was transmuted into a just revenge. He bit and tore till the doubles of
parchment were laid open, and then—it was a sight that made him
pant—there *was* an amulet. It was very small, but it was as blue as
those far-off waters; it was an engraved sapphire, which must be
worth some gold ducats. Baldassarre no sooner saw those possible
ducats than he saw some of them exchanged for a poniard. He did
not want to use the poniard yet, but he longed to possess it. If he
could grasp its handle and try[8] its edge, that blank in his mind—that
past which[9] fell away continually—would not make him feel so cruelly
helpless: the sharp steel that despised talents and eluded strength
would be at his side, as the unfailing friend of feeble justice. There
was a sparkling triumph under Baldassarre's black eyebrows as he
replaced the little sapphire inside the bits of parchment and wound
the string tightly round them.

It was nearly dusk now, and he rose to walk back towards
Florence. With his *danari* to buy him some bread, he felt rich: he
could lie out in the open air, as he found plenty more doing in all

7 ⟨hunger would have⟩ thirst would ⟨have prevailed⟩ prevail *MS*
8 try] *3P* feel *MS CM 1 2*   9 which] that *MS*

corners of Florence. And in the next few days he had [1]sold his sapphire, had added to his[2] clothing, had bought a bright dagger, and
had still [3]a pair of gold florins left. But he meant to hoard that treasure carefully: his lodging was an outhouse with a heap of straw in it,
in[4] a thinly inhabited part of Oltrarno, and he[5] thought of looking
about for work as a porter.

He had bought his dagger at Bratti's. Paying his meditated visit
there one evening at dusk, he had found that singular rag-merchant
just returned from one of his rounds, emptying out his basketful of
broken glass and old iron amongst his handsome show of miscel-
laneous[6] second-hand goods. As Baldassarre entered the shop, and
looked towards the smart pieces of apparel, the musical instruments,
and weapons, which[7] were displayed in the broadest light of the window, his eye at once singled out a dagger hanging[8] up high against a
red scarf. By buying that[9] dagger he could not only satisfy a strong
desire[1]; he could open his original errand in a more indirect manner
than by speaking of the onyx ring. In the course of bargaining for the
weapon he let drop, with cautious carelessness, that he came from
Genoa, and had been directed to Bratti's shop by an acquaintance in
that city who had bought a very valuable ring[2] here[3]. Had the
respectable [4]trader any more such rings?

Whereupon Bratti had much to say as to the unlikelihood of such
rings being within reach of many people, with much vaunting of his
own rare connections, due to his known wisdom and honesty. [5]It
might be true that he was a pedlar—he chose to be a pedlar; though
he was rich enough to kick his heels in his shop all day. But those
who thought they had said all there was to be said about Bratti when[6]
they had called him a pedlar, were a good deal further off the truth
than the other side of Pisa. How was it that he could put that ring in
a stranger's way? It was, because he had a very particular knowledge
of a handsome young Signor, who did not look quite so fine a feath-
ered bird when Bratti first set eyes on him as he did at the present
time. And by a question or two Baldassarre extracted, without any

1 ⟨bought⟩ sold *MS*   2 added to his] changed all his *MS*
3 ⟨three gold⟩ a pair of gold *MS*
4 carefully: his lodging . . . in] carefully: he chose for his lodging ⟨a stable room⟩ an
out house with a heap of straw in it, which he hired ⟨of a poor wool-beater in
Oltrarno⟩ for a trifle from an old woman in *MS*
5 he ⟨was preparing⟩ *MS*   6 miscellaneous] *3P* heterogeneous *MS CM 1 2*
7 which] *3P* that *MS CM 1 2*   8 hanging] *3C* that hung *MS CM 1 2*
9 that] the *2 3*
1 {By buying that dagger} He could not only satisfy a strong desire ⟨by buying that
dagger⟩ *MS*
2 ring] onyx ring *MS*   3 here] *3C* there *MS CM 1 2*   4 ⟨Bratti⟩ trader *MS*
5 ⟨He might be a pedlar⟩ It *MS*   6 Bratti when] *3P* Bratti, when *MS CM 1 2*

trouble, such a rough and rambling account of Tito's life[7] as the pedlar could give, since the time when he had found him sleeping under
the Loggia de' Cerchi. It never occurred to Bratti that the[8] decent
man (who was rather deaf, apparently, asking him to say many things
twice over) had any curiosity about Tito; the curiosity was doubtless
about himself, as a truly remarkable pedlar.

And Baldassarre left Bratti's shop, not only with the dagger at his
side, but also[9] with a general knowledge of Tito's conduct and position—of[1] his early sale of the jewels, his immediate quiet settlement
of himself at Florence, his marriage, and his great prosperity.

"What story had he told about his previous life—about his father?"

It would be difficult for Baldassarre to discover the answer to that
question.[2] Meanwhile, he wanted to learn all he could about Florence.
But he found, to his acute distress, that of the new details he learned
he could only retain a few, and those only by continual repetition;
and he began to be afraid of listening to any new discourse, lest it
should obliterate what he was already striving to remember.

The day he [3]was discerned by Tito in the Piazza del Duomo, he
had the fresh anguish of this consciousness in his mind, and Tito's
ready speech fell upon him like the mockery of a glib, defying demon.

As he went home to his heap of straw, and passed by the booksellers' shops in the Via del Garbo, he paused to look at the volumes
spread open. Could he by long [4]gazing at one of those books lay hold
of the slippery threads of memory? Could he by striving get a firm
grasp somewhere, and lift himself above these waters that flowed over
him?

He was tempted, and bought the cheapest Greek book he could
see. [5]He carried it home and sat on his heap of straw, looking at the
characters by the light of the small window; but no inward light arose
on them. Soon the evening darkness came; but it made little
difference to Baldassarre. [6]His strained eyes seemed still to see the
white pages with the unintelligible black marks upon them.

---

7 account {of Tito's life} MS   8 the ⟨stranger had an⟩ MS
9 but also] 3P but MS CM 1 2   1 of] with MS
2 It would . . . question.] 3C That was a question to which it would be difficult for
⟨him to find out⟩ Baldassarre to discover the answer. MS CM 1 2
3 ⟨had been⟩ was MS   4 ⟨looking⟩ gazing MS
5 ⟨And⟩ He MS   6 ⟨He seemed⟩ His MS

CHAPTER XXXI.

FRUIT IS SEED

"My Romola," said Tito, the second [1]morning after he had made his speech in the Piazza del Duomo, "I am to receive grand visitors to-day; the Milanese Count is coming again, and the Seneschal de Beaucaire,* the great favourite of the Cristianissimo. I know you don't care to go through [2]smiling ceremonies with these rustling magnates, whom we are not likely to see again; and as they will want to [3]look at the antiquities and the library, perhaps you had better give up your work[4] to-day, and go to see your cousin Brigida."

Romola discerned a wish in this intimation, and immediately assented. But presently, coming back in her hood and mantle, she said[5], "Oh, what a long breath Florence will take when the gates are flung open, and the last Frenchman is walking out of them! Even you are getting tired, with all your patience, my Tito; confess it. Ah, your head is hot."

He was leaning over his desk, [6]writing, and she had laid her hand on his head, meaning to give a parting caress[7]. The attitude had been a frequent one, and Tito was accustomed, when he felt her hand there, to raise his head, throw himself a little backward, and look up at her. But he felt now as unable to raise his head as if her hand had been a leaden [8]cowl. He spoke instead, in a light [9]tone, as his pen still ran along.

"The French are as ready to go from Florence as the wasps to leave a ripe pear when they have just fastened on it."[1]

Romola, keenly sensitive to the absence of the usual response, took away her hand and said,[2] "I am going, Tito."

"[3]Farewell, my sweet one. I must wait at home. Take Maso with you."

Still Tito did not look up, and Romola went out without saying any more. Very slight things make epochs in married life, and this

---

1 ⟨day⟩ morning *MS*   2 ⟨rustl[ing]⟩ smiling *MS*
3 ⟨see⟩ look at the {antiquities and the} library *MS*   4 work] work there *MS*
5 presently {⟨when⟩ coming back in her hood and mantle, she} said *MS*
6 ⟨with a pen in his hand⟩ writing *MS*
7 caress ⟨before she prepared to go out⟩ *MS*   8 ⟨weight⟩ cowl *MS*
9 ⟨tongue⟩ tone *MS*
1 it." ⟨It is expected the Signoria will have to try the Frate's thunder and threaten the Most Christian King with the pestilence if he doesn't march off to Rome or his high kinsmen⟩ *MS*
2 said, ⟨rather timidly⟩ *MS*   3 ⟨*Addio* Romola mia⟩ Farewell *MS*

morning for the first time she [4]admitted to herself not only that Tito
had changed, but that he had changed towards her. Did the reason lie
in herself? She might perhaps have thought so, if there had not been
the facts of the armour and the picture to suggest some external event
which was an entire mystery to her.

But Tito no sooner believed that Romola was out of the house than
he laid down his pen and looked up, in delightful security from seeing anything else than parchment and broken marble. He was rather
disgusted with himself that he had not been able to look up at
Romola and behave to her just as usual. He would have chosen, if he
could, to be even more than usually kind; but he could not, on a sudden, master an involuntary shrinking from her, which, by a subtle
relation, depended on those very characteristics in him that made him
desire not to fail in his marks of affection.[5] He was about to take a
step which he knew would arouse her deep indignation: he [6]would
have to encounter much that was unpleasant before he [7]could win her
forgiveness. And Tito could never find it easy to face displeasure and
anger; his nature was one of those most remote from defiance or
impudence, and all his inclinations leaned towards preserving
Romola's tenderness. He was not tormented by sentimental scruples
which[8], as he had demonstrated to himself by a very rapid course of
argument, had no relation to solid utility; but his freedom from
scruples did not release him from the dread of what was disagreeable.
Unscrupulousness gets rid of much, but not of toothache, or
wounded vanity, or the sense of loneliness, against which, as the
world at present stands, there is no security but a thoroughly healthy
jaw, and a just, loving soul. And Tito was feeling intensely at this
moment that no devices could save him from pain in the impending
collision with Romola; no persuasive blandness could cushion him
against the shock[9] towards which he was being driven like a timid
animal urged to a desperate leap by the terror of the tooth and the
claw that are close behind it.

The secret feeling he had [1]previously had that the tenacious adherence to Bardo's wishes about the library had become under existing
difficulties a piece of sentimental folly, which deprived himself and
Romola of substantial advantages, might perhaps never have wrought
itself into action but for the events of the past week, which had
brought at once[2] the pressure of a new motive and the outlet of a rare

4 ⟨said⟩ admitted to herself ⟨distinctly⟩ {not only} that Tito had ⟨not only⟩ changed
MS
    5 kind. {but he . . . affection.} {¶} ⟨Tito⟩ He MS   6 ⟨should⟩ would MS
    7 ⟨had won⟩ could win MS   8 which ⟨had no relation to⟩ MS
    9 shock ⟨of that collision⟩ MS   1 ⟨long⟩ previously MS
    2 brought {at once} MS

opportunity. Nay, it was not till[3] his dread had been aggravated by
the sight of Baldassarre looking more like his sane self, not until he
had begun to feel that he[4] might be compelled to flee from Florence,
that he had brought himself to resolve on using his legal right to sell
the library before the great opportunity offered by French and
Milanese bidders slipped through his fingers. For if he had to leave
Florence he did not want to leave it as a destitute wanderer. He had
been used to an agreeable existence,[5] and he wished to carry with him
all the means at hand for retaining the same agreeable conditions. He
wished among other things to carry Romola with him, and *not*, if possible, to carry any infamy. Success had given him a growing appetite
for all the pleasures that depend on an advantageous social position,
and at no moment could it look like a temptation to him, but only
like a hideous alternative, to decamp under dishonour, even with a
bag of diamonds, and incur the life of an adventurer. [6]It was not possible for him to make himself independent even of those Florentines
who only greeted him with regard; still less was it possible for him to
make himself independent of Romola. She was the wife of his first
love—he loved her still; she belonged to [7]that furniture of life which
he shrank from[8] parting with. He winced under her judgment, he felt
uncertain how far the revulsion of her feeling towards him might go;
and all that sense of power over a wife which makes a husband risk
betrayals that a lover never ventures on[9], would not suffice to counteract Tito's uneasiness. This was the leaden weight which had been
too strong for his will, and kept him from raising his head to meet
her eyes. Their pure light brought too near him the prospect of a
coming struggle. But it was not to be helped: if they had to leave
Florence, they must have money; indeed, Tito could not arrange life
at all to his mind without a considerable sum of money. And that
problem of arranging life to his mind had been the source of all [1]his
misdoing. He would have been equal to any sacrifice that was not
unpleasant.

The rustling magnates came and went, the bargains had been concluded, and[2] Romola returned home; but nothing grave[3] was said that
night. Tito was only gay and chatty, pouring forth to her, as he had

3 till ⟨the newly quickened ⟨⟨fear⟩⟩ sight⟩ *MS*   4 he ⟨must flee⟩ *MS*
5 existence, ⟨he had an⟩ *MS*
6 ⟨If life had not demanded something unpleasant from his [1 word]⟩ It was ⟨imposs-
ible⟩ not possible *MS*
7 ⟨the⟩ that *MS*
8 from ⟨thinking of. And he now had a dread overcome by that other greater dread
of Baldassarre⟩ *MS*
9 that a lover never ventures on] on which a lover would never venture *MS*
1 ⟨Tito's⟩ his *MS*   2 {the bargains had been concluded} and *MS*
3 nothing {grave} *MS*

not done before, stories and descriptions of what he had witnessed during the French visit. Romola thought she discerned[4] an effort in his liveliness, and, attributing it to [5]the consciousness in him that she had been wounded in the morning, accepted the effort as an act of penitence, inwardly aching a little at that sign of growing distance between them—that there was an offence about which neither of them dared to speak[6].

The next day Tito remained away from home until [7]late at night. It was [8]a marked day to Romola, for Piero di Cosimo, stimulated to greater industry on her behalf by the fear that he might have been the cause of pain to her in the past week, had sent home her father's portrait. She had propped it against the back of his old chair, and had been looking at it for some time, when the door opened behind her, and Bernardo del Nero came in.

"It is you, godfather! How I wish you had come sooner: it is getting a little dusk," said Romola, going towards him.

"I have just looked in to tell you the good news, for I know Tito is[9] not come yet," said Bernardo. "The French King moves off tomorrow; not before it is high time. There has been another tussle between our people and his soldiers this morning. But there's a chance now of the city getting into order once more and trade going on."

"That is joyful," said Romola. "But it is sudden, is it not? Tito seemed to think yesterday that there was little prospect of the King's going soon."

"He has been well barked at, that's the reason," said Bernardo, smiling. "His own generals opened their throats pretty well, and at last our Signoria sent the mastiff of the city,* Fra Girolamo. The Cristianissimo was frightened at that thunder, and has given the order to move. I'm afraid there'll be small agreement among us when he's gone, but, at any rate, all[1] parties are agreed in being glad not to have Florence stifled with soldiery any longer, and the Frate has barked this time to some purpose. Ah, what is this?" he added, as Romola, clasping him by the arm, led him in front of the picture. "Let us see[2]."

He began to unwind his long scarf while she placed a seat for him.

"Don't you want your spectacles, godfather?" said Romola, in anxiety that he should see just what she saw.

"No, child, no," said Bernardo, uncovering his grey head, as he seated himself with firm erectness. "For seeing at this distance, my

4 {thought she} discerned *MS*   5 ⟨some⟩ the *MS*
6 speak ⟨because it depended on some secret⟩. *MS*
7 ⟨the evening⟩ late at night *MS*   8 ⟨an eventful⟩ a marked *MS*
9 is] has *3*   1 all ⟨of us⟩ *MS*   2 see ⟨, Let us see⟩." *MS*

old eyes are perhaps better than your young ones. Old men's eyes are like old men's memories; they are strongest for things a long way off."

"It is better than having no portrait," said Romola, apologetically, after Bernardo had been silent a little while. "It[3] is less like him now than the image I have in my mind, but then that might fade with the years." She rested her arm on the old man's shoulder as she spoke, drawn towards him strongly by their common interest in the dead.

"I don't know," said Bernardo. "I almost think I see Bardo as he was when he was young, better than that picture shows him to me as he was when he was old. Your father had a great deal of fire in his eyes when he was young. It[4] was what I could never understand, that he, with his fiery spirit, which seemed much more impatient than mine, could hang over the books and live with shadows all his life. However, he had put his heart into that."

Bernardo gave a slight shrug as he spoke the last words, but Romola discerned in his voice a feeling that accorded with her own.

"And he was disappointed to the last," she said, involuntarily. But immediately fearing lest her words should be taken to imply an accusation against Tito, she went on almost hurriedly, "If we could only see his longest, dearest wish fulfilled just to his mind!"

"Well, so we may," said Bernardo, kindly, rising and [5]putting on his cap. "The times are cloudy now, but fish are caught by waiting. Who knows? When the wheel has turned often enough, I may be Gonfaloniere yet before I die; and no creditor can touch these things." He looked round as he spoke. Then, turning to her, and patting her cheek, said, "And you need not be afraid of my dying; my ghost will claim nothing. I've taken care of that in my will."

Romola seized the hand that was against her cheek, and put it to her lips in silence.

"Haven't you been scolding your husband for keeping away from home so much lately? I see him everywhere but here," said Bernardo, willing to change the subject.

[6]She felt the flush spread over her neck and face as she said, "He has been very much wanted; you know he speaks so well. I am glad to know that his value is understood."

"You are contented, then, Madonna Orgogliosa?" said Bernardo, smiling as he moved to the door.

"Assuredly."

Poor Romola! There was one thing that would have made the pang of disappointment in her husband harder to bear: it was, that any one

---

3 It ⟨seems now very much⟩ MS   4 young. It] young: that MS
5 ⟨taking⟩ putting on his cap ⟨again⟩ MS   6 ⟨Romola⟩ She MS

should know he gave her cause for disappointment. This might be a woman's weakness, but it is[7] closely allied to a woman's nobleness. She who willingly lifts up the veil of her married life has profaned it from a sanctuary into a vulgar place.

7 is ⟨a feeling inseparable from⟩ *MS*

CHAPTER XXXII.

A REVELATION

THE next day Romola, like every other Florentine, was excited about the departure of the French. Besides her other reasons for gladness, she had a dim hope, which she was conscious was half superstitious, that those new anxieties about Tito, having[1] come with the burthensome guests, might perhaps vanish with them. The French had been in Florence [2]hardly eleven days, but[3] in that space she had felt more acute unhappiness than she had known in her life before. Tito had adopted [4]the hateful armour on the day of their arrival, and though she could frame no distinct notion why their departure should remove the cause of his fear—though, when she thought of that cause, the image of the prisoner grasping him, as she had seen it in Piero's sketch,[5] urged itself before her and excluded every other—still, when the French were gone, she would be rid of something that was strongly associated with her pain.

Wrapped in her mantle she waited under the loggia at the top of the house, and watched for the glimpses of the troops and the royal retinue passing the bridges on their way to the Porta San Piero, that looks towards Siena and Rome. She even returned to her station when the gates had been closed, that she might feel herself vibrating with the great peal of the bells. It was dusk then, and when at last she descended into the library, she lit her lamp, with the resolution that she would overcome the agitation which[6] had made her idle all day, and sit down to work at her copying of the catalogue. Tito had left home early in the morning, and she did not expect him yet. Before he came she intended to leave the library, and sit in the pretty saloon, with the dancing nymphs and the birds. She had done so every evening since he had objected to the library as chill and gloomy.

To her great surprise, she had not been at work long before Tito entered. Her first thought was, how cheerless he would feel[7] the wide darkness of this great room, with one little oil-lamp burning at the farther[8] end, and the fire nearly out. She almost ran towards him.

"Tito, dearest, I did not know you would come so soon," she said, nervously, putting[9] up her white arms to unwind his *becchetto*.

1 Tito, having] Tito which had *MS*   2 ⟨only⟩ hardly *MS*
3 but ⟨that space had been the unhappiest⟩ *MS*
4 ⟨that [?chain]⟩ the hateful *MS*   5 prisoner {grasping him . . . sketch,} *MS*
6 which] *3P* that *MS CM 1 2*   7 feel] feel in *2 3*
8 farther] further *2 3*   9 nervously, putting] *MS 1 2 3* nervously putting *CM*

"I am not welcome then?" he said, with one of his brightest smiles, clasping her, but playfully holding his head back from her.

"Tito!" She uttered the word in a tone of pretty, loving reproach, and then he kissed her fondly, stroked her hair, as his manner was, and seemed not to mind about taking off his mantle yet. Romola quivered with delight. All the emotions of the day had been preparing in her a keener sensitiveness to the return of this habitual manner. "It will come back," she was saying to herself, "the old happiness will perhaps come back. He is like himself again."

Tito was taking great pains to be like himself; his heart was palpitating with anxiety.

"If I had expected you so soon," said Romola, as she at last helped him to take off his wrappings, "I would have had a little festival prepared[1] to this joyful ringing of the bells. I did not mean to be here in the library[2] when you came home."

"Never mind, sweet," he said, carelessly. "Do not think about the fire. Come—come and sit down."

There was a low stool against Tito's chair, and that was Romola's habitual seat when they were talking together. She rested her arm on his knee, as she used to do on her father's, and looked up at him while he spoke. He had never yet noticed the presence of the portrait, and she had not mentioned it—thinking of it all the more.

"I have been enjoying the clang of the bells for the first time, Tito," she began. "I liked being shaken and deafened by them: I [3]fancied I was something like a Bacchante possessed by a divine rage. [4]Are not the people looking very [5]joyful to-night?"

"[6]Joyful after a sour and pious fashion," said Tito, with a shrug. "But, in truth, those who are left behind in Florence have little cause to be [7]joyful; it seems to me, the most reasonable ground of gladness would be to have got out of Florence."

Tito had sounded the desired key-note without any trouble, or appearance of premeditation. He spoke with no emphasis, but he looked grave enough to make Romola ask rather anxiously,

"Why, Tito? Are there fresh troubles?"

"No need of fresh ones, my Romola. There are three strong parties in the city, all ready to fly at each other's throats. And if the Frate's party is strong enough to frighten the other two into silence, as seems most likely, life will be as pleasant and amusing as a funeral. They have the plan of a great Council simmering already; and if they get it,

1 prepared ⟨after that⟩ MS   2 here⟨, in the library,⟩ MS
3 ⟨think⟩ fancied MS
4 ⟨It is delicious to have thoughts quite driven out of one sometimes⟩ ⟨Is not Florence⟩ Are not MS
5 ⟨merry⟩ joyful MS   6 ⟨Merry⟩ Joyful MS   7 ⟨glad⟩ joyful MS

the man[8] who sings sacred lauds the loudest will be the most eligible for office. And besides that, the city will be so drained by the payment of this great subsidy* to the French King, and by the war to get back Pisa, that the prospect would be dismal enough without the rule of fanatics. On the whole, Florence will be a delightful place for those worthies who entertain themselves in the evening by going into crypts and lashing themselves; but for everything else, the exiles have the best of it. For my own part, I have been thinking seriously that we should be wise to quit Florence, my Romola."

[9]She started. "Tito, how could we leave Florence? Surely you do not think I could leave it—at least, not yet—not for a long while." She had turned cold and trembling, and did not find it quite easy to speak. Tito must know[1] the reasons she had in her mind.

"That is all [2]a fabric of your own imagination, my sweet one. Your secluded life has made you lay such false stress on a few things. You know I used to tell you, before we were married, that I wished we were somewhere else than in Florence. If you had seen more places and more people, you would know what I mean when I say that there is something in the Florentines that reminds me of their cutting spring winds. I like people who take life less eagerly; and it would [3]be good for my Romola, too, to see a new life. I should like to dip her a little in the soft waters of forgetfulness."

He leaned forward and kissed her brow, and laid his hand on her fair hair[4] again; but she felt his caress no more than if he had [5]kissed a mask.* She was too much agitated by the sense of the distance between their minds to be conscious that his [6]lips touched her.[7]

"Tito, it is not because I suppose[8] Florence is the pleasantest place in the world that I desire not to [9]quit it. It is because I—because we have to see my father's wish fulfilled. My godfather is old—he is seventy-one[1]—we could not leave it to him."

"It is precisely[2] those superstitions which hang about your mind like bedimming clouds, my Romola, that make one great reason why I could wish we were two hundred leagues from Florence. I am obliged to take care of you in opposition to your own will: if those dear eyes,

---

8 They have the . . . man] They will get their Grand Council with a thousand shop-keeping voters in it to settle everything, and the man *MS*

9 ⟨Romola⟩ She started ⟨: she felt a shock of surprize that made her turn quite cold ¶⟩. "Tito *MS*

1 know ⟨why she could not leave⟩ *MS*   2 ⟨the⟩ a *MS*

3 ⟨suit⟩ be good for *MS*   4 fair hair] hair *MS*   5 ⟨touched⟩ kissed *MS*

6 ⟨hand⟩ lips *MS*

7 her. ⟨She was still cold and tremulous—still afraid to say all she was thinking⟩ *MS*

8 because {I suppose} *MS*   9 ⟨leave⟩ quit *MS*

1 old—{he is seventy one} *MS*

2 precisely ⟨because of⟩ those superstitions ⟨that⟩ which *MS*

that look so tender[3], see falsely, I must see for them, and save my wife from wasting her life in disappointing herself [4]by impracticable dreams."

Romola sat silent and motionless: she could not [5]blind herself to the direction in which Tito's words pointed: he wanted to persuade her that they might get the library deposited in some monastery, or take some other ready means to rid themselves of a task, and of a[6] tie to Florence; and she[7] was determined never to submit her mind to his judgment on this question of duty to her father; she was inwardly prepared to encounter any sort of pain in resistance. But the determination was kept latent in these first moments by the heart-crushing sense that now at last she and Tito must be confessedly divided in their wishes.[8] He was glad of her silence;[9] for, much as he had feared[1] the strength of her feeling, it was impossible for him, shut up in the narrowness that hedges in all merely clever, unimpassioned men, not to over-estimate the [2]persuasiveness of his own arguments[3]. His conduct did not look ugly to himself, and his imagination did not suffice to show him exactly how it would look to Romola. He went on in [4]the same gentle, remonstrating tone.

"You know, dearest—your own clear judgment always showed you—that the notion of isolating a collection of books and antiquities, and attaching a single[5] name to them for ever, was one that had no valid, substantial good for its object: and yet more, one that was liable to be defeated in a thousand ways. See what has become of the Medici collections!* And, for my part, I consider it even blameworthy to entertain those petty views of appropriation: why should any one be reasonably glad that Florence should possess the benefits of learned research and taste more than any other city? I understand your feeling about the wishes of the dead; but wisdom puts a limit to these sentiments, else [6]lives might be continually wasted[7] in that sort of futile devotion—like praising deaf gods for ever. You gave your life to your father while he lived; why should you demand more of yourself?"

"Because it was a trust," said Romola, in a low but distinct voice. "He trusted me, he trusted you, Tito. [8]I did not expect you to feel

---

3 eyes {that look so tender} *MS*   4 ⟨with⟩ by *MS*
5 ⟨be blind⟩ blind herself *MS*   6 of a] *1 2 3* a *MS CM*
7 pointed {—he wanted . . . Florence. And} She *MS*
8 divided {in their ⟨efforts⟩ wishes}. ⟨A feeling⟩ ⟨Tito⟩ ⟨Tito⟩ He *MS*
9 silence;] *3P* silence, *MS CM 1 2*   1 he {had} feared *MS*
2 ⟨force⟩ persuasiveness *MS*   3 arguments ⟨against⟩ *MS*
4 ⟨a⟩ the same *MS*   5 a single] one *MS*   6 ⟨life⟩ lives *MS*
7 {continually} wasted *MS*
8 ⟨If I felt nothing else about it, I should feel that⟩ I *MS*

anything else about it—to feel [9]as I do—but I did expect you to feel that."

"Yes, dearest, of course I should feel it on a point where your father's real welfare or happiness was concerned; but[1] there is no question of that now. If we believed in Purgatory, I should be as anxious as you to have masses said; and if I believed it could now[2] pain your father to see his library preserved and used in a rather different way from what he had set his mind on, I should share the strictness of your views. But a little philosophy[3] should teach us to rid ourselves of those air-woven fetters that mortals hang round themselves, spending their lives in misery under the mere imagination of weight[4]. Your mind, which seizes ideas so readily, my Romola, is able to discriminate between substantial good and these brain-wrought fantasies. Ask yourself, dearest, what possible good can these books and antiquities do[5] stowed together under your father's name in Florence, more than they would do [6]if they were divided or carried elsewhere? Nay, is not the very dispersion of such things in hands that know how to value them, one[7] means of extending their useful-ness? This rivalry of Italian cities is very petty and illiberal. The loss of Constantinople was the gain of the whole civilized world."

Romola was still too thoroughly under the painful pressure of the new revelation Tito was making of himself, for her resistance to find any strong vent. As[8] that fluent talk fell on her ears there was a rising contempt within her, [9]which only made her more conscious of her bruised despairing love, her love for the Tito she had married and believed in. Her nature, [1]possessed with the energies of strong emo-tion, recoiled from this hopelessly shallow readiness which professed to appropriate the widest sympathies and had no pulse for the near-est. She still spoke like one who was restrained from showing all[2] she felt. She had only drawn away her arm from his knee and sat with her hands clasped before her, cold and motionless as locked waters.

"[3]You talk of substantial good, Tito! Are faithfulness, and love, and sweet grateful memories, no good? Is it no good that we should keep our silent promises on which others build because they believe in our love and truth? Is it no good that a just life should be justly [4]honoured? Or, is it good[5] that we should harden our hearts against all the wants and hopes of those who have depended on us?[6] What good can belong to men who have such souls? To talk cleverly, perhaps, and find soft couches for themselves, and live and die with their base selves as their best companions."

Her voice had gradually risen till there was a ring of scorn in the last words; she made a slight pause, but[7] he saw there were other words quivering on her lips, and he chose to let them come.

"I know of no good for cities or the world if they are to be made up of such beings. But I am not thinking of other Italian cities and the whole civilized world—I am thinking of my father, and of my love and sorrow for him, and of his just claims on us. I would give up anything else, Tito,—I would leave Florence,—what else did I live for but for him and you? But I will not give up that duty. What have I to do with your arguments? It was a yearning of *his* heart, and therefore it[8] is a yearning of mine."

Her voice, from having been [9]tremulous, had become full and firm. She felt[1] that she had been urged on to say all that it was needful for her to say. She thought, poor thing, there was nothing harder to come[2] than this struggle against Tito's suggestions as against the meaner part of herself.

He had begun to see clearly that he could not persuade her into assent: he must take another course, and show her that the time for resistance was past. That, at least, would put an end to further struggle; and[3] if the disclosure were not made by himself to-night, to-morrow it must be made in another way. This[4] necessity nerved his courage; and[5] his experience of her affectionateness and unexpected submissiveness, ever since[6] their marriage until now, encouraged him to hope that, at last, she would accommodate herself to what had been his will.

"I am sorry to hear you speak in that spirit of blind persistence, my Romola," he said, quietly, "because it obliges me to give you pain. But I partly foresaw your opposition, and as a prompt decision was necessary, I avoided that obstacle, and decided without consulting you. The very care of a husband for his wife's interest compels him

4 ⟨remembered⟩ honoured *MS*   5 good] a good *MS*
6 us ⟨to fulfil them⟩? *MS*   7 but ⟨not long enough for him to⟩ *MS*
8 {and therefore} it *MS*   9 ⟨low and⟩ tremulous *MS*
1 felt ⟨now⟩ that *MS*

2 come, ⟨and now she [2 words] herself to live with the [?dirtiest] [1 word] that Tito was the meaner part of herself⟩ *MS*

3 and ⟨the disclosure must be made by himself tonight, for tomorrow,⟩ *MS*

4 This] *3P* That *MS CM 1 2*

5 {That necessity nerved his courage and} His *MS*   6 {ever} since *MS*

to that separate action sometimes—even when he has such a wife as you, my Romola."

She turned her eyes on him in breathless inquiry.

"I mean," he said, answering her look, "that I have arranged for the transfer, both of the books and of the[7] antiquities, where they will find the highest use and value. The books have been bought for the Duke of Milan, the marbles and bronzes and the rest are going to France: and both will be protected by the stability of a great [8]Power, instead of remaining in a city which is exposed to ruin."

Before he had finished speaking, Romola had started from her seat, and stood up[9] looking down at him, with tightened hands falling before her, and, for the first time in her life, with a [1]flash of fierceness in her scorn and anger.

"You have *sold* them?" she asked, as if she distrusted her ears.

"I have," said Tito, quailing a little. The scene was unpleasant[2]— the descending scorn already scorched him.

"You are a treacherous man!" she said, with something grating in her voice, as she looked down at him.

She was silent for a minute, and he sat still, feeling that ingenuity was powerless just now. Suddenly she turned away, and said, in an agitated tone[3], "It may be hindered—I am going to my godfather."

In an instant Tito started up, went to the door, locked it, and took out the key. It was time for all the masculine predominance that was latent in him to show itself. But he was not angry; he only felt that the moment was eminently unpleasant, and that when this scene was at an end he should be glad to keep away from Romola for a little while. But it was absolutely necessary first that she [4]should be reduced to passiveness.

"Try to calm yourself a little, Romola," he said, [5]leaning in the easiest attitude possible against a pedestal under the bust of a grim old Roman. Not that he was inwardly easy: his heart palpitated[6] with a moral dread, against which no chain armour could be found. He had locked-in[7] his wife's anger and scorn, but he had been obliged to lock himself in with it; and his blood did not rise with contest—his olive cheek was perceptibly paled.

Romola had paused and turned her eyes on him as she saw him

7 and of the] *3P* and *MS CM 1 2*
9 stood up ⟨close to him⟩ *MS*
2 unpleasant; ⟨it was his first⟩ *MS*
3 said, in an agitated tone] said {in an agitated voice} *MS*
4 ⟨must⟩ should *MS*
5 ⟨standing at some distance from her—in the easiest attitude possible leaning against a pedestal.⟩ leaning *MS*
6 palpitated] *3C* palpitated a little *MS CM 1 2*
7 locked-in] *3P* locked in *MS CM 1 2*

8 ⟨nation⟩ power *MS*
1 ⟨look almost⟩ flash *MS*

take his stand and lodge the key in his scarsella. Her eyes were flashing, and her whole frame seemed to be possessed by impetuous force
that wanted to leap out in some deed. All the crushing pain of disappointment in her husband, which had made the strongest part of her
consciousness a few minutes before, was annihilated[8] by the vehemence of her indignation. She could not care in this moment that the
man [9]she was despising as he leaned there in his loathsome beauty—
she could not care that he was[1] her husband; she could only feel that
she despised him. The pride and fierceness of the old Bardi[2] blood
had been thoroughly awaked[3] in her for the first time.

"Try at least to understand the facts[4]," said Tito, "and do not seek
to take futile steps which[5] may be fatal. It is of no use for you to go
to your godfather. Messer Bernardo cannot reverse what I have done.
Only sit down. You would hardly wish, if you were quite yourself, to
make known to any third person what passes between us in private."

Tito knew that he had touched the right fibre there. But she did
not sit down; she was too unconscious of her body voluntarily to
change[6] her attitude.

"Why can it not be reversed?" she said, after a [7]pause. "Nothing is
moved yet."

"Simply because the sale has been concluded by written agreement;
the purchasers have left Florence, and I hold the bonds for the
purchase-money."

"If my father had suspected you of being a faithless man," said
Romola, in a tone of bitter scorn, which insisted on darting out before
she could say anything else, "he would have placed the library safely
out of your [8]power. But death overtook him too soon, and when you
were sure his ear was deaf, and his hand stiff, you robbed him." She
paused an instant, and then said, with gathered passion, "Have you
robbed somebody else, who is *not* dead? Is that the reason you wear
armour?"

Romola had been driven to utter the words as men are driven to
use the lash of the horsewhip. At first, Tito[9] felt horribly cowed; it
seemed to him that the disgrace he had been dreading would be
worse than he had imagined it. But[1] soon there was a reaction: such
power of dislike and resistance as there was within him was beginning

8 annihilated ⟨for the moment⟩ *MS*
9 ⟨she desp[ised]⟩ ⟨who leaned there in his loathsome beauty⟩ she was despising *MS*
1 {she could not care that he} was *MS*   2 Bardi] Bardo *2 3*
3 {thoroughly} awaked *MS*   4 facts] *MS* fact *CM 1 2 3*
5 steps which] steps—which *MS*
6 voluntarily to change] to have {voluntarily} changed *MS*
7 ⟨slight⟩ pause *MS*   8 ⟨hands⟩ power *MS*
9 {At first} Tito *MS*   1 But ⟨such power of dislike⟩ *MS*

to rise against a wife[2] whose voice seemed like the herald of a retributive fate. Her, at least, his quick mind told him that he might master.

"It is useless," he said, coolly, "to answer the words of madness, Romola. Your peculiar feeling about your father has made you mad at this moment. Any rational person looking at the case from a due distance will see that I have taken the wisest course. Apart from the influence of your exaggerated feelings on him, I am convinced that Messer Bernardo would be of that opinion."

"He would not!" said Romola. "[3]He lives in the hope of seeing my father's wish exactly fulfilled. We spoke of it together only yesterday. He will help me yet. Who are these men to whom you have sold my father's property?"

"There is no reason why you should not be told, except that it signifies little. The Count di San Severino* and the Seneschal de Beaucaire are now on their way with the King to Siena."

"They [4]may be overtaken and persuaded to give up their purchase," said Romola, eagerly, her anger beginning to be surmounted by anxious thought.

"No, they [5]may not," said Tito, with cool decision.

"Why?"

"Because I do not choose that they should."

"But if you were paid the money?—we will pay you the money," said Romola. No words could have disclosed more fully her sense of alienation from Tito; but they were spoken with less of bitterness than of anxious pleading. And he [6]felt stronger, for he saw that the first impulse of fury was past.

"No, my Romola. Understand that such thoughts as these are impracticable. You would not, in a reasonable moment, ask your godfather to bury three thousand florins in addition to what he has already paid on the library. I think your pride and delicacy would shrink from that."

She began to tremble and turn cold again with discouragement, and sank down on the carved chest near which she was standing. He went on in a clear voice[7], under which she shuddered, as if it had been a narrow cold stream coursing over[8] a hot cheek.

"Moreover, it is not my will that Messer Bernardo should advance the money, even if the project were not an utterly wild one. And I beg you to [9]consider, before you take any step or utter any word on the subject, what will be the consequences of your placing yourself in

---

2 wife ⟨who was⟩ MS   3 ⟨My godfather⟩ He MS   4 ⟨can⟩ may MS
5 ⟨cannot⟩ may not MS   6 ⟨began to feel⟩ felt MS
7 clear voice] ⟨soft⟩ clear mellow voice MS
8 a {narrow} cold stream coursing over ⟨her hot cheeks⟩ a hot cheek MS
9 ⟨reflect⟩ consider MS

opposition to me, and trying to exhibit your husband in the odious light which your own distempered feelings cast over him. What object will you serve by injuring me with Messer Bernardo? The event is irrevocable, the library is sold, and you are my wife."

Every word was spoken for the sake of a calculated effect, for his intellect was urged into the utmost activity by the danger of the crisis. He knew that Romola's mind would take in rapidly enough all the wide meaning of his [1]speech. He waited and watched her in silence.

She had turned her eyes from him and was looking on the ground, and in that way she sat for several minutes. When she spoke, her voice was quite altered,—it was quiet and cold.

"I have one thing to ask."

"Ask anything that I can do without injuring us both, Romola."

"That you will give me that portion of the money which belongs to my godfather, and let me pay him."

"I must have some assurance from you, first,[2] of the attitude you intend to take towards me."

"Do you believe in assurances, Tito?" she said, with a tinge of returning bitterness.

"From you, I do."

"I will do you no harm. I shall disclose nothing. I will say nothing to pain him or you. You say truly, the event is irrevocable."

"Then I will do what you desire to-morrow morning."

"To-night, if possible[3]," said Romola, "that we may not speak of it again."

"It is possible," he said, moving towards the lamp, while she sat still, looking away from him with absent eyes.

Presently he came and bent down over her, to put a piece of paper into her hand. "You will receive something in return, you are aware, my Romola[4]?" he said, gently, not minding so much what had passed, now he was secure; and feeling able to try and propitiate her.

"Yes," she said, taking the paper, without looking at him, "I understand."

"And you will forgive me, my Romola, when you have had time to reflect." He just touched her brow with his lips, but she took no notice, and seemed really unconscious of the act.

She was aware that he unlocked the door and went out. She moved her head and listened. [5]The great door of the court opened and shut again. She started up as if some sudden freedom had come, and going to her father's chair where his picture was propped, fell on her knees before it, and burst into sobs.

1 ⟨words⟩ speech *MS*   2 first, ⟨my Romola,⟩ *MS*
3 Tonight {if possible} *MS*   4 my Romola] Romola mia *MS*
5 ⟨She heard the⟩ The *MS*

CHAPTER XXXIII.

BALDASSARRE MAKES AN ACQUAINTANCE

WHEN Baldassarre was wandering about Florence in search of a spare outhouse where he might have the cheapest of sheltered beds, his steps had been attracted towards that sole portion of ground within the walls of the city which is not perfectly level, and where the spectator, lifted above the roofs of the houses, can see beyond the city to the protecting hills and far-stretching valley, otherwise shut out from his view except along the welcome opening made by the course of the Arno. Part of that ground has been already seen by us as the Hill of Bogoli, at that time a great stone quarry; but the side towards which Baldassarre directed his steps was the one that sloped down behind the Via de' Bardi, and was most commonly called the Hill of San Giorgio. Bratti had told him that Tito's dwelling was in the Via de' Bardi; and, after surveying that street, he turned up the slope of the hill which he had observed as he was crossing the bridge. If he could find a[1] sheltering outhouse on that hill, he would be glad: he had now for some years been accustomed to live with a broad sky about him; and, moreover, the narrow passes of the streets, with their strip of sky above, and the unknown labyrinth around them, seemed to intensify his sense of loneliness and feeble[2] memory.

The hill was sparsely inhabited, and covered chiefly by gardens; but in one spot was a piece of rough ground jagged with great stones, which had never been cultivated since a landslip had ruined some houses there towards[3] the end of the thirteenth century. Just above the edge of this broken ground stood a queer little square building, looking like a truncated tower roofed in with fluted tiles, and close by was a small outhouse[4], apparently built up against a piece of ruined stone wall. Under a large half-dead mulberry-tree that was now sending its last fluttering leaves in at the open doorways, a shrivelled, hardy old woman was untying a goat with two kids, and Baldassarre could see that part of the outbuilding was occupied by live stock[5]; but the door of the other part was open, and it was empty of everything

---

1 a] his *MS*   2 feeble] of feeble *MS*
3 towards] in *MS*
4 a small outhouse] a little line of outhouses *MS*
5 live stock] that live stock *MS*

'You didn't think it was so pretty did you?'

but some tools and straw. It was just the sort of place he wanted. He spoke to the old woman; but it was not till he got close to her and shouted in her ear, that he succeeded in making her understand his want of a lodging, and his readiness to pay for it. At first, he could get no answer beyond shakes of the head and the words, "No—no lodging," uttered in the muffled tone of the deaf. But, by dint of persistence, he made clear to her that he was a poor stranger from a long way over seas, and could not afford to go to hostelries; that he only wanted to lie on the straw in the outhouse, and would pay her a quattrino or two[6] a week for that shelter. She still looked at him dubiously, shaking her head and talking low to herself; but presently, as if a new thought occurred to her, she fetched a hatchet from the house, and, showing him a chump that lay half covered with litter in a corner, asked him if he would chop that up for her: if he would, he might lie in the outhouse for one night. He agreed, and Monna Lisa stood with her arms akimbo to watch him, with a smile of gratified cunning, saying low to herself,

"It's lain there ever since my old man died. What then?[7] I might as well have put a stone on the fire. He chops very well, though he does speak[8] with a foreign tongue, and looks odd. I couldn't have got it done cheaper. And if he only wants a bit of straw to lie on, I might make him do an errand or two up and down the hill. Who need know? And sin that's hidden's half forgiven.* He's a stranger: he'll take no notice of *her*. And I'll tell her to keep her tongue still."

The antecedent to these feminine pronouns[9] had a pair of blue eyes, which at that moment were applied to a large round hole in the shutter of the upper window. The shutter was closed, not[1] for any penal reasons, but because only the opposite window had[2] the luxury of glass in it: the weather was not warm, and a round hole four inches in diameter served all the purposes of observation. The whole was unfortunately a little too high, and obliged the small observer to stand on a [3]low stool of a rickety character; but Tessa would have stood a long while in a much more inconvenient position for the sake of seeing a little variety in her life. She had been drawn to the opening at the first loud tones of the strange voice speaking to Monna Lisa; and darting gently across her room every now and then to peep

---

6 quattrino {or two} *MS*

8 he does speak] he speaks *MS*

I not ⟨because⟩ *MS*

7 What then?] *Ma che? MS*

9 {feminine} pronouns *MS*

2 because only the opposite window had] because it was only the opposite window that ⟨was glazed⟩ had *MS*

3 ⟨small⟩ low stool of a rickety ⟨disposition⟩ character but Tessa would have stood {a long while} in a much more inconvenient position for ⟨a very long⟩ the sake *MS*

at something, she continued to stand there until[4] the wood had been chopped, and she saw Baldassarre enter the outhouse, as the dusk was gathering, and seat himself on the straw.

A great temptation had [5]laid hold of Tessa's mind; she would go and take that old man part of her supper, and talk to him a little. He was not deaf like Monna Lisa, and besides she could say a great many things to him[6] that it was no use to shout at Monna Lisa who knew them already. And he was a stranger—strangers came from a long way off and went away again, and lived nowhere in particular. It was naughty, she knew, for obedience made the largest part in Tessa's idea of duty; but it would be something to confess to the *padre* next Pasqua, and there was nothing else to confess except going to sleep sometimes over her beads, and being a little cross with Monna Lisa because she was so deaf; for she had as much idleness as she liked now, and was never frightened into telling white lies. She turned away from her shutter with rather an excited expression in her childish face, which was as pretty and pouting as ever. Her garb was still that of a simple contadina, but of a contadina prepared for a Festa: her gown of dark green serge, with its red girdle, was very clean and neat, she had the string of red glass beads round her neck, and her brown hair, rough from curliness, was duly knotted up and fastened with the silver pin. She had but one new ornament, and she was very proud of it, for it was a fine gold ring.

Tessa[7] sat on the low stool, nursing her knees, for a minute or two, with her little soul poised in fluttering excitement on the [8]edge of this pleasant transgression. It was quite irresistible. She[9] had been commanded to make no acquaintances, and warned that if she did, all her new happy lot would vanish away, and be like a hidden treasure[1] that turned to lead as soon as it was brought to the daylight; and she had been so obedient that when she had to go to church she had kept her face shaded by her hood and had pursed up her lips quite tightly. It was true her obedience had been a little helped by her own dread lest the [2]alarming step-father Nofri should turn up even in this quarter, so far from the Por' del Prato, and beat her at least, if he did not drag her back to work for him. But this old man was not an acquaintance; he was a poor stranger going to sleep in the outhouse, and he probably knew nothing of [3]step-father Nofri; and, besides, if she took

---

4 and darting . . . until] and she ⟨stood⟩ continued to stand there, only darting gently across her room every now and then to peep at something, until *MS*

5 ⟨taken⟩ laid *MS*   6 things {to him} *MS*

7 Tessa] *3C* She *MS CM 1 2*   8 ⟨verge⟩ edge *MS*

9 irresistible. She] *3P* irresistible: she *MS CM* irresistible; she *1 2*

1 {hidden} treasure *MS*   2 ⟨patrigno⟩ alarming step-father Nofri *MS*

3 ⟨father-in-law⟩ step-father *MS*

him some supper, he would like her, and not want to tell anything about her. Monna Lisa would say she must not go and talk to him, therefore Monna Lisa must not be consulted. It did not signify what she found out after it had been done.

Supper was being prepared, she knew—a mountain of macaroni flavoured[4] with cheese—fragrant enough to tame any stranger. So [5]she tripped downstairs with a mind full of deep designs, [6]and first asking with an innocent look[7] what that noise of talking had been, without waiting for an answer, knit her brow with a peremptory air, something like a kitten trying to be formidable, and sent the old woman upstairs; saying, she[8] chose to eat her supper down below. In three minutes Tessa, with her lantern in one hand and a [9]wooden bowl of macaroni in the other, was kicking gently at the door of the outhouse, and Baldassarre, roused from sad reverie, [1]doubted in the first moment whether he were [2]awake[3] as he opened the door and saw this surprising little handmaid, with delight in her wide eyes, breaking in on his dismal loneliness.

"I've brought you some supper," she said, [4]lifting her mouth towards his ear and shouting, as if he had been deaf like Monna Lisa. "Sit down and eat it, while I stay with you."

[5]Surprise and distrust surmounted every other feeling in Baldassarre, but, though he had no smile or word of gratitude ready, there could[6] not be any impulse to push away this visitant, and he sank down passively on his straw again, while Tessa placed herself close to him, put the wooden bowl on his lap, and set down the lantern in front of them, crossing her hands before her, and nodding at the bowl with a significant smile, as much as to say, "Yes, you may really eat it." For, in the excitement of carrying out her deed, she had forgotten her previous thought that the stranger would not be deaf, and had fallen into her habitual alternative of dumb show and shouting.[7]

The invitation was not a disagreeable one, for he had been gnawing a [8]remnant of dried[9] bread, which had left plenty of appetite for anything warm and relishing. Tessa watched the disappearance of two[1] or

4 macaroni flavoured] *3C* macaroni, flavoured *MS CM 1 2*

5 ⟨Tessa⟩ she *MS*　　　6 ⟨and knitting her⟩ and *MS*　　　7 look] air *MS*
8 saying, she] *3C* she *MS CM 1 2*　　　9 ⟨plate⟩ wooden bowl *MS*
1 ⟨rubbed his eyes as if he distrusted⟩ ⟨after he had⟩ doubted *MS*
2 ⟨waking⟩ awake *MS*　　　3 were awake] *3C* was awake *MS CM 1 2*
4 ⟨putting⟩ lifting *MS*
5 ⟨The sense of⟩ surprize and ⟨of⟩ distrust ⟨towards everything⟩ surmounted *MS*
6 could ⟨be no⟩ *MS*　　　7 shouting.] shouting with Monna Lisa. *MS*
8 ⟨piece⟩ remnant *MS*　　　9 dried] dry *2 3*
1 watched the disappearance of two] watched him take two *MS*

three mouthfuls without speaking, for she had thought [2]his eyes rather fierce at first; but now she ventured to put her mouth to his ear again and cry[3]—

"I like my supper, don't you?"

It was not a smile, but rather the milder look of a dog touched by kindness but unable to smile, that Baldassarre turned on this round blue-eyed thing that was caring about him.

"Yes," he said; "but I can hear well—I'm not deaf."

"It is true; I forgot," said Tessa, lifting her hands and clasping them. "But Monna Lisa is deaf, and I live with her. She's a kind old woman, and I'm not frightened at her. And we live very well: we have plenty of nice things. I can have nuts if I like. And I'm not obliged to work now. I used to have to work, and I didn't like it; but I liked feeding the mules, and I should like to see poor Giannetta, the little mule, again. We've only got a goat and two kids, and I used to talk to[4] the goat a good deal, because there was nobody else but Monna Lisa. But now I've got something else—can you guess what it is?"

She drew her head back, and looked with a challenging smile at Baldassarre, as if she had proposed a difficult riddle to him.

"No," said he, putting aside his bowl, and looking at her dreamily. It seemed as if this young prattling thing were some memory come back out of his own youth.

"You like me to talk to you, don't you?" said Tessa, "but you must not tell anybody. Shall I fetch you a bit of cold sausage?"

He shook his head, but he looked so mild now that Tessa felt quite at her ease.

"Well, then, I've got a little baby. Such a pretty *bambinetto*, with little fingers and nails! Not old yet; it was born at the Natività,* Monna Lisa says. I was married one Natività, a long, long while ago, and nobody knew. O Santa Madonna! I didn't mean to tell you that!"

Tessa set up her shoulders and bit her lip, looking at Baldassarre as if this betrayal of secrets must have an exciting effect on him too. But he seemed not to care much; and perhaps that was in the nature of strangers.

"Yes," she said, carrying on her thought aloud, "you are a stranger; you don't live anywhere or know anybody, do you?"

"No," said Baldassarre, also thinking aloud, rather than consciously answering, "I only know one man."

"His name is not Nofri, is it?" said Tessa, anxiously.

"No," said Baldassarre, noticing her look of fear. "Is that your hus-

2 ⟨him⟩ his eyes MS   3 cry] say MS
4 I {used to} talk to ⟨them⟩ the goat a good deal, ⟨else I've got⟩ because there was nobody ⟨to talk to⟩ else MS

band's name?"

That mistaken supposition was very amusing to Tessa. She laughed and clapped her hands as she said,—

"No, indeed! But I must not tell you anything about my husband. You would never think what he is—not at all like Nofri!"

She laughed again at the delightful incongruity between the name of Nofri—which was not separable from the idea of the cross-grained step-father—and the idea of her husband.

"But I don't see him very often," she went on, more gravely. "And sometimes I pray to the Holy Madonna to send him oftener, and once she did. But I must go back to my bimbo[5] now. I'll bring it to show you to-morrow. You would like to see it. Sometimes it cries and makes a face, but only when it's hungry, Monna Lisa says. You wouldn't think it, but Monna[6] Lisa had babies once, and they are all dead old men. My husband says she will never die now, because she's so well dried. I'm glad of that, for I'm fond of her. You would like to stay here to-morrow, shouldn't you?"

"I should like to have this place to come and rest in, that's all," said Baldassarre. "I would pay for it, and harm nobody."

"No, indeed; I think you are not a bad old man. But you look sorry about something. Tell me, is there anything you shall cry about when I leave you by yourself? *I* used to cry once."

"No, child; I think I shall cry no more."

"That's right; and I'll bring you some breakfast, and show you the bimbo[7]. Good-night[8]."

Tessa took up her bowl and lantern, and closed the door behind her. The pretty loving apparition had been no more to Baldassarre than a faint rainbow on the blackness to the man who is wrestling in deep waters. He hardly thought of her again till his dreamy waking passed into the more vivid images of disturbed sleep.

But Tessa thought much of him. She had no sooner entered the house than she told Monna Lisa what she had done, and insisted that the stranger should be allowed to come and rest in the outhouse when he liked. The old woman, who had had her notions of making him a useful tenant, made a great show of reluctance, shook her head, and urged that Messer Naldo would be angry if she let[9] any one come about the house. Tessa did not believe that. Naldo[1] had said nothing against strangers who lived nowhere; and this old man knew nobody except one person, who was not Nofri.

5 bimbo] *1 2 3 Bambinetto MS bambinetto CM*
6 it, but Monna] it—Monna *MS*   7 bimbo] *1 2 3 Bambino MS bambino CM*
8 breakfast {and show you the *Bambino*}. Good night *MS*
9 angry if she let] angry at her letting *MS*
1 Naldo] *1 2 3 Messer Naldo MS CM*

"Well," conceded Monna Lisa, at last, "if I let him stay for awhile[2] and carry things up the hill for me, thou must keep thy counsel and tell nobody."

"No," said Tessa, "I'll only tell the bimbo[3]."

"And then," Monna Lisa went on, in her thick under-tone, "God may love us well enough not to let Messer Naldo find out anything about it. For he never comes near[4] but at dark; and[5] as he was here two days ago, it's likely he'll never come at all till the old man's gone away again."

"Oh, me! Monna," said Tessa, clasping her hands, "I wish Naldo had not to go such a long, long way sometimes[6] before he comes back again."

"Ah, child, the world's big, they say. There are[7] places behind the mountains, and if people go night and day, night and day, they get to Rome, and see the Holy Father."

Tessa looked submissive in the presence of this mystery, and began to rock her baby, and sing syllables of[8] vague loving meaning, in tones that imitated a triple chime.

The next morning she was unusually industrious in the prospect of more dialogue and of the [9]pleasure she should give the poor old stranger by showing him her baby. But before she could get ready to take Baldassarre his breakfast, she found that Monna Lisa had been employing him as a drawer of water. She deferred her paternosters, and hurried down to insist that Baldassarre should[1] sit[2] on his straw, so that she might come and sit by him again while he ate his breakfast. That attitude made the new companionship all the more delightful to Tessa, for she had been used to sitting on straw in old days along with her goats and mules.

"I will not let Monna Lisa give you too much work to do," she said, bringing him some [3]steaming broth and soft bread. "I don't like much work, and I dare say you don't. I like sitting in the sunshine and feeding things. Monna Lisa says work is good, but she does it all herself, so I don't mind. She's not a cross old woman—you needn't be afraid of her being cross. And now, you eat that, and I'll go and fetch my baby and show it you."

Presently she came back with the small mummy case in her arms. The mummy looked very lively,[4] having unusually large dark eyes, [5]though no more than the usual indication of a future nose.

2 awhile] a while *3*
4 near] *MS* here *CM 1 2 3*
6 long way {sometimes} *MS*
8 rock {her baby} and sing syllables of ⟨unrevealed⟩ vague loving meaning in ⟨silver-soft⟩ tones *MS*
9 ⟨comfort⟩ pleasure *MS*
2 sit ⟨down⟩ on *MS*
4 lively, ⟨with⟩ *MS*

3 bimbo] *1 2 3 bambino MS CM*
5 and ⟨perhaps he'll⟩ *MS*
7 There are] ⟨There are⟩ There's *MS*

1 should] would *MS*
3 ⟨polenta⟩ steaming broth and soft bread *MS*
5 ⟨but⟩ though *MS*

"This is my baby," said Tessa, seating herself close to Baldassarre. "You didn't think it was so pretty, did you? It is like the little Gesù, and I should think the Santa Madonna would be kinder to me now, is it not true? But I have not much to ask for, because I have every thing now—only that I should see my husband oftener. You may hold [6]the *bambino* a little if you like, but I think you must not kiss him, because you might hurt him."

She spoke this [7]prohibition in a tone of soothing excuse, and Baldassarre could not refuse to hold the small package. "Poor thing! poor thing!" he said, in a deep voice which had something strangely threatening in its apparent pity. It did not seem to him as if this [8]guileless loving little woman could reconcile him to the world at all, but rather that she was with him against the world[9], that she was a creature who would need to be avenged.

"Oh, don't you be sorry for me," she said; "for though I don't see him often, he is more beautiful and good than anybody else in the world. I say prayers to him when he's away.[1] You couldn't think what he is!"

She looked at Baldassarre with a wide glance of mysterious meaning, taking the baby from him again, and almost wishing he would question her[2] as if he wanted very much to know more.

"Yes, I could," said Baldassarre, rather bitterly.

"No, I'm sure you never could," said Tessa, earnestly. "You thought he might be Nofri," she added with a triumphant air of conclusiveness. "But never mind; you couldn't know. What is your name?"

He rubbed his hand over his knitted brow, then looked at her blankly and said, "Ah, child, what is it?"

It was not that he did not often remember his name well enough; and if he had had presence of mind now to remember it, he would have chosen not to tell it. But a sudden question appealing to his memory, had a paralyzing effect, and in that moment he was conscious of nothing but helplessness.

Ignorant as Tessa was, the pity stirred in her by his blank look taught her to say,

"Never mind: you are a stranger, it is no matter about your having a name. Good-by now, because I want my breakfast. You will come here and rest when you like; Monna Lisa says you may. And don't you be unhappy, for we'll be good to you."

"Poor thing!" said Baldassarre again.

6 ⟨him⟩ the *bambino* MS
7 ⟨last⟩ prohibition MS
8 ⟨innocent⟩ guileless loving ⟨little woman⟩ ⟨little thing⟩ little woman MS
9 world—⟨something⟩ MS
1 world: {I say prayers ⟨every⟩ to him, when he's away MS
2 question her ⟨and tempt her⟩ MS

CHAPTER XXXIV.

NO PLACE FOR REPENTANCE

MESSER NALDO came again sooner than was expected: he came on the evening of the twenty-eighth of November, only eleven days after his previous visit, proving that he had not gone far beyond the mountains; and a scene which we have witnessed as it took place that evening in the Via de' Bardi may help to explain the impulse which turned his steps towards the Hill of San Giorgio.

When Tito had first found this home for Tessa, on his return from Rome, more than a year and a half ago, he had acted, he persuaded himself, simply under the constraint imposed on him by his own kindliness after the unlucky incident which had made foolish little Tessa imagine him to be her husband. It was true that the kindness was manifested towards a pretty trusting thing whom it was impossible to be near without feeling inclined to caress and pet her; but it was not less true that Tito had movements of kindness towards her apart from any contemplated gain to himself. Otherwise, charming as her prettiness and prattle were in a lazy moment, he might have preferred to be free from her; for he was not in love with Tessa—he was in love for the first time in his life with an entirely different woman, whom he was not simply inclined to shower caresses on, but whose presence possessed him so that the simple sweep of her long tresses across his cheek seemed[1] to vibrate through the hours. All the young ideal passion he had in him had been stirred by Romola, and his fibre was too fine, his intellect too bright, for him to be tempted into the habits of a gross pleasure-seeker. But he had spun a web about himself and Tessa, which he felt incapable of breaking: in the first moments after the mimic marriage he had been prompted to leave her under an illusion by a distinct calculation of his own possible need, but since that critical moment it seemed to him that the web had gone on spinning itself[2] in spite of him, like a growth over which he had no power. The elements of kindness and self-indulgence are hard to [3]distinguish in a soft nature like Tito's; and the annoyance he had felt under Tessa's pursuit of him on the day of his betrothal,[4] the thorough intention of revealing the truth to her with which he set out

1 so that . . . seemed] so that a single caress—the simple sweep of her long tresses across his cheek—seemed MS
2 spinning itself] *1 2 3* spinning CM spreading MS
3 ⟨separate⟩ distinguish MS
4 betrothal, ⟨was a strong argument to him that in fulfilling his promise to seek her again⟩ MS

to fulfil his promise of seeing her again, were a sufficiently strong argument to him that in ultimately leaving Tessa under her illusion, and providing a home for her, he had been overcome by his own kindness. And in those[5] days of his first devotion to Romola he needed a self-justifying argument. He had learned to be glad that she was deceived about some things. But every strong feeling makes to itself a conscience of its own—has it own piety; just as much as that[6] feeling of the son towards the mother which will sometimes survive amid the worst fumes of depravation; and Tito could not yet be easy in committing a secret offence against his wedded love.

But he was all the more careful in taking precautions to preserve the secrecy of the offence. Monna Lisa, who, like many of her class, never left her habitation except to go to one or two particular shops, and to confession once a year, knew nothing of his real name and whereabout: she only knew that he paid her so as to make her very comfortable, and minded little about the rest, save that she got fond of Tessa, and found pleasure in[7] the cares for which she was paid. There was some mystery behind, clearly, since Tessa was a contadina, and Messer Naldo was a signor; but, for aught [8]Monna Lisa knew, he might be a real husband[9]. For Tito had thoroughly frightened Tessa into silence about the circumstances of their marriage, by telling her that if she broke that silence she would never see him again; and Monna Lisa's deafness, which made it impossible to say anything to her without some premeditation, had saved Tessa from any incautious revelation to her, such as had run off her tongue in talking with Baldassarre. For[1] a long while Tito's visits were so rare, that it seemed likely enough he took journeys between them. They were prompted chiefly by the desire to see that all things were going on well with Tessa; and though he always found his visit pleasanter than the prospect of it—always felt anew the charm of that pretty ignorant lovingness and trust—he had not yet any real need of it. But he was determined, if possible, to preserve the simplicity on which the charm depended; to keep Tessa a genuine contadina, and not [2]place the small field-flower among conditions that would rob it of its grace. He would have been shocked to see her in the dress of any other rank than her own; the piquancy of her talk would be all gone if things began to have new relations for her, if her world became wider, her pleasures less [3]childish; and the squirrel-like enjoyment of nuts at discretion marked the standard of the luxuries he provided[4] for her. By

5 those] MS these CM 1 2 3
7 found pleasure in] 3C liked MS CM 1 2
9 husband; for ⟨Tessa⟩ Tito MS
2 ⟨put⟩ place MS
4 provided] had provided 2 3

6 that] MS the CM 1 2 3
8 ⟨she⟩ Monna Lisa MS
1 For] 3P And for MS CM 1 2
3 ⟨childlike⟩ childish MS

this means, Tito saved Tessa's charm from being sullied; and he also, by a convenient coincidence, saved himself from aggravating expenses that were already rather importunate to a man whose money was all required for his avowed [5]habits of life.

This, in brief, had been the history of Tito's relation to Tessa up to a very recent date[6]. It is true that once or twice before Bardo's death, the sense that there was Tessa up the hill, with whom it was possible to [7]pass an hour agreeably, had been an [8]inducement to him to escape from a little weariness of the old man, when, for lack of any positive engagement[9], he might otherwise have borne the weariness patiently and shared Romola's burthen. But the moment when he had first felt a real hunger for Tessa's ignorant lovingness and belief in him had not come till quite lately, and it was distinctly marked out by circumstances as little to be forgotten as the oncoming of a malady that has permanently vitiated the sight and hearing. It was[1] the day when he had first seen Baldassarre, and had bought the armour. Returning across the bridge that night, with the coat of mail in his hands, he had felt an [2]unconquerable shrinking from an immediate encounter with Romola[3]. She, too, knew little of the actual world; she, too, trusted him; but he had an uneasy consciousness that behind her frank eyes there was a nature that could judge him, and that any ill-founded trust of hers sprang not from[4] pretty brute-like incapacity, but from a nobleness which might prove an alarming touchstone. He wanted a little ease, a little repose from self-control, after the agitation and exertions of the day; [5]he wanted to be where he could adjust his mind to the morrow, without caring how he behaved at the present moment. And there was a sweet[6] adoring creature within reach whose presence was as safe and unconstraining as[7] that of her own kids,— who would believe any fable, and remain quite unimpressed by public opinion. And so on that evening when Romola was waiting and listening for him, he turned his steps up the hill.

No wonder, then, that the steps took the same course on this evening, eleven days later, when he had had to recoil under Romola's first outburst of scorn. He could not wish Tessa in his wife's place, or refrain from wishing that his wife should be thoroughly reconciled to

---

5 ⟨expenses⟩ habits *MS*   6 date] *1 2 3* day *MS CM*
7 ⟨spend⟩ pass *MS*   8 ⟨additional⟩ inducement *MS*
9 when {for lack of any ⟨other real⟩ ⟨frenchmen⟩ positive engagement} *MS*
1 was ⟨only⟩ *MS*   2 ⟨insurmountable⟩ unconquerable *MS*
3 Romola ⟨but he⟩. *MS*
4 from ⟨any⟩ pretty, brute-like incapacity, but ⟨precisely⟩ from ⟨that⟩ a ⟨special⟩
nobleness which ⟨when once undeceived would have a terrible lucidity of vision⟩ *MS*
5 ⟨he knew where he could find that ?ease⟩ he *MS*
6 sweet ⟨little⟩ adoring *MS*   7 as ⟨a⟩ *MS*

him; for it was Romola[8], and not Tessa, that belonged to the world where all the larger desires of a man who had ambition and effective faculties must necessarily lie. But he wanted a refuge from a standard disagreeably rigorous, of which he could not make himself independent simply by thinking it folly; and Tessa's little soul was that inviting refuge.

It was not much more than eight o'clock when he went up the stone steps to the door of Tessa's room. Usually she heard his entrance into the house, and ran to meet him, but not to-night; and when he opened the door he saw the reason. A single dim light was burning above the dying fire, and showed[9] Tessa in a kneeling attitude by the head of the [1]bed where the baby lay. Her head had fallen aside on the pillow, and her brown rosary, which usually hung above the pillow over the picture of the Madonna and the golden palm branches, lay in the loose grasp of her right hand. She had gone fast asleep over her beads. Tito stepped lightly across the little room, and sat down close to her. She had probably heard the opening of the door as part of her dream, for he had not been looking at her two moments before she opened her eyes. She opened them without any start, and remained quite motionless looking at him, as if the sense that he was there smiling at her shut out any impulse which could disturb that happy passiveness. But when he put his hand under her chin, and stooped to kiss her, she said:—

"I dreamed it, and then I said it was dreaming—and then I awoke, and it was true."

"Little sinner!" said Tito, pinching her chin, "[2]you have not said half your prayers. I will punish you by not looking at your baby; it is ugly."

Tessa did not like those words, even though Tito was smiling. She had some pouting distress in her face, as she said, [3]bending anxiously over the baby,

"Ah, it is not true! He is prettier than anything. You do not think he is ugly. You *will*[4] look at him. He is even prettier than when you saw him before—only he's asleep, and you can't see his eyes or his tongue, and I can't show you his hair—and it grows—isn't that wonderful? Look at him! It's true his face is very much all alike when he's asleep, there is not much to see as when he's awake. If you kiss him very gently, he won't wake: you want to kiss him, is it not true?"

He satisfied her by giving the small mummy a butterfly kiss, and then putting his hand on her shoulder and turning her face towards

8 Romola ⟨alone who belonged⟩ MS
9 showed ⟨the baby sleeping with⟩ Tessa MS   1 ⟨cradle⟩ bed MS
2 ⟨thou hast⟩ you have not said half ⟨thy⟩ your MS
3 ⟨turning anxiously towards⟩ bending MS   4 *will*] MS will CM *1 2 3*

him, said, "You like looking at the baby better than looking at your husband, you false one!"

She was still kneeling, and [5]now rested her hands on his knee, looking up at him like one of Fra Lippo Lippi's round-cheeked adoring angels.*

"No," she said, shaking her head; "I love you always best,[6] only I want you to look at the *bambino* and love him; I used only to want you to love me."

"And did you expect me to come again so soon?" said Tito, inclined to make her prattle. He still felt the effects of the agitation he had undergone, still felt[7] like a man who has been violently jarred, and this[8] was the easiest relief from silence and solitude.

"Ah, no," said Tessa, "I have counted the days—to-day I began at my right thumb again—since you put on the beautiful chain coat, that[9] Messer San Michele[1] gave you to take care of you on your [2]journey. And you have got it on now," she said, peeping through the opening in the breast of his tunic. "Perhaps it made you come back sooner."

"Perhaps it did, Tessa," he said. "But don't[3] mind the coat now. Tell me what has happened since I was here. Did you see the tents in the Prato, and the soldiers and horsemen when they passed the bridges—did you hear the drums and trumpets?"

"Yes,[4] and I was rather frightened, because I thought the soldiers might come up here. And Monna Lisa was a little afraid too, for she said they might carry our kids [5]off; she said it was their business to do mischief. But the Holy Madonna[6] took care of us, for we never saw one of them up here. But something has happened, only I hardly dare tell you, and that is what I was saying more [7]*aves* for."

"What do you mean, Tessa?" said Tito, rather anxiously. "Make haste and tell me."

"Yes, but will you let me sit on your knee? because then I think I shall not be so frightened."

He took her on his knee, and put his arm round her, but looked grave: it seemed that something unpleasant must pursue him even here.

"At first, I didn't mean to tell you," said Tessa, speaking almost in a whisper, as if that would mitigate the offence; "because we thought

5 ⟨had now⟩ now *MS*   6 {I love you always best,} only *MS*
7 felt ⟨as if he had⟩ *MS*
8 this ⟨easy relief from silence and solitude was just what he wanted⟩ *MS*
9 that ⟨was to take care of you⟩ *MS*
1 San Michele] *1 2 3* Saint Michael *MS CM*   2 ⟨journeys⟩ journey *MS*
3 don't] do not *MS*   4 Yes, ⟨I saw something every day⟩ *MS*
5 ⟨away⟩ off *MS*   6 Madonna ⟨kept them away⟩ *MS*
7 ⟨paternosters⟩ *aves MS*

the old man would be gone away before you came again, and it would
be as if it had not been. But now he is there, and you are come, and I
never did anything you told me not to do before. And I want to tell
you, and then you will perhaps forgive me, for it is a long while
before I go to confession."

"Yes, tell me everything, my Tessa." He began to hope it was after
all a trivial matter.

"Oh, you will be sorry for him: I'm afraid he cries about something
when I don't see him. But that was not the reason I went to him first;
it was because I wanted to talk to him and show him my baby, and
he was a stranger that lived nowhere, and I thought you wouldn't
care so much about my talking to him. And I think he is not a bad
old man, and he wanted to come and sleep on the straw next to the
goats, and I made Monna Lisa say, 'Yes, he might,' and he's away all
the day almost, but when he comes back I[8] talk to him, and take him
something to eat."

"Some beggar, I suppose. It was naughty of you, Tessa, and I am
angry with Monna Lisa. I must have him sent away."

"No, I think he is not a beggar, for he wanted to pay Monna Lisa,
only she asked him to do work for her instead. And he gets himself
shaved, and his clothes are tidy: Monna Lisa says he is a decent man.
But sometimes I think he is not in his right mind. Lupo, at Peretola,
was not in his right mind: and he looks a little like Lupo sometimes,
as if he didn't know where he was."

"What sort of face has he?" said Tito, his heart beginning to beat
strangely. He was so haunted by the thought of Baldassarre, that it
was already he whom he saw in imagination sitting on the straw not
many yards from him. "Fetch your stool, my Tessa, and sit on it."

"Shall you not forgive me?" she said, timidly, moving from his
knee.

"Yes, I will not be angry—only sit down, and tell me what sort of
old man this is."

"I can't think how to tell you: he is not like my stepfather, Nofri[9],
nor anybody. His face is yellow, and he has deep marks in it; and his
hair is white, but there is none on the top of his head: and his eyebrows are black, and he looks from under them at me, and says, 'Poor
thing!' to me, as if he thought I was [1]beaten as I used to be; and that
seems as if he couldn't be in his right mind, doesn't it? And I asked
him his name once, but he couldn't tell it me: yet everybody has a
name,—is it not true? And he has a book now, and keeps looking at it
ever so long, as if he were a Padre[2]. But I think he is not saying

prayers, for his lips never move;—ah, you are angry with me, or is it because you are sorry for the old man?"

Tito's eyes were still fixed on Tessa; but he had ceased to see her, and was only seeing the objects her words suggested. It was this absent glance which frightened her, and she could not help [3]going to kneel at his side again. But he [4]did not heed her, and she dared not touch him, or speak to him: she knelt, trembling and wondering; and this state of mind [5]suggesting her beads to her, she took them from the floor, and began to tell them again, her pretty lips moving silently, and her blue eyes wide with anxiety and struggling tears.

Tito was quite unconscious of her movements—unconscious of his own attitude: he was in that wrapt state in which a man will grasp painful roughness, and press, and press it closer, and never feel it. A new possibility had risen before him, which might dissolve at once the [6]wretched conditions of fear and [7]suppression that were marring his life. Destiny had brought within his reach an opportunity of retrieving that moment on the steps of the Duomo, when the Past had grasped him with living quivering hands, and he had disowned it. A few steps, and he might be face to face with his father, with[8] no witness by; he might seek forgiveness and reconciliation; and there was money now, from the sale of the library, to enable them to leave Florence without disclosures[9], and go into Southern Italy, where, under the probable French rule, he had already laid a foundation for patronage. Romola need never know the whole truth, for she could have no certain means of identifying that prisoner in the Duomo with Baldassarre,[1] or of learning what had taken place on the steps, except from Baldassarre himself; and if his father forgave, he would also consent to bury, that offence. But with this possibility of relief, by an easy spring, from present evil[2], there rose the other possibility, that the fierce-hearted man might refuse to be propitiated. Well—and if he did, things would only be as they had been before; for there would be *no witness by*. It was not repentance with a white sheet round it and taper in hand, [3]confessing its hated sin in the eyes of men, that Tito was preparing for: it was a repentance that would make all things pleasant again, and [4]keep all past unpleasant things secret. And Tito's

3 ⟨leaving⟩ going *MS*   4 ⟨took no notice of⟩ did not heed *MS*
5 ⟨suggested⟩ suggesting *MS*   6 ⟨irksome⟩ wretched *MS*
7 ⟨secrecy⟩ suppression *MS*   8 with] and *MS*
9 disclosures] *MS* disclosure *CM 1 2 3*
1 no {certain} means of identifying that prisoner {in the Duomo} with Baldassarre, ⟨and⟩ or *MS*
2 {by an easy spring} from present evil ⟨by an easy spring⟩ *MS*
3 ⟨that⟩ ⟨declaring⟩ confessing its {hated} sin *MS*
4 ⟨make⟩ keep all {past} unpleasant *MS*

[5]soft-heartedness, his indisposition to feel himself in harsh relations with any creature, was in strong activity towards his father, now his father was brought near to him. It [6]would be a state of ease that his nature could not but desire, if the[7] poisonous hatred in Baldassarre's glance could be replaced by something of the old [8]affection and complacency. Tito longed to have his world once [9]again completely cushioned with good-will, and longed for it the more eagerly because of [1]what he had just suffered from the collision with Romola. It was not difficult to him to smile pleadingly on[2] those whom he had injured, and offer to do them much kindness: and no quickness of intellect could tell him exactly the taste of that honey on the lips of the injured. The opportunity was there, and it raised an inclination which hemmed in the calculating activity of his thought. He started up, and stepped towards the door; but Tessa's [3]cry, as she dropped her beads, roused him from his absorption. He turned and said,

"My Tessa, get me a lantern; and don't cry, little pigeon, I am not angry."

They went down the stairs, and Tessa [4]was going to shout the need of the lantern in Monna Lisa's ear, when Tito, who had opened the door, said, "Stay, Tessa—no, I want no lantern:[5] go upstairs again, and keep quiet, and say nothing to Monna Lisa."

In half a minute he [6]stood before the closed door of the outhouse, where the moon was shining white on the old paintless wood.

In this last decisive moment, Tito felt a tremor upon him—a sudden instinctive shrinking from a possible tiger glance, a possible tiger leap. Yet why should he, a young man, be afraid of an old one? a young man with armour on, of an old man without a weapon? It[7] was but a moment's hesitation, and Tito laid his hand on the door. Was his father asleep? Was there nothing else but the door that screened him from the voice and the glance which no magic could turn into ease?

Baldassarre was not asleep. There was a square opening high in the wall[8] of the hovel, through which the moonbeams sent in a stream of

5 ⟨kindliness⟩ soft heartedness *MS*　　　6 ⟨was⟩ would be *MS*
7 the] *3C* that *MS CM 1 2*　　　8 ⟨good-will⟩ affection *MS*
9 ⟨more⟩ again *MS*
1 ⟨the jar he⟩ what he had {just} suffered from the collision with Romola ⟨to which he had been ?urged⟩. It *MS*
2 smile {pleadingly} on ⟨one⟩ those *MS*　　　3 ⟨little scream⟩ cry *MS*
4 ⟨shouted⟩ was going to shout *MS*
5 lantern: ⟨go up I don't want a lantern⟩ ¶ "Go upstairs again ⟨Tessa⟩, and keep quiet," ⟨he said as he took the lantern, "Say nothing to Monna Lisa⟩ and say *MS*
6 ⟨was in front of the closed⟩ stood before the closed door of the outhouse ⟨with the lantern in his hand⟩ where *MS*
7 weapon? It] weapon, too poor to have bought a weapon yet? It *MS*
8 wall] *1 2 3* walls *MS CM*

pale light; and if Tito could have looked through the opening, he
would have seen his father seated on the straw, with something that
shone like a white star in his hand. Baldassarre was feeling the edge
of his poniard[9], taking refuge in that sensation from a hopeless blank
of thought that seemed to lie like a great gulf between his passion and
its aim. He was in one of his most wretched moments of conscious
helplessness: he had been poring, while it was light, over the book
that lay open beside him; then he had been trying to recall the names
of his jewels, and the symbols engraved on them; and though at certain other times he had recovered some of those [1]names and symbols,
to-night they were all gone into darkness. And this effort at inward
seeing had seemed to end in utter paralysis of memory. He was
reduced to a sort of mad consciousness that he was a solitary pulse of
just rage in a world filled with defiant[2] baseness. He had clutched and
unsheathed his dagger, and for a long while had been feeling its edge,
his mind narrowed to one image, and the dream of one sensation—
the sensation of plunging that dagger into a base heart, which he was
unable to pierce in any other way.

Tito had his hand on the door and was pulling it: it dragged
against the ground as such old doors often do, and Baldassarre,
startled out of his dream-like state, rose from his sitting posture in
vague amazement, not knowing where he was. He had not yet risen to
his feet, and was still kneeling on one knee, when the door came wide
open and he saw, dark against the moonlight, with the rays falling on
one bright mass of curls and one rounded[3] olive cheek, the image of
his reverie—not shadowy—close and real like water at the lips after
the thirsty dream of it. No thought could come athwart that eager
thirst. In one moment, before Tito could start back, the old man,
with the preternatural force of rage in his limbs, had sprung forward
and the dagger had flashed out. In the next moment the dagger had
snapped in two, and Baldassarre, under the parrying force of Tito's
arm, had fallen back[4] on the straw, clutching the hilt with its bit of
broken blade. The pointed end lay shining against Tito's feet.

Tito had felt one great heart-leap of terror as he had staggered
under the weight of the thrust[5]: he felt now the triumph of deliverance and safety. His armour had been proved, and vengeance lay
helpless before him. But the triumph raised no devilish impulse; on
the contrary the sight of his father close to him and unable to injure
him, made the effort at reconciliation easier. He was free from fear,

9 his poniard] that white thing *MS*   1 ⟨images⟩ names and symbols *MS*
2 defiant] *3P* defying *MS CM 12*   3 rounded] *1 2 3* round *MS CM*
4 Baldassarre {under the parrying force of Tito's arm} had fallen back ⟨helpless⟩ on
MS
5 the {weight of the} thrust *MS*

but he had only the more unmixed and direct want to be free from the sense that he was hated. After they had looked at each other a little while[6], Baldassarre lying motionless in despairing rage, Tito said in his soft tones, just as they had [7]sounded before the last parting on the shores of Greece,

"*Padre mio!*" There was a pause after those words, but no movement or sound till he said,—

"I came to ask your forgiveness![8]"

Again he paused, that the healing balm of those words might have time to work. But there was no sign of change in Baldassarre: he lay as he had fallen, leaning on one arm: he was trembling, but it was from the shock that had thrown him down.

"I was taken by surprise that morning. I wish now to be a son to you again. I wish to make the rest of your life happy, that you may forget what you have suffered."

He paused again. He had used the clearest and strongest words he could think of.[9] It was useless to say more, until he had some sign that Baldassarre understood him. Perhaps [1]his mind was too distempered or too imbecile even for that: perhaps the shock of his fall and his disappointed rage might have quite suspended the use of his faculties.

Presently Baldassarre began to move. He threw away the broken dagger, and slowly and gradually, still trembling, began to raise himself from the ground. Tito put out his hand to help him,[2] and so strangely quick are men's souls that in this moment when he began to feel his atonement was accepted, he [3]had a darting thought of the irksome efforts it entailed. Baldassarre clutched the hand that was held out, raised himself and clutched it still, going close up to Tito till their faces were not a foot off each other. Then he began to speak, in a deep trembling voice,

"I saved you—I nurtured you—I loved you. You forsook me—you robbed me—you denied me. [4]What can you give me? You have made the world bitterness to me; but there is one draught of sweetness left—*that you shall know agony*[5]."

He let fall[6] Tito's hand, and going backward[7] a little, first rested his arm on a projecting stone in the wall, and then sank again in a sitting posture on the straw. The outleap of [8]fury in the dagger-thrust had evidently exhausted him.

6 while ⟨as Baldassarre lay⟩ *MS*   7 ⟨fallen on his⟩ sounded *MS*
8 forgiveness!] forgiveness. *MS*   9 again. {He had . . . of.} *MS*
 1 ⟨he⟩ his mind was ⟨even⟩ too *MS*
 2 him, ⟨believing that his atonement had been accepted⟩ *MS*   3 ⟨also⟩ had *MS*
 4 ⟨You are terrible⟩—what *MS*
 5 *that you shall know agony*] *3P* that you shall know agony *MS CM 1 2*
 6 let fall] let go *MS*   7 backward] *MS* backwards *CM 1 2 3*
 8 ⟨physical effort⟩ fury *MS*

Tito stood silent. If it had been a deep, yearning[9] emotion which had brought him to ask his father's forgiveness, the denial of it might have caused him a pang which would have excluded the rushing train of thoughts[1] that followed those decisive words. As it was, though[2] the sentence of unchangeable hatred grated on him and jarred him terribly, his mind glanced round with a self-preserving instinct to see how far those words could have the force of a substantial threat. [3]When he had come down to speak to Baldassarre, he had said to himself that if his effort at reconciliation failed, things would only be as they had been before. The first glance of his mind was backward to that thought again, but the future possibilities of danger[4] that were conjured up along with it brought the [5]perception that things were *not* as they had been before, and the perception came as a triumphant relief. There was not only the broken dagger, there was the certainty from what Tessa had told him[6], that Baldassarre's mind was broken too, and had no edge that could reach him. Tito felt he had no choice now: he must defy Baldassarre as a mad, imbecile old man; and the chances were so strongly on his side that there was hardly room for fear[7]. No, except the fear of having to do many unpleasant things in order to save himself from what was yet more unpleasant. And one of those unpleasant things must be done immediately: it was very difficult.

"Do you mean to stay here?" he said.

"No," said Baldassarre, bitterly, "you mean to turn me out."

"Not so," said Tito. "I only ask."

"I tell you, you have turned me out. If it is your straw, you turned me off it three years ago."

"Then you mean to leave this place?" said Tito, more anxious about this certainty than the ground of it.

"I have spoken," said Baldassarre.

Tito turned and re-entered the house. Monna Lisa was nodding[8]: he went up to Tessa, and found her crying by the side of her baby.

"Tessa," he said, sitting down, and taking her head between his hands. "Leave off crying, little goose, and listen to me."

[9]He lifted her chin upward, that she might look at him, while he spoke very distinctly and emphatically.

9 deep, yearning] *MS* deep yearning *CM 1 2 3*
1 thoughts] *MS* thought *CM 1 2 3*
2 As it was {, though} the ⟨words⟩ sentence . . . terribly, ⟨but⟩ his mind *MS*
3 ⟨Before⟩ When *MS*   4 possibilities {of danger} *MS*
5 ⟨joyful flash of conviction⟩ perception *MS*
6 certainty {from what Tessa had told him} *MS*
7 fear: ⟨for fear—no⟩ no, ⟨not for⟩ except *MS*
8 nodding ⟨, having of course heard nothing⟩ *MS*
9 ⟨She looked up at⟩ He *MS*

"You must never speak to that old man again. He is a mad old man, and he wants to kill me. Never speak to him or listen to him again."

Tessa's tears had ceased, and[1] her lips were pale with fright.

"Is he [2]gone away?" she whispered.

"He will go away. Remember what I have said to you."

"Yes; I will never speak to a stranger any more," said Tessa, with a sense of guilt.

He told her, to comfort her, that he would come again to-morrow; and then went down to Monna Lisa to rebuke her severely for letting a dangerous man come about the house.

Tito felt that these were odious tasks; they were very evil-tasted morsels, but they were forced upon him. He heard Monna Lisa fasten the door behind him, and turned away, without looking towards the open door of the hovel. He felt secure that Baldassarre would go, and he could not wait to see him go. Even *his* young frame and elastic spirit were shattered by the agitations that had been crowded into this single evening.

Baldassarre was still sitting on the straw when the shadow of Tito passed by. Before him lay the fragments of the broken dagger; beside him lay the open book, over which he had pored in vain. They looked like mocking symbols of his utter helplessness; and his body was still too trembling for him to rise and walk away.

But the next morning very early, when Tessa peeped anxiously[3] through the hole in her shutter, the door of the hovel was open, and the strange old man was gone.

---

1 and ⟨she was⟩ *MS*   2 ⟨going⟩ gone *MS*   3 peeped {anxiously} *MS*

CHAPTER XXXV.

WHAT FLORENCE WAS THINKING OF

FOR several days Tito saw little of Romola. He told her gently, the [1]next morning, that it would be better for her to remove any small articles of her own from the library, as there would be agents coming to pack up the antiquities. Then, leaning to kiss her on the brow, he suggested that she should [2]keep in her own room where the little painted tabernacle was, and where she was then sitting, so that she might be away from the noise of strange footsteps. Romola assented quietly, making no sign of emotion: the night had been one long waking to her, and, in spite of her healthy frame, sensation had become a dull continuous pain, as if she had been stunned and bruised. Tito divined that she felt ill, but he dared say no more; he only dared, perceiving that her hand and brow were stone cold, to fetch a furred mantle and throw it lightly round her. And in every brief interval that he returned to her, the scene was nearly the same: he tried to propitiate her by some unobtrusive act or word of tenderness, and she seemed to have lost the power of speaking to him, or of looking at him. "Patience!" he said to himself. "She will recover it, and forgive[3] at last. The tie to me must still remain the strongest." When the stricken person is slow to recover and look as if nothing had happened, the striker easily glides into the position of the aggrieved party; he feels no bruise himself, and is strongly conscious of his own amiable behaviour since he inflicted the blow. But Tito was not naturally disposed to feel himself aggrieved; the constant bent of his mind was towards propitiation, and he would have submitted to much for the sake of feeling Romola's hand resting on his head again, as it did that morning when he first shrank from looking at her.

But[4] he found it the less difficult to wait patiently for the return of his home happiness, because his life out of doors was more and more interesting to him. [5]A course of action which is in strictness a slowly-prepared outgrowth of the entire character, is yet almost always traceable to a single impression as its point of apparent origin; and since that moment in the Piazza del Duomo, when Tito, mounted on the bales, had tasted a keen pleasure in the consciousness of his ability to

1 ⟨morning after the disclosure about the library⟩ next morning *MS*
2 ⟨remain⟩ keep in her own ⟨little⟩ room *MS*
3 forgive] forgive me *MS*
4 But ⟨it was that less difficult to him⟩ *MS*
5 ⟨Since that moment in the Piazza del Duomo⟩ ⟨A course of action which is strictly⟩ A course *MS*

tickle the ears of men with any phrases that pleased them, his imagination had glanced continually towards a sort of political activity which the troubled public life of Florence was likely enough to find occasion for. But the [6]fresh dread of Baldassarre, waked in the same moment, had lain like an immovable rocky obstruction across that path, and had urged him into the sale of the library, as a preparation for the possible necessity of leaving Florence, at the very time when he was beginning to feel that it had a new attraction for him. That dread was nearly removed now: he must wear his armour still, he must prepare himself for possible demands on his coolness and ingenuity, but he did not feel obliged to take the inconvenient step of leaving Florence and seeking new fortunes. His father had refused the offered atonement—had forced him into defiance; and an old man in a strange place, with his memory gone, was weak enough to be defied.

[7]Tito's implicit desires were working themselves out now in very explicit thoughts. As the freshness of young passion faded, life was taking more and more decidedly for him the aspect of a game in which there was an agreeable mingling of skill and chance.

And the game that might be played in Florence promised to be rapid and exciting; it was a game of revolutionary and party struggle, sure to include plenty of that unavowed action in which brilliant ingenuity, able to get rid of all inconvenient beliefs except that "ginger is hot in the mouth,"* is apt to see the path of superior wisdom.

No sooner were the French guests gone than Florence was as agitated as a colony of ants when an alarming shadow has been removed, and the camp has to be repaired. "How are we to raise the money for the French King? How are we to manage the war with those obstinate Pisan rebels? [8]Above all, how are we to mend our plan of government[9], so as to hit on the best way of getting our magistrates chosen and our laws voted?" Till those questions were well answered trade was in danger of standing still, and [1]that large body of the working men who were not counted as citizens and had not so much as a vote to serve as an anodyne to[2] their stomachs were likely to get impatient. Something must be done.

And first the great bell was sounded, to call the citizens to a parliament in the Piazza de' Signori; and when the crowd was wedged close, and hemmed in by armed men[3] at all the outlets, the Signoria (or Gonfaloniere and eight Priors for the time being) came out and stood by the stone lion on the platform in front of the Old Palace,

6 ⟨new⟩ fresh MS
7 ⟨As the freshness of young passion faded, life⟩ Tito's MS
8 ⟨And how⟩ Above all how MS   9 {plan of} Government MS
1 ⟨the hungry monster Plebs⟩ ⟨that large mass of voting⟩ that large body MS
2 to ⟨its endless⟩ MS   3 armed men] armed men as a sort of sheep-dogs MS

and proposed that twenty chief men of the city should have dictatorial authority given them, by force of which they should for one year choose all magistrates, and set the frame of government in order. And the people shouted their assent, and felt themselves the electors of the Twenty. This kind of "parliament" was a very old Florentine fashion, by which the will of the few was made to seem the choice of the many.

The shouting in the Piazza was soon at an end, but not so the debating inside the Palace: was Florence to have a [4]Great Council after the Venetian mode, where all the officers of government might be elected, and all laws voted by a wide number of citizens of a certain age and of ascertained qualifications, without question of rank or party; or, was it to be governed on a narrower and less popular scheme, in which the hereditary influence of good families would be less adulterated with the votes of shopkeepers? Doctors of law disputed day after day, and far on into the night; Messer Pagolantonio Soderini alleged excellent reasons on the side of the popular scheme; Messer Guidantonio Vespucci alleged reasons equally excellent on the side of a more aristocratic form. It was a question of boiled or roast, which had been prejudged by the palates of the disputants, and the excellent arguing might have been protracted a long while without any other result than that of deferring the cooking. The majority of the men inside the Palace, having power already in their hands, agreed with Vespucci, and thought change should be moderate; the majority outside the palace, conscious of little power and many grievances, were less afraid of change.

And there was a force outside the Palace which was gradually tending to give the vague desires of [5]that majority the character of a determinate will. That force was the preaching of Savonarola. Impelled partly by the [6]spiritual necessity that was laid upon him to guide the people, and partly by the prompting of public men who could get no measures carried without his aid, he was rapidly passing in his daily sermons from the general to the special—from telling his hearers that they must postpone their private passions and interests to the public good, to telling[7] them precisely what sort of government they must[8] have in order to promote that good—from "Choose whatever is best for all" to "Choose the Great Council," and "the Great Council is the will of God."

To Savonarola these were as good as identical propositions. The Great Council was the only practicable plan for giving an expression to the public will large enough to counteract the vitiating influence of party interests; it was a plan that would make honest impartial public action at least possible. And the purer the government of Florence could[9] become—the more secure from the designs of men who saw their own advantage in the moral debasement of their fellows—the nearer would the Florentine people approach the character of a pure community, worthy to lead the way in the renovation of the Church and the world. And Fra Girolamo's mind never stopped short of that sublimest end: the objects towards which he felt himself working had always the same moral magnificence. He had no private malice, he sought no petty gratification. Even in the last terrible days, when ignominy, torture, and the fear of torture, had laid bare every hidden weakness of his soul, he could say to his importunate judges, "Do not wonder if it seems to you that I have told[1] but few things; for my purposes were few and great."[*]

9 could] would 2 3   1 told ⟨you⟩ MS

CHAPTER XXXVI.

ARIADNE DISCROWNS HERSELF

IT was more than three weeks before the contents of the library were all packed and carried away. And Romola, instead of shutting her eyes and ears, had watched the process. [1]The exhaustion consequent on violent emotion is apt to bring a dreamy disbelief in the reality of its cause; and in the evening, when[2] the workmen were gone, Romola took her hand-lamp, and walked slowly round amongst the confusion of straw and wooden cases[3], pausing at every vacant pedestal, every well-known object laid prostrate, with a sort of bitter desire to assure herself that there was a sufficient reason why her love was gone and the world was barren for her. And still, as the evenings came, she went and went again; no longer to assure herself, but because this vivifying of pain and despair about her father's memory was the strongest life left to her affections. On[4] the 23rd of December, she knew that the last packages were going. She ran to the loggia at the top of the house that she might not lose the last pang of seeing the slow wheels move across the bridge.

It was a cloudy day, and nearing dusk[5]. Arno ran dark and shivering; the hills were mournful; and [6]Florence with its girdling stone towers had that silent, tomblike look, which unbroken shadow gives to a city seen from above. Santa Croce, where her father lay, [7]was dark amidst that darkness, and slowly crawling over the bridge, and slowly vanishing up the narrow street, was the white load, like a cruel, deliberate fate carrying away her father's life-long hope to bury it in an unmarked grave. [8]Romola felt less that she was seeing this herself than that her father was conscious of it as he lay helpless[9] under the imprisoning stones, where her hand could not reach his to tell him that he was not alone.

She stood still even after the load had disappeared, heedless of the cold, and soothed by the gloom which seemed to cover her like a mourning garment and shut out the discord of joy. When suddenly the great bell in the palace tower rang[1] out a mighty peal: not the hammer-sound of alarm, but an agitated peal of triumph; and one after another every other bell in every other tower seemed to catch

1 ⟨After any great strain on the emotions there⟩ The *MS*
2 {in the evening} when *MS*   3 {wooden} cases *MS*
4 On] *3C* And on *MS CM 1 2*   5 day {and nearing dusk} *MS*
6 ⟨the city⟩ Florence *MS*   7 ⟨looked⟩ was *MS*
8 ⟨At first⟩ Romola felt less ⟨as if she were⟩ that *MS*
9 lay {helpless} *MS*   1 rang] swung *MS*

the vibration and join the chorus. And as the chorus swelled and swelled till the air seemed made of sound,[2] little flames, vibrating too, as if the sound had caught fire, burst out [3]between the turrets of the palace and on the girdling towers.

That sudden clang, that leaping light, fell on Romola like sharp wounds. They were the triumph of demons at the success of her husband's treachery, and the desolation of her life. Little more than three weeks ago she had been intoxicated with the sound of these[4] very bells; and in the gladness of Florence she had heard a prophecy of her own gladness. But now [5]the general joy seemed cruel to her; she stood aloof from that common life—that Florence which was flinging out its loud exultation to stun the ears of sorrow and loneliness. She could never join hands with gladness again, but only with those whom it was in the hard nature of gladness to forget. And in her bitterness she felt that all rejoicing was mockery. Men shouted pæans with[6] their souls full of heaviness, and then looked in their neighbours' faces to see if there was really such a thing as joy. Romola had lost her belief in the happiness she had once thirsted for: it was a hateful, smiling, soft-handed thing, with a narrow, selfish heart.

She ran down from the loggia, with her hands pressed against her ears, and was[7] hurrying across the ante-chamber, when she was startled by unexpectedly meeting her husband, who was coming to seek her.

His step was elastic, and there was a radiance of satisfaction about him not quite usual.[8]

"What! the noise was a little too much for you?" he said; for Romola, [9]as she started at the sight of him, had[1] pressed her hands all the closer against her ears. He took her gently by the wrist, and drew her arm within his, leading her into the saloon surrounded with the dancing nymphs and fauns, and then went on speaking: "Florence is gone quite mad at[2] getting its Great Council, which is to [3]put an end to all the evils under the sun—[4] especially to the vice of merriment. You may well look[5] stunned, my Romola, and you are cold. You must not stay so late under that windy loggia[6] without wrappings. I was coming to tell you that I am suddenly called to Rome—about[7] some learned business for Bernardo Rucellai. I am going away imme-

---

2 sound,] *MS* sound; *CM 1* sound—*2 3*   3 ⟨on⟩ between *MS*
4 these] *MS* those *CM 1 2 3*   5 ⟨that⟩ the *MS*
6 with ⟨aching hearts⟩ *MS*   7 was ⟨still in that attitude when,⟩ *MS*
8 seek her. {His step . . . usual.} *MS*   9 ⟨though⟩ as she ⟨had⟩ started *MS*
1 had ⟨only⟩ pressed *MS*   2 at ⟨the⟩ getting *MS*
3 ⟨remedy⟩ put an end to *MS*   4 sun—] *MS* sun; *CM 1 2 3*
5 ⟨But I was coming to tell you⟩ You may {well} look *MS*
6 {windy} loggia *MS*   7 Rome—about] *MS* Rome about *CM 1 2 3*

diately, for I [8]am to join my party at San Gaggio* to-night, that we may start early in the morning. I need give you no trouble; I have had my packages made already. It will not be very long before I am back again."

He knew he had nothing to expect from her but quiet endurance of what he said and did. He [9]could not even venture to kiss her brow this evening, but just pressed her hand to his lips, and left her. Tito felt that Romola was[1] a more unforgiving woman than he had imagined; her love was not that sweet clinging instinct, stronger than all judgments, which, he began to see now, made the great charm of a wife. Still, this [2]petrified coldness was better than a passionate, futile opposition.[3] Her pride and capability of seeing where resistance was useless had their convenience[4].

But when the door had closed on Tito, Romola lost the look of cold immobility which came over her like an inevitable frost whenever he approached her. Inwardly she was very far from being in a state of quiet endurance, and the days that had passed since the scene which had divided her from Tito had been days of active planning and preparation for the fulfilment of a purpose.

The first thing she did now was to call old Maso to her.

"Maso," she said, in a decided tone, "we take our journey to-morrow morning. We shall be able now to overtake that first convoy of cloth, while they are waiting at San Piero.* See about the two mules to-night, and be ready to set off with them at break of day, and wait for me at Trespiano."*

She meant to take Maso with her as far as Bologna, and then send him back with letters to her godfather and Tito, telling them that she was gone and never meant to return. She had planned her departure so that its secresy might be perfect, and her broken love and life might be[5] hidden away unscanned by vulgar eyes. Bernardo del Nero had been [6]absent at his villa, willing to escape from political suspicions to his favourite occupation of attending to his land, and she had paid him the debt without a personal interview. He did not even know that the library was sold, and was left to conjecture that some

8 ⟨shall⟩ ⟨am going to⟩ am to MS   9 ⟨did⟩ could MS

1 her. Tito felt that Romola was] her. {The laws of substances are often inconvenient: we make a slight mistake with jars and crucibles, ⟨and that which was soft and yielding becomes of a⟩ something subtle escapes, that which was soft and yielding becomes of a rocky hardness, and nature has no magic that will reverse the change.} {Tito felt that} Romola ⟨, he felt,⟩ was MS

2 ⟨immovable⟩ petrified coldness was better than ⟨active opposition and⟩ a passionate MS

3 opposition: ⟨Romola's⟩ her MS   4 convenience] ⟨convenience⟩ advantage MS

5 might be] MS be CM 1 2 3   6 ⟨away⟩ absent MS

sudden piece of good fortune[7] had enabled Tito to [8]raise this sum of money. Maso had been taken into her confidence only so far that he knew her intended journey was a secret; and to do just what she told him was the thing he cared most for in his [9]withered wintry age.

Romola did not mean to go to bed that night. When she had fastened the door she took her [1]taper to the carved and painted chest which contained her wedding-clothes. The white silk and gold lay there, the long white veil and the circlet of pearls. A great sob rose as she looked at them: they seemed[2] the shroud of her dead happiness. In a tiny gold loop of the circlet a sugar-plum had lodged—a pink hailstone from the shower of sweets: Tito had detected it first, and had said that it should always remain there. At certain moments—and this was one of them—Romola was carried, by a sudden wave of memory, back again into the[3] time of perfect trust, and felt again the presence of the husband whose love made the world as fresh and wonderful to her as to a little child that sits in stillness among the sunny flowers: heard the gentle tones and saw the soft eyes without any lie in them, and breathed again[4] that large freedom of the soul which comes from the faith that the being who is nearest to us is greater than ourselves. And in those brief moments the tears always rose: the woman's lovingness felt something akin to what the bereaved mother feels when the tiny fingers seem to lie warm on her bosom, and yet are marble to her lips as she bends over the silent bed.

But there was something else lying in the chest besides the wedding-clothes: it was something dark and coarse, rolled up in a close bundle. She turned away her eyes from the white and gold to the dark bundle, and as her hands touched the serge, her tears began to be checked. That coarse roughness recalled her fully to the present, from which love and delight were gone. She unfastened the thick white cord and spread the bundle out on the table. It was the grey serge dress of a Sister belonging to the Third order of St. Francis, living in the world but specially[5] devoted to deeds of piety—a personage whom the Florentines were accustomed to call[6] a Pinzochera. Romola was going to put on this dress as a disguise, and she determined to put it on at once, so that[7], if she needed sleep before the morning, she might wake up in perfect readiness to be gone. She put off her black garment, and as she thrust her soft white arms into the harsh sleeves

7 conjecture {that} some sudden {piece of} good fortune *MS*
8 ⟨find⟩ raise *MS*   9 ⟨old age⟩ withered wintry ⟨days⟩ age *MS*
1 ⟨lamp⟩ taper *MS*   2 them: they seemed] it: it seemed *MS*
3 the] that *MS*   4 breathed again] *3P* breathed over again *MS CM 1 2*
5 specially] especially *2 3*
6 accustomed to call] accustomed, with no complimentary intention, to call *MS*
7 {so} that *MS*

of the serge mantle and felt the hard [8]girdle of rope hurt her
fingers as she tied it, she courted those rude sensations: they were in
keeping with her new scorn of that thing called pleasure which made
men base—that dexterous contrivance for selfish ease, that shrinking
from endurance and strain, when others were bowing beneath
burthens too heavy for them, which now made one image with her
husband.

Then she gathered her long hair together, [9]drew it away tight from
her face, [1]bound it in a great hard knot at the back of her head, [2]and
taking a square piece of black silk, [3]tied it in the fashion of a kerchief
[4]close across her head and under her chin; and over that she drew the
cowl. She lifted the candle to the mirror. Surely her disguise would
be complete to any one who had not lived very near to her. [5]To herself she looked strangely like her brother Dino: the full oval of the
check had only to be wasted; the eyes, already sad, had only to
become a little sunken[6]. Was she getting more like him in anything
else? Only in this, that she understood now how men could be
prompted to rush away for ever from earthly delights, how they could
be prompted to dwell on images of sorrow rather than of beauty and
joy.[7]

But she did not linger at the mirror: she set about collecting and
packing all the relics of her father and mother that were too large to
be carried in her small travelling wallet. They were all to be put in
the chest along with her wedding-clothes, and the chest was to be
committed to her godfather when she was safely gone. First she laid
in the portraits; then one by one every little thing that had a sacred
memory clinging to it was put into her wallet or into the chest.

She paused. There was still something else to be stript away from
her, belonging[8] to that past on which she was going to turn her back
for ever. She put her thumb and forefinger[9] to her betrothal ring; but
they rested there, without drawing it off. Romola's mind had been
rushing with an impetuous current towards this act for which she was
preparing: the act of quitting a husband who had disappointed all her
trust, the act of breaking an outward tie that no longer represented
the inward bond of love. But that force of outward symbols by which
our active life is knit together so as to make an inexorable external
identity for us, not to be shaken by our wavering consciousness, gave

8 ⟨cord⟩ girdle MS   9 ⟨and⟩ drew MS   1 ⟨and⟩ bound MS
2 ⟨then she took⟩ and taking MS   3 ⟨and⟩ tied MS
4 ⟨over⟩ ⟨under her chin⟩ close across her head MS   5 ⟨But to⟩ To MS
6 {a little} sunken ⟨and her face would be almost like⟩. Was MS
7 joy. ⟨In every thing else that {visionary} life was as remote from her {, as repulsive to her} as ever.⟩ ¶ But MS
8 her, belonging] MS 3P her belonging CM 1 2
9 forefinger] MS her forefinger CM 1 2 3

a strange effect to this simple movement towards taking off her ring—
a movement which was but a small sequence of her energetic resolution. It brought a vague but arresting sense that she was somehow
violently rending[1] her life in two: a presentiment[2] that the strong
impulse which had seemed to exclude doubt and make her path clear
might after all be blindness, and that there was something in human
bonds which must prevent them from being broken with the breaking
of illusions.

If that beloved Tito who had placed the betrothal ring on her
finger was not in any valid sense the same Tito whom she had ceased
to love, why should she return to him the sign of their union, and
not rather retain it as a memorial? And this act, which came as a palpable demonstration of her own and his identity, had a power, unexplained to herself, of shaking Romola. It is the way with half the
truth amidst which we live, that it only haunts us and makes dull
pulsations that are never born into sound. [3]But there was a passionate
voice speaking within her that presently nullified all such muffled
murmurs.

"It cannot be! I cannot be subject to him. He is false. I shrink from
him. I despise him!"

She snatched the ring from her finger and laid it on the table
against the [4]pen with which she meant to write. Again she felt that
there could be no law for her but the law of her affections. That [5]ten-
derness and keen fellow-feeling for the near and the loved which are
the main outgrowth of the affections[6], had made the religion of her
life: they had made her patient in spite of natural impetuosity; they
would have sufficed to make her heroic. But now all that strength was
gone, or, rather, it was converted into the strength of repulsion. She
had recoiled from Tito in proportion to the energy of that young
belief and love which he had disappointed, of that life-long devotion
to her father against which he had committed an irredeemable
offence. And now it[7] seemed as if all motive had slipped away from
her, except the indignation and scorn that made her tear herself asunder from him. She was not acting after any precedent, or obeying any
adopted maxims. The grand severity of the Stoical philosophy in
which her father had taken care to instruct her, was familiar enough
to her ears and lips, and[8] its lofty spirit had raised certain echoes
within her; but she had never used it, never needed it as a rule of
life. She had endured and forborne* because she loved: maxims which

---

1 {violently} rending *MS*
2 a presentiment] *1 2 3* a palpitating presentiment *MS CM*   3 ⟨And⟩ But *MS*
4 ⟨paper on⟩ pen with which *MS*   5 ⟨pity⟩ tenderness *MS*
6 {the} affections *MS*   7 And now it] And it *1 2 3*
8 and ⟨had⟩ its lofty spirit had raised ⟨its⟩ certain *MS*

told her to [9]feel less, and not to cling close lest the onward course of
great Nature should jar her, had been as powerless on her tenderness
as they had been on her father's yearning for just fame. She had
appropriated no theories: she had simply felt strong in the strength of
affection, and life without that energy came to her as an entirely new
problem.

She was going to solve the problem in a way that seemed to her
very simple. Her mind had never yet bowed to any obligation apart
from personal love and reverence; she had no keen sense of any other
human relations, and all she had to obey now was the instinct to
sever herself from the man she loved no longer.

Yet the unswerving resolution was accompanied with continually
varying phases of anguish. And now that the active preparation for
her departure was almost finished, she lingered: she deferred writing
the irrevocable words of parting from all her little world. The emotions of the past weeks[1] seemed to rush in again with cruel hurry,
and take possession even of her limbs. She was going to write and her
hand fell. Bitter tears came now at the delusion which had blighted
her young years: tears very different from the sob of remembered
happiness with which she had looked at the circlet of pearls and the
pink hailstone. And now she felt a tingling shame at the words of
ignominy she had cast at Tito—"Have you robbed some one else who
is *not* dead?" To have had such words wrung from her—to have
uttered them to her husband seemed a degradation of her whole life.
Hard speech between those who have loved is hideous in the
memory, like the sight of greatness and beauty sunk into vice and
rags.

That heart-cutting comparison of the present with the past urged
itself upon Romola till it even transformed itself into wretched sensations: she seemed benumbed to everything but inward throbbings,
and began to feel the need of some hard contact. She drew her hands
tight along the harsh knotted cord[2] that hung from her waist. She[3]
started to her feet and seized the rough lid of the chest[4]: there was
nothing else to go in? No. She closed the lid, pressing her hand upon
the rough carving, and locked it.

Then she remembered that she had still to complete her equipment
as a Pinzochera. The large leather purse or scarsella, with small coin
in it, had to be hung on the cord at her waist (her florins and small
jewels, presents from her godfather and cousin Brigida, were safely
fastened[5] within her serge mantle)—and on the other side must hang

---

9 ⟨love⟩ feel *MS*   1 weeks ⟨repeated themselves with⟩ *MS*
2 knotted cord] cord *MS*   3 She] Then she *MS*   4 chest] *cassone MS*
5 {presents from her godfather and cousin Brigida,} were safely fastened ⟨inside⟩
within *MS*

the rosary. It did not occur to Romola as she hung that rosary by her side that something else besides the mere garb would perhaps be necessary to enable her to pass as a Pinzochera, and that her whole air and expression were as little as possible like those of a sister whose eyelids were used to be bent and whose lips were used to[6] move in silent iteration. Her inexperience prevented her from picturing distant details, and it helped her proud courage in shutting out any foreboding of danger and insult. She did not know that any Florentine woman had ever done exactly what[7] she was going to do: unhappy wives often took refuge[8] with their friends, or in the cloister, she knew, but both those courses were impossible to her; she had invented a lot for herself—to go to the most learned woman in the world,[9] Cassandra Fedele, at Venice, and ask her how an instructed woman could support herself in a lonely life there. She was not daunted by the practical difficulties in the way or the dark uncertainty at the end. Her life could never be happy any more, but it must not, could not be ignoble. [1]And by a pathetic mixture of childish romance with her woman's trials, the philosophy which had nothing to do with this great decisive deed of hers had its place in her imagination of the future: so far as she conceived her solitary loveless life at all, she saw it animated by a proud stoical heroism, and by an indistinct but strong purpose of labour, that she might be wise enough to write something which would rescue her father's name from oblivion. After all, she was only[2] a young girl—this poor Romola, who had found herself at the end of her joys.

There [3]were other things yet to be done. There was a small key in a casket on the table—but now Romola perceived that her taper was dying out, and she had forgotten to provide herself with any other light. In a few moments the room was in total darkness. Feeling her way to the nearest chair, she sat down to wait for the morning.

[4]Her purpose in seeking the key had called up certain memories which had come back upon her during the past week with the new vividness that remembered words always have for us when we have learned to give them a new meaning. [5]Since the shock of the revelation which had seemed to divide her for ever from Tito, that last interview with Dino had never been for many hours together out of her mind. And it solicited her all the more, because while its

6 and whose lips were used to] and her lips to *MS*   7 {exactly} what *MS*
8 refuge ⟨from their husbands⟩ with their friends {or in the cloister} *MS*
9 to {the most learned woman in the world,} *MS*
1 ⟨And one [?smiles] to think that⟩ And *MS*
2 After all, she was only] She was after all, only *MS*
3 ⟨was one thing⟩ were other things *MS*
4 ⟨The purpose with which she had sought⟩ Her *MS*
5 ⟨That⟩ Since the shock of ⟨that⟩ the *MS*

remembered images pressed upon her almost with the imperious force of sensations, they raised struggling thoughts which resisted their influence. She could not prevent herself from hearing inwardly the dying prophetic voice saying again and again,—"The man whose face was a blank loosed thy hand and departed; and as he went, I could see his face, and it was the face of the Great Tempter. . . . And thou, Romola, didst wring thy hands and seek for water, and there was none. . . . and the plain was bare and stony again, and thou wast alone in the midst of it. . . . and[6] then it seemed that the night fell, and I saw no more." She could not prevent herself from dwelling with a sort of agonized fascination on [7]the wasted face; on the straining gaze at the crucifix; on the awe which had compelled her to kneel; on the last [8]broken words and then the unbroken silence—on all the details of [9]the death-scene, which had seemed like a sudden opening into a world apart from that of her life-long knowledge.

But her mind was roused to resistance of impressions that, from being obvious phantoms, seemed to be getting solid in the daylight. As a strong body struggles against fumes with the more violence when they begin to be stifling, a strong soul struggles against phantasies with all the more alarmed energy when they threaten to govern in the place of thought. What had the words of that vision to do with her real sorrows? That fitting of certain words was a mere chance; the rest was all vague—nay, those words themselves were vague; they were determined by nothing but her brother's memories and beliefs. He believed there was something fatal in pagan learning; he believed that celibacy was more holy than marriage; he remembered their home, and all the objects in the library; and of these threads the vision was woven. What reasonable warrant could she have had for believing in such a vision and acting on it? None. True as the voice of foreboding had proved, Romola saw with unshaken conviction that to have renounced Tito in obedience to a warning like that, would have been meagre-hearted folly. Her trust had been delusive, but she would have chosen over again to have acted on it rather than be a creature led by [1]phantoms and disjointed whispers in a world where there was the large music of reasonable speech, and the warm grasp of living hands.

But the persistent presence of these memories, linking themselves in her imagination[2] with her actual lot, gave her a glimpse of understanding into the lives which had before lain utterly aloof from her sympathy—the lives of the men[3] and women who were led by such inward images and voices.

6 it . . . and] *MS* it. And *CM 1 2 3*   7 ⟨that⟩ the wasted face, ⟨that⟩ the *MS*
8 ⟨struggling⟩ broken *MS*   9 ⟨that scene⟩ the death scene *MS*
1 ⟨disjointed⟩ phantoms *MS*   2 linking themselves {in her imagination} *MS*
3 {the} men *MS*

"If they were only a little stronger in me," she said to herself, "I should lose the sense of what that vision really was, and take it for a prophetic light. I might in time get to be a seer[4] of visions myself, like the Suora Maddalena,* and Camilla Rucellai[5], and the rest."

Romola shuddered at the possibility. All the instruction, all the main influences of her life had gone to fortify her scorn of that sickly superstition which led men and women, with eyes too weak for the daylight, to sit in dark swamps and try to read human destiny by the chance flame of wandering vapours.

And yet she was conscious of something deeper than that coincidence of words which made the parting contact with her dying brother live anew in her mind, and gave her a[6] new sisterhood to the wasted face. If there were much more of such experience as his in the world, she would like to understand it—would even like to learn the thoughts of men who sank in ecstasy before the pictured agonies of martyrdom. There seemed to be something more than madness in that supreme fellowship with suffering. The springs were all dried up around her: she wondered what other waters there were at which men drank and found strength in the desert. And those moments in the Duomo when she had sobbed with a mysterious mingling of rapture and pain, while Fra Girolamo offered himself a willing sacrifice for the people, came back to her as if they had been a transient taste of some such far-off fountain. But again she shrank from impressions that were alluring her within the sphere of visions and narrow fears which compelled men to outrage natural affections as Dino had done.

This was the tangled web that Romola had in her mind as she sat weary in the darkness. No radiant angel came across the gloom with a clear message for her. In those times, as now, there[7] were human beings who never saw angels or heard perfectly clear messages. Such truth as came to them was brought confusedly in the voices and deeds of men not at all like the seraphs of unfailing wing and piercing vision—men who[8] believed falsities as well as truths, and did the wrong as well as the right. The helping hands stretched out to them were the hands of men who stumbled and often saw[9] dimly, so that these beings unvisited by angels had no other choice[1] than to grasp that stumbling guidance along the path of reliance and action which is the path of life, or else to pause in loneliness and disbelief, which is no path, but the arrest of inaction and death.

And so Romola, seeing no ray across the darkness, and heavy with conflict that changed nothing, sank at last to sleep.

4 seer] seeress *MS*   5 Maddalena, {and Camilla Rucellai} *MS*
6 gave her a] gave a *1 2 3*
7 In those times, as now, there] Even in times gone by there *MS*
8 {men} who *MS*   9 {often} saw *MS*   1 no {other} choice *MS*

CHAPTER XXXVII.

THE TABERNACLE UNLOCKED

ROMOLA was waked by a tap at the door. The cold [1]light of early morning was in the room, and Maso was come for the travelling wallet. The old man could not help starting when she opened the door, and showed him, instead of the graceful outline he had been used to, crowned with the brightness of her hair, the thick folds of the grey mantle and the pale face[2] shadowed by the dark cowl.

"It is well, Maso," said Romola, trying to speak in the calmest voice, and make the old man easy. "Here is the wallet quite ready. You will go on quietly, and I shall not be far behind you. When you get out of the gates, you may go more slowly, for I shall perhaps join you before you get to Trespiano."

She closed the door behind him, and then[3] put her hand on the key which she had taken from the casket the last thing in the night. It was the original key of the little painted tabernacle: Tito had forgotten to [4]drown it in the Arno, and it had lodged, as such small things will, in the corner of the embroidered scarsella which he wore with the purple tunic. One day, long after their marriage, Romola had found it there, and had put it by, without using it, but with a sense of satisfaction that the key was within reach. The cabinet on which the tabernacle stood had been moved to the side of the room, close to one of the windows, where the pale morning light[5] fell upon it so as[6] to make the painted forms discernible enough to Romola, who knew them well,—the triumphant Bacchus, with his clusters and his vine-clad spear, clasping the[7] crowned Ariadne; the Loves showering roses, the wreathed vessel[8], the cunning-eyed dolphins, and the rippled sea; all encircled by a flowery border, like a bower of paradise. Romola looked at the familiar images with new bitterness and repulsion: they seemed a more pitiable [9]mockery than ever on this chill morning, when she had waked up to wander in loneliness. They had been no tomb of sorrow, but a lying screen. Foolish Ariadne! with her gaze of love, as if that bright face, with its hyacinthine curls like tendrils among the vines, held the deep secret of her life!

---

1 ⟨morning⟩ light *MS*
2 face ⟨with no halo but the cowl.⟩ ⟨with the dark cowl for a halo⟩ *MS*
3 then ⟨took up⟩ *MS*   4 ⟨bury⟩ drown *MS*
5 {pale} morning light *MS*   6 so as ⟨to [?show] the painting distinctly⟩ *MS*
7 {clasping ⟨with the right⟩} the *MS*
8 vessel] *MS 2 3* vessels *CM 1*   9 ⟨lying⟩ mockery *MS*

"Ariadne is [1]wonderfully transformed," thought Romola. "She would look strange among the vines and the roses now."

She took up the mirror, and looked at herself [2]once more. But the sight was so startling in this morning light that she laid[3] it down again, with a sense of shrinking almost as strong as that with which she had turned from the joyous Ariadne. The recognition of her own face, with the cowl about it, brought back the dread lest she should be drawn at last into fellowship with some wretched superstition—into the company of the howling fanatics[4] and weeping nuns who had been her contempt from childhood till now. She thrust the key into the tabernacle hurriedly: hurriedly she opened it, and took out the crucifix, without looking at it; then, with trembling fingers, she passed a cord through the little ring, hung the crucifix round her neck, and hid it in the bosom of her mantle. "For Dino's sake," she said to herself.

Still there were the letters to be written which Maso was to carry back from Bologna. They were very brief. The first said,

"Tito, my love for you is dead; and therefore, so far as I was yours, I too am dead. Do not try to put in force any laws for the sake of fetching me back: that would bring you no happiness. The Romola you married can never return. I need explain nothing to you after the words I uttered to you the last time we spoke long together. If you supposed them to be words of transient anger, you will know now that they were the sign of an irreversible change.

"I think you will fulfil my wish that my bridal chest[5] should be sent to my godfather, who gave it me. It contains my wedding clothes and the portraits and other relics of my father and mother."

She folded the ring inside the letter, and wrote Tito's name outside. The next letter was to Bernardo del Nero:—

"DEAREST GODFATHER,—If I could have been any good to your life by staying, I would not have gone away to a distance. But now I am gone. Do not ask the reason; and if you loved[6] my father, try to prevent any one from seeking me. I could not bear my life at Florence. I cannot bear to tell any one why. Help to cover my lot in silence. I have asked that my bridal chest[7] should be sent to you: when you open it, you will know the reason[8]. Please to give all the things that were my mother's to my cousin Brigida, and ask her to forgive me for not saying any words of parting to her.

"Farewell, my second father. The best thing I have in life is still to remember your goodness and be grateful to you.

ROMOLA.

1 ⟨?strangely⟩ wonderfully *MS*   2 ⟨again⟩ once more *MS*
3 laid ⟨down the mirror⟩ *MS*   4 {the} howling fanatics *MS*
5 bridal chest] *cassone MS*   6 loved] love *3*
7 bridal chest] *cassone MS*   8 reason ⟨why⟩ *MS*

Romola put the letters, along with the crucifix, within the bosom of her mantle, and then felt that everything was done. She was ready now to depart.

[9]No one was stirring in the house, and she went almost as quietly as a grey phantom down the stairs and into the silent street. Her heart was palpitating violently, yet she[1] enjoyed the sense of her firm tread on the broad flags—of the swift movement, which was like a chained-up resolution set free at last. The anxiety to carry out her act, and the dread of any obstacle, averted sorrow; and as she reached the Ponte Rubaconte, she felt less that Santa Croce was in her sight than that the [2]yellow streak of morning which parted the grey was [3]getting broader and broader, and that, unless she hastened her steps, she should have to encounter faces. Her simplest road was to go right on to the Borgo Pinti, and then along by the walls to the Porta San Gallo, from which she must leave the city;[4] and this road carried her by the Piazza di Santa Croce. But she walked as steadily[5] and rapidly as ever though the piazza, not trusting herself to look towards the church. The thought that any eyes might be turned on her with a look of curiosity and recognition, and that indifferent minds might be set speculating on her private sorrows, made Romola shrink physically as from the imagination of torture. She felt degraded even by that act of her husband from which she was helplessly suffering[6]. But there was no sign that any eyes looked forth from windows to notice this [7]tall grey sister, with the firm step, and proud attitude of the cowled head. Her road lay aloof from the stir of early traffic, and when she reached the Porta San Gallo, it was easy to pass while a dispute was going forward about the toll for[8] panniers of eggs and market produce which were just entering.

Out! Once past the houses of the *Borgo* and she[9] would be beyond the last fringe of Florence, the sky would be broad above her, and she would have entered on her new life—a life of loneliness and endurance, but of freedom. She had been strong enough to snap asunder the bonds she had accepted in blind faith: whatever befel her, she would no more feel the breath of soft, hated lips warm upon her cheek, no longer feel the breath of an odious mind stifling her own. The bare wintry morning, the chill air, were welcome in their

9 ⟨The house was in [?perfect] quietness and Romola⟩ No *MS*
1 she ⟨trod the still pavement with resolute⟩ *MS*
2 ⟨broad streak⟩ yellow streak *MS*   3 ⟨widening⟩ getting broader *MS*
4 city;] *3P* city, *MS CM 1 2*   5 {as} steadily *MS*
6 suffering ⟨, and would have had her lips sealed against⟩. *MS*
7 ⟨singular⟩ tall grey sister with ⟨her tall [?frame] and⟩ {the} firm step *MS*
8 for ⟨a load of hay⟩ *MS*
9 *Borgo* and ⟨she would be quite beyond the [?breath] of Florence⟩ she] *MS Borgo*, she *CM Borgo*, she *1 2 3*

Escaped

severity: the leafless trees, the sombre hills, were not haunted by the gods of beauty and joy, whose worship she had forsaken for ever.

But presently the light burst forth with sudden strength, and shadows were thrown across the road. It seemed that the sun was going to chase away the greyness. The light is perhaps never felt more strongly as a divine presence stirring all those inarticulate sensibilities which are our deepest life, than in these moments when it [1]instantaneously awakens the shadows. A certain awe which inevitably accompanied this most momentous act of her life became a more conscious element in Romola's feeling as she found herself in the sudden presence of the impalpable golden glory and the long shadow of herself that was not to be escaped. Hitherto she had met no one but an occasional contadino with mules, and the many turnings of the road on the level prevented her from seeing that Maso was not very far ahead of her. But when she had passed Pietra* and was on rising ground, she lifted up the hanging roof of her cowl and looked eagerly before her.

The cowl was dropped again immediately. She had seen, not Maso, but—two[2] monks, who were approaching within a few yards of[3] her. The edge of her cowl making a penthouse on her brow had shut out the objects above the level of her eyes, and for the last few moments she had been looking at nothing but the brightness on the path and at her own shadow, tall and shrouded like a dread spectre. She wished now that she had not looked up. Her disguise made her especially dislike to encounter monks: they might expect some pious passwords of which she knew nothing, and she walked along with a careful appearance of unconsciousness till she had seen the skirts of the black mantles pass by her. The encounter had made her heart beat disagreeably, for Romola had an uneasiness in her religious disguise, a shame at this studied concealment, which was made more distinct by a special effort to appear unconscious under actual glances.

But the black skirts would be gone the faster because they were going down hill; and seeing a great flat stone against a cypress that rose from a projecting green bank, she yielded to the desire which the slight shock had given her, to sit down and rest.

She turned her back on Florence, not meaning to look at it till the monks were quite out of sight; and raising the edge of her cowl again when she had seated herself, she discerned Maso and the mules at a distance where it was not hopeless for her to overtake them, as the old man would probably linger in expectation of her.

Meanwhile she might pause a little. She was free and alone.

---

1 ⟨suddenly⟩ instantaneously *MS*   2 but—two] but two *MS*
3 of] before *MS*

CHAPTER XXXVIII.

[1]THE BLACK MARKS BECOME MAGICAL

THAT journey of Tito's to Rome, which had removed many difficulties from Romola's departure, had been resolved on quite suddenly, at a supper, only the evening before.

Tito had set out towards that supper with agreeable expectations. The meats were likely to be delicate, the wines choice, the company distinguished; for the place of entertainment was the Selva, or Orto de' Rucellai, or, as we should say, the Rucellai Gardens; and the host, Bernardo Rucellai, was quite a typical Florentine grandee. Even his family name has a significance which is [2]prettily symbolic: properly understood, it may bring before us a little lichen, popularly named *orcella* or *roccella*, which grows on the rocks of Greek isles and in the Canaries; and having drunk a great deal of light into its little stems and button-heads, will, under certain circumstances,* give it out again as a reddish purple dye, very grateful to the eyes of men. By bringing the excellent secret of this dye, called *oricello*, from the Levant to Florence, a certain merchant, who lived nearly a hundred years before our Bernardo's time, won for himself[3] and his descendants much wealth, and the pleasantly suggestive surname of Oricellari, or Roccellari, which on Tuscan tongues speedily became Rucellai. And our Bernardo,* who stands out more prominently than the rest on this purple background, had added all sorts of distinction to the family name: he had married the sister of Lorenzo de' Medici, and had had the most splendid wedding in the memory of Florentine upholstery; and for these and other virtues he had been sent on embassies to France and Venice, and had been chosen Gonfaloniere; he had not only built himself a fine palace, but had finished putting the black and white marble façade to the church of Santa Maria Novella;* he had planted a garden with rare trees,* and had made it classic ground by receiving within it the meetings of the Platonic Academy,

---

1 ⟨[2 or 3 words] Supper⟩ The *MS*   2 ⟨pregnant⟩ prettily symbolic *MS*
3 lichen, popularly named *orcella* . . . himself] lichen which grows on the rocks of Greek isles and in the Canaries . . . very grateful to the eyes of men. The said little lichen is called *oricella* or *roccella*, and by bringing the excellent secret of its dye from the Levant to Florence, a certain ⟨Giovanni⟩ merchant who lived nearly a hundred years before our Bernardo's time won ⟨much wealth⟩ for himself *MS*

'Father, I will be guided'

orphaned by the death of Lorenzo; he had written [4]an excellent, learned book,* of a new topographical sort, about ancient Rome; he had collected antiquities; he had a pure Latinity. The simplest account of him, one sees, reads like a laudatory epitaph, at the end of which the Greek and Ausonian Muses might be confidently requested to tear their hair,* and Nature to desist from any second attempt to combine so many virtues with one set of viscera.

His invitation had been conveyed to Tito through Lorenzo Tornabuoni, with an emphasis which would have suggested that the object of the gathering was political, even if the public questions of the time had been less absorbing. As it was, Tito felt sure that some party purposes were to be furthered by the excellent flavours of stewed fish and old Greek wine; for Bernardo Rucellai was not simply an influential personage, but he was one of the elect Twenty who for three weeks had held the reins of Florence. This assurance put Tito in the best spirits as he made his way to the Via della Scala, where the classic garden was to be found: without it, he might have had some uneasy speculation as to whether the [5]high company he would have the honour of meeting was likely to be dull as well as distinguished; for he had had experience of various dull suppers even in the Rucellai gardens, and especially of the dull-philosophic[6] sort, wherein he had not only been called upon to accept an entire scheme of the universe (which would have been easy to him[7]), but to listen to an exposition of the same, from the origin of things to their complete ripeness in the tractate of the philosopher then speaking.

It was a dark evening, and it was only when Tito crossed the occasional light of a lamp suspended before an image of the Virgin, that the outline of his figure was discernible enough for recognition. At such [8]moments any one caring to watch his passage from one of these lights to another might have observed that the tall and graceful personage with the mantle folded round him was followed constantly by a very different form, thick-set and elderly, in a serge tunic and felt hat. The conjunction might have been taken for mere chance, since there were many passengers along the streets at this hour. But when Tito stopped at the gate of the Rucellai gardens, the figure behind stopped too. The *sportello*, or [9]smaller door of the gate, was already being held open by the servant, who, in the distraction of attending to some question, had not yet closed it [1]since the last arrival, and Tito turned in rapidly, giving his name to the servant, and passing on

4 ⟨a very⟩ an excellent *MS*
5 ⟨distinguished assemblage was⟩ high company *MS*
6 dull-philosophic] *MS* dull philosophic *CM 1 2 3*   7 easy {to him} *MS*
8 ⟨times⟩ moments *MS*
9 ⟨small door within⟩ smaller *MS*   1 ⟨after⟩ since *MS*

between the evergreen bushes that shone like metal in the torchlight. The follower turned in too.

"Your name?" said the servant.

"Baldassarre Calvo," was the immediate answer.

"You are not a guest; the guests have all passed."

"I belong to Tito Melema, who has just gone in. I am to wait in the gardens."

The servant hesitated. "I had orders to admit only guests. Are you a servant of Messer Tito?"

"No, friend, I am not a servant; I am a scholar."

There are men to whom you need only say, "I am a buffalo," in a certain tone of quiet confidence, and they will let you pass. The porter gave way at once, Baldassarre entered, and heard the door closed and chained behind him, as he too [2]disappeared among the shining bushes.

Those ready and firm answers argued a great change in Baldassarre since [3]the last meeting face to face with Tito, when the dagger broke in two. The change had declared itself in a startling way.

At the moment when the shadow of Tito passed in front of the hovel as he departed homeward, Baldassarre was sitting in that state of after-tremor [4]known to every one who is liable to great outbursts of passion: a state in which physical powerlessness is sometimes accompanied[5] by an exceptional lucidity of thought, as if that disengagement of excited passion[6] had carried away a fire-mist and left clearness behind it. He felt unable to rise and walk away just yet; his limbs seemed benumbed[7]; he was cold, and his hand[8] shook. But in that bodily helplessness he sat[9] surrounded, not by the habitual dimness and vanishing shadows, but by the clear images of the past: he was living again in an unbroken course through that life[1] which seemed a long preparation for the taste of bitterness. For some minutes he was[2] too thoroughly absorbed by the images to reflect on the fact that he saw them, and note the fact as a change. But when that sudden clearness had travelled through the distance, and came at last to rest on the scene just gone by, he felt fully where he was: he remembered Monna Lisa and Tessa. Ah! *he* then was the mysterious husband; he who had another wife in the Via de' Bardi. It was time to pick up the broken dagger and go—go and leave no trace of himself; for to hide his feebleness seemed the thing most like power that

2 ⟨passed⟩ disappeared *MS*   3 ⟨that⟩ the *MS*
4 ⟨liable⟩ known *MS*   5 accompanied ⟨or followed⟩ *MS*
6 {excited} passion *MS*   7 {be}numbed *MS*   8 hand] hands *1 2 3*
9 sat ⟨without reflecting on the fact so as to [?note] that it was⟩ *MS*
1 life ⟨with and for Tito⟩ *MS*
2 bitterness. {For some ⟨moments⟩ minutes} He was *MS*

was left to him. He leaned to take up the fragments of the dagger; then he turned towards the book which lay open at his side. It was a fine large manuscript, an odd volume of Pausanias. The moonlight was upon it, and he could see the large letters at the head of the page:

ΜΕΣΣΗΝΙΚΑ. ΚΒ'*

In old days he had known Pausanias familiarly; yet[3] an hour or two ago he had been looking hopelessly at that page, and it had suggested no more meaning to him than if the letters had been black weather-marks on a wall; but at this moment they were once more the magic signs that conjure up a world. That moonbeam falling on the letters had raised Messenia before him, and its struggle against the Spartan oppression. He snatched up the book, but the light was too pale for him to read further by. No matter; he knew that chapter; he read inwardly. He saw the stoning of the traitor Aristocrates*—stoned by a whole people, who cast him out from their borders to lie unburied, and set up a pillar with verses upon it, telling how Time had brought home justice to the unjust. The words arose within him, and stirred innumerable vibrations of memory. He forgot that he was old: he could almost have shouted. The light was come again, mother of knowledge and joy![4] In that exultation his limbs recovered their strength: he started up with his broken dagger and book, and went out under the broad moonlight. It was a nipping frosty air, but Baldassarre could feel no chill—he only felt the glow of conscious power. He walked about and paused on all the open spots of that high ground, and looked down on the domed and towered city, sleeping darkly under its sleeping guardians, the mountains; on the pale gleam of the river; on[5] the valley vanishing towards the peaks of snow; and felt himself master of them all. That sense of mental empire which belongs to us all in moments of exceptional clearness was intensified for him by the long days and nights in which memory had been little more than the consciousness of something gone. That city, which had been a weary labyrinth, was material that he could subdue to his purposes now: his mind glanced through its affairs with flashing conjecture; he was once more a man who knew cities, whose sense of vision[6] was instructed with large experience, and who[7] [8]felt the keen delight of [9]holding all things in the grasp of language. Names! Images!—his mind rushed through its wealth without pausing, like one who enters on a great inheritance.

But admist all that rushing eagerness there was one End[1] presiding

3 yet] but MS   4 unjust. {The words arose . . . joy.} MS
5 river; on] river and on MS   6 {sense of} vision MS
7 and who] who MS   8 ⟨knew⟩ felt MS   9 ⟨grasping⟩ holding MS
1 End] 3C end MS CM 1 2

in Baldassarre's consciousness,—a dark deity in the inmost cell, who only seemed forgotten while his hecatomb* was being prepared. And when the first triumph in the certainty of recovered power had[2] had its way, his thoughts centred themselves on Tito. That fair slippery viper could not escape him now: thanks to struggling justice, the heart that never quivered with tenderness for another had its sensitive selfish fibres that could be reached by the sharp point of anguish. The soul that bowed to no right, bowed to the great lord of mortals, Pain.

He could search into every secret of Tito's life now: he knew some of the secrets already, and [3]the failure of the broken dagger, which seemed like frustration, had been the beginning of achievement. Doubtless that sudden rage had shaken away the obstruction which stifled his soul. Twice before, when his memory had partially returned, it had been in consequence of sudden excitation: once when he had had to defend himself from an enraged dog; once when he had been overtaken by the waves and had had to scramble up a rock to save himself.

Yes, but if this time, as then, the light were to die out, and the dreary conscious blank come back again! This time the light was stronger and steadier; but what security was there that before the morrow the dark fog would not be round him again? Even the fear seemed like the beginning of feebleness: he thought with alarm that he might sink the faster for this excited vigil of his on the hill, which was expending his force; and after seeking anxiously for a sheltered corner where he might lie down, he nestled at last against a heap of warm garden straw, and so fell asleep.

When he opened his eyes again it was daylight. The first moments were filled with strange bewilderment: he was a man with a double[4] identity; to which had he awaked?—to the life of dim-sighted sensibilities, like[5] the said heirship of some fallen greatness, or to the life of recovered power? Surely the last, for the events of the night all came back to him: the recognition of the page in Pausanias, the crowding resurgence of facts and names, the sudden wide prospect which had given him such a moment as that of the Mænad in the glorious amaze of her morning waking on the mountain top.* He took up the book again, he read, he remembered without reading. He saw a name, and the images of deeds rose with it; he saw the mention of a deed, and he linked it with a name. There were stories of inexpiable crimes, but stories also of guilt that seemed successful. [6]There were sanctuaries

2 had ⟨spent itself⟩ MS
3 ⟨that⟩ the failure of the broken dagger ⟨had been⟩ which MS
4 {a} double MS
5 sensibilities, like] MS sensibilities like CM 1 2 3
6 ⟨The avenging gods were not all powerful⟩ There MS

for swift-footed miscreants; baseness had its armour, and the weapons of justice sometimes broke against it. What then? If baseness triumphed everywhere else, if it could heap to itself all the goods of the world, and even hold the keys of hell, it would never triumph over the hatred which it had itself awakened[7]. It could devise no torture that would seem greater than the torture of submitting to its smile. Baldassarre felt the indestructible independent force of a supreme emotion, which knows no terror, and asks for no motive—which is itself an ever-burning motive, consuming all other desire. And now, in this morning light, when the assurance came again that the fine fibres of association were active still, and that his recovered self had not departed, all his gladness was but the hope of vengeance.

From that time till the evening on which we have seen him [8]enter the Rucellai gardens, he had been incessantly, but cautiously, inquiring into [9]Tito's position and all his circumstances, and there was hardly a day on which he did not contrive to follow his movements. But he wished not to arouse any alarm in Tito: he wished to secure a moment when the hated favourite of blind fortune was at the summit of confident ease, surrounded by chief men on whose favour he depended. It was not any retributive payment or recognition of himself for his own behoof, on which Baldassarre's whole soul was bent: it was to find the sharpest edge of disgrace and shame by which a selfish smiler could be pierced; it was to[1] send through his marrow the most sudden shock of dread[2]. He was content to lie hard, and live stintedly—he had spent [3]the greater part of his remaining money in buying another poniard: his hunger and his thirst were after nothing exquisite but an exquisite vengeance. He had avoided addressing himself to any one whom he suspected of intimacy[4] with Tito, lest[5] an alarm raised in Tito's mind should urge him either to flight, or to some other counteracting measure which hard-pressed ingenuity might devise. For this reason he had never entered Nello's shop, which he observed that Tito frequented, and he had turned aside to avoid meeting Piero di Cosimo.

The possibility of frustration gave added eagerness to his desire that the great opportunity he sought should not be deferred. The desire was eager in him on another ground:[6] he trembled lest his memory should go again. Whether from the agitating presence of that

---

7 hatred which it had itself awakened] *3C* hatred itself awaked *MS CM 1 2*
8 ⟨follow Tito into⟩ enter *MS*   9 ⟨his circumstances⟩ Tito's *MS*
1 to ⟨make him know⟩ *MS*
2 dread, ⟨at the apparition of a Nemesis not to be escaped.⟩ *MS*
3 ⟨most⟩ the greater part *MS*   4 intimacy] any intimacy *MS*
5 lest ⟨some⟩ an alarm ⟨should be⟩ raised *MS*
6 ground:] *MS* ground; *CM 1 2 3*

fear, or from some other causes, he had twice felt a sort of mental dizziness, in which the inward sense or imagination[7] seemed to be losing the distinct forms of things. Once he had attempted to enter the Palazzo Vecchio and make his way into a council-chamber where Tito was, [8]and had failed. But now on this evening, he felt that his occasion was come.[9]

7 sense {or imagination} *MS*   8 ⟨but⟩ and *MS*
9 come. ⟨Fortune had favoured him. Standing under the Loggia d'Orcagna to watch Tito's ⟨⟨issuing⟩⟩ departure from the Palazzo, he had heard some politicians discussing party measures. Their talk was strongly anti-Medicean, and they were especially bitter against those men amongst the elect Twenty who were suspected of Medicean inclinations. Such men were not to suppose that the eye of Florentine vigilance was closed upon them. There was Bernardo Rucellai giving a Medicean supper in his gardens this very evening—secretly as he supposed—but the speaker could furnish any honest Florentine with a list of the company; and the list was forthwith given. It contained the name of Tito Melema. Baldassarre knew enough of Florence now to know what sort of person Bernardo Rucellai was; he made his resolution at once, and from the moment of Tito's issuing from the Palazzo never lost sight of him till, as we have seen, he vanished among the evergreens of the Rucellai gardens.⟩*MS*

CHAPTER XXXIX.

A [1]SUPPER IN THE RUCELLAI GARDENS

On entering the handsome pavilion, Tito's quick glance soon discerned in the selection of the guests the confirmation of his conjecture that the object of the gathering was political[2], though, perhaps, nothing more distinct than that strengthening of party which comes from good fellowship. Good dishes and good wine were at that time believed to heighten [3]the consciousness of political preferences, and in the inspired ease of after-supper talk it was supposed that people ascertained their own opinions with a clearness quite inaccessible to uninvited stomachs. The Florentines were a sober and frugal people; but wherever men have gathered wealth, Madonna della Gozzoviglia[4] and San Buonvino* have had their worshippers; and the Rucellai were among the few Florentine families who kept a great table and lived splendidly.[5] It was not probable that on this evening there would be any attempt to apply high philosophic theories; and there could be no objection to the bust of Plato looking on, or even to the modest presence of the cardinal virtues in fresco on the walls.

That bust of Plato had been long used to look down on conviviality of a more transcendental sort, for it had been brought from Lorenzo's villa after his death, when the meetings of the Platonic Academy* had been transferred to these gardens. Especially on every thirteenth of November, reputed anniversary of Plato's death,* it had looked down from under laurel leaves on[6] a picked company of scholars and philosophers, who met to eat and drink with moderation, and to discuss and admire, perhaps with less moderation, the doctrines of the great master:—on Pico della Mirandola, once a Quixotic young genius with[7] long curls, astonished at his own powers, and astonishing Rome with heterodox theses;* afterwards a more humble student, with a consuming passion for inward perfection, having come to find the universe more astonishing than his own cleverness:—on innocent, laborious Marsilio Ficino, picked out young to be reared as a Platonic philosopher, and fed on Platonism in all its stages till his mind was perhaps a little pulpy from that too exclusive diet:*—on Angelo

---

1 A ⟨Political⟩ Supper {in the Rucellai Gardens} *MS*
2 political ⟨. The guests were⟩, though *MS*   3 ⟨men's⟩ the *MS*
4 Madonna della Gozzoviglia] Madonna Gozzoviglia *MS*
5 stomachs. {The Florentines . . . splendidly.} *MS*
6 looked down from under laurel leaves on] *1 2 3* looked from under laurel leaves at *MS CM*
7 genius with] *MS 1 2 3* genius, with *CM*

Poliziano, chief literary genius of that age, a born poet, and a scholar without dulness, whose phrases had blood in them and are alive still:—or, farther[8] back, on Leon Battista Alberti,* a reverend senior when those three were young, and of a much grander type than they, a robust, universal mind, at once practical and theoretic, artist, man of science, inventor, poet:—and on many more valiant workers whose names are not registered where every day we turn the leaf to read them, but whose labours make a part, though an unrecognized part, of our inheritance, like the ploughing and sowing of past generations.

Bernardo Rucellai was a man to hold a distinguished place in that Academy even before he became its host and patron. He was still in the prime of life, not more than four and forty,* with a somewhat haughty, cautiously dignified presence; conscious of [9]an amazingly pure Latinity, but, says Erasmus,* not to be caught speaking Latin— no word of Latin to be sheared off him by the sharpest of Teutons. He welcomed Tito with more marked favour than usual, and gave him a place between Lorenzo Tornabuoni and Giannozzo Pucci,* both of them accomplished young members of the Medicean party.

Of course the talk was the lightest in the world while the brass bowl filled with scented water was [1]passing[2] round, that the company might wash their hands, and rings flashed on white fingers under the wax-lights, and there was the pleasant fragrance of fresh white damask newly come from France. The tone of remark was a very common one in those times. Some one asked what Dante's pattern old Florentine would think if the life could come into him again under his leathern belt and bone clasp,* and he could see the silver[3] forks on the table? And it was agreed on all hands that the habits of posterity would be very surprising to ancestors, if ancestors could only know them. And while the silver forks were just dallying with the appetizing delicacies that introduced the more serious business of the supper—such as morsels of liver, cooked to that exquisite point that they would melt in the mouth—there was time to admire the designs on the enamelled silver centres of the brass service, and to say something, as usual, about the silver dish for *confetti*, a masterpiece of Antonio Pollajuolo, whom patronizing Popes had seduced from his native Florence to more gorgeous Rome.*

"Ah, I remember," said Niccolò Ridolfi, a middle-aged man, with that negligent ease of manner which, seeming to claim nothing, is really based on the life-long consciousness of commanding rank—"I

8 farther] further *2 3*   9 ⟨a pure⟩ an amazingly pure *MS*
ı ⟨being passed⟩ passing *MS*
2 bowl filled with scented water was passing] *MS ı 2 3* bowl, filled with scented water, was passing *CM*
3 the silver] *MS* silver *CM ı 2 3*

remember our Antonio getting bitter about his chiselling and enam-elling of these metal things, and taking in a fury to painting, because, said he, 'the artist who puts his work into gold and silver, puts his brains into the melting-pot.'"*

"And that is not unlikely to be a true foreboding of Antonio's," said Giannozzo Pucci. "If this pretty war with Pisa goes on, and the revolt only spreads a little to our other towns, it is not only our silver dishes that are likely to go; I doubt whether Antonio's silver saints* round the altar of San Giovanni will not some day vanish from the eyes of the faithful to be worshipped more devoutly in the form of coin."

"The Frate is preparing us for that already," said Tornabuoni. "He is telling the people that God will not have silver crucifixes and starv-ing stomachs; and that the church is best adorned with the gems of holiness and the fine gold of brotherly love."

"A very useful doctrine of war-finance, as many a Condottiere has found," said Bernardo Rucellai, drily. "But politics come on after the *confetti*, Lorenzo, when we can drink wine enough to wash them down; they are too solid to be taken with roast and boiled."

"Yes, indeed," said Niccolò Ridolfi. "Our Luigi Pulci would have said this[4] delicate boiled kid must be eaten with an impartial mind. I remember one day at Careggi, when Luigi was in his rattling vein, he was maintaining that nothing perverted the palate like opinion. 'Opinion,' said he, 'corrupts the saliva—that's why men took to pep-per. Scepticism is the only philosophy that doesn't bring a taste in the mouth.' 'Nay,' says poor Lorenzo de' Medici, 'you must be out there, Luigi. Here is this untainted sceptic, Matteo Franco,* who wants hotter sauce than any of us.' 'Because he has a strong opinion of *himself*,' flashes out Luigi, 'which is the original egg of all other opinion. *He* a sceptic? He believes in the immortality of his own verses. He is such a logician as that preaching friar who described the pavement of the bottomless pit.' Poor Luigi! his mind was like sharpest steel that can touch nothing without cutting."

"And yet a very gentle-hearted creature," said Giannozzo Pucci. "It seemed to me his talk was a mere blowing of soap bubbles.* What dithyrambs he went into about eating and drinking! and yet he was as temperate as a butterfly."

The light talk and the solid eatables were not soon at an end, for after the roast and boiled meats came the indispensable capon and game, and, crowning glory of a well-spread table, a peacock cooked according to the receipt of Apicius* for cooking partridges, namely, with the feathers on, but not plucked afterwards, as that great author-ity ordered concerning his partridges; on the contrary, so disposed on

4 said ⟨that⟩ this *MS*

the dish that it might look as much as possible like a live peacock taking its unboiled repose. Great was the skill required in that confidential servant who was the official carver, respectfully to turn[5] the classical though insipid bird on its back[6], and expose the plucked breast from which he was to dispense a delicate slice to each of the honourable company, unless any one should be of so independent a mind as to decline that [7]expensive toughness and prefer the vulgar digestibility of capon.

Hardly any one was so bold. Tito quoted Horace,* and dispersed his slice in small particles over his plate; Bernardo Rucellai made a learned observation about the ancient price of peacocks' eggs[8], but did not pretend to eat his slice; and Niccolò Ridolfi held a mouthful on his fork while he told a favourite story of Luigi Pulci's,* about a man of Siena, who, wanting to give a splendid entertainment at moderate expense, bought a wild goose, cut off its beak and webbed feet, and boiled it in its feathers, to pass for a pea-hen.

In fact, very little peacock was eaten; but there was the satisfaction of sitting at a table where peacock was served up in a remarkable manner, and of knowing that such caprices were not within reach of any but those who supped with the very wealthiest men. And it would have been rashness to speak slightingly of peacock's flesh, or any other venerable institution, at a time when Fra Girolamo was teaching the disturbing doctrine that it was not the duty of the rich to be luxurious for the sake of the poor.

Meanwhile, in the chill obscurity that surrounded this centre of warmth, and light, and savoury odours, the lonely disowned man was walking in gradually narrowing circuits. He paused among the trees, and looked in at the windows, which made brilliant pictures against the gloom. He could hear the laughter; he could see Tito gesticulating with careless grace, and hear his voice, now alone, now mingling in the merry confusion of interlacing speeches. Baldassarre's mind was highly strung. He was preparing himself for the moment when he could win his entrance into this brilliant company; and he had a savage satisfaction in the sight of Tito's easy gaiety, which seemed to be preparing the unconscious victim for more effective torture.

But the men seated among the branching [9]tapers and the flashing cups could know nothing of the pale fierce face that watched them from without. The light can be a curtain as well as the darkness.

And the talk went on with more eagerness as it became less disconnected and trivial. The sense of citizenship was just then strongly forced even on[1] the most indifferent minds. What the over-mastering

5 {respectfully} to turn MS   6 back ⟨adroitly to slit the⟩ MS
7 ⟨classical⟩ expensive MS   8 eggs ⟨and allowed his plate to be⟩ MS
9 ⟨lights⟩ tapers MS   1 {even} on MS

A Supper in the Rucellai Gardens

Fra Girolamo was saying and prompting was really uppermost in the thoughts of every one at table; and before the stewed fish was removed, and while the[2] favourite sweets were yet to come, his name rose to the surface of the conversation, and, in spite of Rucellai's previous prohibition, the talk again became political. At first, while the servants remained present, it was mere gossip: what had been done in the Palazzo on the[3] first day's voting for the Great Council; how hot-tempered and domineering Francesco Valori was, as if he were to have everything his own way by right of his austere virtue; and how it was clear to everybody who [4]heard Soderini's speeches in favour of the Great Council, and also heard the Frate's sermons, that they were both kneaded in the same trough.*

"My opinion is," said Niccolò Ridolfi, "that the Frate has a longer head for public matters than [5]Soderini or any Piagnone among them: you may depend on it that Soderini is his mouthpiece more than he is Soderini's."

"No, Niccolò; there I differ from you," said Bernardo Rucellai: "the Frate [6]has an acute mind, and readily sees what will serve his own ends; but it is not[7] likely that Pagolantonio Soderini, who has had long experience of affairs, and has specially studied the Venetian Council, should be much indebted to a monk* for ideas on that subject.[8] No, no: Soderini loads the cannon; though, I grant you, Fra Girolamo brings the powder and lights the match. He is master of the people, and the people are getting master of us. Ecco!"

"Well," said Lorenzo Tornabuoni, presently, when the room was clear of servants, and nothing but wine was passing round[9], "whether Soderini is indebted or not, *we* are indebted to the Frate for the general amnesty* which has gone along with the scheme of the Council. We might have done without the fear of God and the reform of [1]morals being passed by a majority of black beans; but that excellent proposition, that our Medicean heads[2] should be allowed to remain comfortably on our shoulders, and that we should not be obliged to hand over our property in fines,[3] has my warm approval, and it is my belief that nothing but the Frate's predominance could have procured that for us. And you may rely on it that[4] Fra Girolamo is as firm as a rock on that point of promoting peace. I have had an interview with him."

2 while the] the *MS*   3 the] *3C* this *MS CM 1 2*
4 ⟨compared⟩ heard *MS*
5 ⟨he⟩ ⟨Soderini and Valore are his mouthpieces more than he is theirs⟩ Soderini *MS*
6 ⟨is⟩ has *MS*   7 not ⟨a man like⟩ *MS*
8 indebted {to a monk} for ideas on that subject ⟨to a monk⟩ *MS*
9 Tornabuoni {presently, when . . . round} *MS*
1 ⟨manners⟩ morals *MS*   2 {Medicean} heads *MS*
3 fines, ⟨a political measure that⟩ *MS*   4 rely on {it that} *MS*

There was a [5]murmur of surprise and curiosity at the further[6] end of the table; but Bernardo Rucellai simply nodded, as if he knew what Tornabuoni had to say, and wished him to go on.

"Yes," [7]proceeded Tornabuoni, "I have been favoured with an interview in the Frate's own cell, which, let me tell you, is not a common favour; for I have reason to believe that even Francesco Valori very seldom sees him in private. However, I think he saw me the more willingly because I was not a ready-made follower, but had to be converted. And, for my part, I see clearly enough that the only safe and wise policy for us Mediceans to pursue is to throw our strength into the scale of the Frate's party. We are not strong enough to make head on our own behalf; and[8] if the Frate and the popular party were upset, every one who hears me knows perfectly well what other party would be uppermost just now: Nerli, Alberti[9], Pazzi, and the rest—*Arrabbiati*,* as somebody [1]christened them the other day— who, instead of giving us an amnesty, would be inclined to fly at our throats like mad dogs, and not be satisfied till they had banished half of us."

There were strong interjections of assent to this last sentence of Tornabuoni's, as he paused and looked round a moment[2].

"A wise dissimulation," he went on, "is the only course for moderate rational men in times of violent party feeling. I need hardly tell [3]this company what are my real political attachments: I am not the only man here who has strong personal ties to the banished family; but, apart from [4]any such ties, I agree with my more experienced friends, who are allowing me to speak for them in their presence, that the only lasting and peaceful state of things for Florence [5]is the predominance of some single family interest. This theory of the Frate's, that we are to have a popular government, in which every man is to strive only for the general good, and know no party names, is a theory that may do for some isle of Cristoforo Colombo's finding, but will never do for our fine old quarrelsome Florence. A change must come before long, and with patience and caution we have every chance of determining the change in our favour. Meanwhile, the best thing we can do will be to keep the Frate's flag flying, for if any other were to be hoisted just now it would be a black flag for us."

"It's true," said Niccolò Ridolfi, in a curt decisive way. "What you say is true, Lorenzo. For my own part, I am too old[6] for anybody to

5 ⟨slight⟩ murmur *MS*   6 further] *MS* farther *CM 1 2 3*
7 ⟨he went⟩ proceeded *MS*
8 and ⟨there are but two alternatives before us⟩ *MS*   9 Alberti] Albizzi *MS*
1 ⟨has⟩ christened *MS*   2 moment ⟨before going on with his⟩. *MS*
3 ⟨the present⟩ this *MS*   4 ⟨those⟩ any such ties *MS*
5 ⟨will be⟩ is *MS*   6 old ⟨to be⟩ *MS*

believe that I've changed my feathers. And there are certain of us—
our old Bernardo del Nero for one—whom you would never persuade
to borrow another man's shield. But we can lie still, like sleepy old
dogs; and it's clear enough that barking would be of no use just now.
As for this psalm-singing party, who vote for nothing but the glory of
God, and want to make believe we can all love each other, and talk as
if vice could be swept out with a besom by the Magnificent Eight,
their day will not be a long one. After all the talk of scholars[7], there
are but two sorts of government: one where men show their teeth at
each other, and one where men show their tongues and lick the feet
of the strongest. They'll get their Great Council finally voted to-
morrow*—that's certain enough—and they'll think they've found out
a new plan of government; but as sure as there's a human skin under
every *lucco* in the Council, their new plan will end like every other, in
snarling or in licking. That's my view of things as a plain man. Not
that I consider it becoming in men of family and following, who have
got others depending on their constancy and on their sticking[8] to
their colours, to go a hunting with a fine net to catch reasons in the
air,* like doctors of law. I say frankly that, as the head of my family, I
shall be true to my old alliances; and I have never yet seen any chalk-
mark on political reasons to tell me which is true and which is false.
My friend Bernardo Rucellai here is a man of reasons, I know, and
I've[9] no objection to anybody's finding fine-spun reasons for me, so
that they don't interfere with my actions as a man of family who has
faith to keep with his connections."

"If that is an appeal to me, Niccolò," said Bernardo Rucellai, with
a formal dignity, in amusing contrast with Ridolfi's curt and pithy
ease, "I may take this opportunity of saying, that while my wishes are
partly determined by long-standing personal relations, I cannot enter
into any positive schemes with persons over whose actions I have no
control. I myself[1] might be content with a restoration of the old order
of things; but with modifications—with important modifications. And
the one point on which I wish to declare my concurrence with
Lorenzo Tornabuoni is, that the best policy to be pursued by our
friends is, to throw the weight of their interest into the scale of the
popular party. For myself, I condescend to no dissimulation; nor do I
at present see the party or the scheme that commands my full assent.
In all alike there is crudity and confusion of ideas, and of all the
twenty men who are my colleagues in the present crisis, there is not
one with whom I do not find myself in wide disagreement."

Niccolò Ridolfi shrugged his shoulders, and left it to some one
else[2] to take up the ball. As the wine went round the talk became

7 scholars ⟨that I've⟩ MS   8 {on their} sticking MS   9 I've] I have 2 3
1 I {myself} MS   2 else ⟨in the company⟩ MS

more and more frank and lively, and the desire of [3]several at once to be the chief speaker, as usual caused[4] the company to break up into small knots of two and three. It was a result which had been foreseen by Lorenzo Tornabuoni and Giannozzo[5] Pucci, and they were[6] among the first to turn aside from the high-road of general talk and enter into a special conversation with Tito, who sat between them; gradually pushing away their seats, and turning their backs on the table and wine.

[7]"In truth, Melema," Tournabuoni was saying at this stage, laying one hose-clad leg across the knee of the other, and caressing his ancle, "I know of no man in Florence who can serve our party better than you. You see what most of our friends are: men who can no more hide their prejudices than a dog can hide the natural tone of his bark, or else men whose[8] political ties are so notorious, that they must always be objects of suspicion. Giannozzo here, and I,[9] I flatter myself, are able to overcome that suspicion; we have that power of concealment and finesse[1], without which a rational cultivated man, instead of having any prerogative, is really at a disadvantage compared with a wild bull or a savage. But, except yourself, I know of no one else on whom we could rely[2] for the necessary discretion."

"Yes," said Giannozzo Pucci, laying his hand on Tito's shoulder, "the fact is, [3]*Tito mio*, you can help us better than if you were Ulysses himself, for I am convinced that Ulysses often made himself disagreeable.* To manage men one ought to have a sharp mind in a velvet sheath. And there is not a soul in Florence who could undertake a business like this journey to Rome, for example, with the same safety that you can. There is your scholarship, which may always be a pretext for such journeys; and what is better, there is your talent, which it would be harder to match than your scholarship. Niccolò Macchiavelli might have done for us if he had been on our side,* but hardly so well. He is too much bitten with notions, and has not your powers[4] of fascination. All the worse for him. He has lost a great chance in life, and you have got it."

"Yes," said Tournabuoni, lowering his voice in a significant manner, "you have only to play your game well, Melema, and the future belongs to you. For the Medici, you may rely upon it, will keep a foot in Rome as well as in Florence, and the[5] time may not be far off

3 ⟨half a dozen men⟩ several *MS*   4 {as usual} caused *MS*
5 Gianozzo] Giovanni *MS*   6 Pucci, and they were] Pucci who were *MS*
7 ⟨The fact is, Melema;" said Tornabuoni⟩ "In *MS*
8 {men} whose ⟨ties are so strong that they [1 word] them to be anything but⟩ political ties are ⟨too notorious for⟩ *MS*
9 I, ⟨I ?feel⟩ *MS*   1 concealment {and finesse} *MS*
2 rely ⟨with the same confidence⟩ for *MS*   3 ⟨Melema⟩ *Tito mio MS*
4 powers] *MS* power *CM 1 2 3*   5 the ⟨day may come⟩ *MS*

when they will be able to make a finer career for their adherents[6]
even than they did in old days. Why shouldn't you take orders some
day[7]? There's a cardinal's hat at the end of that road, and you would
not be the first Greek who has worn [8]that ornament."

Tito laughed gaily. He was too acute not to measure Tornabuoni's
exaggerated flattery, but still the flattery had a pleasant flavour.

"My joints are not so stiff yet," he said, "that I can't be induced to
run without such a high prize as that. I think the income of an abbey
or two held 'in commendam,'[9]* without the trouble of getting my
head shaved, would satisfy me at present."

"I was not joking," said Tournabuoni, with grave suavity; "I think
a scholar would always be the better off for taking orders. But we'll
talk of that another time. One of the objects to be first borne in mind,
is that you should win the confidence of the men who hang about San
Marco; that is what Giannozzo and I shall do, but you may carry it
farther than we can, because you are less observed. In that way you
can get a thorough knowledge of their doings, and you will make a
broader screen for [1]your agency on our side. Nothing of course can
be done before you start for Rome, because this bit of business
between Piero de' Medici and the French nobles must be effected at
once. I mean when you come back, of course; [2]I need say no more. I
believe you could make yourself the pet votary of San Marco, if you
liked; but you are wise enough to know that effective dissimulation is
never immoderate."

"If it were not that an adhesion to the popular side is necessary to
your safety as an agent of our party, *Tito mio*," said Giannozzo Pucci,
who was more fraternal and less patronizing in his manners[3] than
Tornabuoni, "I could have wished your skill to have been employed
in another way, for which it is still better fitted[4]. But now we must
look out for some other man among us who will manage to get into
the confidence of our sworn enemies, the Arrabbiati; we need to know
their movements more than those of the Frate's party, who are strong
enough to play above board. Still, it would have been a difficult thing
for you, from your known relations with the Medici a little while
back, and that sort of kinship your wife has with Bernardo del Nero.
We must find a man who has no distinguished connexions, and who
has not yet taken any side."

Tito was pushing his hair backward[5] automatically, as his manner

6 adherents ⟨now⟩ *MS*   7 day ⟨as other scholars have done⟩—there's *MS*
8 ⟨the [?red] [?hat]⟩ that ornament *MS*
9 abbey {or two held *in commendam*} *MS*   1 ⟨any⟩ your *MS*
2 ⟨but I need suggest nothing more to you⟩ I need *MS*
3 manners] manner *2 3*   4 way {for which it is still better fitted} *MS*
5 backward] *3C* back *MS CM 1 2*

was, and looking straight at Pucci with a scarcely perceptible smile on his lip.

"No need to look out for any one else," he said promptly. "I can manage the whole business with perfect ease. I will engage to make myself the special confidant of that thick-headed Dolfo Spini, and know his projects before he knows them himself."

Tito seldom spoke so confidently of his own powers, but he was in a state of exaltation at the sudden opening of a new path before him, where Fortune seemed to have hung higher prizes than any he had thought of hitherto. Hitherto he had seen success only in the form of favour; it now flashed on him in the shape of power—of such power as is possible to talent without traditional ties, and without beliefs. Each party that thought of him as a tool might become dependent on him[6]. His position as an alien, his indifference to the ideas[7] or prejudices of the men amongst whom he moved, were suddenly transformed into advantages; he became newly conscious of his own adroitness in the presence of a game that he was called on to play. And all the motives which might have made Tito shrink from the triple deceit that came before him as a tempting game, had been slowly strangled[8] in him by the successive falsities of his life.

Our lives make a moral tradition for our individual selves, as the life of mankind at large makes a moral tradition[9] for the race; and to have once acted nobly[1] seems[2] a reason why we should always be noble. But Tito was feeling the effect of an opposite tradition: he had won no [3]memories of self-conquest and perfect faithfulness from which he could have a sense of falling.

[4]The triple colloquy went on with growing spirit till it was interrupted[5] by a call from the table. Probably the movement came from the listeners in the party, who were afraid lest the talkers should tire themselves. At all events it was agreed that there had been enough of[6] gravity, and Rucellai had just ordered new flasks of Montepulciano.*

"How many minstrels are there among us?" he said, when there had been a general rallying round the table. "Melema, I think you are the chief: Matteo will give you the lute."

"Ah, yes!" said Giannozzo Pucci; "lead the last chorus from

6 without ⟨strong⟩ ⟨any⟩ beliefs: {each . . . dependent on him} MS
7 ideas ⟨of the men around⟩ MS   8 {slowly} strangled ⟨for him long ago⟩ MS
9 a {moral} tradition, for our {individual} selves, as the life of ⟨the⟩ mankind at large makes a {moral} tradition MS
1 nobly] 3C greatly MS CM 1 2   2 seems] 1 2 3 seems to make MS CM
3 ⟨memory⟩ memories MS   4 ⟨His⟩ The triple colloquy ⟨with⟩ MS
5 interrupted ⟨. Every one was tired of gravity⟩ by MS
6 enough of] 1 2 3 enough MS CM

Poliziano's *Orfeo*, that you have found such an excellent measure for, and we will all fall in:

> Ciascun segua, o Bacco, te:
> Bacco, Bacco, evoè, evoè!"*

The servant put the lute into Tito's hands, and then said something in an under-tone to his master. A little subdued questioning and answering went on between them, while Tito touched the lute in a preluding way to the strain of the chorus, and there was a confusion of speech and musical humming all round the table. Bernardo Rucellai had said, "Wait a moment, Melema;" but the words had been unheard by Tito, who was leaning towards Pucci, and singing low to him the phrases of the Mænad-chorus[7]. He noticed nothing until the buzz round the table suddenly ceased, and the notes of his own voice, with its soft low-toned triumph, "Evoè, evoè!" fell in startling isolation[8].

It was a strange moment. Baldassarre had moved round the table till he was opposite Tito, and as the hum ceased there might be seen for an instant Baldassarre's fierce dark eyes bent on [9]Tito's bright smiling unconsciousness, while the low notes of triumph dropped from his lips into the silence.

Tito looked up with a slight start, and his lips turned[1] pale, but he seemed hardly more moved than Giannozzo Pucci, who had looked up at the same moment—or even than several others round the table; for that sallow deep-lined face with the hatred in its eyes seemed a terrible apparition across the wax-lit ease and gaiety. And Tito quickly recovered some self-command. "A mad old man—he looks like it—he *is* mad!" was the instantaneous thought that brought some courage with it; for he could conjecture no inward change in Baldassarre[2] since they had met before. He just let his eyes fall and laid the lute on the table with apparent ease; but his fingers pinched the neck of the lute hard while he governed his head and his glance sufficiently to look with an air of quiet appeal towards Bernardo Rucellai, who said at once,—

"Good man, what is your business? What is the important declaration that you have to make?"

"Messer Bernardo Rucellai, I wish you and your honourable friends to know in what sort of company you are sitting. There is a traitor among you."

There was a general movement of alarm. Every one present, except Tito, thought of political danger, and not of private injury.

---

7 Mænad-chorus] Menad's chorus *MS*   8 isolation ⟨into the silence⟩ *MS*
9 ⟨the⟩ Tito's *MS*   1 {his lips} turned *MS*
2 change in Baldassarre] change *MS*

Baldassarre[3] began to speak as if he were thoroughly assured of what he had to say; but, in spite of his long preparation for this moment, there was the tremor of overmastering excitement in his voice. His passion shook him. He went on, but he did not say what he had meant to say. As he fixed his eyes on Tito again the[4] passionate words were like blows—they defied premeditation.

"There is a man among you who is a scoundrel, a liar, a robber. I was a father to him. I took him from beggary when he was a child. I reared him, I cherished him, I taught him, I made him a scholar. My[5] head has lain hard that his might have a pillow. And he left me in slavery; he sold the gems that were mine, and when I came again, he denied me."

The last words had [6]been uttered with almost convulsed agitation, and Baldassarre paused, trembling. All glances were turned on Tito, who was now looking straight at Baldassarre. It was a moment of desperation that annihilated all feeling in him, except the determination to risk anything for the chance of escape. And he gathered confidence from the agitation by which Baldassarre was evidently shaken. He had ceased to pinch the neck of the lute, and had thrust his thumbs into his belt, while his lips had begun to assume a slight curl. He had never yet done an act of murderous cruelty even to the smallest animal that could utter a cry, but at that moment he would have been capable of treading the breath from a smiling child for the sake of his own safety.

"What does this mean, Melema?" said Bernardo Rucellai, in a tone of cautious surprise. He, as well as the rest of the company, felt relieved that the tenor of the accusation was not political[7].

"Messer Bernardo," said Tito, [8]"I believe this man is mad. I did not recognize him the first time he encountered me in Florence, but I know now that he is the servant who years ago accompanied me and my adoptive father to Greece, and was dismissed on account of misdemeanours. His name is Jacopo di Nola. Even at that time I believe his mind was unhinged, for, without any reason, he had conceived a strange hatred towards me; and now I am[9] convinced that he is labouring under a mania which causes him to mistake his identity. He has already attempted my life since he has been in Florence; and I am in constant danger from him. But he is an object of pity rather than

3 you. {There was a general . . . private injury.} Baldassarre ⟨spoke⟩ began to speak *MS*

4 say: {as he fixed his eyes on Tito again,} the *MS*

5 {I made him a scholar}—my *MS*   6 ⟨come⟩ been uttered *MS*

7 surprize. {He . . . political} *MS*

8 ⟨"I must first of all beg you to let this man depart in safety. I have no wish that he should be punished.⟩ I believe ⟨he⟩ this man *MS*

9 unhinged {⟨and⟩ for without . . . now} I am *MS*

of indignation. It is too certain that my father is dead. You have only my word for it; but I must leave it to your judgment how far it is probable that a man of intellect and learning would have been lurking about in dark corners for the last month with the purpose of assassinating me; or how far it is probable that, if this man were my second father, I could have any motive for denying him. That story about my being rescued from beggary, is the vision of a diseased brain. But it will be a satisfaction to me at least if you will demand from him proofs of his identity, lest any malignant person should choose to make[1] this mad impeachment a reproach to me."

Tito had felt more and more confidence as he went on: the lie was not so difficult when it was once begun; and as the words fell easily from his lips, they gave him a sense of power such as men [2]feel when they have begun a muscular feat successfully. In this way he acquired boldness enough to end with a challenge for proofs.

Baldassarre[3], while he had been walking in the gardens, and afterwards waiting in an outer room of the pavilion with the servants, had been making anew the digest of the evidence he would bring to prove his identity and Tito's baseness, recalling the description and history of his gems, and assuring himself by rapid mental glances that he could attest his learning and his travels. It might be partly owing to this nervous strain that the new shock of rage he felt as Tito's lie fell on his ears brought a strange [4]bodily effect with it: a cold stream seemed to rush over him, and the last words of the speech seemed to be drowned by ringing chimes. Thought gave way to a dizzy horror, as if the earth were slipping away from under him. Every one in the room was looking at him as Tito ended, and saw that the eyes which håd had such fierce intensity only a few minutes before had now[5] a vague fear in them. He clutched the back of [6]a seat, and was silent.

Hardly any evidence could have been more in favour of Tito's assertion.

"Surely I have seen this man before, somewhere," said Tornabuoni.

"Certainly you have," said Tito, readily, in a low tone.[7] "He is the escaped prisoner[8] who clutched me on the steps of the Duomo. I did not recognize him then; he looks now more as he used to do, except that he has a more unmistakable air of mad imbecility."

"I cast no doubt on your word, Melema," said Bernardo Rucellai, with cautious gravity, "but you are right to desire some positive test of the fact." Then turning to Baldassarre, he said, "If you are the person you claim to be, you can doubtless give some description of

---

1 {choose to} make *MS*   2 ⟨have⟩ feel *MS*   3 proofs. {¶} Baldassarre *MS*
4 ⟨physical⟩ bodily *MS*   5 had now] *3C* had *MS CM 1 2*
6 ⟨the⟩ a *MS*   7 readily {in a low tone} *MS*
8 {escaped} prisoner *MS*

the gems which were your property. I myself was the purchaser of
[9]more than one gem from Messer Tito—the chief rings, I believe, in
his collection. [1]One of them is a fine sard[2],* engraved with a subject
from Homer. If, as you allege, you are a scholar, and the rightful
owner of that ring, you can doubtless turn to the noted passage in
Homer from which that subject is taken. Do you accept this test,
Melema? or have you anything to allege against its validity? The
Jacopo you speak of, was he a scholar?"

It was a fearful crisis for Tito. If he [3]said, "Yes," his quick mind
told him that he would shake the credibility of his story: if he said,
"No," he risked everything on the uncertain extent of Baldassarre's
imbecility. But there was no noticeable pause before he said, "No. I
accept the test."

There was a dead silence while Rucellai moved towards the recess
where the books were, and came back with the fine Florentine Homer
in his hand. Baldassarre, when he was addressed, had turned his head
towards the speaker, and Rucellai believed that he had understood
him. But he chose to repeat what he had said, that there might be no
mistake as to the test.

"The ring I possess," he said,[4] "is a fine sard[5], engraved with a
subject from Homer. There was no other at all resembling it in
Messer Tito's collection. Will you turn to the passage in Homer from
which that subject is taken? Seat yourself here," he added, laying the
book on the table, and pointing to his own seat while he stood beside
it.

Baldassarre had so far recovered from the first confused horror
produced by the sensation of rushing coldness and chiming din in the
ears[6] as to be partly aware of what was said to him; he was aware that
something was being demanded from him to prove his identity, but
he formed no distinct idea of the [7]details. The sight of the book
recalled the habitual longing and faint hope[8] that he could read and
understand, and he moved towards the chair immediately. The book
was open before him, and he bent his head a little towards it, while
everybody watched him eagerly. He turned no leaf. His eyes wandered over the pages that lay before him, and then fixed on them
with[9] a straining gaze. His lasted for two or three minutes in dead
silence. [1]Then he lifted his hands to each side of his head, and said,
in a low tone of despair, "Lost, lost!"

There was something so piteous in the wandering look and the low

---

9 ⟨a⟩ more than one *MS*   1 ⟨It⟩ One of them *MS*   2 sard] sardonyx *MS*
3 ⟨had⟩ said *MS*   4 said, ⟨as he held out the Homer towards Baldassarre⟩ *MS*
5 sard] sardonyx *MS*   6 din {in the ears} *MS*   7 ⟨ring⟩ details *MS*
8 {faint} hope *MS*   9 them with] them 2 3   1 ⟨At length⟩ Then *MS*

cry, that while they confirmed the belief in his madness they raised compassion. Nay, so distinct sometimes[2] is the working of a double consciousness within us, that Tito himself, while he triumphed in the apparent verification of his lie, wished that he had never made the lie necessary to himself—wished he had recognized his father on the steps—wished he had gone to seek him—wished everything had been different. But he had borrowed from the terrible usurer Falsehood, and the loan had mounted and mounted with the years, until he belonged to the usurer, body and soul.

The compassion excited in all the witnesses was not without its danger to Tito; for conjecture is constantly guided by feeling, and more than one person suddenly conceived that this man might have been a scholar and have lost his faculties. On the other hand, they had not present to their minds the motives which could have led Tito to the denial of his benefactor, and having no ill-will towards him, it would have been difficult to them to believe that he had been uttering the basest of lies. And [3]the originally common type of Baldassarre's person, coarsened by years of hardship, told as a confirmation of Tito's lie. If Baldassarre, to begin with, could have uttered precisely the words he had premeditated, there might have been something in the form of his accusation which would have given it the stamp not only of true experience but of mental refinement. But there had been no such testimony in his impulsive agitated words; and there seemed the very opposite testimony in the rugged face and the coarse hands that trembled beside it, standing out in strong contrast in the midst of that velvet-clad, fair-handed company. His next movement, while he was being watched in silence, told against him too. He took his hands from his head, and felt for something under his tunic[4]. Every one guessed what that movement meant—guessed that there was a weapon at his side. Glances were interchanged; and Bernardo Rucellai said, in a quiet tone, touching Baldassarre's shoulder:—

"My friend, this is an important business of yours. You shall have all justice. Follow me into a private room."

Baldassarre was still in that half-stunned state in which he was susceptible to any prompting, in the same way as an insect[5] that[6] forms no conception of what the prompting leads to. He rose[7] from his seat, and followed Rucellai out of the room.

In two or three minutes Rucellai came back again, and said,—

"He is safe under lock and key. Piero Pitti, you are one of the

2 distinct {sometimes} *MS*
3 ⟨that original [?commonness] of ⟨⟨physique⟩⟩ ⟨⟨person⟩⟩ Baldassarre's⟩ the *MS*
4 tunic—⟨apparently for something that was⟩ ⟨with a look of frustration⟩. *MS*
5 ⟨a dim-sighted animal⟩ an insect *MS*
6 insect that] *MS 3P* insect, that *CM 1 2*
7 Baldassarre was still . . . leads to. He rose] Baldassarre, still . . . leads to, rose *MS*

Magnificent Eight, what do you think of our sending Matteo to[8] the palace for a couple of *sbirri*, who may escort him to the Stinche?* If there is any danger in him, as I think there is, he will be safe there; and we can inquire about him to-morrow."

Pitti assented, and the order was given.

"He is certainly an ill-looking fellow," said Tournabuoni. "And you say he has attempted your life already, Melema?"

And the talk turned on the various forms of madness, and the fierceness of the Southern blood. If[9] the seeds of conjecture unfavourable to Tito had been planted in [1]the mind of any one present, they were hardly strong enough to grow without the aid of much daylight[2] and ill-will. The common-looking, wild-eyed old man[3], clad in serge, might have won belief without very strong evidence, if he had accused a man who was envied and disliked. As it was, the only congruous and probable view of the case seemed to be the one that sent the unpleasant accuser safely out of sight, and left the pleasant serviceable Tito just where he was before.

The subject gradually floated away, and gave place to others, till a heavy tramp, and something like the struggling of a man who was being dragged away, were heard outside. The sounds soon died out, and the interruption seemed to make the last hour's conviviality more resolute and vigorous. Every one was willing to forget a disagreeable incident.

Tito's heart was palpitating, and the wine tasted no better to him[4] than if it had been blood.

To-night he had paid a heavier price than ever to make himself safe. He did not like the price, and yet it was inevitable that he should be glad of the purchase.

And after all he led the chorus. He was in a state of excitement in which oppressive sensations, and the wretched consciousness of something hateful but irrevocable, were mingled with a feeling of triumph which seemed to assert itself as the feeling that would subsist and be master of the morrow.

And it *was*[5] master. For on the morrow, as we saw, when he was about to start on his mission to Rome, he had the air of a man well satisfied with the world.

---

8 sending {Matteo} to *MS*   9 If ⟨there were⟩ *MS*   1 ⟨any⟩ the *MS*
2 {much} daylight *MS*   3 {wild-eyed} old man *MS*
4 better {to him} *MS*   5 *was*] was *MS*

CHAPTER XL.

AN ARRESTING VOICE

WHEN Romola sat down on the stone under the cypress, [1]all things conspired to give her the sense of freedom and solitude: [2]her escape from the accustomed walls and streets; the widening distance from her husband, who was by this time riding towards Siena, while every hour would take her farther on the opposite way; the morning stillness; the great dip of ground on the roadside making a gulf between her and the sombre calm of the mountains. For the first time in her life she felt alone in the presence of the earth and sky, with no human [3]presence interposing and making a law for her.

Suddenly a voice close to her said,—

"You are Romola de' Bardi, the wife of Tito Melema."

She knew the voice: it had vibrated through her more than once before; and because she knew it, she did not turn round or look up. She sat shaken by awe, and yet inwardly rebelling against the awe. It was one of those black-skirted monks who was daring to speak to her, and interfere with her privacy: that was all.[4] And yet she was shaken, as if [5]that destiny which men thought of as a sceptred deity had come to her, and grasped her with fingers of flesh.

"You are fleeing from Florence in disguise. I have a [6]command from God to stop you. You are not permitted to flee."

Romola's anger at the intrusion mounted higher at these imperative words. She would not turn round to look at the speaker, whose [7]examining gaze she resented. Sitting quite motionless, she said,—

"What right have you to speak to me, or to hinder me?"

"The right of a messenger. You have put on a religious garb, and you have no religious purpose. You have sought the garb as a disguise. But you were not suffered to pass me without being discerned. It was declared to me who you were: it is declared to me that you are seeking to escape from the lot God has laid upon you. You wish your true name and your true place in life to be hidden, that you may choose for yourself a new name and a new place, and have no rule but your own will. And I have a command to call you back. My daughter, you must return to your place."

Romola's mind rose in stronger rebellion with every sentence. She was the more determined not to show any sign of submission, because

1 ⟨everything around her⟩ all things *MS*   2 ⟨the⟩ her *MS*
3 ⟨bond⟩ presence *MS*   4 privacy. {That was all.} *MS*
5 ⟨destiny had grasped her bodily.⟩ that destiny *MS*
6 ⟨commission⟩ command *MS*   7 ⟨?curt⟩ examining *MS*

the consciousness of being inwardly shaken made her dread lest she should fall into irresolution. She spoke with more irritation than before.

"I will not return. I acknowledge no right of priests and monks to interfere with my actions. You have no power over me."

"I know—I know you have been brought up in scorn of obedience. But it is not the poor monk who claims to interfere with you: it is the truth that commands you. And you cannot escape it. Either you [8]must obey it, and it will lead you; or you must disobey it, and it will hang on you with the weight of a chain which[9] you will drag for ever. But you will obey it, my daughter. Your old servant will return to you with the mules: my companion is gone to fetch him; and you will go back to Florence."

She started up with anger in her eyes, and faced the speaker. It was Fra Girolamo: she knew that well enough before. She was nearly as tall as he was, and their faces were almost on a level. She had started up with defiant words ready to burst from her lips, but they fell back again without utterance. She had met Fra Girolamo's calm glance, and the impression from it was so new to her, that her anger sank ashamed as something irrelevant.

There was nothing transcendent[1] in Savonarola's [2]face. It was not beautiful. It was strong-featured, and owed all its refinement to habits of mind and rigid discipline of the body.[3] The source of the impression [4]his glance produced on Romola was the sense it conveyed to her of interest in her and care for her apart[5] from any personal feeling. It was the first time she had encountered a gaze in which simple human fellowship expressed itself as a strongly-felt bond. Such a glance is half the vocation of the priest or spiritual guide of men, and Romola felt it impossible again to question his authority to speak to her. She stood silent, looking at him. And he spoke again.

"You assert your freedom proudly, my daughter. But who is so base as the debtor that thinks himself free?"

There was a sting in those words, and Romola's countenance changed as if a subtle pale flash had gone over it.

"And you are flying from your debts: the debt of a Florentine woman; the debt of a wife. You are turning your back on the lot that[6] has been appointed for you—you are going to choose another. But can man or woman choose duties? No more than they can choose their birthplace or their father and mother. My daughter, you are fleeing from the presence of God into the wilderness."

As the anger melted from Romola's mind, it had given place to a new presentiment of the [7]strength there might be in submission, if this man, at whom she was beginning to look with a [8]vague reverence, had some valid law to show her. But no—it was impossible; he could not know what determined her. Yet she could not again[9] simply refuse to be guided; she was constrained to plead; and in her new[1] need to be reverent while she resisted, the title which she had never given him before came to her lips without forethought.

"My father, you cannot know the reasons which compel me to go. None can know them but myself. None can judge for me. I have been driven by great sorrow. I am resolved to go."

"I know enough, my daughter: my mind has been so far illuminated concerning you, that I know enough. You are not happy in your married life; but I am not a confessor, and I seek to know nothing that should be reserved for the seal of confession. I have a divine warrant to stop you, which does not depend on such knowledge. You were warned by a message from heaven, delivered in my presence— you were warned before marriage, when you might still have lawfully chosen to be free from the marriage bond. But you chose the bond; and in wilfully breaking it—I speak to you as a pagan, if the holy mystery of matrimony is not sacred to you—you are breaking a pledge. Of what wrongs will you complain, my daughter, when you yourself are committing one of the greatest wrongs a woman and a citizen can be guilty of—withdrawing[2] in secrecy and disguise from a pledge which you have given in the face of God and your fellow-men? Of what wrongs will you complain, when you yourself are breaking the simplest law that lies at the foundation of the trust which binds man to man—faithfulness to the spoken word? This, then, is the wisdom you have gained by scorning the mysteries of the Church?—not to see the bare duty of integrity, where the Church would have taught you to see, not integrity only, but religion."

The blood had rushed to Romola's face, and she shrank as if she had been stricken. "I would not have put on a disguise," she began; but she could not go on,—she was too much shaken by the suggestion in the Frate's words of a possible affinity between her own conduct and Tito's.

"And to break that pledge you fly from Florence: Florence, where

---

7 ⟨possible delight⟩ strength *MS*
8 ⟨kind of open-eyed expectancy⟩ vague reverence *MS*   9 not {again} *MS*
1 and in her new] and feeling a new *MS*
2 are {committing one . . . guilty of} withdrawing *MS*

there are the only men and women in the world to whom you owe
the debt of a fellow-citizen."

"I should never have quitted Florence," said Romola, tremulously,
"as long as there was any hope of my fulfilling a duty to my father
there."

"And do you owe no tie but that of a child to her father in the
flesh? Your life has been spent in blindness, my daughter. You have
lived with those who sit on a hill aloof, and look down on the life of
their fellow-men.* I know their vain discourse. It is of what has been
in the times which they fill with their own fancied wisdom, while
they scorn God's work in the present.³ And doubtless you were
taught how there were pagan women who felt what it was to live for
the Republic; yet you have never felt that you, a Florentine woman,
should live for Florence. If your own people are wearing a yoke, will
you slip from under it, instead of struggling with them to lighten it?
There is hunger and misery in our streets, yet you say, 'I care not; I
have my own sorrows; I will go away, if peradventure I can ease
them.' The servants of God are struggling after a law of justice,
peace, and charity, that the hundred thousand citizens among whom
you were born may be governed righteously; but you think no more
of this⁴ than if you were a bird, that may spread its wings and fly
whither it will in search of food to its liking. And yet you have
scorned the teaching of the Church, my daughter. As if you, a wilful
wanderer, following your own blind choice, were not below the hum-
blest Florentine woman who stretches forth her hands with her own
people, and craves a blessing for them; and feels a close sisterhood
with the neighbour who kneels beside her and is not of her own
blood; and thinks of the ⁵mighty purpose that God has for Florence;
and waits and endures because the promised work⁶ is great, and she
feels herself little."

"I was not going away to ease and self-indulgence," said Romola,
raising her head again, with a prompting to vindicate herself. "I was
going away to hardship. I expect no joy: it is gone from my life."

"You are seeking your own will, my daughter. You are seeking
some good other than the law you are bound to obey. But how will
you find good? It is not a thing of choice: it is a river that flows from
the foot of the Invisible Throne, and flows by the path of obedience.
I say again, man cannot choose his duties. You may choose to forsake
your duties, and choose not to have the sorrow they bring. But you
will go forth; and what will you find, my daughter? Sorrow without
duty—bitter herbs, and no bread with them."

3 wisdom {while they scorn God's work in the present.} MS
4 this] *1* *2* *3* that MS CM   5 ⟨great⟩ mighty MS
6 work ⟨of God⟩ MS

"But if you knew," said Romola, clasping[7] her hands and pressing them tight, as she[8] looked pleadingly at Fra Girolamo; "if you knew what it was to me—how impossible it seemed to me to bear it."

"My daughter," he said, pointing to the cord round Romola's neck, "you carry something within your mantle; draw it forth, and look at it."

Romola gave a slight start, but her impulse now was to do just what Savonarola told her. Her self-doubt was grappled by a stronger will and a stronger conviction than her own. She drew forth the crucifix. Still pointing towards it, he said,

"There, my daughter, is the image of a Supreme Offering, made by Supreme Love, because the need of man was great."

He paused, and she held the crucifix trembling—trembling under a sudden impression of the wide distance between her present and her past self. What a length of road[9] she had travelled through since she first took that crucifix from the Frate's hands! Had life as many secrets before her still as it had for her then, in her young blindness? It was a thought that helped all other subduing influences; and at the sound of Fra Girolamo's voice again, Romola, with a quick involuntary movement, pressed the crucifix against her mantle, and looked at him with[1] more submission than before.

"Conform your life to that image, my daughter; make your sorrow an offering: and when the fire of divine charity burns within you, and you behold the need of your fellow-men by the light of that flame, you will not call your offering great. You have carried yourself proudly, as one who held herself not of common blood or of common thoughts; but you have been as one unborn to the true life of man. What! you say your love for your father no longer tells you to stay in Florence? Then, since that tie is snapped, you are without a law, without religion: you are no better than a beast of the field when she is robbed of her young. If the yearning of a fleshly love is gone, you are without love, without obligation. See, then, my daughter, how you are below the life of the believer who worships that image of the Supreme Offering, and feels the glow of a common life with the lost multitude for whom that offering was made, and beholds the history of the world as the history of a great redemption in which he is himself a fellow-worker, in his own place and among his own people![2] If you held that faith, my beloved daughter, you would not be a wanderer flying from suffering, and blindly seeking the good of a freedom which is lawlessness. You would feel that Florence was the home of your soul as well as your birthplace, because you would see the work

7 clasping] involuntarily, clasping *MS*   8 she ⟨spoke⟩ *MS*
9 length of road] long road *MS*   1 with ⟨child-like expectancy⟩ *MS*
2 people!] people. *MS*

that was given[3] you to do there. If you forsake your place, who will
fill it? You ought to be in your place now, helping in the great work
by which God will purify Florence, and raise it to be the guide of the
nations. What! the earth is full of iniquity—full of groans—the light
is still struggling with a mighty darkness, and you say, 'I cannot bear
my bonds; I will burst them asunder; I will go where no man claims
me'? My daughter, every bond of your life is a debt: the right lies in
the payment of that debt; it can lie nowhere else. In vain will you
wander over the earth; you will be wandering forever away from the
right."

Romola was inwardly struggling with strong forces: that immense
personal influence of Savonarola, which[4] came from the energy of his
emotions and beliefs; and her consciousness, [5]surmounting all prejudice, that his words implied a higher[6] law than any she had yet
obeyed. But the[7] resisting thoughts were not yet overborne.

"How then could Dino be right? He broke ties. He forsook his
place."

"That was a special vocation. He was constrained to depart, else he
could not have attained the higher life. It would have been stifled
within him."

"And I too"—said Romola, raising her hands to her brow, and
speaking in a tone of anguish, as if she were being dragged to some
torture. "Father, you may be wrong."

"Ask your conscience, my daughter. You have no vocation such as
your brother had. You[8] are a wife. You seek to break your ties in
[9]self-will and anger, not because the higher life calls upon you to
renounce them. The higher life begins for us, my daughter, when we
renounce our own will to bow before a divine law. That seems hard
to you. [1]It is the portal of wisdom, and freedom, and blessedness.
And the symbol of it hangs before you. That wisdom is the religion
of the cross. And you stand aloof from it: you are a pagan; you[2] have
been taught to say, 'I am as the wise men who lived before the time
when the Jew of Nazareth was crucified.' And that is your wisdom!
To be as the dead whose eyes are closed, and whose ear is deaf to the
work of God that has been since their time. What has your dead wisdom done for you, my daughter? It has left you without a heart for
the neighbours among whom you dwell, without care for the great
work by which Florence is to be regenerated and the world made
holy; it has left you without a share in the divine life which quenches

3 that was given] God has given *MS*
4 Savonarola, which] Savonarola which *MS*   5 ⟨in spite⟩ surmounting *MS*
6 higher ⟨and higher⟩ *MS*   7 {But} The *MS*   8 You ⟨break⟩ *MS*
9 ⟨pride⟩ self will *MS*   1 ⟨My daughter,⟩ It *MS*   2 you ⟨say⟩ *MS*

the sense of suffering[3] Self in the ardours of an ever-growing love. And now, when the sword has pierced your soul, you say, 'I will go away; I cannot bear my sorrow.' And you think nothing of the sorrow and the wrong that are within[4] the walls of the city where you dwell: you would leave your place empty, when it ought to be filled with your pity and your labour. If there is wickedness in the streets, your steps should shine with the light of purity: if there is a cry of anguish, you, my daughter, because you know the meaning of the cry, should be there to still it. My beloved daughter[5], sorrow has come to teach you a new worship: the sign of it hangs before you."

Romola's mind was still torn by conflict. She foresaw that she should obey Savonarola and go back: his words had come to her[6] as if they were an interpretation of [7]that revulsion from self-satisfied ease, and of that new fellowship with suffering, which had already been awakened in her. His arresting voice had brought a new condition into her life, which made it seem impossible to her that she could go on her way as if she had not heard it; yet she shrank as one who sees the path she must take, but sees, too, that the hot lava lies there. And the instinctive shrinking from a return to her husband brought doubts. She turned away her eyes from Fra Girolamo, and stood for a minute or two with her hands hanging clasped before her, like a statue[8]. At last she spoke, as if the words were being wrung from her, still looking on the ground,

"My husband. . . . he is not. . . . my love is gone![9]"

"My daughter, there is a bond of a higher love. Marriage is not carnal only, made for selfish delight. See what that thought leads you to! It leads you to wander away in a false garb from all the obligations of your place and name. That would not have been, if you had learned that it is a sacramental vow, from which none but God can release you. My daughter, your life is not as a grain of sand, to be blown by the winds; it is a thing of flesh[1] and blood, that dies if it be sundered. Your husband is not a malefactor?"

Romola started[2]. "Heaven forbid! No; I accuse him of nothing."

"I did not suppose he was a malefactor. I meant, that if he were a malefactor, your place would be in the prison beside him. My daughter, if the cross comes to you as a wife, you must carry it as a wife. [3]You may say, 'I will forsake my husband,' but you cannot cease to be a wife."

3 {the sense of} suffering *MS*   4 are within] is ⟨about⟩ within *MS*
5 {beloved} daughter *MS*   6 to her ⟨only as the [?piping] of⟩ *MS*
7 ⟨her⟩ that revulsion from {self-}satisfied *MS*
8 statue] *1 2 3* pale statue *MS CM*   9 gone!] gone. *MS*
1 a thing of flesh] *1 2 3* as flesh *MS CM*
2 Romola started] *1 2 3* Romola flushed and started *MS CM*
3 ⟨You cannot cease to be⟩ You *MS*

"Yet if—oh, how could I bear—" Romola had involuntarily begun[4] to say something which she sought to banish from her mind again.

"Make your marriage-sorrows an offering too, my daughter: an offering to the great work by which sin and sorrow are being made to cease. The end is sure, and is already beginning. Here in Florence it is beginning, and the eyes of faith behold it. And it may be our blessedness to die for it: to die daily by the crucifixion of our selfish will—to die at last by laying our bodies on the altar. My daughter, you are a child of Florence; fulfil the duties of that[5] great inheritance. Live for Florence—for your own people, whom God is preparing to bless the earth. Bear the anguish and the smart. The iron is sharp—I know, I know—it rends the tender flesh. The draught is bitterness on the lips. But there is rapture in the cup—there is the vision which makes all life below it dross for ever. Come, my daughter, come back to your place!"

While Savonarola spoke with growing intensity, his arms tightly folded before him still, as they had been from the first, but his face alight as from[6] an inward flame, Romola felt herself surrounded and possessed by the glow of his passionate faith. The chill doubts all melted away; she was subdued by the sense of something unspeakably great to which she was being called by a strong being who roused a new strength within herself. In a voice that was like a low, prayerful cry, she said—

"Father, I will be guided. Teach me![7] I will go back."

Almost unconsciously she sank on her kness. Savonarola stretched out his hand over her; but feeling would no longer pass through the channel of speech, and he was silent.

4 {involuntarily} begun MS
5 fulfil the duties of that] God has given you that MS   6 {as} from MS
7 guided. Teach me!] guided. MS

CHAPTER XLI.

COMING BACK

"Rise, my daughter," said Fra Girolamo at last. "Your servant is waiting not far off with the mules. It is time that I should go onward to Florence."

Romola arose from her knees. That silent attitude had been a sort of sacrament to her, confirming the state of yearning passivity on which she had newly entered. By the one act of renouncing her resolve to quit her husband, her will seemed so utterly bruised that she felt the need of direction even in small things. She lifted up the edge of her cowl, and saw Maso and the second Dominican standing with their backs towards her on the edge of the hill about ten yards from her; but she looked at Savonarola again without speaking, as if the order to Maso to turn back must come from him and not from her.

"I will go and call them," he said, answering her glance of appeal; "and I will recommend you, my daughter, to the Brother who is with me. You desire to put yourself under guidance, and to learn that wisdom which has been hitherto as foolishness to you. A chief gate of that wisdom is the Sacrament of Confession. You will need a confessor, my daughter, and I desire to put you under the care of Fra Salvestro,[1] one of the brethren of San Marco in whom I most confide."

"I would rather have no guidance but yours, father," said Romola, looking anxious.

"My daughter, I do not act as a confessor. The vocation I have withdraws me from offices that would force me into frequent contact with the laity, and interfere with my special duties."

"Then shall I not be able to speak to you in private? if I waver. . . . if—" Romola broke off from rising agitation. She felt a sudden alarm lest her new strength in renunciation should vanish if the immediate personal influence of Savonarola vanished.

"My daughter, if your soul has need of the word in private[2] from my lips, you will let me knew it through Fra Salvestro, and I will see you in the sacristy or in the choir of San Marco. And I will not cease to watch over you. I will instruct my brother concerning you, that he may guide you into that path of labour for the suffering and the hungry to which you are called as a daughter of Florence in these times of hard need. I desire to behold you among the feebler and more

1 ⟨brothers⟩ brethren *MS*   2 word in private] word *MS*

ignorant sisters as the apple-tree among the trees of the forest, so that your fairness and all natural gifts may be but as a lamp through which the divine light shines the more purely. I will go now and call your servant."

When Maso had been sent a little way in advance, Fra Salvestro came forward, and Savonarola led Romola towards him. She had beforehand felt an inward shrinking from a new guide who was a total stranger to her; but to have resisted Savonarola's advice would have been to assume an attitude of independence at a moment when all her strength must be drawn from the renunciation of independence. And the whole bent of her mind now was towards doing what was painful rather than what was easy. She bowed reverently to Fra Salvestro before looking directly at him; but when she raised her head and saw him fully, her reluctance became a palpitating[3] doubt. There are men whose presence infuses trust and reverence; there are others to whom we have need to carry our trust and reverence ready made; and that difference flashed on Romola as she ceased to have Savonarola before her, and saw in his stead Fra Salvestro Maruffi. It was not that there was anything manifestly repulsive in Fra Salvestro's face and manner, any air of hypocrisy, any tinge of coarseness; his face was handsomer than Fra Girolamo's, his person a little taller. He was the long-accepted confessor of many among the chief personages in Florence, and had therefore had large experience as a spiritual director. But his face had the vacillating expression of a mind unable to concentrate itself strongly in the channel of one great emotion or belief, an expression which is fatal to influence over an ardent nature like Romola's. Such an expression is not the stamp of insincerity; it is the stamp simply of a shallow soul, which will often be found sincerely striving to fill a high vocation, sincerely composing its countenance to the utterance of sublime formulas, but finding the muscles twitch or relax in spite of belief, as prose insists on[4] coming instead of poetry to the man who has not the divine frenzy. Fra Salvestro had a peculiar liability to visions, dependent apparently on a constitution given to somnambulism[5].* Savonarola believed in the supernatural character of these visions, while Fra Salvestro himself had originally resisted such an interpretation of them, and had even rebuked Savonarola for his prophetic preaching. Another[6] proof, if one were wanted, that the relative greatness of men is not to be gauged by their tendency to disbelieve the superstitions of their age. For of these two there can be no question which was the great man and which the small.

The difference between them was measured very accurately by the

3 palpitating] chill palpitating *MS*   4 on] *MS CM 1 3C* in *2*
5 somnambulism ⟨, and with a characteristic that⟩. *MS*
6 preaching. Another] preaching: another *2 3*

change in Romola's feeling as Fra Salvestro began to address her in words of exhortation and encouragement. After her first angry resistance of Savonarola had passed away, she had lost all remembrance of the old dread lest any influence should drag her [7]within the circle of fanaticism and sour monkish piety. But now again, the chill breath of that dread stole over her. It could have no decisive effect against the impetus her mind had just received; it was only like the closing of the grey clouds over the sunrise, which made her returning path monotonous and sombre.

And perhaps of all sombre paths that on which we go back after treading it with a strong resolution is the one that most severely tests the fervour of renunciation. As they re-entered the city gates the light snow-flakes fell about them, and as the grey sister walked hastily homeward from the Piazza di San Marco, and trod the bridge again, and turned in at the large door in the Via de' Bardi, her footsteps were marked darkly on the thin carpet of snow, and her cowl fell laden and damp about her face.

She went up to her room, threw off her serge, destroyed the parting letters, replaced all her precious trifles, unbound her hair, and put on her usual black dress. Instead of taking a[8] long exciting journey, she was to sit down in her usual place. The snow fell against the windows, and she was alone.

She felt the dreariness, yet her courage was high, like that of a seeker who has come on new signs of gold. She was going to thread life by a [9]fresh clue. She had thrown all the energy of her will into renunciation. [1]The empty tabernacle remained locked, and she placed Dino's crucifix outside it.

Nothing broke the outward monotony of her solitary home, till the night came like a white ghost at the windows. Yet it was the most memorable Christmas-eve in her life to Romola, this of 1494.

END OF BOOK II

7 ⟨into⟩ within *MS*   8 {taking} a *MS*   9 ⟨new⟩ fresh *MS*
1 ⟨She looked up⟩ The *MS*

BOOK III

*

CHAPTER XLII.

ROMOLA IN HER PLACE

It was the thirtieth of October, 1496. The sky that morning was clear enough, and there was a pleasant autumnal breeze. But the Florentines just then thought very little about the land breezes: they were thinking of the gales at sea, which seemed to be uniting with all other powers to disprove the Frate's declaration that Heaven [1]took special care of Florence.

For those terrible gales had driven away from the coast of Leghorn certain ships from Marseilles, freighted with soldiery and corn; and Forence was in the direst need, first of food, and secondly of fighting men. Pale Famine was in her streets, and her territory was threatened on all its borders.

For the French King, that new Charlemagne, who had entered Italy in anticipatory triumph, and had conquered Naples without the least trouble, had gone away again fifteen months ago, and was even, it was feared, in his grief for the loss of a new-born son,* losing the languid intention of coming back again to redress grievances and set the Church in order. A league had been formed* against him—a Holy League, with Pope Borgia at its head, to "drive out the barbarians," who still garrisoned the fortresses[2] of Naples. That had a [3]patriotic sound; but, looked at more closely, the Holy League seemed very much like an agreement among certain wolves to drive away all other wolves and then to see which among themselves could snatch the largest share of the prey. And there was a general disposition to regard Florence not as a fellow wolf, but rather as a desirable carcase. Florence, therefore, of all the chief Italian States, had alone declined to join the League, adhering still to the French alliance.

She had declined at her peril. At this moment Pisa, still fighting savagely for liberty, was being encouraged not only by strong forces from Venice and Milan, but by the presence of the German Emperor Maximilian, who had been invited by the League, and was joining the

---

1 ⟨had⟩ took special care ⟨of⟩ ⟨for⟩ of *MS*   2 fortresses] *MS* fortress *CM 1 2 3*
3 ⟨very⟩ patriotic *MS*

The Visible Madonna

Pisans with such troops as he had in the attempt to get possession of Leghorn, while the coast was invested by Venetian and Genoese ships. And if Leghorn should fall into the hands of the enemy, woe to Florence! For if that one outlet towards the sea were closed, hedged in as she was on the land by the bitter ill-will of the Pope and the jealousy of smaller Sates, how could succours reach her?

The government of Florence had shown a great heart in this urgent need, meeting losses and defeats with vigorous effort, raising fresh money, raising fresh soldiers, but not neglecting the good old method of Italian defence—conciliatory embassies. And while the scarcity of food [4]was every day becoming greater, they had resolved, in opposition to old precedent, not to shut out the starving country people, and the mendicants driven from the gates of other cities, who came flocking to Florence like birds from a land of snow. These acts of a government in which the disciples of Savonarola made the strongest element were not allowed to pass without criticism. The disaffected were plentiful, and they saw clearly that the government took the worst course for the public welfare. Florence ought to join the League and make common cause with the other great Italian States, instead of drawing down their hostility by a futile adherence to a foreign ally. Florence ought to take care of her own citizens, instead of opening her gates to famine and pestilence in the shape of starving contadini and alien mendicants.

Every day the distress became sharper: every day the murmurs became louder. And, to crown the difficulties of the government, for a month and more—in obedience to a mandate from Rome—Fra Girolamo had ceased to preach. But on the arrival of the terrible news that the ships from Marseilles had been driven back, and that no corn was coming, the need for the voice that could infuse faith and patience into the people became too imperative to be resisted. In defiance of the Papal mandate the Signoria requested Savonarola to preach. And two days ago* he had mounted again the pulpit of the Duomo, and had told the people only to wait and be steadfast, and the divine help would certainly come. It was a bold sermon: he consented to have his frock stripped off him if, when Florence persevered in fulfilling the duties of piety and citizenship, God did not come to her rescue.

Yet at present, on this morning of the thirtieth, there[5] were no signs of rescue. Perhaps if the precious Tabernacle of the Madonna dell' Impruneta were brought into Florence and carried in devout procession to the Duomo, that Mother, rich in sorrows and therefore

4 ⟨became⟩ was every day becoming *MS*
5 Yet at present . . . there] It was now the thirtieth of the month, yet at present there *MS*

in mercy, would plead for the suffering city? For a century and a half there were records of how[6] the Florentines, suffering from drought, or flood, or famine, or pestilence, or the threat of wars, had fetched the potent image within their walls, and had found deliverance. And grateful honour had been done to her and her ancient church[7] of L'Impruneta; the high house of Buondelmonti, patrons of the church, had to guard her hidden Image with bare sword; wealth had been poured out for prayers at her shrine, for chantings, and chapels, and ever-burning lights; and lands had been added, till there was much quarrelling for the privilege of serving her. The Florentines were deeply convinced of her graciousness to them, so that the sight of her Tabernacle within their walls was like the parting of the cloud, and the proverb ran, that[8] the Florentines had a Madonna who would do what they pleased. When were they in more need of her pleading pity than now? And already, the evening before, the Tabernacle containing the [9]miraculous hidden image had been brought with high and reverend escort from L'Impruneta, the privileged spot six miles beyond the gate of San Piero that looks towards Rome, and had been deposited in the church of San Gaggio, outside the gate, whence it was to be fetched in solemn procession by all the fraternities,[1] trades, and authorities of Florence.

But the Pitying Mother had not yet entered within the walls, and the morning arose on unchanged misery and despondency. Pestilence was hovering in the track of famine. Not only the hospitals were full, but the courtyards of private houses had been turned into refuges and infirmaries; and still there was unsheltered want. And early this morning, as usual, members of the various fraternities who made it part of their duty to bury the unfriended dead, were bearing away the corpses that had sunk by the wayside. As usual, sweet womanly forms, with the refined air and carriage of the well-born, but in the plainest garb, were moving about the streets on their daily errands of tending the sick and relieving the hungry.

One of these forms was easily distinguishable as Romola de' Bardi. Clad in the simplest garment of black serge, with a plain piece of black drapery drawn over her head, so as to [2]hide all her hair, except the bands of gold that rippled apart on her brow, she was advancing from the Ponte Vecchio towards the Por' Santa Maria—the street in a direct line with the bridge—when she found her way obstructed by

---

6 of how] *MS* how *CM 1 2 3*   7 church] {parish} church *MS*
8 that ⟨then Florentines⟩ ⟨Florence⟩ the Florentines had a Madonna who would do what ⟨they⟩ ⟨it⟩ they pleased. When ⟨had they had⟩ were they more in need of her {pleading pity} than now? *MS*
9 ⟨angel[ic]⟩ miraculous *MS*   1 fraternities, ⟨and⟩ trades {and authorities} *MS*
2 ⟨hold⟩ hide *MS*

the pausing of a bier, which was being carried by members of the company of San Jacopo del Popolo,* in search for the unburied dead. The brethren at the head of the bier were stooping to examine something, while a group of idle workmen, with features paled and sharpened by hunger, were clustering round³ and all talking at once.

"He's dead, I tell you! Messer Domeneddio has loved him well enough to take him."

"Ah, and it would be well for us all if we could have our legs stretched out and go with our heads two or three *bracci* foremost!* It's ill standing upright with hunger to prop you."

"Well, well, he's an old fellow. Death has got a poor bargain. Life's had the best of him."

"And no Florentine, ten to one! A beggar turned out of Siena. San Giovanni defend us! They've no need of soldiers to fight us. They send us an army of starving men."

"No, no! This man is one of the prisoners turned out of the Stinche. I know by the grey patch where the prison badge was."

"Keep quiet! Lend a hand! Don't you see the brethren are going to lift him on the bier?"

"It's likely he's alive enough if he could only look it. The soul may be inside him if it had only a drop of *vernaccia* to warm it."

"In truth, I think he is not dead," said one of the brethren, when they had lifted him on the bier. "He has perhaps only sunk down for want of food."

"Let me try to give him some wine," said Romola, coming forward. She loosened the small flask which she carried at her belt, and, leaning towards the prostrate body, with a deft hand she applied a small ivory implement between the teeth, and poured into the mouth a few drops of wine. The stimulus acted: the wine was evidently swallowed. She poured more, till the head was moved a little towards her, and the eyes of the old man opened full upon her with the vague look of returning consciousness. Then for the first time a sense of complete recognition came over Romola. Those wild dark eyes opening in the sallow deep-lined face, with the white beard, which was now long again, were like an unmistakable signature to a remembered handwriting. The light of two summers had not made that image any fainter in Romola's memory: the image of the escaped prisoner, whom she had seen in the Duomo the day when Tito first wore the armour—at whose grasp Tito was paled with terror in the strange sketch she had seen in Piero's studio. A wretched tremor and palpitation seized her. Now at last, perhaps, she was going to know some secret which might be more bitter than all that had gone before. She

3 round] around *1 2 3*

felt an impulse to dart away as from a sight[4] of horror; and again, a more imperious need to keep close by the side of this old man whom, the divination of keen feeling told her, her husband had injured. In the very instant of this conflict she still leaned towards him and kept her right hand ready to administer more wine, while her left was passed under his neck. Her hands trembled, but their habit of soothing helpfulness would have served to guide them without the direction of her thought.

Baldassarre was looking at *her* for the first time. The close seclusion in which Romola's trouble had kept her in the weeks preceding her flight and his arrest, had denied him the opportunity he had sought of seeing the Wife who lived in the Via de' Bardi: and at this moment the descriptions he had heard of the fair golden-haired woman were all gone, like yesterday's waves.

"Will it not be well to carry him to the steps of San Stefano?" said Romola. "We shall cease then to stop up the street, and you can go on your way with your[5] bier."

They had only to move onward for about thirty yards before reaching the steps of San Stefano, and by this time Baldassarre was able himself to make some efforts towards getting off the bier, and propping himself on the steps against the church doorway. The charitable brethren passed on, but the group of interested spectators, who had nothing to do and much to say, had considerably increased. The feeling towards the old man was not so entirely friendly now it was quite certain that he was alive, but the respect inspired by Romola's presence caused the passing remarks to be made in a rather more subdued tone than before.

"Ah, they gave him his morsel every day in the Stinche—that's why he can't do so well without it. You and I, Cecco, know better what it is to go to bed fasting."

"*Gnaffè!* that's why the Magnificent Eight have turned out some of the prisoners, that they may shelter honest people instead. But if every thief is to be brought to life with good wine and wheaten bread, we Ciompi had better go and fill ourselves in Arno while the water's plenty."

Romola had seated herself on the steps by Baldassarre, and was saying, "Can you eat a little bread now? perhaps by and by you will be able, if I leave it with you. I must go on, because I have promised to be at the hospital. But I will come back, if you will wait here, and then I will take you to some shelter. Do you understand? Will you wait? I will come back."

He looked dreamily at her, and repeated her words, "come back."

4 a sight] 3P some sight *MS CM 1 2*   5 your] the *MS*

It was no wonder that his mind was enfeebled by his bodily exhaustion, but she hoped that he apprehended her meaning. She opened her basket, which was filled with pieces of soft bread, and put one of the pieces into his hand.

"Do you keep your bread for those that can't swallow, madonna?" said a rough-looking fellow, in a red night-cap[6], who had elbowed his way into the inmost circle of spectators—a circle that was pressing rather closely on Romola.

"If anybody isn't hungry," said another, "I say, let him alone. He's better off than people who've got craving stomachs and no breakfast."

"Yes, indeed; if a man's a mind to die, it's a time to encourage him, instead of making him come back to life against his will. Dead men want no trencher."

"Oh, you don't understand the Frate's charity," said a young man[7] in an excellent cloth tunic, whose face showed no signs of want. "The Frate has been preaching to the birds, like Saint Anthony,* and he's been telling the hawks they were made to feed the sparrows, as every good Florentine citizen was made to feed six starving beggarmen from Arezzo or Bologna.* [8]Madonna, there, is a pious Piagnone: she's not going to throw away her good bread on honest citizens who've got all the Frate's prophecies to swallow."

"Come, madonna," said he of the red cap, "the old thief doesn't eat the bread, you see: you'd better try us[9]. We fast so much, we're half saints already."

The circle had narrowed till the coarse men—most of them gaunt from privation—had left hardly any margin round Romola. [1]She had been taking from her basket a small horn cup, into which she put the piece of bread and just moistened it with wine; and hitherto she had not appeared to heed them. But now she rose[2] to her feet, and looked round at them. Instinctively the men who were nearest to her pushed backward a little, as if their rude nearness were the fault of those behind. Romola held out the basket of bread to the man in the nightcap, looking at him without any reproach in her glance, as she said,—

"[3]Hunger is hard to bear, I know, and you have the power to take this bread if you will. [4]It was saved for sick women and children. You are strong men; but if you do not[5] choose to suffer because you are strong, you have the power to take everything from the weak. You

6 fellow {in a red ⟨cap⟩ nightcap} MS   7 {young} man MS
8 ⟨Madonna ⟨⟨most pities the⟩⟩ leaves on Florentines nothing⟩ Madonna MS
9 us] us MS
1 ⟨Hitherto she had not appeared to heed them and⟩ She had been taking ⟨a small horn cup⟩ from her basket a small {horn} cup MS
2 rose ⟨from⟩ MS
3 ⟨This bread was saved for sick women and children⟩ "Hunger MS
4 ⟨But⟩ It MS   5 do not ⟨feel⟩ MS

can take the bread from this basket; but I shall watch by this old man; I shall resist your taking the bread from *him*."

For a few moments there was perfect silence, while Romola looked at the faces before her, and held out the basket of bread. Her own pale face had the slightly pinched look and the deepening of the eye-socket which indicate unusual fasting in the habitually temperate, and the large direct gaze of her hazel eyes was all the more impressive. [6]The man in the night-cap [7]looked rather silly, and backed, thrusting his elbow into his neighbour's ribs with an air of moral rebuke. The backing was general, every one wishing to imply that he had been pushed forward against his will; and the young man in the fine cloth tunic[8] had disappeared.

But at this moment the armed servitors of the Signoria, who had begun to patrol the line of streets through which the procession was to pass, came up to disperse the group which was obstructing the narrow street. The man addressed as Cecco retreated from a threatening mace up the church steps, and said to Romola, in a respectful tone,—

"Madonna, if you want to go on your errands, I'll take care of the old man."

Cecco was a wild-looking figure: a very ragged tunic, made shaggy and variegated by cloth-dust and clinging fragments of wool, gave relief to a pair of bony arms and a long sinewy neck; his square jaw shaded by a bristly black beard, his bridgeless nose and low forehead, made his face look as if it had been crushed down for purposes of packing, and a narrow piece of red rag tied over his ears seemed[9] to assist in the compression. Romola looked at him with some hesitation.

"Don't mistrust me, madonna," said Cecco, who understood her look perfectly; "I'm[1] not so pretty as you, but I've got an old mother who eats my porridge for me. What! there's a heart inside me, and I've bought a candle for the Most Holy Virgin before now. Besides, see there, the old fellow is eating his sop. He's [2]hale enough: he'll be on his legs as well as the best of us by and by."

"Thank you for offering to take care of him, friend," said Romola, rather penitent for her doubting glance. Then leaning to Baldassarre, she said, "Pray wait for me till I come again."

He assented with a slight movement of the head and hand, and Romola went on her way towards the hospital of San Matteo,* in the Piazza di San Marco.

6 ⟨There is a rebuke so strong in the presence⟩ The man *MS*
7 ⟨thrust his hands behind him and backed⟩ looked *MS*
8 in {the} fine cloth {tunic} *MS*   9 seemed ⟨intended to secure⟩ *MS*
1 I'm] I am *2 3*   2 ⟨pale⟩ hale *MS*

CHAPTER XLIII.

THE UNSEEN [1]MADONNA

In returning from the hospital, more than an hour later, Romola took a different road, making a wider circuit towards the river, which she reached at some distance from the Ponte Vecchio. She turned her steps towards that bridge, intending to hasten to San Stefano* in search of Baldassarre. She dreaded to know more about him, yet she felt as if, in forsaking him, she would be forsaking some near claim upon her.

But when she approached the meeting of the roads where the Por' Santa Maria would be on her right hand and the Ponte Vecchio on her left, she found herself involved in a crowd who suddenly fell on their knees; and she immediately knelt with them. The Cross was passing—the Great Cross of the Duomo—which headed the procession. Romola was later than she had expected to be, and now she must wait till the procession had passed. As she rose from her knees, when the Cross had disappeared, the return to a standing posture, with nothing to do but gaze, made her more conscious of her fatigue than she had been while she had been walking and occupied. A shop-keeper by her side said,—

"Madonna Romola, you will be weary of standing: Gian Fantoni will be glad to give you a seat in his house. Here is his door close at hand. Let me open it for you. What! he loves God and the Frate as we do. His house is yours."

Romola was accustomed now to be addressed in this fraternal way by ordinary citizens, whose faces were familiar to her from her having seen them constantly in the Duomo. The idea of home had come to be identified for her less with the house in the Via de' Bardi, where she sat in frequent loneliness, than with the towered[2] circuit of Florence, where there was hardly a turn of the streets at which she was not greeted with looks of appeal or of friendliness. She was glad enough to pass through the opened[3] door on her right hand and be led by the fraternal hose-vendor to an upstairs window, where a stout woman with three children, all in the plain garb of Piagnoni, made a place for her with much reverence above the bright hanging draperies. From this corner station she could see, not only the

---

1 ⟨Mother⟩ Madonna *MS*
2 The idea of home . . . towered] *1 2 3* The word "home" had come to mean, for her, less the house . . . than the towered *MS CM*
3 opened] open *1 2 3*

procession pouring in solemn slowness between the lines of houses on
the Ponte Vecchio, but also the river and the Lung' Arno on towards
the bridge of the Santa Trinità.

In sadness and in stillness came the slow procession. Not even a
wailing chant[4] broke the silent appeal for mercy: there was only the
tramp of footsteps, and the faint sweep of woollen garments. They
were young footsteps that were passing when Romola first looked
from the window—a long train of the Florentine youth, bearing high
in[5] the midst of them the white image of the youthful Jesus, with a
golden glory above his head, standing by the tall cross where the
thorns and the nails lay ready.

After that train of fresh beardless faces came the mysterious-
looking Companies of Discipline,* bound by secret rules to self-
chastisement, and devout praise, and special acts of piety; all wearing
a garb which concealed the whole head and face except the eyes.
Every one knew that these mysterious forms were Florentine citizens
of various ranks, who might be seen at ordinary times going about the
business of the shop, the counting-house, or the State; but no member now was discernible as son, husband, or father. They had
dropped their personality, and walked as symbols of a common vow.
Each company had its colour and its badge, but the garb of all was a
complete shroud, and left no expression but that of fellowship.

In comparison with them, the multitude of monks seemed to be
strongly distinguished individuals, in spite of the common tonsure
and the common frock. First came a white stream of reformed
Benedictines;* and then a much longer stream of the Frati Minori, or
Franciscans, in that age all clad in grey, with the knotted cord round
their waists, and some of them with the *zoccoli*, or wooden sandals,*
below their bare feet;—perhaps the most numerous order in
Florence,[6] and owning[7] many zealous members who loved mankind
and hated the Dominicans. And after the grey came the black of the
Augustinians of San Spirito, with more cultured human faces above
it—men who had inherited the library of Boccaccio, and had made
the most learned company in Florence when learning was rarer;* then
the white over dark of the Carmelites; and then again the unmixed
black of the Servites, that famous Florentine order[8] founded by seven
merchants who forsook their gains to adore the Divine Mother.*

4 chant] chant raised at intervals *MS*   5 {high} in *MS*
6 Florence, ⟨holding the great monasteries of Santa Croce and San ?Danielo⟩ *MS*
7 and owning] *MS* owning *CM 1 2 3*
8 order {⟨which had come to possess the great church and monastery of the
Annunziata, though it was founded in a very humble way⟩} founded by ⟨twelve⟩ seven
merchants who forsook their gains to adore the Divine Mother ⟨in small huts in Monte
Senario⟩. *MS*

And now the hearts of all on-lookers began to beat a little faster, either with hatred or with love, for there was a stream of black and white coming over the bridge—of black mantles over white scapularies; and every one knew that the Dominicans were coming. Those of Fiesole passed first. One black mantle parted by white after another, one tonsured head after another, and still expectation was suspended. They were very coarse mantles, all of them, and many were threadbare, if not ragged; for the Prior of San Marco had reduced the fraternities under his rule[9] to the strictest poverty and discipline. But in the long line of black and white there was at last singled out a mantle only a little more worn than the rest, with a tonsured head above it which might not have appeared supremely remarkable to a stranger who had not seen it on bronze medals, with the sword of God as its obverse; or surrounded by an armed guard on the way to the Duomo; or transfigured by the inward flame of the orator as it looked round on a rapt multitude.

[1]As the approach of Savonarola was discerned, none dared conspicuously to break the stillness by a sound which would rise above the solemn tramp of footsteps and the faint sweep of garments; nevertheless his ear, as well as other ears, caught a mingled sound of low[2] hissing that longed to be curses, and murmurs that longed to be blessings. Perhaps it was the sense that the hissing predominated which made two or three of his disciples in the foreground of the crowd, at the meeting of the roads, fall on their knees as if something divine were passing. The movement of silent homage spread: it went along the sides of the streets like a subtle shock, [3]leaving some unmoved, while it made the most bend the knee and bow the head. But the hatred, too, gathered a more intense expression; and as Savonarola passed up the Por' Santa Maria, Romola could see that some one at an upper window spat upon him.

Monks again—Frati Umiliati, or Humbled Brethren, from Ognissanti, with a glorious tradition of being the earliest workers in the wool trade;* and again more monks—Vallombrosan* and other varieties of Benedictines, reminding the instructed eye by niceties of form and colour that in ages of abuse, long ago, reformers had arisen who had marked a change of spirit by a change of garb; till at last the shaven crowns were at an end, and there came the train of untonsured secular priests.[4]

9 the fraternities under his rule] the two fraternities MS

1 ⟨At⟩ As MS   2 low] slow 3

3 ⟨leaving⟩ ⟨which left⟩ leaving some unmoved, ⟨making them⟩ while MS

4 priests ⟨and then all⟩ {. Then followed} the twenty one incorporated Arts of Florence, ⟨beginning⟩ in long array, ⟨from the bakers to the judges and notaries⟩ with their banners floating above them, ⟨and then⟩ in ⟨prouder⟩ proud declaration MS

Then followed the twenty-one incorporated Arts of Florence* in long array, with their banners floating above them in proud declaration that the bearers had their distinct functions, from the bakers of bread to the judges and notaries. And then all the secondary officers of state, beginning with the [5]less and going on to the greater, till the line of [6]secularities was broken by the Canons of the Duomo, carrying a sacred relic—the very head, enclosed in silver, of San Zenobio,* immortal bishop of Florence, whose virtues were held to have saved the city perhaps a thousand years before.

Here was the nucleus of the procession. Behind the relic came the Archbishop in gorgeous cope, with canopy held above him; and after him the mysterious hidden Image—hidden first by rich curtains of brocade enclosing an outer painted tabernacle, but within this, by the more ancient tabernacle which had never been opened in the memory of living men, or the fathers of living men. In that inner shrine was the [7]image of the Pitying Mother,* found ages ago in the soil of L'Impruneta, uttering a cry as the spade struck it. Hitherto the unseen Image had hardly ever been carried to the Duomo without having rich gifts borne before it. [8]There was no reciting the list of precious offerings made by emulous men and communities, especially of veils and curtains and mantles. But the richest of all these, it was said, had been given by a poor abbess and her nuns, who, having no money to buy materials, wove a mantle of gold brocade with their prayers, embroidered it and adorned it with their prayers, and, finally, saw their work presented to the Blessed Virgin in the great Piazza by two beautiful youths who spread out white wings and vanished in the blue.

But to-day there were no gifts carried before the Tabernacle: no donations were to be given to-day except to the poor. That had been the advice of Fra Girolamo, whose preaching never insisted on gifts to the invisible powers, but only on help to visible need; and altars had been raised at various points in front of the churches, on which the oblations for the poor were deposited. Not even a torch was carried. Surely the hidden Mother cared less for torches and brocade than for the wail of the hungry people. Florence was in extremity: she had done her utmost, and could only wait for something divine that was not in her own power.

The Frate in the torn mantle had said that help would certainly come, and many of the faint-hearted were clinging more to their faith in the Frate's word, than to their faith in the virtues of the unseen

5 ⟨least⟩ less MS   6 ⟨secular officials⟩ secularities MS

7 ⟨unseen⟩ image MS

8 ⟨Mantles and ornaments and all precious things offered by emulous men and communities⟩ There MS

Image. But there were not a few of the fierce-hearted who thought with secret rejoicing that the Frate's word might be proved false.

Slowly the Tabernacle moved forward, and knees were bent. There was profound stillness; for the train of priests and chaplains from L'Impruneta stirred no passion in the on-lookers[9]. The procession was about to close with the Priors and the Gonfaloniere; the long train of companies and symbols, which have their silent music and stir the mind as a chorus stirs it, was passing out of sight, and now a faint yearning hope was all that struggled with the accustomed despondency.

Romola, whose heart had been swelling, half with foreboding, half with that enthusiasm of fellowship which the life of the last two years had made as habitual to her as the consciousness of costume to[1] a vain and idle woman, gave a deep sigh, as at the end of some long mental tension, and remained on her knees for very languor; when suddenly there flashed from between the houses on to the distant bridge something bright-coloured. In the instant, Romola started up and stretched out her arms, leaning from the window, while the black drapery fell from her head, and the golden gleam of her hair[2] and the flush in her face seemed the effect of one illumination. A shout arose in the same instant; the last troops of the procession paused, and all faces were turned towards the distant bridge.

But the bridge was passed now; the horseman was pressing at full gallop along by the Arno; the sides of his bay horse, just streaked[3] with foam, looked all white from swiftness; his cap was flying loose by his red *becchetto*, and he waved an olive branch in his hand. It was a messenger—a messenger of good tidings! The blessed olive branch spoke afar off. But the impatient people could not wait. They rushed to meet the on-comer, and seized his horse's rein, pushing and trampling.

And now Romola could see that the horseman was her husband, who had been sent to Pisa a few days before on a private embassy. The recognition brought no new flash of joy into her eyes. She had checked her first impulsive attitude of expectation; but her governing anxiety was still to know what news of relief had come for Florence.

"Good news!" "Best news!" "News to be paid with hose (*novelle da calze*)!" were the vague answers with which Tito met the [4]importunities of the crowd, until he had succeeded in pushing on his horse to the spot at the meeting of the ways where the Gonfaloniere and the Priors were awaiting him. There he paused, and, bowing low, said:—

9 on-lookers ⟨and now, as the⟩. The *MS*   1 to ⟨the vain and idle⟩ *MS*
2 and {⟨her golden hair and⟩ the golden gleam of her hair} *MS*
3 {just} streaked *MS*   4 ⟨inquiries⟩ importunities *MS*

"Magnificent Signori! I have to deliver to you the joyful news that the galleys from France, laden with corn and men[5], have arrived safely in the port of Leghorn, by favour of a strong wind, which kept the enemy's fleet at a distance."

The words had no sooner left Tito's lips than they seemed to vibrate up the streets. A great shout rang through the air, and rushed along the river; and then another, and another; and the shouts were heard spreading along the line of the procession towards the Duomo; and then there were fainter answering shouts, like the intermediate plash of distant waves in a great lake whose waters obey one impulse.

For some minutes there was no attempt to speak further: the Signoria themselves lifted up their caps, and stood bare-headed in the presence of a rescue which had come from outside the limit of their own power—from that region of trust and resignation which has been in all ages called divine.

At last, as the signal was given to move forward, Tito said, with a smile—

"[6]I ought to say, that any hose to be bestowed by the Magnificent Signoria in reward of these tidings, are due, not to me, but to another man who had ridden hard to bring them, and would have been here in my place if his horse had not broken down just before he reached Signa. Meo[7] di Sasso will doubtless be here in [8]an hour or two, and may all the more[9] justly claim the glory of the messenger, because he has had the chief labour and has lost the chief delight."

It was a graceful way of putting a necessary statement, and after a word of reply from the *Proposto*, or spokesman[1] of the Signoria, this dignified extremity of the procession passed on, and Tito turned his horse's head to follow in its train, while the great bell of the Palazzo Vecchio was already beginning to swing, and give a louder voice to the people's joy.

In that moment, when Tito's attention has ceased to be imperatively directed, it might have been expected that he would look round and recognize Romola; but he was apparently engaged with his cap, which, now the eager people were leading his horse, he was able to seize and place on his head, while his right hand was still encumbered with[2] the olive branch. He had a becoming air of lassitude after his exertions; and Romola, instead of making any effort to be recognized by him, threw her black drapery over her head again, and remained perfectly quiet. Yet she felt almost sure that Tito had seen her; he had the power of seeing everything without seeming to see it.

5 France {laden with corn and men} *MS*
6 ⟨The⟩ ⟨I should⟩ I ought *MS*   7 Meo] Good Meo *MS*
8 ⟨a few hours⟩ an hour or two *MS*   9 {all the} more *MS*
1 spokesman] "foreman" *MS*   2 with] by *2 3*

CHAPTER XLIV.

THE VISIBLE MADONNA

THE crowd had no sooner passed onward than Romola descended to the street, and hastened to the steps of San Stefano. Cecco had been attracted with the rest towards the Piazza, and she found Baldassarre standing alone against the church door, with the horn cup in his hand, waiting for her. There was a striking change in him: the blank, dreamy glance of a half-returned consciousness had given place to a fierceness which, as she advanced and spoke to him, flashed upon her as if she had been its object. It was the glance of caged fury that sees its prey passing safe beyond the bars.

Romola started as the glance was turned on her, but her immediate thought was that he had seen Tito. And as she felt the look of hatred grating on her, something like a hope arose that this man might be the criminal, and that her husband might not have been guilty towards him. If she could learn that now, by bringing Tito face to face with him, and have her mind set at rest!

"If you will come with me," she said, "I can give you shelter and food until you are quite rested and strong. Will you come?"

"Yes," said Baldassarre, "I shall be glad to get my strength. I want to get my strength," he repeated, as if he were muttering to himself, rather than speaking to her.

"Come!" she said, inviting him to walk by her side, and taking the way by the Arno towards the Ponte Rubaconte as the more private road.

"I think you are not a Florentine," she said, presently, as they turned on to the bridge.

He looked round at her without speaking. [1]His suspicious caution was more strongly upon him than usual, just now[2] that the fog of confusion and oblivion was made denser by bodily feebleness. But she was looking at him too, and there was something in her gentle eyes which at last compelled him to answer her. But he answered cautiously,—

"No, I am no Florentine; I am a lonely man."

She observed his reluctance to speak to her, and dared not question him further, lest he should desire to quit her. As she glanced at him from time to time, her[3] mind was busy with thoughts which

---

1 ⟨The state of timid suspicion which belonged to the sense that his mental power was gone⟩ His *MS*

2 {just} now *MS*   3 {As she glanced at him from time to time} Her *MS*

quenched the faint hope that there was nothing painful to be revealed about her husband. If this old man had been in the wrong, where was the cause for dread and secrecy? They walked on in silence till they reached the entrance into the Via de' Bardi, and Romola noticed that he turned and looked at her with a sudden movement as if some shock had passed through him. A [4]few moments after, she[5] paused at the half-open door of the court and turned towards him.

"Ah!" he said, not waiting for her to speak, "you are his wife."

"Whose wife?" said Romola.[6]

It would have been impossible for Baldassarre to recall any name at that moment. The very force with which the image of Tito pressed upon him seemed to expel any verbal sign. He made no answer, but looked at her with strange fixedness.

She opened the door wide and showed the court covered with [7]straw, on which lay four or five sick people, while some little children crawled or sat on it at their ease—tiny pale creatures, biting straws and gurgling.

"If you will come in," said Romola, tremulously. "I will find you a comfortable place, and bring you some more food."

"No, I will not come in," said Baldassarre. But he stood still, arrested by the burthen of [8]impressions under which his mind was too confused to choose a course.

"Can I do nothing for you?" said Romola. "Let me give you some money that you may buy food. It will be more plentiful soon."

She had put her hand into her scarsella as she spoke, and held out her palm with several grossi in it. She purposely offered him more than she would have given to any other man in the same circumstances. He looked at the coins a little while, and then said,—

"Yes[9], I will take them."

She poured the coins into his palm, and he grasped them tightly.

"Tell me," said Romola, almost beseechingly. "What shall you—"

But Baldassarre had turned away from her, and was walking again towards the bridge. Passing from it[1], straight on up the Via del Fosso, he came upon the shop of Niccolò Caparra,* and turned towards it without a pause, as if it had been the very object of his search. Niccolò was at that moment in procession with the Armourers of Florence, and there was only [2]one apprentice in the shop. But there were all sorts of weapons in abundance hanging there, and Baldassarre's eyes discerned what he was more hungry for than for

---

4 ⟨minute⟩ few moments *MS*   5 after, she] *3C* after she *MS CM 1 2*
6 said Romola.] *1 2 3* said Romola, flushing and trembling. *MS CM*
7 ⟨beds of⟩ straw *MS*   8 ⟨ideas⟩ impressions *MS*   9 "Yes: ⟨it is just⟩ *MS*
1 Passing {from it} *MS*   2 ⟨an⟩ one *MS*

bread[3]. Niccolò himself would probably have refused to sell[4] anything that might serve as a weapon to this man with signs of the prison on him, but the apprentice, less observant and scrupulous, took three grossi for a sharp hunting-knife without any hesitation. It was a conveniently small weapon, which Baldassarre could easily thrust [5]within the breast of his tunic, and he walked on, feeling stronger. That sharp edge might give deadliness to the thrust of an aged arm: at least it was a companion, it was [6]a power in league with him, even if it failed. It would break against armour, but was the armour sure to be always there[7]? In those long months while vengeance had lain[8] in prison, baseness had perhaps become forgetful and secure. The knife had been bought with [9]the traitor's own money. That was just. Before he took the money, he had felt what he should do with it—buy a weapon. Yes, and if possible, [1]food too: food to nourish the arm that would grasp the weapon, food to nourish the body which was the temple of vengeance. When he had had enough bread, he would[2] be able to think and act—to think first how he could hide himself, lest Tito[3] should have him dragged away again. With that idea of hiding in his mind, Baldassarre turned up the narrowest streets, bought himself some meat and bread, and sat down under the first loggia to eat[4]. The bells [5]that swung out louder and louder peals of joy[6], laying hold of him and making him vibrate along with all the air, seemed to him simply part of that strong world which was against him.

Romola had watched Baldassarre until he had disappeared round the turning into the Piazza de' Mozzi, half feeling that his departure was a relief, half reproaching herself for not seeking with more decision to know the truth about him, for not assuring herself whether there [7]were any guiltless misery in his lot which she was not helpless to relieve. Yet what could she have done if the truth had proved to be the burthen of some painful secret about her husband, in addition to the anxieties that already weighed upon her? Surely a wife [8]was permitted to desire ignorance of a husband's wrong-doing, since she alone must not protest[9] and warn men against him. But that thought stirred too many intricate fibres of feeling to be pursued now in her weariness. It was a time to rejoice, since help had come to Florence; and she turned into the [1]court to tell the good news to her patients

3 than {for} bread MS   4 sell ⟨a [?dagger] to this old⟩ MS
5 ⟨into⟩ within MS   6 ⟨something⟩ a power MS
7 {always} there MS   8 lain ⟨forgotten⟩ MS
9 ⟨Tito's⟩ the traitor's MS
1 ⟨bread⟩ food too, ⟨bread⟩ food . . . weapon, ⟨bread⟩ food MS
2 ⟨should⟩ would] MS should CM 1 2 3   3 Tito] 1 2 3 the traitor MS CM
4 eat] eat it MS   5 ⟨which⟩ that MS
6 joy ⟨making all the⟩ MS   7 ⟨was⟩ were MS   8 ⟨is⟩ was MS
9 protest ⟨against it⟩ MS   1 ⟨courtyard⟩ court MS

on their straw beds[2]. She closed the door after her, [3]lest the bells should drown her voice, and then[4] throwing the black drapery from her head, that the women might see her better, she stood in the midst and told them that corn was coming, and that the bells were ringing for gladness at the news. They all sat up to listen, while the children trotted or crawled towards her, and pulled her black skirts, as if they were impatient at being all that long way off her face. She yielded[5] to them, weary as she was, and sat down on the straw, while the little pale things peeped into her basket and pulled her hair down, and the feeble voices around her said, "The Holy Virgin be praised!" "It was the procession!" "The Mother of God has had pity on us!"

At last Romola rose from the heap of straw, too tired to try and smile any longer, saying as she turned up the stone steps,—

"I will come by and by, to bring you your dinner."

"Bless you, madonna! bless you!" said the faint chorus, in much the same tone as that in which they had a few minutes before praised and thanked the unseen Madonna.

Romola cared a great deal for that music. She had no innate taste for tending the sick and clothing the ragged, like some women to whom the details of such work are welcome in themselves, simply as an occupation. Her early training had kept her aloof from such womanly labours; and if she had not brought to them the inspiration of her deepest feelings, they would have been irksome to her. But they had come to be the one unshaken resting-place of her mind, the one narrow pathway on which the light fell clear. If the gulf between herself and Tito which[6] only gathered a more perceptible wideness from her attempts to bridge it by submission, brought a doubt whether, after all, the bond to which she had laboured to be true might not itself be false—if she came away from her confessor, Fra Salvestro, or from some contact with the disciples of Savonarola amongst whom she worshipped, with a sickening sense that these people were miserably narrow, and with an almost impetuous reaction towards her old contempt for their superstition—she found herself recovering a firm footing in her works of womanly sympathy. Whatever else made her doubt, the help she gave to her fellow-citizens made her sure that[7] Fra Girolamo had been right to call her back. According to his unforgotten words, her place had not been empty: it had been filled with her love and her labour[8]. Florence had had need of her, and the more her own sorrow pressed upon her, the more gladness she felt in the

2 beds ⟨and tell them that corn was coming and that the bells were ringing for gladness⟩ MS

3 ⟨that the bells might not⟩ lest MS   4 then ⟨standing in⟩ MS

5 yielded] gave way MS   6 Tito which] MS 1 2 3 Tito, which CM

7 sure that] sure, that MS   8 {her} labour MS

memories, stretching through the two long years, of hours and moments in which she had lightened the burthen of life to others. All that ardour of her nature which could no longer spend itself in the woman's tenderness for father and husband, had transformed itself into an enthusiasm of sympathy with the general life. She had ceased to think that her own lot could be happy—had ceased to think of happiness at all: the one end of her life seemed to her to be the diminishing of sorrow.

Her enthusiasm was continually stirred to fresh vigour by the influence of Savonarola. In spite of the wearisome visions and allegories from which she recoiled in disgust when they came as stale repetitions from other lips than his, her strong affinity for his passionate sympathy and the splendour of his aims had[9] lost none of its power. His burning indignation against the abuses and oppression that made the daily story of the Church and of States had kindled the ready fire in her too. His special care for liberty and purity of government in Florence, with his constant reference of this immediate[1] object to the wider end of a universal regeneration, had created in her a new consciousness of the great drama of human existence in which her life was a part; and through her daily helpful contact[2] with the less fortunate of her fellow-citizens this new consciousness became something stronger than a vague sentiment; it grew into a more and more definite motive of self-denying practice[3]. She thought little about dogmas, and shrank from reflecting closely on the Frate's prophecies of the immediate scourge and closely following regeneration. She had submitted her mind to his and had[4] entered into communion with the Church, because in this way she had found an immediate satisfaction for moral needs which all the previous culture and [5]experience of her life had left hungering. Fra Girolamo's voice had waked in her mind a reason for living, apart from personal enjoyment and personal affection; but it was a reason that seemed to need feeding with greater forces than she possessed within herself, and her[6] submissive use of all offices of the Church was simply a watching and waiting if by any means fresh strength might come. The pressing problem for Romola just then was not to settle questions of controversy, but to[7] keep alive that flame of unselfish emotion by which a life of sadness might still be a life of active love.

9 aims had] MS 1 2 3 aims, had CM   1 immediate] more immediate MS
2 {helpful} contact MS
3 citizens this new . . . practice] citizens brought that consciousness from the region of vague sentiment into that of self-denying practice MS
4 his and had] his, she had MS   5 ⟨satisfaction⟩ experience MS
6 herself, and her] herself, she trembled under the weight of a large effort, and ⟨in the⟩ her MS
7 to ⟨find the energies⟩ MS

Her trust in Savonarola's nature as greater than her own made a large part of the strength she had found. And [8]the trust was not to be lightly shaken. It is not force of intellect which causes ready repulsion from the aberrations[9] and eccentricities of greatness, any more than it is force of vision that causes the eye to explore the warts on a face bright with human expression; it is simply the negation of high sensibilities. Romola was so deeply moved by the grand energies of Savonarola's nature, that she found herself listening patiently to all dogmas and prophecies, when they came in the vehicle of his ardent faith and believing utterance.*

No [1]soul is desolate as long as there is a human being for whom it can feel trust and reverence. Romola's trust in Savonarola was something like a rope suspended securely[2] by her path, making her step elastic while she grasped it; if it were suddenly removed, no firmness of the ground she trod could save her from staggering, or perhaps from falling.

8 ⟨her⟩ the *MS*   9 aberrations] aberration *2 3*   1 ⟨life⟩ soul *MS*
2 securely ⟨from a ?block⟩ *MS*

CHAPTER XLV.

AT THE BARBER'S SHOP

AFTER that welcome appearance as the messenger with the olive branch, which was an unpromised favour of Fortune, Tito had other commissions to fulfil of a more premeditated character. He paused at the Palazzo Vecchio, and awaited there the return of the Ten[1], who managed external and war affairs, that he might duly deliver to them the results of his private mission to Pisa, [2]intended as a preliminary to an avowed embassy of which Bernardo Rucellai was to be the head, with the object of coming, if possible, to a pacific understanding with the Emperor Maximilian and the League.*

Tito's talents for diplomatic work had been well ascertained, and as he gave with [3]fullness and precision the results of his inquiries and interviews, Bernardo del Nero, who was at that time one of the Ten[4], could not withhold his admiration. He would have withheld it if he could; for his original dislike of Tito had returned, and become stronger, since the sale of the library. Romola had never uttered a word to her godfather on the [5]circumstances of the sale, and Bernardo had understood her silence as a prohibition to him to enter on the subject, but he felt sure that the breach of her father's wish had been a blighting grief to her, and the old man's observant[6] eyes discerned other indications that her married life was not happy.

"Ah," he said, inwardly, "that doubtless is the reason she has taken to listening to Fra Girolamo, and going amongst the Piagnoni, which I never expected from her. These women, if they are not happy, and have no children, must either take to folly or to some overstrained religion that makes them think they've got all heaven's work on their shoulders. And as for my poor child Romola, it is as I always said—the cramming with Latin and Greek has left her as much a woman as if she had done nothing all day but prick her fingers with the needle. And this husband of hers, who gets employed everywhere, because he's a tool with a smooth handle, I wish Tornabuoni and the rest may not [7]find their fingers cut. Well, well, *solco torto, sacco dritto*—many a full sack comes from a crooked furrow; and he who will be captain of none but honest men will have small hire to pay."

With this long-established conviction that there could be no moral sifting of political agents, the old Florentine abstained from all

1 the Ten] the *Dieci* or Ten *MS*
3 ⟨much⟩ fullness *MS*
5 ⟨subject⟩ circumstances of the sale *MS*
7 ⟨get⟩ find *MS*

2 ⟨which had been⟩ intended *MS*
4 the Ten] the *Dieci MS*
6 observant] *1 2 3* keen *MS CM*

interference in Tito's disfavour. Apart from what must be kept sacred and private[8] for Romola's sake, Bernardo had nothing distinct[9] to allege against the useful Greek, except that he was a Greek, and that he, Bernardo, did not like him; for the doubleness of feigning attachment to the popular government, while at heart a Medicean, was common to Tito with more than half the Medicean party. [1]He only feigned with more skill than the rest: that was all. So Bernardo was simply cold to Tito, who returned the coldness with a scrupulous, distant respect. And it was still the notion in Florence that the old tie between Bernardo and Bardo made any service done to Romola's husband an acceptable homage to her godfather.

After delivering himself of his charge at the Old Palace, Tito felt that the avowed official work of the day was done. He was tired and adust with long riding; but he did not go home. There were certain things in his scarsella and on his mind from which he wished to free himself as soon as possible, but the opportunities must be found so skilfully that they must not seem to be sought. [2]He walked from the Palazzo in a sauntering fashion towards the Piazza del Duomo. The procession [3]was at an end now, but the bells were still ringing, and the people were moving about the streets restlessly, longing for some more definite vent to their joy. If the Frate could have stood up in the great Piazza and preached to them, they might have been satisfied, but now, in spite of the new discipline which declared Christ to be the special King of the Florentines and required all pleasures to be of a Christian sort, there was a secret longing in many of the youngsters who shouted "Viva Gesù!" for a little vigorous stone-throwing in sign of thankfulness.

Tito as he passed along could not escape being recognized by some[4] as the welcome bearer of the olive branch, and could only rid himself of an inconvenient ovation, chiefly in the form of eager questions, by telling those who pressed on him that Meo di Sasso, the true messenger from Leghorn[5], must now be entering, and might certainly be met towards the Porta San Frediano. He could tell much more than Tito knew.

[6]Freeing himself from importunities in this adroit manner, he made his way to the Piazza del Duomo, casting his long eyes round the space with an air of the utmost carelessness, but really seeking to

---

8 sacred and private] sacredly private *MS*   9 distinct] direct *2 3*
1 ⟨Tito⟩ He only feigned ⟨better⟩ with more skill *MS*
2 ⟨No one must be able to prove that on the day of his return from Pisa he had sought ⟨⟨an⟩⟩ a private interview with any particular man⟩ He *MS*
3 ⟨was at an end⟩ ⟨was all dispersed⟩ was at an end *MS*
4 recognized {by some} *MS*   5 Leghorn] Lioverno *MS*
6 ⟨Having freed⟩ Freeing himself {from importunities} *MS*

detect some presence which might furnish him with one of his desired opportunities. The fact of the procession having terminated at the Duomo made it probable that there would be more than the usual concentration of loungers and talkers in the Piazza and round Nello's shop. It was as he expected. There was a group leaning against the rails near the north gates of the Baptistery, so exactly what he sought, that he looked more indifferent than ever, and seemed to recognize the tallest member of the group entirely by chance as he had half passed him, just turning his head to give him a slight greeting, while he tossed the end of his *becchetto* over his left shoulder.

Yet the tall, broad-shouldered personage greeted in that slight way looked like one who had considerable claims. He wore a richly embroidered tunic, with a great show of linen, after the newest French mode, and at his belt there hung a sword and poniard of fine workmanship. His hat, with a red plume in it, seemed a scornful protest against the gravity of Florentine costume, which had been exaggerated to the utmost under the influence of the Piagnoni. Certain undefinable indications of youth made the breadth of his face and the large diameter of his waist appear [7]the more emphatically a stamp of coarseness, and his eyes had that rude desecrating stare at all men and things which to a refined mind is as intolerable as a bad odour or a flaring light.

He and his companions, also young men dressed expensively and wearing arms, were[8] exchanging jokes with that sort of ostentatious laughter which implies a desire to prove that the laugher[9] is not mortified though some people might suspect it. There were good reasons for such a suspicion; for this broad-shouldered man with the red feather was Dolfo Spini, leader of the *Compagnacci*,* or Evil Companions—that is to say, of all the dissolute young men belonging to the old aristocratic party, enemies of the Mediceans, enemies[1] of the popular government, but still more bitter enemies of Savonarola. Dolfo Spini, heir of the great house with the loggia, over the bridge of the Santa Trinità[2],* had organized these young men into an armed band, as sworn champions of extravagant suppers and all the pleasant sins of the flesh, against reforming pietists who threatened to make the world chaste and temperate to so intolerable a degree that[3] there would soon be no reason for living, except the extreme unpleasantness of the alternative. Up to this very morning he had been loudly

7 ⟨the more emphatic stamp⟩ the more emphatically a stamp *MS*
8 light. {¶} He ⟨was ex[changing]⟩ and his companions {also young . . . wearing arms} were *MS*
9 laugher] laughter *3*
1 party, enemies of the Mediceans, enemies] party, enemies *MS*
2 {the} Santa Trinità *MS*   3 degree that] *MS 1 2 3* degree, that *MS*

declaring that Florence was given up to famine and ruin entirely
through its blind adherence to the advice of the Frate, and that there
could be no salvation for Florence but [4]in joining the League and driving the Frate out of the city—sending him to Rome, in fact, whither
he ought to have gone long ago in obedience to the summons of the
Pope. It was suspected, therefore, that Messer Dolfo Spini's heart was
not aglow with pure joy at the unexpected succours which had come
in apparent fulfilment of the Frate's prediction, and the laughter,
which was ringing out afresh as Tito joined the group at Nello's door,
did not serve to dissipate the suspicion. For leaning against the door-
post in the centre of the group was a close-shaven, keen-eyed personage, named Niccolò Macchiavelli, who, young as he was, had
penetrated all the small secrets of egoism.

"Messer Dolfo's head," he was saying, "is more of a pumpkin than
I thought. I measure men's dulness by the devices they trust in for
deceiving others. Your dullest animal of all is he who grins and says
he doesn't mind just after he has had his shins kicked. If I were a
trifle duller now," he went on, smiling as the circle opened to admit
Tito, "I should pretend to be fond of this Melema, who has got a
Secretaryship that would exactly suit me—as if Latin ill-paid could
love better Latin that's better paid! Melema, you are [5]a pestiferously
clever fellow, very much in my way, and I'm sorry to hear you've had
another piece of good luck to-day."

"Questionable luck, Niccolò," said Tito, touching him on the
shoulder in a friendly way; "I have got nothing by it yet but being
laid hold of and breathed upon by wool-beaters, when I am as soiled
and [6]battered with riding as a *tabellario* (letter-carrier) from Bologna."

"Ah! you want a touch of my art, Messer Oratore," said Nello,
who had come forward at the sound of Tito's voice; "your chin, I
perceive, has yesterday's crop upon it. Come, come—consign yourself
to the priest of all the Muses. Sandro, quick with the lather!"

"In truth, Nello, that is just what I most desire at this moment,"
said Tito, seating himself; "and that was why I turned my steps
towards thy shop, instead of going home at once, when I had done
my business at the Palazzo."

"Yes, indeed, it is not fitting that you should present yourself to
Madonna Romola with[7] a rusty chin and a tangled *zazzera*. Nothing
that is not dainty ought to approach the Florentine lily; though I see
her constantly going about like a sunbeam amongst the rags that line
our corners—if indeed she is not more like a moonbeam now, for I

4 ⟨by⟩ in *MS*   5 ⟨an [?oppressively]⟩ a pestiferously *MS*
6 ⟨?hardridden⟩ battered with riding as a {*tabellario* (} letter-carrier{)} from Bologna.
"⟨Nello, *amico mio*⟩ "Ah, you want a touch of my art, ⟨I perceive⟩ Messer *MS*
7 Madonna {Romola} with ⟨a chin of this rustiness⟩ a rusty chin *MS*

thought yesterday, when I met her, that she looked as pale and worn as that[8] fainting Madonna of Fra Giovanni's.* You must see to it, my *bel erudito*: she keeps too many fasts and vigils in your absence."

Tito gave a melancholy shrug. "It is too true, Nello. She has been depriving herself of half her proper food every day during this famine. But what can I do? Her mind has been set all aflame. A husband's influence is powerless against the Frate's."

"As every other influence is likely to be, that of the Holy Father included," said Domenico Cennini, one of the group at the door, who had turned in with Tito. "I don't know whether you have gathered anything at Pisa about the way the wind sits[9] at Rome, Melema?"

"Secrets of the council chamber, Messer Domenico!" said Tito, smiling and opening his palms in a deprecatory manner. "An envoy must be as dumb as a father confessor."

"Certainly, certainly," said Cennini. "I ask for no breach of that rule. Well, my belief is, that if his Holiness were to drive Fra Girolamo to extremity, the Frate would move heaven and earth to get a General Council of the Church[1]—ay, and would get it too; and I, for one, should not be sorry, though I'm no Piagnone."

"With leave of your greater experience, Messer Domenico," said Macchiavelli, "I must differ from you—not in your wish to see a General Council which might reform the Church, but in your belief that the Frate will checkmate his Holiness. The[2] Frate's game is an impossible one. If he had contented himself with preaching against the vices of Rome, and with prophesying that in some way, not mentioned, Italy would be scourged, depend upon it Pope[3] Alexander would have allowed him to spend his breath in that way as long as he could find hearers. Such spiritual blasts as those knock no walls down. But the Frate wants to be something more than a spiritual trumpet: he wants to be a lever, and what is more, he *is* a lever. He wants to spread the doctrine of Christ by maintaining a popular government in Florence, and the Pope, as I know, on the best authority, has private views to the contrary."

"Then Florence will stand by the Frate," [4]Cennini broke in, with some fervour. "I myself should prefer that he would let his prophesying alone, but if our freedom to choose our own government is to be attacked—I am an obedient son of the Church, but I would vote for resisting Pope Alexander the Sixth, as our forefathers resisted Pope Gregory the Eleventh."*

"But pardon me, Messer Domenico," said Macchiavelli, sticking

8 that] *MS CM 1 3C* the 2   9 sits] *MS 1 2 3* sets *CM*
1 Council of the Church] Council *MS*
2 you—not in your . . . Holiness. The] you. The *MS*
3 it Pope] *3C* it, Pope *MS CM 1 2*   4 ⟨said⟩ Cennini *MS*

his thumbs into his belt, and speaking with that cool enjoyment of exposition which surmounts every other force in discussion. "Have you correctly seized the Frate's position? How is it that he has become a lever, and made himself worth attacking by an acute man like his Holiness? Because he has got the ear of the people: because he gives them threats and promises[5], which they believe come straight from God, not only about hell, purgatory, and paradise, but about Pisa and our Great Council[6]. But let events go against him, so as to shake the people's faith, and the cause of his power will be the cause of his fall. He is accumulating three sorts of hatred on his head—the hatred of average mankind against every one who wants to lay on them a strict yoke of virtue; the hatred of the stronger powers in Italy, who want to farm Florence for their own purposes; and the hatred of the people, to[7] whom he has ventured to promise good in this world, instead of confining his promises to the next. If a prophet is to keep his power, he must be a prophet like Mahomet, with an army at his back, that when the people's faith is fainting it may be frightened into life again."

"Rather sum up the three sorts of hatred in one," said Francesco Cei, impetuously, "and say he has won the hatred of all men who have sense and honesty, by inventing hypocritical lies. His proper place is among the false prophets in the Inferno, who walk with their heads turned hind foremost."[*]

"You are too angry, my Francesco," said Macchiavelli, smiling; "you poets are apt to cut the clouds in your wrath. I am no votary of the Frate's, and would not lay down my little finger for his veracity. But veracity is a plant of paradise, and the seeds have never flourished beyond the walls. You yourself, my Francesco, tell poetical lies only; partly compelled by the poet's fervour, partly to please your audience; but you object to lies in prose. Well, the Frate differs from you as to the boundary of poetry, that's all. When he gets into the pulpit of the Duomo[8], he has the fervour within him, and without him he has the audience to please. Ecco!"

"You are somewhat lax there, Niccolò," said Cennini, gravely. "I myself believe in the Frate's integrity, though I don't believe in his prophecies, and as long as his integrity is not disproved, we have a popular party strong enough to [9]protect him and resist foreign interference."

"A party that seems strong enough," said Macchiavelli, with a shrug, and an almost imperceptible glance towards Tito, who [1]was

5 threats and promises] promises and threats *MS*
6 not only about . . . Council] not about ⟨[?hell] or heaven but⟩ paradise, purgatory and hell, but about Pisa and the Great Council *MS*
7 people, to] *1 2 3* people to *MS CM*   8 the {pulpit of the} Duomo *MS*
9 ⟨defend⟩ protect *MS*   1 ⟨seemed to be⟩ was *MS*

abandoning himself with much enjoyment to Nello's combing and scenting. "But how many Mediceans are there among you? How many who will not be turned round by a private grudge?"

"As to the Mediceans," said Cennini, "I believe there is very little genuine feeling left on behalf of the Medici. Who would risk much for Piero de' Medici? A few old staunch friends[2], perhaps, like Bernardo del Nero; but even some of those most connected with the family are hearty friends of the popular government, and would exert themselves for the Frate; I was talking to Giannozzo Pucci only [3]a little while ago, and I'm[4] convinced there's nothing he would set his face against more than against any attempt to alter the new order of things."

"You are right there, Messer Domenico," said Tito, with a laughing meaning in his eyes, as he rose from the shaving-chair; "and I fancy the tender passion came in aid of hard theory there. I am persuaded there was some jealousy at the bottom of Giannozzo's alienation from Piero de' Medici; else so amiable a creature as he[5] would never feel the bitterness he sometimes allows to escape him in that quarter. He was in the procession with you, I suppose?"

"No," said Cennini; "he is at his villa—went there three days ago."

Tito was settling his cap and glancing down at his splashed hose as if he hardly heeded the answer. In reality he had obtained a much-desired piece of information. He had at that moment in his scarsella a crushed gold ring which he had engaged to deliver to Giannozzo Pucci. He had received it from an envoy of Piero de' Medici, whom he had ridden out of his way to meet at Certaldo on the [6]Siena road. Since Pucci was not in the [7]town, he would send the ring by Fra Michele, a [8]Carthusian lay brother in the service of the Mediceans, and the receipt of that sign would bring Pucci back to hear the verbal part of Tito's mission.

"Behold him!" said Nello, [9]flourishing his comb and pointing it at Tito, "the handsomest scholar in the world or in the wolds,* now he has passed through my hands! A trifle thinner in the face, though, than when he came in his first bloom to Florence—eh? and, I vow, there are some lines just faintly hinting themselves about your mouth, Messer Oratore! Ah, mind is an enemy to beauty! I myself was thought beautiful by the women at one time—when I was in my swaddling-bands. But now—*oimè*! I carry my unwritten poems in cipher on my face!"

Tito, laughing with the rest as Nello looked at himself tragically in

2 friends ⟨of the family⟩ MS
3 ⟨just now⟩ a little while ago MS
5 as he ⟨looked at the ⟨⟨?ground⟩⟩ ?ceiling⟩ MS
6 ⟨road towards Siena⟩ Siena road MS
8 ⟨father⟩ Carthusian lay brother MS

4 I'm] I am 2 3
7 ⟨city⟩ town MS
9 ⟨pointing⟩ flourishing MS

the hand-mirror, made a sign of farewell to the company generally, and took his departure.

"I'm of our old Piero di Cosimo's mind," said Francesco Cei. "I don't half like Melema. That trick of smiling gets stronger than ever—no wonder he has lines about the mouth."

"He's too successful," said Macchiavelli, playfully. "I'm sure there's something wrong about him, else he wouldn't have that Secretaryship."

"He's an able man," said Cennini, in a tone of judicial fairness. "I and my brother have always found[1] him useful with our Greek sheets[2], and he gives great satisfaction to the Ten[3]. I like to see a young man work his way upward by merit. And the Secretary Scala, who befriended him from the first, thinks highly of him still, I know."

"Doubtless," said a notary in the background. "He writes Scala's official letters for him, or corrects them, and gets well paid for it too."

"I wish Messer Bartolommeo would pay *me* to doctor his gouty Latin," said Macchiavelli, with a shrug. "Did *he*[4] tell you about the pay, Ser Ceccone, or was it Melema himself?" he added, looking at the notary with a face ironically innocent.

"Melema? no, indeed," answered Ser Ceccone. "He is as close as a nut. He never brags. That's why he's employed everywhere. They say he's getting rich with doing all sorts of underhand work."

"It *is* a little too bad," said Macchiavelli, "and so many able notaries out of [5]employment!"

"Well, I must say I thought that was a nasty story a year or two ago about the man who said he had stolen jewels," said Cei. "It got hushed up somehow; but I remember Piero di Cosimo said, at the time, he believed there was something in it, for he saw Melema's face when the man laid hold of him,[6] and he never saw a visage so 'painted with fear,' as our sour old Dante says."[*]

"Come, spit no more of that venom, Francesco," said Nello, getting indignant, "else I shall consider it a public duty to cut your hair awry the next time I get you under my scissors. That story of the stolen jewels was a lie. Bernardo Rucellai and the Magnificent Eight knew all about it. The man was a dangerous madman, and he was very properly kept[7] out of mischief in prison. As for our Piero di Cosimo, his wits are running after the wind of Mongibello: he has such an extravagant fancy that he would take a lizard for a crocodile. No[8]: that story has been dead and buried too long—our noses object to it."

---

1 {have always} found *MS*
3 the Ten] the Dieci *MS*
5 ⟨work⟩ employment *MS*
7 kept ⟨in prison⟩ *MS*

2 sheets: ⟨when⟩ *MS*
4 *he*] *1 2 3* ⟨*he*⟩ he *MS CM*
6 in it ⟨. And⟩ {for he saw . . . him,} *MS*
8 No ⟨Francesco⟩ *MS*

"It is true," said Macchiavelli. "You forget the danger of the precedent, Francesco. The next mad beggarman may accuse you of stealing his verses, or me, God help me! of stealing his coppers. Ah!" he went on, turning towards the door, "Dolfo Spini has carried his red feather out of the Piazza. That captain of swaggerers would like the republic to lose Pisa just for the [9]chance of seeing the people tear the frock off the Frate's back. With your pardon, Francesco—I know he is a friend of yours—there are[1] few things I should like better than to see him play the part of Capo d'Oca, who went out to the tournament blowing his trumpets and returned with them in a bag."[*]

9 ⟨sake⟩ chance *MS*
1 back. With your pardon . . . are] *1 2 3* back. There are *MS CM*

CHAPTER XLVI.

BY A STREET LAMP

THAT evening, when it was dark and threatening rain, Romola, returning with Maso and the lantern by her side,[1] from the hospital of San Matteo, which she had visited after vespers, encountered her husband just issuing from the monastery of San Marco. Tito[2], who had gone out again shortly after his arrival in the Via de' Bardi, and had seen little of Romola during the day[3], immediately proposed to accompany her home, dismissing Maso, whose [4]short steps annoyed him. It was only usual for him to pay her such an [5]official attention when it was obviously demanded from him. Tito and Romola never jarred, never remonstrated with each other. They were too hopelessly alienated in their inner life ever to have that contest which is an effort towards agreement. They talked of all affairs, public and private, with careful adherence to an adopted course. If Tito wanted a supper prepared in the old library, now pleasantly furnished as a banqueting-room, Romola assented, and saw that everything needful was done; and Tito, on his side, left her entirely uncontrolled in her daily habits, accepting the help she offered him in transcribing or making digests, and in return meeting her conjectured want of supplies for her charities. Yet he constantly, as on this very morning, avoided exchanging glances with her:[6] affected to believe that she was out of the house, in order to avoid seeking her in her own room; and playfully attributed to her a perpetual preference[7] of solitude to his society.

In the first ardour of her self-conquest, after she had renounced her resolution of flight, Romola had made many timid efforts towards the return of a frank relation between them. But to her such a relation could only come by open speech about their differences, and the attempt to arrive at a moral understanding; while Tito could only be saved from alienation from her by [8]such a recovery of her effusive tenderness as would have presupposed[9] oblivion of their differences. He cared for no explanation between them; he felt any thorough explanation impossible: he would have cared to have Romola fond again, and to her, fondness was impossible. She could be submissive

---

1 {returning} with Maso . . . side, ⟨was returning⟩ from . . . vespers, ⟨when she⟩ encountered *MS*

2 Marco. Tito] Marco. It was an unexpected encounter on both sides, but Tito *MS*

3 Romola {during the day} *MS*　　　　4 ⟨tottering⟩ short *MS*

5 ⟨obvious⟩ official *MS*　　　　　　6 her:] *3P* her; *MS CM 1 2*

7 {perpetual} preference *MS*　　　　8 ⟨a return of⟩ such a recovery of *MS*

9 presupposed] *3C* ⟨required⟩ supposed *MS CM 1 2*

and gentle, she could repress any sign of repulsion; but tenderness was not to be feigned. She was [1]helplessly conscious of the result: her husband was [2]alienated from her.

It was an additional reason why she should be carefully kept[3] outside of secrets which he would in no case have chosen to communicate to her. With regard to his political action he sought[4] to convince her that he considered the cause of the Medici hopeless; and that on that practical ground, as well as in theory, he heartily served the popular government, in which she had now a warm interest. But impressions subtle as odours made her uneasy about his relations with San Marco. She was painfully divided between the dread of seeing any evidence to arouse her suspicions, and the impulse to watch lest any harm should come that she might have arrested.

As they walked[5] together this evening, Tito said:—"The business of the day is not yet quite ended for me. I shall conduct you to our door, my Romola[6], and then I must fulfil another commission, which will take me an hour, perhaps, before I can return and rest, as I very much need to do."

And then he talked amusingly of what he had seen at Pisa, until they were[7] close upon a loggia, near which there hung a lamp before a picture of the Virgin.* The street was a quiet one, and hitherto they had passed few people; but now there was a sound of many approaching[8] footsteps and confused voices.

"We shall not get home without a wetting, unless[9] we take shelter under this convenient loggia," Tito said[1], hastily, hurrying Romola, with a slightly startled movement, up the step of the loggia.

"Surely it is useless to wait for this small drivelling[2] rain," said Romola, in surprise.

"No; I felt it becoming heavier. Let us wait a little." With that wakefulness to the faintest indications[3] which belongs to a mind

---

1 ⟨thoroughly⟩ helplessly *MS*
2 ⟨daily more⟩ alienated from her. ⟨She had lost all power over him⟩ *MS*
3 {carefully} kept *MS*
4 {With regard to his political action} He sought *MS*
5 walked ⟨home⟩ together *MS*   6 my Romola] *Romola mia MS*
7 Pisa, until they were] Pisa—of the Emperor's wretched band of soldiery befitting a third-rate condottiere, and of the small probability that he would carry on his enterprise, seeing that the Venetians and Milanese on whom it depended were too jealous to fight ⟨for⟩ consistently for a common object ¶ "So I think you may sing a 'Laudamus' beforehand, my Romola" . . . ¶ At that moment they were *MS*
8 {many} approaching *MS*
9 We shall not . . . unless] Not for our getting home without a wetting though, unless *MS*
1 said] added *MS*   2 drivelling] *MS* drizzling *CM 1 2 3*
3 indications] *MS* indication *CM 1 2 3*

habitually in a state of caution, Tito had detected[4] by the glimmer of
the lamp that the leader of the advancing group wore a red feather
and a glittering sword-hilt—in fact, was almost the last person in the
world he would have chosen to meet at this hour with Romola by his
side. He had already during the day had one momentous interview
with Dolfo Spini, and the business he had spoken of to Romola as yet
to be done was a second interview with that personage,[5] a sequence of
the visit he had paid at San Marco. Tito, by a long preconcerted
plan, had been the bearer of letters to Savonarola—carefully forged[6]
letters, one of them, by a strategem, bearing the very signature and
seal of the Cardinal of Naples, who of all the Sacred College had[7]
most exerted his influence at Rome in favour of[8] the Frate. The purport of the letters was to state that the Cardinal was on his progress
[9]from Pisa, and, unwilling for strong reasons to enter Florence, yet
desirous of taking counsel with Savonarola at this difficult juncture,
intended to pause this very day at San Casciano, about ten miles from
the city, whence he would ride out the next morning in the plain
garb of a priest, and meet Savonarola, as if casually, five miles on the
Florence road, two hours after sunrise. The plot, of which these
forged letters were the initial step, was that Dolfo Spini with a band
of his Compagnacci was to be posted in ambush on the road, at a
lonely spot about five miles from the gates; that he was to seize
Savonarola with the Dominican Brother who would accompany him
according to rule, and deliver him over to a small detachment[1] of
Milanese horse in readiness near San Casciano, by whom he was to
be carried into the Roman territory.

There was a strong chance that the penetrating Frate would suspect a trap, and decline to incur the risk, which he had for some time
avoided, of going beyond the city walls. Even when he preached, his
friends held it necessary that he should be attended by an armed
guard; and here he was called on to commit himself to a solitary road,
with no other attendant than a fellow monk. On this ground the minimum of time had been given him for decision, and the chance in
favour of his acting [2]on the letters was, that the eagerness with which
his mind was set on the combining of interests within and without
the Church towards the procuring of a General Council, and also the
expectation of immediate service from the Cardinal in the actual junc-

4 detected ⟨by his ear and⟩ by the ⟨distant⟩ glimmer *MS*
5 personage, ⟨according to engagement,⟩ *MS*   6 {carefully} forged *MS*
7 Cardinal of Naples, who of all the Sacred College had] *1 2 3* Cardinal di Napoli
⟨that member of the Sacred College⟩ the Cardinal who had *MS* Cardinal of Naples, the
Cardinal who had *CM*
8 influence {at Rome} in favour of ⟨Savonarola⟩ the Frate *MS*
9 ⟨towards⟩ from *MS*   1 {small} detachment *MS*   2 ⟨according to⟩ on *MS*

ture of his contest with the Pope, would triumph over his shrewdness and caution in the brief space allowed for deliberation.

Tito had had an audience of Savonarola, having declined to put the letters into any hands but his, and with consummate art had admitted that incidentally, and by inference, he was able so far to[3] conjecture their purport as to believe they referred to a rendezvous outside the gates, in which case he urged that the Frate should seek an armed guard from the Signoria, and offered his services in· carrying the request with the utmost privacy. Savonarola had replied briefly that this was impossible: an armed guard was incompatible with privacy. He spoke with a flashing eye, and Tito felt convinced that he meant to incur the risk.

Tito himself did not much care for the result. He managed his affairs so cleverly, that all results, he considered, must turn to his advantage. Whichever party came uppermost, he was secure of favour and money. That is an indecorously naked statement[4]; the fact, clothed as Tito habitually clothed it, was that his acute mind, discerning the equal hollowness of all parties, took the only rational course in making them subservient to his own interest.

If Savonarola fell into the snare, there were diamonds in question and papal patronage; if not, Tito's adroit agency had strengthened his position with Savonarola and with Spini, while [5]any confidence[6] he obtained from them made him the more valuable as an agent of the Mediceans.

But Spini was an inconvenient colleague. He had cunning enough to delight in plots, but not the ability or self-command necessary to so complex an effect as secrecy. He frequently got excited with drinking, for even sober Florence had its "Beoni,"* or topers[7], both lay and clerical, who became loud at taverns and private banquets; and in spite of the agreement between him and Tito, that their public recognition of each other should [8]invariably be of the coolest sort, there was always the possibility that on an evening encounter he would be suddenly blurting and affectionate. The delicate sign of casting the *becchetto* over the left shoulder was understood in the morning, but the strongest hint short of a threat might not suffice to keep off [9]a fraternal grasp of the shoulder in the evening.

Tito's chief hope now was that Dolfo Spini had not caught sight of him, and the hope would have been well-founded if Spini had had no clearer view of him than he had caught of Spini. But, himself[1] in shadow, he had seen Tito illuminated for an instant by the direct rays

3 {so far} to *MS*   4 statement: ⟨clothed⟩ *MS*   5 ⟨the⟩ any *MS*
6 confidence] *MS* confidences *CM 1 2 3*   7 "Beoni," or topers] "Beoni" *MS*
8 ⟨always⟩ invariably *MS*   9 ⟨Spini's⟩ a fraternal grasp of ⟨Tito's⟩ the *MS*
1 But, himself] *MS 1 2 3* But himself *CM*

A Dangerous Colleague

of the lamp, and Tito in his way was as strongly-marked a personage as the Captain of the Compagnacci. Romola's black-shrouded[2] figure had escaped notice, and she now stood behind her husband's shoulder in the [3]corner of the loggia. Tito was not left to hope long. "Ha! my carrier-pigeon!" grated Spini's harsh voice, in what he meant to be an under-tone[4], while his hand grasped Tito's shoulder; "what did you run into hiding for? You didn't know [5]it was comrades who were coming. It's well I caught sight of you; it saves time. What of the chase to-morrow morning? Will the bald-headed game[6] rise? [7]Are the falcons to be got ready?"

If it had been in Tito's nature to feel an access of rage, he would have felt it against this bull-faced accomplice, unfit either for a leader or a tool. His lips turned white, but his excitement came from the pressing difficulty of choosing a safe device. If he attempted to hush Spini, that would only deepen Romola's suspicion, and he knew her well enough to know that if some strong alarm were roused in her, she was neither to be silenced nor hoodwinked; on the other hand, if he repelled Spini angrily the wine-breathing Compagnaccio might become savage, being more ready at resentment than at the divination of [8]motives. He adopted a third course, which proved that Romola [9]retained one sort of power over him—the power of dread.

He pressed her hand, as if intending a hint to her, and said in a good-humoured tone of comradeship,—

"Yes, my Dolfo, you may prepare in all security. But take no trumpets with you."

"Don't be afraid," said Spini, a little piqued. "No need to play Ser Saccente* with me. I know where the devil keeps his tail* as well as you do. What! he swallowed the bait whole? The prophetic nose didn't scent the hook at all?" he went on, lowering his tone a little, with a blundering sense of secrecy.

"The brute will not be satisfied till he has emptied the bag," thought Tito; but aloud he said,—"Swallowed all as easily as you swallow a cup of Trebbiano.* Ha! I see torches: there must be a dead body coming.[1] The pestilence has been spreading, I hear."

"Santiddio![2] I hate the sight of those biers. Good night," said Spini, hastily moving off.

2 black-shrouded] *MS 3C* black shrouded *CM 1 2*
3 ⟨narrow loggia⟩ corner *MS*
4 voice, {in what he meant to be an under-tone} *MS*
5 ⟨we were⟩ it was comrades ⟨all⟩ *MS*   6 {bald headed} game *MS*
7 ⟨Shall the falcons be⟩ Are *MS*   8 ⟨causes⟩ motives *MS*
9 ⟨had⟩ retained *MS*
1 I see . . . coming.] There must be a dead body coming. I see torches. *MS*
2 "Santiddio!] *1 2 3* "Suffocation! ⟨said Spini⟩ *MS CM*

The torches were really coming, but they preceded a church digni-
tary, who was returning homeward; the suggestion of the[3] dead body
and the pestilence was Tito's device for getting rid of Spini without
telling him to go. The moment he had moved away, Tito turned to
Romola and said, quietly,—

"Do not be alarmed by anything that *bestia* has said, my Romola.
We will go on now: I think the rain has not increased."

She was quivering with indignant resolution: it was of no use for
Tito to speak in that unconcerned way. She distrusted every word he
could utter.

"I will not go on," she said[4]. "I will not move nearer home until I
have some security against this treachery being perpetrated."

"Wait, at least, until these torches have passed," said Tito, with
perfect self-command, but with a new rising of dislike to a wife who
this time, he foresaw, might have the power of thwarting him in spite
of the husband's predominance.

The torches passed, with the Vicario dell' Arcivescovo,* and due
reverence was done by Tito[5], but Romola saw nothing outward. If for
the defeat of this treachery, in which she believed with all the force
of long presentiment[6], it had been necessary at that moment for her
to spring on her husband and hurl herself with him down a precipice,
she felt as if she could have done it. Union with this man! At that
moment the self-quelling discipline of two years seemed to be
nullified: she felt nothing but that they were divided.

They were nearly in darkness again, and could only see each
other's faces dimly.

"Tell me the truth, Tito—this time tell me the truth," said
Romola, in a low quivering voice. "It will be safer for you."

"Why should I desire to tell you anything else, my angry saint?"
said Tito, with a slight touch of contempt, which was the vent of his
annoyance; "since the truth is precisely that over which you have
most reason to rejoice—namely, that my knowing a plot of Spini's
enables me to secure the Frate from falling a victim to it."

"What is the plot?"

"That I decline to tell," said Tito. "It is enough that the Frate"s
safety will be secured."

"It is a plot for drawing him outside the gates that Spini may murder him."

"There has been no intention of murder. It is simply a plot for
compelling him to obey the Pope's summons to Rome. But as I serve
the popular government, and think the Frate's presence here is a

---

3 {the suggestion of} the *MS*   4 on {" she said} *MS*
5 done {by Tito} *MS*   6 treachery {in which . . . presentiment} *MS*

necessary means of maintaining it at present, I choose to prevent his departure. You may go to sleep with entire ease of mind to-night."

For a moment Romola was silent. Then she said, in a voice of anguish, "Tito, it is of no use: I have no belief in you."

She could just discern his action as he shrugged his shoulders, and spread out his palms in silence. That cold dislike which is the anger of unimpassioned beings was hardening within him.

"If the Frate leaves the city—if any harm happens to him," said Romola, after a slight pause, in a new tone of indignant resolution,— "I will declare what I have heard to the Signoria, and you will be disgraced. What if I am your wife?" she went on, impetuously; "I will be digraced with you. If we are united, I am that part of you that will save you from crime. Others shall not be betrayed."

"I am quite aware of what you would be likely to do, *anima mia*," said Tito, in the coolest of his liquid tones; "therefore if you have a small amount of reasoning at your disposal just now, consider that if you believe me in nothing else, you may believe me when I say I will take care of myself, and not put it in your power to ruin me."

"Then you assure me that the Frate is warned—he will not go beyond the gates?"

"He shall not go beyond the gates."

There was a moment's pause, but distrust was not to be expelled.

"I will go back to San Marco now and find out," Romola said, making a movement forward[7].

"You shall not!" said Tito, in a bitter whisper, seizing her wrists with all his masculine force. "I am master of you. You shall not set yourself in opposition to me."

There were passers-by approaching. Tito had heard them, and that was why he spoke in a whisper. Romola was too conscious of being mastered to have struggled, even if she had remained unconscious that witnesses were at hand. But she was aware now of footsteps and voices, and her habitual sense of personal dignity made her at once yield to Tito's movement towards leading[8] her from the loggia.

They walked on in silence for some time, under the small drizzling rain. The first rush[9] of indignation and alarm in Romola had [1]begun to give way to more complicated feelings, which rendered speech and action difficult. In that simpler state of [2]vehemence, open opposition to the husband from whom she felt her soul revolting, had had the

7 {and find out}" Romola said, making a movement forward, ⟨"and find out."⟩ *MS*
8 personal dignity . . . leading] personal dignity and shrinking from remark, made her at once yield to Tito's movement towards placing her arm within his and leading *MS*
9 {first} rush *MS*   1 ⟨given⟩ begun to give *MS*
2 ⟨passion⟩ vehemence *MS*

aspect of a temptation[3] for her; it seemed the easiest of all courses. But now, habits[4] of self-questioning,[5] memories of impulse subdued, and that proud reserve which all discipline had left unmodified, began to emerge from the flood of passion. The grasp of her wrists, which asserted her husband's physical predominance, instead of arousing a new fierceness in her, as it might have done if her impetuosity had been of a more vulgar kind, had given her a momentary shuddering horror at this [6]form of contest with him. It was the first time they had been in declared hostility to each other since her flight and return[7], and the check given to her ardent resolution then, retained[8] the power to arrest her now. In this altered condition her mind began to dwell on the probabilities that would save her from any desperate course: Tito would not risk betrayal by her; whatever had been his original intention, he must be determined now by the fact that she knew of the plot. She was not bound now to do anything else than to hang over him that certainty that if he deceived her, her lips would not be closed. And then, it[9] was possible—yes, she must cling to that possibility till it was disproved—that Tito had never meant to aid in the betrayal of the Frate.

Tito, on his side, was busy with thoughts, and did not speak again till they were near home. Then he said—

"Well, Romola, have you now had time to recover [1]calmness? If so, you can supply your want of belief in me by a little rational inference: you can see, I presume, that if I had had any intention of furthering Spini's plot I should now be aware that the possession of a fair Piagnone for my wife, who knows the secret of the plot, would be a serious obstacle in my way."

Tito assumed [2]the tone which was just then the easiest to him, conjecturing that in Romola's present mood persuasive deprecation would be lost upon her.

"Yes, Tito," she said, in a low [3]voice, "I think you believe that I would guard the Republic from further treachery. You are right to believe it:[4] if the Frate is betrayed, I will denounce you." She paused a moment, and then said with an effort, "But it was not so. I have perhaps spoken too hastily—you never meant it. Only, why will you seem to be that man's comrade?"

3 a temptation] temptation *1 2 3*   4 now, habits] *1 2 3* now habits *MS CM*
5 self-questioning, ⟨and proud reserve⟩ memories of impulse subdued, {and that . . .
unmodified} began to emerge from ⟨that⟩ the *MS*
6 ⟨new⟩ form *MS*
7 since her flight and return] since the disclosure about the library *MS*
8 then, retained] *3P* then retained *MS CM 1 2*   9 then, it] ⟨then⟩ it *MS*
1 ⟨a little⟩ calmness *MS*   2 ⟨that⟩ the *MS*   3 ⟨tone⟩ voice *MS*
4 it:] *MS 1 2 3* it; *CM*

"Such relations are inevitable to practical men, my Romola," said Tito, gratified by discerning the struggle within her. "You fair creatures live in the clouds. Pray go to rest with an easy heart," he added, opening the door for her.

Monna Brigida's Conversion

CHAPTER XLVII.

CHECK

TITO's clever arrangements[1] had been unpleasantly frustrated by trivial incidents which could not enter into a clever man's calculations. It was [2]very seldom that he walked with Romola in the evening, [3]yet he had happened to be walking with her precisely on[4] this evening when her presence was supremely inconvenient. Life was so complicated a game that the devices of skill were liable to be defeated at every turn[5] by air-blown chances, incalculable as the descent of thistle-down.

It was not that he minded about the failure of Spini's plot, but he felt an awkward difficulty in so adjusting his warning to Savonarola on the one hand, and to Spini on the other, as not to incur [6]suspicion. Suspicion roused in the popular party might be fatal to his reputation and ostensible position in Florence: suspicion roused in Dolfo Spini might[7] be as disagreeable in its effects as the hatred of a fierce dog not to be chained.

If Tito went forthwith to the monastery to warn Savonarola before the monks went to rest, his warning would follow so closely on [8]his delivery of the forged letters that he could not escape unfavourable surmises. [9]He could not warn Spini at once without telling him the true reason, since he could not immediately allege the [1]discovery that Savonarola had changed his purpose; and he knew Spini well enough to know that his understanding would discern nothing but that Tito had "turned round" and frustrated the plot. On[2] the other hand, by deferring his warning to[3] Savonarola until the early morning[4], he would be almost sure to lose the opportunity of warning Spini that the Frate had changed his mind; and the band of Compagnacci[5] would come back [6]in all the rage of disappointment. This last, however, was[7] the risk he chose, trusting to his power of soothing Spini by assuring him that the failure was due only to the Frate's caution.

1 Tito{'s clever arrangements} *MS*   2 ⟨so⟩ very *MS*   3 ⟨and⟩ yet *MS*
4 {precisely} on *MS*   5 defeated {at every turn} *MS*
6 ⟨the⟩ suspicion. ⟨And⟩ suspicion *MS*
7 {Dolfo} Spini might ⟨have effects⟩ *MS*   8 ⟨the⟩ his *MS*
9 ⟨On the other hand⟩ He *MS*   1 ⟨knowledge⟩ discovery *MS*
2 plot. On] plot. Romola's threat to denounce Tito would not seem a ground of alarm to Spini. On *MS*
3 to] of *MS*   4 early morning] morning *2 3*
5 the band of Compagnacci] the Compagnacci *MS*   6 ⟨with the⟩ in all the *MS*
7 last, however, was] last ⟨risk⟩ was *MS*

Tito was annoyed. If[8] he had had to smile it would have been an unusual effort to him. He was determined not to encounter Romola again, and he did not go home that night.

She watched through the night, and never took off her clothes. She heard the rain become heavier and heavier. She liked to hear the rain: the stormy heavens seemed a safeguard against men's devices, compelling them[9] to inaction. And Romola's mind was again assailed, not only by the utmost doubt of her husband, but by doubt as to her own conduct. What lie might he not have told her? What project might he not have, of which she was still ignorant? Every one who trusted Tito was in danger; it was useless to try and persuade herself of the contrary[1]. And[2] was not she selfishly listening to the promptings of her own pride, when she shrank from warning men against him? "If her husband was[3] a malefactor, her place was in the prison by his side"— that might be; she was contented to fulfil that claim. But was she, a wife, to allow[4] a husband to inflict the injuries that would make him a malefactor, when it might be in her power to prevent them? Prayer seemed impossible to her. The activity of her thought excluded a mental state of which the essence is expectant passivity.

The excitement[5] became stronger and stronger. Her imagination, in a state of morbid activity, conjured up possible schemes by which, after all, Tito would have eluded her threat; and towards daybreak the rain became less violent, till at last it ceased, the breeze rose again and dispersed the clouds, and the morning fell clear on all the objects around her. It made her uneasiness all the less endurable. She wrapped her mantle round her, and ran up to the loggia,[6] as if there could be anything in the wide landscape that might determine her action; as if there could be anything but roofs hiding the line of street along which Savonarola might be walking[7] towards betrayal.

If she went to her godfather, might[8] she not induce him,[9] without any specific revelation, to take measures for preventing Fra Girolamo[1]

---

8 annoyed. If] annoyed 〈. If〉, and if *MS*

9 devices, compelling them] devices: it would compel them *MS*

1 Every one . . . contrary] It was useless to try and persuade herself of the contrary—every one who trusted Tito was in danger. *MS*

2 And 〈had not she been〉 *MS*   3 was] were *MS*

4 she {a wife} to allow 〈him〉 a husband *MS*

5 {The activity of her thought 〈seemed to〉 excluded . . . passivity.} The excitement 〈produced by this thought〉 became *MS*

6 loggia, 〈with the vague wild hope of seeing something〉 *MS*

7 roofs hiding . . . walking] roofs which might be hiding the line of street along which Savonarola was walking *MS*

8 godfather, might] godfather?—might *MS*

9 him, {〈as one of the Dieci〉} without any specific revelation to 〈prevent〉 *MS*

1 Fra Girolamo] Savonarola *MS*

from passing the gates? But that might be too late. Romola[2] thought, with new distress, that she had failed to learn any guiding details from Tito, and it was already long past seven.[3] She must go to San Marco: there was nothing else to be done.

She hurried down the stairs, she went out into the street without looking at her sick people, and walked [4]at a swift pace along the Via de' Bardi towards the Ponte Vecchio. She would go through the heart of the city; it was the most direct road, and, besides, in the great Piazza there was a chance of encountering her husband, who, by some possibility to which she still clung might satisfy her[5] of the Frate's safety, and leave no need for her to go to San Marco. When she arrived in front of the Palazzo Vecchio, she looked eagerly into the pillared court; then her eyes swept the Piazza; but the well-known figure, once painted in her heart by young love, and now branded there by eating pain, was nowhere to be seen. She hurried straight on to the Piazza del Duomo. It was already full of movement: there were worshippers passing up and down the marble steps[6], there were men pausing for chat, and there were[7] market people carrying their burthens. Between these[8] moving figures Romola caught a glimpse of her husband. On his way from San Marco he had turned into Nello's shop, and was now leaning against the door-post. As Romola approached she could see[9] that he was standing and talking, with the easiest air in the world, holding his cap[1] in his hand, and shaking back his freshly-combed hair. The contrast of this ease with the bitter anxieties he had created convulsed her with indignation: the new vision of his hardness heightened her dread. She recognized Cronaca and two other frequenters of San Marco standing near her husband. It flashed through her mind—"I will compel him to speak before those men." And her light step brought her close upon him before he had time to move, while Cronaca was saying, "Here comes Madonna Romola."

A slight shock passed through Tito's frame as he felt himself face to face with his wife.[2] She was haggard with her anxious watching, but there was a flash of something else than anxiety in her eyes as she said,—

"Is the Frate gone beyond the gates?"

"No," said Tito, feeling completely helpless before this woman, and needing all the self-command he possessed to preserve a countenance in which there should seem to be nothing stronger than surprise.

2 late. Romola] *1 2 3* late; and Romola *MS* late: Romola *CM*
3 {guiding} details from Tito {, and it was already long past seven}. *MS*
4 ⟨with⟩ at *MS*   5 satisfy her ⟨without⟩ of the Frate's safety ⟨without⟩ and *MS*
6 {marble} steps ⟨of the cathedral⟩ *MS*   7 and there were] and *MS*
8 these] those *3*   9 see ⟨him⟩ *MS*   1 cap] *beretta MS*
2 face to face with his wife.] face to face. *MS*

"And you are certain that he is not going?" she insisted.

"I am certain that he is not going."

"That is enough," said Romola, and she turned[3] up the steps, to take refuge in the Duomo, till she could recover from her agitation.

Tito never had a feeling so near hatred as that with which his eyes followed Romola retreating up the steps.

There were present not only genuine followers of the Frate, but Ser Ceccone, the notary, who at that time, like Tito himself, was secretly an agent of the Mediceans. Ser Francesco di Ser Barone, more briefly known to infamy as Ser Ceccone,* was not learned[4], not handsome, not successful, and the reverse of generous. He was a traitor without charm. It followed that he was not fond of Tito Melema.

3 turned ⟨without another glance around her⟩ *MS*
4 Ser Francesco . . . learned] Ser Ceccone was not learned *MS*

CHAPTER XLVIII.

COUNTER CHECK

It was late in the afternoon when Tito returned home. Romola, seated opposite the cabinet in her narrow room, copying documents, was about to desist from her work because the light was getting dim, when her husband entered. He had come straight to this room to seek her, with a thoroughly defined intention, and there was something new to Romola in his manner and expression as he looked at her silently on entering, and, without taking off his cap and mantle, leaned one elbow on the cabinet, and stood directly [1]in front of her.

Romola, fully assured during the day of the Frate's safety, was feeling the reaction of some penitence for the access of distrust and indignation which had impelled her to address her husband publicly on a matter that she knew he wished to be private. She told herself that she had probably been wrong. The scheming duplicity which she had heard even her godfather allude to as inseparable from party tactics might be sufficient to account for the connexion with Spini, without the supposition that Tito had ever meant to further the plot. She wanted to atone for her impetuosity by confessing that she had been too hasty, and for some hours her mind had been dwelling on the possibility that this confession of hers might lead to other frank words breaking the two years' silence of their hearts. The silence had been so complete, that Tito was ignorant of her having fled from him and come back again; they had never approached an avowal of that past which, both in its young love and in the shock that shattered the love, lay locked away from them like a banquet-room where death had once broken the feast.

She looked up at him with that submission in her glance which belonged to her state of self-reproof; but the subtle change in his face and manner arrested her speech. For a few moments they remained silent, looking at each other.

Tito himself felt that a crisis was come in his married life. The husband's determination to mastery, which lay deep below all blandness and beseechingness, had risen permanently to the surface now, and seemed to alter his face, as a face is altered by [2]a hidden muscular tension with which a man is secretly throttling[3] or stamping out the life from something feeble, yet dangerous.

---

1 ⟨opposite to⟩ in front of *MS*   2 ⟨some secret⟩ a hidden *MS*
3 {secretly} throttling *MS*

"Romola," he began, in the cool liquid tone that made her shiver, "it is time that we should understand each other." He paused.

"That is what I most desire, Tito," she said, faintly. Her sweet pale face, with all its anger gone and nothing but the timidity of self-doubt in it, seemed to give a marked predominance to her husband's dark strength.

"You took a step this morning," Tito went on, "which you must now yourself perceive to have been useless—which exposed you to remark and may involve me in serious practical difficulties."

"I acknowledge that I was too hasty[4]; I am sorry for any injustice I may have done you." Romola spoke these words in a fuller and firmer tone; Tito, she hoped, would look less hard when she had expressed her regret, and then she could say other things.

"I wish you once for all to understand," he said, without any change of voice, "that such collisions are incompatible with our position as husband and wife. I wish you to reflect on the mode in which you were led to[5] that step, that the process may not be repeated."

"That depends chiefly on you, Tito," said Romola, taking fire slightly. It was not what she had at all thought[6] of saying, but we see a very little way before us in mutual speech.

"You would say, I suppose[7]," answered Tito, "that nothing is to occur in future which can excite your unreasonable suspicions. You were frank enough to say last night that you have no belief in me. I am not surprised at any exaggerated conclusion you may draw from slight premises, but I wish to point out to you what is likely to be the fruit of your making such exaggerated conclusions a ground for interfering in affairs of which you are ignorant. Your attention is thoroughly awake to what I am saying?"

He paused for a reply.

"Yes," said Romola, flushing in [8]irrepressible resentment at this cold tone of superiority.

"Well, then, it may possibly not be very long before some other chance words or incidents set your imagination at work devising crimes for me, and you may perhaps rush to the Palazzo Vecchio to alarm the Signoria and set the city in an uproar. Shall I tell you what may be the result? Not simply the disgrace of your husband, to which you look forward with so much courage, but the arrest and ruin of many among the chief men in Florence, including Messer Bernardo del Nero."

Tito had meditated a decisive move, and he had made it. The flush died out of Romola's face, and her very lips were pale—an unusual

4 hasty ⟨Tito⟩ MS   5 led to] 3C led to take MS CM 1 2
6 not what she had at all thought] not at all what she had thought 2 3
7 say {I suppose} MS   8 ⟨wonder and⟩ irrepressible resentment MS

effect with her, for she was [9]little subject to fear. Tito [1]perceived his success.

"You would perhaps flatter yourself," he went on, "that you were performing a heroic deed of deliverance; you might as well try to turn locks with fine words as apply such notions to the politics of Florence. The question now is, not whether you can have any belief in me, but whether, now you have been warned, you will dare to rush, like a blind man with a torch in his hand, amongst intricate affairs of which you know nothing."

Romola felt as if her mind were held in a vice by Tito's: the possibilities he had indicated were rising before her with terrible clearness. "I am too rash," she said. "I will try not to be rash."

"Remember," said Tito, with unsparing insistance, "that your act of distrust towards me this morning might, for aught you knew, have had more fatal effects than that sacrifice of your husband which you have learned to contemplate without flinching."

"Tito, it is not so," Romola burst forth in a pleading tone, rising and going nearer to him, with a desperate resolution to speak out. "It is false that I would willingly sacrifice you. It has been the greatest effort[2] of my life to cling to you. I went away in my anger two years ago, and I came back again because I was more bound to you than to anything else on earth. But it is useless. You shut me out from your mind. You affect to think of me as a being too unreasonable to share in the knowledge of your affairs. You will be open with me about nothing."

She looked like his good angel pleading with him, as she bent her face towards him with dilated eyes, and laid her hand upon[3] his arm. But Romola's touch and glance no longer stirred any fibre of tenderness in her husband. The good-humoured, tolerant Tito, incapable of hatred, incapable almost of impatience, disposed always to be gentle towards the rest of the world, felt himself becoming strangely hard towards this wife whose presence had once been the strongest influence he had known. With all his softness of disposition, he had a masculine [4]effectiveness of intellect and purpose which, like sharpness of edge, is itself an energy, working its way without any strong momentum[5]. Romola had an energy of her own which thwarted his, and no man, who is not exceptionally feeble, will endure being thwarted by his wife. Marriage must be a relation either of sympathy or of conquest.

No emotion darted across his face as he heard Romola for the first time speak of having gone away from him. His lips only looked a little harder as he smiled slightly and said—

9 ⟨little⟩ ⟨rarely⟩ little *MS*   1 ⟨saw⟩ perceived *MS*   2 {greatest} effort *MS*
3 upon] on *MS*   4 ⟨strength⟩ effectiveness *MS*
5 purpose {which, like . . . momentum} *MS*

"My Romola, when certain conditions are ascertained we must make up our minds to them. No amount of wishing will fill the Arno, as your people say, or turn a plum into an orange.* I have not observed even that prayers have much efficacy that way[6]. You are so constituted as to have certain strong impressions inaccessible to reason: I cannot share those impressions, and you have withdrawn all trust from me in consequence. You have changed towards me; it has followed[7] that I have changed towards you. It is useless to take any retrospect. We have simply to adapt ourselves to altered conditions."

"Tito, it would not be useless for us to speak openly," said Romola, with[8] the sort of exasperation that comes from using living muscle against some lifeless insurmountable resistance. "It was the sense of deception in you that changed me, and that has kept us apart. And it is not true that I changed first. You changed towards me the night you first wore that chain armour. You had some secret from me—it was about that old man—and I saw him again yesterday. Tito," she went on, [9]in a tone of agonized entreaty, "if you would once tell me every thing, let it be what it may—I would not mind pain—that there might be no wall between us! Is it not possible that we could begin a new life?"

This time there was a flash of emotion across Tito's face. He stood perfectly still; but the flash seemed to have whitened him. He took no notice of Romola's appeal, but after a moment's pause said, quietly,

"Your impetuosity about trifles, Romola, has a freezing influence[1] that would cool the baths of Nero."* At these cutting words Romola shrank and drew herself up into her usual self-sustained attitude. Tito went on. "If by 'that old man'[2] you mean the mad Jacopo di Nola who attempted my life and made a strange accusation against me, of which I told you nothing because it would have alarmed you to no purpose, he, poor wretch, has died in prison. I saw his name in the list of dead."

"I know nothing about his accusation," said Romola. "But[3] I know he is the man[4] whom I saw with the rope round his neck in the

6 that way] in that way MS   7 it {has} followed MS
8 Romola, with] 1 2 3 Romola, flushing with MS CM
9 ⟨speaking⟩ in MS   1 influence] influence {on me} MS
2 'that old man'] 1 2 3 that old man MS CM
3 Nero." At these cutting words . . . "But] Nero. If by that old man you mean the mad Jacopo di Nola who {attempted my life and} made a strange accusation against me, of which I told you nothing because it would have alarmed you to no purpose, he, poor wretch, has died in prison. I saw his name in the list of the dead." ¶ "I know nothing about his accusation," said Romola shrinking and drawing herself up into her usual self-sustained attitude at Tito's cutting ⟨sarcasm⟩ words. "But MS
4 the man ⟨who laid hold of your arm the day you wore the armour—the man⟩ whom MS

Duomo—the man whose portrait Piero di Cosimo painted, grasping
your arm as he saw him grasp it the day the French entered, the day
you first wore the armour."

"And where is he now, pray?" said Tito, still pale, but governing
himself.

"[5]He was lying lifeless in the street from [6]starvation," said Romola.
"I revived him with bread and wine. I brought him to our door, but
he refused to come in. Then I gave him some money, and he went
away without telling me anything. But he had found out that I was
your wife. *Who* is he?"

"A man, half mad, half imbecile, who was once my father's servant
in Greece, and who has a rancorous hatred towards me because I got
him dismissed for theft. Now you have the whole mystery, and the
further satisfaction of knowing that I am again in danger of assassina-
tion. The fact of my wearing the armour, about which you seem to
have thought so much, must have led you to infer that I was in danger from this man. Was that the reason you chose to cultivate his
acquaintance and invite him into the house?"

Romola was mute. To speak was only like rushing with bare breast[7]
against a shield.

Tito moved from his leaning posture, slowly took off his cap and
mantle, and pushed back his hair. He was collecting himself for some
final words. And Romola stood upright looking at him as she might
have looked at some on-coming deadly force, to be met only by silent
endurance.

"We need not refer to these matters again, Romola," he said, precisely in the same tone as that in which he had spoken at first. "It is
enough if you will remember that the next time your generous ardour
leads you to interfere in political affairs, you[8] are likely, not to save
any one from danger, but to be raising scaffolds and setting houses on
fire. You are not yet a sufficiently ardent Piagnone to believe that
[9]Messer Bernardo del Nero is the prince of darkness[1], and Messer
Francesco Valori the archangel Michael. I think I need demand no
promise from you?"

"I have understood you too well, Tito."

"It is enough," he said, leaving the room.

Romola turned round with despair in her face and sank into her
seat. "Oh, God, I have tried—I cannot help it. We shall always be
divided." Those words passed silently through her mind. "Unless",

5 ⟨I don't know," said Romola.⟩ He *MS*   6 ⟨want of food⟩ starvation *MS*
7 breast] bosom *MS*   8 you ⟨may⟩ are likely, ⟨instead of saving⟩ not to save *MS*
9 ⟨your godfather⟩ {Messer} Bernardo *MS*
1 prince of darkness] *3P* Prince of Darkness *MS CM 1 2*

she said aloud, as if some sudden vision had startled her into speech—"unless misery should come and join us!"

Tito, too, had a new thought in his mind after he had closed the door behind him. With the project of leaving Florence as soon as his life there had become a high enough stepping-stone[2] to a life elsewhere, perhaps at Rome or Milan[3], there was now for the first time[4] associated a desire to be free from Romola, and to leave her behind him. She had ceased to belong to the desirable furniture of his life: there was no possibility of an easy relation between them without genuineness on his part. Genuineness implied confession of the past, and confession involved a change of purpose. But Tito had as little bent that way as a leopard has to lap milk when its teeth are grown. From all relations that were not easy and agreeable, we know that Tito shrank: why should he cling to them?

And Romola had made his relations difficult with others besides herself. He had had a troublesome interview with Dolfo Spini[5], who had come back in a rage after an ineffectual soaking with rain and long waiting in ambush, and that scene between Romola and himself at Nello's door, once reported in Spini's ear, might be a seed of something more unmanageable than suspicion. But now, at least, he believed that he had mastered Romola by a terror which appealed to the strongest forces of her nature. He had alarmed her affection and her conscience by the shadowy image of consequences; he had arrested her intellect by hanging before it the idea of a hopeless complexity in affairs, which[6] defied any moral judgment.

Yet Tito was not at ease. The world was not yet quite cushioned with velvet, and, if it had been, he could not have abandoned himself to that softness with thorough enjoyment; for before he went out again this evening he put on his [7]coat of chain armour.

2 {high enough} stepping stone *MS*   3 Rome or Milan] Rome *MS*
4 {With} The project . . . Rome, {there was} now for the first time ⟨associated itself with⟩ associated *MS*
5 Spini ⟨today⟩ *MS*   6 affairs, which] *MS* affairs which *CM 1 2 3*
7 ⟨suit⟩ coat *MS*

CHAPTER XLIX.

[1]THE PYRAMID OF VANITIES

THE wintry days passed for Romola as the white ships pass one who is standing lonely on the shore—passing in silence and sameness, yet each bearing a hidden burthen of coming change. Tito's hint had mingled so much dread with her interest[2] in the progress of public affairs that she had begun to court ignorance rather than knowledge. The threatening German Emperor* was gone again; and, in other ways besides, the position of Florence was alleviated; but so much distress remained that Romola's active duties were hardly diminished, and in these, as usual, her mind found a refuge from its doubt.

She dared not rejoice that the relief which had come in extremity and had appeared to justify the policy of the Frate's party was making that party so triumphant, that Francesco Valori, hot-tempered chieftain of the Piagnoni, had been elected[3] Gonfaloniere at the beginning of the year, and was making haste to have as much of his own liberal way[4] as possible during his two months of power. That seemed for the moment like a strengthening of the party most attached to freedom, and a reinforcement of protection to Savonarola; but Romola was now alive to every suggestion likely to deepen her foreboding, that whatever the present might be, it was only an unconscious brooding over the mixed germs of Change which[5] might any day become tragic. And already by Carnival time, a little after mid-February, her presentiment was confirmed by the signs of a very decided change: the Mediceans had ceased to be passive, and were openly exerting themselves to procure the election of Bernardo del Nero as[6] the new Gonfaloniere.

On the last day of the Carnival, between ten and eleven in the morning, Romola walked out, according to promise, towards the Corso degli Albizzi, to fetch her cousin Brigida, that they might both be ready to start from the Via de' Bardi early in the afternoon, and take their places at a window which Tito had had reserved for them in the Piazza della Signoria, where there was to be a scene of so new and striking a sort, that all Florentine eyes must desire to see it. For

---

1 ⟨A Carnival Scene⟩ The Pyramid of Vanities *MS*
2 interest] *MS CM 1 3C* interests 2   3 elected] made *MS*
4 {liberal} way *MS*   5 which] that *MS*
6 Nero as] *3C* Nero, as *CM 1 2*

the Piagnoni[7] were having their own way thoroughly about the mode of keeping the Carnival. In vain Dolfo Spini and his companions had struggled to get up the dear old masques and practical jokes, well spiced with indecency. Such things were not to be in a city where Christ has been declared King.*

Romola set out[8] in that languid state of mind with which every one enters on a long day of sight-seeing, purely for the sake of gratifying a child, or some dear childish friend. [9]The day was certainly an epoch in Carnival-keeping; but this phase of reform had not touched her enthusiasm: and she did not know that it was an epoch in her own life, when another[1] lot would begin to be no longer secretly but visibly[2] entwined with her own.

She chose to go through the great Piazza that she might take a first survey of the unparalleled sight there while she was still alone. Entering[3] it from the south, she saw something monstrous and many-coloured in the shape of a pyramid, or, rather, like a huge fir-tree, sixty feet high, with shelves [4]on the branches, widening and widening towards the base till they reached a circumference of eighty yards. The Piazza was full of life: slight young figures, in white garments,

---

7 a little after mid-February . . . Piagnoni] a little after mid-February, the signs of a very decided change were declaring themselves. Men had almost left off finding fault with the actual chief magistrates and had begun to debate who were to be the new ones—especially who was to be the new Gonfaloniere. Wet handbills found their way from a printing house in the Via del Garbo in the dark hours and were seen fixed and well dried at the street corners in the early morning, recommending all Florentines who loved their city to use their influence for Bernardo del Nero. The Mediceans had ceased to be passive: they were exerting themselves to get a government specifically favourable to them, and there was no man on their side who had the weight of years and character that belonged to Bernardo del Nero. The popular party was getting alarmed: the laity who frequented San Marco and gossiped mildly on politics with their confessor Fra Salvestro, said with growing emphasis that they were afraid of getting a "bad Signoria"; other lovers of popular government were perhaps a little consoled by the probable vexation of the too-⟨predominating⟩ arrogant Francesco Valori at seeing the man he most detested elected as his successor; and certain women given to a strictly inward illumination were feeling themselves instructed by the angels as to the best way of determining the proportion of black and white beans against the Mediceans. ¶ Meanwhile the Piagnoni MS

8 King. ¶ Romola set out] King. Nevertheless on the last ⟨evening⟩ day of the Carnival there was to be a scene in the great Piazza of so new and striking a sort that every one, whether Piagnone or not, must desire to see it; and soon after ten o'clock in the morning Romola walked out according to promise towards the Corso degli Albizzi to fetch her cousin Brigida, that they might both be ready to start from the Via de' Bardi {to the Piazza} early in the afternoon and take {their} places {at a window} which Tito had ⟨set apart⟩ reserved for them. Romola set out MS

9 ⟨It⟩ The day MS   1 another] another MS   2 {secretly but} visibly MS
3 {She chose to ⟨take her way through⟩ go through . . . still alone.} Entering ⟨the Piazza⟩ it from the South, ⟨Romola⟩ she MS
4 ⟨for⟩ on the MS

with olive wreaths on their heads, were moving to and fro about the base of the pyramidal tree, carrying baskets full of bright-coloured things; and maturer forms, some in the monastic frock, some in the loose tunics and dark-red caps of[5] artists, were helping and examining, or else retreating to various points in the distance to survey the wondrous whole; while a considerable group, amongst whom Romola [6]recognized Piero di Cosimo, [7]standing on the marble steps of Orgagna's Loggia, seemed to be keeping aloof in discontent and scorn.

Approaching nearer, she paused to look at the multifarious objects ranged in gradation from the base to the summit of the pyramid. There were tapestries and brocades of immodest design, pictures and sculptures held too likely to incite to vice; there were boards and tables for all sorts of games, playing-cards along with the blocks for printing them, dice, and other apparatus for gambling; there were worldly music-books, and musical instruments in all the pretty varieties of lute, drum, cymbal, and trumpet; there were masks and masquerading dresses used in the old carnival shows; there were handsome copies of Ovid, Boccaccio[8], Petrarca[9], Pulci, and other books of a vain or impure sort; there were all the implements of feminine vanity—rouge-pots, false hair, mirrors, perfumes, powders, and transparent veils intended to provoke inquisitive glances: lastly, at the very summit, there was the unflattering effigy of a probably mythical Venetian merchant, who was understood to have offered a heavy sum* for this collection of marketable [1]abominations, and, soaring above him in surpassing ugliness, the symbolic figure of the old debauched Carnival.

This was the preparation for a new sort of bonfire—the Burning of Vanities. Hidden in the interior of the pyramid was a plentiful store of dry fuel and gunpowder; and on this last day of the festival, at evening, the pile of vanities was to be set ablaze to the sound of trumpets, and the ugly old Carnival was to tumble into the flames amid the songs of reforming triumph.

This crowning act of the new festivities could hardly have been prepared but for a peculiar organization which had been started by Savonarola two years[2] before. The mass of the Florentine boyhood and youth was no longer [3]left to its own genial promptings towards street mischief and crude dissoluteness. Under the training of Fra Domenico,* a sort of lieutenant to Savonarola, lads and striplings, the hope of Florence, were to have none but pure words on their lips,

---

5 {dark-}red caps of ⟨the⟩ artists *MS*   6 ⟨descried⟩ recognized *MS*
7 ⟨leaning against⟩ standing on *MS*   8 {Ovid} Boccaccio *MS*
9 Petrarca] *1 2 3* Petrarch *MS CM*   1 ⟨goods⟩ abominations *MS*
2 two years] a year *MS*   3 ⟨to be⟩ left *MS*

were to have a zeal for Unseen Good[4] that should put to shame the lukewarmness of their elders, and were to know no pleasures save of an angelic sort—singing divine praises and walking in white robes. It was for them that the ranges of seats had been raised high against the walls of the Duomo; and they had been used to hear Savonarola appeal to them as the future glory of a city specially appointed to do the work of God.

These fresh-cheeked troops were the chief agents in the regenerated merriment of the new Carnival, which was a sort of sacred parody of the old. Had there been bonfires in the old time? There was to be a bonfire now, consuming impurity from off the earth. Had there been symbolic processions? There were to be processions now, but the symbols were to be white robes and red crosses and olive wreaths—emblems of peace and innocent gladness—and the banners and images held aloft were to tell the triumphs of goodness. Had there been dancing in a ring under the open sky of the Piazza, to the sound of choral voices chanting loose songs? There was to be dancing in a ring now, but dancing of monks and laity in fraternal love and divine joy, and the music was to be the music of hymns. As for the collections from street passengers, they were to be greater than ever—not for gross and superfluous suppers, but—for the benefit of the hungry and needy; and, besides, there was the collecting of the *Anathema*, or the Vanities to be laid on the great pyramidal bonfire.

Troops of young inquisitors went from house to house on this exciting business of asking that the *Anathema* should be given up to them. Perhaps after the more avowed vanities had been [5]surrendered, Madonna, at the head of the household, had still certain little reddened balls brought from the Levant, intended to produce on a sallow cheek a sudden bloom of the most ingenuous falsity? If so, let her bring them down and cast them into the basket of doom. Or, perhaps, she had ringlets[6] and coils of "dead hair"?*—if so, let her bring them to the street-door, not on her head, but in her hands, and publicly renounce the *Anathema* which hid the respectable signs of age under a ghastly mockery of youth. And, in reward, she would hear fresh young voices pronounce a blessing on her and her house.

The beardless inquisitors, organized into little regiments, doubtless took to their work very willingly. To coerce people by shame[7], or other spiritual pelting, into[8] the giving up of things it will probably vex them to part with, is a form of piety to which the boyish mind is

---

4 Unseen Good] *3P* unseen good *MS CM 1 2*   5 ⟨given up⟩ surrendered *MS*
6 doom. Or, perhaps, she had ringlets] doom:—or perhaps ringlets *MS*
7 shame ⟨moral dread⟩ or *MS*   8 into] *3P* to *MS CM 1 2*

most readily converted; and if some obstinately wicked men[9] got enraged and threatened the whip or the cudgel, this also was exciting. Savonarola himself evidently felt about the training of these boys the difficulty weighing on all minds with noble yearnings towards great ends, yet with that imperfect perception[1] of means which forces a resort to some supernatural constraining influence as the only sure hope. The Florentine youth had had very evil habits and foul tongues: it seemed at first an unmixed blessing when they were got to shout "*Viva Gesù!*" but Savonarola was forced at last to say from the pulpit, "There is a little too much shouting of '*Viva Gesù!*' This constant utterance of sacred words brings them into contempt. [2]Let me have no more of that shouting till the next Festa."

Nevertheless, as the long stream of white-robed youthfulness, with its little red crosses and olive wreaths, had gone to the Duomo at dawn this morning to receive the communion from the hands of Savonarola, it was a sight of beauty; and, doubtless, many of those young souls were[3] laying up memories of hope and awe that might save them from ever resting in a merely vulgar view of their work as men and citizens. There is no kind of conscious obedience that is not an advance on lawlessness, and these boys became the generation of men who fought greatly and endured greatly in the last struggle of their Republic.* Now, in the intermediate hours between the early communion and dinner-time, they were making their last perambulations to collect alms and vanities, and this was why Romola saw the slim white figures moving to and fro about the base of the great pyramid.

"What think you of this folly, Madonna Romola?" said a brusque voice close to her ear. "Your Piagnoni will make *Ninferno*[4]* a pleasant prospect to us, if they are to carry things[5] their own way on earth. It's enough to fetch a cudgel over the mountains to see painters, like Lorenzo di Credi and young Baccio* there, helping to burn colour out of life in this fashion."

"My good Piero," said Romola, looking up and smiling at the grim man, "even you must be glad to see some of these things burnt. Look at those gew-gaws and wigs and [6]rouge-pots: I have heard you talk as indignantly against those things as Fra Girolamo himself."

"What then?" said Piero, turning round on her sharply. "I never said a woman should make a black patch of herself against the back-

9 obstinately wicked men] men *MS*
1 ends, yet with that imperfect perception] ends and that dim perception *MS*
2 ⟨I will⟩ Let me *MS*
3 many of those young souls were] many young souls there were *MS*
4 *Ninferno*] *MS* *l'inferno CM 1 2 3*
5 carry things ⟨on earth in this fashion⟩ *MS*   6 ⟨paint⟩ rouge pots *MS*

ground. [7]*Va!* Madonna Antigone, it's a shame for a woman with your hair and shoulders to run into such nonsense—leave it to women who are not worth painting. What! the most holy Virgin herself has always been dressed well; that's the doctrine of the Church:—talk of heresy, indeed! And I should like to know what the excellent Messer Bardo would have said to the burning of the divine poets by these Frati, who are no better an imitation of men than if they were onions with the bulbs uppermost. Look at that Petrarca sticking up beside a rouge-pot: do the idiots pretend that the heavenly Laura was a painted harridan? And Boccaccio, now: do you mean to say, Madonna Romola—you who are fit to be a model for a wise Saint[8] Catherine of Egypt*—do you mean to say you have never read the stories of the immortal Messer Giovanni[9]?"

"It is true I have read them, Piero," said Romola. "Some of them a great many times over, when I was a little girl. I used to get the book down when my father was asleep, so that I could[1] read to myself."

"*Ebbene?*" said Piero, in a fiercely challenging tone.

"There are some things in them I do not[2] want ever to forget," said Romola[3], "but you must confess, Piero, that a great many of those stories are only about low deceit for the lowest ends. Men do not[4] want books to make them think lightly of vice, as if life were a vulgar joke. And I cannot[5] blame Fra Girolamo for teaching that we owe our time to something better."

"Yes, yes, it's very well to say so now you've read them," said Piero, bitterly, turning on his heel and walking away from her.

Romola too walked on, smiling at Piero's innuendo, with[6] a sort of tenderness towards the odd[7] painter's anger, because she knew that her father would have felt something like it. For herself, she was conscious of no inward collision with the strict and sombre view of pleasure which tended to repress poetry in the attempt to repress vice. Sorrow and joy have each their peculiar narrowness; and a religious enthusiasm like Savonarola's, which ultimately blesses mankind by giving the soul a strong propulsion towards sympathy with pain, indignation against wrong, and the subjugation of sensual desire, must always incur the reproach of a great negation. Romola's life had given her an affinity for sadness which inevitably made her unjust towards merriment. That subtle result of culture which we call Taste was subdued[8] by the need for deeper motive; just as the nicer demands of the

7 ⟨Deh⟩ *Va MS*
8 Saint] *MS 1 2 3* St. *CM*   9 {the immortal} Messer Giovanni *MS*
1 so that I could] *1 2 3* and I could *MS CM*   2 do not] don't *MS*
3 Romola ⟨smiling at that [?clear] utterance⟩ *MS*
4 do not] don't *MS*   5 cannot] can't *MS*   6 with ⟨a feeling⟩ *MS*
7 odd] old *3*   8 subdued ⟨in her⟩ *MS*

palate are annihilated by urgent hunger. Moving habitually among scenes of suffering, and carrying [9]woman's heaviest disappointment in her heart, the severity which allied itself with self-renouncing [1]beneficent strength had no dissonance for her.

9 ⟨the⟩ woman's *MS*
1 ⟨strength and beneficence⟩ beneficent strength *MS*

CHAPTER L.

[1]TESSA ABROAD AND AT HOME

ANOTHER figure easily recognized by us—a figure not clad in black, but in the old red, green, and[2] white—was approaching the Piazza that morning to see the Carnival. She came from an opposite point, for Tessa no longer lived on the Hill of San Giorgio.* After what had happened there with Baldassarre, Tito had thought it best for that and other reasons to find her a new home, but still in a quiet airy quarter, in a house bordering on the wide garden grounds north of the Porta Santa Croce.

Tessa was not come out sight-seeing without special leave. Tito had been with her the evening before, and she had kept back the entreaty which she felt to be swelling her heart and throat until she saw him in a state of radiant ease, with one arm round the sturdy Lillo, and the other resting gently on her own shoulder as she tried to make the tiny Ninna steady on her legs. She was sure then that the weariness with which he had come in and flung himself into his chair had quite melted away from his brow and lips. Tessa had not been slow at learning a few small stratagems by which she might avoid vexing Naldo and yet have a little of her own way. She could read nothing else, but she had learned to read a good deal in her husband's face.

And certainly the charm of that bright, gentle-humoured Tito who woke up under the Loggia de' Cerchi on a Lenten morning five years before, not having yet given any hostages to deceit, never returned so nearly as in the person of Naldo, seated in that straight-backed, carved arm-chair which he had provided for his comfort when he came to see Tessa and the children. Tito himself was surprised at the growing sense of relief which he felt in these moments. No guile was needed towards Tessa: she was too ignorant and too innocent to suspect him of anything. And the little voices calling him "Babbo" were very sweet in his ears for the short while that he heard them. When he thought of leaving Florence, he never thought of leaving Tessa and the little ones behind. He was very fond of these round-cheeked, wide-eyed human things that clung about him and knew no evil of him. And wherever affection can spring, it is like the green leaf and the blossom—pure, and breathing purity, whatever soil it may grow in. Poor Romola, with all her self-sacrificing effort, was really helping

---

1 ⟨A Carnival Scene⟩ Tessa Abroad and at Home *MS*
2 green, and] *1 2 3* green and *MS CM*

to harden Tito's nature by chilling it with a positive dislike which had beforehand seemed impossible in him; but Tessa kept open the fountains of kindness.

"Ninna is very good without me now," began Tessa, feeling her request rising very high in her throat, and letting Ninna seat herself on the floor. "I can leave her with Monna Lisa any time, and if she is in the cradle and cries, Lillo is as sensible as can be—he goes and thumps Monna Lisa[3]."

Lillo, whose great dark eyes looked all the darker because his curls were of a light brown like his mother's, jumped off Babbo's knee, and went forthwith to attest his intelligence by thumping Monna Lisa, who was shaking her head slowly over her spinning at the other end of the room.

"A wonderful boy!" said Tito, laughing.

"Isn't he?" said Tessa, eagerly[4], getting a little closer to him, "and I might go and see the Carnival to-morrow, just for an hour or two, mightn't I?"

"Oh, you wicked pigeon!" said Tito, pinching her cheek; "those are your longings, are they? What have you to do with Carnivals now you are[5] an old woman with two children?"

"But old women like to see things," said Tessa, her lower lip hanging a little. "Monna Lisa said she should like to go, only she's so deaf she can't hear what is behind her, and she thinks we couldn't take care of both the children."

"No, indeed, Tessa," said Tito, looking rather grave, "you must not think of taking the children into the crowded streets[6], else I shall be angry."

"But I have[7] never been[8] into the Piazza without leave," said Tessa, in a frightened, pleading tone, "since the[9] Holy Saturday, and Nofri I think[1] is dead, for you know the poor madre died; and I shall never forget the carnival I saw once; it was so pretty—all roses and[2] a king and queen under them—and singing. I liked it better than the San Giovanni."

"But there's nothing like that now, my Tessa. They are going to make a bonfire in the piazza—that's all. But I cannot let you go out by yourself in the evening."

"Oh, no, no! I don't want to go in the evening. I only want to go and see the procession by daylight. There *will* be a procession—is it not true?"

3 Lisa ⟨to wake her⟩ MS   4 said Tessa, {eagerly} MS
5 you are] you're MS   6 {crowded} streets MS
7 I have] I've MS   8 been ⟨out without⟩ MS
9 since the ⟨[2 words] with the [1 word] began to talk to me and laugh at me⟩ MS
1 Nofri I think] I think Nofri *1 2 3*   2 roses and] MS *1 2 3* roses, and CM

"Yes, after a sort," said Tito, "as lively as a flight of cranes. You must not expect roses and glittering kings and queens, my Tessa. However, I suppose any string of people to be called a procession will please your blue eyes. And there's a thing they have[3] raised in the Piazza de' Signori for the bonfire. You may like to see that. But come home early, and look like[4] a grave little old woman; and if you see any men with feathers and swords, keep out of their way: they are very fierce, and like to cut old women's heads off."

"Santa Madonna! where do they come from? Ah! you are laughing; it is[5] not so bad. But I will keep away from them. Only," Tessa went on in a whisper, putting her lips near Naldo's ear, "if I might take Lillo with me! He is very sensible."

"But who will thump Monna Lisa then, if she doesn't hear?" said Tito, finding it difficult not to laugh, but thinking it necessary to look serious. "No, Tessa, you could not take care of Lillo if you got into a crowd, and he's too heavy for you to carry him."

"It is true," said Tessa, rather sadly, "and he likes to run away. I forgot that. Then I will go alone. But now look at Ninna—you have not looked at her enough."

Ninna was a blue-eyed thing, at the tottering, tumbling age—a fair solid, which, like a loaded die, found its base with a constancy that warranted prediction. Tessa went to snatch her up, and when Babbo was paying due attention to the recent teeth and other marvels, she said, in a whisper, "And shall I buy some *confetti* for the children?"

Tito drew some small coins from his scarsella, and poured them into her palm.

"That will buy no end," said Tessa, delighted at this abundance. "I shall not mind going without Lillo so much, if I bring him something."

So Tessa set out in the morning towards the great Piazza where the bonfire was to be. She did not think the February breeze cold enough to demand further covering than her green woollen dress. A mantle would have been oppressive, for it would have hidden a new necklace and a new clasp, mounted with silver, the only ornamental presents Tito had ever made her. Tessa did not think at all of showing her figure, for no one had ever told her it was pretty; but she was quite sure that her necklace and clasp were of the prettiest sort ever worn by the richest contadina, and she arranged her white hood over her head so that the front of her necklace[6] might be well displayed. These ornaments, she considered, must inspire [7]respect for her as the wife of some one who could afford to buy them.

She tripped along very cheerily in the February sunshine, thinking

3 they have] they've *MS*   4 look like] look *MS*   5 it is] it's *MS*
6 {the front of} her necklace *MS*   7 ⟨some⟩ respect *MS*

much of the purchases for the little ones[8], with which she was to fill her small basket, and not thinking at all of any one who might be observing her. Yet her descent from her upper story into the street had been watched, and she was being kept in sight as she walked by a person who had often waited in vain to see if it were not Tessa who lived in that house to which he had more than once dogged Tito. Baldassarre was carrying a package of yarn: he was constantly employed in that way, as a means of earning his scanty bread, and keeping[9] the sacred fire of vengeance alive; and he had come out of his way this morning, as he had often done before, that he might pass by the house to which he had followed Tito in the evening. [1]His long imprisonment had so intensified his timid suspicion and his belief in some diabolic fortune favouring Tito, that he had not dared to pursue him, except under cover of a crowd or of the darkness; he felt with instinctive horror, that if Tito's eyes fell upon him, he should again be held up to obloquy, again be dragged away; his weapon would be taken from him, and he should be[2] cast helpless into a prison-cell. His fierce purpose had become as stealthy as a serpent's, which depends for its prey on one dart of the fang. Justice was weak and unfriended; and [3]he could not hear again the voice that pealed the promise of vengeance in the Duomo: he had been there again and again[4], but that voice, too, had apparently been stifled by cunning strong-armed wickedness. For a long while, Baldassarre's ruling thought was to ascertain whether Tito still wore the armour, [5]for now at last his fainting hope would have been contented with a successful stab on this side the grave; but he would never risk his precious knife again. It was a weary time he had had to wait for the chance of answering this question by touching Tito's back in the press of the street. Since then, the knowledge that the sharp steel was useless, and that he had no hope but in some new device, had fallen with leaden weight on his enfeebled mind. A dim vision of winning one of those two wives to aid him came before him continually, and continually slid away[6]. The wife who had lived on the hill was no longer there. If he could find her again[7], he might grasp some thread of a project, and work his way to more clearness.

And this morning he had succeeded. He was quite certain now where this wife lived, and as he walked bent a little under his burthen

8 purchases {for the little ones} *MS* 9 keeping ⟨sacred vengeance⟩ *MS*
1 ⟨This morning for the first time, he was fortunate: he had assured himself⟩ His *MS*
2 be ⟨helpless in⟩ *MS* 3 ⟨he⟩ ⟨Baldassarre⟩ he *MS*
4 again {and again} *MS*
5 ⟨for⟩ ⟨but he would never risk breaking his precious knife again. In his present state of fainting hope he would have been contented⟩ for *MS*
6 slid away ⟨again⟩ *MS* 7 find her {again} *MS*

of yarn, yet keeping the green and white figure in sight, his mind was dwelling upon her and her circumstances as feeble eyes dwell on lines and colours, trying to interpret them into consistent significance.

Tessa had to pass through various long streets without seeing any other sign of the Carnival than unusual groups of the country people in their best garments, and that disposition in everybody to chat and loiter which marks the early hours of a holiday, before[8] the spectacle has[9] begun. Presently, in her disappointed search for remarkable objects, her eyes fell on a man with a [1]pedlar's basket before him, who seemed to be selling nothing but little red crosses to all the passengers. [2]A little red cross would be pretty to hang up over the bed; it[3] would also help to keep off harm, and would perhaps make Ninna stronger. Tessa [4]went to the other side of the street that she might ask the pedlar the price of the crosses, fearing[5] that they would cost a little too much for her to spare from her purchase of sweets. [6]The pedlar's back had been turned [7]towards her hitherto, but when she came near[8] him she recognized an old acquaintance of the Mercato, Bratti Ferravecchi, and accustomed to feel that she was to avoid old acquaintances, she turned away again and passed to the other side of the street. But [9]Bratti's eye was too well practised in looking out at the corner after possible customers, for her movement to have escaped him, and she was presently arrested by a tap on the arm from one of the red crosses.

"Young woman," said Bratti,[1] as she unwillingly turned her head, "you come from some castello a good way off, it seems to me, else you'd never think of walking about, this blessed Carnival, without a red cross in your hand. Santa Madonna! Four white quattrini[2] is a small price to pay for your soul—prices rise in purgatory, let me tell you."

"Oh, I should like one," said Tessa, hastily, "but I couldn't spare four white quattrini."

Bratti had at first regarded Tessa too abstractedly as a mere customer to look at her with any scrutiny, but when she began to speak he exclaimed, "By the head of San Giovanni, it must be the little Tessa, and looking as fresh as a ripe apple! What, you've done none the worse, then, for running away from father Nofri? You were in the right of it, for he goes on crutches now, and a crabbed fellow with

8 holiday, before] *3C* holiday before *MS CM 1 2*
9 spectacle has] spectacles have *MS*   1 ⟨large⟩ pedlar's basket *MS*
2 ⟨Tessa thought⟩ A little red cross would be pretty ⟨[?for] a procession⟩ *MS*
3 it] *MS 1 2 3* and it *CM*   4 ⟨crossed the street⟩ went *MS*
5 fearing ⟨however⟩ that *MS*   6 ⟨But⟩ The *MS*   7 ⟨on⟩ towards *MS*
8 near ⟨enough to see⟩ him *MS*   9 ⟨Bratti's⟩ ⟨the⟩ Bratti's *MS*
1 said Bratti, ⟨holding up the red cross before her⟩ as she {unwillingly} turned *MS*
2 {white} *quattrini MS*

crutches is dangerous; he can reach across the house and beat a woman as he sits."

"I'm married," said Tessa, rather demurely, remembering Naldo's command that she should behave with gravity; "and my husband takes great care of me."

"Ah, then you've fallen on your feet! Nofri said you were good-for-nothing vermin; but what then? An ass may bray a good while before he shakes the stars down.* I always said you did well to run away, and it isn't often Bratti's in the wrong. Well, and so you've got a husband and plenty of money? Then you'll never think much of giving four white quattrini for a red cross. I get no profit; but what with the famine and the new religion, all other merchandise is gone down. You live in the country where the chestnuts are plenty, eh? You've never wanted for polenta, I can see."

"No,³ I've never wanted anything," said Tessa, still on her guard.

"Then you can afford to buy a cross. I got a *padre* to bless them, and you get blessing and all for four quattrini. It isn't for the profit; I hardly get a danaro by the whole lot. But then they're holy wares, and it's getting harder and harder work to see your way to Paradise: the very Carnival is like Holy Week, and the ⁴least you can do to keep the devil from getting the upper hand is to buy a cross. God guard you! think what the devil's tooth is! ⁵You've seen him biting the man in San Giovanni,* I should hope?"

Tessa felt much teased and frightened. "Oh, Bratti, she said, with a discomposed face, "I want to buy a great many *confetti*: I've got little Lillo and Ninna at home. And nice coloured sweet things cost a great deal. And they will not like the cross so well, though I know it would be good to have it."

"Come, then," said Bratti⁶, fond of laying up a store of merits by imagining possible extortions and then heroically renouncing them, "Since you're an old aquaintance, you shall have it for two quattrini. It's making you a present of the cross, to say nothing of the blessing."

Tessa ⁷was reaching out her two quattrini with trembling hesitation, when Bratti said, abruptly, "Stop a bit! Where do you live?"

"Oh, a long way off," ⁸she answered, almost automatically, being preoccupied with her quattrini; "beyond San Ambrogio, in the Via Piccola, at the top of the house where the wood is stacked below."

"Very good," said Bratti, in a patronizing tone; "then I'll let you

3 ⟨"No," ⟨said Tessa, still on her guard,⟩ *MS*   4 ⟨very⟩ least *MS*
5 ⟨When⟩ You've *MS*
6 Bratti ⟨who was⟩ fond of laying up a store of merits by ⟨cheating people less than he had [?assured] himself it was possible to cheat them⟩ imagining {possible} extortions *MS*
7 ⟨reached⟩ was reaching *MS*   8 ⟨said Tessa⟩ she answered *MS*

have the cross on trust, and call for the money. So you live inside the gates? Well, well, I shall be passing."

"No, no![9]" said Tessa, frightened lest Naldo should be angry at this revival of an old aquaintance. "I can spare the money. Take it now."

"No," said Bratti, resolutely; "I'm not a hard-hearted pedlar. I'll call and see if you've got any rags, and you shall make a bargain. See, here's the cross; and there's Pippo's shop, not far behind you: you can go and fill your basket, and I must go and get mine empty. *Addio, piccina.*"

Bratti went on his way, and Tessa, stimulated to change her money into *confetti* before further accidents[1], went into Pippo's shop, a little fluttered by the thought that she had let Bratti know more about her than her husband would approve. There were certainly more dangers in coming to see the Carnival than in staying at home; and she would have felt this more strongly if she had known that the wicked old man, who had wanted to kill her husband on the hill, was still keeping her in sight. But she had not noticed the man with the burthen on his back.[2]

The consciousness of having a small basketful of things to make the children glad, dispersed her anxiety, and as she entered the Via de' Libraj* her face had its usual expression of child-like content. And now she thought there was [3]really a procession coming, for she saw white robes and a banner, and her heart began to palpitate with expectation. She stood a little aside, but in that narrow street there was the pleasure of being obliged to look very close. The banner was [4]pretty: it was the Holy Mother with the Babe, whose love for her Tessa had believed in more and more since she had had her babies; and the figures in white had not only green wreaths on their heads, but little red crosses by their side, which caused her some satisfaction that she also[5] had her red cross. Certainly, they looked as beautiful as the angels on the clouds, and to Tessa's mind they too had a background of cloud, like everything else that came to her in life. How and whence did they come? She did not mind much about knowing. But one thing surprised her as [6]newer than wreaths and crosses; it was that some of the[7] white figures carried baskets between them. What could the baskets[8] be for?

But now they were very near, and, to her astonishment, they wheeled aside and came straight up to her. She trembled as she

9 No, no!] O no *MS*   1 accidents] accident 2 3
2 Staying at home {and she . . . back.} *MS*   3 ⟨actually⟩ really *MS*
4 ⟨very⟩ pretty: it was the Holy ⟨Madonna with the Babe⟩ Mother *MS*
5 also] too *MS*   6 ⟨much⟩ newer *MS*
7 {some of} the ⟨foremost⟩ white figures *MS*   8 the baskets] they *MS*

would have done if St. Michael in the picture had shaken his head at her, and was conscious of nothing but terrified wonder till she [9]saw close to her a round boyish face, [1]lower than her own, and heard a treble voice saying, "Sister, you carry the *Anathema* about you. Yield it up to the blessed Gesù, and he will adorn you with the gems of his grace."

Tessa was only more frightened, understanding nothing. Her first conjecture settled on her basket of sweets. They wanted that, these alarming angels. Oh, dear, dear! She looked down at it.

"No, sister," said a taller youth, pointing to her necklace and the clasp of her belt, "it is those vanities that are the *Anathema*. Take off that necklace and unclasp that belt, that they may be burned in the holy Bonfire of Vanities, and save *you* from burning."

"It is [2]the truth, my sister," said a still taller youth[3], evidently the archangel of this band. "Listen to these [4]voices speaking the divine message. You already carry[5] a red cross: let that be your only adornment. Yield up your necklace and [6]belt, and you shall obtain grace."

This was too much. Tessa, overcome with awe, dared not say "no," but she was equally unable to render up her beloved necklace and [7]clasp. Her pouting lips were quivering, the tears rushed to her eyes, and a great drop fell. For a moment she ceased to see anything; she felt nothing but confused terror and misery. Suddenly[8] a gentle hand was laid on her arm, and a soft, wonderful voice, as if the Holy Madonna were speaking, said, "Do not be afraid; no one shall harm you."

Tessa looked up and saw a lady in black, with a young heavenly face[9] and loving hazel eyes. She had never[1] seen any one like this lady before, and under other circumstances might have had awe-struck thoughts about her; but now everything else was overcome by the sense that loving protection was near her. The tears only fell the faster, relieving her swelling heart, as she looked up at the heavenly face, and, putting her hand to her necklace, said sobbingly,

"I can't give them to be burnt. My husband—he bought them for me—and they are so pretty—and Ninna—Oh, I wish I'd never come!"

"Do not ask her for them," said Romola, speaking to the white-robed boys[2] in a tone of mild authority. "It [3]answers no good end for

---

9 ⟨heard⟩ saw *MS*   1 ⟨much⟩ lower *MS*   2 ⟨true⟩ the truth *MS*
3 youth] personage *MS*   4 ⟨young⟩ voices *MS*   5 {already} carry *MS*
6 ⟨clasp⟩ belt *MS*   7 ⟨belt⟩ clasp *MS*
8 Suddenly ⟨she felt a gentle hand laid⟩ *MS*   9 {a young} heavenly face *MS*
1 never ⟨been near to⟩ *MS*   2 boys] youths *MS*
3 ⟨would answer⟩ answers no good {end} *MS*

people to give up such things[4] against their will. That is not what Fra
Girolamo approves: he would have such things given up freely."

Madonna Romola's word was not to be resisted, and the white
train moved on. They even moved with haste, as if some new object
had caught their eyes; and Tessa felt with bliss that they were gone,
and that her necklace and clasp were still with her.

"Oh, I will go back to the house," she said, still agitated[5]; "I will
go nowhere else. But if I should meet them again, and you not be
there?" she [6]added, expecting everything from this heavenly lady.

"Stay a little," said Romola. "Come with me under this doorway, and
we will hide the necklace and clasp, and then you will be in no danger."

She led Tessa under the archway, and said, "Now, can we find
room for your necklace and belt in your basket? Ah! your basket is
full of crisp things that will break: let us be careful, and lay the heavy
necklace under them."

It was like a change in a dream to Tessa—[7]the escape from night-
mare into floating safety and joy—to find herself taken care of by this
lady, so lovely, and powerful, and gentle. She let Romola unfasten her
necklace and clasp, while she herself did nothing but look up at the
face that bent over her.

"They are sweets for Lillo and Ninna," she said, as Romola carefully lifted up the light parcels in the basket[8], and placed the ornaments below them.

"Those are your children?" said Romola, smiling. "And you would
rather go home to them than see any more of the Carnival? Else you
have not far to go to the Piazza de' Signori, and there you[9] would see
the pile for the great bonfire."

"No; oh, no!" said Tessa, eagerly; "I shall never like bonfires again.
I will go back."

"You live at some castello, doubtless," said Romola, not waiting for
an answer. "Towards which gate do you go?"

"Towards Por' Santa Croce."

"Come, then," said Romola, taking her by the hand and leading
her to the corner of a street nearly opposite. "If you go down there,"
she said, pausing, "you will soon[1] be in a straight road. And I must
leave you now, because some one else expects me. You will not be
frightened. Your pretty things are quite safe now. Addio."

"Addio, Madonna," said Tessa, almost in a whisper, not knowing
what else it would be right to say; and in an instant the heavenly lady
was gone. Tessa turned to catch a last glimpse, but she only saw the
tall gliding figure vanish round the projecting stonework. So she went

4 give up such things] give such things up MS   5 said {still agitated} MS
6 ⟨said⟩ added MS   7 ⟨to have escape[d]⟩ the escape MS
8 basket] small basket MS   9 and {there} you MS   1 will {soon} MS

on her way in wonder, longing to be once more safely housed with Monna Lisa, undesirous of Carnivals for ever more.

Baldassarre had kept Tessa in sight till the moment of her parting with Romola: then he went away with his bundle of yarn. It seemed to him that he had discerned a clue which might guide him if he could only grasp the necessary details firmly enough. He had seen the two wives together, and the sight had brought[2] to his conceptions that vividness which had been wanting before. His[3] power of imagining facts needed to be reinforced continually by the senses. The tall wife was the noble and rightful wife; she had the blood in her that would be readily kindled to resentment; she would know what scholarship was, and how it might lie locked in by the obstructions of the stricken body, like a treasure buried by earthquake. She could believe him: she would be *inclined*[4] to believe him, if he proved to her that her husband was unfaithful. Women cared about that: they would take Vengeance for that. If this wife of Tito's loved him, she would have a sense of injury which Baldassarre's mind dwelt on with keen longing, as if it would be the strength of another will added to his own, the strength of another mind to form devices.

Both these wives had been kind to Baldassarre, and their acts towards him, being bound up with the very image of them, had not vanished from his memory; yet the thought of their pain could not present itself to him as a check. To him it seemed that pain was the order of the world for all except the hard and base. If any were innocent, if any were noble, where could the utmost gladness[5] lie for them? Where it lay for him—in unconquerable hatred and triumphant vengeance. But he must be cautious: he must watch this wife in the Via de' Bardi[6], and learn more of her; for even here frustration was possible.[7] There was no power for him now but in patience.

2 brought ⟨that vividness⟩ to *MS*
3 His ⟨memory of relative⟩ power of imagining {facts} *MS*
4 *inclined*] inclined *MS*   5 {the utmost} gladness *MS*
6 this wife {in the Via de' Bardi} *MS*
7 here frustration was possible.] here there might be possible frustration. *MS*

CHAPTER LI.

MONNA BRIGIDA'S CONVERSION

WHEN Romola said that some one else expected her, she meant her cousin Brigida, but she was far from suspecting how much that good kinswoman was in need of her. Returning together[1] towards the Piazza, they had descried the company of youths coming to a stand before Tessa, and when Romola, having approached near enough to see the simple little contadina's distress, said, "Wait for me a moment, cousin," Monna Brigida said hastily, "Ah, I will not go on: come for me to Boni's shop,—I shall go back there."

The truth was, Monna Brigida had a consciousness on the one hand of certain "vanities" carried on her person, and on the other of a growing alarm lest the Piagnoni should be right in holding that rouge, and false hair, and pearl embroidery[2], endamaged the soul. Their serious view of things filled the air like an odour; nothing seemed to have exactly the same flavour as it used to have[3]; and there was the dear child Romola, in her youth and beauty, leading a life that was uncomfortably suggestive of rigorous demands on woman. A widow at fifty-five whose satisfaction has been largely drawn from what she thinks of her own person, and what she believes others think of it, requires a great fund of imagination to keep her spirits buoyant. And Monna Brigida had begun to have frequent struggles at her toilet. If her soul would prosper better without them, was it really worth while to put on the rouge and the braids? But when she lifted up the hand-mirror and saw a sallow face with baggy cheeks[4], and crows' feet that were not to be dissimulated by any simpering of the lips—when she[5] parted her grey hair, and let it lie in simple Piagnone fashion round her face, her courage failed. Monna Berta would certainly burst out laughing at her, and call her an old hag, and as Monna Berta was really only fifty-two, she had a superiority which [6]would make the observation cutting. Every woman who was not a Piagnone would give a shrug at the sight of her, and the men would accost her as if she were their grandmother. Whereas, at fifty-five a woman was not so very old—she only required making up a little. So the rouge and the braids and the embroidered berretta went on again, and Monna Brigida was satisfied with the accustomed effect; as for

1 Returning {together} *MS*   2 {pearl} embroidery *MS*
3 have. {⟨the sight of Romola's life touched her very closely⟩ there was the dear child Romola ⟨with⟩ in her youth . . . woman} *MS*
4 a {sallow} face with {baggy} cheeks ⟨bagging⟩ *MS*
5 she ⟨let⟩ *MS*   6 ⟨made⟩ would make *MS*

her neck, if she covered it up, people might suppose it was too old to show, and on the contrary, with the necklaces round it, it looked better than Monna Berta's. This very day, when she was preparing for the Piagnone Carnival, such a struggle had occurred, and the conflicting fears and longings which caused the struggle, caused her to turn back and seek refuge in the druggist's shop rather than encounter the collectors of the *Anathema* when Romola was not by her side.

But Monna Brigida was not quite rapid enough in her retreat. She had been descried, even before she turned away, by the white-robed boys in the rear of those who wheeled round towards Tessa, and the willingness with which[7] Tessa was given up was, perhaps, slightly due to the fact that part of the troop had already accosted [8]a personage carrying more markedly upon her the dangerous weight of the *Anathema*. It happened that[9] several of this troop were at the youngest age taken into peculiar training; and a small fellow of ten[1], his olive wreath resting above cherubic cheeks and wide brown eyes, his imagination really possessed with a hovering awe at existence as something in which great consequences impended on being good or bad, his longings nevertheless running in the direction of mastery and mischief, was the first to reach Monna Brigida and place himself across her path. She felt angry, and looked for an open door, but there was not one at hand, and by attempting to escape now, she would only make things worse. But it was not the cherubic-faced young one who first addressed her; it was a youth of fifteen, who held one handle of a wide basket[2].

"Venerable mother!" he began, "the blessed Jesus commands you to give up the *Anathema* which you carry upon you. That cap embroidered with pearls, those jewels that fasten up your false hair— let them be given up and sold for the poor; and cast the hair itself away from you, as a lie that is only fit for burning. Doubtless, too, you have other jewels under your silk mantle[3]."

"Yes, lady," said the youth at the other handle, who had many of Fra Girolamo's phrases by heart, "they are too heavy for you: they are heavier than a millstone, and are weighting you for perdition. Will you adorn yourself with the hunger of the poor, and be proud to carry God's curse upon your head?"

"In truth you are old, buona madre," said the cherubic boy, in a sweet soprano. "You look very ugly with the red on your cheeks and that black glistening hair, and those fine things. It is only Satan who

7 with which ⟨Tessa's ornaments were abandoned⟩ *MS*
8 ⟨Monna Berta⟩ a personage *MS*
9 happened that ⟨this troop had amongst it some of the youngest boys⟩ *MS*
1 ten] twelve *MS*   2 {wide} basket *MS*
3 burning. {Doubtless . . . mantle} *MS*

can like to see you. Your Angel is sorry. He wants you to rub away
the red."

The little fellow snatched a soft silk scarf from the basket, and held
it towards Monna Brigida, that she might use it as her guardian angel
desired. Her anger and mortification were fast giving way to spiritual
alarm. Monna Berta, and that cloud of witnesses, highly-drest society
in general[4], were not looking at her, and she was surrounded by
young monitors, whose white robes, and wreaths, and red crosses, and
dreadful candour, had something awful in their unusualness. Her
Franciscan confessor, Fra Cristoforo, of Santa Croce, was not at hand
to reinforce her distrust of Dominican teaching, and she was helplessly possesed and shaken by a vague sense that a supreme warning
was come to her. Unvisited by the least suggestion of any other
course that was open to her, she took the scarf that was held out[5],
and rubbed her cheeks, with trembling submissiveness.

"It is well, Madonna," said the second youth. "It is a holy beginning. And when you have taken those vanities from your head, the
dew of heavenly grace will descend on it." The infusion[6] of mischief
was getting stronger, and putting his hand to one of the jewelled pins
that fastened her braids to the berretta, he drew it out. The heavy
black plait fell down over Monna Brigida's face, and dragged the rest
of the [7]head-gear forward. It was a new reason for not hesitating: she
put up her hands hastily, undid the other fastenings, and flung down
into the basket of doom her beloved crimson-velvet berretta,* with all
its unsurpassed embroidery of seed-pearls, and stood an unrouged
woman[8], with grey hair pushed backward from a face where certain
deep lines[9] of age had triumphed over embonpoint.

But the berretta was not allowed to lie in the basket. With impish
zeal, the youngsters lifted it[1], and held it up[2] pitilessly[3], with the false
hair dangling.

"See, venerable mother," said the taller youth, "what ugly lies you
have delivered yourself from! And now you look like the blessed Saint
Anna, the mother of the Holy Virgin."

[4]Thoughts of going into a convent forthwith, and never showing
herself in the world again, were rushing through Monna Brigida's

4 Monna Berta {and that ⟨imaginary⟩ cloud of witnesses} and highly drest society
{in general} *MS*
5 held out ⟨to her⟩ *MS*   6 infusion] mixture *MS*   7 head ⟨dress⟩ gear *MS*
8 an unrouged woman] a pale ⟨old⟩ woman *MS*
9 {deep} lines *MS*   1 lifted it] *3C* lifted it up *MS CM 1 2*
2 held it up] *1 2 3* held it *MS CM*
3 held it {pitilessly} *MS*
4 ⟨The thought that she would go into a convent forthwith and never show herself
again⟩ Thoughts *MS*

mind. There was[5] nothing possible for her but to take care of her soul. Of course, there were spectators laughing: she had no need to look round to assure herself of that. Well! it would[6], perhaps, be better to be forced to think more of paradise. But[7] at the thought that the dear accustomed world was no longer in her choice, there gathered some of those hard tears which just moisten elderly eyes, and[8] she could see but dimly a large rough hand holding a red cross, which was suddenly thrust before her over the shoulders of the boys, while a strong guttural voice said, "Only four quattrini, Madonna, blessing and all! Buy it. You'll find a comfort in it now your wig's gone. Deh! what are we sinners doing all our lives? Making soup in a basket, and getting nothing but the scum for our stomachs. Better buy a blessing, Madonna! Only four quattrino; the profit is not so much as the smell of a danaro, and it goes to the poor."

Monna Brigida, in dim-eyed confusion, was proceeding to the further submission of reaching money from her embroidered scarsella, at present hidden by her silk mantle[9], when the group round her, which she had not yet entertained the idea of escaping, opened before a figure as welcome as an angel loosing prison bolts.*

"Romola, look at me!" [1]said Monna Brigida, in a piteous tone, putting out both her hands[2].

The white troop was already moving away, with a slight consciousness that [3]its zeal about the head-gear had been [4]superabundant enough to afford a dispensation from any further demand for penitential offerings.

"Dear cousin, don't be distressed," said Romola, smitten with pity, yet hardly able to help smiling at the sudden apparition of her kinswoman in a genuine, natural guise, strangely contrasted with all memories of her. She took the black drapery from her own head, and threw it over Monna Brigida's. "There," she went on, soothingly, "no one will remark you now. We will turn down the Via del Palagio* and go straight to our house."

They hastened away, Monna Brigida grasping Romola's hand tightly as if to get a stronger assurance of her being actually there.

"Ah, my Romola, my dear child," said the short fat woman,

---

5 There was] There was no need for her to forsake folly now, for it had been ⟨taken⟩ stripped from her: there was *MS*

6 would] could *MS*

7 But ⟨those hard tears which just moisten elderly eyes had gathered⟩ at the thought *MS*

8 choice, there gathered . . . eyes, and] choice those hard tears which just moisten elderly eyes had gathered, and *MS*

9 silk mantle] mantle *MS*   1 ⟨she⟩ said *MS*

2 tone {, putting out both her hands} *MS*   3 ⟨their⟩ its *MS*

4 ⟨abundant⟩ superabundant *MS*

hurrying with frequent steps to keep pace with the majestic young figure beside her. "What an old scarecrow I am! I must be good—I mean to be good!"

"Yes, yes; buy a cross!" said the guttural voice, while the rough hand was thrust once more before Monna Brigida; for Bratti was not to be abashed by Romola's presence into renouncing a probable customer, and had quietly followed up their retreat. "Only four quattrini, blessing and all—and if there was any profit, it would all go to the poor."

Monna Brigida would have been compelled to pause, even if she had been in a less submissive mood. She put up one hand deprecatingly to arrest Romola's remonstrance, and with the other reached out a grosso, worth many white quattrini, saying, in an entreating tone—

"Take it, good man, and begone."

"You're in the right, Madonna," said Bratti, taking the coin quickly, and thrusting the cross into her hand, "I'll not offer you change, for I might as well rob you of a mass. What! we must all be scorched a little, but you'll come off the easier; better fall from the window than the roof.* A good Easter[5] and a good year to you!"

"[6]Well, Romola," cried[7] Monna Brigida, pathetically, as Bratti left them, "if I'm to be a Piagnone, it's no matter how I look!"

"Dear cousin", said Romola, smiling[8] at her affectionately, "you don't know how much better you look than you ever did before. I see now how good-natured your face is, like yourself. That red and finery seemed to thrust themselves forward and hide expression. Ask our Piero[9] or any other painter if he would not rather paint your portrait now than before. I think all lines of the human face have something either touching or grand, unless they seem[1] to come from low passions. How fine old men are, like my godfather! Why should not old women look grand and simple?"

"Yes, when one gets to be sixty, my Romola," said Brigida, relapsing a little; "but I'm only fifty-five, and Monna Berta and everybody—but it's no use: I will be good, like you. Your mother, if she'd been alive, would have been as old as I am—we were cousins together. One *must* either die or get old. But it doesn't matter about being old, if one's a Piagnone[2]."

5 easier; better fall . . . Easter] easier. A Good Easter *MS*
6 ⟨Ebbene⟩ Well *MS*　　　7 cried] said *MS*　　　8 smiling] *1 2 3* looking *MS CM*
9 Piero ⟨di Cosimo⟩ *MS*　　　1 unless they seem] when they don't seem *MS*
2 Piagnone ⟨does it?⟩ *MS*

CHAPTER LII.

A PROPHETESS

THE incidents of that Carnival day seemed to Romola to carry no other personal consequences to her than the new care of supporting poor cousin Brigida in her fluctuating resignation to age and grey hairs; but they introduced a Lenten time in which she was kept at a high pitch of mental excitement and active effort.

Bernardo del Nero had been elected Gonfaloniere[1]. By great exertions the Medicean party had so far triumphed, and that triumph had deepened Romola's presentiment of some secretly prepared scheme likely to ripen either into success or betrayal during these two months of her godfather's authority. Every morning the dim daybreak as it peered into her room seemed to be that haunting fear coming back to her. Every morning the fear went with her as she passed through the streets on her way to the early sermon in the Duomo: but there she gradually lost the sense of its chill presence, as men lose the dread of death in the clash of battle.

[2]In the Duomo she felt herself sharing in a passionate conflict[3] which had wider relations than any enclosed within the walls of Florence. For Savonarola was preaching—preaching the last course of Lenten sermons he was ever allowed to finish in the Duomo: he [4]knew[5] that excommunication was imminent, and he had reached the point of defying it. He held up the condition of the Church in the terrible mirror of his unflinching speech, which called things by their right names and dealt in no polite periphrases; he proclaimed with heightening confidence the advent of renovation—of a moment when there would be a general revolt against corruption. As to his own destiny, he seemed to have a double and alternating prevision: sometimes he saw himself taking a glorious part in that revolt, sending forth a voice that would be heard through all Christendom, and making the dead body of the Church tremble into new life, as the body of Lazarus trembled when the divine voice pierced the sepulchre;* sometimes he saw no prospect for himself but persecution and [6]martyrdom:—this

1 Gonfaloniere ⟨and this triumph of the Medicean party⟩. *MS*
2 ⟨For⟩ In *MS*   3 {passionate} conflict *MS*
4 ⟨felt excommunication to be⟩ knew that ⟨his⟩ excommunication *MS*
5 the last course . . . knew] his last course of Lenten sermons: he knew *MS*
6 ⟨death, and again life⟩ martyrdom *MS*

'But you will help me'

life for him was only a vigil, and only after death would come the dawn.

The position was one which must have had its impressiveness for all minds that were not of the [7]dullest order, even if they were inclined, as Macchiavelli was, to interpret the Frate's character by a key that presupposed no loftiness.* [8]To Romola, whose kindred ardour gave her a firm belief in Savonarola's genuine greatness of purpose, the crisis was as stirring as if it had been part of her personal lot. It blent itself as an exalting[9] memory with all her daily labours; and those labours were calling not only for difficult perseverance, but for new courage. Famine had never yet taken its flight from Florence,[1] and all distress, by its long continuance, was getting harder to bear; disease was spreading in the crowded city, and the Plague [2]was expected. As Romola walked, often in weariness, among the sick, the hungry, and the murmuring, she felt it good to be inspired by something more than her pity—by the belief in a heroism struggling for sublime ends, towards which the daily action of her pity could only tend feebly, as the dews that freshen the weedy ground to-day tend to prepare an unseen harvest in the years to come.

But that mighty music which stirred her in the Duomo was not without its jarring notes. Since those first days of glowing hope when the Frate[3], seeing the near triumph of good in the reform of the Republic and the coming of the French deliverer, had preached peace, charity, and oblivion of political differences, there had been a marked change of conditions: political intrigue had been too obstinate to allow of the desired oblivion; the belief in the French deliverer[4], who had turned[5] his back on his high mission, seemed to have wrought harm; and hostility, both on a petty and on a grand scale, was attacking the Prophet with new weapons and new determination. It followed that the spirit of contention and self-vindication pierced more and more conspicuously in his sermons; that he was urged to meet the popular demands not only by increased insistance and detail concerning visions and private revelations, but by a tone of defiant confidence against objectors; and from having denounced the desire for the miraculous, and declared that miracles had no relation to true

7 ⟨?vilest⟩ dullest *MS*   8 ⟨For⟩ To *MS*

9 exalting ⟨strengthening⟩ memory *MS*

1 Florence; ⟨trade to⟩ and all distress {by its long continuance} was getting harder to bear ⟨by its long continuance⟩ *MS*

2 ⟨had appeared⟩ was expected *MS*

3 Frate ⟨had⟩, seeing the near triumph of good in the ⟨expulsion of the Medici government⟩ reform of the ⟨Florentine⟩ republic *MS*

4 French deliverer] *3P* deliverer *CM 1 2*

5 the {belief in the} Deliverer {who} had turned *MS*

faith, he had come to [6]assert that at the right moment the divine power would attest the truth of[7] his prophetic preaching by a miracle. And continually, in the rapid transitions of excited feeling, as the vision of triumphant good receded behind the actual predominance of evil, the threats of coming vengeance against vicious tyrants and corrupt priests gathered some impetus from personal exasperation, as well as from indignant zeal. In the career of a great public orator who yields himself to the inspiration of the moment[8], that conflict of selfish and unselfish emotion which [9]in most men is hidden in the chamber of the soul, [1]is brought into terrible evidence: the language of the inner voices is written out in letters of fire.

But if the tones of [2]exasperation jarred on Romola, there was [3]often another member of Fra Girolamo's audience to whom they were the only thrilling tones, like the vibration of deep[4] bass notes to the deaf. Baldassarre had found out that the wonderful Frate was preaching again, and as often as he could, he went to hear the Lenten sermon, [5]that he might drink in the threats of a voice which[6] seemed like a power on the side of justice. He went the more because he had seen that Romola went too; for he was waiting and watching for a time when not only outward circumstance[7], but his own varying mental state[8], would mark the right moment for seeking an interview with her. Twice Romola had caught sight of his face in the Duomo—once when its dark glance was fixed on hers. She wished not to see it again, and yet she looked for it, as men look for the reappearance of a portent. But any revelation that might be yet to come[9] about this old man was a subordinate fear[1] now: it referred, she thought, only to the past, and her anxiety was almost absorbed by the present.

Yet the stirring Lent passed by; April, the second and final[2] month of her godfather's supreme authority, was [3]near its close; [4]and nothing had occurred to fulfil her presentiment. In the public mind, too, there had been fears, and rumours had spread from Rome of a menacing activity on the part of Piero de' Medici; but in a few days the suspected Bernardo would go out of power[5].

6 ⟨declare his confidence that⟩ assert that MS   7 attest {the truth of} MS
8 orator {who yields himself to the inspiration of the moment} MS
9 ⟨for⟩ in MS   1 ⟨becomes terribly audible⟩ is brought MS
2 ⟨irritation⟩ exasperation MS   3 ⟨frequently⟩ often MS
4 like the vibration of deep] like deep MS   5 ⟨to⟩ that he might MS
6 which] that MS   7 circumstance] circumstances 2 3
8 {varying} mental state MS   9 {yet} to come MS
1 fear ⟨when⟩ MS   2 second {and final} MS
3 ⟨advancing to⟩ near MS   4 ⟨yet⟩ and MS
5 power ⟨and a bitter *Arrabbiato*, enemy alike of the Medici⟩ {¶} Romola was ⟨gathering⟩ trying to gather some ⟨comfort from this⟩ courage MS

Romola was trying to gather some courage from the review of her futile fears, when on the twenty-seventh, as she was walking out on[6] her usual errands of mercy in the afternoon, she was met by a messenger from Camilla Rucellai, chief among the feminine seers of Florence, desiring her presence forthwith on matters of the highest moment. Romola, who shrank with unconquerable repulsion from the shrill volubility[7] of those illuminated women, and had just now a special repugnance towards Camilla because of a [8]report that she had announced revelations hostile to Bernardo del Nero, was at first inclined to send back a flat refusal. [9]Camilla's message might refer to public affairs, and Romola's immediate prompting was to close her ears against knowledge that might only make her mental burthen heavier. But it had become so thoroughly her habit to reject her impulsive choice, and to obey passively the guidance of outward claims, that, reproving herself for allowing her presentiments to make her cowardly and selfish, she ended by compliance, and went straight to Camilla. She found the nervous grey-haired woman in a chamber arranged as much as possible like a convent cell. The thin fingers clutching Romola as she sat, and the eager voice addressing her at first[1] in a loud whisper, caused [2]her a physical shrinking that made it difficult for her to keep her seat.

Camilla had a vision to communicate—a vision in which it had been revealed to her by Romola's Angel, that Romola knew certain secrets concerning her godfather, Bernardo del Nero, which, if disclosed, might save the Republic from[3] peril. Camilla's voice rose louder and higher as she narrated her vision, and ended by exhorting Romola to obey the command of her Angel, and separate herself from the enemy of God.

Romola's impetuosity was that of a massive nature, and, except in moments when she was deeply stirred, her manner was calm and self-controlled. She had a constitutional disgust for the shallow excitability of women like Camilla, whose [4]faculties seemed all wrought up into [5]fantasies, leaving nothing for emotion and thought. [6]The exhortation was not yet ended when she started up and attempted to wrench her arm from Camilla's tightening grasp. It was of no use. The

6 {out} on *MS*
7 repulsion from the shrill volubility] *3C* disgust from the shrill excitability *MS CM 1 2*
8 ⟨rumour⟩ report *MS*
9 ⟨If, as was possible, Camilla's message referred⟩ Camilla's message *MS*
1 at first] *MS CM 1 3P* first 2   2 ⟨Romola⟩ her *MS*
3 from ⟨the curse of having him elected Gonfaloniere⟩ *MS*
4 ⟨nature⟩ faculties *MS*   5 ⟨fantasy⟩ fantasies *MS*
6 ⟨She had compelled herself to come lest she should be neglecting some call of duty, but the⟩ The exhortation was ⟨hardly at an end⟩ not yet ended *MS*

prophetess kept her hold like a crab, and, [7]only incited to more eager exhortation by Romola's resistance, was carried beyond her own intention into a shrill statement of other visions which were to corroborate this. Christ himself had appeared to her and ordered her to send his commands to certain citizens in office that they should throw Bernardo del Nero from the window of the Palazzo Vecchio. Fra Girolamo himself knew of it, and had not dared this time to say that the vision was not of divine authority.

"And since then," said Camilla, in her excited treble, straining upward with wild eyes towards Romola's face, "the [8]Blessed Infant has come to me and laid a wafer of sweetness on my tongue in token of his pleasure that I had done his will."

"Let[9] me go!" said Romola, in a deep voice of anger[1]. "God grant you are mad! else you are detestably wicked!"

The violence of her effort to be free was too strong for Camilla now[2]. She wrenched away her arm and rushed out of the room, not pausing till she had hurriedly gone[3] far along the street, and found herself close to the church of the Badia. She had but to pass behind the curtain under the old stone arch, and she would find a sanctuary shut in from the noise and hurry of the street, where all objects and all uses suggested the thought of an eternal peace subsisting in the midst of turmoil. She turned in, and sinking down on the step of the altar in front of [4]Filippino Lippi's serene Virgin* appearing to St. Bernard, she waited in hope that the inward tumult[5] which agitated her would by and by subside.

The thought which pressed on her the most acutely, was that[6] Camilla could allege Savonarola's countenance of her wicked folly. Romola did not for a moment believe that he had sanctioned the throwing of Bernardo del Nero[7] from the window as a divine suggestion; she felt certain that there was falsehood or mistake in that allegation. Savonarola had become more and more severe in his views of resistance to malcontents; but the ideas of strict law and order were fundamental to all his political teaching. Still, since he knew the possibly fatal effects of visions like Camilla's, since he had a marked distrust of such spirit-seeing women, and kept aloof from them as much

7 ⟨impeded by⟩ ⟨incited⟩ only incited *MS*
8 ⟨blessed⟩ Blessed ⟨Gesù⟩ Infant has come to me ⟨again⟩ *MS*
9 Let] Woman, let *MS*
1 anger ⟨while her face and neck were⟩ ⟨with her face and neck flushing and her eyes shooting fire⟩ *MS*
2 now] *3P* this time *MS CM 1 2*
3 hurriedly gone] *3P* gone hurriedly *MS CM 1 2*   4 ⟨Fra Lippo⟩ Filippino *MS*
5 {inward} tumult ⟨of painful thoughts and feelings⟩ *MS*
6 acutely, was that] *MS* acutely was, that *CM 1 2* acutely was that *3*
7 Bernardo {del Nero} *MS*

as possible, why, with his readiness to denounce wrong from the pulpit, did he[8] not publicly denounce these pretended revelations which
brought new darkness instead of light across the conception of a
Supreme Will? Why? The answer came with painful clearness: he was
fettered inwardly by the consciousness that such revelations were not,
in their basis, distinctly separable from his own visions; he was fettered outwardly by the foreseen consequence of raising a [9]cry against
himself even among members of his own party, as one who would
suppress all divine inspiration of which he himself was not the vehicle
—he or his confidential and supplementary[1] seer of visions, Fra
Salvestro.

Romola, kneeling with buried face on the altar step, was enduring
one of those sickening moments, when the enthusiasm which had
come to her as the only energy strong enough to make life worthy,
seemed to be inevitably bound up with vain dreams and wilful eye-
shutting. Her mind rushed back with a new attraction towards the
strong worldly sense, the dignified prudence, the [2]untheoretic virtues
of her godfather, who was to be treated as a sort of Agag* because he
held that a more restricted form of government was better than the
Great Council, and because he would not pretend to forget[3] old ties
to the banished family. But[4] with this last thought rose the presentiment of some plot to restore the Medici; and then again she felt that
the popular party was half justified in its fierce suspicion. Again she
felt that to keep the Government of Florence pure, and to keep[5] out
[6]a vicious rule, was a sacred cause; the Frate was right there, and had
carried her understanding irrevocably with him. But at this moment
the assent of her understanding went alone; it was given unwillingly.
Her heart was recoiling from [7]a right allied to so much narrowness; a
right apparently entailing that hard systematic judgment of men
which measures them by assents and denials quite superficial to the
manhood within them. Her affection and respect were clinging with
new tenacity to her godfather,[8] and with him to those memories of
her father which were in the same opposition to the division of men
into sheep and goats by the easy mark of some political or religious
symbol.[9]

After all has been said that can be said about the widening

8 why ⟨then⟩ {with his readiness . . . pulpit,} did he *MS*   9 ⟨fanatical⟩ cry *MS*
1 confidential {and supplementary} *MS*   2 ⟨unimpassioned⟩ untheoretic *MS*
3 {pretend to} forget *MS*   4 But ⟨again⟩ with *MS*
5 to keep] keep *MS*
6 ⟨the⟩ a vicious rule ⟨of a vicious Piero de' Medici⟩ *MS*
7 ⟨that⟩ a right ⟨which was⟩ allied to so much narrowness, ⟨and to⟩ *MS*
8 godfather, ⟨inseparable to her from the memory of her father⟩ and {with him} *MS*
9 same opposition to . . . symbol.] ⟨same⟩ ⟨equal⟩ same opposition to the political
⟨and⟩ or religious division of ⟨Florentines⟩ men into sheep and goats. *MS*

influence of ideas, it remains true that they would hardly be such strong agents unless they were taken in a solvent of feeling. The great world-struggle of[1] developing thought is continually foreshadowed in the struggle of the affections, seeking a justification for love and hope. If[2] Romola's intellect had been less capable of discerning the complexities in human things, all the early loving associations of her life would have forbidden her to accept implicitly the denunciatory exclusiveness of Savonarola. She had simply felt that his mind had suggested deeper and more efficacious truth to her than any other, and the large breathing-room which she found[3] in his grand view of human duties had made her patient towards that part of his teaching which she could not absorb, so long as its practical effect came into collision with no strong force in her. But now a sudden insurrection of feeling had brought about that collision. Her indignation[4], once roused by Camilla's visions, could not pause there, but ran like an illuminating fire over all the kindred facts in Savonarola's teaching, and for the moment she felt what was true in the scornful sarcasms she heard continually flung against him, more keenly than she felt what[5] was false.

But it was an illumination that made all life look ghastly to her. Where were the beings to whom she could cling, with whom she could work and endure, with the belief that she was working for the right? On the side from which moral energy came lay a fanaticism from which she was shrinking with [6]newly startled repulsion; on the side to which she was drawn by affection and memory, there was the presentiment of some secret plotting, which her judgment told her would not be unfairly called crime. And still surmounting every other thought was the dread inspired by Tito's hints, lest that presentiment should be converted into knowledge, in such a way that she would be torn by irreconcilable claims.

1 struggle of ⟨individual⟩ MS
2 love and hope. If] love and hope, and the most effective stimulus to argument that a given heresy is not damnable is a strong unwillingness to believe that the dear heretic will be damned. If MS
  3 which she found] MS she found CM 1 2 3
  4 collision. Her indignation] collision. ⟨Her indignation could not pause upon Camilla's visions⟩ Romola's generous energy had its corresponding imperfection: her intellectual discernment, though powerful, had its ⟨direction⟩ action confined by the deep channel of her predominant emotion, and under a strong revulsion of feeling she was liable to as strong a revulsion of judgment. In petty beings such a result seems ⟨but⟩ an intensified pettiness, but it is only by this narrowing concentration that human nature whether in ⟨the individual⟩ individuals or in the mass rises high enough for deeds of ⟨heroic resistance⟩ heroism or for earth-shaking ⟨revolutions⟩ movements of enterprise and reform. ¶ Romola's indignation MS
  5 than she felt what] 3P than what MS CM 1 2
  6 ⟨renewed⟩ newly startled MS

Calmness would not come even on the altar step[7]; it would not come from looking at the serene picture where the saint, writing in the rocky solitude, was being visited by faces with celestial peace in them. Romola was[8] in the hard press of human difficulties, and that rocky solitude was too far off. She [9]rose from her knees that she might hasten to her sick people in the courtyard, and, by some immediate beneficent[1] action, revive that sense of worth in life which at this moment was unfed by any wider faith[2]. But when she turned round, she found herself face to face with a man who was standing[3] only two yards off her. The man was Baldassarre.

7 step] steps *3*   8 Romola was ⟨not in rocky solitude⟩ *MS*
9 ⟨was rising⟩ rose *MS*   1 {immediate} beneficent *MS*
2 faith ⟨, when the touch of a hand on her shoulder⟩. *MS*
3 standing ⟨with⟩ only ⟨a⟩ two *MS*

CHAPTER LIII.

ON SAN MINIATO

"I WOULD speak with you," said Baldassarre, as Romola looked at him in silent expectation. It was plain that he had followed her, and had been waiting for her. She was going at last to know the secret about him.

"Yes," she said, with the same sort of submission that she might have shown[1] under an imposed penance. "But you wish to go where no one can hear us.[2]"

"Where *he* will not come upon us," said Baldassarre, turning and glancing behind him timidly. "Out—in the air—away from the streets."

"I sometimes go to San Miniato* at this hour," said Romola. "If you like, I will go now, and you can follow me. It is far, but we can be solitary there."

He nodded assent, and Romola set out. [3]To some women it might have seemed an alarming risk to go to a comparatively solitary spot with a man who had some of the outward signs of that madness which Tito attributed to him. But Romola was not given to personal fears, and she was glad of the distance that interposed some delay before another blow fell on her. The afternoon was far advanced, and the sun was already low in the west, when she paused on some rough ground in the shadow of the cypress trunks, and looked round for Baldassarre. He was not far off, but when he reached her, he was glad to sink down on [4]an edge of stony earth. His thick-set frame had no longer the sturdy vigour which belonged to it when he first appeared with the rope round him in the Duomo; and under the transient tremor caused by the exertion of walking up the hill, his eyes seemed to have a more helpless vagueness.

"The hill is steep," said Romola, with compassionate gentleness, seating herself by him. "And I fear you have been weakened by want."

He turned his head and [5]fixed his eyes on her in silence[6], unable, now the moment for[7] speech was come, to seize the words that would convey [8]the thought he wanted to utter: and she remained as motionless as she could, lest he should suppose her impatient. He looked like nothing higher than a common-bred, neglected old man; but she

---

1 shown ⟨to⟩ MS
3 ⟨She was glad of the distance⟩ To MS
5 ⟨looked fixedly at⟩ fixed MS
7 for] of 2 3

2 us.] MS us? CM 1 2 3
4 ⟨the⟩ an MS
6 silence—⟨He was⟩ unable MS
8 ⟨his⟩ the MS

was used now to be very near to such people, and to think[9] a great deal about their troubles. Gradually his glance gathered a more definite expression, and at last he said with abrupt emphasis—

"Ah! you would have been my daughter!"

The swift flush came in Romola's face and went back again as swiftly, leaving her with white lips a little apart, like a marble image of horror. For her mind, this[1] revelation was made. She divined the facts that lay behind that single word, and in the first moment there could be no check to the impulsive belief which sprang from her keen [2]experience of Tito's nature. The sensitive response of her face was a stimulus to Baldassarre; for the first time his words had wrought their right effect[3]. He went on with gathering eagerness and firmness, laying his hand on her arm.

"You are a woman of proud blood—is it not true? You go to hear the preacher; you hate baseness—baseness that smiles and triumphs. You hate your husband?"

"Oh, God! were you really his father?[4]" said Romola, in a low voice, too entirely possessed by the images of the past to take any note[5] of Baldassarre's question. "Or was it as he said? Did you take him when he was little?"

"Ah, you believe me—you know what he is!" said Baldassarre, exultingly, tightening the pressure on her arm, as if the contact gave him power. "You will help me.[6]"

"Yes," said Romola, not interpreting the words as he meant them. She laid her palm gently on the rough hand that grasped her arm, and the tears came to her eyes as she looked at him. "Oh! it is piteous! Tell me—why, you[7] were a great scholar; you taught him. How[8] is it?"

She broke off. Tito's allegation of this man's madness [9]had come across her; and where were the signs even of[1] past refinement? But she had the self-command not to move her hand. She sat perfectly still, waiting to listen with new caution.

"It is gone!—it is all gone!" said Baldassarre; "and they would not believe me, because he lied, and said I was mad; and they had me dragged to prison. And I am old—my mind will not come back. And the world is against me."

He paused a moment, and his eyes sank as if he were under a wave of despondency. Then he looked up at her again, and said with renewed eagerness—

9 {to} think *MS* 1 this] the *2 3* 2 ⟨sense⟩ experience *MS*
3 {right} effect *MS* 4 father?] *3P* father! *MS CM 1 2*
5 {any} note *MS* 6 me.] *MS* me? *CM 1 2 3* 7 why, you] you *2 3*
8 him. *How*] him—how *MS* 9 ⟨came⟩ had come *MS*
1 {even} of *MS*

"But *you*[2] are not against me. He made you love him, and he has been false to you; and you hate him. Yes, he made *me* love him: he was beautiful and gentle, and I was a lonely man. I took him when they were beating him[3]. He slept in my bosom when he was little, and I watched him as he grew, and gave him all my knowledge, and everything that was mine I meant to be his. I had many things: money, and books, and gems. He had my gems—he sold them; and he left me in slavery. He never came to seek me, and when I came back poor and in misery, he denied me. He said I was a madman."

"He told us his father was dead—was drowned," said Romola, faintly. "Surely he must have believed it then. Oh! he could not have been so base *then!*"

A vision had risen of what Tito was to her in those first days when she thought no more of wrong in him than a child thinks of poison in flowers. The yearning regret that lay in that memory brought some relief from the tension of horror. With one great sob the tears rushed forth.

"Ah, you are young, and the tears come easily," said Baldassarre, with some impatience. "But tears are no good; they only put out the fire within, and it is the fire that works. Tears will hinder us. Listen to me."

Romola turned towards him with a slight start. Again the possibility of his madness had darted through her mind, and checked the rush of belief. If, after all, this man were only a mad assassin? But her deep belief in his[4] story still lay behind, and it was more in sympathy than in fear that she[5] avoided the risk of paining him by any show of doubt.

"Tell me," she said, as gently as she could, "how did you lose your memory—your scholarship?"

"I was ill. I can't tell how long—it was a blank. I remember nothing, only at last I was sitting in the sun among the stones, and everything else was darkness. And slowly, and by degrees, I felt something besides that: a longing for something—I did not know what—that never came. And when I was in the ship on the waters I began to know what I longed for; it was for the Boy[6] to come back—it was to find all my thoughts again, for I was locked away outside them all. And I am outside now. I feel nothing but a wall and darkness."

Baldassarre had become dreamy again, and sank into silence, resting his head [7]between his hands; and again Romola's belief in him had submerged all cautioning doubts. The pity with which she dwelt on his words seemed like the revival of an old pang. Had she not

2 *you*] you *MS*   3 him, ⟨I [?nursed] him⟩ he *MS*
4 his] this 2 3   5 {it was} more in sympathy than in fear {that} she *MS*
6 Boy] boy *MS*   7 ⟨on⟩ between *MS*

daily seen how her father missed Dino and all the future[8] he had dreamed of in that son?

"It all came back once," Baldassarre went on presently. "I was master of everything. I saw all the world again, and my gems, and my books; and I thought I had him in my power, and I went to expose him where—where the lights were and the trees; and he lied again, and said I was mad, and they dragged me away to prison. . . . Wickedness is strong, and he wears armour."

The fierceness had flamed up again. He spoke with his former intensity, and again he grasped Romola's arm[9].

"But you will help me.[1] He has been false to you[2] too. He has another wife, and she has children. He makes her believe he is her husband, and she is a foolish, helpless thing. I will show you where she lives."

The first shock that passed through Romola was visibly one of anger. The woman's sense of indignity was inevitably foremost. Baldassarre instinctively felt her in sympathy with him.[3]

"You hate him," he went on. "Is it not true? There is no love between you; I know that. I know women can hate; and you have proud blood. You hate falseness, and you can love revenge."

Romola sat paralysed by the shock of conflicting feelings. She [4]was not conscious of the grasp that was bruising her tender arm.

"You[5] shall contrive it,' said Baldassarre, presently, in[6] an eager whisper. "I have learned by heart that you are his rightful wife. You are a noble woman. You go to hear the preacher of vengeance; you will help justice. But you will think for me. My mind goes—everything goes sometimes—all but the fire. The fire is God: it is justice: it will not die. You believe that—is it not true?[7] If they will not hang him for robbing me, you will take away his armour—you will make him go without it, and I will stab him. I have a knife, and my arm is still strong enough."

He put his hand under his tunic, and reached out the hidden knife, feeling the edge abstractedly, as if he needed the sensation to keep alive his ideas.

It seemed to Romola as if every fresh hour of her life were to become more difficult than the last. Her [8]judgment was too vigorous and rapid for her to fall into the mistake of using futile deprecatory

8 all the future] MS the future CM 1 2 3
9 and again he grasped Romola's arm] 1 2 3 and grasped Romola's arm again MS CM
1 me.] MS me? CM 1 2 3   2 you] you MS
3 lives." {The first shock . . . him.} MS
4 ⟨did not feel⟩ was not conscious of MS   5 You] You MS
6 {presently} in MS   7 die. {You believe that—is it not true?} MS
8 ⟨intellect⟩ judgement MS

words to a man in Baldassarre's state of mind. She chose not to answer his last speech. She would win time for [9]his excitement to allay itself by asking something else that she cared to know. She spoke rather tremulously—

"You say she is foolish and helpless—that other wife—and believes him to be her real husband. Perhaps he is: perhaps he married her before he married me."

"I cannot tell," said Baldassarre, pausing in that action of feeling the knife, and looking bewildered. "I can remember no more. I only know where she lives. You shall see her. I will take you; but not now," he added, hurriedly, "*he* may be there. The [1]night is coming on."

"It is true," said Romola, starting up with a sudden consciousness that the sun had set, and the hills were darkening; "but you will come and take me—when?"

"In the morning," said Baldassarre, dreaming that she, too, wanted to hurry to her vengeance.

"Come to me, then, where you came to me to-day, in the church. I will be there at ten; and if you are not there, I will go again towards[2] midday. Can you remember?"

"Midday," said Baldassarre—"only midday. The same place, and midday. And, after that," he added, rising, and grasping her arm again with his left hand, while he held the knife in his right[3]; "we will have our revenge. He shall feel the sharp edge of justice. The world is against me, but you will help me."

"I would help you in other ways," said Romola, making a first, timid effort to dispel his illusion about her. "I fear you are in want; you have to labour, and get little. I should like to bring you comforts, and make you feel again that there is some one who cares for you."

"Talk no more about that," said Baldassarre, fiercely. "I will have nothing else. Help me to wring one drop of [4]vengeance on this side of the grave. I have nothing but my knife. It is sharp; but there is a moment after the thrust when men see the face of death,—and it shall be *my* face that he will see."

He loosed his hold, and sank down again in a sitting posture. Romola felt helpless: she must defer all intentions till the morrow.

"Midday, then," she said, in a distinct voice.

"Yes," he answered, with an air of exhaustion. "Go; I will rest here."

She hastened away. Turning at the last spot [5]whence he was likely to be in sight, she saw him seated still.

9 ⟨the⟩ his *MS*
2 towards] at *MS*
4 ⟨revenge⟩ vengeance *MS*

1 ⟨darkness⟩ night *MS*
3 again {with his left . . . right} *MS*
5 ⟨where⟩ whence *MS*

CHAPTER LIV.

THE EVENING AND THE MORNING

ROMOLA had a purpose in her mind as she was hastening away; a purpose which had been growing through the afternoon hours[1] like a side-stream, rising higher and higher along with the main current. It was less a resolve than a necessity of her feeling. Heedless of the darkening streets, and not caring to call for Maso's slow escort, she hurried across the bridge where the river showed itself black before the distant dying red, and took the most direct way to the Old Palace. She might encounter her husband there. No matter. She could not weigh probabilities; she must discharge her[2] heart. She did not know what she passed in the pillared court or up the wide stairs; she only knew that she asked an usher for [3]the Gonfaloniere, giving her name, and begging to be shown into [4]a private room.

She was not left long alone with the frescoed figures and the [5]newly-lit tapers. Soon the door opened, and Bernardo del Nero entered, still[6] carrying his white head erect above his silk *lucco*.

"Romola, my child, what is this?" he said, in a tone of anxious surprise as he closed the door.

She had uncovered her head and went towards him without speaking. He laid his hand on her shoulder, and held her a little way from him that he might see her better. Her face was haggard from fatigue and long agitation[7], her hair had rolled down in disorder; but there was an excitement in her eyes that seemed to have triumphed over the bodily consciousness.

"What has he done?" said Bernardo, abruptly[8]. "Tell me everything, child; throw away pride. I am your father."

"It is not about myself—nothing about myself," said Romola, hastily. "Dearest godfather, it is about you. I have heard things—some I cannot tell you. But you are in danger in the palace; you are in danger everywhere. There are fanatical men who would harm you, and—and there are traitors. Trust nobody. If you trust, you will be betrayed."

Bernardo smiled.

"Have you worked yourself up into this agitation, my poor child,"

---

1 growing {through the afternoon hours} *MS*   2 discharge her ⟨soul of⟩ *MS*
3 ⟨Bernardo del Nero⟩ the Gonfaloniere *MS*   4 ⟨his⟩ a *MS*
5 ⟨candle⟩ ⟨dim oil lamp⟩ newly lit tapers *MS*   6 still ⟨erect⟩ *MS*
7 {long} agitation *MS*   8 said Bernardo {abruptly} *MS*

he said, raising his hand [9]to her head, and patting it gently, "to tell[1] such old truths[2] as that to an old man like me?"

"Oh, no, no! they are not old truths I mean[3]," said Romola, pressing her clasped hands painfully together, as if that action would help her to suppress what must not be told. "They are fresh things that I know, but cannot tell. Dearest godfather, you know I am not foolish. I would not come to you without reason. Is it too late to warn you against any one, *every* one who seems to be working on your side? Is it too late to say, Go to your villa and keep away in the country when these three more days of office are over? Oh, God! perhaps it is too late! and if any harm comes to you, it will be as if I had done it!"

The last words had burst from Romola involuntarily: a[4] long-stifled feeling had found spasmodic utterance. But she herself was startled and arrested.

"I mean," she added, hesitatingly, "I know nothing positive. I only know what fills me with fears."

[5]"Poor child!" said Bernardo, looking at her with[6] quiet penetration for a moment or two. Then he said—"Go, Romola, go home and rest. These fears may be only big ugly shadows of something very little and harmless. Even traitors must see their interest in betraying; the rats will run where they smell the cheese, and there is no knowing yet which way the scent will come."

He paused[7], and turned away his eyes from her with an air of abstraction, till, with a slow shrug, he added—

"As for warnings, they are of no use to me, child. I enter into no plots, but I never forsake my colours. If I march abreast with obstinate men, who will rush on guns and pikes, I must share the consequences. Let us say no more about that. I have not many years left at the bottom of my sack for them to rob me of. Go, child; go home and rest."

He put his hand on her head again caressingly, and she could not help clinging to his arm, and pressing her brow against his shoulder. Her godfather's caress seemed the last thing that was left to her out of that young filial life, which now looked so happy to her even in its troubles, for they were troubles untainted by anything hateful.

"Is silence best, my Romola?" said the old man.

"Yes, now; but I cannot tell whether it always will be," she answered, [8]hesitatingly, raising her head with an appealing look.

"Well, you have a father's ear while I am above[9] ground"—he

9 ⟨from her shoulder⟩ to her head *MS*   1 tell ⟨an⟩ *MS*
2 truths] truth *2 3*   3 I mean] that I mean *2 3*
4 involuntarily: a] *MS 1 2 3* involuntarily; a *CM*   5 ⟨The old man⟩ "Poor *MS*
6 with] *1 2 3* {silently} with *MS CM*   7 paused ⟨a moment and⟩ and *MS*
8 ⟨with some hesitation⟩ hesitatingly *MS*   9 {while I am} above *MS*

lifted the black drapery and folded it round her head, adding—"and a father's home; remember that." Then opening the door, he said: "There, hasten away. You are like a black ghost; you will be safe enough."

When Romola fell asleep that night, she slept deep. Agitation had reached its limits; she must gather strength before she could suffer more; and, in spite of rigid habit, she slept on far beyond sunrise.

When she awoke, it was to the sound of guns. Piero de' Medici[1], with thirteen hundred men[2*] at his back, was before the gate that looks towards Rome.

So much Romola learned from Maso, with many circumstantial additions of dubious quality. A countryman had come in and alarmed the Signoria before it was light, else the city would have been taken by surprise. His master was not in the house, having been summoned to the Palazzo long ago. She sent out the old man again, that he might gather news, while she went up to the loggia from time to time to try and discern any signs of the dreaded entrance having been made, or of its having been effectively repelled. Maso brought her word that the great Piazza was full of armed men, and that many of the chief citizens suspected as friends of the Medici had been summoned to the Palace and detained there. Some of the people[3] seemed not to mind whether Piero got in or not, and some said the Signoria itself[4] had invited him; but however that might be, they were giving him an ugly welcome; and the soldiers from Pisa were coming against him.

In her memory of those morning hours, there were not many things that Romola could distinguish as actual external[5] experiences standing markedly out above the tumultuous waves of retrospect and anticipation. She knew that she had really walked to the Badia by the appointed time in spite of street alarms; she knew that she had waited there in vain. And the scene she had witnessed when she came out of the church[6], and stood watching on the steps while the doors were being closed behind her for the afternoon interval, always came back to her like a remembered waking.

There was a change in the faces and tones of the people[7], armed and unarmed, who were pausing or hurrying along the streets. The guns were firing again, but the sound[8] only provoked laughter. She soon knew the cause of the change. Piero de' Medici and his horse-

---

1 Piero de' Medici ⟨was before the gate of San Piero that looks towards Rome, with thirteen hundred⟩ MS

2 men] horsemen MS   3 Some {of the people} MS

4 itself] themselves MS   5 {actual} external MS

6 Church ⟨at [?noon]⟩ MS

7 people ⟨who were pausing or hurrying⟩ MS   8 sound ⟨stirred no alarm⟩ MS

men had turned their backs on Florence, and were galloping as fast as they could along the Siena road. She learned this from a substantial shopkeeping Piagnone[9], who had not yet laid down his pike.

"It is true," he ended, with a certain bitterness in his emphasis. "Piero is gone, but there are those left behind who were in the secret of his coming—we all know that; and if the new Signoria does its duty we shall soon know *who* they are."

The words darted through Romola like a sharp spasm; but the evil they foreshadowed was not yet close upon her, and as she entered her home again, her most pressing anxiety was the possibility that she had lost sight for a long while of Baldassarre.

9 shopkeeping Piagnone] Piagnone shopkeeper *MS*

CHAPTER LV.

WAITING

THE lengthening sunny days went on without bringing either what Romola most desired or what she most dreaded. They brought no sign from Baldassarre, and, in spite of special watch on the part of the Government, no revelation of the suspected conspiracy. But they brought other things which touched her closely, and bridged the phantom-crowded space of anxiety[1] with active sympathy in immediate trial. They brought the [2]spreading Plague and the Excommunication of Savonarola.

Both those[3] events tended to arrest her incipient alienation from the Frate, and to rivet again her attachment to the man who had opened[4] to her the new life of duty, and who seemed now to be worsted in the fight for principle against profligacy. For Romola could not [5]carry from day to day into the abodes of pestilence and misery[6] the sublime excitement of a gladness that, since such[7] anguish existed, she too existed to make some of the anguish[8] less bitter, without remembering that she owed[9] this transcendent moral life to Fra Girolamo. She could not witness the silencing and excommunication of a man whose distinction from the great mass of the clergy lay, not in any heretical belief, not in[1] his superstitions, but in the energy with which he sought to make the Christian life a reality, without feeling herself drawn strongly to his side.

Far on in the hot days of June the[2] Excommunication, for some weeks arrived from Rome, was solemnly published in the Duomo.* Romola went to witness the scene, that the resistance it inspired might invigorate [3]that sympathy with Savonarola which[4] was one source of her strength. It was in memorable contrast with the scene she had been accustomed to witness there. Instead of upturned citizen-faces filling the vast area under the morning light, the youngest rising amphitheatre-wise towards the walls and making a garland of

---

1 space {of anxiety} *MS*   2 ⟨spread of the Plague⟩ spreading Plague *MS*
3 those] these *2 3*   4 {had} opened *MS*
5 ⟨carry⟩ ⟨be carried with a sublime excitement⟩ carry *MS*
6 pestilence {and misery} *MS*   7 such] this *MS*
8 {some of} the anguish *MS*   9 owed ⟨it to⟩ *MS*
1 not in any heretical belief, not in] not in his theological beliefs, not {even} in *MS*
2 Far on in the hot days of June the] *1 2 3* It was far on in the hot days of June before the *MS CM*
3 ⟨her⟩ that sympathy with ⟨the denounced Frate⟩ Savonarola *MS*
4 Savonarola which] *MS 2 3* Savonarola, which *CM 1*

hope around the memories of age—instead of the mighty voice thrilling all hearts with the sense of great things, visible and invisible, to be struggled for—there were the bare walls at evening made more sombre by the glimmer of tapers, there was the black and grey flock of monks and secular clergy with bent unexpectant faces, there was[5] the occasional tinkling of little bells in the pauses of a monotonous voice reading a sentence which had already been long hanging up in the churches[6], and at last there was the extinction of the tapers, and the slow shuffling tread of [7]monkish feet departing in the dim silence.

Romola's ardour on the side of the Frate was doubly strengthened, by[8] the gleeful triumph she saw in hard and coarse faces, and by the[9] fear-stricken confusion[1] in the faces and speech of many among his strongly attached friends. The question where the duty of obedience ends, and the duty of resistance begins, [2]could in no case be an easy one; but it was made overwhelmingly difficult by the belief that the Church [3]was—not a compromise of parties to secure a more or less approximate[4] justice in the appropriation of funds, but—a living organism instinct with divine power [5]to bless and to curse. To most of the pious Florentines, who had hitherto felt no doubt in their adherence to the Frate, that belief in the Divine potency of the Church was[6] not an embraced opinion, it was an inalienable impression, like the concavity of the blue firmament; and the boldness of Savonarola's written arguments that the Excommunication was unjust, and that, being unjust, it was not valid, only made them tremble the more,[7] as a defiance cast at a mystic image, against whose subtle immeasurable power there was neither weapon nor defence.

But Romola, whose mind had not been allowed to draw its early nourishment from the traditional associations of the Christian community, in which her father had lived a life apart, felt her relation to the Church only through Savonarola; his moral force had been the only authority to which she had bowed; and in his excommunication she only saw the menace of hostile vice: on one side she saw a man whose life was devoted to the ends of public virtue and spiritual purity, and on the other the assault of alarmed selfishness, headed by a lustful, greedy, lying, and murderous old man, once called Rodrigo Borgia, and now lifted to the pinnacle of infamy as Pope Alexander the Sixth. The finer shades of fact which soften the edge of such

5 there was ⟨a monotonous⟩ *MS*   6 churches ⟨. Finally⟩, and at last *MS*
7 ⟨departing⟩ monkish *MS*   8 strengthened, by] *MS* strengthened by *CM 1 2 3*
9 {by} the *MS*
1 confusion ⟨in the faces of many who had loved the Frate⟩ *MS*
2 ⟨is never a very⟩ could *MS*   3 ⟨is⟩ was *MS*
4 {a more or less} approximate *MS*   5 ⟨independently⟩ to bless *MS*
6 belief in the Divine potency of the Church was] *3P* belief was *MS CM 1 2*
7 more, ⟨it was⟩ ⟨they seemed⟩ *MS*

antitheses are not apt to be seen except by neutrals, who are not distressed to discern some folly in martyrs and some judiciousness in the men who burn[8] them. But Romola required a strength[9] that neutrality could not give; and this Excommunication, which simplified and ennobled the resistant position of Savonarola by bringing into prominence its wider relations, seemed to come to her like a rescue from the threatening isolation of criticism and doubt. The Frate was now withdrawn from that smaller antagonism against Florentine enemies into which he continually fell in the unchecked excitement of[1] the pulpit, and presented himself simply as appealing to the Christian world against[2] a vicious exercise of ecclesiastical power. He was a standard-bearer leaping into the breach. Life never seems so clear and easy[3] as when the heart is beating faster at the sight of some generous self-risking deed. We feel no doubt then what is the highest prize the soul can win; we almost believe in our own power to attain it. By[4] a new current of such enthusiasm Romola was helped through these difficult summer days.

She had ventured on no words to Tito that would apprise him of her late interview[5] with Baldassarre, and the revelation he had made to her. What would such agitating, difficult words[6] win from him? No admission of the truth; nothing, probably, but a cool sarcasm about her sympathy with his assassin. Baldassarre was evidently helpless: the thing to be feared was, not that he should injure Tito, but that Tito, coming upon his traces, should carry out some new scheme for ridding himself of the injured man who was a haunting dread to him. Romola felt that she could do nothing decisive until she had seen Baldassarre again, and learned the full truth about that "other wife"— learned whether she were[7] the wife to whom Tito was first bound.

The possibilities about that other wife, which involved the worst wound to her hereditary pride, mingled themselves as a newly embittering suspicion with the earliest memories of her illusory love, eating away the lingering associations of tenderness with the past image of her husband; and her irresistible belief[8] in the rest of Baldassarre's revelation made her shrink from Tito[9] with a horror which would perhaps have urged some passionate speech in spite of herself if he had not been more than usually absent from home. Like many of the

---

8 burn] burnt *3*

9 strength ⟨which neutrality could not give, and⟩ ⟨that can never come from neutrality but only from sympathy and trust, and⟩ *MS*

1 {unchecked} excitement of ⟨preaching⟩ the pulpit *MS*

2 world against] world for a General Council against *MS*   3 easy ⟨to us⟩ *MS*

4 By] *1 2 3* And by *MS CM*   5 {late} interview *MS*

6 {agitating, difficult} words *MS*   7 were] was *MS*

8 The possibilities about . . . belief] Meanwhile, her irresistible belief *MS*

9 Tito] her husband *MS*

wealthier citizens in that time of pestilence, he spent the intervals of business chiefly in the country: the agreeable Melema was welcome at many villas, and [1]since Romola had refused to leave the city, he had no need to provide a country residence of his own.

But at last, in the later days of July, the [2]alleviation of those public troubles which had absorbed her activity and much of her thought, left Romola to a less counteracted sense of her personal lot. The plague had almost disappeared, and the position of Savonarola was made more hopeful by a favourable magistracy, who were writing urgent vindicatory letters to Rome on his behalf, entreating the withdrawal of the Excommunication.

[3]Romola's healthy and vigorous frame was undergoing the reaction of languor inevitable after continuous excitement and over-exertion; but[4] her mental restlessness would not allow her to remain at home without peremptory occupation, except during the sultry hours. In the cool of the morning and evening she walked out constantly, varying her direction as much as possible, with the vague hope that if Baldassarre were still alive she might encounter him. Perhaps some illness had brought a new paralysis of memory, and he had forgotten where she lived—forgotten even her existence. That was her most sanguine explanation of his non-appearance. The explanation she felt to be most probable was, that he had died of the Plague.

1 ⟨as⟩ since *MS*   2 ⟨diminution⟩ ⟨lightening⟩ alleviation *MS*
3 ⟨Romola in spite⟩ Romola's *MS*
4 but ⟨in the day-time, it was only during the sultry hours that⟩ her mental restlessness would {not} allow *MS*

CHAPTER LVI.

THE OTHER WIFE

THE morning warmth was already beginning to be rather oppressive to Romola, when, after a walk along by the walls on her way from San Marco, she turned towards the intersecting streets again at the Gate of Santa Croce.

The Borgo La Croce was so still, that she listened to her own footsteps on the pavement in the sunny silence, until, on approaching a bend in the street[1], she saw, a few yards before her, a little child not more than three years old, with no other clothing than his white shirt, pause from a waddling run and look around him. In the first moment of coming nearer she could only see his back—a boy's back, square and sturdy, with a cloud of reddish-brown curls above it; but in the next he turned towards her, and she could see his [2]dark eyes wide with tears, and his lower lip pushed up and trembling, while his fat brown fists clutched his shirt helplessly. The glimpse of a tall black figure sending a shadow over him brought his bewildered fear to a climax, and[3] a loud crying sob sent the big tears rolling.

Romola, with the ready maternal instinct which was one hidden source of her passionate tenderness, instantly uncovered her head, and, stooping down on the pavement, put her arms round him, and her cheek[4] against his, while she spoke to him in caressing tones. At first his sobs were only the louder, but he made no effort to get away, and presently the outburst ceased with that strange abruptness which belongs to childish joys and griefs: his face lost its distortion, and was fixed in an open-mouthed gaze at Romola.

"You have lost yourself, little one," she said, kissing him. "Never mind! we will find the house again. Perhaps Mamma will meet us."

She divined that he had made his escape at a moment when the mother's eyes were turned away from him, and thought it likely that he would soon be followed.

"Oh, what a heavy, heavy boy!" she said, trying to lift him. "I cannot carry you. Come, then, you must toddle back by my side."

The parted lips remained motionless in awed silence, and one brown fist still clutched the shirt with as much tenacity as ever; but the other yielded itself quite willingly to the wonderful white hand, strong but soft.

"You *have* a Mamma?" said Romola, as they set out, looking down

1 street ⟨before the church⟩ *MS*   2 ⟨great⟩ dark *MS*
3 and ⟨the big tears fell with⟩ *MS*   4 cheek] cheeks *2 3*

at the boy with a certain yearning. But he was mute. A girl under those circumstances might perhaps have chirped abundantly; not so this square-shouldered little man with the big cloud of curls.

He was awake to the first sign of his whereabout, however. At the turning by the front of San Ambrogio he dragged Romola towards it, looking up at her.

"Ah, that is the way home, is it?" she said, smiling at him. He only thrust his head forward and pulled, as an admonition that they should go faster.

There was still another turning that he had a decided opinion about, and then Romola found herself in a short street leading to open garden ground. It was in front of a house at the end of this street that the little fellow paused, pulling her towards some stone stairs. He had evidently no wish for her to loose his hand, and she would not have been willing to leave him without[5] being sure that she was delivering him to his friends. They mounted the stairs, seeing but dimly in that sudden withdrawal from the sunlight, till, at the final landing place, an extra stream of light came from an open doorway. Passing through a small lobby they came to another open door, and there Romola paused. Her approach had not been heard.

On a low chair at the farther end of the room, opposite the light, sat Tessa, with one hand on the [6]edge of the cradle, and her head hanging a little on one side, fast asleep. Near[7] one of the windows, with her back turned towards the door, sat Monna Lisa at her work of preparing salad[8], in deaf unconsciousness. There was only an instant for Romola's eyes to take in that still scene; for Lillo snatched his hand away from her and ran up to his mother's side, not making any direct effort to wake her, but only leaning his head back against her arm, and surveying Romola seriously from that distance.

[9]As Lillo pushed against her Tessa opened her eyes, and looked up in bewilderment; but[1] her glance had no sooner rested on the figure at the opposite doorway than she started up[2], blushed deeply, and began to tremble a little, neither speaking nor moving forward.

"Ah! we have seen each other before," said Romola, smiling, and coming forward. "I am glad it was *your*[3] little boy. He was crying in the street; I suppose he had run away. So we walked together a little way, and then he knew where he was, and brought me here. But you had not missed him? That is well, else you would have been frightened."

The shock of finding that Lillo had run away overcame every other feeling in Tessa for the moment. Her colour went again, and, seizing

5 without ⟨landing him safely amongst⟩ *MS*   6 ⟨side⟩ edge *MS*
7 Near ⟨the window⟩ *MS*   8 Lisa {at her work of preparing salad} *MS*
9 ⟨On feeling⟩ As *MS*   1 but ⟨when her glance rested⟩ *MS*
2 she {started up} *MS*   3 *your*] your *MS*

Tessa at Home

Lillo's arm, she ran with him to Monna Lisa, saying, with a half sob, loud in the old woman's ear—

"Oh, Lisa, you are wicked! Why will you stand with your back to the door? Lillo ran away ever so far into the street."

"Holy Mother!" said Monna Lisa, in her meek, thick tone[4], letting the spoon fall from her hands. "Where were *you*, then? I thought you were there, and had your eye on him."

"But you *know* I go to sleep when I am[5] rocking," said Tessa, in pettish remonstrance.

"Well, well, we must keep the outer door shut, or else tie him up," said Monna Lisa, "for he'll be as cunning as Satan before long, and that's the holy truth. But how came he back, then?"

This question recalled Tessa to the consciousness of Romola's presence. Without answering, she turned towards her, blushing and timid again, and Monna Lisa's eyes followed[6] her movement. The old woman made a low reverence, and said—

"Doubtless the most noble lady brought him back." Then, advancing a little nearer to Romola, she added, "It's my shame for him to have been found with only his shirt on; but he kicked, and wouldn't have his other clothes on this morning, and the mother, poor thing, will never hear of his being beaten. But what's an old woman to do without a stick when the lad's legs get so strong? Let your nobleness look at his legs."

Lillo, conscious that his legs were in question, pulled his shirt up a little higher, and looked down at their olive roundness with a dispassionate and curious air. Romola laughed, and stooped to give him a caressing shake and a kiss, and this action helped the reassurance that Tessa had already gathered from Monna Lisa's address to Romola. For when Naldo had been told about the adventure at the Carnival, and Tessa had asked him who the heavenly lady that had come just when she was wanted, and had vanished so soon, was likely to be— whether she could be the Holy Madonna herself?—he had answered, "Not exactly, my Tessa; only one of the saints," and had not chosen to say more. So that in the dream-like combination of small experience which made up Tessa's thought, Romola had remained confusedly associated with the pictures in the churches, and when she reappeared, the grateful remembrance of her protection was slightly tinctured with religious awe—not deeply, for Tessa's dread was chiefly of ugly and evil things. It seemed unlikely that good beings would be angry and punish her, as it was the nature of Nofri and the devil to do. And now that Monna Lisa had spoken freely about Lillo's legs and Romola had laughed, Tessa was more at her ease.

4 Lisa, {in her meek thick tone} *MS*   5 I am] I'm *MS*
6 followed ⟨in the same direction⟩ *MS*

"Ninna's in the cradle," she said. "*She's* pretty too."

Romola went to look at the sleeping Ninna, and Monna Lisa, one of the exceptionally meek deaf, who never expect to be spoken to, returned to her salad.

"Ah! she is waking: she has opened her blue eyes," said Romola. "You must take her up, and I will sit down in this chair—may I?—and nurse Lillo. Come, Lillo!"

She had sat[7] down in Tito's chair, and put out her arms towards the lad, whose eyes had followed her. He hesitated, and, pointing his small fingers at her with a half-puzzled, half-angry feeling, said, "That's Babbo's chair," not seeing his way out of the difficulty if Babbo came and found Romola in his place.

"But Babbo is not here, and I shall go soon. Come, let me nurse you as he does," said Romola, wondering to herself for the first time what sort of Babbo he was whose wife was dressed in[8] contadina fashion, but had a certain daintiness about her person that indicated idleness and plenty. Lillo consented to be lifted up, and, finding the lap exceedingly comfortable, began to explore her dress and hands, to see if there were any ornaments besides her[9] rosary.

Tessa, who had hitherto been occupied in coaxing Ninna out of her waking peevishness, now sat down in her low chair, near Romola's knee, arranging Ninna's tiny person to advantage, jealous that the strange lady too seemed[1] to notice the boy most, as Naldo did.

"Lillo was going to be angry with me because I sat in Babbo's chair," said Romola, as she bent forward to kiss Ninna's little foot. "Will he come soon and want it?"

"Ah, no!" said Tessa; "you can sit in it a long while. I shall be sorry when you go. When you first came to take care of me at the Carnival, I thought it was wonderful; you came and went away again so fast. And Naldo said, perhaps you were a saint, and that made me tremble a little, though the saints are very good, I know; and you were good to me, and now you have taken care of Lillo. Perhaps you will always come and take care of me. That was how Naldo did a long while ago; he came and took care of me when I was frightened, one San Giovanni. I couldn't think where he came from—he was so beautiful and good. And so are you," ended Tessa, looking up at Romola with devout admiration.

"Naldo is your husband. His eyes are like Lillo's," said Romola, looking at the boy's darkly-pencilled eyebrows, unusual at his age. She did not speak interrogatively, but with a quiet certainty of inference which was necessarily mysterious to Tessa.

---

7 had sat] sat 2 3   8 dressed {in} *MS*   9 besides her] beside the 2 3
1 seemed ⟨to take most⟩ *MS*

"Ah! you know him![2]" she said, pausing a little in wonder. "Perhaps you know Nofri and Peretola, and our house on the hill, and everything. Yes, like Lillo's; but not his hair. His hair is dark and long—" she went on, getting rather excited. "Ah! if you know it, ecco!"

She had put her hand to a thin red silk cord that hung round her neck, and drew from her bosom the tiny old parchment *Breve*, the horn of red coral, and a long dark curl carefully tied at one end and suspended with those mystic treasures. She held them towards Romola, away from Ninna's snatching hand.

"It is a fresh one. I cut it lately. See how bright it is!" she said, laying it against the white background of Romola's fingers. "They get dim, and then he lets me cut another when his hair is grown; and I put it with the *Breve*, because sometimes he is away a long while, and then I think it helps[3] to take care of me."

A slight shiver passed through Romola as [4]the curl was laid across her fingers. At [5]Tessa's first mention of her husband as having come mysteriously she knew not whence, a possibility had risen before Romola that made her heart beat faster; for to one who is anxiously in search of a certain object, the faintest suggestions have[6] a peculiar significance. And when the curl was held towards her, it seemed for an instant like a mocking phantasm of the lock she herself had cut to wind with one of her own five years ago. But she preserved her outward calmness, bent not only on knowing the truth, but also on coming to that knowledge in a way that would not pain this poor, trusting, ignorant thing, with the child's mind in the woman's body. "Foolish and helpless:" yes; so far she corresponded to Baldassarre's account.

"It is a beautiful curl," she said, resisting the impulse to withdraw her hand. "Lillo's curls will be like it, perhaps, for *his* cheek, too, is dark. And you never know where your husband goes to when he leaves you?"

"No," said Tessa, putting back her treasures out of the children's way. "But I know Messer San Michele[7] takes care of him, for he gave him a beautiful coat, all made of little chains; and if he puts that on, nobody can kill him. And, perhaps, if—" Tessa hesitated a little, under a recurrence of [8]that original dreamy wonder about Romola which had been expelled by chatting contact—"if you *were* a saint, you would take care of him, too, because you have taken care of me and Lillo."

2 him! {she said, pausing a little in wonder.} perhaps you know Nofri and {Peretola and} our little house on the hill ⟨where we had the goats⟩ and everything" ⟨she ⟨⟨said⟩⟩ went on, getting rather excited,⟩ "Yes *MS*

3 I think it helps] *1 2 3* it helps *MS CM*   4 ⟨Tessa laid⟩ the curl was laid *MS*

5 ⟨the⟩Tessa's *MS*   6 have] seem to have *MS*

7 San Michele] *1 2 3* Saint Michael *MS CM*

8 ⟨her⟩ that original ⟨vague⟩ dreamy *MS*

[9]An agitated flush came over Romola's face in the first moment of certainty, but she had bent her cheek against Lillo's head. [1]The feeling that leaped out in that flush was something like exultation at the thought that the wife's burthen might be about to slip from her overladen shoulders; that this little ignorant creature might prove to be Tito's lawful wife. [2]A strange exultation for a proud and high-born woman to have been brought to! But it seemed to Romola as if that were the only issue that would make duty anything else for her than an unsolvable[3] problem. [4]Yet she was not deaf to Tessa's last appealing words; she raised her head, and said, in her clearest tones,—

"I will always take care of you, if I see you need me. But that beautiful coat? your husband did not wear it when you were first married? Perhaps he[5] used not to be so long away from you then?"

"Ah, yes! he was. Much—much longer. So long, I thought he would never come back. I used to cry. Oh, me! I was beaten then; a long, long while ago at Peretola, where we had the goats and mules."

"And how long had you been married before your husband had that chain-coat?" said Romola, her heat beating faster and faster.

Tessa looked meditative, and began to count on her fingers, and Romola watched the fingers as if they would tell the secret of her destiny.

"The chestnuts were [6]ripe when we were married," said Tessa, marking off her thumb and fingers again as she spoke; "and then again they were ripe at Peretola before he came back, and then again[7], after that, on the hill. And soon the soldiers came and we heard the trumpets, and then Naldo had the coat."

"You had been married more than two years. In which church were you married?" said Romola, too entirely absorbed by one thought to put any question that was less direct. Perhaps before the next morning she might go to her godfather and say that she was not Tito Melema's lawful wife—that the vows which had bound her to strive after an impossible union had been made void beforehand.

Tessa gave a slight start at Romola's new tone of inquiry, and looked up at her with a hesitating expression. Hitherto she had prattled on without consciousness that she was making revelations, any more than when she said old things over and over again to Monna Lisa.

9 〈There was a momentary flush in Romola's face〉 An *MS*
1 〈If she had had any〉 〈If there had been the slightest [?remnant] of love for Tito, she would not have felt herself in danger of 〈〈hoping that this〉〉 asking the question〉 The *MS*
2 〈It was a〉 A *MS*   3 unsolvable] *MS* insoluble *CM 1 2 3*
4 〈But〉 Yet *MS*   5 he 〈was〉 *MS*   6 〈just〉 ripe *MS*
7 then {again} *MS*

"Naldo said I was never to tell about that," she said, doubtfully. "Do you think he would not be angry if I told you?"

"It is right that you should tell me. Tell me everything," said Romola, looking at her with mild authority.

If the impression from Naldo's command had been much more recent than it was, the constraining effect of Romola's mysterious authority would have overcome it. But the sense that she was telling what she had never told before made her begin with a lowered voice.

"It was not in a church—it was at the Natività, when there was the[8] fair, and [9]all the people went overnight to see the Madonna in the Nunziata, and [1]my mother was ill and couldn't go, and I took the bunch of cocoons for her; and then he came to me in the church and I heard him say, 'Tessa!' I knew him because he had taken care of me at the San Giovanni, and then we went into the Piazza where the fair was, and I had some *berlingozzi*, for I was hungry and he was very good to me; and at the end of the Piazza there was a holy father and an altar like what they have at the processions outside the churches. So he married us, and then Naldo took me back into the church and left me; and I went home, and my mother died, and Nofri began to beat me more, and Naldo never came back. And I used to cry, and once at the Carnival I saw him and followed him, and he was angry, and said he would come some time, I must wait. So I went and waited; but, oh! it was a long while before he came; but he would have come if he could, for he was good; and then he took me away, because I cried and said I could not bear to stay with Nofri. And, oh! I 'was so glad, and since then I have been always happy, for I don't mind about the goats and mules, because I have Lillo and Ninna now; and Naldo is never angry, only I think he doesn't love Ninna so well as Lillo, and she *is* pretty."

Quite forgetting that she had thought her speech rather momentous at the beginning, Tessa fell to devouring Ninna with kisses, while Romola sat in silence with absent eyes. It was inevitable that in this moment she should think of the three beings before her chiefly in their relation to her own lot, and she was feeling the chill of disappointment that her difficulties were not to be solved by external law. She had relaxed her hold of Lillo, and was leaning her cheek against her hand, seeing nothing of the scene around her. Lillo was quick in perceiving a change that was not agreeable to him; he had[2] not yet made any return to her caresses, but he objected to their withdrawal, and putting up both his brown arms to pull her head towards him, he said, "Play with me again!"

Romola, roused from her self-absorption, clasped the lad [3]anew,

8 the] a *2 3*   9 ⟨we⟩ all the people *MS*   1 ⟨the madre⟩ my mother *MS*
2 had ⟨made no return⟩ ⟨not returned⟩ *MS*   3 ⟨again⟩ anew *MS*

and looked from him to Tessa, who had now paused from her shower of kisses, and seemed to have returned to the more placid delight of contemplating the heavenly [4]lady's face. That face was undergoing a [5]subtle change, like the gradual oncoming of a warmer, softer light. Presently Romola took her scissors from her scarsella, and cut off one of her long wavy locks, while the three pair of wide eyes followed her movements with kitten-like observation.

"I must go away from you now," she said, "but I will leave this lock of hair that it may remind you of me, because if you are ever in trouble you can think that perhaps God will send me to take care of you again. I cannot tell you where to find me, but if I ever know that you want me, I will come to you. Addio!"

She had set down Lillo hurriedly, and held out her hand to Tessa, who kissed it with a mixture of awe and sorrow at this parting. Romola's mind was oppressed with thoughts; she needed to be alone as soon as possible, but with her habitual care for the least fortunate, she turned aside to put her hand in a friendly way on Monna Lisa's shoulder and[6] make her a farewell sign. Before[7] the old woman had finished her deep reverence, Romola had disappeared.

Monna Lisa and Tessa moved towards each other by [8]simultaneous impulses, while the two children[9] stood clinging to their mother's skirts as if they, too, felt the atmosphere of awe.

"Do you think she *was* a saint?" said Tessa, in Lisa's ear, showing her the lock.

Lisa rejected that notion very decidedly by a backward movement[1] of her fingers, and then[2] stroking the rippled gold, said,—

"She's a great and noble lady. I saw such in my youth."

Romola [3]went home and sat alone through the sultry hours of the day with the heavy [4]certainty that her lot was unchanged[5]. She was thrown back again on the conflict between the demands of an outward law which she recognized as a widely ramifying obligation, and[6] the demands of inner moral facts which were becoming more and more peremptory. She had drunk in deeply the spirit of that teaching by which Savonarola had urged her to return to her place. She felt that the sanctity attached to all close relations, and, therefore, pre-eminently to the closest, was but the expression in outward law of that result towards which all human goodness and nobleness must

4 ⟨lady⟩ lady's face. ⟨Presently Romola took⟩ That MS
5 ⟨gradual⟩ subtle MS   6 and ⟨look a goodbye to the old woman⟩ MS
7 Before] But before MS   8 ⟨a common impulse⟩ simultaneous impulses MS
9 {two} children MS   1 backward movement] movement MS
2 then ⟨said⟩, stroking the rippled gold, ⟨she said⟩ said MS
3 ⟨hastened⟩ went MS   4 ⟨?consciousness⟩ certainty MS
5 unchanged ⟨and that⟩. She MS
6 obligation, and] MS 2 3 obligation and CM 1

spontaneously tend; that the light abandonment of ties, whether
inherited or voluntary, because they had ceased to be pleasant, was
the uprooting of social and personal virtue. What else had Tito's
crime towards Baldassarre been but that abandonment working itself
out to the most hideous extreme of falsity and ingratitude?

And the inspiring consciousness [7]breathed into her by Savonarola's
influence that her lot was vitally united with the general lot had
exalted even the minor details of obligation into religion. She was
marching with a great army; she was feeling the stress of a common
life. If victims were needed, and it was uncertain on whom the lot
might fall, she would stand ready to answer to her name. She had
stood long; she had striven hard to fulfil the bond; but she had seen
all the conditions which made the fulfilment possible gradually forsaking her. The one effect of her marriage-tie seemed to be the stifling
predominance over her of a nature that she despised. All her efforts at
union had only made its impossibility more palpable, and the relation
had become for her simply a degrading servitude. The law was
sacred.[8] Yes, but rebellion might be sacred too. It flashed upon her
mind that the problem before her was essentially the same as that
which had lain before Savonarola—the problem where the sacredness
of obedience ended and where the sacredness of rebellion began.[9] To
her, as to him, there had come one of those moments in life when the
soul must dare to act on its own warrant, not only without external
law to appeal to, but in the face of a law which is not unarmed with
divine lightnings—lightnings that may yet fall if the warrant has been
false.[1]

Before the sun had gone down she had adopted a resolve. She
would ask no counsel of her godfather or of Savonarola until she had
made one determined effort to speak freely with Tito and obtain his
consent that she should live apart from him. She desired not to leave
him clandestinely again, or to forsake Florence. She would tell him
that if[2] he ever felt a real need of her, she would come back to him.
Was not that the utmost faithfulness to her bond that could be
required of her? A shuddering anticipation came over her that he
would clothe a refusal in a sneering suggestion that she should enter a
convent as the only mode of quitting him that would not be scandalous[3]. He knew well that her mind revolted from that means of
escape, not only because of her own repugnance to a narrow rule, but
because[4] all the cherished memories of her father forbade that she

---

7 ⟨which had been⟩ breathed *MS*   8 sacred.] sacred? *MS*
9 before Savonarola {: the problem . . . began.} *MS*
1 false. ⟨She could not ask counsel from her⟩ *MS*
2 that if] *MS 1 2 3* that, if *CM*   3 scandalous; ⟨knowing⟩ He knew *MS*
4 because ⟨it seemed forbidden by her father's memory⟩ *MS*

should adopt a mode of life which was associated with his deepest griefs and his bitterest dislike.

Tito had announced his intention of coming home this evening. She would wait for him, and say what she had to say at once, for it was difficult to get his[5] ear during the day. If he had the slightest suspicion that personal words were coming, he slipped away with an appearance of unpremeditated ease. When she sent for Maso to tell him that she would wait for his master, she observed that the old man looked at her and lingered[6] with a mixture of hesitation and wondering anxiety; but finding that she asked him no question, he slowly turned away. Why should she ask questions? Perhaps Maso only knew or guessed something of what she knew already.

It was late before Tito came. Romola had been pacing up and down the long room which had once been the library, with the windows open and a loose white linen robe on instead of her usual black[7] garment. She was glad of that change after the long hours of heat and motionless meditation; but the coolness and exercise made her more intensely wakeful, and as she went with the lamp in her hand to open the door for Tito he might well have been startled by the vividness of[8] her eyes and the expression of painful resolution which was in contrast with her usual self-restrained quiescence before him. But[9] it seemed that this excitement was just what he expected.

"Ah! it is you, Romola. Maso is gone to bed," he said, in a grave, quiet tone, interposing to close the door for her.[1] Then, turning round, he said, looking at her more fully than he was wont, "You have heard it all, I see.[2]"

Romola quivered. *He*, then, was inclined to take the initiative. He had been to Tessa. She led the way through the nearest door, set down her lamp, and turned towards him again.

"You must not think despairingly of the consequences," said Tito, in a tone of soothing encouragement, at which Romola stood wondering, until he added, "The accused have too many family ties with all parties not to escape; and Messer Bernardo del Nero has other things in his favour besides his age."

Romola started, and gave a cry as if she had been suddenly stricken by a sharp weapon.

"What! you did not know it?" said Tito, putting his hand under her arm that he might[3] lead her to a seat; but she seemed to be unaware of his touch.

5 his] Tito's *MS* 6 {looked at her and} lingered *MS*
7 {usual} black *MS* 8 vividness of ⟨expression⟩ *MS*
9 But ⟨he seemed not to be ⟨⟨surprized⟩⟩ ?perplexed⟩ *MS*

1 {Maso is gone to bed} he said in a grave quiet tone, {interposing to close the door for her} ⟨Then ⟨⟨I will⟩⟩ ⟨⟨turning to⟩⟩ pushing the bolt to like [1 word]⟩ Then *MS*
2 see.] see? *MS* 3 that he might] as if he would *MS*

"Tell me," she said, hastily—"tell me what it is."

"A man, whose name you may forget—Lamberto dell' Antella—
who was banished, has been seized within the territory: a[4] letter has
been found on him of very dangerous import to the chief Mediceans,
and the scoundrel, who was once a favourite hound of Piero de'
Medici, is ready now to swear what any one pleases against him or
his friends.* Some have made their escape, but five are now in
prison."

"My godfather?" said Romola, scarcely above a whisper, as Tito
made a slight pause.

"Yes; I grieve to say it. But along with him there are three, at
least, whose names have a commanding interest even among[5] the popular party—Niccolò Ridolfi, Lorenzo Tornabuoni, and Giannozzo
Pucci."

The tide of Romola's feeling[6] had been violently turned into a new
channel. In [7]the tumult of that moment there could be no check to
the words which came as the impulsive utterance of her long-accumu-
lating horror. When Tito had named the men of whom she felt certain he was the confederate, she said[8], with a recoiling gesture and
low-toned bitterness—

"And *you*—you are safe?"

"You are certainly an amiable wife, my Romola," said Tito, with
the coolest[9] irony. "Yes; I am safe."

They turned away from each other in silence.

---

4 territory: a] territory and a *MS*   5 even among] among *MS*
6 feeling] *MS* feelings *CM 1 2 3*   7 ⟨that⟩ the *MS*
8 When Tito . . . said] When Tito had uttered the names of ⟨his most intimate asso-
ciates⟩ men whom she knew to be his intimate associates, she said *MS*
9 coolest] *MS* coldest *CM 1 2 3*

CHAPTER LVII.

WHY TITO WAS SAFE

TITO had good reasons for saying that he was safe. In the last three months, during which he had foreseen the discovery of the Medicean conspirators as a probable event, he had had plenty of time to[1] provide himself with resources. He had been strengthening his influence at Rome and at Milan, by being the medium of secret information and indirect measures against the Frate and the popular party; he had cultivated more assiduously than ever the regard of this party by showing subtle evidence that his political convictions were entirely on their side; and all the while, instead of withdrawing his agency from the Mediceans, he had sought to be more actively employed and exclusively trusted by them. It was easy to him to keep up this triple game. The principle of duplicity admitted by the Mediceans on their own behalf deprived them of any standard by which they could measure the trustworthiness of a colleague who had not, like themselves, hereditary interests, alliances, and prejudices, which were intensely Medicean. In their minds to deceive the opposite party was fair stratagem, to deceive their own party was a baseness to which they felt no temptation; and in using Tito's facile ability they were not keenly awake to the fact that the absence of traditional attachments which made him a convenient agent was also the absence of what among themselves was the chief guarantee of mutual honour. Again, the Roman and Milanese friends[2] of the aristocratic party, or Arrabbiati, who were the bitterest enemies of Savonarola, carried on a system of underhand correspondence and espionage, in which the deepest hypocrisy was the best service, and demanded the heaviest pay; so that to suspect an agent because he played a part strongly would have been an absurd want of logic. On the other hand, the [3]Piagnoni of the popular party, who[4] had the directness that belongs to energetic conviction, were the more inclined to credit Tito with sincerity in his political adhesion[5] to them, because he affected no religious sympathies[6].

1 to ⟨meditate on possible⟩ *MS*
2 {Roman and Milanese} friends *MS*
3 ⟨popular party⟩ Piagnoni *MS*
4 party, who] *MS* 2 3 party who *CM 1*
5 {political} adhesion *MS*
6 sympathies, ⟨they had the tendency, common to religious politicians in all times, to pet an unbeliever who was on their side in public measures, and almost to regard his

Drifting Away

By virtue of these conditions the last three months had been a time of flattering success to Tito. The result he most cared for was the securing of a future position for himself at Rome or at Milan, for he had a growing determination, when the favourable moment should come, to quit Florence for one of those great capitals where life was easier, and the rewards of talent and learning were more splendid. At present, the scale dipped in favour of Milan; and if within the year he could render certain services to Duke Ludovico Sforza, he had the prospect of a place at the Milanese court, which outweighed the advantages of Rome.

The revelation of the Medicean conspiracy, then, had been a subject of forethought to Tito; but he had not been able to foresee the mode in which it would be brought about. The arrest of Lamberto dell' Antella with a tell-tale letter on his person, and a bitter rancour against the Medici in his heart, was an incalculable event. It was not possible, in spite of the careful pretexts with which his agency had been guarded, that Tito should escape implication: he had never expected this in case of any wide discovery concerning the Medicean plots.[7] But [8]his quick mind had soon traced out the course that would secure his own safety with the [9]fewest unpleasant concomitants. It is agreeable to keep a whole skin; but the skin still remains an organ sensitive to the atmosphere.

His reckoning had not deceived him. That night before he returned home, he had secured the three[1] results for which he most cared: he was to be freed from all proceedings against him on account of complicity with the Mediceans; he was to retain his Secretaryship for another year, unless he previously resigned it; and, lastly, the price by which he had obtained these guarantees was to be kept as a State secret. The price would have been thought heavy by most men; and Tito himself would rather not have paid it.

He had applied himself first to win the mind of Francesco Valori, who was not only one of the Ten under whom he immediately held his Secretaryship, but one of the special council appointed to investigate the evidence of the plot. Francesco Valori, as we have seen, was the head of the Piagnoni, a man with certain fine qualities that were not incompatible with violent partisanship, with an arrogant temper that alienated [2]his friends, nor with bitter personal animosities—one of the bitterest being directed against Bernardo del Nero. To him, in a brief private interview, after obtaining a pledge of secrecy, Tito

laxity as providentially arranged to show that mere worldly wit, if it were only strong enough would inevitably strike the balance in their favour.⟩ *MS*

7 an incalculable event. {It was . . . plots.} *MS*   8 ⟨Tito's⟩ his *MS*
9 ⟨least⟩ fewest *MS*   1 {the} three *MS*   2 ⟨even⟩ his friends *MS*

avowed his own[3] agency for the Mediceans—an agency induced by motives about which he was very frank, declaring at the same time that he had always believed their efforts futile, and that he sincerely preferred the maintenance of the popular government; affected to confide to Valori, as a secret,[4] his own personal dislike for Bernardo del Nero; and after this preparation, came to the important statement that[5] there was another Medicean plot, of which, if he obtained certain conditions from the government, he could, by a journey to Siena, and into Romagna* where Piero de' Medici was again trying to gather forces,[6] obtain documentary evidence to lay before the council. To this end it was essential that his character as a Medicean agent should be unshaken for all Mediceans, and hence the fact that he had been a source of information to the authorities must be wrapped in profound secrecy. Still, some odour of the facts might escape in spite of precaution, and before Tito could incur the unpleasant consequences of acting against [7]his friends, he must be assured of immunity from any prosecution as a Medicean, and from deprivation of office for a year to come.

These propositions did not sound in the ear of Francesco Valori precisely as they sound to us. Valori's mind was not intensely bent on the estimation of Tito's conduct; and it *was* intensely bent on procuring an extreme sentence against the five prisoners. There were sure to be immense efforts to save them; and it was to be wished (on public grounds) that the evidence against them should be of the strongest, so as to alarm all well-affected men at the dangers of clemency. The character of legal proceedings at that time implied that evidence was one of those desirable things which could only be come at by foul means. To catch a few people and torture them into confessing everybody's guilt[8] was one step towards justice; and it was not always easy to see [9]the next unless a traitor turned up. Lamberto dell' Antella had been tortured in aid of his previous willingness to tell more than he knew; nevertheless,[1] additional and stronger facts were desirable, especially against Bernardo del Nero, who, so far as appeared hitherto, had simply refrained from [2]betraying the late plot after having tried

3 {after obtaining a pledge of secrecy} Tito avowed his own ⟨active⟩ agency for the Mediceans ⟨to⟩ ⟨induced by motives which he made no effort to conceal⟩ an agency MS
4 secret, ⟨that he⟩ MS
5 that ⟨he had⟩ there was another Medicean plot ⟨not yet [7 or 8 words]⟩ ⟨of which he possessed⟩ MS
6 Siena ⟨and Rome⟩ {and into . . . gather forces} MS
7 ⟨former colleagues⟩ his friends MS
8 torture them {into confessing everybody's guilt} MS   9 ⟨another⟩ the next MS
1 nevertheless, ⟨more decisive evidence was⟩ MS
2 ⟨disclosing an attempt⟩ betraying the late plot ⟨of Piero de' Medici⟩ after having tried in vain to ⟨hinder⟩ discourage MS

in vain to discourage it; for the welfare of Florence demanded that the guilt of Bernardo del Nero should be put in the strongest light. So Francesco Valori zealously believed[3]; and perhaps he was not himself aware that the strength of his [4]zeal was determined by his hatred. He decided that Tito's proposition ought to be accepted, laid it before his colleagues without [5]disclosing Tito's name, and won them over to his opinion. Late in the day Tito was admitted to an audience of the special council, and produced a deep sensation among them by revealing another plot for insuring the mastery of Florence to Piero de' Medici, which was to have been carried into execution in the middle of this very month of August.* Documentary evidence on this subject would do more than anything else to make the right course clear. He received a commission to start for Siena by break of day; and, besides this[6], he carried away with him from the council-chamber a written guarantee of his immunity and of his retention[7] of office.

Among the twenty [8]Florentines who bent their grave eyes on Tito, as he stood gracefully before them, speaking of startling things with easy periphrasis, and with that apparently unaffected admission of being actuated by motives short of the highest which is often the intensest affectation, there were several whose minds were not too entirely preoccupied for them to pass[9] a new judgment on him in these new circumstances; they silently concluded that this ingenious and serviceable Greek was in future rather to be used for public needs than for private intimacy. Unprincipled men were [1]useful, enabling those who had more scruples to keep their hands tolerably clean in a world where there was much dirty work to be done. Indeed, it was not clear to respectable Florentine brains, unless they held the Frate's extravagant belief[2] in a possible purity and loftiness to be striven for on this earth, how life was to be carried on in any department without human instruments whom it would not be unbecoming to kick or to spit upon in the act of handing them their wages. Some of these very men who passed [3]a tacit judgment on Tito were shortly to be engaged in a [4]memorable transaction that could by no means have been carried through without the use of [5]an unscrupulousness* as decided as his; but, as their own bright poet

3 {zealously} believed *MS*   4 ⟨belief⟩ zeal *MS*
5 ⟨revealing its author⟩ disclosing *MS*   6 and {besides this} *MS*
7 {of his} retention *MS*   8 ⟨citizens⟩ Florentines *MS*
9 for them to pass] to pass 2 3   1 ⟨clearly⟩ useful, enabling ⟨men of⟩ those *MS*
2 {extravagant} belief *MS*
3 ⟨an unfavourable⟩ ⟨a severe⟩ a tacit judgement *MS*
4 ⟨world famous⟩ memorable *MS*
5 ⟨a much uglier turpitude⟩ an unscrupulousness *MS*

Pulci[6] had said for them, it is one thing to love the fruits of treachery, and another thing to love traitors.

> "Il tradimento a molti piace assai,
> Ma il traditore a gnun non piacque mai[7]."*

The same society has had a gibbet for the murderer and a gibbet
for the martyr, an execrating hiss for a dastardly act, and as loud a
hiss for many a word of generous truthfulness or just insight: a mixed
condition of things which is the sign, not of hopeless confusion, but
of struggling order.

For Tito himself, he was not unaware that he had sunk a little in
the estimate of the men who had accepted his services. He had that
degree of self-contemplation which necessarily accompanies the habit
of acting on well-considered reasons, of whatever quality; and if he
could have chosen, he would have declined to see himself disapproved
by men of the world. He had never meant to be disapproved; he had
meant always to conduct himself so ably that if he acted in opposition
to the standard of other men they should not be aware of it; and the
barrier between himself and Romola had been raised by the impossibility of such concealment with her. He shrank from condemnatory
judgments[8] as from a climate to which he could not adapt himself.
But[9] things were not so plastic in the hands of cleverness as could be
wished, and events had turned out inconveniently[1]. He had really no
rancour against Messer Bernardo del Nero; he had a personal liking
for Lorenzo Tornabuoni and Giannozzo[2] Pucci. He had served them
very ably, and in such a way that if their party had been winners he
would have merited high reward; but was he to relinquish all the
agreeable fruits of life because their party had failed? His proffer of a
little additional proof against them would probably have no influence
on their fate; in fact, he felt convinced they would escape any extreme
consequences; but if he had not given it, his own fortunes, which
made a promising fabric, would have been utterly ruined.[3] And what
motive could any man really have, except his own interest?
Florentines whose passions were engaged in their petty and precarious

6 poet Pulci] *3P* Pulci *MS CM 1 2*   7 mai] *MS* mai *CM 1 2 3*
8 judgements ⟨: they implied⟩ *MS*
9 But ⟨the adroitness could not control events and if they⟩ *MS*
  1 inconveniently ⟨, as they had done several times before in his life⟩ ⟨it was not
Tito's fault that they left him no alternative which was quite free from disagree-
ables⟩. *MS*   2 Gianozzo] *1 2 3* Giovanni *MS CM*
  3 ruined. ⟨If men with their opposing schemes, one as futile as the other, came to
ask for his services, he gave them and earned his pay: when their schemes failed his
work was at an end. He had ⟨⟨never⟩⟩ not meant ⟨⟨from the first⟩⟩ to furnish information against ⟨⟨any one—no⟩⟩ his friend any more than he had meant beforehand to deny
his father. Circumstances had forced that ⟨⟨course⟩⟩ upon him as the only apparent
means of self preservation.⟩ *MS*

political schemes might have no self-interest separable from family pride and tenacity in old hatred and attachments; a modern simpleton who swallowed whole one of the old systems of philosophy, and took the indigestion it occasioned for the signs of a divine afflux or the voice of an inward monitor, might see his interest in a form of self-conceit which he called self-rewarding virtue; fanatics who believed in the coming Scourge and Renovation[4] might see their own interest in a future palm branch and white robe: but no man of clear intellect allowed his course to be determined by such puerile impulses or questionable inward fumes. Did not Pontanus, poet and philosopher of unrivalled Latinity, make the finest possible oration at Naples[5] to welcome the French King,* who had come to dethrone the learned orator's royal friend and patron? and still Pontanus held up his head and prospered. Men did not really care about these things, except when their personal spleen was touched. It was weakness only that was despised; power of any sort carried its immunity; and no man, unless by very rare good fortune, could mount high in the world without incurring a few unpleasant necessities which laid him open to enmity, and perhaps to a little hissing, when enmity wanted a pretext.[6]

It was a faint prognostic of that hissing, gathered by Tito from certain indications when he was before the council, which gave his present conduct the character of an epoch to him, and made him dwell on it with argumentative vindication. It was not that he was taking a deeper step in wrong-doing, for it was not possible that he should feel any tie to the Mediceans to be stronger than the tie to his father; but his conduct to his father had been hidden by successful lying:[7] his present act did not admit of total concealment—in its very nature it was a revelation. And Tito winced under his new liability to disesteem.

Well! a little patience, and in another year, or perhaps in half a year, he might turn his back on these hard, eager Florentines, with their futile quarrels and sinking fortunes. His brilliant success at Florence had had some ugly flaws in it: he had fallen in love with the wrong woman, and Baldassarre had come back under incalculable circumstances. But as Tito galloped with a loose rein towards Siena, he saw a future before him in which he would no longer be haunted by those mistakes. He had much money safe out of Florence already; he

4 Scourge and Renovation] *3P* scourge and renovation *MS CM 1 2*
5 oration {at Naples} *MS*
6 pretext. ⟨Unpleasant? yes: things were not so plastic in the hands of cleverness as might have been wished. Enmity sometimes forced a man to wear inconvenient armour, and hissing, even to a small amount, seemed even worse than a dagger, for there was no buying armour against it.⟩ *MS*
7 lying: ⟨it was not possible⟩ *MS*

was in the fresh ripeness of eight-and-twenty; he was conscious of well-tried skill. Could he not strip himself of the past, as of rehearsal clothing, and throw away the old bundle, to robe himself for the real scene?

It did not enter into Tito's meditations on the future, that, on issuing from the council chamber and descending the stairs, he had brushed against a man whose face he had not stayed to recognize in the lamplight. The man was Ser Ceccone—also willing to serve the State by giving information against unsuccessful employers.

CHAPTER LVIII.

A FINAL UNDERSTANDING

[1]TITO soon returned from Siena, but almost immediately set out on another journey, from which he did not return till the seventeenth of August. Nearly a fortnight had passed since the arrest of the accused[2], and still they were in prison, still their fate was uncertain. Romola had felt during this interval as if all cares were suspended for her, other than watching the fluctuating probabilities concerning that fate. Sometimes they seemed strongly in favour of the prisoners; for the chances of effective interest[3] on their behalf were heightened by delay, and an indefinite prospect of delay was opened by the reluctance of all persons in authority to incur the odium attendant on any decision. On the one side there was a loud cry that the Republic was in danger, and that lenity to the prisoners would be the signal of attack for all its enemies; on the other, there was the[4] certainty that a sentence of death and confiscation of property passed on five citizens of distinguished name, would entail the rancorous hatred of their relatives on all who were conspicuously instrumental to such a sentence.

The final judgment properly lay with the Eight, who presided over the administration of criminal justice; and the sentence depended on a majority of six votes. But the Eight shrank from their onerous responsibility, and asked in this exceptional case to have it shared by the Signoria (or the Gonfaloniere and the eight Priors[5]). The Signoria in its turn shrugged its shoulders, and proposed the Appeal to the Great Council. For, according to a law passed by the earnest persuasion of Savonarola nearly three years before,* whenever a citizen was condemned to death by the fatal six votes (called the *sei fave* or *six beans*, beans being in more senses than one the political pulse of Florence), he had the right of appealing from that sentence to the Great Council.

But in this stage of the business, the friends of the accused resisted the Appeal, determined chiefly by the wish to gain delay; and, in fact, strict legality required that sentence should have been passed prior to the Appeal. Their resistance prevailed, and a middle course was taken: the sentence was referred to a large assembly convened on the

---

1 ⟨On the seventeenth⟩ Tito *MS*
2 passed {since the arrest of the accused}—and still ⟨the accused⟩ they *MS*
3 interest] *MS CM 1 3C* interests 2
4 the] a 3
5 the Gonfaloniere and the eight Priors] Eight Priors and Gonfaloniere *MS*

seventeenth, consisting of all the higher magistracies, the smaller council or senate[6] of eighty,* and a select number of citizens.[7]

On this day Romola, with anxiety heightened by the possibility that before its close her godfather's fate might be decided, had obtained leave to see him for the second time, but only in the presence of witnesses. She had returned to the Via de' Bardi in company with her cousin Brigida, still ignorant whether the council had come to any decisive issue; and Monna Brigida had gone out again to await the momentous news at the house of a friend belonging to one of the magistracies, that she might bring back authentic tidings as soon as they were to be had.

Romola had sunk on the first seat in the bright saloon, too much agitated, too sick at heart to care about her place, or be conscious of discordance in the objects that surrounded her. She sat with her back to the door, resting her head on her hands. It seemed a long while since Monna Brigida had gone, and Romola was expecting her return. But when the door opened she knew it was not Monna Brigida who entered.

Since she had parted from Tito on that memorable night, she had had no external proof to warrant her belief that he had won his safety by treachery; on the contrary, she had had evidence that he was still trusted by the Miceans and was believed by them to be accomplishing certain errands of theirs in Romagna, under cover of fulfilling a commission of the government. For the obscurity in which the evidence concerning the conspirators was shrouded allowed it to be understood that Tito had escaped any implication.

But Romola's suspicion was not to be dissipated: her horror of his conduct towards Baldassarre projected itself over every conception of his acts; it was as if she had seen[8] him committing a murder and had had a diseased impression ever after that his hands were covered with fresh blood.

As she heard his step on the stone floor, a chill shudder passed through her; she could not turn round, she could not rise to give any greeting. He did not speak, but after an instant's pause took a seat on the other side of the table just opposite to her. Then she raised her

6 council {or senate} *MS*

7 citizens. ⟨In this assembly much heat of temper was evolved on one side, much timidity on the other; but the Eight were constrained to deposit their decisive beans, and gave the majority of six for the sentence of death. In this desperate moment there was but one resource for those who desired to save the prisoners: they demanded the Appeal to the Great Council. New tumult, new indecision. The assembly was prorogued till the twenty first, when it was to deliberate anew on the question of according or denying the Appeal.⟩ *MS*

8 seen] *1 2 3* witnessed *MS CM*

eyes and looked at him; but she was mute. He did not show any irritation, but said, coolly—

"This meeting corresponds with our parting, Romola. But I understand that it is a moment of terrible suspense. I am come, however, if you will listen to me, to bring you the relief of hope."

She started, and altered her position, but looked at him dubiously.

"It will not be unwelcome to you to hear—even though it is I who tell it—that the council is prorogued till the twenty-first. The Eight have been frightened at last into passing a sentence of condemnation, but the demand has now been made on behalf of the condemned for the[9] Appeal to the Great Council."

[1]Romola's face lost its dubious expression; she asked eagerly—
"And when is it to be made?"

"It has not yet been granted; but[2] it *may* be granted. The Special Council[3] is to meet again on the twenty-first to deliberate whether the Appeal shall be allowed or not. In the meantime there is an interval of three days in which chances may occur in favour of the prisoners—in which interest may be used on their behalf."

Romola started from her seat. The colour had risen to her face like a visible thought, and her hands trembled. In that moment her feeling towards Tito was forgotten.

"Possibly," said Tito, also rising, "your own intention may have anticipated what I was going to say. You are thinking of the Frate."

"I am," said Romola, looking at him with surprise. "Has he done anything? Is there anything to tell me?"

"Only this. It was Messer Francesco Valori's bitterness and violence which chiefly determined the course of things in the council to-day. Half the men who gave in their opinion against the prisoners were frightened into it, and there are numerous friends of Fra Girolamo both in[4] this Special Council and out of it who are strongly opposed to the sentence of death—Piero Guicciardini,* for example, who is one member of[5] the Signoria that made the stoutest resistance[6]; and there is[7] Giovan Battista Ridolfi, who, Piagnone as he is, will not lightly forgive* the death of his brother Niccolò."

"But how can the Appeal be denied," said Romola, indignantly, "when it is the law—when it was one of the chief glories of the popular government to have passed the law?"

9 the] *1 2 3* an *MS CM*
1 ⟨Romola started from her seat⟩ Romola's face lost its dubious expression. {she asked eagerly,} And ⟨it has been granted? she asked eagerly,⟩ And when *MS*
2 granted; but] granted ¶ "No; but *MS*
3 Special Council] *1 2 3* Council *MS* council *CM*   4 both in] within *MS*
5 one member of] the one of *MS*   6 resistance] resistance to it *MS*
7 and {there is} *MS*

"They call this an exceptional case. Of course there are ingenious arguments, but there is much more of loud bluster about the danger of the republic. But, you see, no opposition could prevent the assembly from being prorogued, and a certain powerful influence[8] rightly applied during the next three days might determine the wavering courage of those who desire that the Appeal should be granted, and might even give a check to the headlong enmity of Francesco Valori. It happens to have come to my knowledge that the Frate has so far interfered as to send a message* to him in favour of Lorenzo Tornabuoni.[9] I know you can sometimes have access to the Frate: it might at all events be worth while to use your privilege now."

"It is true," said Romola, with an air of abstraction. "I cannot believe that the Frate would approve denying the Appeal."

"I heard it said by more than one person in the court of the Palazzo, before I came away, that it would be to the everlasting discredit of Fra Girolamo if he allowed a government which is almost entirely made up of his party, to deny the Appeal, without entering his protest, when he has been boasting in his books and sermons that it was he who got the law passed.* But, between ourselves, with all respect for your Frate's ability, my Romola, he has[1] got into the practice of preaching that form of human sacrifices called killing tyrants and wicked malcontents which some of his followers are likely to think inconsistent with lenity in the present case."

"I know, I know," said Romola, with a look and tone of pain. "But he is driven into those excesses of speech. It used to be different. I *will* ask for an interview. I cannot rest without it. I trust in the greatness of his heart."

She was not looking at Tito; her eyes were bent with a vague gaze towards the ground, and she had no distinct consciousness that the words she heard came from her husband.

"Better lose no time, then," said Tito, with unmixed suavity, moving his cap round in his hands as if he were about to put it on and depart. "And now, Romola, you will perhaps be able to see, in spite of prejudice, that my wishes go with yours in this matter. You will not regard the misfortune of my safety as an offence."

Something like an electric shock passed through Romola: it was the full consciousness of her husband's presence returning to her. She looked at him without speaking.

"At least," he added, in a slightly harder tone, "you will endeavour to base our intercourse on some other reasoning[2] than that because an evil deed is possible, *I* have done it. Am I alone to be beyond the pale of your extensive charity?"

8 {powerful} influence *MS*   9 Valori. {It happens . . . Tornabuoni.} *MS*
1 has] 2 3 had *MS CM 1*   2 reasoning] reasonings 2 3

The feelings[3] which had been driven back from Romola's lips a fortnight before rose again with the gathered force of a tidal wave. She spoke with a decision which told him that she was careless of consequences.

"It is too late, Tito. There is no killing the suspicion that deceit has once begotten. And now I know everything. I know who that old man was: he was your father, to whom you owe everything—to whom you owe more than if you had been his own child. By the side of that, it is a small thing that you broke my trust and my father's. As long as you deny the truth about that old man, there is a horror rising between us: the law that should make us one can never be obeyed. I too am a human being. I have a soul of my own that abhors your actions. Our union is a pretence—as if a perpetual lie could be a sacred marriage."

Tito did not answer immediately. When he did speak it was with a calculated caution, that was stimulated by alarm.

"And you mean to carry out that independence by quitting me, I presume?"

"I desire to quit you," said Romola, impetuously.

"And supposing I do not submit to part with what the law gives me some security for retaining? You will then, of course, proclaim your reasons in the ear of all Florence. You will bring forward your mad assassin[4], who is doubtless ready to obey your call, and you will tell the world that you believe his testimony because he is so rational as to desire to assassinate me. You will first inform[5] the Signoria that I am a Medicean conspirator, and then you will inform the Mediceans that I have betrayed them, and in both cases you will offer the excellent proof that you believe me capable in general of everything bad. It will certainly be a striking position for a wife to adopt. And if, on such evidence, you succeed in holding me up to infamy, you will have surpassed all the heroines of the Greek drama[6]."

He paused a moment, but she stood mute. He went on with the sense of mastery.

"I believe you have no other grievance against me[7]—except[8] that I have failed in fulfilling some lofty indefinite conditions on which you gave me your wifely affection, so that, by withdrawing it, you have gradually reduced me to the careful supply of your wants as a fair Piagnone of high condition and liberal charities. I think your success in gibbeting me is not certain. But doubtless you would begin by winning the ear of Messer Bernardo del Nero?"

3 ⟨words⟩ feelings] MS feeling CM 1 2 3   4 assassin ⟨and he⟩ MS
5 {first} inform MS   6 Greek drama] drama MS
7 me ⟨that the public will recognize⟩ MS
8 me—except] 3P me except MS CM 1 2

[9]"Why do I speak of anything?" cried Romola, in anguish, sinking on her chair again. "It is hateful in me to be thinking of myself!"

She did not notice when Tito left the room, or know how long it was before the door opened to admit Monna Brigida. But in that instant she started up and said—[1]

"Cousin, we must go to San Marco directly. I must see my confessor, Fra Salvestro."

9 ⟨"O God"⟩ {"Why do I speak of anything} cried . . . chair again {"Why do I speak of anything?⟩ MS

1 said—] 3P said, MS CM 1 said,—2

CHAPTER LIX.

PLEADING

THE morning was in its early brightness when Romola was again on her way to San Marco, having obtained through Fra Salvestro, the evening before, the promise of an interview with Fra Girolamo in the chapter-house of the convent. The rigidity with which Savonarola guarded his life from all the pretexts of calumny made[1] such interviews very rare, and whenever they were granted, they were kept free from any appearance of mystery. For this reason the hour chosen was one at which there were likely to be other visitors in the outer cloisters of San Marco.

She chose to pass through the heart of the city that she might notice the signs of public feeling. Every loggia, every convenient corner of the piazza, every shop that made a rendezvous for gossips, was astir with the excitement of gratuitous debate; a languishing trade tending to make political discussion all the more vigorous. It was clear that the parties for and against the death of the conspirators[2] were bent on making the fullest use of the three days' interval[3] in order to determine the popular mood. Already handbills were in circulation; some presenting, in large print, the alternative of Justice on the Conspirators or Ruin to the Republic, others in equally large print urging the observance of the Law and the granting of the Appeal. Round these jutting islets of black capitals there were lakes of smaller characters setting forth arguments less necessary to be read; for it was an opinion entertained at that time (in the first flush of triumph at the discovery of printing), that there was no argument more widely convincing than question-begging phrases in large type.

Romola, however, cared especially to become acquainted with the arguments in smaller type, and though obliged to hasten forward she looked round[4] anxiously as she went that she might miss no opportunity of securing copies. [5]For a long way she saw none but such as were in the hands of eager readers, or else fixed on the walls, from which in some places the *sbirri* were tearing them down. But at last, passing behind San Giovanni with a quickened pace that she might avoid the many acquaintances who frequented the piazza, she saw Bratti with a stock of handbills which he appeared to be exchanging

1 made ⟨it⟩ *MS*
2 conspirators ⟨had already begun to use⟩ were ⟨determined⟩ bent on *MS*
3 interval ⟨of suspense⟩ *MS*   4 looked round {⟨eagerly⟩ anxiously} *MS*
5 ⟨But⟩ For *MS*

for small coin with the passers-by. She was too familiar with the
humble life of Florence for Bratti to be any stranger to her, and
[6]turning towards him she said, "[7]Have you two sorts of handbills,
Bratti? Let me have them quickly."

"Two sorts," said Bratti, separating the wet sheets with a slowness
that tried Romola's patience. "There's 'Law,' and there's 'Justice.'"

"Which sort do you sell most of?"

"'Justice'—'Justice' goes the quickest[8],—so I raised the price and
made it two danari. But then I bethought me the 'Law' was good
ware too, and had as good a right to be charged for as 'Justice;' for
people set no store by cheap things, and if I sold the 'Law' at one
danaro, I should be doing it a wrong. And I'm a fair trader. 'Law,' or
'Justice,' it's all one to me; they're good wares. I get[9] 'em both for
nothing, and I sell 'em at a fair profit. But you'll want more than one
of a sort?"

"No, no: here's a white quattrino for the two," said Romola, folding up the bills and[1] hurrying away.

She was soon [2]in the outer cloisters[3] of San Marco, where Fra
Salvestro was awaiting her under the cloister, but did not notice the
approach of her light step.[4] He was chatting, according to his habit,
with lay visitors; for under the auspices of a government friendly to
the Frate, the timidity about frequenting San Marco, which had followed on the first shock of the excommunication, had been gradually
giving way.[5] In one of these lay visitors she recognized a well-known
satellite of Francesco Valori, named Andrea Cambini,* who was narrating or expounding with emphatic gesticulation, while Fra Salvestro
was listening with that air of trivial curiosity which tells that the listener cares [6]very much about news and very little about its quality.
This characteristic of her confessor, which was always repulsive to
Romola, was made exasperating to her at this moment by the certainty she gathered, from the disjointed words which reached her ear,
that Cambini was narrating something relative to the fate of the conspirators. She chose not to approach the group, but as soon as she
saw that she had arrested Fra Salvestro's attention[7], she turned
towards the door of the chapter-house, while he, making a sign of

6 ⟨she turned⟩ turning MS
7 ⟨I have no money with me, Bratti⟩ Have MS
8 quickest—⟨I didn't know which was which myself but⟩ MS
9 get] MS got CM 1 2 3
1 and ⟨putting them in her scarsella as she hurried⟩ MS
2 ⟨at⟩ in MS   3 cloisters] cloister MS
4 but ⟨he⟩ {did not notice ⟨her⟩ the approach of her light step.} He was . . . lay visitors ⟨and did not notice . . . step.⟩ MS
5 visitors, {for under . . . way.} MS   6 ⟨simply⟩ very much MS
7 that {she had arrested} Fra Salvestro's attention ⟨was directed towards her⟩ MS

approval, [8]disappeared within the inner cloister. A [9]lay Brother stood ready to open the door of the chapter-house for her, and closed it behind her as she entered.

[1]Once more looked at by those [2]sad frescoed figures* which had seemed to be [3]mourning with her at the death of her brother Dino, it was inevitable that something of that[4] scene should come back to her; but the intense occupation of her mind with the present made the remembrance less a retrospect than an indistinct recurrence of impressions which blended themselves with her agitating fears, as if her actual anxiety were a revival of the strong yearning she had once before brought to this spot—to be repelled by marble rigidity. She gave no space for the remembrance to become more definite, for she at once opened the handbills, thinking she should perhaps be able to read them in the [5]interval before Fra Girolamo appeared. But by the time she had read to the end of the one that recommended the observance of the law,[6] the door was opening, and doubling up the papers she stood expectant.

When the Frate had entered she knelt, according to the usual practice of those who saw him in private; but as soon as he had uttered a benedictory greeting she rose and stood opposite to him at a few yards' distance. Owing to his seclusion since he had been excommunicated, it had been an unusually long while since she had seen him, and the late months had visibly deepened in his face the marks of overtaxed mental activity and bodily severities; and yet Romola was [7]not so conscious of this change as of another, which was less definable. Was it that the expression of serene elevation and pure human fellowship which had once moved her was no longer present in the same force, or was it that the sense of his being divided from her in [8]her feeling about her godfather roused the slumbering sources of alienation, and marred her own vision? Perhaps both causes were at work. Our relations with our fellow-men are most often determined by coincident currents of that sort[9]; the inexcusable word or deed seldom comes until after affection or reverence has been already enfeebled by the strain of repeated excuses.

It was true that Savonarola's glance at Romola had [1]some of that hardness which is caused by an egoistic[2] prepossession. He divined that the interview she had sought was to turn on the fate of the

8 ⟨turned⟩ disappeared *MS*   9 ⟨*Fra Converso*⟩ lay Brother *MS*

1 ⟨In the presence of⟩ Once *MS*   2 ⟨pale⟩ sad *MS*

3 ⟨looking on and⟩ mourning *MS*   4 {something of} that *MS*

5 ⟨space⟩ interval *MS*   6 law, ⟨which happened to come first⟩ *MS*

7 ⟨less conscious of this than⟩ not so conscious of this change as of another ⟨change⟩ which *MS*

8 ⟨this⟩ her *MS*   9 sort ⟨, and⟩: the *MS*   1 ⟨something⟩ some *MS*

2 egoistic] egotistic *3*

conspirators, [3]a subject on which he had already had to quell inner voices that might become loud again when encouraged from without. Seated in his cell, [4]correcting the sheets of his "Triumph of the Cross"[5],* it was easier to repose on a resolution of neutrality.

"It is a question of moment, doubtless, on which you wished to see me, my daughter," he began, in a tone which was gentle rather from self-control than from [6]immediate inclination. "I know you are not wont to lay stress on small matters."

"Father, you know what it is before I tell you," said Romola, forgetting everything else as soon as she began to pour forth her plea. "You know what I am caring for—it is for the life of the old man I love best in the world. The thought of him has gone [7]together with the thought of my father as long as I remember the daylight. That is my warrant for coming to you, even if my coming should have been needless. Perhaps it is: perhaps you have already determined that your power over the hearts of men shall be used to prevent them from denying to Florentines a right which you yourself helped to earn for them."

"I meddle not with the functions of the State, my daughter," said Fra Girolamo, strongly disinclined to reopen externally a debate which he had already gone through inwardly. "I have preached and laboured that Florence should have a good government, for a good government is needful to the perfecting of the Christian life; but I keep away my hands from particular affairs, which it is the office of experienced citizens to administer."

"Surely, father—" Romola broke off. She had uttered this first word almost impetuously, but she was checked by the counter agitation of feeling herself in an attitude of remonstrance towards the man who had been the source of guidance and strength to her. In the act of rebelling she was bruising her own reverence.

Savonarola was too keen not to divine something of the conflict that was arresting her—too noble, deliberately to assume in calm speech that self-justifying evasiveness into which he was often hurried in public by the crowding impulses of the[8] orator.

"Say what is in your heart; speak on, my daughter," he said, standing with his arms laid one upon the other, and looking at her with quiet expectation.

"I was [9]going to say, father, that this matter is surely of higher

---

3 ⟨and that was⟩ a subject *MS*
4 ⟨busying himself with correcting⟩ correcting *MS*
5 "Triumph of the Cross"] *MS 1 2 3 Triumph of the Cross CM*
6 ⟨the⟩ immediate *MS*   7 ⟨along⟩ together *MS*
8 hurried {in public} by the crowding impulses of the ⟨public⟩ orator *MS*
9 ⟨about⟩ going *MS*

moment than many about which I have heard you preach and exhort fervidly. If it belonged to you to urge that men condemned for offences against the State should have the right to appeal to the Great Council—if—" Romola was getting eager again—"if you count it a glory to have won that right for them, can it less belong to you to declare yourself against the right being denied to almost the first[1] men who need it? Surely that touches the Christian life more closely than whether you knew beforehand* that the Dauphin would die, or whether Pisa will be conquered."

There was a subtle movement, like a subdued sign of pain, in Savonarola's strong lips, before he began to speak.

"My daughter, I speak as it is given me to speak—I am not master of the times when I may become the vehicle of knowledge beyond the common lights of men. [2]In this case I have no illumination beyond what wisdom may give to those who are charged with the safety of the State. As to the Law of Appeal against the Six Votes, I laboured to have it passed in order that no Florentine should be subject to loss of life and goods through the private hatred of a few who might happen to be in power; but these five men, who have desired to overthrow a free government and restore a corrupt tyrant, have been condemned with the assent of a large assembly of their fellow-citizens. They refused at first to have their cause brought before the Great Council. They have lost the right to the Appeal."

"How can they have lost it?" said Romola. "[3]It is the right to appeal against condemnation, and they have never been condemned till now; and, forgive me, father, it *is* private hatred that would deny them the Appeal; it *is* the violence of the few that frightens others; else why was the assembly divided again directly, after it had seemed to agree? And if anything weighs against the observance of the Law, let this weigh *for* it—this, that you used to preach more earnestly than all else,[4] that there should be no place given to hatred and bloodshed because of these party strifes, so that private ill-will should not find its opportunities in public acts. Father, you[5] *know* that there is private hatred concerned here: will it not dishonour you not to have interposed on the side of mercy, when there are many who hold that it is also the side of law and justice?"

"My daughter," said Fra Girolamo, with more visible emotion than before, "there is a mercy which is weakness, and even treason against the common good. The safety of Florence, which means even more than the welfare of Florentines, now demands severity, as it once demanded mercy. It is not only for a past plot[6] that these men are

---

1 {almost} the first *MS*   2 ⟨But when⟩ In *MS*
3 ⟨They had not been condemned⟩ It *MS*   4 else, ⟨father⟩ *MS*
5 {Father} You *MS*   6 not only {for} a past plot ⟨for which⟩ that *MS*

condemned, but also for a plot[7] which has not yet been executed; and the [8]devices that were leading to its execution are not put an end to: the tyrant is still gathering his forces in Romagna, and the enemies of Florence, that[9] sit in the highest places of Italy, are ready to[1] hurl any stone that will crush her."

"What plot?" said Romola, reddening, and trembling with alarmed surprise.

"You carry papers in your hand, I see," said Fra Girolamo, pointing to the handbills. "One of them will, perhaps, tell you that the government has had new information."

Romola hastily opened the handbill[2] she had not yet read, and saw that the government had now[3] positive evidence of a second plot, which was to have been carried out in this August time. [4]To her mind it was like reading a confirmation that Tito had won his safety by foul means; his pretence of wishing that the[5] Frate should exert himself on behalf of the condemned only helped the [6]wretched conviction. She crushed up the paper in her hand, and, turning to Savonarola, she said, with new passion, "Father, what safety can there be for Florence when the worst man[7] can always escape? And,[8]" she went on, a sudden flash of remembrance coming from the thought about her husband, "have not you yourself encouraged this deception which corrupts the life of Florence, by wanting more favour to be shown to Lorenzo Tornabuoni, who has worn two faces, and flattered you with[9] a show of affection, when my godfather has always been honest? [1]Ask all Florence who of those five men has the truest heart, and there will not be many who will name any other name than Bernardo del Nero. You did interpose with Francesco Valori for the sake of one prisoner: you have *not*[2] then been neutral; and you know that your word will be powerful."

"I do not desire the death of Bernardo," said Savonarola, colouring deeply. "It would be enough if he were sent out of the city."*

"Then why do you not speak to save an old man of seventy-five from dying a death of ignominy—to give him at least the fair chances of the law[3]?" burst out Romola, the impetuosity of her nature so

7 {also for} a plot *MS*   8 ⟨preparation⟩ devices *MS*
9 that] who 2 3   1 to ⟨lay there⟩ *MS*
2 handbill ⟨headed 'Justice on the conspirators⟩ *MS*   3 had {now} *MS*
4 ⟨It was as if she had read⟩ To *MS*
5 the ⟨prisoners might escape only helped the odium⟩ *MS*
6 ⟨odious⟩ wretched *MS*   7 man] men *MS*
8 And ⟨have not you yourself encouraged⟩, she went ⟨on with⟩ on, *MS*
9 with ⟨the belief that⟩ a ⟨false⟩ show *MS*
1 ⟨It belongs to your nobleness to feel the most regard for the noblest enemy⟩ Ask *MS*
2 *not*] not *MS*   3 ignominy {—to give . . . law} *MS*

roused[4] that she forgot everything but her indignation. "It is not that you feel bound to be neutral; else why did you speak for Lorenzo Tornabuoni? You spoke for him because he is more friendly to San Marco; my godfather feigns no friendship. It is not then as[5] a Medicean that my godfather is to die; it is as a man you have no love for!"

[6]When Romola paused, with cheeks glowing, and with quivering lips, there [7]was dead silence. As she saw Fra Girolamo standing motionless before her, she seemed to herself to be hearing her own words over again; words that in this echo of consciousness were in[8] strange, painful dissonance[9] with the memories that made part of [1]his presence to her.* The moments of silence were expanded by gathering compunction and self-doubt. She had committed sacrilege in her passion. And even the sense that she could retract nothing of her plea, that her mind could not submit itself to Savonarola's negative, made it the more needful to her to satisfy those reverential memories. With a sudden movement towards him, she said,

"Forgive me, father; it is pain to me to have spoken those words— yet I cannot help speaking. I am little and feeble compared with you; you brought me light and strength. But I submitted because I felt the proffered strength—because I saw the light. *Now* I cannot see it. Father, you yourself declare that there comes a moment when the soul must have no guide but the voice within it, to tell whether the consecrated thing has sacred virtue. And therefore I must speak."

Savonarola had that readily roused resentment towards opposition, hardly separable from a power-loving and powerful nature, accustomed to seek great ends that[2] cast a reflected grandeur on the means by which they are sought. His sermons have much[3] of that red flame in them. And if he had been a meaner man his susceptibility might have shown itself in irritation at Romola's accusatory [4]freedom, which was in strong contrast with the deference he habitually received from his disciples. But at this moment such feelings were nullified by that hard struggle which made half the tragedy of his life—the struggle of a mind possessed by a never-silent hunger after purity and simplicity, yet caught in a tangle of egoistic demands, false ideas, and difficult outward conditions, that made simplicity impossible. Keenly alive to

4 {so} roused ⟨to its utmost, so⟩ that *MS*
5 as ⟨Mediceans dangerous to Florence that these men⟩ *MS*
6 ⟨It was a position⟩ When *MS*
7 ⟨came⟩ was dead silence. ⟨She seemed⟩ As *MS*
8 words that in this echo of consciousness were in] *3C* words that seemed in this echo of consciousness to be in *MS CM 1 2*
9 {painful} dissonance *MS*
2 that] which *MS*
4 ⟨?frankness⟩ freedom *MS*
1 ⟨Savonarola⟩ his presence *MS*
3 much] a great deal *MS*

all the suggestions of Romola's remonstrating words, he was rapidly surveying, as he had done before, the courses of action that were open to him, and their probable results. But it was a question on which arguments could seem decisive only in proportion as they were charged with [5]feeling, and he had received no impulse that could alter his bias. He looked at Romola and said—

"You have full pardon for your frankness, my daughter. You speak, I know, out of the fullness of your family affections. But these affections must give way to the needs of the Republic. If those men who have a close acquaintance with the affairs of the State believe[6], as I understand they do, that the public safety requires the extreme punishment of the law to fall on the[7] five conspirators, I cannot control their opinion, seeing that I stand aloof from such affairs."

"Then you desire that they should die? You desire that the Appeal should be denied them?" said Romola, feeling anew repelled by a vindication which seemed to her to have the nature of a subterfuge.

"I have said that I do not desire their death."

"Then," said Romola, her indignation rising again, "you can be indifferent that Florentines should inflict death which you do not desire, when you might have protested against it—when you might[8] have helped to hinder it, by urging the observance of a law which you held it good to get passed. Father, you used not to stand aloof: you used not to shrink from protesting. Do not say you cannot protest where the lives of men are concerned; say rather, you desire their death. Say rather, you hold it good for Florence that there shall be more blood and more hatred. Will the death of five Mediceans put an end to parties in Florence? Will the death of a noble old man like Bernardo del Nero save a city that holds such men as Dolfo Spini?"

"My daughter, it is enough. The cause of freedom, which is the cause of God's kingdom upon earth, is often[9] most injured by the enemies who carry within them the power of certain human virtues. The wickedest man is often not the most insurmountable obstacle to the triumph of Good."

"Then why do you say again, that you do not desire my godfather's death?" said Romola, in mingled anger and despair. "Rather, you hold it the more needful he should die because he is the better man. I cannot unravel your thoughts, father; I cannot hear the real voice of your judgment and conscience."

5 ⟨?personal⟩ feeling *MS*
6 men who have . . . State believe] *MS 3P* men, who have . . . State, believe *CM 1 2*
7 the] *3P* those *MS CM 1 2*   8 might ⟨help to save them⟩ *MS*
9 is {often} *MS*

There was a moment's pause. Then Savonarola said, with keener emotion than he had yet shown,

"Be thankful, my daughter, if your own soul has been spared perplexity; and judge not those to whom a harder lot has been given. *You* see one ground of action in this matter. I see many. I have to choose that which will further the work entrusted to me. The end I seek is one to which minor respects must be sacrificed. The death of five men—were they less guilty than these—is a light matter weighed against the withstanding of the vicious tyrannies which stifle the life of Italy, and[1] foster the corruption of the Church; a light matter weighed against the furthering of God's Kingdom upon earth, the end for which I live and am willing myself to die."

Under any other circumstances, Romola would have been sensitive to the appeal at the beginning of Savonarola's speech; but at this moment she was so utterly in antagonism with him, that what he called perplexity seemed to her sophistry and doubleness; and as he went on, his words only fed that flame of indignation, which now again, more fully than ever before, lit up the memory of all[2] his mistakes, and made her trust in him seem to have been a purblind delusion. She spoke almost with bitterness.

"Do you then know so well what will further the coming of God's Kingdom, father, that you will dare to despise the plea of mercy—of justice—of faithfulness to your own teaching? Has the French King then [3]brought renovation to Italy? Take care, father, lest your enemies have some reason when they say, that in your visions of what will further God's Kingdom you see only what will strengthen your own party."

"And that is true!" said Savonarola, with flashing eyes. Romola's voice[4] had seemed to him in that moment the voice of his enemies. "The cause of my party *is*[5] the cause of God's Kingdom."

"I do not believe it!" said Romola, her whole frame shaken with passionate repugnance. "God's Kingdom is something wider—else, let me stand outside it with the beings that I love."

The two faces[6] were lit up, each with an opposite emotion,[7] each with an opposite certitude. Further words were impossible. Romola hastily covered her head and went out in silence.

1 which {stifle the life of Italy, and} *MS*
2 than ever {before} lit up {the memory of} all *MS*
3 ⟨furthered the renovation of⟩ brought *MS*   4 Romola{'s voice} *MS*
5 *is*] is *MS*   6 The {two} faces *MS*   7 emotion, ⟨which was⟩ *MS*

CHAPTER LX.

THE SCAFFOLD

THREE days later the[1] moon that was just surmounting the buildings of the piazza in front of the Old Palace within the hour of midnight, did not make the usual broad lights and shadows on the pavement. Not a hand's breadth of pavement was to be seen, but only the heads of an eager struggling multitude. And instead of that background of silence on[2] which the pattering footsteps and buzzing voices, the lute-thrumming [3]or rapid scampering of the many night-wanderers of Florence stood out in obtrusive distinctness, there was the background of a roar from mingled shouts and imprecations, tramplings and pushings, and accidental clashing of weapons, across which nothing was distinguishable but a darting shriek or the heavy dropping[4] toll of a bell.

Almost all who could call themselves the public of Florence were awake at that hour, and either enclosed within the limits of that piazza, or struggling to enter it. Within the palace were still assembled in the council chamber all the chief magistracies, the eighty members of the senate, and the other select citizens who had been in hot debate through long hours of daylight and torchlight whether the Appeal should be granted or whether the sentence of death should be executed on the prisoners forthwith, to forestal the dangerous chances of delay. And the debate had been so much like fierce quarrel that the noise from the council chamber had reached the crowd outside. Only[5] within the last hour had the question been decided: the Signoria had remained divided, four of them standing out resolutely for the Appeal in spite of the strong argument that if they did not give way their houses should be sacked, until Francesco Valori, in brief and furious speech, made the determination of his party more ominously distinct by declaring that if the Signoria would not defend the liberties of the Florentine people by executing those five perfidious citizens, there would not be wanting others who would take that cause in hand to the peril of all who opposed it. The Florentine Cato* triumphed. When the votes were counted again, the four obstinate [6]white beans no longer appeared; the whole nine were of the fatal affirmative [7]black, deciding the death of the five prisoners without delay—

1 the ⟨?rising⟩ moon that was ⟨rising above⟩ just surmounting {the buildings of} the Piazza in front of the Old Palace {within the hour of midnight} *MS*
    2 on] *MS* in *CM 1 2 3*   3 ⟨and⟩ or *MS*   4 {heavy} dropping *MS*
    5 delay. And the debate . . . Only] delay. Only *MS*
    6 ⟨black⟩ white *MS*   7 ⟨white⟩ black *MS*

deciding also, only tacitly and with much more delay, the death of Francesco Valori.[8]

And now, while the judicial Eight were gone to the Bargello to prepare[9] for the execution, the five condemned men were being led barefoot and in irons through the midst of the council. It was their friends who had contrived this: would not Florentines be moved by the visible association of such cruel ignominy with two venerable men like Bernardo del Nero and Niccolò Rodolfi, who had taken their bias long before the new order of things had come to make Mediceanism retrograde—with two brilliant popular young men like Tornabuoni and Pucci, whose absence would be felt as a haunting vacancy wherever there was a meeting of chief Florentines? [1]It was useless: such pity as could be awakened now was of that hopeless sort which leads not to rescue, but to the tardier action of revenge.[2]

While this scene was passing upstairs Romola stood below against one of the massive pillars in the court of the [3]palace, expecting the moment when her godfather would appear, on his way to execution. By the use of strong interest she had gained permission to visit him in the evening of this day, and[4] remain with him until the result of the council should be determined. And now she was waiting with his confessor to follow the guard that would lead him to the Bargello. Her heart was bent on clinging to[5] the presence of the childless old man to the last moment, as her father would have done, and she had overpowered all remonstrances. Giovan Battista Ridolfi, a disciple of Savonarola, who[6] was going in bitterness to [7]behold the death of his elder brother Niccolò, had promised that she should be guarded, and now stood by her side.

Tito, too, was in the palace; but Romola had not seen him. Since the evening of the seventeenth they had avoided each other, and Tito only knew by inference from the report of the Frate's neutrality that her pleading had failed. He was now surrounded with official[8] and other personages, both Florentine and foreign, who had been awaiting the issue of the long-protracted council, maintaining, except when he was directly addressed, the subdued air and grave silence of a man whom actual events are placing in a painful state of strife between public and private feeling. When an allusion was made to his wife in relation to those events, he implied that, owing to the violent excitement of her mind,[9] the mere fact of his [1]continuing to hold office

8 delay {deciding also . . . Valori.} MS
9 gone to {the Bargello to} prepare MS   1 ⟨But such⟩—It MS
2 {the tardier action of} revenge. MS   3 ⟨Palazzo⟩ Palace MS
4 {visit him in the evening of this day and} remain MS
5 clinging to ⟨his presence⟩ MS   6 who ⟨?like ?her⟩ MS   7 ⟨witness⟩ behold MS
8 official] officials MS   9 {owing to} the violent excitement of her mind, ⟨made⟩ MS
1 ⟨holding⟩ continuing to hold MS

under a government concerned in her godfather's condemnation, roused in her a diseased hostility towards him; so that for her sake he felt it best not to approach her.

"Ah, the old Bardi blood!" said Cennini, with a shrug. "I shall not be surprised if this business shakes *her* loose from the Frate, as well as some others I could name."

"It is excusable in a woman, who is doubtless beautiful, since she is the wife of Messer Tito[2]," said a young French envoy, smiling and bowing to Tito, "to think that her affections must overrule the good of the State, and that nobody is to be beheaded who is anybody's cousin; but such a view is not to be encouraged in the male population. It seems to me your Florentine polity is much weakened by it."

"That is true," said Niccolò Macchiavelli; "but where personal ties are strong, the hostilities they raise must be taken due account of. Many of these halfway severities are mere hot-headed blundering. The only safe blows to be inflicted on men and parties are the blows that are too heavy to be avenged."*

"Niccolò," said Cennini, "there is a clever wickedness in thy talk sometimes that makes me mistrust thy pleasant young face as if it were a mask of [3]Satan."

"Not at all, my good Domenico," said Macchiavelli, smiling, and laying his hand on the elder's shoulder. "[4]Satan was a blunderer, an introducer of *novità*, who made a stupendous failure. If he had succeeded, we should all have been worshipping him, and his portrait would have been more flattered."

"Well, well," said Cennini, "I say not thy doctrine is not too clever for Satan: I only say it is wicked enough for him."[5]

"I tell you," said Macchiavelli, "[6]my doctrine is the doctrine of all men who seek an end a little farther off than their own noses. Ask our Frate, our Prophet, how his universal renovation is to be brought about: he will tell you, first, by getting a free and pure government; and since it appears that cannot[7] be done by making all Florentines love each other, it must be done by cutting off every head that happens to be obstinately in the way. Only if a man incurs odium by sanctioning a severity that is not thorough enough to be final, he commits a blunder. And something like that blunder, I suspect, the Frate has committed.[8] It was an occasion on which he might have

2 beautiful, {since she is ⟨Messer's wife⟩ the wife of Messer Tito} *MS*
3 ⟨Satanasso⟩ Satan *MS*   4 ⟨Satanasso himself⟩ Satan *MS*
5 been {more} flattered." {"Well, well," said Cennini, I say not thy ⟨doctrines are⟩ doctrine is not too clever for Satan: I only say ⟨they are⟩ it is wicked enough for him."} *MS*
6 "I tell you {" said Machiavelli "} my *MS*   7 that cannot] that this cannot 2 3
8 committed. ⟨" ¶ Before any one else could speak there came the expected announcement that the⟩ It *MS*

won some lustre by exerting himself to maintain the Appeal; instead of that, he has lost lustre, and has gained no strength."

Before any one else could speak, there came the expected announcement that the prisoners were about to leave the council chamber; and the majority of those who were present hurried [9]towards the door, intent on securing the freest passage to the Bargello in the rear of the prisoners' guard; for the scene of the execution was one that drew alike those who were moved by the deepest passions and those who were moved [1]by the coldest curiosity.

Tito was one of those who remained behind. He had a native repugnance to sights of death and pain, and five days ago whenever he had thought of this execution as a possibility he had hoped that it would not take place, and that the utmost sentence would be exile: [2]his own safety demanded no more. But[3] now he felt that it would be a welcome guarantee of his security when he had learned that Bernardo del Nero's head was off the shoulders. The new knowledge and new attitude towards him disclosed by Romola on the day of his return, had given him a new dread of the power she possessed to make his position insecure. If any act of hers only succeeded in making him an object of suspicion and odium, he foresaw not only frustration, but frustration under unpleasant circumstances. [4]Her belief in Baldassarre had clearly determined[5] her wavering feelings against further submission, and if her godfather lived she[6] would win him to share her belief without much trouble. Romola seemed more than ever an unmanageable fact in his destiny. But if Bernardo del Nero were dead, the difficulties that would beset[7] her in placing herself in opposition to her husband would probably be insurmountable to her shrinking pride. Therefore Tito had [8]felt easier when he knew that the Eight had[9] gone to the Bargello to order the instant erection of the scaffold. Four other men—his intimates and confederates—were to die, besides Bernardo del Nero. But a man's own safety is a god that sometimes makes very grim demands. Tito felt them to be grim: even in the pursuit of what was agreeable, this paradoxical life forced upon him the desire for what was disagreeable. But he had had other experience of this sort, and as he heard through the open doorway the shuffle of many feet and the clanking of metal on the stairs, he was able to answer the questions of the young French envoy without showing signs of any other feeling than that of sad resignation to State necessities.

9 ⟨?eagerly⟩ towards *MS*   1 ⟨with⟩ by *MS*   2 ⟨that⟩ his *MS*
3 But ⟨the new knowledge and new [?attitude] towards him disclosed by Bernardo on the day of his return⟩ *MS*
4 ⟨And he saw that her⟩ Her *MS*   5 {clearly} determined *MS*
6 lived she] *3P* lived, she *MS CM 1 2*   7 {would} beset *MS*
8 ⟨been glad⟩ felt easier *MS*   9 had ⟨descended the ?stair ?surveying⟩ *MS*

Those sounds fell on Romola as if her power of hearing had been exalted along with every other sensibility of her nature. She needed no[1] arm to support her; she shed no tears. She felt that intensity of life which seems to transcend both grief and joy—in which the mind seems to itself akin to elder forces[2] that wrought out existence before the birth of pleasure and pain. Since her godfather's fate had been decided, the previous struggle of feeling in her had given way to an identification of herself with him in these supreme moments: she was inwardly asserting for him that, if he suffered the punishment of treason, he did not deserve the name of traitor; he was the victim to a collision between two kinds of faithfulness. It was not given to him[3] to die for the noblest cause, and yet he died because of his nobleness. He might have been a meaner man and found it easier not to incur this guilt. [4]Romola was feeling the full force of that sympathy with the individual lot [5]that is continually opposing itself to the formulæ by which actions and parties are judged. She was treading the way[6] with her second father to the scaffold, and nerving herself to defy ignominy by the consciousness that it was not deserved.

The way was fenced in by three hundred armed men, who had been placed as a guard by the orders of Francesco Valori, for among the apparent contradictions that[7] belonged to this event, not the least striking was the alleged alarm on the one hand at the popular rage against the conspirators, and the alleged alarm on the other lest there should be an attempt to rescue them in the midst of a hostile crowd. When they had arrived within the court of the Bargello, Romola was allowed to approach Bernardo with his confessor for a moment of farewell. Many eyes were bent on them even in that struggle of an agitated throng[8], as the aged man, forgetting that his hands were bound with irons, lifted them towards the golden head that was bent towards him, and then, checking that movement, leaned to kiss her. She seized the fettered hands that were hung down again, and kissed them as if they had been sacred things.

"My poor Romola," said Bernardo, in a low voice, "I have only to die, but thou hast to live—and I shall not be there to help thee."

"Yes," said Romola, hurriedly, "you *will* help me—always—because I shall remember you."

She was taken away and conducted up the flight of steps[9] that led to the loggia surrounding the grand old court. She took her place there, determined to look till the moment when her godfather laid his

---

1 no ⟨support⟩ MS   2 forces ⟨than pleasure and pain⟩ MS
3 to him] him 2 3   4 ⟨She⟩ Romola MS   5 ⟨which⟩ that MS
6 treading {the way} MS   7 that ⟨accompanied this execution⟩ MS
8 them {even in that struggle of an agitated throng} MS
9 {flight of} steps MS

head on the block. Now while the prisoners were allowed a brief interval with their confessors[1], the spectators were pressing into the court[2] until the crowd became dense around the black scaffold, and the torches fixed in iron rings against the [3]pillars threw a varying startling light at one moment on passionless stone carvings, at another on some pale[4] face agitated with suppressed rage or suppressed grief—the face of one among the many near relatives of the condemned, who were presently to receive their dead and carry them home.

Romola's face looked like a marble image against the dark arch as she stood watching for the moment when her godfather would appear at the foot of the scaffold. He was to suffer first, and Battista Ridolfi, who was by her side, had promised to take her away through a door behind them when she should[5] have seen the last look of the man who alone in all the world had shared her [6]pitying love for her father. And still, in the background of her thought, there was the possibility striving to be a hope, that[7] some rescue might yet come, something that would keep that scaffold [8]unstained by blood.[9]

For a long while there was constant movement, lights flickering, heads swaying to and fro, confused voices within the court, rushing waves of sound[1] through the entrance from without. It seemed to Romola as if she were in the midst of a storm-troubled sea[2], caring nothing about the storm, caring only to hold out[3] a signal till the eyes that looked for it could seek it no more.

Suddenly there was stillness, and the very tapers seemed to tremble into quiet. The executioner was ready on the scaffold, and Bernardo del Nero was seen ascending it with a slow firm step. Romola made no visible movement, uttered not even a suppressed sound: she[4] stood more firmly, caring for *his* firmness. She saw him pause, saw the white head kept erect, while he said in a voice distinctly audible,

"It is but a short space of life that my fellow-citizens have taken from me."

She perceived that he was gazing slowly round him as he spoke. She felt that his eyes were resting on her, and that she was stretching out her arms towards him. Then she saw no more till—a long while after as it seemed—a voice said, "My daughter, all is peace now. I can conduct you to your house."

1 confessors] *MS* confessor *CM 1 2 3*　　　2 the court] court *2 3*
3 ⟨stone⟩ pillars *MS*　　　4 pale ⟨agitated face⟩ *MS*　　　5 should] would *2 3*
6 ⟨compassionate⟩ pitying *MS*　　　7 that ⟨something might yet⟩ *MS*
8 ⟨bloodless⟩ unstained by blood *MS*　　　9 father. {And still . . . blood.} *MS*
1 sound ⟨from⟩ *MS*
2 a storm-troubled sea] *1 2 3* a storm on a troubled sea *MS CM*
3 storm, caring only to hold out] *3P* storm, but only about holding out *MS CM 1 2*
4 she ⟨felt herself⟩ *MS*

She uncovered her head and saw her godfather's confessor standing by her, in a room where there were other grave men talking in subdued tones.

"I am ready," she said, starting up. "Let us lose no time."

She thought all clinging was at an end for her: all her strength now should be given to escape from a grasp under which she shuddered.

CHAPTER LXI.

DRIFTING AWAY

ON the eighth day from that memorable night Romola was standing on the brink of the Mediterranean, watching the gentle summer pulse of the sea just above what was then the little fishing village of Viareggio.*

Again she had fled from Florence, and this time no arresting voice had called her back. Again she wore the grey religious dress; and this time, in her heart-sickness, she did not care that it was a disguise. A new rebellion had risen within[1] her, a new despair. Why should she care about wearing one badge more than another, or about being called by her own name? She despaired of finding any consistent duty belonging to that name. What force was there to create for her that supremely hallowed motive[2] which men call duty, but which can have no inward constraining existence [3]save through some form of believing love? The bonds of all strong affection were snapped. In her marriage, the highest bond of all, she had ceased to see the mystic union which is its own guarantee of indissolubleness, had ceased even to see the obligation of a voluntary pledge: had she not proved that the things to which she had pledged herself were impossible? The impulse to set herself free had risen again with overmastering force; yet the freedom could only be an exchange of calamity. There is no compensation for the woman who feels that the chief relation of her life has been no more than a mistake. She has lost her crown. The deepest secret of human blessedness has half whispered itself to her, and then for ever passed her by.

And now Romola's best support under that supreme woman's sorrow had slipped away from her. The[4] vision of any great purpose, any end of existence which could ennoble endurance and [5]exalt the common deeds of a dusty life with divine ardours, was utterly eclipsed for her now by the sense of a confusion in human things which made all efforts[6] a mere dragging at tangled threads; all fellowship, either for resistance or advocacy, mere unfairness and exclusiveness. What, after all, was the man who had represented for her the highest heroism: the heroism not of hard self-contained endurance,

1 within] *1 2 3* in *MS CM*
2 supremely hallowed motive] *1 2 3* hallowed supreme motive *MS CM*
3 〈but〉 save *MS*
4 And now Romola's . . . The] And now Romola had lost her 〈[?]long refuge] under〉 best support under that supreme woman's sorrow. The *MS*
5 〈thrill〉 exalt *MS*   6 efforts] *MS* effort *CM 1 2 3*

but of willing, self-offering love? What was the cause he was struggling for? Romola had lost her [7]trust in Savonarola, had lost that
fervour of [8]admiration which had made her unmindful of his aberrations, and[9] attentive only to the grand curve of his orbit. And now
that her[1] keen feeling for her godfather had thrown her into antagonism with the Frate, she saw all the repulsive and inconsistent details
in his teaching with a painful lucidity which exaggerated their proportions. In the bitterness of her disappointment she said that his striving after the renovation of the Church and the world was a striving
after a mere name which told no more than the title of a book: a
name that had come to mean practically the measures that would
strengthen his own position in Florence; nay, often questionable
deeds and words, for the sake of saving his influence from suffering
by his own errors. And that political reform which had once made a
new interest in her life seemed now to reduce itself to narrow devices
for the safety of Florence, in contemptible contradiction with the
alternating professions of blind trust in the Divine care.

It was inevitable that she should judge the Frate unfairly on a
question of individual suffering, at which *she* looked with the eyes of
personal tenderness, and *he* with the eyes of theoretic conviction. In
that declaration of his, that the Cause of his party was the Cause of
God's kingdom, she heard only the ring of [2]egoism. Perhaps such[3]
words have rarely been uttered without that meaner ring in them[4];
yet they are the implicit formula of all energetic belief. And if[5] such
energetic belief, pursuing a grand and remote end, is often in danger
of becoming a demon-worship, in which the votary lets his son and
daughter pass through the fire with a readiness that hardly looks like
sacrifice; tender fellow-feeling for the nearest has its danger too, and
is apt to be timid and sceptical towards the larger aims without which
life cannot rise into religion. In this way poor Romola was being
blinded by her tears.

No one who has ever known what it is thus to lose faith in a fellow
man whom he has profoundly loved and reverenced, will lightly say
that the shock can leave the faith in the invisible goodness unshaken.
With the sinking[6] of high human trust, the dignity of life sinks too;
we cease to believe in our own better [7]self, since that also is part of
the common nature which is degraded in our thought; and all the
finer impulses of the soul are dulled. Romola felt even the springs of
her once active pity drying up, and leaving her to barren [8]egoistic

7 ⟨?high⟩ trust *MS*   8 ⟨sympathy with him⟩ admiration *MS*
9 and ⟨had attended⟩ *MS*   1 {And now that} Her *MS*
2 ⟨?hard⟩ egoism *MS*   3 Perhaps such] Doubtless ⟨?those⟩ such *MS*
4 ring {in them}: ⟨nevertheless⟩ yet *MS*   5 if ⟨the believing pursuit of a great⟩ *MS*
6 sinking] loss *MS*   7 ⟨selves⟩ self *MS*   8 ⟨selfish⟩ egoistic *MS*

complaining. Had not *she* had her [9]sorrows too? And few had cared
for her, while she had cared for many. She had done enough; she had
striven after the impossible, and[1] was weary of this stifling crowded
life. She longed for that repose in mere sensation which she had
sometimes dreamed of in the sultry afternoons of her early girlhood,
when she had fancied herself floating naiad-like in the waters.

The clear waves seemed to invite her: she wished she could lie
down to sleep on them and pass from sleep into death. But Romola
could not directly seek death; the fulness of young life in her forbade
that. She could only wish that death would come.

At the spot where she had paused there was a deep bend in the
shore and a small boat with a sail was moored there. In her longing to
glide over the waters that were getting golden with the level sun-rays,
she thought of [2]a story which had been one of the things she had
loved to dwell on in Boccaccio, when her father fell asleep and she
glided from her stool to sit on the floor and read the *Decamerone*. It
was the story of[3] that fair Gostanza* who in her love-lornness desired
to live no longer, [4]but not having the courage to attack her young life,
had put herself into a boat and pushed off to sea; then,[5] lying down
in the boat, had wrapt her mantle round her head, hoping to be
wrecked, so that her fear would be helpless to flee from death. The
memory had remained a mere thought in Romola's mind, without
budding into any distinct wish; but now, as she paused again in her
walking to and fro, she saw gliding black against the red gold another
boat with [6]one man in it, making[7] towards the bend where the first
and smaller boat was moored. Walking on again, she at length saw the
man land, pull his boat ashore, and begin to unlade something from
it. He was perhaps the owner of the smaller boat also: he would be
going away soon, and her opportunity would be gone with him—her
opportunity of buying that smaller boat. She had not yet admitted to
herself that she meant to use it, but she felt a sudden eagerness to
secure [8]the possibility of using it, which disclosed the half-
unconscious growth of a thought into a desire.

"Is that little boat yours also?" she said to the fisherman, who had
looked up, a little startled by the tall grey figure, and had made a reverence to this holy sister wandering thus mysteriously in the evening
solitude.

It *was* his boat; an old one, hardly sea-worthy, yet worth repairing
to any man who would buy it. By the blessing of San Antonio, whose

9 ⟨?heavy⟩ sorrows *MS*   1 {she had striven after the impossible,} and *MS*
2 ⟨that girl whose story⟩ a story which *MS*
3 Decamerone ⟨—⟩ {. It was the story} of *MS*   4 ⟨yet⟩ but *MS*
5 then, ⟨covering her head, had lain down with⟩ *MS*   6 ⟨a⟩ one *MS*
7 making ⟨for the spot where⟩ *MS*   8 ⟨that⟩ the *MS*

chapel was in the village yonder, his fishing had prospered, and he had now a [9]better boat, which had once been Gianni's who died. But he had not yet sold the old one. Romola asked him how much it was worth, and then, while he was busy, thrust[1] the price into a little satchel lying on the ground and containing the remnant of his dinner. After that, she[2] watched him furling his sail and asked him how he should set it if he wanted to go out to sea, and then, pacing up and down again, waited to see him depart.

The imagination of herself gliding away in that boat on the darkening waters was growing more and more into a longing, as the thought of a cool brook in sultriness becomes a painful thirst. To be freed from the burthen of choice when all motive was bruised, to commit herself, sleeping, to destiny which would either bring death or else new necessities that might rouse a new life in her!—it was a thought that beckoned her the more because the soft evening air made her long to rest in the still solitude, instead of going back to the noise and heat of the village.

At last the slow fisherman had gathered up all his moveables and was walking away. Soon the gold was shrinking and getting duskier in sea and sky, and there was no living thing in sight, no sound but the lulling monotony of the [3]lapping waves. In this sea there was no tide that would help to carry her away if she waited for its ebb; but Romola thought the breeze from the land was rising a little. She got into the boat, [4]unfurled the sail, and fastened it as she had learned in that first brief lesson. She saw that it caught the light breeze, and this[5] was all she cared for. Then she loosed the boat from its moorings, and tried to urge it with an oar, till she was far out from the land, till [6]the sea was dark even to the west, and the stars were disclosing themselves like a palpitating life over the wide heavens. Resting at last, she threw back her cowl, and, taking off the [7]kerchief underneath, which confined her hair, she doubled them both under her head for a pillow on one of the boat's ribs. The fair head was still very young and could bear a hard pillow.

And so she lay, with the soft night air breathing on her while she glided on the waters[8] and watched the deepening quiet of the sky. She was alone now: she had freed herself from all claims, she had freed herself even from that burthen of choice which presses with heavier and heavier weight when claims have loosed their guiding hold.

9 ⟨new⟩ better MS
1 thrust ⟨more than⟩ the price into a little satchel ⟨which he had thrown⟩ lying on the ground, and ⟨which contained⟩ containing MS
2 she ⟨?paced⟩ watched him ⟨untying his sail⟩ furling MS
3 ⟨plashing⟩ lapping MS   4 ⟨and⟩ unfurled MS   5 this] that MS
6 ⟨it⟩ the sea MS   7 ⟨white linen⟩ kerchief MS   8 waters] water 2 3

Had she found anything like the dream of her girlhood? No. Memories hung upon her like the weight of broken wings that could never be lifted—memories of human sympathy which even in its pains leaves a thirst that[9] the Great Mother has no milk to still. Romola felt orphaned in those wide spaces of sea and sky. She read no message of love for her in that far-off symbolic writing of the heavens, and with a great sob she wished that she might be gliding into death.

She drew the cowl over her head again and covered her face, choosing darkness rather than the light of the stars, which seemed to her like the hard light of eyes that looked at her without seeing her. Presently she felt that she was in the grave, but not resting there: she was touching the hands of the beloved dead beside her, and trying to wake them.[1]

9 that] which *MS*
1 wake them.] wake them. She was gliding not into death, but into sleep. *MS*

'Will his eyes open?'

CHAPTER LXII.

THE BENEDICTION

ABOUT ten o'clock on the morning of the twenty-seventh of February the current of passengers along the Florentine streets set decidedly towards San Marco. It was the last morning of the Carnival, and every one knew there was a second Bonfire of Vanities being prepared in front of the Old Palace; but at this hour it was evident that the centre of popular interest lay elsewhere.

The Piazza di San Marco was filled by a multitude who showed no other movement than that which proceeded from the pressure of new comers trying to force their way forward from all the openings; but the front ranks were already close-serried and resisted the pressure. Those ranks[1] were ranged around a semicircular barrier in front of the church, and within this barrier were already assembling the Dominican Brethren of San Marco.

But the temporary wooden pulpit erected over the church door was still empty. It was presently to be entered by the man whom the Pope's command had banished from the pulpit of the Duomo, whom the other ecclesiastics of Florence had been forbidden to consort with, whom the citizens had been forbidden to hear on pain of excommunication. This man had said,* "A wicked, unbelieving Pope who has gained the pontifical chair by bribery is not Christ's Vicar. His curses are broken swords: he grasps a hilt without a blade. His commands are contrary to the Christian life: it is lawful to disobey them—nay, *it is not lawful to obey them.*" And the people still flocked to hear him as he preached in his own church of San Marco, though the Pope was hanging terrible threats over Florence if it did not renounce the pestilential schismatic and send him to Rome to be "converted"—still, as on this very morning, accepted the communion from his excommunicated hands. For how if this Frate had really more command over the divine lightnings than that official successor of Saint Peter? It was a momentous question, which for the mass of citizens could never be decided by the Frate's ultimate test, namely, what was and what was not accordant with the highest spiritual law. No: in such a case as this, if God had chosen the Frate as his Prophet to rebuke the High Priest who carried the mystic raiment unworthily, he would attest his choice by some unmistakable sign. As long as the belief in the

1 ranks] front ranks *MS*

Prophet carried no threat of outward calamity, but rather the confident hope of exceptional safety, no sign was needed: his preaching was a music to which the people felt themselves marching along the way they wished to go; but now that belief meant an immediate blow to their commerce, the shaking of their position among the Italian States, and an interdict on their city, there inevitably came the question, "What miracle showest thou?" Slowly at first, then faster and faster, that fatal demand had been swelling in Savonarola's ear, provoking a response, outwardly in the declaration that at the fitting time the miracle would come; inwardly in the faith—not unwavering, for what faith is so?—that if the need for miracle became urgent, the work he had before him was too great for the divine power to leave it halting. His faith wavered, but not his speech: it is the lot of every man who has to speak for the satisfaction of the crowd, that he must often speak in virtue of yesterday's faith, hoping it will come back tomorrow.

It was in preparation for a scene which was really a response to the popular impatience for some supernatural guarantee of the Prophet's mission[2] that the wooden pulpit had been erected above the church door. But while the ordinary Frati in black mantles were entering and arranging themselves, the faces of the multitude were not yet eagerly directed towards the pulpit: it was felt that Savonarola[3] would not appear just yet, and there was some interest in singling out the various monks, [4]some of them belonging to high Florentine families, many of them[5] having fathers, brothers, or cousins among the artisans and shopkeepers who made the majority of the crowd. It was not till the tale of monks was complete, not till they had fluttered their books and had begun to chant, that people said to each other, "Fra Girolamo must be coming now."

That expectation rather than any spell from the accustomed wail of psalmody was what made silence and expectation seem to spread like a paling solemn light over the multitude of upturned faces, all now directed towards the empty pulpit.

The next instant the pulpit was no longer empty. A figure covered from head to foot in black cowl and mantle had entered it, and was kneeling with bent head and with[6] face turned away. It seemed a weary time to the eager people while the black figure knelt and the monks chanted. But the stillness was not broken, for the Frate's audiences with heaven were yet charged with electric awe for that mixed multitude, so that those who had already the will to stone him felt their arms unnerved.

2 Prophet's mission] Frate's ⟨inspiration⟩ mission *MS*
3 Savonarola] *the* Frate *MS*   4 ⟨many⟩ some *MS*   5 them ⟨sons⟩ *MS*
6 and with] and *MS*

At last there was a vibration among the multitude, each seeming to give his neighbour a momentary aspen-like touch, as when men who have been watching for something in the heavens see the [7]expected presence silently disclosing itself. The Frate had risen, turned towards the people, and partly pushed back his cowl. The monotonous wail of psalmody had ceased, and to those who stood near the pulpit, it [8]was as if the sounds which had just been filling their ears had suddenly merged themselves in the force of Savonarola's flashing glance, as he looked round him in the silence. Then he stretched out his hands, which, in their exquisite delicacy, seemed transfigured from an animal organ for grasping into vehicles of sensibility[9] too acute to need any gross contact: hands that came like an appealing speech from that part of his soul which was masked by his strong passionate face, [1]written on now with deeper lines about the mouth and brow than are made by forty-four years* of ordinary life.

At the first stretching out of the hands some of the crowd in the front ranks fell on their knees, and here and there a devout disciple farther off; but the great majority stood firm, some resisting[2] the impulse to kneel before this excommunicated man (might not a great judgment fall upon him even in this act of blessing?)—others jarred[3] with scorn and hatred of the ambitious deceiver who was getting up this new comedy, before which, nevertheless, they felt themselves impotent, as before the triumph of a fashion.

But then came the voice, clear and low at first, uttering the words of absolution—"*Misereatur vestri*[4]"—and more fell on their knees; and as it rose higher and yet clearer, the erect heads became fewer and fewer, till, at the words "*Benedicat vos omnipotens Deus*[5]," it rose to a masculine cry, as if protesting its power to bless under the clutch of a demon that wanted to stifle it: it rang like a trumpet to the extremities of the Piazza, and under it every head was bowed.

After the utterance of that blessing Savonarola himself fell on his knees and hid his face in temporary exhaustion. Those great jets of emotion were a necessary part of his life: he himself had said to the people long ago, "Without preaching I cannot live."* But it was a life that shattered him.

In a few minutes more, some had risen to their feet, but a larger number remained kneeling, and all faces were intently watching him. He had taken into his hands a crystal vessel, containing the consecrated Host, and was about to address the people.

7 ⟨silent⟩ expected *MS*   8 ⟨sounded⟩ was *MS*
9 vehicles of sensibility] vehicles simply of ⟨an acute⟩ sensibility *MS*
1 ⟨marked⟩ written on *MS*   2 {some} resisting ⟨any impulse they might feel⟩ *MS*
3 jarred] all ajar *MS*   4 *Misereatur vestri*] *3P* Misereatur vestri *MS CM 1 2*
5 *Benedicat . . . Deus*] *3P* Benedicat . . . Deus *MS CM 1 2*

"You remember, my children, three days ago I besought you, when I should hold this Sacrament in my hand in the face of you all, to pray [6]fervently to the Most High that if this work of mine does not come from Him, He will send a fire and consume me,* that I may vanish into the eternal darkness away from His light which I have hidden with my falsity. Again I beseech you to make that prayer, and to make it *now*."

It was a breathless moment: perhaps no [7]man really prayed, if some in a spirit of devout obedience made the effort to pray. Every consciousness was chiefly possessed by the sense that Savonarola was praying, in a voice not loud but distinctly audible in the wide stillness.

"Lord, if I have not wrought in sincerity of soul, if my word cometh not from Thee, strike me in this moment with Thy thunder, and let the fires of Thy wrath [8]enclose me."

He ceased to speak, and stood motionless, with the consecrated Mystery in his hand, with eyes uplifted and a quivering excitement in his whole aspect. Every one else was motionless and silent too, while the sunlight, which for the last quarter of an hour had here and there been piercing the greyness, made fitful streaks across the convent wall, causing some awe-stricken spectators to start timidly. But soon there was a wider parting, and with a gentle quickness, like a smile, a stream of brightness poured itself on the crystal vase, and then spread itself over Savonarola's face with mild glorification.

An instantaneous shout rang through the Piazza, "Behold the answer!"

The warm radiance thrilled through Savonarola's frame, and so did the shout. It was his last [9]moment of troubled triumph, and in its rapturous confidence he felt carried to a grander scene yet to come, before an audience that would represent all Christendom, in whose presence he should[1] again be sealed as the messenger of the supreme righteousness, and feel himself full charged with divine strength. It was but a moment that expanded itself in that prevision. While the shout was still ringing in his ears he turned away within the church, feeling the strain too great for him to bear it longer.

But when the Frate had disappeared, and the sunlight seemed no longer to have anything special in its illumination, but was spreading itself impartially over all things clean and unclean, there began, along with the general movement of the crowd, a confusion of voices in which certain strong discords and varying scales of laughter made it evident that, in the previous silence and universal kneeling, hostility and scorn had only submitted unwillingly to a momentary spell.

6 ⟨fervidly⟩ fervently *MS*   7 ⟨soul⟩ man *MS*   8 ⟨consume⟩ enclose *MS*
9 ⟨experience⟩ moment *MS*   1 should] *1 2 3* would *MS CM*

"It seems to me the plaudits are giving way to criticism," said Tito, who had been watching the scene attentively from an upper loggia in one of the houses opposite the church. "Nevertheless it was a striking moment, eh, Messer Pietro? Fra Girolamo is a man to make one understand that there was a time when the monk's frock was a symbol of power over men's minds rather than over the keys of women's cupboards."

"Assuredly," said Pietro Cennini. "And until I have seen proof that Fra Girolamo has much less faith in God's judgments than the common run of men, instead of having considerably more, I shall not believe that he would brave heaven in this way if his soul were laden with a conscious lie."

CHAPTER LXIII.

RIPENING SCHEMES

A MONTH after that Carnival, one morning near the end of March, Tito descended the marble steps of the Old Palace, bound on a pregnant errand to San Marco. For some reason, he did not choose to take the direct road, which was but a slightly bent line from the Old Palace; he chose rather to make a circuit by the Piazza di Santa Croce, where the people would be pouring out of the church after the early sermon.

It was in the grand church of Santa Croce that the daily Lenten sermon had of late had the largest audience. For Savonarola's voice had ceased to be heard even in his own church of San Marco, a hostile Signoria having imposed silence on him in obedience to a new letter from the Pope, threatening the city with an immediate interdict if this "wretched worm" and "monstrous idol"* were not forbidden to preach, and sent to demand pardon at Rome. And next to hearing Fra Girolamo himself, the most exciting Lenten occupation was to hear him argued against and vilified. This excitement was to be had in Santa Croce, where the Franciscan appointed to preach the Quaresimal sermons had offered to clench his arguments by walking through the fire with Fra Girolamo. Had not that schismatical Dominican said, that his prophetic doctrine would be proved by a miracle at the fitting time? Here, then, was the fitting time. Let Savonarola walk through the fire, and if he came out unhurt, the divine origin of his doctrine would be demonstrated; but if the fire consumed him, his falsity would be manifest; and that he might have no excuse for evading the test, the Franciscan declared himself willing to be a victim to this high logic, and to be burned for the sake of securing the necessary minor premiss[1].

Savonarola, according to his habit, [2]had taken no notice of these pulpit attacks. But it happened that the zealous preacher of Santa Croce was no other than the Fra Francesco di Puglia[3], who at Prato the year before had been engaged in a like challenge with Savonarola's fervent follower Fra Domenico, but had been called home by his superiors while the heat was simply oratorical.* Honest Fra Domenico, then, who was preaching Lenten sermons to the women in the Via del Cocomero,* no sooner heard of this new challenge, than he took up the gauntlet for his master and declared himself ready to

---

1 premiss ⟨to the conclusion that Fra Girolamo was a deceiver⟩ MS
2 ⟨took⟩ had taken MS   3 Fra Francesco {di Puglia} MS

walk through the fire with Fra Francesco. Already the people were beginning to take a strong interest in what seemed to them a short and easy method of argument ([4]for those who were to be convinced), when Savonarola, keenly alive to the dangers that lay in the mere discussion of the case, commanded Fra Domenico to withdraw his acceptance of the challenge and secede from the affair. The Franciscan declared himself content: he had not directed his challenge to any subaltern, but to Fra Girolamo himself.

After that, the popular interest in the Lenten sermons had flagged a little. But this morning, when Tito entered the Piazza di Santa Croce, he found, as he expected, that the people were pouring from the church in [5]large numbers. Instead of dispersing, many of them concentrated themselves towards a particular spot near the entrance of the Franciscan monastery, and Tito took the same direction, threading the crowd with a careless and leisurely air, but keeping careful watch on that monastic entrance, as if he expected some object of interest to issue from it.

It was no such expectation that occupied the crowd. The object they were caring about was already visible to them in the shape of a large placard, affixed by order of the Signoria, and covered with very legible official handwriting. But curiosity was somewhat baulked by the fact that the manuscript was chiefly in Latin; and though nearly every man knew beforehand approximately what the placard contained, he had an appetite for more exact knowledge, which gave him an irritating sense of his neighbour's ignorance in not being able to interpret the learned tongue. For that aural acquaintance with Latin phrases which the unlearned might pick up from pulpit quotations constantly interpreted by the preacher could help them little when they saw written Latin; the spelling even of the modern language being in an unorganized and scrambling condition for the mass of people who could read and write,* while[6] the majority of those assembled nearest to the placard were not in the dangerous predicament of possessing that little knowledge.

"It's the Frate's doctrines that he's to prove by being burned," said that large public character Goro, who happened to be among the foremost gazers. "The Signoria has taken it in hand, and the writing is to let us know. It's what the Padre has been telling us about in his sermon."

"Nay, Goro," said a sleek shopkeeper, compassionately, "thou hast got thy legs into twisted hose there. The Frate has to prove his doctrines by *not* being burned: he is to walk [7]through the fire, and come out on the other side sound and whole."

4 ⟨at least⟩ for *MS*   5 ⟨unusual⟩ large *MS*   6 while] *2 3* and *MS CM 1*
7 ⟨into⟩ through *MS*

"Yes, yes," said a young sculptor, who wore his white-streaked cap and tunic with a jaunty air. "But [8]Fra Girolamo objects to walking through the fire. Being sound and whole already, he sees no reason why he should walk through the fire to come out in just the same condition. He leaves such odds and ends of work to Fra Domenico."

"Then I say he flinches like a coward," said Goro, in a wheezy treble. "Suffocation! that was what he did at the Carnival. He had us all in the piazza to see the lightning strike him, and nothing came of it."

"Stop that bleating," said a tall shoemaker, who had stepped in to hear part of the sermon, with [9]bunches of slippers[1] hanging over his shoulders. "It seems to me, friend, that you are about as wise as a calf with water on its brain. The Frate will flinch from nothing: he'll say nothing beforehand, perhaps, but when the moment comes he'll walk through the fire without asking any grey-frock to keep him company. But I would[2] give a shoestring to know what this Latin all is."

"[3]There's so much of it," said the shopkeeper, "else I'm pretty good at guessing. Is there no scholar to be seen?" he added, with a slight expression of disgust.

There was a general turning of heads, which caused the talkers to descry Tito approaching in their rear.

"Here is one," said the young sculptor, smiling and raising his cap.

"It is the secretary of the Ten: he is going to the convent, doubtless; make way for him," said the shopkeeper, also doffing, though that mark of respect was rarely shown by Florentines except to the highest officials. The exceptional reverence[4] was really exacted by the splendour and grace of Tito's appearance, which made his black mantle, with its gold fibula, look like a regal robe, and his ordinary black velvet cap like an entirely exceptional head-dress. The hardening of his cheeks and mouth, which was the chief change in his face since he came[5] to Florence, seemed to a superficial glance only to give his beauty a more masculine character. He raised his own cap immediately and said,

"Thanks, my friend, I merely wished, as you did, to see what is at the foot of this placard—ah, it is as I expected. I had been informed that the government permits any one who will to subscribe his name as a candidate to enter the fire—which is an act of liberality worthy of the magnificent Signoria—reserving of course the right to make a selection. And doubtless many believers[6] will be eager to subscribe their names. For what is it to enter the fire, to one whose faith is

---

8 ⟨the Frate⟩ Fra Girolamo *MS*   9 ⟨a bunch⟩ bunches *MS*
1 slippers] *pianelle* or walking-slippers *MS*   2 would ⟨?fain ?know⟩ *MS*
3 ⟨There seems⟩ There's *MS*
4 exceptional reverence] {⟨exceptional⟩} reverence *MS*   5 came] first came *MS*
6 many {believers} *MS*

firm? A man is afraid of the fire, because he believes it will burn him; but if he believes the contrary?"—here Tito lifted his shoulders and made an oratorical pause— "for which reason I have never been one to disbelieve the Frate, when he has said that he would enter the fire to prove his doctrine. For in his place,[7] if you believed the fire would not burn you, which of you, my friends, would not enter it as readily as you would walk along the dry bed of the Mugnone?"*

As Tito looked round him during this appeal, there was a change in some[8] of his audience very much like the change in an eager dog when he is invited to smell something pungent. Since the question of burning was becoming practical, it was not every one who would rashly commit himself to any general view of the relation between faith and fire. The scene might have been too much for [9]a gravity less under command than Tito's.

"Then, Messer Segretario," said the young [1]sculptor, "it seems to me Fra Francesco is the greater hero, for he offers to enter the fire for the truth, though he is sure the fire will burn him."

"I do not deny it," said Tito, blandly. "But if it turns out that Fra Francesco is mistaken, he will have been burned for the wrong side, and the Church has never reckoned such victims to be[3] martyrs. We must suspend our judgment until the trial has really taken place."

"It is true, Messer Segretario," said the shopkeeper, with subdued impatience. "But will you favour us by interpreting the Latin?"

"Assuredly," said Tito. "It does but express the conclusions or doctrines which the Frate specially teaches, and which the Trial by Fire is to prove true or false. They are doubtless familiar to you. First, that Florence—"

"Let us have the Latin bit by bit, and then tell us what it means," said the shoemaker, who had been a frequent hearer of Fra Girolamo.

"Willingly," said Tito, smiling. "You will then judge[4] if I give you the right meaning."

"Yes, yes; that's fair," said Goro.

"*Ecclesia Dei indiget renovatione*, that is, the Church of God needs purifying or regenerating."

"It is true," said several voices at once.

"That means, the priests ought to lead better lives; there needs no miracle to prove that. That's what the Frate has always been saying," said the shoemaker.

"*Flagellabitur*," Tito went on. "That is, it will be scourged. *Renovabitur:* it will be [5]purified. *Florentia quoque post flagella*[6] *renov-*

7 place, ⟨which of you, my friends⟩ *MS*   8 some ⟨faces⟩ *MS*
9 ⟨the⟩ a *MS*   1 ⟨painter⟩ sculptor *MS*   2 ⟨on⟩ for *MS*
3 such victims to be] *3P* such as *MS CM 1 2*   4 judge ⟨of my⟩ *MS*
5 ⟨renewed or⟩ purified *MS*   6 *flagella*] *flagellam 2 3*

abitur et prosperabitur: Florence also, after the scouring, shall be purified and shall prosper."

"That means, we are to get Pisa again," said the shopkeeper.

"And get[7] the wool from England as we used to do,* I should hope," said an elderly man, in an old fashioned berretta, who had been silent till now. "There's been scourging enough with the sinking of the trade."

At this moment, a tall [8]personage, surmounted by a red feather, issued from the door of the convent, and exchanged an indifferent glance with Tito; who, tossing his becchetto carelessly over his left shoulder, turned to his reading again, while the bystanders, with more timidity than respect, shrank to make a passage for Messer Dolfo Spini.

"*Infideles convertentur ad Christum,*" Tito went on. "That is, the Infidels shall be converted to Christ."

"Those are the Turks and the Moors. Well, I've nothing to say against that," said the shopkeeper, dispassionately.

"*Hæc autem omnia[9] erunt temporibus nostris:*[1] and all these things shall happen in our times."

"Why, what use would they be, else?" said Goro.

"*Excommunicatio nuper lata contra Reverendum Patrem nostrum Fratrem Hieronymum nulla est:*[2] the excommunication lately pronounced against our Reverend Father, Fra Girolamo, is null. *Non observantes eam non peccant:*[3] those who disregard it are not committing a sin."

"I shall know better what to say to that when we have had the Trial by Fire," said the shopkeeper.

"Which doubtless will clear up everything," said Tito. "That is all the Latin—all the conclusions that are to be proved true or false by the trial. The rest you can perceive[4] is simply a [5]proclamation of the Signoria in good Tuscan, calling on such as are eager to walk through the fire, to come to the Palazzo and subscribe their names.* Can I serve you further? If not—"

Tito, as he turned away, raised his cap and bent slightly, with so easy an air that the movement seemed a natural prompting of deference.

[6]He quickened his pace as he left the Piazza, and after two or three turnings he paused in a quiet street before a door at which he gave a light and peculiar knock. It was opened by a young woman whom he

---

7 And get] And *MS*
9 *Hæc* {*autem*} *omnia MS*
2 *est:*] *MS 3P est*—*CM 1 2*
4 can perceive] ⟨can⟩ perceive *MS*
6 ⟨Tito⟩ He *MS*

8 ⟨figure⟩ personage *MS*
1 *nostris:*] *MS 3P nostris*—*CM 1 2*
3 *peccant:*] *MS 3P peccant*—*CM 1 2*
5 ⟨an invitation from⟩ a proclamation of *MS*

chucked under the chin as he asked her if the Padrone was within, and he then passed, without further ceremony, through another door which stood ajar on his right hand. It admitted him into a handsome but untidy room, where Dolfo Spini sat playing with a fine staghound which alternately snuffed at a basket of pups and licked his hands with that affectionate disregard of [7]her master's morals sometimes held to be[8] one of the most agreeable attributes of her sex. He just looked up as Tito entered, but continued his play, simply from that[9] disposition to persistence in some irrelevant action, by which slow-witted sensual [1]people seem to be continually counteracting their own purposes. Tito was [2]patient.

"A handsome *bracca* that," he said quietly, standing with his thumbs in his belt. Presently he added, in that cool liquid tone which seemed mild, but compelled attention, "When you have finished such caresses as cannot possibly be deferred, my Dolfo, we will talk of business, if you please. My time[3], which I could wish to be eternity at your service, is not entirely my own this morning."

"Down, Mischief, down!" said Spini, with sudden roughness. "Malediction!" he added, still more gruffly, pushing the dog aside; then, starting from his seat, he stood close to Tito, and put [4]a hand on his shoulder as he spoke.

"I hope your sharp wits see all the ins and outs of this business, my fine necromancer, for it seems to me no clearer than the bottom of a sack."

"What is your difficulty, my cavaliere[5]?"

"These accursed Frati Minori at Santa Croce. They are drawing back now. Fra Francesco himself seems afraid of sticking to his challenge; talk of the Prophet being likely to use magic to get up a false miracle—thinks he himself[6] might be [7]dragged into the fire and burned, and the Prophet might come out whole by magic, and the Church be none the better[8]. And then, after all our talking, there's not so much as a blessed lay brother who will offer himself to pair with that pious sheep Fra Domenico[9]."

"It is the peculiar stupidity of the tonsured skull that prevents them from seeing of how little consequence it is whether they are burned or not," said Tito. "Have you sworn well to them that they shall be in no danger of entering the fire?"

7 ⟨his⟩ her master's *MS*
8 morals sometimes held to be] *1 2 3* morals which in the fifteenth century was ⟨regarded as⟩ felt to be *MS CM*
9 that] ⟨that⟩ the *MS*   1 ⟨men⟩ people *MS*   2 ⟨silent⟩ patient *MS*
3 My time ⟨is not⟩ *MS*   4 ⟨his⟩ a *MS*   5 cavaliere] cavalier *1 2 3*
6 he himself] *3P* he *MS CM 1 2*   7 ⟨burned⟩ dragged *MS*
8 magic {and the Church be none the better}. *MS*
9 {that pious sheep} Fra Domenico *MS*

"No," said Spini, looking puzzled; "because one of them will be obliged to go in with Fra Domenico, who thinks it a thousand years till the fagots are ready."

"Not at all. Fra Domenico himself is not likely to go in. I have told you before, my Dolfo, only your [1]powerful mind is not to be impressed without more repetition than suffices for the vulgar—I have told you that now you have got the Signoria to take up this affair and prevent it from being hushed up by Fra Girolamo, nothing is necessary but that on a given day the fuel should be prepared in the Piazza, and the people got together with the expectation of seeing something prodigious. If, after that, the Prophet quits the Piazza without any appearance of a miracle on his side, he is ruined with the people: they will be ready to pelt him out of the city, the Signoria will find it easy to banish him from the territory, and his Holiness may do as he likes with him. Therefore, my Alcibiades,* swear to the Franciscans that their grey frocks shall not come within singeing distance of the fire."

Spini rubbed the back of his head with one hand, and tapped his sword against his leg with the other, to stimulate his power of seeing these intangible combinations[2].

"But," he said presently, looking up again, "unless we fall on him in the Piazza,* when the people are in a rage, and make an end of him and his lies[3] then and there, Valori and the Salviati[4] and the Albizzi* will take up arms and raise a fight for him. I know that was talked of when there was the hubbub on Ascension Sunday. And the people may turn round again: there may be a story raised of the French King coming again, or some other cursed chance in the hypocrite's favour. The city will never be safe till he's out of it."

"He *will* be out of it before long, without your giving yourself any further trouble than this little comedy of the Trial by Fire. The wine and the sun will make vinegar without any shouting to help them, as your Florentine sages would say. You will have the satisfaction of delivering your city from an incubus by an able strategem, instead of risking blunders with sword-thrusts."

"But suppose he *did* get magic and the devil to help him, and walk through the fire after all?" said Spini,[5] with a grimace intended to hide a certain shyness in trenching on this speculative ground. "How do you know there's nothing in those things? Plenty of scholars believe in them, and this Frate is bad enough for anything."

---

1 ⟨large⟩ powerful *MS*

2 combinations ⟨, necessarily difficult to a man who had never been able to understand why chess should be a slow game, since it was but moving pieces from one square to another.⟩ *MS*

3 him {and his lies} *MS*   4 {the} Salviati *MS*

5 said Spini, ⟨shyly⟩ ⟨shyly⟩ with a grimace *MS*

"Oh, of course there are such things," said Tito, with a shrug; "but I have particular reasons for knowing that the Frate is not on such terms with the devil as[6] can give him any confidence in this affair. The only magic he relies on is his own ability."

"Ability!" said Spini. "Do you call it ability to be setting Florence at loggerheads with the Pope and all the powers of Italy—all to keep beckoning at the French King who never comes? You may call him able, but I call him a hypocrite, who wants to be master of everybody, and get himself made Pope."

"You judge with your usual penetration, my captain, but[7] our opinions do not clash. The Frate, wanting to be master, and to carry out his projects against the Pope, requires the lever of a foreign power, and requires Florence as a fulcrum. I used to think him a narrow-minded bigot, but now I think him a shrewd ambitious man who knows what he is aiming at, and directs his aim as skilfully as you direct a ball when you are playing at *maglio*."*

"Yes, yes," said Spini, cordially, "I can aim a ball."

"It is true," said Tito, with bland gravity; "and I should not have troubled you with my trivial remark on the Frate's ability, but that you may see how this will heighten the credit of your success against him at Rome and at Milan, which is sure to serve you in good stead when the city comes to change its policy."

"Well, thou art a good little demon, and shalt have good pay," said Spini, patronizingly; whereupon he thought it only natural that the useful Greek adventurer should smile with gratification as he said,—

"Of course, any advantage to me depends entirely on your[8]—"

"We shall have our supper at my palace to-night," interrupted Spini, with a significant nod and an affectionate [9]pat on Tito's shoulder, "and I shall expound the new scheme* to them all."

"Pardon, my magnificent patron," said Tito; "the scheme has been the same from the first—it has never varied except in your memory. Are you sure you have fast hold of it now?"

Spini rehearsed.

"One thing more," he said, as Tito was hastening away. "There is that sharp-nosed notary, Ser Ceccone; he has been handy of late. Tell me, you who can see a man wink when you're behind him, do you think I may go on making use of him?"

Tito dared not say "no." He knew his companion too well to trust him with advice when all Spini's vanity and self-interest were not engaged in concealing the adviser.

---

6 as ⟨to⟩ *MS*   7 penetration, my captain, but] penetration but *MS*
8 your"—⟨Spini nodded significantly and patted Tito's shoulder.⟩ *MS*
9 ⟨patting⟩ pat *MS*

"Doubtless," he answered, promptly. "I have nothing to say against Ceccone."

That suggestion of the notary's intimate access to Spini [1]caused Tito a passing twinge, interrupting [2]his amused satisfaction in the success with which he made a tool of the man who fancied himself a patron. For he [3]had been rather afraid of Ser Ceccone. Tito's nature made him peculiarly alive to circumstances that might be turned to his disadvantage; his memory was much haunted by such possibilities, stimulating him to contrivances by which he might ward them off. And it was not likely that he should forget that October morning more than a year ago, when Romola had appeared suddenly before him at the door of Nello's shop, and had compelled him to declare his certainty that Fra Girolamo was not going outside the gates. The fact that Ser Ceccone had been a witness of that scene, together with Tito's perception that for some reason or other he was an object of dislike to the notary, had received a new importance from the recent turn of events. For after having been implicated in the Medicean plots, and having found[4] it advisable in consequence to [5]retire into the country for some time, [6]Ser Ceccone had of late, since his reappearance in the city, attached himself to the Arrabbiati, and cultivated the patronage of Dolfo Spini. Now that captain of the Compagnacci was much given, when in the company of intimates, to confidential narrative about his own doings, and if Ser Ceccone's powers of combination were sharpened by enmity, he might gather some knowledge which he could use against Tito with very unpleasant results.

It would be pitiable to be baulked in well-conducted schemes by an insignificant notary; to be lamed by the sting of an insect whom he had offended unawares. "But," Tito said to himself, "the man's dislike to me can be nothing deeper than the ill-humour of a dinnerless dog; I shall conquer it if I can make him prosperous." And he had been very glad of an opportunity which had presented itself to [7]providing the notary with a temporary post as an extra *cancelliere* or registering secretary [8]under the Ten, believing that with this sop and the expectation of more, the waspish cur must be quite cured of the disposition to bite him.

But perfect scheming demands omniscience, and the notary's envy had been stimulated into hatred by causes of which Tito knew nothing. That evening when Tito, returning from his critical audience with the Special Council, had brushed by Ser Ceccone on the stairs,

---

1 ⟨was only⟩ caused Tito *MS*   2 ⟨the⟩ his *MS*   3 ⟨was⟩ had been *MS*
4 having found] *3P* found *MS CM 1 2*
5 ⟨disappear⟩ retire into the country *MS*   6 ⟨he⟩ Ser Ceccone *MS*
7 ⟨giving⟩ providing *MS*   8 ⟨under himself⟩ under the Ten *MS*

the notary, who had only just[9] returned from Pistoja, and learned the arrest of the conspirators, was bound on an errand which bore a humble resemblance to Tito's. He also, without giving up a show of popular zeal, had been putting in the Medicean lottery. He also had been privy to the unexecuted plot, and was willing to tell what he knew, but knew much less to tell. He also would have been willing to go on treacherous errands, but a more eligible agent had forestalled him. His propositions were received coldly; the council, he was told, was already in possession of the needed information, and since he had been thus busy in sedition, it would be well for him to retire out of the way of mischief, otherwise the government might be obliged to take note of him. Ser Ceccone wanted no evidence to make him attribute his failure to Tito, and his spite was the more bitter because the nature of the case compelled him to hold his peace about it. Nor was this the whole of his grudge against the flourishing Melema. On issuing from his hiding-place, and attaching himself to the Arrabbiati, he had earned some pay as one of the spies who reported information on Florentine affairs to the Milanese court, but his pay had been small, notwithstanding his pains to write full letters, and he had lately been apprised that his news was seldom more than a late and imperfect edition of what was known already. Now Ser Ceccone had no positive knowledge that Tito had an underhand connection with the Arrabbiati and the Court of Milan, but he had a suspicion of which he chewed the cud with as strong a sense of flavour as if it had been a certainty.

This fine-grown vigorous hatred could swallow the feeble opiate[1] of Tito's favours, and be as lively as ever after it. Why should Ser Ceccone like Melema any the better for [2]doing him favours? Doubtless the suave secretary had his own ends to serve; and what right had he to the superior position which made it possible for him to show favour? But since he had tuned his voice to flattery, Ser Ceccone would pitch his in the same key, and it remained to be seen who would win at the game of outwitting.

To have a mind well oiled with that sort of argument which prevents any claim from grasping it, seems eminently convenient sometimes; only the oil becomes objectionable when we find it anointing other minds on which we want to establish a hold.

Tito, however, not being quite omniscient, felt now no more than a passing twinge of uneasiness at the suggestion of Ser Ceccone's power to hurt him. It was only for a little while that he cared greatly about keeping clear of suspicions and hostility[3]. He was now playing his final game in Florence, and the skill he was conscious of applying

9 {only} just *MS*   1 {feeble} opiate *MS*   2 ⟨showing⟩ doing *MS*
3 {suspicions and} hostility *MS*

gave him a pleasure in it even apart from the expected winnings. The errand on which he was [4]bent to San Marco was a stroke in which he felt so much confidence that he had already given notice to the Ten of his desire to resign his office at an indefinite period within the next month or two, and had obtained permission to make that resignation suddenly, if his affairs needed it, with the understanding that Niccolò Macchiavelli was to be his provisional substitute,* if not his successor[5]. He was acting on hypothetic grounds, but this was the sort of action that had the keenest interest for his diplomatic mind. From a combination of general knowledge concerning Savonarola's purposes with diligently observed details he had framed a conjecture which he was about to verify by this visit to San Marco. If he proved to be right, his game would be won, and he might soon turn his back on Florence. He looked eagerly towards that consummation, for many circumstances besides his own weariness of the place told him that it was time for him to be gone.

4 ⟨now⟩ bent *MS*   5 {his} successor *MS*

CHAPTER LXIV.

THE PROPHET IN HIS CELL

TITO's visit to San Marco had been announced beforehand, and he was at once conducted by Fra Niccolò, Savonarola's secretary, up the spiral staircase into the long corridors lined with cells—corridors where Fra Angelico's frescoes, delicate as the rainbow on the melting cloud, startled the unaccustomed eye here and there, as if they [1]had been sudden reflections cast from an etherial world, where the Madonna sat crowned in her radiant glory, and the divine Infant* looked forth with perpetual promise.

It was an hour of relaxation in the monastery, and most of the cells were empty. The light through the narrow windows [2]looked in on nothing but bare walls, and the hard pallet, and the crucifix. And even behind that door at the end of a long corridor, in the inner cell opening from an ante-chamber where the Prior usually sat[3] at his desk or received private visitors, the high jet of light fell on only one object more[4] that looked quite as common a monastic sight as the bare walls and hard pallet. It was but the back of a figure in the long white Dominican [5]tunic and scapulary, kneeling with bowed head before a crucifix. It might have been any ordinary Fra Girolamo, who had nothing worse to confess than thinking of wrong things when he was singing *in coro*, or feeling a spiteful joy when Fra Benedetto* dropped the ink over his own miniatures in the breviary he was illuminating—who had no higher thought than that of climbing safely into paradise up the narrow ladder of prayer, fasting, and obedience. But under this particular white tunic there was a heart beating with a consciousness inconceivable[6] to the average monk, and perhaps hard to be conceived by any man who has not arrived at self-knowledge through a tumultuous inner life: a consciousness in which irrevocable errors and lapses from veracity were so entwined with noble purposes and sincere beliefs, in which self-justifying expediency was so inwoven with the tissue of a great work which the whole being seemed as unable to abandon as the body was unable to abandon glowing and trembling before the objects of hope and fear, that it was perhaps impossible, whatever course might be adopted, for the conscience to find perfect repose.

1 ⟨were⟩ had been *MS*   2 ⟨looking⟩ looked *MS*   3 {usually} sat *MS*
4 one object more] *MS* one more object *CM 1 2 3*
5 ⟨frock⟩ tunic and scapulary *MS*
6 inconceivable ⟨not only⟩ to the average monk ⟨but perhaps also to all men who have⟩ *MS*

Savonarola was not only in the attitude of prayer, there were Latin words of prayer on his lips;[7] and yet he was not praying. He had entered his cell, had fallen on his knees, and burst into words of supplication, seeking in this way for an influx of calmness which would be a warrant to him that the resolutions urged on him by crowding thoughts and passions were not wresting him away from the divine support; but the previsions and impulses which had been at work within him for the last hour were too imperious; and while he pressed his hands against his face, and while his lips were uttering audibly, "*Cor mundum crea in me*[8],"* his mind was still filled with the images of the snare his enemies had prepared for him, was still busy with the arguments by which he could justify himself against their taunts and accusations.

And it was not only[9] against his opponents that Savonarola had to defend himself. This morning he had had new proof that his friends and followers were as [1]much inclined to urge on the Trial by Fire as his enemies; desiring and tacitly expecting that he himself would at last accept the challenge and evoke the long-expected miracle which was to dissipate doubt and triumph over malignity. Had he not said that God would [2]declare Himself at the fitting time? And to the understanding of plain Florentines, eager to get party questions settled, it seemed that no time could be more fitting than this. Certainly, if Fra Domenico walked through the fire unhurt, *that* would be a miracle, and the faith and ardour of that good brother were felt to be a cheering augury; but Savonarola was acutely conscious that the secret longing of his followers to see him accept the challenge had not been dissipated by any reasons he had given for his refusal.

Yet it was impossible to him to satisfy them; and with bitter distress he saw now that it was impossible for him any longer to resist the prosecution of the trial in Fra Domenico's case. Not that Savonarola had uttered and written[3] a falsity when he declared his belief in a future supernatural attestation of his work; but his mind was so constituted that while it was easy for him to believe in a miracle which, being distant and undefined, was screened behind the strong reasons he saw for its occurrence, and yet easier for him to have a belief in inward miracles such as his own prophetic inspiration[4] and divinely wrought intuitions; it was at the same time insurmountably difficult to him to believe in the probability of a miracle which[5], like this of being carried unhurt through the fire, pressed

7 lips;] *MS 1 2 3* lips, *CM*
8 *Cor mundum crea in me*] *3P* Cor mundum crea in me *MS CM 1 2*
9 not only ⟨his enemies against whom⟩ *MS*   1 ⟨eager⟩ much inclined *MS*
2 ⟨show⟩ declare *MS*   3 uttered {and written} *MS*
4 {his own} prophetic inspiration *MS*   5 which ⟨pressed⟩ *MS*

in all its details on his imagination and involved a demand not only for belief but for exceptional action.

Savonarola's nature was one of those in which opposing tendencies co-exist in almost equal strength: the passionate sensibility which, impatient of definite thought, floods every idea with emotion and tends towards contemplative ecstasy, alternated in him with a keen perception of outward facts and a vigorous practical judgment of men and things. And in this case of the Trial by Fire, the latter characteristics were stimulated into unusual activity by an acute physical sensitiveness which gives overpowering force to the conception of pain and destruction as a necessary sequence of facts which have already been causes of pain in our experience.[6] The promptitude[7] with which men will consent to touch red-hot iron with a wet finger is not to be measured by their theoretic acceptance of the impossibility that the iron will burn them: practical belief depends on what is most strongly represented [8]in the mind at a given moment. And with the Frate's constitution, when the Trial by Fire was urged on his imagination as an immediate demand, it was impossible for him to believe that he or any other man could walk through the flames unhurt—impossible for him to believe that even if he resolved to offer himself, he would not shrink at the last moment.

But the Florentines were not likely to make these fine distinctions. To the common run of mankind it has always seemed a proof of mental vigour to find moral questions easy, and judge conduct according to concise alternatives. And nothing was likely to seem plainer than that a man who at one time declared that God would not leave him without the guarantee of a miracle, and yet drew back when it was proposed to test his declaration, had said what he did not believe. Were not Fra Domenico and Fra Mariano, and scores of Piagnoni besides, ready to enter the fire? What was the cause of their superior courage, if it was not[9] their superior faith? Savonarola could not have explained his conduct satisfactorily to [1]his friends, even if he had been able to explain it thoroughly to himself. And he was not. Our naked feelings make haste to clothe themselves in propositions which lie at hand among our store of opinions, and to give a true account of what passes within us something else is necessary besides sincerity, even when sincerity is unmixed. In these very moments, when Savonarola was kneeling in audible prayer, he had ceased to hear the words on his lips. They were drowned by argumentative voices within him that shaped their reasons more and more for an outward audience.

"To appeal to heaven for a miracle by a rash acceptance of a challenge, which is a mere snare prepared for me by ignoble foes, would be a tempting of God, and the appeal would not be responded to. Let the Pope's Legate come, let the ambassadors of all the great Powers come and promise that the calling of a General Council and the reform of the Church shall hang on the miracle, and I will enter the flames, trusting that God will not withhold His seal from that great work.* Until then I reserve myself for higher duties which are directly laid upon me: it is not permitted to me to leap from the chariot for the sake of wrestling with ²every loud vaunter. But Fra Domenico's invincible zeal to enter into the trial may be the sign of a Divine vocation, may be a pledge that the miracle—"

But no! when Savonarola brought his mind close to the threatened³ scene in the Piazza, and imagined a human body entering the fire, his belief recoiled again. It was not an event that his imagination could simply see: he felt it with shuddering vibrations to the extremities of his sensitive fingers. The miracle could not be. Nay, the trial itself was not to happen: he was warranted in doing all in his power to hinder it. The fuel might be got ready in the Piazza, the people might be assembled, the preparatory formalities might be gone through: all ⁴this was perhaps inevitable now, and he could no longer resist it without bringing dishonour on—himself? Yes, and therefore on the cause of God. But it was not really intended that the Franciscan should enter the fire, and while *he*⁵ hung back there would be the means of preventing Fra Domenico's entrance. At the very worst, if Fra Domenico were compelled to enter, he should carry the consecrated Host with him, and with that Mystery in his hand, there ⁶might be a warrant for expecting that the ordinary effects of fire would be stayed; or, more probably, this demand would be resisted, and might thus be a final obstacle to the trial.

But these intentions could not be avowed: he must appear frankly to await the trial, and to trust in its issue. That dissidence between inward reality⁷ and outward seeming was not the Christian simplicity after which he had striven through years of his youth and prime, and which he had preached as a chief fruit of the divine life. In the stress and heat of the day, with cheeks burning, with shouts ringing in the ears, who is so blest as to remember⁸ the yearnings he had in the cool and silent morning and⁹ know that he has not belied them?

"O God, it is for the sake of the people—because they are blind—because their faith depends on me. If I put on sackcloth and cast

---

2 ⟨a⟩ every *MS*   3 the threatened ⟨—the now inevitable⟩ scene *MS*
4 ⟨that⟩ this *MS*   5 *he*] he *MS*   6 ⟨was⟩ might be *MS*
7 {inward} reality *MS*   8 remember ⟨his yearnings⟩ *MS*
9 morning and] *MS 3P* morning, and *CM 1 2*

myself among the ashes, who will take up the standard and head the battle? Have I not been led by a way which I knew not to the work that lies before me?"

The conflict was one that could not end, and in the effort at prayerful pleading the uneasy mind laved its smart continually in thoughts of the greatness of that task which there was no man else to fulfil if he forsook it. It was not a thing of every day that a man should be inspired with the vision and the daring that made a sacred rebel. Even the words of prayer had died away[1]. He continued to kneel, but his mind was filled with the images of results to be felt through all Europe; and the sense of immediate difficulties was being lost in the glow of that vision, when the knocking at the door announced the expected visit.

Savonarola drew on his mantle before he left his cell[2], as was his custom when he received visitors; and with that immediate response to any appeal from without which belongs to a power-loving nature accustomed to make its power felt by speech, he met Tito with a glance as self-possessed and strong as if he had risen from resolution instead of conflict.

Tito did not kneel, but simply made a greeting of profound deference, which Savonarola received quietly without any sacerdotal words, and then desiring him to be seated, said at once,

"Your business is something of weight, my son, that could not be conveyed through others?"

"Assuredly, father, else I should not have presumed to ask it. I will not trespass on your time by any proem. I gathered from [3]a remark of Messer Domenico Mazzinghi that you might be glad to make use of the next special courier who is sent to France with despatches from the Ten. I must intreat you to pardon me if I have been too officious; but inasmuch as Messer Domenico is at this moment away at his villa, I wished to apprise you that[4] a courier carrying important letters is about to depart for Lyons [5]at daybreak to-morrow."

The muscles of Fra Girolamo's face were eminently under command, as must be the case with all men whose personality is powerful, and in deliberate speech he was habitually cautious, confiding his intentions to none without necessity. But under any strong mental stimulus, his eyes were liable to a dilation[6] and added brilliancy that no strength of will could control. He looked steadily at Tito, and did not answer immediately, as if he had to consider whether the information he had just heard[7] met any purpose of his.

---

1 away ⟨, and though he⟩. He *MS*
2 mantle {before he left his cell} *MS*
3 ⟨a word let fall by⟩ a remark of *MS*
4 that ⟨there is⟩ *MS*
5 ⟨this evening⟩ at daybreak *MS*
6 dilation] dilatation *3*
7 heard ⟨was any busine[ss]⟩ *MS*

Tito, whose glance never seemed observant, but rarely let anything escape it, had expected precisely that dilation[8] and [9]flash of Savonarola's eyes which he had noted on other occasions. He saw it, and then immediately busied himself in adjusting his gold fibula, which had got wrong; [1]seeming to imply that he awaited an answer patiently.

The fact was that Savonarola had expected to receive this intimation from Domenico Mazzinghi,* one of the Ten, an ardent disciple of his whom he had already employed to write a private letter to the Florentine ambassador in France, to prepare the way for a letter to the French King himself in Savonarola's handwriting,* which now lay ready in the desk at his side. It was a letter calling on the King to[2] assist in summoning a General Council, that might reform the abuses of the Church, and begin by deposing Pope Alexander, who was not rightfully Pope, being a vicious unbeliever, elected by corruption, and governing by simony.

This fact was not what Tito knew, but what his constructive talent, guided by subtle[3] indications, had led him to guess and hope.

"It is true, my son," said Savonarola, quietly, "It is true I have letters which I would gladly send [4]by safe conveyance under cover to our ambassador. Our community of San Marco, as you know, has affairs in France, being, amongst other things, responsible for a debt to[5] that singularly wise and experienced Frenchman, Signor Philippe de Comines,* on the library of the Medici, which we purchased;* but I apprehend that Domenico Mazzinghi himself may return to the city before evening, and[6] I should gain more time for preparation of the letters if I waited to deposit them in his hands."

"Assuredly, reverend father, that might be better on all grounds except one, namely, that if anything occurred to hinder Messer Domenico's return, the despatch of the letters would require either that I should [7]come to San Marco again at a late hour, or that you should send them to me by your secretary; and I am aware that you[8] wish to guard against the false inferences which might be drawn from a too frequent communication between yourself and any officer of the government." In throwing out this difficulty Tito felt that the more unwillingness the Frate showed to trust him, the more certain he would be of his conjecture.

8 dilation] dilatation *3*   9 ⟨brillian[t]⟩ flash *MS*
1 ⟨and seemed⟩ seeming *MS*   2 to ⟨summon⟩ *MS*
3 constructive talent, guided by subtle] *3P* hypothetic talent, constructing from subtle *MS CM 1 2*
4 ⟨under⟩ by *MS*   5 to ⟨the Signor Philippe de Comines⟩ *MS*
6 and ⟨if so can deposit the letters with him gaining⟩ *MS*
7 ⟨return⟩ come *MS*
8 {that} you ⟨object to⟩ wish to guard against *MS*

Savonarola was silent[9]; but while he kept his mouth firm, a slight glow rose in his face with the suppressed excitement that was growing within him. It would be a critical moment—that in which he delivered the letter out of his own hands.

"It is[1] most probable that Messer Domenico will return in time," said Tito, affecting to consider the Frate's determination settled, and rising from his chair as he spoke. "With your permission, I will[2] take my leave, father, not to trespass on your time when my errand is done; but as I may not be favoured with another interview, I venture to confide to you what is not yet known to others except to the magnificent Ten, that[3] I contemplate resigning my secretaryship, and leaving Florence shortly. Am I presuming too much on your interest in stating what relates chiefly to myself?"

"Speak on, my son," said the Frate; "I desire to know your prospects."

"I find, then, that I have mistaken my real vocation in forsaking the career of pure letters, for which I was brought up. The politics of Florence, father, are worthy[4] to occupy the greatest mind—to occupy yours—when a man is in a position to execute his own ideas; but when, like me, he can only hope to be the mere instrument of changing schemes, he requires to be animated by the minor attachments of a born Florentine: also, my wife's unhappy alienation from a Florentine residence since the painful events of August naturally influences me. I wish to join her."

Savonarola inclined his head approvingly.

"I intend, then, soon to leave Florence,[5] to visit the chief courts of Europe, and to widen my acquaintance with the men of letters in the various universities. I shall go first to the court of Hungary[6], where scholars are eminently welcome;* and I shall probably start in a week or ten days. I have not concealed from you, father, that I am no religious enthusiast; I have not my wife's ardour; but[7] religious enthusiasm, as I conceive, is not necessary in order to appreciate the grandeur and justice of your views concerning the [8]government of nations and the Church. And if you condescend to intrust me with any commission that will further the relations you wish to establish, I shall feel honoured. May I now take my leave?"

"Stay, my son. When you depart from Florence I will send a letter to your wife, of whose spiritual welfare[9] I would fain be assured,

9 silent ⟨for a little while⟩ MS   1 It is ⟨after all⟩ MS
2 {With your permission} I will MS
3 you what is not yet known to others except to the magnificent Ten, that] you—
what is not yet known to others, except to the magnificent Ten—that 1 2 3
4 worthy ⟨of⟩ MS   5 {soon} to leave Florence, ⟨and⟩ MS
6 {the court of} Hungary MS   7 {I have not my wife's ardour;} but MS
8 ⟨welfare⟩ government MS   9 {spiritual} welfare MS

for she left me in anger. As for the letters to France, such as I have ready—"

Savonarola rose and turned to his desk as he spoke. He took from it a letter on which Tito could see, but not read, an address in the Frate's own minute and exquisite handwriting, still to be seen* covering the margins of his Bibles. He took a large sheet of paper, enclosed the letter, and sealed it.

"Pardon me, father," said Tito, before Savonarola had time to speak, "unless it were your decided wish, I would rather not incur the responsibility of carrying away the letter. Messer Domenico Mazzinghi will doubtless return, or, if not, Fra Niccolò can convey it to me at the second hour of the evening, when I shall place the other despatches in the courier's hands."

"At present, my son," said the Frate, waiving that point, "I wish you to address this packet to our ambassador in your own handwriting, which is preferable to my secretary's."

Tito sat down to write the address while the Frate stood by him with folded arms, the glow mounting in his cheek, and his lip at last quivering. Tito rose and was about to move away, when Savonarola said abruptly,

"Take it, my son. There is no use[1] in waiting. It does not please me that Fra Niccolò should have needless errands to the Palazzo."

As Tito took the letter, [2]Savonarola stood in suppressed excitement that forbade further speech. There seems to be a subtle emanation from passionate natures like [3]his, making their mental states tell immediately on others; when they are absent-minded and inwardly excited[4] there is silence in the air.

Tito made a deep reverence and went out with the letter under his mantle.

The[5] letter was duly delivered to the courier and carried out of Florence. But before that happened another messenger, privately employed by Tito, had conveyed information in cipher, which was carried by a series of relays to armed agents of[6] Ludovico Sforza, Duke of Milan, on the watch for the very purpose of intercepting despatches on the borders of the Milanese territory.

---

1 use] end *MS*
2 ⟨and seeing Savonarola stand with that air of⟩ Savonarola stood *MS*
3 ⟨the Frate's⟩ his making their ⟨states of mind⟩ mental states *MS*
4 absent{-minded} and {inwardly} excited *MS*
5 The] That *MS*   6 of ⟨the Duke⟩ *MS*

CHAPTER LXV.

THE TRIAL BY FIRE

LITTLE more than a week after, on the seventh of April, the great Piazza della Signoria presented a stranger spectacle even than the famous Bonfire of Vanities. And a greater multitude had assembled to see it than had ever before tried to find place for themselves in the wide Piazza, even on the day of San Giovanni.

It was near midday, and since the early morning there had been a gradual swarming of the people at every coign of vantage or disadvantage* offered by the façades and roofs of the houses, and such spaces of the pavement as were free to the public. Men were seated on iron rods that made a sharp angle with the rising wall, were clutching slim pillars with arms and legs, were astride on the necks of the rough [1]statuary that here and there surmounted [2]the entrances of the grander houses, were finding a palm's breadth of seat on a bit of architrave, and a footing on the rough projections of the rustic stone-work,* while they clutched the strong iron rings or staples[3] driven into the walls beside them.

For they were come to see a miracle: cramped limbs and abraded flesh [4]seemed slight inconveniences with that prospect close at hand. It is the ordinary lot of mankind to hear of miracles, and more or less believe[5] in them; but now the Florentines were going to see one. At the very least they would see half a miracle; for if the monk did not come whole out of the fire, they would see him enter it, and infer that he was burned in the middle.

There could be no reasonable doubt, it seemed, that the fire would be kindled, and that the monks would enter it. For there, before their eyes, was the long platform, eight feet broad, and twenty [6]yards long, with a grove of fuel heaped up terribly,[7] great branches of dry oak as a foundation,[8] crackling thorns above, and well-anointed tow and rags, known to make fine flames in Florentine illuminations. The platform began at the corner of the marble terrace in front of the Old Palace, close to Marzocco, the stone lion, whose aged visage looked frowningly along the grove of fuel that stretched obliquely across the Piazza.

Besides that, there were three large bodies of armed men: five hundred hired soldiers[9] of the Signoria stationed before the Palace;[1]

---

1 ⟨statues⟩ statuary *MS* 2 ⟨an entrance⟩ the entrances *MS*
3 rings {or staples} *MS* 4 ⟨were⟩ seemed *MS* 5 believe] to believe *2 3*
6 ⟨feet⟩ yards *MS* 7 terribly, ⟨with⟩ *MS* 8 foundation, ⟨with⟩ *MS*
9 {hired} soldiers *MS* 1 palace;] *3P* palace, *MS CM 1 2*

five hundred Compagnacci under Dolfo Spini, far off on the opposite side of the Piazza;[2] and [3]three hundred armed citizens of another sort, under Marco Salviati, Savonarola's friend, in front of Orgagna's Loggia, where the [4]Franciscans and Dominicans were to be placed with their champions.

Here had been [5]much expense of money and labour, and high dignities were concerned. There could be no reasonable doubt that something great was about to happen; and it would certainly be a great thing if the two monks were simply burned, for in that case too God would have spoken, and said very plainly that Fra Girolamo was not his prophet.

And there was not much longer to wait, for it was now near midday. Half the monks were already at their post, and that half of the Loggia that lies towards the Palace was already filled with grey mantles; but the other half, divided off by boards, was still empty of everything except a small altar. The Franciscans had entered and taken their places in silence. But now, at the other side of the Piazza, was heard loud chanting from two hundred voices, and there was general satisfaction, if not in the chanting, at least in the evidence that the Dominicans were come. That loud chanting repetition of the prayer, "Let God arise, and let his enemies be scattered,"* was unpleasantly suggestive to some impartial ears of a desire to vaunt confidence and excite dismay; and so was the flame-coloured velvet cope in which Fra Domenico was arrayed as he headed the procession, cross in hand, his simple mind really exalted with faith, and with the genuine intention to enter the flames for the glory of God and Fra Girolamo. Behind him came Savonarola in the white vestment of a priest, carrying in his hands a vessel containing the consecrated Host. He too was chanting loudly, he too looked firm and confident, and as all eyes were turned eagerly on him either in anxiety, curiosity or malignity, from the moment when he entered the Piazza till he mounted the steps of the loggia and deposited the Sacrament on the altar, there was an intensifying flash and energy in his countenance responding to that scrutiny.

We are so made, [6]almost all of us, that the false seeming which we have thought of with painful shrinking when beforehand in our solitude it has urged itself on us as a necessity, will possess our muscles and move our lips as if nothing but that were easy when once we have come under the stimulus of expectant eyes and ears. And the strength of that stimulus to Savonarola can hardly be measured by

2 Piazza;] *3P* Piazza, *MS CM 1 2*
3 ⟨five⟩ three hundred armed ⟨Florentines⟩ citizens *MS*
4 ⟨two bodies of monks⟩ Franciscans and Dominicans *MS*   5 ⟨great⟩ much *MS*
6 ⟨perhaps⟩ almost *MS*

the experience of ordinary lives. Perhaps no man has ever had a [7]mighty influence over his fellows without having the innate need to dominate, and this need [8]usually becomes the more imperious in proportion as the complications of life make self[9] inseparable from a purpose which is not selfish. In this way it came to pass that on the day of the Trial by Fire, the doubleness which[1] is the pressing temptation in every public career, whether of priest, orator, or statesman, was more strongly defined[2] in Savonarola's consciousness as the acting of a part, than at any other period in his life. He was struggling not against impending martyrdom, but against impending ruin.

Therefore he looked and acted as if he were thoroughly confident, when all the while foreboding was pressing with leaden weight on his heart, not only because of the probable issues of this trial, but because of another event already past—an event which was spreading a sunny satisfaction through the mind of a man who was looking down at the passion-worn prophet from[3] a window of the Old Palace. It was a common turning-point towards which those widely sundered lives had been converging, that two evenings ago the news had come that the Florentine courier of the Ten had been arrested and robbed of all his despatches, so that Savonarola's letter was already in the hands of the Duke of Milan, and would soon be in the hands of the Pope, not only heightening rage but[4] giving a new justification to extreme measures. There was no malignity in Tito Melema's satisfaction: it was the mild self-gratulation of a man who has won a game that has employed hypothetic skill, not a game that has stirred the muscles and heated the blood. Of course that bundle of desires and contrivances called human nature, when moulded into the form of a plain-featured Frate Predicatore,[5] more or less of an impostor, could not be a pathetic object to a brilliant-minded scholar who understood everything.[6] Yet this tonsured Girolamo with the high nose and large under lip was[7] an immensely clever Frate, mixing with his absurd superstitions or fabrications very remarkable notions about government: no babbler, but a man who could keep his secrets. Tito had no more spite against him than against Saint Dominic. On the contrary, Fra Girolamo's existence had been highly convenient to Tito Melema, furnishing him with that round of the ladder from which he was about to leap on to a new and smooth footing very much to his heart's content. And everything now was in forward preparation for that leap: let one more

7 ⟨strong⟩ mighty *MS*   8 ⟨only⟩ usually *MS*   9 self] Self *2 3*
1 that {on the day of the Trial by Fire} the doubleness which ⟨besets⟩ *MS*
2 defined ⟨as conscious histrionism than at any other period in Savonarola's life⟩ *MS*
3 from ⟨amidst a group stationed at⟩ a window *MS*
4 but ⟨justifying⟩ *MS*   5 Predicatore, ⟨who was⟩ *MS*
6 heated the blood. {Of course . . . everything.} *MS*
7 {Yet} This tonsured Girolamo {with the high nose and large under lip} was *MS*

[8]sun rise and set, and Tito hoped to quit Florence. He had been so industrious that he felt at full leisure to amuse himself with[9] to-day's comedy, which the thick-headed Dolfo Spini could never have brought about but for him.

Not yet did the loud chanting cease, but rather swelled to a deafening roar, being taken up in all parts of the Piazza by the Piagnoni, who carried their little red crosses as a badge and, most of them[1], chanted the prayer for the confusion of God's enemies with the expectation of [2]an answer to be given through the medium of a more signal personage than Fra Domenico. This good Frate in his flame-coloured cope was now kneeling[3] before the little altar on which the Sacrament was deposited, awaiting his summons.

On the Franciscan side of the Loggia there was no chanting and no flame-colour: only silence and greyness. But there was this counter-balancing difference, that the Franciscans had two champions: a certain Fra Giuliano* was to pair with Fra Domenico, while the original champion, Fra Francesco, confined his challenge to Savonarola.

"Surely," thought the men perched uneasily on rods[4] and pillars, "all must be ready now. This chanting might stop, and we should see better when the Frati are moving towards the platform[5]."

But the Frati were not to be seen moving yet. Pale Franciscan faces were looking uneasily over the boarding at that flame-coloured cope. It had an evil look and might be enchanted, so that a false miracle would be wrought by magic. Your monk may come whole out of the fire, and yet it may be the work of the devil.

And now there was passing to and fro between the Loggia and the marble terrace of the Palazzo, and the roar of chanting became a little quieter, for every one at a distance was beginning to watch more eagerly. [6]But it soon appeared that the new movement was not a beginning, but an obstacle to beginning. The dignified Florentines appointed to preside over this affair as moderators on each side, went in and out of the Palace, and there was much debate with the Franciscans. But at last it was clear that Fra Domenico, conspicuous in his flame-colour, was being fetched towards the Palace. Probably the fire had already been kindled—it was difficult to see at a distance—and the miracle was going to begin.

Not at all. The flame-coloured cope disappeared within the Palace;

---

8 ⟨day⟩ sun *MS*
9 {full} leisure to amuse himself with ⟨the⟩ today's comedy ⟨in the Piazza⟩ *MS*
1 most of them ⟨looked forward to a [?curse] against the enemies of God⟩ *MS*
2 ⟨a yet more signal answer⟩ an answer *MS*
3 {now} kneeling *MS*   4 rods] the rods 2 3
5 platform ⟨when the Fire is being kindled⟩ *MS*
6 ⟨[?Some] difficulty⟩ But *MS*

then another Dominican was fetched away; and[7] for a long while everything went on as before—the tiresome chanting, which was not miraculous, and Fra Girolamo in his white vestment standing just in the same place. But at last something happened: Fra Domenico was seen coming out of the Palace again, and returning to his brethren. He had changed all his clothes with a brother monk, but he was guarded on each flank by a Franciscan, lest coming into the vicinity of Savonarola he should be enchanted again.

"Ah, then," thought the distant spectators, a little less conscious of cramped limbs and hunger, "Fra Domenico is not going to enter the fire. It is Fra Girolamo who offers himself after all. We shall see him move presently, and if he comes out of the flames we shall have a fine view of him!"

But Fra Girolamo did not move, except with the ordinary action accompanying speech. The speech was bold and firm, perhaps somewhat ironically remonstrant, like that of Elijah to the priests of Baal,* demanding the cessation of these trivial delays. But speech is the most irritating[8] kind of argument for those who are out of hearing, cramped in the limbs, and empty in the stomach. And what need was there for speech? If the [9]miracle did not begin, it could be no one's fault but Fra Girolamo's, who might put an end to all difficulties by offering himself now the fire was ready, as he had been forward enough to do when there was no fuel in sight.

More movement to and fro, more discussion; and the afternoon seemed to be [1]slipping away all the faster because the clouds had gathered, and changed the light on everything, and sent a chill [2]through the spectators, hungry in mind and body.

Now it was the crucifix which Fra Domenico wanted to carry into the fire and must not be allowed to profane in that manner. After some little resistance Savonarola gave way to this objection, and thus had the advantage of making one more concession; but he immediately placed in Fra Domenico's hands the vessel containing the consecrated Host. The idea that the presence of the sacred mystery might in the worst extremity avert the ordinary effects of fire hovered in his mind as a possibility; but the issue on which he counted was of a more positive kind. In taking up the Host he said quietly, as if he were only doing what had been presupposed from the first,

"Since they are not willing that you should enter with the crucifix, my Brother, enter simply with the Sacrament."

New horror in the Franciscans; new firmness in Savonarola. "It was impious presumption to carry the Sacrament into the fire: if it

7 {then another Dominican was fetched away}; and *MS*
8 most irritating ⟨of arguments⟩ *MS*   9 ⟨trial⟩ miracle *MS*
1 ⟨advancing⟩ slipping away *MS*   2 ⟨over⟩ through *MS*

were burned the scandal would be great in the minds of the weak and ignorant." "Not at all: even if it were burned, the Accidents only would be consumed, the Substance* would remain." Here was a question that might be argued till set of sun and remain as elastic as ever; and no one could propose settling it by proceeding to the trial, since it was essentially a preliminary question. It was only necessary that both sides should remain firm—that the Franciscans should persist in not permitting the Host to be carried into the fire, and that Fra Domenico should persist in refusing to enter without it.

Meanwhile the clouds were getting darker, the air chiller. Even the chanting was missed now it had given way to inaudible argument; and the confused sounds of talk from all points of the Piazza, showing that expectation was everywhere relaxing, contributed[3] to the irritating presentiment that nothing decisive would be done. Here and there a dropping shout was heard; then, more frequent shouts in a rising scale of scorn.

"Light the fire and drive them in!" "Let us have a smell of roast— we want our dinner!" "Come, Prophet, let us know whether anything is to happen before the twenty-four hours are over!" "Yes, yes, what's your last vision?" "Oh, he's got a dozen in his inside; they're the small change for a miracle!" "Olà, Frate, where are you? Never mind wasting the fuel!"

Still the same movement to and fro between the Loggia and the Palace; still the same debate, slow and [4]unintelligible to the multitude as the colloquies of insects that touch antennæ to no other apparent effect than that of going and coming. But an interpretation was not long wanting to unheard debates[5] in which Fra Girolamo was constantly a speaker: it was he who was hindering the trial; everybody was appealing to him now, and he was hanging back.

Soon the shouts ceased to be distinguishable, and were lost in an uproar not simply of voices, but of clashing metal and trampling feet. The suggestions of the irritated people had stimulated old impulses in Dolfo Spini and his band of Compagnacci; it seemed an opportunity not to be lost for putting an end to Florentine difficulties by getting possession of the arch-hypocrite's person; and there was a vigorous rush of the armed men towards the Loggia, thrusting the people aside, or driving them on to the file of soldiery stationed in front of the Palace. At this movement, everything was suspended both with monks and embarrassed magistrates [6]except the palpitating watch to see what would [7]come of the struggle.

But the Loggia was well guarded by the band under the brave

3 {showing that expectation was everywhere relaxing} contributed *MS*
4 ⟨uninteresting⟩ unintelligible *MS*   5 {unheard} debates *MS*
6 ⟨but⟩ except *MS*   7 ⟨become⟩ come *MS*

Salviati; the soldiers of the Signoria assisted in the repulse; and the trampling and rushing were all backward again towards the Tetto[8] de' Pisani,* when the blackness of the heavens seemed to intensify in this moment of utter confusion, and the rain, which had[9] already been felt in scattered drops, began to fall with rapidly growing violence, wetting the fuel, and running in streams off the platform[1], wetting the weary, hungry people to the skin, and driving every man's disgust and rage inwards to ferment there in the damp darkness.

Everybody knew now that the Trial by Fire was not to happen. The Signoria was doubtless glad of the rain, as an obvious reason, better than any pretext, for declaring that[2] both parties might go home. It was the issue which Savonarola had expected and desired[3]; yet it would be an ill description of what he felt to say that he was glad. As that rain fell, and plashed on the edge of the Loggia, and sent spray over the altar and all garments and faces, the Frate knew that the demand for him or his[4] to enter the fire was at an end. But he knew too, with a certainty as irresistible as the damp chill that had taken possession of his frame, that the design of his enemies was fulfilled, and that his honour was not saved. He knew that he should have to make his way to San Marco again through the enraged crowd, and that the hearts of many friends who would once have defended him with their lives would now be turned against him.

When the rain had ceased he asked for a guard from the Signoria, and it was given him. Had he said that he was willing to die for the work of his life? Yes, and he had not spoken falsely. But to die in dishonour—held up to scorn as a hypocrite and a false prophet? "O God![5] *that* is not martyrdom! It is the blotting out of a life that has been a [6]protest against wrong. Let me die because of the worth that is in me, not because of my weakness."

The rain had ceased, and the light from the breaking clouds fell on Savonarola as he left the Loggia in the midst of his guard, walking, as he had come, with the Sacrament in his hand. But there seemed no glory in the light that fell on him now, no smile of heaven:[7] it was only that light which shines on, patiently and impartially, justifying or condemning by simply showing all things in the slow history of their [8]ripening. He heard no blessing, no tones of pity, but only taunts and threats. He knew this was but[9] a foretaste of coming bitterness; yet

8 Tetto] Tetta *MS*   9 had ⟨fallen⟩ *MS*
1 violence, {wetting . . . platform} *MS*
2 declaring that ⟨negative officially⟩ *MS*
3 expected and desired] desired and expected *MS*   4 him or his] him *2 3*
5 God!] God, *MS*   6 ⟨struggle⟩ protest *MS*
7 heaven: ⟨rather it seemed⟩ *MS*
8 ⟨growth and ripeness⟩ ripening *MS*   9 was but] was *2 3*

his courage mounted under all moral attack, and he showed no sign of dismay.

"Well parried, Frate!" said Tito, as Savonarola descended the steps of the Loggia. "But I fear your career at Florence is ended. What say you, my Niccolò?"

"It is a pity his falsehoods were not all of a wise sort," said Macchiavelli, with a melancholy shrug. "With the times so much on his side as they are about Church affairs[1], he might have done something great."

---

1 ⟨were⟩ are {about church affairs} *MS*

CHAPTER LXVI.

A MASQUE OF THE FURIES

THE next day was Palm Sunday, or Olive Sunday, as it was chiefly called in the olive-growing Valdarno; and the morning sun shone with a more delicious clearness for the yesterday's rain. Once more Savonarola mounted the pulpit in San Marco, and saw a flock around him whose faith in him was still unshaken; and this morning in calm and sad sincerity he declared himself ready to die: in the front[1] of all visions he saw his own doom. Once more he uttered the benediction, and saw the faces of [2]men and women lifted towards him in venerating love. Then he descended the steps of the pulpit and turned away from that sight for ever.

For before [3]the sun had set Florence was in an uproar. The passions which had been roused the day before had been smouldering through that quiet morning, and had now burst out again with a fury not unassisted by design, and not without official connivance[4]. The uproar had begun at the Duomo in an attempt of some Compagnacci to hinder the evening sermon, which the Piagnoni had assembled to hear[5]. But no sooner had men's blood mounted and the disturbance[6] had become an affray than the cry arose, "To San Marco! the fire to San Marco!"*

And long before[7] the daylight had died, both the church and convent were being besieged by [8]an enraged and continually increasing multitude. Not without resistance. For[9] the monks, long conscious of growing hostility without, had arms within their walls, and some of them fought as vigorously in their long white tunics as if they had been Knights Templars.* Even the command of Savonarola could not prevail against the impulse to self-defence in arms that were still muscular under the Dominican serge. There were laymen too who had not chosen to depart, and some of them fought [1]fiercely: there was firing from the high altar close by the great Crucifix[2], there was pouring of stones and hot embers from the convent roof, there was close fighting with swords[3] in the cloisters. Notwithstanding the force of the assailants the attack lasted till deep night.

---

1 in the front] in front *2 3*   2 ⟨a multitude⟩ men and women *MS*
3 ⟨that⟩ the *MS*   4 design {and not without official connivance} *MS*
5 hear ⟨from a {Dominican} Brother of San Marco⟩ *MS*
6 disturbance] *MS* disturbances *CM 1 2 3*   7 {long} before *MS*
8 ⟨a furious⟩ an enraged *MS*
9 resistance. For] *1 2 3* resistance; for *MS CM*   1 ⟨like tigers⟩ fiercely *MS*
2 {great} Crucifix *MS*   3 swords ⟨when the assailants got into⟩ *MS*

The[4] demonstrations of the Government had all been against the convent; early in the attack guards had been sent for[5], not to disperse the assailants, but to command all within the convent to lay down their arms, all laymen to depart from it, and Savonarola himself to quit the Florentine territory [6]within twelve hours. [7]Had Savonarola quitted the convent then, he could hardly have escaped being torn to pieces; he was willing to go, but his friends hindered him. It was felt to be a great risk even for some laymen of high name to depart by the garden wall, but among those who had chosen to do so was Francesco Valori, who hoped to raise rescue from without.

And now when it was deep night—when the struggle could hardly have lasted much longer, and the Compagnacci might soon have carried their swords into the library, where Savonarola was praying with the Brethren who had either not taken up arms or had laid them down at his command—there came a second body of guards, commissioned by the Signoria to demand the persons of Fra Girolamo and his two coadjutors, Fra Domenico and Fra Salvestro.

Loud was the roar of triumphant hate when the[8] light of lanterns showed the Frate issuing from the door of the convent with a guard who promised him no other safety than that of the prison. The [9]struggle now was, who should get first in the stream that rushed up the narrow street to see the [1]Prophet carried back in ignominy to the Piazza where he had braved it yesterday—who should be in the best place for reaching his ear with insult, nay, if possible, for smiting him and kicking him. This was not difficult for some of the armed Compagnacci who were not prevented from mixing themselves with the guards.

When Savonarola felt himself dragged and pushed along in the midst of that hooting multitude; when lanterns were lifted to show him deriding faces; when he felt himself spat[2] upon, smitten and kicked with grossest words of insult, it seemed to him[3] that the worst bitterness of life was past. If men judged him guilty, and were bent on having his blood, it was only death that awaited him. But the worst drop of bitterness can never be wrung on to our lips from without: the lowest depth of resignation is not to be found in martyrdom; it is only to be found when we have covered our heads in silence and felt, "I am not worthy to be a martyr: the Truth[4] shall prosper, but not by me."

But that brief imperfect triumph of insulting the Frate, who had

4 night. {¶} The *MS*   5 sent for] *1 2 3* sent *MS CM*
6 ⟨in⟩ within *MS*   7 ⟨For Savonarola to have quitted⟩ Had *MS*
8 the ⟨Frate was seen⟩ *MS*   9 ⟨rivalry⟩ struggle *MS*
1 ⟨Frate⟩ Prophet *MS*   2 spat] spit *2 3*   3 seemed {to him} *MS*
4 Truth] *3P* truth *MS CM 1 2*

soon disappeared under the doorway of the Old Palace, was only like the taste of blood to the tiger. Were there not the houses of the hypocrite's friends to be sacked? Already one half of the armed multitude, too much in the rear to share greatly in the siege of the convent, had been employed in the more profitable work of [5]attacking rich houses, not with planless desire for plunder, but with that discriminating selection of such as belonged to chief Piagnoni, which showed that the riot was under guidance, and that the rabble with clubs and staves was well officered by sword-girt Compagnacci. Was there not—next criminal after the Frate—the ambitious Francesco Valori, suspected of wanting with the Frate's help[6] to make himself a Doge or Gonfaloniere for life? And the grey-haired man who, eight months ago, had lifted his arm and his voice in such ferocious demand for justice on five of his fellow-citizens, only escaped from San Marco to experience what *others* called justice—to see his house surrounded by an angry, greedy multitude, to see his wife shot dead with an arrow, and to be himself murdered, as he was on his way to answer a summons to the Palazzo, by the swords of men named Ridolfi and Tornabuoni.*

In this way that Masque of the Furies, called Riot, was played on in Florence[7] through the hours of night and early morning.

But the chief director was not visible: he had his reasons for issuing his orders from a private retreat, being of rather too high a name to let his red feather be seen waving amongst all the work[8] that was to be done before the dawn. The retreat was [9]the same house and the same room in a quiet street between Santa Croce and San Marco, where we have seen Tito paying a secret visit to Dolfo Spini. Here the Captain of the Compagnacci sat through his memorable night, receiving visitors who [1]came and went, and went and came, some of them in the guise of armed Compagnacci, others[2] dressed obscurely and without visible arms. There was abundant wine on the table, with drinking cups for chance comers; and though Spini was on his guard against excessive drinking, he took enough from time to time to heighten the excitement produced by the news that was being brought to him continually.

Among the obscurely dressed visitors Ser Ceccone was one of the most frequent, and as the hours advanced towards the morning twilight he had[3] remained as Spini's constant companion, together with

---

5 ⟨breaking into⟩ attacking *MS* 6 wanting {with the Frate's help} *MS*
7 played on {in Florence} *MS* 8 {all} the work *MS*
9 ⟨that house⟩ the same house {and the same room} *MS*
1 ⟨went and⟩ came *MS*
2 others ⟨in the dress of obscurer⟩ ⟨not visibly armed⟩ *MS*
3 had ⟨taken the place of another⟩ *MS*

Francesco Cei, who was then in rather careless hiding in Florence, expecting to have his banishment revoked[4] when the Frate's fall had been accomplished.

The tapers had burnt themselves into low shapeless masses, and[5] holes in the shutters were just marked by a sombre outward light, when Spini, who had started from his seat and walked up and down with an angry flush on his face at some talk that had been going forward with those two unmilitary companions, burst out—

"The devil spit him![6] he shall pay for it, though. Ha, ha! the claws shall be down on him when he little thinks of them. So *he* was to be the great man after all! He's been pretending to chuck everything towards my cap, as if I were a blind beggarman, and all the while he's been winking and filling his own scarsella. [7]I should like to hang skins about him and set my hounds on him! And he's got that fine ruby* of mine, I was fool enough to give him yesterday. Malediction! And he was laughing at me in his sleeve two years ago, and spoiling the best plan that ever was laid. I was a fool for trusting myself with a rascal who had long-twisted[8] contrivances that nobody could see to the end of but himself."

"A Greek, too, who dropped into Florence with [9]gems packed about him," said Francesco Cei, who had a slight smile of amusement on his face at Spini's fuming. "You did *not* choose your confidant[1] very wisely, my Dolfo."

"He's a cursed deal cleverer than you, Francesco, and handsomer too," said Spini, turning on his associate with a general desire to worry[2] anything that presented itself.

"I humbly conceive," said Ser Ceccone, "that Messer Francesco's poetic genius will outweigh— "

"Yes, yes, rub your hands! I hate that notary's trick of yours," interrupted Spini, whose patronage consisted largely in this sort of frankness. "But there comes Taddeo, or somebody: now's the time! What news, eh?" he went on, as two Compagnacci entered with heated looks.

"Bad!" said one. "The people had[3] made up their minds they were going to have the sacking of Soderini's house, and now they've[4] been baulked we shall have them turning on us, if we don't take care. I suspect there are some Mediceans buzzing about among them, and we

---

4 revoked ⟨by the present Signoria⟩ *MS*
5 and ⟨there was a faint gray lig[ht]⟩ *MS*
6 The devil spit him!] Suffocation! *MS*   7 {⟨Ecco⟩} I *MS*
8 long-twisted] such long-twisted *MS*   9 ⟨jewels⟩ gems *MS*
1 confidant] *MS CM 1 3P* confident 2   2 worry ⟨no matter what⟩ *MS*
3 had] have 3   4 they've] they have 2 3

may see them attacking your palace over the bridge before long, unless we can find a bait for them another way."

"I have it," said Spini, and seizing Taddeo by the belt he drew him aside to give him directions, while the other went on telling Cei how the Signoria had interfered about Soderini's house.

"Ecco!" exclaimed Spini, presently,[5] giving Taddeo a slight push towards the door. "Go and make quick work."

5 presently, ⟨pushing⟩ *MS*

CHAPTER LXVII.

WAITING BY THE RIVER

ABOUT the time when the two Compagnacci went on their errand, there was another man who, on the opposite side of the Arno, was also going out into the chill grey twilight. His errand, apparently, could have no relation to theirs; he was making his way to the brink of the river at a spot which, though within the city walls, was overlooked by no dwellings, and which only seemed the more shrouded and lonely for the warehouses and granaries which at some little distance backward turned their shoulders to the river. There was a sloping width of long grass and rushes made all the more dank by broad gutters which here and there emptied themselves into the Arno.

The gutters and the loneliness were the attraction that drew this man to come and sit down among the grass, and bend over the waters[1] that ran swiftly in the channelled slope at his side. For he had once had a large piece of bread brought to him by one of those friendly runlets, and more than once a raw carrot and apple parings. It was worth while to wait for [2]such chances in a place where there was no one to see, and often in his restless wakefulness he came to watch here before daybreak;[3] it might save him for one day the need of that silent begging which consisted in sitting on a church step or by[4] the wayside out beyond the Porta San Frediano.

For Baldassarre hated begging so much that he would have perhaps[5] chosen to die rather than make even that silent appeal, but for one reason that made him desire to live. It was no longer a hope; it was only that possibility which clings to every idea that has taken complete possession of the mind: the sort of possibility that makes a woman watch on a headland for the ship which held something dear, though all her neighbours are certain that the ship was a wreck long years ago. [6]After he had come out of the convent hospital[7], where the monks of San Miniato* had taken care of him as long as he was helpless; [8]after he had watched in vain for the Wife who was to help him, and had begun to think that she was dead of the pestilence that seemed to fill all the space since the night he parted from her, he had been unable to conceive any way in which sacred vengeance could satisfy itself through his arm. His knife was gone, and he was too feeble in body to win another by work, too feeble in mind[9], even if he had

---

1 waters] stained waters *MS*   2 ⟨these⟩ such *MS*
3 to see {and often . . . daybreak:} ⟨for⟩ it might *MS*   4 or by] by *2 3*
5 would have perhaps] would perhaps have *1 2 3*   6 ⟨Since⟩ After *MS*
7 {convent} hospital *MS*   8 ⟨since⟩ after *MS*   9 mind, ⟨to⟩ *MS*

had the knife, to contrive that it should serve its one purpose. He was a shattered, bewildered, lonely old man; yet he desired to live: he waited for something of which he had no distinct vision—something dim[1], formless—that startled him, and made strong pulsations within him, like that unknown thing [2]which we look for when we start from sleep, though no voice or touch has waked us. Baldassarre desired to live; and therefore he crept out in the grey light and seated himself in the long grass and watched the waters[3] that had a faint promise in them.

Meanwhile the Compagnacci were busy at their work. The formidable bands of armed men, left to do their will, with very little interference from an embarrassed if not conniving Signoria, had parted into two masses, but both were soon making their way by different roads towards the Arno. The smaller [4]mass was making for the Ponte Rubaconte, the larger for the Ponte Vecchio;* but in both the same words had passed from mouth to mouth as a signal, and almost every man of the multitude knew that he was going to the Via de' Bardi to sack a house there. If he knew no other reason, could he demand a better?

The armed Compagnacci knew something more, for a brief word of command flies quickly, and the leaders of the two streams of rabble had a perfect understanding that they would meet before a certain house a little towards the eastern end of the Via de' Bardi, where the master would probably be in bed, and be surprised in his morning sleep.

But the master of that house was neither sleeping nor in bed: he had not been in bed that night. For Tito's anxiety to quit Florence had been stimulated by the events of the previous day: investigations [5]would follow in which appeals might be made to him delaying his departure; and in all delay he had an uneasy sense that there was danger. Falsehood had prospered and waxed strong; but it had nourished the twin life[6], Fear. He no longer wore his armour, he was no longer afraid of Baldassarre; but from the corpse of that dead fear a spirit had risen—the undying *habit* of fear. [7]He felt he should not be safe till he was out of this fierce, turbid Florence; and now he was ready to go. Maso was to deliver up his house to the new tenant; his horses and mules were awaiting him in San Gallo; Tessa and the children had been lodged for the night in the Borgo outside[8] the gate, and would be dressed in readiness to mount the mules and join him. He

---

1 dim ⟨and formless⟩ *MS*   2 ⟨that⟩ which *MS*
3 waters] muddy waters *MS*   4 ⟨number⟩ mass *MS*   5 ⟨might⟩ would *MS*
6 life] growth *MS*
7 ⟨But he⟩ He felt he should ⟨be safe when⟩ not be safe till *MS*
8 {in the Borgo} outside *MS*

descended the stone steps into the courtyard, he passed through the great doorway, not the same Tito, but nearly as brilliant as[9] on the day when he had first entered that house and made the mistake of [1]falling in love with Romola. The[2] mistake was remedied now, [3]the old life was cast off, and was soon to be far behind him.

He[4] turned with rapid steps towards the Piazza dei Mozzi, intending to pass over the Ponte Rubaconte; but as he went along certain sounds came upon his ears that made him turn round and walk yet more quickly in the opposite direction. Was the mob coming into Oltrarno? It was a vexation, for he would have preferred the [5]more private road. He must now go by the Ponte Vecchio; and unpleasant sensations made him draw his mantle close round him, and walk at his utmost speed. There was no one to see him in that grey twilight. But before he reached the end of the Via de' Bardi like sounds fell on his ear again, [6]and this time they were much louder and nearer. Could he have been deceived before? The mob must be coming over the Ponte Vecchio. Again he turned, from an impulse of fear that was stronger than reflection; but it was only to be assured that the mob was actually entering the street from the opposite end. He chose not to go back to his house: after all, they would not attack *him*. [7]Still, he had some valuables about him; and all things [8]except reason and order are possible with a mob. But necessity does the work of courage. He went on towards the Ponte Vecchio, the rush and the trampling and the confused voices getting so loud before him that he had ceased to hear them behind.

For he had reached the end of the street, and the crowd pouring from the bridge met him at the turning and hemmed in his way. He had not time to wonder[9] at a sudden shout before he felt himself surrounded, not, in the first instance, by an unarmed rabble, but by armed Compagnacci; the next sensation was that his cap fell off, and that he was thrust violently forward[1] amongst the rabble, along the narrow passage of the bridge. Then he distinguished the shouts, "Piagnone! Medicean! Piagnone! Throw him over the bridge!"

His mantle was being torn off him with strong pulls that would have throttled him if the fibula had not given way. Then his scarsella was snatched at[2]; but all the while he was being hustled and dragged; and the snatch failed—his scarsella still hung at his side[3]. Shouting,

---

9 nearly as brilliant as] *1 2 3* as brilliant, as *MS CM*
1 ⟨loving⟩ falling in love *MS*   2 The] But the *MS*   3 ⟨that⟩ the *MS*
4 He ⟨was about⟩ *MS*   5 ⟨shorter⟩ more private *MS*
6 ⟨but they⟩ and this time they *MS*   7 ⟨But⟩ Still *MS*
8 ⟨but order⟩ except *MS*   9 wonder ⟨that⟩ *MS*
1 violently {forward} *MS*   2 snatched at ⟨and his belt⟩ *MS*
3 dragged {and the snatch . . . side} ⟨he⟩ ⟨that horrible moment⟩ {Shouting, yelling . . . to be reviled.} Tito's {horrible} dread *MS*

yelling, half-motiveless execration rang stunningly in his ears, spreading even amongst those who had not yet seen him, and only knew there was a man to be reviled. Tito's horrible dread was that he should be struck down or trampled on[4] before he reached the open arches that surmount the centre of the bridge. There was one hope for him—that they might throw him over before they had wounded him or beaten the [5]strength out of him; and his whole soul was absorbed in that one hope and its obverse terror.

Yes—they *were* at the arches. In that moment Tito, with bloodless face and eyes dilated, had one of the self-preserving inspirations[6] that come in extremity. [7]With a sudden desperate effort he mastered the clasp of his belt, and flung belt and scarsella forward towards a yard of clear space against the parapet, crying in a ringing voice,—

"There are diamonds! there is gold!"

In the instant the hold on him was relaxed, and there was a rush towards the scarsella. He threw himself on the parapet with a desperate leap, and the next moment [8]plunged—plunged with a great plash into the dark river far below.

[9]It was his chance of salvation; and it was a good chance. His life had been saved once before by his fine swimming, and as he rose to the surface again after his long dive he had a sense of deliverance. He struck out with all the energy of his strong prime, and the current helped him. If he could only swim beyond the Ponte alla Carraja* he might land in a remote part of the city, and even yet reach San Gallo. Life was still before him. And the idiot mob, shouting and bellowing on the bridge there[1], would think he was drowned.

They did think so. Peering over the parapet along the dark stream, they could not see afar off the moving blackness of the floating hair, and the velvet tunic-sleeves.

It was only from the other way that a pale olive face could be seen looking white above the dark water: a face not easy even for the indifferent to forget, with its square forehead, the long low arch of the eyebrows, and the long lustrous agate-like eyes. Onward the face went on the dark current, with inflated quivering nostrils, with blue veins distended on the temples. One bridge was passed—the bridge of Santa Trinità. Should he risk landing now rather than trust to his strength? No. He heard, or fancied he heard, yells and cries pursuing him.[2] Terror pressed him most from the side of his fellow-men: he was less afraid of indefinite chances, and he swam on,

---

4 trampled on] trampled *MS*
6 {self-preserving} inspirations *MS*
7 ⟨He mastered the clasp of his belt⟩ With {a} sudden *MS*
8 ⟨fell—fell⟩ plunged—plunged *MS*
1 mob {shouting . . . there} *MS*

5 ⟨life⟩ strength *MS*

9 ⟨It was what he desired⟩ It *MS*
2 No. {He heard . . . him.} *MS*

panting and straining. He was not so fresh as he would have been if he had passed the night in sleep.

Yet the next bridge—the last bridge*—was passed. He was conscious of it; but in [3]that[4] tumult of his blood, he could only feel vaguely that he was safe and might land. But where? The current was having its way with him: he hardly knew where he was: exhaustion was bringing on the dreamy state that precedes unconsciousness.[5]

But now there were eyes that discerned him—aged eyes, strong for the distance. Baldassarre, looking up blankly from the search in the runlet[6] that brought him nothing, had seen a white object coming along the broader stream. Could that be any fortunate chance for *him*[7]? He looked and looked till the object[8] gathered form: then he leaned forward with a start as he sat among the rank green stems, and his eyes seemed to[9] be filled with a new light. Yet he only watched—motionless. Something was being brought to him.

The next instant a man's body was cast violently on the grass two yards from him, and he started forward like a panther, clutching the velvet tunic as he fell forward on the body and flashed a look in the man's face.

Dead—was he dead? The eyes were rigid. But no, it could not be—Justice[1] had brought him. Men looked dead sometimes, and yet the life came back into them. Baldassarre did not feel feeble in that moment. He knew just what he could do. He got his large fingers within the neck of the tunic and held them there, kneeling on one knee beside the body and watching the face. There was a fierce hope in his heart, but it was mixed with trembling. [2]In his eyes there was only fierceness: all the[3] slow-burning remnant of life within him seemed to have leaped into flame.

Rigid—rigid still. Those eyes with the half-fallen lids were locked against [4]vengeance. *Could* it be that he was dead? There was nothing to measure the time: it seemed long enough for hope to freeze into despair.

Surely at last the eyelids were quivering: the eyes were no longer rigid. There was a vibrating light in them:[5] they opened wide.[6]

"Ah, yes! You see me—you know me!"

Tito knew him; but he did not know whether it was life or death that had brought him into the presence of his injured father. It might be death—and death might mean this chill gloom with the face of the hideous past hanging over him for ever.

3 ⟨the⟩ that *MS*   4 that] the *2 3*
5 was {: exhaustion . . . unconsciousness.} *MS*   6 runlet] muddy runlet *MS*
7 *him*] him *MS*   8 the object] it *MS*   9 to ⟨gather⟩ *MS*
1 Justice] *3P* justice *MS CM 1 2*   2 ⟨But in⟩ In *MS*
3 all the ⟨[?stored] life⟩ *MS*   4 ⟨?terror⟩ vengeance *MS*
5 them:] *3P* them—*MS CM 1 2*   6 quivering: {the eyes . . . wide.} *MS*

But now Baldassarre's only dread was, lest the young [7]limbs should escape him. He pressed his knuckles against the round throat and knelt upon the chest with all the force of his aged frame. Let death come now! Again he kept his watch on the face. And when the eyes were rigid again, he dared not trust them. He would never loose[8] his hold till some one came and found them. Justice would send some witness, and then, he, Baldassarre, would declare that he had killed[9] this traitor,[1] to whom he had once been a father. They would perhaps believe him now, and then he would be content with the struggle of justice on earth—then he would desire to die with his hold on this[2] body, and follow the traitor to hell that he might clutch him there.

And so he knelt, and so he pressed his knuckles against the round throat, without trusting to the seeming death, till the light [3]got strong and[4] he could kneel no longer. Then he sat on the body, still clutching the neck of the tunic. But the hours went on, and no witness came. No[5] eyes descried afar off the two human bodies among the tall grass by the river side. Florence was busy with greater affairs, and the preparation of a deeper tragedy.

Not long after those[6] two bodies were lying in the grass, Savonarola was being tortured and crying out in his agony, "I will confess!"

It was not until the sun was [7]westward that a waggon drawn by a mild grey ox came to the edge of the grassy margin, and as the man who led it was leaning to gather up the round stones that lay heaped in readiness to be carried away, he detected [8]some startling object in the grass. The aged man had fallen forward, and his dead clutch was on the garment of the other. It was not possible to separate them: nay, it was better to put them into the waggon and carry them as they were into the great Piazza, that notice might be given to the Eight.

As the waggon entered the frequented streets there[9] was a growing crowd escorting [1]it with its strange burthen. [2]No one knew the bodies for a long while, for the aged face had fallen forward, half hiding the younger. But before they had been moved out of sight, they had been recognized.

"I know that old man," Piero di Cosimo had testified. "I painted

7 ⟨body⟩ limbs MS   8 loose] lose 3   9 killed] murdered MS
1 traitor, ⟨and [?demand] to be killed⟩ MS   2 this] MS CM 1 3C his 2
3 ⟨had come⟩ got strong MS   4 strong and] 3P strong, and MS CM 1 2
5 No ⟨human⟩ eyes MS   6 Not long after those] While those MS
7 ⟨going down⟩ westward MS
8 ⟨those startling objects⟩ some startling object MS
9 {As the waggon entered the frequented streets} there MS
1 ⟨the body⟩ it MS   2 ⟨For a long while⟩ No one MS

his likeness once. He is the prisoner who clutched Melema on the steps of the Duomo."

"He is perhaps[3] the same old man who appeared at supper in my gardens," said Bernardo Rucellai, one of the Eight. "[4]I had forgotten him. I[5] thought he had died in prison. But there is no knowing the truth now."

Who shall put his finger on the work of Justice, and say, "It is there"? Justice is like the Kingdom of God—[6]it is not without us as a fact, it is within[7] us as a great yearning.

---

3 He is {perhaps} *MS*   4 ⟨That man said he was Melema's benefactor⟩ I *MS*
5 him. I] *3P* him—I *MS CM 1 2*
6 ⟨It is within us as a great yearning⟩ it *MS*   7 it is within] but within *MS*

CHAPTER LXVIII.

ROMOLA'S WAKING

ROMOLA in her boat passed from dreaming into long deep sleep, and
then again from deep sleep into busy dreaming, till at last she felt herself stretching out her arms in the court of the Bargello, where the
flickering flames of the tapers seemed to get stronger and stronger till
the dark scene was blotted out with light. Her eyes opened, and she saw
it was the light of morning. Her boat was lying still in a little creek: on
her right hand lay the speckless sapphire-blue of the Mediterranean; on
her left one of those scenes which were and still are repeated again and
again, like a sweet rhythm, on the shores of that loveliest sea.

In a deep curve of the mountains lay a breadth of green[1] land, cur-
tained by gentle tree-shadowed slopes leaning towards the rocky
heights. [2]Up these slopes might be seen here and there, gleaming
between the tree-tops[3], a pathway leading to a little irregular mass of
building that seemed to have clambered in a hasty way up the mountain side, and taken a difficult stand there for the sake of showing the
tall belfry as a sight of beauty to the scattered and clustered houses of
the village below. The rays of the newly-risen sun fell obliquely on
the westward horn of this crescent-shaped nook: all else lay in dewy
shadow. No sound came across the stillness; the very waters seemed
to have curved themselves there for rest.

The delicious sun-rays fell on Romola and thrilled her gently like a
caress. She lay motionless, hardly watching the scene; rather, feeling
simply the presence of peace and beauty. While we are still in our
youth there can always come, in our early waking, moments when
mere passive existence is itself a Lethe, when the exquisiteness of
subtle indefinite sensation creates a bliss which is without memory
and without desire. As the soft warmth penetrated Romola's young
limbs, as her eyes rested on this sequestered luxuriance, it seemed[4]
that the agitating past had glided away like that dark scene in the
Bargello, and that the afternoon dreams of her girlhood had really
come back to her. For a minute or two the oblivion was untroubled;
she did not even think that she could rest here[5] for ever, she only felt

1 green ⟨corn-covered⟩ land *MS*   2 ⟨Above⟩ Up *MS*
3 there {gleaming between the tree tops} *MS*   4 seemed ⟨as if all⟩ *MS*
5 rest {here} *MS*

that she rested. Then she became distinctly conscious that she was lying in the boat which had been bearing her over the waters all through the night. [6]Instead of bringing her to death, it had been the gently lulling cradle of a new life. And in spite of her evening despair she was glad that the morning had come to her again—glad[7] to think that she was resting in the familiar sunlight rather than in the unknown regions of death. *Could* she not rest here? No sound from Florence would reach her. Already oblivion was troubled; from behind the golden haze were piercing domes and towers and walls, parted by a river and enclosed by the green hills.

She rose from her reclining posture and sat up in the boat, willing, if she could, to resist the rush of thoughts that urged themselves along with the conjecture how far the boat had carried her. Why need she mind? This was a sheltered nook where there were simple villagers who would not harm her. For a little while, at least, she might rest and resolve on nothing. Presently she would go and get some bread and milk, and then she would nestle in the green quiet, and feel that there was a pause in her life. She turned to watch the crescent-shaped valley, that she might get back the soothing sense of peace and beauty which she had felt in her first waking.

She had not been [8]in this attitude of contemplation more than a few minutes when[9] across the stillness there came a piercing cry[1]; not a brief cry, but continuous and more and more intense. Romola felt sure it was the cry of a little child in distress that no one came to help. She started up and put one foot on the side of the boat ready to leap on to the beach; but she paused there and listened—the mother of the child must be near, the cry must soon cease. But it went on, and drew Romola so irresistibly, seeming the more piteous to her[2] for the sense of peace which had preceded it, that she jumped on to the beach and walked many paces before she knew what direction she would take. The cry, she thought, came from some rough garden growth many yards on her right hand, where she saw a half-ruined hovel. She climbed over a low broken stone fence, and made her way across patches of weedy green crops and ripe but neglected corn. The cry grew plainer, and, convinced that she was right she[3] hastened towards[4] the hovel; but even in that hurried walk she felt an oppressive change in the air as she left the sea behind. Was there some taint lurking amongst the green luxuriance that had seemed such an

6 ⟨It had {not} brought⟩ Instead *MS*
7 glad ⟨that rest seemed to have⟩ to think that she ⟨could ?watch⟩ *MS*
8 ⟨seated⟩ in *MS*   9 when ⟨she heard⟩ *MS*   1 cry ⟨. It did not⟩, not *MS*
2 piteous {to her} *MS*   3 right she] *3P* right, she *CM 1 2*
4 corn. The cry grew . . . towards] corn. She felt sure that she was right for the cry grew plainer and she hurried towards *MS*

inviting shelter from the heat of the coming day? She could see the opening into the hovel now, and the cry was darting through her like a pain. The next moment her foot was within the doorway, but the sight she beheld in the sombre light arrested her with a shock of awe and horror. On the straw, with which the floor was scattered, lay three dead bodies, one of a tall man, one of a girl about eight years old, and one of a young woman whose long black hair was being clutched and pulled by a living child—the child that was sending forth the piercing cry. Romola's experience in the haunts of death and disease made thought and action prompt: she lifted the little living child, and in trying to soothe it on her bosom, still bent to look at the bodies and see if they were really dead. The strongly marked type of race in their features and their peculiar garb made her conjecture that they were Spanish or Portuguese Jews, who had perhaps been put ashore and abandoned there by rapacious sailors, to whom their property remained as a prey. Such things were happening continually to Jews compelled to abandon their homes by the Inquisition:* the cruelty of greed thrust them from the sea, and the cruelty of superstition thrust them back to it.

"But surely," thought Romola, "I shall find some woman in the village whose mother's heart will not let her refuse to tend this helpless child—if the real mother is indeed dead."

This doubt remained, because while the man and girl looked emaciated and also showed signs of having been long dead, the woman seemed to have been hardier, and had not quite lost the robustness of her form. Romola, kneeling, was about to lay her hand on the heart; but as she lifted the piece of yellow woollen drapery that lay across the bosom, she saw the purple spots which marked the familiar pestilence. Then it struck her that if the villagers knew of this, she[5] might have more difficulty than she had expected in getting help from them; they would perhaps shrink from her with that child in her arms. But she had money to offer them, and they would not refuse to give her some goats' milk in exchange for it.

She set out at once towards the village, her mind filled now with the effort to soothe the little dark creature, and with wondering how she should win some woman to be good to it. She could not help hoping a little in a certain awe she had observed herself to inspire, when she appeared, unknown and unexpected, in her religious dress. As she passed across a breadth of cultivated ground, she noticed, with wonder, that little patches of corn mingled with the other crops had been left to over-ripeness untouched by the sickle, and that golden apples and dark figs lay rotting on the weedy earth[6]. There were

5 she ⟨would have more difficulty in⟩ MS   6 earth] 3C ground MS CM 1 2

grassy spaces within sight, but no cow, or sheep, or goat. The stillness began to have something fearful in it to Romola; she hurried
along towards the thickest cluster of houses, where there would be
the most life to appeal to on behalf of the helpless life she carried in
her arms. But she had picked up two figs, and bit little pieces from
the sweet pulp to still the child with.

She entered between two lines of dwellings. It was time that villagers should have been stirring long ago, but not a soul was in sight.
The air was becoming more and more oppressive, laden, it seemed,
with some horrible impurity. There was a door open; she looked in,
and saw grim emptiness. Another open door; and through that she
saw a man lying dead with all his garments on, his head lying athwart
a spade handle, and an earthenware cruise in his hand, as if he had
fallen suddenly.

Romola felt horror taking possession of her. Was she in a village of
the unburied dead? She wanted to listen if there were any faint
sound, but the child cried out afresh when she ceased to feed it, and
the cry filled her ears. At last she saw a figure crawling slowly out of
a house, and soon sinking back in a sitting posture against the wall.
She hastened towards the figure; it was a young woman in fevered
anguish, and she, too, held a pitcher in her hand. As Romola
approached her she did not start; the one need was too absorbing for
any other idea to impress itself on her.

"Water! get me water!" she said, with a moaning utterance.

Romola stooped to take the pitcher, and said gently in her ear,
"You shall have water; can you point towards the well?"

The hand was lifted towards the more distant end of the little
street, and Romola set off at once with as much speed as she could
use under the difficulty of carrying the pitcher as well as feeding[7] the
child. But the little one was getting more content as the morsels of
sweet pulp were repeated, and ceased to distress her with its cry, so
that she could give a less distracted attention to the objects around
her.

The well lay twenty yards or more beyond the end of the street,
and as Romola was approaching it her eyes were directed to the
opposite green slope immediately below the church. High up, on a
patch of grass between the trees, she had descried a cow and a couple
of goats, and she tried to trace a line of path that would lead her
close to that cheering sight, when once she had done her errand to
the well. Occupied in this way, she was not aware that she was very
near the well, and that some one approaching it [8]on the other side
had fixed a pair of astonished eyes upon her.

7 as well as {feeding} *MS*   8 ⟨from⟩ on *MS*

Romola certainly presented a sight which, at that moment and in
that place, could hardly have been seen without some pausing and
palpitation. With her gaze fixed intently on the distant slope, the long
lines of her thick grey garment giving a gliding character to her rapid
walk, her hair rolling backward and illuminated on the left side by the
sun-rays, the little olive baby on her right arm now looking out with
jet-black eyes, she might well startle that youth of fifteen,
accustomed[9] to swing the censer in the presence of a Madonna less
fair and marvellous than this.

"She carries[1] a pitcher in her hand—to fetch water for the sick. It
is the Holy Mother, come to take care of the people who have the
pestilence."

It was a sight of awe: she would, perhaps, be angry with those who
fetched water for themselves only. The youth flung down his vessel
in terror, and Romola, aware now of some one near her, saw the black
and white figure [2]fly as if for dear life towards the slope she had just
been contemplating. But remembering the parched sufferer, she half
filled her pitcher quickly and hastened back.

Entering the house to look for a small cup, she saw salt meat and
meal: there[3] were not signs of want in the dwelling. With nimble
movements[4] she seated baby on the ground, and lifted a cup of water
to the sufferer, who drank eagerly and then closed her eyes and
leaned her head backward, seeming to give herself up to the sense of
relief. Presently she opened her eyes, and, looking at Romola, said
launguidly,—

"Who are you?"

"I came over the sea," said Romola. "I only came this morning.
Are all the people dead in these houses?"

"I think they are all ill[5] now—all that are not dead. My father and
my sister[6] lie dead upstairs, and there is no one to bury them: and
soon I shall die."

"Not so, I hope," said Romola. "I am come to take care of you. I
am used to the pestilence; I am not afraid. But there must be some
left who are not ill. I saw a youth running towards the mountain
when I went to the well."

"I cannot tell. When the pestilence came, a great many people went
away, and drove off the cows and goats. Give me more water!"

Romola, suspecting that if she followed the direction of the youth's
flight, she should find some men and women who were still healthy
and able, determined to seek them out at once, that she might at least

---

9 accustomed] an acolyth accustomed *MS*   1 carries] carried *MS*
2 ⟨flying⟩ fly *MS*   3 there ⟨was no want⟩ *MS*
4 movements] movement *1 2 3*   5 {all} ill *MS*
6 My father {and my sister} *MS*

win them to take care of the child, and leave her free to come back and see how many living needed help, and how many dead needed burial. She trusted to her powers of persuasion to conquer the aid of the timorous, when once she knew what was to be done. Promising the sick woman to come back to her, she lifted the dark bantling again, and set off towards the slope. She felt no burthen of choice on her now, no longing for death. She was thinking how she would go to the other sufferers, as she had gone to that fevered woman.

But, with the child on her arm, it was[7] not so easy to her as usual to walk up a slope, and it seemed a long while before the winding path took her near the cow and the goats. She was beginning herself to feel faint from heat, hunger, and thirst, and as she reached a double turning, she paused to consider whether she would not wait near the cow, which some one was likely to come and milk soon, rather than toil up to the church before she had taken any rest. Raising her eyes to measure the steep distance, she saw peeping between[8] the boughs, not more than five yards off, a broad round face, watching her attentively, and lower down the black skirt of a priest's garment, and a hand grasping a bucket. She stood mutely observing, and the face, too, remained motionless. Romola[9] had often witnessed the over-powering force of dread in cases of pestilence, and she was cautious.

Raising her voice in a tone of gentle pleading, she said, "I came over the sea[1]. I am hungry, and so is the child. Will you not give us some milk?"

Romola had divined part of the truth, but she had not divined that preoccupation of the priest's mind which[2] charged her words with a strange significance. Only a little while ago, the young acolyte had brought word to the Padre that he had seen the Holy Mother with the Babe, fetching water for the sick: she was as tall as the cypresses, and had a light about her head, and she looked up at the church. The *pievano*[3]* had not listened with entire belief: he had been more than fifty years in the world [4]without having any vision of the Madonna, and he thought the boy might have misinterpreted the unexpected appearance[5] of a villager. But he had been made [6]uneasy, and before

7 But {with the ⟨heavy⟩ child on her arm} it was . . . up a slope ⟨with the ⟨⟨heavy⟩⟩ child on her arm⟩ *MS*
8 {peeping} between *MS*
9 Romola ⟨was at a loss to divine the truth. She⟩ had *MS*
1 {Raising her voice in a tone of gentle pleading she said} I came over the sea ⟨Padre⟩—I am hungry and so is the child ⟨she said raising her voice . . . pleading⟩ *MS*
2 which ⟨caused⟩ charged her words with a {strange} significance. Only ⟨a quarter of an hour⟩ ⟨half an⟩ a little while *MS*
3 *pievano*] priest *MS*   4 ⟨and had never had⟩ without having any *MS*
5 {unexpected} appearance *MS*   6 ⟨?wary⟩ uneasy *MS*

venturing to come down and milk his cow, he had repeated many Aves. The pievano's conscience tormented him a little: he [7]trembled at the pestilence, but he also trembled at the thought of the mild-faced [8]Mother, conscious that that Invisible Mercy might demand something more of him than prayers and "Hails." In this state of mind—unable to banish the image the boy had raised of the Mother with the glory about her tending the sick[9]—the pievano had come down to milk his cow, and had suddenly caught sight of Romola pausing at the parted way. Her pleading words, with their strange refinement of tone and accent, instead of being explanatory, had a preternatural sound for him. Yet he did not quite believe he saw the Holy Mother: he was in a state of alarmed hesitation. If anything miraculous were happening, he felt there was no[1] strong presumption that the miracle would be in his favour. He dared not run away; he dared not advance.

"Come down," said Romola, after a pause. "Do not fear. Fear rather to deny food to the hungry when they ask you."

A moment after, the[2] boughs were parted, and the complete figure of a thick-set priest with[3] a broad, harmless face, his black frock much worn and soiled, stood, bucket in hand, looking at her timidly, and still keeping aloof as he took the path towards the cow in silence.

Romola followed him and watched him without speaking again, as he seated himself against the tethered cow, and, when he had nervously drawn some milk, gave it to her in a brass cup he carried with him in the bucket. As Romola put the cup to the lips of the eager child, and [4]afterwards drank some milk herself, the Padre observed her from his wooden stool with a timidity that changed its character a little. He recognized the Hebrew baby, he was certain that he had a substantial woman before him; but there was still something strange and unaccountable in Romola's presence in this spot, and the Padre had a presentiment that things were going to change with him. Moreover, that Hebrew baby was terribly associated with the dread of pestilence.

Nevertheless, when Romola smiled at the little one sucking its own milky lips, and stretched out the brass cup again, saying, "Give us more, good father," he obeyed less nervously than before.

Romola, on her side, was not unobservant; and when the second supply of milk had been drunk, she looked down at the round-headed man, and said with mild decision,

7 ⟨was afraid of⟩ trembled at *MS*　　　　8 ⟨Madonna⟩ Mother *MS*
9 sick, ⟨from whom he their pastor had fled—⟩ the Pievano had ⟨begun to descend the slope⟩ *MS*
1 felt {there was} no *MS*　　　2 after, the] *3P* after the *MS CM 1 2*
3 priest with] *MS 3P* priest, with *CM 1 2*
4 ⟨then⟩ afterwards drank some {milk} herself, the ⟨priest⟩ Padre *MS*

"And now tell me, father, how this pestilence came, and why you let your people die without the Sacraments, and lie unburied. For I am come over the sea to help those who are left alive—and you[5], too, will help them now."

He told her the story of the pestilence: and while he was telling it, the youth, who had fled before, had come peeping and advancing gradually, till at last he stood and watched the scene from behind a neighbouring bush.

Three families of Jews, twenty souls in all, had been put ashore [6]many weeks ago, some of them already ill of the pestilence. The villagers, said the priest, had of course refused to give shelter to the miscreants, otherwise than in [7]a distant hovel, and under heaps of straw. But when the strangers had died of the plague, and some of the people had thrown the bodies into the sea, the sea had brought them back again in a great storm, and everybody was smitten with terror. A grave was dug, and the bodies were buried; but then the pestilence attacked the Christians, and the greater number of the villagers went away over the mountain, driving away their few cattle, and carrying provisions. The priest had not [8]fled; he had stayed and prayed for the people, and he had prevailed on the youth Jacopo to stay with him; but he confessed that a mortal terror of the plague had taken hold of him, and he had not dared to go down into the valley.

"You will fear no longer, father," said Romola, in a tone of encouraging authority; "you will come down with me, and we will see who is living, and we will look for the dead to bury them. I have walked about for months where the pestilence was, and see, I am strong. Jacopo will come with us," she added, [9]motioning to the peeping lad, who came slowly from behind his defensive bush, as if invisible threads were dragging him.

"Come, Jacopo," said Romola again, smiling at him, "you will carry the child for me. See! your arms are strong, and I am tired."

That was a dreadful proposal to Jacopo, and to the priest also; but they were both under a peculiar influence forcing them to obey. The suspicion that Romola was a supernatural form was dissipated, but their minds were filled instead with the more effective sense that she was a human being whom God had sent over the sea to command them.

"Now we will carry down the milk," said Romola, "and see if any one wants it."

So they went all together down the slope, and that morning the sufferers saw help come to them in their despair. There were hardly[1]

5 you ⟨will repent now and⟩ *MS*   6 ⟨some⟩ many *MS*
7 ⟨hovels⟩ a distant hovel *MS*   8 ⟨gone⟩ fled *MS*
9 ⟨beckoning⟩ motioning *MS*   1 hardly ⟨thirty⟩ *MS*

more than a score alive in [2]the whole valley; but all of these were comforted, most were saved, and the dead were buried.

In this way,[3] days, weeks, and months passed with Romola, till the men were digging and sowing again, [4]till the women smiled at her as they carried their great vases on their heads to the well, and the Hebrew baby was a tottering tumbling Christian, Benedetto by name, having been baptized in the church [5]on the mountain side. But by that time she herself was suffering from the fatigue and languor that must come after[6] a continuous strain on mind and body. She had taken for her dwelling one of the houses abandoned by their owners, standing a little aloof from the village street, and here on a thick heap of clean straw—a delicious bed for those who do not dream of down—she felt glad to lie still through most of the daylight hours, taken care of along with the little Benedetto[7] by a woman whom the pestilence had widowed.

Every day the Padre and Jacopo and the [8]small flock of surviving villagers paid their visit to this cottage to see the Blessed Lady[9], and to bring her of their best as an offering—[1]honey, fresh cakes, eggs, and polenta. It was a sight they could none of them forget, a sight they all told of in their old age—how the[2] sweet and sainted Lady with her fair face[3], her golden hair, and [4]her brown eyes that had a blessing in them, [5]lay weary with her labours[6] after she had been sent over the sea to help them in their extremity, and how the queer little black Benedetto used to crawl about the straw by her side and want everything that was brought to her, and she always gave him a bit of what she took, and told them if they loved her they must be good to Benedetto.

Many legends were afterwards told in that valley about the blessed Lady who came over the sea, but they were legends by which all who heard might know that in times gone by a woman had done beautiful loving deeds there, rescuing those who were ready to perish.

2 ⟨all the⟩ the whole *MS*   3 way ⟨the time⟩ *MS*   4 ⟨and⟩ till *MS*
5 ⟨by⟩ on *MS*   6 {that must come} after *MS*
7 care of {along with the little Benedetto} *MS*   8 ⟨little⟩ small *MS*
9 Blessed Lady—⟨La Beata Donna⟩ and *MS*
1 ⟨their⟩ honey, ⟨their⟩ fresh cakes, ⟨their⟩ eggs *MS*   2 {how} the *MS*
3 face ⟨and⟩ *MS*   4 ⟨the eyes⟩ her brown eyes *MS*
5 ⟨as she⟩ lay *MS*   6 labours ⟨for them⟩ *MS*

CHAPTER LXIX.

HOMEWARD

IN those silent wintry hours when Romola lay resting from her weariness, her mind, travelling back over[1] the past, and gazing across the undefined distance of the future, saw all objects from a new position[2]. Her experience since the moment of her waking in the boat had come to her[3] with as strong an effect as that of the fresh seal on the dissolving wax. She had felt herself without bonds, without motive; sinking in mere egoistic complaining that life could bring her no content; feeling a right to say, "I am tired of life; I want to die." That thought had sobbed within her as she fell asleep, but from [4]the moment after her waking when the cry had drawn her, she had not even reflected, as she used to do in Florence, that she was glad to live because she could lighten sorrow—she had simply lived, with so energetic an impulse to share the life around her, to answer the call of need and do the work which cried aloud to be done, that the reasons for living, enduring, labouring, never took the form of argument.

The[5] experience was like a new baptism to Romola. In Florence the simpler relations of the human being to his fellow-men had been complicated for her with all the special ties of [6]marriage, the State, and religious discipleship, and when these had disappointed her trust the shock seemed to have shaken her aloof from life and stunned her sympathy. But now she said, "It was mere baseness in me[7] to desire death. If everything else is doubtful, this suffering that I can help is certain; if the glory of the cross is an illusion, the sorrow is only the truer. While the strength is in my arm I will stretch it out to the fainting; [8]while the light visits my eyes they shall seek the forsaken."

And then the past arose with a fresh appeal to her. Her work in this green valley was done, and the emotions that were disengaged from the people immediately around her rushed back into the old deep channels of use and affection. That rare possibility of self-contemplation which comes in any complete[9] severance from our wonted life made her judge herself as she had never done before: the compunction which is inseparable from a sympathetic nature keenly alive to the possible experience of others, began to stir in her with growing

---

1 travelling {back} over ⟨all⟩ the past *MS*
2 position ⟨which gave them a ⟨⟨changed⟩⟩ new aspect⟩. *MS*
3 come to her ⟨as the fresh seal comes to⟩ *MS*   4 ⟨that⟩ the *MS*
5 argument. {¶} The *MS*   6 ⟨the family⟩ marriage *MS*
7 baseness {in me} *MS*   8 ⟨and⟩ while *MS*   9 {any} complete *MS*

force. She questioned the justness[1] of her own[2] conclusions, of her own deeds: she had been rash, arrogant, always dissatisfied that others were not good enough, while she herself had not been true to what her soul had once recognized as the best. She began to condemn her flight: after all, it had been cowardly self-care; the grounds on which Savonarola had once taken her back were truer, deeper than the grounds she had had for her second flight. How could she feel the needs of others and not feel above all the needs of the nearest?

But then[3] came reaction against such self-reproach. The memory of her life with Tito, of the conditions which made their real union impossible, while their external union imposed a set of false duties on her which were [4]essentially the concealment and sanctioning of what her mind revolted from, told her that flight had been her only resource. All minds, except such as are delivered from doubt by dulness of sensibility, must be subject to this recurring conflict where the [5]many-twisted conditions of life have forbidden the fulfilment of a bond. For in strictness there is no replacing of relations: the presence of the new does not nullify the failure and breach of the old. Life has lost its perfection: it has been[6] maimed; and until the wounds are quite scarred, conscience continually casts backward doubting glances.

Romola shrank with dread from the renewal of her proximity to Tito, and yet she was uneasy that she had put herself out of reach of knowing what was his fate—uneasy that the moment might yet come when he would be in misery and need her. There was still a thread of pain within her, testifying to those words of Fra Girolamo, that she could not cease to be a wife. Could anything utterly cease for her that had once mingled itself with the current of her heart's blood?

Florence, and all her life there, had come back to her like hunger; her feelings could not go wandering after the possible and the vague: their living fibre was fed with the memory of familiar things. And the thought that she had divided herself from them for ever became more and more importunate in these hours that were unfilled with action. What if Fra Girolamo had been wrong? What if the life of Florence was a web of inconsistencies? Was she, then, something higher, that she should shake the dust from off her feet, and say, "This world is not good enough for me"? If she had been really higher, she would not so easily have lost all her trust.

[7]Her indignant grief for her godfather had no longer complete possession of her, and her sense of debt to Savonarola was recovering

---

1 justness] justice *MS*   2 {the justice of} her own *MS*
3 then ⟨again⟩ *MS*   4 ⟨in reality⟩ essentially *MS*
5 ⟨complicated facts⟩ many-twisted conditions *MS*
6 {it} has been ⟨[?]lopped] by⟩ maimed *MS*   7 ⟨For now her⟩ Her *MS*

predominance. Nothing that [8]had come, or was to come, could do away with the fact that there had been a great inspiration in him which had waked a new life in her. Who, in all her experience, could demand the same gratitude from her as he? His errors—might they not bring calamities?

She could not rest. She hardly knew whether it was her strength returning with the budding leaves that made her active again, or whether it was her eager longing to get nearer[9] Florence. She did not imagine herself daring to enter Florence, but the desire to be near enough to learn what was happening there urged itself with a strength that excluded all other purposes.

And one March morning the people in the valley were gathered together to see the blessed Lady depart. Jacopo had fetched a mule for her, and was going with her over the mountains. The Padre, too, was going with her to the nearest town, that he might help her in learning the [1]safest way by which she might get to Pistoja. Her store of trinkets and money, untouched in this valley, was abundant for her needs.

If Romola had been less drawn by the longing that was taking her away, it would have been a hard moment for her when she walked along the village street for the last time, while the Padre and Jacopo, with the mule, were awaiting her near the well. Her steps were hindered by the wailing people, who knelt and kissed her hands, then clung to her skirts and kissed the grey folds, crying, "Ah, why will you go, when the good season is beginning and the crops will be plentiful? Why will you go?"

"Do not be sorry," said Romola, "you are well now, and I shall remember you. I must go and see if my own people want me."

"Ah, yes, if they have the pestilence!"

"Look at us again, Madonna!"

"Yes, yes, we will be good to the little Benedetto!"

At last Romola mounted her mule, but a vigorous screaming from Benedetto as he saw her turn from him in this new position, was an excuse for all the people to follow her and insist that he must ride on the mule's neck to the foot of the slope.

The parting must come at last, but as Romola turned continually before she passed out of sight, she saw the little flock lingering to catch the last waving of her hand.

CHAPTER LXX.

MEETING AGAIN

On the fourteenth of April Romola was once more within the walls of Florence. Unable to rest at Pistoja, where contradictory reports reached her about the Trial by Fire, she had gone on to Prato; and [1]was beginning to think that she should be drawn on to Florence in spite of dread, when she encountered that monk of San Spirito who had been her godfather's confessor. From him she learned the full story of Savonarola's arrest, and of her husband's death. This Augustinian monk had been in the stream of people who had followed the waggon with its awful burthen into the Piazza, and he could tell her what was generally known in Florence—that Tito had escaped from an assaulting mob by leaping into the Arno, but had been murdered on the bank by an old man who had long had an enmity against him. But Romola understood the catastrophe as no one else did. Of Savonarola the monk told her, in that tone of unfavourable prejudice which was usual in the Black Brethren (Frati Neri) towards the Brother who showed white under his black, that he had confessed himself a deceiver of the people.

Romola paused no longer. That evening she was in Florence, sitting in agitated silence under the exclamations of joy and wailing, mingled with exuberant narrative, which were poured into her ears by Monna Brigida, who had backslided into[2] false hair in Romola's absence, but now drew it off again and declared she would not mind being grey, if her dear child would stay with her.

Romola was too deeply moved by the main events which she had known before coming to Florence, to be wrought upon by the doubtful gossiping details added in Brigida's narrative. The tragedy of her husband's death, of Fra Girolamo's confession of duplicity under the coercion of torture, left her hardly any power of apprehending minor circumstances. All the mental activity she could exert under that load of awe-stricken grief, was absorbed by two purposes which must supersede every other; to try and see Savonarola, and to learn what had become of Tessa and the children.

"Tell me, cousin," she said abruptly, when Monna Brigida's tongue had run quite away from troubles into projects of Romola's living with her, "has anything been seen or said since Tito's death of a young woman with two little children?"

Brigida started, rounded her eyes, and lifted up her hands.

1 ⟨she⟩ was *MS* 2 backslided into] *3P* retrograded to *MS CM 1 2*

"Cristo! no. What! was he so bad as that, my poor child? Ah, then, that was why you went away and left me word only that you went of your own free will. Well, well, if I'd known that, I shouldn't have thought you so strange and flighty. For I did say to myself, though I didn't tell anybody else, 'What was she to go away from her husband for, leaving him to mischief, only because they cut poor Bernardo's head off? She's got her father's temper,' I said, 'that's what it is.' Well, well, never scold me, child: Bardo *was* fierce, you can't deny it. But if you had only told me the truth, that[3] there was a young hussey and children, I should have understood it all. Anything seen or said of her? No; and the less the better. They say enough of ill about him without that. But since that was the reason you went—"

"No, dear cousin," said Romola, interrupting her earnestly, "pray do not talk so. I wish above all things to find that young woman and her children, and to take care of them. They are quite helpless. Say nothing against it; that is the thing I shall do first of all."

"Well," said Monna Brigida, shrugging her shoulders and lowering her voice with an air of puzzled discomfiture, "if that's being a Piagnone, I've been taking peas for paternosters.* Why, Fra Girolamo said as good as that widows ought not to marry again.* Step in at the door and it's a sin and a shame, it seems; but come down the chimney and you're welcome. *Two* children—Santiddio!"

"Cousin, the poor thing has done no conscious wrong: she is ignorant of everything. I will tell you—but not now."

Early the next morning Romola's steps were directed to the house beyond San Ambrogio where she had once found[4] Tessa; but it was as she had feared: Tessa was gone. Romola conjectured that Tito had sent her away beforehand to some spot where he had intended to join her, for she did not believe that he would willingly part with those children. It was a painful conjecture, because, if Tessa were out of Florence, there was hardly a chance of finding her, and Romola pictured the childish creature waiting and waiting at some wayside spot in wondering helpless misery. Those who lived near could tell her nothing except that old deaf Lisa had gone away a week ago with her goods, but no one knew where[5] Tessa had gone. Romola saw no further active search open to her; for she had no knowledge that could serve as a starting-point for inquiry, and not only her innate reserve but a more noble sensitiveness made her shrink from assuming an attitude of generosity in the eyes of others by publishing Tessa's relation to Tito along with her own desire to find her. Many days passed in anxious inaction. Even under strong solicitation from other thoughts Romola found her heart palpitating if she caught sight of a

3 that ⟨your husband⟩ *MS*   4 {once} found *MS*
5 where] ⟨where⟩ when *MS*

pair of round brown legs, or of a short woman in the contadina dress.

She[6] never for a moment told herself that it was heroism or exalted charity in her to seek these beings; she needed something that she was bound specially to care for; she yearned to clasp the children and to make them love her. This at least would be some sweet result, for others as well as herself, from all her past sorrow. It appeared there was much property of Tito's to which she had a claim; but she distrusted the cleanness of that money, and she had determined to make it all over to the State, except so much as was equal to the price of her father's library. This would be enough for the modest support of Tessa and the children. But Monna Brigida threw such planning into the background by clamorously insisting that Romola must live with her and never forsake her till she had seen her safe in Paradise—else why had she persuaded her to turn Piagnone?—and if Romola wanted to rear other people's children, she, Monna Brigida, must rear them too. Only they must be found first.

Romola felt the full force of that innuendo. But strong feeling unsatisfied is never without its superstition, either of hope or despair. Romola's was the superstition of hope: *somehow* she was to find that mother and the children. And at last another direction [7]for active inquiry suggested itself. She learned that Tito had provided horses and mules to await him in San Gallo; he was therefore going to leave Florence by the gate of San Gallo, and she determined, though without much confidence in the issue, to try and ascertain from the gatekeepers if they had observed any one corresponding to the description of Tessa, with her children, to have passed the gates before the morning of the ninth of April. Walking along the Via San Gallo, and looking watchfully about her through her long widow's veil, lest she should miss any object that might aid her, she descried Bratti chaffering with a customer. That roaming man, she thought, might aid her: she would not mind talking of Tessa to *him*. But as she put aside her veil and crossed the street towards him, she saw something hanging from the corner of his basket which made her heart leap with a much stronger hope.

"Bratti, my friend," she said abruptly, "where did you get that necklace?"

"Your servant, Madonna," said Bratti, looking round at her very deliberately, his mind not being subject to surprise. "It's a necklace worth money, but I shall get little by it, for my heart's too tender for a trader's; I've[8] promised to keep it in pledge."[9]

6 dress. {¶} She *MS*   7 ⟨of⟩ for *MS*
8 I've] I have *1 2 3*   9 trader's: {I've promised to keep it in pledge."} *MS*

"Pray tell me where you got it:—from a little woman named Tessa, is it not true?"

"Ah! if you know her," said Bratti, "and would [1]redeem it of me at a small profit, and give it her again, you'd be doing a charity, for she cried at parting with it—you'd have thought she was running into a brook. It's a small profit I'll charge you. You shall have it for a florin, for I don't like to be hard-hearted."

"Where is she?" said Romola, giving him the money, and unclasping the necklace from the basket in joyful agitation.

"Outside the gate there, at the other end of the Borgo, at old Sibilla Manetti's: anybody will tell you which is the house."

Romola went along with winged feet, blessing that incident of the Carnival which had made her learn by heart the [2]appearance of this necklace. Soon she was at the house she sought. The young woman and the children were in the inner room—were to have been fetched away a fortnight ago and more—had no money, only their clothes, [3]to pay a poor widow with for their food and lodging. But since Madonna knew them—[4]Romola waited to hear no more, but opened the door.

Tessa was seated on the low bed: her crying had passed into tearless sobs[5], and she was looking with sad blank eyes at the two children, who were playing in an opposite corner—Lillo covering his head with his skirt and roaring at Ninna to frighten her, then peeping out again to see how she bore it. The door was a little behind Tessa, and she did not turn round when it opened, thinking it was only the old woman: expectation was no longer alive. Romola had thrown aside her veil and paused a moment, holding the necklace in sight. Then she said, in that [6]pure voice that used to cheer her father,[7]—

"Tessa!"

Tessa started to her feet and looked round.

"See," said Romola, clasping the beads on Tessa's neck, "God has sent me to you again."

The poor thing screamed and sobbed, and clung to the arms that fastened the necklace. She could not speak. The two children came from their corner, laid hold of their mother's skirts, and looked up with wide eyes at Romola.

That day they all went home to Monna Brigida's, in the Borgo degli Albizzi[8]. Romola had made known to Tessa by gentle degrees, that Naldo could never come to her again; not because he was cruel, but because he was dead.

1 ⟨buy⟩ redeem MS
2 ⟨look⟩ appearance MS
3 ⟨with⟩ to pay a {poor} widow⟨-woman⟩ with MS
4 them—⟨¶⟩ Romola MS
5 sobs] {convulsive} sobs MS
6 ⟨clear⟩ pure MS
7 father, ⟨clearing the air and resting in the ear,⟩ MS
8 Brigida's {in the Borgo degli Albizzi} MS

"But be comforted, my Tessa," said Romola. "I am come to take care of you always. And we have got Lillo and Ninna."

Monna Brigida's mouth twitched in the struggle between her awe of Romola and the desire to speak unseasonably.

"Let be, for the present," she thought; "but it seems to me a thousand years till I tell this little contadina, who seems not to know how many fingers she's got on her hand, who Romola is. And I *will* tell her some day, else she'll never know her place. It's all very well for Romola; nobody will call their souls their own when she's by; but if I'm to have this puss-faced minx living [9]in my house, she must be humble to me."

However, Monna Brigida wanted to give the children too many sweets for their supper, and confessed to Romola, the last thing before going to bed, that it would be a shame not to take care of such cherubs.

"But you must give up to me a little, Romola, about their eating, and those things. For you have never had[1] a baby, and I had twins, only they died [2]as soon as they were born."

9 ⟨with me⟩ in my house *MS*   1 {have} never had *MS*
2 ⟨before⟩ as soon as *MS*

CHAPTER LXXI.

THE CONFESSION

WHEN Romola brought home Tessa and the children April was already near its close, and the other great anxiety on her mind had been wrought to its highest pitch by the publication in print of Fra Girolamo's Trial, or rather of the confessions drawn from him by the sixteen Florentine citizens commissioned to interrogate him. [1]The appearance of this document, issued by order of the Signoria, had called forth such strong expressions of public suspicion and discontent, that severe measures were immediately taken for recalling it. Of course there were copies accidentally mislaid, and a second edition, *not* by order of the Signoria, was soon in the hands of eager readers.

Romola, who began to despair of ever [2]speaking with Fra Girolamo, read this evidence again and again, desiring to judge it by some clearer light than the contradictory impressions that were taking the form of assertions in the mouths of both partisans and enemies. In the more devout followers of Savonarola his want of constancy under torture, and his retractation of prophetic claims, had produced a consternation too profound to be at once displaced as it ultimately was by the suspicion, which soon grew into a positive datum, that any reported words of his which were in inexplicable contradiction to their faith in him, [3]had not come from the lips of the Prophet, but from the falsifying pen of Ser Ceccone,* that notary of evil repute, who had made the digest of the examination. But there were obvious facts that at once threw discredit on the printed document. Was not the list of sixteen examiners half made up of the Prophet's bitterest enemies? Was not the notorious Dolfo Spini one of the new Eight prematurely elected, in order to load the dice* against a man whose ruin had been determined on by the party in power? It was but a murder with slow formalities that was being transacted in the Old Palace. The Signoria had resolved to drive a good bargain with the Pope and the Duke of Milan, by extinguishing the man who was as great a molestation to vicious citizens and greedy foreign tyrants as to a corrupt clergy. The Frate had been doomed beforehand, and the only question that was pretended to exist now was, whether the Republic, in return for a permission to lay a tax on ecclesiastical property,* should deliver him alive into the hands of the Pope, or whether the Pope should further concede to the Republic what its

1 ⟨No sooner had the Signoria issued this document than⟩ The *MS*
2 ⟨seeing⟩ speaking with *MS*　　　　　　　　　3 ⟨were⟩ had *MS*

dignity demanded—the privilege of hanging and burning its own Prophet on its own Piazza.

Who, under such circumstances, would give full credit to this so-called confession? If the Frate had denied his prophetic gift, the denial had only been wrenched from him by the agony of torture—agony that, in his sensitive frame, must quickly produce raving. What if these wicked examiners declared that he had only had the torture of the rope and pully thrice, and[4] only on one day, and that his confessions had been made when he was under no bodily coercion—was that to be believed? He had been tortured much more; he had been tortured in proportion to the distress his confessions had created in the hearts of those who loved him.

Other friends of Savonarola, who were less ardent partisans, did not doubt the substantial [5]genuineness of the confession, however it[6] might have been coloured by the transpositions and additions of the notary; but they argued indignantly that[7] there was nothing which could warrant a condemnation to death, or even to grave punishment. It must be clear to all impartial men that if this examination represented the only evidence against the Frate, he would die, not for any crime, but because he had made himself inconvenient to the Pope, to the rapacious Italian States that wanted to dismember their Tuscan neighbour, and to those unworthy citizens who sought to gratify their private ambition in opposition to the common weal.

Not[8] a shadow of political crime had been proved against him. Not one stain had been detected on his private conduct: his fellow monks, [9]including one who had formerly been his secretary* for several years, and who[1], with more than the average culture of his companions, had a disposition to criticize Fra Girolamo's rule as Prior, bore testimony, even after the shock of his retractation, to an unimpeachable purity and consistency in his life, which had commanded their unsuspecting veneration. The Pope himself had not been able to raise a charge of heresy against the Frate, except on the ground of disobedience to a mandate, and disregard of the sentence of excommunication. It was difficult to justify that breach of discipline by argument, but[2] there was a moral insurgence in the minds of grave men against the court of Rome, which tended to confound the theoretic distinction between the Church and churchmen, and to lighten the scandal of disobedience.

4 and ⟨that⟩ only MS
5 ⟨verity⟩ genuineness of the ⟨documents⟩ confessions MS
6 confession, however it] confessions however they MS
7 that ⟨it contained⟩ ⟨this [?provided] that Examination⟩ MS
8 weal. {¶} Not MS   9 ⟨even⟩ including one who had {formerly} been MS
1 and {who} MS   2 but ⟨the state of⟩ MS

Men of ordinary morality and public spirit felt that[3] the triumph of the Frate's enemies was really the triumph of gross licence. And keen Florentines like Soderini and Piero Guicciardini may well have had an angry smile on their lips at a severity which dispensed with all law in order to hang and burn a man in whom the seductions of a public career had warped the strictness of his veracity; may well have remarked that if the Frate had mixed a much deeper fraud with a zeal and ability less inconvenient to high personages, the fraud would have been regarded as an excellent oil for ecclesiastical and political wheels.

Nevertheless such shrewd men were forced to admit that, however poor a figure the Florentine government made in its clumsy pretence of a judicial warrant for what had in fact been predetermined as an act of policy, the measures of the Pope against Savonarola were necessary measures[4] of self-defence. Not to try and rid himself of a man who wanted to stir up the powers of Europe to summon a General Council and depose him, would have been adding ineptitude to iniquity. There was no denying that towards Alexander the Sixth Savonarola was a rebel, and what was much more, a dangerous rebel. Florence had heard him say, and had well understood what he meant, that he would not *obey the devil*.* It was inevitably a life and death struggle between the Frate and the Pope; but it was less inevitable that Florence should make itself the Pope's executioner.

Romola's ears were filled in this way with the suggestions of a faith still ardent under its wounds, and the suggestions of worldly discernment, judging things according to a very moderate standard of what is possible to human nature. She could be satisfied with neither. She brought to her long meditations over that printed document[5] many painful observations, registered more or less consciously through the years of her discipleship, which[6] whispered a presentiment that Savonarola's retractation of his prophetic claims was not merely a spasmodic effort to escape from torture. But, on the other hand, her soul cried out for some explanation of his lapses which would make it still possible for her to believe that the main striving of his life had been pure and grand. The recent memory of the [7]selfish discontent which had come over her like a blighting wind along with the loss of her trust in the man who had been for her an incarnation of the highest motives, had produced[8] a reaction which is known to many as a sort of faith [9]that has sprung up to them out of the very depths of

---

3 Men of . . . that] It was felt by men of ordinary morality and public spirit that *MS*

4 {necessary} measures *MS*   5 document ⟨of the Examination⟩ *MS*
6 which ⟨forbade her to believe⟩ *MS*
7 ⟨cold⟩ selfish discontent ⟨into⟩ which ⟨she⟩ had *MS*   8 produced ⟨in her⟩ *MS*
9 ⟨which⟩ that *MS*

their despair. It was impossible, she said now, that the negative[1] dis-
believing thoughts which had made her soul arid of all good, could be
founded in the truth of things: impossible that[2] it had not been a living spirit, and no hollow pretence, which had once breathed in the
Frate's words, and kindled a new life in her. Whatever falsehood
there had been in him, had been a fall[3] and not a purpose; a gradual
entanglement in which he struggled, not a contrivance encouraged by
success.

Looking at the printed confessions she saw many sentences which
bore the stamp of bungling fabrication: they had that emphasis and
repetition in self-accusation which none but very low hypocrites use
to their fellow-men. But the fact that these sentences were in striking
opposition, not only to the character of Savonarola, but also to the
general tone of the confessions, strengthened the impression that the
rest of the text represented in the main what had really fallen from
his lips. Hardly a word was dishonourable to him except what turned
on his prophetic annunciations. He was unvarying in his statement of
the ends he had pursued for Florence, the Church, and the world;
and, apart from the mixture of falsity in that claim to special inspiration by which he sought to gain hold of men's minds, there was no
admission of having used unworthy means. Even in this confession,
and without expurgation of the notary's malign phrases, Fra Girolamo
shone forth as a man who had sought his own glory indeed, but
sought it by labouring for the very highest end—the moral welfare of
men—not by vague exhortations, but by striving to turn beliefs into
energies that would work in all the details of life.

"Everything that I have done," said one memorable passage,* which
may perhaps have had its erasures and interpolations, "I have done
with the design of being for ever famous, in the present and in future
ages; and that I might win credit in Florence; and that nothing of
great import should be done without my sanction. And when I had
thus established my position in Florence, I had it in my mind to do
great things in Italy and beyond Italy, by means of those chief personages with whom I had contracted friendship and consulted on high
matters, such as this of the General Council. And in proportion as
my first efforts succeeded, I should have adopted further measures.
Above all, when the General Council had once been brought about, I
intended to rouse the princes of Christendom, and especially those
beyond the borders of Italy, to subdue the infidels. It was not much
in my thoughts to get myself made a Cardinal or Pope; for when I

1 {the} negative *MS*
2 that ⟨the spirit⟩ {it had not . . . pretence} which had . . . life in her, ⟨had not been
a living spirit and no hollow pretence.⟩ *MS*
3 fall ⟨and a gradual entanglement⟩ *MS*

should have achieved the work I had in view, I should, without being Pope, have been the first man in the world in the authority I should have possessed, and the reverence that would have been paid me. If I had been made Pope, I would not have refused the office: but it seemed to me that to be the head of that work was a greater thing than to be Pope; because a man without virtue may be Pope, but *such a work as I contemplated demanded a man of excellent virtues.*"

That blending of ambition with belief[4] in the supremacy of goodness made no new tone to Romola, who had been used to hear it in the voice that rang through the Duomo. It was the habit of [5]Savonarola's mind to conceive great things, and to feel that he was the man to do them. Iniquity should be brought low; the cause of justice, purity, and love should triumph; and it should triumph by his voice, by his work, by his blood. In moments of ecstatic contemplation, doubtless, the sense of self melted in the sense of the Unspeakable[6], and in that part of his experience lay the elements of genuine self-abasement; but in the presence of his fellow-men for whom he was to act, pre-eminence seemed a necessary condition of his life.

[7]And perhaps this confession, even when it described a doubleness that was conscious and deliberate, really implied no more than that wavering of belief[8] concerning his own impressions and motives which most human beings who have not a stupid inflexibility of self-confidence must be liable to under a marked change of external conditions?[9] In[1] a life where the experience was so tumultuously mixed

4 That blending of ambition with belief] That blended ambition and belief *MS*

5 ⟨his⟩ Savonarola's *MS*   6 Unspeakable] *MS 3P* unspeakable *CM 1 2*

7 ⟨Neither was that part of his confession quite unforeshadowed for Romola, in which he declared that he had begun to preach the coming scourge and renovation without the suggestions of visions or any supernatural teaching, but solely from a conviction founded on arguments drawn from Scripture and reason, and that finding his doctrine lay hold on men's minds, he sought to tighten its grasp by affirming still higher evidence than he possessed. ⟨⟨Notwithstanding Romola's ardour, her⟩⟩ Romola's habitual contact with minds sarcastically critical of the Frate, made her keenly sensitive to whatever seemed to justify their criticism. She had again and again felt uneasy, when he was preaching, at the perception that he was being urged into impromptu statements, and even when he narrated his great vision of the {divine} sword hanging from the sky, which she did not doubt to have been originally a ⟨⟨spontaneous mental impression⟩⟩ vision, she always felt inclined to shut her ears when he went on amplifying it by an elaborate accompaniment of articulate voices.⟩ ¶ And ⟨yet⟩ perhaps this confession, {even when . . . conscious and deliberate,} really *MS*

8 wavering {of} belief *MS*

9 conditions? ⟨Romola remembered how she herself had been subject to continual fluctuations in surveying her own impulses and conduct in the years she had lived through with Tito. Often, if some one had condemned her, that condemnation would have turned the scale, and she would have said, "I was driven more by pride and anger than by anything better." And in⟩ In *MS*

1 conditions? In] conditions. In *2 3*

as it must have been in the Frate's, what a possibility was opened for a change of self-judgment, when, instead of eyes that venerated and knees that knelt, instead of a great work on its way to accomplishment, and in its prosperity stamping the agent as a chosen instrument, there came the hooting and the spitting and the curses of the crowd; and then the hard faces of enemies [2]made judges; and then the horrible torture, and with the torture the irrepressible cry, "It is true, what you would have me say: let me go, do not torture me again: yes, yes, I am guilty. O God! [3]Thy stroke has reached me!"

As Romola thought of the anguish that must have followed the confession—whether, in the subsequent solitude of the prison, conscience retracted or confirmed[4] the self-taxing words—that anguish seemed to be pressing on her own heart and urging the slow bitter tears. Every vulgar self-ignorant person in Florence was glibly pronouncing on this man's demerits, while he[5] was knowing a depth of sorrow which can only be known to the soul that has loved and sought the most perfect thing, and beholds itself fallen.

She had not then seen—what she saw afterwards—the evidence of the Frate's mental state after he had had thus to lay his mouth in the dust. As the days went by, the reports of new unpublished examinations, eliciting no change of confessions, ceased; Savonarola was left alone in his prison and allowed pen and ink for a while, that, if he liked, he might use his poor bruised and strained right arm to write with. He wrote; but what he wrote was no vindication of his innocence, no protest against the proceedings used towards him: it was a continued colloquy with that divine purity with which he sought complete reunion; it was the outpouring of self-abasement; it was one long cry for inward renovation. [6]No lingering echoes of the old vehement[7] self-assertion, "Look at my work, for it is good, and those who set their faces against it are the children of the devil!" The voice of Sadness tells him, "God placed thee in the midst of the people even as if thou hadst been one of the excellent. In this way thou hast taught others, and hast failed to learn thyself. Thou hast cured others: and thou thyself hast been still diseased. Thy heart was [8]lifted up at the beauty of thy own deeds, and through this thou hast lost thy wisdom and art become, and shalt be to all eternity, nothing. . . . After so many benefits with which God has honoured thee, thou art fallen into the depths of the sea; and after so many gifts bestowed on thee, thou, by thy pride and vainglory, hast scandalized all the world." And when Hope speaks and argues that the divine love has not forsaken him, it says nothing now of a great work to be done, but

2 (turned) made *MS*   3 (at last) thy *MS*   4 confirmed (the suffering) *MS*
5 while *he*] *3P* and he *MS CM 1 2*   6 (The old tone) No *MS*
7 the old vehement] vehement *MS*   8 (exalted) lifted *MS*

only says, "Thou art not forsaken, else why is thy heart bowed in penitence? That too is[9] a gift."

There is no jot of worthy evidence that from the time of his imprisonment to the supreme moment, Savonarola thought or spoke of himself as a martyr. The idea of martyrdom had been to him a passion dividing the dream of the future with the triumph of beholding his work achieved. And now, in place of both, had come a resignation which he called by no glorifying name.

But therefore he may the more fitly be called a martyr by his fellow-men to all time[1]. For power rose against him not because of his sins, but because of his greatness—not because he sought to deceive the world, but because he sought to make it noble. And through[2] that greatness of his he endured a double agony: not only the reviling, and the torture, and the death-throe, but the agony of sinking from the vision of glorious achievement into that deep shadow where he could only say, "I count as nothing: darkness encompasses me: yet the light I saw was the true[3] light."

9 That too is] *MS 1 2 3* That, too, is *CM*
1 *But therefore . . . time*] *3P* But therefore . . . time *MS CM 1 2*
2 through] for *MS*   3 the true] {a} true *MS*

CHAPTER LXXII.

THE LAST SILENCE

ROMOLA had seemed to hear, as if they had been a cry, the words repeated to her by many lips—the words uttered by Savonarola when he took leave of those Brethren of San Marco who had come to witness his signature of the Confession: "Pray for me, for God has withdrawn from me the spirit of prophecy."

Those words had shaken her with new doubts as to the mode in which he looked back at the past in moments of complete self-possession. And the doubts were strengthened by more piteous things still, which soon reached her ears.

The nineteenth of May had come, and by that day's sunshine there had entered into Florence the two Papal Commissaries, charged with the completion of Savonarola's trial. They entered amid the acclamations of the people, calling for the death of the Frate. For now the popular cry was, "It is the[1] Frate's deception that has brought[2] on all our misfortunes; let him be burned, and all things right will be done, and our evils will cease."

The next day it is well certified that there was fresh and fresh torture of the shattered sensitive frame; and now, at[3] the first threat and first sight[4] of the horrible implements, Savonarola, in convulsed agitation, fell on his knees, and in brief, passionate words, *retracted his confession*, declared that he had spoken falsely in denying his prophetic gift, and that if he suffered[5], he would suffer for the truth—"The things that I have spoken, I had them from God."

But not the less the torture was laid upon him, and when he was under it he was asked why he had uttered those retracting words. Men were not demons in those days, and yet nothing but confessions of guilt were held a reason for release from torture. The answer came: "I said it that I might seem good; tear me no more, I will tell you the truth."*

There were Florentine assessors at this new trial, and those words of twofold retraction[6] had soon spread. They filled Romola with dismayed uncertainty.

"But"—it flashed across her—"there will come a moment when he may speak. When there is no dread hanging over him but the dread

---

1 the ⟨Frate who deceived⟩ *MS*   2 has brought] brought *MS*
3 {now} at *MS*   4 first threat and first sight] first sight *2 3*
5 declared that . . . suffered] declared that if he suffered *MS*
6 words of twofold retraction] words {of retractation} *MS*

of falsehood, when they have brought him into the presence of death, when he is lifted above the people, and looks on them for the last time, they cannot hinder him from speaking a last decisive word. I will be there."

Three days after, on the 23rd of May, 1498, there was again a long narrow platform stretching across the great Piazza, from the Palazzo Vecchio towards the Tetto* de' Pisani. But there was no grove of fuel as before: instead of that, there was one great heap of fuel placed on the circular area which made the termination of the long narrow platform. And above this heap of fuel rose a gibbet with three halters on it; a gibbet which, having two arms, still looked so much like a cross as to make some beholders uncomfortable, though one arm had been truncated to avoid the resemblance.

On the marble terrace of the Palazzo were three tribunals; one near the door for the Bishop, who was to perform the ceremony of degradation on Fra Girolamo and the two Brethren who were to suffer as his followers and accomplices; another for the Papal Commissaries, who were to pronounce them heretics and schismatics, and deliver them over to the secular arm; and a third, close to Marzocco, at the corner of the terrace where the platform began, for the Gonfaloniere, and the Eight who were to pronounce the sentence of death.

Again the Piazza was thronged with expectant faces: again there was to be a great fire kindled. In the majority of the crowd that pressed around the gibbet the expectation was that of ferocious hatred, or of mere hard curiosity to behold a barbarous sight. But there were still many spectators on the wide pavement, on the roofs, and at the windows, who, in the midst of their bitter grief and their own endurance of insult as hypocritical Piagnoni, were not without a lingering hope, even at this eleventh hour, that God would interpose, by some sign, to manifest their beloved Prophet as His servant. And there were yet more who looked forward with trembling eagerness, as Romola did, to that final moment when Savonarola might say, "O people, I was innocent of deceit."

Romola was at a window on the north side of the Piazza, far away from the marble terrace where the tribunals stood; and near her[7], also looking on in painful doubt concerning the[8] man who had won his [9]early reverence, was a young Florentine[1] of two-and-twenty, named Jacopo Nardi,* afterwards[2] to deserve honour as one of the very few[3] who, feeling Fra Girolamo's eminence, have written about him with

---

7 near her ⟨was a youth of seventeen named Iacopo Nardi⟩ MS   8 the] a MS
9 ⟨young⟩ early reverence—was a ⟨youth⟩ young man of ⟨seventeen⟩ two and twenty MS
1 Florentine] man MS   2 Nardi, afterwards] Nardi, who was afterwards MS
3 few] few men MS

the simple desire to be veracious. He had said to Romola, with respectful gentleness, when he saw the struggle in her between her shuddering horror of the scene and her yearning to witness what might happen in the last moment,

"Madonna, there is no need for you to look at these cruel things. I will tell you when he comes out of the Palazzo. Trust to me; I know what you would see."

Romola covered her face, but the hootings that seemed to make the hideous scene still visible could not be shut out. At last her arm was touched, and she heard the words, "He comes." She looked towards the Palace, and could see Savonarola led out in his Dominican garb; could see him standing before the Bishop, and being stripped of the black mantle, the white scapulary, and long white tunic, till he stood in a close woollen under-tunic, that told of no sacred office, no rank. He had been degraded, and cut off from the Church Militant.

The baser part of the multitude delight in degradations, apart from any hatred; it is the satire they best understand[4]. There was a fresh hoot of triumph as the three degraded Brethren passed on to the tribunal of the Papal Commissaries, who were to pronounce them schismatics and heretics. Did not the Prophet look like a schismatic and heretic now? It is easy to believe in the damnable state of a man who stands stripped and degraded.

Then the third tribunal was passed—that of the Florentine officials who were to pronounce sentence, and amongst[5] whom, even at her distance, Romola could discern the odious figure of Dolfo Spini, indued in the grave black *lucco*, as one of the Eight.

Then the three figures, in their close white raiment, trod their way along the platform, amidst yells and grating tones of insult.

"Cover your eyes, madonna," said Jacopo Nardi; "Fra Girolamo will be the last."

It was not long before she had to uncover them again. Savonarola[6] was there. He was not far off her now. He had mounted the steps; she could see him look round on the multitude.

But in the same moment expectation died, and she only saw what he was seeing—torches waving to kindle the fuel beneath his dead body, faces glaring with a yet worse light; she only heard what *he* was hearing—gross jests, taunts, and curses.

The moment was past. Her face was covered again, and she only knew that Savonarola's voice had passed into eternal silence.

4 understand ⟨and delight in⟩ *MS*
5 amongst ⟨them⟩ *MS*   6 Savonarola] The Frate *MS*

EPILOGUE

On the evening of the twenty-second of May, 1509[1], five persons, of whose history we have known something, were seated in a handsome upper room opening on to a loggia which, at its right-hand corner, looked all along the Borgo Pinti, and over the city gate towards Fiesole, and the solemn heights beyond it.

At one end of the room was an archway opening into [2]a narrow inner room, hardly more than a recess, where the light fell from above on a small altar covered with fair white linen. Over the altar was a picture, discernible at the distance where the little party sat only as the small full-length portrait of a Dominican Brother. For it was shaded from the light above by overhanging branches and wreaths of flowers, and the fresh tapers below it were unlit. But it seemed that the decoration of the altar and its recess was[3] not complete. For part of the floor was [4]strown with a confusion of flowers and green boughs, and among them sat a delicate blue-eyed girl of thirteen[5], tossing her long light-brown hair out of her eyes, as she made selections for the wreaths she was weaving, or looked up at her mother's work in the same kind, and told her how to do it with a little air of instruction.

For that mother was not very clever at weaving flowers or at any other work. Tessa's fingers had not become more adroit with the years—only very much fatter. She got on slowly and turned her head about a good deal, and asked Ninna's opinion with much deference; for Tessa never ceased to be astonished at the wisdom of her children. She still wore her contadina gown: it was only broader than the old one; and there was the silver pin in her rough curly brown hair, and round her neck the memorable necklace, with a red cord under it, that ended mysteriously in her bosom. Her rounded face wore even a more perfect look of childish content than in her younger days: everybody was so good in the world, Tessa thought; even Monna Brigida never found fault with her now, and did little else than sleep, which was an amiable practice in everybody, and one that Tessa liked for herself.

Monna Brigida was asleep at this moment, in a straight-backed arm-chair, a couple of yards off. Her hair, parting backward under her black hood, had that soft whiteness which is not like snow or anything else, but is simply the lovely whiteness of aged hair. Her chin

---

1 1509] 1510 *MS*   2 ⟨an inner⟩ a narrow inner *MS*
3 was] were *MS*   4 ⟨strewed⟩ strown *MS*
5 thirteen] fourteen or fifteen *MS*

had sunk on her bosom, and her hands rested on the elbow of her chair. She had not been weaving flowers or doing anything else: she had only been looking on as usual, and as usual had fallen asleep.

The other two figures were seated farther off, at the wide doorway that opened on to the loggia. Lillo sat on the ground with his back against the angle of the door-post, and his long legs stretched out, while he held a large book open on his knee and occasionally made a dash with his hand at an inquisitive fly, with[6] an air of interest stronger than that excited by the finely-printed copy of Petrarch which he kept open at one place, as if he were learning something by heart.

Romola sat nearly opposite Lillo, but she was not observing him. Her hands were crossed on her lap and her eyes were fixed absently on the distant mountains: she was evidently unconscious of anything around her. An eager life had left its marks upon her: the finely moulded cheek had sunk a little, the golden crown was less massive; but there was a placidity in Romola's face which had never belonged to it in youth. It is but once that we can know our worst sorrows, and Romola had known them while life was new.

Absorbed in this way, she was not at first aware that Lillo had ceased to look at his book, and was watching her with a slightly impatient air, which meant that he wanted to talk to her, but was not quite sure whether she would like that entertainment just now. But persevering looks make themselves felt at last. Romola did presently turn away her eyes from the distance and met Lillo's impatient dark gaze with a brighter and brighter smile. He shuffled along the floor, still keeping the book on his lap, till he got close to her and lodged his chin on her knee.

"What is it, Lillo?" said Romola, pulling his hair back from his brow. Lillo was a handsome lad, but his features were turning out to be more massive and less regular than his father's. The blood of the Tuscan peasant was in his veins.

"Mamma Romola, what am I to be?" he said, well contented that there was a prospect of talking till it would be too late to con "Spirto gentil"* any longer.

"What should you like to be, Lillo? You might be a scholar. My father was a scholar, you know and taught me a great deal. That is the reason why I can teach you."

"Yes," said Lillo, rather hesitatingly. "But he is old and blind in the picture. Did he get a great deal of glory?"

"Not much, Lillo. The world was not always very kind to him, and he saw meaner men than himself put into higher places, because they could flatter and say what was false. And then his dear son thought it right to leave him and become a monk; and after that, my father being blind and lonely, felt[7] unable to do the things that would have made his learning of greater use[8] to men, so that he might still have lived in his works after he was in his grave."

"I should not like that sort of life," said Lillo. "I should like to be something that would make me a great man, and very happy besides—something that would not hinder me from having a good deal of pleasure."

"That is not easy, my Lillo. It[9] is only a poor sort of happiness that could ever come by caring very much about our own narrow pleasures. We can only have the highest happiness, such as goes along with being a great man, by having wide thoughts, and much feeling for the rest of the world, as well as ourselves; and this sort of happiness often brings so much pain with it, that we can only tell it from pain by its being what[1] we would choose before everything else, [2]because our souls see it is good. There are so many things wrong and difficult in the world, that no man can be great—he can hardly keep himself from wickedness—unless he gives up thinking much about pleasures[3] or rewards, and gets strength to endure what is hard and painful. My father had the greatness that belongs to integrity; he chose poverty and obscurity rather than falsehood. And there was Fra Girolamo—you know why I keep to-morrow sacred: *he* had the greatness which belongs to a life spent in struggling against powerful wrong, and in trying to raise men to the highest deeds they are capable of. And so, my Lillo, if you mean to act nobly and seek to know the best things God has put within reach[4] of men, you must learn to fix your mind on that end, and not on what will happen to you because of it. And remember, if you were to choose something lower, and make it the rule of your life to seek your own pleasure and escape from what is disagreeable, calamity might come just the same; and it would be calamity falling on a base mind, which is the one form of sorrow that has no balm in it, and that may well make a man say,—'It would have been better for me if I had never been born.' I will tell you something, Lillo."

Romola paused a moment[5]. She had taken Lillo's cheeks between her hands, and his young eyes were meeting hers.

"There was a man to whom I was very near, so that I could see a

7 father {being blind and lonely} felt ⟨that he would not⟩ unable to do the things ⟨he had wanted to do to make⟩ that *MS*

8 {greater} use *MS*   9 It] For it *MS*

1 by its being what] because it is what *MS*   2 ⟨since⟩—because *MS*

3 pleasures] pleasure *2 3*   4 {God has put} within reach *MS*

5 a moment] for a moment *2 3*

great deal of his life, who made almost every one fond of him, for he was young, and clever, and beautiful, and his manners to all were gentle and kind. I believe, when I first knew him, he never thought of doing anything[6] cruel or base. But because he tried to slip away from everything that was unpleasant, and cared for nothing else so much as his own safety, he came at last to commit some of the basest deeds—such as make men infamous. He denied his father, and left him to misery; he betrayed every trust that was reposed in him, that he might keep himself safe and get rich and prosperous. Yet calamity overtook[7] him."

Again Romola paused. Her voice was unsteady, and Lillo was looking up at her [8]with awed[9] wonder.

"Another time, my Lillo—I will tell you another time. See, there are our old Piero di Cosimo and Nello coming up the Borgo Pinti, bringing us their flowers. Let us go and wave our hands to them, that they may know we see them."

"How queer old Piero is," said Lillo, as they stood at the corner of the loggia, watching the advancing figures. "He abuses you for dressing the altar, and thinking so much of Fra Girolamo, and yet he brings you the flowers."

"Never mind," said Romola. "There are many good people who did not love Fra Girolamo. Perhaps I should never have learned to love him if he had not helped me when I was in great need."

THE END.

6 of doing anything] of anything 2 3   7 overtook] came upon MS
8 ⟨in⟩ with MS   9 awed] pale MS

EXPLANATORY NOTES

Writing to John Blackwood in December 1861 about George Eliot's researches into 15th-cent. Florentine history, George Henry Lewes announced 'as a matter of fact I know that she has immensely more knowledge of the particular period than any other writer who has touched it'. He was exaggerating only slightly: George Eliot's reading in the subject (see App. B), and her accumulation of information about it, were alike prodigious. Nor was the knowledge she thus acquired worn lightly: few historical novels are as closely tied to documentary sources as *Romola*. From the notes that follow it will be clear quite how much of her preparatory research found its way bodily into the novel, where it tends on occasions to weigh down the text with what the *Saturday Review* characterized as 'instructive antiquarianism'.

The geography of Florence as laid out in the novel is precise and almost always accurate. I point out George Eliot's very occasional error; otherwise the reader should assume that all details and directions are correct as described. Though it is unlikely that anyone today would seek to use *Romola* as a guidebook to the city, I also indicate when the names of streets have changed since the 1860s. In fact, however, it seems that at the height of its popularity the novel was used for just such a purpose; in an article entitled 'Two Cities—Two Books' in *Blackwood's Edinburgh Magazine* in 1874, Margaret Oliphant reports that a Florentine bookseller had assured her that he sold as many as 500 copies a year to foreign tourists. She goes on to observe that 'if there could be anything more quaint and strange than the invasion of the jealous and proud old town by Mr Cook's excursionists, it would be the vision thus suggested to us of an excursionist sallying forth with "Romola" instead of Baedeker in his hand to "do" Florence'. (Ironically, Mrs Oliphant comforts herself with the reflection that 'If London should ever fall into decadence and decay, it is a consolation to think that there is nothing in it which will bring wandering hordes across the Atlantic, or tempt the Continental to dare the dangers of the Channel.')

For convenience of text layout, George Eliot's own *foot*notes (and her single *end*note) to the novel are interspersed in sequence with my own explanatory notes; they are given in inverted commas, followed by the designation [GE] in square brackets. Occasionally I interpolate explanatory remarks of my own within quotations given in the notes; these are indicated by square brackets.

3 **Pillars of Hercules** The rocks on either side of the straits of Gibraltar, supposedly joined together until Hercules tore them apart, and in ancient times thought to mark the end of the habitable world. There are at least two notable references to them in the Italian literature that GE read in her preparations for *Romola*, each offering a rather different perspective on the legend. In canto 26 of Dante's *Inferno* (ll. 107–9), Ulysses talks of 'quella foce stretta | dov' Ercule segnò li suoi riguardi, | acciò che l'uom più oltre non si metta' (that narrow outlet where Hercules set up his

landmarks so that men should not pass beyond). On the other hand, in canto 26 of Luigi Pulci's *Il morgante maggiore*, in a passage underlined by GE in her own copy of the poem, Rinaldo is told by Astarotte (stanza 228) that 'Uno error lungo e fioco . . . fa che si dice d'Ercul le colonne | e che più la molti periti sonne' (it is an old and foolish error that those columns should be called those of Hercules, and that beyond them many should have been thought to have perished). Astarotte goes on to explain that one can indeed sail beyond, and reach another hemisphere where there are cities, castles, and empires. GE's novel, of course, opens in the year 1492, and she goes on to refer to Columbus about to make his journey to the new world.

4 **Palos** Columbus sailed from Palos in Andalucia on 3 Aug. 1492.

4 **revisit the glimpses** Cf. 'What may this mean, | That thou, dead corse, again in complete steel | Revisits thus the glimpses of the moon' (*Hamlet*, 1. 4. 51–3).

4 **encircled the city as with a regal diadem** The metaphor is probably borrowed from Varchi's *Storia fiorentina*—'le torri, le quali a guisa di ghirlanda le mura di Firenze intorno incoronovano'. *Murray's Handbook for Travellers in Northern Italy* had quoted the same description: '"These towers," says the historian Varchi, who had seen them in his younger days, "encircled the city like a garland."'

4 **the Old Palace** In fact, a late 15th-cent. Florentine would have known the building, begun 200 years earlier by Arnolfo di Cambio, as 'the Palace of the People' (as it is called on p. 84). It was not known as 'the Old Palace' until the mid-16th cent., when Cosimo I removed his court from it to the Pitti Palace.

4 **great dome . . . daring thought** The cupola of the Duomo (1420–36), by Brunelleschi, was the highest and largest of its time, and the first dome designed so as not to require a wooden frame to support the vault during construction. Numerous consulting architects had presented plans for the design of the cupola, but none was judged adequate from an engineering or aesthetic point of view. Brunelleschi's own plans were so daring and relied on so many novel structural features that they initially encountered still more vigorous opposition than those of his rivals, assailable simply on grounds of calculable error. Only gradually, and then with great difficulty, did he manage to infuse the commission charged to decide with something of his own visionary confidence in the project.

5 **Giotto's** The bell tower of the Duomo was begun by Giotto (*c*.1266–1337) in 1334, continued by Andrea Pisano, and completed by Francesco Talenti in 1359. Like the Duomo itself, it is built of coloured marbles.

5 **Badia** The church of an ancient Benedictine abbey, rebuilt, probably by Arnolfo di Cambio, in the late 13th cent.

5 **Santa Croce . . . famous dead** The Franciscan church of Santa Croce was begun in 1294 by Arnolfo di Cambio and soon became the fashionable place to be buried. By the 15th cent. the floor was entirely covered

with tombstones of the Florentine nobility, and the walls lined with commemorative monuments and plaques. In her journal 'Recollections of Italy' GE notes that Dante, Machiavelli, and Michelangelo were all buried in Santa Croce. Romola's father is buried there in 1494 (see p. 250).

5 **it is a great thing . . . communia** [cancelled *MS* reading] The quotation, from Cicero's *De Officiis* (1. 17. 55), is incomplete. It should read 'magnum est enim eadem habere monumenta maiorum, eisdem uti sacris, sepulcra habere communia' (for it means much to share the same family traditions, the same forms of domestic worship, and the same ancestral tombs). GE jots down the complete phrase in *WN*, in a selection of 10 quotations from *De Officiis*.

5 **Santa Croce had no spire then** The spired bell tower was not added until the 1840s. From its 1847 edition onward *Murray's Handbook* described it as 'a monument of bad taste, and entirely out of keeping with the style of the church', an opinion with which GE's Florentine Spirit evidently concurred.

5 **Frati Minori** 'The Franciscans.' [GE: n. added in *CM*]

5 **Brunelleschi or Michelozzo** Filippo Brunelleschi (1377–1446) was the architect of San Lorenzo, Santo Spirito, the Pazzi chapel, and, most famously, the cupola of the Duomo. Among the buildings of his pupil Michelozzo di Bartolommeo Michelozzi (1396–1472) were the convent of San Marco and the Medici Palace in the Via Larga.

5 **the church of Arnolfo** Santa Croce, whose architect, Arnolfo di Cambio (*c*.1245–1302), was also responsible for the designs of the Duomo and the Palace of the People or Old Palace. The *MS* reading here, 'something as grand as the campanile of San Spirito', was presumably changed by GE because of its historical inaccuracy: the bell tower of Santo Spirito, built, as GE records in *BL*, by Baccio d'Agnolo, dates from 1503—more than a decade after the Spirit of the Proem had 'closed his eyes for the last time'.

5 **gates been closed** There were in fact 12 principal gates in the circuit of walls designed by Arnolfo in the late 13th cent. By GE's time, as the Spirit notices, only 6 were still in use, the others having been overrun by the city's expansion.

5 **towers . . . that were once a glory and defence** The towers on the walls had been built in the early 14th cent. Again the Spirit's verdict coincides with that of *Murray's Handbook*, which explains that they were designed 'as well for beauty as for defence'. They were demolished in 1527, by which time it was believed that they in fact diminished the city's defensive capabilities.

5 **Bogoli** 'Now Boboli.' [GE: footnote added in *CM*]

5 **Oltrarno** The area of the city on the south bank of the Arno, one of the 6 *sestieri* into which Florence was divided in the 13th cent. following the building of the second circuit of the city's walls.

5 **too ambitious palace** The Pitti Palace, begun by Luca Fancelli in 1458 but whose original design is attributed to Brunelleschi some 20 years earlier, was intended by Luca Pitti to show off his wealth and importance. It was to be greater than all others in Florence, and in particular the first-floor windows were to be as large as the doors of the Medici Palace. In 1466, however, following an abortive conspiracy against the Medici, Pitti was disgraced and effectively bankrupted; work on the palace ceased and it was still incomplete when he died in 1472. The hill from which the stone was quarried is now the site of the adjacent Boboli gardens, which date from the 16th cent.

5 **anxious voting with black and white beans** The 'Magnificent Eight' (see p. 175), the *Otto di Guardia*, who presided over the State's legal and judicial business, were empowered to pass sentence of confiscation of property, imprisonment, exile, or death on a citizen. Voting on such matters was carried out with black and while beans; 6 black beans (*sei fave*: see p. 485) were required for a verdict of guilty. Alternatively, GE may be referring to the *scrutinio* (see three notes below).

6 **the *Priori*** Members of the 21 guilds (see p. 382) were eligible for election to the Signoria, the State executive, consisting of nine *Priori* (priors: chief officers), each holding office for just two months.

6 **Orgagna's Loggia** The Loggia dei Lanzi or Loggia della Signoria, also known after its probable designer, Andrea Orcagna (fl. 1344–68), was constructed (1376–82) beside the Palazzo Vecchio and used for State ceremonial. The 'significant banners' were those of the 9 priors who constituted the Signoria (for a period of two months at a time). The name is mentioned three times in the novel. On each occasion GE clearly writes it as Or*c*agna in *MS*. On this first occurrence all printed states, too, give it as Or*c*agna. On its second occurrence (p. 423), however, all printed states have Or*g*agna, and on its third (p. 538), though *CM* reads Or*c*agna, *1*, *2*, and *3* again have Or*g*agna. The 'g' is an acceptable period alternative to the 'c'; e.g. Burchiello (see p. 32) regularly spells the name with a 'g', while Ruskin uses both forms in *Modern Painters* (1843). It seems unlikely that a *CM* compositor miscopied the name at p. 423, and that a compositor of *1* then did the same at p. 538—in each case without GE noticing the change on the proofs. The more logical explanation is that GE herself marked the changes on the proofs of *CM* and *1* respectively, but in neither case bothered to ensure that the other occurrences of the name should be similarly altered. (Indeed, when she read proof for *CM* of the chapter in which the name occurs for the second time, the first mention (here in the Proem) had already been published.) In the Clarendon edition I have silently emended to Or*g*agna throughout.

6 **keep a hated name out of the *borsa*** From the early 14th cent., public officials in Florence were elected by lot. The names of those eligible for the various magistracies were selected by a complicated procedure, known as the *scrutinio*, from the membership of the 21 guilds (see p. 659) and put into *borse* (leather bags or purses) from which the required number were then drawn. Voting in the *scrutinio* was carried

out with black and white beans (black for, white against); a successful candidate required a minimum of 68 black beans out of a possible total of 97.

6 **satisfactory marriage . . . game at chess** In her notes from Lastri in *BL* GE writes: 'Borghini mentions fifteen *Loggie* existing in his time (16th century). Marriages arranged under them by fathers. Challenges to games at chess and *tavola reale* [i.e. backgammon] (?)' She also found information about chess-playing in public in Sacchetti (*Trecentonovelle*, no. 68, which she refers to in *BL*).

6 **the "Ten" . . . the "Eight" . . . the *Priori* . . . *Gonfaloniere*** The committee of ten, the *Dieci di Guerra*, was elected only in time of war. For the committee of 8 and the *Priori*, see pp. 175–6. The *Gonfaloniere* (i.e. standard-bearer) *di Giustizia* was the city's chief magistrate. Like the priors, he served for just two months. Government policy was largely determined by the party to which he belonged.

6 **bloodless battles . . . casual falls and tramplings** In his *History of Florence* Machiavelli remarks that the 1400s were the least dangerous times ever for waging war. Referring to the 'great rout and protracted engagement' of the Battle of Anghiari, he notes that only one man was killed and that even he perished 'non di ferite o d'altro virtuoso colpo, ma caduto da cavallo e calpesto' (not from a blow dealt in combat or any other honourable wound, but from being trampled after falling off his horse).

7 *truncis naribus* Martial, *Epigrams*, 2. 83. 3: 'trunci naribus auribusque voltus' (a face shorn of nose and ears). In *BL* GE records a remark by Poggio about Niccolò Niccoli's collection of antique busts: 'some "truncis naribus" but others perfect'.

7 **that fine Homer** The *editio princeps* of Homer, edited by Demetrius Chalcondylas, was printed in 1488.

7 **waxen image** See pp. 16 and 147.

7 **Unseen Powers . . . pressed the finger** In *WN*, in a section headed 'Superstitions in Medicine' (consisting of notes from John Paris's *Pharmacologia*), GE records that 'Every disease the origin and cause of which did not immediately strike the senses, has in all ages been attributed by the ignorant to the wrath of heaven, to the resentment of some invisible demon, or to some malignant aspect of the stars; & hence the introduction of a rabble of superstitious remedies . . . [P]recious stones . . . from their being the residence of spirits . . . were . . . used as amulets, or external charms'.

7 **Lucretius might be right** The Roman poet Lucretius contended in *De Rerum Natura* that the order of the world could be explained without recourse to divine intervention. Denouncing all forms of superstition, he thus sought to liberate men from the credulous awe of controlling deities.

7 **Luigi Pulci** A popular Florentine poet (1432–84), considered a master of idiomatic vernacular expression, best known for his comic epic *Il mor-*

gante maggiore. His interest in magic and his avowed religious scepticism, notably concerning the immortality of the soul, led to accusations of heresy, and he was denied burial in consecrated ground. *Morgante*'s mockery of orthodox Christian beliefs prompted Savonarola's supporters to burn all available copies of the book on the 'Pyramid of Vanities' (see p. 423). The supper-table referred to by the Spirit was probably that of Lorenzo de' Medici, of whose circle Pulci was a colourful member.

7 **dal tetto in su** In *Pf* GE jots down two lines from Lastri's *Osservatore fiorentino*: 'io mi maravigliavo del voto, ch'io so bene che tu non credi dal tetto in su' (I was amazed at the vow because I know very well you don't believe in it at all). She might also have come across the phrase in the *Cedrus Libani* of Fra Benedetto (see p. 529), who, describing the lax morals and unbelieving temper of the 1490s, writes: 'Papa Alessandro Sesto alla regnava, | Ripien d'ogn avarizia e di lussuria: | L'esemplo del pastor ogn' uom pigliava. | Fatt'era Italia come infernal furia, | . . . La verità non se dicea più, | Ogni predicator buffoneggiava | Nè quasi si credea dal tetto in su' (Pope Alexander VI was then on the throne, full of avarice and licentiousness. The pastor's example was followed by everyone. Italy was made like an infernal fury. No one spoke the truth any more. Every preacher behaved like a buffoon and people hardly believed anything from the roof upward).

7 **Aristotle . . . was a thoroughly irreligious philosopher** Following the publication in 1438 of a pamphlet by Gemistos Plethon, *De Platonicae atque Aristoteliae Philosophia Differentia*, a debate sprang up in 15th-cent. Italy between the respective claims of the two philosophers. Florence became the seat of the Platonic school; indeed, according to Marsilio Ficino it was Plethon who, while visiting Florence, gave the idea of a Platonic Academy to Cosimo de' Medici. Aristotle was championed in the north of Italy, notably in Bologna, Padua, and Pavia. It proved harder, however, to make Aristotle's doctrines accord with the Christian creed than those of Plato.

7 **circling hours** In classical mythology the Horae—Eunomia, Dice, and Irene—were three sisters, daughters of Zeus and Themis, who presided over the seasons of spring, summer, and winter.

7 **baptized in San Giovanni . . . coming judgment** Peculiar to Florence, there were no baptismal fonts in the city's churches. All baptisms were carried out in the central Baptistery of San Giovanni, adjacent to the Duomo. The ceiling of the Baptistery is decorated with mosaics of Byzantine influence, one of which depicts the Last Judgement.

8 **Pope Angelico** That such a religious leader would emerge, heralding a new, spiritual age, was a common belief throughout medieval and renaissance times. In Q, in a section headed 'Prophetic Powers', GE writes: 'Burlamacchi mentions a certain messer Prospero Pitti, canonico di Santa Maria del Fiore, who prophesied many years beforehand, the expulsion of the Medici, the coming of Savonarola, the chastisement of Italy, & *il Papa Angelico* . . . In 1491, according to Muratori, a man went preaching

about the streets of Rome, prophecying tribulations to Italy especially to Florence, Milan, and Venice—and that this was all to come in the present year & two following, together with the advent of a Pastore Angelico. Again, a partisan of the Medici, anonymous writer of two letters, accuses Savonarola of wishing to make himself *Papa Angelico'*.

8 **Innocent the Eighth** Pope, 1484–92.

8 **Lent of 1492** Savonarola's Lenten sermons in the church of San Lorenzo in 1492 were on Noah's Ark (see p. 209). GE may be confusing them with those of 1491, delivered in the Duomo, when he specifically attacked the corruption of the clergy.

8 **sold for the benefit of the needy** The contemporary chroniclers do indeed record that one course of Savonarola's sermons had this effect on its hearers, but the series concerned was that of Advent 1494—more than two years after the death of the Proem's Spirit.

8 **denunciations of speedy vengeance** A reference to Savonarola's often-repeated warning (as he put it in the *Compendium Revelationum*) 'la Chiesa se aveva a renovare in questi tempi; . . . che innanzi a questa renovazione Dio darebbe un grande flagello a tutta la Italia; . . . che queste cose sarebbono presto'—or as GE transl. this in ch. 24; *'in these times God will regenerate his Church*, and that *before the regeneration must come the scourge over all Italy*, and that *these things will come quickly.'*

8 *Iddio non paga il Sabato* '"God does not pay on a Saturday."' [GE]

8 **Frate Predicatore** A preaching friar—a Dominican.

8 **makers of San Marco** Cosimo de' Medici had commissioned Michelozzo to rebuild the Dominican convent of San Marco in the mid-15th cent.

8 **Careggi** The Medici villa at Careggi, just to the north of Florence, had been built by Lorenzo's grandfather, Cosimo. It was one of Lorenzo's favourite retreats, and the house in which he died.

8 **play the part of Rehoboam** Rehoboam was the son of Solomon, who, when he succeeded his father, rejected the advice of the elders and instead followed that of his young, reckless friends, saying to the people 'My father chastised you with whips, but I will chastise you with scorpions' (1 Kings 12: 14).

9 **rare animals . . . fugitive enemies** Among Lorenzo's gifts from Sultan Mahomet II were a lion and a giraffe; he was also sent the person of Bernardo Bandini, the murderer of his brother Giuliano, who had taken refuge at Constantinople.

9 **famous scholar . . . Latin letters of the Republic . . . lecturing on Dante . . . bitter invectives** The senior posts in the government of most 15th-cent. Italian states were held by classical scholars, for they alone were sufficiently fluent in the Latin used for all official documents and negotiations with other states. In 15th-cent. Florence the position of Secretary, or Chancellor, of the Republic was held, in sequence, by Coluccio Salutati (described by Poggio as 'the common father and

instructor of all the learned'), Leonardo Aretino, Carlo Marsuppini, Poggio himself, Benedetto Accolti, and, beneath the sway of Lorenzo de' Medici, Bartolommeo Scala. A chair for the explanation of Dante was established at Florence in the mid-14th cent. when it was first held by Boccaccio. Subsequently it was commonly united with the chair of philology and rhetoric, as when Francesco Filelfo held it. For examples of critics' 'bitter invectives', see p. 65.

9 *Regno* 'The name given to Naples by way of distinction among the Italian States.' [GE]

9 **trade in the Calimala** The Via de Calimala is just to the west of Orsanmichele. I have adjusted the spelling here—all states of the text (including *MS*) have the incorrect 'Calimara'. On the only other mention of the name (p. 90), though *MS* reads 'Calimala', all printed states misspell it 'Calimara'.

10 **Bratti Ferravecchi** *Ferravecchio* is Italian for scrap (literally, old) iron dealer. Bratti, as GE notes in *BL*, is a colloquial contraction of *barattare* (to exchange)—as in '*Chi abbaratta—baratta—b'ratta*' (see p. 12). The name, in other words, is derived from the street cry. The street of the *Ferravecchi*, which no longer exists, led into the Mercato Vecchio. In the same set of notes GE records that 'a Ferravecchio . . . commonly called Bratti Ferravecchio, died very rich'. In *MS* and *CM* the name is spelt 'Ferraveccj' throughout. On the assumption that it was GE who decided to drop the archaism (on the proofs of *1*), I have emended to 'Ferravecchi'.

11 **San Giovanni** Midsummer Day: the Feast of St John the Baptist, patron saint of Florence.

11 **money** [changed from *testoni* on *3P*] GE's change here, though consistent with her general trend of translating Italian words and phrases, also corrects an error: the small silver coins known as *testoni* (so called because they bore the impression of a large head of Cosimo I, Grand Duke of Tuscany) were not minted until the mid-16th cent.

11 **can't tell a hook from a hanger** Hooks and hangers were basic shapes practised by children learning to write. It is perhaps surprising that so distinctly *English* a remark should be put into the mouth of Bratti.

12 **Rovezzano** Some 2½ miles to the east of the city.

12 **Mercato Vecchio** The market was demolished at the end of the 19th cent. to make way for the Piazza Vittorio Emanuele, now the Piazza della Repubblica.

12 **San Niccolò** As always, GE has attended to the smallest background detail: as well as being a patron of travellers and a protector against robbery, St Nicholas of Myra was patron saint of the city of Bari, Tito's birthplace (see p. 29).

12 "*Chi abbaratta . . . vecchi?*" '"Who wants to exchange rags, broken glass, or old iron?"' [GE]

12 a **Ridolfi** The Ridolfi were one of the great Florentine families. Two of them, Niccolò and Giovan Battista, appear in the novel.

12 a **raven to . . . mind the stock** Ravens were commonly kept in shops to deter thieves by the noise they would make if anyone entered while the owner was not there.

12 **win no hose** The Florentine custom of rewarding the bringer of good tidings with hose (*novelle da calze*) was recorded by GE in *Pf.* It is referred to again in ch. 43.

13 **not born of a Sunday—the salt shops were open** GE has taken this phrase, signifying that the person concerned is very shrewd, from *Decameron*, 8. 9.

13 **as hot as Spain . . . all the profits of usury** For the persecution of Spanish Jews by the Inquisition in the 1490s (when Naples too was a Spanish dominion) see p. 560. By an ordinance of 1437 only Jews were permitted to act as money-lenders and pawnbrokers in Florence.

13 **grey cloth is against yellow cloth** The Franciscans were known as grey friars from the colour of their habit. As GE notes in *BL*, Jews were obliged to wear a piece of yellow cloth as a distinguishing badge—men on their hats, women on their sleeves. For the Franciscans' enmity towards Jews see p. 176.

13 **hose for Saint Christopher . . . sight of him** St Christopher was a giant. It was commonly believed that to see a picture of him would bring good luck for the rest of the day (see p. 150).

13 **Fesulean ancestors** It was believed that Florence was founded by merchants from the ancient city of Fiesole, some three miles distant, who erected buildings on the plain between the 'high fastness' of Fiesole and the Arno to facilitate trade with the population of the valley.

13 **the old poet Antonio Pucci accounts a . . .** *dignità* The popular poet Antonio Pucci (*c.*1310–88) was for most of his life the town crier of Florence. Much of his verse is on patriotic, civic, and historic themes. GE alludes here to l. 25 of his *terza rima* poem 'La proprietà di Mercato Vecchio', which she copied out entire in Q. The butchers' stalls were located in a pavilion in the very centre of the market.

14 **E vedesi . . . ingoffi** 'La Proprietà di Mercato Vecchio', ll. 91–3 ('You can see the losers panting heavily, cursing with hands to the jaw, and the exchanging of many blows').

14 **brood-rabbits . . .** *gattuccio,* or "Tom,"* GE's catalogue of the livestock for sale in the market follows that of Pucci's poem: 'v'arrivano uccellini | Si da tenere in gabbia da cantare, | E pe' fanciu' frusoni, e passerini; | E colombi, a conigli da figliare, | E dimolte vi son gatte, e gattucci' (there were birds put in cages to sing, and finches for children, and little sparrows, and doves, and brood rabbits, and numerous tom cats and kittens). GE translates *gattuccio* as 'Tom': strictly speaking it means a tom kitten.

14 **castello** 'Walled village.' [GE]

14 **high on a pillar** . . . **statue of Plenty** The Colonna dell' Abbondanza, a granite Roman pillar, had been moved to the Mercato Vecchio from the Baptistery in the early 15th cent. The statue by Donatello (1384–1466), known as 'La Dovizia' (Abundance, Plenty) was probably executed in the early 1430s; it was subsequently damaged, and replaced in 1721 by a copy by Foggini. The figure had a basket of fruit on her head and carried a cornucopia.

14 **says old Pucci** In 'La Proprietà di Mercato Vecchio', ll. 212–16. In *MS* GE quotes l. 216: 'Ma pe' mariti voglian risparmiare' (But because they wanted to economize for their husbands).

15 **very sour crabs** Possibly an allusion to Dante, *Inferno*, 15. 61–5: 'quello ingrato popolo maligno | che discese di Fiesole ab antico [see p. 13] . . . ti si farà . . . nemico: | ed è ragion, che tra li lazzi sorbi | si disconvien fruttar lo dolce fico' (those thankless and malignant people who came down of old from Fiesole . . . shall become your enemy: and with reason, for among the bitter sorbs it is not natural that the sweet fig should fruit). In some translations the word *sorbi* is given as 'crab-apples'.

15 **excommunicated us again** A papal interdict had last been laid upon Florence by Sixtus IV in 1478.

15 **it seems a thousand years** . . . **till** A translation of the Italian expression *parer mill'anni che* . . .

16 **A bad Easter and a bad year** The expression is almost certainly taken from Boccaccio. In *Bod* GE writes: ' "Va' via". "Dio gli dia il buono anno e le boune calendi." Bocc.' She appears to have run together two lines from *Decameron*, 8. 3: 'Iddio gli déa il buono anno a messer Domenedio' and 'Prego Iddio che vi déa il buono anno e le boune calendi'. On the same page of the notebook she writes: 'Che Dio ti dia il malanno e male pasqua' (a phrase also jotted down in *Pf*). Again, this is not a direct quotation, but its constituent elements can be found in the *Decameron*: 'Via, che Dio vi metta in malanno, rea femina' (7th day, 7th story) and 'La donna . . . vide bene nel viso al marito che ella gli aveva data la mala pasqua' (7th day, 5th story).

16 **The woman started up** . . . In his *Storie fiorentina*, Guicciardini reports that 'A mad woman in Santa Maria Novella had cried out that a bull with horns was burning the whole city.' This incident and the other portents are recorded also by Politian in a letter of 1 June 1492, by Machiavelli in his *Discorsi*, and, in a passage from which GE made notes in *Q*, by Giovanni Cambi in his diary.

16 *Palle* 'Arms of the Medici.' [GE] Six red balls (*palle*) on a gold background.

16 **Lantern of the Duomo struck** . . . **Lions tearing each other to pieces** On 5 Apr. 1492 the lions in the city menagerie had inexplicably turned on each other and killed one of their number. That night, as Luca Landucci records in his diary, 'the lantern of the cupola of Santa Maria del Fiore was struck by a thunderbolt and split almost in half . . . It was considered a great marvel, and one that signified some extraord-

inary event, especially as it happened suddenly, when the weather was calm, and the sky without a cloud . . . It was said that when [Lorenzo de' Medici] heard the news of the effects of the thunderbolt, being so ill, he asked on which side [the debris] had fallen; and when he was told, he said: "Alas! I shall die, because it fell towards my house." '

16 **Boto** 'A votive image of Lorenzo, in wax, hung up in the church of the Annunziata, supposed to have fallen at the time of his death. *Boto* is popular Tuscan for *Voto*.' [GE] The 2nd sentence of the n. was added in *CM* after T. A. Trollope had queried the word *Boto* in his letter to GE about the proofs of the first instalment of the novel (see n. on '*netto di specchio*', below). In her reply GE explained that she had been attracted by the 'colloquial stamp' of the usage, adding 'I think I may venture to keep it, having a weakness for those indications of the processes by which language is modified' (*Letters*, iii. 432). Trollope later observed that '*Boto* for *voto* is a Florentinism which may be heard to the present day, though the vast majority of strangers would never hear it, or understand it if they did. George Eliot no doubt met with it in some of those old chroniclers who wrote exactly as not only the lower orders, but the generality of their fellow citizens, were speaking around them. And her use of it testifies to the minuteness of her care to reproduce the form and pressure of the time of which she was writing' (*What I Remember*, 2 vols. (1887), ii. 303).

17 **Frati Serviti** The Santissima Annunziata was the church of the Servite order of friars (Servants of the Blessed Virgin Mary; see p. 380).

17 **a greater poet than Dante** An allusion to Pico della Mirandola's outrageously flattering praise of Lorenzo (expressed in a letter to him) as a more accomplished writer than either Dante or Petrarch.

17 **Florentines are blind** See p. 88.

17 *netto di specchio* 'The phrase used to express the absence of disqualification—*i.e.*, the not being entered as a debtor in the public book (*specchio*).' [GE] The *specchio* (literally 'mirror') was a register of citizens who had not paid their taxes and who were therefore disqualified from taking part in public life. The wording of the n. was changed to this form in *CM*; in *MS* (and evidently in the proofs of *CM*) it had read ' "Mirror-proof"—the phrase used to express the absence of disqualification.' On 2 June 1862 GE had sent a set of the proofs of the first instalment to T. A. Trollope, which he had agreed to check—presumably for just such matters of historical detail. His letter about has not survived, but her reply to it leaves no doubt as to the nature of his comments here: 'I am very grateful to you for your notes. Concerning *netto di specchio*, I have found a passage in Varchi [i.e. in the *Storia fiorentina*] which decides the point according to *your* impression. My inference had been gathered from the vague use of the term to express disqualification. But I find from Varchi b.viii, that the *specchio* in question was a public book, in which the names of all debtors to the *Commune* were entered. Thus your doubt has been a very useful caveat to me' (*Letters*, iii. 431). Trollope comments that 'Passages equally

decisive might be found *passim* in the old Florentine historians, and I ought to have referred her to them. But as she had altogether mistaken the meaning of the phrase, I had insinuated my correction as little presumptuously as I could' (*What I Remember*, ii. 301). Trollope, writing long after the event, notes that GE's letter is undated, but suggests that 'the subject of it dates it with considerable accuracy'. Gordon Haight surmises June 1861, but it surely dates from June of the following year—written as it must have been after Trollope had read the proofs of the first part of the novel.

17 **bawdy songs at the Carnival** In *BL* GE writes: 'In an ancient collection of *Laude* or hymns printed at Venice in 1512, I find several of these devout pieces are directed to be sung to the air of *Ben venga Maggio*, a *canzone a ballo* of Lorenzo [de' Medici]. From this collection it appears that it was a general custom in Italy, as it now is or lately was, the practice of a certain sect in this country, to sing pious hymns to the most profane and popular melodies, for the purpose of stimulating the languid piety of the performers, by an association with the vivacity of sensual enjoyment.' Lorenzo de' Medici's *Canti carnascialeschi* are described by Roscoe—the staunchest apologist for their author—as 'carnival songs . . . calculated for the gratification of the multitude, and devoted only to the amusement of an evening'.

17 **raise a riot over your *quattrini bianchi*** In 1490 the government of Florence called in the small coins known as *quattrini neri* (each worth 4 *danari*) and issued new ones, the *quattrini bianchi*, in their place, of one-fifth greater value. Then, while insisting on all payments to itself being made in the new coinage, it made its own payments in the old, which caused widespread dissatisfaction. GE marked the passage dealing with these disturbances in her own copy of Nardi's *Istorie*.

18 **saddled and bridled Milan** On the death of the last Visconti Duke of Milan in 1447 a republic had been established, but it lasted only three years before the Sforza family took control. First Francesco, then Galeazzo, and, by the time this remark is made, Ludovico, proved cruel tyrants.

18 **Ser Cioni** In Q GE notes that 'Ser' was a title given to notaries of good family.

18 **Balaam's ass** Balaam's ass was given the power of speech by God (see Numbers 22: 21–34). In referring thus sarcastically to a 'pious notary' GE may also have in mind the term 'Balaamite'—i.e. someone who follows religion for personal gain.

18 **into the piazza** Both *MS* and *CM* here read '*in piazza*' (much as they had read '*in Mercato*' at p. 13, which in *1* becomes '*in the Mercato*'). T. A. Trollope evidently queried these usages in the *CM* proofs he had been sent to check. GE responded that 'Concerning the phrase *in piazza*, and *in mercato*, my choice of them was partly founded on the colloquial usage as represented by Sacchetti [i.e. in the *Trecentonovelle*], whose dialogue is intensely idiomatic. Also, *in piazza* is, I believe, used by the his-

torians (I think even by Macchiavelli), when speaking of popular *turn-outs*. The ellipse took my fancy because of its colloquial stamp. But I gather from your objections that it seems too barbarous in a modern Italian ear. Will you whisper your final opinion in Mr. Lewes' ear on Monday?' (*Letters*, iii. 432). Trollope comments 'As regards the use of the phrase *in piazza* she is perfectly right. The term keeps the same meaning to the present day, and is equivalent in political language to *the street*' (*What I Remember*, ii. 302). Whatever his final opinion at the time may have been, however, it would seem that GE subsequently decided that both ellipses were 'too barbarous', for both were opened out and anglicized in *1*.

19 **Fra Menico** Fra Domenico da Ponzo, a Franciscan, was a prominent enemy of Savonarola. The change, made by GE on *3P*, from 'Fra Menico da Ponzo' to plain 'Fra Menico' is an interesting one. Presumably she was no longer concerned—or aware—that, thus named, he might be confused with the other Fra Domenico in the novel: Fra Domenico da Pescia, the zealous disciple of Savonarola, who was executed along with him (see p. 423).

19 **Mongibello** An alternative name for the Sicilian volcano Mount Etna. The proverbial expression 'Andare dietro al vento di Mongibello' (signifying to indulge in a wild-goose chase) is jotted down by GE in *Bod*.

19 **certain swine** For the story of the Gadarene swine, which, possessed by devils, drowned themselves in the Sea of Galilee, see Matthew 8: 28–32; Mark 5: 1–13; Luke 8: 26–33.

19 **Niccolò Grosso surnamed Caparra** [cancelled *MS* reading] See p. 241.

19 **Domenico Ghirlandajo . . . life of Florence** A reference to the frescos by Ghirlandaio (1449–94) in Ognissanti, Santa Maria Novella, and the Sassetti Chapel in Santa Trinità, in which many of the figures are portraits of the artist's contemporaries (including Lorenzo de' Medici, Marsilio Ficino, Demetrius Chalcondylas, Cristoforo Landino, and Angelo Poliziano).

20 **San Gallo** The area of parkland, on the north-east of the city, around the Augustinian convent of San Gallo, a favourite summer resort.

20 **Marzocco** 'The stone Lion, emblem of the Republic.' [GE: n. added in *CM*] There were numerous such statues in the city; the most famous, by Donatello, was in the Piazza della Signoria.

21 **the Abbot Joachim** Joachim of Fiore (*c*.1135–1202), a Cistercian abbot in Calabria who subsequently founded the community of hermits at San Giovanni in Fiore from which the Florensian order arose, argued that the history of the world was divided into three ages. The first, the period of the Old Testament, was that of the Father, dominated by law and fear. The second, from the birth of Christ to the year 1260, was that of the Son, a period of grace and faith. The third age was that of the Holy Ghost, characterized by love and spirituality. Each age had a precursor and an initiator; the birth throes of each were violent, and produced a series of Antichrists. Around the year 1260 the Saracens and the Jews

would be converted and mankind would enter on its highest destiny—a spiritual age led by *viri spirituales*, namely monks. In Q GE records details about the Abbate Gioacchino's prophecies and their reception by contemporary commentators. She also notes that Savonarola invoked him in his sermons (specifically that of 13 Jan. 1495), referring to his prophecy of the scourge and renovation to come. For Savonarola's vision of 'the sword hanging from the sky', see p. 211.

21 **the Magnifico sent for the Frate at the last** There are several, and by degrees conflicting, accounts of this interview in GE's primary sources, notably by Poliziano and Burlamacchi and later by Roscoe, Sismondi, and Villari. The burden of the story is that on his deathbed at Careggi, and despite his previous antipathy to the Frate, Lorenzo de' Medici sent for Savonarola hoping to receive absolution at his hands. Savonarola insisted that he could offer this only if Lorenzo would agree to restore to Florence the republican government and liberty of which he had despoiled it. Even *in extremis* Lorenzo could not bring himself to submit to such a condition, and Savonarola accordingly refused to grant him absolution; the 'Magnifico', in other words, did indeed die without the Frate's blessing.

22 **tell peas from paternosters** In *Pf* GE jots down ' "s'io non conosco il bacello da' paternostri!" "If I don't know peas from paternosters"'. The phrase is from Sacchetti's *Trecentonovelle* (no. 209). The comparison is between a pea and a single rosary bead from a 'paternoster'.

22 **Ognissanti** The area around the church of All Saints, where one of the main centres of the city's woollen industry was located.

23 **obolus** An ancient Greek coin, worth half a drachma. Later, the word was used allusively for any coin of small value: cf. 'Inquire what lowest offering may suffice, | Cheapen it meanly to an obolus' (*The Spanish Gypsy*). Tito presumably spoke to himself in the Italianate Greek of his native Apulia.

25 **the first and last requisite of eloquence** Cicero records (*Brutus*, 38. 142) that when Demosthenes was asked to list the first, second, and third requisites of oratory, he replied 'action' to all three.

26 **the excellent Demetrio** Born in Athens, the celebrated scholar Demetrius Chalcondylas (1424–1511) was invited to Florence in 1479 by Lorenzo de' Medici and remained there as professor of Greek until (as Bardo notes on p. 65) 1492. Among his many accomplishments was the great edition of Homer referred to in the Proem.

26 **Bernardo Rucellai** See ch. 38.

28 **carries his skin** St Bartholomew was martyred by being flayed alive. He is often represented in paintings carrying his own skin over his arm.

28 **the Muses are tearing their hair** See p. 337.

29 **the accomplished Marullo . . . Alessandra Scala** In Q GE makes several pages of notes about Michael Marullus Tarchaniota, who came to Italy as a boy following the fall of Constantinople in 1453, and won fame

there as both a poet and a soldier. His fortunes were assured when in 1487 he married the 'learned and lovely' Alessandra Scala, daughter of the Secretary of the Florentine Republic, who had been taught Latin by Johannes Lascaris and Greek by Demetrius Chalcondylas. Marullo was drowned near Volterra in 1500.

29 **Greek stock . . . peaches are Persian** The Florentine silk trade, as GE recorded in *BL*, began in the early 15th cent. and was subsequently encouraged by Lorenzo de' Medici, who planted mulberry trees (native to Asia) on his estate. The ancient and much-fought-over city of Bari, in Apulia in south-east Italy, had had a mixed Greco–Roman population since classical times. The Latin name for peach, as GE noted in *Pf*, is *persicum malum*—persian apple. The line 'in fact, I am a Greek very much as your peaches are Persian' was changed to this reading by GE on *3P*. All previous states of the text read 'in fact, may rather be called a Græculus than a Greek'. The Latin word *Græculus* ('Greekling'), however, was often used in a pejorative or even contemptuous sense. The revised reading here is less derogatory: signifying, presumably, that Tito's pedigree is a familiar and well-established one—that he is an import fully acclimatized to Italy, with no hint of the fraudulent or meretricious about him.

29 **Minerva** The Roman goddess of wisdom, equivalent to the Greek Athena; 'fallacious' here since the information given to Tito proves false. The underlying allusion is probably to the episode in the *Odyssey* in which the disguised Athena counsels Telemachus to fit out a ship and go in search of his father, Odysseus.

29 **Alamanno Rinuccini** The Rinuccini were one of the great Florentine mercantile families. Alamanno (1426–1504), a close friend of Lorenzo de' Medici, was a notable scholar and historian, and one of the earliest members of the Platonic Academy (see p. 343).

30 **Messer Angelo** Angelo Poliziano, 1454–94. The celebrated humanist, scholar, and poet was born in the Tuscan village of Montepulciano (whence his Latinized name derives) and went to study in Florence at the age of 10. While still in his teens he wrote Greek poems, edited Catullus, and began to transl. Homer into Latin. In 1473 Lorenzo de' Medici appointed him tutor to his son Piero, and in 1480 to a chair of Greek and Latin, in which post he lectured on a wide range of classical authors. He transl. works by Epictetus, Hippocrates, Plutarch, and Plato, among others, and ed. the *Pandects* of Justinian (see p. 52). His compositions in Italian include the *Stanze di Messere Angelo Poliziano cominciate per la giostra di Giuliano de' Medici* and the lyric pastoral *Orfeo* (see p. 354).

30 **a sgherro, or a man of evil repute** In BL, in a section of notes headed 'Florentine costume' taken from Agostino Ademollo's *Marietta de' Ricci*, GE records that 'Chi portava i capelli lunghi e non si radeva la barba era tenuto per sgherro o uomo di mal-affare' (see cancelled *MS* reading at 'man of evil repute').

30 **Pietro Crinito** *c.*1465–1505. The transcriber of numerous classical texts and the author of a commentary on Cicero, his second name is the Latinized form of *riccio* ('curly-locks'), a nickname given to his father. Nello's unflattering portrait of him follows that of Paulus Jovius' unreliable *Elogia Virorum Literis Illustrium,* which records that his fondness for wine, 'uncircumscribed by the reliable bounds of dignity and modesty, opened the way to insults and to ruin'. Jovius goes on to note, doubtless apocryphally, that he died as a result of 'the unaccustomed outrage' of a homosexual advance made towards him while drunk at a friend's country house.

30 **hyacinthine locks** The phrase is from *Paradise Lost,* 4. 301, describing the appearance of Adam. If GE is not being anachronistic, however, Nello must be referring to Homer's description of Ulysses (*Odyssey,* 6. 231), whose hair flowed 'like the hyacinth flower'.

30 **Pico di Mirandola** Giovanni Pico, Prince of Mirandola (1463–94), was celebrated alike for his learning and his beauty. According to Poliziano, he was a man 'on whom Nature had lavished all the endowments both of body and mind; erect and elegant in his person, there was something in his appearance almost divine'. Unlike Tito, he had fair hair, but contemporary portraits show it hanging in thick curls on his shoulders (see p. 343). He was a close friend and zealous supporter of Savonarola and was buried in San Marco.

30 **gates of storied bronze** The octagonal Baptistery of San Giovanni has three sets of bronze doors. The south doors are by Andrea Pisano and date from the mid-14th cent. Those on the north (1403–24) and the east (1425–52) are the work of Lorenzo Ghiberti; the latter are reported to have been described by Michelangelo as worthy of the gates of Paradise.

30 **the façade . . . ignominious in faded stucco** The original marble façade of the Duomo, left uncompleted by Giotto, was removed in the 16th cent. Its replacement, the 'ignominious' stucco seen by GE (and described by her in her journal 'Recollections of Italy' as 'the wretched unfinished façade'), was itself removed in the 1870s, whence the present façade dates.

31 **rough with imagery** The words deleted in *MS* at this point—*signis extantibus asper* (rough with high-wrought figures) are from Ovid, *Metamorphoses,* 12. 235.

32 **half a century ago . . . hardly so many years as you do** Nello's remark is not strictly accurate. The east doors were indeed completed exactly 50 years previously, but by then Ghiberti, who died in 1455, was 74 years old. The north doors were begun when Ghiberti was 25.

32 **Poliziano . . . in spite of his canonicate** Poliziano, who accumulated various benefices in the course of his career—rather as a source of income than as a result of any strong religious vocation—took a degree in canon law and in 1486 was appointed a canon of Santa Maria del Fiore, the Cathedral of Florence. The remark attributed to him by Nello about the (ancient) gods awaking, though not taken from his own writings, is

appropriately suggestive of the rediscovery of classical sources of inspiration. The 'quotation' that follows about the vulgar speaking Latin is equally in character, though it too is almost certainly made up.

32 **Burchiello** The celebrated barber and vernacular poet Domenico di Giovanni (1404–49) was known as 'Il Burchiello' because he had the sign of a small barge (*burchio* = barge; *burchiello* = wherry) outside his shop in the Via Calimala, where many of the leading Florentine poets and artists of the day congregated. Nello is plainly modelled on Burchiello, details of whose character and works GE recorded at length in *BL*. Following the account in Domenico Manni's *Vita di Burchiello*, the layout of Nello's shop closely follows that of his predecessor's. One of Burchiello's sonnets, 'La Poesia contende col Rasajo' ('Poetry argues with the Razor'), in which he contrasts his high artistic vocation with his lowly tonsorial profession, probably prompted GE's choice of 'Apollo and the Razor' as the sign for Nello's shop. Nello's boast that his shop is 'the navel of the earth' is based on another of Burchiello's sonnets, which begins 'Nel bilicato centro della terra' (*bilicato* = umbilical, navel), and in which he maintains that *his* shop should be thus termed since it stood at the centre of Florence, which in turn was at the centre of Tuscany, and therefore at the centre of the world. More significantly, perhaps, as Felicia Bonaparte has pointed out (in *The Triptych and the Cross: The Central Myths of George Eliot's Poetic Imagination*, New York, 1979), 'the navel of the earth' was a term used by the Greeks about Delphi, the site of the most important of Apollo's temples; it is appropriate that Nello's barber's mirror should, later in this chapter, be referred to as 'the true *nosce teipsum*', the admonition of the Delphic oracle.

32 **Triptolemus** According to Greek legend the Eleusinian hero Triptolemus taught men the art of ploughing. By implication Nello suggests a similar, though anonymous, patron for *reaping*.

32 **adytum** The innermost or most secret part of a temple.

33 **a fancy of Piero di Cosimo's . . . looking at a mouldy wall** The sketch is in fact a fancy of GE's. It resembles no known work by the artist, who is to play an important role in the novel; nor do the portraits of Tito as Sinon (see p. 191) or of Bardo and Romola as Oedipus and Antigone (see p. 261). Vasari notes that Piero 'would sometimes stand beside a wall, against which various impurities were cast, and from these he would image forth the most singular scenes'.

34 **'The Moor' . . . a doctor of physic** In *BL* GE notes 'Custom of doctors to wait in chemists' shops for patients—or stand at the door on horseback. See Sacchetti, Nov. 155 and 168.' Both tales concern the comic exploits of a doctor from Prato called Maestro Gabbadeo (see p. 141). Later in the notebook, in a list headed 'Hints and Queries', she jots down 'Chemist and doctor—(sign *Il Moro*)'.

34 **the e hath the stronger following in Florence** In 1488 Landino (see p. 62) had pronounced that Virgil should in fact be spelt with an 'e', and the case had subsequently been taken up by Poliziano in his *Miscellanea*, 1489 (ch. 77: 'Quo argumento dicendum Vergilius non Virgilius').

34 **young Niccolò Macchiavelli** Machiavelli was 22 in Apr. 1492.

34 **keen enough to discern** *il pelo nell' uovo* In *Pf* GE writes '*Conoscere il pelo nell' uovo*—To know the bird's feather by the egg'. The Italian expression *cercare il pelo nell' uovo* (literally, to look for the hair in the egg) is broadly equivalent to the English 'to split hairs'—to be excessively fussy.

35 **Venetian mirror from Murano, the true** *nosce teipsum* Murano, in the Venetian lagoon, became the centre of the Venetian glass industry in the late 13th cent. *Nosce teipsum* (know thyself) was the admonition of the Delphic oracle.

35 **Poliziano . . . had a younger beard than yours** Poliziano was barely 25 when he was appointed to the chair of Greek and Latin Eloquence at Florence.

35 **an Apulian Greek** See p. 603.

37 **the old Furies** The Roman name (*Furiae*) for the Greek *Erinyes* (also known as *Eumenides*: see p. 118–19), the merciless goddesses of vengeance who pursued and punished all transgressors, especially those who neglected filial or familial duty.

37 **leaven . . . Doxology** Nello is alluding to liturgical and theological differences between the Greek and Roman Churches. Leavened bread is used during the Mass in the Greek Church, unleavened in the Roman. The dispute over doxology—the form of offering of glory to God— specifically concerned the *Filioque* section of the Nicene Creed, the Roman Church holding that the Holy Ghost proceeds from the Father and the Son, the Greek that it proceeds from the Father alone. Both issues were debated by representatives of the two Churches at the Council of Florence in 1439.

38 **Ingenium velox . . . torrentior** Juvenal, *Satires*, 3. 73–4: 'quick witted and of unbounded impudence, they are as ready of speech as Isaeus [an Assyrian rhetorician] and more garrulous'.

38 **Giovanni Argiropulo, who ran full tilt against Cicero** Johannes Argyropylus (1404–74) was a Greek scholar brought to Florence by Cosimo de' Medici in 1459. He served as tutor to, among others, Lorenzo de' Medici and Poliziano. The latter records his criticism of Cicero in the first chapter of the *Miscellanea*, though GE may well have come across it also in Roscoe's *Life of Lorenzo de' Medici*: 'Argyropylus had professed an open hostility to the reputation of Cicero, whom he represented as a sciolist in the Greek tongue . . . and Politiano, in his riper years, seems to shudder at the recollection of the time when the ignorance of Tully was a matter taken for granted by him and his fellow-students.'

38 **a fine Cleopatra cut in sardonyx . . . intaglios and cameos** King describes just such a stone in *Antique Gems*: 'a bust of Cleopatra, given in exact accordance with the prescribed type of the Queen . . . worked out with extreme delicacy in the black layer of Onyx in very flat relief'. An intaglio, like Tito's Cleopatra, is a precious stone with a design cut

into it. A cameo is a stone with two layers of contrasting colour; the design is carved in relief from the upper layer, while the lower serves as a background.

39 **another sort of Cleopatra that he covets most** The allusion is somewhat cryptic. GE may possibly be thinking of the famous classical statue of a reclining female figure generally thought (including by Vasari) to be of Cleopatra until well into the 19th cent., when it was reclassified as of Dido or Ariadne. The original was acquired (it is not known whence) by Pope Julius II in 1512, and not long afterwards a copy was placed in the Villa Medici in Rome—perhaps by Piero de' Medici's younger brother Giovanni, who became Pope in 1513 (it is highly unlikely that Piero himself, who died in 1503, had anything to do with its purchase). In ch. 19 of *Middlemarch*, Ladislaw and Naumann, visiting the Vatican, pass through 'the hall where the reclining Ariadne, then [i.e. during the reign of George IV] called the Cleopatra, lies in the marble voluptuousness of her beauty'. The only other Cleopatra associated with the Medici family at this time was the portrait by Piero di Cosimo, mentioned by Vasari, of Simonetta Vespucci (the mistress of Piero de' Medici's uncle Giuliano) as the Egyptian Queen. Vasari describes the picture as 'a most beautiful head of Cleopatra . . . with the asp twined round her neck'. Alternatively, of course, Nello may simply be alluding to a mistress of Piero himself, using the name Cleopatra to signify a woman of luxurious tastes and dubious morals.

39 **'branny monster'** On at least two occasions (see p. 78) Poliziano described Scala as *monstrum furfuraceum*. 'Furfur' is Latin for bran.

39 **such a steed as Ser Benghi's** Ser Benghi was a corruption of or nickname for Ser Gherardo, a Florentine whose comic antics on an old hack under whose tail a thistle had been surreptitiously placed are recounted in no. 64 of Sacchetti's *Trecentonovelle*.

39 **the halving of a fennel seed** In *Bod* GE notes that 'Finocchio = fennel seed, is used in the same way as "mustard seed" to express the minimum.' The expression signifies that the person concerned will be scrupulous to a fault.

39 **Florentine lily . . . got quarrelsome, and turned red** Until the middle of the 13th cent. the Florentine banner consisted of a white lily on a red field. In the year 1251, at the height of the conflict between the Guelfs and the Ghibellines, a group of the latter faction committed treason and joined forces with the city's enemies, but still flew the white lily at the head of their column, whereupon the government of Florence promptly changed its emblem to a *red* lily on a *white* field. Cf. Dante, *Paradiso*, 16. 151–4: 'con queste genti vid' io glorioso | e giusto il popol suo, tanto che 'l giglio | non era ad asta mai posto a ritroso, | nè per division fatto vermiglio' (with these I saw her [Florence's] people so glorious and so just that the lily had never been reversed on the spear, nor by dissension changed to red).

40 **'raggia come stella per sereno'** 'Shines likes a star in a clear sky': Pulci, *Il morgante maggiore*, 3. 17.

41 **like cheese ready grated** In *MS* and *CM* this phrase reads 'like *cacio alla lasagna*', an expression jotted down by GE in *Bod*. The more common form of the idiom (meaning to turn up at the right time) is *essere come il cacio sui maccheroni*, which she had already used, in transl., in the 2nd sentence of the chapter.

41 **Menico Cennini . . . Bernardo Cennini** Bernardo Cennini (1415–98) was a Florentine engraver and goldsmith (he assisted Lorenzo Ghiberti with one of the doors of the Baptistery of San Giovanni) who became interested in printing, built a press, and cut his own type. The first book from his press was Servius' Commentary on Virgil (1471–2). His son Domenico (1452–1504) carried on the family business. 'Grave' Domenico may have been, but in 1492, aged 40, he was scarcely 'elderly'. Later in the novel (p. 85) his brother Piero, a notary and copyist, appears; this is an odd slip by GE: Piero, Bernardo's eldest son, had died in 1484.

41 **juvenile learning . . . Francesco Filelfo** Filelfo (1398–1481) was appointed to the chair of Rhetoric at Padua at the age of 18. He subsequently studied Greek at Constantinople under Johannes Chrysoloras, bringing back numerous important MSS with him, before becoming professor of Eloquence at Venice, of Moral Philosophy at Bologna, and then of Rhetoric at Florence (1429–34). At Florence, he declared, 'the whole State is turned to look at me, and praise me to the skies. My name is on every lip. Not only the leaders of the city, but women also of the noblest birth make way for me'. He went on to hold chairs at Siena, Bologna again, Milan, and then Rome; he returned to Florence to die, and was buried in the Santissima Annunziata. He frequently boasted that no other man alive had mastered the whole of ancient literature as he had.

41 **A second Guarino . . . shipwrecked** Guarino of Verona (1374–1460), sometime professor of Rhetoric at Florence, was a noted collector of ancient MSS. GE records in *Pf* that 'Catullus was discovered by Guarino di Verona, covered with dust in a [?grenier]'. As she notes in *BL*, his hair is reputed to have turned white from grief following a shipwreck in which he lost all the treasures he had acquired on a trip to Greece.

41 **man . . . about fifty** GE's source is presumably Vasari, who gives Piero's birthdate as 1441. (In *Pf* she writes that he died in 1521 aged 80.) In fact, he was born in 1462 (he did indeed die in 1521), which would have made him 30 at this point in the novel.

42 **Sinon deceiving old Priam** It was Sinon who persuaded King Priam to bring the wooden horse into the city of Troy.

42 **Saint Sebastian . . . troops of devout women** Sebastian was a Roman soldier martyred for his Christian belief by the Emperor Diocletian, who ordered him shot to death with arrows. The scene became a popular one with artists in the 15th cent., supposedly because it afforded the opportunity of displaying the almost naked body of a young man in an unimpeachably religious context.

42 **thy chatter and the bells together** Vasari records that Piero 'was

much disturbed by the cries of children, the sound of bells, the singing of monks, and even by the coughing of men'.

43 **a curious and valuable ring . . . may have lost** In her notes from King's *Antique Gems* in *WN* GE writes: '*Onyx* has two layers, usually in strong contrast with each other, but of various combinations. There is a variety according to Pliny containing spots of various colours surrounded by white veins, like so many eyes. By cutting out these spots—or a blue spot with a black zone,—the so-called *Niccolo* (Onicolo, little onyx), is obtained.' In *Bod*, in a passage also taken from King, she records that 'the figure of a big fish with bent tail & wide mouth . . . cut on a stone with a large crested serpent with a long mane above it . . . gives good luck at sea, & restores lost things'.

44 **horoscopes are all a nonsensical dream** Pico della Mirandola's *De Astrologia* was one of the first books systematically to deny the power of astrological influences over human lives. The term 'Phoenix', denoting a person of unique excellence or matchless beauty, was commonly applied to Pico by his contemporary admirers.

44 **made his Judas as beautiful as St. John** Nello is presumably referring to Leonardo's famous painting of the Last Supper, in Milan, which includes representations of both Judas and John. In fact, however, the painting was not commissioned until 1494 (i.e. two years after Nello's remark; the *MS* reading here—'to make his Judas'—might in one sense have been less inaccurate). GE's spelling of the painter's name as 'Lionardo' follows Vasari.

45 **world-famous quarrels** See p. 81.

45 **high towers of the nobles** Prior to the mid-13th cent. the city of Florence, considerably smaller than in the 15th cent., was notable for the extremely narrow streets at its centre, and for the towers—of between 200 and 300 feet in height—of its noble families. In 1250 it was decreed that the towers should be reduced to a height of less than 100 feet; subsequently most were either demolished altogether or incorporated in other buildings. Only the 'labyrinth of narrow streets' (p. 10) at the heart of the city remained.

45 **old tutelar God Mars . . . his rival, the Baptist** In ancient times Mars was honoured as patron of Florence until, with the coming of Christianity, he was gradually replaced by St John the Baptist. Dante describes Florence as 'tra Marte e 'l Batista' (*Paradiso*, 16. 47) and remarks 'I' fui de la città chel nel Batista | mutò il primo padrone' (*Inferno*, 13. 143–4). A ruined statue of Mars stood at the northern end of the Ponte Vecchio (see p. 81).

45 **their original condition of *popolani*** The accuracy of this statement was another of the questions raised by T. A. Trollope in his comments on the proofs of the first part of the novel's serialization. GE replied: 'Concerning the Bardi, my authority for making them originally *popolani* is G. Villani. He says, c. xxxix, "*e gia cominciavano a venire possenti i Frescobaldi e Bardi e Mozzi ma di piccolo cominciamento.*" And c. lxxxi.

"*e questi furono le principale case de' Guelfi che uscirono di Firenze. Del Sesto d'Oltr' Arno, i Rossi, Nerli, e parte de' Manelli, Bardi, e Frescobaldi de' Popolani dal detto Sesto*, case nobili *Canigiani*," etc. These passages corrected my previous impression that they were originally Lombard nobles' (*Letters*, iii. 431). Trollope remarks: 'It needs some familiarity with the Florentine chroniclers to understand that the words quoted by no means indicate that the families named were not of a patrician origin . . . But the passage is interesting as showing the great care she took to make her Italian novel historically accurate. And it is to be remembered that she came to the subject absolutely new to it. She would have known otherwise, that the *Case* situated in the Oltr' Arno quarter, were almost all noble. That ward of the city was the Florentine *quartier St. Germain*' (*What I Remember*, ii. 302).

45 **furnish specie for the wars of our Edward the Third** GE's review of the Bardi family history is drawn largely from Lastri. Also, in Q she jots down a reference from Ammirato's *Delle famiglie nobili fiorentine* to Taldo Valori, a partner in the banking house of the Bardi in England, lending 30,000 florins to Edward III. In his notes to Ademollo's *Marietta de' Ricci*, Luigi Passerini records a loss ('*fallimento*' = bankruptcy) of 900,000 florins by the Bardi and Peruzzi loaned to Edward III.

46 **certain noteworthy circumstances** In the tumult following the expulsion from Florence, in Aug. 1343, of Gaultier de Brienne, Duke of Athens, the Frankish adventurer who had effectively controlled the city for the past year, a number of noble Florentine families, including the Bardi, sought to acquire power by force of arms. In the ensuing struggle with the people they were roundly defeated; the Bardi, barricaded in between the Ponte Vecchio and the Ponte Rubaconte, held out longer than any of their allies, but were eventually overcome by an attack from the rear launched from the hill of San Giorgio.

46 **the honest pages of Giovanni Villani** In the *Historie universale de suoi tempi*.

46 **palagi e case grandi** Villani, *Historie universale*, bk. 12, ch. 21 ('arsonvi 22 tra palagi e case grandi e ricche').

46 **kinship** 'A sign that such contrasts were peculiarly frequent in Florence, is the fact that Saint Antonine, Prior of San Marco, and afterwards Archbishop, in the first half of this fifteenth century, founded the Society of Buonuomini di San Martino (Good Men of St. Martin) with the main object of succouring the *poveri vergognosi*—in other words, paupers of good family. In the Records of the famous Panciatichi family we find a certain Girolamo in this century who was reduced to such a state of poverty that he was obliged to seek charity for the mere means of sustaining life, though other members of his family were extremely wealthy.' [GE: in *MS* the phrase 'to seek charity' reads 'to apply to the Opera di Sant' Jacopo'.]

47 **Scheldt . . . Euxine** The Scheldt is the river on which both Ghent and Antwerp stand. Pontus Euxinus is the Latin name for the Black Sea, which was commonly thus named on Italian maps of the 15th cent.

47 **Maso** In *MS* the name of the Bardi servant was originally Ambrogio; GE crossed this out and substituted, in turn, Tonio, Maso, and then Totto. He remained Totto for his next five appearances, GE finally settling on Maso only at p. 63.

47 **Magna Græcia** The name given to the Greek colonies in Southern Italy.

48 **Politian's *Miscellanea*** According to Poliziano's own preface to the work—which consists principally of philosophical and philological observations on the writings of ancient authors—these fugitive pieces or 'miscellanies' had their origin in remarks made to Lorenzo de' Medici as he and Poliziano took their daily ride together. It was Lorenzo, to whom the book (published in 1489) was dedicated, who encouraged him to commit them to paper. The transl. of the passage quoted is GE's own.

49 **Actæon exclaiming . . . in his soul** Nonnos, *Dionysiaca*, 5. 337–42.

50 *mens divinior* Cf. Horace, *Satires*, 1. 1. 43–4: 'cui mens divinior atque os | magna sonaturum, des nominis huius honorem' (if one has a divine soul and a tongue of noble utterance, to such give honour of that name).

50 "Ὄλβιε Τειρεσία [cancelled MS reading] 'Happy Teiresias': *Dionysiaca*, 5. 337.

50 **the four verses** In ch. 80 of the *Miscellanea*, headed 'Fabula ignotior de Tiresia & Pallade, qua sensus aperitur Propertianus', Poliziano quotes only 4 of the 6 lines from bk. 5 of Nonnos' *Dionysiaca* which contain the exclamation of Actæon. He omits ll. 339–40: 'You did not die! you did not get the shape of a stag, no poking horns raised themselves on your brow.'

51 **those Lamiæ** According to legend, Lamia was a Libyan queen with whom Zeus fell in love. The jealous Hera robbed her of her children, and in vengeful despair Lamia then stole and murdered the children of others. Her savage cruelty distorted her once beautiful face, and to mitigate this effect Zeus gave her the power of taking her eyes out of her head and putting them back again. Poliziano's *Lamia* was the prolusion, or essay preparatory, to the course of lectures on Aristotle's *Prior Analytics* which he delivered in Florence during the academic year 1492–3, and constitutes a defence against criticism of him by other scholars for venturing into the field of philosophy. Bardo is referring to the humorous opening passage of the work in which Poliziano, citing Plutarch as his source, emphasizes that Lamiae could take out or put in their eyes at will—whichever suited them. They wear them, he says, when they are out of doors and are thus alert to every detail; at home, however, they remove them and thus are totally blind. Florence too, he continues, has its Lamiae, who point him out in the streets as 'that braggart who has suddenly turned philosopher'. He thus refers not to the Florentines in general, as Bardo would have it, but specifically to his own critics—and not so much to their native inquisitiveness as to their malicious sniping and backstabbing. In the idea that they remove their eyes when at home, Poliziano insinuates that they are hypercritical of others (of himself in particular) but ignorant of their own shortcomings.

51 **saying with Petrarca** . . . **junguntur** The quotation, from a letter of Petrarch to Giovanni dell' Incisa (*Rerum Familiarium*, 3. 18), may be transl. 'books delight our inmost being; they converse with us, advise us, and become living companions to us'.

51 **the Greek was a dead letter to him** Gibbon (whom, according to her journal, GE consulted on 'the revival of learning') records that when the 50-year-old Petrarch was given a copy of Homer he replied: 'you should have given me . . . a guide who could lead me into the fields of light, and disclose to my wondering eyes the specious miracles of the Iliad and Odyssey. But, alas! Homer is dumb, or I am deaf; nor is it in my power to enjoy the beauty which I possess'.

51 **the younger Crisolora** GE is presumably thinking of Johannes, the nephew of Emmanuel Chrysoloras, who did indeed teach Greek in Florence (to Filelfo and Guarino among others). Johannes died in 1426, however, so for Bardo to have studied with him, even as a youth, would mean that Bardo must now be around 80 years old—as opposed simply to 'rather more than seventy', as he is described on p. 55.

51 **try to be a pentathlos** . . . **limbs of a nymph** Bardo is alluding to Epictetus, *Encheiridion*, 29—'do you wish to be a pentathlos, or a wrestler? Look to your arms, your thighs; see what your limbs are like'. (The word *palaestra* means wrestling-place or wrestling-school.) In *Pf* GE writes out a passage from *Encheiridion*, 29 (not so much a straight transl. as a précis of 20 ll. or so) as follows: ' "If you would undertake anything", says Epictetus, "consider the antecedents & the consequences. If you would win in the Olympic games, consider the discipline you will have to go through beforehand. Would you be a Πένταθλος or a wrestler? Would you be great in all the five exercises; in hurling the discus, in running, in leaping, in wrestling, in throwing? Look well at your limbs & see whether they be fit for that work." '

52 **energumen** Someone possessed by a devil.

52 **Panhormita** . . . **Poggio** The poet and classical scholar Antonio Beccadelli (1394–1471), known as Panhormita from his birthplace of Palermo (Latin: Panormus), was the first president of the Neapolitan literary academy. A number of his letters were dated 'ex mediis poculis' (in the midst of a drinking session), and he is supposed to have claimed that the Trojan War could have been averted if Menelaeus had given Helen to Paris for a month. His poem *Hermaphroditus* (dedicated to Cosimo de' Medici and praising, in the manner of Catullus, the pleasures of physical love between two young men) was publicly burnt in several Italian cities on grounds of indecency; Pope Eugenius IV proscribed the reading of it under penalty of excommunication. The Florentine Poggio Bracciolini (1380–1459) was one of the most distinguished scholars of his day. While in the papal service he travelled widely in Europe, and discovered and edited MSS of several classical authors (hence, presumably, Bardo's admiration), including Quintilian and Vitruvius. He also published philosophical dialogues and a history of Florence. In 1453 he became Chancellor of the Florentine Republic. Bardo's disapproval is probably

on account of his bawdy collection of stories, the *Facetiae*, widely considered to be an outrage against good taste and decorum.

52 **not yet born . . . Thomas of Sarzana** Poliziano was born in 1454. Thommaso Parentucelli, from Sarzana near Spezia, became Pope Nicholas V in 1447 and died in 1455. An accomplished scholar and an enthusiastic collector of classical MSS, he was responsible for the founding of the Vatican Library. Bardo's use of his secular name implies that the 'discussion' between them took place prior to his election to the papacy (see p. 122), probably when Parentucelli was in Florence, engaged by Cosimo de' Medici to catalogue his books.

52 **a commentator on the Pandects** The *Digesta seu Pandectae* was a compendium of writings on civil law by Roman jurists, ordered by the Emperor Justinian in the year 533. Poliziano's celebrated edn. of the work was commissioned by Lorenzo de' Medici.

53 **Ficino . . . high priest of Platonism** The philosopher and scholar Marsilio Ficino (1433–99) was the son of Cosimo de' Medici's doctor. Himself a student of medicine, he started reading Plato in his 20s. He went on to transl. most of Plato's works into Latin, to teach him to Lorenzo de' Medici, and to become the central figure of the Florentine Platonic Academy. (In 1462 Cosimo gave him a villa at Careggi—where meetings of the Academy were subsequently held—on the understanding that he would devote himself to the interpretation and exposition of Platonic philosophy.) A believer in astrology and the magic arts, he translated the occult *Corpus Hermeticum* of Hermes Trismegistus from Greek into Latin. His major philosophical work, *Theologica Platonicae de Immortalitate Animarum*, was designed in part to reconcile the tenets of Platonism and Christianity (he became a priest in 1473). In his commentary on the *Symposium* he developed the concept of Platonic love. His Latin style ('an offence' to the donnish Bardo) was fluent but inelegant; he wrote a number of his works in the Tuscan vernacular.

53 **massive prophylactic rings** See p. 7.

53 **Niccolò Niccoli** Like Bardo, Niccoli (1363–1437) was a member of a rich Florentine mercantile family who devoted his life to scholarship and to acquiring antiquities. In *BL* GE records Poggio's remark that Niccoli's collection of pictures, seals, busts, and so on 'attracted so many beholders that the house seemed like a public place'. He bequeathed his collection to the city, but left so many debts that there was insufficient money to found the library he had desired. In fact, Cosimo de' Medici paid off the debts (much as Bardo hoped that Lorenzo would do his) and gave the collection of antiquities to San Marco.

54 **Cassandra Fedele** A Venetian, Cassandra Fedele (1465–1558) was renowned throughout Italy for her Greek and Latin learning. Poliziano hailed her as much a prodigy among women as was Pico della Mirandola among men.

54 **the divine Petrarca . . . alia pejor sit** Bardo's quotation is from *Rerum Familiarium*, 4. 19. The passage in Plautus' *Aulularia* referred to

by Petrarch reads (ll. 138–9) 'nam optimam nulla potest eligi: | alia alia peior, frater est' (there is no such thing as picking out the best woman: it's only a question of comparative badness, brother). The 'supreme Greek intellect' in this context is probably Hesiod: in *Bod* GE writes 'Hesiod's Works & Days for opinions about women'; l. 375 of *Works and Days* reads 'The man who trusts womankind trusts deceivers'; and ll. 695–705 give some hard-headed advice about marriage, concluding 'a man wins nothing better than a good wife, and, again, nothing worse than a bad one'. In *WN* GE writes 'Petrarch, out of his sonnets, is a bitter misogynist. In his philosophical dialogue "De remediis utriusque fortunae," he makes *Ratio* denounce marriage & wives in reply to *Gaudium* [saying] . . . Inter mundi taedia nullum importunius procaci faemina et tacere nescia' (among the vexations of the world none is more wearisome than a woman who is insolent and incapable of silence).

54 **the choice words of Quintilian** The quotation is from Quintilian's *Institutio Oratoria*, 11. 3. 40: 'sweet, enduring, resonant, clear, pure, carrying far and penetrating the ear'.

55 **Boccaccio** Boccaccio bequeathed his important collection of ancient MSS to the Augustinian monastery of Santo Spirito in Florence.

55 **Aldo Manunzio when he sets up his press at Venice** In Q GE notes that Aldus Manutius (1449–1515) set up his press there in 1494. An editor and printer of classical texts, he had arrived in Venice in 1490; his first dated book was issued 1494–5.

55 **Hymettus** A mountain to the east of Athens, famous for its honey.

55 **Pontanus or Merula** Giovanni Pontano (1429–1503) was a driving force behind the Neapolitan academy, within which he adopted the Latinized name of Jovianus Pontanus. The celebrated patron of scholarship Alfonso I of Naples, known as 'the Magnanimous', made Pontano tutor to his children and then showered him with numerous gifts and honours. When Charles VIII of France entered Naples in 1494 to depose Alfonso's dynasty, Pontanus greeted him with a panegyrical oration. In Q GE writes: 'Note the baseness of Pontanus, making an oration in honour of Charles VIII on his entrance as conqueror into Naples, he being deeply indebted to the Aragonese dynasty.' The textual scholar Georgius Merula (*c.* 1424–94) devoted his career primarily to the emendation of classical MSS, though in his quest to produce readable texts he introduced frequent inaccuracies. He spent much of his life at the Milanese court, and repaid the favour he was shown there by an unduly flattering account of the ruling house of Sforza in his history of the city.

55 **Platina** [cancelled *MS* reading] Born near Cremona, Bartolommeo Platina (*c.*1421–81) had studied Greek under Argiropulo in Florence, where he became the friend of both Cosimo and Lorenzo de' Medici. He then moved to Rome, corrected sheets for the press of Swynheim and Pannartz, and was appointed prefect of the Vatican Library by Pope Sixtus IV. Among his many books were a treatise on the Latin language and a dictionary of Greek words in Virgil.

55 **from the client's basket** Bardo is alluding to the practice, common in republican Rome, whereby a wealthy noble would have numerous clients or dependants attached to his household, whom he would support and on whose allegiance he in turn could always count. In later, Imperial times, however, the institution of the *clientela* was so much abused that many so-called clients were mere hangers-on who presented themselves at stated times at their patron's house simply to receive food, which was dispensed to them in baskets.

56 **a Promethean word** The word 'Promethean' may be used to signify something 'vital', 'kindling', or 'inspiriting'—as in the fire which Prometheus gave to mortals. Here, though, it may be that Bardo is more specifically alluding to the 'Promethean unguent', made from a herb on to which some of Prometheus's blood had dripped, given by Medea to Jason to render his body safe from fire and weapons. Romola's 'Promethean word' makes Bardo feel proof against the '*shafts* of Fortune' and reminds him that he has the '*armour . . .* of a clear conscience'.

56 **æs triplex** Horace, *Odes*, 1. 3 ('To Virgil setting out for Greece'), ll. 9–10: 'illi robur et aes triplex | circa pectus erat' (oak and triple bronze must have girt the breast).

56 **says Epictetus** *Encheiridion*, nos. 5 and 14.

56 **wavering in his philosophy** Bardo may be thinking of Horace, *Epistles*, 1. 1. 15–19: 'quo me cumque rapit tempestas, deferor hospes. | nunc agilis fio et mersor civilibus undis, | virtutis verae custos rigidusque satelles; | nunc in Aristippi furtim praecepta relabor | et mihi res, non me rebus, subiungere conor' (wherever the storm drives me I turn in for comfort. Now I become all action and plunge into the tide of civil life, stern champion and follower of true Virtue; now I slip back stealthily into the rules of Aristippus and would bend the world to myself, not myself to the world). Though neither Zeno nor Epicurus is mentioned by name, the opposition suggested between action and the 'stern' pursuit of virtue on the one hand and the (Aristippean) attempt to control circumstances to suit oneself on the other, may in general terms be associated with the Stoic school (of which Zeno of Citium was the founder) and the Epicurean respectively.

56 **'duabus sellis sedere'** To sit on two stools; to sit on the fence. Seneca employed the phrase when referring to Cicero's attempt to keep in with both Pompey and Caesar (*Controversiae*, 7. 3. 9). GE originally wrote the incorrect 'sellibus' in *MS*, but then crossed it out and substituted 'sellis'.

56 **Sunt qui non habeant . . . habere.** 'Some people don't have these things and there is someone who doesn't want to have them' (Horace, *Epistles*, 2. 2. 182).

56 **'inanis'** Bardo is probably alluding to Horace, *Satires*, 2. 3. 212–13: 'cum prudens scelus ob titulos admittis inanis, | stas animo et purum est vitio tibi, cum tumidum est, cor?' (when you deliberately commit a crime for empty glory, are you sound of mind, and is your heart, when swollen with pride, free from fault?).

56 **parchment . . . in a sealed bag** See p. 276.

59 **panther-skin and . . . thyrsus** Traditional accoutrements of Bacchus.

60 **Manuelo Crisolora** The Greek scholar Emmanuel Chrysoloras (c.1350–1415) was a pioneer in spreading the knowledge of Greek literature in the West. Born in Constantinople, where he was a pupil of Gemisthos Plethon, he was sent to Italy by the Byzantine Emperor Manuel II Palaeologus to secure assistance against the Ottoman Turks. He taught Greek in Florence for a while in the 1390s, transl. Homer and Plato, and wrote a Greek grammar.

60 *lippi* Latin: near-sighted, blear-eyed.

61 **Nauplia** Nauplia (now Nauplion) was the port and chief town of Argolis, at the head of the Gulf of Argos.

62 **two things not to be hidden—love and a cough** Cf. 'Vero è pur, che l'uom non possa | Celar per certo l'amore e la tossa' (Pulci, *Il morgante maggiore*, 4. 88). These lines are written out by GE in *Bod*.

62 *tonsor inequalis* The unskilful barber. The phrase should properly be 'inaequali tonsore' (Horace, *Epistles*, 1. 1. 94).

62 **Perdonimi . . . latino** 'May I be forgiven if I make a mistake: the person who hears me can understand my vulgar tongue with his Latin' (Pulci, *Il morgante maggiore*, 2. 57. 2–3).

62 *grylli* The Latin word *gryllus*, meaning cricket or grasshopper, was used figuratively to signify a comic caricature. Bardo may possibly be thinking of Pliny's *Natural History*, 35. 114: 'idem [Antiphilus, a 4th-cent. BC painter] iocosco nomine Gryllum derediculi habitus pinxit, unde id genus picturae grylli vocantur' (he also painted a figure in an absurd costume known by the joking name of Gryllus, the name consequently applied to every picture of that sort). In her notes from King's *Antique Gems* in *WN* GE records that '*Chimerae*, also called Grylli, from the Italian word signifying both cricket and caprice, are grotesque figures formed of portions of various animals combined into the outline of a monster which generally bears the shape of a bird or a horse. Paintings of similar "capricci" were common among the ancients . . . Their first origin must have been those combinations of masks where the engraver sought to produce effect by putting together the strongest contrasts.'

62 **Landino** Cristoforo Landino (1424–98), who held the chair of Poetry and Rhetoric at Florence from 1458, was the author of a notable commentary on the *Aeneid*. One of the most eminent intellectuals at the court of Lorenzo de' Medici, he was a leading member of the Platonic Academy.

62 **the example of Lorenzo** See p. 17.

62 **an age worse than that of iron** The period between the death of Charlemagne and the end of the Carlovingian dynasty (814–987) was sometimes called the 'age of iron' because of its ceaseless wars. Bardo's contemptuous description of the Laurentian period as 'an age of tinsel and gossamer' may be an allusion to Marsilio Ficino's famous remark

that 'this is an age of gold . . . at Florence', or to that of Jacopo Nardi that 'from iron was born a golden age [at Florence]'.

63 **Aurispa and Guarino . . . laden with manuscripts** The scholar and collector Giovanni Aurispa (1370–1459), who spent some years teaching at Florence, is said to have brought back to Italy, in a single year, over 200 MSS of works—by Plato and other ancient writers—many of which were hitherto unknown. For Guarino see p. 41.

63 **eager to borrow . . . not always willing to restore** In *BL* GE writes 'Filelfo scolds his friends in his letters because they don't return his books.' In Q she quotes from and transl. one of Filelfo's Latin letters to Niccolò Niccoli, excusing himself from not sending a book as requested on the grounds that 'it is in the hands of that harpy, John Aurispa, who borrows books on the condition of never returning them'. Later in the same notebook she jots down a reference from Filelfo to lending books for a month and then having them kept for years despite repeated requests for their return.

63 **erudite Greeks . . . for a refuge** Bardo is referring to the period immediately following the fall of Constantinople to the Turks in 1453, when many Greek scholars sought refuge in Italy and gave added impetus to the renascent interest in antiquity.

63 **Ciriaco** Born in Ancona and largely self-educated (he began life as a shipping-clerk), Ciriaco de Filippo Pizzicolli (*c.*1391–*c.*1450) spent many years travelling in Greece, Asia Minor, and Egypt in search of classical inscriptions and antiquities. (It was from him that Florence received first-hand knowledge of the Pyramids.) When asked why he had devoted himself to these labours, he replied 'I go to awake the dead'. He wrote various accounts of his travels; one of them took the form of a long letter to Pope Eugenius IV entitled *Itinerarium*, which is presumably the book referred to by Bardo (see p. 65).

64 **Ancona** A seaport on the Adriatic coast of central Italy.

64 **plains of the Eurotas . . . Mycenæ and Tyryns** The Eurotas is the river on which Sparta stood. The ancient cities of Mycenae and Tiryns, about 9 miles apart, both had massive walls which were said to have been built by the Cyclopes.

65 **the *Isolario* of Cristoforo Buondelmonte** A Florentine merchant turned priest, Buondelmonte (?–1422) travelled widely among the Greek islands in search of MSS for Cosimo de' Medici. He described his voyages in *De Insulis Archipelago*, the book referred to by Bardo as the *Isolario* (*isola* = island).

65 **Ambrogio Traversari** 1386–1439, a Camaldolensian monk who had studied Greek at Constantinople. Later, as General of the Camaldolensian order, he made an extended inspection tour of monasteries throughout Italy, where he discovered a number of important ancient MSS. He wrote an account of his travels in the *Hodoeporicon*—the book referred to by Bardo as an *Itinerarium*.

65 **charged with forgery** . . . **hideous crimes** Of the transcribers and editors of ancient MSS in the 15th cent. Villari writes: 'Then came discussions on the authenticity and interpretation of the manuscripts; there were hot disputes on philological and grammatical details, and the strife overleaping the limits of debate, these learned scholars tore one another to pieces in violent onslaughts on their respective honour and reputation.' In his *Life of Lorenzo de' Medici* Roscoe notes that in his *Invectivae* against Filelfo, Poggio accuses his fellow-scholar first of meanness of birth (he branded him the bastard son of a country priest and a tripe-seller) and then of 'fraud, ingratitude, theft, adultery, and yet more scandalous crimes'. Poggio also feuded with Lorenzo Valla for writing *illi* instead of *sibi*—the occasion, perhaps, of the reference here to Bardo being attacked 'for having shown error in a single preposition'.

66 **Setine** A Turkish corruption of the name Athens. In *Bod* GE writes: 'Corruption du nom d'Athènes, en Athina, Setine, etc. C'est la fausse interprétation que les oreilles occidentales donnaient à la contraction du grec moderne, εἰς ταἰς 'Αθηναἰς—εἰς τ' θηναἰς—Σθηναἰς. Stamboul s'est formé de la même maniere.' The passage is from Léon de Laborde's *Athènes aux XVᵉ, XVIᵉ et XVIIᵉ siècles*.

66 **conquered rival** . . . **philosopher Aristotle** Athens was named for Athena, who had successfully disputed with Poseidon for the honour of being the city's patron. Tito may perhaps be alluding also to a more specific (though obscurely erudite) topographical relationship between the two gods. In his history of Athens, Laborde quotes a MS from the Imperial library at Vienna written by an anonymous Greek in 1460 describing a visit to Athens; part of the account, in Laborde's transl., is as follows: 'près de ces palais subsiste encore à présent l'école dite d'Aristote. Au dessus de cette école s'élève deux colonnes: sur celle qui est au levant était placée la statue de Minerve; et sur celle qui est au couchant, la statue de Neptune'. (Minerva and Neptune, of course, are the Roman equivalents of Athena and Poseidon.)

66 **where St. Philip baptized the Ethiopian eunuch** Acts 8: 26–39 records that the baptism took place on the road from Jerusalem to Gaza. The anonymous Greek MS quoted by Laborde refers to 'la première place de la ville, où l'apôtre Philippe plongea le scribe dans l'eau'; in his commentary Laborde talks of 'La légende violemment transplantée du texte des Actes des apôtres'.

66 **voice of the muezzin** . . . **prayers** In *Bod* GE writes: 'Minaret with its gallery rising above the [?entablature] of the Parthenon: "C'est de là que le muezzin appela dès lors, et a pu appeler pendant quatre cent ans, les fidèles mussulmans à la prière."' The sentence in French is from Laborde's *Athènes*.

66 **the Parthenon** . . . **the temple of the Unknown God** [cancelled *MS* reading] In Q GE records two references in Laborde's *Athènes* to the Parthenon being known as the temple of the Unknown God: one from the anonymous Greek MS of 1460 and one from a letter by another Greek, Simeon Kabasilas, of 1578.

66–7 temple which had once been won . . . the Moslem The chief temple of Athena on the Acropolis, the Parthenon was originally associated with the cult of Athena Parthenos the Virgin. It was transformed into a church in the 5th cent. and dedicated to the Virgin Mary in 662. The Turks turned it into a mosque after the fall of Athens in 1458.

67 walls of the Acropolis . . . Piræus Cf. 'les marins . . . apercevaient les murs de l'Acropole d'Athènes par-dessus le bastinage de leur navire, à l'ancre dans le port du Pirée' (Laborde, *Athènes*). This passage is written out by GE in Q.

67 'old stones' . . . Venetian spies Cf. 'Quant aux archéologues, s'ils eûssent existé, ils auraient été malvenus à Athènes, on les eût traités comme des espions vénitiens, nul alors n'eût compris qu'un homme de sens se détournât de la route suivie pour venir voir ce qui était déjà pour les Turcs, et ce qu'ils n'ont cessé d'appeler de *vieilles pierres*' (Laborde, *Athènes*).

67 Pausanias and Pliny described In the *Periegesis* and the *Historia Naturalis* respectively.

67 groves of Helicon . . . fountain Hippocrene Mount Helicon, in Boestia, was the seat of the Muses. The fountain Hippocrene was on Helicon. Both were commonly used to suggest poetic inspiration.

67 French or Italian marquis When the crusaders conquered Greece in the early 13th cent., they divided it into duchies ruled over, for the most part, by Frankish and Italian knights.

68 girl of eighteen Bardo says that Romola was 6 when he went blind (p. 55), and that his sight was 'fast failing' in 1477 (p. 49), which suggests that in 1492 Romola should have been 20 or 21.

69 the ill-famed Margites Margites—'the booby'—is the hero of a lost Greek comic poem that was widely believed to have been written by Homer. A ludicrous figure, he displayed conceit and ignorance in equal measure.

69 'abnormis sapiens' 'Strangely wise', 'an unschooled scholar' (Horace, *Satires*, 2. 2. 3). GE jots down the phrase in *WN*, with the gloss 'For a description of the frugal rich farmer, see this satire'.

69 Con viso che tacendo dicea, Taci 'With a look that silently said "Be silent"' (Dante, *Purgatorio*, 21. 104). The word *dicea* should in fact be *disse*.

70 sanctioned by Pliny See *Historia Naturalis*, bk. 37.

70 Camillo Leonardi The author of *Speculum Lapidum* ('The Mirror of Stones'), a book—dedicated to Cesare Borgia—on the mystic properties of gems, which GE consulted in her preparations for the novel.

73 'To wish ill or well . . . wrongs or kindness' In *Pf* jots down the original of this statement (quoted by Villani in his *Istorie fiorentine*) by Farinata degli Uberti, a prominent Florentine Ghibelline in the 13th cent.: 'Volere e disvolere, per oltraggi e grazie riceviste.'

75 **now known as the Casa Gherardesca** In 1558 the Scala Palace was sold to Cardinal Alessandro de' Medici. He died shortly after being elected Pope Leo XI, and the palace descended to his sister Constanza, wife of Ugo della Gherardesca.

75 *Gradatim* Step by step.

75 **long since made his orations** In Q GE records a passage from Rico Spinelli's diary (quoted by Domenico Manni in his *Bartholomaei Scalae, Collensis*, about Scala's official oration on the *ringhiera* on 4 Oct. 1481 to invest Constanza Sforza as Captain-General of Florence). Spinelli notes that it was 'una lunga e degna orazione' and that 'tutto il populo' cried out 'Viva Messer Bartolommeo!'

75 **embassy to Rome . . . Gonfaloniere** Scala went to Rome in Dec. 1484 to deliver the Florentine Republic's official oration in honour of the new Pope, Innocent VIII—as a result of which the Pope conferred on him the various dignities mentioned in the novel. As to the date of Scala's election to the office of Gonfaloniere, GE has made an uncharacteristic slip. As she records in Q, he was elected in 1486; however, 'eight years ago' from this point in the novel would be 1484.

76 **a very typical and pretty quarrel** In fact, though Scala and Poliziano had crossed swords on previous occasions, the specific quarrel which GE goes on to describe in such close detail took place early in 1494—some 18 months after this point in the action of the novel.

76 **a lucky man** When Scala had been elected Gonfaloniere in 1486, Poliziano had written an ode declaring that neither nobility of birth nor virtue, but simply good fortune, had been responsible for his advancement. The insult was repeated by Poliziano in a letter of 1494 during the 'learned squabble' described in this chapter.

76 **the terrible Joseph Scaliger** Joseph Justus Scaliger (1540–1609) was celebrated alike for his learning and his vituperative criticisms of fellow scholars. GE found his remarks about Scala in Domenico Manni's *Bartholomaei Scalae, Collensis*, where he is quoted as saying 'nam de Scala illo nihil dicam aliud, quam totius latinitatis hominem ignarum fuisse' (I shall say nothing about that man Scala, except that he didn't have the remotest clue about Latin).

76 **Ineffable moment!** The whole of this paragraph, and the one that follows, amounts to a close paraphrase of the published correspondence between Scala and Poliziano. GE has not reproduced the entire interchange, but the salient and representative details she has selected are taken directly from the letters.

76 **(egi liberius cum te, ita enim soleo)** [cancelled *MS* reading] Poliziano's letter to Scala opens with the words 'Egi tecum liberius (ita enim soleo)'—'I'm very free with you since that's the way I'm used to being'.

76 **Latin epigram . . . feminine gender** The word *culex* is indeed almost always masculine, though it appears in the feminine gender in Plautus'

Casina (239) and at l. 413 of one MS of the poem *Culex* (see below). Poliziano's epigram, written as if from the culex itself, reads: 'Non sum fœmina Scala nec Latinis, | Nec Græcis, ideo placet puella' (I am not a woman, Scala, neither in Latin nor Greek, and therefore I like girls).

77 **a lively conceit about Venus, Cupid, and the** *culex* The 'conceit' was about the gnat in the role of a lover, rising like Venus from breeding waters and flying like Cupid to suck the blood of sleeping women while singing 'what man bears as many marks of love as the gnat?' The reading in *MS* and *CM* here (presumably changed by GE on the proofs of *1*) is: 'a lively conceit . . . unhappily founded partly on the zoological mistake that the flea, like the gnat, was born from the waters'. The word *culex* means mosquito, gnat, or midge, but *not* flea. Mosquitos, gnats, and midges do breed in water, but fleas do not, so the 'conceit' as originally represented by GE would indeed have been founded on a 'zoological mistake'—though it was not a mistake made by Poliziano. The mistake, rather, appears to have been GE's, in misunderstanding *culex* to mean flea (in Q she jots down a note of the 'dispute between Politian & Scala about the gender of "flea"')—an error, it would seem, she later recognized and corrected.

77 **the doctrine of Thales** The philosopher Thales (6th cent. BC), one of the so-called 'Seven Wise Men' of ancient Greece, was credited by Aristotle with having suggested that all matter has its origin in water.

78 **the gnat . . .** *"alumnus* **of the waters"** Until well into the 20th cent. the poem *Culex* was generally believed to be an early work of Virgil; l. 183 of the poem refers to the gnat as 'umoris alumnus' (nursling of the damp).

78 **"nihil ad rem"** Not to the point, irrelevant. To be precise, Poliziano accused Scala's remarks of being 'frivola & nihil ad rem'.

78 **a Homeric sentiment** Poliziano's quotation was from *Iliad*, 9. 312–13 (Achilles to Odysseus): 'hateful to me even as the gates of hell is he that hides one thing in his heart and says another'.

78–9 **branny monster . . .** *dignissimus* Poliziano's letter reads: 'At ego monstru vocavi te furfuraceum. Monstrum quide, quod ex colluvione monstrorum compositus es. Furfuraceum vero, quod in pistrini sordibus natus, & quidem pistrino dignissimus.' (I've called you a branny monster. A monster certainly, since created from the droppings of monsters. Branny indeed because born amid the filth of a mill, and entirely suited to a mill.)

79 **assuming to be a Hercules . . . miraculous revelations** In *Pf* GE writes: 'Says Scala of Politian. "He sends letters to me without signing them, as if they were miraculous revelations." He thinks himself the Hercules who will destroy all the literary monsters of the age.' Scala did indeed criticize Poliziano in these terms in one of the letters of their correspondence.

79 **thought they wrote like Cicero . . . "esse videtur"** Cicero's preferred ending was in fact '*esse videatur*'; the hexameter verse ending '*esse*

videtur' would have been inappropriate to a prose sentence. What I take
to be GE's mistake here (though conceivably she intends it as a remarkably erudite joke at Scala's expense) is the stranger in that she appears to
be alluding to Quintilian's *Institutio Oratoria*, 10. 2. 18 (as did Poliziano
himself in a letter to Paulus Cortesius): 'Noveram quosdam, qui se pul-
chre expressisse genus illud caelestis huius in dicendo viri sibi videren-
tur, si in clausula posuissent *Esse videtur*' (I have known some who
thought that they had produced a brilliant imitation of the style of that
divine orator, by ending their periods with the phrase *esse videtur*).
Though they argued at length about Ciceronian style, and whose Latin
was closest to it, neither Scala nor Poliziano invoked this comparison in
their correspondence.

79 **O wise young judge!** Cf. *The Merchant of Venice*, 4. 1. 222–3: 'A
Daniel come to judgement! Yea, a Daniel! O wise young judge, how I do
honour thee!'

80 *lusus naturæ* . . . **Cupid riding on the lion** . . . the "Jew's Stone,"
with the lion-headed serpent In her notes from King's *Antique Gems*
in *WN* GE records that 'Among the gems at Strawberry Hill was "a
lusus naturae [a freak of nature: here referring to a gemstone of particularly unusual markings], a rare Egyptian pebble . . . set in gold."' The
emerald signet of Polycrates (a Greek tyrant of the 6th cent. BC), of
which King reproduces a line drawing, was engraved with an image of
Cupid astride a lion. GE goes on to note that '*Gnostic Gems* . . . are the
sole glyptic monuments we possess of the last centuries of Roman
dominion in the West . . . The earliest are those of purely Egyptian
types; a very frequent one being a serpent, erect, with a lion's head surrounded by seven rays . . . This is Chneph the good genius of the
Egyptian religion, the type of life & of the sun . . . When the art had
expired, the Gnostic amulets were ascribed to the ancient Hebrews, &
thence called *Jew's stones*'.

81 **says old Villani** The remainder of this sentence amounts almost to a
direct transl. of a passage from Villani's *Istorie fiorentine* (1. 60): 'i
Fiorentini levarono il loro idolo, il quale appelavano Iddio Marte, e pos-
serlo in su una alta torre appresso al fiume d'Arno, e non vollono
rompere nè spezzare, però che per loro antiche memorie trovavano, che il
detto loro Iddio Marte era consecrato sotto ascendente di tal pianeta, che
come fosse rotto e commosso in vile luogo, la città arebba gran danno, e
gran mutazione . . . E ciò fatto il detto loro tempio consecrarono ed ordi-
narono ad onore d'Iddio, e del beato messere s.Giovanni Battista, e chia-
maronlo duomo di s. Giovanni.'

81 **Theodolinda . . . Constantine the Great and Pope Sylvester**
Theodelinda was queen of the Lombards in the late 6th cent. The
Roman Emperor Constantine was supposedly cured of leprosy by St
Sylvester in the early 3rd cent. The story goes that as a result he
bestowed upon Sylvester and his heirs (i.e. the Popes) the sovereignty of
Rome, and himself founded a new capital in the east (Constantinople).

81 **the man-destroyer** Ares, the Greek equivalent of Mars, is described by Homer as 'murderous' (*Odyssey*, 8. 115) and as 'blood-stained bane of mortals' (*Iliad*, 5. 31).

81 **Guelf and Ghibelline . . . heretic Paterini** The Guelphs and Ghibellines were political factions whose most violent clashes occurred in the 13th cent. The former aligned themselves with the Pope, the latter with the Holy Roman Emperor, though in due course the Guelphs became associated simply with the popular cause and the Ghibellines with the aristocratic. The Blacks and the Whites (*Bianchi e Neri*) were rival factions in the 14th cent., whose quarrel initially derived from a family feud. The common ancestor of the two houses concerned had had two wives; one was called Bianca, and the descendants of that branch were therefore known as *Bianchi*, whereupon their rivals took the name of *Neri*. As the quarrel spread and became political, the *Bianchi* were associated with the Ghibellines and the *Neri* with the Guelphs. *Paterini* (from Pattaria, a poor quarter of Milan) was originally the name given to the followers of deacon Arialdi in 11th-cent. Milan, who opposed the marriage of priests; it was subsequently applied to Albigensians and Cathars, and then became a general term of religious opprobrium directed at Manichaeans and other 'heretical' sects.

81–2 **conquests . . . over hated Pisa** After decades of bitter struggle Florence finally conquered Pisa in 1406, thus gaining direct access to the sea for the first time.

82 **"the fifth element"** On the occasion of the first Jubilee, or Plenary Indulgence, instituted by Pope Boniface VIII in the year 1300, no fewer than 12 European states sent Florentines to Rome as their ambassadors, leading the Pope to remark that Florentines were 'a fifth element of the world'.

82 **Madonna dell' Impruneta** See p. 382.

82 **a clever Cecca** Francesco d'Angelo (1447–88), known as Cecca—a variant of Cecco, from Francesco—was a noted Florentine engineer, builder of siege engines, and improver of the city's defensive walls and towers. He was also responsible for designing the spectacular 'special effects' associated with the celebration of major religious festivals, such as that of San Giovanni. Those described by GE in this paragraph and on p. 84 are taken from Vasari's account in his Life of Cecca. Cecca himself, of course, had been dead for 4 years at the time of this particular episode.

82 **saints . . . in the pictures of Perugino** GE is probably thinking of Perugino's *Assumption of the Virgin* with Saints Giovanni Gualberto, Benedict, Bernardo degli Uberti, and Michael (*c.*1500: now in the Uffizi, though GE saw it in the Accademia delle Belle Arti, describing it in her journal 'Recollections of Italy' as 'an assumption by Perugino which I like well for its cherubs and angels, and for some of the adoring figures below'; Lewes described it as a painting 'of surpassing excellence').

83 **says an old chronicler** Goro Dati, whose chronicle, dating from the year 1400, is quoted thus by Lastri: 'per tutta la città si fa quel di nozze e gran conviti, con tanti pifferi, souni e canti, e balli, feste; e letizia e ornamento, che pare che quella Terra sia il Paradiso'.

84 **Pope Innocent was dying . . . set Italy by the ears** Innocent VIII died almost exactly a month after Midsummer Day 1492, on 25 July. Charles VIII of France was being encouraged by the ambitious Ludovico Sforza of Milan (see p. 212) to invade Italy and claim the house of Anjou's 'hereditary right' (p. 208) to the throne of Naples.

84 **the Bargello** In 1492 the building, which had been begun in 1255, would in fact have been known as the Palazzo del Podestà. It did not become the headquarters of the Bargello (Chief of Police) until the mid-16th cent.

85 **the Valdarno** The valley of the R. Arno in the countryside outside Florence.

86 **'hound of the Lord'** 'A play on the name of the Dominicans (*Domini Canes*) which was accepted by themselves, and which is pictorially represented in a fresco painted for them by Simone Memmi.' [GE: this footnote was added in *CM*; in *MS* the text reads '"hound of the Lord" (Domini Cane)'.] The fresco of the Church Militant, showing St Dominic sending forth the hounds of the Lord, is in the Spanish Chapel of the Dominican church of Santa Maria Novella, and is in fact by Andrea di Bonaiuto (fl. 1343–77), who is also known as Andrea da Firenze. The fresco was formerly thought to be by the Sienese painter Simone Martini (*c*.1283–1344), who in the 19th cent. was sometimes confused with his brother-in-law Lippo Memmi (fl. 1317–47). Andrea di Bonaiuto, a Florentine, was clearly influenced by the Sienese School.

86 **Francesco Cei** 1471–1505, a minor poet. Among the foremost of the *Compagnacci* (see p. 393), he was instrumental in precipitating a riot in San Marco on the occasion of Savonarola's Ascension Day sermon there in 1497. Dissolute and irreverent, he wrote numerous poems against the Church in general and Savonarola in particular.

87 **Cronaca . . . Frate's doctrines into stone** The architect Simone Masi (1455–1509), more generally known as Simone del Pollaiuolo from his being related to the sculptor Antonio Pollaiuolo, was also known as 'Il Cronaca' (the chronicler) because of the vivid and detailed accounts he would give of the antiquities he had seen while living in Rome. Among his most important works are the Strozzi Palace, the sacristy of Santo Spirito, and the Salone dei Cinquecento in the Palazzo Vecchio. During the last years of his life, according to Vasari, 'he became possessed with such a frenzy for the discourses of Fra Girolamo Savonarola, and his head was so filled with them, that he would speak of nothing else'.

87 **Orators** Ambassadors (the usage is now obsolete; the first English use of the word recorded by *OED* is in 1494).

87 **Venetian . . . at home on the back of a dolphin** The speaker being

Cennini, the printer, the allusion here is perhaps to Aldus Manutius' (see p. 55) typographical device of an anchor and dolphin, which appeared as a logo on the title-pages of his books. The anchor represented solidity, the dolphin rapidity.

87 **the Madonna Nunziata** Nello is referring to the 'miraculous fresco' of the Annunciation in the church of the Annunziata, popularly believed to have been painted by a friar under the guidance of an angel or, according to a variant of the legend, by the angels themselves.

88 **'Pisans false, Florentines blind'** From the Tuscan proverb 'Fiorentini ciechi, Senesi matti [crazy], Pisani traditori, Luchesi signori'.

88 **Minerva with her peplos** The Greek counterpart of Minerva, Athena, was patroness of Athens as San Giovanni was patron of Florence. A new robe was woven each year for her statue in Athens.

88 **says the old chronicler, "all things . . . , heart"** Goro Dati, as quoted by Lastri: '. . . quivi sono uomini a cavallo armeggiando, e quali sono perdoni con lance, e quale con palvesi correndo, e quali sono donzelle, che danzano a rigoletto; in su essi sono scolpiti animali, e uccelli e diverse ragioni di alberi, pome e tutte le cose, che anno a dilettare il vedere, e il cuore.'

88 **Mugello . . . Casentino** Rural districts of Tuscany.

88 **grotesque sketches** Vasari records that Leonardo was so fascinated by 'faces of extraordinary character, or heads, beards or hair of unusual appearance' that he would follow their owners about the streets all day and then go home and draw them. He is also reported to have invited a number of peasants to supper on one occasion and then told them funny stories to make them laugh so that he could sketch their faces in extravagant contortions.

89 **Romagnole** From Romagna, the northern part of the Papal States, between the Apennines and the Po.

89 **Saint Anthony's swine** St Anthony (251–356), also known as St Anthony the Abbot, is commonly represented in paintings with a pig—a symbol of sensuality, which he subdued. In her notes from Mrs Jameson's *Sacred and Legendary Art* in *WN* GE records that this image 'gave rise to the superstition that the pig was under his special protection. The monks of the order of St. Antony kept herds of consecrated pigs, which were allowed to feed at the public cost, & which it was sacrilege to kill'.

89 **The car of the Zecca** GE's description of the 'car' (really 'cart' or 'waggon'—from the Italian *carro*) is taken, in close detail, from Vasari's Lives of Cecca and Jacopo da Pontormo, from Luca Chiari's 'Priorista', and above all from the chronicle of Goro Dati as quoted by Lastri.

89 **ill-painted figure . . .** *fantoccio da cero* The line is taken from Vasari's Life of Cecca: 'onde si dice alle cattive pitture "fantocci da ceri"'.

89 **St. John the Baptist . . . the Holy Family** By the mid-15th cent. the figure of St John as a solitary hermit (deriving perhaps from Fra

Domenico Cavalca's *Vita di San Giovanni Battista*) was well established
in Florentine religious iconography—as in Donatello's statue known as
the *Giovanni Martelli*, and Desiderio da Settignano's profile relief bust of
the saint, both in the Bargello; Alesso Baldovinetti's *Madonna and Saints*,
in the Uffizi; and the (slightly later) lunette in Santa Maria Novella
attributed to Botticelli. It was not until the latter part of the century that
the tendency arose to intensify the relationship between John and Jesus
(as children, or infants), whereby John was introduced into the family
group rather than, as before, kept relatively distant or represented alone.
The 'garment of tiger-skins' seems a 'vernacular' and peculiarly
Florentine tradition. Matthew 3: 4 relates that John wore a 'raiment of
camel's hair, and a leathern girdle about his loins'; Mark 1: 6 reads:
'John was clothed in camel's hair, and with a girdle of skin about his
loins'. In almost all 14th- and 15th-cent. representations, Florentine and
otherwise, he is duly shown, whether as a hermit or as a member of the
Holy Family, wearing a garment fashioned of camel hair. GE's source
here is Lastri, who reports that until the mid-18th cent. St John was
represented in the Midsummer Day procession in Florence by 'un uomo
fermato con cigne ad una sbarra di ferro, *vestito di due pelli di tigre*, con
braccia e gambe nude, nimbo in testa, e croce alta di ferro in mano,
affissa alla base. Così rappresentavasi il Precursore.' (My italics.) Lastri
goes on to relate that the said representative's remuneration consisted of
'lire dieci' (see original reading, changed by GE on *3C*); 'una gran
ciambella di circa 14 libbre di pane, con 2 caraffe . . . uno pieno di vin
bianco e l'altro di rosso, ed alcune paste e confetti'; and notes that these
offerings were traditionally presented from a window on the second floor
of the Casa Vannini in the Via de' Balestrieri.

89 **"beautiful sheepfold"** Dante, *Paradiso*, 25. 5 ('bello ovile').

90 **corporation of Calimala** ' "Arte di Calimala," "arte" being, in this use
of it, equivalent to corporation.' [GE]

90 **Art of money-changers** See p. 382.

90 **matriculated** A citizen could be matriculated, i.e. admitted to membership in a guild, only after giving evidence of suitable skills.

90 **Diogenes-fashion** The Cynic philosopher Diogenes of Sinope (4th cent.
BC) was known for his eccentric behaviour. His namesake Diogenes
Laertius, in his *Lives of Eminent Philosophers*, 6. 41, records that on one
occasion he lit a lamp in broad daylight and announced that he was
going in search of an honest man. 400 candle-bearing members of the
Calimala Guild traditionally accompanied the car of the Zecca in processions.

90 **the Feast of Fools** A form of clerical saturnalia or burlesque mass with
indecent songs and obscene dances, common throughout the middle ages
and usually held between 26 and 28 Dec.

90 **Donatello's statue of Judith** Maestro Vaiano's monkeys could not in
fact have seen the statue at all in 1492 unless they had access to the gardens of the Medici Palace. It was removed from there to a site outside

the Palazzo Vecchio in 1495 following the expulsion of the Medici from Florence, and then placed in Orcagna's Loggia—where GE would have seen it—in 1506. The statue was cast in the late 1450s. For Maestro Vaiano, see ch. 10.

91 **ancients . . . gravity and jest** Cei may be alluding to Juvenal (*Satires*, 10. 28–30): 'iamne igitur laudas quod de sapientibus alter | ridebat, quotiens a limine moverat unum | protuleratque pedem, flebat contrarius auctor?' (So won't you commend the two sages [Democritus of Abdera and Heraclitus of Ephesus], one of whom laughed while the other wept each time he set foot outside the door?).

91 **foreign *Podestà*** The office of Podestà or chief magistrate, abolished in Florence by the Medici in the 1470s, was common to most Lombard and Tuscan cities from the early 13th cent. onwards. The Podestà was a non-Florentine, elected for a period of one year, as an impartial arbiter. As well as the 'judge in civil [and criminal] causes', he acted as commander-in-chief of the army and as the city's representative in dealings with foreign powers. He received a fixed salary from the State and had his official residence in the Bargello (see p. 84).

91 **Proposto** 'Spokesman or Moderator.' [GE: n. added in *CM*] The position rotated among the Priors, generally being changed twice a week, and sometimes every second day.

91 **dragon that guards . . . Bardo's gold** The golden apples received by Hera as a marriage-gift were guarded by a dragon in the Garden of the Hesperides.

91 **Pactolus** The Pactolus is a river in Asia Minor believed to have gold in the sands beneath its waters after Midas bathed in it to rid himself of his fatal gift of turning all that he touched to gold.

92 **singular good fortune** Endymion was a shepherd with whom Selene, the moon goddess, fell in love.

92 **Da quel giorno . . . cortese** From the very day when love enflamed me I have become through her both gentle and courteous (Pulci, *Il morgante maggiore*, 2. 68. 7–8).

93 **under our four eyes that I talk** A transl. of the Italian expression 'parlare a quattr' occhi'.

93 **he can see a buffalo in the snow** Cf. 'elli non averebbe veduto la bufola nelle neve' (Sacchetti, *Trecentonovelle*, no. 209).

94 **Corso degli Adimari** Now the Via de' Calzaioli.

96 **forbidden by the Signory to wear the richest brocade** In Q there are 2 pp. of closely written notes giving details of Florence's sumptuary laws in the 15th cent. (designed to check extravagance, particularly in the lower classes, and generally ignored by the nobility). Among the items of dress GE notes as proscribed is 'any brocade of silver or gold, or embroidery'.

97 *morgen cap* 'A sum given by the bridegroom to the bride the day after the marriage (*Morgengabe*).' [GE: n. added in *CM*]

97 **more than a man's ransom** In Q *GE* notes a passage from Laborde's *Athènes* about the payment of 300 gold ducats to ransom an Englishman from the Turks in 1510.

102 **hostelry of the *Bertucce*** In his notes to Ademollo's *Marietta de' Ricci*, Passerini records that one of the most celebrated inns of 15th-cent. Florence (one frequented by Lorenzo de' Medici) was the 'osterìa delle Bertucce', located behind the church of San Martino del Vescovo (between the Duomo and the Badia). GE would also have found information about it in Lastri.

104 **Vaiano** In *MS* the conjuror's name is given as 'Vaio' throughout.

104 **she'll come back presently, as the toad said to the harrow** GE has taken this expression, which she jots down in *Bod*, from Machiavelli's *La mandragola* (3. 6). In a letter of Sept. 1525 to Francesco Guicciardini, Machiavelli explains that it is used to signify that the person has absolutely no wish to return at all.

104 **father-in-law** GE uses the word in its archaic sense of 'step-father'.

104 **San Pulinari** A church just off the Piazza della Signoria.

105 **Peretola** A village some 3½ miles to the north-west of the city.

106 **badge of the yellow veil** Prostitutes were obliged to wear this as a sign of their profession.

106 **Lorenzo de' Medici's *Nencia da Barberino*** The poem tells the story of the wooing by a young peasant (Vallera) of a peasant girl (Nencia).

106 **a Theocritus** Theocritus (3rd cent. BC) created, in his *Idylls*, the model for bucolic poetry in Greek, and later, through imitators such as Virgil, in Latin. The form enjoyed a revival in late 15th-cent. Italy, as in Lorenzo de' Medici's *Nencia da Barberino*.

108 ***Breve*** A charm; more specifically, a bag worn round the neck containing a relic or prayer on a scrap of paper.

108 **Prato** A town about 7 miles north-west of Florence.

111 **bit of red coral . . . a 'buon fortuna'** In her notes from Paris's *Pharmacologia* in *WN* GE writes: 'it was even supposed that coral would drive away devils & evil spirits; hence arose the custom of wearing coral amulets round the neck . . . In Sicily it is also commonly worn as an amulet by persons of all ranks as a security against an evil eye: a small twisted piece, resembling a horn, is worn at the watchchain, under the name of "Buon Fortuna," & is occasionally pointed at those who are supposed to have evil intentions.'

117 **Via del Cocomero** Now the Via Ricasoli.

117 ***nidus*** Latin: a nest.

118–19 **sing the old Eumenides, in Æschylus** *Eumenides*, ll. 517–25.

121 **the poet has wisely said** Cf. Horace, *Satires*, 1. 9. 59–60: 'nil sine magno | vita labore dedit mortalibus' (life grants no reward to man without much toil).

121 'palma sine pulvere' The precise phrase (from Horace, *Epistles*, 1. 1. 51) is 'condicio dulcis sine pulvere palmae'. In Bod GE jots down 'palma sine pulvere' and transl. it as 'honours got without struggle'.

121 what says the Greek? Bardo's quotation is from an untitled fragment by Hesiod (see no. 321 of *Fragmenta Hesioda*, ed. R. Merkelbach and M. L. West (Oxford, 1967).

122 Calderino . . . their own mistakes Domizio Calderino (*c.*1447–78) was professor of Rhetoric at Rome and a celebrated editor of classical texts. In the preface to his *Miscellanea*, Poliziano attacks, in general terms, the widespread malpractices among contemporary scholars who 'freely invent whatever evidence suits their case, ascribe to classical authorities words which are not theirs, quote non-existent classical authors, cite ancient manuscripts which are nowhere to be found, and fill their books with painstaking vanities'. Though Calderino is not referred to here by name, he is the most frequent target of Poliziano's invective in the ensuing chapters; in ch. 9 e.g. he notes Calderino's determination to defend his reputation by fair means or foul ('per aequa, per iniqua famam captans').

122 Lorenzo Valla 1407–57, classical scholar, philologist, and moral philosopher. As Apostolic Secretary to Nicholas V he transl. Thucydides, and Herodotus, into Latin. His famous treatise *De Falso Credita et Emendita Constantini Donatione* proved that the so-called 'Donation of Constantine' was a forgery, and thereby undermined the traditional papal claim to temporal sovereignty. (The document described how the Emperor Constantine presented Pope Sylvester with his diadem and assigned to him, and his successors, Rome and all the provinces of Italy and the West. Valla's examination of the text revealed a Latin style uncommon until several centuries after the supposed date of the MS.) Equally influential in scholarly circles was Valla's *Elegentiae Linguae Latinae*, which sought to establish the correct usage of the ancient Romans on numerous points of grammar and style. Its aim, according to the preface, was to restore the Latin language to the purity that marked it before its corruption by the barbarians—something which Bardo would clearly have applauded. Valla was certainly held 'in dubious fame' by the Church: his exposure of the 'Donation', his attacks on celibacy and monasticism, and his denial of the authenticity of the Apostles' Creed led to furious recriminations; he was branded a heretic and eventually summoned to appear before the Inquisition. Nor was he a popular figure with many of his fellow-scholars, with whom he indulged in rancorous literary feuds (see p. 65). The epigram referred to by Bardo was anonymous; it read 'Dopo che morto il Valla giunse fra le ombre, Plutone non ardisce di parlare in latino.'

124 petticoat . . . seed-pearl arabesques . . . coral rosary . . . *niello* In a letter to Frederic Leighton of June 1862 GE writes that 'the best authority' she had found for women's costume in the 1490s was 'the very incomplete one of a certain Ginevra's *trousseau* in the Ricordi of the Rinuccini family of rather an earlier period, but marking even there the rage for embroidery and pearls which grew instead of diminishing'. In Q

in a list headed 'Trousseau of Ginevra' (which, in *BL* is written out in the original Italian), she notes down: '1 under petticoat (or ciopa) of crimson damask with pearls & fringe' and 'a coral rosary'. The notes are from the *Ricordi storici de Filippo Cino Rinuccini* and concern the trousseau of Ginevra d'Ugolino di Niccolò Martelli, who married Cino di Filippo Rinuccini in Florence in 1461. GE also notes that in 1462 Cino Rinuccini paid Maso di Finiguerra 'for a belt (or clasp?) of silver [the *Ricordi*, as noted in *BL*, refers to 'un fornimento da cintola d'ariento'] pierced and wrought in niello'. Niello is a black alloy of silver, lead, copper, and sulphur, used to fill in engraved designs on silver and gold.

125 **I know how many legs go into one boot** In *Bod*, in a section consisting of proverbial expressions written out in Italian, GE jots down (in English) 'He doesn't know how many fingers he has on his hand—doesn't know how many legs go into one boot.'

125 **I've been at the wedding to-day** So far as I can tell, this wedding is an invention of GE's. According to Ammirato's *Delle famiglie nobili fiorentine*, there was a marriage between a Dianora Acciajoli and Paolo Luca degli Albizzi, but at a quite different date. In *BL*, in a list of prominent Piagnoni, GE notes that Luca Antonio degli Albizzi (Brigida mentions that her 'husband was Luca Antonio's uncle by the mother's side') and Alessandro Acciajoli were 'de primi della setta Fratesca' (among the foremost of the monkish fraternity) and that they each had a 'parentado grande' (a great wedding), but she gives no further details.

125 **as solemn as San Giuseppe** Though later adopted as patron saint of the dying, St Joseph was not generally represented in renaissance art as looking especially solemn (neither does the Bible describe him as such); GE may perhaps be thinking of the figure of Joseph in Gentile da Fabriano's *Adoration of the Magi* which she saw in the Accademia di Belle Arti (now in the Uffizi), whose face might be described as 'solemn' in the sense of 'sad' or 'thoughtful'—and which she noted in her journal was 'masterly in the delicate rendering of expression'. It is of course possible that the reference is to Joseph of Arimathea rather than to the husband of the Virgin, though solemnity is not an attribute particularly associated with him either.

125 **Piagnoni** 'Funereal mourners: properly, paid mourners.' [GE: in 2 and 3 the word 'Funereal' becomes 'Funeral'] The term, meaning 'weepers' or 'snivellers', was applied to members of the popular party because, like Savonarola himself, they continually bewailed the sins of the city.

125 **Pinzochera** 'A Sister of the Third Order of St. Francis: an uncloisterd nun.' [GE] The third order of Franciscans consisted of *lay* brothers and sisters. The word has since come to signify any kind of religious zealot—or bigot.

125 **the Frate's book about widows** Savonarola's pamphlet 'Libro della Vita Viduale' was published in 1491. In it, though acknowledging that widows might remarry under certain circumstances, he declares that the most fitting life for them is to renounce the world, devote themselves

entirely to God, and become 'even as the dove, which is a chaste creature, and therefore, having lost its mate, never couples with another, but spends the rest of its life in lonely lamentation'.

125 **the three doctrines** See pp. 521–2.

126 **Francesco Valori . . . fond of the Medici** Like many of the supporters of Savonarola and the popular party, Valori had been a close associate of Lorenzo de' Medici (whose palace was in the Via Larga). Along with Domenico Bonsi, Guidantonio Vespucci, Pagolantonio Soderini, and Bernardo Rucellai (all of whom appear in the novel), he had been one of the group of prominent citizens sent to Savonarola by Lorenzo in 1491 to urge the newly appointed Prior of San Marco to modify the antagonistic tone of his sermons. Like many of Lorenzo's adherents, however, he became thoroughly disaffected with the wilful and incompetent Piero de' Medici, and transferred his allegiance to Savonarola.

126 **spend on . . . a giostra** In her notes from Vincenzo Borghini's *Discorsi* in Q GE records that in 1467 'Benedetto Salutati grandson of [the scholar] Coluccio, who was not of enormous wealth, spent a treasure in arraying two horses for a giostra, in silver & pearls.'

127 **scarcity of our plate . . . furniture of the table** In her journal for 19 Feb. 1862 GE records that she went to the British Museum and 'picked some details . . . from Borghini's Discorsi, about the simplicity of Florentine table equipage'. In her notes from Lastri in *BL* she jots down 'Plate, scarce in private families: lent on great occasions', and in Q she copies down a passage to this effect from Borghini.

127 **Franco Sacchetti's book** Sacchetti (?1332–1400) was a prolific poet and *novelliere*, whose prose masterpiece, the *Trecentonovelle*, modelled on Boccaccio's *Decameron*, consists of brief moral tales on all aspects of contemporary men and manners. Monna Brigida is probably referring to novella 136: 'E qual artista, o di panni, o di lana, o dipintore è, che del nero possa far bianco . . . Serà una figura pallida e gialla, con artificiati colori la fanno in forma di rosa . . . avrà il naso torto, tosto il faranno diritto . . . ' (And what artist is there, or dyer, or painter, who can turn black into white . . . a pale and yellow face with artificial colours is made into the likeness of a rose . . . a crooked nose is immediately straightened). In *Pf* GE writes: 'Clear that in Sacchetti's time the women painted & stuffed & used as many devices as at any later age to make fowl seem fair.'

127 **come a pulcini bagnati** (superseded *MS* reading) GE underlined the phrase 'come un pulcin bagnato' in her copy of Giuseppe Giusti's *Proverbi Toscani*.

127 **last Quaresima in San Lorenzo** i.e. Savonarola's Lenten sermons of 1492, delivered in the church of San Lorenzo.

127 **the Befana** 'The name given to the grotesque black-faced figures, supposed to represent the Magi, carried about or placed in the windows on Twelfth Night: a corruption of *Epifania*.' [GE] The phrase 'as ugly as the *Befana*' may be an echo of 'Che quest' orrida Befana', from Lippi's *Malmantile racquistato*, 5. 28.

128 **the good men of St. Martin** See p. 610.

128 **my confessor . . . at Santa Croce** The original (cancelled) *MS* reading here was 'my confessor . . . at San Miniato' (a Benedictine foundation). GE presumably decided to make the change since Santa Croce was a Franciscan church, and the Franciscans were implacable opponents of Savonarola. Santa Croce was also a more fashionable church, and one with which the Bardi family had connections (see p. 203).

128 **the great preachers Fra Mariano and Fra Menico** The Augustinian Fra Mariano de Gennazzano was a fashionable preacher known for his ornately eloquent style of delivery. In 1491, alarmed at the growing influence of Savonarola's denunciations of State and Church corruption, Lorenzo de' Medici encouraged Fra Mariano to preach against him. Villari records that he 'instantly and eagerly accepted the task', and that all the leading citizens of Florence were present at the resultant sermon (delivered not in the Duomo but in the convent church at San Gallo, on Ascension Day 1491). According to Villari, however, 'Fra Mariano was betrayed by his own zeal. He began by hurling all manner of accusations against Savonarola, styling him a false prophet, a vain disseminator of scandal and disorder among the people, and this with so much insolence and coarseness of language as to disgust all his hearers.' For Fra Menico see p. 19.

128 **the Pope's dream** In 1210 Pope Innocent III is reported to have had a dream in which he saw Francis of Assisi propping up the wall of the Lateran church, which seemed about to fall down. He promptly sent for Francis and approved the *Regula Prima* which governed the newly formed Franciscan order. The dream became a favourite subject for artists.

132 *mora* A game for *two* players: one holds up a random number of fingers while the other simultaneously guesses the number. Either Sandro is remarkably dim-witted, or GE has misunderstood the nature of the game.

132 **Quant' è bella . . . certezza.** ' "Beauteous is life in blossom! | And it fleeteth—fleeteth ever; | Whoso would be joyful—let him! | There's no surety for the morrow."—*Carnival Song by Lorenzo de' Medici*.' [GE: n. added in *CM*] It is appropriate that Tito should choose these particular lines, which form the opening of Lorenzo's song *Trionfo di Bacco e Arianna* (see p. 188).

132 **like a *trovatore*** Nello's designation of alliteration as a characteristic of Italian (or even provençal) troubadour verse is not strictly accurate. He (or GE) may be thinking of the *cantastorie*, or popular minstrels, whose indulgence in such word play was parodied by his favourite Luigi Pulci.

132 **as the sublime poet says** Cf. Dante, *Purgatorio*, 21. 37–8: '. . . per la cruna | del mio disio'.

133 **young Bernardo Dovizi of Bibbiena** Dovizi (1470–1520) was a tutor to Giovanni de' Medici (see p. 135) though he was barely five years

older than his pupil—on whose election to the papacy in 1513 he was created a cardinal (see p. 196).

133 **carry a net out to catch the wind** GE jots down the Tuscan proverb 'pigliare il vento con le reti' in *Bod*.

133 **Ser Piero** Piero Dovizi da Bibbiena had been chancellor to Lorenzo de' Medici, and subsequently acted in the manner of a vizier to Piero de' Medici. His arrogance and high-handed behaviour (see p. 168) made him widely unpopular.

133 **touch the sky with your forefinger** A transl. of the Italian expression 'toccare il cielo con un dito' (to be beside oneself with joy). In *Bod* GE jots down 'Toccava il ciel col ditto'.

133 **or something else** See p. 265.

133 **ears double-waxed** A reference to Ulysses' device of filling his companions' ears with wax to prevent them from hearing the song of the sirens.

134 **overthrown . . . like cavaliers in heavy armour** The origin of this remark is probably to be found in Tacitus (*Histories*, 1. 79), describing a battle in which the Sarmatian cavalry suffered just such a fate at the hands of the Romans. The expression 'not a herb out of his own garden' is a transl. of the Italian 'non è erba del suo orto' (jotted down by GE in *Bod* as 'non è erba di tua orta').

134 **feeding one with an empty spoon** In *Bod* GE jots down the old Italian expression 'Imboccare col cucchiajo voto' (to feed with an empty spoon—'cucchiaio vuoto' in contemporary usage).

134 **win my Alcestis** When Admetus asked Pelias for the hand of his daughter Alcestis, he was told that she would be given only to a man who arrived at Pelias' court in a chariot drawn by a lion and a boar. Admetus accomplished this feat with the aid of Apollo. Alcestis later gave up her life for her husband.

134 **Pleiad . . . marrying any mortal** The Pleiades were the seven daughters of Atlas, who were transformed into stars. One of them, Merope, is invisible, supposedly out of shame at having married a mortal.

134 **'prettier than the turnip-flower,' 'with a cheek more savoury than cheese.'** The quotations are from the 25th octave of Lorenzo de' Medici's 'well-rhymed' *Nencia da Barberino*: 'tu se' piú bella che 'l fior della rapa'; 'ch'è saporita piú che non è il caccio'.

134 **the mountains of Pistoia** The town of Pistoia is some 20 miles to the north-west of Florence; a range of hills begins just to the north of it.

135 **the Fierucola** 'The Little Fair.' [GE: n. added in *3P*; in all previous states the text reads 'Fierucola (petty fair)'.] Cf. 'quando vengono alla visita del devoto tempio della Nonziata le donne del vicino contado, e quelle del Casentino, e della Montagna di Pistoia. In tale occasione la fiera, o mercato di varie merci che vi si fa, accresce la frequenza dell'allegro popolo. Il filato che portano in vendita le dette donne, il

pannolino, ed i funghi secci, hanno procurato loro il nome di Fierucolone, quasi contribuenti alla fiera' (Lastri, *Osservatore fiorentino*).

135 **Giovanni de' Medici** . . . **Pope Leo the Tenth** Giovanni, the second son of Lorenzo the Magnificent, became a cardinal at the age of 13 in 1489, and was elected Pope in 1513. His 'broad dark cheek' is most famously represented in Raphael's portrait of him as Leo X.

135 **Via del Maglio** Now the Via Alfonso Lamarmora.

137 **as old as Sant' Anna** Luke 11: 36 records that the prophetess Anna, a widow, was 84 years old.

137 **a sign of reverence rarely made** Varchi, in a passage marked by GE in her own copy of the *Storia fiorentina*, records that the 'reverenza' of raising the 'cappuccio' was commonly accorded only to the Gonfaloniere or to a bishop or cardinal.

138 **Via San Sebastiano** Now the Via Gino Capponi.

140 **Via de' Febbrai** I can locate no such street—or any evidence that one so named ever existed. There is a Via de *Fibbiai* running into the Piazza dell' Annunziata, and it may be that GE misremembered or miscopied this name (*MS* clearly has it as *Febbrai*).

141 **Maestro Gabbadeo** See p. 605.

142 **a pumpkin on my shoulders** In *Pf* GE jots down the phrase 'Testa di Zucca', meaning pumpkin-head. The word *zucca* is widely used in certain idioms and in slang to mean head.

142 **Arno run broth** . . . **dipping your finger** In *Bod*, in a series of notes of proverbial expressions, GE writes 'If Arno ran broth you'd never dip your finger—think of dipping'.

144 **Alexander the Sixth** . . . **peculiar piety** Rodrigo Borgia—'a lustful, greedy, lying, and murderous old man' (p. 462)—was elected Pope in 1492.

146 **paint her** . . . **youth of seventeen** . . . **Mariotto** Probably the Florentine painter Mariotto Albertinelli (1474–1515), who, as GE records in Q, was 17 in 1492.

147 **the miraculous fresco of the Annunciation** See p. 87.

147 **dark with excess of light** In both *Bod* and *WN* GE writes out 'E col suo lume se medesmo cela. Dark with excess of light.' The line is from *Purgatorio*, 17. 57; a more literal transl. would be 'and hides itself with its own light'. Another phrase she might have had in mind is 'Si come il sol che si cela elli stessi | per troppa luce' (like the sun which conceals itself by excess of light: *Paradiso*, 5. 133–4).

147 **waxen images** The church had to be enlarged to accommodate these statues; there were over 600 of them by the mid-14th cent.

148 **altar-piece** Surprisingly, perhaps, it would seem that GE has invented this. The only altar-piece in the church with an image of St Michael was the one by Antonio del Ceraiuolo in the eighth chapel of the circular Tribune at the east end—a long way from the 'sacred image' of the

Annunciation, and at the opposite end from the cloisters through which
Tito leads Tessa. It was, moreover, not executed until the early 16th
cent. In fact, the description here of St Michael 'in his armour, with
young face and floating hair, amongst bearded and tonsured saints' is
strikingly reminiscent of Perugino's altar-piece of the Assumption, to
which GE had apparently referred earlier in the novel (see p. 82), though
this was never in the Annunziata and was not executed until c.1500.
There is another Perugino Assumption (c.1506) in the fourth chapel on
the north side of the nave (i.e. roughly at the spot where it seems Tessa
was seen by Tito), but there is no representation of St Michael in it.

149 **cloisters surrounding the atrium** . . . **Andrea del Sarto** There are
12 frescos in the atrium, or Chiostrino dei Voti, of the Santissima
Annunziata, all dating from the early 16th cent.; 7 are by Andrea del
Sarto (1486–1530), and 1 each by Rosso Fiorentino, Pontormo,
Franciabigio, Baldovinetti, and Cosimo Roselli. The cloisters were roofed
over in the 1830s.

150 **Saint Christopher** . . . **little *Gesù*** The story goes that St Christopher
was a giant who one day carried a little child across a river. The child
was Jesus, and when Christopher (= Christ-bearer) exclaimed (in Mrs
Jameson's account of the story in *Sacred and Legendary Art*) 'Had I carried the whole world upon my shoulders, the burthen had not been
heavier!' the child replied 'Wonder not, Christopher, for thou hast not
only borne the world, but him who made the world'. The St Christopher
sighted by Tessa in the streets was evidently one of the 'saints of gigantic size . . . balancing themselves on stilts' who formed part of the procession in honour of San Giovanni described in ch. 8. The St
Christopher 'on the wall of the church' was probably the painting by
Pollaiuolo on the side of San Miniato-tra-le torri, which, as GE records
in her notes from Mrs Jameson in *WN*, was 'a gigantic figure . . . about
twenty feet in height'. There was another huge representation of the
saint on a wall *inside* the church of San Miniato al Monte.

155 **no woman being allowed admission** This was still the case when GE
visited San Marco in 1860; her description of the interior is based on
notes made by Lewes.

158 **roll myself among thorns** When St Benedict, a hermit, was tempted
by the memory of a beautiful woman he had once known, he took off his
clothes and flung himself into a thicket of thorns until his whole body
was lacerated—to rid himself of the impure mental image by physical
pain.

166 **ordeal of swallowing bread and cheese pills** The allusion is to the
medieval superstition (to which Tito clearly does not subscribe) that men
who know themselves to be guilty will be unable to swallow, and may
therefore be tested by being given bread and cheese to eat.

167 **ortolans** An ortolan is a small bird, a species of bunting, found in
southern Europe and prized for its delicate taste.

167 **Bernardo Rucellai's rare trees** See p. 335.

167–8 **Have you heard the news . . . punishment?** The staunch Medicean
Paulo Antonio (or Pagolantonio) Soderini had requested leave from
Piero de' Medici to marry his son to the daughter of Filippo Strozzi,
and Piero had duly given his permission. Piero's close advisor, Piero
Dovizi, remonstrated that such a union of powerful and wealthy families was contrary to Medicean interests, insisting that old Lorenzo de'
Medici would never have allowed it. On learning that the wedding had
taken place notwithstanding, Dovizi berated Soderini so violently that
he received a slap in the face. In revenge he promptly had Soderini
removed from Florence by sending him to Venice as ambassador (a
position he had earlier held under Lorenzo de' Medici: see p. 646).
The story is recounted by both Nardi and Nerli in their histories of
Florence. Nardi refers to the blow as a *gotata* (*gota* = cheek).

169 **got your Fra Girolamo back again** Presumably a reference to
Savonarola's visit to Venice that May.

170 **new Jonah** Jonah was the prophet who warned Nineveh of impending
destruction if it did not mend its wicked ways. Savonarola himself
.invokes this parallel on p. 213.

170 **the fine oration** Cei is referring to Poliziano's *Pro Oratoribus
Senensium ad Alexandrum VI. Pont. Max.* He wrote only one such
address—hence my preference for the reading in *CM* and *1* ('oration')
to that in *MS*, *2*, and *3* ('orations').

170 **'non *o*ratorem, sed *a*ratorem'** 'Not an orator, but a ploughman'.
The remark is from a letter of 1440 from Filelfo to Giovanni
Tuscanella about Quintilian. In *Pf* GE writes: 'Movendi tamen,
delectandique vim nullam habet. Quae quidem duo qui oratori traverit,
non *o*ratorem illum, sed *a*ratorem demonstrabit (Filelfus of
Quintilian).' The word 'traverit' should be 'subtraxerit'.

170 **what says Luigi Pulci?** *Il morgante maggiore*, 17. 101: 'Prese Don
Bruno una sua scimitarra, | la qual già disse alcun ch'era incantata, |
benché 'l nostro aüttor questo non narra: | credo più tosto forte tem-
perata'. These lines are written out by GE in *Bod*. Don Bruno was a
saracen giant defeated by Orlando.

171 **Boccaccio's Maestro Simone** *Decameron*, 8. 9. In *Pf* GE writes: 'For
a picture of the Doctor of Physic see Boccaccio, Gior. ix, Nov. 3.'
This tale also concerns the exploits of Maestro Simone, but it is in the
earlier one that he is thrown into a ditch.

171 **Maestro Tacco** In Q GE notes that 'Maestro' was a title given to
physicians.

173 **Antonio Benevieni** Ben*i*vieni (1443–1502) was a celebrated Florentine
doctor and author of a treatise on the causes of disease.

173 **fasten in the wheel of Fortune** In *Pf* GE writes: 'Story of Valore
Buondelmonte bringing a nail to the feast of Piero degli Albizzi, recommending him to fix it in the wheel of Fortune. Sacchetti'; and
later in the same notebook: '"Putting a nail in the wheel of Fortune,"

to fix it, v. Sacchetti'. In no. 193 of his *Trecentonovelle* Sacchetti tells the story of Buondelmonte, who, though uninvited, turned up at the Albizzi feast carrying a large nail, and suggested that the host, a very successful man, should fasten it in the wheel of Fortune while he was at the top, lest he soon came down in the world. Albizzi replied that to do so would be unfair on those whose fortunes were then at a low point on the wheel, and besides he did not feel that he himself was yet at the top.

173 **San Cosmo and San Damiano** Cosmas and Damian were twin brothers who practised medicine in Cilicia. Christians, they were martyred in the year 303 during the persecutions of Diocletian. They are patron saints of barbers, druggists, dentists, and doctors (and hence of the Medici family).

174 **Canto di Paglia** 'Straw corner', a particularly sordid slum at the corner of the Borgo San Lorenzo and the Via dei Cerretani.

174 **Cecco d'Ascoli** Francesco (or Cecco) Stabili, known as d'Ascoli from his birthplace, was an astrologer who was burnt at the stake for heresy in Florence in 1327.

175 *tussis* Latin: a cough.

175–6 **Frate Minore who preached against the Jews** As Bratti had explained to Tito (see p. 13), the Franciscans were implacable enemies of the Jews and had frequently urged their eviction from the city. The specific event to which Nello alludes here is presumably the expulsion from Florence in 1488 of the rabble-rousing Franciscan Bernardino da Feltre, who denounced the government for permitting Jews to live in the city and practise usury. In her notes from Lastri in *BL* GE jots down 'Firmness of the Florentine government in punishing a friar who preached in favour of spoliating the Jews'. She may have found information about Bernardino da Feltre in the *Ricordanze* of Tribaldo d'Amerigo de' Rossi.

176 **wondrous Florentine device!** In *BL* GE notes that spectacles were invented by a Florentine named Salvino d'Armato, who died in 1317. In fact, though the earliest recorded comment on the use of optical lenses in the West is by Roger Bacon in 1268, it is now generally believed that eyeglasses were introduced into Europe in the late 13th cent. by Alessandro di Spina, also a Florentine. Whatever, the *MS* reading of this line ('wondrous Florentine device of the last generation') is incorrect, and was presumably altered by GE as such on the proofs of *CM*.

178 **a scene such as Florentines loved** Writing to Alexander Main in 1871, GE noted: 'The general ignorance of old Florentine literature, and the false conceptions of Italy bred by idle travelling . . . have caused many parts of "Romola" to be entirely misunderstood—the scene of the quack doctor and the monkey for example, which is a specimen, not of humour as I relish it, but of the practical joking which was the amusement of the gravest old Florentines, and without

which no conception of them would be historical. The whole piquancy of the scene in question was intended to lie in the antithesis between the puerility which stood for wit and humour in the old Republic, and the majesty of its front in graver matters' (*Letters*, v. 174).

178 **potent and reverend signor** Cf. *Othello*, 1. 3. 76: 'potent, grave, and reverend signiors'. *MS* here originally read 'grave signor'. See also p. 6— 'those potent signors'.

178 **licking marble** In *Bod* GE jots down 'As vain as licking marble "Leccar marmo"'.

182 **Aurora** Though Aurora was of course the Roman goddess of the dawn, Tito is clearly alluding to a Greek source—the 'fair-tressed Dawn' of *Odyssey*, 5. 390.

184 **'ingenia acerrima Florentina'** 'Very sharp Florentine minds'. The full quotation ('nam ingenia Florentina acerrima sunt, et in omnem partem strenua'), from a letter of 1432 from Filelfo to Niccolò Cardinal Bononiensi, is written out by GE in *Bod*. It also forms one of the unused epigraphs to the first chapter of the novel (see App. A).

187 **Via Gualfonda** 19th-cent. edns. of Vasari suggest that Piero di Cosimo's house was in the Via Gualfonda (now the Via Valfonda), but according to Piero's own declaration, in the 1498 rent rolls, he lived in the Via della Scala.

187 **pre-eminent in . . . fantastic mythological design** Vasari records that no 'master could produce more extraordinary effects than Piero di Cosimo', and that he delighted in painting 'fantastic objects' and 'entirely fabulous representations'. He goes on to suggest that one of Piero's best pictures was that of Perseus and Andromeda, commissioned by Filippo Strozzi. For Piero's painting of Cupid, Mars, and Venus—a painting which Vasari himself owned—see p. 190.

187 **a basket of eggs** Vasari notes that Piero would often 'allow himself no better food than hard eggs', and that he 'boiled them by fifties; he would set them apart in a basket, and ate them at any moment when he felt the necessity for food'.

188 **a favourite subject with . . . Florentines** GE herself owned a copy of Francesco Redi's poem *Bacco in Toscana*; see also p. 632. In Greek mythology, Dionysus (with whom the Romans identified Bacchus) found and married the Cretan princess Ariadne on the island of Naxos, where she had been abandoned by Theseus after helping him escape from the Minotaur's labyrinth.

188 **a story in Ovid** Cf. *Metamorphoses*, 3. 664–9: 'But ivy twines and clings about the oars, creeps upward . . . and decks the sails with heavy, hanging clusters. [Bacchus] himself, with his brow garlanded with clustering berries, waves a wand wreathed with ivy-leaves. Around him lie tigers . . . lynxes and fierce spotted panthers.' The marriage of Bacchus and Ariadne is described in bk. 8 of the *Metamorphoses*.

189 **tangled, trailing wildness** Cf. Vasari's account of Piero di Cosimo's

garden—'he would not have the soil of his garden cultivated, or the fruit-trees pruned, but suffered the vines to grow wild, and permitted their shoots to extend over the paths, neither would he have the fig or other trees properly trained and attended to, preferring to see all things wild and savage about him'.

189 **mænads . . . Saint Margaret's resurrection out of the devouring dragon** Maenads were female votaries of Bacchus who became possessed by the god. Legend has it that St Margaret (or Marina) of Antioch was swallowed by the devil in the form of a dragon but promptly disgorged when she made the sign of the cross in its stomach.

189 **sketches of fantastic sea-monsters . . . grotesque heads** Vasari notes Piero's pictures of a 'fantastic' and 'unearthly' sea-monster painted for Giuliano de' Medici; of 'fawns, satyrs, and sylvan deities of various kinds' for Giovanni Vespucci; of a Madonna (commissioned by the Tebaldi family for the Santissima Annunziata) who 'turns her head towards the heavens', and above whom 'is seen the Holy Spirit, by whose light she is illuminated'. On the predella of this Madonna, Vasari records, Piero 'executed small historical representations, which are extremely well done, among others that of Saint Margherita escaping from the stomach of the dragon'. Vasari also mentions Piero's studies of plants, strange animals, and 'fantastic', 'fanciful', and 'fabulous' beings.

190 **the picture of Mars and Venus** Vasari himself owned this picture (now in the Staatliche Museen in Berlin), in which, in his description of it, 'there is a Cupid, alarmed at the sight of a rabbit; the doves of Venus are also depicted'.

190 **Giovanni Vespucci . . . Colonos** The portrait of Oedipus and Antigone is an invention of GE. Piero, however, was commissioned by Giovanni's father Guidantonio Vespucci (and according to Vasari— wrongly—by Giovanni himself) to paint two Bacchanalian scenes for the Vespucci Palace in Florence.

193 **"sitting with a certain grandeur . . . queenliness;"** ' "Quando una donna e grande, ben formata, porta ben sua persona, siede con una certa grandezza, parla con gravita, ride con modestia, a finalmente getta quasi un odor di Regina; allora noi diciamo quella donna pare una maesta, ella ha una maesta."—FIRENZUOLA: *Della Bellezza delle Donne*.' [GE] The Florentine writer Agnolo Firenzuola (1493–1543) is best known for his *Ragionamente d'amore*, an unfinished imitation of Boccaccio's *Decameron*, and for his *Discorsi delle bellezze donne*, which offers a portrait of the ideal renaissance woman. The quotation here is from the first of the discorsi.

196 **boys and striplings . . . was killed** Of the Carnival activities before the reforms of Savonarola, Villari writes: 'the boys of Florence took special delight in these revels. They were accustomed, during those days, to continually stop people in the streets by barring the road with long poles, and refusing to remove them until they had extorted enough money to pay for their mad feastings by night. After these carousals they made bonfires in the squares, round which they danced and sang, and

finally pelted one another with stones in so brutal a fashion that no year passed without some of the combatants being left dead on the ground.'

197 **Ponte Rubaconte** This bridge was destroyed in 1944 and replaced by a new one called the Ponte alle Grazie.

201 **young faun . . . by a promising youth** Michelangelo was born in 1475. Vasari records that at the age of 14 he was encouraged by Lorenzo de' Medici to copy the head of an 'old Faun' from a classical statue in the Medici gardens. A later work of which GE may be thinking (not inappropriately in the light of one of the novel's most persistent metaphors) is the statuette of Bacchus commissioned by Jacopo Galli in Rome *c.*1497 and subsequently brought to Florence by the Medici (it is now in the Bargello).

203 **two hundred on each side** GE found information about this practice in Lastri.

203 **that scholarly Benedict, Leonardo Bruno** Leonardo Bruni (not Bruno), 1370–1444, served as Chancellor of the Florentine Republic from 1427 until his death. One of the most learned men of his time, and known in particular for his Latin transls. of Aristotle, Demosthenes, Aeschylus, and Plutarch, his largest work was the incompleted *Historiae Florentini Populi*. He thought of taking holy orders, but in his early 40s renounced his canonry and married. His wife brought him a large dowry—some compensation for the cost of their wedding celebrations, of which he remarked 'In one night I have consummated my marriage and consumed my patrimony'. The term 'Benedict', from the character Benedick in *Much Ado About Nothing*, denotes an erstwhile confirmed bachelor now married.

203 **the little church of Santa Lucia** The church of Santa Lucia dei Magnoli towards the eastern end of the Via de Bardi.

204 **an invention of Piero di Cosimo** Tito is correct in his attribution of the origin of the spectacle, but GE is anticipating the event. The details of the scene are taken from Vasari's account of a procession mounted by Piero di Cosimo for the Carnival in 1511. Vasari notes that 'those by whom the procession . . . was witnessed . . . never weary of extolling the extraordinary spectacle presented by it'.

205 **Care-dispeller** One of the many names by which Dionysus/Bacchus was known was Luaios or Lyaeus—the 'loosener' of care.

207 **after the ancient Greek fashion** GE would have found information about this tradition in W. A. Becker's *Charikles*.

207 **arrogant, exasperating Piero** Piero de' Medici had taken it upon himself to visit Charles VIII of France, who was advancing on Pisa, on 31 Oct. 1494. Having acceeded to Charles's outrageous demands—that Florence should 'loan' the French 200,000 ducats and surrender to them a number of its outlying strategic fortresses (see pp. 213–14)—he returned to the city on 8 Nov. to give an account of the meeting and personally to assume the reins of government. The Signoria, however, received him with outright contempt; encouraged by this attitude, the people began to

riot and sacked the Medici Palace. Piero retreated to the gate of San Gallo and attempted to raise the inhabitants of that quarter (traditional supporters of the Medici) on his behalf. When this failed he fled the city and, according to Villari, 'before he had made a dozen steps beheld the city gates closed behind him'. The Signoria promptly put a price on the heads of both Piero and his brother, the Cardinal Giovanni de' Medici (who had disguised himself as a Franciscan friar to escape the mob): 2,000 florins dead and 5,000 alive.

208 **rich new tunics after the French mode** Nardi reports that on the occasion of Charles VIII's entry a number of Florentine youths went about 'riccamente vestiti di diversi drappi alla franzese'.

208 **canon of bronze . . . the first ball** GE probably took these details about the French artillery from Guicciardini's *Storia d'Italia*: cf. 'The defenders of the place under attack [by the huge iron 'bombards' common in the late 15th cent.] had time calmly to make the necessary repairs and fortifications [between each shot, so slow-firing and unwieldy were the pieces] . . . But the French developed many infantry pieces which were more maneuverable, constructed only of bronze. These were called canons and they used iron cannonballs instead of stone as before, and this new shot was incomparably larger and heavier than that which had been previously employed. Furthermore, they were hauled on carriages drawn not by oxen as was the custom in Italy, but by horses, with such agility . . . that they . . . were led right up to the walls and set in position there with incredible speed; and so little time elapsed between one shot and another . . . that in a few hours they could accomplish what previously in Italy used to require many days.'

208 **reputed rebuilder of Florence** Charlemagne was supposed to have rebuilt the city around the year 800, following its destruction by the Goths, while on his way to Rome to be crowned first Holy Roman Emperor. The parallel between Charles VIII and Charlemagne was invoked by numerous French and Italian politicians of the time. In his drive down the Italian peninsula, Charles himself reputedly dreamt of receiving the crown of Charlemagne in Rome at Christmas, and then of putting the Turks to flight in Greece and reclaiming the ancient throne of Constantine.

208 **Cyrus . . . restorer of the Temple** Following his conquest of Babylon in 538 BC, Cyrus the Great, King of Persia, allowed the captive Israelites to return to their homeland and decreed that the temple at Jerusalem should be rebuilt. Savonarola himself was one of the many who hailed Charles as a 'new Cyrus'.

208 **hereditary right** Charles's father, Louis XI, by crushing the house of Anjou in the late 1470s, had gained for the French crown the Angevin claim to the kingdom of Naples, over which the Counts of Anjou had ruled from 1266–1442.

209 **Most Christian King** The title 'Rex Christianissimus' had been granted to Charles's father, Louis XI, by Pope Paul II in 1469.

209 **widely spread conviction . . . monstrous births** Cf. 'With no less terror did rumours spread everywhere that . . . in the territory of Arezzo an infinite number of armed men on enormous horses were seen for many days passing through the air with a terrible clamour of drums and trumpets. In many places in Italy the sacred images and statues had openly sweated. Everywhere monsters of men and other animals were being born' (Guicciardini, *Storia d'Italia*). GE may have been thinking also of *Julius Caesar*: 'A lioness hath whelpèd in the streets, | And graves have yawned, and yielded up their dead; | Fierce fiery warriors fought upon the clouds | In ranks and squadrons and right form of war' (2. 2. 17–20).

209 **"Behold . . . upon the earth."** Genesis 6: 17, the text of Savonarola's sermon on 21 Sept. 1494. In the *Compendium Revelationum*, recalling his Lenten sermons on Noah's Ark earlier that year, Savonarola writes: 'by God's will and guidance, leaving off where it reads, "Make it with lower, second, and third decks" [Genesis 6: 16], the following September, on the Feast of St Matthew the Apostle, I resumed with the new text, "For behold, I will bring a flood of waters upon the earth". As soon as I began my sermon . . . many were astonished, suddenly realizing that God's secret impulse had given this part of Genesis to fit the times, since everyone knew then that the King of the French had invaded Italy with his army. Among them was Count Giovanni della Mirandola, a man unique in our times for his intellect and breadth of learning, who was terrified upon hearing these words and later told me that his hair had stood on end'.

210 **The idea of prophetic gifts** In Q, under the heading 'Prophetic Powers', GE writes: 'Nerli complains of his fellow-citizens that in his time still [i.e. the 16th century], they were strongly given to crediting prophets & believing any prediction, provided it foreshadowed terrible evils'. She goes on to make notes about the prophecies of the Abbot Joachim (see p. 21) and concludes: 'People, says Nardi, were not afraid or ashamed to discuss the reality of Savonarola's prophetic power'.

210 **the fear of the Turk had ceased to be active** This had reached its zenith in 1480, when a Turkish army landed at Otranto, sacked the city and massacred the inhabitants. In the following year, however, the city was retaken by the Duke of Calabria, and the Turks expelled from Italy.

210 **bribes . . . for a little prospective poisoning** Prince Djem, the brother of Bajazet II, had been captured by Innocent VIII and was subsequently held by Alexander VI, to whom the Sultan paid 40,000 ducats a year to keep him prisoner, offering much larger sums for his murder. When Charles VIII arrived in Rome in 1494 Djem was transferred to his keeping but soon died, reportedly having been given slow poison by the Pope in return for a bribe of 300,000 ducats.

211 **a sword hanging** In the *Compendium Revelationum* Savonarola records that the night before his last Advent sermon of 1492 he had a vision, which he took to be a divine revelation, of a sword in the sky inscribed with the words *Gladius Domini super terram cito et velociter* ('the sword of

God upon the earth, swift and sudden': see p. 230). He heard voices threatening that the wrath of God was about to descend on a corrupt world, which would be given over to war, famine, and pestilence. Finally, he was commanded to warn his flock of the impending scourge and to enjoin them to pray that good shepherds might be sent to purify God's Holy Church.

212 **Ludovico Sforza . . . a Lombard usurper** When Galeazzo Maria Sforza, Duke of Milan, was murdered in 1476, he was succeeded by his son Gian Galeazzo, a minor. His uncle Ludovico, however, under the pretence of protecting him, usurped the power and property of the ducal crown, which he retained even after his nephew's majority. But Gian Galeazzo had married a granddaughter of Ferdinand of Aragon, King of Naples, and her father, the Crown Prince Alfonso, was understandably unhappy with the situation in Milan. In time his remonstrances and threats became such that Ludovico realized he would be unable to maintain his position unless he could find a way of disabling Ferdinand and Alfonso. It was with this in view that he encouraged Charles VIII to invade Italy and claim his right to the throne of Naples. His unfortunate nephew died in 1494 (probably from natural causes).

212 **a recusant Cardinal** Giuliano della Rovere, Cardinal of St Peter in Vincoli, had been defeated by his sworn enemy Rodrigo Borgia in the papal election of 1492. Having defied the new Pope, he took refuge in France, where he urged Charles VIII to invade Italy in order to embarrass and weaken his rival. Villari, following Guicciardini, records that 'his fiery words swept away all Charles's doubts, and at last decided him to set forth towards Italy'.

213 **repent . . . like Nineveh** Jonah was commanded by God to give Nineveh 30 days' notice of destruction if it did not abandon its evil ways. The people repented and the city was spared, though Jonah disapproved strongly of God's compassion.

213 **The greatest of Italian poets** [cancelled *MS* reading] Cf. Dante, *Paradiso*, 30. 137–8: '. . . alto Arrigo, ch'a drizzare Italia | verrà in prima ch'ella sia disposta' (lofty Henry, who shall come to set Italy straight before she is ready).

213 **"orators," even with a prophet at their head** On 5 Nov. 1494 Savonarola had led an embassy to Charles VIII at Pisa to ascertain what his intentions were toward Florence.

213–14 **ignominious surrender of the fortresses** To the universal fury of his fellow-citizens, Piero de' Medici had given up to Charles VIII the strategic fortresses of Pietrasanta, Serenaza, and Serezanello, along with those of Pisa and the port of Leghorn.

214 **chalk . . . to mark Italian doors** Following the contemporary chroniclers, Villari records that groups of French soldiers 'were seen roving about the town unarmed, jaunty, and gallant, bearing pieces of chalk

in their hands to mark the houses on which their troops were to be billeted', and that King Charles entered Florence 'chalk in hand and lance to hip'.

216 **Galli** The speaker is punning on the word *Gallo*, which means both 'a cockerel' and 'a Gaul'.

216 **the old cow lowed** '*"La vacca muglia"* was the phrase for the sounding of the great bell in the tower of the Palazzo Vecchio.' [GE]

216 **the Medici coming back** On 15 Nov. a rumour spread through Florence that Piero de' Medici was approaching the gates. The bell of the Palazzo Vecchio was rung; armed citizens poured into the streets and threw up barricades. Villari records that in the ensuing mêlée with the French who were in the city to pick out their billets 'the foreign soldiers were forced to acknowledge that their tactics and their stout battalions would be almost powerless, hemmed in those streets, against this new and unknown mode of warfare'.

216 **Ciompi** 'The poorer artisans connected with the wool trade—wool-beaters, carders, washers, &c.' [GE: the wording of this n. was changed in *CM*; in *MS* it read 'The poorer artisans: a corruption of *compare* (companion).'] In *Bod* she writes out a passage, probably from the *Delizie degli eruditi toscani*, about the derivation of the word.

217 **Lorenzo Tornabuoni** The Tornabuoni were a prominent Florentine family with strong Medicean connections (Lucrezia Tornabuoni was the mother of Lorenzo the Magnificent). Young Lorenzo Tornabuoni, though indeed 'a Medicean in his heart' (he was one of the 5 conspirators executed in 1497 for plotting the return of Piero de' Medici—see ch. 60), 'pretends to look well satisfied' since he feigned adherence to Savonarola and the popular party, who had invited the French into Florence.

217 **Signa** 6 miles to the west of Florence.

218 **hoof-shaped shoes . . . royal superfluity in toes** Nardi records that Charles VIII had an extra toe on one foot (he refers to him as 'sedigito'), that he wore peculiarly shaped shoes to disguise this deformity, and that his soldiers adopted the same ungainly style in deference to him.

219 **prisoners in Lunigiana** Following Nardi, and the MS chronicles of Parenti and Cerretani, Villari records that some Italian prisoners taken in Lunigiana (a province in northern Tuscany) were brought into the city by French soldiers to beg their ransom money; that their ropes were cut by the crowd, and that they escaped in the ensuing mêlée.

221 **tardigrade fashion** Nardi relates that when the prisoners' bonds were cut the French soldiers were unable to pursue their quarry 'con la medesima velocità' because they were hampered by their ill-shaped shoes.

223 **Fivizzano** A town some 90 miles to the north-west of Florence. It was assaulted and sacked by the French in Oct. 1494.

228 **the Shechinah** The visible glory of God, a manifestation of the divine presence, often symbolized by a refulgent light as in the light over the 'mercy-seat', or cover, placed above the Ark of the Covenant.

229 **it is written** Cf. Amos 3: 7: 'Surely the Lord God will do nothing, but he revealeth his secret unto his servants the prophets'.

229 **smote the sons of Eli** Hophni and Phineas, the sons of the High Priest Eli, and priests themselves, were killed for abusing their position and showing contempt for God (see 1 Samuel 2–4).

230 **there was a pause** In AD 66 the Jews rebelled against Rome. Nero sent Vespasian to subdue them and he duly reconquered most of Judea, but before he could take Jerusalem itself his campaign was interrupted by Nero's death and his own promotion to the throne. This gave Jerusalem a respite of almost 2 years before it was again besieged and eventually destroyed by Vespasian's son, Titus, in AD 70.

231 **while you suffer the accursed thing to lie in the camp** Following Joshua's destruction of Jericho, an absolute ban was placed upon bringing anything from the city into the Israelite camp. Achan, however, disobeyed the order and hid some plunder among his own possessions, as a result of which God caused the Israelites to be defeated in a battle with the Amorites. Achan confessed his sin and was stoned to death; the offending items were thrown out of the camp, and the Israelites immediately triumphed over their enemies. (See Joshua 6–7.) In his sermon on 14 Dec. 1494 Savonarola urged that the Signoria should extirpate from Florence everything hostile to the *culto divino*: vices should be suppressed, gaming and drinking banned, and women forced to reform the manner of their dress.

232 **. . . prosper for ever."** 'The sermon here given is not a translation, but a free representation of Fra Girolamo's preaching in its more impassioned moments.' [GE: n. introduced by GE in *3P*, and set as an endnote to Vol. I of *3*.] The 'free representation' is a skilfully woven one: the vocabulary is distinctly biblical, redolent especially—and appropriately—of Isaiah, Jeremiah, Ezekiel, and Revelation. In fact, though individual words are clearly biblical, and are combined to produce biblical-sounding phrases, they generally make phrases which never actually occur in the Bible. For example, there are cups of wrath and cups of abomination in the Bible, but no 'cup of iniquity' (p. 228). The closest GE comes to direct quotation is probably on the following occasions: 'God is near and not afar off' (p. 229; cf. 'Am I a God at hand, saith the Lord, and not a God afar off?' Jeremiah 23: 23); 'they shall be mown down as stubble' (p. 230; cf. 'thou sentest forth thy wrath, which consumed them as stubble', Exodus 15: 7); 'I would willingly live as a turtle in the depths of the forest, singing low to my Beloved, who is mine and I am His' (p. 231; cf. 'and the voice of the turtle is heard in our land', 'I am my beloved's, and my beloved is mine', Song of Solomon 2: 12; 6: 3); 'let them wag their heads and shoot out the lip at me: let the thorns press upon my brow' (p. 231; cf. 'All they that see me laugh me to scorn: they shoot out the lip, they shake the head', 'And when they had platted a crown of thorns, they put it upon his head . . . And they that passed by reviled him, wagging their heads', Psalms 27: 7—a passage that might also have been known to GE from its use in her favourite

oratorio *Messiah*; Matthew 27: 29 and 27: 39). The possible connection with *Messiah* suggests at least one further reference: 'He shall break in pieces mighty men without number' (p. 229)—cf. 'Thou shalt break them with a rod of iron; thou shalt dash them in pieces like a potter's vessel' (Psalms 2: 9), which forms the text of the tenor aria immediately preceding the 'Hallelujah' chorus.

234 **a hospital . . . outside all our gates** In Q GE notes: 'In all the *Borghi* of the different gates, says Varchi [in his *Storia fiorentina*] there were hospitals for poor travellers, & also for harbouring or feeding one night or more the poor of the city.'

235 **the gate of Santa Croce** The site of the Porta alla Croce is now the Piazza Beccaria.

235 **faces such as Masaccio had painted** GE is probably thinking of the frescos (1428) by Masaccio (1401–28) in the Brancacci Chapel in Santa Maria del Carmine. For Ghirlandaio see p. 19.

235 **another Samuel** The Old Testament prophet who became also a civil ruler and law-giver.

235 **Soderini** Pagolantonio Soderini, a doctor of law, had been Lorenzo de' Medici's ambassador to Venice. It was he who first proposed the scheme of a 'Great Council' for Florence along Venetian lines (see p. 348).

236 **Piero Capponi . . . kept out the Medici** A prominent merchant and erstwhile supporter of Lorenzo de' Medici, Capponi had been sent as an ambassador to France by Piero de' Medici to defend Medicean policies to Charles VIII. However, impatient with Piero's feeble and vacillating rule, he advised the King to expel all Florentine merchants from the country; by thus dealing a severe blow to Florentine commercial interests, he hoped to raise the people against the Medici. Villari writes: 'Capponi had done well in exchanging commerce for diplomacy, but he did still better in forsaking the latter for the business of war, and then realized that his true mission was neither to sit in a banking office, nor negotiate treaties, but rather to fight, sword in hand.' For Capponi's further exploits, see ch. 29.

236 **Accursius** The Latinized name of Francesco Accorso (1182–1260), professor of Law at Bologna and author of the celebrated *Glossa Magistralis*, a commentary on the laws of Justinian.

236 **Luca Corsini . . . the Frate** One of those who shut the gate of San Gallo on Piero de' Medici (see p. 207), and the person deputed to deliver the Latin oration welcoming Charles VIII to Florence (see p. 208 and p. 239), Corsini was a prominent supporter of the Law of Appeal and of Savonarola. The 'memorable occasion' refers to the burning of the Pyramid of Vanities (see ch. 49), when Corsini is reported to have thrown stones at the *Compagnacci* who were attempting to disrupt the procession of Florentine boys organized by Savonarola.

236 **join the community of San Marco** Villari records that under Savonarola's rule 'the number of brethren wearing the robe of St. Mark

was incredibly multiplied . . . Many of the new monks were scions of the leading houses of Florence, such as six brothers of the Strozzi family; several of the Gondi, Salviati, and Acciaiuoli; others were men of mature age and of high standing in literature, science, and statesmanship, such as . . . Zanobi Acciaiuoli'. Alessandro Strozzi was the 'brother monk' with whom Fra Domenico was obliged to change clothes during the Trial by Fire (see p. 541).

236 **young painter** . . . **Fra Bartolommeo** The Florentine painter Baccio della Porta (1475–1517) was a lay follower of Savonarola, and was with him at San Marco when the convent was besieged in 1498 (see ch. 66). According to Vasari, he was so frightened by the mob that he swore he would himself take holy orders as a Dominican if he was safely delivered. He was, and he did; he is better known to history by his religious name of Fra Bartolommeo. Not being allowed access to San Marco herself, GE relied on Lewes's account for her description of its interior. In his journal for 22 May 1860 Lewes noted that 'In the chapel beside Savonarola's rooms there is a much defaced Mother and Child by *Bartolommeo*, the child more lifelike and noble than any but Rafael's Sistine children.' In *BL* GE notes that the room concerned was not a chapel in the 1490s, but one of the set of rooms occupied by Savonarola.

236 **Girolamo Benevieni** . . . **another morning** Like Pico a zealous supporter of Savonarola, and with him a member of the so-called 'Accademia Marciana'—a group of intellectuals who met for discussion in the Greek Library at San Marco—Benevieni wrote many of the hymns sung by the youth of Florence on the occasion of the burning of the vanities (see ch. 49). Pico died on 17 Nov. 1494, the day of Charles VIII's entry into Florence. The day before, Savonarola had visited his bedside, received his vows, and accepted him into the Dominican order. The 'Frate's speedy coming'—a further (undocumented) visit which GE suggests that Benevieni may 'perhaps' be going to announce—would have been in vain.

237 **write reports to friends** In Q GE has an entry, perhaps as an *aide-mémoire*, reading simply 'Letter of Macchiavelli, Mar. 8. 1498'. Villari, who quotes from this letter, refers to it as 'a letter *to a friend*' and notes that 'the writer shows himself decidedly unfavourable to Savonarola'. The friend concerned was Ricciardo Becchi.

237 **Dolfo Spini** Ridolfo (known as Dolfo or Doffo) Spini, leader of the *Compagnacci* (see p. 393), a violent faction of the aristocratic party opposed to Savonarola and the Medici alike. Villari described him as a 'depraved . . . youth of noted audacity' whose 'band met together at nightly banquets, and amid the cheerful clinking of wine cups, laid fresh plots against Savonarola'.

239 **Tall and tough Scotch archers** . . . **gallant meaning** Cf. Villari's account of the King's retinue: 'the Swiss vanguard, resplendent and parti-coloured, bearing halberds of burnished steel . . . Gascon infantry, small, light, agile men . . . the cavalry, comprising the flower of the French aristocracy, and displaying finely-wrought weapons, mantles of

gorgeous brocade, velvet banners embroidered with gold, chains of gold, and other precious ornaments . . . The archers were men of extraordinary height . . . they came from Scotland and other northern countries, and—in the words of a contemporary historian [Cerretani]—*seemed to be beast-like men (parevano uomini bestiali).*'

239 *fù gran magnificenza* The 'old diarist' is Giovanni Cambi, whose account (written out by GE in Q) records that 'El Re Charlo di Francia entrò in Firenze addì 10 di Novenbre 1494 . . . con gran magnificemza di fanteria . . . chom gran numero de' ciptadini amtichi, che fu gran magnificemza'.

240 **Luca Corsini . . . Francesco Gaddi . . . "You, Melema."** The contemporary chroniclers relate that just as Luca Corsini began to read his written address it began to rain; the horses grew restless and the company was thrown into confusion. At this point Francesco Gaddi, one of the two secretaries of the department of external affairs, pushed his way forward and made an impromptu but appropriate speech in French.

240 **the young monarch . . . exorbitant outline** GE's description of Charles's appearance seems to have been modelled on Villari's: 'The monarch's appearance was in strange contrast with that of the numerous and powerful army behind him. He seemed almost a monster, with his enormous head, long nose, wide, gaping mouth, big, white, purblind eyes, very diminutive body, extraordinarily thin legs, and misshapen feet. He was clad in black velvet, and a mantle of gold brocade; bestrode a tall and very beautiful charger, and entered the city riding with his lance levelled—a martial attitude then considered as a sign of conquest. All this rendered the meanness of his person the more grotesquely conspicuous.'

241 **Niccolò Caparra . . . iron-work** The celebrated smith Niccolò Grosso, as he is called in a cancelled *MS* reading on p. 19, was given the sobriquet 'Caparra' ('earnest-money') by Lorenzo de' Medici since he refused to do any work on credit. Vasari records that the burning books on the sign over his shop (see p. 244) were to signify that he could inscribe the names of no more debtors therein. GE's sketch of his character follows that of Vasari, who describes him as 'an upright and religious man, but very whimsical and obstinate', and as one who refused to do business with anyone whose motives he suspected. His most famous commission was for the ornamental iron-work and torch holders on the Strozzi Palace. Vasari hailed him as unequalled in his skill at such work.

242 **block or "isle" of houses** The Italian for block (of houses) is *isolato*.

244 **Maso of Brescia** In *Bod* GE notes: 'Brescia celebrated for the manufacture of arms'.

245 **the cardinal** Presumably Giovanni de' Medici, to whom, following the death of Lorenzo, Bardo has apparently transferred his hopes for the establishment of a Bardi Library.

249 **a lien on the collection as a security** A lien is the right to retain possession of another's property until the owner repays his debt.

258 **Mysteries** i.e., mystery plays. On 23 Nov. 1494 the traditional Florentine mystery play of the Annunciation was performed for Charles VIII at San Felice in Piazza.

258 **his lance in rest** In his *Storia d'Italia*, Guicciardini records that Charles, having entered Florence with 'both himself and his horse in armour, and with his lance on his thigh . . . he had, according to the military rules of the realm of France, legitimately gained dominion' over the city. Lastri notes that Charles rode in 'con la lancia in sulla coscia'.

259 **Chi promette . . . mai bene** 'The soul of one who promises and fails to keep his word does not prosper': Lippi, *Il malmantile racquistato*, 1. 5.

261 **swan-egg** A variety of pear.

263 **seemed to be planting a vine** In *Bod* GE writes: 'Those who don't listen & are distrait are said to *piantare una vigna*'. The expression is roughly equivalent to the English 'to be miles away'.

264 **well-authenticated vision . . . piece of honeycomb** In its context here, and the speaker being Francesco Cei—a particularly vicious enemy of Savonarola—I take this 'vision' (unauthenticated by any of the contemporary biographers or historians) to be made up by GE, and Cei's remark to be intended sarcastically. Besides being the god of war, Mars would carry an added symbolic value for Florentines as their erstwhile 'tutelar deity' (p. 81), as would a liaison with his successor, San Giovanni, above their principal civic building. The 'piece of honeycomb' may be a reference to the Baptist's famous diet of locusts and wild honey.

264 **hide . . . as soon as a storm comes on** Vasari reports that Piero was terrified of lightning, and that during storms he would cover himself with a cloak and hide in a corner.

265 **not two months since** Poliziano died in late Sept. 1494. The Malebolge (literally, the 'evil pits') are the 10 galleries which comprise the lowest circle of Dante's *Inferno*. According to Paulus Jovius, whose account is generally agreed to be preposterously inaccurate in detail (though probably based on a vestige of truth), Poliziano died from a paroxysm of amorous fever while singing the praises on a lute of a male pupil for whom he had conceived a passionate attraction. (Nello has already shown himself susceptible to the kind of prurient gossip in which Jovius dealt—in his reference to Piero Crinito: see p. 604).

265 **Camilla Rucellai** Born Camilla Davanzi in 1465, she married Rodolfo Rucellai in 1484. Later, under the influence of Savonarola's preaching, she divorced her husband, became a sister of the third order of Dominicans, founded a convent in the Via del Cocomero dedicated to St Catherine of Siena, and acquired a considerable reputation as a prophetess. Her prophecy about Pico della Mirandola's death 'in the time of lilies' is widely reported by the contemporary chroniclers.

265 **Euge** Greek (and Latin): 'bravo', 'well done'.

266 **Dido's bull's hide** The story goes that Dido was sold as much land as could be measured by the hide of a single bull. By cutting the hide into

strips, joining them together, and stretching them out, she was able to enclose a sufficient area to found what would become the city of Carthage.

266 **Franco Sacchetti says** *Trecentonovelle*, no. 164.

267 **sent from Herod to Pilate** See Luke 23: 7–12.

269 **Guidantonio Vespucci . . . Domenico Bonsi** Vespucci (143?–1501) was an eminent lawyer and champion of the aristocratic party. Bonsi (1430–1502), also trained as a lawyer, is perhaps best known to history as the ambassador sent to plead Savonarola's cause at Rome in 1497 but who, incensed at Savonarola's increasing intransigence in his dealings with the Pope, gradually turned against him.

269 **two years later . . . died in fight** Capponi was killed in Sept. 1496 fighting against the Pisans. In Q GE records details of his state funeral, from the account in Giovanni Cambi's diary. Villari writes: 'His corpse was . . . followed by all the magistrates and a countless multitude of people . . . Eulogistic speeches were pronounced over his bier, extolling the deeds and lamenting the loss of this valiant solider and eminent citizen.'

275 **men love their own delights** Possibly an echo of Virgil, *Eclogues*, 2. 65: 'trahit sua quemque voluptas' (each is led by his own delight), which is itself adapted from Theocritus, *Idylls*, 10. 30–1.

279 **the Milanese Count . . . and the Seneschal de Beaucaire** The Milanese Count is probably Galeazzo di Sanseverino, a lieutenant of Ludovico Sforza and a favourite of Charles VIII. Etienne de Vesc, Seneschal of Beaucaire, was one of Charles's most trusted advisors.

282 **the mastiff of the city** Possibly an allusion to Savonarola as leader of the Dominicans—the 'hounds of the Lord' (see p. 86). Alarmed that Charles showed no sign of departing from Florence, in late Nov. the Signoria persuaded Savonarola to intercede. Following Savonarola's own account of the ensuing interview (as recollected in his sermon of 28 Oct. 1496), Villari records his (apparently decisive) words to the King: 'Most Christian Prince, thy stay here is causing great injury both to our city and thine own enterprise. Thou losest time, forgetful of the duty imposed on thee by Providence, and to the serious hurt of thy spiritual welfare and worldly fame. Hearken now the voice of God's servant! Pursue thy journey without delay. Seek not to bring ruin on this city and thereby rouse the anger of the Lord against thee.'

287 **great subsidy** One of the provisions of the treaty whose signing is described in ch. 29 was that Florence should loan Charles the sum of 120,000 gold florins—a figure negotiated down from the original sum of 200,000 agreed by Piero de' Medici (see p. 640).

287 **kissed a mask** In *Bod* GE writes, without giving a source, '"Kiss me then—but you kiss a mask!"' The entry, however, probably post-dates her notes for *Romola*.

288 **the Medici collections** The Medici collections of books and antiquities, with the exception of those that had been transferred to San Marco, were plundered by the French.

293 **Count di San Severino** See p. 279.

297 **sin that's hidden's half forgiven** ' "Peccato celato è mezzo perdonato." ' [GE] The expression, from Boccaccio, *Decameron*, 1. 4, signifies—ingeniously—that such a transgression is more worthy of forgiveness than one that is generally known about.

300 **the Natività** Tessa was 'married' on the feast-day of the Nativity of the Blessed Virgin Mary (see p. 139), i.e. 8 Sept., in 1492. Lillo, who is clearly an infant at this point in the novel, and who is described as 'not more than three' in late July 1497 (see p. 465), was presumably born exactly two years later.

308 **Fra Lippo Lippi's round-cheeked adoring angels** GE may be thinking of the angels in the *Coronation of the Virgin* or in the *Madonna and Child* by Filippo Lippi (*c.*1406–69); both paintings are mentioned by Vasari.

317 **"ginger is hot in the mouth"** Cf. *Twelfth Night*, 2. 3. 116–17 ('ginger shall be hot i' th' mouth too').

319 **"Do not wonder . . . few and great."** ' "Se vi pare io abbia detto poche cose, non ve ne maravigliate, perchè le mie cose erano poche e grandi." ' [GE] The words are from Savonarola's interrogation on 21 May 1498—two days before his execution.

322 **San Gaggio** A village barely a mile to the south of the Porta Romana.

322 **San Piero** A town some 8 miles north-west of Florence.

322 **Trespiano** About 2½ miles from Florence on the road to Bologna.

325 **She had endured and forborne** The allusion is to Epictetus, in the 'grand severity' of whose 'Stoical philosophy', as the previous sentence reminds us, Romola had been instructed by her father. More specifically, GE is referring to the account of Epictetus' maxims given by Aulus Gellius in his *Noctes Atticae* (17. 19. 5–6): 'Epictetus . . . used to say that there were two faults which were by far the worst and most disgusting of all: lack of endurance and lack of self-restraint, when we cannot put up with or bear the wrongs which we ought to endure, or cannot restrain ourselves from actions or pleasures from which we ought to refrain. "Therefore," said he, "if anyone would take these two words to heart and use them for his own guidance and regulation, he will be almost without sin and will lead a very peaceful life. These two words," he said, "are ἀνέχου (bear) and ἀπέχου (forbear)." '

329 **the Suora Maddalena** Presumably Maddalena de' Medici, the youngest daughter of Lorenzo the Magnificent.

334 **Pietra** The village of La Pietra is about a mile north of the Porta San Gallo.

335 **under certain circumstances** In his edn. of *Marietta de' Ricci* (almost certainly GE's source) Luigi Passerini notes that to produce the dye the lichen had to be mixed with urine.

335 **our Bernardo** The prosperous merchant, diplomat, scholar, and poet Giovanni Bernardo Rucellai (1448–1514) had been one of Lorenzo de'

Medici's most trusted lieutenants, sharing many of his master's political aims and intellectual interests. His marriage to Lorenzo's sister Nannina had indeed been a splendid affair—at which 500 guests feasted in the piazza in front of the Rucellai Palace, seated on a triangular platform beneath a sumptuously ornamented awning of dark blue cloth (hence, presumably, the reference to 'Florentine upholstery'). Subsequently, however, Rucellai broke with the Medici and, like many of Lorenzo's adherents, became an implacable enemy of Piero. His antipathy to the Medicean cause espoused by his dinner guests is alluded to on p. 350.

335 **a fine palace . . . Santa Maria Novella** In fact both the Rucellai Palace in the Via della Vigna Nuova (designed by Leon Battista Alberti and built by Bernadino Rosellino, c. 1446–51) and the completion of the façade of Santa Maria Novella (also by Alberti, 1456–70) were commissioned by Bernardo's father, Giovanni Rucellai (1403–81).

335 **planted . . . rare trees** Rucellai's aim, as described in Piero Crinito's *De Sylva Oricellaria*, was to represent in his garden all species of trees mentioned in classical literature.

337 **an excellent, learned book** Rucellai's *De Urbe Roma*, on the classical antiquities of Rome, was one of the first topographical studies of its kind.

337 **laudatory epitaph . . . tear their hair** In *Pf* GE records the Latin epitaph on the monument in Santa Croce (by Desidero da Settignano) to the scholar Carlo Marsuppini (1398–1453), which she transl. as 'Tear your hair, O Greek and Ausonian Muses'.

339 **ΜΕΣΣΗΝΙΚΑ. ΚΒ' Messenia. XXII**—ch. 22 of bk. 4 of Pausanias' *Periegesis*, concerning the treachery and death of Aristocrates.

339 **the traitor Aristocrates** Aristocrates, the leader of the Arcadians, formed an alliance with the Messenians against Sparta. Bribed by the Spartans, however, he fled the battlefield and brought about a crushing defeat of his allies. Later, when his treachery was revealed, he was stoned to death by his own people, who set up a tablet inscribed 'Truly time hath declared justice upon an unjust King and with the help of Zeus hath easily declared the betrayer of Messene. Hard it is for a man forsworn to hide from God.'

340 **hecatomb** The sacrifice of a large number of victims.

340 **the Mænad . . . on the mountain top** The allusion is presumably to Horace's ode 'Quo me, Bacche, rapis tu' (*Odes*, 3. 25. 8–12); cf. 'non secus in iugis | exsomnis stupet Euhias, | Hebrum prospiciens et nive candidam | Thracen ac perde barbaro | lustratem Rhodopen': (just so does the sleepless Bacchanal stand rapt on the mountain-tops, looking out over Hebrus, and Thrace glistening with snow, and Rhodope trodden by barbarian feet).

343 **Madonna della Gozzoviglia and San Buonvino** 'Our Lady of Feasting and St Good-Wine'.

343 **the Platonic Academy** An informal group of kindred spirits who gathered to celebrate and discuss the master, the Academy had met both at

Lorenzo de' Medici's villa at Careggi and at the neighbouring one of Marsilio Ficino (see p. 613). At the banquets on Plato's birthday each of the guests made a philosophical oration or read aloud from Plato's works. No such meetings, however, were held in the Rucellai gardens until 1498, and it was not until 1502 that they became a regular occurrence (though Ademollo's *Marietta de' Ricci*, almost certainly GE's source here, incorrectly states that meetings were held in the gardens during the 1490s).

343 **reputed anniversary of Plato's death** In her designation of this date as 13 Nov. GE is apparently following Lastri. She jots it down in her notes from Lastri in *BL*, though later in the same notebook she writes '7 November, Plato's birth and death day, says Heeren(?). Elsewhere, 13th Nov.' Roscoe too gives the date as 7 Nov., Villari as 27 Nov.

343 **Astonishing Rome with heterodox theses** In Dec. 1486 Pico caused a sensation in Rome by proclaiming 900 conclusions or theses of a controversial nature, and offering to pay the travelling expenses of anyone who wished to debate them publicly. The theses ranged from Arabic, Hebrew, Egyptian, and Greek and Latin quotations imparting what he termed 'perennial' truths, to opinions of his own on subjects as diverse as magic and mathematics.

343 **Ficino . . . too exclusive diet** (See also p. 53.) Villari records that 'Ficino was so completely absorbed by his feverish passion for study, that he became a species of living dictionary of ancient philosophy'. Roscoe writes that 'Habituated from his earliest youth to the study of this philosophy, and conversant only with Plato and his followers, their doctrines occupied his whole soul. Even his epistles breathe nothing but Plato, and fatigue us with the endless repetition of opinions'.

344 **Leon Battista Alberti** An accomplished Florentine mathematician and classical scholar, a poet and author of several books on architecture and painting, Alberti (1404–72) is best known as an innovative architect. Among his most important commissions were those for the completion of the marble façade of Santa Maria Novella and for the Rucellai Palace (see p. 335). GE's description of his cast of mind follows that of Vasari, who suggests that in him 'theory and practice [were] happily united in the same person'. In *Bod* GE jots down a passage from Giammaria Mazzuchelli Bresciano's *Gli scrittori d'Italia* concerning Alberti's prominence at the early meetings of Lorenzo de' Medici's Platonic Academy.

344 **not more than four and forty** Rucellai was in fact 46 in Dec. 1494.

344 **says Erasmus** In bk. 8 of his *Apothegms*, referring to his meeting with Rucellai in Venice (Erasmus spoke no Italian, and Rucellai obstinately refused to speak Latin): 'Verbum latinum nunquam quivi ab eo extundere' (Not one word of Latin could I squeeze out of him).

344 **Lorenzo Tornabuoni and Gianozzo Pucci** Tito is appropriately seated by his host. Following Nardi, Villari describes Pucci as 'a youth of great talent' (Nardi refers to his 'arte e astuzia') and recounts that Tornabuoni (see also p. 644) 'was the general admiration of Florence as a

model of grace and fashion'. Both were executed with Bernardo del Nero in 1497 for plotting the return of the Medici (see ch. 60).

344 **Dante's pattern old Florentine . . . leathern belt and bone clasp** Cf. *Paradiso*, 15. 112–13: 'Bellincion Berti . . . cinto di cuoio e d'osso'. Berti was Dante's great-great grandfather. Silver forks were a late 15th-cent. development.

344 **Antonio Pollajuolo . . . seduced . . . to more gorgeous Rome** The Florentine sculptor, silversmith, and painter Antonio Benci (1433–98), known as Pollaiuolo, went to Rome in 1484 to work on the tomb of Sixtus IV and on the trappings of the coronation of Innocent VIII.

345 **the artist who puts . . . melting-pot** Ridolfi's 'quotation' from Pollaiuolo is probably based on Vasari's account of the artist's life, which records that he decided to forsake the sculpting of precious metals for painting since the former activity produced works that could all too readily be melted down to raise money.

345 **Antonio's silver saints** Probably a reference to Pollaiuolo's panel (1477–85), depicting the birth of John the Baptist, in the silver altar in the Baptistery in Florence.

345 **Luigi Pulci . . . Matteo Franco** Pulci's characteristic scepticism is alluded to in the Proem. His quarrel with the minor poet and philosopher Matteo Franco dates from the 1470s, when he apparently felt himself supplanted by Franco in Lorenzo de' Medici's affections. GE was evidently familiar with the details of their antagonism, though Pulci's precise words as 'quoted' here seem to be of her own invention. In *WN* she copies out a sonnet of Pulci's ('Luigi Pulci a un suo amico per ridere') addressed to Pandolfo Rucellai, which, though specifically attacking Marsilio Ficino, in its use of metaphors concerning food may have prompted the words she gives Pulci in the novel. As for the 'preaching friar' (i.e. a Dominican) who 'described the pavement of the bottomless pit', GE may be conflating one of Franco's sonnets to Pulci— in which he suggests that Pulci's brother Luca, who had died a few years earlier, was preparing for him a place in the lowest circle of hell—with Pulci's complaint, in his poem 'La Confessione', that he had been violently upbraided for his unbelief by 'un Cherubino' (i.e. a Dominican: possibly Savonarola himself).

345 **a mere blowing of soap bubbles** The phrase *bolla di sapone* (a soap bubble) is commonly used in Italian to signify something insubstantial.

345 **the receipt of Apicius** Apicius was the proverbial cognomen of several Roman gourmets, most notably of Marcus Gavius Apicius who lived during the reigns of Augustus and Tiberius. The collection of recipes entitled *De Re Coquinaria*, ascribed by its MSS to a certain Caelius Apicius, was probably compiled in the 4th cent. GE's description of the recipe for partridge is accurate (see *De Re Coquinaria*, bk. 4, s. 3). In *BL* she notes the appearance at a Florentine banquet of a 'peacock boiled with the feathers on'. Strictly speaking, the use of any recipe from Apicius at this date would have entailed the cook's having had access to a MS version of

it: the first known printing of *De Re Coquinaria* was at Milan in Jan. 1498, though subsequently it was wrongly recorded that there had been an edn. in 1490.

346 **Tito quoted Horace** Presumably *Satires*, 2. 2. 23–30: about the folly of thinking a peacock tastes better than a pullet because it costs more and looks exotic with its (inedible) tail feathers spread out.

346 **a favourite story of Luigi Pulci's** The episode provides the story for Pulci's *Novella dello sciocco senese* (Tale of the Sienese Fool), a story quoted from by Lastri; it is also referred to in *Il morgante maggiore* (14. 53).

348 **kneaded in the same trough** A literal transl. of the Italian expression for 'made in the same mould'—*impastati nella stessa madia*.

348 **studied the Venetian Council . . . indebted to a monk** Soderini had been Florentine ambassador to Venice, and the *Consiglio Maggiore* he proposed for Florence was based on that of the Venetians. In his sermon on Haggai on 12 Dec. 1494 Savonarola had urged that 'the form of government best adapted to this city would be that of a Grand Council on the Venetian plan'.

348 **the general amnesty** Along with his advocacy, early in 1495, of a law of appeal against the condemnation of citizens by 'a majority of black beans' (see pp. 5 and 485), Savonarola successfully urged a general pardon for all political crimes.

349 *Arrabbiati* Literally, the furious or rabid ones.

350 **Great Council finally voted to-morrow** The supper in the Rucellai gardens evidently took place on 22 Dec. 1494 ('the evening before' (p. 335) 'the 23rd of December' (p. 320)). The *Consiglio Maggiore*, or Great Council, was indeed formally established on 23 Dec. It was empowered to create all the city's chief magistrates and approve all laws, thus making it the sovereign body of the State. Citizens were eligible to be members if they were at least 29 years old, if they were *netto di specchio* (see p. 17) and *beneficiati* (i.e. if they or their fathers, grandfathers, or great-grandfathers had held one of the city's higher magistracies).

350 **a fine net to catch reasons in the air** Probably an adaptation of the Tuscan proverb 'pigliare il vento con le reti' (see p. 133).

351 **Ulysses often made himself disagreeable** It was Ulysses who, with Sinon, devised the ruse of the Trojan horse—a scheme to which Pucci may be alluding here (cf. *3 Henry VI*, 3. 2. 189–90: 'Deceive more slily than Ulysses could, | And, like Sinon, take another Troy'). As for his being 'disagreeable', though characterized by Homer as being tactful, energetic (and at times cunning), Ulysses is less favourably represented by Horace. *Satires*, 2. 5, takes the form of a burlesque continuation of the scene in the *Odyssey* where Ulysses in the underworld learns from the seer Tiresias that he will regain his home, but only after being reduced to poverty; in the satire Ulysses wants to know how to become rich, and Tiresias instructs him in the lucrative ways of fortune-hunting in polite society.

351 **if he had been on our side** Though not a supporter of Savonarola or the popular party, at this point in his career Machiavelli's political leanings were toward the *Arrabbiati* rather than the Mediceans.

352 **'in commendam'** An ecclesiastical benefice is held *in commendam* by a temporary stand-in until a full-time incumbent is appointed. Tito here alludes to the common practice of a layman being granted the income of a benefice without having to undertake any of the duties.

353 **Montepulciano** A wine from the Montepulciano region, south of Florence.

354 **Ciascun . . . evoè!** 'Let everyone follow thee, O Bacchus'. *Evoè* (from the verb *evoeggiare*: to cry out) was used specifically as an invocation to Bacchus. Poliziano's *Orfeo* (1480) was designed as an entertainment to be performed during a banquet. In late 15th-cent. Italy Orpheus was widely regarded as the archetype of the inspired artist as described by Plato in the *Phaedrus*. The art of Orphic, or declamatory, singing to one's own accompaniment on the lyre was introduced to the West by Gemistos Plethon and subsequently hailed by Marsilio Ficino as—together with the revival of Platonic philosophy—one of the supreme accomplishments of the Florentine renaissance.

357 **sard** A type of cornelian, varying in colour from pale yellow to reddish orange.

359 **the Stinche** 'The largest prison in Florence.' [GE]

363 **those who sit on a hill aloof . . . fellow-men** In that Savonarola is criticizing scholars like Bardo whose vain sense of superiority derives from their familiarity with the classics, it is ironic that the form of words he uses should be an allusion to a famous remark by just such an ancient writer—Lucretius (*De Rerum Natura*, 2. 7 ff.): 'sed nihil dulcius est bene quam munita tenere | edita doctrina sapientum templa serena, | despicere unde queas alios passimque videre | errare atque viam palantis quaerere vitae' (but nothing is more delightful than to possess lofty and serene sanctuaries, well fortified by the teachings of the wise, whence you may look down upon others and behold them all astray, wandering abroad and seeking the path of life').

369 **Fra Salvestro . . . somnambulism** Properly Fra S*i*lvestro Maruffi; according to Villari, he was 'subject, even by day, to attacks of somnambulism, during which he saw curious visions and uttered strange words'. Villari goes on to relate that 'Savonarola began to regard Maruffi with an almost reverential esteem totally unmerited by that weak and frivolous man. His blind faith in Silvestro's hysteric utterances involved him in a maze of error and confirmed his strange belief in the truth of his own visions'. Fra Silvestro was eventually executed along with Savonarola and Fra Domenico da Pescia.

371 **grief for the loss of a new-born son** Charles's son, born in Sept. 1496, died when barely a month old. The King was so overwhelmed by grief that he lost all interest in his Italian campaign and abandoned the remains of his army in Naples.

371 **A league had been formed** Ludovico Sforza's plan to use the French
invasion to secure his own position (see p. 643) was beginning to
backfire. King Ferdinand of Naples had died in Jan. 1494 and had been
succeeded by Alfonso, his son. Alfonso, however, was so unpopular with
his subjects that at the news of Charles VIII's approach they rebelled.
Alfonso abdicated and fled to Sicily. Charles entered Naples in Feb.
1495. Gian Galeazzo, the rightful Duke of Milan, had died in Oct. 1494.
With Ludovico's antagonist and the cause of the antagonism both out of
the way, the continued French presence in Italy became unnecessary and
even threatening. Accordingly, in Mar. 1495 Sforza engineered an
alliance between Milan, Venice, Spain, the German Emperor
Maximilian, and the Pope—supposedly against the Turks (hence a 'Holy
League'), but really designed to expel the French from Italy. In advocat-
ing the league, Sforza announced that its purpose was 'to drive away the
barbarians'.

373 **two days ago** i.e. 28 Oct. 1496; in fact Savonarola recommenced his
preaching in the Duomo on 27 Oct.

375 **San Jacopo del Popolo** As GE notes in Q, this was one of the charitable religious societies of Florence dating from the 13th cent.

375 **two or three *bracci* foremost** *Braccio* (= arm) was a common unit of
measurement. In *BL* GE notes that 'The Florentine Braccio is 22' 8
English inches = nearly 2 ft.' The phrase here seems to mean something
like 'at two or three arms' lengths'.

377 **preaching to the birds, like Saint Anthony** It was St Francis who is
reported to have preached to the birds. St Anthony of Padua (1195–1231),
a friend of St Francis, is said to have preached to fishes in the river at
Rimini after the heretics in the city had refused to listen to him.

377 **beggarmen from Arezzo or Bologna** In Q, in a long section of notes
from Nardi, GE writes: 'At this time [Autumn 1496] there was an
immense concourse of beggars at Florence, they having been chased from
the neighbouring cities on account of the scarcity. But at Florence it was
decided that they should be received & treated with the same charity as
natives. On this account the scarcity increased, & the people were in the
depth of despondency from the reported failure of the vessels conveying
provisions &c. from Marseilles to arrive in any Italian port.'

378 **hospital of San Matteo** The hospital, on the south-east corner of the
Piazza di San Marco, is now the site of the Accademia di Belle Arti.

379 **San Stefano** The church of San Stefano al Ponte is just to the north of
the river off the Por' Santa Maria.

380 **Companies of Discipline** The first of these fraternities was founded in
1244 by the Dominican St Peter Martyr in order to combat the Patarine
heresy (see p. 81). Other groups were soon formed, some devoted simply
to communal prayer, others to performing acts of charity. In 1419 a law
was passed to dissolve all existing companies, but a select few were
allowed to reorganize with the consent of the Signoria. Three of the
most prominent were the Arcifraternita della Misericordia, which

specialized in tending the sick and burying the indigent; the Compagnia di Santa Maria del Bigallo, which cared for orphans and foundlings; and the Societa di Santa Maria della Pieta, which distributed bread and wine to the beggars of the city.

380 **reformed Benedictines** The Benedictine order was reformed on a number of occasions during the middle ages in order to make its rules stricter. In *WN* GE makes extensive notes on the varieties, reforms, and garb of the order (see p. 381) from Pierre Helyot's *Histoire des ordres monastiques*. Most Benedictines wore black; certain 'reformed' branches of the order, such as the Cluniacs, wore white; the Vallombrosans (see below) wore grey; the *Umiliati* (see below) first grey, then white.

380 **zoccoli, or wooden sandals** In her notes from Helyot in *WN* GE notes that a reformed branch of the Franciscans 'instituted 1368 at Bruliano . . . were called Zoccolanti because of their wooden sandals'.

380 **when learning was rarer** In the late 14th cent., Luigi Marsili headed a regular colloquium at San Spirito at which scholars and citizens debated moral and philosophical issues. After his death in 1394, leadership of the group passed to Coluccio Salutati, an early champion of the classics in Florence and a leading figure in the city's development as a centre of the new learning. His disciples included some of the most prominent humanist scholars of the next generation—Leonardo Bruni, Poggio, and Niccolò Niccoli.

380 **seven merchants . . . the Divine Mother** The Servite order of mendicant friars was founded in 1233 by St Bonfilius of Florence and 6 fellow Florentine merchants who, as GE records in *WN*, 'renounced the vanities of the world to live in poverty. They were of noble Tuscan families & all belonged to a confraternity in Florence called *de' Laudesi*, whose perpetual obligation it was to sing praises to the Virgin. They went to their oratory for this purpose the day of the Assumption of the B. V. & were all seven divinely inspired to renounce the world. Seeing them in their hair shirts & chains, *the infants at the breast cried*, "See there the Servants of the Blessed Virgin." And hence they took the name of *Serviti*. They built their first monastery on M. Senario; then, to give them shelter when they went to seek alms in Florence, which was ten miles off, they built a small hut which afterwards grew to be the monastery of Annunziata.' (See cancelled *MS* reading on p. 380, n. 8.)

381 **Frati Umiliati . . . wool trade** Founded as an independent order in the 12th cent. (by a group of Lombard nobles who, taken prisoner by the Emperor Henry V, devoted themselves to a life of penitence and piety), the *Umiliati* later came under Benedictine rule. They were skilled in the manufacture of woollen goods and founded the Church of Ognissanti in 1256.

381 **Vallombrosan** The Vallombrosans were an order of Benedictines founded by San Giovanni Gualberto in 1038. The town of Vallombrosa, where their monastery was located, is some 20 miles to the east of Florence.

382 **the twenty-one incorporated Arts of Florence** These 'Arts' or guilds comprised: cloth dealers, bankers and money-changers, wool merchants, silk merchants, lawyers and notaries, physicians and apothecaries, furriers, armourers, locksmiths, shoemakers, strapmakers, leather-workers and tanners, linen-makers and second-hand dealers, blacksmiths, stone- and wood-carvers, carpenters, bankers, butchers, wine merchants, olive-oil dealers, and innkeepers.

382 **San Zenobio** d. 424, Bishop of Florence and one of the city's patron saints. His prayers are reputed to have saved Florence from the Goths in the year 405. His skull was discovered beneath the apse of the Duomo in 1331; it is kept in a reliquary in the Duomo.

382 **image of the Pitying Mother** A miraculous painting of the Virgin, attributed to St Luke, ploughed up in a field near the village of L'Impruneta and taken into Florence to help the city in times of trouble.

386 **the shop of Niccolò Caparra** There is an inconsistency here. Earlier (p. 241) we are told that Caparra's shop is located at the angle between the Borgo Santa Croce and the Via dei Benci. Now it is said to be off the Via del Fosso, the northern continuation of the Ponte Rubaconte, which is the best part of a mile away.

390 **believing utterance** 'He himself had had occasion enough to note the efficacy of that vehicle. "If," as he says in the *Compendium Revelationum*, "you speak of such as have not heard these things from me, I admit that they who disbelieve are more than they who believe, because it is one thing to hear him who inwardly feels these things, and another to hear him who feels them not; . . . and, therefore, it is well said by St. Jerome, 'Habet nescio quid latentis energiae vivae vocis actus, et in aures discipuli de auctoris ore transfusa fortis sonat.'"' [GE] In the *Compendium Revelationum* (which, as the title implies, comprises a summary of its author's visions and prophecies) Savonarola writes: 'ma se voi parlate di quegli che non hanno udite queste cose da me, concedo che più sono quegli che non credono, perché altra cosa è udire colui che queste cose sente dentro che colui che non le sente . . . e però ben disse santo Ieronimo: "Habet nescio quid latentis energiae vivae vocis actus et in aures discipuli, de auctoris ore transfusa, fortius sonat".' The quotation, from an epistle of Jerome to Paulinus, may be transl.: 'The effect of the living voice has an indefinable hidden force, and sounds more strongly in the ears of a disciple when it comes from the mouth of the author himself.'

391 **avowed embassy . . . the League** Rucellai, entrusted by the new government with its most crucial diplomatic missions, was sent to Milan to persuade Ludovico Sforza (who had convened the League) to exert his influence with Charles VIII against any plan to restore Piero de' Medici to Florence.

393 *Compagnacci* A derivative of *compagno* (comrade) used specifically to refer to the younger *Arrabbiati*, who went about the streets armed, provoking quarrels and committing acts of violence.

393 **great house . . . Santa Trinità** In the Via Tornabuoni, overlooking the Ponte Santa Trinità, the Palazzo Spini-Feroni is one of the largest medieval houses in the city, built for Geri degli Spini in 1289.

395 **that fainting Madonna of Fra Giovanni's** Nello is referring to the figure of the Virgin in the fresco of the Crucifixion by Fra Angelico (Giovanni da Fiesole) in the chapter house at San Marco. Lewes recorded in his journal for 22 May 1860: 'we went to St Marco, and Polly remained in a room where the great Fra Angelico—Crucifixion— may be seen by ladies while I went over the monastery and took notes for her'. In her own journal 'Recollections of Italy' GE writes: 'The frescoes I cared for most at Florence were the few of Fra Angelico's that a *donna* was allowed to see in the Convent of San Marco. In the Chapterhouse, now used as a guard-room, is a large crucifixion, with the inimitable group of the fainting mother, upheld by St John and the younger Mary, and clasped round by the kneeling Magdalen. The group of adoring, sorrowing saints on the right hand are admirable for earnest truthfulness of representation.'

395 **forefathers resisted Pope Gregory the Eleventh** During the famine of 1374 Pope Gregory, in an attempt to gain control over Tuscany, refused Florence's request for grain and attacked the city. Florence, however, bribed his army to raise the seige and then allied itself with numerous other cities in a war which lasted for three years and ended only with the Pope's death.

396 **false prophets . . . heads turned hind foremost** See Dante, *Inferno*, 20.

397 **in the world or in the wolds** '"Del mondo o di maremma."' [GE: n. added in *1*; in *MS* and *CM* the text reads 'in the world or in Maremma'] In *Bod* she jots down '"Più gentili uomini del mondo o di maremma". Bocc.' The phrase is from the summary at the beginning of the 6th story of the 6th day of the *Decameron*. GE's transl. is ingenious: *Maremma* is the marshland in southern Tuscany; its juxtaposition with *mondo* is jocular, and GE has effectively reproduced the wordplay in English.

398 **as our sour old Dante says** In both *Bod* (in a section headed 'Dantesque phrases') and *WN* (also in the midst of numerous quotations in Italian from Dante) GE writes 'My visage was painted with fear', but in neither case does she give the Italian original. There are two possible sources. One is *Inferno*, 4. 19–21: 'L'angoscia delle genti | che son qua giù, nel viso mi dipigne | quella pietà che tu per tema senti' (the anguish of the people down here paints my face with that pity which you take for fear). The more likely source, however, is *Purgatorio*, 2. 82: 'Di maraviglia, credo, mi dipinsi' (wonder, I think, was painted on my face). Despite the unusual transl. of 'maraviglia' as 'fear', there is strong circumstantial evidence for this latter line being the source, for in both notebooks 'My visage was painted with fear' appears in a sequence of quotations (many of which are common to both notebooks) drawn exclusively from the *Purgatorio*, and arranged in strict order of cantos and lines

within cantos. In both cases, therefore, it would seem odd if GE were referring to the *Inferno* rather than the *Purgatorio*.

399 **trumpets . . . in a bag** The proverbial expression 'tornare con le pive nel sacco' (to come back with one's bagpipes in a bag, i.e. empty-handed, deflated) has a variant which substitutes *trombe* (trumpets) for *pive*. In *Bod* GE jots this down as 'Ritornare con le trombe in sacco'. Capo d'Oca means 'Goose Head'.

401 **a lamp before a picture of the Virgin** Even the light by which Tito is spotted by Spini has its historical basis: in her notes from Lastri in *BL* GE writes 'Sacred images illuminated by a candle at night-time . . . were found useful as a means of lighting the streets.'

403 **"Beoni"** One of Lorenzo de' Medici's Carnival Songs was entitled 'I Beoni' (The Winebibbers); it is possible that this accounts for the capital 'B' on the word here.

405 **Ser Saccente** 'Mr Know-All'.

405 **know where the devil keeps his tail** By tradition, a tail is a sign by which the devil may be recognized. The better to disguise himself, therefore, he carefully hides his tail. A man who knows where the devil keeps his tail (from the Italian 'sapere dove il diavolo tiene la coda') is one who is particularly astute. In *Bod* GE jots down ' "Egli sa dove il diavol tien la coda"—he is a knowing fellow'. She may have come across the expression in Boccaccio: 'Sanno dove il diavol tien la coda' (*Decameron*, 8. 7).

405 **Trebbiano** A white wine from east central Italy.

406 **Vicario dell' Arcivescovo** The Archbishop's vicar, or vicar general, in charge of the legal affairs of the Florentine archdiocese.

414 **Ser Ceccone** Originally a Medicean, on the discovery of Piero de' Medici's conspiracy Ser Francesco (or Ceccone) di Ser Barone, a Florentine notary of some ability, had sought refuge at San Marco, where he pretended to support the *Piagnone* party while in fact acting as a Milanese spy and an agent of the *Arrabbiati*. He declared his true colours publicly only after Savonarola's arrest (see ch. 71).

418 **turn a plum into an orange** In *Bod* GE jots down 'Fare di un pruno un melarancia', without giving a source. The phrase is from Boccaccio (*Decameron*, 4. 8): 'fare del pruno un mel rancio'.

418 **cool the baths of Nero** Cf. Martial, *Epigrams*, 3. 25. 4: 'Neronianas is refrigerat thermas'. In *Bod* GE jots down 'Neronianas thermas refrigeravit', and in *Pf* 'Neronias thermas refrigeraverit', without giving a source in either case.

421 **threatening German Emperor** Following the unexpected arrival of the French galleys in Leghorn and the subsequent wreck of his own fleet, in late Nov. 1496 the Emperor Maximilian declared himself weary of fighting 'against God and man' and hastily retreated from Italy.

422 **Christ had been declared King** In the last of his Advent sermons on Haggai in 1494, Savonarola had declared that it was God's will that Florence should have a new ruler, and that that ruler was to be Jesus

Christ. Luca Landucci records in his diary that at the head of the procession ordered by Savonarola on Palm Sunday 1495 there was a tabernacle with a painting of Christ upon the ass, and that as it passed the people cried out 'Viva Cristo ch'è 'l nostro Re!' In the same year the city struck a new coin, on one side of which was the Florentine lily, and on the other a cross and the words 'Jesus Christus Rex Noster'.

423 **Venetian merchant . . . heavy sum** The offer—of the astonishing sum of 20,000 crowns—is mentioned by Burlamacchi in his biography of Savonarola, but Villari (so often GE's source of information) regards his account of the burning of the vanities with extreme suspicion: hence, presumably, GE's qualification 'probably mythical'.

423 **Fra Domenico** Fra Domenico da Pescia, described by Villari as Savonarola's 'most sincere and zealous disciple'. According to Burlamacchi, Savonarola 'thought it well to furnish [Florentine children] with some rules, so that they might persevere in righteous living; and being [in 1497] unable to attend to the matter himself by reason of his weighty occupations, committed the care of it to Fra Domenico da Pescia'.

424 **reddened balls . . . "dead hair"** In *BL* GE records that 'Among the *Anatema* collected by the children at Florence were women's false hair ['dead hair' is from the Italian *capelli morti*] and head-ornaments, *pezzelle di Levante*, *i.e.* cotton balls coloured red for rouging the cheeks.'

425 **the last struggle of their Republic** The Florentine Republic finally fell to the forces of Pope Clement VII in 1530 after a long siege, during which, according to Sismondi, the people were 'animated by preachers who inherited the zeal of Savonarola'. The Pope re-established the Medici as rulers of Florence.

425 *Ninferno* A colloquial alternative to *l'inferno*, found in Boccaccio and other writers of the 14th cent. In restoring the *MS* reading here I have assumed that the compositor of *CM* changed the word to its more common form without authority.

425 **Lorenzo di Credi and young Baccio** The Florentine artists Lorenzo di Credi (*c.*1458–1537) and Baccio della Porta (Fra Bartolommeo: see p. 647) were both devoted followers of Savonarola. Vasari records that the latter burnt his sketches of nudes on the Bonfire of Vanities, and that his example was followed by Lorenzo di Credi and other *Piagnoni* painters.

426 **wise Saint Catherine of Egypt** St Catherine of Alexandria (supposedly 4th cent.) was renowned for her learning and beauty. She thus became the patron saint of young girls and of philosophers. GE had seen Titian's painting of *The Marriage of St Catherine* in the Pitti Palace, and had described it as 'a work of supreme beauty'.

428 **the Hill of San Giorgio** Remarkably, if conveniently, Tessa had initially been lodged no more than half a mile from the Via de' Bardi.

433 **an ass may bray . . . shakes the stars down** The Tuscan proverb 'raglio d'asino non arrivò mai in cielo' is underlined by GE in her copy of Giusti's *Proverbi toscani* and then jotted down in *Bod*.

433 **biting the man in San Giovanni** Depicted in the mosaic of the Last Judgement on the interior of the Baptistery roof (see p. 594).

434 **Via de' Libraj** Now the Via dei Proconsolo.

440 **her beloved crimson-velvet berretta** Among the items GE listed from the 'Trousseau of Ginevra' (see pp. 629–30) was '1 cap of Alexandrian velvet, embroidered with pearls and silver' ('berretta di velluta alessandrino, ricamento con perle e ariento'). In her letter to Frederic Leighton of June 1862 about women's costume in the 1490s, GE talks of 'the woman's *berretta*, frequently of velvet embroidered with pearls, and apparently almost as prevalent as our bonnet'.

441 **an angel loosing prison bolts** Cf. Acts 5: 19: 'the angel of the Lord by night opened the prison doors, and brought them forth'.

441 **Via del Palagio** Now the Via Ghibellina.

442 **better fall from the window than the roof** Probably an adaptation of the Tuscan proverb 'meglio cascar dall' uscio, che dalla finestra' (better fall from the doorstep than the window).

443 **body of Lazarus trembled . . . sepulchre** Villari records that in one of his Lenten sermons in 1497 Savonarola promised to 'send forth a mighty cry that shall resound throughout Christendom, and make the corpse of the Church to tremble even as trembled the body of Lazarus at the voice of our Lord'. There is no mention of the body trembling by St John, the only one of the evangelists to recount the story of the raising of Lazarus.

445 **a key that presupposed no loftiness** On two separate occasions in Q GE jots down 'Macchiavelli, Discorsi l. i cap xi al fine: passage concerning Savonarola'. The passage concerned, however, is hardly critical in its attitude to Savonarola: 'It did not seem to the people of Florence that they were either ignorant or rude, yet they were persuaded by Friar Girolamo Savonarola that he had converse with God. I do not propose to decide whether or not this was so, because of so great a man one ought to speak with reverence; but I do say that vast numbers believed it was so, without having seen him do anything out of the ordinary whereby to make them believe; for his life, his teaching, and the topic on which he preached, were sufficient to make them trust him.' In fact, Machiavelli's attitude to Savonarola—at least in his written remarks—was distinctly ambiguous. In bk. 1, ch. 45, of the *Discorsi* he notes the 'learning, prudence, and virtue of his mind' but declares that his refusal to allow the five conspirators the benefit of the Appeal (see ch. 56) showed him to be 'ambitious and a party-man'. In a letter of May 1521 to Francesco Guicciardini he refers to him as a 'crafty monk', while in the first of the *Decannale* poems he describes him as 'inspired with heavenly goodness'. GE's remark in the novel here may perhaps derive from Villari's comment that Savonarola and Machiavelli were 'two almost antagonistic characters—the one, all spontaneous enthusiasm and faith; the other, all analysis, doubt, and inquiry. Both were great men, but each was singularly unfitted to comprehend the other.'

448 **Filippino Lippi's serene Virgin** In fact this painting, dating from the early 1480s, was at this time in the convent at Campora outside the city. It was not removed to the Badia until 1529.

449 **a sort of Agag** Agag was the King of the Amalekites 'hewed to pieces before the Lord' by Samuel (see 1 Samuel 15: 33).

452 **San Miniato** See p. 671.

459 **Piero de' Medici, with thirteen hundred men** When word reached Piero that Bernardo del Nero, a noted Medicean, had been elected Gonfaloniere for the months of Mar. and Apr. 1497, he wrote to him announcing his intention of returning immediately to Florence. Bernardo wisely cautioned against this precipitate course, but Piero set out none the less, arriving with 1,400 troops early on 28 Apr. Finding the gates barred against him, he waited outside the city all day, and then marched back to his base at Siena.

461 **hot days of June . . . published in the Duomo** In fact the Excommunication was promulgated (on 18 June 1497) only in 5 churches of orders hostile to Savonarola: Santa Croce, the Badia, Santissima Annunziata, Santa Maria Novella, and Santo Spirito. It was not read in the Duomo, though Villari (evidently GE's source here) incorrectly states that it was.

476 **Lamberto dell' Antella . . . his friends** A prominent Medicean, Lamberto dell' Antella had been banished along with Piero de' Medici in 1494 and had subsequently accompanied him on his abortive march to Florence in Apr. 1497. Following this venture, relations with his master, already strained, broke down altogether, and Piero ordered his imprisonment in Siena. Having made his escape he returned to Florence bent on revenge. On 1 Aug. 1497 he was arrested with a letter on his person giving details of another plot to restore Piero and incriminating numerous leading citizens. Most of those implicated promptly fled the city, but Bernardo del Nero, Niccolò Ridolfi, Lorenzo Tornabuoni, Gianozzo Pucci, and Giovanni Cambi were arrested. The letter, and the subsequent revelations made by Antella under torture, were crucial to the condemnation of the conspirators.

480 **Romagna** See p. 625.

481 **another plot . . . August** As elsewhere in the novel, GE attributes to Tito an action which history gives to another (minor) character. Following his arrest and torture, and in return for a free pardon, Lamberto dell' Antella, according to Villari (whose own account is drawn from that of Nardi), 'revealed certain preliminaries of a fresh plot, by which Piero was to be secretly brought into Florence on the night of the approaching 15th of August'.

481 **memorable transaction . . . unscrupulousness** Presumably a reference to the trial of Savonarola and the manipulation of the evidence therein (see p. 575).

482 **Il tradimento . . . piacque mai.** Treason is very pleasing to many, but a traitor has never pleased anyone (*Il morgante maggiore*, 17. 69).

483 **oration . . . to welcome the French King** See p. 614.

485 **a law passed . . . nearly three years before** Savonarola had argued the need for such legislative reform in his sermons on the Psalms in Jan. and Feb. 1495. The law of appeal against the *sei fave* was actually passed on 18 Mar.

486 **the smaller council or senate of eighty** The Great Council instituted by Savonarola had over 1,400 members. The 'Senate of Eighty' was an executive body elected by the Council to be in permanent attendance on the Signoria.

487 **Piero Guicciardini** A Florentine aristocrat and father of the historian Francesco Guicciardini. One of several leading Mediceans who transferred their allegiances to Savonarola and the popular party, Piero had known the five conspirators from his days as a prominent official in the government of Lorenzo de' Medici.

487 **Piagnone as he is, will not lightly forgive** In fact, quite soon after his brother Niccolò's death Giovan Battista Ridolfi argued publicly against the Pope's command that Savonarola be prohibited from preaching. He was one of the commanders of the official forces which kept the peace during the Trial by Fire (ch. 65); later, during the attack on San Marco (ch. 66), he narrowly escaped being murdered by an anti-Piagnoni mob.

488 **send a message** Villari records that, during his interrogation by the papal commissioners in the following year, Savonarola explained that 'regarding those five citizens he had taken no special concern; save that he had slightly recommended Lorenzo Tornabuoni to Valori's mercy'.

488 **it was he who got the law passed** 'The most recent, and in some [*MS*: several] respects the best, biographer of Savonarola, Signor Villari, endeavours to show that the Law of Appeal ultimately enacted, being wider than the law originally contemplated by Savonarola, was a source of bitter annoyance to him, as a contrivance of the aristocratic party for attaching to the measures of the popular government the injurious results of licence. But in taking this view the estimable biographer lost sight of the fact that, not only in his sermons, but in a deliberately prepared book (the *Compendium Revelationum*) written long after the Appeal had become law, Savonarola enumerates among the benefits secured to Florence, "*the Appeal from the Six Votes, advocated by me, for the greater security of the citizens.*" ' [GE] Villari's main point concerning the difference between the law as proposed by Savonarola and as actually passed is that 'instead of establishing, as he had proposed, a right of appeal to a limited Court composed of wise experts in legal matters, appeal was to be made to the Greater Council, whose decisions would be influenced by party spirit rather than justice, and where the ignorance of the many would prevail against the wisdom of the few . . . Yet, no sooner had men begun to calumniate Savonarola's memory, than all declared that it was chiefly owing to him that right of appeal had been denied to the prisoners, although he himself had been the most energetic promoter of the law conferring that right. No one chose to remember

that Vespucci not Savonarola had been the proposer of that law in the form in which it was ultimately carried, or that the Friar had not only been dissatisfied with it, but caused his followers to oppose it, since his own object was to establish the right of appeal to a limited council instead of to the Consiglio Maggiore.' In Q GE writes: 'Note, concerning the *Apello*, that Savonarola, in the Comp. Rev. speaks of this law with complacency as having been brought about by himself. What then becomes of Villari's argument that S. did not approve of the law in the form in which it was passed?'

492 **Andrea Cambini** A prominent political supporter of Savonarola and the popular government, his house—like that of his friend Valori—was sacked and burnt by the mob following the attack on San Marco (see ch. 71).

493 **sad frescoed figures** Another referenece to Fra Angelico's *Crucifixion* (see p. 395).

494 **his "Triumph of the Cross"** A treatise in four books designed to demonstrate the truth of the Christian faith, printed in 1497 in both Latin and Italian.

495 **knew beforehand** Savonarola was said to have foretold the Dauphin's death, as well as those of Lorenzo de' Medici and Pope Innocent VIII.

496 **sent out of the city** Villari notes that Savonarola only once expressed any view about the trial of Bernardo del Nero. This was after the event, during his own trial by the papal commissioners, when he said: 'His death gave me no satisfaction; I should have been well pleased had he been banished.'

497 **. . . presence to her** In *MS* 1½ lines are crossed out at this point and are entirely illegible, except for the interesting final words: 'she fell on her knees again'.

500 **the Florentine Cato** The phrase is not GE's own. Valori was commonly thus referred to by the contemporary chroniclers, presumably in allusion to Marcus Porcius Cato (95–46 BC), known as 'Uticensis', a staunch Republican and opponent of Julius Caesar, who argued for the execution of the Catiline conspirators in 63 BC.

502 **blows that are too heavy to be avenged** Machiavelli's remark here is based on a statement in ch. 3 of *Il principe*, marked by GE in her own copy of the book and then written out by her in *Bod*, as follows: 'Si ha a notare, che gli uomini si debbano o vezzeggiare o spegnere; perche si vendicano delle leggieri offese, i delle gravi non possono' (One has to point out that men should either be well treated or totally crushed, because they can avenge themselves of lighter injuries but not of more serious ones). The next sentence in *Il principe* reads 'Sì che l'offesa che si fa all'uomo debba essere in modo che la non tema la vendetta' (Therefore the injury that is to be done to a man should be of such a kind that one does not fear revenge).

507 **Viareggio** Some 50 miles from Florence.

509 **fair Gostanza** See *Decameron*, 5. 2. Believing that the man she loves is dead, Gostanza decides to kill herself; but, lacking the strength to do the deed by violent means, she resolves to drift out to sea—with the expectation of being drowned. She goes to a port, finds a small fishing boat, and rows away from land, but is carried by the wind to the coast of North Africa.

513 **This man had said** In his sermon in the Duomo in Septuagesima Sunday (11 Feb.) 1498—though as usual the words given to Savonarola in the novel are a paraphrase rather than a direct quotation of his actual address. In this instance e.g. the phrases 'broken swords' and 'a hilt without a blade' are representations of Savonarola's repeated characterization of the Pope as *ferro roto*—a broken iron, tool, or sword: powerless because he was not acting as the instrument of God.

515 **forty-four years** In Feb. 1498 Savonarola, who was born in Sept. 1452, was in fact 45 years old.

515 **"Without preaching I cannot live."** In *Bod* GE jots down the original of this phrase (from one of Savonarola's sermons on Ruth and Micah in May 1496): 'senza predicara, io non posso vivere'.

516 **three days ago . . . send a fire and consume me** In his Quinquagesima sermon that year Savonarola had pronounced: 'E vogliomi mettere il sacramento in mano, e che ognuno allora facci forte orazione che se questa cosa è da me, e se io inganno, che Cristo facci venire un fuoco dal cielo sopra di me, che mi assorba allora nello Inferno'. The address outside San Marco, as described at this point in the novel, took place on 'the morning of the twenty-seventh of February', the final day of the Carnival. During it Savonarola again invited God to send a fire from heaven and strike him dead if his words were insincere or his deeds uninspired. He did not, however, refer to his earlier sermon. GE's narrative concision, in its attempt to elide the burden of both addresses, has led her into an error of detail. She has Savonarola say 'three days ago I besought'; if he had in fact thus alluded to his previous imprecation, he would have had to say 'two days ago', for Quinquagesima Sunday in 1498 fell on 25 Feb.

518 **this "wretched worm" and "monstrous idol"** The words quoted (*isto vermiculo . . . isti monstruoso idolo*) are from a letter of the Pope of Mar. 1498 to the Florentine Signoria.

518 **while the heat was simply oratorical** Following Burlamacchi, Villari records that 'on the appointed day the Franciscan, notwithstanding that he was the aggressor and had even proposed the ordeal by fire, hurried from the city, under the pretext of having been summoned to Florence by his superiors'.

518 **preaching . . . to the women in the Via del Cocomero** According to Burlamacchi, in the church of San Niccolò, located in the Via del Cocomero.

519 **spelling . . . read and write** 'The old diarists throw in their consonants with a regard [scrupulous regard *MS CM*] rather to quantity than

position, well typified by the *Ragnolo Braghiello* (Agnolo Gabriello) of Boccaccio's Ferondo.' [GE] See *Decameron*, 3. 8, in which the foolish Ferondo, with his slurred speech, talks of a revelation made '*per la bocca de ragnolo Braghiello*' (by the mouth of the Angel Gabriel).

521 **the Mugnone** A tributary flowing into the Arno just to the west of Florence.

522 **get the wool from England as we used to do** Throughout the middle ages Florence, as a major cloth-producing centre, had imported English wool, but in the late 15th cent. Edward IV had imposed export restrictions to protect English weavers from foreign competition.

522 **proclamation of the Signoria . . . subscribe their names** The 'conclusions or doctrines which the *Frate* specially teaches'—'*Ecclesia Dei indiget renovatione . . . Non observantes eam non peccant*'—though certainly echoing Savonarola's favourite message from the pulpit, were in fact drawn up by Fra Domenico as part of his acceptance, in place of Savonarola, of the challenge by Fra Francesco di Puglia to trial by fire. Villari recounts that the Signoria, urged on by the *Compagnacci*, 'caused the disputed "Conclusions" to be transcribed by the Government notary, and publicly invited the signature of all who wished to maintain or contest them by the ordeal of fire'.

524 **Alcibiades** Wealthy, dissolute, unscrupulous, and untrustworthy, Alcibiades (*c*.450–404 BC) was an Athenian general and statesman who provoked the sharp political antagonisms which led to the final defeat of Athens in the Peloponnesian War.

524 **got the Signoria to take up this affair . . . he is ruined with the people . . . fall on him in the Piazza** The interview between Tito and Spini embellishes Villari's account of the *Compagnacci*'s councils, itself drawn from Burlamacchi and Cerretani: 'The Compagnacci were gathered together at one of their accustomed banquets . . . and decided to do their utmost to bring the ordeal to pass. "If Savonarola enters the fire," they said, "he will undoubtedly be burnt; if he refuses to enter it, he will lose all credit with his followers; we shall have an opportunity of rousing a tumult, and during the tumult shall be able to seize on his person" . . . They accordingly applied to the Signory and found its members not only willing to help, but even to assume the direction of their shameful plot.'

524 **the Salviati and the Albizzi** Marcuccio Salviati commanded the armed guard that protected Savonarola at the trial by fire (see p. 538); according to Burlamacchi, during the ensuing riot in the piazza he drew a line on the ground with his sword and declared 'Whoever dares to cross this line shall taste the steel of Marcuccio Salviati'. Francesco Salviati was one of the two Dominicans flanking Savonarola as he arrived for the trial. Francesco degli Albizzi's was among the loudest voices to demand the execution of the five Medicean conspirators. One of the Frate's most zealous adherents, Luca degli Albizzi urged the armed defence of San Marco (see p. 545) despite Savonarola's insistence on non-violence.

525 *maglio* The word literally means 'mallet'. Here it is short for *pallamaglio* (English: pall-mall), a precursor of croquet. The mallet is used to hit a wooden ball (*palla*) through an iron ring. The street in London so named was originally an alley where the game was played in the 16th cent.

525 **no danger of entering the fire** (p. 523); **the Franciscans . . . shall not come within singeing distance** (p. 524); **supper at my palace . . . expound the new scheme** Again GE embellishes her sources. Burlamacchi writes that 'a few days before [the trial] there had been a supper at the Pitti Palace, whereat the chief enemies of the Friar were present; and it was here settled by them that the Minorites should not enter the fire . . . The Compagnacci and their leader, Doffo Spini, had promised [Fra Giuliano Rondinelli—chosen as a substitute for Fra Francesco di Puglia] that the trial by fire would not be made unless it suited them to allow it; and that it would be enough for this Friar Rondinelli to declare himself ready to enter the fire, but that, in fact and truth, he would not be required to do so.'

528 **his provisional substitute** Machiavelli became Secretary to the Ten early in 1498, succeeding the grammarian Marcello Virgilio Adriani.

529 **the Madonna . . . and the divine Infant** GE's description of the interior of San Marco was based on what Lewes reported to her. In this instance it seems that she may not have followed his account in absolute detail. In his journal for 22 May 1860 he records that in the monks' *cells* on the upper floor of San Marco 'I saw several frescos by Angelico, among them a *bambino* of ideal beauty, and in another a Virgin (in the coronation of the Virgin) more graceful in attitude and the flow of drapery than anything I remember.' (The '*bambino*' is probably that in *The Presentation in the Temple* in cell no. 10.) In *BL*, in notes presumably based on Lewes's, GE herself refers to the fresco (in cell no. 9) of 'the lovely Coronation of the Virgin'. However, the passage in the novel here suggests that the frescos concerned were in the *corridors* rather than the cells. There is indeed one fresco by Fra Angelico of *The Virgin and Child enthroned with Eight Saints* (mentioned by GE in *BL* as 'the Mother & Bambino') on the inner wall of the eastern corridor, but her description of the Virgin, 'crowned in her radiant glory', is rather more appropriate to *The Coronation of the Virgin* (certainly as it is described by Lewes) in the cell than to *The Virgin and Child* in the corridor.

529 **Fra Benedetto** A prominent socialite and successful miniaturist who was inspired by Savonarola's sermons to take holy orders as a Dominican in 1495. GE may have seen an example of his illumination in the Rinuccini codex in the National Library in Florence. In his autobiographical poem *Cedrus Libani* he recounts that during the assault on San Marco it was he who was ordered by Savonarola to lay down his arms (see p. 546). And it is he who, in the same poem, records the 'loud . . . roar of triumphant hate' (p. 546) when Savonarola left the convent under guard. In Q GE writes out several passages from *Cedrus Libani* concerning Fra Benedetto's appearance and character.

530 *Cor mundum crea in me* Vulgate, Psalm 50: 10.

532 **To appeal to heaven for a miracle** . . . **great work** A papal brief to Savonarola in Sept. 1495 had declared (though not in reference to a trial by fire): 'It is not enough for anyone simply to declare that he has been sent by God . . . He must confirm this claim to a Divine mission either by a miracle, or by some special testimony of Holy Scripture.' GE's representation of Savonarola's thoughts here may perhaps be based on his response to this brief, in his sermon of 27 Feb. 1496: 'Seek not a miracle . . . Whoever asks for manifestations of that kind asks only from curiosity. And then the Lord will give answer "A depraved generation seeks a sign". Those who demand miracles are wicked men . . . though I say of a truth that whenever the need shall arise I have such faith in our Saviour that He will certainly provide one.'

534 **Domenico Mazzinghi** When Savonarola decided to call for a General Council of the Church, in defiance of the Pope, he drafted a series of letters to the sovereigns of France, Spain, England, Hungary, and Germany. Before sending these he showed them to certain influential supporters of his who were to urge their friends at the respective European courts to support the convocation of the Council. It was Domenico Mazzinghi's task to brief Giovanni Guasconi, the Florentine ambassador to France. It was Mazzinghi's letter to Guasconi that was intercepted by agents of Ludovico Sforza (see p. 536) and forwarded by Sforza to the Pope.

534 **a letter** . . . **in Savonarola's handwriting** GE appears to be following Burlamacchi here, in whose account the intercepted letter was Savonarola's own to the King of France as opposed to that of Mazzinghi to Guasconi.

534 **Philippe de Comines** Philippe de Commynes (*c.*1446–1511) had been sent by Louis XI to Florence in 1478 to offer condolences and aid to the Medici family on the occasion of the Pazzi conspiracy. He subsequently accompanied Charles VIII on his Italian expedition, of which, in bks. 7 and 8 of his *Mémoires*, he was one of the most notable contemporary chroniclers.

534 **library of the Medici, which we purchased** For all his wealth Lorenzo the Magnificent left heavy debts. His library was sold to help pay his creditors and Savonarola was instrumental in its purchase by the convent of San Marco.

535 **Hungary, where scholars are eminently welcome** Tito's information is somewhat out of date: the scholar-king of Hungary, Matthias Corvinus, who had made his court a centre of European learning, had died in 1490, and his successor had failed to continue the tradition. In his *Life of Lorenzo de' Medici* Roscoe notes that Matthias Corvinus was 'eminently distinguished by his encouragement of learned men', and quotes a letter to him from Poliziano: 'From a humble situation I have . . . been raised to some degree of rank and celebrity, without any other recommendation than my proficiency in literature.'

536 **still to be seen** Two of Savonarola's Bibles, thus annotated, are preserved in Florence, one in the Riccardi Library, one in the National Library.

537 **every coign of vantage or disadvantage** Cf. *Macbeth*, 1. 6. 6–8: 'No jutty, frieze, buttress, nor coign of vantage, but this bird hath made his pendent bed and procreant cradle.'

537 **rustic stone-work** 'Rustication' is the architectural style—common in renaissance Florence—of cutting stone in large blocks separated by deep joints.

538 **"Let God arise, and let his enemies be scattered"** The opening of Psalm 68.

540 **Fra Giuliano** The Franciscan Giuliano Rondinelli was originally supposed to enter the fire alongside the Dominican Fra Mariano Ughi (see p. 531), but was subsequently paired with Fra Domenico instead.

541 **Elijah to the priests of Baal** Elijah challenged King Ahab to a public contest to determine whether Baal or Jehovah were the true God. Two bulls were slaughtered and placed on altars on Mount Carmel, and the priests of Baal invited to call upon their god to light the fire. All morning they invoked Baal, but with no response, whereupon Elijah taunted them sarcastically about the delay before successfully calling upon Jehovah to ignite the other altar, thus proving his case (see 1 Kings 18).

542 **Accidents . . . Substance** The accidents are the material form of the bread used in the Sacrament, the substance that essence which through transubstantiation becomes the body of Christ.

543 **Tetto de' Pisani** A projecting roof built by Pisan prisoners on the west side of the Piazza della Signoria in 1362. It was demolished in 1866.

545 **"To San Marco! the fire to San Marco!"** In his 'halting diction' (see p. 239) Giovanni Cambi records the cry of the mob as 'Assamarcho, assamarcho col fuocho'.

545 **Knights Templars** The Knights Templar (also known simply as 'the Templars') were a military order founded in the early 12th cent. to protect pilgrims on their way to the Holy Land. Their name derived from their headquarters being on the site of Solomon's Temple at Jerusalem. They were renowned for their bravery—and savagery—in battle.

547 **men named Rifolfi and Tournabuoni** Valori was killed by Vincenzo Ridolfi and Simone Tornabuoni in revenge for their kinsmen who were executed along with Bernardo del Nero.

548 **that fine ruby** In her notes from King's *Antique Gems* in *WN* GE records that in the mid-16th cent. a ruby was the most valuable of all gemstones, worth twice as much as an emerald of the same size, and eight times as much as a diamond.

550 **San Miniato** The ancient Benedictine monastery of San Miniato al Monte, located on the hill to the south-east of the city where Romola and Baldassarre had met in ch. 53.

551 **Ponte Rubaconte . . . Ponte Vecchio** i.e. the eastern and western ends, respectively, of the Via de' Bardi.

553 **Carraja** I have emended this spelling. Though the name is spelt correctly on p. 112, all states of the text here have the incorrect 'Carrara'. The *j* is archaic, as in the *MS* spelling of 'Ferraveccj'. Today the accepted spelling is 'Carraia'.

554 **the last bridge** In the 15th cent. the Ponte alla Carraja was the last bridge downstream, though several more have since been constructed.

560 **the Inquisition** In 1492 the Jewish community was banished from Spain on the orders of the Grand Inquisitor Torquemada. Many of its members took refuge in Portugal, whence they were in turn expelled in 1497.

563 *pievano* 'Parish priest.' [GE: n. added in *CM*]

571 **taking peas for paternosters** See p. 602.

571 **Fra Girolamo said . . . widows ought not to marry again** See p. 630.

575 **falsifying pen of Ser Ceccone** Burlamacchi records Ser Ceccone as saying, of Savonarola's interrogation, that if no real case existed it would be necessary to invent one and that he was not afraid to do so. Contemporary historians agree that his digest of the examination was not a faithful one, and Villari suggests that 'the whole deposition merely proves that Savonarola had the fullest confidence in the goodness and sincerity of the disciple [see p. 414] who now so basely betrayed him and vainly endeavoured to blacken his fame!'

575 **sixteen examiners . . . prematurely elected, in order to load the dice** GE follows Burlamacchi's count of the number of these special examiners. (Nardi states that there were 12, Villari 17.) The 'new Eight' were elected at the beginning of Mar. 1498, before the expiry of the existing Eight's term of office in order to remove supporters of Savonarola from this, the judicial body of the Signoria that would pronounce sentence on him. Of Spini's election Villari writes, quoting Burlamacchi: 'The intention to violate all principles of law and justice was so plainly evident, even from the first, that one of the examiners [Bartolo dei Zati] indignantly threw up his appointment the moment after receiving it, declaring "that he would have no share in this homicide".'

575 **lay a tax on ecclesiastical property** The Signoria had been requesting permission from the Pope to levy such a tax for some time, in order to raise revenue for prosecuting the war against Pisa.

576 **one who had formerly been his secretary** GE appears to be referring to Pacifico Burlamacchi, who, according to Villari, 'had been one of the most constant of Savonarola's hearers, and was moved by his discourses to assume the Dominican frock'—though not until 1499, the year after Savonarola's martyrdom. Burlamacchi writes: 'Della castità del suo purissimo corpo, e della sua mente santissima non accade dubitare, perciocchè

non fu mai uomo che pure ne suspicasse.' Cf. 'his fellow-monks . . . bore testimony . . . to an unimpeachable purity and consistency in his life, which had commanded their unsuspecting veneration'.

577 **he would not** *obey the devil* Probably a reference to Savonarola's sermon on Quinquagesima Sunday 1498, when he declared: 'This excommunication is hostile to godly living, and therefore proceedeth from the devil . . . it then becomes thy duty to disregard it'.

578 **one memorable passage** As the context implies, this quotation is a direct transl. of part of Savonarola's 'confession', quoted by Villari exactly as it was taken down: 'Tutto che io ho facto ho designato di fare come disopra lho facto p. essere sempre famoso nel presente et nel futuro: et p. avere tale credito nella cipta di Firenze; et che tutte le cose di grande importantia non facessino senza la mia volunta. Et poi che io fusse stato stabilito in Firenze a questo modo havevo animo a far cose grande in Italia et fuora de Italia p. forza di Signori co equali havevo contratto amicitia: et trattato cose grande: come e questo del concilio. Et secondo che le cose fusseno passate haremo pensato delaltre. Et maxime havevo intentione suscitare iprincipi christiani et principalmente quelli fuori di Italia dopo il concilio a sogiogare glinfedeli e di farmi Cardinale o Papa non pensava molto: perche quando havessi conducto questa opera senza esser Papa sarei stato di auctorita et reverentia il primo huomo del mondo: et quando io fussi stato facto Papa non lharei ricusato: benche mi paresse essere maggiore cosa essere capo di decta opera che esser Papa: perche uno huomo senza virtu puo essere Papa: ma tale opera si richiede a huomo di excellente virtu.'

582 **if he suffered, he would suffer for the truth—"The things that I have spoken, I had them from God"** . . . **"I said it that I might seem good; tear me no more, I will tell you the truth"** Savonarola's confession, taken down by Ser Ceccone, is printed by Villari as one of the many corroborative documents appended to his biography. The above words are direct translations therefrom: 'siatemi testimoni, che io ho negato per paura dei tormenti; se io ho patire, voglio patire per la verità; ciò che io ho detto l'ho avuto da Dio . . . per parer buono: non mi lacerate, che io vi dirò il vero certo, certo'.

583 **Tetto** I have emended this spelling from 'Tetta' (= teat), as the word is misspelt in all states of the text. GE wrote 'Tetta' in *MS* at p. 543 also, though all printed states have 'Tetto' on that occasion.

583 **Jacopo Nardi** (1476–1563). The author of several political discourses, a collection of Carnival songs, and a popular transl. of Livy, his most important work was the posthumously published *Istorie della città de Firenze*, which analysed Florentine affairs between the 1494 and 1538 from the viewpont of an anti-Medicean, pro-Savonarolian republican.

586 **"Spirto gentil"** The opening words of the 53rd poem of Petrarch's *Rime sparse*: 'Noble spirit [, you who control those limbs within which, on his pilgrimage of life, dwells a man who is valorous, knowing, and wise]'.

APPENDIX A

THE CANCELLED EPIGRAPHS TO *ROMOLA*

In the manuscript of the novel chapters 1, 2, 4, and 5 have epigraphs (in Italian and Latin, untranslated), none of which appears in any of the printed states, presumably having been deleted by GE on the proofs of the *Cornhill* serialization. Chapter 1 opened with three epigraphs. The first is the phrase 'Firenze, città di parlar avida' ('Florence, city eager to talk'). GE attributes this to 'Macchiavelli, *Istorie*', but I have been unable to trace its source in the *Istorie fiorentine* or in any other of his works. GE jots down a longer version in the Pforzheimer Notebook: 'Firenze, città di parlar avida, e che le cose dai successi e non dai consigli giudica' ('Florence, city eager to talk, where things are judged by how they turn out rather than by how well advised they were'). Here again she attributes it to 'Macchiavelli, Istorie'. The second epigraph, part of which is later quoted in chapter 17 (see p. 184), is from a letter of 1432 from Francesco Filelfo to Niccolò Cardinal Bononiensi: 'Nam igenia Florentina acerrima sunt, et in omnem partem strenua' ('Florentine minds are very sharp, and their enterprise takes all forms'). GE attributes it simply to '*Filelfus*, Epistolae'. The final epigraph to chapter 1 reads 'E già si dice vulgarmente, che i cervelli fiorentini non hanno mezzo nè nell'una nè nell'altra qualità; onde come gli sciocchi sono stoltissimi, così i savi sono sapientissimi.' The sentence, as attributed by GE, is from Varchi's *Storia fiorentina*, and may be translated 'And indeed it is commonly said that Florentine minds know no middle point between extremes; thus the foolish ones are remarkably stupid and the clever ones extremely wise.'

Chapter 2 had a single epigraph–

> Com'anima gentil che non fa scusa,
> Ma fa sua voglia della voglia altrui,
> Tosto com'è per segno fuor dischiusa
> *Dante*, Purgatorio

The quotation (from *Purgatorio*, 33. 130–2) may be translated 'As a gentle spirit, that makes no excuse, but makes its own will that of another as soon as it is disclosed by a sign'.

The single epigraph to chapter 4 read

> Cascan le rose, e restan poi le spine,
> Non guidicar nulla innanzi alla fine.

The quotation, unattributed by GE (both here and in the Bodleian Notebook, where she also jots it down as above), is from Luigi Pulci's *Il morgante maggiore* (19. 26), and should in fact read

> Cascon le rose, e reston poi le spine:
> Non guidicate nulla innanzi al fine.

The lines may be translated 'Roses wither away, and then the thorns are left: don't judge until the end is reached.'

Chapter 5 opened with two epigraphs. The first, '"Novissima omnium cupido gloriae". *Tacitus*', is almost certainy a garbled version of 'Etiam sapientibus cupido gloriae novissima exuitur' (Tacitus, *Histories*, 4. 6: 'The desire for fame is the last thing from which even philosophers divest themselves').

The second read

> Era tutta cortese, era gentile,
> Onesta, savia, pura, e vergognosa,
> Nelle promesse sue sempre virile,
> Alcuna volta un poco disdegnosa,
> Con un atto magnalmo e signorile,
> Ch'era di sangue e di cor generosa.
>
> *Pulci*
> Morgante Maggiore

The quotation, from canto 15, lines 103–8, of Pulci's poem, may be translated as follows: 'She was all courtesy and gentility; honest, wise, pure, and modest. She kept her word like a man would, sometimes a little haughty in her magnanimous and noble attitude. She was kind-hearted and of a generous nature.'

APPENDIX B

GEORGE ELIOT'S PREPARATORY READING FOR *ROMOLA*

The following list comprises the titles of all the books which we can be reasonably sure George Eliot consulted as part of her preparations for *Romola*. The large majority of them are referred to in her notebooks, journals, or letters; that she consulted the remaining handful can reliably be inferred from the text of the novel itself. When the nature of the work concerned (or her reasons for consulting it) are unclear from the title, and when neither the introduction nor the notes to this edition provides clarification, I offer a brief explanatory gloss. I have not included the numerous classical authors cited or referred to in the novel, most or all of whom it is probable that George Eliot was already familiar with, except when it is clear from the evidence of her notebooks and journals that she reread them while preparing for *Romola*.

ACCIAJOLI, VINCENZIO, *Vita di Piero di Gino Capponi* (1853), published in *Archivio storico italiano*, 1st ser. (1842–57).

ADEMOLLO, AGOSTINO, *Marietta de' Ricci* (1841; ed. Luigi Passerini, 1845).

AIZZI, G. (ed.), *Ricordi storici di Filippo di Cino Rinuccini dal 1282 al 1460* (1840).

AMMIRATO, SCIPIONE, *Delle famiglie nobili fiorentine* (1615).

BECKER, W. A., *Charikles* (1840).

FRA BENEDETTO DA FIRENZE, *Cedrus Libani* (15th century).

BOCCACCIO, GIOVANNI, *Decamerone* (14th century).

BOIS-REYMOND, EMIL DU, *Gedächtnissrede auf Johannes Müller* (1860; consulted Dec. 1862 'à propos of visions': GE: journal).

BORGHINI, VINCENZO, *Discorsi* (1584).

BRADY, JOHN, *Clavis Calendaria; or, a Compendious Analysis of the Calendar: Illustrated with Ecclesiastical, Historical and Classical Anecdotes* (1842).

BRUNI, LEONARDO, *Historiae Florentini Populi* (15th century).

BUHLE, J. G., *Geschichte der neueren Philosophie seit der Epoche der Wiederherstellung der Wissenschaften* (1800–4).

BULWER LYTTON, EDWARD, *Rienzi: The Last of the Tribunes* (1835).

BUONACCORSI, BIAGIO, *Diario de' successi più importanti seguiti in Italia, & particolarmente in Fiorenza dall'anno 1498 in sino all'anno 1512* (1568).

BUONDELMONTE, CRISTOFORO, *Librum Insularum Archipelagi* (15th century).

BURLAMACCHI, PACIFICO (attrib.), *Vita del Girolamo Savonarola* (15th century).

CAMBI, GIOVANNI, *Diario* (15th century).

CAPPONI, GINO, *Chronichette antiche della città di Firenze* (15th century; ed. Domenico Manni, 1733).

CAVALCANTI, GIOVANNI, *Istorie fiorentine* (15th century; ed. Filippo Polidori, 1838).

CHIARI, LUCA, 'Priorista' (15th century MS chronicle, consulted at the Magliabecchian Library in Florence, May 1861, for its information about the Feast of San Giovanni).

CICERO, *De Officiis*.

COINDET, FRANÇOIS, *Histoire de la peinture en Italie* (1849).

COMMYNES, PHILIPPE DE, *Mémoires* (15th century).

COMTE, AUGUSTE, *Cours de philosophie positive* (1830–42).

CORNIANI, GIOVANNI BATTISTA, *I secoli della letteratura italiana dopo il suo risorgimento* (1804–13).

DANTE ALIGHIERI, *La divina commedia* (14th century).

DONI, ANTONIO, *I marmi* (1552).

DOVIZI, BERNARDO, *La calandria* (1521).

EPICTETUS, *Encheiridion*.

FERRARIO, GIULIO, *Il costume antico e moderno* (1816–34).

FILELFO, FRANCESCO, *Epistolae* (15th century).

FINLAY, GEORGE, *The History of Greece from its Conquest by the Crusaders to its Conquest by the Turks* (1851).

FLAVIUS BLONDUS, *Italia Illustrata* (1453).

GIAMBULLARI, PIER FRANCESCO, *Origine della lingua fiorentina* (1549).

GIANNOTTI, DONATO, *Della repubblica fiorentina* (1721).

GIBBON, EDWARD, *The History of the Decline and Fall of the Roman Empire* (1776–88).

GIUSTI, GIUSEPPE, *Raccolta di proverbi toscani* (1853).

GRAZZINI, ANTONIO, *Tutti i trionfi, carri, mascherate, o canti carnascialeschi, andati per Firenze, dal tempo del magnifico Lorenzo de' Medici, fino all'anno 1559* (1750).

GUICCIARDINI, FRANCESCO, *Storia d'Italia* (1561–4).

——*Storie fiorentine* (16th century; published 1859).

GUINGÉMÉ, PIERRE LOUIS, *Histoire littéraire d'Italie* (1811–35).

GUIZOT, FRANÇOIS, *Histoire de la civilisation en France depuis la chute de l'empire romain jusqu'à la révolution française* (1829–32).

HALLAM, HENRY, *View of the State of Europe during the Middle Ages* (1818).

HARFORD, JOHN, *The Life of Michael Angelo Bounarroti* (1857).

HEEREN, ARNOLD, *Geschichte des Studiums der classischen Litteratur seit dem Wiederaufleben der Wissenschaften* (1796).

HÉLYOT, PIERRE, *Histoire des ordres religieux* (1714–21).

HODY, HUMPHREY, *De Graecis Illustribus* (1742).

JAMESON, ANNA, *Sacred and Legendary Art* (1848).

——*Legends of the Monastic Orders* (1850).

JOVIUS, PAULUS (or Paolo Giovio), *Elogia Virorum Literis Illustrium* (16th century).

JUVENAL, *Satires*.

KING, CHARLES WILLIAM, *Antique Gems: Their Origin, Uses, and Value as Interpreters of Ancient History* (1860).

KUGLER, FRANZ, *Handbook of Painting: The Italian Schools* (1837; English transl. 1841).

LABORDE, LÉON DE, *Athènes au XVe, XVIe, et XVIIe siècles* (1854).

LANDUCCI, LUCA, *Diario fiorentino dal 1450 al 1516* (16th century).

LASTRI, MARCO, *Osservatore fiorentino* (1776–8).

LEONARDI, CAMILLO, *Speculum Lapidum* (1502).

LESSING, GOTTHOLD, *Briefe, Antiquarischen Inhalts* (1765; consulted for information about precious gems).

LIPPI, LORENZO, *Il malmantile racquistato* (1676).

LITTA, POMPEO, *Celebri famiglie italiane* (1819–99).

MACHIAVELLI, NICCOLO, *Il principe* (1516).

——*La mandragola* (1518).

——*Istorie fiorentine* (16th century).

MADDEN, R. R., *The Life and Martyrdom of Savonarola* (1853).

MANNI, DOMENICO, *Le veglie piacevoli, ovvero notizie de' più bizzari e giocondi uomini toscani* (1762–3).

——*Bartholomaei Scalae, Collensis, Equitis Florentini ac Romae Senatoris, Vita* (1768).

MARCHESE, VINCENZO, *Memorie dei più insignie pittori, scultori et architteti domenicani* (1845–6).

——*Storia di San Marco* (1854).

MARULLUS, MICHAEL TARCHANIOTA, *Hymni et Epigrammati* (1497).

MAURY, LOUIS FERDINAND ALFRED, *Croyance et légendes de l'Antiquité* (1863).

MAZZUCHELLI, GIOVANNI MARIA, *Gli scrittori d'Italia* (1753–63).

MEIER, FREDERICH KARL, *Girolamo Savonarola, aus grossen Theils Handschriftlichen Quellen* (1836).

MEINERS, CHRISTOPH, *Lebensbeschreibungen berühmter Männer aus den Zeiten der Wiederherstellung der Wissenschaften* (1795–7).

MICHELANGELO BUONARROTI, *La tancia* (16th century).

MIDDLETON, CONYERS, *A Letter from Rome, Showing an Exact Conformity between Popery and Paganism; or, the Religion of the Present Romans to be Derived Entirely from that of their Heathen Ancestors* (1729).

MIGLIORE, LEOPOLDO DEL, *Firenze illustrata* (1684).

MONTALEMBERT, RENÉ DE, *Les Moines d'Occident* (1860).

MONTEIL, A. A., *Histoire des Français des divers états aux cinq derniers siècles* (1828–44).

MURATORI, LUDOVICO ANTONIO, *Dissertazione sopra le antichità italiane* (1750).

Murray's Handbook for Travellers in Northern Italy (1847).

NARDI, JACOPO, *Le istorie della città di Fiorenza* (16th century).

NERLI, FILIPPO, *Commentari de' fatti civili occorsi dentro la città di Firenze dall'anno 1215 al 1537* (16th century).

NISARD, JEAN MARIE, *Études de mœurs et de critique sur les poètes latins de la décadence* (1834).

PALMIERI, MATTEO, *Della vita civile* (15th century).

PANIZZI, SIR ANTHONY, Introductory essay to an edn. (1830) of Boiardo's *Orlando innamorato* and Ariosto's *Orlando furioso*.

PARIS, JOHN AYRTON, *Pharmacologia; or the History of Medicinal Substances* (1820).

PERRENS, F. T., *Jérome Savonarole, sa vie, ses prédications, ses écrits* (1854).

PETRARCA, FRANCESCO, *Epistolae* (14th century).

PETTIGREW, THOMAS, *On Superstitions Connected with the History and Practice of Medicine and Surgery* (1844).

PITTI, JACOPO, *Istoria fiorentina* (16th century).

[POGGIO BRACCIOLINI], *Poggiana, ou la vie, le caractère, les sentences, et les bons mots de Pogge Florentin, avec son histoire de la République de Florence*, ed. J. Lenfant (1720).

POLIZIANO, ANGELO, *Epistolae* (15th century).

——*Lamia* (15th century).
——*Opere volgari* (15th century).
——*Orfeo* (15th century).
PUCCI, ANTONIO, *La proprietà di Mercato Vecchio* (14th century).
PULCI, LUIGI, *Il morgante maggiore* (1483).
——*Novella dello sciocco senese* (15th century).
QUADRIO, FRANCESCO SAVERIO, *Della storia e della ragione d'ogni poesia* (1739–52).
RASTRELLI, MODESTO, *Firenze antica e moderna* (1789–1802).
REDI, FRANCESCO, *Bacco in Toscana* (1685).
RENAN, ERNEST, *Études d'histoire religieuse* (1857).
REPETTI, EMMANUELE, *Dizionario geografico-fisico-storico della Toscana* (1833–46).
ROCK, DANIEL, *Hierurgia; or the Holy Sacrifice of the Mass* (1833).
ROSCOE, WILLIAM, *Life of Lorenzo de' Medici* (1795).
ROSSI, TRIBALDO AMERIGO DE', *Ricordanze* (15th century).
RUSKIN, JOHN, *The Stones of Venice* (1851–3).
SACCHETTI, FRANCO. *Trecentonovelle* (14th century).
SAVONAROLA, GIROLAMO, *Compendio di revelatione* (1495).
——*De Veritate Prophetica* (1497).
——*Trattato circa il reggimento e governo della città di Firenze* (1498).
——*Poesie* ed. Audin de Rians (1847).
——*Sermons* (15th century).
SELDEN, JOHN, *Titles of Honour* (1614).
SISMONDI, JEAN, *Histoire des républiques italiennes du Moyen Age* (1809–18).
STEFANI, MARCHIONNE DI COPO (ed.), *Delizie degli eruditi toscani* (1770–89).
SYBEL, HEINRICH VON, *Geschichte des ersten Kreuzzugs* (1841).
TENNEMANN, W. G., *Geschichte der Philosophie* (1798–1819).
TIARBOSCHI, GIROLAMO, *Storia della letteratura italiana* (1772–82).
TROLLOPE, THOMAS ADOLPHUS, *La Beata: A Tuscan Romeo and Juliet* (1861).
VALLA, LORENZO, *De Elegantiae Linguae Latinae* (1444).
VARCHI, BENEDETTO, *Storia fiorentina* (16th century).
——*L'Ercolano* (1570).
VASARI, GIORGIO, *Le vite de' più eccellenti architettori, pittori, e scultori italiani* (1550–68).
VELLUTI, DONATO, *Cronica di Firenze dal'anno MCCC, in circa sino al MCCCLXX* (14th century).
VESPASIANO DA BISTICCI, *Le vite d'uomini illustri de secolo XV* (15th century).
VILLANI, GIOVANNI, *Cronica* (14th century), also known as *Historie universali de' suoi tempi* (published mid-16th century).
VILLARI, PASQUALE, *Storia di Fra Girolamo Savonarola e de' suoi tempi* (1859–61).
WINCKELMANN, JOHANN JOACHIM, *Description des pierres gravées du feu Baron de Stosch* (1760).
WORDSWORTH, CHRISTOPHER, *Athens and Attica: Journal of a Residence There* (1836).

APPENDIX C

LIST OF PARAGRAPHING VARIANTS

There are twenty-one paragraph breaks (i) in *MS* which are not followed in *CM*, and twenty-eight new breaks (ii) in the *CM* text which were not in *MS*. The Clarendon edition follows *CM* in all instances.

(i) In *MS* there are paragraph breaks at the following points (page and line references are to the Clarendon edition):

104. 24 manner, ¶ "Now	388. 36 back. ¶ According
186. 6 foresight. ¶ He	405. 32 said, – ¶ "Swallowed
200. 24 plain. ¶ When	413. 27 mind – ¶ "I
213. 30 Florence. ¶ Still	421. 21 tragic. ¶ And
228. 13 saying – ¶ "The	435. 4 saying, ¶ "Sister
311. 20 lantern: ¶ go	459. 2 that." ¶ Then
321. 30 speaking: ¶ "Florence	475. 32 added, ¶ "The
339. 18 memory. ¶ He	481. 7 opinion. ¶ Late
339. 20 joy! ¶ In	485. 4 uncertain. ¶ Romola
383. 17 bright-coloured. ¶ In	552. 13 twilight. ¶ But
387. 6 stronger. ¶ That	

(ii) The following paragraph breaks in *CM* were not in *MS* (page and line references are to the Clarendon edition): 21. 34; 98. 30; 99. 26; 100. 26; 111. 9; 135. 17; 140. 24; 211. 31; 212. 19; 214. 2; 229. 7; 229. 34; 300. 3; 321. 23; 353. 20; 354. 38; 354. 40; 381. 38; 389. 8; 412. 19; 455. 14; 455. 17; 462. 26; 502. 25; 502. 27; 545. 19; 546. 27; 570. 17.

Fifty new paragraph breaks were introduced between *CM* and *1*. Some have the effect of dividing up particularly long stretches of uninterrupted prose, and may reflect the different design priorities of the first edition (with *c.*300 words per page) and the serial (*c.*600). In the absence of proofs, however, one can only guess which may have been marked by George Eliot for narrative purposes and which introduced by the printer on his own authority. Under the circumstances, therefore, it seems the most sensible course to reproduce the *CM* (i.e. copy text) version here. The rejected paragraph breaks in *1* are as follows (page and line references are to the Clarendon edition):

100. 3 demand? ¶ He	262. 19 him." ¶ There
138. 18 Annunziata. ¶ he	268. 2 way. ¶ Tito
160. 16 Luca's. ¶ The	293. 23 Romola. ¶ No
164. 15 obligations. ¶ But	310. 28 offence. ¶ But
166. 27 nerves. ¶ But	311. 6 complacency. ¶ Tito
167. 25 Caparra. ¶ That	312. 6 aim. ¶ He
218. 16 native. ¶ Arrived	325. 34 him. ¶ She
227. 15 hand. ¶ For	327. 1 rosary. ¶ It
227. 26 sermon. ¶ Among	327. 14 there. ¶ She
229. 20 *quickly*. ¶ But	328. 21 thought. ¶ What

332. 13 faces. ¶ Her
334. 23 spectre. ¶ She
335. 19 Rucellai. ¶ And
338. 30 bitterness. ¶ For
339. 12 oppression. ¶ He
339. 22 moonlight. ¶ He
339. 28 all. ¶ That
340. 35 top. ¶ He
344. 29 them. ¶ And
351. 3 three. ¶ It
357. 32 immediately. ¶ The
358. 26 company. ¶ His
373. 14 snow. ¶ These
373. 34 come. ¶ It
374. 14 pleased. ¶ When

375. 32 consciousness. ¶ Then
378. 7 impressive. ¶ The
386. 3 secrecy? ¶ They
387. 18 again. ¶ With
388. 1 beds. ¶ She
414. 9 Mediceans. ¶ Ser
441. 9 said, ¶ "Only
445. 29 determination. ¶ It
446. 7 zeal. ¶ In
447. 17 Camilla. ¶ She
448. 22 turmoil. ¶ She
449. 21 family. ¶ But
450. 4 hope. ¶ If
463. 3 them. ¶ But
507. 14 love? ¶ The

In *MS* and *CM* there was a paragraph break on p. 463. 17 ('days. ¶ She'); this was dropped in *1* but is restored in the Clarendon edition. On p. 446. 33 the paragraph break in *MS* at 'power. ¶ Romola' was dropped in *CM* and then reinstated in *1* (and in the Clarendon edition).

There are three paragraphing variants between *1* and *2*, as follows:
21. 26 crucifix." "And] *MS CM 1* crucifix." ¶ "And *2 3*
439. 7 side. ¶ But] *MS CM 1* side. But *2 3*
536. 20 abruptly, ¶ Take] *MS CM 1* abruptly,—Take *2 3*
In all cases the Clarendon edition follows the reading of *MS CM 1*.

The paragraph break in the Clarendon edition on p. 163. 11 ('aloud. ¶ It') was introduced by George Eliot on *3C*.

APPENDIX D

THE ILLUSTRATED CAPITALS TO THE FOURTEEN SERIAL PARTS

Frederic Leighton's vignettes framing the capitals at the start of each of the fourteen *Cornhill* serial parts are reproduced here in order. Each includes the appropriate capital letter at the top right-hand corner. Also reproduced, below these, are Leighton's tailpiece to the Proem (see p. xxxiv) and his illustrated title-page for the 1865 edition.